THE
HANDBOOK
~OF~
TEXAS MUSIC

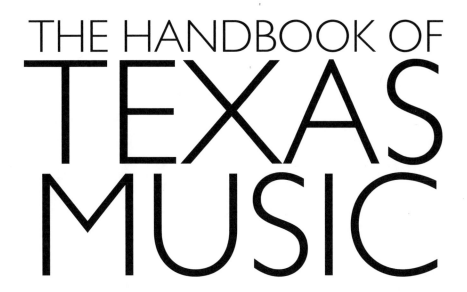

THE HANDBOOK OF TEXAS MUSIC

Editorial Board

Roy Barkley, *Texas State Historical Association*

Douglas E. Barnett, *Texas State Historical Association*

Cathy Brigham, *Concordia University of Austin*

Gary Hartman, *Center for Texas Music History, Southwest Texas State University*

Casey Monahan, *Texas Music Office, Office of the Governor*

Dave Oliphant, *University of Texas at Austin*

George B. Ward, *Texas State Historical Association*

Texas State Historical Association
Austin

Published by the Texas State Historical Association
in cooperation with the Center for Studies in Texas History
at the University of Texas at Austin

Library of Congress Cataloging-in-Publication Data

The handbook of Texas music / editorial board, Roy Barkley ... [et
al.].— 1st ed.
  p. cm.
Includes bibliographical references (p.   ) and index.
  ISBN 0-87611-193-2 (alk. paper) — ISBN 0-87611-194-0 (pbk.)
  1. Music—Texas—Encyclopedias. I. Barkley, Roy R., 1941– II. Texas
State Historical Association.
  ML106.U4 T35 2003
  780'.9764'03—dc21

2003012756

Cover photographs: Buddy Holly: photo by Dick Cole. Janis Joplin: *Texas Rhythm, Texas Rhyme: A Pictorial History of Texas Music*,
Austin, Texas: Texas Monthly Press, 1984; courtesy Larry Willoughby. Mance Lipscomb: CAH; CN 07486. Lydia Mendoza:
photo © by Chris Strachwitz (www. arhoolie.com).

Frontispiece: "The Original Texas Cowboy Pianist" A. O. Babel was born in Seguin, Texas, in 1858. Before becoming a musician, he
worked as a guide, scout, cowboy, and interpreter. He discovered his gift as a pianist while convalescing at Fort Sill, Indian Territory.
During his career, he played in New York City and for European royalty. Gianfranco Spellman Collection.

INTRODUCTION

Like its predecessors, the *Handbook of Texas Music* results from the cooperation of many people. The *Portable Handbook of Texas*—together with, previously and preeminently, the *New Handbook of Texas*—represented the work of numerous cheerful and unpaid contributors. Many of these are experts for whose pro bono work the Texas State Historical Association is deeply grateful. Others are amateurs in the true sense of the word—people who love the subject they pursue and who have, by dint of devoted work, become authoritative; to these also the association is greatly indebted.

The *Handbook of Texas Music* exemplifies this collaborative approach. It is the product of a multi-year series of regular editorial meetings in which institutions and individuals from outside the TSHA donated their time and talent to help shape the finished product. The association gratefully acknowledges the generous cooperation of the Texas Music Office, Office of the Governor; the Center for Texas Music History at Southwest Texas State University; and all the members of the editorial board, both those who represent these institutions and those who as individuals contributed their help.

In 1998 Casey Monahan, director of the Texas Music Office, proposed a joint venture between the Texas State Historical Association and his office. That project was to be a book about Texas music modeled on the *New Handbook of Texas*. It was to be encyclopedic in scope, generality, and editorial features; richly illustrated; and handsomely produced.

In a short time the project enlisted the support of the Center for Texas Music History, whose director, Gary Hartman, joined the editorial staff. Hartman, the tireless leader of a vibrant research center with distinguished archival resources, as well as a professor with graduate-student researchers, brought an unstinting supply of good ideas and well-done articles to this book.

As the concept of the project became clearer, additional distinguished individuals completed the editorial roster. Dave Oliphant, whose publications on Texas music are standards in their field, came aboard. He was followed by Cathy Brigham, whose Ph.D. in ethnomusicology made her vital to the effort. George Ward of the TSHA joined the board to aid in editorial and production decisions.

Donna Coates served as illustrations editor, and the *Handbook of Texas Music* has benefited immensely from her wide knowledge of Texas photographic archives. Finally, David Timmons, who has brought to splendid completion a large number of TSHA publications, designed and laid out the book.

The beginning collection of articles in the *Handbook of Texas Music* comes from the *New Handbook of Texas*. These entries have been updated when possible and corrected when necessary. The topics of "Jazz" and "Blues," for instance, have been so treated. The *NHOT* entries are supplemented by a large number of additional articles—"Country and Western Music" and "Zydeco," for example. Numerous biographies have been added to the original collection. As in the *New Handbook of Texas*, only deceased figures are given separate articles. Though we are aware that many more subjects from the world of music might have been included, we are confident that we have covered the most important ones—if not by separate articles, then by substantial mention in other entries. The index—ably prepared by Linda Webster and Kay Banning—will point the way.

The entries in the *Handbook of Texas Music* were contributed by a wide range of volunteers—musicians, teachers, musicologists, managers of musical enterprises, and others in the music industry, as well as music buffs, some of whom have devoted a lifetime to the study of their subject. To all who contributed to this book, the editorial staff and the staff of the Texas State Historical Association extend their deep gratitude.

Illustration acknowledgements

The editors and staff also extend their heartfelt thanks to all of the individual collectors and institutions who contributed illustrations and information about images. The following in particular gave much of their time and expertise to this project:

John Anderson, Texas State Library, Austin
Joe Carr, South Plains College, Levelland
Alan Govenar, Documentary Arts, Dallas
Lawrence T. Jones III, Austin
Shoshanna Lansberg, Bob Bullock Texas State History Museum
Tary Owens, Austin
Linda Peterson, John Wheat and Steve Williams, Center for American History, University of Texas at Austin
Paisley Robertson, Austin
Clay Shorkey, Austin
Tom Shelton, Institute of Texan Cultures, San Antonio
Larry Willoughby, Austin Community College

Note: The letters CAH in illustration captions designate the Center for American History, University of Texas at Austin. ITC designates the Institute of Texan Cultures, San Antonio.

Roy R. Barkley
Texas State Historical Association

TEXAS MUSIC

GEORGE B. WARD

Texas music was born at the crossroads of America. And it has reached out from there to touch the world. Texas has been a remarkably fertile seedbed for music coming from every point of the compass, and few places on any continent have produced musical styles and musicians whose artistic and cultural impact have been so profound on a national and international scale. Name virtually any style of music and there is a Texas musician whose popularity and influence have been enormous and pivotal in that genre—from the ragtime of Scott Joplin to the Tejano music of Selena, the electrifying blues guitar of T-Bone Walker to the distinctive country vocal styling of Willie Nelson, the bluesy wail of rocker Janis Joplin to the frantic rockabilly drive of Buddy Holly and the subtle piano jazz of Teddy Wilson. The *Handbook of Texas Music* documents all of these and many more. It is a comprehensive, authoritative source on Texas music—an encyclopedia and biographical dictionary that covers all aspects of Texas music, including over 125 striking illustrations of performers and musical artifacts.

For centuries Texas has been a musical and cultural crossroads, and the *Handbook of Texas Music* carefully documents the complex convergence of numerous musical and cultural traditions in this state where east meets west, southern plantations meet high plains ranches, and where an ethnically diverse American culture shares an international border with Mexico. The music of American Indians, Anglo-Americans, African Americans, Mexican Americans, and numerous immigrant groups—Germans, Czechs, Cajuns, among many others—was brought to Texas from every direction. These groups crossed paths, and for centuries have been swapping songs and styles ranging from ancient fiddle tunes to lively polkas and boogie-woogie piano stomps. All cultures and regions of Texas are represented in the *Handbook of Texas Music*, from the East Texas fusion of French Cajun music and African-American rhythm-and-blues known as Zydeco to Mexican-American conjunto music, which in turn borrows heavily from German and Czech accordion polkas. Nineteenth-century German singing societies are treated along with the twenty-first century rap producer DJ Screw.

The *Handbook of Texas Music* tells a compelling story of music that deeply reflects the many distinctive groups that have created Texas music and used it as a means of entertainment, expression, solace, and identity. The recorded country blues of Blind Lemon Jefferson were so popular and influential in the 1920s that his name has come to represent all down-home bluesmen. Gene Autry's singing cowboy music on record and radio and his image on the silver screen and early television had a profound impact on the development of country music and the image of the cowboy in American life. Van Cliburn on stage in Moscow, where he won the Tchaikovsky Piano Competition during the depths of the Cold War, was an important moment in classical musical his-

tory and artistic diplomacy. Music pioneers Bob Wills and Milton Brown brought together the country string-band tradition with jazz, blues, pop, mariachi, and other styles, to help create Western Swing—an eclectic music that changed the face of country music, helped pave the way for rock-and-roll, and stands as a perfect symbol of the musical and cultural complexity of Texas.

In addition to these prominent Texas figures, many significant musicians from elsewhere have spent important parts of their lives and careers in Texas. They too are part of the *Handbook of Texas Music*. Oklahoma-born folk poet Woody Guthrie spent formative years making music with relatives in the Texas Panhandle near Pampa. Jimmie Rodgers, often called the father of country music, moved from Mississippi to Texas for the last years of his short life. Clifton Chenier left Louisiana for Houston and brought to fruition the once obscure musical gumbo known as Zydeco. Early visitors to Texas are featured in this book as well, including Scotsman John McGregor, who died at the Alamo in 1836, and was reported to have entertained the defenders with his bagpipes while Davy Crockett played the fiddle. The famous nineteenth-century poet and critic Sidney Lanier, also a composer of some note, makes an appearance in the pages of the *Handbook of Texas Music*.

Articles also touch on significant issues and institutions related to music, ranging widely over topics as diverse as the Armadillo World Headquarters, the Austin music club that helped bring together hippies and rednecks and gave birth to progressive country music, and WBAP, the Fort Worth radio station that began the country music "barn dance" concept in 1923 and paved the way for the WLS "National Barn Dance" in Chicago, WSM's "Grand Ole Opry" in Nashville, and KWKH's "Louisiana Hayride" in Shreveport. Other articles discuss the important business end of Texas music: Gordon McLendon, whose career in radio influenced media nationwide; the Stamps–Baxter Company of Dallas, which was a leading national purveyor of gospel music; record producer Norman Petty, who helped develop and record Buddy Holly; musician and philanthropist Ima Hogg, who founded the Houston Symphony Orchestra; and Don Robey, owner of Duke–Peacock Records in Houston, which featured artists including Bobby "Blue" Bland and Willie Mae "Big Mama" Thornton, who recorded the original version of "Hound Dog."

Important places on the musical map are given full treatment, from Luckenbach, Texas, the tiny Hill Country town that was immortalized by Waylon Jennings, to Gruene Hall, an old German dance hall that has assumed a new life as a favorite live-music venue, and Deep Ellum, the black entertainment district of Dallas that gave birth to many great Texas musicians. Musical styles that developed in Texas are also covered in numerous articles, including the hard-driving Texas tenor saxophone sound developed by the likes of

Arnett Cobb, Buddy Tate, and Illinois Jacquet, and the hard-drinking honky-tonk style of country music brought to national attention through the singing and songwriting of Ernest Tubb, Lefty Frizzell, George Jones, and a host of others. Sacred music is discussed in articles on gospel music, sacred harp shape-note singing, and pioneering figures in recorded gospel music such as Blind Willie Johnson and Blind Arizona Dranes. Influential singer–songwriters such as Phil Ochs and Townes Van Zandt are given their due, as are the creative guitar wizards Bob Dunn and Leon McAuliffe, who made their electric steel guitars prominent features in the heyday of Western Swing.

Scholars and music fans alike will be interested to learn about the many Texans—and Texas connections—found in music that has traveled far beyond the borders of the state. The rosters are long and impressive: country (George Jones, Johnny Horton, Jim Reeves, Buck Owens), blues (Gatemouth Brown, Albert Collins, Lightnin' Hopkins, Charles Brown), rock-and-roll (Roy Orbison, Bobby Fuller, Stevie Ray Vaughan, ZZ Top), jazz (Jack Teagarden, Eddie Durham, Oran "Hot Lips" Page, Ornette Coleman), música Tejana (Narciso Martínez, Lydia Mendoza, Santiago Jiménez, Valerio Longoria, Selena). And the list goes on. Although the *Handbook of Texas Music* devotes separate biographical articles only to deceased musicians, important living artists such as Willie Nelson are treated in overview articles on topics such as "Country and Western Music," "Willie Nelson's Fourth of July Picnic," and others.

The stories of Texas musicians are important barometers of the political, social, and cultural world around them. Blues guitarist Freddy King was a major influence on Eric Clapton. Jazz piano virtuoso Peck Kelly turned down offers from the jazz greats of his day to play in their bands. Dooley "Play It Again, Sam" Wilson sat at the piano and sang "As Time Goes By" in the famous scene from *Casablanca*. Roger Miller wrote devilishly clever lyrics in songs such as "Dang Me" and won Grammy awards for composing the musical *Big River*. Moon Mullican pounded out boogie-woogie riffs at the piano while wearing a cowboy hat and buckskin fringe jacket, recording everything from truck-driving songs to early rock-and-roll. Wilbert Lee "Pappy" O'Daniel won the governorship of Texas while promoting a great western swing band named the Light Crust Doughboys. Country singer Kenneth Threadgill learned to yodel from Jimmie Rodgers in the 1920s and served as a father figure to Janis Joplin (and a generation of Austinites) many decades later while running a music and beer joint in Austin. Black guitar virtuoso Charlie Christian died at the age of twenty-five, but not before pioneering the electric jazz guitar and recording with the jazz greats of the 1930s. It is these stories and more that form the heart of the *Handbook of Texas Music*

The crossroads that is Texas has produced ground-breaking musicians whose legacy is impossible to pigeonhole simply because it draws on so many musical and cultural strains. Huddie "Leadbelly" Ledbetter, a folk musician brought to national attention through the efforts of folklorists John and Alan Lomax, reflected numerous music styles, black and white, folk and popular. Although Mance Lipscomb, a black Texas sharecropper, is often referred to as a bluesman, he considered himself a "songster" because his music, like that of Leadbelly, was an accumulation of styles learned from a variety of cultural sources. Doug Sahm, a white San Antonio native, who mastered nearly every Texas musical style from country and blues to conjunto and rock, and brought them all to the world through the Sir Douglas Quintet and the Texas Tornados, produced a body of distinctively Texas music perhaps unmatched for its soulful character and variety.

All of these talented and complex figures are part of the story of Texas music that has so enriched the music of the nation and the world. When Blind Lemon Jefferson recorded "Matchbox Blues" in the 1920s, it would have been hard to imagine that decades later the rock-and-roll pioneer Carl "Blue Suede Shoes" Perkins would record a version of the song, and that in the 1960s the Beatles would do the same, inspired by the music of a blind, black entertainer from rural Texas. The stories of Texas music are as powerful as the music itself, and the *Handbook of Texas Music* tells those stories well.

THE
HANDBOOK
∽OF∽
TEXAS MUSIC

A

Akins, Elmer. Radio announcer and gospel music promoter; b. Pilot Knob, Travis County, Texas, March 10, 1911; d. Austin, December 9, 1998; fifth child of sharecroppers Jim and Hattie Akins; known to family members as Dale. After a move to Hornsby Bend, in the Webberville area, his parents sent him to live with an uncle in Austin, so that Akins could attend Gregory School (now Blackshear Elementary School), on East Eleventh Street, at that time an all-black school. In the mid-1920s, Akins moved back to the country and tried cotton farming.

In 1930 poor crops and low prices forced him to leave his ten acres and move back to Austin, where he worked near the old Varsity Theater on Guadalupe for ten years as a porter, janitor, and shoeshine man. During the early 1940s, Akins listened to WLAC Radio, Nashville, and developed a passion for the live broadcasts of such gospel quartets as the Fairfield Four. He began singing in choirs and quartets and hosted live gospel programs at KNOW radio. In 1942 he went to work at the Texas Supreme Court as a janitor and clerk. His employment at the Capitol lasted thirty-four years, until his retirement in 1976. While working at the Varsity Theater, Akins had befriended Jake Pickle and John Connally, and he continued his relationship with them after he took employment at the Capitol.

In 1947 Akins persuaded Pickle to sell him a fifteen-minute slot on KVET Radio, Pickle and Connally's upstart station. The one-time Sunday-morning airing developed into a twelve-week agreement, which blossomed into a fifty-one-year institution. Akins's Sunday morning gospel program, "Gospel Train," expanded to a ninety-minute show. In 2002, KVET's "Gospel Train" was the oldest continuously running American radio show. The Texas Association of Broadcasters recognized Akins as the longest-continuing radio host in the United States and, in 1998, honored him as a "Texas Broadcast Legend." Akins also wore the titles "Voice of Austin" and "Deacon of Austin Gospel Music" during his half-century of broadcasting.

His many accomplishments include his formation of the Royal Gospel Quartet in the early 1940s; his founding of the Austin Quartet Association; his partnership with Bill "the Mailman" Martin, which resulted in the booking and hosting of hundreds of visiting gospel talents at Central Texas venues; his fifty-one-year commitment to providing religious information; his distinction as a founding member of the Austin Christian Relief Board; and his ACTV broadcast of the "Gospel Train" television program. Akins's contributions inspired Austin mayor Roy Butler to declare an Elmer Akins Day in 1975, which afterward evolved into an annual weeklong community and church celebration. Akins's work also gave rise to a fiftieth anniversary celebration at Bass Concert Hall and the production of a television documentary entitled "Elmer Akins: Radio Man." During the celebration, which was sponsored by Texas Folklife Resources, the Texas Gospel Announcers Guild, and the University of Texas Performing Arts Center, several major gospel record labels paid tribute to Akins.

Akins married Mattie Lee Watson in 1931. The couple's first home was an old toolhouse that they bought from a construction crew and moved from the Varsity Theater lot to Chestnut Avenue. They lived there for twelve years. Akins was a member of David Chapel Missionary Baptist Church. His wife of sixty-four years died in 1995. After her death he suffered a broken hip and a series of strokes. He died of pneumonia and was survived by a son, Charles Akins, two grandchildren, and two great-grandchildren.

BIBLIOGRAPHY: Akins obituary, Corpus Christi *Caller Times, Corpus Christi Online* (http://www.caller2.com/autoconv/newstexmex173.html), accessed December 14, 2001. "Best of 1994," Austin *Chronicle* (http://www.austinchronicle.com/issues/annual/bestof/94/critics/boa94.C.arts.html), accessed December 15, 2001. Jay Hardwig, "The Gospel Mission of Elmer Akins," Austin *Chronicle* 18.26 (http://www.austinchroncle.com/issues/vol18/issue 26/music.akins.html, accessed December 15, 2001. *It's All Here. The Performing Arts Center UT College of Fine Arts* (http://www.utexas.edu/admin/erwin/applause/feb97ap/pac.html), accessed December 15, 2001. *Texas Gospel Announcers Guild Newsletter,* March 2001 (http://www.texasgag.com/News.htm), accessed December 14, 2001.

Cheryl L. Simon

Alessandro, Victor Nicholas. Orchestra conductor; b. Waco, November 27, 1915; d. San Antonio, November 27, 1976; son of a prominent music teacher and conductor, Victor Alessandro Sr. The Alessandros moved to Houston in 1919. Victor was introduced to music at an early age and studied horn with his father. He is said to have made his conducting debut at age four, when he led a children's band in a performance of Victor Herbert's "March of the Toys."

In 1932 he entered the Eastman School of Music in Rochester, New York, where he studied composition with Howard Hanson. He afterward studied at the Salzburg Mozarteum and St. Cecilia Academy in Rome, where he studied with Ildebrando Pizzetti. In 1938 he became conductor of the Oklahoma City Symphony Orchestra, an organization that he led from a WPA project to an accomplished ensemble with broad civic support. When Max Reiter, conductor of the San Antonio Symphony Orchestra, died in December 1950, Alessandro took over much of the remaining season; he signed a contract as permanent conductor in April 1951. The next year he also assumed leadership of the San Antonio Symphony Society's Grand Opera Festival. In 1955 he married flutist Ruth Drisko; they had two children.

Alessandro was at his best in works by Tchaikovsky and Richard Strauss. He was a sympathetic interpreter of Brahms and the odd-numbered symphonies of Beethoven.

He introduced works by Bruckner, Mahler, and Berg to San Antonio audiences before they became fashionable elsewhere. He conducted memorable performances of *Elektra*, *Salome*, *Nabucco*, *Boris Godunov*, *Susannah*, *Die Meistersinger*, and the standard operas of Verdi and Puccini. In building the San Antonio orchestra he was an exacting, often irascible taskmaster of high musical standards. But he was capable of less formidable moments as well; in February 1962, for instance, he dedicated a performance of *Ein Heldenleben* to the memory of Bruno Walter.

Alessandro received honorary doctorates from the Eastman School and Southern Methodist University and the Alice M. Ditson Award for service to American music. Recordings of his work include Claude Debussy's *Martyrdom of St. Sebastian* (1950), light accompaniments (ca. 1953), Vivaldi and Rodrigo guitar concertos and works by Richard Strauss and John Corigliano (1967–68). With his health declining, Alessandro retired in 1976. He died on his sixty-first birthday.

BIBLIOGRAPHY: Theodore Albrecht, "101 Years of Symphonic Music in San Antonio," *Southwestern Musician / Texas Music Educator*, March, November 1975. *Baker's Biographical Dictionary of Musicians*, 1978. Hope Stoddard, *Symphony Conductors of the U.S.A.* (New York: Crowell, 1957).   *Theodore Albrecht*

Alexander, Birdie. Music teacher; b. Lincoln County, Tennessee, March 24, 1870; d. El Paso, August 2, 1960; daughter of George Washington and Mary Jane (Shores) Alexander. The family moved to Texas, where Birdie attended school in Forney and studied at Mary Nash College in Sherman. She then attended Ward Seminary in Nashville, Tennessee, where she majored in piano and voice, and graduated with honors in 1891.

After her family moved to Dallas she began teaching in the public schools, where she became supervisor of music in 1900. In Dallas she is credited with having laid the foundation for the system of music education in the public schools. She established the teaching of singing in all grades and was the first to form citywide choral groups for public performance. Under her direction the first operetta was performed at Turner Hall on May 24 and 25, 1901, to raise funds for the children's department of the Dallas Public Library. She produced and directed the music festival in May 1912 at the coliseum and the first cantatas given by the schools. In 1910 she organized the Dallas High School Orchestra, which continued to function with annual concerts. In the same year she inaugurated music-appreciation lessons in the schools with the purchase of the first record player and recordings with funds subscribed by interested citizens. She instituted folk-dancing classes to teach rhythm in the lower grades.

Miss Alexander was a charter member of the first board of directors of the Music Supervisors' National Conference, and as chairman of the MSNC was responsible for the formation of the music department of the Texas State Teachers Association. In the summers of 1908, 1909, and 1910 she organized and taught courses in music education at the University of Texas. She also taught on the summer faculty at Northwestern University in Evanston, Illinois. In 1912 she edited *Songs We Like to Sing*. Because of her health she moved to El Paso in 1913, and there until her death she taught piano and was a leader in musical activities. In 1941 the Texas Music Teachers' Association made her a life member "in recognition of her distinguished contribution to American music."

BIBLIOGRAPHY: Dallas *Morning News*, May 16, 1966.
Lelle Swann

Alexander, "Texas." Blues singer; b. Alger Alexander, Jewett, Texas, September 12, 1900; d. Richards, Texas, April 16, 1954 (buried in Longstreet Cemetery, Grimes County); son of Sam "Ernie" Alexander and Jennie Brooks. Alger was raised by his grandmother, Sally Beavers, in Richards. He spent most of his life working as a railroad section hand or on farms in East Texas. He was a short, stocky man who sang with a deep, booming voice. He often shouted out his lyrics in the tradition of field slaves, although this sometimes made his words difficult to understand. He always carried a guitar with him, but could not play it. When he sang in migrant work camps, in honkytonks, or on the streets, he sought out a guitar player to accompany him. His accompanists included Blind Lemon Jefferson, Lowell Fulson, "Funny Papa" Smith, Dennis "Little Hat" Jones, and Alexander's cousin, "Lightnin'" Hopkins.

Pianist Sam Price discovered Alexander in the early 1920s and arranged a recording session for him. Alexander recorded extensively after that, collaborating with other blues legends, including Lonnie Johnson, the Mississippi Sheiks, Lightnin' Hopkins, and Little Hat Jones. Between 1927 and 1934 he recorded over sixty sides on the Okeh and Vocalion labels. His extensive recording helped him become one of the most popular blues singers of that era. He also served at least two prison terms, including a stint in Paris, Texas, for allegedly killing his wife. Alexander's songs reflected his prison and work experiences. After his release from jail in the mid-1940s, he performed with Hopkins on Houston street corners and busses for tips. After moving back to Richards in 1951, he spent the last years of his life in poor health. He died of syphilis.

BIBLIOGRAPHY: Michael Erlewine, ed., *All Music Guide to the Blues* (San Francisco: Miller Freeman, 1999). Sheldon Harris, *Blues Who's Who* (New Rochelle, New York: Arlington House, 1979). H. Wiley Hitchcock and Stanley Sadie, eds., *The New Grove Dictionary of American Music* (New York: Macmillan, 1986). Frank Scott, *The Down Home Guide to the Blues* (Chicago: Cappella, 1991).
James Head

Alley, Shelly Lee. Fiddler and western swing pioneer; b. Alleyton, Texas, July 6, 1894; d. Houston, June 1, 1964; son of John Ross and Eliza (Hoover) Alley. Alley, considered one of the greatest bandleaders of the 1930s and 1940s, was descended from the original Austin colony settlers after whom Alleyton was named. His father owned a cotton gin. Alley learned to read music when he was a child. That skill enabled him to lead the base orchestra in San Antonio, where he was stationed during World War I. In the 1920s he led several different orchestras that played

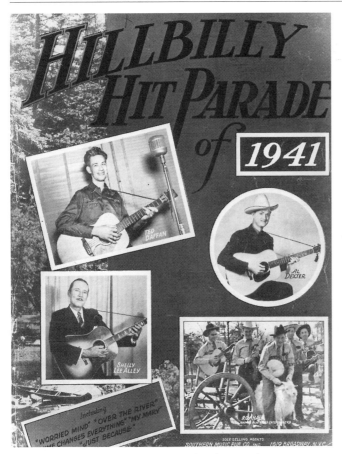

Sheet music cover "Hillbilly Hit Parade of 1941" featuring western swing pioneer Shelly Lee Alley. Bill Boyd Papers, CAH; CN11492.

primarily pop and jazz. He became a pioneer in radio broadcasting when his bands got airtime on numerous Texas radio stations, including KRLD in Dallas.

In the late 1920s Alley began to move away from the orchestra sounds and toward a blues and pop sound that featured guitars and fiddles. In 1936 he formed the Alley Cats, based in Houston and Beaumont. The band featured several members who became famous in their own right, including "Pappy" Selph, Ted Daffan, Floyd Tillman, Cliff Bruner, and Alley's stepson, Clyde Brewer. In the late 1930s the Alley Cats recorded fifty-four sides, primarily for the Vocalion Label. Although Alley himself never had much commercial recording success, some of his songs became huge hits for other artists. In 1933 fellow Texan Jimmy Rodgers recorded Alley's song "Gamblin' Barroom Blues." Alley's most famous song was "Travelin' Blues." Rodgers, accompanied by Shelly and his brother Alvin on the "twin fiddles," first recorded the song in 1931. More than twenty different artists have since recorded "Travelin' Blues," including Merle Haggard, Bob Wills, Ernest Tubb, Lefty Frizzell, and, more recently, Jimmie Dale Gilmore.

During World War II, Alley disbanded the Alley Cats and played with the Beaumont band Patsy and the Buckaroos for a short time. Although he re-formed the Alley Cats again after the war, the band was short-lived. The group

recorded a single on the Globe label before it was permanently disbanded in 1946. After poor health forced Alley to retire from performing, he continued to write music, including several gospel tunes. He also did some session work with Benny Hess and others. He is a member of the Western Swing Hall of Fame. He is buried in the Alley family cemetery in Alleyton. He was survived by his wife of twenty-two years, Velma; a son, Shelly Alley Jr.; and his stepson, Clyde Brewer.

BIBLIOGRAPHY: Clyde Brewer, telephone interview by author, July 23, 2000. Barry McCloud, *Definitive Country* (New York: Berkley Publishing Group, 1995). Houston *Chronicle*, April 14, 1994.   *James Head*

Allison, Irl Sr. Pianist, music educator, and founder of the National Guild of Piano Teachers; b. Warren, Texas, April 8, 1896; d. Austin, September 6, 1979; son of John Van and Mary (Richardson) Allison. He attended Bryan Military Academy and in 1915 received an A.B. from Baylor University. After studying at Chicago Music College and Columbia University he returned to Baylor, where he received an A.M. in 1922. He was awarded honorary doctorates in music by Southwestern Conservatory, Dallas, in 1947 and by the Houston Conservatory of Music in 1955. He also received an honorary law degree from Hardin–Simmons University. As a young man Allison was

Irl Allison, director and founder of the National Guild of Piano Teachers, and his chauffeur Jack Moats after San Antonio detectives stopped their car thinking they had captured the bank robber Clyde Barrow, of "Bonnie and Clyde" fame. Allison and Moats had been stopped several times because Barrow was using a fake auto license plate with the same number as Allison's. UT Institute of Texan Cultures at San Antonio No.0381-C.

a silent-film pianist in a Waco theater. He later studied piano with Rudolph Hoffman, Joseph Evans, Percy Grainger, Ernest Hutchinson, Harold von Mickwitz, and Walter Gilewicz. He married Jessie Johnson on July 3, 1918, and they had four children. A son, Irl Jr., succeeded his father as president of the National Guild of Piano Teachers.

Although Allison was best known to hundreds of thousands of music teachers and their pupils by his signature on certificates awarded by the National Guild for participation in the Annual National Piano Playing Auditions, he was also a renowned music teacher. He served as dean of music at Rusk College in 1918–19, was a piano instructor at Baylor College for Women from 1921 to 1923, and was dean of fine arts at Montezuma College from 1923 to 1927. From 1927 to 1934 he was dean of music at Hardin–Simmons University, where he organized the National Guild and began the National Guild Auditions in 1929. He was also the founder and president of the guild-sponsored American College of Musicians and of the National Fraternity of Student Musicians. Allison edited the guild yearbook from 1936 to 1945 and *Piano Guild Notes* from 1951 to 1963. He contributed to several musical publications and newspapers and wrote *Through the Years* (1925). He also founded the Golden Rule Peace Movement and began the World Peace Programs for radio in 1948. Under the auspices of the guild, Allison compiled and edited the Irl Allison Library of Music (thirty-three volumes); he also initiated and promoted into an international event the Van Cliburn International Piano Competition. In Austin, where the Allisons made their home after 1943, he was largely responsible for developing the Azalea Trail, and presented to Lady Bird Johnson azaleas for the Lyndon B. Johnson Library.

BIBLIOGRAPHY: Austin *American–Statesman*, June 12, 1949, October 14, 1962. *The Guild Syllabus*, 1986–87. *Who's Who in America*, 1980–81.   *Craig H. Roell*

Amster, Pearl. Classical pianist and teacher; b. Pearl Salzman, Brooklyn, New York, May 17, 1917; d. Austin, September 22, 2000; daughter of Joseph and Dorothy Salzman. Pearl Amster was a beloved performer and patron of many Austin youth music programs. Her accomplishments include her debut at Town Hall, New York City, at age sixteen, her recognition as the first woman awarded an artist diploma from the National Guild of Music and Teachers, her performance at Steinway Concert Hall (a part of Carnegie Hall) in 1953, and her CD *An Inspired Collection*, recorded on her eightieth birthday. She studied under Rose Raymond and Rosalyn Tureck and performed as a concert pianist and taught music for many years before she and her husband, Gus, moved to Austin in 1967.

After moving to Austin, she continued to perform and teach piano. For twenty-eight years she hosted such social events as the Austin Gilbert and Sullivan Society's monthly soirees. She performed for many years at the Wednesday Morning Music Club; volunteered as an usher at Capitol City Playhouse, Zachary Scott Theatre, the Paramount, and the University of Texas Performing Arts Center; served on the board of the Violet Crown Players and the Austin

Civic Orchestra; and operated two music stores, Amster Music and Art and Amster Piano Barn. In 1984 the Austin Civic Orchestra named its annual youth concerto competition and scholarship in honor of Pearl Amster for her support of youth performance opportunities.

Mrs. Amster gave piano lessons and held recitals in her Austin home, where she lived for thirty-three years. She treated her students like family members and maintained contact with many of them long after they left her tutelage. Gus Amster, to whom Pearl was married for forty-five years, died in 1986. Pearl Amster died of kidney failure at age 83. The couple was survived by two daughters.

BIBLIOGRAPHY: Austin *American–Statesman*, September 29, 2000; March 10, 2001. Austin *Chronicle*, September 29, 2000.   *Cheryl L. Simon*

Anderson Fair Retail Restaurant. On Grant Street in the Montrose section of Houston; opened in January 1970 as a folk and original music venue. Though the management and ownership have gone through many changes, it is still operating today with virtually the same physical layout and music format as the day it opened. The main room is small, seating about eighty, and it has great acoustics. Not much PA equipment is needed to fill the room. Memorable performances there have included Townes Van Zandt, Richard Dobson, Vince Bell, Lucinda Williams, Steven Fromholz, Eric Taylor, Don Sanders, the Hemma-Ridge Mt. Boys, Bill and Bonnie Hearne, Lyle Lovett, John Vandiver, Katy Moffatt, Butch Hancock, Shake Russell, Dana Cooper, Dan Hicks, and others.

The "A–Fair" serves good "down-home cookin'," maintains a reading room, and has a courtyard for those who want to discuss any topic known to man. Backstage, players meet and talk while waiting their turn, pass a bottle, and smoke (the rest of the establishment is Smoke Free). Anderson Fair has also contributed to some great block parties, since it is on a short street from which traffic is easily excluded. With the side street blocked, the setting is perfect for the street parties at which the bands have often performed on a flatbed truck—all day and often into the night. Release parties for several Buttermilk Records artists—Richard Dobson, Fevertree, the Hemma-Ridge Mt. Boys, Bruce McElheny—have taken place at Anderson Fair. In the 1970s, at the invitation of owners Walter Spinks, Roger Ruffcorn, and Tim Leatherwood, Buttermilk made recordings that included Lucinda Williams, Eric Taylor, Don Sanders and Linda Lowe at Anderson Fair.

Small changes over the years have included construction of a new stage, built by resident songwriters Ken Gaines and Wayne Wilkerson, who host the songwriters' night on Thursdays. A recording studio has been added in the retail space adjoining the club, which does independent projects but can also record live shows from the stage. Tim Leatherwood is still in charge and you can still hear great acoustic music in a non-smoking, serious-listening environment. Patrons who talk during performances or allow a cell phone to ring will get their cover charge back and be asked to leave.

BIBLIOGRAPHY: Anderson Fair website (www.andersonfair.com), accessed January 29, 2003.   *Charles Bickley*

Anhalt Hall. A dance hall and community center on Anhalt Road in southwestern Comal County, a mile off Highway 46 and twenty-eight miles west of New Braunfels. The first part of the hall was constructed in 1879, and additions were completed in 1898 and 1908.

German immigrants first settled the area around Anhalt in 1855. The site was known as Krause Settlement by 1859. The general store there was built by Conrad and Louis Krause in 1856 and became the post office in 1879. The community grew quickly, since it was situated at the midpoint on the trail between New Braunfels and Boerne. Krause Settlement became a place where travelers could water their animals, do business at the freight station, and rest before traveling on. When the post office was established in 1879, the name of the community was changed to Anhalt at the suggestion of local settler Heinrich Wehe. There have been two explanations offered for the name Anhalt. One, that it designates "stopping place" in German, and the other, that it refers to a region of the same name in Germany.

Wehe maintained the freight station on his place; a number of residents were freighters who transported goods between the Gulf Coast and communities inland. Anhalt Hall became the meeting place for the Germania Farmer Verein (German Farmer Association), an association formed in 1875 to protect cattle from thieves and Indians. The residents branded their cattle with the association brand G and began to alert residents and law officers to rustling. The program was successful, and, by February 7, 1876, members received a state charter and adopted bylaws.

When the first part of Anhalt Hall was completed in 1879, the association used it as a meetingplace. This part of the hall is now the old office and the ladies' restroom. In 1887 the German Farmer Association began building a larger meeting hall connected to the original structure. It was completed in 1898 and is the present-day seating area for the dance hall. In 1908 a 6,000-square-foot oak dance floor was added to the hall. The bandstand and center stage were added to the hall after 1908. The hall has high ceilings and large fans at each end. In 1993 the association spent $60,000 to replace the tin roof, which had been damaged by leaks, and to make other structural repairs. A lean-to added to the south side of the building provides covered seating. The dance floor was refurbished during the renovation.

The first six-piece brass band in Comal County, the William Specht Spring Branch Band, was formed in 1880 and played at Anhalt Hall. George Strait, as part of the Ace in the Hole Band, played at Anhalt Hall for the Smithson Valley High School FFA dance in 1978. Country singers such as Clay Blaker, Gary P. Nunn, Johnny Rodriguez, Geronimo Treviño, Chris Wall, and Jerry Jeff Walker have performed at Anhalt Hall. The movie *All the Pretty Horses*, which starred Matt Damon and Penelope Cruz and was directed by Billy Bob Thornton, includes a scene filmed at Anhalt Hall.

The German Farmer Association still gathers three times a year at the hall, for Mayfest, Summerfest, and Oktoberfest. Mayfest and Oktoberfest are held on the third Sunday in May and October. After holding a successful picnic in May 1877, the association decided to hold a planting festival in the fall that would exhibit field and garden products and livestock. This event became known as Oktoberfest and has been held at Anhalt since 1877. Oktoberfest features entertainment and dances and a traditional meal of pot roast, peas, potato salad, and sauerkraut. Summerfest is held in June or July, depending on when entertainment is available, and features a barbeque cookoff.

BIBLIOGRAPHY: Brenda Anderson–Lindemann, *Spring Branch and Western Comal County, Texas* (San Antonio: Omni, 1998). Geronimo Treviño III, *Dance Halls and Last Calls: The History of Texas County Music* (Plano, Texas: Republic of Texas Press, 2002). *David DeKunder*

Antone's Nightclub. A haven for blues music on West Fifth Street in Austin; opened by Clifford Antone on July 15, 1975. Antone feared that blues was in danger of disappearing. From its inception, his club has attracted a variety of influential musicians. "Me and my friends," Antone said, "wanted to hear blues before these [musicians] died." The first act to perform at the club was zydeco legend Clifton Chenier and His Red-Hot Louisiana Band. In the weeks that followed, both Sunnyland Slim and Big Walter Horton, blues legends in their own right, attracted large crowds to the club.

Antone's has hosted an impressive number of other blues masters, including Muddy Waters, B. B. King, John Lee Hooker, Jimmy Reed, Otis Rush, and Albert King. The sounds of blues, however, are not the only ones heard at Antone's. Musicians of all types are frequently on the playbill. Stevie Ray Vaughan and Doug Sahm regularly performed at Antone's. In recent years Bonnie Raitt, Lucinda Williams, and Bono joined local bands to perform there.

In 1986 Antone used his nightclub to establish Antone's Records, which records both live shows and studio sets. The nightclub and the record label have produced recordings of guitarist Eddie Taylor, James Cotton (whose record was nominated for a Grammy Award), Mel Brown, and Memphis Slim. Antone was awarded a Lifetime Achievement Award by the National Blues Foundation for his contributions to music.

BIBLIOGRAPHY: "A Brief History of Antone's" (*www. antones.com/antones/history.html*), accessed November 1, 2002. "Antone's Records" (*www.pressnetwork.com/bios/ Antonbio.htm*), accessed November 1, 2002.
Ryan A. Kashanipour

Archia, Tom. Tenor saxophonist; b. Ernest Alvin Archie Jr., Groveton, Texas, November 26, 1919; d. Houston, January 16, 1977; son of Ernest and Henrietta (McDade) Archie Sr. His father modified his last name to Archia. Ernest Jr.'s parents were both schoolteachers, and while he was still a child, the family moved to Rockdale and then to Houston and lived in the city's Fifth Ward. He took violin lessons, but was playing saxophone by the time he was a teenager. At some point early in his musical career Archia adopted the nickname Tom, and he was billed as "Texas Tom" for a time. He graduated from Prairie View A&M in 1939 and taught school in East Texas in 1939–40.

Micael Priest poster advertising the last performance at the Armadillo World Headquarters, December 31, 1980. Courtesy George B. Ward.

In 1940 Tom Archia joined the Milt Larkin band and played in Houston with tenorists Arnett Cobb and Illinois Jacquet, having also been with the tenorists in the school orchestra in Phyllis Wheatley High School. He continued with Larkin at the Rhumboogie Club in Chicago in 1942–43, and in the mid '40s recorded with trumpet star Roy Eldridge. Archia lived in Los Angeles during part of 1945 and played in Howard McGhee's combo but was back in Chicago in 1946. He made a name for himself primarily during tenor battles with Gene Ammons and Claude McLin in Chicago between 1946 and 1950. In 1947–48 he formed part of fellow Texan Oran Hot Lips Page's band, and during this same period Archia was recorded by the Aristocrat label; a Classics CD reissued this recording in 2001 in its Blues & Rhythm Series.

Archia's style is in a bluesy R&B vein, which has been called a familiar sound even if his name is not familiar to most listeners. He was known as "the Devil" because he could "play the hell out of his horn." The Classics CD describes his recording as "the real deal street wailing and jive." According to Armin Büttner and Robert L. Campbell, Archia's style, "influenced by Lester Young, was characterized by a sense of youthful exuberance and a set of personalized licks that had a discernible influence on Ammons."

Archia was in a common-law marriage with Freda Kelln from 1949 to about 1960, and they had three children. He remained active in Chicago until 1967, when he returned to Texas and settled in Houston. He continued to perform in that city in the 1970s.

BIBLIOGRAPHY: *The Chronological Tom Archia, 1947–1948* (Classics 5006, 2001). Barry Kernfield, ed., *The New Grove Dictionary of Jazz*, Second Edition (New York: Grove's Dictionaries, 2002). *The Tom Archia Discography* (http://hubcap.clemson.edu/~campber/archia.html), accessed November 21, 2002.   *Dave Oliphant*

Armadillo World Headquarters. During the 1970s the Armadillo World Headquarters, a concert hall in Austin, became the focus of a musical renaissance that made the city a nationally recognized music capital. Housed in a converted national guard armory by a group of local music entrepreneurs, the "Armadillo" provided a large and increasingly sophisticated alternative venue to the municipal auditorium across the street. This venture, which capped several years of searching by young musicians and artists to find a place of their own, reflected the emergence nationwide of a counterculture of alternative forms of music, art, and modes of living. The name Armadillo World Headquarters evoked both a cosmic consciousness and the image of a peaceable native critter, the armadillo, often seen on Texas highways as the victim of high-speed technology.

The Armadillo opened its doors in August 1970, and quickly became the focus for much of the city's musical life. With an eventual capacity of 1,500, the hall featured a varied fare of blues, rock, jazz, folk, and country music in an informal, open atmosphere. By being able to host such top touring acts as Frank Zappa, the Pointer Sisters, Bruce Springsteen, and the Grateful Dead, the Armadillo brought to Austin a variety of musical groups that smaller clubs or other local entities might never have booked. Since outstanding local or regional artists often opened these shows, the Armadillo also gave vital exposure to such future stars as Joe Ely, Marcia Ball, and Stevie Ray Vaughan. The Armadillo's eclectic concert calendar brought together different, sometimes disparate, sectors of the community. The most dramatic fusion mixed traditional country-music culture with that of urban blues and rock to produce a Texas hybrid character known as the "cosmic cowboy" and a hybrid music called "progressive country" (sometimes referred to as "redneck rock"). The acknowledged godfather of this movement was singer-songwriter Willie Nelson, who made his Armadillo debut in 1972.

To promote its concerts, the Armadillo maintained a staff of poster and mural artists, including Jim Franklin, Micael Priest, Guy Juke, and Danny Garrett. Given free reign for their creative impulses, these and other artists explored many new images and techniques in poster making. The hundreds of Armadillo concert posters they made during the 1970s contributed to the flowering of poster art in Austin. The Armadillo operated on a shoestring budget and much volunteer labor, on a month-to-month basis in an atmosphere of perpetual financial crisis. By 1980 the demands of downtown real estate signaled the end of an era. As its lease expired, the Armadillo World Headquarters held one final New Year's Eve blowout (December 31, 1980), then closed its doors to await demolition. Though the building is gone, the Armadillo's legacy as a vital center of musical and artistic creativity lives on in Texas music history.

BIBLIOGRAPHY: Armadillo World Headquarters Archives, Center for American History, University of Texas at Austin. David L. Menconi, Music, Media, and the Metropolis: The Case of Austin's Armadillo World Headquarters (M.A. thesis, University of Texas at Austin, 1985). Jan Reid, *The Improbable Rise of Redneck Rock* (New York: Da Capo Press, 1974). Vertical files, Center for American History, University of Texas at Austin.

                    John Wheat

Armstrong, Robert Wright. Railroad executive, soldier, and musician; b. Brownwood, Texas, December 18, 1892; d. Fort Worth, September 15, 1966 (buried in Greenwood Cemetery, Fort Worth); son of Walter David and Mary Elizabeth (Wright) Armstrong. He received his education in the Brownwood public schools, at Kemper Military Academy in Boonville, Missouri, and at the Missouri Military Academy in Mexico, Missouri. He played in the school bands at Brownwood and at the Missouri Military Academy, where he also directed the band and orchestra. After graduation he performed with the Kryl Concert Band, the Honey Boy Evans Minstrels, and the Al G. Fields Minstrels. When he was tired of performing he moved to the Neil O'Brien Minstrels to become first the assistant manager and then the manager. Later, while working as manager of the Brownwood Chamber of Commerce (1919–24), he organized the Old Gray Mare Band, which became the official band of the West Texas Chamber of Commerce.

Although he joined the Brownwood Chamber of Commerce after World War I, Armstrong did not remain there for long. In 1924, at the request of John A. Hulen, whom he had met during military training at Camp Bowie in Fort Worth, he worked for the Trinity and Brazos Valley Railway as general agent, with assignments in Fort Worth (1924–28), Houston (1928–32), and New Orleans (1932–36). Afterwards he was general freight agent for the Chicago, Burlington and Quincy in Denver (1936–38) and St. Louis (1938–43). After active duty in World War II, Armstrong served as executive assistant from 1945 to 1948 with the Burlington lines. Finally, he served as vice president of the Fort Worth and Denver Railway Company (1948–62). He retired in December 1962. In addition to his connection with the Fort Worth and Denver, he was a director of the Houston Belt and Terminal Company of Dallas, and a member of the Board of Control of the Port Terminal Railroad Association of Houston.

The former military-school cadet was active in both world wars. He served overseas with the 142nd Infantry, Thirty-sixth Division, of the U.S. Army during World War I, and achieved the rank of lieutenant. During World War II he was commissioned a major in the Transportation Corps and then assigned to the Twenty-sixth Regulating Station as rail officer. He was awarded the Bronze Star for meritorious service overseas. He was also active in the National Guard.

Armstrong was a member of civic clubs in Fort Worth and Houston and the Western Railway Club of Chicago. He was active in the Fort Worth Chamber of Commerce and was president of the West Texas Chamber of Commerce from 1952 to 1954. In addition, he belonged to the Sons of the American Revolution and the Thirty-sixth Division Association (of which he was president in 1947–48). He also served from 1961 to 1966 on the board of directors of Texas Technological College (now Texas Tech University) and was chairman of that board from 1964 to 1966. Armstrong was a Methodist. He married Nannie Pauline Lusher on April 23, 1918, and they had three children.

BIBLIOGRAPHY: Seymour V. Connor, ed., *Builders of the Southwest* (Lubbock: Southwest Collection, Texas Technological College, 1959). Fort Worth *Star–Telegram*, August 7, 1949. Lubbock *Avalanche–Journal*, September 16, 1966. Vertical files, Center for American History, University of Texas at Austin.   *Michael Q. Hooks*

Arrington, Joseph Jr. Soul singer; b. Rogers, Texas, August 8, 1935; d. Navasota, Texas, August 12, 1982; son of Joseph and Cherie (Jackson) Arrington Sr. Arrington, who later took the pseudonyms Joe Tex and Yusef Hazziez, was taken to Baytown at the age of five by his mother, after her divorce from his father, and attended school there. While in Baytown, Arrington performed song and dance routines to enhance his business as a shoeshine and paper boy. He also sang in the G. W. Carver school choir and the McGowen Temple church choir.

During his junior year of high school he entered a talent search at a Houston nightclub. He took first prize over such performers as Johnny Nash, Hubert Laws, and Acquilla Cartwright, an imitator of Ben E. King. He performed a skit called "It's in the Book" and won $300 and a week's stay at the Hotel Teresa in Harlem. There, Arrington performed at the Apollo Theater. During a four-week period he won the Amateur Night competition four times. After graduating from high school in 1955, he returned to New York City to pursue a music career. While working odd jobs, including caretaking at a Jewish cemetery, he met talent scout Arthur Prysock, who paved the way for him to meet record-company executive Henry Glover and get his first record contract with King Records.

Arrington, now known as Joe Tex, introduced a style of music that has been copied by Isaac Hayes, Barry White, and others. In songs and ballads, in particular, he slowed the tempo slightly and started "rapping," that is, speaking verse that told the story in the middle of the song, before repeating the refrain and ending the song. The biggest hits of Joe Tex included "Hold On to What You Got," "Papa Was Too," "Skinny Legs and All," and *South Country*, an album of Country and Western songs; his biggest seller was "I Gotcha," which went platinum (made 1,000,000 sales) in 1971.

In 1972 Arrington gave up show business and began a three-year speaking ministry for the Nation of Islam, which he joined in 1968. He became known as Yusef Hazziez or Minister Joseph X. Arrington. He said he was through with singing, and he would follow Allah and Elijah Muhammad. But after Muhammad's death in 1975, and with the approval and blessing of the Nation of Islam, Arrington returned to show business in order to deliver the Nation of Islam's message to his fans. He achieved moderate success, with no hit singles, until the 1977 smash hit "I Ain't Gonna Bump no More (With no Big Fat Woman)" put him back on the top of the charts. After that, he left the music scene and performed at local clubs and benefits. Arrington died of heart failure at his home in Navasota. He was survived by his wife, Belilah, and six children.

BIBLIOGRAPHY: H. Wiley Hitchcock and Stanley Sadie, eds., *The New Grove Dictionary of American Music* (New York: Macmillan, 1986). Vertical files, Center for American History, University of Texas at Austin. "Westward," Dallas *Times Herald*, December 13, 1981.   *Kirvin Tillis*

Arthur, Charline. Honky-tonk musician; b. Charline Highsmith, in a railroad boxcar in Henrietta, Texas, September 2, 1929; d. in a trailer home in rural Idaho, November 27, 1987; second of twelve children of Jefferson Benjamin and Edna Mae (Wortham) Highsmith. Her father was a harmonica-playing Pentecostal preacher; and her mother sang and played piano and guitar.

The family moved to Paris, Texas, when she was four years old, and Charline was already showing musical talent at a young age. She made her first guitar out of a wooden cigar box when she was five. She sold soda bottles collected from the roadside to buy her first real guitar for six dollars two years later. She and her sister Dottie wowed audiences with their big voices when they performed at church, barn dances, and rodeos. Charline wrote her first song, "I've Got the Boogie Blues," at age twelve. She was inspired to start a musical career when she met Ernest Tubb, and she landed her first gig singing for radio station KPLT in Paris by the age of fifteen. When a traveling medicine show came to town, she left with it. Her act included slapstick comedy as well as country music. She married Jack Arthur on April 17, 1948, and he became her manager and bass player. Charline was not only a talented country vocalist; she also played lead guitar, rhythm guitar, fiddle, steel guitar, mandolin, piano, five-string banjo, and harmonica.

She was performing in Texas clubs and honky-tonks in 1949, when she recorded two songs for Bullet Records, one of which was "I've Got the Boogie Blues." She moved to Kermit, Texas, where she worked as a deejay and singer for KERB, and made a record for Imperial Records. There she was "discovered" by the legendary Colonel Tom Parker, who later managed Elvis Presley. He signed her with RCA Victor in January 1953. She recorded twenty-eight songs with RCA.

Charline's dynamic stage performances during this time were groundbreaking and controversial. She moved to Dallas to headline the "Big 'D' Jamboree," an unusual honor for a woman at the time. She was the first female country singer to perform on stage wearing pants, and was the only one photographed with a cigarette. While other female country performers stood demurely to sing, Charline pranced across stage, climbed on top of amplifiers, or sang lying down. Her shows were rowdy and sometimes racy. "I was shakin' that thing on stage," she said, "long before Elvis even thought about it." Her reputation as a hard-drinking, cigarette-smoking performer with a hot temper contrasted with that of gingham-dress-clad Kitty Wells. She also performed for the "Louisiana Hayride," Red Foley's "Ozark Jubilee," and the "Grand Ole Opry" (which censored her music). She toured with artists such as Elvis Presley, Johnny Cash, Roy Orbison, and Jerry Lee Lewis. In 1955 she was named runner-up (to Kitty Wells) as the year's Best Female Singer in *Country and Western Jamboree* magazine's DJ's Choice poll. Elvis Presley paid her tribute as "one of the finest entertainers on stage I've ever seen."

In spite of her entertaining stage presence, however, Charline's records were only moderately successful, and her relationship with RCA was tempestuous. She and RCA producer Chet Atkins had very vocal disagreements about what songs Charline should record, as well as about artistic style. She preferred bluesy, assertive, and sometimes sexually suggestive songs. Atkins attempted to mold her to the "Nashville Sound" of a subdued "prim and proper lady." Although Atkins won out, when her RCA contract expired in 1956, it was not renewed.

Her music career never recovered. She recorded several songs in her trailer home in Dallas for the Coin label in 1957. She separated from her husband about that time, and continued to play in honky-tonks and clubs throughout the western United States, later joined by her sisters Dottie, Bettie Sue, and Mary. In 1960 she found herself broke in Salt Lake City. Nightclub owner Ray Pellum helped her get a job at a club in Chubbuck, Idaho. For the next five years Charline performed there and recorded for Pellum's Eldorado Records. From 1965 to 1968 she performed at Myrtle's Club in Pocatello, Idaho. She continued playing in various clubs across the West, including Califor-

nia, and recording for small labels through the 1960s, '70s, and occasionally in the early '80's. Disillusioned with the music industry, she battled problems with alcohol and drugs and suffered from severe arthritis. During her last years she lived on a $335 monthly disability pension in a trailer home in rural Idaho. She died in her sleep of atherosclerosis and was buried in Fort Worth.

Charline's bluesy, rocking country sound, and her wild stage antics, are considered to have influenced Patsy Cline and Elvis Presley. She is now considered a precursor to rockabilly music. She was the first female country musician to attempt to express a unique, "unladylike" style that was not accepted in Nashville. Although she died in relative obscurity, recent CD releases have brought renewed interest in her: *Welcome to the Club* (Bear Family Records, 1986), a compilation of her work; and *The Gals of the Big 'D' Jamboree* (Dragon Street Records, 2001), which features her music. Charline Arthur is also one of the subjects of the PBS documentary *Welcome to the Club: The Women of Rockabilly*, directed by Beth Harrington.

BIBLIOGRAPHY: Bob Allen, "Charline Arthur," *Journal for the Society of the Preservation of Old Time Country Music* 1.3 (June 1991). Bob Allen and Colin Escott, notes to Charline Arthur's *Welcome to the Club* (Bear Family CD, 1986). Mary A. Bufwack and Robert K. Oermann, *Finding Her Voice: The Saga of Women in Country Music* (New York: Crown, 1993). Kevin Coffey, notes to *The Gals of the Big 'D' Jamboree* (Dragon Street Records, 2001). Paul Kingsbury, ed., *The Encyclopedia of Country Music: The Ultimate Guide to the Music* (Oxford University Press 1998). Emily Neely, "Up Beat Down South: Charline Arthur: The Unmaking of a Honky-Tonk Star," *Southern Cultures* 8.3 (Fall 2002). *Tresi Weeks*

Asbury, Samuel Erson. Chemist and Texas historian who proposed using music as a medium of historical narrative; b. Charlotte, North Carolina, September 26, 1872; d. Bryan, Texas, January 10, 1962 (buried in City Cemetery, College Station); one of eight children of Sidney Monroe and Felicia Swan (Woodward) Asbury. In the fall of 1889 Asbury enrolled at North Carolina State College of Agriculture and Engineering, at Raleigh, where he worked his way through school as a janitor in the chemistry building. He graduated in 1893 with a B.S. in chemistry and the next year was employed as an instructor in the chemistry department. At the same time he began work toward a master's degree, which he completed in 1896.

He became assistant state chemist in the North Carolina Experiment Station in 1895 and continued in this capacity until July 1897. During the ensuing years he worked as a chemist in a succession of jobs. He then returned to his old job in the North Carolina Experiment Station in 1899 and worked at the station until November 1, 1904, when he accepted the position of assistant state chemist with the Texas Agricultural Experiment Station on the campus of the Agricultural and Mechanical College of Texas (now Texas A&M University). He held this position until he retired partially in 1940 and completely in 1945. While at A&M he helped put his brothers and sisters through college. He also took a year's leave of absence to do advanced study in physical chemistry at Harvard. As assistant state chemist, Asbury tested seed, feed, and fertilizers and experimented with growing roses. By a judicious combination of aluminum sulfate and water, he succeeded in making roses grow to a height of more than forty feet.

Soon after coming to Texas, he became interested in the early history of the state and became a collector of Texana and of stories about early Texas leaders. After 1930 he became more and more absorbed in historical research; the Texas Revolution became his chief interest. He planned the production of a musical drama to tell the story of that event. In 1951 he published a pamphlet, entitled *Music as a Means of Historical Research*, in which he discussed music as a medium for the presentation of historical narrative. He proposed to produce an opera to interpret the Texas Revolution through a cycle of music dramas, but it was never completed. At the time of his death he held membership in the Southern Historical Association and was a fellow of the Texas State Historical Association. He was the author of one article and the editor of another in the *Southwestern Historical Quarterly*. He was a member of the Bryan–College Station Poetry Society. He attended the First Methodist Church in Bryan.

BIBLIOGRAPHY: Samuel Erson Asbury Papers, Center for American History, University of Texas at Austin. Samuel Erson Asbury Papers, University Archives, Texas A&M University. Austin *American*, October 17, 1952. *Battalion*, September 20, 1945; October 1, 1952. Bryan *Daily Eagle*, May 26, 1953; December 29, 1957; January 11, 12, 1962. Dallas *Morning News*, December 18, 1937. *Extension Service Farm News*, January 1938. Houston *Post*, January 12, 21, 1962. *Joseph Milton Nance*

Ashlock, Jesse. Fiddle player; b. 1915; d. Austin, August 9, 1976. Ashlock started playing violin at age nine. In 1930 he began going to the Crystal Springs Club in Fort Worth, where the Bob Wills Fiddle Band played. Wills bought Jesse a fiddle, taught him to play, and included him in a few of the band's performances at Crystal Springs. In 1932 Ashlock joined Milton Brown and His Musical Brownies. Brown was Wills's chief competition in Western Swing.

In 1935 Ashlock joined Wills's Original Texas Playboys as a fiddle player. He stayed with Bob Wills throughout the rest of Wills's career and continued playing shows until three days before his death. While playing for Wills he became an integral part of the band. He was known as a practical joker. He once told Bob Wills during a performance that his pants were unzipped, causing Bob to stop playing his chorus and double over trying to cover up the offending opening. During his career with Wills, Ashlock was also involved with the movies that Wills made.

Ashlock's playing style had its roots in jazz. His fiddle style was characterized by hot breaks and hot choruses. His idol was jazz violinist Joe Venuti. Ashlock's attempt to play his fiddle like a horn earned him placement in the category of the "hot fiddlers." He moved from Claremore, Oklahoma, to Austin the year before his death. At the age of sixty-one he had performed at the Broken Spoke, a country and western club, three days before his death from cancer.

Dan Del Santo playing with Johnny Gimble on "Austin City Limits," 1979. The promotional description for this program describes Del Santo's music as "jazzy arrangements with traditional materials." Photograph by Scott Newton/Austin City Limits.

BIBLIOGRAPHY: Charles R. Townsend, *San Antonio Rose: The Life and Music of Bob Wills* (Urbana: University of Illinois Press, 1976). Vertical files, Center for American History, University of Texas at Austin.

Matthew Douglas Moore

"Austin City Limits." A television program of concert performances featuring uniquely American styles of music; founded in 1974 by PBS affiliate KLRN–TV (later KLRU–TV) in Austin and carried by hundreds of stations nationwide. The program has showcased performers such as Jimmy Buffett, Rosanne Cash, Ray Charles, Leonard Cohen, B. B. King, Lyle Lovett, Willie Nelson, Roy Orbison, Bonnie Raitt, George Strait, and Tanya Tucker. The show's success was credited with contributing to the rise of several major country performers and coincided with the growing popularity of country music.

The program, known particularly for its "redneck rock" or "progressive country" music, resulted in the mid-1970s from the desire of Bill Arhos, then program director at KLRN, to develop locally produced programming that could attract national attention. With producer Paul Bosner and director Bruce Scafe, Arhos approached PBS's Station Program Cooperative (a program fostered by the network to help individual system stations produce national programming) for funding for a pilot program. Despite resistance from KLRN upper management, the SPC granted support in 1974. The initial show starred Willie Nelson and was an immediate success. Arhos and Bosner sold the show to PBS by convincing station executives, accustomed to shows like "Masterpiece Theater" and "Sesame Street," that "Austin City Limits" was not too far outside the mainstream.

In 1975 Arhos persuaded Greg Harney, program acquisition head for the PBS's annual national membership drive, to show the pilot at the Station Independence Project meeting, a forum for planning the next year's national pledge drive. Thirty-four stations aired the show; subsequently, PBS and Arhos agreed that if five stations would support it, the program could remain in the market for at least a year. With the help of KQED–TV in San Francisco, Arhos got the five stations only minutes before the network deadline. Videotaping began in September 1975 with a reunion of Bob Wills's Original Texas Playboys. Despite technical glitches and limited audiences, the 1976 season defined the show's unique "progressive country" style, a combination of traditional country music with folk and rock influences that flourished in Austin at that time. The show drew on this growing Austin music scene, challenged the dominance of Nashville, and later competed with MTV, the Nashville Network, and Country Music Television. Although "progressive country" and mainstream country have been staples of the program, it has also featured an eclectic mix of American music: jazz, blues, and folk.

Program highlights have included the premiere of the "Austin City Limits" theme song (Gary P. Nunn's "London Homesick Blues") and the return of Willie Nelson's album *Red-Headed Stranger* to the *Billboard* charts for forty-eight weeks after his performance on the show (both in 1977); appearances by Ray Charles and Chet Atkins (1979); the adoption of the Austin-skyline backdrop (1981); and the three-hour special *Down Home Country Music*, which won Best Network Music Program in the New York International Film and Television Festival (1982). Other high points have been the tenth-anniversary show taping, featuring the Texas Playboys, before an open-air crowd of more than 5,000 in Austin (1984); the first all-female "Songwriters Special" (with Emmylou Harris, Rosanne Cash, and others) and the first show appearance by Fats Domino (both in 1986); appearances by Johnny Cash and by Reba McEntire (both in 1987); Garth Brooks's first appearance on the show (1990); the featuring of Nanci Griffith, the Indigo Girls, Mary Chapin Carpenter, and Julie Gold in another "Songwriters Special" (1992); and appearances by humorist Garrison Keillor and the Hopeful Gospel Quartet (1993).

After losing Budweiser as an underwriter in 1990, "Austin City Limits" faced a declining PBS budget and network demands that the series raise more than a quarter of its own funding. Performers on the show have always been paid on a union scale. In 2003, advertising its content as

Uncle Walt's Band (left to right: Walter Hyatt, David Ball, Deschamps "Champ" Hood) performing on "Austin City Limits," 1980. Photograph by Scott Newton/Austin City Limits.

"live music, pure and simple," the show was sponsored by such companies as Chevrolet and Michelob. By its nineteenth network season (1993), "Austin City Limits" was focusing less on mainstream country music and more on songwriters and the "new folk movement," and had introduced a variety of new formats to supplement its traditional stage-show settings.

"Austin City Limits" produced an enormously successful Tribute to Stevie Ray Vaughan in 1995, which featured B. B. King, Buddy Guy, Bonnie Raitt, Eric Clapton, and others. The show also filmed a memorable tribute to Townes Van Zandt in late 1997 that included Willie Nelson, Guy Clark, Lyle Lovett, and Nanci Griffith. In 2000, after facing competition from other music programming on public television such as New York City's "Sessions at West 54th," producers made the decision to offer "Austin City Limits" to PBS affiliates free of charge. By 2003 "Austin City Limits" was in its twenty-eighth season and had featured hundreds of artists performing in such genres as zydeco and Tejano, in addition to its foundation of folk–rock–country–bluegrass. Longtime producer and program director Terry Lickona had been with the show since the mid-1970s.

BIBLIOGRAPHY: Austin *American–Statesman*, January 14, 1993. Austin City Limits homepage (http://www.pbs.org/klru/austin/about/index.html), accessed February 27, 2003. John T. Davis, *Austin City Limits: 25 Years of American Music* (New York: Billboard, 2000). Clifford Endres, *Austin City Limits* (Austin: University of Texas Press, 1987). Houston *Chronicle*, January 14, 1990.

Damon Arhos

During World War II, recording and movie star Gene Autry enlisted in the Army Air Corps and served as a technical sergeant assigned to various duties such as riding in the Washington Birthday Celebration Parade in Laredo, Texas, February 22, 1943. Texas State Library and Archives Commission.

Austin, Gene. Singer and composer; b. Eugene Lucas, Gainesville, Texas, June 24, 1900; d. Palm Springs, California, January 24, 1972; son of Serena Belle (Harrell) Lucas. Eugene took the surname of his stepfather, Jim Austin. He grew up in small towns in Louisiana, joined the United States Army when he was fifteen, participated in the expedition sent to capture Pancho Villa in 1916, and served in France during World War I. He studied both dentistry and law in Baltimore, but decided on a singing career. Though he composed more than 100 songs, Austin never learned to read music. He was one of the original crooners, and his tenor voice was well known in the early days of radio and on the hand-cranked phonographs of the 1920s and 1930s. His RCA Victor recordings sold a total of more than 86 million copies; one of the recordings, "My Blue Heaven" (1927), sold over 12 million records.

Austin started his recording career in 1923, and the next year Jimmy McHugh produced his first hit song, "When My Sugar Walks Down the Street," with lyrics by Austin and Irving Mills. Other hit songs Austin introduced were "My Melancholy Baby," "Girl of My Dreams," "Ramona," "Carolina Moon," and "Sleepy Time Gal." His compositions included "How Come You Do Me Like You Do?" and "Lonesome Road." Austin debuted in the movies in 1932 and ultimately made three: *Sadie McKee,*

Gift of Gab, and *Melody Cruise.* Over the years he was also featured on numerous radio programs. In 1939 he began working with Billy Wehle in a musical-comedy tent show that spent the winter in Gainesville and opened in 1940 during the Circus Roundup of the Gainesville Community Circus.

Austin was a nightclub entertainer in the 1930s, but then his career waned. After his life was dramatized in a television special in the late 1950s, he resumed nightclub appearances. He continued to write songs until the last ten months of his life, when he developed lung cancer. Austin spent most of his adult life in Las Vegas, Nevada, and in 1962 he ran for governor there, but lost badly to the incumbent, Grant Sawyer. He was married five times. He was survived by his wife Gigi and two daughters from a previous marriage.

BIBLIOGRAPHY: Austin *American–Statesman,* January 25, 1972. Dallas *Morning News,* August 6, 1956. New York *Times,* January 24, 1972. *Newsweek,* May 6, 1957. *Saturday Evening Post,* August 31, 1957.

Autry, Gene. Movie star known as the "Singing Cowboy"; b. Tioga, Texas, September 29, 1907; d. Los Angeles, October 3, 1998; first child of cattle rancher Delbert Autry. A few years after his birth, the family moved to Ravia, Oklahoma. At age five Gene began singing in the church choir where his grandfather was a minister. At the age of twelve he received his first guitar lessons from his mother on an instrument ordered from the Sears and Roebuck catalog. As a young man, Autry was hired to work as a telegraph operator for the Frisco Railroad in Chelsea, Oklahoma. One evening in 1927, during Autry's shift, Will Rogers overheard the young telegraph operator singing and playing guitar. Rogers was so impressed that he suggested Autry move to New York and try to find work on radio. Autry heeded Rogers's advice and left for New York. However, he was unable to establish a successful radio career and soon returned to Oklahoma.

In Tulsa, Autry was billed as the "Oklahoma Yodeling Cowboy" on local radio station KVOO. In 1929 he signed his first record deal and returned to New York. Two years later he recorded his first hit, "That Silver-Haired Daddy of Mine," which eventually sold a million copies. The recording set an industry record for sales and became part of the first album in history to go gold. The next year Autry married Ina Spivey, a schoolteacher from Oklahoma. In 1934 he began his Hollywood career as a singing cowboy in the B western movie *In Old Santa Fe*, starring Ken Maynard. The following year, Autry played the lead in another western named after his hit song "Tumbling Tumbleweeds." By 1942 he had established a successful career in recording, touring, and moviemaking. All of these projects were put on hold, however, when he enlisted in the Army Air Corps during World War II. Autry returned in 1946 to his singing and acting career. He also began to invest some of his new-found fortune in television, radio, real estate, and other ventures. In addition, he formed his own publishing company in order to retain the rights to all of his songs.

As the popularity of B westerns declined, Autry soon broke new ground as the first film actor ever to become a major television star. In 1949 he recorded "Rudolph the Red-Nosed Reindeer," which became the first record in history to go platinum. In 1960 he expanded his financial empire further by purchasing the California Angels baseball franchise. In 1978 he published his autobiography, *Back in the Saddle Again*. In 1981, following the death of his first wife, Autry married Jackie Ellam. He sold 25 percent of his baseball franchise to the Disney Corporation in 1995. When he died at home at the age of 91, he had earned an unprecedented five stars on the Hollywood Walk of Fame.

BIBLIOGRAPHY: *Daily Variety*, October 5, 1998. *Hollywood Reporter*, October 5, 1998.   *Jarad Brown*

Aves, Dreda. Operatic soprano; b. Etheldreda Aves, Norwalk, Ohio, 1890s; d. Newark, Ohio, April 17, 1942; daughter of Rev. Charles S. and Jessie Olivia (Hughes) Aves. Dreda was taken as a child to Galveston, where her father was rector of Trinity Episcopal Church. She first studied singing with H. T. Huffmeister, director of the Galveston Choral Club and organist at her father's church. Her father reportedly had "vigorous moral objections" to Dreda's singing in public, with the result that she sang only at church services until she left Texas. She attended the University of Texas in 1913–14, during which time Madame Ernestine Schumann-Heink, a renowned contralto, encouraged her to study in the East. Aves attended Columbia University in 1916 and studied for two years at the Damrosch Institute of Musical Art in New York.

She debuted with the De Foe Carlin Opera Company in the title role of *Carmen* in Baltimore in 1922. She sang for a season with the Havana Opera Company, toured with the San Carlo Opera Company in 1924 and 1925, and was a guest artist with the Philadelphia Civic Opera in 1927 and the Dresden Opera in 1928. Although she began her career as a contralto, with the advice and help of Vilonat, her last teacher, she became a dramatic soprano. Aves joined the Metropolitan Opera in 1927 and made her debut there in *Aïda* in 1928. She remained with the Metropolitan through the end of the 1931–32 season and later sang with the San Carlo Opera, an American touring company. During her career she also appeared with the Friends of Music (New York), the Detroit Symphony Orchestra, the Cleveland Symphony Orchestra, and other groups. She moved from New York City to Buckeye Lake in Ohio in 1940 or 1941. She died after an illness of several months and was survived by three brothers and a sister.

BIBLIOGRAPHY: *Alcalde* (magazine of the Ex-Students' Association of the University of Texas), April 1928. *Musical America*, April 25, 1942. New York *Times*, April 18, 1942. *Who Was Who in America*, Vol. 2.   *Mary M. Standifer*

B

Babasin, Harry. Jazz musician; b. Dallas, March 19, 1921; d. California, May 21, 1988. His father was a dentist who had immigrated to Texas from Armenia, and his mother was a Texas native who taught music at the public school in Vernon, Texas. Harry was eventually featured on more than 1,500 recordings.

Harry "the Bear" grew up in Vernon, became intrigued with music at a young age, and became proficient on numerous instruments. In high school he played bassoon, bass, cello, and clarinet. After graduating he enrolled at North Texas State Teachers College, Denton, where he was first introduced to jazz. He and his friend Herb Ellis often attended jazz concerts and showcases. At one such show in 1942 they saw the Charlie Fisk Orchestra, and, confident in their musicianship, told Fisk afterward that they could outplay any member of his orchestra. When Fisk asked them to prove it, Ellis and Babasin embarked on a staggering bit of showmanship. Impressed, Fisk hired them. A few months later, Babasin joined the Jimmy Joy Orchestra and was based in Chicago while he toured the Midwest.

In 1943 he joined the Bob Strong Orchestra and headed to New York City. He also worked with various other groups on the scene, including Gene Krupa and Boyd Raeburn, with whom he recorded *Boyd Meets Stravinsky*. He joined up with Charlie Barnet, with whom he moved to California in 1945.

Situated in Los Angeles, Babasin continued to work with several musicians, including Benny Goodman, Charlie Parker, Louis Armstrong, and Chet Baker. In 1947 he appeared in the movie *A Song Is Born*, which starred Danny Kaye and Virginia Mayo. During the filming, Babasin began experimenting with playing the cello in the role of the bass. This led to his development of the pizzicato jazz cello, possibly his most significant contribution to jazz. He recorded the first-ever jazz cello tracks with the Dodo Marmarosa Trio in December 3, 1947, which can be heard on the CD *Up in Dodo's Room*. While on the movie set, he also met a Brazilian musician, Laurindo Almeida, and this association led to another pioneering effort, the first "bossa nova" jazz recordings, in 1954. This fusion of modern jazz with traditional Brazilian rhythms was released on two LPs that were later remastered into a compilation entitled *Brazilliance, Volume 1*.

Throughout the 1950s and 1960s, Babasin freelanced for radio and television and served as a session player. He and drummer Roy Harte formed their own record company, Nocturne Records, in the early 1950s and went on to produce ten albums. Babasin also formed his own ensemble, the Jazz Pickers. In 1974 he helped to establish the Los Angeles Theaseum, an archive specializing in the preservation of jazz and other music recordings as well as instruments and other artifacts donated by musicians. Babasin died of emphysema.

BIBLIOGRAPHY: Leonard Feather and Ira Gitler, *Biographical Encyclopedia of Jazz* (New York: Oxford University Press, 1999). *Harry "the Bear" Babasin* (http://www.onoffon.com/harrythebear.html), accessed February 6, 2003. Chuck Kelly, "Talking Jazz with Harry Babasin: An Interview," *International Musician* 80.7 (January 1982). Dave Oliphant, *Texan Jazz* (Austin: University of Texas Press, 1996). *Bradley Shreve*

Bacas of Fayetteville. The first Baca Family Band—a Czech musical group—was formed in 1892 in Fayetteville, Texas, by Frank Baca. Prior to this, Frank had been a member of the Fayetteville city band and a member of an informal family band. These groups performed traditional Czech polka and waltz music. In addition to attracting the talents of all thirteen of Frank Baca's children, the Baca Family Band drew participants from around Central Texas. Upon Frank's death in 1907 his son Joe, who had won local and national cornet competitions, assumed leadership of the band. Demand for the group throughout the area as entertainment for festivals and special events increased. Among the most notable of their appearances was the band's participation in an enormous celebration at the Fayetteville SPJST (Slavonic Benevolent Order of the State of Texas) at the end of World War I.

In 1920 Joe Baca died and his brother John assumed leadership of the band. Under John, the Baca Band played on Houston radio station KPRC in 1926, and made phonograph recordings on the Okeh, Columbia, and Brunswick labels during the 1930s. By 1937, two other Baca bands had appeared apart from the original group led by John Baca. Ray Baca's "New Deal" Band and the L. B. Baca Band entertained audiences across the state. Although the Baca Band had already made plans for a national tour in 1907 (canceled by the death of Frank Baca), the band did not make its first out-of-state appearance until 1968, when it performed at the Smithsonian Institution's American Folklife Festival. The Bacas of Fayetteville remain the state's best-known family Czech folk band.

BIBLIOGRAPHY: W. Phil Hewitt, *The Czech Texans* (San Antonio: University of Texas Institute of Texan Cultures, 1983). Clinton Machann and James W. Mendl, *Krasna Amerika: A Study of the Texas Czechs, 1851–1939* (Austin: Eakin Press, 1983). *Brandy Schnautz*

Bailey, Mollie Arline Kirkland. "Circus Queen of the Southwest"; b. on a plantation near Mobile, Alabama, probably on November 2, 1844; d. Houston, October 2, 1918 (buried there in Hollywood Cemetery); daughter of William and Mary Arline Kirkland. As a young woman she eloped with James A. (Gus) Bailey, who played the cornet in his father's circus band, and was married on March 21, 1858. With Mollie's sister Fanny and Gus's brother Alfred, the young couple formed the Bailey Family Troupe, which traveled through Alabama, Mississippi, and Arkansas acting, dancing, and singing.

In the Civil War, Gus served as bandmaster for a company of Hood's Texas Brigade. Leaving their child Dixie, the first of nine children, with friends in Richmond, Virginia, Mollie traveled with the brigade as a nurse and, according to some sources, as a spy for Gen. John Bell Hood and Jubal A. Early. Mrs. Bailey disguised herself as an elderly woman, passed through Federal camps pretending to be a cookie seller, and claimed to have taken quinine through enemy lines by hiding packets of it in her hair. She joined her husband and brother-in-law in Hood's Minstrels and on April 5, 1864, performed a "musical and dancing program" with them near Zillicoffer. During this period Gus wrote the words for "The Old Gray Mare," based on a horse who almost died after eating green corn but revived when given medicine. A friend set it to music, and it was played as a regimental marching song. It was later used as the official song of the Democratic national convention of 1928; the West Texas Chamber of Commerce named its Old Gray Mare Band after the song. When the war was over, the couple traveled throughout the South and then toured by riverboat with the Bailey Concert Company.

Their career in Texas began in 1879 when the troupe traded the showboat for a small circus that enjoyed immediate success as the Bailey Circus, "A Texas Show for Texas People." The show became the Mollie A. Bailey Show after Gus's health forced him to retire to winter quarters in Blum, Texas. Mollie came to be known as "Aunt Mollie." Her circus was distinguished by the United States, Lone Star, and Confederate flags that flew over the bigtop and Mollie's practice of giving war veterans, Union or Confederate, free tickets. At its height, the one-ring tent circus had thirty-one wagons and about 200 animals; it added elephant and camel acts in 1902.

After her husband's death in 1896, Mollie Bailey continued in the business, buying lots in many places where the circus performed to eliminate the high "occupation" taxes levied on shows by most towns. When the circus moved on, she allowed these lots to be used for ball games and camp meetings and later let many of them revert to the towns. She is also credited for her generosity to various churches and for allowing poor children to attend the circus free. In 1906, when the circus began traveling by railroad, Bailey entertained such distinguished guests as governors James Stephen Hogg and Oscar Branch Colquitt and senators Joseph Weldon Bailey and Morris Sheppard, along with members of Hood's Brigade, in a finely appointed parlor car. She was also said to be a friend of Comanche chief Quanah Parker.

In 1906 she married A. H. (Blackie) Hardesty, a much younger man, who managed the circus gas lights and who was subsequently known as Blackie Bailey. According to some sources, Mollie Bailey showed the first motion pictures in Texas in a separate circus tent, including a one-reel film of the sinking of the USS *Maine*. After her youngest child, Birda, died in 1917, Mollie ran the circus from home, communicating with the road by telegram and letter. She was survived for nineteen years by her husband, who became a jitney driver between Houston and Goose Creek and resided in Baytown.

BIBLIOGRAPHY: Francis Edward Abernethy, ed., *Legendary Ladies of Texas*, Publications of the Texas Folklore Society 43 (Dallas: E-Heart, 1981). Olga Bailey, *Mollie Bailey: The Circus Queen of the Southwest*, ed. Bess Samuel Ayres (Dallas: Harben–Spotts, 1943). Marj Gurasich, *Red Wagons and White Canvas: A Story of the Mollie Bailey Circus* (Austin: Eakin Press, 1988). *Diana J. Kleiner*

Ballew, Smith. Singer, actor, and bandleader; b. Sykes Ballew, Palestine, Texas, January 21, 1902; d. Longview, Texas, May 2, 1984 (buried in Fort Worth); son of May and William Y. Ballew. After attending Sherman High School in Sherman, Ballew attended Austin College and the University of Texas from 1920 to 1922. At UT he organized a jazz combo, Jimmie's Joys, in which he first played banjo and later became the vocalist. He left the university after the fall 1922 semester, and continued with the combo until forming the Texajazzers in March 1925.

By then primarily a vocalist, Ballew accepted work with a number of noted bandleaders, including Ted Weems, Hal Kemp, and Tommy and Jimmy Dorsey. In 1929 he organized the Smith Ballew Orchestra, which highlighted his singing and included associations with jazzmen such as Glenn Miller and Bunny Berigan. In the same year he signed his first recording contract, with Okeh Records of Chicago. Ballew's recording career as vocalist and bandleader spanned some twenty years, during which he cut records for more than thirty labels, including Okeh, Victor, Brunswick, Columbia, and Decca.

From 1936 to 1950 he mixed an acting career with singing. In 1936, after moving his family to Hollywood and landing a contract with Paramount Pictures, he made his acting debut in the motion picture *Palm Springs*. He appeared in twenty-four films, primarily Westerns. Among his pictures were *Western Gold* (1937), *Roll Along Cowboy* (1937), *Under Arizona Skies* (1946), *Panamint's Bad Man* (1938), *Hawaiian Buckeroos* (1938), and *The Red Badge of Courage* (1951). During World War II, as his singing and film career waned, and until his retirement in 1967, Ballew worked in the aircraft industry, including stints at Northrup and at Convair (which later became part of General Dynamics). In 1952, after living in California and Arizona, he settled in Fort Worth. He was married twice, first in 1924 to Justine Vera, with whom he had a daughter. Justine died in 1960, and that same year Ballew married Mary Ruth Clark, who died in 1972.

BIBLIOGRAPHY: Geoffrey J. Orr, *Texas Troubador: A Bio-Discography of the Life and Times of Smith Ballew, 1902–1984* (Melbourne: Exact Science Press, 1985).

John H. Slate

Barclay, William Archibald. Organist and professor of organ; b. Temple, Texas, February 26, 1907; d. Fort Worth, January 28, 1969; son of Rigsby Ledbetter and Louzelle Rose Barclay. Gifted from his earliest days, Barclay began playing the piano almost as soon as his hands could reach the keys. His mother, a talented pianist and organist, was his first piano teacher. On the organ, Barclay began with Mrs. W. A. Harrell in Temple. As a teenager he traveled alone on the train to Dallas to study under Harold Van Katwick.

Barclay had the ability to play by ear any music he heard. As a result, he played in church as early as age ten. He entered Burleson College in Greenville, Texas, the year he graduated from Temple High School (1923). The next year, he transferred to Baylor University in Waco, from which he graduated in 1927. During the summers he studied in New York—at Columbia University, and at Guilmant Organ School with William Carl and Ernest Hutchinson. After graduation, Barclay moved to Fort Worth, where he accepted the position of professor of organ at Southwestern Baptist Theological Seminary. He was well liked by the students, and his performances were always well attended. One commentator at a commencement service for which Barclay played wrote, "President Scarborough presided, Prof. I. E. Reynolds had charge of the music and Prof. William Barclay was at the pipe organ. How that boy can play! He gets a wonderful amount of music out of that great instrument."

Barclay had come to the seminary as a result of his friendship with I. E. Reynolds, director of the School of Gospel Music. He remained with the seminary from 1928 to 1948. He held numerous other positions in and around Fort Worth, including: staff organist, WBAP radio, Fort Worth (1928–42); professor of organ, Trinity University, Waxahachie (1933–36); organist, Hemphill Presbyterian Church, Fort Worth (1933–36); organist, First Presbyterian Church, Fort Worth (1942–46); minister of music, First Presbyterian Church, Fort Worth (1946–69); staff organist, WBAP TV, Fort Worth (1949–53); and "director of serious music," WBAP FM, Fort Worth (1955–57). Barclay was married in 1948 to Dora Poteet. The couple had no children. At the time of his death, Barclay was married to a woman named Louise. He died of cancer and was buried in the family plot in Temple.

BIBLIOGRAPHY: Fort Worth *Star–Telegram*, January 29, 1969. F. M. McConnell, "Seminary Commencement," *Baptist Standard*, May 29, 1930. William J. Reynolds, *The Cross & the Lyre: The Story of the School of Church Music, Southwestern Baptist Theological Seminary, Fort Worth, Texas* (Southwestern Baptist Theological Seminary, 1994). Vertical files, Archives and Special Collections Department, Roberts Library, Southwestern Baptist Theological Seminary, Fort Worth.   *Michael Pullin*

Baromeo, Chase. Operatic bass-baritone; b. Chase Baromeo Sikes, Augusta, Georgia, August 19, 1892; d. Birmingham, Michigan, August 7, 1973; son of Clarence Stevens and Medora (Rhodes) Sikes. He received B.A. (1917) and M.M. (1929) degrees from the University of Michigan. Before going to the University of Texas in 1938 to head the voice faculty in the music department of the new College of Fine Arts, he had a highly successful operatic career. He made his debut in 1923 at the Teatro Carcano in Milan. From 1923 to 1926 he was a member of La Scala in Milan, where he sang under Arturo Toscanini.

Because of the Italians' difficulty in pronouncing his last name, Sikes became known professionally as Chase

Baromeo, and he used that name for the rest of his life. He also sang at the Teatro Colón in Buenos Aires in 1924, with the Chicago Civic Opera Company from 1926 to 1931, and with the San Francisco Opera Company in 1935. From 1935 to 1938 he was with the Metropolitan Opera Company in New York. He also performed with many of the leading symphony orchestras in the United States. He was married to Delphie Lindstrom on May 12, 1931; they had three children, one of whom predeceased him. At UT, Baromeo directed and performed in many university-staged operas. He left the university in 1954 to join the University of Michigan faculty.

BIBLIOGRAPHY: Austin *American–Statesman*, August 8, 1973. Vertical files, Center for American History, University of Texas at Austin.   *Eldon S. Branda*

Baxter, J. R. Gospel music composer and publisher; b. Jesse Randall Baxter Jr., Lebanon, Alabama, December 8, 1887; d. January 21, 1960. Baxter, a "Sand Mountain native," was a prolific song composer and co-founder of the Stamps–Baxter Music Company. He was known as "Pap" to his close friends. He learned the fundamentals of harmony and gospel music from T. B. Mosley and A. J. Showalter, and began teaching while he was still a student. He subsequently learned hymn writing from James Rowe, Charles H. Gabriel, and others. By 1943 he had composed more than 500 songs; by the time of his death his song lyrics numbered in the thousands. Several gospel quartets were named for him. As a publisher, he put out thousands of songs and sold hundreds of thousands of songbooks. Numerous singers and directors learned from him.

In 1918 Baxter married Clarice Howard, later called "Ma" Baxter. Not long afterward, Baxter became manager of the A. J. Showalter office in Texarkana, Texas. In 1926 he and V. O. Stamps started the Stamps–Baxter Company, which had offices in Chattanooga, Tennessee; Jacksonville, Texas; and, later, Pangburn, Arkansas. Stamps–Baxter, which published hymnals and sponsored traveling quartets and radio programs, grew to be the world's largest gospel music business. After Stamps died (1940), Baxter moved the business headquarters to Dallas and became president and general manager, a position he held until his death.

BIBLIOGRAPHY: Mrs. J. R. (Ma) Baxter and Videt Polk, comps., *Gospel Song Writers Biography* (Dallas: Stamps–Baxter Music and Printing Company, 1971). Shirley L. Beary, The Stamps–Baxter Music and Printing Company: A Continuing Tradition, 1926–1976 (D.M.A. dissertation, Southwestern Baptist Theological Seminary, 1977).
          Greg Self

Beard, Dean. Rockabilly pioneer; b. Santa Anna, Texas, August 31, 1935; d. Coleman, Texas, April 4, 1989; son of Raymond and Opal (Baker) Beard. He was sometimes called the "West Texas Wild Man" because of his frantic stage presence and piano-playing style.

Beard, a lifelong resident of Coleman County, moved to Coleman in 1953 and graduated from Coleman High School. While in high school, he started doing session work in Abilene for Key City media mogul and record producer Slim Willet. He briefly attended Tarleton State College, but soon opted to pursue a music career. He made his first recordings in 1955 in Abilene with the Fox Four Sevens. The same year he shared the stage with Elvis Presley, whose star was rising. The two became friends, and they spent a day together in Coleman, where Presley's Cadillac created quite a stir.

Intent on duplicating Presley's success, Beard cut two demo sessions in Memphis for Sun Records in 1956, but Sam Phillips decided not to sign him. One of the demos was "Rakin' and Scrapin'," which Beard recorded again the next year in Abilene for Willet's Edmoral label. His popular West Texas band, Dean Beard and the Crew Cats, included area teenagers Jimmy Seals and Dash Crofts. A tenor sax and piano–driven pounder, "Rakin' and Scrapin'" was leased to Atlantic Records for national distribution but failed to break out. A high energy follow-up on Atlantic, "Party Party," suffered a similar fate.

In 1958 Beard, along with Seals and Crofts, joined the Champs (of "Tequila" fame) and journeyed to the West Coast. After recording several sessions with the group for Challenge Records, he was fired and returned to Texas in 1959. Beard continued to record for Slim Willet and then for a variety of other small labels throughout the 1960s. He remained a popular live act into the 1970s, despite having to battle crippling arthritis, the results of an auto accident that broke his back.

BIBLIOGRAPHY: Coleman *Chronicle & Democratic–Voice*, April 6, 1989. Clay Glover, "The Legend of Dean Beard," *Rockin' Fifties* 52 (June 1994). Wayne Russell, "Dean Beard," *New Kommotion* 23 (1980). Abilene *Reporter–News*, April 11, 1989.   *Joe W. Specht*

Beck, Carl. Choir, orchestra, and band conductor; b. Ilmenau, Thuringia, April 26, 1850; d. San Antonio, October 2, 1920; first name appears as Karl in some sources. Beck was educated as a musician in Germany, came to the United States as part of a music group in 1875, and settled in New Orleans. In May 1884 he moved to San Antonio to become conductor of the Beethoven Männerchor and the Mendelssohn Mixed Chorus. An energetic and progressive leader, Beck conducted excerpts from Richard Wagner's *Tannhäuser* and *Lohengrin* at the 1885 State Sängerfest in Houston. This may have been the first performance of Wagner in Texas. When San Antonio hosted the festival in 1887, Beck organized a forty-six-member orchestra that performed Mendelssohn's *Italian Symphony*, possibly the first complete symphony to be heard in Texas.

Beck had an orchestra of more than two dozen players to complement his choruses and also to perform independently. The orchestra played a subscription series of six concerts at Muth's Garden in 1894, with concertmaster Wilhelm Marx as soloist. The need for a concert hall was satisfied in 1895, when the Beethoven Männerchor built the 1,200-seat Beethoven Hall on South Alamo Street. Beck programmed the music of Wagner whenever he could muster the forces necessary. During the 1896 State Sängerfest, hosted by the Beethoven Männerchor, he presented four concerts that included six Wagnerian works, in addition to music by Verdi, Beethoven, Saint-Saëns, Weber, and Grieg. The combined forces united to perform the

"Spring" section of Haydn's oratorio *The Seasons*. By the 1890s Beck had also developed an accomplished band, an addition that enabled him to promote popular music. Even with the band, Beck programmed Wagner in potpourri arrangements, and a wider audience than usual came to hear the performances.

In 1904, after twenty years in San Antonio, he moved to Odessa, where he organized a band of fourteen members that played from Toyah to Abilene. When enthusiasm waned, Beck moved to Pecos and later to Kingsville. In July 1919, after Arthur Claassen had left San Antonio, Beck again accepted conductorship of the Beethoven Männerchor and returned to the Alamo City.

BIBLIOGRAPHY: Theodore Albrecht, "101 Years of Symphonic Music in San Antonio," *Southwestern Musician / Texas Music Educator*, March, November 1975.
Theodore Albrecht

Beckham, Garland Wayne. Country music journalist, photographer, and publisher; b. Lantham, Kansas, March 21, 1929; d. Arlington, Texas, October 15, 2001; son of William Charles and Viola Beckham. He began his publishing career at the age of twelve working in the press room of the *Daily Oklahoman*. Beckham served in the United States Navy during World War II and afterwards in the Norfolk, Virginia, press room of NATO.

During the 1960s and 1970s he worked in the Fort Worth area as a publisher and photojournalist and also owned his own talent agency, Way-Beck Talent. In addition to publishing the magazine *Country Music Reporter*, Beckham was a staff photographer at Panther Hall, one of the Dallas–Fort Worth area's most popular dance halls of the time. He photographed numerous country music performers both on and off stage at Panther Hall, including Willie Nelson, Charley Pride, Bob Wills, and Tanya Tucker. He also played harmonica and occasionally sat in with some of the bands at Panther Hall.

Beckham died of congestive heart failure at Arlington Memorial Hospital and is buried at the DFW National Cemetery in Dallas. He was survived by his father, William Charles Beckham, a daughter, Patricia Jo McCubbin, and four sons, Larry Wayne, William Charles, Donald Ned, and Patrick James. Beckham's collection of photos and other related materials is archived at Southwest Texas State University in San Marcos.

BIBLIOGRAPHY: Fort Worth *Star-Telegram*, October 18, 2001.   *Gary Hartman*

Beers, Iola Barns. Civic leader and music patron; b. New Orleans, December 17, 1852; d. Galveston, November 13, 1925; daughter of Thomas and Antoinette Barns. She moved to Galveston with her parents in 1875 and in 1879 or 1880 married William Francis Beers, a Galveston insurance agent and civic leader. They had one son.

In 1890 Iola Beers founded the Girl's Musical Club in Galveston, which, with the aid of trained musicians, educated talented young women and assisted them in their musical studies regardless of income. The club presented concerts and held biweekly meetings to study the history of music and the work of great composers. Galveston's example became the model for the Girl's Musical Club of Houston, founded by a Galveston member. Mrs. Beers also served on the executive committee of the Ladies' Musical Club of Galveston.

She represented Texas at the Chicago World's Fair in 1893 and later was on the Texas committee at the St. Louis World's Fair. She raised $2,000 for the Galveston public school's representation at the Chicago fair. In addition she raised $5,000 for equipment for the Galveston public schools through such productions as *H.M.S. Pinafore*, performed at the Grand Opera House. After the Galveston hurricane of 1900, she joined the relief efforts of the American Red Cross Association. Clara Barton appointed her chairman of the Eleventh Ward distribution committee. She continued her Red Cross work during World War I.

Mrs. Beers joined many progressive women's organizations and was on the board of directors of the Galveston Orphan's Home and the Galveston Art League. She belonged to the Wednesday Club and the Galveston Equal Suffrage Association. Perhaps her greatest civic contribution came through helping to found, with Anna Maxwell Jones, the Women's Health Protective Association in 1901. Within the first year she and sixty-five other women had the bodies of hastily buried storm victims moved to a gravesite at the west end of the island and began beautifying the area. Throughout her years of association with the WHPA she demonstrated her commitment to music and public education by chairing the Education and Art Committee, the Public Schools Committee, and the School Hygiene Committee of the WHPA.

BIBLIOGRAPHY: Galveston *Daily News*, November 14, 15, 1925. S. C. Griffin, *History of Galveston, Texas* (Galveston: Cawston, 1931). Elizabeth Hayes Turner, Women's Culture and Community: Religion and Reform in Galveston, 1880–1920 (Ph.D. dissertation, Rice University, 1990). *Elizabeth Hayes Turner*

Beethoven Männerchor. A San Antonio German men's chorus. The heaviest influx of German immigrants to Texas, fleeing political and economic problems in their homeland, began arriving in 1845. They brought with them their love of music, *Gemütlichkeit* (fellowship) and *das deutsche Lied* (German song).

The Beethoven Männerchor was formed as an offshoot of the San Antonio Maennergesang-Verein, which was founded by Simon Menger in July 1847. Menger was the musical director until March 1853, when Adolf Douai, publisher of the San Antonio *Zeitung*, took over. W. C. A. Thielepape was elected president on October 16, 1854. With the approach of the Civil War and the demands it brought on the members of the Maennergesang-Verein, the group ceased its activity until about 1865. The members re-formed on February 24, 1867, and chose the name Beethoven Männerchor following an *Abend Unterhaltung* (evening of entertainment) held at the old San Antonio Casino Hall.

The poet and musician Sidney Lanier visited San Antonio in 1873 and was invited to attend a Männerchor practice by his friend Andreas Schiedemantel (then Beethoven president), on January 29. He subsequently wrote in a letter:

Last night at 8 o'clock came Mr. Schiedemantel, a genuine lover of music and a fine pianist, to take me to the Maennerchor, which meets every Wednesday night for practice....Presently seventeen Germans were seated at the singing table. Great pipes were all afire. The leader, Herr Thielepape, an old man with a white beard and mustache, formerly mayor of the city, rapped his tuning fork vigorously, gave the chords by arpeggios of his voice (a wonderful high tenor …) and off they all swung into such a noble, noble old full-voice *lied* [song] that imperious tears rushed to my eyes.

As the German population grew in prominence in San Antonio before 1900, so did German music. The Beethoven had been meeting in several different locations until 1894, when it built its own concert and club hall on South Alamo Street. Architect Albert Beckmann designed the building, which was formally dedicated on October 12, 1895. This building burned down on October 31, 1913, and a new hall was designed by prominent San Antonio architect Leo M. J. Dielmann with Jacob Wagner supervising the construction. Beethoven Hall is now owned by the city of San Antonio and still serves as a concert hall. Several prominent musicians and ensembles have performed at this hall: Sarah Bernhardt, John Philip Sousa, and the Chicago Symphony under Arthur Claassen, who in response to his well-received performance moved to San Antonio to serve for a time as the Männerchor Director.

In 1932 women from the Mozart Society organized by Arthur Claassen formed the Beethoven Damenchor (ladies' choir); in 1943 the Beethoven Concert Band was formed, and in 1977 the Beethoven Kinderchor (childrens' choir). After World War I the Beethoven sold its concert hall and in July 1920 purchased the new location at 422 Pereida Street in the historic King William area, where it still holds rehearsals and concerts. Over the last 135 years, the Männerchor has had several notable musical directors: Carl Beck (popular director of the 1880s and 1890s), Carl Hahn, Alfred Schaefer (depression years and World War II), and Otto Wick (renowned New York conductor and composer in the 1950s.)

In more recent years the Beethoven Männerchor and Damenchor have hosted visiting choirs from the Republic of Germany visiting Texas on nationwide concert tours. The Beethoven participates each year in the Staats-Saengerfest (State Singing Festival), which brings together German choirs from throughout Texas. The singing festivals are hosted by a different city each year, as they have been since the first Saengerfest on October 15, 1853, in New Braunfels. The Beethoven Männerchor has banded together with these societies to form two separate statewide organizations: the Texanischer Gebirgs Saengerbund (Texas Hill Country Singers League, founded in 1881), and the Deutsch Texanischer Saengerbund (German Texas Singers League, founded in 1854). The Beethoven also is a member of the Nord Amerikanischer Saengerbund (North American Singers Association).

In 1948 president Guido Ransleben explained the group's philosophy:

The expression of one's innermost feelings through song is the direct expression of the joy of living, and the happiness one experiences through freedom. Freedom from toils and cares of everyday life, freedom from illness or despair, freedom from the oppression of tyrannous rulers, freedom from oneself. This freedom is best expressed in an outburst of song which comes to a neighborly understanding when several voices are combined in harmonious unison, an understanding which the human soul alone appreciates and loves. It propagates a happier more joyful well-being, a more congenial view of life. It conquers the dark retiring character of Puritanism and sows the seeds of harmony and understanding between people of all nations, races or creeds in the only universal language, the language of music.

BIBLIOGRAPHY: *Beethoven Maennerchor Centennial, 1867–1967: San Antonio, Texas, February 25 and 26, 1967* (San Antonio: Hemisfair '68, 1968). Howard R. Driggs and Sarah S. King, *Rise of the Lone Star* (New York: Frederick A. Stokes, 1936). Lee Gastinger, "125 Years Beethoven Maennerchor," program for the 125th State Saengerfest, 1992. Cecilia Steinfeldt, *San Antonio Was: Seen Through a Magic Lantern: Views from the Slide Collection of Albert Steves, Sr.* (San Antonio Museum Association, 1978). Moritz Tiling, *History of The German Element in Texas from 1820–1850* (Houston, 1913).

Jean M. Heide

Belle Plain College. An institution in Belle Plain, Callahan County, noted for its music department; established in 1881 by the Northwest Conference of the Methodist Church. John Day gave the new school ten acres of land, and local citizens donated generously in the beginning. During its first year (1881–82) the college operated in conjunction with the public school. F. W. Chatfield served as its first president. After a state charter was granted to the institution in the spring of 1882, Rev. J. T. L. Annis took over as president for two years. During his administration enrollment reached 122. Other presidents at Belle Plain College were John W. McIllhenny (1884–85), C. M. Virdel (1885–87), and I. M. Onins (1887–92).

From the beginning, the college advertised a department of music. By the end of the decade the school had fifteen pianos, a brass band, and an orchestra. By 1885 the institution had two buildings on its land, but the entire plant had been mortgaged to pay for classroom furnishings and musical instruments. Operating funds came only from the local school district, a fact that hastened the institution's demise. The railroad skipped Belle Plain, Baird became the Callahan county seat in 1883, and the population declined. Two years of bad weather further eroded the college's financial base. By 1887 the trustees of Belle Plain College were unable to make mortgage payments. Judge I. M. Onins took over the school with its debts in 1887 after a successful school year, but the mortgage company foreclosed on the property in 1889. The company allowed the school to continue to operate until the president's death in 1892.

BIBLIOGRAPHY: Brutus Clay Chrisman, *Early Days in Callahan County* (Abilene, Texas: Abilene Printing and Stationery, 1966). Thomas Robert Havins, *Belle Plain, Texas: Ghost Town in Callahan* (Brownwood, Texas: Brown Press, 1972). Russell F. Webb, History of Early Colleges of Callahan County, Texas (M.A. thesis, Hardin-Simmons University, 1949).

Larry Wolz

Beneke, Tex. Swing-band tenor saxophonist and vocalist; b. Gordon Beneke, Fort Worth, February 12, 1914; d. Costa Mesa, California, May 30, 2000. Beneke started playing the saxophone at the age of nine. He worked with various bands until 1935, when he joined the Ben Young band. In 1937, on a recommendation by drummer Gene Krupa, Glenn Miller hired Beneke for his band. During the first rehearsal, while playing the tune "Doin' the Jive," Miller changed the lyric, "Hi, there, Buck, what'cha say?" to "Hi, there, Tex, what'cha say?" From that time on, Beneke was known as Tex.

He became one of Miller's favorites, even though the other tenor saxophonist in the band, Al Klink, was considered to be the better musician. Miller considered Beneke to be "not merely a musician but also a commercial personality," and so he never missed a chance to showcase him. Beneke was often featured on vocals with the Modernaires. Some of his biggest vocal successes were "I've Got a Gal in Kalamazoo," "Ida," "Don't Sit Under the Apple Tree," and "Chattanooga Choo Choo." Jazz critic Gunther Schuller tepidly praised Beneke as "a consistent player, reliable within his limitations, and never really embarrassing." Nevertheless, according to Dave Oliphant, Beneke "became 'world famous' as the most prominent musician during the heyday of Miller's hugely successful swing-era band." He won both the *Down Beat* and *Metronome* polls for the most popular tenor saxophonist of 1941 and 1942.

During World War II Beneke served in the U.S. Navy Band. After demobilization, he led a band first billed as the "Glenn Miller Orchestra under the Direction of Tex Beneke," subsequently called "Tex Beneke and the Glenn Miller Orchestra," then "Tex Beneke and his Music in the Miller Manner," and finally "Tex Beneke and his Orchestra." During this time, Beneke tried to modernize the band's style, but met resistance from Don Haynes, the band's longtime manager. Eli Oberstein, RCA Victor recording chief, and Miller's widow, Helen, also wanted the band to stick to the "old Miller style." In December 1950 Beneke left the Miller organization. His dispute with the Miller estate may have been the reason that he was noticeably absent from the 1953 film *The Glenn Miller Story*, even though he had played a very prominent role in the band's success. Beneke continued to perform with his own band for many years, playing Miller pieces as well as those of other swing bands. He died at a convalescent home.

BIBLIOGRAPHY: John Chilton, *Who's Who of Jazz: Storyville to Swing Street*, Fourth Edition (New York: Da Capo Press, 1985). Leonard Feather, ed., *The Encyclopedia of Jazz* (New York: Horizon Press, 1955). New York

Times, June 1, 2000. Dave Oliphant, *Texan Jazz* (Austin: University of Texas Press, 1996). Gunther Schuller, *The Swing Era: The Development of Jazz, 1930–1945* (New York: Oxford University Press, 1989). George T. Simon, *Glenn Miller and His Orchestra* (New York: Bigbee Productions, 1974). *Roy G. Scudday*

Big Bopper. Disc jockey, songwriter, and singer; b. Jiles Perry Richardson, Sabine Pass, Texas, October 24, 1930; d. Mason County, Iowa, February 3, 1959. Some sources claim Richardson's first name was Jape rather than Jiles, but in any case he usually went by the initials J. P. He is best known for his hit "Chantilly Lace," which reached number one on the charts in 1958, and for dying in a plane crash with Richie Valens and Buddy Holly.

While still a teenager Richardson began working as a disc jockey at KTRM radio in Beaumont. After a stint in the army, he returned in 1955 to the station, where he eventually became program director while still working as a disc jockey.

Richardson was influenced early by country and western singers. In 1957 he sent some songs to Pappy Dailey at Mercury Records in Houston, and the company signed him as a country and western act. He left Mercury when the records proved to be unsuccessful and began working with Shelby Singleton, who also had Johnny Preston and Bruce Channel under contract. The switch also indicated Richardson's move from traditional country to the new and extremely popular rockabilly music.

His first single was "Chantilly Lace," which he followed with "Little Red Riding Hood" and "Big Bopper's Wedding." The latter songs were also hits, but not of the same caliber as "Chantilly Lace." Other songs written by Richardson included "The Purple People Eater Meets the Witch Doctor" and "Running Bear." In 1960 fellow Texan Johnny Preston made a recording of "Running Bear" that became an international hit.

The Bopper wrote about thirty-eight songs and recorded twenty-one of them. Most of his recordings were of novelty songs that did not have lasting popularity. His appeal was largely in his flamboyant stage performances. He wore checkered jackets and zoot suits and used a prop phone during "Chantilly Lace" to talk to his girl. In order to maintain his showman image, he did not wear his wedding ring in public and generally kept his marriage to Adrian Richardson a secret from his fans. The couple had two children.

On February 2, 1959, Richardson, Holly, and Valens played a show at the Surf Ballroom in Clear Lake, Iowa. They were scheduled to play in North Dakota the next day, but they and their pilot died in a crash at about 1:00 A.M. In the late 1980s the Port Arthur Historical Society commissioned sculptor Donald Clark to create a memorial to the musicians. The piece was initially displayed at a Fabulous Thunderbirds benefit concert on February 3, 1989, thirty years after the crash.

BIBLIOGRAPHY: Colin Larkin, ed., *The Guinness Encyclopedia of Popular Music* (Chester, Connecticut: New England Publishing Associates, 1992). Norm N. Nite, *Rock On: The Illustrated Encyclopedia of Rock n' Roll* (New York: Crowell, 1974–). Irwin Stambler, *Encyclopedia of Pop, Rock, and Soul* (New York: St. Martin's Press, 1974). Vertical Files, Center for American History, University of Texas at Austin. *Alan Lee Haworth*

"Big 'D' Jamboree." A Dallas-based barn dance and radio program. Building on the success of country music radio programs like WSM's "Grand Ole Opry" (Nashville) and WLS's "National Barn Dance" (Chicago), regional barn dances sprouted up across the country throughout the 1940s. By the end of that decade, more than 600 American radio stations tried this live country music format.

One of the biggest such shows was KRLD's "Big 'D' Jamboree." This revered radio show grew out of a weekly live-music program called the "Texas State Barn Dance," which began in Dallas in 1946. This show was strictly a live-audience program and was not broadcast over the radio until 1948. The program then spent a few months on WFAA, where it was called the "Lone Star Jamboree," but finally found its home on KRLD and was permanently renamed "Big 'D' Jamboree." The show first aired on KRLD on October 16, 1948. Its immediate popularity came partly because its debut coincided with the State Fair of Texas, held each fall in Dallas. Johnny Hicks was the primary host.

The "Jamboree" aired from a multi-purpose arena at the corner of Cadiz and Industrial boulevards, a center of country music nightclubs in Dallas. This building, the Sportatorium, also hosted other major events, most notably the professional wrestling matches produced by building owner and "Jamboree" co-producer Ed McLemore. The original building was noted for its octagonal design and also for its seating capacity of more than 6,000. The original Sportatorium burned down in a 1953 blaze rumored to have been set by a rival wrestling promoter. A new Sportatorium was built four months later, and the "Jamboree" was broadcast from this new venue for its remaining years.

The "Big 'D' Jamboree" was inspired by other radio programs of the time, including the "Grand Ole Opry" and the "Louisiana Hayride." Though the "Big 'D' Jamboree" was never as prominent as either of these two shows, it was important in Texas and served as a springboard to fame. The show also provided weekly entertainment for as many as 5,000 attending patrons and countless radio listeners within KRLD's 50,000-watt broadcast range, which could reach listeners in forty states. During its peak the show aired four hours each Saturday night and featured between twenty and fifty performers a week.

The "Jamboree" managed to bring in an amazing array of country performers, including Johnny Cash, Ronnie Dawson, Lefty Frizzell, Merle Haggard, Homer and Jethro, Wanda Jackson, Ray Price, Rose Maddox, Moon Mullican, Carl Perkins, Webb Pierce, Elvis Presley, Hank Thompson, Floyd Tillman, Hank Snow, and Hank Williams. It vigorously promoted local talent as well, in no small part because it could not afford to fill its air-time with well-known artists. Presenting local talent was slightly against the grain of radio barn dances, which tended to promote national, more-recognizable acts. In this practice and others the "Jamboree" broke with an established formula in programming in order to create a strong marketing niche for itself.

When the show first started in 1948, the most popular form of country music in North Texas was western swing. But the "Jamboree" preferred artists who played other styles of country music, styles more geared towards pop and honky-tonk. The show thus served as an alternative venue for country music within the region, and also prepared itself for reaching audiences outside of north Texas. In the mid-1950s, the "Jamboree" continued bucking proven formulas by playing a different type of country music than the other radio barn dances. The "Jamboree" catered to youth by featuring rockabilly artists. This kept the program successful throughout the burgeoning years of rockabilly.

Although the show never reached the heights of the "Opry" or the "Hayride," the "Jamboree" was picked up by the CBS radio network and incorporated into the network's weekly "Saturday Night Country Style" program. This nationally broadcast radio show alternated various regional country music radio programs (including both the "Opry" and the "Hayride") in its Saturday night spot. "Saturday Night Country Style" was also broadcast on the Armed Forces Radio Network.

"Big 'D' Jamboree" ended in 1959. Throughout the latter years of that decade, the show's audience had dwindled and the format and medium had become increasingly outdated. Americans were more fascinated by television in their homes and by rock-and-roll music than by locally produced country music variety shows broadcast over the radio. Producers unsuccessfully tried to revive the show in the 1960s.

BIBLIOGRAPHY: Kevin Coffey and David Dennard, notes to CD *The Big "D" Jamboree Live! Volumes 1 & 2* (2000). Dallas *Observer*, January 6, 2000. Bill C. Malone, *Country Music, U.S.A.* (Austin: University of Texas Press, 1985). *Cathy Brigham*

Billy Bob's Texas. Billed as the "World's Largest Honky-Tonk"; in the historic Fort Worth Stockyards district. Billy Bob's Texas, which comprises a total area of 127,000 square feet or almost seven acres, is one of the most popular tourist attractions in the state. Many of the brightest stars in country and western music have played on its stage. In addition to nightly musical performances, Billy Bob offers live bull riding, dancing, drinking, games, and more to a capacity crowd of 6,000 (the same capacity as that of the other "world's largest," the now-defunct Gilley's).

Billy Bob's has been nominated eight times and has won five titles as the country music "Club of the Year" by the Academy of Country Music. The Country Music Association also has recognized the nightclub three times—with the "Club of the Year" title in 1992 and 1994 and "Venue of the Year" in 1997.

Billy Bob's Texas was the brainchild of Texas A&M University graduate and professional football player Billy Bob Barnett. Joining Barnett in the venture was nightclub owner Spencer Taylor, a former car salesman. The two chose an abandoned 100,000-square-foot department store that had once been an open-air cattle barn in the Fort Worth Stockyards. The original structure was built in 1910 and underwent several transformations through the years. Additional animal stalls and an auction ring were constructed in 1936, and during World War II the Globe Aircraft Corporation used the building as an airplane factory. With the additional help of investment partners Thomas and Mitt Lloyd, Barnett renovated the facility and opened the doors for business on April 1, 1981.

Following on the heels of the early 1980s *Urban Cowboy* craze and subsequent country music boom, Billy Bob's Texas was an instant hit. The first week featured Larry Gatlin and the Gatlin Brothers, Waylon Jennings, Janie Fricke, and Willie Nelson. A host of others followed, including rockers ZZ Top and the Beach Boys and country music legends Marty Robbins and Ernest Tubb. Billy Bob's Texas helped foster many new musical acts. As the club's marketing director, Pam Minick, wrote, "Billy Bob's became the place for country music musicians to hone their skills, build a fan following, and possibly secure a recording contract." George Strait, for example, played first as an opening act at Billy Bob's. Rick Treviño placed in a talent contest at the nightclub. Ty Herndon was a member of the house band, Southern Thunder.

However, problems eventually beset the nightclub. In the late 1980s, country music, Billy Bob's biggest draw, declined in popularity. Financial mismanagement and unrealized projects drained the nightclub. Billy Bob's Texas was bankrupt, and on January 8, 1988, it closed, causing great loss to the tourism industry of Fort Worth, especially the Stockyards district. Soon afterward, however, entrepreneur Holt Hickman, a Fort Worth native, sought to revive the Stockyards. Hickman's long-time friend and businessman Steve Murrin encouraged him to reopen Billy Bob's Texas. Hickman and Murrin, along with Donald K. Jury, an original Billy Bob's Texas investor, reopened the place on November 28, 1988. In February 1989, Billy Minick, now CEO, became a partner and manager of the nightclub.

When Billy Bob's Texas reopened, new headliners took the stage, including Garth Brooks, Tim McGraw, and Texans LeAnn Rimes and Clint Black. As country music regained popularity, Billy Bob's focused on native talent, especially musicians who had crossover appeal. Such Texas acts as Robert Earl Keen and Pat Green became some of the club's biggest draws. The high-energy environment and close setting of Billy Bob's Texas allowed these performers to interact more with their fans. According to Pam Minick, most stars know they have made it when they have played the main stage at Billy Bob's. The club has a Handprint Wall of Fame that displays impressions of every performer who has played onstage.

Several artists have recorded live at Billy Bob's. Among the first to do so were Chris LeDoux and David Allen Coe. In 1998 the nightclub, in partnership with Smith Music Group, started the "Live at Billy Bob's" label. Singers performing on this label include Lynn Anderson, Moe Bandy and Joe Stampley, Roy Clark, John Conlee, Pat Green, Merle Haggard, Eddy Raven, and Kevin Fowler. Many country music videos, television shows, and movies have featured Billy Bob's Texas. Videos have been shot at the club for Collin Raye, Chris LeDeux, Billy Dean, and Aaron Tippin, among others. Billy Bob's Texas has been the setting for CBS's "Happy New Year America," "TNN Onstage," CBS's "This Morning," and "Walker, Texas Ranger." Movies such as *Over The Top* (1980) starring Sylvester Stallone; *Baja Oklahoma* (1988) staring Lesley Ann Warren, Peter Coyote, and Willie Nelson; *Necessary Roughness* (1991); and George Strait's *Pure Country* (1992) include scenes filmed at Billy Bob's.

BIBLIOGRAPHY: "Academy of Country Music Selects Billy Bob's Texas as Country Music Club of the Year for 2000" (http://www.billybobstexas.com/acm_club.htm), accessed November 8, 2002. *Billy Bob's Texas: 20 Years of Astonishing Entertainment* (Fort Worth: Country Media, 2001). "Billy Bob's Texas: The World's Largest Country Music Nightclub" (http://www.billybobstexas.com), accessed November 8, 2002. Fort Worth *Star–Telegram*, April 1, 2001. John T. Davis, "The World's Largest Honky-Tonk: Billy Bob's Texas," *Texas Highways*, January 2003.

Tanya Krause

Blackie Simmons and the Blue Jackets. An early Western Swing band organized under the leadership of Fort Worth fiddle player Tumpie Lee "Blackie" Simmons. The band was short-lived, but played an important role in the development of several prominent musical careers, as well as providing entertainment at the historic Fort Worth Frontier Centennial exposition, alongside such notables as Billy Rose, Paul Whiteman, and Sally Rand.

The band's membership was fluid, but the primary lineup included Blackie Simmons, his brother Luther Wayne "Brownie" Simmons on standup bass, Jesse Ashlock on bass fiddle, John W. "Knocky" Parker on piano, Bruce Pierce on guitar, Sam Graves on tenor banjo, and Albert Brant on bass. From time to time, the band may have also included another banjo player and a saxophonist. Ashlock was a future member of Bob Wills's Texas Playboys, and Knocky Parker was a future member of the Light Crust Doughboys.

Tumpie Lee Simmons was the oldest of five children, born to Henry R. and Elizabeth Cornelia Simmons in 1901. The exact date of his birth is unknown, even to his family members. Wayne Luther "Brownie" Simmons, Blackie's partner and also a member of the Blue Jackets, was born February 12, 1909. Other siblings include brother Thomas Edison Simmons and sisters Ruth Simmons Hooten and Gertrude "Gertie" Simmons Stewart Whittier. Blackie Simmons's mother and his maternal aunt, Edna (maiden name unknown) married two brothers. Blackie's father, Henry R. Simmons, was involved in bootlegging and other illicit activities and was killed by a county sheriff's deputy when the children were very young. The family grew up in the Fort Worth area, primarily in Burleson, Everman, and Fort Worth proper.

Tumpie Lee and Luther Wayne Simmons's musical careers began with singing "medicine shows" and a black-faced minstrel show. It was during this time period that the brothers adopted their peculiar nicknames, Blackie and Brownie, taken as stage names as a part of their minstrel act. Blackie Simmons became so enamored of his nickname

that he used it formally for his entire life, even having it engraved on his tombstone in place of his real name.

Luther Wayne Simmons was not a full-time musician, but a sign painter and neon sculptor by trade. However, his talent on the fiddle, upright bass, and guitar enabled him to supplement his income by working with his older brother, who was a professional performer by trade. Little is known about the brothers' early musical development, only that they were musicians from childhood. By the mid-1930s, Blackie was making his living playing dances. By December 1935 he and his brother were performing the first radio show of the morning (5:45 to 6:15 AM) on KRLD radio in Dallas, appearing under the name Uncle Ezra and the Boys.

At the time, KRLD radio (an abbreviation for Radio Laboratories of Dallas) broadcast from the Adolphus Hotel on Commerce Street. Initially, Wayne Simmons refused to perform the radio show because he feared riding on the hotel's elevators to reach the broadcasting room. While the morning show was airing, a chance encounter between Blackie Simmons and Marvin A. "Smokey" Montgomery helped to mold the future of Texas music. In an oft-told tale, Montgomery later credited this encounter with Simmons as his reason for staying in Texas. After playing throughout Texas in a tent show, Montgomery had become homesick and ready to return to his native Iowa. He had saved enough money to take him as far as Dallas. On his arrival in Dallas at 4 AM, he went to the Adolphus Hotel, where he knew Simmons was playing, hoping to land a job. Simmons got Montgomery a job playing a gig that night at a country club, along with the band's piano player (most likely Knocky Parker). Montgomery later recounted, "That night the piano player picked me up, and we went out to the Dallas Country Club, of all places. It was a stag party, and I'd never seen a stag party. This gal took off things she didn't even have on. We played the music, and I was crosseyed looking at the girl." From that point on, Montgomery chose to stay in Texas. He had a long and distinguished career as one of the pillars of Texas music, remaining a part of the Light Crust Doughboys for more than sixty-five years.

On December 30, 1935, Blackie Simmons and his band began appearing on KRLD as Uncle Tumpie and the Boys. On February 12, 1936, the band appeared for the first time as Blackie's Blue Jackets. Simmons took the band's name from the blue coats he had his sidemen wear while playing dances. At this time, other notable Western Swing bands of the era were also appearing on Dallas radio, most prominent of which was Milton Brown and his Musical Brownies, who came on at 1:15 PM. On April 16, 1936, the Blue Jackets gave their last known radio performance.

That year, the state of Texas was engaged in festivities celebrating one hundred years of independence from Mexico. The official Centennial celebration, dubbed the Texas Centennial Exposition, was set to take place in Dallas. However, Fort Worth city leaders, chief among them Amon G. Carter, planned their own rival celebration, dubbed the Texas Frontier Centennial. A large exposition ground was set aside for the celebration, and a theater-in-the-round, called the Casa Mañana or "House of Tomorrow," was constructed to accommodate stage performances. Famed

New York promoter Billy Rose was hired to coordinate the event. Rose brought a version of his Broadway production *Jumbo* to the Casa Mañana. Other events included a midway, restaurant, and Sally Rand's "Nude Ranch," a risqué burlesque theatre.

The Frontier Centennial was highly controversial. The nude performances, as well as bawdy advertising, stirred a wealth of indignation against the Centennial by local residents, as is evidenced by newspaper editorials of the day. However, the celebration was popular and enjoyable. Amon Carter said of the celebration, "Go to Dallas for education; come to Fort Worth for entertainment."

A central part of the Frontier Centennial was the performance of Texas music. Newspaper articles of the era highlight Rose's insistence on giving the music a Texas flare. As a result, he wanted the "best fiddle band in the business" to play the Pioneer Palace, one of the attractions at the Centennial. Initially Milton Brown and His Musical Brownies were to be the Pioneer Palace Band, but Rose did not hire them because they cost too much.

By 1937, band members Parker and Ashlock had moved on to other projects. From 1937 to 1939, Parker was piano player for the Light Crust Doughboys. Before his death on September 3, 1986, he had recorded numerous albums and made a strong contribution to jazz. He also earned a Ph.D. in English and spent much of his life as a university professor. Jesse Ashlock had come to the Blue Jackets by way of Milton Brown and His Musical Brownies. He was already playing with Bob Wills as early as 1935, and work with the Blue Jackets appears to have only been a brief interlude. Ashlock went on to build a stellar career under Wills. He died on August 9, 1976.

Following the Frontier Centennial, Blackie Simmons continued to perform dances and shows. He moved to California for some time. In addition to his musical career, he was involved in the ownership of several clubs around Fort Worth, as well as a drapery shop run by his wife, Alvena. Simmons finally retired to a ranch near Coppell, Texas, where he spent his last years raising horses and cattle and playing the fiddle. He passed away on December 21, 1966, and is buried in Bluebonnet Hills Memorial Park in Colleyville. Wayne Luther "Brownie" Simmons continued to perform music for the rest of his life, playing in a band at a cafeteria near his home in Haltom City until his death, on August 31, 1981; he is buried at Prairie Springs Cemetery in Burleson.

BIBLIOGRAPHY: Dallas *Morning News*, December 28, 30, 1935; February 12, 1936; April 16, 1936. John Dempsey, "Marvin 'Smokey' Montgomery: A Life in Texas Music," *Journal of Texas Music History* 1.2 (Fall 2001). Cary Ginell, *Milton Brown and the Founding of Western Swing* (Chicago: University of Illinois Press, 1994). Marvin A. "Smokey" Montgomery, interview by John Daniels, University of North Texas Oral History Collection, No. 1152, September 8, 1996. "Parker, John W., 'Knocky'," *Musiweb Encyclopedia of Popular Music* (http://www.musicweb.uk.net/encyclopaedia/p/P18.HTM), accessed February 3, 2003. Vertical file, Fort Worth Public Library ("Frontier Exposition"). *Jerry C. Drake*

Bledsoe, Jules. African-American baritone and composer; b. Julius Lorenzo Cobb Bledsoe, Waco, Texas, December 29, 1897; d. Hollywood, California, July 14, 1943 (buried in Greenwood Cemetery, Waco); son of Henry L. and Jessie (Cobb) Bledsoe. Bledsoe attended Central Texas Academy in Waco from about 1905 until his graduation as class valedictorian in 1914. He then attended Bishop College in Marshall, where he earned a B.A. in 1918. He was a member of the ROTC at Virginia Union University in Richmond in 1918–19 and studied medicine at Columbia University between 1920 and 1924. While attending Columbia, he studied voice with Claude Warford, Luigi Parisotti, and Lazar Samoiloff. He was sponsored by the impresario Sol Hurok for his professional singing debut on April 20, 1924, at Aeolian Hall in New York. As a concert artist Bledsoe performed in the United States and Europe. He was praised for his ability to sing in several languages, for his vocal control and range, and for his power to communicate through music.

His best-known achievement was his portrayal of Joe in Florenz Ziegfeld's 1927 production of Jerome Kern's *Showboat*. His interpretation of "Ol' Man River" made the song an American classic. In his versatile career of nearly twenty years Bledsoe performed with such distinguished musical organizations as the Boston Symphony Chamber Players (1926), the BBC Symphony in London (1936), and the Concertgebouw Orchestra of Amsterdam (1937). He also sang for vaudeville and radio and in opera. He sang the role of Amonasro in Verdi's *Aïda* with the Cleveland Stadium Opera (1932), the Chicago Opera Company at the Hippodrome in New York (1933), and the Cosmopolitan Opera Company, also at the Hippodrome (1934). A highlight of his career was his performance in the title role for the European premiere, in Amsterdam, of Louis Gruenberg's opera *The Emperor Jones* (1934). In 1940 and 1941 Bledsoe worked in films in Hollywood. He played the part of Kalu in *Drums of the Congo*, and, although his name did not appear in the credits, he probably played in *Safari*, *Western Union*, and *Santa Fe Trail*.

He wrote several patriotic songs and songs in spiritual and folk styles. Some of his compositions were "Does Ah Luv You?" (1931); "Pagan Prayer" (date unknown), on a poem by Countee Cullen; "Good Old British Blue" (1936); and "Ode to America" (1941). He wrote an opera, *Bondage* (1939), based on Harriet Beecher Stowe's novel *Uncle Tom's Cabin*. Bledsoe's *African Suite*, a set of four songs for voice and orchestra, was featured with the Concertgebouw Orchestra, directed by Wilhelm Mengelberg. Bledsoe died of a cerebral hemorrhage after a war-bond tour.

BIBLIOGRAPHY: *Baker's Biographical Dictionary of Musicians*. Jules Bledsoe Papers, Texas Collection, Baylor University, Waco. Maud Cuney–Hare, *Negro Musicians and Their Music* (Washington: Associated Publishers, 1936). Lynnette Geary, The Career and Music of Jules Bledsoe (M.Mus. thesis, Baylor University, 1982). Dayton Kelley, ed., *The Handbook of Waco and McLennan County, Texas* (Waco: Texian, 1972). *Lynnette Geary*

Blitz, Julien Paul. String player, professor, and conductor; b. Ghent, Belgium, May 21, 1885; d. Dallas, July 17, 1951;

Cellist Julien Blitz and his wife, pianist Flora Blitz, performing in Galveston, ca. early 1900s. Julien Paul Blitz Scrapbook, CAH; CN 11489.

son of Edouard E. and Mattie Louise (Miller) Blitz. His father was a renowned violinist, music teacher, and conductor, and his mother, from Ohio, was an acclaimed pianist. Blitz arrived in the United States when he was two years old and studied piano and violin as a child. He returned to Belgium for study and graduated from the Royal Conservatory in Ghent in 1905. In 1906–07 he was a music professor at Baylor Female College in Belton, Texas. In 1907, in Belton, he wrote the "Bell County March," a piano solo dedicated to county sheriff D. C. Burkes. As a young man Blitz also performed as soloist with several orchestras, including ensembles in Chicago and New York, and received recognition in the United States and abroad.

By 1912 he was director of the Treble Clef Club, a women's singing organization in Houston. He was founding conductor of the Houston Symphony Orchestra and conducted the orchestra's first trial concert on June 21, 1913, at the 600-seat Majestic Theatre (now part of the Houston Chronicle) at Texas and Milam. The original ensemble consisted of thirty-five musicians, with Benjamin Steinfelt serving as concertmaster. The performance garnered enough support that the orchestra could open its first season on December 19, 1913. Blitz continued in his position as conductor until 1916. During his time in Houston he taught music and also conducted the Blitz Orchestra at the Rice Hotel. From 1917 to 1922 he was conductor of the San Antonio Symphony. In 1920 he was co-director of the San Antonio College of Music.

On January 24, 1921, Blitz married Flora Briggs, a San Antonio pianist. They had one son, Edouard. Blitz and his wife gave many performances together and are credited as the first two professional instrumentalists to play on radio in Texas (San Antonio, 1922). From 1930 to 1934 Blitz was director of music at Kidd–Key College in Sherman. In

the 1930s and 1940s he headed the music department at Texas Tech in Lubbock. He moved to Dallas in 1950, conducted workshops in cello, and performed as guest cellist with the Dallas Symphony Orchestra. In 1997 the "Bell County March" was given to the Bell County Museum by Dewitt J. Lorenz, Noema Dahlke, and Catherine Jean Duncan, grandchildren of Sheriff Burkes.

BIBLIOGRAPHY: Blitz (Julien Paul) Papers, Center for American History, University of Texas at Austin. Hubert Roussel, *The Houston Symphony Orchestra, 1913–1971* (Austin: University of Texas Press, 1972). Vertical file, Center for American History, University of Texas at Austin.

Susan Love Fitts

Blues. The earliest reference to what might be considered blues in Texas was made in 1890 by collector Gates Thomas, who transcribed a song titled "Nobody There." Thomas doesn't mention whether the singing was accompanied by an instrument, but he does indicate that it was a pentatonic tune containing tonic, minor, third, fourth, fifth, and seventh chords, all of which combined to produce something similar to a blues tune. Later, Thomas published other song texts that he had collected from African Americans in South Texas. Some of these included verses that had been noted by other writers in different areas of the South. The song "Baby, Take a Look at Me," for example, was transcribed both by Thomas and Charles Peabody in Mississippi. And "Alabama Bound" and "C. C. Rider" are variants of blues songs that Jelly Roll Morton sang in New Orleans.

Geographically diffuse sources suggest that blues musicians were itinerant and that blues was part of an oral tradition that developed in different areas of the South. By all accounts, the blues was widespread in the early 1900s. Thousands of blacks during this period were migratory, looking for work and escape from all too prevalent racism. Blues singers were often migrant workers who followed the crop harvests or lived in lumber camps and boomtowns. Some settled down and labored as sharecroppers, leasing small tracts of land controlled by white landowners. Others continued roving from town to town, working odd jobs in the growing urban centers—Dallas, Houston, Shreveport, and Atlanta—cities where black migrant populations were crowded into neighborhoods of shotgun shacks and pasteboard houses.

Blues music expressed the hardships of newly freed black slaves. The freedoms offered by Reconstruction were hard-won. Racism, Jim Crow laws, and the Ku Klux Klan were major obstacles to economic independence and self-determination. Still, leisure, even under the most desolate circumstances, was vitally new and served as a catalyst in the development of the blues. Early blues answered the need for a release from everyday life. The blues is an intensely personal music; it identifies itself with the feelings of the audience—suffering and hope, economic failure, the break-up of the family, the desire to escape reality through wandering, love, and sex. In this way, blues is somewhat different from African songs, which usually concern the lives and works of gods, the social unit (tribe and community), and nature.

With its emphasis on individual experience, blues reflects a Western concept of life. Yet, as a musical form it shows little Western influence. The traditional three-line, twelve-bar, *aab* verse form of the blues arises from no apparent Western source, although some blues does incorporate Anglo-American ballad forms that have six, ten, or sixteen bar structures. Early blues drew from the music of its time: field hollers and shouts, which it most closely resembles melodically; songster ballads, from which it borrows imagery and guitar patterns; spirituals and gospel, which trained the voices and ears of black children. These, with exception of the ballad, were the descendants of African percussive rhythms and call-and-response singing.

Although blues drew from the religious music of both African and Western cultures, it was often considered sinful. Blues singers were stereotyped as "backsliders" in their own communities. In many areas blues was known as the devil's music. As historian Larry Levine points out, blues blended the sacred and the secular. Like the spirituals and folktales of the nineteenth century, blues was a plea for release, a mix of despair, hope, and humor that had a cathartic effect upon the listener. The blues singer had an expressive role that mirrored the power of the preacher, and because of this power, blues was both embraced and rejected by blacks and their churches.

In Texas, blues musician Lil Son Jackson explained to British blues aficionado Paul Oliver that it was, in effect, the spiritual power of the blues that made the music sinful. "If a man hurt within and he sing a church song then he's askin' God for help....if a man sing the blues it's more or less out of himself....He's not askin' no one for help. And he's really not really clingin' to no one. But he's expressin' how he feel. He's expressin' to someone and that fact makes it a sin, you know....you're tryin' to get your feelin's over to the next person through the blues, and that's what make it a sin." Because of the frequent lack of centralized authority in black churches, however, community opposition to the blues varied from place to place. Rarely were blues singers completely ostracized. They lived on the margins of what was acceptable and derived their livelihood from itinerant work at house parties and dances.

With the growth of the recording industry during the 1920s the audience for blues expanded among blacks nationwide. For example, demographic studies indicate that Blind Lemon Jefferson's records sold thousands of copies to blacks in the urban ghettos of the North, but in Dallas Jefferson was recognized primarily as street singer who performed daily with a tin cup at the corner of Elm Street and Central Avenue. Despite his limited commercial success in Dallas, he had a great influence on the development of Texas blues. Huddie (Leadbelly) Ledbetter credited him as an inspiration, as did Aaron Thibeaux (T-Bone) Walker. What distinguishes Jefferson from the other blues performers of his generation was his singular approach to the guitar, which established the basis of what is today known as the Texas style. He strummed or "hammered" the strings with repetitive bass figures and produced a succession of open and fretted notes, using a quick release and picking single-string, arpeggio runs. T-Bone Walker later applied this technique to the electric guitar and, combined

Early blues music was derived from African-American field hollers, shouts, and call-and-response singing. Folklorist John A. Lomax collected black American songs in Texas and took this picture of "Lightnin' and his gang singing at the Darrington State Prison Farm, Sandy Point, Texas in 1934." Library of Congress, AFS L13.

with the influences of the jump and swing blues of the regional or "Territory" jazz bands of the 1920s and 1930s, produced the modern sound.

In the Territory jazz bands of the Southwest, the guitar was used as a rhythm instrument to underlie the voice and horn sections. The introduction of the electric guitar occurred first in these bands, pioneered by Eddie Durham of San Marcos and Charlie Christian of Fort Worth. By using electric amplification, jazz guitarists were able to increase the resonance and volume of their sound. Charlie Christian is credited with teaching T-Bone Walker about the electric guitar and its potential as a solo instrument. In the rhythm-and-blues of T-Bone Walker the electric guitar assumed a role that superseded the saxophone, which had until then been the prominent solo instrument in jazz. The interplay between the saxophone and the guitar remained important in rhythm-and-blues, but the relationship between the instruments was transformed. The rhythm-and-blues band sound became tighter and depended more on the interplay of the electric guitar with the horn section, piano, and drums.

In Texas, blues has developed a unique character that results not only from the introduction of the electric guitar, but also from the cross-pollination of musical styles—itself a result of the migratory patterns of African Americans—

Blues Boy Hubbard, a long-time proponent of Austin rhythm and blues, and a member of the Austin Jazz Hall of Fame. Photo by Steve Goodson, courtesy Diana and Paul Ray.

as well as the impact of the recording industry and mass-media commercialization. Not only is the black population of Texas less concentrated than that of other states in the South, but blues music in Texas also evolved in proximity to other important musical traditions: the rural Anglo, the Cajun and Creole, the Hispanic, and the Eastern and Central European.

The white crossover to blues in Texas began in the nineteenth century, when black fiddlers and guitar songsters played at white country dances. Eddie Durham recalled in interviews that his father was a fiddler who played jigs and reels as well as blues. Mance Lipscomb's and Gatemouth Brown's fathers were songsters who played fiddle and guitar. White musicians were exposed to blues at country dances and minstrel shows and among black workers in the fields, road gangs, turpentine camps, and railroad yards. Country singer Bill Neely said that he first heard blues when he picked cotton in Collin County north of Dallas in the 1920s, but he learned to play blues by listening to Jimmie Rodgers. Though known as a country singer, "Jimmie Rodgers was a bluesman," Neely maintained. "A lot of those songs Jimmie Rodgers didn't write. He got them from the blacks he heard when he was growing up in Mississippi and when he worked as a brakeman on the railroad." The influence of blues and jazz is also apparent in the early western swing bands of Bob Wills and Milton Brown, where the horn sections of the Territory jazz bands

were imitated and developed through different instrumentation. In addition, blues and jazz influenced Hispanic as well as Anglo-European popular music.

In the 1920s Dallas became a recording center primarily because it is a geographical hub. The major race labels, those catering to a black audience, held regular sessions in Dallas. Okeh, Vocalion, Brunswick, Columbia, RCA, and Paramount sent scouts and engineers to record local artists once or twice a year. Engineers came into the city, set up their equipment in a hotel room, and put the word out. Itinerant musicians found their way to Dallas, among them the legendary Delta bluesman Robert Johnson, who recorded there in 1937 (but was also recorded in San Antonio). In part, the intense recording activity in Dallas was spurred by the commercial success of Blind Lemon Jefferson, who was discovered by a Paramount record company executive on a Deep Ellum sidewalk and invited to Chicago to make race records. Between 1926 and 1929 Jefferson made more than eighty records and became the biggest-selling country bluesman of his generation.

As a result of Jefferson's commercial success, blues singers from around the south flocked to Dallas with the hope of being recorded. Generally, these musicians lived and worked in the area around Deep Ellum and Central Tracks. Deep Ellum was the area of Dallas north and east of downtown, where black newcomers to the city came. Branching off from Elm Street was Central Tracks, a stretch of railroad near the Union Depot, where the Texas and Pacific line crossed the Houston and Texas Central line. Lying east of the downtown business district and north of Deep Ellum, Central Tracks was the heart of the black community. In the area were Ella B. Moore's Park Theater, with vaudeville, minstrel, and touring blues and jazz shows, the Tip Top, Hattie Burleson's dance hall, the Green Parrot, and the Pythian Temple, designed by the black architect William Sidney Pittman.

In addition to Blind Lemon Jefferson, other important blues musicians recorded in Dallas during the heyday of Deep Ellum and Central Tracks. These included Lonnie Johnson, Lillian Glinn, Little Hat Jones, Texas Alexander, Jesse Thomas, Willard (Ramblin) Thomas, Sammy Hill, Otis Harris, Willie Reed, Buddy Woods, Babe Kyro (Black Ace) Turner, and the young T-Bone Walker. With the Great Depression of the 1930s, race recording declined, but the Dallas area remained a center of blues activity. In the 1940s the railroad tracks on Central Avenue were torn up to make room for Central Expressway, which was built in the 1950s, and for R. L. Thornton Freeway in the 1960s. These changes choked Deep Ellum off from downtown, and the area became a warehouse district with industrial suppliers and small businesses mixed in.

In the 1980s the redevelopment of Deep Ellum stimulated commercial activity, street life, and a club scene that has become an important venue for contemporary blues. Among blacks in Dallas, the locus of blues activity in the 1940s and 1950s shifted from Central Tracks to North and South Dallas. The Rose Ballroom, opened by T. H. Smith in March 1942 and reopened as the Rose Room in April 1943, became a showplace for the best of the local and nationally known blues artists. T-Bone Walker performed there, as did

Big Joe Turner, Pee Wee Crayton, Lowell Fulson, Eddie Vinson, Jimmy Nelson, and Henry (Buster) Smith. The Rose Room was renamed the Empire Room in 1951 and continued to feature the most popular R&B of the day: Zuzu Bollin, Lil Son Jackson, Clarence (Nappy Chin) Evans, Mercy Baby, Frankie Lee Sims, and Smoke Hogg.

In the 1960s, Chris Strachwitz of Arhoolie Records worked in earnest to release contemporary recordings of these and other blues musicians in Dallas and elsewhere in Texas. Since 1985, Documentary Arts, a nonprofit organization in Dallas, has been involved in the documentation and preservation of Texas blues through the production of radio features, films, videos, audiocassettes, and compact discs. The Dallas Blues Society has also worked to heighten public knowledge of the blues through the promotion of concerts and the production of recordings. In 1987 Dallas pianist Alex Moore became the first black blues musician from Texas to receive a National Heritage Fellowship from the Folk Arts Program National Endowment for the Arts.

African Americans in Houston settled mostly in four segregated wards: the Third, Fourth, Fifth, and Sixth. It was in the Third Ward where Lightnin' Hopkins accompanied his cousin Texas Alexander in the late 1920s, and where Hopkins returned by himself in the 1940s to play on Dowling Street. The Santa Fe Group gathered in the Fourth Ward. They were a loosely knit association of itinerant black pianists in the 1920s and 1930s that included Robert Shaw, Black Boy Shine, Pinetop Burks, and Rob Cooper, who performed in the roadhouses and juke joints along the Santa Fe tracks, playing their distinctive style of piano, which combined elements of blues with the syncopation of ragtime. In the Fifth Ward also there were black blues pianists, but their style of performance was even more eclectic. Probably the most well-known of these were members of the George W. Thomas family. The eldest, George Thomas Jr., was born about 1885, followed by his sister, Beulah, better known as Sippie Wallace, and her brother, Hersal.

In Houston there were fewer opportunities for recording than in Dallas until after World War II, when several independent labels were started. The earliest to record blues was Gold Star, founded by Bill Quinn in 1946 as a hillbilly label to record Harry Choates. In 1947 Quinn decided to enter the race market by recording Lightnin' Hopkins. By the early 1950s, competition among independent record labels in Houston was intense. Macy's, Freedom, and Peacock (as well as Bob Shad's New York-based Sittin-In-With label) were all involved in recording local and regional blues musicians, including Lightnin' Hopkins, Goree Carter, Lester Williams, Little Willie Littlefield, Peppermint Harris, Grady Gaines, and Big Walter Price.

Of the Houston-based independent labels, Peacock emerged as the most prominent. Houston businessman Don Robey founded Peacock Records in 1949 to record Gatemouth Brown, who was the headliner at Robey's Bronze Peacock club. The first rhythm-and-blues singer with whom Robey made the charts was Marie Adams, whose song "I'm Gonna Play the Honky Tonks" was a hit in 1952. With this success, Robey expanded his recording interests by acquiring the Memphis label Duke Records.

Through this acquisition Robey secured the rights to the musicians who were then under contract to Duke. These included Johnny Ace, Junior Parker, and Bobby Blue Bland. In addition to Peacock and Duke, Robey started the Songbird and Back Beat labels, as well as the Buffalo Booking Agency, which was operated by his associate, Evelyn Johnson. Robey's business began to wane in the early 1960s, but benefited greatly from the influx of British rock 'n' roll and the revival of interest in rhythm-and-blues. In 1973 Robey sold his recording and publishing interests to ABC/Dunhill.

Concurrent with the growth of Peacock Records, a new generation of Houston-bred rhythm-and-blues musicians began their careers, but were not recorded by Don Robey. These musicians included Albert Collins, Johnny Copeland, Joe Hughes, Johnny Watson, Clarence and Cal Green, and Pete Mayes. Playing at the Club Matinee, Shady's Playhouse, the Eldorado Ballroom, and other nightspots around Houston, these musicians emulated the music of T-Bone Walker and eventually developed their own distinctive performance styles.

Austin was slower to develop as a recording center than Dallas or Houston, although there is a long history of blues in Central Texas. The relatively small black population of Austin made the capital unappealing for record producers until the 1960s, when the "Austin Sound" began to attract national attention. With the influx of white musicians, including Jimmie Vaughan, Stevie Ray Vaughan, Joe Ely, Angela Strehli, and Kim Wilson, the enthusiasm for blues grew significantly. The success of these musicians also benefited many older African-American blues musicians who gained a larger audience outside of their own community and performed at Antone's, the Continental Club, and other venues near the University of Texas campus. In Austin, T-Bone Walker clearly had the biggest influence upon aspiring black blues musicians, including Dooley Jordan, Jewel Simmons, and T. D. Bell. Bell himself also inspired younger blues artists, such as Herbert (Blues Boy) Hubbard and W. C. Clark. In the 1950s the Victory Grill on East Eleventh Street was an important venue for local musicians as well as for nationally touring acts.

In addition to R&B, Austin has also been the home of barrelhouse blues pianists Grey Ghost, Robert Shaw, and Lavada Durst, and for country blues guitarist Alfred (Snuff) Johnson. Texas Folklife Resources in Austin has presented some of these performers in touring programs. The Center for American History, University of Texas at Austin, possesses an important sound archive collected by John Wheat, including the Texas Music Collection, the John A. Lomax Family Papers, the Mance Lipscomb / Glen Alyn Collection, the William A. Owens Collection, and other blues recordings, posters, and memorabilia.

BIBLIOGRAPHY: William Barlow, "Looking Up at Down": The Emergence of Blues Culture (Philadelphia: Temple University Press, 1989). Lawrence Cohn, Nothing but the Blues: The Music and the Musicians (New York: Abbeville Press, 1993). Francis Davis, The History of the Blues (New York: Hyperion, 1995). David Evans, ed., Journal of Black Music Research 20.1 (Spring 2000). Alan B. Govenar, The Early Years of Rhythm and Blues: Focus

Boerne Band in Fredericksburg, 1885. Today, the band is acclaimed as the "Oldest Continuously Organized German Band in the World outside Germany Itself." Courtesy Robert H. Thonhoff.

on Houston (Houston: Rice University Press, 1990). Alan Govenar, *Meeting the Blues* (New York: Da Capo Press, 1995). Alan Govenar and Jay Brakefield, *Deep Ellum and Central Track: Where the Black and White Worlds of Dallas Converged* (Denton: University of North Texas Press, 1998). Paul Oliver, *The New Grove Gospel, Blues and Jazz: With Spiritual and Ragtime* (London: Macmillan, 1986). Roger Wood, *Down in Houston: Bayou City Blues* (Austin: University of Texas Press, 2003).   *Alan Govenar*

Boerne Village Band. From Boerne, Texas, county seat of Kendall County; organized in 1860 by Karl Dienger. Having previously organized the Boerne Gesang Verein (singing club), Dienger organized the band to complement the singing festivals in Boerne with band music. He coordinated both musical groups from 1860 to 1885. Ottmar von Behr, who moved with his family to Sisterdale in the 1840s, was a strong influence in the band. Two of his children, Jennie and Ottmar, played with the group, and Jennie's husband, Fritz Fisher, taught his nephews, Ottmar Jr, Arthur, and Oscar to play musical instruments. In time, both Oscar and Ottmar Behr became directors of the band. Later, Oscar's daughter Roma married Alvin Herbst, and their son, Kenneth, a veterinarian, became the band director. In turn, Dr. Herbst's sons, Kenneth, Jr., and Clint, also became members. In all, the descendants of the Behr family have included four generations of musicians and three generations of directors of the Boerne Village Band.

The band managed to stay organized during the difficult Civil War period. After the war it continued to practice and play at various events in and around Boerne. During the world wars the group was less active but remained organized. After World War II Ottmar Behr, despite losing his son Calvin in Normandy, reassembled the group with Erhard Ebner, Henry Schrader, Eugene Ebell, Alvin Grosser, Fritz Grosser, Harry Grosser, and others participating.

In 1988 the Federal Republic of Germany recognized the Boerne Village Band for its contribution to the German heritage in Texas and America by donating to it much traditional German music and a magnificent tenor horn. For the band's 130th anniversary in 1990, Peter Fihn, a noted German composer, dedicated and presented his march "Grüsse an Texas" ("Greetings to Texas") to the band. In 1991 the Texas legislature adopted a resolution to recognize the Boerne Village Band for "keeping alive German music as a part of our heritage." The city of Boerne and the Boerne Area Historical Preservation Society have also recognized the band for its contribution to the German heritage of Boerne.

Additionally, in 1988 the Federal Republic of Germany presented Dr. Kenneth C. Herbst Sr., director of the band since 1972, with its Friendship Award. Otto Schicht, a special friend in Bavaria, helped obtain authentic uniforms for the band, which were first worn during its 1986 Texas Sesquicentennial performances. On May 2, 1992, Dr. and Mrs. Herbst and other invited guests attended a luncheon given by the president of Germany, Richard von Weizsäcker, during his state visit to Houston, where he commended the German musical tradition in Boerne. In 1996, Germany's most distinguished award for folk music, the Pro-Musica Plakette, given only to German Bands with more than 100 years of continuous existence, was presented to the Boerne Village Band by German president Roman Herzog.

Over the years, the German government has graciously donated several hundred pieces of sheet music to the band. German composers Hans Freivogel, Peter Fihn, and Alfred Fischer have dedicated march and waltz music to the band.

For fifteen years, 1985–2000, band members Rudolf and Lia Scheffrahn maintained the musicians' folders, which in the year 2001 held more than 300 selections of authentic German music.

Acclaimed as the "Oldest Continuously Organized German Band in the World outside Germany Itself," the Boerne Village Band celebrated its 140 anniversary on October 15, 2000. With sixteen members and several associates, the band continued in 2001 to practice weekly and perform regularly at the Texas Folklife Festival, the New Braunfels Wurstfest, the Kendall County Fair, the Boerne Berges Fest, Boerne Abendkonzerte (summer evening concerts) and many other area events. Additionally, it has traveled each year since 1995 to Monterrey, Mexico, to perform for the Deutscher Club and the Cuauhtémoc Moctezuma Brewery. In 1999 and 2000 the band played for the Germanfest at Robert's Cove, Louisiana.

In 1994, 1997, and 2000, the Boerne Village Band toured Germany and Austria, where it presented a series of concerts. A highlight of the year 2000 tour was performing a concert in honor of the 1000th anniversary of Bad Camberg, a small town near Runkel, Germany, where the band performed another concert at the Runkel Castle.

BIBLIOGRAPHY: *Boerne Village Band History* (City of Boerne, Texas, 2000). Garland Perry, *Historic Images of Boerne, Texas* (Boerne: Perry Enterprises, 1982).

Robert H. Thonhoff

Boles, John. Stage and screen star; b. Greenville, Texas, October 27, 1895; d. San Angelo, February 27, 1969; son of John Monroe and Mary Jane (Love) Boles. In early childhood Boles demonstrated an affection and talent for acting and singing. After graduating from the University of Texas in 1917, he returned to Greenville, where he was one of many "locals" selected by an out-of-town producer to act in an opera at the King Opera House. This experience convinced him that he preferred music and the stage to the preference of his parents, a medical degree and a doctor's practice. On June 21, 1917, Boles married Marielite Dobbs and, submitting to his parents' wishes, decided to attend medical school. For two years in World War I he served in the army intelligence service.

Afterward, he studied music in New York. His voice, physique, and handsome face led to his selection as the lead in the 1923 Broadway musical *Little Jesse James*. Boles quickly became an established star of Broadway and attracted the attention of Hollywood producers and actors. Gloria Swanson persuaded him to travel to Hollywood and star in the film *Loves of Sunya* (1926). After portraying Capt. Jim Stewart in *Rio Rita* (1929) he accepted the lead of Red Shadow in *The Desert Song* (1930) and became a matinee idol.

His arrival in Hollywood coincided with the introduction of talkies. Unlike many of his colleagues, Boles made the transition from silent to sound films with few problems. He acted in over a dozen films during the 1930s, normally playing a successful, sophisticated, urban businessman. He played opposite Barbara Stanwyck in *Stella Dallas* (1937), Rosalind Russell in *Craig's Wife* (1936), and Shirley Temple in *Curley Top* (1935), *Littlest Rebel*

(1935), and *Stand Up and Cheer* (1934). He also had roles in *Frankenstein* (1931) and *Back Street* (1932).

By the end of the decade, however, Boles's fame waned, and he left movie-making for eleven years. Over the decades he had saved his money and invested it in the oil business in Texas. In 1943 he starred with fellow Texan Mary Martin in *One Touch of Venus* on Broadway. He returned to the screen in *Babes in Baghdad* in 1952. From the mid-1950s, however, he lived and worked in San Angelo, where he died of a stroke. He was survived by his wife and two daughters.

BIBLIOGRAPHY: San Angelo *Standard Times*, February 28, 1969. Vertical files, Center for American History, University of Texas at Austin.

David Minor

Bollin, Zuzu. Blues singer; b. A. D. Bollin, Frisco, Texas, September 5, 1923; d. October 19, 1990. His social security records say he was born in 1923, though most music references give his birth year as 1922. As a boy, Bollin was influenced by two uncles, amateur guitarists, who played the records of Blind Lemon Jefferson and other early blues musicians.

He moved to Dallas with his mother by the 1930s, served in the navy from 1944 to 1946, and started performing professionally in the postwar years. In 1947 he was living in Denton, where he played in the band of Texan E. X. Brooks. During this time he took the nickname "Zuzu" from his favorite brand of gingersnap cookies. He also performed in bands with such illustrious Texas reedmen as Buster Smith, Booker Ervin, and Adolphus Sneed.

In 1949 Bollin formed a group with renowned saxists Leroy Cooper and David "Fathead" Newman. Both of these musicians played on his 1951 recording of one of the true classics of Texas blues, "Why Don't You Eat Where You Slept Last Night?" (flip side "Matchbox Blues"), for the short-lived label Torch. Bollin's voice was deep and strong, his guitar break in the jazzy T-Bone Walker style. The 1951 piece garnered a bit of regional fame for Bollin, so he figured he was entitled to raise his performance price a bit. Reputedly this irked Dallas nightclub boss Jack Ruby, who used his influence to quash the record.

In the 1950s and early 1960s Bollin traveled around Texas and the United States touring with various bands, including the band of Joe Morris, which backed such performers as Jackie Wilson. About 1964 he left the music business and went into dry cleaning. He fell into obscurity that lasted until 1987, when blues enthusiast Chuck Nevitt found him in a poverty-row roominghouse near downtown Dallas. Nevitt took Bollin down the comeback trail, acting as his manager and producing the acclaimed LP *Zuzu Bollin: Texas Bluesman*, sponsored by the Dallas Blues Society and released on the Antone's label in 1989. Bollin was suddenly ubiquitous in Dallas nightspots. The friendly, personable bluesman sometimes performed with the Juke Jumpers, but his most empathic accompanist was Brian "Hash Brown" Calway. In 1989 Bollin played at the Chicago Blues Festival and toured Europe, playing at Holland's prestigious Blues Estafette. His impressive comeback was curtailed by cancer, from which he died.

BIBLIOGRAPHY: Michael Erlewine et al., ed., *All Music*

Houston bluesman Juke Boy Bonner performing at Kerrville, Texas, 1975. Courtesy Brian Kanof.

1960s. In the late 1960s and early 1970s he toured Europe, where he recorded on the Flyright and Storyville labels (British). His best work, however, came in the late 1960s on the Arhoolie label. Songs such as "Going Back to the Country," "Struggle Here in Houston," and "Life Is a Nightmare" reflected his impoverished youth and the dangers he had faced living in big cities. Bonner continued to tour, work local venues, and record. He was married in 1950 and was later divorced. He died of cirrhosis of the liver. Five children survived him.

BIBLIOGRAPHY: Michael Erlewine, ed., *All Music Guide To The Blues* (San Francisco: Miller Freeman, 1999). Sheldon Harris, *Blues Who's Who* (New Rochelle, New York: Arlington House, 1979). Colin Larkin, ed., *The Guinness Encyclopedia of Popular Music* (New York: Guinness, 1995). Frank Scott, *The Down Home Guide To The Blues* (Chicago: Cappella,1991). *James Head*

Bonner, Moses J. Fiddle player and recording artist; birth date and place unknown; d. Fort Worth, September 2, 1939. Bonner was one of the earliest Texas country musicians to record and one of the first to play a radio "barn dance."

His family moved to Texas in 1854. Bonner joined the Twelfth Texas Cavalry (Confederate) in May 1864 and served until the end of the Civil War. Little is known of his life until 1901, when he, with Henry Gilliland and others, formed the Old Fiddlers' Association in Fort Worth.

Bonner participated in local and regional fiddle contests during the early twentieth century. In 1911 he tied with Gilliland and Jesse Roberts for the world's championship. On January 4, 1923, he broadcast a program of old-time fiddle music over WBAP, Fort Worth, thus becoming one of the earliest radio fiddle players. His radio popularity led to a recording session with Victor on March 17, 1925. Accompanied by Fred Wagoner on harp-guitar, Bonner waxed medleys of "Yearlings in the Canebrake" / "The Gal on the Log" and "Dusty Miller" / "Ma Ferguson." His rendition of "Dusty Miller" has become a classic of old-time fiddling.

Like Gilliland, Bonner was active in Confederate veterans' affairs and was eventually elevated to the rank of lieutenant general in the United Confederate Veterans.

BIBLIOGRAPHY: Keith Chandler, notes to *Texas Fiddle Bands* (Document Records DOCD-8038), which contains Bonner's complete recordings. Kevin S. Fontenot, "Country Music's Confederate Grandfather: Henry C. Gilliland," *Country Music Annual 2001* (Lexington: University Press of Kentucky, 2001). Bill C. Malone, *Country Music U.S.A.* (Austin: University of Texas Press, 1985).

Kevin S. Fontenot

Border Radio. The American broadcasting industry that sprang up on Mexico's northern border in the early 1930s and flourished for half a century. High-powered transmitters on Mexican soil, beyond the reach of U.S. regulators, blanketed North America with unique programming. Mexico accommodated these "outlaw" media operators, some of whom had been denied broadcasting licenses in the United States, because Canada and the United States

Guide to the Blues, Second Edition (San Francisco: Backbeat Books, 1999). *Living Blues*, January–February 1991.

Tim Schuller

Bonner, Juke Boy. Blues guitarist, vocalist, and harmonica player; b. Weldon Philip H. Bonner, Bellville, Texas, March 22, 1932; d. Houston, June 29, 1978; one of nine children of sharecroppers Emanuel and Carrie (Kessee) Bonner. His parents died when he was young, so he was raised by another family on a nearby farm. Bonner became interested in music when he was six and sang with a local spiritual group when he was in elementary school. By the time he was twelve, he had taught himself to play the guitar. He quit school when he was a teenager and moved to Houston to find a job. When he was fifteen, he won a talent contest held by Trummy Cain, a local talent coordinator. This led to an appearance on KLEE radio.

For the next decade, Bonner worked as a one-man band in lounges, bars, and clubs throughout the South and in California. He frequently worked in juke joints accompanied only by jukebox music; hence his nickname. In 1956 he cut his first record, "Rock Me Baby," with "Well Baby" as the flipside, on Bob Geddins's Irma label. Bonner made his next record for Goldband Records in 1960 and continued to record for Liberty, Sonet, and other labels during the

had divided the long-range radio frequencies between themselves, allotting none to Mexico. Though the "borderblaster" transmitters were always in Mexico, studios (especially in the early 1930s) were sometimes in the United States, and the stations were often identified by the American town across the border. For instance, in his classic poem, "Clem Maverick, the Life and Death of a Country Singer," R. G. Vliet has Clem reminisce: "We was on the radio at Del Rio." Early on, hillbilly music proved to be one of the most effective mediums for pulling mail and moving merchandise; in turn, the border stations played a significant role in popularizing country music during the genre's crucial growth years before and after World War II.

The stations also familiarized American listeners with Mexican and Mexican-American artists. Lydia Mendoza's future husband first heard the "Lark of the Border" from Piedras Negras station XEPN in 1937. "The highlight of the [XER] program, for me," recalled a South Dakota listener in 1995, "was the beautiful voice of the 'Mexican Nightingale' [Rosa Domínguez], especially when she would sing 'Estrellita'—this farm boy thought that must be how the angels would sound in heaven."

The first border station, XED, began broadcasting from Reynosa, Tamaulipas, in 1930. Owned for a time by Houston theater owner and philanthropist Will Horwitz, XED hosted occasional performances by Horwitz's friend Jimmie Rodgers. Horwitz, who dressed up as Santa Claus each year and distributed Christmas presents to Houston's underprivileged children, was sent to prison by the U.S. government for broadcasting the Tamaulipas state lottery over XED.

Dr. John R. Brinkley, originator of "the goat gland transplant" as a sexual rejuvenation treatment, opened XER (later called XERA) in Villa Acuña, Coahuila, in 1931. Brinkley also obtained XED, changing the name to XEAW. In 1939 he sold XEAW to Carr Collins, Dallas insurance magnate and owner of Crazy Water Crystals, a laxative product derived from the fabled Crazy Water in Mineral Wells. According to Collins's son Jim, Texas governor (and later U.S. senator) W. Lee "Pappy" O'Daniel was part-owner of the station. The Mexican government confiscated XERA in 1941 and tried to confiscate XEAW shortly thereafter, but Collins moved his equipment north of the border.

Engineer Bill Branch and businessman C. M. Bres operated XEPN in Piedras Negras in the 1930s. And Iowan Norman Baker, whose experimental cancer treatments made him a controversial figure, broadcast from his station XENT in Nuevo Laredo. Texas governor Ma Ferguson once dispatched Texas Rangers to Laredo to arrest Baker on a charge of practicing medicine without a license, but the defiant broadcaster could not be lured across the Rio Grande.

Border station power generally ranged from 50,000 to 500,000 watts. Sometimes listeners claimed to hear broadcasts without a radio, receiving the powerful signal on dental work, bedsprings, and barbed wire. American network programs were often lost in the ether when a Mexican border station was broadcasting near an American station's frequency.

Hank Thompson, who grew up in Waco in the 1930s, said the American-Mexican stations on the Rio Grande "were about the only ones where you could hear country-and-western music most all the time." (Later, as a navy radio engineer during World War II, Hank piped border-station programming through his ship on the high seas.) Thompson and other listeners heard Cowboy Slim Rinehart, Patsy Montana, the Carter Family, the Pickard Family, the Shelton Brothers, the Callahan Brothers, the International Hot Timers, Pappy O'Daniel's Hillbilly Boys, Roy "Lonesome Cowboy" Faulkner, Shelly Lee Alley, and countless others. Performers broadcast live and via transcription disc, sometimes syndicating a show on several of the maverick stations. Border radio pitchman and ad executive Don Baxter, aka Major Kord, recorded many artists with this technology in San Antonio. Later, many of the transcription discs made good roofing material for homes in Acuña and other border-station towns.

Important postwar stations included XEG in Monterrey and XERF in Ciudad Acuña. Webb Pierce, Jim Reeves, and other stars appeared live in the studio with XERF deejay Paul Kallinger, known from "coast to coast and border to border" as "Your Good Neighbor Along the Way." In a colorful exaggeration that could hold a nugget of truth, Pierce said that country music "might not have survived if it hadn't been for border radio."

The Good Neighbor turned down an appearance on his show by the future King of Rock, Elvis Presley. But in the early 1960s, a young platter-spinner from Brooklyn named Bob Smith metamorphosed into XERF's late-night saint of radio naughtiness, Wolfman Jack. From his border lair the Wolfman tantalized American listeners with rock-and-roll, rhythm-and-blues, and blues. Joe Ely recalls listening to the Wolfman while drinking beer in Lubbock cottonfields: "it was the first time any of us heard John Lee Hooker, Muddy Waters, Lightnin' Hopkins, Mance Lipscomb, all these guys." Delbert McClinton remembers the border airwave as a mysterious force. "With border radio," he explains, "you could hear race music and funky stuff, and it only existed through this secret channel you could pick up from across the border."

Some border musicians played several roles, such as singing cowboy, evangelist, and pitchman. "Only three things will sell on the border," says Dallas "Nevada Slim" Turner—"health, sex, and religion." Often, border radio programming combined all three. The stations also became known for incessant, long-winded advertisements that pitched Hillbilly Flour, Crazy Water Crystals, the cold remedy Peruna, the hair-dye Kolorbak, Hadacol, vinyl tablecloths depicting the Last Supper, razor blades, genuine simulated diamonds, ballpoint pens, horoscopes, rosebushes, baby chicks, records, and many other products. Some folks even claim to have heard commercials for "autographed photos of Jesus Christ."

In 1986, XERF was seized by the Mexican government, and all border stations were dealt a crippling blow by an international broadcasting agreement between the United States and Mexico that allowed both Mexican and American broadcasters to use the other country's clear-channel frequencies for low-powered stations in the evening. That meant that the signals of the border stations would be drowned out in many communities by local broadcasts. The agreement effectively ended the era of high-powered, far-ranging radio.

Or not. It may be that efforts at a revival, in the hands of such enthusiasts as Arturo Gonzalez, may succeed. In the early years of the new millennium, Del Rio attorney Gonzalez, a force at XERF since the 1940s, was, in his nineties, laying plans to regain control of the station and contacting engineering firms to shop for a new super-power transmitter.

BIBLIOGRAPHY: Gene Fowler and Bill Crawford, *Border Radio—Quacks, Yodelers, Psychics, Pitchmen, and Other Amazing Broadcasters of the American Airwaves* (Austin: University of Texas Press, 2002). San Francisco *Chronicle*, November 29, 1987.

Gene Fowler and Bill Crawford

Bowman, Euday Louis. Composer of the famed "Twelfth Street Rag"; b. Fort Worth, November 9, 1887; d. New York City, May 26, 1949 (buried in Oakwood Cemetery, Fort Worth); son of George A. Bowman and Marguerite Olivia Estee Landin. Bowman was raised with his older brother and sister on his grandfather's (Isaac Gatewood Bowman's) farm, east of Mansfield, Texas. He most likely attended Webb School or Lloyd School in eastern Tarrant County. He apparently told many people that, when his parents were divorced in 1905, he left home and went to Kansas City. But the evidence indicates that he moved to Fort Worth to live with his sister, Mary, a school and piano teacher who taught her brother to play the piano. Euday played at local night spots and worked as a junk dealer. In 1920 he married Geneva Morris, but she left him after a couple of months, and they were divorced in 1926.

Bowman had a reputation as a local celebrity and entertained by invitation in private livingrooms and fire halls, as well as at such public venues as the Meadow Brook and the Garland. He wrote sheet music and made a few trips to Kansas City to promote his songs and attempt to sell his music. He probably wrote "Twelfth Street Rag" while playing in a Main Street shoe-shine parlor located between Tenth and Eleventh streets in Fort Worth. Though he wrote several original compositions between 1914 and 1917, including "Fort Worth Blues," "Tipperary Blues," and "Kansas City Blues," the unusual combination of a repeating three-note melody and duple-metered bass made "Twelfth Street Rag" his most popular hit. It inspired jazz musicians for decades. Despite the popularity of the catchy tune, Bowman made very little money from it. In 1916 he had sold the copyright and royalties to Jenkins Music Company for a price between $50 and $100. In 1941 he renewed the copyright and sold it to Shapiro, Bernstein & Company of New York City.

Although first published in 1914, "Twelfth Street Rag" had a profound influence on jazz from the late 1920s through the 1940s. Among the dozens of musicians, groups, and arrangers who interpreted Bowman's rag are Louis Armstrong and his Hot Seven (1927), the Bennie Moten band (1927), Duke Ellington with Benny Payne (1931), Fats Waller and his Rhythm (1935), Count Basie

with Lester Young (1939), Andy Kirk and his Twelve Clouds of Joy with Mary Lou Williams (1940), Sidney Bechet and his New Orleans Feetwarmers (1941), and Walter "Pee Wee" Hunt (1948). Jazz critics and enthusiasts credit "Twelfth Street Rag" with helping re-ignite an interest in ragtime. Because of their musical features—descending and ascending arpeggios, exaggerated syncopation, call-and-response motifs, sophisticated swing and stride styles, cool and bop interpretations—the various recordings of the piece chronicle the progression of jazz over the decades. Besides the more than 120 versions recorded by other artists, Bowman recorded his rag in 1924 and in 1938, although his interpretation was never issued until he released his own recording of the song in 1948.

Other pieces published or copyrighted by Bowman include "Colorado Blues," "Petticoat Lane," "Old Glory on Its Way," "Shamrock Rag," "Eleventh Street Rag," "Water Lily Dreams" and "Jubilee Ball." Bowman's songs appear on many albums by various artists, including Albert Ammons, Louis Armstrong and his All Stars, Count Basie, Teddy Buckner and his Dixieland Band, Al Caiola, Duke Ellington, Lionel Hampton, Fats Waller, Bob Wills, and Lester Young.

Bowman married again on February 6, 1949, but he filed for divorce the next month, claiming that his wife, Ruth Emma Thompson, treated him cruelly. In May 1949 he made his only trip to New York City to appeal for royalties earned by "Twelfth Street Rag." After three days he caught pneumonia and died. He left an automobile and royalties amounting to about $11,000 to his sister, Mary. Most of his hand-notated sheet music is in an extensive Bowman collection at the Pate Museum of Transportation, near Cresson, Texas.

BIBLIOGRAPHY: *ASCAP Biographical Dictionary*, Fourth edition (New York: Bowker, 1980). Barbara Cohen–Stratyner, ed., "Twelfth Street Rag," *Popular Music 1900–1919: An Annotated Guide* (Detroit: Gale Research, Inc., 1988). Fort Worth *Star–Telegram*, December 20, 1992; January 7, 2001. H. Wiley Hitchcock and Stanley Sadie, eds., *The New Grove Dictionary of American Music* (New York: Macmillan, 1986). Dave Oliphant, *Texan Jazz* (Austin: University of Texas Press, 1996).

Cheryl L. Simon

Bowser, Erbie. Blues, jazz, and boogie-woogie pianist; b. Davila, Texas, May 5, 1918; d. Austin, August 15, 1995; youngest of ten children. Bowser's parents moved the family to Palestine, Texas, when he was five. His father played the violin, and his mother played piano, violin, and accordion. Erbie began playing piano and singing in the church choir, as his musical parents expected.

While still attending Lincoln High School, he joined the North Carolina Cotton Pickers Review and began performing throughout the South during summer vacations. After high school he joined the Sunset Entertainers and toured Texas with the Tyler-based band, playing blues, jazz, and big band tunes. He soon toured Europe and North Africa with the Special Services Band, playing at USO shows in England, Sicily, Italy, and Africa. Upon his discharge from military service he worked as a brick mason, and then attended Jarvis Christian College in Hawkins, Texas, for two years. His parents' death prevented him from finishing college. He married a woman from Greenville, Texas, in 1948. Around 1949 the couple moved to Odessa. There Bowser found a job with Midwestern Drilling Company, while his wife went to work at the local hospital.

Bowser met guitarist T. D. Bell working in the oilfields of West Texas. The two began playing together with Johnny Holmes at nightspots in West Texas and New Mexico. Their musical partnership lasted five decades. Bowser and his wife moved to Austin in the mid-1950s, so she could attend Huston–Tillotson College. In Austin Bowser began a twenty-year career with the National Cash Register Company. He also participated in jam sessions with musicians from nearby colleges, performed with fraternity bands such as the Sweetarts, and played solo at the Commodore Perry Hotel. When Bell moved to Austin around 1960, he and Bowser began playing together at the Victory Grill, the Club Petit, and Charlie's Playhouse. Eventually, various combinations of Bowser, Bell, and such musicians

Pianist Erbie Bowser performing for the Texas Folklife Resources program "Texas Piano Professors" (1992–94). Along with his longtime collaborator T. D. Bell, Bowser played a mix of jazz, blues, and boogie-woogie from the 1950s to the 1970s. Photograph by Jane Levine, courtesy Texas Folklife Resources.

as the Grey Ghost, Mel Davis, James Jones, Lem Nichols, and Fred Smith became known as the Blues Specialists.

Bowser and the Blues Specialists were regular fixtures on the Austin music scene throughout the 1960s and 1970s. After a hiatus, in the late 1980s Bowser and Bell returned to the stage. In 1991 they released an LP entitled *It's About Time* (Spindletop). Sponsored by folklorists and blues and jazz enthusiasts such as Tary Owens, and by organizations such as the Texas Commission on the Arts, Bowser made national and international appearances, including performances at the Smithsonian Institution and Carnegie Hall. This return from semiretirement resulted in a revival of the Blues Specialists, and Bowser and Bell became regular performers at venues such as the Continental Club.

Bowser credited the influence of his parents, his wife, and a high school music teacher, B. G. Bradley, for his success and his early interest in music. His wife of forty-seven years coached him through difficult songs, because, although he had an excellent ear, he could not read music. Bradley, who had played with Erskin Hawkins before becoming a teacher, encouraged Bowser to play from his heart. Other influences included Dorothy Campbell, Nat Williams, Ella Fitzgerald, Louis Armstrong, and the Ink Spots. During his fifty-year career, Bowser worked with many other fine performers, such as Jim Watts, George Rains, Mark Kazanoff, Ed Guinn, Jonathan Foose, Long John Hunter, Little Daddy Lot, Spec Hicks, and Marcia Ball.

Among the honors and recognitions extended to Bowser are a proclamation of honor from the Texas Commission on the Arts and induction into the Texas Music Hall of Fame. Displays and holdings honoring him include biographical and charcoal portraits in the "Texas Piano Professors" exhibit at the Texas Music Museum in Austin and interviews and biographical sketches in the keeping of the Austin Blues Family Tree Project. Bowser died of cancer at St. David's Hospital, Austin. His piano can be heard on such recordings as Tary Owens's *Texas Piano Professors* (1987), the *Blues Specialists Liveset: January, 15, 1989*, Long John Hunter's *Ride with Me* (1992), and *Blues Routes: Heroes & Tricksters* (1999).

BIBLIOGRAPHY: Austin *American–Statesman*, August 16, 1995. Harold McMillan, "Hometown Cats: Interview with Erbie Bowser" (http://www.klru.org/Jazz/Jazz_hometowncats_bowserBio.html), accessed May 16, 2002.

Cheryl L. Simon

Boxcar Willie. Country music performer; b. Lecil Travis Martin, Sterrett, Texas, September 1, 1931; d. Branson, Missouri, April 12, 1999; eldest son of Birdie Brown and Edna (Jones) Martin. Martin developed a love of country and gospel music during his childhood through singing with his family while his father played the fiddle. He cultivated that love by listening to the "Grand Ole Opry" on the radio. In his early teens he began performing in country music clubs near Dallas.

At the age of seventeen, he garnered an appearance on "Big D Jamboree," a country music show broadcast by Dallas radio station KRLD. Despite reports to the contrary, however, Martin wrote that he never became a regular on the show. Another influence during his early years was his family's close connection to trains. Birdie Martin worked for the railroad in 1931, and the family lived in a small, company-owned house near the tracks. Frequently, Lecil's mother would give hobos that knocked on her door a meal in exchange for doing some small task such as sharpening her knives. After he was laid off during the Great Depression, Birdie occasionally traveled with some of these hobos, riding freight trains to find work.

Lecil himself rode the rails as a teenager. In 1949 he joined the air force, where he served as a flight engineer for twenty years. During his service, he occasionally worked in small clubs under the name Marty Martin. He also spent several years on military reserve status working at various jobs including television and radio positions. For a short time he owned and operated Martin's Auto Repair Service in Midlothian. These years constituted a relatively unsettled period in the performer's life. He married and divorced several times, and became the father of seven children and stepchildren.

Eventually, Martin's life grew more settled, and he resumed his stage career. In the mid-seventies, he began appearing as Boxcar Willie, a singing hobo sporting striped overalls, a ragged jacket, and a crumpled fedora. Although this hobo persona came from his childhood memories of Texas, Martin stated that Boxcar Willie was "born" several years earlier in Lincoln, Nebraska. In a 1997 interview, he told an Associated Press reporter that he was waiting in Lincoln for a freight train to clear the tracks when he saw a hobo in a passing boxcar. The man reminded Martin of a friend named Willie Wilson. "I said, 'There's Willie in a boxcar,'" the singer stated, "and that's where [the idea] came from."

The performer's first appearance as Boxcar Willie took place at a club in Corpus Christi. In October 1979 he retired from the military in order to concentrate on his musical career. Soon, the hobo was also appearing regularly at several clubs in the Dallas–Fort Worth area. Martin's new look proved popular, especially in Britain, where he toured successfully several times. Through the 1980s, he supplemented his repertoire of traditional country and gospel melodies with train songs such as "Wabash Cannonball" and his most popular tune, "Train Medley." His realistic imitation of a train whistle and his unique hobo persona helped him to build a large and devoted following in the United States and the United Kingdom. In 1981, after several successful appearances on the "Grand Ole Opry," he became a member of the show. He also became a regular guest on the long-running television show "Hee Haw." His *King of the Road* album, released in 1982, was number one on the British country music chart for nineteen weeks and eventually sold nearly a million copies in the UK. Despite these successes, however, Martin never had a hit record in the United States.

In 1986 he and his fourth wife, Lloene (Davis Johnson) Martin, bought a theater in Branson, Missouri. The Boxcar Willie Theater opened the following May, and Willie retired from the road. He continued to perform at the successful theater through 1998, often appearing in as many

as six shows a week during the town's nine-month tourist season. Soon, he expanded his business in Branson, adding a train museum and two motels. In 1996 he was diagnosed with leukemia. Although he enjoyed a brief remission after treatment, he eventually died of the disease.

BIBLIOGRAPHY: Fred Deller, et al., *The Harmony Illustrated Encyclopedia of Country Music* (New York: Harmony, 1997). "Lecil Travis Martin," in *Fuller Up: The Dead Musician Directory* (*http://elvispelvis.com/boxcarwillie.htm*), accessed September 5, 1999. Lecil Travis Martin, *Box Car Willie: My Life Story* (Springfield, Missouri: Cantrell-Barnes Printing, 1997). New York *Times*, April 14, 1999. *Constance M. Bishop*

Boyd, William Lemuel. Western swing bandleader; b. near Ladonia, Fannin County, Texas, September 29, 1910; d. Dallas, December 7, 1977; one of thirteen children of Lemuel and Molly (Jared) Boyd. Boyd was a pioneer who led the Cowboy Ramblers, an influential band associated with the music scene in Dallas. Recording for the Victor record label from 1934 to 1951, Bill Boyd's Cowboy Ramblers maintained a western swing feel while remaining basically a country string band and recording enormously influential songs such as "Under the Double Eagle"(1935) and "Lone Star Rag" (1949).

The Boyd family moved to Texas from Tennessee around 1902. The children were exposed to music through their parents, both of whom sang, as well as by the singing and playing of the ranchhands. After purchasing a guitar through a mail-order catalog, Bill and his younger brother, Jim (born in 1914), were performing country music on radio KFPM in Greenville as early as 1926. The Boyd family moved in 1929 to Dallas, where Bill worked a number of odd jobs such as laborer and salesman while pursuing his musical career. He quickly became active as a local musician and played on Jimmie Rodgers's Dallas recording session in 1932.

In that same year Bill organized the Cowboy Ramblers. The original lineup of his band included Jim Boyd on bass, Art Davis on fiddle, and Walter Kirkes on tenor banjo. They soon found regular radio work on station WRR and in 1934 were signed to Victor's budget label, Bluebird. The band continued to record for them until 1951, during which time they recorded more than 229 singles. Though they moved toward the performance of jazz and swing music, the Cowboy Ramblers basically remained a string band, not using brass instruments like many bands of that era. While their recorded output includes blues, cowboy songs, and novelty tunes, waltzes and fiddle tunes were their staples. The Cowboy Ramblers were influential recording musicians, with songs that remained country standards long after being recorded in the 1930s. "Under the Double Eagle," for instance, became one of the most popular instrumentals in all of country music.

Unlike many bands, the Cowboy Ramblers didn't spend much time touring. With most of their performances coming in the recording studio and on radio stations, they were basically a recording band. Their members, however, often played with other groups. Although Bill and Jim Boyd were the mainstays, the Cowboy Ramblers had a number of

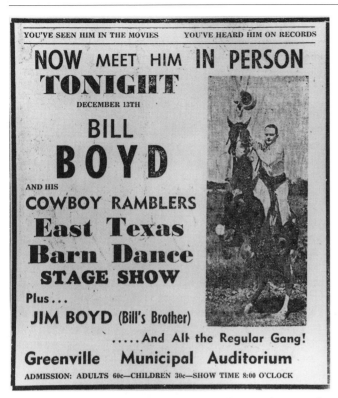

YOU'VE SEEN HIM IN THE MOVIES   YOU'VE HEARD HIM ON RECORDS

NOW MEET HIM **IN PERSON**
TONIGHT
DECEMBER 13TH
BILL
BOYD
AND HIS
COWBOY RAMBLERS
East Texas
Barn Dance
STAGE SHOW
Plus...
JIM BOYD (Bill's Brother)
.....And All the Regular Gang!
Greenville Municipal Auditorium
ADMISSION: ADULTS 60c—CHILDREN 30c—SHOW TIME 8:00 O'CLOCK

Greenville, Texas, newspaper advertisement for a performance by Bill Boyd and his Cowboy Ramblers, December 13, 1947. Bill Boyd Papers, CAH; CN 11493

important sidemen pass through their ranks, such as Art Davis, Jesse Ashlock, Cecil Brower, and Knocky Parker. A younger Boyd brother, John, also played steel guitar on later recordings as well as forming his own band, the Southerners, in the late 1930s. John continued to perform until his death in 1942. Jim Boyd, as well as playing with the Cowboy Ramblers and several other bands, also formed his own group, the Men of the West, and continued to work part-time as late as 1975.

Bill Boyd and his Ramblers also appeared in six western films in the 1940s, including *Raiders of the West* (1942) and *Texas Man Hunt* (1942), and is often mistakenly confused with William Boyd—Hopalong Cassidy. In the 1950s, as live music broadcasts on the radio were edged out by the playing of records, Bill Boyd switched to working as an announcer and disc jockey, continuing his long-time association with station WRR. He retired after he suffered a stroke in 1973. He was survived by his wife, Mildred, and two daughters.

BIBLIOGRAPHY: Richard Carlin, *The Big Book of Country Music: A Biographical Encyclopedia* (New York: Penguin, 1995). Patrick Carr, ed., *The Illustrated History of Country Music* (New York: RandomHouse / Times Books, 1995). Dallas *Morning News*, December 9, 1977. Michael Erlewine, *All Music Guide to Country: The Expert's Guide to the Best Recordings in Country Music* (San Francisco: Miller Freeman, 1997). Bill C. Malone, *Country Music, U.S.A.*, revised edition (Austin: University of Texas Press, 1985).

Linc Leifeste

Boze, Calvin. Rhythm-and-blues musician; b. Trinity County, Texas, October 15, 1916; d. West Los Angeles, California, June 18, 1950; son of Calvin Boze Sr., a day laborer, and Sarah (Taylor) Boze. The younger Calvin Boze is best known as a formative member of the rhythm-and-blues scene in Los Angeles during the early 1950s. In the mid-1930s, he was a trumpet leader in the Wheatley High band that included such future music luminaries as Illinois and Russell Jacquet, Arnett Cobb, Tom Archia, and Richard Dell.

Boze attended college at Prairie View A&M and was a member of the Prairie View Collegians band. By the 1940s he had become a vocalist for the Southwestern Territory Band of Marvin Johnson. He was later a trumpeter for the Milton Larkin Orchestra. During this period he developed his noted vocal style, patterned after Louis Jordan.

By 1949 Boze was in Los Angeles and recording for Aladdin Records. His songs have been described as solid, jive-talking rhythm-and-blues. His best-known numbers are "Safronia B" and "Angel City Blues." He also wrote "Texas Blues" and "Hot Lips and Seven Kisses" for fellow Aladdin artist Charles Brown. Starting in January 1950, Boze formed his own group, the Calvin Boze Combo, and had an extended gig at Georgia's Playroom in Los Angeles. By April 1950, Boze's band, rechristened the Calvin Boze All-Stars, was touring the West Coast with the Ravens. In summer 1950 they began a tour of the East Coast, including an appearance at the Apollo Theater.

Boze returned to Los Angeles to record more songs with Aladdin in 1952, including "Looped," which did well on the rhythm-and-blues charts. For unknown reasons, in 1953 Boze completely and permanently dropped out of the music scene.

BIBLIOGRAPHY: "Remembering Calvin Boze" (http://home.earthlink.net/~jaymar41/cboze.html), accessed October 24, 2002. Colin Larkin, *The Encyclopedia of Popular Music* (New York; Grove's Dictionaries, 1998).

Mike Reaves

Britain, Radie. Composer, pianist, writer, and teacher; b. near Silverton, Texas, March 17, 1899; d. Palm Desert, California, May 23, 1994; daughter of Edgar Charles and Katie (Ford) Britain. She was one of the most successful Texas-born composers of symphonic music in the twentieth century.

By 1905 the family had moved to a ranch near Clarendon; Radie began her piano studies in earnest at Clarendon College. Even though the family later moved to Amarillo, Radie remained in Clarendon to finish high school and all the music curriculum offered there. After high school, she studied one year at Crescent College near Eureka Springs, Arkansas. All her early studies were with good European-trained teachers who recognized her superior talents and predicted success for her in the music world. In the fall of 1919 she enrolled at the American Conservatory in Chicago, where she studied piano with Heniot Levy. She completed her B.M. degree in 1921. She then spent a year (1921–22) as music teacher at Clarendon College and set up her own teaching studio in Amarillo (1922–23), saving as much money as possible for a trip to Europe for further

Sheet music cover "Lasso of Time (The End of the Trail)" by Radie Britain (Neil A. Kjos Music Co., Chicago). Lota Harrigan Spell Papers, CAH: CN 11519.

study. During the summer of 1922, she studied in Dallas with the organist Pietro Yon.

Britain made her first trip to Europe during the summer of 1923. She settled in Paris, where she studied organ with Marcel Dupré. After another year teaching privately in Amarillo, she set her sights on Germany. She moved to Berlin and studied piano with Adele aus der Ohre (1924), but soon moved to Munich to study with Albert Noelte (1924–26), who encouraged her to pursue composition seriously. She had her first compositions published there and made a successful debut as a composer in May 1926. The death of her younger sister in Amarillo forced Britain to return to the U.S., but she continued studying with Noelte in Chicago (1926–27), where he had moved. Britain herself moved to Chicago permanently to teach with Noelte at Girvin Institute of Music and Allied Arts.

During these years she began to compose orchestral works, the genre that produced her greatest successes. Her training as an organist gave her insights as an orchestrator, and she began to produce a long series of programmatic orchestral works in the tradition of German post-romanticism. Her *Heroic Poem* (1929) was inspired by Charles Lindbergh's flight and won the Juilliard National Publication Prize in 1930. With the help of her mentor Noelte and encouragement from the Federal Music Project, her works were played by symphony orchestras all over the country during the next decade.

Her career underway, Britain finally pursued marriage.

Her first husband, Leslie Edward Moeller, was a Chicago businessman with little interest in his wife's career. They married in June 1930, and Britain's only child, Lerae, was born in 1932. An earlier-generation woman composer, Amy Beach, made it possible for Britain to spend the summers of 1935 and 1936 at the famed MacDowell Colony. During the 1930s Britain fell in love with the Italian sculptor Edgardo Simone (1889–1949). After divorcing her first husband in 1939, she moved to California and married Simone (1940). After Simone's death, Britain married Theodore Morton, an aviation pioneer, in 1959. Morton died in 1993.

In 1941 Britain settled in Hollywood. There she taught piano and composition and continued a distinguished career as a composer. She is undoubtedly the most honored Texas composer in history. More than fifty of her works received international or national awards. She was given an honorary doctorate by the Musical Arts Conservatory in Amarillo in 1958. Throughout her career she maintained a connection to her native Southwest. One of her first published piano pieces in Munich was *Western Suite* (1925), and she returned to her roots many times for inspiration and titles. Among her orchestral works are *Southern Symphony* (1935), *Drouth* (1939), *Paint Horse and Saddle* (1947), *Cowboy Rhapsody* (1956), and *Texas* (1987). Similar titles can be found in her piano, vocal, and chamber music works.

For decades Radie Britain was associated with the National League of American Pen Women. She wrote numerous articles in magazines and journals. In 1959 she wrote an unpublished autobiographical novel, *Bravo*, based on her relationship with Edgardo Simone. Her other published writings include *Major and Minor Moods* (Hollywood, 1970), a collection of autobiographical and inspirational short stories; *Composer's Corner* (Hollywood, 1978), a collection of her articles from *National Pen Women Magazine*; and *Ridin' Herd to Writing Symphonies: an Autobiography* (Lanham, Maryland, 1996), a fascinating memoir published posthumously.

Collections of Radie Britain's music (published and manuscript) are housed in several locations: the Amarillo Public Library; the American Music Center, New York; the Edwin A. Fleisher Collection of Orchestral Music, Philadelphia; the Moldenhauer Collection at Harvard University; the Texas Composers Collection at the Center for American History, University of Texas at Austin; and the Radie Britain Collection in the UCLA Music Library's Archival Collection. The composer's original music scores, manuscripts, and tapes are at the Indiana University School of Music. The Radie Britain Papers (scrapbooks, letters, programs, notes, newspaper articles,citations, and photos) are housed at the Center for American History, University of Texas at Austin.

BIBLIOGRAPHY: Christine Ammer, *Unsung: A History of Women in American Music*, Century Edition, Second Edition (Portland, Oregon: Amadeus Press, 2001). Walter B. and Nancy Gisbrecht Bailey, *Radie Britain: A Bio-Bibliography* (New York: Greenwood Press, 1990). Radie Britain, *Ridin' Herd to Writing Symphonies: An Autobiography* (Lanham, Maryland: Scarecrow Press, 1996). Jane Weiner

Micael Priest poster advertising "Genuine Texas Swing" with members of the original Texas Playboys and Alvin Crow and the Pleasant Valley Boys at the Broken Spoke, September 17, 1975. Courtesy George B. Ward.

LePage, *Women Composers, Conductors, and Musicians of the Twentieth Century: Selected Biographies* (Metuchen, New Jersey: Scarecrow Press, 1980). *New Grove Dictionary of Music and Musicians*, Second Edition (Washington, D.C., 2000).   *Larry Wolz*

Broken Spoke. On South Lamar in Austin; established in 1964 by proprietor James White; claims to be the "last of the true Texas dance halls." The Broken Spoke is a bastion for traditional country music. Its standard honky-tonk decor—red-checkered tablecloths, low ceilings, pool tables, and neon lights—appeals to city folk as well as those from the country. As one reporter stated, "Here, on the skating rink–type dance floor, cowpokes mix with city slickers and good ol' gals gather with alternachicks—with lots of intermingling going on." Owner White says the Broken Spoke is about showing people a good time in a safe, family-friendly atmosphere. "It doesn't matter if you are a millionaire or a ditch digger, all can have a good time at the Spoke."

The Broken Spoke opened for business as a cafe on November 10, 1964. The name was inspired by the owner's memories of a radio program called "Broken Arrow," combined with his fondness for wagon wheels. When customers started dancing to music from the jukebox, White moved the pool tables and added more room. People were still dancing anywhere they could, including out on the dirt parking lot underneath the big oak tree. Other customers played a few of the songs they had written. Never one to pass up an opportunity, White expanded the Broken Spoke to its current size in 1966, when he added a dance floor.

Local groups started performing at the Spoke as early as 1964. White was later able to book more well-known acts, including Bob Wills and His Texas Playboys, Roy Acuff, Tex Ritter, Ray Price, Floyd Tillman, and Ernest Tubb. In the 1970s, he booked the "outlaw" bands that had gained notoriety by rebelling against Nashville's more mainstream sound. Leading this brigade were Kris Kristofferson and Willie Nelson. Such Texas favorites as the Dixie Chicks and George Strait also played the Broken Spoke when they were just starting out. Although these superstars moved on, other well-loved performers such as Jerry Jeff Walker and Gary P. Nunn continued to play the Broken Spoke in the third millennium. Local favorites included the Geezinslaw Brothers, Chris Wall, Don Walser, the Derailers, and Alvin Crow.

In 1988 Crow and White formed a record label, the Broken Spoke Company, which White states is "all for fun. There's no fancy recording studio—just the stage at the Broken Spoken on Monday when it's closed." A singer and songwriter himself, White has performed with many of the Spoke's acts, including Willie Nelson and the Sons of the Pioneers. He has also written songs such as "Where There's a Willy, There's a Way" and "The Broken Spoke Legend," which appears on Alvin Crow's album *Pure Country*.

The Broken Spoke has been featured on PBS's "Austin City Limits" and the Country Music Television special "Honky Tonk Sounds." Nelson filmed parts of his movie *Honeysuckle Rose* (1980) there, and the Dolly Parton–Gary Busey film *Wild Texas Wind* (1991), featuring Broken Spoke mainstay Asleep at the Wheel, was partly filmed there. The Spoke is also known for showcasing young Texas country talent. According to White, "We like the cover stuff, but we like original songs more. We like to have the steel guitar and fiddles. They define Texas country from other country music."

The Broken Spoke features live music nightly, Tuesday through Saturday. The kitchen, source of the Spoke's famous Chicken Fried Steak, is open from 10:30 in the morning until 10:30 at night. *Texas Highways*, *National Geographic*, and *Entertainment Weekly* have honored the Broken Spoke for its down-home cooking and traditional Texas honky-tonk atmosphere.

Ernest Tubb once told White to "keep it country." "I've always kept it country," White said, "for him and myself. The Broken Spoke ain't fancy, but it sure is country."

BIBLIOGRAPHY: *Broken Spoke* (http://www.lone-star.net/bspoke/), accessed January 28, 2003. "Broken Spoke," *Austin Chronicle Live Music Venue Guide* (http://www.austinchronicle.com/issues/vol18/issue25/xtra.live_music_guide/feature.brokenspoke.html), accessed January 28, 2003. James White, telephone interview by Tanya Krause, November 14, 2002.   *Tanya Krause*

Brown, Charles. Pianist and vocalist; b. Tony Russell Brown, Texas City, September 13, 1922 (some accounts say 1920); d. January 21, 1999; son of John (Mose) Brown, a cotton picker, and Mattie Evelyn Simpson Brown. Mattie Brown died when the boy was six months old, and his father was killed by a train in 1928. Charles was raised by his maternal grandparents, Conquest and Swanee Simpson. Mrs. Simpson, a church choir director, encouraged him to learn classical music and provided him with piano training.

Brown played in the band at Central High School in Galveston, and also at various local clubs with saxophonist Costello James, his science teacher at the high school. Brown enrolled at Prairie View A&M College in 1939 and graduated in 1942 with a degree in chemistry. During his college years he played with the Prairie View Collegians, and in 1942 he was voted the most popular student on the campus. After college he worked as a chemistry teacher at George Washington Carver High School in Baytown, at the federal arsenal in Pine Bluff, Arkansas, manufacturing mustard gas, and as an apprentice electrician in a shipyard in Richmond, California, before settling in Los Angeles in 1943.

In Los Angeles he worked briefly as a church organist and as an elevator operator in a downtown department store. In 1944 he won first prize in an amateur talent show at the Lincoln Theater, and was hired by Mark Neal, the husband of jazz singer Ivie Anderson, to play at Ivie's Chicken Shack, a local nightclub. Brown quit the job when he was denied a raise, and was working part-time at the Lincoln Theater playing the piano for rehearsals when Johnny Moore, who had also been in the audience when Brown won the amateur contest, invited him to join Moore's band, the Three Blazers. Brown debuted with the group at the Talk of the Town, a Beverly Hills nightclub, in September 1944. The Three Blazers quickly became a popular attraction at local clubs, and Eddie Mesner, the head of Philo Records, signed them to a recording contract. In 1946 their song "Driftin' Blues," featuring Brown's smooth vocals, became one of the nation's top rhythm-and-blues hits. The Three Blazers had a string of hits, including "So Long," "Sunny Road," "Groovy Movie Blues," and "Merry Christmas Baby," the last of which was released during the 1947 Christmas season.B

Brown left the Blazers in 1948 for a solo career following a financial disagreement with Moore. He recorded over 200 sides with Aladdin Records and had several hits, including "Black Night," "Trouble Blues," and "Seven Long Days," but a dispute with the label over royalties and the advent of the rock-and-roll era caused Brown's musical popularity to wane. In 1958 he retired from touring, unable to pay his musicians' union dues in the wake of a legal dispute with his booking agency. In 1959 he found work in a casino in Newport, Kentucky.

Although Brown continued to record sporadically, the buying public largely ignored his albums. For most of the next two decades he worked as a janitor, window washer, and music teacher to make ends meet. In the late 1970s two events helped resurrect his career: in 1978 the country-rock band the Eagles recorded his song "Please Come Home For Christmas," which reached number eighteen on the national charts, and in 1979 he played a lengthy engagement at Tramps, a nightclub in New York City, which led to several European tours. In 1988 he was featured in the documentary film *That Rhythm . . .Those Blues,* and the following year he opened for Grammy-winning singer Bonnie Raitt on her national tour. In the 1980s and 1990s Brown recorded a number of albums, including *One More for the Road* (1986), *All My Life* (1990), *Someone to Love* (1992), *These Blues* (1994), *Just a Lucky So and So* (1994), *Honeydripper* (1996), and *So Goes Love* (1998). In addition, the Rhythm & Blues Foundation awarded him its Lifetime Achievement Award in 1989, and he received a National Endowment for the Arts Heritage Award in 1997. Two months after his death from congestive heart failure, Brown was inducted into the Rock and Roll Hall of Fame in Cleveland, Ohio. Both of his marriages, to singer Mabel Scott in 1948 and to Eva McGhee in 1959, ended in divorce. He left no children.

BIBLIOGRAPHY: Michael Erlewine, ed., *All Music Guide To The Blues* (San Francisco: Miller Freeman, 1999). Sheldon Harris, *Blues Who's Who* (New Rochelle, New York: Arlington House, 1979). *The Independent* (London), January 27, 1999. Colin Larkin, ed., *The Guinness Encyclopedia of Popular Music* (New York: Guinness, 1995). San Francisco *Chronicle,* January 23, 1999. *Living Blues* 118 (November–December 1994), no. 144 (March–April 1999). *Martin Donell Kohout*

Brown, Milton. Western swing bandleader and singer; b. William Milton Brown, Stephenville, Texas, September 8, 1903; d. Fort Worth, April 18, 1936; son of B. L. "Barty" and Martha Annie (Hueford) Brown. Milton's parents were cotton sharecroppers who were determined that Milton and his older sister, Era Lee, would get an education and not spend their lives in the cottonfields. Milton and Era attended the Smith Springs school. Both were good and popular students who showed a talent for singing at an early age. Stephenville's entertainment center, known as the Stephenville Jokey Yard, served as a marketplace as well as performance venue for the traveling medicine shows that came to town. The tent-show patter and musical numbers performed there may well have influenced the stage presence Brown developed later. His early vocal repertoire included church songs and sentimental ballads learned at home. In September 1915 a second son, Melvin Durwood, was born to the Brown family.

In May 1918, Era died. Devastated by her death, the family moved to Fort Worth a few months later. They settled on the city's west side close to the Bain Peanut Company, where Barty found work. Another son, Roy Lee, was born in Fort Worth in February 1921. Over the next several years Milton attended school, but dropped out periodically to help support the family by working with his father. As a result of this sporadic school attendance, he did not graduate from Arlington Heights High School until 1925. He was not sure what direction his talents would take him, but he was sure that he wanted to make his living in music. Although Barty Brown was an accomplished fiddle player and Milton's brothers both became musicians, Milton never showed an interest in any musical expression besides singing.

By 1927 Brown was singing with his friends Roy McBride and Ellis Fagan in a group called the Rock Island Rockets. Advertised on radio and in newspapers, the group received good responses at their performances around town for various organizations and businesses. Before long, young Durwood started playing guitar with his brother at singing engagements. The Brown brothers met fiddler Bob Wills and guitarist Herman Arnspiger in the spring of 1930 at a Fort Worth house dance. They formed a band, the Wills Fiddle Band, which played every Saturday night at the Eagles' Fraternal Hall in downtown Fort Worth. After winning a fiddle contest in the summer of 1930, the band performed on KFJZ radio, Fort Worth, and later on WBAP, Dallas. The group also played at the Crystal Springs dance hall, a popular club near Fort Worth. Wills hired tenor banjoist Clifton "Sleepy" Johnson and a second fiddler, Jesse Ashlock, to fill out the band's sound. With the help of friends and fans in Fort Worth, Wills persuaded W. Lee O'Daniel, general sales manager of Burrus Mills and Elevator Company, to sponsor the group on a KFJZ radio show by advertising the mill's Light Crust Flour. The program and the band became a huge success, but when O'Daniel ordered the band to quit playing dances and placed other restrictions on the group, Brown left.

Seeking creative freedom in a band of his own, Brown organized the Musical Brownies in 1932 and shaped them into the first western swing band. Original members of the group were Jesse Ashlock (fiddle), Ocie Stockard (tenor banjo), Wanna Coffman (bass fiddle), Durwood Brown (guitar), and Milton Brown (vocals). Pianist Fred "Papa" Calhoun and fiddler Cecil Brower were soon added. In 1934 steel guitarist Bob Dunn was invited to join, and in 1935 fiddler Cliff Bruner. Brown had assembled the prototype western swing band—two fiddles, guitar, banjo, bass,

Light Crust Doughboys Sleepy Johnson, Bob Wills, and Milton Brown at the home of future governor W. Lee "Pappy" O'Daniel, 1932. Sleepy Johnson Collection, courtesy Dr. Charles Townsend.

steel guitar, and piano—to accompany his pop vocal styling and occasional scat-singing. Milton Brown and His Musical Brownies began broadcasting in Fort Worth on KTAT and playing at the Crystal Springs dance hall. The band became extremely popular in North and Central Texas and was highly influential for other swing bands. Bob Wills once said of Brown that he had "the finest voice I'd ever heard."

Brown married Mary Helen Hames in Marietta, Oklahoma, on September 17, 1934. A son, Buster Lee, was born to the couple in December 1935. Tensions soon arose, however, with Mary's insistence that her husband quit the music business, get off the road, and lead a more traditional life, an accommodation Brown was unwilling to make. The couple were divorced in 1936.

But Brown's professional career was going strong. His band became the first western swing organization to record. Between 1934 and 1936 it made more than 100 recordings for RCA Victor / Bluebird and Decca. The group played Saturday night dances at Crystal Springs and out-of-town engagements on a regular circuit that included Waco, Corsicana, Weatherford, Mineral Wells, and other towns around Fort Worth. Brown was on his way to national prominence when he died. Early on the morning of April 13, 1936, while driving a young lady home from an evening out with friends at Crystal Springs and another Fort Worth nightspot, he evidently fell asleep at the wheel. The woman was killed instantly in the crash. Brown died at Methodist Hospital of pneumonia brought on by the acci-

dent. His funeral, held at Lucas Funeral Home, was attended by as many as 3,500 people, according to newspaper accounts. Brown was buried next to his sister in the little cemetery in Smith Springs. He was survived by his parents, two brothers, and a son. If he had not died so young, he might have achieved the national prominence of Bob Wills, Spade Cooley, Tex Williams, and others whom he influenced.

BIBLIOGRAPHY: Jean A. Boyd, *The Jazz of the Southwest: An Oral History of Western Swing* (Austin: University of Texas Press, 1998). Cary Ginell, *Milton Brown and the Founding of Western Swing* (Urbana and Chicago: University of Illinois Press, 1994).   *Ruth K. Sullivan*

Bruner, Cliff. Western swing fiddler and bandleader; b. Clifton Lafayette Bruner, Texas City, April 25, 1915; d. Houston, August 25, 2000. Bruner's father worked as a longshoreman on the Houston docks but dreamed of being a farmer. Periodically he would take his dock money and lease land or share-crop. On one such venture, when Cliff was five years old, the family moved to Arkansas. While playing in their farmhouse, Cliff found a fiddle. As he recalled later, "I got the thing out and I was sawing on it and my grandmother, who was living with us at the time, said, 'That sounds like a tune that I've heard before.'...That's when I started playing. I was playing fiddle before I could talk good."

The Arkansas farm eventually failed, and the family moved to Tomball, Texas. Bruner's playing ability led him to perform for family and friends. Like many western swing violinists from a rural background, Bruner learned to play by listening, watching, and improvising. The only formal music training he ever received was from a Texas-Mexican musician who spoke no English and played only Mexican music. Through this training, however, Bruner was exposed to one of the distinctive threads of Texas musical culture woven into Texas jazz.

While still in school, Bruner played at local dances and eventually toured with Doc Scott's medicine show. In 1935 he joined Milton Brown's Musical Brownies, a swing band based in Fort Worth. Brown was the first Texas bandleader to use twin fiddlers. He paired Bruner with Cecil Brower, and this duo became the trademark sound of Brown's music. Bruner recorded forty-eight sides with the Brownies on the Decca label. The band's promising future ended with Brown's untimely death in 1936, when Bruner moved to Houston and formed his own band, the Texas Wanderers. Musicians who played with this band included steel guitarist Bob Dunn, electric mandolinist Leo Raley, fiddler J. R. Chatwell, guitarist and vocalist Dickie McBride, and country boogie pianist Moon Mullican. The band became one of the most popular and successful Texas Gulf Coast ensembles. It broadcast regularly on radio station KXYZ, Houston, and later on KFDM, Beaumont. Between 1937 and 1941, in numerous recordings for Decca Records, the Wanderers turned out such hits as a version of Floyd Tillman's "It Makes No Difference Now" and the first truck-driving song, "Truck Driver's Blues," with vocals by Bruner and Mullican.

During his long career, Bruner formed several bands, most called the Texas Wanderers. He also played with other groups, including those of W. Lee "Pappy" O'Daniel and Jimmy Davis, who used their bands to promote their political campaigns. In the 1950s, due to his wife Ruth's illness, Bruner dissolved the Wanderers and sought a more stable occupation in the insurance business. The Bruners were living in Amarillo when Ruth died. Left with two small children to raise, Bruner returned to Houston, married a second woman named Ruth, and continued to work in his own insurance company. He pursued music on the side, playing on weekends with local musicians. He died of cancer and was survived by his wife, six daughters, seventeen grandchildren, sixteen great-grandchildren, and five great-great-grandchildren.

BIBLIOGRAPHY: Jean A Boyd, *The Jazz of the Southwest: An Oral History of Western Swing* (Austin: University of Texas Press, 1998). Houston *Chronicle*, August 27, 2000.   *Ruth K. Sullivan*

Buckner, John Edward. Dixieland jazz trumpeter, known as Teddy Buckner; b. Sherman, Texas, July 16, 1909; d. Los Angeles, September 22, 1994. Buckner spent five years of his childhood in Silver City, New Mexico, then grew up in the Los Angeles area. His first musical experience came from an uncle who taught him to play the drums and ukulele; later he studied the trumpet under Harold Scott. By the age of fifteen Buckner was playing with the band of Buddy Garcia, then with "Big Six" Reeves and Speed Webb. In the early 1930s he joined Sonny Clay, and in 1934 he went to Shanghai with the Buck Clayton big band.

Buckner reportedly played with several bands in the mid-1930s, including a stint with the Brownskin Models Revue, before joining Lionel Hampton in the summer of 1936. In November of that year, when Hampton left to join Benny Goodman, Buckner took over as leader. Also in 1936 he stood in for his idol, Louis Armstrong, in the film *Pennies from Heaven*. Hampton recalled that Armstrong once gave Buckner a horn, saying, "Man, you're a real trumpet player!" Armstrong's influence may have been a mixed blessing, however; one latter-day critic has averred that Buckner, while a technically impressive player, never developed "a sound of his own."

After the former Hampton band broke up during World War II, Buckner worked and recorded with Benny Carter, Kid Ory, and Hampton's new band in the 1940s and 1950s. In the mid-1950s he formed his own group to record and tour the West Coast, and he released ten albums during the 1950s and early 1960s, including *A Salute to Louis Armstrong* (1957). Buckner also gained national attention for his solo work on "Just a Closer Walk with Thee" while playing with Ory's band on live radio broadcasts from New Orleans in the mid-1950s. During that decade, he worked with Texas guitarist Aaron (T-Bone) Walker and the legendary New Orleans clarinetist–saxophonist Sidney Bechet. His trumpet playing was featured in the film *Pete Kelly's Blues* (1955), and he also appeared in *D.O.A.* (1950), *The Wild Party* (1956), *St. Louis Blues* (1958), *4 for Texas* (1963), the short film *The Legend of Jimmy Blue Eyes* (1964), and *They Shoot Horses, Don't They?* (1969). Into the 1980s he continued to lead his own band, which worked regularly at Disneyland from 1965 to 1981.

BIBLIOGRAPHY: *All Music Guide* website (http://www.allmusic.com/cg/amg.dll?p=amg&sql=B7ddnvwrva9uk), accessed February 12, 2002. *American Big Bands Database* (http://nfo.net/.WWW/b9.html), accessed February 5, 2002. John Chilton, *Who's Who of Jazz: From Storyville to Swing Street*, Fourth Edition (New York: Da Capo Press, 1985).   *Martin Donell Kohout*

Burden, Omega. Guitarist; b. near Gordonville, Grayson County, Texas, January 28, 1913; d. November 25, 1973 (buried in nearby Cedar Mills Cemetery); son of Finis and Meda (Cook) Burden. Burden is recognized by many as the originator of "Texas Style" guitar. He worked for various railroads and spent much of his free time competing in fiddle contests and jamming with friends—Major Lee Franklin, Benny Thomason, Joe Hughes, William Orville Burns, and Ervin, Vernon, and Norman Solomon. Burden is reported to have participated in an all-night fiddle session on October 31, 1947, followed by an all-day session the next day. His late-night jam sessions at friends' houses extended through the 1960s. He was reputed to be one of the finest rhythm guitarists in the Southwest. Many believed that his guitar provided the heartbeat that kept the Texas State Old Time Fiddlers Association vibrant during the decade between the early 1960s and early 1970s.

Affectionately referred to as "Biggun" by his friends, Burden played at fiddle contests throughout Texas, and such fiddlers as Jimmy Henley and Garland Gainer came from New Mexico and Oklahoma to jam with him. He played at events such as the Yamboree in Gilmer, the Fiddlers' World Championship in Crockett, the Saint Paddies Day Jam in Shamrock, and at such venues as Hale Center and the Seminary in Fort Worth. Burden influenced Larry Franklin, Carl Hopkins, and Randy Elmore, and his guitar students included Bobby Christman of Pottsboro, Steve Williams of Houston, and Anthony Mature of New Waverly.

In the late 1930s, Burden farmed cotton and corn in Trenton, Texas. In 1941 he moved to Dallas, where he worked for the Southern Pacific for two years. He worked for the next thirty-one years as a switchman and yardmaster for the Katy (Missouri, Kansas and Texas), until his retirement in the early 1970s. He married twice. His first marriage, to Jane Short, ended in divorce in the 1940s, and the second, to Amy Crawford, ended in the early 1970s. He had two children by his first marriage and one child by his second. In late 1973 his long-time friend Major Franklin found him unconscious in his apartment in Gordonville; he died without recovering consciousness.

Burden left his 1943 Gibson Southern Jumbo guitar to Christman, and Christman subsequently played "Maybelle," the legendary and beloved instrument, at fiddlers' competitions regularly. In November 1978, Major Franklin received the "Omega Burden" award at the Fiddlers' Super Bowl Invitational at Durant, Oklahoma. Burden was inducted into the Texas Fiddlers Hall of Fame during the 1999 Texas State Championship Fiddlers Frolic in Hallettsville, Texas.

BIBLIOGRAPHY: Cheryl Dill, "William Orville Burns," *Fiddlers Frolics* (http://www.fiddlersfrolics.com/halloffame/oburns.htm), accessed November 4, 2002. "Larry Franklin Biography" (http://www.larry-franklin.com/bio.htm), accessed November 4, 2002. "Major Lee Franklin Biography," *Fiddlers Frolics*, (http://www.fiddlersfrolics. com/halloffame/mfranklin.htm), accessed November 4, 2002. *The Texas Fiddler: Newsletter of the Texas Old Time Fiddlers Association*, 23.10 (October 1995).
Cheryl L. Simon and Bobby Christman

Bureau, Allyre. Political writer, Texas colonizer, musician, and composer; b. Cherbourg, France, 1810; d. Kellum Springs, Texas, late 1859. Bureau studied at the École Polytechnique and the Paris Conservatory, fought against the king in the July Revolution (1830), and was briefly an artillery officer. He was a Fourierist and friend of Victor P. Considérant. He wrote for *Démocratie pacifique*, a Fourierist publication, urged social changes in other publications, ran unsuccessfully for national office in 1848 and 1849, and spent some time in prison after the Paris riots of June 1848. He also translated English novels into French.

On September 26, 1854, in Brussels, he signed as a director the charter of the Société de Colonisation Europeo-Americaine au Texas, which founded La Réunion, a colony of French and Swiss emigrants near Dallas

and experiment in the practical application of Fourier's theory. Bureau worked as part of the central agency in Paris and served on a subcommittee to initiate the society's operation. When the colony's financial problems became dire, he traveled to America with his wife, three sons, and daughter. They arrived at La Réunion on January 17, 1857. Upon the resignation of François J. Cantagrel, Bureau assumed the directorship of the colony, but, unable to reverse its deterioration, he dissolved the society on January 28, 1857. He remained at the settlement, where his musical talent contributed much to the colony's reputation for good musical entertainment. He brought the first piano to Dallas and composed songs including "Clang, Clang, Clang," and "Choose a Flower." One of his compositions appeared in a songbook used in the Dallas public schools. While beginning a trip to France with his wife and daughter for an extended visit, he contracted yellow fever and died in a sanitarium about fifty miles north of Houston.

BIBLIOGRAPHY: *Dictionnaire de biographie française* (13 vols., Paris: Letouzey et Ane, 1933–75). George H. Santerre, *White Cliffs of Dallas: The Story of La Reunion* (Dallas: Book Craft, 1955). Lota M. Spell, *Music in Texas* (Austin, 1936; rpt., New York: AMS, 1973).
Joan Jenkins Perez

Byrd, Bobby. Rhythm-and-blues singer and bandleader; b. Robert James Byrd, Fort Worth, July 2, 1929; d. Los Angeles, July 27, 1990; son of Julia Jennings. In 1947 Byrd moved to Los Angeles and began his performing career under the stage name Bobby Day at Johnny Otis's Barrelhouse Club. By 1950 he had formed the Hollywood Flames, with whom he made a hit recording, "Buzz Buzz Buzz" (1957). In 1957 he formed a second musical group, the Satellites, that backed him on his hit "Little Bitty Pretty One," which Day wrote. He was also the first to perform Jimmie Thomas's "Rockin' Robin" (1958), the song by which most pop music lovers recognize Day.

As Bobby Day, Byrd performed with Earl Nelson from 1957 to 1959 as the original Bob in the R&B duo Bob and Earl. Day and Nelson had met in 1957, when the latter joined the Hollywood Flames. As the Flames' lead singer, Nelson was spotlighted on Day's "Buzz Buzz Buzz." Byrd's unique baritone voice kept him in demand with a variety of recording labels, including Rendezvous, RCA, and Sureshot. For Jama records he sang lead with the Day Birds. His "doo-wop" style was revived by performers of the 1960s and 1970s. The Jackson 5 and the Dave Clark Five rerecorded, respectively, "Rockin' Robin" and "Over and Over." Byrd established Byrdland Attractions and Quiline Publishing, songwriting enterprises. He was survived by his wife, Jackie, and four children.

BIBLIOGRAPHY: Colin Larkin, ed., *The Guinness Encyclopedia of Popular Music* (Chester, Connecticut: New England Publishing Associates, 1992). Norm N. Nite, *Rock On: The Illustrated Encyclopedia of Rock n' Roll* (New York: Crowell, 1974–).
Peggy Hardman

C

Caceres, Emilio. Jazz violinist; b. ca. 1900; d. ca. 1973; elder brother of Ernesto Caceres, who was born in Rockport, Texas. Little biographical information on Emilio is available, except with reference to his more famous brother. But it was through Emilio's Trio that the two brothers first gained national attention when they appeared on the Benny Goodman radio show in 1937. Prior to this date, the trio, which included Emilio on violin, Ernesto on clarinet and baritone sax, and a cousin, Johnny Gomez, on guitar, had performed "some of the hottest music around San Antonio."

After appearing on the Goodman show, the Trio recorded, in the words of critic Gunther Schuller, "six splendid small group sides" that were "astonishing" for "the violin and clarinet blended and, even more surprisingly, how Ernie's gutty, burly baritone functioned so successfully with the violin." In 1969, after returning to San Antonio, Emilio and Ernesto recorded a final album, entitled simply *Ernie and Emilio Caceres*.

BIBLIOGRAPHY: Tony Baldwin, liner notes to *Hot Violins* (ABC Records 836 049-2, 1988). Gunther Schuller, *The Swing Era: The Development of Jazz, 1930–1945* (New York: Oxford University Press, 1989).

Dave Oliphant

Caceres, Ernesto. Multi-instrumentalist; b. Rockport, Texas, November 22, 1911; d. San Antonio, January 10, 1971. He studied clarinet from an early age and worked with local bands beginning in 1928. In a family trio led by his elder brother, violinist Emilio Caceres, and including a cousin, Johnny Gomez, on guitar, he performed in San Antonio and appeared on the Benny Goodman radio show in 1937. The trio subsequently recorded six sides called "splendid" by critic Gunther Schuller.

Ernesto became a member of the Jack Teagarden Orchestra in 1939, and in 1940 he joined the Glenn Miller Orchestra, with which he remained until 1942, performing solos on alto saxophone and forming part of the famous Miller saxophone sound. Ernesto was with the Tommy Dorsey Orchestra in 1943 and the Benny Goodman and Woody Herman orchestras in 1944, before serving in the U.S. Army until 1945. He played with Louis Armstrong's All-Stars in 1947 and led his own quartet at the Hickory Log in New York in 1949. Between 1950 and 1956 Ernesto worked regularly with the orchestra of the Garry Moore television show. He also worked with the bands of Bobby Hackett and Billy Butterfield before moving back to San Antonio.

BIBLIOGRAPHY: John Chilton, *Who's Who of Jazz: Storyville to Swing Street*, Fourth Edition (New York: Da Capo Press, 1985). Gunther Schuller, *The Swing Era: The Development of Jazz, 1930–1945* (New York: Oxford University Press, 1989). *Dave Oliphant*

Violinist Emilio P. Caceres playing for WCAR radio, San Antonio, December 1925. A trio including his brother Ernesto on clarinet and baritone sax, and his cousin Johnny Gomez on guitar was very popular in San Antonio. UT Institute of Texan Cultures at San Antonio, No. 0501-E.

Callahan, Homer. Bluegrass, hillbilly, and western musician, aka Bill Callahan; b. Laurel, North Carolina, March 27,1912; d. Dallas, September 12, 2002. Callahan's most significant impact on Texas music was his role in one of the state's most popular radio shows, the "Big 'D' Jamboree." At the time of his birth, Laurel was a small town in the largely Scots-Irish region of western North Carolina. This area was rich in musical traditions from the British Isles that undoubtedly influenced Callahan's musical development.

Callahan came from a musical family. His father taught voice in his spare time to supplement his income as a postman and grocery clerk. His mother was an accomplished organist. Callahan's sister Alma and especially his brother Walter were also talented musicians. A great deal of Callahan's future success in the music industry came from working with his brother. Callahan was skilled with several musical instruments and singing styles. He played the guitar, the string bass, and the mandolin. In addition to playing instruments, he was an accomplished singer and yodeler. His principal styles borrowed from the native sounds of his home state, bluegrass and hillbilly music. In addition, he listened to the popular singers of traditional country music, such as Ernest Stoneman, Riley Puckett, and Jimmie Rodgers.

His first break in the music business came in 1933 while he was performing at the annual Rhododendron Festival in Asheville, North Carolina. At this festival Callahan and his brother publicly demonstrated their yodeling ability, and their success led to their first recording session for ARC records in New York in January 1934. Homer and Walter recorded fourteen songs, including their most famous hit "She's My Curly Headed Baby." In addition to his work with his brother on the album, Callahan recorded solo numbers, such as "Rattlesnake Daddy" and "My Good Gal Has Thrown Me Down." He also completed a few tracks with his sister. The Callahan brothers embarked on successful careers in radio, working first at WWNC in Asheville, North Carolina, and then at jobs in Louisville, Wheeling, Cincinnati, Tulsa, and Springfield, Missouri. They published songbooks and continued making recordings, including one of the first recorded versions of the classic folk song "The House of the Rising Sun" in 1935.

The Callahan brothers moved to Texas by 1941. They achieved their greatest fame through their part on "Big 'D' Jamboree" on KRLD in Dallas. This early, successful barn dance was broadcast every Saturday night from the Dallas Sportatorium and included other well-known performers, such as Charline Arthur, Roy Acuff, and Johnny Carroll. During this time, Homer and his brother Walter altered their musical style to accommodate the growing popularity of cowboy music made popular by Roy Rogers and Gene Autry. As a part of their move away from their hillbilly and bluegrass roots, the Callahan brothers changed their names. Homer became Bill, and Walter took the name Joe. In 1941 the two signed a contract with Decca Records and cut seven songs. But their change in style resulted in only moderate success. The brothers achieved the majority of their success during this time as sidemen for performers such as Wesley Tuttle and Marty Robbins. They quit recording together in October 1951.

During the latter part of his career, Homer Callahan undertook a variety of projects. In 1945 he teamed with his brother in the movie *Springtime in Texas* with Jimmy Wakely and went on a nationwide tour to promote the film. He later went on a tour of the east coast with Ray Whitely, and in 1947 he recorded a solo for Cowboy Records in Philadelphia. For a period starting in 1951, Callahan worked as the opening act for the young Lefty Frizzell and served briefly as Frizzell's manager.

Eventually, both Homer and his brother retired from the music industry and took up other careers. Walter went back to Asheville and became a grocer like his father. Homer remained in Dallas and made a living as a photographer. Walter died on September 10, 1971. Homer was survived by his son Buddy, his grandsons Kelly and Michael, and five great grandchildren. Homer Callahan, along with his brother Walter, represented the rapid expansion and popularity of country music on the radio from the 1940s to the 1960s and played a key role in its development.

BIBLIOGRAPHY: Richard Carlin, *The Big Book of Country Music: A Biographical Encyclopedia* (New York: Penguin, 1995). Paul Kingsbury, ed., *The Encyclopedia of Country Music: The Ultimate Guide to the Music* (New York: Oxford University Press, 1998). Mickey Newbury

and Tony Martinez, obituary of Homer Callahan (http://mailman.xmission.com/pipermail/exotica/2002-September/006 167.html), accessed November 22, 2002. *The Story of the Big "D" Jamboree* (originally published as notes to the CD *The Big "D" Jamboree Live! Volumes 1 &2*, February 2000). *Michael S. Morawski*

Carroll, Johnny. Guitarist, composer, and "Wild Rockabilly Singer"; b. John Lewis Carroll, Cleburne, Texas, October 23, 1937; d. Dallas, February 18, 1995. Carroll bought his first guitar at age nine with money he had earned by working as a waterboy at a World War II POW camp. His mother, who played the fiddle, taught her son basic music skills. By listening to the radio, he learned to play country-and-western music. Carroll later was introduced to rhythm-and-blues when a cousin in the jukebox business gave him some old 78 RPM R&B records. By 1955 he had formed his own high school band, the Moonlighters. His group sometimes shared the stage with the South's newest singing sensation, Elvis Presley, as they performed on the "Big 'D' Jamboree" and the "Louisiana Hayride" circuit.

During a performance of the "Ferlin Husky Show," Carroll gained the attention of local radio operator Jack "Tiger" Goldman, who helped him get a contract with Decca Records. In 1956 Carroll recorded for Decca in Nashville. During this two-day recording session he was encouraged to sing in a dark and husky voice, a trademark he carried throughout his career. At the session he recorded his own "Crazy, Crazy Lovin'" along with "Hot Rock," written by Goldman. With moderate sales, Carroll embarked on a series of tours. In 1957 he appeared in the motion picture *Rock, Baby, Rock It*, in which he performed several songs with his old high school band.

After a dispute with Goldman, Carroll left him and rejoined the "Louisiana Hayride." He enlisted Ed McLemore as his new manager in 1958 and recorded two singles for Warner Brothers, including his biggest hit, "Bandstand Doll." In 1962 he recorded his last single for more than ten years. In 1974, after leaving the nightclub business, Carroll returned to performing and recorded "Black Leather Rebel." Three years later, he re-released three of his Decca singles, the success of which led to several tours across Europe, where he was a rock-and-roll icon. A year later, Carroll rekindled his 1950s rock-and-roll sound with the release of *Texabilly*, an album recorded in a twenty-eight-hour marathon session. By the 1990s he had completed eleven European tours and was a popular draw on the American music festival circuit. He died of liver failure.

BIBLIOGRAPHY: Craig Morrison, *Go Cat Go!: Rockabilly Music and its Makers* (Chicago: University of Illinois Press, 1996). *Juan Carlos Rodríguez*

Carter, John. Jazz composer and clarinetist; b. Fort Worth, 1929; d. Los Angeles, March 31, 1991. Carter was influenced by the music at his Baptist church and by recordings his parents owned of jazz greats such as Duke Ellington, Count Basie, and Cab Calloway. He began playing clarinet at the age of twelve; he also played flute and saxophone. He performed with Ornette Coleman in Fort Worth. He received his B.A. in music in 1949 at Lincoln University in Jefferson, Missouri, and his M.A. at the University of Colorado in 1956.

Carter taught music in the Fort Worth public schools from 1949 to 1961, when he secured a position as a traveling elementary school music teacher in Los Angeles. There he and Bobby Bradford, also from Texas, collaborated to form the New Art Jazz Ensemble. Some of their music was released as "West Coast Hot" in 1969. In Los Angeles, Carter opened a jazz establishment, Rudolph's, where progressive musicians met. He was critics' choice for best jazz clarinetist for most of the 1980s.

Between 1985 and 1990 Carter composed and recorded "Roots and Folklore: Episodes in the Development of American Folk Music," in five albums focused on African-Americans—*Dauwhe* (1985), *Castles of Ghana* (1985), *Dance of the Love Ghosts* (1986), *Fields* (1988), and *Shadows on a Wall* (1989). The complete set was acclaimed by jazz critics as containing some of the best releases of the 1980s. In February 1990 Carter had a nonmalignant tumor that resulted in the removal of his left lung. He made an appearance in Los Angeles in September of that year, in which he stated that he expected a full recovery. But he developed lung cancer, from which he died. He was survived by his wife, Gloria, three sons, and a daughter.

BIBLIOGRAPHY: Austin *Chronicle*, April 12, 1991. Barry Kernfeld, ed., *The New Grove Dictionary of Jazz* (London: Macmillan, 1988). Los Angeles *Times*, September 5, 1990, April 14, 1991. New York *Times*, February 5, 1988.

Kristi Strickland

The Cellar. One of the most unusual clubs in Texas; owned by Pat Kirkwood and managed by Jim Hill. Four cities had a Cellar—Houston, Fort Worth, Dallas, and San Antonio. The club appeared on the Texas music scene beginning about 1958, first in Fort Worth and then in Houston. These two cities were the most successful locations; the San Antonio Cellar lasted only a few years, and the Dallas location was never as busy as the first two.

The original Cellar in Fort Worth opened on Houston Street about 1958 and was subsequently moved several times in the early 1960s. "House bands" rotated periodically from one Cellar to another. The resident music director in Houston was a rockabilly singer–guitarist named Johnny Carroll, who helped get the Houston club rolling.

All the clubs were equally strange and had the same format. There were four bands playing each night (or three on some week nights), alternating one-hour sets. The Cellar was open from 6 P.M. to 6 A.M. This was before "liquor by the drink" was passed in Texas, so no alcohol was served, just setups. If a band played fourth, its first set was at 9 PM and its last was at 5 A.M.—an all-night break between performances. The cover charge was one dollar. For that small price a customer could hear four bands and watch the pretty waitresses (they wore bikinis) serve Cokes all night long.

Another unique feature was that there was no dance floor. The space in front of the stage was covered with old couch cushions where the clientele could lie down and listen to the music. The rest of the club was filled with tables, and sofas lined the walls. The lack of dancing encouraged the customers to listen, and the music was great. Bands played cutting-edge rock, blues, R&B, country rock, and the Beatles, mixed with their own originals. There was also a two-foot-high and two-foot-wide partition separating the band from the sofa-cushion area. This was often used as a "runway" by female dancers, who sometimes stripped spontaneously. Stripping was not legal in the Cellar, but it wasn't the only shady thing going on. The Cellar also later had the dubious distinction of being frequented by rival club owner Jack Ruby, who killed Lee Harvey Oswald. Secret Service agents patronized the club on the night before the Kennedy assassination.

The Cellar had an undertone of violence. Five or six bouncers were usually on hand to throw out anyone who passed out on the cushions (a side door that opened onto the street was the portal used, and the bouncers would really rough people up badly), to keep anyone not welcome in the club from getting in, to break up fights (of which there were many, some instigated by the bouncers), and to protect the waitresses and musicians. On stage above the musicians, out of sight of the audience, were three bulbs in a row—one white, one blue, and one red. The white light meant that all was okay; the blue meant that the police were in the club, so performers had to watch their language and behavior; and the red meant to start playing a song immediately and continue playing until the light went out (the music was meant to distract the audience from a fight). Since all the Cellars were in rough parts of town, some of the bouncers' actions were justified, though fighting was a poor fit with the hippie attitudes in the music scene at the time.

Nevertheless, the main focus of the Cellar was music. Dusty Hill, Frank Beard of ZZ Top, and Rocky Hill had a band called the American Blues, and they had blue hair. Other groups—the Cellar Dwellers, the Neurotic Sheep, the Geeks—were made up of great session players from around town who could play any type of music. The Dream Machine (later called Deerfield) did half Beatle songs and half originals—the Sergeant Pepper album from start to finish in one set, and the band's original Texas "psychedelic rock" in another. It was like two different bands.

The various locations of the Cellar began to close in the mid-1970s, mainly because of the legalization of liquor by the drink and the rise of clubs with light shows and long jams catering more to young music fans. The Cellar was a strange mix of old-style club management and the innovative music of the '70s. It was a place to hear hours of music for just a dollar, with no boundaries on style or genre, and it was a great training ground for young musicians tough enough to survive all the strange things going on around them. Cellar music director Johnny Carroll died in 1995, and owner Pat Kirkwood died in 2000. The CD *The Cellar Tapes Volume One* (2000) features live recordings from the club.

BIBLIOGRAPHY: *The Cellar* homepage (http://www.ask4music.com/cellarhome.html), accessed February 7, 2003. Joe Nick Patoski, "The King of Clubs," *Texas Monthly* 28.4 (April, 2000).

Charles Bickley

Center for Texas Music History. At Southwest Texas State University in San Marcos; established in 1999 as the Institute for the History of Texas Music; approved by the Texas State University System Board of Regents on August 20, 1999. In the fall of 2001 the institute was officially renamed Center for Texas Music History.

The center's primary goal, under founder and director Gary Hartman, is to help students and the general public better understand how music reflects the richly varied ethnic and cultural heritage of the American Southwest. Through a variety of activities and projects, the center strives to increase awareness and appreciation for the important role music plays in shaping and reflecting the historical development of American society.

Headquartered in the university's history department, the center offers graduate and undergraduate courses on the musical history of Texas and the Southwest. Students examine the many different ethnic musical influences involved in the development of the region, including Hispanic, Anglo, African-American, Irish, German, Polish, Czech, French, and others. Students also look at how other social, economic, and political factors have helped shape the region, its people, and its music, as well as how Texas and the Southwest have made important contributions to larger American musical idioms, such as blues, ragtime, jazz, conjunto, Tejano, western swing, and rock-and-roll.

The center publishes the *Journal of Texas Music History*, the first academic journal to focus on the entire spectrum of Southwestern music history. It has worked with the Bob Bullock Texas State History Museum, public schools, and other entities to organize exhibits, musical performances, and other educational programs. Events include an annual Texas Music History Unplugged concert. By 2002 the center had released three volumes of a compilation CD titled *Travelin' Texas*, which featured current Texas musicians. The center also collects archival materials related to Texas music history and adds them to the larger Texas music collection housed in the university's Southwestern Writer's Collection. These materials include holdings from Willie Nelson and the Western Swing Hall of Fame.

BIBLIOGRAPHY: Center for Texas Music History website (http://www.history.swt.edu/Music/TexasMusic.htm), accessed January 30, 2003. *Gary Hartman*

Central Plains College and Conservatory of Music. The first junior college in Plainview, established in 1907 as Central Plains Holiness College on land given by Ferd Falkner. Although the school was intended to serve students from the Nazarene Church, L. L. Gladney of Mississippi, the first president, persuaded the governing board to accept students of other denominations. The college was renamed Central Plains College and Conservatory of Music before opening on September 18, 1907. In the first year some 159 students enrolled. The institution was coeducational but stressed military training. Students wore blue uniforms and kept strict schedules. Classes were taught from grade school through college; tuition ranged from $35 a term for grades one through eight to $150 for nine months of college. Campus facilities included a three-story main building, two three-story dormitories, and a smaller music building. The college was set up to be self-sufficient and thus maintained a laundry and several barns and stables.

By 1910 the campus had grown to about fifty acres. College classes included music, business, theology, liberal arts, and dressmaking. The enrollment was estimated at 152 in 1908 and 225 in 1909. After three years, however, the task of running the school became too great for the Nazarenes, who sold the college for $32,000 to the Methodist Church of Plainview on December 27, 1910. The institution was renamed Seth Ward College and reduced its music emphasis.

BIBLIOGRAPHY: Mary L. Cox, *History of Hale County, Texas* (Plainview, Texas, 1937). Vera D. Wofford, ed., *Hale County Facts and Folklore* (Lubbock, 1978).
Charles G. Davis

Chabot, Frederick Charles. Diplomat, historian, and musician; b. San Antonio, May 11, 1891; d. Mexico, January 18, 1943; son of Charles Jasper and Pauline Minter (Waelder) Chabot. After graduating from San Antonio High School in 1909 (with the "highest honors any graduate had received up to that time," according to his obituary), he embarked upon studies overseas at the Sorbonne and the University of Berlin, where he focused on music and languages.

After returning to Texas, he had a brief career as a concert pianist and organist. He also apparently tried his hand in the insurance and real estate businesses, as well as doing historical research in 1915–16. Perhaps because his grandfather, George S. Chabot, had served in the British Foreign Service, Chabot decided to prepare for a career in the State Department by attending classes at George Washington University in Washington. In 1917 he found his first government employment working for the Library of Congress; by April of that year he was performing duties as a special agent of the Department of Justice.

In June 1917 he embarked upon his career in the diplomatic service. During the next eight years he moved from posting to posting—Paris, Athens, Sofia, Rio de Janeiro, San Salvador, San José, and finally, in 1923, Caracas. His service in the diplomatic corps was not smooth: he had conflicts with superiors, was reprimanded several times for infractions of State Department rules, and, while serving in San Salvador, was arrested by local officials on what appeared to be trumped-up charges of being drunk and disorderly. His last chance for saving his diplomatic career had been in Caracas, but his poor and sometimes incoherent reports from the field eventually moved the State Department to ask him to resign or face being fired. Despite protests that he was a victim of "Republican politics," Chabot tendered his resignation in December 1924.

After returning to Texas he made a more positive contribution in the field of historical research. He published his first book, *The Alamo, Altar of Texas Liberty*, in 1931, and continued his writing and research on Texas and Mexican history for the remainder of his life. Through the auspices of the Yanaguana Society, founded by Chabot in 1933 and devoted to promoting the study of Texas history, he published and edited a number of brief books on a variety of topics. His most notable works are *With the Makers of San Antonio* (1937); *Excerpts from the Memorias for the History of Texas, by Father J. A. Morfi* (1932), a translation of those parts of Juan A. Morfi's work that dealt with Indians in Texas; and *Texas in 1811*, a translation done in 1941. He also contributed articles dealing with the history of Texas to a local newspaper, the San Antonio *Light*. Other significant contributions made by Chabot include his locating thirteen original paintings by Theodore Gentilz, which were later placed in the Alamo, helping in the restoration of La Villita and San José Mission in San Antonio, and compiling an album entitled *Pictorial Sketch of Mission San José* (1935). Chabot died of uremic poisoning while on a research trip in Mexico, and was buried in San Luis Potosí. At the time of his death, he had been preparing four more books for publication.

BIBLIOGRAPHY: Florence Elberta Barns, *Texas Writers of Today* (Dallas: Tardy, 1935). San Antonio *Light*, January 22, 1943. Vertical files, Center for American History, University of Texas at Austin. *Michael L. Krenn*

Chambers, Iola Bowden. Music teacher and director of the Negro Fine Arts School; b. Holder, Texas, October 18, 1904; d. Brownwood, Texas, December 14, 1978 (buried in May, Texas); daughter of Andrew Mack and Amanda (Heflin) Bowden. Her father was a doctor, and Iola was a fifth-generation Texan.

She developed an early interest in music and studied privately while attending the public schools at Holder and May. She attended the last two years of high school at Daniel Baker Academy in Brownwood and graduated in 1921. After receiving a diploma in piano from Daniel Baker College in 1923, she studied piano at the Washington Conservatory of Music, where she received a graduate diploma in piano in 1926. She returned to Texas and taught piano in May, Rotan, and Breckenridge, as well as at Baylor University, before moving to Georgetown in 1933 to teach at Southwestern University and complete her degrees, a B.F.A. (1935) and a B.A. (1936). She subsequently stayed at Southwestern University as instructor of music, teaching piano and harmony. She later taught piano pedagogy. She began a master's program at the Cincinnati Conservatory of Music in the summer of 1938 and completed it in the summer of 1941.

Iola Bowden was an early white proponent of black education. In 1946 she and several of her piano students founded the Negro Fine Arts School, in which students from Southwestern University taught local African-American children to play the piano. The program was sponsored by the Student Christian Association at Southwestern University and was conducted at the First Methodist Church of Georgetown. The project, in operation from 1946 to 1966, added vocal music and art in later years.

The Negro Fine Arts School provided generations of black children an opportunity to learn music. It staged an annual recital, complete with a printed program, to showcase the students' accomplishments. It awarded scholarships to students going to college or pursuing other higher education. The school also helped to ease the transition from segregation to integration both in the Georgetown ISD and at Southwestern University. The first black student to enroll at Southwestern University was a student of Iola Bowden and an alumnus of the Negro Fine Arts School.

Charles Miller, one of the first students in the Negro Fine Arts School and in 1993 an administrator for the Georgetown Independent School District, characterized Iola Bowden as "the one that came across the railroad tracks and helped us all. Miss Bowden was to Georgetown what Eleanor Roosevelt was to the United States, because she was one of the first."

Bowden was promoted to assistant professor in 1948 and to associate professor in 1960. In addition to her work as a member of the music faculty and as director of the Negro Fine Arts School, she supervised the Junior Music Department at the university for years and was organist for the First Methodist Church in Georgetown for more than twenty years. She was active in state and national professional organizations, including the American Guild of Organists, the National Federation of Music Clubs (in which she was a district officer), the Texas Music Teachers' Association, the National Guild of Piano Teachers (she served as a judge in the National Piano Playing Auditions), and the American College of Musicians. She was one of the founders of the Delta Nu chapter of Delta Omicron at Southwestern University and served as a national officer in that organization. She was a member of the Alpha Chi honor society. She published an article, "Musical Phrasing," in *Southwestern Musician* in June 1949.

In 1955 Iola Bowden married Walter R. Chambers. She retired from Southwestern University in 1966, and the couple moved to Brownwood. After her retirement she continued to be active professionally and endowed a scholarship in music at Southwestern University.

BIBLIOGRAPHY: Estill Franklin Allen, *Methodist History of May, Texas* (Brownwood, Texas: Howard Payne University, 1980). *Histories of Pride: Thirteen Pioneers Who Shaped Georgetown's African American Community* (Georgetown, Texas, 1993). Ralph W. Jones, *Southwestern University, 1840–1961* (Austin: Jenkins, 1973). *Martha Mitten Allen*

Chance, John Barnes. Composer and arranger, nicknamed Barney Chance; b. Beaumont, Texas, November 20, 1932; d. Lexington, Kentucky, August 16, 1972. Chance was purportedly a descendant of Robert Chance, a Mississippi gambler who settled in Southeast Texas in the late 1800s. His parents, Mr. and Mrs. Robert Floyd Chance, were natives of Southeast Texas.

Chance was a prolific composer for band and wind ensemble. His music became known for its tonal and romantic style and its dependence on unique rhythms and a secure command of instrumentation. Chance attended the University of Texas (B.Mus., M.Mus.), where he studied composition with James Clifton Williams, Kent Kennan, and Paul Pick. In 1956–57 he was honored with the Carl Owens Award for student composition. After college he played timpani for the Austin Symphony Orchestra before becoming an arranger for the Fourth and Eighth United States Army bands.

While serving in Seoul, South Korea, as a member of the Eighth U.S. Army Band, Chance came across a pentatonic Korean folk song that served as the inspiration for his 1965 composition *Variations on a Korean Folk Song*, which became his best-known work. It featured gong, temple blocks, and other exotic equipment in the percussion section. The Northwestern University Band premiered the work in March 1966 at the American Bandmasters Association convention, where the composition won the Ostwald Award. Some of Chance's other important works include *Incantation and Dance*, *Elegy*, *Blue Lake Overture*, and *Symphony No. 2*. After leaving the army, Chance held the position of composer-in-residence at the Ford Foundation Young Composers Project in Greensboro, North Carolina, from 1960 to 1962. He joined the faculty of the University of Kentucky in 1966 and taught there until his untimely death. He was accidentally electrocuted while working in the backyard of his home in Lexington, Kentucky.

BIBLIOGRAPHY: John Barnes Chance, "Variations on a Korean Folk Song," *Journal of Band Research* 3 (Autumn 1966). William H. Rehrig, *The Heritage Encyclopedia of Band Music*, Vol. 1 (Westerville, Ohio: Integrity Press, 1991). Stanley Sadie, ed., *The New Grove Dictionary of Music and Musicians*, Second Edition (New York: Grove, 2001). *William Pugatch*

Chatwell, J. R. Fiddle player, also called "Chat the Cat"; b. James Robert Chatwell, Weatherford, Texas, May 27, 1915; d. San Antonio, June 18, 1983 (buried in San Antonio); son of Edward Isaac and Sudie Chatwell. J. R. was part of a large farming family that encouraged and appreciated music. Although all members of the family played piano, none showed the affinity for the fiddle that he possessed. When he started playing violin at age eight, Chatwell became daddy's "fiddlin' boy" and soon was the pride of the family.

Chatwell always played by ear, and at age fifteen or sixteen was sneaking out the back window of the family's home to play local dances after the Chatwells moved to Sudan, Texas. During one of his late-night forays he met and heard Cliff Bruner, the lead fiddler for the famous western swing group Milton Brown and the Musical Brownies. Brown allowed good local musicians to sit in with his group, and Chatwell was asked to sit in with the Brownies. Bruner was impressed with the youth and helped get him a gig with fiddler Elmer Scarborough, who was putting together a group called the Hi-Flyers and needed a fiddling partner. A month later, Bruner persuaded Chatwell to join his own Houston-based group, the Texas Wanderers—not as a fiddler, but as a piano player. Although Chatwell preferred playing fiddle and did not want to play piano, Bruner reminded him of who it was that discovered him. Soon Chatwell joined Bruner to play a boogie-woogie, blues, and barrelhouse piano for the group.

His love of fiddling made it difficult to stay with the group for very long as a piano player, though, and soon Chatwell had picked up and moved on to join the Modern Mountaineers. Although the Mountaineers switched personnel frequently, at the time Chatwell joined, they had a largely jazz combo sound that perfectly fitted Chatwell's interest in jazz. Chatwell was greatly influenced by the jazz-violin style of Stuff Smith. He picked up on Smith's jazz licks and applied them to country, thus creating a unique sound that influenced swing fiddlers to come,

including Johnny Gimble of the Texas Playboys. Chatwell recorded with the Modern Mountaineers in 1937.

Through the years, he played with a variety of popular Texas bands, including Johnny Thames, Bill Boyd's Country Ramblers, and the Light Crust Doughboys, before signing up for an on-and-off twenty-five-year stint with Adolph Hofner. Between tours with Hofner, Chatwell also played with other groups, including the Village Boys from 1945 to 1948, and Smiley Whitley's Texans and Walter Kleypas's Lone Star Boys in the early 1950s. "He played good notes, and good passages, but the way he phrased them—it was like a good comedian – there's pauses, you know, like Jack Benny's routine," said Johnny Gimble of Chatwell's playing. "It's hard to explain—you have to feel it."

Chatwell married Jewell Grace in 1937. They had two children, Joyce Ann Chatwell in 1938 and James Robert Chatwell in 1945. Although Chatwell recorded in California, he never did move to the West Coast as so many other Texas musicians at the time were doing, preferring to raise his family in Texas, even if it meant he would never make it big. "I've been quoted as saying that I didn't think J. R. was in the music for the money," said Gimble of Chatwell's relative obscurity. "He'd go play where the rhythm was good. If you're playing swing or improvising, you just get on top of that wave and ride."

A stroke in 1968 ended Chatwell's fiddling career, although he still managed to play piano with his right hand and sing. He found a new generation of musicians that appreciated his western swing style, including Asleep at the Wheel, Willie Nelson, and Doug Sahm. Sahm's parents took him to the Chatwell house when Doug was a child, and Sahm virtually grew up with Chatwell as his musical mentor. Consequently, it was no surprise when Sahm later took the elderly musician under his wing and had him perform piano at several of his own gigs.

Chatwell continued to play and cross over the line between jazz, blues, and country when he played on Yusef Lateef's jazz album *Part of the Search"* (1971), on several Johnny Gimble albums, and finally on his own album, *Jamming with J. R. and Friends"* (1982). *Jamming* featured appearances by Sahm, Nelson, Augie Meyers, and Ernie Durawa, as Chatwell played his romping one-handed barrelhouse blues. Chatwell was survived by his wife, Jewell, who moved after his death to Devine, Texas.

BIBLIOGRAPHY: Eugene Chadbourne, "J. R. Chatwell – Biography," *All Music Guide* (http://www.allmusic.com), accessed November 1, 2002. San Antonio *Express–News*, June 19, 1983. *Jackie Potts*

Cheatham Street Warehouse. On Cheatham Street in San Marcos. The building originally functioned as Reed Grocery Warehouse, a distribution center that received goods by train and sold supplies to local grocers. Kent Finlay purchased the structure and in June 1974 opened a music hall to serve as a venue for a variety of genres, including country, blues, rock, and folk. The honky-tonk soon provided an outlet for area talent, and many musicians, both famous and lesser known, began their performing careers on the stage at Cheatham Street. Southwest Texas State University student George Strait and the Ace in the Hole band played their first shows at the club in the 1970s. A young Stevie Ray Vaughan performed there every Tuesday night.

Throughout the 1970s and 1980s the music hall played host to an impressive roster of musicians. Patrons heard country legends such as Ernest Tubb and Willie Nelson, the blues of Omar and the Howlers and Lou Ann Barton, the songwriting prowess of Townes Van Zandt and Jerry Jeff Walker, as well as notable players such as country fiddler Alvin Crow, accordionist Flaco Jiménez, and guitarist Eric Johnson. Over the years the wealth of artists has also included Doug Sahm and Augie Meyers, Marcia Ball, Gatemouth Brown, Charlie and Will Sexton, Gary P. Nunn, Joe "King" Carrasco, Ponty Bone, and Ray Benson's Asleep At The Wheel.

In 1988 Finlay sold Cheatham Street Warehouse, and during the next few years the building changed hands between Finlay and other buyers. For a time in the early 1990s the establishment hosted primarily Tejano bands. In 1999 Finlay bought back the club, which returned to its original honky-tonk format. The official reopening occurred on December 31, 1999.

A mainstay of the hall throughout its existence has been Finlay's songwriter nights on Wednesdays, when both professional and novice players are encouraged to perform their original compositions. Finlay, called the "Godfather of Texas Songwriters," has endeavored to cultivate new tunesmiths and musicians, and his establishment has gained the reputation as a premier songwriter venue in Central Texas. The club has also been the scene for many live recordings, from early demos of players like George Strait and Todd Snider to full-length albums for commercial release. In 2003 Cheatham Street Warehouse continued to present musical acts every night of the week.

BIBLIOGRAPHY: *Kent Finlay's Cheatham Street Warehouse* (http://www.cheathamstreet.com), accessed January 27, 2003. *Laurie E. Jasinski*

Choates, Harry H. Cajun musician; b. either Rayne or New Iberia, Louisiana, December 26, 1922; d. Austin, July 17, 1951. Choates moved with his mother, Tave Manard, to Port Arthur, Texas, during the 1930s. He apparently received little formal education and spent much of his childhood in local bars, where he listened to jukebox music.

By the time he reached the age of twelve he had learned to play a fiddle and performed for tips in Port Arthur barbershops. As early as 1940 he was playing in Cajun-music bands for such entertainers as Leo Soileau and Leroy "Happy Fats" LeBlanc. Choates, who also played accordion, standard guitar, and steel guitar, preferred to play on borrowed instruments and may never have owned a musical instrument of his own.

Around 1946 he organized a band, the Melody Boys. Perhaps in honor of his daughter, Linda, he rewrote an old Cajun waltz, "Jolie Blone" (Pretty Blonde) and renamed it "Jole Blon." He recorded the song in 1946 for the Gold Star label, owned by Bill Quinn of Houston. "Jole Blon" became a favorite in the field of country and western music and a standard number in Texas and Louisiana clubs and dance halls. A year after Choates's recording, Moon Mullican, a Texas-born singer and piano player, made an even

bigger hit with the song. "Jole Blon," which Choates performed in the key of A instead of the traditional G, featured slurred fiddle notes and has been sung with both Cajun French and English romantic lyrics as well as nonsense lyrics with references to the "dirty rice" and "filé gumbo" of Cajun cuisine. Choates, who suffered from chronic alcoholism, sold "Jole Blon" for $100 and a bottle of whiskey.

He and his Melody Boys recorded over two dozen other songs for Gold Star in 1946 and 1947, including "Baisile Waltz," "Allans a Lafayette," "Lawtell Waltz," "Bayou Pon Pon," and "Poor Hobo," but none of those records earned Choates the success he achieved with "Jole Blon." He also recorded for the Mary, DeLuxe, D, O.T., Allied, Cajun Classics, and Humming Bird labels during his brief career. His recordings have been preserved on *Jole Blon*, an album by D Records of Houston that contains the Gold Star issues, and *The Fiddle King of Cajun Swing*, a compilation of Choates's works released by Arhoolie Records of El Cerrito, California, in 1982. Rufus Thibodeaux, a well-known Cajun fiddler, recorded an album entitled *A Tribute to Harry Choates* in the mid-1960s on the Tribute label. Choates remained popular fare on Cajun French radio stations in Jennings, Crowley, and Ville Platte, Louisiana.

Choates, who could sing in French or English, became famous for his "Eh...ha, ha!" and "aaiee" vocal cries. A real crowd pleaser, he frequently played his amplified fiddle while dancing on the floor with his audience and stood on tiptoe while reaching for high notes. He merged traditional French Cajun music with the western swing music pioneered by such musicians as Bob Wills. He played jazz and blues as well as country music, including instrumental tunes like "Rubber Dolly," "Louisiana Boogie," "Draggin the Bow," and "Harry Choates Blues." As songwriter, instrumentalist, singer, and bandleader he raised Cajun music to national prominence.

One observer has characterized Choates as "a Cajun Janis Joplin." Like her, he achieved a great deal of notoriety for his raucous lifestyle. Often performing while intoxicated and oblivious of his personal appearance, he wore a formerly white hat which, according to one of his band members, "looked like a hundred horses had stomped on it and then it had been stuck in a grease barrel." Choates was virtually illiterate and incurred the ire of musicians' union locals for ignoring contracts. Consequently, after the union in San Antonio blacklisted him and forced a cancellation of his bookings, his band broke up.

By 1951 he had moved to Austin, where he appeared with Jessie James and His Gang, a band at radio station KTBC. His estranged wife, Helen (Daenen), whom he had married in 1945, filed charges against Choates for failing to make support payments of twenty dollars a week for his son and daughter. Authorities in Austin jailed him pursuant to an order from a Jefferson County judge who found Choates in contempt of court. After three days in jail, Choates, unable to obtain liquor and completely delirious, beat his head against the cell bars, fell into a coma, and died, at the age of twenty-eight. Although some of his fans believe his jailers may have killed him while attempting to calm him, Travis County health officer Dr. H. M.

Williams determined that liver and kidney ailments caused his death. The James band played a benefit to raise money for Choates's casket, and Beaumont disk jockey Gordon Baxter secured funds to bury him in a Catholic cemetery in Port Arthur. Baxter and music historian Tim Knight of Groves raised money in 1979 and 1980 to purchase a granite grave marker with the inscription in Cajun French and English: "Parrain de la Musique Cajun"—"The Godfather of Cajun Music."

BIBLIOGRAPHY: John Broven, *South to Louisiana: The Music of the Cajun Bayous* (Gretna, Louisiana: Pelican, 1983). Houston *Chronicle*, July 23, 1989. Bill C. Malone and Judith McCulloh, eds., *Stars of Country Music* (Urbana: University of Illinois Press, 1975). John Morthland, *The Best of Country Music* (Garden City, New York: Doubleday, 1984). Irwin Stambler and Grelun Landon, *Encyclopedia of Folk, Country and Western Music* (New York: St. Martin's, 1969). *Paul M. Lucko*

Christian, Ben. Fiddler and band leader; b. Benjamin Theodore Christian, on a farm near Rockdale, Texas, June 1, 1885; d. Houston, March 27, 1956; fifth of nine children of Charles S. and Anne E. (Murray) Christian. Affectionately known as "Uncle Ben" to a later generation of country music fans, Christian probably learned to play the fiddle from an older brother. Although most of his siblings played instruments, only his younger brother Elwood (Elmer) also established a musical career.

Before entering the music field, Christian engaged in a number of business activities, including bookkeeping and sales. While performing with a traveling medicine show, he met and married Rose Lee Franklin in Port Neches in 1928. They remained married until his death in 1956. This and a previous marriage produced three sons.

Christian entered the Houston music scene in the early 1930s, when Fort Worth–based western swing was attracting growing audiences over the radio waves. For a time he teamed with guitarists Dave Melton and Lynn Henderson at house parties. Ben and Henderson organized the Bar X Cowboys, named by radio announcer Harry Greer, as a commonwealth band with Ben as business manager and lead fiddler and Elwood on fiddle and bass. Although offering no pay for the band, the live programs, variously on KTRH, KPRC, and KXYZ, provided free advertising for dances within the approximate 200-mile range of the radio stations.

Performing cowboy and country songs in addition to western swing, the Bar X Cowboys became one of the most popular aggregations in the vibrant coastal region, competing with such major talents as Pappy Selph, Cliff Bruner, Moon Mullican, and Shelly Lee Alley. Ted Daffan, a pioneer in the electrification of instruments and charter member of the Nashville Song Writers Association Hall of Fame for compositions "Born To Lose," "Truck Driver's Blues," and a host of other hits, played steel guitar for the band before organizing his Texans in 1940. Although primarily a dance band, the Bar X Cowboys made a number of records with Decca, including Christian's "Rockdale Rag," in Dallas studios. Some of the selections have been reproduced recently in country music albums.

In 1940 Christian turned over the Bar X Cowboys to Elwood to form the Texas Cowboys, which he managed until his retirement. The new band continued the success of its predecessor, with (Richard) "Jerry" Jericho, a later performer on Shreveport's "Louisiana Hayride," as principal vocalist. Christian broadcast on KNUZ and KLEE until disk jockeys replaced the local live bands in the late forties. During that decade the Texas Cowboys performed at leading Houston venues, such as Cook's Hoedown, Eagles' Hall, and Polish Hall (now Fitzgerald's), in addition to rural communities. Hank Thompson, Hank Locklin, Floyd Tillman, Hank Snow, and Elton Britt made guest appearances with the band. The Texas Cowboys shared the bandstand in "battle dances" with Bob Wills, Adolph Hofner, and Jesse James. Christian and the band provided instrumentation for Hank Williams on one of his last area tours and permitted a young Elvis Presley to gain experience with them before an audience at Magnolia Gardens.

Declining health and lessening opportunities for local bands persuaded Christian to transfer the Texas Cowboys to Jericho in 1954. Ben Christian's death, at his Houston residence, closed a musical career that had spanned the golden age of string dance bands on the Texas Gulf Coast.

BIBLIOGRAPHY: Garna L. Christian, *Stay A Little Longer: The First Generation of Houston Country Music* (Houston: Houston Center for the Humanities, 1985). Colin Escott and Kira Florita, *Hank Williams, Snapshots from the Lost Highway* (Cambridge, Massachusetts: Da Capo Press, 2001). Bill C. Malone, *Country Music U.S.A.* (Austin: University of Texas Press, 1985). "They Brightened the Corner: The Era of Gulf Coast Swing," *Houston Review* 9.1 (1987). *Garna L. Christian*

Christian, Charles. Jazz guitarist; b. Dallas, July 29, 1916; d. Staten Island, New York, March 2, 1942. Charlie spent much of his youth in Oklahoma City, where he lived with his father and played bass and guitar in various small groups. He made his first experiments with an amplified guitar in 1937. When music critic John Hammond heard him in 1939, he persuaded Benny Goodman to employ Christian. Although barely twenty years old, Christian immediately became known among professional jazzmen for his new sounds and new ideas. Only one other electric guitar had been recorded on jazz records when the first Christian– Goodman records were issued.

After that, his large creative contribution to modern jazz was widely recognized. Christian featured a down-stroke technique almost exclusively. His single-string solos, with altered chords, new melodic lines, rows of even beats, and contrasting dramatic aspects became the base from which musicians constructed an entirely new approach to jazz. Christian won *Down Beat* polls from 1939 through 1941 and in the *Encyclopedia Year Book* poll of 1956 was chosen "Greatest Ever." Always in delicate health, he died of tuberculosis in a Staten Island sanitarium, leaving behind a contribution that belies the brevity of his career.

BIBLIOGRAPHY: Arrigo Polillo, "Charlie Christian," in *I Grande del Jazz*, Vol. 48 (Milan: Fabbri, 1982). Audio Archives, Center for American History, University of Texas at Austin). *Joe B. Frantz*

Dallas-born Charlie Christian played electric guitar with Benny Goodman. Christian is recognized for his creative contributions to modern jazz. (*Texas Rhythm, Texas Rhyme: A Pictorial History of Texas Music*, Austin, Texas: Texas Monthly Press, 1984). Courtesy Larry Willoughby.

Claassen, Arthur. Choral and orchestral conductor; b. Stargard, Prussia, February 19, 1859; d. San Francisco, March 16, 1920. Claassen studied at the Music School in Weimar, and as early as 1878 his youthful compositions aroused the attention of Franz Liszt, who gave him encouragement. From 1880 to 1884, Claassen was opera conductor in Göttingen and Magdeburg. Upon the recommendation of Leopold Damrosch, a disciple of Wagner, Claassen was chosen conductor of the New York Eichenkranz and, in 1890, of the Brooklyn Arion—both male singing societies.

In nearly a quarter century under Claassen's baton, the Arion became one of the most celebrated choruses in the United States, earning him an audience with Kaiser Wilhelm II in 1900. Claassen conducted important American performances of Wagner's *Liebesmahl der Apostel*, Mendelssohn's *Midsummer Night's Dream*, and Bruch's *Frithjof*, as well as a number of German operas. With the New York Liederkranz, he made recordings for Columbia Records after about 1910, and these were marketed in Texas.

In May 1913 Claassen was guest festival conductor for the Texas State Sängerfest, held in Houston. The Beethoven Männerchor of San Antonio was so impressed by his musicianship that in the spring of 1914 they invited him to become their permanent conductor. Thus Claassen became the first conductor of international reputation to assume full responsibility for a Texas musical organization. He took over the forty-three-voice male chorus and organized a sixty-voice women's chorus (the Mozart Society) to complement it. He also assumed charge of the sixty-member San Antonio Philharmonic (later the San Antonio Symphony Orchestra). In a newly refurbished Beethoven Hall he gave concerts of unprecedented sophistication in the Alamo City.

An orchestral concert of March 15, 1917, is typical of Claassen's programming: Weber's *Euryanthe* Overture, Schumann's Piano Concerto, and Beethoven's Symphony No. 7, as well as light numbers by Liszt and himself. For the 1916 State Sängerfest, Claassen had combined all his forces for extensive excerpts from Wagner's *Die Meistersinger*. World War I signaled the decline of German ethnic prestige, however, and the influenza epidemic during the winter of 1918–19 brought concert life in San Antonio to a standstill.

Claassen's own compositions include the cantatas *The Battle* and *Festival Hymn*, the symphonic poem *Hohenfriedberg*, the *Waltz–Idyll* for string orchestra, and many songs and choruses. Claassen moved to San Francisco in July 1919.

BIBLIOGRAPHY: Theodore Albrecht, German Singing Societies in Texas (Ph.D. dissertation, North Texas State University, 1975). Theodore Albrecht, "101 Years of Symphonic Music in San Antonio," *Southwestern Musician / Texas Music Educator*, March, November 1975. *Baker's Biographical Dictionary of Musicians*, Seventh Edition. W. L. Hubbard, ed., *American History and Encyclopedia of Music* (12 vols., New York: Irving Squire, 1910), Vol. 5.

Theodore Albrecht

Classical Music. It is truly said that music of virtually every Western genre has flourished in Texas, from before the advent of Europeans through the times of colonization, settlement, and revolution, until the present—the outgrowth of a fusion of races and nations. Classical music found such a congenial culture in Texas that it flourished and grew, from small beginnings among European colonists of numerous nations to an important pursuit of countless citizens. During the twentieth century, the proliferation of musical activities in Texas mirrored that of the entire country. The town bands and scattered opera houses of 1900 yielded to a handful of sophisticated orchestral ensembles and opera projects by 1950, and by the year 2000 virtually every standard metropolitan statistical area in the state had one or more professional or semiprofessional musical organizations.

Along with this growth, however, came a significant blurring of the boundaries between "classical" music and other forms. The crossing-over that "crossover" musicians chose to participate in became ever more athletic, ever more of a stretch. At the beginning of the new millennium, for instance, the Texas Wind Symphony was performing with the Light Crust Doughboys (or vice versa), and the Dallas Symphony Orchestra, which produced an "Amazing Jazz" television show in 1999, was accompanying the "folk" trio Peter, Paul and Mary. The softening attitude of the *haute couture* crowd toward lower-brow music had long before been adumbrated by such composers as Gershwin, Charles Ives, and Claude Bolling. "Classical," always hard to define, had become even more elusive. But even with these caveats in place, it is possible to trace the beginnings of classical music in Texas, and its development in various important musical activities and persons.

Beginnings. Prescinding from later concepts of "classical," one may say that Texas music began with Texas Indians. When the Spaniards arrived on Texas soil, they found Native American peoples whose ceremonies employed the music of singing, rattles and percussion devices, and simple wind instruments. The first European music was that of the Catholic Church, which came by way of Mexico City, where a European music school was established in 1525. The work of University of Texas at Austin musicologist Robert Joseph Snow toward the end of the twentieth century helped to illuminate this music. In the missions around El Paso, in East Texas, and near San Antonio, music attracted Indians to the Church and formed an integral part of the liturgy. Spanish folk music and guitars came with soldiers and settlers to the missions.

The French music that came to Texas first around the beginning of the nineteen century—with the opening of the West after the Louisiana Purchase—came mainly from New Orleans, where a sophisticated culture had developed, but also from a black Creole culture that has had an incalculable effect on Texas music. Later in the century came colonies of French and Swiss that included musicians; for example, Allyre Bureau, a Parisian composer and director, settled in the Dallas area.

After 1820 Anglo-Americans introduced music from the United States, especially songs of the English, Scots, and Irish. Following the first fiddles and flutes, the first heavy instruments, especially pianos, came during the 1830s. In 1834 the elder Robert Justus Kleberg imported a piano and

Van Cliburn in recital at the Moscow conservatory, 1962. Courtesy Van Cliburn Foundation. A classical pianist of international renown, Cliburn helped found the international piano competition in Fort Worth that bears his name.

music books to Harrisburg (now part of Houston). On the more portable side, at the battle of San Jacinto, musicians played "Yankee Doodle" and "Will You Come to the Bower?" Dick the Drummer was one of two free blacks who participated in that decisive battle. He and three fifers constituted the Texas army's band. Dick also played the drums during the Mexican War at the battles of Monterrey and Buena Vista.

A scant two years later, classical music was becoming more formalized, especially in urban centers and in the Church. In the theater opened at Houston in 1838 an orchestra and singers from Europe and the United States performed excerpts from popular operas and other music. Sacred music societies were organized in several towns. Bishop Jean Marie Odin, the first bishop of the Catholic Diocese of Galveston—which at the time encompassed all of Texas—had an organ for his cathedral in 1848.

But the Germans brought more musical activities than the other national groups, beginning about 1845. Though such individual German immigrants as Kleberg had brought their music with them, the big impetus to German music in Texas began with the Adelsverein, the colonization project of the Society of Nobles, after 1844. The Germans formed singing societies, beginning in New Braunfels in 1850, and held biennial singing festivals beginning in 1853. As early as 1840 they had introduced operatic per-

formances to Houston. Their support of opera continued in such centers of German settlement as San Antonio. Numerous German music teachers worked in the state's population centers as well as in the smaller German settlements. Their influence was long-lasting. About 1879, for instance, a native of Saxony, Julius Weiss, moved to Texarkana, where he taught a young student named Scott Joplin, destined to become "King of Ragtime."

Texas culture became a potpourri of national cultures. Among Hispanics, singing and dancing to stringed orchestras was common in the homes and on the plazas. German music centers were the beer gardens as well as the Casino Club in San Antonio, the Turnverein Hall in Austin, and later the Scholz Garten in Austin, where William Besserer directed operettas and choral productions. The Anglo-Americans brought visiting concert groups in the early 1840s; a few small opera companies came from New Orleans and Mexico before 1860. Local bands, sometimes military, played in the larger communities before 1850; by 1900 most of the towns had bands.

The subsequent history of music in Texas is largely a reflection of the cultural boom that swept the United States in the twentieth century, slowly gathering force in the early part of the century and accelerating greatly after World War II. Musical activities of every type increased, resident opera and ballet companies were founded, symphonies were formed, reorganized, and expanded, choral groups were established. All played to larger audiences in more sophisticated halls, and received more financial support than ever before. At the same time each of these groups has suffered from rising costs and, in many cases, general public apathy. Foundation grants, the Texas Commission on the Arts, and generous support from civic-minded individuals and businesses have made possible much of the progress achieved by musical organizations in the state.

Education. Private pedagogy is the classic mode of imparting the arts of classical music. Among early Texans, the Germans excelled in music education; many civic leaders among them were also music teachers. Somewhat later than the large wave of German immigration, the first institutions of higher learning that featured training in music included Kidd–Key College and Belle Plain College. Since their time, virtually every college or university has developed a music department. The leading Texas universities—Texas Tech, Texas A&M, the University of Texas at Austin, Rice University, Texas Christian University, Baylor, Southern Methodist University—all have successful classical music programs. Among smaller institutions, Prairie View A&M University has a significant music program. The University of North Texas is especially noted for music.

In the cultural flowering that followed World War II—and partly as a result of the Federal Music Program—numerous smaller Texas towns initiated music programs that introduced children to classical music and brought world-renowned performers to their civic auditoriums. In Brownwood, for instance, during the 1950s an enterprising violinist and conductor, Chester Parks, taught children beginning in the fifth grade the art of playing violin, viola, cello, and string bass. The result in a few years was a high school string orchestra, with piano accompaniment, that consistently won top ratings in University Interscholastic League contests. Meanwhile, the Brownwood Community Concert series brought such leading musicians as clarinetist Reginald Kell and conductor Walter Susskind to town. Brownwood also had a Schubert Music Club and a Piano Teachers' Association. Brownwood was typical of many such mid-sized communities.

The Texas Music Educators Association is the leading professional association of music teachers in the state. Among numerous other activities, the association sponsors the All State Orchestra, the All State Band, and several All State choruses, all of which are composed of talented Texas high school students.

Ensembles. After the establishment of the San Antonio Symphony Orchestra (1904), the Dallas Symphony Orchestra (1911), and the Houston Symphony Orchestra (1933), numerous city ensembles developed, while the pioneer orchestras became truly professional and attained international distinction. The Houston Symphony, for example, grew phenomenally. At the middle of the century, the Houston orchestra was more and more associated with world-renowned conductors—Sir Thomas Beecham, Leopold Stokowski, Sir John Barbirolli, André Previn, Christoph Eschenbach. During the 1963–64 season, Barbirolli took the group on a three-week tour of the East, whereupon the Houston Symphony became the first

orchestra from the Southwest to play in New York and Washington, D.C. The great patroness of the arts Miss Ima Hogg was long a principal supporter of the Houston Symphony, which began performing in the splendid Jesse H. Jones Hall in 1966.

The Dallas Symphony Orchestra also had considerable success under such conductors as Antal Dorati, Walter Hendl, Paul Kletzki, George Solti, and Anshel Brusilow. Between 1950 and 1960 the symphony grew from seventy to ninety-two musicians, and the number of concerts increased from thirty a year to 150. After ten seasons in McFarlin Auditorium, the orchestra, under Anshel Brusilow's baton, returned to the State Fair Music Hall, although the facilities there were judged inadequate. Eduardo Mata became music director in 1977, and in September 1989 the Morton H. Meyerson Symphony Center opened to wide acclaim. Since that time the Meyerson has been home base for the orchestra. Thirty-four-year-old Andrew Litton was named conductor of the Dallas Symphony Orchestra in 1994, thus becoming the first native-born musician appointed head of a major American orchestra in a decade.

When the founder and initial director of the San Antonio Symphony, Max Reiter, died in December 1950, Victor N. Alessandro, a native of Waco, became that orchestra's head; at the time, Alessandro was the only native-born Texan to serve as musical director of a major symphony orchestra. Under his leadership the San Antonio Symphony's budget more than doubled, and its artistic accomplishments revealed a similar growth. The annual San Antonio Grand Opera festival, which imported stars from such houses as the Metropolitan Opera to perform with the San Antonio orchestra, flourished under Alessandro. In 1961 Alessandro initiated an annual Rio Grande Valley International Music Festival, which attracted music lovers from South Texas and northern Mexico for a week of concerts, operas, and student performances. After Alessandro's retirement in 1976, François Huybrechts, Lawrence Leighton Smith, Zdenek Macal, and Christopher Wilkins served successively as music directors of the orchestra, and innovative programming remained a pattern. Larry Rachleff was hired to replace Wilkins in the 2003–2004 season, and Wilkins became director emeritus.

City and suburban orchestras abound, in Fort Worth, Austin, Wichita Falls, Corpus Christi, Beaumont, Lubbock, and numerous other places. A few random examples are suggestive of the whole. The El Paso Symphony Orchestra, one of the oldest in the state, traces its roots back to 1893. In 2000 the Richardson Symphony Orchestra, under the direction of Anshel Brusilow, celebrated its fortieth season. The Plano Symphony Orchestra was first established in 1983 as the Plano Chamber Orchestra. The Abilene Philharmonic Orchestra gave its first performance in 1950, and in 2003 was under the direction of Korean Shinik Hahm, who was in his tenth season with the ensemble. The Amarillo Symphony in 1967 consisted of eighty-five members, all local talent. This orchestra was formed in 1924 by conductor–pianist Grace Hamilton and in 2003 was under the direction of James Setapen, who assumed the post in 1988. Midland and Odessa strengthened their musical resources in 1964 by combining their two symphonies into an interurban orchestra.

Each of the state's symphonic groups has played a significant role in bringing live concerts to its area—often with high artistic results and despite sharp financial limitations. In a highly competitive entertainment market, virtually all of the ongoing ensembles have broadened their offerings to include pops concerts, children's concerts, and such crossover concerts as were mentioned in the beginning of this article. In 2003 the Fort Worth Symphony, for instance, under the direction of Miguel Harth–Bedoya, in addition to its traditional classical offerings, took part in a *Star–Telegram* Pops Series (which included such features as Larry Gatlin and the Gatlin Brothers) and a grab-bag Subscriber Special series (which offered, for instance, both a Tchaikovsky Gala and an appearance by Kenny Rogers). The Fort Worth Symphony also is the host orchestra for the Van Cliburn International Piano Competition. In addition to its regular season, the Austin Symphony offers pops concerts and supports an innovative youth program aimed at primary school students.

In addition to the larger ensembles, chamber music groups and societies multiplied in the latter decades of the twentieth century. In 2003 the Chamber Music Society of Fort Worth, for instance, featured a concert series of performances by ensembles of two to five musicians who played a wide variety of programs. The state's major university music departments—at the University of Texas at Austin, the University of North Texas, and Texas A&M University, for example—sponsored numerous chamber music performances, both by faculty members and by touring artists.

Opera. From its small beginnings—the performance of selected operatic chestnuts in the entertainment halls of frontier towns—opera has grown to be a major cultural feature of Texas urban centers. Dallas, Houston, Austin, San Antonio, and other cities across the state support resident opera companies. Historic Texas operatic singers have included Isabella Maas, Dreda Aves, Chase Baromeo, Lenore Cohron, Josephine Lucchese, May Peterson Thompson, Rafaelo Diaz, Mack Harrell, Vernon Dalhart (a true crossover musician), and Zelma George. Texas opera composers have included Scott Joplin, William John Marsh, Julia Frances Smith, and Merrill Ellis.

The San Antonio Symphony was the first professional resident opera producer in Texas. In 1945 conductor Max Reiter conceived a plan for extending the symphony season by adding a spring opera festival and launched the venture with *La Bohème*, starring Grace Moore. From 1945 until 1983 the San Antonio Symphony presented an annual season of opera—four different works given each year, one performance each, divided between two successive weekends. While stars from the Metropolitan and New York City operas were imported for leading roles, the chorus was drawn largely from three local colleges. Most of the sets were designed by Peter Wolf of Dallas. With few exceptions the opera festival closed its seasons financially in the black, in part because the San Antonio Municipal Auditorium would seat nearly 6,000; symphony officials looked upon a audience of 4,500 as a poor showing. Infla-

tion plus a move into less spacious housing forced a termination of the annual opera festival, but the Lyric Opera of San Antonio, founded in 1997, brought regular high-quality operatic performances back to the Alamo City.

Fort Worth followed San Antonio's resident opera productions in 1946 with the formation of the Fort Worth Opera Association. One of the company's prime ambitions was to provide opportunity for gifted local singers, with professionals used only in stellar roles. *La Traviata* launched the organization in November 1946. From 1955 to 1969 conductor Rudolf Kruger, who formerly worked with the Columbia (South Carolina) Symphony and the Chicago Light Opera, served as the Fort Worth musical director and general manager. Under his supervision four operas were performed each season, spaced over fall, winter, and spring; two performances were given of each work, and most productions were in English. Beginning in the late 1960s more of the company's operas were sung in the original language. Economic constraints in subsequent decades forced the company to reduce its number of yearly productions to three. The Fort Worth Opera—in 2003 the oldest opera company in Texas—performs in Bass Hall, billed as the last great performance hall built in the second millennium.

The busiest Texas resident opera organization, the Houston Grand Opera Association, began in January 1956 with *Salomé*, starring Brenda Lewis. In 1969 the company's musical director was Walter Herbert, who had held similar posts earlier with the New Orleans and Fort Worth operas. Under Herbert's leadership the Houston company presented four or five works annually, usually in the original language. Noted singers were used only for leading roles, and local talent was employed whenever artistically feasible. The Houston company proved dynamic in repertory by presenting such seldom-heard works as Rossini's *La Cenerentola* and *La Donna del Lago*, the Texas premiere of Richard Strauss's *Elektra*, a rare Texas staging of Wagner's *Die Walküre*, Handel's *Rinaldo*, Ralph Vaughan Williams's *Hugh the Drover*, and world premieres of John Adams's *Nixon in China*, Carlisle Floyd's *Willie Stark*, and Thomas Pasatieri's *The Seagull*. In 1987, under general director David Gockley, the Houston Grand Opera moved its productions to the Wortham Center. In 2002, with Gockley still on board, the Houston Grand Opera had mounted twenty-five world premiers in forty-five years and six American premiers, and was the fifth largest opera company in the nation. It was the only opera company in the United States to have earned two Grammies, a Tony, and two Emmies.

The Dallas Opera, founded in 1957 by Lawrence V. Kelly and Nicola Rescigno, formerly of the Chicago Lyric Opera, received immediate national and international acclaim. A concert by legendary soprano Maria Callas got the project off to a brilliant start on November 21, 1957, followed shortly by a production of Rossini's novelty *L'Italiana in Algeri*, with Giulietta Simionato in the title role. "For a couple of nights running," *Newsweek* reported, "Dallas was the operatic capital of the United States." Afterward, Dallas presented a number of remarkable productions and artists. In 1958 Callas returned for *La Travi-*

ata, in a production designed by the renowned Italian stage director Franco Zeffirelli, and highly praised performances of Cherubini's *Medea*, staged by Alexis Minotis of the Greek National Theater—a production later loaned to Covent Garden (London) and La Scala (Milan). The 1960 Dallas season saw the United States debut of Joan Sutherland in Zeffirelli's production of Handel's *Alcina*, an American premiere. Other American premieres for the company have included Monteverdi's seventeenth-century classic *Coronation of Poppea* and Vivaldi's *Orlando Furioso*.

The Dallas Opera also staged the state's first complete cycle of Wagner's *Ring des Nibelungen* and in 1988 gave the world premiere of Dominick Argento's *The Aspern Papers*. Since the city sampled the Metropolitan Opera's tour in the spring from 1939 until 1984, the Dallas Opera tried not to duplicate the New York company's repertoire and artists. Instead, the resident company's aim was to give Texas a look at European productions; each year manager Kelly borrowed at least one production from abroad—in 1960 *Alcina* from La Fenice (Venice) and *Figlia del Regimento* from Palermo, and in 1961 *La Bohème* from Spoleto. In addition to Sutherland's United States debut, the Dallas company benefited from those of Teresa Berganza, Luigi Alva, Denise Duval, Placido Domingo, Montserrat Caballe, Gwyneth Jones, Jon Vickers, Magda Olivero, Linda Esther Gray, and Ghena Dimitrova. Under general director Plato Karayanis, the Dallas Opera expanded its offering to six productions a year, with most performances attracting capacity audiences.

The Austin Lyric Opera was formed in 1985 with Walter Ducloux as artistic director, and within a decade the company had built its season to three productions. In 1995 the annual budget was $2.25 million, and the repertoire included Wagner's *Tannhäuser*, sung in German. The Austin Lyric Opera employs major international artists as well as American talent, and stages its productions in the Bass Concert Hall at the University of Texas.

In addition to grand opera, musical comedy, musicals, and light opera have prospered in Texas. The Starlight Operettas were begun in Dallas in 1941 in an outdoor arena and bandshell on the fairgrounds and were renamed the State Fair Musicals in 1951, when the shows were moved into the Music Hall. Outstanding Broadway and Hollywood talent was imported each summer for musicals of recent vintage, as well as the older "operetta" show. In 1952 the musicals opened with William Warfield and Leontyne Price in Gershwin's *Porgy and Bess*, the premiere of a production that the State Department later sent to Moscow. Each year during the State Fair of Texas the national company of a recent Broadway musical was brought to the Music Hall. Mary Martin began her tour in Irving Berlin's *Annie Get Your Gun* at the fair in October 1947, and succeeding years saw productions of *South Pacific*, *Guys and Dolls*, *The King and I*, *My Fair Lady*, *The Sound of Music*, *A Chorus Line*, *Cats*, and other hits. Houston, Fort Worth, and other Texas cities have hosted similar productions in increasing numbers. Casa Mañana in Fort Worth introduced "musicals-in-the-round" to the Southwest.

Resident ballet companies exist in several Texas cities, including Houston, Dallas–Fort Worth, Austin, and Corpus Christi. Other cities—Lubbock, for instance—have ballet schools and programs that support professional ballet. As an adjunct to musical ensembles, such dance companies are important in bringing the classics to students and other citizens of Texas. Ballet Austin, for instance, presents several annual Christmas performances of *The Nutcracker*, with accompaniment by the Austin Symphony Orchestra, before thousands of schoolchildren.

Composers, pianists, and other personnel. A list of Texas composers—native, immigrant, and transient— would be prohibitively large. Many Texas composers have written both popular and classical music. Some have written partial or complete movie scores. Some have confined themselves to traditional compositions. Others have joined the ranks of such groundbreaking experimentalists as the electronic-music pioneer Edgard Varèse and the tone-row composers Arnold Schoenberg, Alban Berg, and Anton Webern. The experimentalists have worked especially in such academic contexts as the University of North Texas School of Music.

Representative among those who composed more traditional music are Jules Bledsoe, Radie Britain, Allyre Bureau, Roger Edens, Don Gillis, David Guion, Mary Austin Holley, Scott Joplin, William John Marsh, Roger Miller (a wide-ranging talent), Harold Morris, Joseph Eugene Pillot, Leonora Rives–Diaz, Julia Frances Smith, John M. Steinfeldt, James Sudduth, Carl Venth, and Otto Wick. Considerably more experimental were John Barnes Chance and Paul Pisk. Out at the margin of experimentalism were Merrill Ellis and Jerry Hunt.

Olga Samaroff, born in San Antonio in 1882, was recognized as an outstanding pianist, teacher, and music critic. Julia Frances Smith, in addition to her numerous compositions, was a concert pianist. One of the best-known contemporary performers—and a distinguished and tireless promoter of music in the Lone Star State—is James Dick, of the International Festival–Institute in Round Top. Other Texas pianists include Irl Allison Sr., who founded the National Guild of Piano Teachers.

Easily the most famous of Texas piano players, however, is Van Cliburn. In 1958 this Texas pianist, who grew up in Kilgore, won the prestigious Tchaikovsky Piano Competition in Moscow. The resulting acclaim given to the Texan led to Irl Allison's establishment of the Van Cliburn International Piano Competition in Fort Worth in the early 1960s. The quadrennial competition continues to draw world-wide attention to Fort Worth.

Texas musicologists include Fritz Oberdoerffer and Robert J. Snow. The first music publisher in the state was Thomas Goggan and Brothers, established in 1866. Among leading Texas music patrons were Ima Hogg and Stanley Marcus.

Early in the twenty-first century, Texas was said to be "home to more than 10,000 songwriters, 100,000 music business professionals and 6,800 music businesses." A significant number of these were devoted to classical music.

BIBLIOGRAPHY: Ronald L. Davis, *A History of Opera in the American West* (Englewood Cliffs, New Jersey: Prentice–Hall, 1965). "Deep in the Heart of Dallas," *Legacies:*

A History Journal for Dallas and North Central Texas, Fall 1995. Casey Monahan, ed., *Texas Music Industry Directory*, Eleventh Edition (Austin: Texas Music Office, 2001). Hubert Roussel, *The Houston Symphony Orchestra, 1913–1971* (Austin: University of Texas Press, 1972). Lota M. Spell, *Music in Texas* (Austin, 1936; rpt., New York: AMS, 1973). Moritz Tiling, *History of the German Element in Texas* (Houston: Rein and Sons, 1913). Larry Wolz, "Roots of Classical Music in Texas: the German Contribution," in *The Roots of Texas Music*, ed. Lawrence S. Clayton and Joe W. Specht (College Station: Texas A&M University Press, 2003).

Clay, James Earl. Saxophonist; b. Dallas, September 8, 1935; d. Dallas, January 6, 1995. His mother was Jessie Lloyd. Clay attended Lincoln High School. His musical interest began with the flute, but he took up the saxophone during his teenage years and became a sax player in the "Texas tenor" tradition. He refined his playing as a student at Huston–Tillotson College in Austin, and later at North Texas State University in Denton. In 1955 he moved to Los Angeles and established himself in the hard-bop and freestyle jazz styles.

His first commercial breakthrough came when he joined Red Mitchell's band, with which he appeared in the album *Presenting Red Mitchell*. Shortly thereafter, Clay joined the Jazz Messiahs, collaborating with Ornette Coleman. He also cut an album with David "Fathead" Newman in 1960. Later that year he turned down a chance to replace John Coltrane in Miles Davis's band. Instead, Clay returned to his native Dallas to care for his ailing grandmother. Though he performed in the Deep Ellum district, financial strains forced him to work full-time at a record warehouse. He had some commercial success again in the 1960s when he landed a spot in Ray Charles's band, but continued playing primarily in the Dallas area over the next two decades. In the 1990s he reunited with Fathead Newman, and two albums resulted—*Return to the Wide Open Spaces* and *Cookin' at the Continental*. Clay was survived by his wife, Billye, and three children.

BIBLIOGRAPHY: Dallas *Morning News*, January 9, 1995. Rick Koster, *Texas Music* (New York: St. Martin's Press, 1998). Dave Oliphant, *Texan Jazz* (Austin: University of Texas Press, 1996). *Bradley Shreve*

Clay, Sonny. Pianist; b. William Sonny Clay, Chapel Hill, Texas, May 15, 1899; d. California, ca. 1972. The family moved to Phoenix in 1908. In Arizona, Clay began to perform with various groups, before leaving for California around 1916. He is credited with being one of the first important jazz musicians in California during the second decade of the twentieth century.

Around 1920 Clay met Jelly Roll Morton in Tijuana, and by 1922 he was leading one of the earliest jazz bands in Los Angeles, the Eccentric Harmony Six. In 1923 he recorded two titles for the Sunset record label, and in 1925 he recorded four more titles for Sunset with a group called the Stompin' Six. In 1925 he also made recordings for Vocalion, and in 1926 he recorded with his Plantation Orchestra, performing a fine piano solo on "California Stomp."

Clay also is credited with taking "probably the first black jazz group" to Australia, which he did in January 1928. Their tour ended in controversy when they were expelled from the country for allegedly hosting wild, interracial parties. On his return to Los Angeles, Clay organized the Dixie Serenaders. His band broke up around 1933, and he worked as a solo piano player. He served in World War II as a band leader, and resumed his career playing piano in clubs in 1945. He worked in the post office and as a piano tuner for a time, but resumed playing in clubs in the 1950s.

BIBLIOGRAPHY: Albert McCarthy, *Big Band Jazz* (London: Barrie and Jenkins, 1974). John Chilton, *Who's Who of Jazz: Storyville to Swing Street*, Fourth Edition (New York: Da Capo Press, 1985). *Dave Oliphant*

Cliburn, Rildia Bee O'Bryan. Piano teacher, mother of pianist Van Cliburn; b. McGregor, Texas, October 14, 1896; d. Fort Worth, August 3, 1994; daughter of William Carey and Sirrildia (McClain) O'Bryan. Mrs. Cliburn's father was a journalist and lawyer. She studied under Arthur Friedheim, a pupil of Franz Liszt's assistant, and passed the grand nineteenth-century virtuoso tradition on to her son, who revived and personified that tradition for audiences in the second half of the twentieth century.

After early piano lessons from her mother and local teacher Prebble Drake, and after graduating from high school in Richmond, Texas, she studied at the Cincinnati Conservatory and later in New York, but was discouraged from pursuing a concert career by her father, a member of the Texas legislature and an associate of leading politicians of the day. She returned to Texas, where, in 1923, she married Harvey Lavan Cliburn, a native of Mississippi and a railroad employee who, shortly after their marriage, entered the oil business on the advice of his father-in-law.

By the time she became a mother at the age of thirty-seven, Mrs. Cliburn had engaged in activities ranging from teaching piano lessons to running a riverfront mission in Shreveport, Louisiana. She began teaching her son while the family lived in Shreveport, where he was born, and continued teaching him as well as many other young pupils after the family moved to Kilgore, Texas, in 1940. After Van was catapulted to world fame as the winner of the first Tchaikovsky International Competition in Moscow in 1958, his mother frequently traveled with him; she served as his manager until he withdrew from active concertizing in 1978. She resumed traveling with him when he renewed his concert career in the late 1980s. Cliburn always credited his mother as his most influential teacher and as a valued advisor up to the time of her death; he frequently said that she had better hands for playing the piano than his, and that, as his teacher, she could demonstrate anything she required him to do.

After the death of her husband in 1974, Mrs. Cliburn shared Van's New York apartment until 1985, when they moved to the estate that had previously belonged to Kimbell Art Museum benefactor Kay Kimbell in the Westover Hills neighborhood of Fort Worth. There she lived her final years, lionized as the mother of an international concert star and musical celebrity. As long as her health permitted, well into her nineties, she circulated prominently in Fort

Worth society at her son's side at cultural and church events (she was a lifelong, devoted Southern Baptist) and frequently entertained visiting musical artists. She died at the age of ninety-seven, five days after suffering a stroke. The huge Rildia Bee O'Bryan Organ at Broadway Baptist Church in Fort Worth was under construction at the time.

BIBLIOGRAPHY: Abram Chasins and Villa Stiles, *The Van Cliburn Legend* (Garden City, New York: Doubleday, 1959). Fort Worth *Star–Telegram*, February 2, August 4, 1994. Howard Reich, *Van Cliburn* (Nashville: Thomas Nelson, 1993).   *Wayne Lee Gay*

Cobb, Arnett. Jazz tenor saxophonist; b. Arnette Cleophus Cobbs, Houston, August 10, 1918; d. Houston, March 24, 1989. He was taught piano by his grandmother and went on to study violin before taking up tenor saxophone in the Wheatley High School band. When he was fifteen he joined Louisiana band leader Frank Davis's band and performed in the Houston area and throughout Louisiana during the summer. He worked with trumpeter Chester Boone for two years and left to become a founding member of the Milton Larkin Orchestra in 1936.

Cobb worked with Larkin for six years and, with members Eddie Vinson, Cedric Heywood, Wild Bill Davis, Illinois Jacquet, and others, made the band one of the most successful territorial bands from Texas. The band became a regular at venues including the Apollo Theatre in Harlem and boxer Joe Louis's Rhumboogie Club in Chicago.

Originator of the "open prairie" tone and "southern preacher" style, Cobb continually turned down offers from many national bands including Jimmie Lunceford, Count Basie, and Lionel Hampton. However, with his mother's approval, and Gladys Hampton's offer to Elizabeth (Cobb's wife), in 1942 Arnett took the lead saxophone chair in Hampton's band, replacing Illinois Jacquet, who had gotten the position as Arnett's substitute (from an original 1941 offer to Cobb). Jacquet had held his position with Hampton on the condition that he switch from alto to tenor and "play like Cobb." With Cobb as the featured soloist, Hampton re-recorded his theme song, "Flying Home [No. 2]," and the excitement elicited by Cobb's uninhibited, blasting style earned him the label "Wild Man of the Tenor Sax." He was a major asset to the Hampton band for five years as co-writer, writer, reed-section arranger, lead saxophone, featured soloist, and talent scout. Gladys Hampton and Elizabeth Cobb helped manage the band, and Cobb's mother did the tailoring.

Cobb left Hampton in 1947, formed his own combo, and was immediately signed by Ben Bartz of Universal Attractions for management and booking. Under Ben's direction, Cobb toured extensively through 1949, while recording such hits as "Dutch Kitchen Bounce" (Princeton University's theme song), "Big Red's Groove," "Go Red Go," and "Big League Blues" for the Apollo label. He had begun some of his most influential years in American music history with his showmanship (bar walking and circular breathing techniques) and style (predecessor of Texas "swing" blues). Between 1950 and 1956, Cobb produced a string of hits including "Jumpin' the Blues," "Lil Sonny," "The Shy One," and "Smooth Sailing" (Ella Fitzgerald's

signature scat) on the Columbia label; "Night," "Light Like That" and "Flying Home Mambo" on the Atlantic label; and other popular tunes for these and other labels. His combos and support became a career-building platform for Red Garland (playing with Miles Davis), George Rhodes (Sammy Davis Jr.'s music director), George Duvivier (bassist), Dinah Washington, comedian Redd Foxx, Jackie Wilson, Arthur Prysock, and many others. Arnett scouted James Brown, positioned him as his opening act, and took him to New York to sign with agent Ben Bartz at Universal.

In 1956 a car accident interrupted his national prominence. Against doctors' advice, a year later he was back performing and touring coast to coast, although from this time on he could not walk without crutches. Cobb was living in New Jersey at the time, but the long, cold, damp, northeastern winter made working too strenuous, so in 1959 he moved back to Houston permanently. He managed the Club Ebony, organized regional orchestras for touring acts (Sammy Davis, Sarah Vaughn, Ella Fitzgerald, Ray Charles and others), and devoted a lot of time to nurturing young talent. Major recording R&B, soul, and jazz artists of the day called on him constantly for arrangements, band personnel, and gigs. Cobb restricted his touring to Texas from 1959 to 1973, but proceeded with a recording schedule that had continued from 1957 for the Prestige label. He recorded extensively with VeeJay, Prestige, Muse, Black and Blue (France), BeeHive, Progressive, Soul Note, MCA, and the Fantasy labels between 1957 and 1988. Cobb began an international touring schedule in 1973 with his daughter as his personal manager. He toured consistently, in the U.S., Europe, and Japan, with the Lionel Hampton All-stars, as a member of the renowned Texas Tenors, as a featured soloist, and, from 1985 to 1989, with his own ensemble, Texas Jazz and Blues featuring Jewel Brown.

Cobb was a prolific showman, writer, stylist, arranger, and tenor saxophone technician. His saxophone technique and music style directly influenced Illinois Jacquet, Gene Ammons, Johnny Griffin, Red Prysock, Houston Person, Sonny Stitt, Stanley Turrentine, King Curtis, Eddie "Lockjaw" Davis, Rahsaan Roland Kirk, and a generation of musicians in jazz, swing, R&B, soul, and funk music. Cobb received a Grammy nomination in 1979 for best jazz instrumental performance (*Live at Sandy's*, Muse). He shared a Grammy with B. B. King in 1984 for best traditional blues performance (*Blues n' Jazz*, MCA). In 1986 he founded the Jazz Heritage Society of Texas, which established the Texas Jazz Archives at the Houston Public Library. Cobb was survived by his daughter and grandson.

BIBLIOGRAPHY: Larry Birnbaum, "Arnett Cobb: Soul-Wrenching Sax," *Down Beat*, April 1981. "A Feeling for Jazz: An Interview with Arnett Cobb," *Houston Review* 12 (1990). Barry Kernfeld, ed., *The New Grove Dictionary of Jazz* (London: Macmillan, 1988).

Stephen G. Williams and Kharen Monsho

Cohron, Lenore. Operatic soprano, also known as Leonora Corona; b. Dallas, October 14, 1900; place and date of death unknown; daughter of Judge Cicero F. and Annie J.

Arnett Cobb playing with Lionel Hampton's Band at the Trianon Ballroom, Chicago. While playing with Hampton from 1942 to 1947, Cobb became known as the "Wild Man of the Tenor Sax." Duncan Scheidt Collection.

Cohron. Lenore exhibited an interest in singing and acting as a child, but spent most of her youth studying piano with her mother, who remained her mentor and close companion throughout her career. She was considered a child prodigy and gave solo recitals in Dallas. She attended Oak Cliff High School in Dallas before her family moved to Seattle. While living on the West Coast as a teenager, she became increasingly drawn to singing after hearing the Chicago Grand Opera and the Scotti Opera Company perform. These experiences inspired her to write a brief opera entitled "The Egyptian Tragedy," which was performed in Seattle. With some encouragement from prominent opera performers of the time, she determined to change her emphasis from piano to opera. She studied voice in New York and Italy and made her operatic debut around 1924 in Naples, where she changed her name to Leonora Corona.

Corona's career in Italy included singing five operas under Tullio Serafin, a future conductor at the Metropolitan Opera, and performing at La Scala in Milan. She sang in more than twenty-five European theaters before signing a contract with the Bracale Opera Company and touring in Havana and Puerto Rico. She signed a long-term contract with the Metropolitan Opera in 1927 and made her debut there in November of that year as Leonora in Verdi's *Il Trovatore*.

Corona sang at the Met for eight seasons, performing in twelve operas during this time. Known particularly for her performances in Italian operas, she sang the leading roles in *Tosca*, *Aïda*, and *Don Giovanni*. During these years she also performed at Carnegie Hall and at the Opéra Comique in Paris. Critics praised both her vocal and dramatic powers and her picturesque beauty. Her tenure with the Met overlapped with that of two other Texans, Etheldreda Aves of Galveston and Rafaelo Diaz of San Antonio, and followed the career of Texan Lillian Eubank. Throughout this time Corona maintained ties to her hometown by returning to Dallas occasionally for concerts and other special events.

After her career with the Met concluded in 1935, she continued to perform professionally. She sang with such regional opera companies as the San Carlo Opera of Chicago, and presented recitals at both Town Hall and Carnegie Hall in New York. She appeared in a performance of Julia Smith's *Cynthia Parker* at North Texas State Teachers College (now the University of North Texas) in Denton in 1939. Throughout her career she encouraged Americans to take a greater interest in opera. Despite her fame as a singer, virtually no information is available on Leonora Corona after the late 1930s. No obituary for her appeared in Dallas or New York papers, and it is not certain that she remained in this country in her later life.

BIBLIOGRAPHY: Dallas *Morning News*, April 29, May 2, 1928; June 25, 1932; April 7, 1933. Files, Library and Museum of the Performing Arts, Lincoln Center, New York Public Library. New York *Times*, November 16, 25, 1927; October 6, 1937. Vertical files, Center for American History, University of Texas at Austin.

Debbie Mauldin Cottrell

Coker, Henry. Trombonist; b. Dallas, December 24, 1919; d. Los Angeles, November 23, 1979. As a child, Coker lived in Omaha for a time. He began his formal musical training in high school at Washington, Texas, where he studied the piano and harp. He continued with these instruments into his early college career. While studying music at Wiley College in Marshall, Texas, he developed an interest in jazz that led him to switch to the trombone. Inspired by the music of Duke Ellington and others, Coker first worked regularly in the jazz field in 1935, with the band of trumpeter John White. He was with Nat Towles' Band from 1937 to 1939. During this period he began to create for himself a highly distinctive solo style. Abruptly, however, he left the jazz world behind, darting off to Honolulu to play in a series of Hawaiian bands, including a period with drummer Monk McFay.

On returning to the United States in 1945, Coker became a member of Benny Carter's band in California. He later joined the Eddie Heywood Sextet to go on a tour that included important dates in New York City. He stayed with Heywood until 1947. During his time with Heywood he recorded with a number of jazz artists, among them fellow trombonist Vic Dickenson. After leaving the Heywood Sextet, Coker remained on the West Coast freelancing and doing studio work until 1949, when he joined the Illinois Jacquet band. Illness forced him to leave Jacquet around 1950. After he recovered from his sickness, his consequent financial difficulties ended when he landed a job with the Count Basie Orchestra in 1952. Coker so impressed Basie that he was assigned the post of section leader and principal trombone soloist. During his long tenure with the Basie band (1952–63), Coker had countless opportunities for solos on such songs as "No Name," "Redhead," and "Peace Pipe." He also was the principal trombone soloist on the important retrospective album *The Count Basie Story* (1960). Coker spent much of his later career doing studio work in New York City and playing with the Ray Charles orchestra, with which he remained from 1966 through 1971. For most of the seventies he worked as a freelance and studio musician in the Los Angeles area. He played on the soundtrack for the movie *Lady Sings the Blues* (1972), and for four months in 1973 he was back with the Count Basie band. He also was reunited briefly with Ray Charles in 1976.

Coker's career thus featured performances with some of the most important jazz groups from the thirties all the way into the mid-seventies. His longest and most notable engagement was with the Count Basie Orchestra. He was well known for his forceful, imposing musical style, which was mirrored by his massive frame and commanding personality. He was also a musical perfectionist, as is his impressive solos demonstrate. He is especially notable for his ability to combine his roots in thirties-era swing with more modern, improvisational jazz methods. Deliberate, forceful attacks and inventive, technically conscious solos personified Coker's style. His playing possessed a rugged vitality, and owing to this and to his reputation as a self-critic, Coker is regarded as a quite important jazz trombonist.

BIBLIOGRAPHY: John Chilton, *Who's Who of Jazz:*

From Storyville to Swingstreet Fourth Edition (New York: Da Capo Press, 1985). Leonard Feather, *The Encyclopedia of Jazz* (New York: Horizon Press, 1960). Leonard Feather and Ira Gitler, *The Biographical Encyclopedia of Jazz* (New York: Oxford University Press, 1999). Raymond Horricks, *Count Basie and His Orchestra* (London: Jazz Book Club, 1958). Barry Kernfeld, ed., *The New Grove Dictionary of Jazz*, Second Edition (New York: Grove's Dictionaries, 2002). *Alex Daboub*

Coleman, Gary B. B. Blues singer and instrumentalist; b. Paris, Texas, 1947; d. 1994. Coleman grew up listening to the blues. He was inspired by such artists as Slim Harpo, T-Bone Walker, Freddie King, Albert King, and B. B. King. By age 15, Coleman was working as a sideman for fellow Texan Freddie King. He subsequently worked with Lightnin' Hopkins and later formed his own band, in which he sang and played keyboards, guitar, and bass for many years in Texas and Oklahoma. He did not begin his recording career until 1986, when he recorded his debut album, *Nothin' but the Blues*, under his own label, Mr. B's Records. In 1987 Coleman joined Ichiban Records as recording mainstay and producer.

He became a major promoter of blues musicians, booking blues performers into clubs throughout Texas, Oklahoma, and Colorado and producing more than thirty albums for such artists as Clarence Carter, Chick Willis, Little Johnny Taylor, Buster Benton, Travis Haddix, Blues Boy Willie, Vernon Garrett, and the Legendary Blues Band. Besides Ichiban's re-release of *Nothin' but the Blues*, Coleman released six albums between 1988 and 1992, including *If You Can Beat Me Rockin'*, *One Night Stand*, *Dancin' My Blues Away*, *Romance Without Finance Is a Nuisance*, *The Best of Gary B. B. Coleman*, and *Too Much Weekend*. While working with Ichiban, Coleman continued to tour, playing his own songs and popular blues tunes in clubs, colleges, and resort towns across the nation. He achieved national recognition just before his death in 1994, the same year that he recorded his last release, *Cocaine Annie*.

BIBLIOGRAPHY: Denver *Post*, January 11, 1991. Jim O'Neal and Steven Thomas Erlewine, ed., *All Music Guide to the Blues*, Second Edition (San Francisco: Miller Freeman, 1999). *Cheryl L. Simon*

Coleman, George. Street performer, percussionist, and singer, known as Bongo Joe; b. George Coleman, Haines City, Florida, November 28, 1923; d. San Antonio, December 19, 1999. Coleman's father died before he was born, and his mother died when he was seven. After he graduated from high school he moved to Detroit to live with his older sister. There he was exposed to the Detroit jazz scene and began his interest in musical performance with the piano. He played with many local musicians, and even with Sammy Davis Jr.

He moved to Houston by his late twenties and started his career as a percussionist with a local band. Rather than appearing on stage with a full drumset, which he did not own, he fabricated a makeshift kit out of empty fifty-five-gallon oil drums. This led to a unique percussive sound that he developed over the course of his career through spe-

"Bongo Joe" frequently played his oil drums on the streets of Galveston, Houston, and San Antonio from the 1960s until the early 1990s. Photo © by Chris Strachwitz (www.arhoolie.com).

cialized drumming techniques, tuning, and hand-made instruments. He also augmented his sound with his humorous and insightful lyrics.

Coleman started performing more on streets than on stages, hauling his oil drums around the cities of Texas, mounting them with a pick-up microphone and playing through a small amplifier. For fifteen years or so, he played at popular Houston-area tourist spots such as Seawall Boulevard in Galveston, and later moved to more prominent tourist attractions such as HemisFair '68 in San Antonio. He traveled through Mexico playing for tips, but settled in San Antonio. As he continued to travel the state of Texas and its immediate environs, taking his oil drums with him and playing on streetcorners, he acquired the affectionate nickname "Bongo Joe."

Coleman was invited to participate in the New Orleans Jazz & Heritage Festival nine times. There he played piano once with Dizzy Gillespie. In 1976 he played on a ten-city tour as part of Gerald Ford's presidential campaign. In 1991 he appeared on three television programs called "Almost Live from the Liberty Bar" that aired on the San Antonio PBS affiliate. His performances stopped in the early 1990s, when he was diagnosed with diabetes and kidney disease.

Coleman has been alternately viewed as inspired and as a novelty act. Whichever way he is interpreted, he was certainly a cult classic. He was recorded in San Antonio by Chris Strachwitz of Arhoolie Records in 1968. These recordings led to an LP that, in combination with a few later sessions, turned into a CD re-release by Arhoolie entitled *George Coleman: Bongo Joe*. One selection from these original recordings, "Innocent Little Doggy," was an underground classic on independent radio in Texas as well as in England. Associates of Coleman knew him to be an extremely talented musician who performed on the streets by choice, often turning down opportunities to play more respectable, and more lucrative, engagements in order to play for the general public.

BIBLIOGRAPHY: "George Coleman, a.k.a. Bongo Joe" (http://www.arhoolie.com/artists/bongo_joe.shtml), accessed March 6, 2003. San Antonio *Express–News*, Dec. 21, 1999. *Cathy Brigham*

Collins, Albert. Blues musician; b. Albert Gene Drewery, Leona, Texas, October 1, 1932; d. Las Vegas, Nevada, November 24, 1993; son of Andy Thomas. The family moved to Marquez when Albert was seven and to Houston when he was nine. He started his music career in Houston in 1952. Collins recorded his first single, "The Freeze," in 1958 and the first of fifteen albums, *The Cool Sound of Albert Collins*, in 1965. He called his guitar the "Telecaster" and was himself known both as "Master of the Telecaster" and as the "Iceman." He became famous for walking into the audience, and on one occasion into the parking lot, with a 300-foot extension cord, followed by the audience. Collins used his fingers, not a pick, to play the guitar; unorthodox minor tunings and a capo on the fingerboard produced his unusual sounds. In the early 1960s *Frosty* became his first gold album.

In 1968 Collins moved from Texas to California with the group Canned Heat. Although he had numerous regional hits recorded on small labels in the 1960s and 1970s, in the late 1970s he signed with Alligator. His 1979 *Ice Pickin'* won the best blues album award from the Montreux Jazz Festival and was nominated for a Grammy. In 1983 he won the W. C. Handy award for best blues album of the year with *Don't Lose Your Cool*, and in 1986 he shared a Grammy for *Showdown*. By the 1990s he had played in Carnegie Hall and appeared at the Live Aid Television benefit. His last album, *Molten Ice*, was released in 1992. A favorite in Austin, Collins yearly played three or four two-night stands at Antone's, a local club, and in 1991 taped a BBC special there. He also played at the annual Aqua-Fest and appeared on the PBS show "Austin City Limits" in 1991.

BIBLIOGRAPHY: Austin *American–Statesman*, November 25, 29, 1993. Colin Larkin, ed., *The Guinness Encyclopedia of Popular Music* (Chester, Connecticut: New England Publishing Associates, 1992). *Newsweek*, December 6, 1993. *John G. Johnson*

Copeland, Johnny "Clyde." Songwriter and blues guitarist; b. Haynesville, Louisiana, March 27, 1937; d. New York City, July 3, 1997; son of sharecroppers. Copeland developed an interest in the blues at an early age. His parents separated when he was six months old, and his mother took him to Magnolia, Arkansas, with his mother. When his father died a few years later, Copeland inherited a guitar and began learning to play it.

Houston guitarist and singer Johnny Copeland played blues in Texas and New York from the 1950s until the 1990s. He was nicknamed the "Texas Twister" for his energetic showmanship and style of playing. Photograph by Robert Turner. (*Texas Rhythm, Texas Rhyme: A Pictorial History of Texas Music*, Austin: Texas Monthly Press, 1984). Courtesy Larry Willoughby.

When Johnny was thirteen years old, the Copelands moved to Houston, where the boy first saw a performance by guitarist T-Bone Walker. In 1954, influenced by Walker, Copeland and his friend Joe "Guitar" Hughes formed a band, the Dukes of Rhythm. While his musical interest grew, Copeland engaged in boxing and acquired the nickname Clyde. The band played regularly in several leading Houston blues clubs, including Shady's Playhouse and the El Dorado Ballroom. While with the Dukes of Rhythm, Copeland also played back-up for such blues figures as Sonny Boy Williamson II, Big Mama Thornton, and Freddie King.

In 1958 he recorded his first single with Mercury Records, "Rock 'n' Roll Lily," which became a regional hit. In the 1960s he achieved only limited regional success as he recorded with various small and independent labels. His hits included "Please Let Me Know" and "Down on Bending Knees," recorded with the All Boy and the Golden Eagle labels, both based in Houston.

During the early 1970s Copeland toured the "Texas Triangle"—Louisiana, Texas, and Arkansas—and developed a reputation as one of the most frenetic live performers in Texas-style blues. In 1974 he moved to New York City, where he worked days at a Brew 'n' Burger and performed in clubs at night. In a few years Copeland became a major draw, attracting receptive audiences at clubs in Harlem and Greenwich Village, and leaving his mark by "brandishing his sizzling guitar, like a slick, sharp weapon."

In 1981 he signed with Rounder Records, which released the album *Copeland Special*, recorded in 1979 with saxophonists Arthur Blythe and Byard Lancaster. This album inspired Copeland to cut a series of albums with the label in the 1980s, including *Make My Home Where I Hang My Hat* (1982), and *Texas Twister* (1983), which also featured blues guitarist Stevie Ray Vaughan. With this recording success, Copeland toured the United States and Europe. In 1986, while on a ten-city tour in West Africa, he recorded *Bringing It All Back Home*, using local musicians. The album included imaginative hybrids of blues mixed with African idioms. Copeland thus became the first American blues musician to record an album in Africa.

That same year, he won a Grammy for the Best Traditional Blues Recording for *Showdown!* (1985), an album he recorded with fellow blues musicians Robert Cray and Albert Collins. His follow-up album, *Ain't Nothing but a Party [Live]*, earned him a Grammy nomination in 1988. Throughout the decade he played and recorded with a furious Texas-Style blues guitar, performing burning guitar licks that became his trademark and earned him another nickname, the "Fire Maker."

Despite adversity, Copeland continued to perform throughout the 1990s. He showed off his songwriting talents when he released his albums *Flying High* for Verve Records in 1992, and *Catch Up with the Blues*, for Polygram in 1994. The albums included the hits "Life's Rainbow" and "Circumstances." In 1994 he was diagnosed with heart disease, and he spent the next few years checking in and out of hospitals and undergoing a series of open-heart operations. He had been placed on an L-VAD (left ventricular assist device), a battery-powered pump designed for patients suffering from congenital heart defects. He appeared on CNN and ABC-TV's "Good Morning America" wearing the L-VAD, an event that gave both Copeland and the medical device greater national exposure. He lived a remarkable length of time, twenty months, on the L-VAD.

In January 1, 1997, he received a successful heart transplant, and in a few months he resumed touring. During the summer his heart developed a defective valve, and he was admitted to Columbia–Presbyterian Hospital in New York for heart surgery. After complications during the surgery, he died. He was survived by his wife, Sandra, and seven children.

Copeland left a lasting impact on Texas-Style blues and played a major part in the blues boom of the 1980s. In his career he earned a Grammy, four WC Handy awards, and the Best Album of the Year Award from the French National Academy of Jazz (1995). In 1984 he also became one of the few blues musicians to perform behind the Iron Curtain during the Cold War.

BIBLIOGRAPHY: David Dicaire, *Blues Singers: Biographies of 50 Legendary Artists of the Early 20th Century* (North Carolina: McFarland, 1999). New York *Times*, July 4, 1984. Tony Russell, *The Blues: From Robert Johnson to Robert Cray* (New York: Schirmer, 1997). Richard Skelly and Bruce Eder, "Johnny Copeland," in *AMG All Music Guide to the Blues: The Experts' Guide to the Best Blues Recordings*, Second Edition (San Francisco: Miller Freeman, 1999). Vertical files, Center for American History, University of Texas at Austin.

Juan Carlos Rodríguez and Matthew Tippens

Corley, George. Trombonist; b. Austin, September 7, 1912; place and date of death unknown. Corley, scion of a musical family, studied piano and later trombone. As a trombonist he organized his own group, the Royal Aces, probably during high school. He joined the Terrence Holder band in the early 1930s, left to join Troy Floyd, a San Antonio band, in 1932, and subsequently worked with a number of Texas bands, including those of Tommy Brooks, Sammy Holmes, Howard Brown, and Clifford "Boots" Douglas. He can be heard soloing on "Remember" as recorded in 1937 by the San Antonio band Boots and His Buddies (in *Boots and His Buddies, 1937–1938* [Classics 738, 1993]). In the 1940s and early 1950s Corley performed in California. From 1955 to 1962 he worked in Texas and then returned to California, where he worked with singer Jimmy McCraklin.

BIBLIOGRAPHY: John Chilton, *Who's Who of Jazz: Storyville to Swing Street*, Fourth Edition (New York: Da Capo Press, 1985). *Dave Oliphant*

Corridos. The corrido in its usual form is a ballad of eight-syllable, four-line stanzas sung to a simple tune in fast waltz time, now often in polka rhythm. Corridos have traditionally been men's songs. They have been sung at home, on horseback, in town plazas by traveling troubadours, in cantinas by blind *guitarreros* (guitarists), on campaigns during the Mexican Revolution (1910–30), and on migrant workers' journeys north to the fields. Now they are heard frequently on records and over the radio.

These ballads are generally in major keys and have tunes with a short—less than an octave—range. Américo Paredes, the preeminent scholar of the corrido of the lower Rio Grande border area, remarks: "The short range allows the corrido to be sung at the top of the singer's voice, an essential part of the corrido style." In Texas this singing has traditionally been accompanied by a guitar or *bajo sexto*, a type of twelve-string guitar popular in Texas and northern Mexico.

In its literary form the corrido seems to be a direct descendent of the *romance*, a Spanish ballad form that developed in the Middle Ages, became a traditional form, and was brought to the New World by Spanish conquistadors. Like the *romance*, the corrido employs a four-line stanza form with an *abcd* rhyme pattern. Paredes surmises that corrido is ultimately derived from the Andalusian phrase *romance corrido*, which denoted a refrainless, rapidly sung romance. With the noun dropped, the participle corrido, from a verb meaning "to run," itself became a noun.

The corrido, like the romance, relates a story or event of local or national interest—a hero's deeds, a bandit's exploits, a barroom shootout, or a natural disaster, for instance. It has long been observed, however, that songs

Américo Paredes, ca. 1990s. Paredes, the premier scholar of border corridos and a professor at UT Austin, integrated music into his teaching. He often played his guitar and sang for his students. Photograph by Valentino Mauricio, courtesy Texas Folklife Resources.

little dove") often signals the *despedida* on the first line of the penultimate or ultimate stanza of the song.

In the middle to late 1800s several ballad forms—the *romance*, *décima*, and *copla*—existed side by side in Mexico and in the Southwest, and at this time the corrido seems to have had its genesis. By 1848, however, the remote outposts of northern Mexico already belonged to the United States as a result of the Texas Revolution, the Mexican War, and the Treaty of Guadalupe Hidalgo. The *romance* tradition in California dwindled with the Anglo-American migration and takeover, and a native balladry did not develop there until the corrido form was imported by Mexican immigrants in this century. New Mexico, on the other hand, remained somewhat isolated from modern Mexican and Anglo-American currents and retained much of its archaic Spanish tradition.

The border area of the lower Rio Grande and South Texas, however, was different. There the corrido seems to have had a separate and perhaps earlier development than elsewhere. Events in Texas between 1836 and 1848 resulted in the colonization of the lower Rio Grande area by white empresarios. The gradual displacement or subjugation of the Mexican people there provided the basis for more than a century of border conflict between the Anglos and the Mexicans. During the struggle against the Anglos, the corrido form developed in the area and became extremely popular. In Paredes's words, the borderers' "slow, dogged struggle against economic enslavement and the loss of their own identity was the most important factor in the development of a distinct local balladry."

The border corrido developed after 1848 and reached its peak at the height of cultural conflict between 1890 and 1910, at least ten years before the zenith of the Mexican corrido during the Mexican Revolution. The border corridos, in short, dramatic form, picture a heroic struggle against oppression and rival the Mexican corridos in quality, if not in quantity. Border heroes such as Ignacio and Jacinto Treviño and Aniceto Pizaña are depicted in corridos of this time defending their rights against the Americans. But the epitome of the border corrido hero was Gregorio Cortez. In *With His Pistol in His Hand*, Paredes discusses the legend, life, and corridos of Cortez. Despite Cortez's notoriety among South Texas Anglos, the ballads portray him as a peaceful Mexicano living in South Texas at the turn of the century. When Cortez's brother is shot, allegedly for no good reason, Cortez is pursued over South Texas by as many as 300 *rinches*, or Texas Rangers. Following the pattern, the corridos picture Cortez goaded into action, fighting against "outsiders" for his own and the people's independence.

The border ceased to be a distinct cultural area in the early 1900s. Improved communications and means of travel linked the south bank of the Rio Grande more with the interior of Mexico and the north bank more with Texas and the United States. The idea of a boundary caused the borderer to begin to see himself as a Mexican or American. Corridos in Mexico embodied epic characteristics during the revolutionary period. Although these corridos were known in Texas, few if any new corridos of border conflict were composed after about 1930. With the borderer's loss

with little or no narration are still called corridos if they adhere to the corrido's usual literary and musical form.

Besides its music, versification, and subject matter, the corrido also employs certain formal ballad conventions. In *La lírica narrativa de México*, Vicente Mendoza gives six primary formal characteristics or conventions of the corrido. They are: (1) the initial call of the *corridista*, or balladeer, to the public, sometimes called the formal opening; (2) the stating of the place, time, and name of the protagonist of the ballad; (3) the arguments of the protagonist; (4) the message; (5) the farewell of the protagonist; and (6) the farewell of the *corridista*. These elements, however, vary in importance from region to region in Mexico and the Southwest, and it is sometimes difficult to find a ballad that employs all of them. In Texas and the border region, the formal opening of the corrido is not as vital as the balladeer's *despedida* (farewell) or formal close. Often the singer will start the corrido with the action of the story to get the interest of the audience, thus skipping the introduction, but the *despedida* in one form or another is almost never dropped. The phrase *Ya con esta me despido* ("With this I take my leave") or *Vuela, vuela, palomita* ("Fly, fly,

of identity went the corrido of border strife. The corrido tradition itself did not die in Texas, however; it merely changed during and after the 1930s.

At the same time that border strife was waning, labor demands of developing agribusiness in Texas were pulling more and more Texas-Mexican borderers into migrant farmwork. The decades of the 1920s through the 1950s were particularly frustrating for Texas Mexicans, who held the lowest status in the economy of South Texas. In these years were composed and sung hundreds of corridos about bad working conditions, poverty, and the hopelessness of the Texas-Mexican migrant agricultural worker.

In the late 1940s and in the 1950s, as Texas-Mexican music in general became commercialized, so did the corrido. With local *guitarreros* and conjuntos (musical groups), the new Texas-Mexican recording companies produced many corridos. These recorded songs, however, were usually about such sensational subjects as barroom shootings or drug smuggling. Corridos about migrant work were never recorded, for they were considered too politically inflammatory for fledgling recording companies and new radio stations.

Not until the Kennedy assassination did Texas-Mexican corridos have a subject that would reinvigorate the genre. During the months following John Kennedy's death, dozens of Kennedy corridos were composed, recorded, and broadcast on Spanish-language radio stations in Texas and across the Southwest. In contrast to the usual commercial corridos of the time, those about Kennedy often resembled the older, heroic corridos. The new ballads spoke for Mexican Americans who identified with what they saw as Kennedy's struggles and ideas. After the mid-1960s and the beginnings of the Chicano movement, corridos continued to thrive. Their subjects were Chicano leaders and ideals of economic justice and cultural pride.

From the 1970s and into the twenty-first century the biggest factor in corridos in Texas, across the southwestern United States and in northern Mexico was the rise of the genre of *narcocorridos*. Following the early-1970s release of *Contrabando y traición* by the popular group Los Tigres del Norte, the exploits and profits of drug smugglers such as Camelia "la tejana" were chronicled in hundreds of corridos, and this trend shows no signs of tapering off. In the 1980s and 1990s some corridos circulated about famous Texans—some promoted the political aspirations of Henry Cisneros, for instance—and there were outpourings of sadness in *tragedias* about the killing of the popular singer Selena. Disasters over the years such as the space shuttle *Challenger* explosion spawned a few corridos. The 9/11 terrorist attacks received the greatest expression from *corridistas*; at least three corridos about the event circulated in San Antonio, and many more were composed and recorded throughout the Southwest on both sides of the border. In a new development, some corridos are now starting to be diffused through internet sites. The Internet has less impact than recordings played on the radio, but also less censorship.

BIBLIOGRAPHY: Dan W. Dickey, "Tejano Troubadours," *Texas Observer*, July 16, 1976. Dan W. Dickey, *The Kennedy Corridos: A Study of the Ballads of a Mexican American Hero* (Center for Mexican-American Studies, University of Texas at Austin, 1978). Vicente T. Mendoza, *El corrido mexicano* (Mexico City: Fondo de Cultura Económica, 1954). Vicente T. Mendoza, *Lírica narrativa de México: El Corrido* (Mexico City: Universidad Nacional Autónoma de México, Instituto de Investigaciones Estéticas, 1964). Américo Paredes, Ballads of the Lower Border (M.A. thesis, University of Texas, 1953). Américo Paredes, El Corrido de Gregorio Cortez: A Ballad of Border Conflict (Ph.D. dissertation, University of Texas, 1956). Américo Paredes, *A Texas-Mexican Cancionero: Folksongs of the Lower Border* (Urbana: University of Illinois Press, 1976). Américo Paredes, *With His Pistol in His Hand: A Border Ballad and Its Hero* (Austin: University of Texas Press, 1958). Merle Simmons, *The Mexican Corrido as a Source of an Interpretive Study of Modern Mexico, 1870–1950* (Bloomington: University of Indiana Press, 1957). Elijah Wald, *Narcocorrido: A Journey into the Music of Drugs, Guns and Guerillas* (New York: Rayo / Harper Collins, 2001).
Dan W. Dickey

Country and Western Music. Country and western music is rooted in the folk music of the British Isles. English, Irish, Scottish, and Welsh poetry, folklore, ballads, and sea chanteys form the basis for many of the earliest songs that came to be called country and western music in the United States. However, modern country and western music has been profoundly influenced by a variety of other regional and ethnic genres of music during the past few centuries. African Americans, Mexican Americans, German Americans, Polish Americans, French Americans, and several other groups have had a major impact on the development of country and western music over the years.

"Country" music began to emerge in the American South as large numbers of English-speaking settlers moved into the region during the seventeenth and eighteenth centuries. By the early nineteenth century, some of these Anglo pioneers had moved as far west as Texas. As a primarily rural, agrarian society, the South remained somewhat culturally isolated from the increasingly urbanized and industrialized North. Consequently, southerners tended to preserve the traditional folk music of their ancestral homelands. However, even though southern folk songs typically were based on traditional music from the British Isles, they underwent significant transformation according to the particular ethnic and social influences present in different parts of the South. By the beginning of the nineteenth century, "country" music included a wide variety of styles that differed dramatically from region to region across the southern United States.

In Texas, country music developed its own unique characteristics. Beginning with Moses and Stephen Austin's arrangement with the Mexican government to bring English-speaking settlers into the province of Tejas in the 1820s, tens of thousands of white southerners poured into Texas over the next two decades, bringing their southern folk culture with them. These southerners also brought many black slaves along, who also had an important impact on the unique development of country music in Texas.

Texas won its independence from Mexico in 1836, and, by the time it joined the United States in 1845, the original Native American and Hispanic inhabitants had been joined by an astounding array of other immigrant and ethnic groups, including Anglo, Irish, Scottish, Welsh, African, German, French, Czech, Polish, Jewish, and Italian. Partly because Texas was less strictly segregated than the Deep South, and partly because the rugged environment of the western frontier necessitated cooperation among traditionally disparate groups, people of different racial, ethnic, and socioeconomic backgrounds interacted somewhat more freely in Texas than in other parts of the South, exchanging musical ideas and influences in the process. This blending of a variety of rich musical traditions made Texas a fertile ground for the emergence of several new sub-genres of American country music.

The great cattle drives from Texas to the Midwest during the late 1800s made the cowboy a key player in the developing Texas economy and secured his status as an almost mythical character within the folk culture of the Southwest. The music of the cowboys included traditional folksongs that were modified to fit the unique living and working conditions cowboys faced. "Bury Me Not on the Lone Prairie," for example, was based on the old English sailor's song "Ocean Burial." Other songs included humorous anecdotes or spoke of the lonely, difficult nature of life on the open range. Since nearly half of all Texas cowboys were either Hispanic or black, the cowboy's repertoire also reflected lyrical, instrumental, and stylistic influences from these ethnic communities. In some cases, songs widely considered to be traditional cowboy ballads were written years after the great cattle drives by songwriters hoping to recapture what they considered the romance and adventure of a bygone era. Such is the case with the classic tune "Home on the Range," written by Texan David Guion in the early twentieth century.

By the 1920s the increasing availability of radios, phonographs, and moving pictures helped spread country music, which previously had been limited mainly to the South and Southwest, across the nation and even into international markets. The first known commercial recording of country music came in 1922, when Amarillo fiddler Eck Robertson recorded "Arkansas Traveler" and "Sallie Goodin" for Victor Records. In 1924, Vernon Dalhart from Jefferson, Texas, released the first country record to sell over a million copies. Dalhart's phenomenal success with "Wreck of the Old 97" convinced major record companies that there was a lucrative national market for country music. Soon, record companies and Hollywood film producers launched nationwide searches for marketable country singing stars. Among the most influential of these stars who were from or had lived in Texas were Jimmie Rodgers, Gene Autry, Dale Evans, and Tex Ritter. Rodgers, originally from Meridian, Mississippi, helped blend the Deep South country style of his native state with the western style of the Texas prairies to create the music that would come to be called "country and western." The tremendous popularity of such radio and movie singing personalities helped make country and western music an international phenomenon and made the cowboy and his

music a permanent and powerful symbol of the culture of Texas and the Southwest.

During the Great Depression of the 1930s, Texas continued to contribute to the ongoing evolution of country and western music. Folksinger Woody Guthrie, who was born in Oklahoma but spent much of his early life in Texas, became an important spokesman for millions of Texans, Oklahomans, and Arkansans displaced by the great Dust Bowl. Bob Wills, born in Limestone County, Texas, and Milton Brown, born in Stephenville, Texas, joined with a variety of jazz and country musicians to create western swing, one of the most eclectic, exciting, and enduring forms of American music ever to appear. Western swing blended traditional ballads and country fiddle tunes with blues, jazz, ragtime, polkas, schottisches, waltzes, reels, and instrumental arrangements that reflected the influences of every style from mariachi to big band swing. The great versatility of these western swing groups was due in part to the love that Wills, Brown, and the others had for all types of music, regardless of their ethnic or geographical origins. However, economic considerations also played a part in shaping the diverse repertoire of these bands. In order to keep their jobs on radio during the depression, entertainers had to be able to perform an extensive variety of musical styles that would appeal to a broad spectrum of listeners. The end result was a new type of music that introduced an astounding array of musical influences into mainstream country and western music.

The World War II era brought other important changes to country and western music. The rapid mobilization of the civilian population for the war effort resulted in a dramatic increase in urbanization and industrialization, as millions of Americans from rural backgrounds moved to the cities to work in factories and office buildings. This rapid transformation from an agrarian to an urban lifestyle was reflected in the emergence of a new type of country and western music called "honky-tonk." Although still based on the traditional country and western musical structures and instrumentation, honky-tonk music dealt more candidly with the problems of an increasingly urbanized, industrialized, and morally permissive society. Issues such as alcoholism, infidelity, divorce, and other social problems, which formerly were not discussed openly in public, became common themes in honky-tonk songs.

Some of the most influential honky-tonk musicians of this period came from Texas. Ernest Tubb, the first country and western singer to perform at Carnegie Hall, helped pioneer the post–World War II honky-tonk era, along with Floyd Tillman, Lefty Frizzell, Hank Thompson, Ray Price, and George Jones. By the late 1950s, Texas artists were bridging the gap between country and western and pop music, bringing country and western music increasingly into mainstream popular culture. For example, Johnny Horton's "Battle of New Orleans," Jim Reeves's "He'll Have to Go," Jimmy Dean's "Big Bad John," Roger Miller's "King of the Road," and Jeannie C. Riley's "Harper Valley P.T.A." all became major hits on both the country and pop charts. Texas-born Buck Owens even saw one of his songs, "Act Naturally," recorded by the Beatles.

In the 1970s, Texas gave birth to yet another sub-genre

Willie Nelson, pen and ink drawing by John A. Wilson (Austin, Texas) after a photograph by Dick Reeves. Willie Nelson was one of the leaders of the "redneck rock" or progressive country music movement that was centered in Austin in the 1970s.

of country and western music that forever altered the course of American music. Centered in Austin, the phenomenon known as "progressive country" or "redneck rock" sprang from an unlikely combination of traditional honky-tonk music and the hippie counterculture of the late 1960s. Such Austin venues as Armadillo World Headquarters and Soap Creek Saloon provided an environment in which cowboys, hippies, bikers, and college students could mingle freely and hear a great variety of music, including blues, country and western, rock-and-roll, and conjunto. Texas singer–songwriters such as Kris Kristofferson, Waylon Jennings, and Willie Nelson, who had grown tired of the Nashville music scene, returned to their home state to lead the progressive country movement.

Kristofferson, born in Brownsville on June 22, 1936, includes on his resumé such diverse occupations as janitor, Rhodes Scholar, and helicopter pilot. He became a successful songwriter and movie star, recording and performing with Bob Dylan, Johnny Cash, and Barbara Streisand. Jennings, born in Littlefield near Lubbock on June 15, 1937, played bass guitar for Buddy Holly before moving to Nashville to record for RCA Records. Nelson, born on April 30, 1933 in Abbott, Texas, was raised by his grandparents. As a child, he began composing his own songs,

and, by the 1950s, had established a successful songwriting career in Nashville. Some of the biggest stars of country and western music turned Nelson's songs into top hits, including Ray Price with "Night Life," Patsy Cline with "Crazy," and Faron Young with "Hello Walls." However, Nelson and the others found more freedom for their musical creativity back in the Lone Star state.

The phenomenal commercial success of such progressive country hits as "Me and Bobby Mc Gee," "Luckenbach, Texas," and "Mommas, Don't Let Your Babies Grow Up To Be Cowboys," forced the Nashville establishment to acknowledge Nelson, Jennings, Kristofferson, and other "outlaw" artists and incorporate their unconventional musical style into the country and western mainstream. Soon, a flood of younger Texas performers, including Asleep at the Wheel, Guy Clark, Michael Murphey, Rodney Crowell, Johnny Rodriguez, Tanya Tucker, B.J. Thomas, Freddy Fender, Billie Jo Spears, Townes Van Zandt, Don Williams, and transplanted Texan Jerry Jeff Walker, was riding the wave of a new country music market that embraced country and western, folk, blues, pop, rock, and western swing.

The 1980s brought further important developments in country and western music. While native Texans such as

Kenny Rogers, born in Houston in 1938, Barbara Mandrell, born in Houston in 1948, and Larry Gatlin, born in Seminole in 1948, topped the charts with crossover pop–country hits, a group of college friends living in San Marcos was about to turn the country and western world on its head. The Ace in the Hole Band, featuring a young, unknown singer named George Strait, exploded on the scene, inspiring a return to the roots of traditional country and western music. Strait, born in Poteet, Texas, in 1952 and raised in Pearsall, honed his singing skills during a stint in the army and then went on to pursue a degree in agriculture at Southwest Texas State University. Between classes and local gigs, Strait and the band developed a loyal following. In 1981 Strait signed on with MCA Records and quickly became a country and western superstar. With an emphasis on western swing and back-to-basics honky-tonk, his long string of number-one hits, which includes "Fool Hearted Memory," "Right or Wrong," "Amarillo By Morning," and "Does Fort Worth Ever Cross Your Mind?," spawned legions of imitators and reawakened an interest in more traditional-sounding country and western music.

Other Texans, such as Clint Black, Lyle Lovett, LeAnn Rimes, Robert Earl Keen, Jr., and Jimmie Dale Gilmore, have followed in the footsteps of these earlier pioneers to build very successful careers of their own. With exciting new acts, such as Rick Treviño, Pat Green, and the Dixie Chicks, it seems clear that Texas will continue to have a profound and lasting impact on shaping country and western music to reflect the tremendous cultural variety of Texas and the Southwest.

BIBLIOGRAPHY: Joe Carr and Alan Munde, *Prairie Nights to Neon Lights: The Story of Country Music in West Texas* (Lubbock: Texas Tech University Press, 1995). Fred Deller, ed., *The Harmony Illustrated Encyclopedia of Country Music* (New York: Harmony, 1986). Alan B. Govenar and Jay F. Brakefield, *Deep Ellum and Central Track: Where the Black and White Worlds of Dallas Converged* (Denton: University of North Texas Press, 1998). Archie Green, "Austin's Cosmic Cowboys: Words in Collision," in *And Other Neighborly Names: Social Process and Cultural Image in Texas Folklore*, ed. Richard Bauman and Roger D. Abrahams (Austin: University of Texas Press, 1981). Duncan McLean, *Lone Star Swing: On the Trail of Bob Wills and His Texas Playboys* (New York: Norton, 1997). Bill C. Malone, *Country Music U.S.A.* (Austin: University of Texas Press, 1975). Steven Opdyke, *Willie Nelson Sings America* (Austin: Eakin Press, 1998). William A. Owens, *Tell Me a Story, Sing Me A Song: A Texas Chronicle* (Austin: University of Texas Press, 1983). Texas Music Museum, *Waltz Across Texas: An Introduction to the Country and Western Music of Texas* (Austin, 1991). Charles R. Townsend, *San Antonio Rose: The Life and Music of Bob Wills* (Urbana: University of Illinois Press, 1976).

Gary Hartman

Cowboys' Christmas Ball. An annual event in Anson, Texas, based on a nineteenth-century ballad. A frontier dance at Anson impressed William Lawrence Chittenden so much that he later wrote a poem about the event. He was staying overnight at the Star Hotel, where a Christmas dance was held annually in appreciation of the patronage of ranchers and cowboys. He watched the cowboys and their ladies dance the square, the schottische, the heel-and-toe polka, the waltz, and the Virginia reel. From his observations there, and perhaps at later dances, he wrote his poem "The Cowboys' Christmas Ball."

Some uncertainty exists as to which year's dance was the model for the poem; 1885 and 1887 are the most common suggestions. The poem was first published in the Anson *Texas Western* on June 19, 1890, after the Star Hotel had been destroyed by fire earlier in the year and information about the old hotel was being sought. In 1893 the poem appeared in the first volume of *Ranch Verses*, a collection of Chittenden's poems. John A. Lomax and his brother Alan published it in their book *Cowboy Songs and Other Frontier Ballads* in 1910. Gordon Graham, a cowboy folklorist from Colorado, set the poem to music and sang it at the Anson ball in 1946, and it became a common practice to have a soloist sing the ballad before the ball.

The music at the ball in 1885 was from a bass viol, a tambourine, and two fiddles. Both music and vocals have changed over the years, yet ball officials have remained firm that both music and song must conform to the tradition that became clearer over the years. Dances were held at Christmas in Anson at irregular intervals with little regard for the poem for several decades following the poem's publication. In 1934 the event was revived under the title Cowboys' Christmas Ball by Leonora Barrett, Anson teacher and folklorist. This first reenactment was held in the high school gymnasium and continued on an annual basis thereafter. The Anson dancers attempted to retain the old dance customs, steps, and songs. The men bowed and the women curtsied. The music was slow enough to allow the dances to be done in an unhurried manner and with much grace.

Because the Anson group performed dances not done by any other group in the National Folk Festival, they were invited to the festival in Chicago in 1937. Gertrude Knox, Washington folklorist, invited them to the festival in 1938 in Washington; there they danced on the White House lawn. At later dates they performed their folk dances in St. Louis, St. Petersburg, Denver, and various cities in Texas.

The Anson group was incorporated in 1937. A board of directors was named, and the event was copyrighted. In 1940, because of increased interest and attendance, Pioneer Hall was built as a permanent home for the ball, which had become a three-day event before Christmas each year. The dance has brought dignitaries, writers, and visitors from all over the nation to Anson. The Cowboys' Christmas Ball observed its sixty-eighth consecutive year in December 2002, with the music and folkloric dances that have characterized the ball from the beginning. In recent years the ball has employed two separate bands, one on Thursday and Saturday nights and one on Friday. Both bands' performances ratify Anson's claim to be the "Home of the Western Dance."

BIBLIOGRAPHY: Hybernia Grace, "Larry Chittenden and West Texas," West Texas Historical Association *Year Book* 13 (1937). *Juanita Daniel Zachry*

Coy, Eugene. Drummer and pianist; active professionally as early as 1927; died in California in the 1960s. As leader of the Happy Black Aces, Gene Coy worked out of Amarillo with his wife as the band's pianist. It has been reported that Ann Coy "played piano like a *man*." Between 1929 and 1933, Gene's group included some of the most outstanding jazzmen of the Southwest: Ben Webster, Carl "Tatti" Smith, and Dick Wilson. Bassist Junior Raglin was with Coy from 1938 to 1941, after which he replaced Jimmy Blanton in the Duke Ellington Orchestra. Coy's band traveled fairly extensively, even venturing into Mexico and Canada. Headquartered in San Francisco in the early 1940s, the band toured the Pacific Northwest and dubbed themselves "Gene Coy and his Harlem Swing." Unfortunately, Coy only recorded in 1949, long after he had made an impact on those who heard his most talented groups.

BIBLIOGRAPHY: Albert McCarthy, *Big Band Jazz* (London: Barrie & Jenkins, 1974). *Dave Oliphant*

Crawford, Roberta Dodd. African-American contralto also known as Princess Kojo Tovalou–Houenou; b. in the black Tank Town section of Bonham, Texas, 1897; d. Dallas, June 14, 1954 (buried in Gates Hill Cemetery, Bonham); oldest daughter among eight children of Joe and Emma (Dunlap) Dodd. As a child she attended Washington School and later worked as a waitress at Curtis Boarding House.

Roberta's singing talent brought her to the attention of Bonham women who arranged for her to perform at the Alexander Hotel and at several Bonham churches. With help from benefactors, she attended Wiley College at Marshall for two years, then entered Fisk University, where she studied with Roland Hayes. About 1920 she entered the University of Chicago, where for the next six years she studied voice with Madame Herman Devries. In 1926 she debuted at Kimball Hall and received favorable reviews from the Chicago *Tribune* and the Chicago *Defender*. While in Chicago she married Capt. William B. Crawford of the Eighth Illinois Regiment.

Two years later she performed at the First United Methodist Church in Bonham, where her program combined Italian, French, German, Spanish, and English art songs and operatic arias with Negro spirituals and at least one "primitive African melody." She then left for France to become a student of Blanche Marchessi in Paris. In 1931 she made her French debut by singing selections in five languages at the Salle Gaveau. Now widowed, she met Kojo Marc Tovalou–Houenou (or Marc Tovalou Quenum), a doctor and lawyer and Pan-African activist from Porto Novo, the capital of Dahomey in French West Africa. Some sources also refer to him as a prince. They married in 1932; he died about 1938.

After Marc's death, his widow returned to Paris. Unable to secure funds from her African property, she worked in the National Library of Paris and during World War II joined the Red Cross and sang in churches and canteens for American soldiers. Suffering from anemia, she relied on friends for financial help and credited a Fort Worth physician with saving her life by getting surplus food coupons for her. She reportedly spent time in a concentration camp

Roberta Dodd Crawford, ca. 1920s. Courtesy Texas A&M University—Commerce Archives. Crawford was an African-American opera star who sang in both the United States and Europe, but when she appeared in her hometown, Bonham, her family was forced to sit in the balcony of the town's segregated opera house.

during the German occupation of France. In 1948 she returned to Bonham, but her poor physical and emotional health left her unwilling to perform again. She later moved to Dallas. Roberta Crawford sang in several cities in the United States and at Spellman and Tuskegee universities as well as in Europe. She had no children.

BIBLIOGRAPHY: Bonham *Daily Favorite*, June 15, 1954; November 25, 1973. *Fannin County Folks and Facts* (Dallas: Taylor, 1977). Juanita C. Spencer, *Bonham—Town of Bailey Inglish* (Wolfe City, Texas: Henington, 1977). Pat Stephens, ed., *Forgotten Dignity: The Black Community of Bonham...1880–1930* (Bonham, Texas: Progressive Citizens, 1984). *Nancy Baker Jones*

Crayton, Pee Wee. Blues guitarist; b. Connie Curtis Crayton, Rockdale, Texas, December 18, 1914; d. Los Angeles, June 25, 1985. The Craytons moved to Austin while Connie was a child. The boy, whose father called him Pee Wee in honor of a local pianist, began playing music early in life after building a makeshift guitar-like instrument from a cigar box. Later, as a teenager, he received his first formal

Blues guitarist Pee Wee Crayton and Derek O'Brien (left) performing at Antone's, Austin, ca. 1980s. Photograph by Jeff Newman. Jeff Newman Southern Lights/Northern Cross Collection, CAH: CN 11490.

musical training on trumpet and ukulele through his school band.

In 1935 Pee Wee moved to Los Angeles. During the 1940s he performed throughout California in a variety of different venues and was influenced by the playing of T-Bone Walker. One musicologist called him "a shaper of the West Coast blues sound." Among the musicians Crayton toured or recorded with in the 1950s and 1960s were Ivory Joe Hunter, Lowell Fulson, Gatemouth Brown, and Ray Charles. He first charted in 1948 with "Blues After Hours," an instrumental on the Modern label, which reached number one on *Billboard*'s rhythm-and-blues chart. He soon had other successes with "Texas Hop" (1948), which reached number five, and "I Love You So" (1949), which reached number six. Crayton later recorded for other labels, including Vee-Jay, Aladdin, and Imperial, but with less success. Seeing his popularity declining, he moved to the Midwest to play music and try his hand at various other jobs, including golf hustling, before returning to Los Angeles in the 1960s. During this period he drove a truck and occasionally collaborated on songs with his wife, Esther.

Crayton launched a musical comeback in 1970, when he played with Johnny Otis at the Monterey Jazz Festival.

He released his first album, *Things I Used to Do* (Vanguard), the following year. He also performed for albums by Lightnin' Hopkins, Joe Turner, and Dizzy Gillespie. He continued to record and tour throughout the remainder of his life. His performances include an appearance at Antone's in Austin.

BIBLIOGRAPHY: Michael Erlewine, ed., *All Music Guide to the Blues: The Experts' Guide to the Best Blues Recordings*, Second Edition (San Francisco: Miller Freeman, 1999). Sheldon Harris, *Blues Who's Who: A Biographical Dictionary of Blues Singers* (New Rochelle, New York: Arlington House, 1979). Robert Santelli, *The Big Book of Blues: A Biographical Encyclopedia* (New York: Penguin, 1993). *Jarad Brown*

Crockett, Howard. Singer and songwriter; b. Howard Hausey, Yellow Pine, Webster Parish, Louisiana, December 25, 1925; d. Fort Worth, December 27, 1994. Hausey made it into the Brooklyn Dodgers' farm system as a pitcher, but turned to singing and songwriting after a shoulder injury ended his baseball playing.

Of the more than 200 songs he wrote, some of the best known are "Whispering Pines," "Slew Foot," and "Honky Tonk Man." These three, plus several others, were released and made famous by Johnny Horton. According to fellow songwriter Joe Davis, Crockett wrote what might be his most famous song, "Honky Tonk Man," at a club called Yankee's in Mississippi and almost never released it, because he figured someone else had already written something similar. From his numerous songs, four went gold, two platinum, and one double-platinum. As a young man Crockett also performed on the "Louisiana Hayride."

He made several recordings with Dot Records, his first in 1967, as well as with Mercury Records. His "The Last Will and Testament of a Drinking Man" was a hit in 1973. He retired from singing in 1981, though he continued to write songs up until a few months before his death. Dwight Yoakum made a hit recording of "Honky Tonk Man" in 1986.

Crockett died of lung cancer at home. His wife, Patricia Carol Hausey, had died on November 28, 1989. Crockett was survived by three sons and three daughters, as well as four grandchildren. His memorial service was held at Shannon Funeral Chapel, Fort Worth. In 1999 he was inducted into the LSSCMA of Texas Country Music Hall of Fame along with other Texas greats Lefty Frizzell, Lenora Sinistre, Gordon Jones, and Jess Beaumont.

BIBLIOGRAPHY: "Crockett, Howard," *Rockin' Country Style* discography (http://rcs.law.emory.edu/rcs/artists /c/croc 1000.htm), accessed March 4, 2003. Dallas *Morning News*, December 31, 1994. *Family Search* (http:// www.familysearch.org/Eng/Search/frameset_search.asp), accessed March 4, 2003. Fort Worth *Star–Telegram*, December 30, 1994. Houston *Chronicle*, December 31, 1994. *LSSCMA of Texas Halls of Fame* (http://ssrecords. techplanet.net/lsscma_halls_of_fame.htm), accessed March 4, 2003. *Hugh O'Donovan*

Crystal Springs Dance Pavilion. In Fort Worth; the birthplace of western swing. With the help of such performers as Bob Wills and Milton Brown, the dance hall at 5653 White Settlement Road became one of the most popular night spots in the area for dancing, drinking, and most importantly, listening to a new music genre.

The pavilion got its start, however, many years before Brown rocketed it to fame. It opened in March 1916 under the proprietorship of "Papa" Sam Cunningham and continued to remain under family control until fire consumed it in December 1966. It was named for springs at the site. Initially, the dance pavilion was set up in a discarded building from nearby Camp Bowie. Among others, World War I doughboys and their ladies came to swim in the springs and hear music. The music venue grew and in 1925 moved into a new building constructed on the premises. This structure had a capacity of about 1,000 persons and could accommodate approximately 800 on its dance floor.

By 1930, people at the Crystal Springs Dance Pavilion could hear Milton Brown singing popular tunes of the day. After he formed his own band, the Musical Brownies, they became featured performers there. People walked, drove, and even took the Crystal Springs shuttle bus from downtown Fort Worth to hear Milton Brown and His Musical Brownies play a new kind of dance music called hillbilly string music or cowboy jazz. Reportedly, Bonnie Parker

and Clyde Barrow also came to the pavilion. In addition to Brown's famous group, the hall had a modestly successful house band called the Crystal Spring Ramblers. Even though this western swing band had little success on the music charts, it continued to be a live favorite at the dance hall.

By the mid-1930s, Fort Worth was a hub for western swing music, and Crystal Springs was at the center. Brown died on April 18, 1936, but even without its headliner the pavilion continued to prosper as a country music venue until the 1950s. Henry Cunningham Sr. and his wife, Mary, took over the dance hall in 1955 when Papa Cunningham died. Henry kept the place open until January 1956. On New Year's Eve 1955, about 1,800 persons danced there. The hall remained closed until it was leased in 1965 and renamed the Stagecoach Inn. In December 1966 fire completely destroyed the structure.

BIBLIOGRAPHY: Fort Worth *Press*, January 9, 1956. Fort Worth *Star–Telegram*, April 20, 1997; September 25, 2002. Geronimo Treviño III, *Dance Halls and Last Calls: The History of Texas Country Music* (Plano, Texas: Republic of Texas Press, 2002). *Christina H. Wilson*

Cuney–Hare, Maud. Musician and writer; b. Galveston, February 16, 1874; d. Boston, February 13, 1936 (buried beside her parents in Lake View Cemetery, Galveston); daughter of Norris Wright and Adelina (Dowdy) Cuney. After graduating from Central High School in Galveston in 1890, she studied piano at the New England Conservatory of Music, where she successfully resisted the pressure that white students exerted on the school's administrators to have her barred from living in the dormitory. She also studied privately with biographer Emil Ludwig and Edwin Klare. She taught music at the Texas Deaf, Dumb, and Blind Institute for Colored Youths in 1897–98; at the settlement program of the Institutional Church of Chicago, 1900–1901; and at Prairie View State College (now Prairie View A&M University), Texas, 1903–04. She married William P. Hare in 1906.

As a folklorist and music historian she was especially interested in African and early American music. She collected songs in Mexico, the Virgin Islands, Puerto Rico, and Cuba, and was the first music scholar to direct public attention to Creole music. She contributed to *Musical Quarterly*, *Musical Observer*, *Musical America*, and *Christian Science Monitor* and for years edited a column on music and the arts for *The Crisis*, the journal of the NAACP.

After her marriage, she made her home in Boston and traveled in the East to give recitals and lectures. She participated in the artistic life of Boston and founded the Musical Art Studio to promote concerts and a little-theater movement in the black community. *Antar*, her play about an Arabian Negro poet, was staged in Boston under her direction in 1926. She was the author of *Creole Songs* (1921); *The Message of the Trees* (1918), a collection of poetry; and *Norris Wright Cuney: A Tribune of the Black People* (1913), a biography of her father. She is best remembered for the highly regarded *Negro Musicians and Their Music* (1936).

The Bill Naizer Brass Band, Granger, Texas, ca. 1935. Photograph by John Trilica Studio, Granger, Texas. UT Institute of Texan Cultures at San Antonio, No. 97-493. The 1930s was the heyday of Czech music. Dance orchestras played traditional waltzes and polkas and marching bands played for outdoor festivals.

BIBLIOGRAPHY: Rayford W. Logan and Michael R. Winston, eds., *Dictionary of American Negro Biography* (New York: Norton, 1982).   *Judith N. McArthur*

Czech Music. The musical traditions of Czech Texans have long been considered one of the most important and enduring aspects of Czech culture in the state. The themes that distinguish the music as unique are commonly shared by all Czechs, regardless of their religious and ethnic differences, and can easily be traced back in lyrics and style to Bohemia and Moravia, the ancestral homes of most Czech Texans. The "high" musical culture of the Czech homelands found its largest audience among certain Czech communities in the northern United States, but it never reached the same degree of popularity among Czech Texans as did traditional and folk music. However, touring Czech musicians playing the works of composers Antonin Dvořak (1841–1904), Bedřich Smetana (1824–1884), and Leoš Janáček (1854–1928) have found large and enthusiastic audiences in larger Texas cities. Even classical and operatic Czech works often are based on folk music traditions and themes.

For Czechs in Texas, as in other places, folk music was a crucial part of ethnic and national identity and of daily life. Not simply a form of entertainment to be passively enjoyed, it was an activity that invited the participation of all. Family gatherings, social visits, and fraternal meetings all occasioned singing, and in Czech Texas communities, Saturday nights were filled with dancing and Sunday mornings with hymns. Traditional songs ranged from the melancholy *A ja sam* (I Alone) to the drunken *Nemelem, nemelem* (We Are Not Milling). The most popular Czech waltz in Texas was *Louka Zelena* (Green Meadow), and songs celebrating love and the beauty of nature such as *Okolo Libice* (Around Libice), *Na Bilej Hore* (On White Mountain), and *Pod dubem, za dubem* (Over the Oak, Under the Oak). When played instrumentally, most of these tunes require only common instruments such as clarinets, accordions, and horns, but traditional instruments such as the *cymbal* (a Czech dulcimer native to Moravia), or the *flastinet* (a Czech import, which requires a skilled player to turn a crank and produce sound by allowing air to enter and blow past reeds) were utilized occasionally.

Dances were first held among the immigrants in private houses, but once fraternal halls such as those belonging to the SPJST were built, large-scale community dances on Saturday evenings or on special occasions became the norm. Since beer often was not allowed in the hall, men would divide their time between outside drinking and inside dancing, while the women sat on benches around the dance floor chatting and waiting to be asked to dance. The usual entertainment for these occasions included "orchestras" playing traditional Czech tunes, such as waltzes and polkas. These same groups often would be expanded and organized into a more military, marching-band style when playing at larger, outdoor celebrations. The *beseda*, literally "social gathering," was a dance performed at such special events and festivals. Resembling an American square dance, it involved a number of couples dancing in formation, with hands usually kept on the hips, using polka and waltz steps.

Until the 1950s and 1960s, when rock-and-roll and country-and-western influences began to erode traditional themes, folk music survived as the most popular form of music within the Czech communities. In the 1930s, the heyday of Czech music, scores of Czech bands could be found playing in the state on any given Saturday night. The Majek Orchestra could be heard on a station broadcast from Cameron, and the Joe Merlick Orchestra was heard in Fort Worth on KFJZ. Between 1935 and 1940, the polka program "Adolph and the Boys," sponsored by Gold Chain Flour, was broadcast from Schulenburg on weekend mornings. For years, "Lee Roy's Czech Hour" has been broadcast three times weekly from KVLG–AM in La Grange. The most popular of the Texas Czech bands was the Baca Band of Fayetteville. It was founded in 1892 by Frank Baca. He died in 1907, but other family members have kept the band together and touring throughout the state and even in other parts of the country. Adolph Hofner, who grew up in an ethnic Czech family in San Antonio, was an accomplished accordionist who is generally recognized as having introduced the Czech polka into Western Swing music.

Czech Texans continue to celebrate their musical heritage through a variety of festivals and activities. Fayette County, with the highest concentration of ethnic Czechs in Texas, hosts several events each year. Several Texas communities, including Praha, Shiner, and Ennis, still attract sizable crowds to various Czech musical and religious celebrations.

BIBLIOGRAPHY: Clinton Machann and James W. Mendl, *Krasna Amerika: A Study of the Texas Czechs, 1851–1939* (Austin, Eakin Press, 1983).   *Brandy Schnautz*

D

DJ Screw. Rapper, disc jockey, and producer; b. Robert Earl Davis, Jr., Bastrop, Texas, July 20, 1971; d. Houston, November 16, 2000; son of Robert Earl and M. Deary Davis. His popularity was based largely on the unique style of music he performed, which was known as "screwed" or "screwed down" music, because it involved slowing the tempo of songs to half the normal speed or less. His nickname grew out of his practice of taking two records and "screwing" them together, using this method of changing the music's tempo.

As a child Davis lived in Smithville, Texas, and Los Angeles, California. At the age of five he began collecting records. By the age of ten, when he moved to Houston to stay with his truck-driver father, he had out of school to concentrate on music. He began his career as a disk jockey in 1989. He often stayed up until 3:00 or 4:00 in the morning working on tapes for which he gathered a handful of local artists and had them perform. DJ Screw made a major breakthrough in the music scene in 1993 with his album *All Screwed Up!*. Among his best sellers were *June 27th*, *Hellraiser*, *Plots and Schemes*, and *The Final Chapter*. Other albums included three volumes of *3'N the Mornin*, and *No Work, No Play*. In 1996 he opened the Screwed Up Record and Tapes store and record label in Houston. He also organized the Screwed Up Click, a crew of local rappers who provided him with rhymes to complement his beats. He died of a drug overdose in the restroom of his recording studio, just as Houston was becoming nationally recognized as a Mecca for Southern rap.

BIBLIOGRAPHY: "The Slow Life and Fast Death of DJ Screw," *Texas Monthly*, April 2001.   *Jesse J. Esparza*

Daffan, Ted. Early steel guitarist and songwriter; b. Theron Eugene Daffan, Beauregard Parish, Louisiana, September 21, 1912; d. Houston, October 6, 1996; son of Carl and Della Daffan. Ted Daffan pioneered in the electrification of instruments and was an active figure in the Houston-area country-dance-band scene of the 1930s. His most lasting contribution to country music was in songwriting.

The Daffans moved from Louisiana to Houston, where Ted graduated from high school in 1930. Having developed a fascination with electronics at an early age, he opened a repair shop for radios and electric musical instruments. The shop served as a center of experimentation with pickups and amplifiers. Daffan also developed an early interest in Hawaiian guitar and played in a Hawaiian music group called the Blue Islanders that performed on radio station KTRH in Houston in 1933.

Drawn to country music mainly through the influence of Milton Brown, in 1934 Daffan joined the Blue Ridge Playboys, an influential group whose membership included two other legendary early honky-tonk figures, Floyd Tillman and Moon Mullican. He also performed with several other Houston-area bands, including the Bar-X Cowboys and

Ted Daffan publicity photo, ca. 1940s. Daffan first recorded with an amplified steel guitar in 1939. As a songwriter, he was best known for his truck-driving songs. He recorded "Truck Drivers Blues" in 1939. Courtesy Dorothy Daffan Yannuzi.

Shelly Lee Alley's Alley Cats, before he started his own band, the Texans, in 1940. The Texans leaned more toward honky-tonk than swing.

Daffan is generally credited with writing the first truck-driving song, "Truck Driver's Blues," in 1939; the song became a hit for Cliff Bruner's Texas Wanderers, and its success led to Daffan's Texans being signed by Columbia Records in 1940. Among the songs he went on to write and record in the early 1940s, three became honky-tonk classics: "Worried Mind," "Born to Lose," and "Headin' Down the Wrong Highway." Daffan was inducted into the Nashville Songwriters Association International Hall of Fame as a charter member in 1970. Among the artists who recorded his songs were Ray Charles, who performed versions of "Born to Lose" and "No Letter Today," and Les Paul and Mary Ford, who recorded "I'm a Fool to Care."

Daffan moved to California in 1944 and led a band at the Venice Pier Ballroom for a short time, before returning to Texas in 1946. After leading a band in the Dallas–Fort Worth area, he returned to Houston by the early 1950s.

Although his recording career slowed after World War II, he continued a successful career as a songwriter and stayed involved in the music business. From 1955 to 1971 he ran his own record label, Daffan Records, which featured releases by Floyd Tillman, Jerry Irby, and Dickie McBride, among others. Daffan moved to Nashville in 1958 to form a music publishing company with Hank Snow but returned in 1961 to Houston, where he formed his own music-publishing business and continued to live until his death.

Daffan was married to Bobbie Martin Daffan for over fifty years. They had one daughter. He was inducted into the Texas Western Swing Hall of Fame. His song "Born to Lose" received a BMI "one million air play" award in 1992.

BIBLIOGRAPHY: Richard Carlin, *The Big Book of Country Music: A Biographical Encyclopedia* (New York: Penguin, 1995). Patrick Carr, ed., *The Illustrated History of Country Music* (New York: Random House / Times Books, 1995). Houston *Chronicle*, October 7, 1996. Adam Komorowski, notes to CD *Doughboys, Playboys and Cowboys: The Golden Years of Western Swing* (London, Proper Records, 1999). Nashville Songwriters Foundation homepage (http://www.nashvillesongwritersfoundation.com), accessed February 7, 2003. Bill C. Malone, *Country Music, U.S.A.*, revised edition (Austin: University of Texas Press, 1985). Nick Tosches, *Country: The Twisted Roots of Rock 'n' Roll* (New York: Da Capo Press, 1996).

Linc Leifeste

Daily, Pappy. Record producer, music publisher, and promoter of Texas music; b. Harold W. Daily, Yoakum, Texas, February 8, 1902; d. Houston, December 5, 1987 (buried at Forrest Park Lawndale Cemetery, Houston); m. Gladys Andrews; two sons. When Daily was still a child, his father died. His mother soon remarried and moved the family to Houston. At age sixteen, he left Central High School to join the Marine Corps. Discharged after two years, he began working for the Southern Pacific Railroad. Around the same time he began playing baseball. From the mid-1920s until 1931, he dabbled in baseball management and even launched a new baseball team called the Freeport Tarpons.

When the Great Depression forced the Southern Pacific to lay off many of its workers, Daily sought a job with more security. He soon found it in the amusement-machine business. At first he kept his job with the railroad and worked part-time distributing jukeboxes. In 1933, he borrowed $250 from a coworker at Southern Pacific to open a store. Before long, he had his own jukebox distributing company, known as South Coast Amusement Company, in Houston. Although he never read music or played an instrument, Daily developed an ear for country music by listening to the records in his jukeboxes. Although shellac rationing during World War II restricted the production of jukeboxes and records, Daily gathered as many records as he could and opened a record store in Houston. He claimed to have brought the first Capitol record into Texas in 1942. In 1952 Daily and his business partner, Jack Starnes, founded the Starday label. Daily paired artists

with songs and supervised recording sessions. The most notable stars to sign with Starday were George Jones, Roger Miller, the Big Bopper (J. P. Richardson), Jimmy Dean, and Hank Locklin. The Big Bopper's 1958 recording of "Chantilly Lace" was Pappy Daily's biggest seller.

During the 1950s Daily began producing and managing his own Houston-based label, D Records. He hoped this line would serve as a regional subsidiary for Mercury Records, with which he had established a working relationship as George Jones's producer. The two companies reached an agreement by which, if a D Records recording began selling well in Texas, Daily would release the record to Mercury for national distribution. During the next twenty years, D Records released hundreds of songs, including a couple of early recordings by Willie Nelson and George Strait. Although the label typically recorded Texas honky-tonk music, it also covered western swing, rockabilly, Tex-Mex, Cajun, and polka music. Pappy recorded his last session in February 1971 in Nashville with George Jones. During the 1970s and 1980s, he remained active only with his publishing company, Glad Music Company, founded in 1958. Glad is still an active company today, with rights to such classics as "White Lightnin'," "She Thinks I Still Care," "Chantilly Lace," "Night Life," and "The Party's Over."

Several members of the family carried on his musical legacy. In 1958 Pappy sold his record-distributing company, H. W. Daily, Inc., to his sons, Bud and Don, who opened Cactus Music and Video in 1975, now the oldest such store in Houston. After Daily's death Bud and Don also took over the D Records catalog. Pappy's grandson, Mike Daily, began a successful career playing steel guitar for George Strait's Ace in the Hole Band in 1975.

BIBLIOGRAPHY: Houston *Chronicle*, December 7, 1995. John Pugh, "Pappy Daily, A Legend in His Own Time: The Last of the Red Hot Pappies," *Music City News*, January 1971.

Linda Hellinger

Dalhart, Vernon. Singer; b. Marion Try Slaughter II, Jefferson, Texas, probably on April 6, 1883; d. September 14, 1948 (buried in Bridgeport, Connecticut); only child of Robert Marion and Mary Jane (Castleberry) Slaughter. The 1900 census indicates that Try (as he was called) was born in 1881. However, his birth date is listed as April 6, 1883, in his obituaries and on his grave. Due to the family's use of this date it is the generally accepted birthdate. Try's parents had married in 1880 and moved to a ranch run by Bob and his brother. Although Try was born in Jefferson, he grew up on the ranch outside of town, where he learned to ride and shoot at an early age. He also learned to play the harmonica and Jew's harp while still a small child.

Try was named for his grandfather, who was notorious in Jefferson for his violent ways and was almost certainly a member of the Ku Klux Klan. Nonetheless in 1880 the grandfather was appointed a deputy sheriff of Marion County. Later he became the Jefferson town constable, a position he held until his death in 1886. His son, Robert, inherited his father's violent ways. Robert Castleberry, Try's uncle, thought Bob Slaughter was mistreating his sister, and a feud soon developed between the two Bobs. In

1893, one of their violent arguments ended in the death of Bob Slaughter in the alley behind Kahn's Saloon. The shooting seems to have been in self-defense, since Bob Castleberry was never tried for murder. In fact, Slaughter's widow soon moved into Jefferson with her son to live with her brother.

Try attended school in Jefferson for several years and also took singing lessons. As he grew older he spent his summers in West Texas working as a cowboy. He continued his singing during the school year and often sang at local affairs. Legend has it that he often sang at the Kahn Saloon before he left Jefferson. If so, it was at a young age, since he left Jefferson before he was seventeen. Try and his mother moved around 1898 to Dallas, where he continued his musical education at the Dallas Conservatory of Music and worked at various jobs to support himself and his growing family. He married Sadie Lee Moore–Livingston in 1902 and by 1904 had a son, Marion Try III, and a daughter, Janice.

Encouraged by his teachers at the conservatory, Try moved to New York around 1908. After settling in an apartment in the Bronx, he supported his family by working in a piano warehouse and taking singing jobs as a church soloist. Meanwhile he continued studying voice to prepare himself for his eventual goal, opera and the concert stage. By 1910 he was performing with one of the many opera groups operating in the New York area. The following year, he had progressed enough to be hired as one of the minor principals for a six-month tour of Puccini's *Girl of the Golden West*, performed in English. The tour covered eighty-seven cities across the continent. While in rehearsal for the opera, Try made a trial cylinder for Edison Records. The cylinder was filed away by Edison and forgotten. Shortly after the recording attempt, Try picked a stage name to use for his first listing as a principal in *Girl of the Golden West*. He chose the names of two west Texas towns, near where he had worked on a ranch during his teens: Vernon Dalhart.

In the years following *Girl of the Golden West,* Dalhart toured with various opera companies performing tenor roles such as Camilla Jolidon in *The Merry Widow* and Lt. Pinkerton in *Madam Butterfly*. One of his best-known roles was Ralph Rackstraw in Gilbert and Sullivan's *H.M S. Pinafore*. He performed this role at the Hippodrome in New York in 1914 and also toured with the road-show version.

In 1915 he made further record tests—with Edison in January and Columbia in February. Finally, in 1916, Dalhart managed to record for both of those companies and a third, Emerson. His first record release was "Just a Word of Sympathy," issued in December 1916 on Columbia. Emerson released two Dalhart records later the same month. Dalhart's first Edison recording, "Can't You Heah Me Callin', Caroline?" was issued in 1917. On April 30, 1917, before his first Edison record was released, Dalhart signed a contract with Edison; he recorded for the company almost exclusively for the next two years. He also continued concert appearances as well as touring for the famous Edison Tone Tests.

Dalhart was versatile from the beginning of his recording career, doing everything from classical to popular music as well as children's songs and vocal refrains for dance bands. His recording career continued to grow, albeit slowly, and by mid-1924 he had made well over 400 recordings that appeared on more than 800 sides in the United States and at least 200 sides abroad.

In May 1924, Dalhart talked Edison into letting him record a song he had heard and thought he could do well with his native accent. His "The Wreck of the Old Southern 97," made with Frank Ferera on guitar and with Dalhart playing the harmonica between choruses, did well enough that Dalhart asked Victor, a much larger company, to let him do it on trial. This time Carson Robison, a contract artist for Victor, played the guitar along with Dalhart's harmonica and vocal. For the B-side, an old folk song was rearranged and used. Dalhart had heard the song from his cousin, Guy Massey. It was recorded with Robison again playing guitar and Lou Raderman playing viola. Both songs were accepted by Victor and issued in November 1924.

As soon as it showed signs of popularity, Dalhart copyrighted "The Prisoner's Song" under his cousin's name and split the royalties with Guy Massey, 95 percent for himself and 5 percent for Guy. (Years later all rights were returned to the Massey family.) The song became enormously popular. Within a year it was being heard everywhere. Dalhart performed it on radio and recorded it for almost every record company in the United States. His recordings of this song appeared on more than fifty labels. In addition, the song was recorded as a waltz and by dance and jazz bands, often with a vocal refrain by Dalhart, although he was usually not identified on the record.

In 1926 the song was re-recorded electrically by Victor and Columbia and re-released using the original record numbers. The song continued to sell until the late 1930s and became popular in every English-speaking country in the world. It has been said that "The Prisoner's Song" was the biggest-selling record of the acoustical era, but this is difficult to substantiate, since many copies sold were of the electric version. It was certainly the biggest-selling song of the 1920s.

Dalhart and Robison teamed up as soon as Robison's Victor contract expired. Robison performed as singer, whistler, and guitarist on Dalhart's recordings and also became a prolific composer, writing many of Dalhart's hits. Over the next three years, Dalhart and Robison, usually accompanied by violinist Murray Kellner, made records for almost every company in the United States. Among the most popular were "My Blue Ridge Mountain Home," "In The Baggage Coach Ahead," "Golden Slippers," "The Death Of Floyd Collins," and "The Letter Edged In Black."

Although Dalhart started accumulating pseudonyms almost as soon as he began recording, they now began to multiply. Many of the names were used by the record companies without Dalhart's knowledge, usually to avoid the same name appearing on labels selling for seventy-five cents and others selling for twenty-five cents. At least eighty pseudonyms have been verified as used by Dalhart in the United States. At least thirty more were used in England, Australia, and Canada. Dalhart also recorded with many musical groups without being identified on the label.

By 1926 he was doing well enough to purchase a large estate in Mamaroneck, New York, where he had moved in 1922. In addition to real estate purchases, Dalhart also invested a lot of his money in the stock market.

In May 1927, while Robison was on his honeymoon in Kansas, Dalhart replaced their violinist, Murray Kellner, with Adelyne Hood. Dalhart had met her during an early Edison Tone Test tour. She was an accomplished violinist and pianist and also sang. Although Robison respected Hood, he resented Dalhart's making a change in their group without his approval. Robison was already unhappy with Dalhart since Dalhart was claiming a portion of the royalties on Robison's songs that Dalhart recorded. Despite Robison's discontent, the trio of Hood, Robison, and Dalhart recorded together for a year, and some of Dalhart's most popular songs were released during this time. However, in mid-1928, Dalhart signed a contract with Columbia over Robison's objections. This was the end of their partnership. Robison found a new partner in Frank Luther and left Dalhart.

Although the new contract prevented Dalhart from recording for all the record companies as he had in the past, he still managed to record over 200 songs after Robison left. Hood usually backed him, often with additional contract musicians. But the loss of Robison's songwriting, the decline of record sales due to radio and the Great Depression, plus competition from new country artists such as Jimmie Rodgers and the Carter Family, all contributed to the decline in Dalhart's popularity.

Dalhart lost many of his investments in the Crash of '29. Eventually he was forced to sell his large mansion and move to a smaller home in Mamaroneck. By 1931 the record industry had almost disappeared. Many performing artists were now relying on radio, not recordings, for their income. Dalhart had earlier appeared on network radio as a guest star, and in 1931, along with Adelyne Hood, he signed up to host a network show for Barbasol. The show, "Barber Shop Chords," did not do well and left the air after only six months. In the spring of 1931 Dalhart and Hood traveled to England, apparently for a few personal appearances. While there they did two recording sessions, recording eight songs with an English orchestra. Two of the four songs released were never issued in the United States.

Dalhart made only a few records over the next few years. In 1938 he toured upstate New York, where he appeared at a few fairs and conventions. He also performed on a local radio station to generate interest in his personal appearances. In 1939 he signed with RCA Victor and in one recording session cut six songs with a group called Vernon Dalhart and his Big Cypress Boys. Dalhart named the group after Big Cypress Bayou, near Jefferson, Texas, but the musicians were hired only for the session. The six songs, released on the Bluebird label, were not promoted by RCA and sold poorly. Dalhart never recorded again.

In 1943 he moved to Bridgeport, Connecticut, where he took a job as a security guard at a defense plant. After the war ended, he set up as a voice coach in Bridgeport. In addition, he worked as a night baggage clerk at the Barnum Hotel. He had a serious heart attack in January 1948 and was under a doctor's care when he died of a coronary occlusion in September of that year. He is buried along side his wife and son in the family plot at Mountain Grove Cemetery. His daughter is buried with her husband in a nearby section.

Many people, including Carson Robison, have stated Dalhart was a difficult man to work with. However, others say he was easy to get along with and was a gentleman to work for. Two Dalhart protégés, Bobby Gregory and Red River Dave McEnery, always spoke of him with great affection. The Country Music Foundation called Dalhart a one-man recording industry when he was inducted into the Country Music Hall of Fame in 1981. They were not far off. Dalhart recorded over 1,600 songs between 1916 and 1939, for nearly every record company in the United States. He appeared on over 5,200 sides for a total of more than 3,300 records issued under 173 labels. In 1995, during Dalhart Days in Jefferson, Dalhart was belatedly inducted into the Texas Country Music Hall of Fame. In 1998 his recording of "The Prisoner's Song" for Victor was honored with a Grammy Hall of Fame Award.

BIBLIOGRAPHY: Paul Kingsbury, ed., *The Encyclopedia of Country Music* (New York: Oxford University Press, 1998). Colin Larkin, ed., *Encyclopedia of Popular Music* (London: MuzeUK Limited, 1998). Bill C. Malone, *Country Music, U.S.A.* (Austin: University of Texas Press, 1985). Jamey Moore, "From the Hills of Home," *Texas Historian*, 40.1 (September 1979). *Jack Palmer*

Davila, Manuel Gonzales Sr. Tejano radio pioneer; b. San Antonio, May 22, 1918; d. San Antonio, July 12, 1997; son of José Luis and María Davila. As a young man Davila enjoyed boxing. He became involved in radio at the age of eighteen and continued that involvement for the remainder of his life.

He and his brother, José, began broadcasting in 1935 by buying one-hour slots on English-language stations; there were no Spanish stations in San Antonio at the time. Davila found bias against Mexican-American broadcasters—from Anglos, but also from Hispanics who believed that one should be from Mexico in order to broadcast in Spanish.

In 1961, after losing his job when the station at which he worked throughout the 1950s was sold, Davila decided to buy his own station. On March 17, 1966, after a five-year legal fight, he began broadcasting Tex-Mex music on his newly purchased station, KEDA–AM, nicknamed "Radio Jalapeño." The station's competitors called it the "cantina station" because of its accordion-driven South Texas music, although Davila insisted that the station was "all about *familia* and respect and giving newcomers a break." The local nature of the radio station raised skepticism at first, but the major labels that originally bypassed it eventually started calling.

About his career path Davila said, "All I ever wanted to do was play country music, but I wanted to play it in Spanish. I had to show everybody...that a Mexican-American could run a station successfully playing Mexican-American music." Emphasizing local bands, KEDA aired Texas musicians Santiago Jiménez Sr. and Narciso Martínez and later

Tejano newcomers Selena, Emilio, and Los Aguilares. Davila's "Jalapeño Network" came to include KCCT–AM, KBSO–FM, and KFLZ–FM in Corpus Christi. As Davila's broadcasting range expanded, so did the variety of musical styles performed on his radio stations. KCCT is a Spanish Christian station, KBSO plays classic rock, and KFLZ plays international Spanish music. Most of Davila's immediate family has been involved with the radio operations.

In 2003 KEDA was the last remaining family-owned independent radio station in the San Antonio market; along with playing music, it maintained a connection to its roots through community-service programming. These efforts included the reading of obituaries on the air, as well as fundraisers for those who could not afford to bury their dead children.

In October 1943 Davila married Madeline Peña. They had seven children, Manuel, Richard, Marcella, Roy, Joseph, Albert, and Madeline. Davila died of natural causes and is buried in San Fernando Cemetery No. 2. In 1997 he was inducted into the Tejano Music Hall of Fame for Special Achievements and received a lifetime achievement award from the Tejano Conjunto Festival Hall of Fame.

BIBLIOGRAPHY: San Antonio *Express–News*, March 15, 1991; July 15, 1997. *Texas Talent Musicians Association: Tejano Hall of Fame* (http://www.tejanomusicawards.com/fame.html), accessed February 4, 2003. *Lois Smith*

Day, Jimmy. Pedal steel guitar player; b. James Clayton Day, Tuscaloosa, Alabama, January 9, 1934; d. Texas, January 22, 1999 (buried in Austin). Day grew up in Lousiana, moved to Texas and then Nashville, Tennessee, and eventually returned to Texas permanently. After he graduated from high school in 1951 he played non-pedal steel guitar as a teenager on the "Louisiana Hayride."

It was on the Hayride that he performed as a sideman for many future stars, such as Hank Williams, Elvis Presley, Jim Reeves, Faron Young, and Johnny Horton. His first recording was on Beff Pierce's 1952 hit "That Heart Belongs to Me." Day later became a member of Jim Reeves's band and took up the pedal steel guitar. He was influenced by steel guitar innovators such as Shot Jackson and Buddy Emmons. Together, Day, Jackson and Emmons manufactured the Sho-Bud brand of pedal steel in 1957. Day named his own steel guitar "Blue Darlin.'"

Ray Price invited Day to join the Cherokee Cowboys, and Day quickly demonstrated his now legendary style on such songs as "Crazy Arms" and "Heartaches by the Number." Day later teamed up with Willie Nelson on such songs as "Shotgun Willie." He became a member of the International Steel Guitar Hall of Fame in 1982. He is also a member of the Texas Steel Guitar Hall of Fame and the Texas Western Swing Hall of Fame.

Like most sidemen, Jimmy Day never received the fame he deserved for his contribution to shaping Texas country music. However, he helped to make many others famous. They realized the value of his contribution and sought him out. Day played with Webb Pierce, Ernest Tubb, Skeeter Davis, and Patsy Cline, as well as many others stars. He also played with lesser known stars, such as Alvin Crow,

Clay Blaker, and Don Walser. It did not seem to matter to Day who they were or where they were from, as long as he liked their music and could make a contribution.

In 1978, as Nashville studios increasingly eliminated the steel guitar from most recordings, Day returned to Central Texas, where he believed he could find audiences that still appreciated him. He went back to Nashville for a short time in 1991, but returned to Texas for the remainder of his life. He lived in Buda, near Austin. Day and his wife, Marilyn, had two daughters and three sons. He died of cancer. He was inducted into the Country Music Association Hall of Fame on February 25, 1999.

BIBLIOGRAPHY: "James Clayton Day," *Fuller Up: the Dead Musician Directory*" (http://elvispelvis.com/jimmyday.htm), accessed January 30, 2003. Curtis W. Ellison, *Country Music Culture: From Hard Times to Heaven* (Jackson: University Press of Mississippi, 1995). Bill C. Malone, *Country Music, U.S.A.* (Austin: University of Texas Press, 2002). Bob Millard, *Country Music What's What* (New York: Harper Perennial, 1995).

James Kent Cox

Deep Ellum. An entertainment and arts district on Elm Street east of downtown Dallas. The area was settled as a "freedmen's town" by former slaves after the Civil War; its location on Elm Street, just east of the Houston and Texas Central tracks near the depot, was too far from downtown Dallas to be desirable. The area was called Deep Elm or, as early residents pronounced it, "Deep Ellum." Because of the proximity of the railroad it was also called Central Track.

Several industries were located in Deep Ellum at one time. Robert S. Munger invented a new cotton gin in Mexia in 1883 that revolutionized the ginning industry. He built his first factory to manufacture the new gin in Deep Ellum in 1884. His Munger Improved Cotton Machine Company merged with several smaller companies in 1899 to form the Continental Gin Company. In 1913 Henry Ford opened several regional assembly plants to supplement the manufacture of Model Ts at his Detroit plant. One was built in Deep Ellum, the Southwestern Ford Assembly Plant.

The Grand Temple of the Black Knights of Pythias, in Deep Ellum, was designed in 1916 by William Sidney Pittman. In addition to serving as the state headquarters for the Knights, the building held offices of black doctors, dentists, and lawyers. It was therefore the first commercial building built for and by blacks in Dallas. An auditorium–ballroom on the top floor was used for dances, assemblies, and parties. At one time the Dallas *Express*, a weekly black newspaper, was published in the Temple, and the state and local headquarters of the YMCA were there.

By the 1920s the Deep Ellum area had become a retail and entertainment center for Dallas residents, primarily African Americans. Anything could be bought in the stores along Elm: new and used merchandise including furniture, clothing, shoes, and jewelry. Deep Ellum was famous for its "Pawnshop Row," where more than ten pawnshops operated until the 1950s. Entertainment was an important part of the business of Deep Ellum, which became a mecca for

Harlem Theater, ca. 1940s. Courtesy Dallas Public Library. In the 1920s Deep Ellum (East Elm Street) was a Dallas entertainment center where many jazz and blues artists performed. From the collections of the Texas/Dallas History and Archive Division, Dallas Public Library

jazz and blues artists. In 1920 twelve nightclubs, cafes, and domino parlors were open in Deep Ellum, and by 1950 the number had grown to twenty. Many famous jazz and blues musicians played in the neighborhood at some time, including Blind Lemon Jefferson and Lightnin' Hopkins. Huddie Ledbetter began performing in 1920 in Deep Ellum, before he began his career in Greenwich Village, New York. Crap games in the back rooms of the domino parlors necessitated keeping an eye out for the police. Deep Ellum had a red-light district, and murders were frequent near the nightclubs and domino parlors.

Deep Ellum declined throughout the 1940s and 1950s. The Houston and Texas Central tracks and depot were removed. The growth of Dallas suburbs encouraged businesses in the area to move to shopping malls. As cars became more prevalent, the pedestrian traffic decreased, and when the streetcar line was abandoned in 1956 it decreased still further. In 1954 the Uptown Improvement League was formed to improve business in Deep Ellum, including provision of off-street parking, but the area continued to decline. In 1969 the new elevation of Central Expressway bisected Deep Ellum and eliminated the 2400 block of Elm, the center of the community. By the 1970s and early 1980s few businesses remained.

In January 1983 the Near East Side Area Planning Study, or, as it was commonly called, the Deep Ellum Plan, was unveiled. This plan to redevelop the area called for Deep Ellum to be "downzoned" so as to keep the atmosphere on a small, artsy level. The height of buildings was to be limited, the streets would not be widened, and population would be kept down. While this was happening, artists were moving into the area, and art galleries and nightclubs were renovating the vacant buildings. By 1991 Deep Ellum had become popular as a nightspot for young urban dwellers and had more than fifty bars and nightclubs. In addition, a plethora of avant-garde shops sold a variety of merchandise, including clothing, antiques, crafts, and art works.

BIBLIOGRAPHY: Denise M. Ford, Deep Ellum (MS, Dallas / Texas Collection, Dallas Public Library, 1985). Alan Govenar, "Them Deep Ellum Blues," *Legacies: A History Journal for Dallas and North Central Texas* 2 (Spring 1990). Virginia and Lee McAlester, *Discover Dallas–Fort Worth* (New York: Knopf, 1988). William L. McDonald, *Dallas Rediscovered: A Photographic Chronicle of Urban Expansion, 1870–1925* (Dallas: Dallas County Historical Society, 1978). *Lisa C. Maxwell*

Degüello. Music played by the Mexican army bands on the morning of March 6, 1836; the signal for Antonio López de Santa Anna's attack on the Alamo. The word *degüello* signifies the act of beheading or throat-cutting and in Spanish history became associated with the battle music, which, in different versions, meant complete destruction of the enemy without mercy.

BIBLIOGRAPHY: Amelia W. Williams, A Critical Study of

Degüello. Reproduced in Amelia Williams, "A Critical Study of the Siege of the Alamo," *Southwestern Historical Quarterly* 37 (January 1934). The playing of this Mexican bugle call, announcing that no quarter would be given the rebellious Texans, signaled the final assault on the Alamo.

the Siege of the Alamo and of the Personnel of Its Defenders (Ph.D. dissertation, University of Texas, 1931; rpt., *Southwestern Historical Quarterly* 36–37 [April 1933–April 1934]).

DeWitty, Virgie Carrington. Music teacher and choir director; b. Wetumka, Oklahoma, ca. 1913; d. Austin, August 11, 1980; daughter of William and Violet Carrington. The family moved to Austin when Virgie was a small child and joined Ebenezer Baptist Church, where her mother sang in the choir for forty-eight years. Because of a strong musical influence and encouragement at home and at church, Virgie started playing the piano by ear at home. One Sunday when she was five, the Sunday school had no pianist. Her mother led her to the piano, where she played and sang her first solo, "Jesus Wants Me for a Sunbeam." From that time until her death she played for Ebenezer Third Baptist Church.

She received her formal education from the Phillips White Private Academy, Austin public schools, and Tillotson (now Huston–Tillotson) College, where she earned a diploma in education and music. She received a bachelor of science degree in music from Prairie View A&M College and a bachelor of arts degree and teaching certificate in light opera from the American Conservatory of Music in Chicago. She also studied in Boulder, Colorado, at the Juilliard School of Music in New York City, and at the University of Texas. She married Arthur DeWitty, an Austin civic leader, in 1932; they had no children.

Mrs. DeWitty directed the first commercially sponsored radio program over the Texas Quality Network, "The Bright and Early Choir," from 1938 to 1940. She composed more than 100 gospel songs, spirituals, and anthems. One of her most famous pieces was "Magnify the Lord." She taught music at Anderson High School in Austin and composed the school song. She also taught private classes in voice and piano for many years. Her specialty was writing four-part-harmony anthems and religious music for choirs. She was a charter member of the Alpha Kappa Zeta chapter of Zeta Phi Beta sorority and a member of the NAACP and the Douglas Club. She received the 1957 Woman's Day Speaker award from Ebenezer Baptist Church. She was active in the Missionary Baptist General Convention of Texas and the National Baptist Convention of America. She died at Holy Cross Hospital in East Austin. In 1991 a fund for music students was established from her estate.

BIBLIOGRAPHY: Austin *American–Statesman*, August 28, 1980, June 21, 1992. Vertical files, Center for American History, University of Texas at Austin.   *Kharen Monsho*

Dexter, Al. Country and western singer; b. Clarence Albert Poindexter, Jacksonville, Texas, 1902; d. Lewisville, Texas, January 28, 1984. While working as a house painter, Dexter began performing in local bars and clubs. In the early 1930s he collected a band to perform in the outskirts of Longview, Texas. He signed a recording contract with American Recording Corporation in 1936. Dexter's "Honky Tonk Blues," which he wrote with James B. Paris, was the first country song to use the term *honky-tonk*. In the late 1930s Dexter owned a honky-tonk himself, the Roundup Club, in Turnertown, Texas.

Through his experiences there and in other roadhouses, Dexter developed the idea for his future hit, "Pistol Packin' Mama." Art Satherley, Dexter's producer, helped him by arranging a recording session with Gene Autry's backup band, for which Dexter had expressed admiration. Dexter recorded "Pistol Packin' Mama" and "Rosalita" with them at Columbia's Hollywood studios. The record was released in 1943 and in its first six months sold a million copies. The song "Pistol Packin' Mama," a controversial number due to its lyrics, remained at Number One on *Billboard Magazine*'s best-sellers chart for eight weeks. In 1944, when *Billboard* started its "Most Played Juke Box Folk Records" chart for country music, "Pistol Packin' Mama" was still at the top. "Rosalita" also had a week at Number One, and Dexter received such widespread recognition that he launched national tours.

Between 1944 and 1948 Dexter recorded other country hits, including "Too Late to Worry," "Wine, Women and Song," and "Calico Rag." But the popularity of his honky-tonk sound decreased over time. Although he recorded other songs with King, Decca, and Capitol, he never had another hit. In 1971 Dexter was inducted into the Nashville Songwriter's Hall of Fame. He had invested in savings and loan, motel, and real estate businesses in Texas, and died a wealthy man—of a heart attack at his home on Lake Lewisville.

BIBLIOGRAPHY: Vertical Files, Center for American History, University of Texas at Austin. *Jill S. Seeber*

Tenor Rafaelo Diaz performed with the Metropolitan Opera Company of New York from 1917 to 1936. Diaz is dressed in costume as Aetholwold in *The King's Henchman*. From the *San Antonio Express Magazine*, December 16, 1951. UT Institute of Texan Cultures at San Antonio, No. 68-695.

Diaz, Rafaelo. Operatic tenor; b. Francisco Rafael Diaz, San Antonio, May 16, 1883; d. New York City, December 12, 1943; son of Rafaelo and Rosa (Umscheid) Diaz. He received his early schooling at the German-English School in San Antonio and the West Texas Military Academy. He showed musical talent at an early age and began his career as a pianist under the guidance of one of San Antonio's pioneer music teachers, Miss Amalia Hander. After his promising voice was discovered while he was studying at the Stern Conservatory in Berlin, Diaz went to Italy to study under famous Italian maestro Vincenzo Sabatini. He returned to America and made his debut in the Boston Opera Company's production of Verdi's *Otello*. In 1917 he joined the Metropolitan Opera Company and performed leading tenor roles in Massenet's *Thaïs* and Rimski-Korsakov's *Le Coq d'Or*.

His stage presence and magnetic personality, along with his fine lyric tenor voice, kept him with the Metropolitan until 1936. He then toured the country with the Scotti Opera Company, making several stops in San Antonio along the way. In his spare time he made records for a leading phonograph company. He also conducted a series of concerts at the Waldorf–Astoria. Critics praised Diaz for his smooth performance, the depth and richness of his voice, the clarity of his enunciation, and the beauty of his phrasing. He sang in English, French, Spanish, Italian, and German, and was known as the "Lone Star Tenor of the Lone Star State." He never married. He died of a cerebral hemorrhage.

BIBLIOGRAPHY: Vertical files, Center for American History, University of Texas at Austin. *Jeremy Roberts*

Dick the Drummer. Musician, one of two free blacks who participated in the battle of San Jacinto. He was a member of the regular infantry who, with three fifers, constituted the Texas army's band. He is credited with confusing the Mexican troops at the battle. Dick also served as a drummer during the Mexican War at the battles of Monterrey and Buena Vista. He was described as an older man at a dinner honoring San Jacinto veterans in May 1850.

BIBLIOGRAPHY: Harold Schoen, "The Free Negro in the Republic of Texas," *Southwestern Historical Quarterly* 39–41 (April 1936–July 1937). Frank X. Tolbert, *The Day of San Jacinto* (New York: McGraw–Hill, 1959; 2d ed., Austin: Pemberton Press, 1969). *Diana J. Kleiner*

Dorham, Kenny. Trumpet player; b. McKinley Howard Dorham, Fairfield, Texas, August 30, 1924; d. December 5, 1972. Dorham, considered one of the finest trumpet players of his era, played with numerous East Coast jazz giants, including Charlie "Bird" Parker. He grew up in a musically inclined family and learned the piano at a young age. He attended high school in Austin, where he learned the sax and later the trumpet. At Wiley College he studied chemistry and physics before joining the army.

After discharge in 1942, Dorham pursued a career in music that led him to Los Angeles, where he played in a band led by Russell Jacquet, and then to New York City. Upon his arrival in New York, he began playing with the big bands of Dizzy Gillespie and Lionel Hampton. In 1948 he replaced Miles Davis in the Charlie Parker Quintet and helped define the emerging bebop or bop jazz style. Characterized by fast tempos, complex arrangements, driving rhythms, and experimental solos, bebop took New York by storm in the early 1950s.

Dorham was not one to stick with a single band. Through the 1950s he floated about the New York bop scene, playing with Thelonious Monk, Charles Mingus, and Art Blakey. In 1954 Dorham, Blakey, and Horace Silver formed the Jazz Messengers, from which emerged Dorham's side project, the Jazz Prophets. Dorham also played with the Max Roach quintet before forming his own combos in the late 1950s and 1960s. Featuring, at one time or another, the great Cannonball Adderley and Joe Henderson, Dorham's various combos recorded several albums, including *Whistle Stop* (1961), considered by many to be his finest work. Through the 1960s he split his time between playing and attending graduate classes in music at New York University. He also traveled extensively in Europe, taught part-time, and worked as a journalist for *Down Beat* magazine. In 1966 Dorham was honored at the Longhorn Jazz Festival in Austin. His last few years were spent in relative seclusion because of declining health.

BIBLIOGRAPHY: *Down Beat*, February 1, 1973. Len Lyons and Don Perlo, *Jazz Portraits: The Lives and Music of the Jazz Masters* (New York: William Morrow, 1989). Dave Oliphant, *Texan Jazz* (Austin: University of Texas Press, 1996). David H. Rosenthal, *Hard Bop: Jazz and Black Music, 1955–1965* (New York: Oxford University Press, 1992). *Bradley Shreve*

Double Bayou Dance Hall. In the small black community of Double Bayou, Chambers County, sixty miles east of Houston; established in the late 1920s, damaged by a storm in the early 1940s, and reestablished at its present site in 1946 by returning World War II serviceman Manuel Rivers Jr. and his wife, Ella.

The hall served as a gathering place during the week and a dance hall on the weekends. The Riverses operated the dance hall until Manuel's death in 1983, whereupon their nephew, blues guitarist Floyd "Texas Pete" Mayes, inherited the property. The current dance hall was built atop cedar logs and constructed of wood with hogwire for walls; it had a tin roof. Tar paper–covered walls and a low-clearance ceiling were later added. Capacity is 125 people.

From 1946 to the mid-1950s, Double Bayou Dance Hall was home to a thriving live-music scene that operated on the outer edge of the "chitlin circuit." A frequent performer in the early years was Amos Milburn (with Texas Johnny Brown on guitar). Other regular performers were Gatemouth Brown, Lightnin' Hopkins, Albert Collins, Johnny Copeland, Percy Mayfield, Joe Hughes, Barbara Lynn, and Clifton Chenier. Big Joe Turner and T-Bone Walker made rarer appearances, with T-Bone's coming on Thursday nights when he arrived a day early for his weekend tour dates in Houston.

Pete Mayes and the Texas Houserockers played their first professional gig at Double Bayou Dance Hall in 1954, and served thereafter as the house band into the early 1960s. Weekly offerings of live music began to fade at the Double Bayou in the '60s, in part because Mayes began traveling extensively. Nevertheless, the hall remained open as a local gathering spot and watering hole. Pete Mayes and his band routinely performed a Christmas Day matinee dating from 1955. Starting in 1991, they have played for scheduled tour groups from Houston and on other major holidays.

BIBLIOGRAPHY: Aaron Howard, "Pete Mayes' Double Bayou Dance Hall," *Living Blues*, July–August 1994. Houston *Chronicle*, June 11, 1995. *Steve Sucher*

Douglas, Boots. Jazz bandleader; b. Clifford Douglas, Temple, Texas, September 7, 1908; date and place of death unknown. Douglas, known as one of the finest Texas jazz bandleaders of his era, recorded and toured throughout Texas during the big band or Texas swing heyday of the 1930s. He began experimenting on the drums at age fifteen. He played in Central Texas before moving to San Antonio, where he got his start on the emerging jazz scene.

Douglas began by accompanying Millard McNeal's Southern Melody Boys; he played his first show at Turner's Park, San Antonio, in 1926. After earning a reputation as a fine drummer and musician, he formed his own outfit, which he named Boots and His Buddies. Although eclectic in style, the ensemble was successful. The band concentrated most of its energies on playing in Texas, but made forays into surrounding states as well. Although Boots and His Buddies was not famous in New York or other eastern cities, the group garnered a large following in its home region. In 1935 Bluebird signed the band, which cut forty-two sides for the label between 1935 and 1938, including the songs "Ain't Misbehavin'" and "Blues of Avalon."

After reaching a pinnacle of success in the 1930s, the band steadily declined in popularity. Douglas called it quits, and in 1950 packed his belongings and headed to Los Angeles. He continued to play part-time, but his job for the county government replaced music as his primary source of income. By the 1970s he had dropped out of the public eye, and he has since faded into obscurity.

BIBLIOGRAPHY: John Chilton, *Who's Who of Jazz: From Storyville to Swing Street* (New York: Da Capo Press, 1985). Dave Oliphant, *Texan Jazz* (Austin: University of Texas Press, 1996). Gunther Schuller, *The Swing Era: The Development of Jazz, 1930–1945* (New York: Oxford University Press, 1989). *Bradley Shreve*

Draeger, Hans–Heinz. Musicologist; b. Stralsund, Germany, December 6, 1909; d. Austin, November 9, 1968. Draeger, a pioneer in the study of music, was one of the most influential musicologists in Texas. He came from a long musical tradition and studied under some of Europe's most influential composers. He exerted his greatest influence in Texas as a faculty member at the University of Texas in Austin.

He attended the Oberreal Schule in Stralsund from 1920 to 1931. From 1931 to 1937 he studied musicology at the University of Berlin under such giants in German musical scholarship as Friedrich Blume, Erich Moritz von Hornbostel, Curt Sachs, and Georg Schünemann. In 1937 Draeger received his doctorate with a dissertation on the development of the bow and its use in Europe. He subsequently served as an assistant in the history department at the State Institute for German Music Research in Berlin. In 1938 he was an assistant at the State Museum of Musical Instruments, where, in 1939, he was named administrative director. That same year, he was also appointed lecturer of organology at the Hochschule für Musik.

Draeger's career in music continued to grow after the end of World War II. In 1946 he completed his *Habilitation* (appointment as university lecturer) at Kiel, where he wrote an important work on the classification of musical instruments. From 1947 to 1949 he served as professor of musicology at the University of Greiswald and at the University of Rostock. He went on to work at other key universities, such as Humboldt University (1949–53) and Free University (1953–61). For a brief period in 1955 he taught at Stanford University as a Fulbright scholar and visiting professor. In 1961 he made his way to the Lone Star State to work as a visiting professor of musicology at the University of Texas.

Draeger soon distinguished himself as a member of the University of Texas faculty. During his career he published two books and over thirty articles. In addition to his many other publications, he wrote the program notes for the *Fine Arts Booklet*, published by the University of Texas Department of Music from 1961 to 1963, and for the Austin Symphony Orchestra from 1963 to 1968. He concentrated his research on the theoretical and mathematical aspects of intonation and pitch in music. He was also interested in the relation between words and notes. Draeger's background in art history and philosophy led him to explore other avenues in musical research extending into such areas as psychology and computers. In 1966 he became an American citizen.

After his death he was remembered by many in both Germany and the United States as a giant in the study of musicology. He was survived by his wife, Mrs. Helen B. Draeger, a son, Udo–Heyber Vetter, his father, and two brothers and three sisters.

BIBLIOGRAPHY: Austin *American–Statesman*, November 10, 1968. Bruno Nettl, *Theory and Method in Ethnomusicology* (New York, Free Press of Glencoe, 1964). Bruno Nettl and Philip Bohlman, eds., *Comparative Musicology and Anthropology of Music: Essays on the History of Ethnomusicology* (Chicago: University of Chicago Press, 1990). Stanley Sadie, ed., *The New Grove Dictionary of Music and Musicians*, Second Edition (New York: Grove's Dictionaries, 2001). Vertical files, Center for American History, University of Texas at Austin.

Michael S. Morawski

Dranes, Blind Arizona. Gospel singer; b. Arizona Juanita Dranes, Texas (Dallas?), April 4, 1894; d. Signal Hill, California, July 27, 1963; of mixed African-American and Mexican-American heritage. She lost her sight in an influenza outbreak early in her childhood. She grew up in the musically rich Deep Ellum district of Dallas, where she learned piano and developed her own distinct "sanctified" style of playing, known as "gospel beat." It combined the ragtime and barrelhouse traditions to produce a rolling

blues sound. Dranes's piano playing was accompanied by her penetrating singing, which derived from the emotional shout song of traditional gospel.

Eventually, she became a regular pianist and singer for various traveling ministers of the Church of God in Christ, a national black Pentecostal church that has since developed into the largest of its kind. Dranes spent much of this early period with COGIC traveling through Texas and Oklahoma and aiding in the "planting" of new churches. In the mid-1920s she settled back in the Dallas–Fort Worth area and was soon spotted by Okeh Record Company scout Richard M. Jones. The company took Dranes to Chicago for recording sessions in 1926 and again held sessions in Dallas in 1928. During her contract with Okeh, she recorded over thirty tracks, including such gospel standouts as "I Shall Wear a Crown" and "My Soul Is a Witness for the Lord."

With the onset of the Great Depression, Blind Arizona Dranes fell into obscurity, and little is known of her life thereafter. She was one of the most influential and innovative gospel pianists of the twentieth century.

BIBLIOGRAPHY: Horace Clarence Boyer, *How Sweet the Sound: The Golden Age of Gospel* (Washington: Elliot and Clark, 1995). Alan B. Govenar and Jay F. Brakefield, *Deep Ellum and the Central Track: Where the Black and White Worlds Converged* (Denton, Texas: University of North Texas Press, 1998). Rick Koster, *Texas Music* (New York: St. Martin's Press, 1998). *Bradley Shreve*

DuBois, Charlotte Estelle. Music educator; b. Liberty, Indiana, October 26, 1903; d. Austin, Texas, January 1, 1982 (buried in Liberty, Indiana); daughter of Smith and Caroline (Lambert) DuBois. She earned a bachelor of arts degree at Western College in Oxford, Ohio, in 1925, an academic diploma in piano at the Cincinnati Conservatory of Music in 1927, and an M.A. at Teachers College, Columbia University, in 1936. Before moving to Texas she served in Louisiana as supervisor of music for the Shreveport and Caddo Parish schools. In 1940 she joined the music faculty at the University of Texas, where she remained until her retirement in August 1971. She took guest teaching assignments at the University of California at Los Angeles from January to August 1949, the University of Michigan from June to August 1952, and the University of British Columbia for the summer session of 1958.

Charlotte DuBois was the first woman to be named a full professor in the University of Texas music department. In the Music Educators National Conference she served as a member of the Education Research Council and as chairman of the National Committee on Music for the Elementary Teacher. She contributed articles to the *Music Educators Journal*, *The School Musician*, *Southwestern Musician*, and other publications. She wrote *Songs to Play* (1954) and *The Keyboard Way to Music* (1956) and was a coauthor of the widely used elementary textbook series *This Is Music for Today* (1971). She gave lectures and demonstrations at numerous colleges and universities and for conventions of such groups as the National Association of Schools of Music and the Music Educators National

Conference. She was a member of All Saints Episcopal Church in Austin and a Republican.

Professor DuBois was an honorary member of Sigma Alpha Iota, a national fraternity for women in music, and was awarded the fraternity's ring of excellence. She received a Teaching Excellence Award from the Students' Association of the University of Texas and in October 1971 the rarely given Citation of Service, "in recognition of excellence and devotion to the music education profession," from the Texas Music Educators Association.

BIBLIOGRAPHY: Vertical files, Center for American History, University of Texas at Austin. *Who's Who of American Women,* 1958–59.   *Janet M. McGaughey*

Dudley, Sherman H. Black vaudevillian and theater owner; b. Dallas, ca.1870; d. near Oxon Hill, Maryland, March 1, 1940 (buried in nearby Harmony Cemetery). According to various sources Dudley was involved in medicine shows and minstrel groups in his youth. One account reports that his Dudley Georgia Minstrels received a favorable review from the Galveston *News* in 1897. Most sources place him in P. T. Wright's Nashville Students and in the McCabe and Young Minstrels, where he was nicknamed either Happy or Hapsy.

Dudley wrote a play, *The Smart Set,* first staged in 1896. In 1904 he appeared with Billy Kersands in *King Rastus.* Later that year, after Tom McIntosh's death, he took over McIntosh's lead role in *The Smart Set.* The same year he introduced his most famous stage act, a routine in which a mule dressed in overalls would nod his head as Dudley spoke, giving the impression that the mule understood. According to the obituary for Dudley in the Baltimore *Afro-American,* this number "never failed to convulse the house." Dudley introduced the mule act in *The Black Politician,* which he had written with S. B. Cassion. He also contributed material to *His Honor, the Barber,* produced in 1909–11, and, with Henry Troy, wrote *Dr. Beans from Boston,* which was staged in 1911–12.

Dudley reportedly organized the Colored Actors' Union, headquartered in Washington, D.C., and served as its general manager and treasurer. In 1911 he began buying theaters and organized S. H. Dudley Theatrical Enterprises. By 1913 this project had developed the first black theatrical circuit, which, in the beginning, included eight or nine theaters in Washington and Virginia, five or six of which were owned by Dudley. By 1916 more than twenty-eight theaters had joined the Dudley circuit, which extended into the East, South, and Midwest. The circuit enabled black entertainers for the first time to secure contracts for an eight-month season through one office.

Dudley retired from the stage after 1917 and devoted himself to producing musicals. He regularly updated his *Smart Set* productions, which continued to be popular with black audiences. This show was one of a number of musicals written by blacks in the late nineteenth and early twentieth centuries that departed from the older minstrel show. Dudley was a pioneer in writing works about black life that included seriously considered plots and rounded characterization.

He was married to the actress Alberta (Bertie) Ormes

and was a friend of heavyweight boxing champion Jack Johnson, with whom he was once in business. Dudley sold his theaters after the onset of the Great Depression and retired to his farm in Maryland, where he raised thoroughbred cattle and racehorses until his death. He was survived by a son.

BIBLIOGRAPHY: Maud Cuney–Hare, *Negro Musicians and Their Music* (Washington: Associated Publishers, 1936). Tom Fletcher, *One Hundred Years of the Negro in Show Business: The Tom Fletcher Story* (New York: Burdge, 1954). James V. Hatch, *Black Image on the American Stage: A Bibliography of Plays and Musicals, 1770–1970* (New York: D.B.S. Publications, 1970). Rayford W. Logan and Michael R. Winston, eds., *Dictionary of American Negro Biography* (New York: Norton, 1982). Loften Mitchell, *Black Drama: The Story of the American Negro in the Theater* (New York: Hawthorn, 1967). New York *Age,* March 16, 1940. Henry T. Sampson, *Blacks in Blackface: A Source Book on Early Black Musical Shows* (Metuchen, New Jersey: Scarecrow Press, 1980).
        Kharen Monsho

Dufallo, Richard. Clarinetist and conductor; b. Whiting, Indiana, January 30, 1933; d. Denton, Texas, June 16, 2000. Dufallo was considered one of the country's leading exponents of twentieth-century music. He conducted more than eighty major orchestras and festivals in the United States, Canada, and Europe, premiering numerous works by American and European composers, including Karlheinz Stockhausen, Jacob Druckman, Sir Peter Maxwell Davies, and Krzysztof Penderecki.

Although best known as a conductor and teacher, Dufallo began his career as a clarinetist and studied at the American Conservatory of Music in Chicago. When he enrolled at the University of California, Los Angeles, in the 1950s, he was thought such an exceptional talent that the composer and conductor Lukas Foss immediately invited the young clarinetist to join his Improvisation Chamber Ensemble.

Dufallo began his conducting career in the 1960s, when he became associate conductor of the Buffalo Philharmonic; Foss was music director. Dufallo was in Buffalo from 1962 to 1967. He joined the faculty of the Center of Creative and Performing Arts at the State University of New York, and studied under William Steinberg at a New York Philharmonic seminar for conductors. In 1965 Leonard Bernstein appointed him to a two-year position as an assistant conductor of the New York Philharmonic, which he conducted on an Asian tour in 1967. Dufallo served as assistant conductor until 1975. He performed as guest conductor of various orchestras, including the Philadelphia Orchestra, the Chicago Symphony, and the St. Paul Chamber Orchestra. He studied with Pierre Boulez in 1969 and succeeded Darius Milhaud as artistic director of the Conference on Contemporary Music at the Aspen Festival.

Much of Dufallo's career was taken up with teaching at the Juilliard School and at the Aspen Music Festival, where he was in charge of contemporary music during the 1970s and 1980s. At Aspen he was affectionately dubbed "hard-to-follow," because of his insistence that classically trained musicians master new techniques. As a promoter of American works in Europe, he conducted the first European performances of works by Charles Ives, Carl Ruggles, Jacob Druckman, and Elliott Carter, as well as such younger composers as Robert Beaser.

Dufallo was noted throughout his career for guest appearances and recordings that included many premieres by such notable European avantgardists as Iannis Xenakis and George Crumb, and Aribert Reimann. He made his European debut in 1970 with the Orchestre Téléphonique Français of Paris. Among the European orchestras he conducted were the Berlin Philharmonic, the London Symphony, and the National Orchestra of Spain. He was especially associated with the orchestras of the Netherlands. He made his debut with the Royal Concertgebouw Orchestra of Amsterdam in 1975, toured with the Netherlands Wind Ensemble and the Dutch Radio Philharmonic, and made recordings with the Rotterdam Philharmonic. In 1980 he was appointed music director of the Gelders Orchestra of Arnhem.

Dufallo also had an interest in opera. He headed the Metropolitan Opera's short-lived "Mini-Met" from 1972 to 1974, and he was a regular at the Cincinnati Opera and the New York City Opera. In *Trackings: Composers Speak With Richard Dufallo* (Oxford University Press, 1989), a collection of interviews and conversations, Dufallo meets some of the leading figures in contemporary classical music, including Aaron Copland, Stockhausen, John Cage, and Sir Michael Tippett. Dufallo was married to pianist and University of North Texas professor of music Pamela Mia Paul and had two sons and a daughter. He died at home of stomach cancer.

BIBLIOGRAPHY: *New Grove Dictionary of American Music*, Volume 1 (London, 1986). *New Music Box* (http://www.newmusicbox.org/news/juloo/obit_dufallo.html), accessed November 5, 2002.   *Larry S. Bonura*

Duncan, Tommy. Singer and songwriter; b. Thomas Elmer Duncan, Whitney, Texas, January 11, 1911; d. San Diego, California, July 25, 1967. Duncan, a member of a large and impoverished family of truck farmers, worked on the farm with African Americans who indelibly marked his singing style and repertoire. He was influenced, according to his sister, Corrine Andrews, "by the records of colored people and by the recordings of Jimmie Rodgers."

When he was seventeen he left home and moved in with a cousin near Hedley, where residents remembered that Duncan sang Jimmie Rodgers songs as he drove along in an "old stripped-down car." He evidently went broke on a farm he had leased in Hedley and in the early 1930s was still broke, out of work, and living in Fort Worth. But the show-business bug had bitten him, and he was determined to have a career as a singer. Clifton "Sleepy" Johnson, an early member of the Light Crust Doughboys, recalled first seeing Duncan playing a little cheap guitar "about a foot and a half long" and singing at the Ace High root-beer stand for tips. In 1932 Duncan won an audition against sixty-six other singers to join bandleader Bob Wills as the vocalist for the Light Crust Doughboys.

He was versatile in his singing style and repertoire, had a fine voice and range, and was ideal for the kind of dance music Wills performed. In his earliest recording sessions for Wills, he sang everything from ballads and folk to pop, Tin Pan Alley, Broadway, and cowboy songs. Even in songs with sad lyrics he maintained a touch of fun. Duncan had "soul" in his singing like black blues singers, not the sentimentality of some country singers. Like some of his black friends, he appeared to be completely detached from any sad mood or story in the lyrics. His versatility was well-suited to the western swing music that he and Wills pioneered.

When Wills left the Light Crust Doughboys in August 1933 to form the Texas Playboys, Duncan went with him. Alton Stricklin, a member of the group, observed that Duncan remembered the lyrics to more than 4,000 songs and could learn the words to a new song within fifteen minutes. The song that made the Texas Playboys famous was a folk-rooted pop song that Irving Berlin heard Wills play as a fiddle instrumental and published in 1940. Since Berlin wanted lyrics for the selection, Wills asked Duncan and several other band members to help him write words for the fiddle tune. Wills called it "New San Antonio Rose." In 1940 Wills recorded it in Dallas. That recording, with the brilliant Duncan vocals, sold three million copies for Columbia Records. Bing Crosby then recorded it and won his second gold record.

Tommy Duncan was the first member of Wills's band to volunteer for the armed services after the bombing of Pearl Harbor. He rejoined Wills in 1944 as the war neared its end and as Bob Wills was becoming even more famous in music and the movies. Duncan appeared with Wills in several movies, including *Bob Wills and His Texas Playboys* (1944), *Rhythm Roundup* (1945), *Blazing the Western Trail* (1945), *Lawless Empire* (1945), and *Frontier Frolic* (1946). He became not only a movie star but the most famous singer in all of western swing. His voice matured in the middle to late 1940s, and he became a star in his own right, second only to Wills himself in the Texas Playboy band. Duncan, who could also play piano and guitar, joined Wills in writing several numbers, including "New Spanish Two Step" (1945), "Stay a Little Longer" (1945), "Cotton-Eyed Joe" (1946), and "Sally Goodin" (1947).

For various reasons—Wills's periodic drinking and Duncan's own ego and ambition to go on his own, for instance—Duncan left the Texas Playboys in 1948. He organized one of the best western swing bands ever assembled, Tommy Duncan and His Western All Stars. Although the band was technically perfect and Duncan's singing was excellent, the group lacked the spark that had made Wills's group exciting. The band had only minor success with such recordings as "Gambling Polka Dot Blues," "Sick, Sober, and Sorry," "There's Not a Cow in Texas," "Mississippi River Blues," and "Wrong Road Home Blues." Attendance at the Western All Stars' dances ranged from fair to poor, certainly not good enough to sustain a large band for very long. The band lasted less than two years.

Duncan then spent several years recording and entertaining on his own, but in 1959 returned to the Wills band. There was standing-room only as they crisscrossed the country on national tours. In 1960–61 they made three albums that sold much better than either of their recordings had while they worked separately: *Together Again, A Living Legend*, and *Mr. Words and Mr. Music*. In the early 1960s the two pioneers of western swing went their various ways, Wills to Oklahoma and Texas, and Duncan to California. Duncan never had a band of note after his All Stars disbanded in the late 1940s, although he continued to make personal appearances with various bands.

He never compromised his style in order to be more popular and commercial. He would never sing like vocalists of mainstream country-and-western or rock-and-roll or pop, though at times he appealed to almost all audiences. Among the singers who felt his influence were Elvis Presley, Ray Price, Willie Nelson, Waylon Jennings, John Denver, Merle Haggard, Ray Benson, Red Steagall, George Strait, Clint Black, Randy Travis, and Garth Brooks. Duncan died in California after a performance at Imperial Beach.

BIBLIOGRAPHY: *The Illustrated Encyclopedia of Country Music* (New York: Harmony Books, 1977). Ruth Sheldon, *Hubbin' It: The Life of Bob Wills* (Kingsport, Tennessee: Kingsport Press, 1938). Al Stricklin and John McConal, *My Years with Bob Wills* (San Antonio: Naylor, 1976; 2d ed., Burnet, Texas: Eakin Press, 1980). Charles R. Townsend, *San Antonio Rose: The Life and Music of Bob Wills* (Urbana: University of Illinois Press, 1976).

Charles R. Townsend

Dunn, Bob. Western swing musician, first electric steel guitarist to use his instrument for jazz; b. Robert Lee Dunn, Fort Gibson, Oklahoma, February 5, 1908; d. Houston, May 27, 1971. With musical encouragement from his fiddler father, Dunn gained an interest in Hawaiian music at an early age and developed his skills on the steel guitar in his teens. In 1927 he began touring with the Panhandle Cowboys and Indians touring unit. Influenced by the extemporaneous lines played by Texas trombonist Jack Teagarden, he incorporated this style into his Hawaiian music, creating a brassy sound with his steel guitar as the lead instrument.

In 1934, after playing in a number of jazz and blues bands, Dunn arrived in Fort Worth. There he met Milton Brown, who invited him to a studio jam. Dunn made a great impression on Brown and immediately became a member of Milton Brown and His Musical Brownies. In 1935 the band became the first to use an electric guitar to record a country-rooted song, entitled "Taking Off." Dunn fell in love with western swing music. His amplified steel guitar was featured on several recordings. He played and recorded more than ninety tunes with the Brownies before Brown's death in 1936.

After playing and recording with Roy Newman a year later, Dunn got together with ex-Brownie Cliff Bruner and his Musical Wanderers. He cut several tunes, including "It Makes No Difference Now" and "I'll Keep on Loving You." In 1938 he formed his own band, the Vagabonds, and recorded for Decca Records. After serving in the United States Navy during World War II, Dunn played in a number of bands in the late 1940s. In 1950 he retired from performing and opened his own music store in Houston,

where he also taught music. He operated the store for more than twenty years—until he died from lung cancer. Dunn influenced generations of steel guitar players.

BIBLIOGRAPHY: Kevin Coffey, "Bob Dunn," in *The Encyclopedia of Country Music: The Ultimate Guide to the Music* (New York: Oxford University Press, 1998). Rick Koster, *Texas Music* (New York: St. Martin's Press, 1998).

Juan Carlos Rodríguez

Durham, Eddie. One of the most important Swing Era composer–arrangers; b. San Marcos, Texas, August 19, 1906; d. New York City, March 6, 1987; son of Joe Durham. His father played the fiddle at square dances, and his oldest brother, Joe, who played cello briefly with Nat King Cole, took correspondence lessons and in turn taught Eddie and his other brothers to read and notate music. Together with cousins Allen and Clyde Durham, Eddie and his brother Roosevelt formed the Durham Brothers Band around 1920. (In 1929 Allen recorded on trombone with Andy Kirk's Clouds of Joy.) They were later joined in Dallas by another cousin, the great tenor saxophonist Herschel Evans. According to his own account, Eddie began as a professional musician at age ten; at eighteen he was with the 101 Ranch Brass Band playing for circuses in the Southwest and traveling as far as New York City, where he performed in Yankee Stadium. He moved to New York in 1934.

Durham's early training in music theory led to his work during the 1930s and 1940s as a jazz composer and arranger for four important bands from Oklahoma, Missouri, and Tennessee: the Blue Devils, Bennie Moten, Count Basie, and Jimmie Lunceford. The tunes Durham composed or arranged for these bands include such classics as "Moten Swing," "Swinging the Blues," "Topsy," "John's Idea," "Time Out," "Out the Window," "Every Tub," "Sent for You Yesterday," "One O'Clock Jump," "Jumpin' at the Woodside," "Lunceford Special," "Harlem Shout," and "Pigeon Walk." In addition, he arranged music for Artie Shaw and Glenn Miller, among other white big bands of the Swing Era; Durham contributed to one of Miller's greatest hits, "In the Mood." He is primarily considered a key figure in working out arrangements in the famous Kansas City riff style.

As an instrumentalist, Durham was proficient on both guitar and trombone. The 1935 Lunceford recording of Durham's arrangement of "Hittin' the Bottle" features Eddie as one of the first jazz musicians to perform on an amplified guitar. Durham later influenced fellow Texan Charlie Christian, probably the most important guitarist in jazz history. In 1938 Durham was the leader for a historic combo recording session with Lester Young, Count Basie's star tenor saxophonist. In the 1940s Durham organized his own band, directed an all-girl orchestra, and brought together a number of important Texas jazzmen from the Kansas City era, including Joe Keyes, Hot Lips Page, and Buster Smith. During the 1950s and 1960s he performed less but still worked as an arranger for various groups. Durham and Smith appear in conversation on a 1979 video entitled *The Last of the Blue Devils*, on which Durham also plays a trombone solo. In England, albums were

Eddie Durham recording with Lester Young and the Kansas City Six, 1940. Courtesy Alan Govenar, Dallas.

released under Eddie Durham's name in 1974 and 1981; on the latter he can be heard in impressive form at age seventy-five, in particular on "Honeysuckle Rose," where he plays single-string guitar solos in the southwestern style. In the 1980s Durham toured Europe with the Harlem Blues and Jazz Band.

BIBLIOGRAPHY: Stanley Dance, *The World of Count Basie* (New York: Scribner, 1980). George Hoefer, "Held Notes: Eddie Durham," *Down Beat*, July 19, 1962. Barry Kernfeld, ed., *The New Grove Dictionary of Jazz* (London: Macmillan, 1988). Dave Oliphant, "Eddie Durham and the Texas Contribution to Jazz History," *Southwestern Historical Quarterly* 96 (April 1993). *Dave Oliphant*

Durst, Albert Lavada. Pianist and first black disc jockey in Texas, known as "Dr. Hepcat"; b. Austin, January 9, 1913; d. Austin, October 31, 1995. As a youth Lavada taught himself to play piano in the church across the street from his home. Later, influenced by Boot Walden, Baby Dotson, Black Tank, and others, Durst became a master at playing the 1930s and 1940s "barrelhouse" blues.

He also had a talent for a pre-"rap" method of rhythmic

"jive talk." During the mid-1940s this helped land him a job as an announcer for Negro League baseball games at the old Disch Field in Austin. When players such as Jackie Robinson were in Austin some whites attended, including a young World War II veteran, John B. Connally, Jr., who was impressed by the talented, smooth-talking Durst. Connally and another progressive young war veteran, Jake Pickle, owned KVET Radio in Austin. Connally was also the station manager. In the late 1940s the two opened their station to African-American and Mexican-American broadcasts. In 1948 Pickle hired Durst as the first black disc jockey in Texas. "Dr. Hepcat's" cool jive-talk was a hit and made him a celebrity with the local white college students. He can be credited for introducing an entire generation of white Austin listeners to jazz, blues, and R&B sounds. While working as a disc jockey, Durst made two singles, "Hattie Green" and "Hepcat's Boogie." Both were recorded in 1949 for Uptown Records, which was owned by KVET program director Fred Caldwell. During the 1950s, Durst managed a spiritual group, the Charlottes. He also published a pamphlet called *The Jives of Dr. Hepcat*, a dictionary of jive-talk.

The "Texas Piano Professors"—Lavada Durst (Dr. Hepcat), Roosevelt T. Williams (the Grey Ghost) and Erbie Bowser—at Mollberg & Assoc. Piano Restoration, Austin, ca. early 1990s. Photograph by Clay Shorkey, Texas Music Museum.

Durst retired from KVET in the early 1960s and gave up performing the blues to become a minister. He was ordained at Mount Olive Baptist Church in 1965 and was named an associate minister at Olivet Baptist Church in 1972. In the mid-1970s, convinced that God wanted him to use his talents, he returned to performing the blues. For the next several years, he played "boogie-woogie barrelhouse blues" at festivals, museums, and other venues. He also wrote the hit gospel song "Let's Talk About Jesus" for the group Bells of Joy.

In addition to his musical endeavors, Durst worked for the city of Austin as director of athletics for Rosewood Recreation Center. He retired in 1979, after working there for 35 years. He was preceded in death by his wife, Bernice, who died in 1983. They had two sons and numerous grandchildren and great-grandchildren. In 1995 Durst was inducted into the unofficial Rock Radio Hall of Fame.

BIBLIOGRAPHY: Austin *American–Statesman*, November 1 and 4, 1995. Fort Worth *Star–Telegram*, March 2, 1993. Colin Larkin, ed., *The Guinness Encyclopedia of Popular Music* (New York: Guinness, 1995). San Francisco *Chronicle*, September 3, 1989.

James Head

E

Ealey, Robert. Blues musician; b. Texarkana, Texas, December 6, 1924; d. Fort Worth, March 7, 2001. After serving in the army during World War II, Ealey moved to Dallas in 1951 with the hopes of becoming a gospel musician. But under the influence of such blues legends as Lil Son Jackson and Lightnin' Hopkins, he was lured into a life of blues. He teamed up with guitarist U. P. Wilson in the mid-1950s to form Boogie Chillen, and developed a strong following in Fort Worth. The city became his permanent home base. On August 27, 1959, he married Eva Mae Ealey. They had three children.

Ealey began by singing and drumming in a series of bands, including the Boogie Chillen, the Juke Jumpers, and the Five Careless Lovers. He was great at identifying young talent. Popular sax player Johnny Reno sat behind the band for a year at their gigs, without a microphone, learning the changes as if at some kind of blues prep school. Remembered for his boundless energy, Ealey once performed four shows in a single day in Fort Worth—a party in the afternoon, two clubs, and another party after the clubs were closed. He often bragged about knowing more than 400 songs and, always the professional, once escorted an unruly club patron to the exit without interrupting the song he was singing. Ealey was a huge draw in Europe, where his gigs would often turn into all-night jam sessions.

In the late 1970s he began thinking of opening his own nightclub. He wanted to establish a place where local musicians could learn from one another and showcase their talent. Musicians began raising money to revive a popular nightspot on the corner of Horne and Wellesley, in the predominantly black Como neighborhood of Fort Worth. It became the New Bluebird Nite Club, a school for some of the region's most famous musicians. Some of the up-and-comers included Jimmy and Stevie Ray Vaughan, T Bone Burnett, the Fabulous Thunderbirds, and ZZ Top. Ealey co-owned the club from 1977 to 1989.

In addition to his club, Ealey drove a truck for Bruce Alford Lumber and Door Company. He met his second wife, Helen George, while she was singing with another band. They were married in the early 1980s. On December 3, 2000, Ealey was driving in downtown Fort Worth when a car going the wrong direction down a one-way street struck his car. He survived the crash and reportedly refused medical treatment at the scene, but suffered vertebral damage and, subsequently, damage to his renal system. He was in and out of the hospital for weeks following the crash and lost forty pounds from his already small frame. He collapsed at his home on March 4, 2001, and died three days later at John Peter Smith Hospital. He was buried with military honors in Dallas–Fort Worth National Cemetery. He was survived by six children.

Known for his enthusiastic pursuit of the blues and an encyclopedic knowledge of music, Ealey was one of the most influential voices in Texas blues. His discography covers three decades of performances, including a live album entitled *Robert Ealey and His Five Careless Lovers* (1973), *Live at the New Blue Bird Nite Club,* and *Electric Ealey* (2000).

BIBLIOGRAPHY: Dallas *Morning News*, March 12, 2002. Fort Worth *Star–Telegram*, March 10, 13, 2001.

Lance Looper

East Texas Serenaders. A musical group of four East Texans from Smith and Wood counties, one of the most unusual bands of the 1920s and '30s. Their rare left-handed fiddle player, Daniel Huggins Williams, won contests all over East and Central Texas. The guitar player was Cloet Hamman, with a gift of good bass runs and a faultless rhythm. On the group's first recordings Patrick Henry Bogan Sr. played an upright bass, but later played a three-string cello with a bow; the bass didn't travel well on top of the car in bad weather. John Munnerlyn played tenor banjo with a steady colorful style.

The Serenaders first recorded two pieces on December 2, 1927, in Dallas for Columbia Records. They subsequently recorded fourteen songs for Brunswick about 1928. Finally, in 1937 they recorded eight songs for Decca. Munnerlyn left the group about 1930 and was replaced by Shorty Lester, whose brother Henry played second fiddle on later recordings. The rags and breakdowns the group played were clear steps toward swing and string-band music, a departure from the standard fiddle-band tradition. Some critics have given the Serenaders credit for the beginning of western swing. Hamman, Bogan, and Munnerlyn made one of the most forceful rhythm sections in string-band history.

Bogan was born on Jan. 5, 1894, and died on June 24, 1968. He started playing guitar early and then took up the bass fiddle and chorded the piano. He decided to play the cello later because it was smaller; he removed a string, he said, because he didn't need it. He worked for a time on a ranch near Happy, Texas, in the Panhandle, served in the navy during World War I, then worked for Wells Fargo and the post office in Mineola.

Huggins Williams was born in 1900 and died in 1974. His father, originally from Milan, Tennessee, played fiddle, and Huggins would sneak the fiddle off the shelf to practice when he was nine years old. He began to learn several tunes before his father became aware. Since he was left-handed, the boy was reaching over the lower strings to play the upper ones. His father bought him a left-handed fiddle and arranged lessons from a local teacher. Williams played with Lew Preston in the Tyler area in later years. He also tutored one of the really great jazz and swing fiddle players of all time, Johnny Gimble of Nashville—a fact related by Gimble to Bill Malone.

Cloet Hamman was born on May 5, 1899, and died in June 1983; he was the last of the Serenaders to die. His

East Texas Serenaders, ca. 1928–29. Left to right: (front row) Jack Hopper, Patrick Henry Bogan; (second row) John Munnerlyn, Daniel Huggins Williams, Cloet Hamman. Photo courtesy Patrick Bogan Jr.

father, Will, was a famous breakdown fiddler and piano tuner from near Lindale, Texas, who won every contest he entered until he was about seventy years old. Cloet learned guitar backing him up. Cloet lost some fingers in an accident with a saw in his later years and was unable to play thereafter.

John Munnerlyn, of Mineola, worked for the United Gas Pipeline Company west of Mineola. He moved to Houston about 1930. Shorty Lester, on tenor banjo on later recordings, was said to be from the Garden Valley area in Smith County west of Lindale. His brother Henry, second fiddler on later recordings, was from somewhere in northern Texas.

Many of the Serenaders' recorded pieces were written by Williams—"Acorn Stomp," "East Texas Drag," and "Arizona Stomp," for instance. The group got "Shannon Waltz" and "Sweetest Flower Waltz" from a northern fiddler named Brigsley who taught Huggins to play several ragtime tunes as well. Hamman composed "Adeline Waltz." "Mineola Rag" and "Combination Rag" include bits of other tunes. The Serenaders so refined their music that they set the stage for other western and Texas bands by relying on their ragtime, waltzes, and tin-pan-alley style, using syncopations, flatted notes, and a fast tempo. From the radio they picked up some of the influence of Cajun music, Chicago jazz, and the new swinging sounds of popular music.

The members of this band were not full-time musicians and did not care to travel far and wide but preferred playing house parties, social events and Chamber of Commerce functions, rather than honky-tonks. The night spots could get pretty rough, although Bogan had been a bouncer in a dance hall and could handle difficult situations. The group turned down an opportunity to travel the states when an agent named H. M. Barnes offered to represent them and book them into ballrooms around the country. Their popularity, however, did spread as far as Dallas, Houston and Oklahoma. They played some large hotels—the Adolphus and the Baker in Dallas, for example—for a fee of $8 to $15 a night. They also played at the Ashby Cafe in Tyler for a six-month job.

Although their recordings were instrumental, the group occasionally sang such songs as "Five Foot Two," "Roseta," "Somebody Stole My Gal," and other popular tunes of that era. They had no vocalist good enough to record, however. When Bob Wills was asked in an interview about his success in the music business, he said that his only early competition was the East Texas Serenaders. Wills and his Playboys took up western swing where the Serenaders left it. The Serenaders' "Shannon Waltz" is included in the Smithsonian Collection of Classic Country Music, annotated by Bill C. Malone (Washington, 1981).

BIBLIOGRAPHY: Patrick Carr, ed., *The Illustrated History of Country Music* (New York: Random House, 1995). Keith Chandler, notes to *The East Texas Serenaders: Complete Recorded Works in Chronological Order, 1927–1937* (Document Records DOCD-8031, 1998). *The East Texas Serenaders, 1927–1936* (Floyd, Virginia: County Records, ca. 1977). Bill C. Malone, *Country Music, U.S.A.* (Austin: University of Texas Press, 1985). Mineola *Monitor*, March 24, 1976.   *Patrick Henry Bogan Jr.*

Eastwood Country Club. A legendary club on St. Hedwig Road in eastern San Antonio, sometimes called Eastwoods; opened in 1954. The club, owned by Johnnie Phillips, was instrumental in helping young up-and-comers to practice their music, as well as giving well-known black performers a place to play. Eastwood was one of the major San Antonio black clubs during the "Chitlin Circuit" era.

According to saxophonist Spot Barnett, Eastwood Country Club was one of the few places during the social unrest of the 1960s where blacks sat, drank, and danced beside whites in peace. Barnett observes that Phillips probably didn't realize the effect the club would have on race relations in San Antonio. As Phillips once said, "The Eastwood was one of the few places where people, no matter what color they were, were always welcome. Everyone from gamblers to politicians and Texas Rangers came there. We had the most mixed audience of any club."

Without regard to the cost, Phillips booked the top-notch black performers of the era to play Eastwood, including such musicians as Fats Domino, Pearl Bailey, B. B. King, the Drifters, Tyrone Davis, Ike & Tina Turner, Bobby Bland, Gatemouth Brown, T-Bone Walker, Little Richard, Chubby Checker, Bo Diddley, Della Reese, and Big Joe Turner. Comedian Redd Foxx performed at Eastwood for two months and tended bar when he was not on stage.

Many talented local musicians were part of the various house bands that would open for major acts at the club. Those bands included the Fats Martin Band, Shake Snyder's Band, Spot Barnett's Band, and Curly Mays' band. Part of Curly Mays's act was to play the guitar with his toes. Some of the local musicians who helped to shape Eastwood were teachers as well as professional musicians; others were from local military bands. Some went on to international fame. The local instrumentalists and singers included Clifford "Honky Tonk" Scott, Bobbie June Parker, Cora Woods, Mary Parchman, David Hegwood, Jitterbug Webb, and Marcus Adams. A favorite of the Eastwood crowd was Miss Wiggles, a dancing contortionist whose act included standing on her head atop a spinning chair. There was also a popular dancer by the name of Vanilla Wafer.

Phillips operated the Eastwood Country Club until his health began to fail him in 1978.

BIBLIOGRAPHY: Estella Reyes Lopez, "The Chitlin Circuit," San Antonio *Current*, February 15–21, 2001. San Antonio *Light*, November 3, 1985.   *Karla Peterson*

Edens, Roger. Musician, composer, and producer; b. Hillsboro, Texas, November 9, 1905; d. Hollywood, California, July 13, 1970. Edens began his career in the early 1930s as a piano accompanist for ballroom dancers. He played piano in the orchestra pit for the musical *Girl Crazy* in 1930–31. Afterward, he worked with Ethel Merman as accompanist and musical arranger. He also wrote songs for Judy Garland that she performed at the Palace Theater and in concert.

Edens joined the staff at Metro Goldwyn Meyer as a musical supervisor and composer in 1935 and eventually became an associate producer. He worked as musical supervisor or director on many noted films, including *Born to Dance* (1936), *The Wizard of Oz* (1939), *Strike Up the Band* (1940), *Babes on Broadway* (1941), *Ziegfeld Follies* (1944), and *Meet Me in St. Louis* (1944). He received the Academy Award for *Easter Parade* in 1948 and *Annie Get Your Gun* in 1950. Some films he worked on as associate producer include *Show Boat* (1951), *An American in Paris* (1951), *Funny Face* (1957), *The Unsinkable Molly Brown* (1964), and *Hello, Dolly* (1969). Edens helped produce many of the extravagant show numbers that have come to be associated with the great Hollywood musical.

BIBLIOGRAPHY: Roger D. Kinkle, *The Complete Encyclopedia of Popular Music and Jazz: 1900–1950* (4 vols., New Rochelle, New York: Arlington House, 1974). *The International Dictionary of Films and Filmmakers*.

Amanda Oren

El Conjunto Bernal. Founded in 1954 in Kingsville, Texas, by brothers Eloy and Paulino Bernal; one of the most innovative and influential conjunto bands in twentieth-century Mexican-American music.

Eloy (b. March 11, 1937) and Paulino (b. June 22, 1939) were raised in a poor farming family in South Texas. Despite having to quit school to work, the two brothers still found time to hone their musical skills at an early age. Inspired by conjunto pioneers Valerio Longoria and Narciso Martínez, Paulino taught himself accordion, while Eloy learned to play a *bajo sexto* given to him by his father. They launched their musical career as teenagers in 1952, when they formed the band Los Hermanitos Bernal. The brothers soon distinguished themselves, not only by their musical proficiency, but also by their unique style. Paulino made unprecedented use of the full range of notes on the accordion and began experimenting with four and five-row chromatic accordions. The band was one of the first in conjunto music to encourage experimentation with soloing, phrasing, and more sophisticated mixing of instrumentation. By 1955 the brothers had released their first record, "Mujer Paseada," backed by "Desprecio," for Armando Marroquín's Ideal records. In the meantime, they renamed their group El Conjunto Bernal.

In addition to playing backup for such popular artists as Carmen y Laura, the brothers soon began developing a reputation as one of the Southwest's premiere conjunto bands in their own right. Paulino and Eloy became best known for their pioneering work in vocal harmony arrangements. With rich two and three part harmonies, El Conjunto Bernal was the first to incorporate complex vocal harmonics into conjunto music. The group became one of the most technically accomplished bands of the 1950s and 1960s, and one of the most commercially successful of its genre.

In 1960 the conjunto began recording for Marroquín's new label, Nopal Records. Soon afterwards, the Bernal brothers co-founded their own recording company, Bego Records, with Victor González. Eventually, the brothers split from Bego and formed a new label, Bernal Records. Paulino soon stopped performing, however, and the group went through several new singers, including Ruben Perez and Laura Canales. While Eloy continued touring with the band, Paulino underwent a series of troubles. Beset by problems with alcohol and drugs, Paulino became a "born-again" Christian in 1972. He began playing accordion again and founded Bernal Christian Records, quickly establishing himself as one of the most capable and popular Spanish-language gospel singers. Eloy died on April 22, 1998, when his tour bus was involved in an accident near Corpus Christi. Paulino continued performing.

BIBLIOGRAPHY: Ramiro Burr, *The Billboard Guide to Tejano and Regional Mexican Music* (New York: Billboard, 1999). Rick Koster, *Texas Music* (New York: St. Martin's Press, 1998). Manuel Peña, *The Texas-Mexican Conjunto: History of a Working-Class Music* (Austin: University of Texas Press, 1985). Manuel Peña, *Música Tejana: The Cultural Economy of Artistic Transformation* (College Station, Texas: Texas A&M University Press, 1999).

Gary Hartman

"El Corrido de Gregorio Cortez." A corrido, or ballad, is a form of folk song used to tell a story. Typically, corridos are highly stylized and often romantic ballads that celebrate Hispanic history and culture along the Texas–Mexico border. The earliest border corrido can be traced to Juan Nepomuceno Cortina, who became the first border Mexican hero when he shot an American marshal in the late 1850s for mistreating one of his mother's young servants. This incident led to an open conflict with American authorities.

Cortina's actions helped spark a long series of border conflicts, involving legal, political, and cultural clashes between Mexicans and Americans living on both sides of the border. It was during the time of Cortina's revolt that the first such ballads set the general pattern of the border corrido. The subject matter of this genre ordinary involved a Mexican, usually outnumbered, defending his putative rights with a pistol in hand against the evil *rinches* (Texas Rangers).

Probably the best-known corrido of the entire turn-of-the-century period is "El Corrido de Gregorio Cortez." Although this ballad celebrates an event that occurred a century ago, it is still very popular among Spanish-speaking people throughout the American Southwest and northern Mexico. Typical of ballads in all societies, "El Corrido de Gregorio Cortez" is based on fact, but it also has been richly embellished. The event that inspired it occurred on June 12, 1901, in Karnes County, at the W.A. Thulmeyer Ranch. Gregorio Cortez and his brother Romaldo, who worked as ranchhands on the Thulmeyer property, were approached by Karnes County sheriff W. T. Morris and his deputies John Trimmell and Boone Choate. The sheriff and his men went to the ranch to look for a horse thief who had been trailed to Karnes County. As the sheriff interrogated the Cortez brothers, Choate, who acted as interpreter, apparently misunderstood several of Gregorio Cortez's replies. For example, when asked if he had recently traded a horse, Cortez replied "no." Choate seemed unaware that, in Spanish, there is a distinction between a horse (*caballo*) and a mare (*yegua*). Cortez, in fact, had traded a mare but not a horse.

As the misunderstanding escalated, the sheriff became convinced that Cortez was lying. When Morris tried to arrest the brothers, Gregorio refused, telling the sheriff, "*No me puede arrestar por nada*" ("You can not arrest me for nothing"). Choate misinterpreted this statement as well and reported to Morris that Cortez was saying, "No white man can arrest me." Believing the Cortez brothers were unarmed, Morris drew his gun. Romaldo tried to protect his brother by lunging at the sheriff. Morris shot and wounded Romaldo and then fired at Gregorio, narrowly missing him. Cortez shot and killed the sheriff, fled the scene, and headed for the Rio Grande. He was soon pursued by hundreds of men, including several Texas Rangers. He was able to evade his pursuers for several days but eventually was captured after one of his acquaintances, Jesus "El Teco" González, informed a posse that Cortez was hiding at Abrán de la Garza's sheep camp in Cotulla. On June 22, 1901, Cortez was arrested and taken to San Antonio.

The Cortez incident quickly came to symbolize the ongoing border conflicts, and the ballad that it inspired helped establish the Mexican corrido as a means of expressing racial and cultural tensions along the border. As Cortez eluded his captors, they only grew more determined to capture and punish him. However, Cortez also gained a huge following of supporters, especially from within the Hispanic population, many of whom began to view him as a hero. Those who admired him pointed to the fact that, on the run, he had walked nearly 100 miles and ridden more than 400, while being pursued by search parties of up to 300 men. By the time of his arrest, Cortez had killed two sheriffs and evaded capture by numerous posses.

Most of his supporters feared that he would not receive a fair trial. He was sentenced to life in prison. However, when he eventually won early release, many of his admirers saw this as the final triumph of justice. Because of his remarkable ability to prevail against great odds, Cortez came to be seen as an almost mythic symbol of heroism to many Hispanic people in Texas and Mexico. His exploits and his triumph over a legal system that seemed biased against Mexican Americans have been celebrated for decades through "El Corrido de Gregorio Cortez."

Numerous ballads have derived from the original corrido. It was these different variants that were responsible for the growth of Cortez's image as a folk hero. It is widely believed that the original version of the Cortez corrido was written as the drama was unfolding by an unknown *guitarrero* who performed the ballad in cantinas along the border. Soon after Cortez's capture, other variations of the corrido appeared, some of which expressed doubt that he would be given a fair hearing. Between Cortez's capture and his sentencing, from 1901 to 1905, the corrido grew increasingly popular and could be heard on ranches, in bars, and at public gatherings throughout the Southwest. In at least a few cases along the Texas side of the border, singers sometimes were arrested, beaten, or even lost their jobs if they performed it in public. In Mexico City a broadside ballad about him was used to collect funds for his defense. Along the border and in Texas, however, there is no evidence of the ballad's being used to collect funds.

Cortez entered the Huntsville penitentiary on January 1, 1905, to begin serving his life sentence, and the ballad fell into disuse. When he was released from prison in 1913—during the Mexican Revolution—the ballad was revived and generated interest, especially along the lower border. Over the next few years, the original corrido continued to evolve into numerous versions. By the 1920s, details had become less important, and the focus was directed more toward the general story of Cortez. During the 1940s the Cortez corrido continued to be a favorite among Mexican *guitarreros* and the Spanish-speaking public. In 1958 historian Américo Paredes examined the Cortez legend in *With His Pistol in His Hand: A Border Ballad and Its Hero*. This study helped to popularize the story again among the Mexican-American population and to reintroduce Cortez to the Anglo-American public. A riled-up former Texas Ranger claimed that he wanted to "pistol whip the son-of-a-bitch who wrote that book." In 1982 Hollywood made a movie entitled *The Ballad of Gregorio Cortez*.

BIBLIOGRAPHY: Leticia M. Garza–Falcón, *Gente Decente: A Borderlands Response to the Rhetoric of Dominance* (Austin: University of Texas Press, 1998). Richard J. Mertz, "No One Can Arrest Me: The Story of Gregorio Cortez," *Journal of South Texas* 1974:1.

Juan Carlos Rodríguez

Eldorado Ballroom. In Houston. Throughout the middle part of the twentieth century, the Eldorado reigned as one of the finest showcases in Texas for the live performance of black secular music—mostly blues, jazz, and R&B, but occasionally also pop and zydeco. This venue, owned and operated by African Americans, occupied the entire second floor of the Eldorado Building, located across from historic Emancipation Park on the southwest quadrant of the intersection of Elgin and Dowling Streets in the Third Ward, home to the city's largest black population.

From 1939, when it was built, until the early 1970s, the Eldorado was the venue of choice for upscale blues and jazz performances featuring touring stars and local talent, as well as afternoon talent shows and sock-hops. The ballroom was the centerpiece of several profitable enterprises owned by African-American businesswoman and philanthropist Anna Dupree (1891–1977), who had already achieved significant success as a beauty-shop operator before marrying Clarence Dupree in 1914. Together they established the Eldorado Ballroom in order to provide a "class" venue for black social clubs and general entertainment. Almost from the beginning, "the 'rado" (as people sometimes called it) and the large building that housed it became symbols of community pride—the Third Ward's most prestigious focal point, especially for musicians.

Like the more famous Savoy Ballroom in Harlem, the Eldorado Ballroom billed itself as the "Home of Happy Feet"—signifying not only its reputation for lively musical performance but also its large, and reportedly often crowded, dance floor. Among the house orchestras that worked there, providing instrumental backing for locally produced floor shows as well as for featured touring artists, were big bands directed by distinguished Texas bandleaders and instrumentalists such as Ed Golden, Milton Larkin, I. H. "Ike" Smalley, Arnett Cobb, Pluma Davis, and Conrad Johnson. At its heyday as a venue for major touring acts from the postwar years through the early 1960s, the Eldorado regularly headlined nationally known performers such as Ray Charles, Bill Doggett, Guitar Slim (Eddie Jones), Etta James, Jimmy Reed, Big Joe Turner, and T-Bone Walker.

Numerous Houston musicians received valuable early professional experience by playing in the Eldorado Ballroom house bands. Many of them subsequently became famous bandleaders and recording artists in their own right. Noteworthy examples include saxophonist and vocalist Eddie Vinson, saxophonist Don Wilkerson, and trumpeter Calvin Owens. Likewise, for many musically inclined black Houstonians coming of age in the mid-twentieth century, the weekly talent shows at the Eldorado Ballroom provided an initial opportunity to perform in public before large audiences. Among those who reportedly launched their careers there are Peppermint Harris (Harrison Nelson), Johnny "Guitar" Watson, and Joe "Guitar" Hughes.

By 1970, however, the fortunes of the Eldorado, like those of the Third Ward in general, were in decline. Key factors contributing to the ballroom's eventual demise were the negative economic impact for black-owned businesses in the old wards triggered by desegregation, the lack of adequate parking space in an era when more African Americans were starting to own automobiles, and changing musical tastes (as many younger blacks abandoned the classic jazz and blues of their parents' generation for more progressive sounds).

During the last quarter of the twentieth century the Eldorado Building was home to various small business enterprises and much vacant subdivided space for lease. But in December 1999 the massive structure (along with the entire seventeen-lot block on which it sits) was acquired by Third Ward–based Project Row Houses, a non-profit arts and community service organization formed to restore the facility as a special performance venue, archive, and meeting site that will preserve the legacy of the once grand Eldorado Ballroom.

BIBLIOGRAPHY: Houston *Press*, December 16, 1999. Yvette Jones, "Seeds of Compassion," *Texas Historian*, November 1976. Profile of Anna Dupree, "Black History 24/7/365," *African-American News & Issues* 5.35 (October 4–10, 2000). Roger Wood, *Down In Houston: Bayou City Blues* (Austin: University of Texas Press, 2003).

Roger Wood

Ellis, Merrill. Composer, performer, and researcher; b. Cleburne, Texas, December 9, 1916; d. Denton, Texas, July 21, 1981. He studied clarinet as a child and received his higher education (B.A., M.M.) from the University of Oklahoma. He later taught at the University of Missouri. Ellis appeared throughout the central and southwestern United States in numerous performances of electronic and intermedia compositions, and he lectured at different colleges and universities. Interested in the advancement of new music, he carried out research in new compositional techniques, development of new instruments, and exploration of new notation techniques for scoring and performance.

Some of his instrumental works listed by ASCAP include *Kaleidoscope* (for mezzo-soprano, electronic synthesizer, and orchestra), *A Dream Fantasy* (tape, clarinet, percussion, 16mm film, and slides), *Nostalgia* (orchestra, film, and theatrical events), *Mutations* (brass choir, film tape, and slides), *Scintillation* (solo piano), *Celebration* (flute, oboe, clarinet, bassoon, percussion, tape, lasers, and "visual events"), and *Dream of the Rode* (tape and 16 mm film). ASCAP also lists among his scores the opera *The Sorcerer* (solo baritone, tape, film, slides, and chorus) and the TV film *The Choice is Ours* (intermedia work for 2 films, slides, tape, and audience participation). Ellis was a member of many professional organizations, including the Music Teachers National Association. He received several commissions and research grants and won an ASCAP award in 1979.

He began exploring electro-acoustic music when he arrived at the University of North Texas at Denton in 1962. He founded the university's Computer Music Center in 1963 and was director of the Electronic Music Center and professor of composition. In 1963 he established the Electronic Music Center, the precursor to the Center for Experimental Music and Intermedia. He intended the center to be an important part of the Division of Composition, where professors and students could employ experimental technologies to produce art.

During the center's first ten years, participating composers centered their work on the prominent electronic music forms of the time—works for magnetic tape and live performances using analog synthesizers. Ellis induced Robert Moog, who invented the synthesizer, to make a second one for him and his students. Between 1973 and 1983 these composers also integrated elements from other artistic disciplines, such as theater, painting, and dance, to create intermedia compositions.

Ellis died at home after a short illness. His body was cremated at the Roselawn Cemetery in Denton. Instead of funeral services, a concert was held in his honor at the UNT Intermedia School of Music. Ellis bequeathed a fund to commission yearly student concerts of new music, which took place five successive years after his death. He was survived by his wife, Naomi, three sons, and two daughters, as well as nine grandchildren. In 1981, when Phil Winsor joined the North Texas faculty, the Electronic Music Center became the Center for Experimental Music and Intermedia.

BIBLIOGRAPHY: American Society of Composers, Author and Publishers, *ASCAP Biographical Dictionary* (New York: Bowker, 1980). Dallas *Morning News*, July 22, 1981. Special Collections, *Merrill Ellis Collection* (www.library. unt.edu/music/speccol.htm), accessed January 6, 2003.

Elsa Gonzalez

Ervin, Booker. Tenor saxophonist; b. Denison, Texas, October 31, 1930; d. August 31, 1970. Ervin was known primarily for his work with jazz legend Charles Mingus, and was highly regarded in New York jazz circles. His father, who played trombone with Buddy Tate, taught Booker the instrument at an early age. After finishing high school, Booker joined the air force and was stationed in Okinawa, where he learned to play the tenor sax. When his service was completed in 1953, he enrolled at the Berklee School of Music in Boston; there he learned the essentials of music theory. The following year, he moved to Tulsa and joined fellow Texan Ernie Fields.

Though Fields's band was primarily a rhythm-and-blues outfit, Ervin's playing became more refined, and he developed a sense of self-confidence that eventually led him to New York City (1958). Shortly after his arrival he met Mingus, who was impressed with his style. Ervin joined the Mingus Jazz Workshop, and this creative association led to a string of recordings, including the 1959 masterpiece *Mingus Ah-Um.* Mingus was demanding and at times dictatorial, but he nurtured creativity and encouraged his musicians to improvise. Ervin soon developed a reputation as one of New York's finest young sax players. His playing could be explosive, yet his sensitive touch was powerful. Though he continued playing with Mingus through the 1960s, Ervin also recorded several solo albums for Prestige Records, including *The Blues Book, The Space Book, The Freedom Book,* and *The Song Book.* He died of kidney disease.

BIBLIOGRAPHY: Dave Oliphant, *Texan Jazz* (Austin: University of Texas Press, 1996). Brian Priestly, *Mingus: A Critical Biography* (New York: Quartet Books, 1982). Gene Santoro, *Myself, When I Am Real: The Life and Music of Charles Mingus* (New York: Oxford University Press, 2000). *Bradley Shreve*

Escobar, Eligio Roque. Conjunto musician; b. Jim Wells County, Texas, December 1, 1926; d. Corpus Christi, October 4, 1994; fourth son and fifth child of Eleuterio and Andrea (Farías) Escobar Sr. Escobar was reared in Ben Bolt, Texas. He traced his family's origins to Escobares, a small town on the Rio Grande in Starr County. On September 24, 1944, he married Jesusa Koehler, with whom he had two daughters and two sons. He served in the United States Army of Occupation in Japan after World War II. For the first part of his life he worked principally as an oil-field truck driver around Alice.

Through the influence of an uncle, Escobar learned to play guitar and sing as a child. He honed his skills as he grew to adulthood. He became a professional musician, however, after an automobile accident in 1960 injured his legs severely and rendered him unable to pursue his previous employment. He developed his Texas-Mexican conjunto music during his convalescence and thereafter launched his professional career. Beginning in 1962, Escobar recorded more than 250 songs. Although he sang in both English and Spanish, his voice became most familiar to Spanish-language radio listeners. Among his best-known songs were "Cuando dos Almas," "Rosario Nocturno," and "El Gambler." Perhaps his most famous song, "El Veterano," spoke to the feelings of the Mexican-American veteran of World War II and endeared him to a sizable audience of postwar Hispanic music lovers.

He likewise toured extensively with Spanish-language musicians in the United States and Mexico. Escobar helped launch the musical career of his daughter, Linda Escobar, who gained prominence as a singer and recording artist. After eventually moving in with his family in Corpus Christi, Escobar often used his music to benefit such civic organizations as the American G.I. Forum, of which he and his brothers were members.

Firmly rooted in his South Texas culture, Escobar was an avid fisherman and hunter. Toward the end of his life, along with his music, he worked as a wildlife manager on South Texas ranches. He was revered by many for his generous spirit and easygoing manner as well as for his unique musical style. He died of cancer and is buried in Corpus Christi.

BIBLIOGRAPHY: Corpus Christi *Caller-Times*, October 10, 1994. *Thomas H. Kreneck*

Evans, Dale. Actress, singer, and wife of Roy Rogers; b. Frances Octavia Smith, Uvalde, Texas, October 31, 1912; d. Apple Valley, California, February 7, 2001; first child of Walter and Betty Sue Smith, who farmed in Italy, Texas. She discovered in 1954 that her original name was Lucille Wood Smith, according to her birth certificate, but her mother insisted this was a mistake. The same document indicated that she was born on October 30, not October 31, but Dale Evans chose to accept the latter date as her birthday.

The Smith family moved to Osceola, Arkansas, when Frances was seven, and she entered high school at the age of twelve. At the age of fourteen she eloped with Thomas Frederick Fox, two years older, who left her twice within the first six months of their marriage. After the birth of their son, Tom Jr., the following year, she moved back in with her parents, who had relocated to Memphis, Tennessee. She divorced Fox, who had left a third and final time, in 1929, and married August Wayne Johns. The two divorced in 1935.

Her show-business career began in Memphis while she was working as a secretary for an insurance company. Her boss overheard her singing to herself in the office and suggested she appear on a local radio show the company sponsored. The station that aired the show then asked her to become a regular. Evans's efforts to pursue a career as a singer took her from Memphis to Chicago, Louisville, and Dallas over the next few years, but she achieved only marginal success. In Louisville, where she had found work with radio station WHAS using the name Marian Lee, the station manager reportedly suggested she change her name to the more euphonious Dale Evans.

She then moved to Dallas to be near her parents, who had moved back to Italy, Texas, and found a job as a singer on radio station WFAA's "Early Bird" program. In 1937 she married a third time, to Robert Dale Butts, a pianist and bandleader whom she had dated in Louisville. Butts had moved to Dallas and got a job with WFAA as well. The couple moved back to Chicago, where Butts was hired as a composer–arranger with NBC and Evans joined the Anson Weeks Orchestra for a tour of the Midwest and West Coast.

After the tour she returned to Chicago, where she worked for local CBS affiliate WBBS during the day and sang in clubs at night. Hollywood agent Joe Rivkin heard her on the radio and persuaded her to try out for the female lead in the movie *Holiday Inn,* starring Fred Astaire and

Roy Rogers and Dale Evans arriving in San Antonio, ca. 1955. UT Institute of Texan Cultures at San Antonio, No. Z-2492-A-22738. Radio and movie singing personalities like Rogers and Evans helped make "cowboy" music internationally popular and a symbol of Texas and the Southwest.

Bing Crosby. She failed to land the part, supposedly because she wasn't a good enough dancer (it went to Marjorie Reynolds instead), but executives at Twentieth Century Fox saw her screen test and signed her to a one-year contract. She had small parts in *Girl Trouble* and *Orchestra Wives* in 1942.

When her contract with Fox expired, she got a job as a vocalist on the "Chase and Sanborn Hour" radio show, starring Don Ameche, Jimmy Durante, and Edgar Bergen, but her option was not renewed in the fall of 1943. She signed a one-year contract with Republic, and landed a singing part in the country musical *Swing Your Partner*. During the next year she appeared in several films, including *Here Comes Elmer, Hoosier Holiday,* and *In Old Oklahoma* (which starred John Wayne), while performing in numerous USO and Hollywood Victory Committee shows.

In 1943, Republic proclaimed its singing western star Roy Rogers—born Leonard Slye in Duck Run, Ohio—the "King of the Cowboys." Republic head Herbert Yates, inspired by the success of the stage musical *Oklahoma!,* decided that Rogers's next western should feature a more prominent role for a female costar. The film was *The Cowboy and the Señorita,* and Evans won the role, despite her lack of experience riding horses. The movie was an immediate success, and Rogers and Evans were paired in four more movies in 1944: *Yellow Rose of Texas, Lights of Old Santa Fe, Song of Nevada,* and *San Fernando Valley.*

Evans's marriage to Butts ended in divorce in 1945, and Rogers's wife Arline died of an embolism shortly after the birth of their son Roy Jr. in 1946. The following year Rogers proposed to Evans while they were sitting on their horses waiting to appear in a rodeo in Chicago, and they were married on December 31, 1947, at the Flying L Ranch in Oklahoma, where they had just finished filming *Home to Oklahoma.*

Rogers and Evans became probably the most popular husband-and-wife team in American entertainment history. By 1951, when their television series "The Roy Rogers Show" began its seven-year run, they had appeared together in twenty-nine movies; their weekly radio show was a huge hit; and there were more than 2,000 Roy Rogers fan clubs around the world, including one in London with 50,000 members—the largest such club in the world.

Dale Evans also enjoyed considerable success as a songwriter. In addition to Rogers's theme song, "Happy Trails," she also composed such western and gospel standards as "The Bible Tells Me So," "My Heart Went That-a-Way," "I Wish I Had Never Met Sunshine," and "Aha, San Antone."

But Rogers and Evans also had their share of suffering. Their family was a large one—in addition to Evans's son, Tom, Rogers had three children from his first marriage, and the couple adopted three other children and one foster child. They had one child together, a daughter named Robin, who was born in 1950. She was born with Down syndrome and heart defects, and her death two years later inspired Evans to write the first of her many inspirational books, *Angel Unaware.* Their adopted daughter Debbie, twelve, was killed in a bus accident in 1964, and their

adopted son Sandy, eighteen, died the next year after a drinking binge while serving in the military in Germany.

Rogers and Evans attempted to revive their flagging popularity in 1962 with the short-lived "Roy Rogers and Dale Evans Show," but eventually retired to Apple Valley, California, and devoted themselves to the Roy Rogers–Dale Evans Museum there. (The museum moved to neighboring Victorville in 1976.) Evans continued to write books testifying to her Christian faith and appeared at numerous religious meetings. The Texas Press Association named her Texan of the Year in 1970, and she was named to the National Cowgirl Museum and Hall of Fame, Fort Worth, in 1995. She and Rogers were elected to the Western Music Association Hall of Fame in 1989. Her final show-business appearance was as the host of a television show called "A Date with Dale" for the religious Trinity Broadcast Network in 1996. Roy Rogers died in 1998. Dale Evans died of congestive heart failure three years later.

BIBLIOGRAPHY: Official Roy Rogers–Dale Evans Website (http://www.royrogers.com/), accessed March 10, 2003. Roy Rogers and Dale Evans, with Carlton Stowers, *Happy Trails : The Story of Roy Rogers and Dale Evans* (Waco: Word, 1979).   *Martin Donell Kohout*

Evans, Herschel. Musician and composer; b. Denton, Texas, 1909; d. New York City, February 9, 1939. Evans spent some of his childhood in Kansas City, Kansas, where his cousin Eddie Durham was a trombonist and guitarist. Durham persuaded him to switch from alto to tenor sax, the instrument that ultimately established Evans's reputation. After perfecting his craft in famous jam sessions held in the jazz district between Twelfth and Eighteenth streets in Kansas City, Evans returned to Texas in the 1920s and joined the Troy Floyd orchestra in San Antonio in 1929. He stayed with the band until it dispersed in 1932. Evans performed for a time with Lionel Hampton and Buck Clayton in Los Angeles, and in the mid-1930s returned to Kansas City to become a featured soloist in Count Basie's big band.

For the next three years Evans's reputation as a tenor saxophonist was at its peak. His musical duels with fellow band member Lester Young are considered jazz classics. Count Basie's popular "One O'Clock Jump" featured the contrasting styles of the two musicians and brought to each the praise of both critics and the general public. The composition displayed Evans's full-bodied, emotional timbre and Young's high-pitched, light, and buoyant tone, contrasting sounds that highlighted each other. Evans's greatest single success was his featured solo in Basie's hit "Blue and Sentimental."

He also made records with such notable jazz figures as Harry James, Teddy Wilson, and Lionel Hampton. Evans has been credited with influencing fellow tenorists Buddy Tate, Illinois Jacquet, and Arnett Cobb. Although not a prolific composer, he wrote a number of popular works, including the hits "Texas Shuffle" and "Doggin' Around." He died of heart disease at the age of thirty.

BIBLIOGRAPHY: Frank Driggs and Harris Lewine, *Black Beauty, White Heat: A Pictorial History of Classic Jazz,*

Tenor sax player Herschel Evans (right) with trumpeter Don Albert, ca.1930. This photograph was taken when both Albert and Evans played with San Antonio orchestras. Duncan Scheidt Collection.

1920–1950 (New York: Morrow, 1982). Leonard G. Feather, *The Encyclopedia of Jazz* (New York: Horizon, 1955; rev. ed., New York: Bonanza, 1960). Len Lyons, *The 101 Best Jazz Albums* (New York: Morrow, 1980). Ross Russell, *Jazz Style in Kansas City and the Southwest* (Berkeley: University of California Press, 1971).

David Minor

"Eyes of Texas." The official song of the University of Texas at Austin, considered by some a sort of unofficial state song. It was first sung at a minstrel show to benefit the university track team at the Hancock Opera House in Austin on May 12, 1903. William L. Prather, an alumnus of Washington College (Lexington, Virginia) and president of UT from 1899 to 1905, had often in his student days heard Robert E. Lee, then president of Washington College, say to students, "The eyes of the South are upon you." Prather altered the saying for use at the University of Texas.

The best-documented version of the song's origin has Lewis Johnson, director of the band and the person in charge of the show, asking his roommate, John Lang Sinclair, to write the lyrics to a lively song. On the night before the show, Sinclair, recalling Prather's words, wrote lyrics fitted to the melody of "I've Been Working on the Railroad" on a piece of scrap paper. The glee club quartet performed the song repeatedly at the show to great applause, and the band paraded the campus playing and singing the song the next day. Two years later Prather's family requested that the song be sung at his funeral.

Sinclair later revised the words, and the chorus to the revised version is the song now in popular use. The song gradually became the students' favorite school song. It was translated into ten languages on order of university president Harry Y. Benedict in 1930. The UT Students' Association copyrighted the piece in 1936. In 1951 the association set up the John Lang Sinclair Eyes of Texas Scholarship Fund. Royalties were placed in the fund, and half went to the association and the other half to scholarships.

When the copyright expired in 1964, the Students' Association, with the assistance of the Ex-Students' Association and Congressman Jake Pickle, tried to renew the copyright, but the request was refused. Even so, "The Eyes of Texas" continued to be recognized as the official song of the University of Texas at Austin and at times was mistakenly identified as the state song.

UT students and administration were surprised in the late 1970s to hear that a man living in Oregon was claiming ownership of the "Eyes of Texas" and collecting on his version of the composition. A former Fort Worth musician, Wylbert Brown, copyrighted the words in 1928 with the hope that the song would become the official state song during the Texas Centennial in 1936. In 1984 Arthur B. Gurwitz, president of Southern Music Company in San Antonio, set out to honor his son, who had died only five years after graduating from UT. Gurwitz negotiated with Brown, then ninety-one, who agreed to assign the copyright to UT Austin, provided he would continue to draw some royalty until his death. He died in February 1987. The copyright now belongs to UT Austin. Arthur Gurwitz was honored in a special salute on November 14, 1987, before a football game.

BIBLIOGRAPHY: *Alcalde* (magazine of the Ex-Students' Association of the University of Texas), February 1930, March 1936, January 1959. Austin *American–Statesman*, June 8, 1986. Margaret Catherine Berry, *UT Austin: Traditions and Nostalgia* (Austin: Shoal Creek, 1975). *On Campus*, November 9–15, 1987. T. U. Taylor, *Fifty Years on Forty Acres* (Austin: Alec, 1938). *Margaret C. Berry*

F

Federal Music Project. A New Deal project. Before the Great Depression, radio and sound movies had forced thousands of musicians into unemployment; music was being delivered electronically rather than by live musicians. The economic collapse intensified their situation, causing by 1934 a 60 percent displacement (an estimated 20,000 to 70,000 people), compared to a national unemployment rate of 25 percent. Early relief was administered inefficiently under the New Deal's Civil Works Administration and Federal Emergency Relief Administration, forerunners of the Work Projects Administration, until, in mid-1935 the Federal Music Project was organized as an agency of the WPA.

The FMP was directed by Nikolai Sokoloff. It sought to employ professional musicians, to give free concerts, and to educate the public about music. Soon musicians were taken from manual labor and reassigned to work better suited for their talents. The project's relief efforts focused on New York City, Chicago, Los Angeles, San Francisco, and Boston, traditional centers for musical activity. A third of federal relief was divided among the forty-four remaining states. Texas was in Region 8 with Oklahoma, Arkansas, and Louisiana, and received the careful administration of Lucil M. Lyons of Fort Worth, who was well known in Texas musical activities. Although she was appointed by and technically under Sokoloff, she was administratively responsible to the state WPA administrator, H. P. Drought, in San Antonio. Under Mrs. Lyons's direction, city councils, school boards, chambers of commerce, universities, locals of the musicians' union, and especially the Texas Federation of Music Clubs coordinated relief programs with the national office.

Employment in the project peaked in spring 1936. During Sokoloff's tenure (1936–39), Texas FMP units gave 4,077 performances attracting 2,784,823 listeners. Though WPA activity occurred statewide, four centers were San Antonio, Fort Worth, Dallas, and El Paso. The FMP launched the career of the San Antonio Symphony Orchestra's illustrious future conductor, Victor Alessandro, a native Texan. Although Texas lacked a composer's forum, state copyists and arrangers transcribed vernacular folk songs. San Antonio units recorded examples of Mexican, Spanish, and Cuban music and early Texas plains songs for the Library of Congress, thus saving a wealth of folk music.

Although Texas had no assigned FMP opera units, WPA workers in Fort Worth performed operettas and choruses under the direction of Walker Moore. The highlight of the 1936 season was the "Texas under Six Flags" folk festival at Texas Christian University stadium; a chorus of 1,500 voices sang historic songs in celebration of the Texas Centennial. The FMP also encouraged music appreciation in the schools. Moore divided the Fort Worth WPA orchestra into teams to teach schoolchildren all over the city and county.

Similar projects by educational units reached two-thirds of the rural areas having no prior musical instruction.

Not only did WPA orchestras train hundreds of musicians; their programs also emphasized American compositions. Texans also heard works by their own, such as David Guion and Oscar Julius Fox. Most important, the FMP lifted the nation's morale and awakened pride in native music.

Major reorganization followed Sokoloff's resignation in May 1939. Partly because of the uneven distribution of funds under Sokoloff, under Dr. Earl Vincent Moore the FMP lost its charter as a federal agency. This shifted the sponsorship of projects to the state and local level, where it had been in Texas virtually all along. The state thus autonomously preserved the beneficial effects of the FMP. Although the public activities of the project ended in 1941, its effects were notable in Texas musical culture long afterward.

BIBLIOGRAPHY: Cornelius B. Canon, The Federal Music Project of the Works Progress Administration: Music in a Democracy (Ph.D. dissertation, University of Minnesota, 1963). Earl Vincent Moore, *Final Report of the Federal Music Project, October 10, 1939* (Washington, D.C.: Government Printing Office, 1939). Nikolai Sokoloff, *The Federal Music Project* (Washington, D.C.: Government Printing Office, 1936). Texas Reports, Record Group 69, WPA–FMP Files, National Archives, Washington, D.C. Janelle J. Warren, Of Tears and Need: The Federal Music Project, 1935–1943 (Ph.D. dissertation, George Washington University, 1973).
Craig H. Roell

Fields, Ernie. Band leader; b. Nacogdoches, Texas, August 26, 1905; d. May 11, 1997. Fields toured the United States with his band for nearly four decades. In his youth, before turning to a career in music, he studied at the Tuskegee Institute, where he learned the ins and outs of being an electrician. He also played trombone in the school's marching band—a skill he later took with him to Tulsa. There he began playing part-time at clubs in and around the city; he also met his wife, Bernice, to whom he remained married for more than sixty years.

Eventually, around 1930, Fields formed his own jazz big-band outfit and had considerable success. As his popularity grew, he and his band toured the Midwest and Southwest. He made several recordings for various jazz and blues labels, including Frisco, Bullet, and Gotham. In 1939 the group traveled to New York City, where they recorded and played shows at the legendary Apollo Theater. With the advent of rock-and-roll and the decline of big-band jazz in the 1950s, Fields downsized his band and transformed it into a rhythm-and-blues group. He also dabbled in the record industry and served as an arranger in various rock and pop recording sessions. In 1959 he founded his own record label, Rendezvous, and cut a blistering rendition of

Tipica Orchestra, Federal Music Project, Dallas, Texas, April 12, 1936. The purpose of the Federal Music Project was to employ professional musicians, to give free concerts, and to educate the public about music. Courtesy Connie Easley.

Glenn Miller's classic "In the Mood." The single—a huge hit—reached gold-record status and remained on the charts for a staggering 23 weeks.

Shortly after this success, Fields retired from playing and recording. He subsequently worked as a promoter and talent manager in the Tulsa vicinity.

BIBLIOGRAPHY: Colin Larkin, ed., *Encyclopedia of Popular Music* (London: MuzeUK Limited, 1998), Volume 3. Dave Oliphant, *Texan Jazz* (Austin: University of Texas Press, 1996). Tulsa *World*, May 18, 1997.

Bradley Shreve

Fifth Ward, Houston. A musically rich neighborhood east of downtown; bounded by Buffalo Bayou on the south, Lockwood Drive on the east, Liberty Road on the north, and Jensen Drive on the west. The site was sparsely inhabited before the Civil War. It was subsequently settled by freedmen and became known as the Fifth Ward in 1866, when an alderman was elected to represent the community in the Houston city government.

At the time, half the population was black and half white. By 1870 the population of the ward comprised 561 white and 578 black residents. Two schools, one black and one white, corresponded to the roughly equal segments of the ward's population in 1876. Mount Vernon United Methodist Church, founded in 1865 by former slave Rev. Toby Gregg, is the oldest institution in the ward. Five other churches are over 100 years old: Pleasant Grove Baptist, Mount Pleasant Baptist, Sloan Memorial United Methodist, Payne Chapel Methodist, and First Shiloh Baptist. The Fifth Ward was also the site of a saloon named for Carry Nation, which, after considerable damage resulting from a dispute with the owner over the name, was subsequently known as the "Carnation."

In the 1880s the ward enjoyed a boom following the construction of repair shops for the newly built Southern Pacific Railroad. Growth was interrupted by a fire in 1891 at the Phoenix Lumber Mill and another in 1912 that burned 119 houses, 116 boxcars, nine oil tanks, thirteen plants, and St. Patrick's Catholic Church and school.

Eventually, the Fifth Ward population became predominantly black. At Frenchtown, a four-square-block neighborhood in the ward, 500 blacks of French and Spanish descent from Louisiana organized a community in 1922. Black-owned businesses, including a pharmacy, a dentist's office, an undertaking parlor, a theater, and several barbershops, operated after 1900 on Lyons Avenue and numbered forty by 1925. Working-class blacks were primarily employed within walking distance of the ward; many worked for the Southern Pacific Railroad or at the Houston Ship Channel. Others commuted across town to work as domestics and servants for wealthy Houstonians. By 1927 Phillis Wheatley High School in the ward, with 2,600 students and sixty teachers, was one of the largest black high schools in America. Other new businesses developed in the 1930s, including printing plants, photography studios, and the Club Matinee, which came to be known as the Cotton Club of the South. Local businessman Grand Duke Crawford organized the Fifth Ward Civic Club.

Houston's second housing project for African Americans, the Kelly Court Housing Project, opened in the ward after World War II. Early community activists included Lonnie Smith and Lilly Portley. Peacock Records, a black-owned recording company, started in the ward, as did C. F. Smith Electric Company, one of the state's early licensed electrical-contracting companies. Finnigan Park, the second public park for blacks in Houston, opened in the community in the postwar years, and the Julia C. Hester

Troy Floyd Shadowland Orchestra, Plaza Hotel, San Antonio, 1928. Photograph by Crown Art Photo Company. Duncan Scheidt Collection.

House, a black community center, began service. Nat Q. Henderson, long-time principal of Bruce Elementary School, was the mayor of the Fifth Ward and became known for his leadership.

With passage of integration laws in the 1960s, however, many residents left the community seeking wider opportunities. The Fifth Ward is noted for training many prominent athletes. Musicians from the ward include Arnett Cobb, Milton Larkin, and Illinois Jacquet. Barbara Jordan and Mickey Leland, members of Congress, graduated from Wheatley High School.

Bibliography: Marie Phelps McAshan, *A Houston Legacy: On the Corner of Main and Texas* (Houston: Gulf, 1985). David G. McComb, *Houston: The Bayou City* (Austin: University of Texas Press, 1969; rev. ed., *Houston: A History*, 1981). WPA Writers Program, *Houston* (Houston: Anson Jones, 1942). *Diana J. Kleiner*

Floyd, Troy. Jazz bandleader and instrumentalist; b. Texas, January 5, 1901; d. San Diego County, California, July 16, 1953. Floyd led various jazz groups in San Antonio during the late 1920s and early '30s. He played alto and tenor saxophone and clarinet. His first unit was a sextet, organized in 1924 and increased to nine pieces by 1926.

His band broadcast regularly on radio station HTSA from the Plaza Hotel in San Antonio, from which the group took the name Troy Floyd and His Plaza Hotel Orchestra when it recorded for the first time on March 14, 1928. This was one of the first black bands to record in Texas. Floyd's band also appeared at the Shadowland club, from which its 1928 recording of "Shadowland Blues" derived its title. Among the musicians in the Floyd bands

were Claude "Benno" Kennedy, "a trumpeter with a considerable technique and freak style," and Siki Collins, an alto and soprano saxophonist who was praised by a number of his fellow sidemen. Kennedy organized his own band, the Oleanders, in 1927 and later left for California.

In 1928 Floyd's band included trumpeter Don Albert, who later started a unit of his own, which in 1932 he billed as "America's Greatest Swing Band," the first group to use "swing" in its name. Also a member of the 1929 unit was Texas tenor saxophonist Herschel Evans, who recorded with the group its two-part "Dreamland Blues," on which Evans is said to take his first solo. Another Texas tenorist, Buddy Tate, joined the Floyd unit after the 1929 recording session, and in 1932 Texas trombonist George Corley also became a member of the group. But Floyd disbanded the same year.

A CD of all the recordings made by Floyd's bands includes, in addition to "Shadowland Blues" and "Dreamland Blues," a version of "Wabash Blues" that was not released until thirty years after it was made. Jazz critic Albert McCarthy has written that "the impression one receives from these records is that Floyd's was a proficient band with one or two good soloists . . . but that all in all it was undistinguished." Floyd worked in later years as a pool-hall operator in San Diego, California.

Bibliography: *Jazz in Texas, 1924–1930* (Timeless Records, CBC 1-033, 1997). Albert McCarthy, *Big Band Jazz* (New York: Putnam, 1974). *Dave Oliphant*

Foley, Blaze. Blues and folk singer and songwriter; b. Michael David Fuller, Marfa, Texas, December 18, 1949; d. Austin, February 1, 1989 (buried in Austin). Foley grew up in far West Texas singing with his mother, brother, and sisters as the Fuller Family Gospel Singers.

He renamed himself after Red Foley and adopted the name Blaze to suit his personality. He was noted for his honest, uncompromising lyrics, solid picking style, and deep voice. It is believed that he never worked at any job other than songwriting, singing, and guitar picking. In fact, he used to chide musician friends who worked "day jobs," saying they were not true to their craft. Foley lived for music. Perhaps that is why he lived on the charity of others—musicians who had day jobs, mostly. Not having a home of his own, Foley slept on the couches of friends and sometimes under pool tables at places like the Austin Outhouse. His fondness for decorating his clothes with duct tape became well known, and he often joked that the letters BFI (Browning-Ferris Industries) on dumpsters stood for "Blaze Foley Inside."

He performed through the 1970s and 1980s at venues such as Anderson Fair in Houston and at many Austin spots, including Spellman's Lounge, emmajoe's, the Soap Creek Saloon, the Hole in the Wall, and, most regularly, the Austin Outhouse. He also performed at places such as Tipitina's in New Orleans. He counted such performers as Townes Van Zandt, Jubal Clark, Pat and Barbara MacDonald, Mandy Mercier, Kimmie Rhodes, and "Lost John" Casner among his friends and was often backed by quality musicians, such as the Muscle Shoals Horns, bassist–guitarist Gurf Morlix, fiddler Champ Hood, and singer–songwriter Sarah Elizabeth Campbell. Original songs by Foley include "If I Could Only Fly," "Clay Pigeons," "Oh Darlin'," "Small Town Hero," "Faded Loves," "Cold, Cold World," "Oval Room," "Getting Over You," "Picture Cards Can't Picture You," and "Let Me Ride in Your Big Cadillac."

Foley recorded one vinyl album entitled *Blaze Foley* (1983, Vital). In December 1988 he recorded a cassette entitled *Live at the Austin Outhouse and Not There*, and planned to donate a portion of the proceeds to a homeless shelter. He was shot to death at the home of an old friend by the friend's son. The jury ruled that the assailant shot Foley in self-defense. After Foley's untimely death, Deep South Productions, headed by Jon Smith and Ryan Rader and supported by more than seventy-five Austin musicians, released three memorial albums: *In Tribute and Loving Memory* (1998), *BFI Too* (1999), and *Blaze Foley Inside: Volume 3* (2000). In Foley's memory, Townes Van Zandt wrote "Blaze's Blues" and Lucinda Williams wrote "Drunken Angel." Willie Nelson and Merle Haggard recorded Foley's "If I Could Only Fly" on their *Seashores of Old Mexico* album (1987); Haggard later performed the song at Tammy Wynette's memorial service, and rerecorded it as the title track of an album released in 2000. In 2001, two films on Foley were under production—a documentary by Kevin Triplett and a feature film by David Parks.

BIBLIOGRAPHY: *Austin Chronicle Music*, December 24, 1999. Larry Monroe, "Blaze Foley," *Austin Weekly*, February 1989.

Cheryl L. Simon

Folk Festivals. Festivals in Texas, always featuring music or at least garnished by it, reflect a tradition of community

Young fiddler at the Texas Folklife Festival, UT Institute of Texan Cultures, San Antonio, 1983. UT Institute of Texan Cultures at San Antonio, No. TFF-83-22-5

cooperation and celebration that began at least as early as the arrival of permanent settlers. Early European Texans of all faiths, occupations, and ethnic backgrounds brought their traditions with them. Texas festivals reflect this diversity of cultural identity and also demonstrate the wide range of occupations, agricultural products, and historical events that characterize the state. The origins of some celebrations reach far back into history in other lands; others originated in twentieth-century Texas.

In frontier Texas full-scale festivals were sometimes impossible, but groups still gathered frequently to celebrate special occasions with music, dance, and food. Older traditional festivals are rarely called that. Instead, they derive their names from what they celebrate—a saint such as St. Anthony, for instance, or an object that is celebrated, as in the Luling Watermelon Thump. Those festivals that were brought to Texas usually incorporate features from life in the state, especially a heightened awareness of ethnicity.

Traditional festivals based solely on experience in Texas are associated with particular towns, regions, or historical events. The major symbol of these celebrations is often a natural product, such as watermelons, cattle, or trees. All festivals foster the concept of identity based on shared experience. A second group of festivals of more recent origin do use the term *festival* in their names. These have not developed out of a community or ethnic group and are typically sponsored by an institution or an individual. Such festivals are designed to attract masses of people for performance and the display of traditions. The range and variety of festivals in Texas make a listing impossible. The editors of *Texas Highways* keep a file of community events for the year and publish a monthly list of events in the magazine. At any festival an event may be added or removed at any time, and dates can be altered from year to year.

For early settlers traditional festivals celebrated in the country of origin often took on even greater significance in Texas. In the latter half of the nineteenth century Mexican Americans celebrated the full round of religious fiestas throughout the year, with special emphasis on the December holidays. In San Antonio the Feast of Our Lady of Guadalupe (December 12) was observed as early as the 1840s with an elaborate procession. Twelve girls dressed in white carried the image of the Virgin Mary, and fiddlers accompanied the procession to San Fernando de Bexar Cathedral on the Main Plaza. After Mass, people attended all-night dances in their homes. During the Christmas season the Texas-Mexican population, especially in San Antonio, performed the Spanish medieval drama *Los Pastores* and enacted *posadas*, rituals commemorating Joseph and Mary's search for shelter in Bethlehem. Hispanic and other Catholics all over the state have continued to celebrate the various saints days in the twentieth century. Additionally, El Cinco de Mayo, a secular holiday and one of the Fiestas Patrias, is celebrated with parades, floats, folk dancing, and an all-night ball in some parts of Texas.

Germans brought unique celebrations to their new homes in Central Texas. Immigrants came in large numbers between 1845 and 1850 and organized singing societies in most of the German Texas communities. Singers and families assembled on Saturday morning for a *Sängerfest* (singers' festival), at which they sang and ate sausage, sauerkraut, and potato salad and drank beer. The festivals began with parades, included dancing, and concluded with grand finales of song. An older tradition among the Germans are the *Schützenfeste*, or marksmen's festivals. These originated as archery contests in Europe several hundred years ago. They developed into shooting fairs and then folk festivals. In Texas a festival of shooting clubs includes an opening parade, competitive shooting, music, dancing, and feasting. The largest current German festival is the Wurstfest of New Braunfels, held in October and featuring German food and music.

To Czechs the Feast of the Assumption of the Virgin on August 15 has historical, religious, and ethnic value. Czechs from Moravia and Bohemia immigrated to Texas in the 1850s and established the town of Praha, where in 1890 they built a church that became the mother parish for surrounding communities. When Czechs from Central Texas gather in Praha on August 15, Mass is celebrated in the historic church, which is Czech in architectural style; at the gathering Czech food is served, and Texas Czech bands play music for dancing throughout the evening.

For Italians near Bryan, St. Joseph's Day (March 19) is an annual event to honor the saint and bring Italians together. The Italian feast is primarily a domestic celebration with roots in Sicily, but in Texas it is associated with a miraculous cure that occurred in 1938 and is attributed to San Giuseppe.

A date of great importance to African Americans in Texas is June 19, popularly known as Juneteenth, the anniversary of the day in 1865 when Gen. Gordon Granger officially announced in Texas that slavery was ended. This day has been celebrated ever since in Texas, western Louisiana, southern Oklahoma, and southwestern Arkansas by black communities with parades, picnics, music, and sports events, especially baseball. Since 1979 Juneteenth has been an official Texas holiday. Among blacks the occasion is important for reunions and homecomings.

On June 13 the Tigua Indians of Ysleta del Sur Pueblo, located in the mission lands of El Paso, honor their patron saint, San Antonio, in the Fiesta de San Antonio. The Tiguas built their city in the 1680s, when they moved south from their original home on the Rio Grande in northern New Mexico. On June 11 and 12, the two days preceding the fiesta, the reservation becomes the scene for intertribal Indian dances, and the pueblo holds an Indian market. The day of the fiesta is celebrated with processions, feasting, traditional dances, and a Mass, all in honor of San Antonio, whom the Tiguas associate with gods of their pre-Christian religion.

Among the most popular festivals based on the Texas experience are cowboy festivals—events of several days' duration that feature rodeos, barbecue, and fiddle music. In Stamford the Fourth of July is celebrated with three days of rodeo and reunion, known as the Texas Cowboy Reunion. Many individuals hold family or class reunions at the same time as the Cowboy Reunion.

Festivals often honor the fruits of the land and the experience of living on the land. The Luling Watermelon Thump, a popular festival of this type, lasts several days in July and includes a watermelon auction and coronation of a queen. In deep East Texas the town of Winnsboro holds an October festival called Autumn Trails that includes trail rides, gospel singing, and evening dances.

Audiences who attend large so-called folk festivals are frequently unfamiliar with the traditions displayed or have consciously learned the music or acquainted themselves with the food of another culture. Among the most popular of the contemporary festivals is the Kerrville Folk Festival, where visitors can hear country, folk, bluegrass, and gospel music. Amateur banjo players, guitar pickers, and fiddlers are judged in competition at the Bluegrass Festival, and the winners are offered the opportunity to perform the following year. Every year the University of Texas Institute of Texan Cultures in San Antonio hosts the Texas Folklife Festival, which celebrates the many ethnic groups of Texas. Visitors can try ethnic foods such as Cajun boudin, Jewish bagels, or Czechoslovakian kolaches. Costumed musicians and dancers perform tunes and steps from Lebanon, Germany, and other nations. Other traditions demonstrated at the festival reflect pioneer life, and under a large shade tree yarn spinners captivate audiences. In the fall the Chamizal National Memorial in El Paso hosts the Border Folk Festival. Sponsored by the National Park Service, the National Council for the Traditional Arts, and the El Paso Friends of Folk Music, the festival specializes in music and dance of folk traditions around the world and presents performances on three stages.

BIBLIOGRAPHY: Richard Bauman and Roger D. Abra-

Late in November 1941, Mrs. John Lomax recorded fiddler Al Brite, guitarist John Heathercock and dance caller J. M. Mills, in San Antonio for the congressional library. UT Institute of Texan Cultures at San Antonio, No. 2860-F.

hams, eds., *"And Other Neighborly Names": Social Process and Cultural Image in Texas Folklore* (Austin: University of Texas Press, 1981). J. Frank Dobie, ed., *Coffee in the Gourd*, Publications of the Texas Folklore Society 2 (Dallas: Southern Methodist University, 1923). Richard Dorson, ed., *Handbook of American Folklore* (Bloomington: Indiana University Press, 1982). Victor Turner, ed., *Celebration* (Washington: Smithsonian Institution, 1982).

Beverly J. Stoeltje

Folk Music. Musical material that usually originated in the forgotten or dimly remembered past and has been passed from one generation to the next down to the present. It exists in the forms of tunes, songs, and ballads. Folk tunes

are traditional melodies such as those played by fiddlers. Folk songs are melodies with accompanying verses. Ballads are folk songs that tell stories. Some folk music is utilitarian; that is, it accompanies an activity such as work, worship, or dance. Other folk music exists just for the stories it tells or the feelings it expresses. Texas folk music is "Texas" only because it passed through the state during the course of its transmission. Its traditional nature means that it was played or sung long before being brought to Texas.

There are as many varieties of folk music in Texas as there are cultures that came to Texas. Anglo-Texan folk music, the dominant strain, has taken the forms of tunes, songs, and ballads. Much of the history of Texas is accompanied by folk music. "Shoot the Buffalo" and "Texas

Boys" describe early attitudes toward settling Texas. "The Greer County Bachelor" and "Little Old Sod Shanty" tell of life on the Texas frontier. "Buffalo Skinners" is the story of the rigors of a buffalo hunt in the 1870s, and "The Old Chisholm Trail" describes the life of the Texas trail-driving cowboy of the same period. According to tradition, Texans marched into battle at San Jacinto to the tune of "Will You Come to the Bower?" They fought the Mexicans again in 1846, to the sweet strains of "Green Grow the Lilacs." Fifteen years later Hood's Texas Brigade marched off to the Civil War to the "Yellow Rose of Texas." "Texas Rangers" was a song about one of that heroic group's early adventurers, and "Sam Bass" was a ballad about the other side of the law. Later such events as the Galveston hurricane of 1900, the Dust Bowl and Great Depression, and the Kennedy assassination were memorialized in folk songs. Now, however, topical folk songs have generally lost out to news media and copyrighted popular music.

In Texas, as elsewhere, children's songs fall into two categories, songs sung to children and songs sung by children. The first song a child usually hears is a lullaby like "Babes in the Woods," sung to the child to put it to sleep. Then children are patty-caked, bounced, and counted to in chants and songs whose purpose is to entertain. These simple songs and later more complicated traditional songs, such as "Froggie Went a-Courtin'" and "Fox Is on the Town," are sung to children. The songs sung by children are simple and basic. They begin with simple game songs like "London Bridge," grow to elaborate jump-rope chants and songs, and conclude with such crudities as "The Monkey Wrapped His Tail Around the Flagpole." Perhaps the last realization of children's songs is the fraternity-party song.

Love has spawned a world of songs and ballads that have made their ways into the Texas repertoire. The most venerable of these were Child's ballads, so called after Francis James Child's *English and Scottish Popular Ballads* (1882–98). Two of the best known of these in Texas were "Barbara Allen" and "Fair Eleanor." Both of these ballads told stories of love affairs that ended in death. Many other English ballads not blessed with the stamp of Child's approval came to Texas. These included "My Horses Ain't Hungry," "Roving Gambler," and "Little Sparrow." Most Anglo-Saxon love songs, including "Wildwood Flower," "Fond Affection," and "Columbus Stockade Blues," relate in some way to the Old World. "Careless Love" is an Anglo response to the black blues tradition. Such love ballads as "Rosewood Casket" and "Bury Me Beneath the Willow" filtered down into the folk idiom from Tin Pan Alley. Though these late-nineteenth-century weepers were not authentic folk music, they became a much-loved part of the singing traditions of Texas.

One of the most popular forms of folk music on the Texas frontier was square-dance music with a lead fiddle. The tunes played were old jigs and reels and hornpipes that were ancient in the British Isles when the settlers first came to the New World. Many of the tunes, like "Irish Washerwoman," "The Campbells are Coming," and "Sailor's Hornpipe," stayed close to their originals. Most underwent subtle and gradual changes as they were passed along from one fiddler and generation and area to another, and now

only a hint of their Old World ancestry remains. Most of the early dancing was group dancing, for which a leader called the steps and patterns while the music was being played. Sometimes fiddle tunes became songs when lyrics were thrown in between calls. In the evolution of some fiddle-dance songs—"Sally Goodin," "Cindy," "Cotton-Eyed Joe," and "Old Joe Clark," for instance—the calls were dropped and the words became almost as important as the tunes. Fiddlers took their tunes and songs from everywhere, but their richest source during the nineteenth century was black minstrelsy, where they found the classic "Arkansas Traveler," "Turkey in the Straw," "Buffalo Gals," and "Old Dan Tucker." The purest of old-time fiddle music can best be found nowadays at fiddle contests held all over Texas, for instance at the annual Crockett World's Champion Fiddlers' Contests held on the second Friday of June. Some of the favorite tunes played there and at other Texas contests are "Billy in the Low Ground," "Sally Johnson," "Durang's Hornpipe," "Devil's Dream," and "Tom and Jerry." Such fiddling dance music as that played by Bob Wills and Milton Brown in the 1930s became modern country-and-western music.

Another folk song-and-dance tradition is the play party. Many early Texas settlers were fundamentalists who believed that dancing and fiddle music were sinful. They satisfied the universal urge to move to music with the play party, which was song-accompanied dance that allowed no instruments. They called their rhythmical group movements "marches" or "games," they danced in rings or in longways formations but never in squares, and they swung each other by hand, never by the waist. They used many popular dance tunes—"Old Clark," "Old Dan Tucker," "The Gal I Left Behind Me," "Willis Ballroom"—but because of the lack of instrumental music, the words became all-important. Play-party songs have preserved many stanzas that were lost in the fiddle-dance tradition. A play party usually began with a choosing game such as "Needle's Eye" or "Hog Drovers," then progressed to ring-game songs like "Saro Jane" or "Coffee Grows on White Oak Trees," and in full swing went into longways dances like "Weevily Wheat," "Little Brass Wagon," and "Baltimore." Play parties were not only popular among fundamentalists; they were necessary when no musician was around. In spite of the reservations laid on the players by their elders, play-party songs and formations were just as joyful and exuberant as their sinful fiddling square-dance counterparts.

One of the richest veins in Texas folk music is its religious strain, and the particular kind to which the state owes the most is Sacred Harp music, named after B. F. White's 1844 songbook, *Sacred Harp*. The tunes and words in this book, still much used in Texas, go back to the Great Revival on the southern frontier at the turn of the nineteenth century, then beyond to the British Isles. Southern preachers found themselves with vast congregations and no songs, so they took familiar popular tunes and put religious words to them. A ballad about Captain Kidd the pirate became "Wondrous Love," and "Auld Lang Syne" became "Hark! From the Tomb." Music in this tradition also employed easily remembered single lines and repeated refrains, in which substitutions of words prolonged the song and increased its intensity. "We Have Fathers Over Yonder," with its simple refrain "Over yonder ocean," could continue as long as substitutions could be made for "fathers." The same was true with the song that began, "You [or "Father," "Mother," "Jesus," etc.] got to walk that lonesome valley." A final influence on Sacred Harp singing was the eighteenth-century singing schools that taught shaped notation. Because it is written in the shaped notes called, since medieval times, fa, sol, la, etc., Sacred Harp music is also called fasola music. The fasola tradition and the "fuguing tunes," whose counterpoint and joyful play of rounds was popular with early singing masters, lost their popularity in the East but became a vehicle for religious enthusiasm in the South and an integral part of Sacred Harp singing, which often lasted all day and was accompanied with "dinner on the grounds."

A modern outgrowth of early Sacred Harp is gospel music. It is livelier than Sacred Harp, more concerned with the play of tune and tempo, and more optimistic in tone. It started to develop at the beginning of the twentieth century and culminated in 1926 with the founding in Dallas of the Stamps–Baxter Music Company. Stamps–Baxter music used the idioms of jazz and popular music and incorporated most modern instrumentation. All-day gospel singing can be found in just about any county in Texas on any weekend. It is a religious folk-music form that is still growing.

Though cowboy songs were sung all across the cow-country frontier of the United States, these folk songs and ballads are still most closely associated with Texas. The Texas cowboy originated in the 1860s and 1870s, when cattlemen began trailing herds to the newly established railheads in Kansas. His skills were derived from the vaquero, his Spanish and Mexican forbear, who had been working large herds for 300 years. The cowboys' mores were Southern. Many men left their Southern homes after the surrender at Appomattox to start again in Texas, and they brought with them the hymns, minstrel songs, and sentimental ballads that were their tradition. Some of the old songs were rewritten to fit the new way of life. "Little Old Log Cabin" furnished the tune for "Little Joe the Wrangler." An old song about a dying English soldier became "The Streets of Laredo." The sad tale of a sailor buried at sea became "Bury Me Not on the Lone Prairie," and "My Bonnie Lies Over the Ocean" furnished the tune for "The Cowboy's Dream." Some cowboy songs exist in differing versions, one traditional and one written. D. J. O'Malley claimed "When the Work's All Done This Fall," and Jack Thorp wrote "Little Joe the Wrangler." Both men put their lyrics to tunes already traditionally circulating.

In the 1930s, cowboy songs and the cowboy mystique formed the basis for western swing, which was the primary antecedent of modern country-and-western music.

Country-and-western music, the modern heir to traditional Texas folk music, incorporates both the earthy themes of traditional music and the elemental three-chord sounds. Country-and-western bands also regularly include such folk classics as "Cotton-Eyed Joe," "Wildwood Flower," and "Careless Love" in their repertoires. Commercial country music, which developed in the 1920s, combined Anglo folk music, old-time religion, and elements of nineteenth-century show business.

BIBLIOGRAPHY: Francis Edward Abernethy, *Singin' Texas* (Dallas: E-Heart Press, 1983). John A. and Alan Lomax, *Cowboy Songs and Other Frontier Ballads* (New York: Sturgis and Walton, 1910; rev. ed., New York: Macmillan, 1945). Bill C. Malone, *Country Music U.S.A.* (Austin: University of Texas Press, 1968). William A. Owens, *Swing and Turn: Texas Play-Party Games* (Dallas: Tardy, 1936). William A. Owens, *Tell Me a Story, Sing Me a Song* (Austin: University of Texas Press, 1983). William A. Owens, *Texas Folk Songs*, Publications of the Texas Folklore Society 23 (Austin: Texas Folklore Society, 1950; 2d ed., Dallas: Southern Methodist University Press, 1976).
Francis E. Abernethy

Ford, Jimmy. Alto saxophonist; b. James Martin Ford, Houston, June 16, 1927; d. Houston, March 13, 1994. Jimmy Ford was the first Caucasian to join the black band of Houston native Milt Larkin. He played with the orchestra in 1947 and 1948, and was referred to as the "white Bird" because his performance style was patterned on that of Charlie Parker.

Ford toured with trombonist Kai Winding's group in 1948 and later worked at the Royal Roost in New York with bebop pianist–composer–arranger Tadd Dameron, whose band included bebop giants Fats Navarro and Kenny Clarke. For much of 1951 Ford played in New York with Charlie Parker's former trumpeter, Red Rodney, with whom he recorded on tenor. In 1951–52 he also worked at times with another outstanding bebop musician, pianist Bud Powell. Soon afterwards, Ford returned to Houston, but by 1957 he was back in New York, where he joined the Maynard Ferguson big band, with which he played until 1960.

During his tenure with the Ferguson band, which appeared frequently at Birdland, Ford was the featured altoist and "one of the band's most impassioned improvisers." He recorded "breakneck," "searing," and "passionate" solos on such tunes as "Humbug," "Ol' Man River," "Stella by Starlight," "Newport," "Oleo," and the wittily entitled "Back in the Satellite Again." While with Ferguson, Ford also served on occasion as a "boy singer."

After returning to Houston in 1961, he participated in the local jazz scene, which included such musicians as altoist and vocalist Eddie "Cleanhead" Vinson and tenorist Arnett Cobb, the latter a former sideman with the Larkin band and the Lionel Hampton orchestra. In 1971 Ford recorded on alto with Cobb for the tenorist's album *The Wild Man from Texas*, which was not released until 1989, the year of Cobb's death. Ford solos on Cobb's original tune "I Stand Alone," as well as on "Doxy" and "Mr. T." His performances on these last two exhibit his "fiery form" and his "fluent, exciting" execution. One of Ford's rare outings at a slower tempo can be heard in "You Stepped Out of a Dream," where his solo work is beautifully flowing. Ford's final public appearance came in the year of his death, when he joined trumpeter Clark Terry for a February performance in his hometown.

BIBLIOGRAPHY: *The Complete Roulette Recordings of the Maynard Ferguson Orchestra* (Mosaic Records, 3-Box CD set, S210-17683, 1994). Barry Kernfeld, ed., *The New Grove Dictionary of Jazz*, Second Edition (New York: Grove's Dictionaries, 2002). Dave Oliphant, *Texan Jazz* (Austin: University of Texas Press, 1996). *The Wild Man from Texas* (Home Cooking Records, HCS-114, 1989).

Dave Oliphant

Fort Griffin Fandangle. An annual outdoor musical drama produced in Albany, Texas, on Thursday, Friday, and Saturday evenings of the last two weeks in June. Its focus is the historical and cultural development of the area along the Clear Fork of the Brazos River in northern Shackelford County near Fort Griffin, the military outpost that from 1867 to 1881 provided protection for settlers in the region and gave rise to a community in the flat between the fort on the hill and the Clear Fork.

The story is recalled through the memory of an old-timer of the region, a cattleman who sits on the porch of a ranchhouse to reveal the past as he remembers it. The production consists of a series of segments, each based on historical material introduced by the narrators and then interpreted by one or more songs and dancing.

The *Fandangle* had its inception in 1937 when C. B. Downing, superintendent of the Albany schools, asked Alice Reynolds, a local music teacher, if she would write an outdoor musical play for the senior class to present the next spring. She declined but asked another native of Albany, Robert Edward Nail Jr., who responded enthusiastically with *Dr. Shackelford's Paradise*, produced in 1938. The play was so well received that it was expanded to include adults in the cast and was produced that summer under the name *Fort Griffin Fandangle*. A sponsoring organization, the Fandangle Association, was first incorporated in 1947. Nail established three rules: first, anybody with ties in Shackelford County could be in the show; second, the show would have to be publicized by word of mouth, not by paid publicity; and third, there would be no profanity in the show.

Alice Reynolds was active from the beginning in writing songs, in designing sets and the numerous banners associated with the play, particularly the steer-head and fiddle emblem that represents the *Fandangle*, and in sketching some of the elaborate costumes. For many years she also played the organ for the performances. She died in May 1984.

The title of the show was chosen for its alliteration and euphony. *Fandangle* is a provincial version of Spanish *fandango*, a fast dance. Originally only traditional or folk music and dances were used, but as the show was repeated in later years by popular demand, new material was written and included in the performances, a practice that is still followed. Although material is repeated from year to year, each season's version varies from any previous show in both content and focus.

In addition to Nail and Reynolds, numerous others have contributed significantly. Songs written by James Ball, Elsa Turner, and later Luann George, who replaced Reynolds as organist in 1983, have increased the store available to the production. Marge Bray, long-time choreographer for the show, assumed the directorship after James Ball, who served for four years after Nail's death in 1968. Of particular significance to the development of the *Fandangle* over the years is the work of G. P. Crutchfield, local craftsman, who built the authentic replica of the Butterfield stagecoach, the machine representing the Texas Central Railroad train, a self-contained blacksmith shop on wheels, and the steam calliope, which is still played regularly before performances. All of these works and many other entries, bands, and horse units appear in the annual parade, which occurs on Thursday afternoon of the second week.

The early performances were held at the local football stadium. The Prairie Theatre, west of town, was constructed in 1965, on land leased for a dollar a year from the John Alexander Matthews estate. Performances have been held there since that time. Full-scale productions are held only in Albany, but short versions have been given in many locations over the years. These are usually performed in the spring and serve as the core around which the major show is built during late May and early June. These "samplers" were performed in Europe in 1967 and 1976 and in Washington, D.C., in 1984.

BIBLIOGRAPHY: Fane Downs, "Fandangle: Myth as Reality," West Texas Historical Association *Yearbook* 54 (1978). Vertical files, Center for American History, University of Texas at Austin. *Lawrence Clayton*

Fox, Oscar Julius. Composer of western songs; b. Burnet County, Texas, October 11, 1879; d. Charlottesville, Virginia, July 29, 1961 (buried in Mission Burial Park, San Antonio); son of Bennie and Emma (Kellersberger) Fuchs and grandson of Adolph Fuchs. Oscar's mother died five months after his birth, and he was reared in the home of an uncle, Hermann T. Fuchs. He attended school in Marble Falls until 1893, when he went to San Antonio and began to study music. In 1896 he was sent to Zürich, Switzerland, by his grandfather, Getuli Kellersberger, to study piano, violin, and choral direction. After three years in Switzerland, he studied in New York City for two years before going to Galveston in 1902 as choirmaster of the First Presbyterian Church and later of St. Mary's Cathedral. He resigned in 1904 to accept a similar position at the First Presbyterian Church in San Antonio, where he served for ten years. He was conductor of the San Antonio Choir Club (1913–15) and director of the men's and girls' glee clubs and the University Choral Society at the University of Texas (1925–28).

Fox was a member of the Texas Music Teachers Association, the Sinfonia Fraternity of America, the American Society of Composers, Authors, and Publishers, the Composers–Authors Guild, and the Sons of the Republic of Texas. He published the first of his more than fifty songs in 1923. He never wrote lyrics but set existing poems to music. He first achieved fame through setting to music the cowboy songs collected by John A. Lomax. He drew strongly on his Texas background, as his best-known compositions illustrate: "The Hills of Home" (1925), "Old Paint" (1927), "The Old Chisholm Trail" (1924), "Whoopee Ti Yi Yo, Git

Cover of sheet music "The Cowboy's Lament" (G. Shirmer, Inc., New York, 1923), one of Fox's best-known compositions. Lota May Harrigan Spell Papers, CAH; CN 11498.

Along, Little Dogies" (1927), "Will You Come to the Bower?" (1936), and "The Cowboy's Lament" (1923).

Fox married Nellie Tuttle in 1905; they had three daughters. The last fifteen years of his life he taught voice and was organist and choir director at Christ Episcopal Church, San Antonio. On May 27, 1962, the state honored him by placing a red granite marker a mile south of Marble Falls on Highway 281. Inscribed on the marker beneath his name is the first line of "The Hills of Home," his own favorite song and one that has continued to be popular around the world.

BIBLIOGRAPHY: *Daily Texan*, October 18, 1925. Dallas *Morning News*, July 30, 1961. San Antonio *Express*, December 8, 1931. Lota M. Spell, *Music in Texas* (Austin, 1936; rpt., New York: AMS, 1973). Vertical files, Center for American History, University of Texas at Austin. Carl Weaver, "Oscar J. Fox and His Heritage," *Junior Historian*, December 1963.　　　　　　*S. W. Pease*

Frantz, Dalies Erhardt. Pianist and teacher; b. Lafayette, Colorado, January 9, 1908; d. Austin, December 1, 1965 (buried at Capital Memorial Gardens, Austin); son of William Henry and Amalia (Lueck) Frantz. He grew up in Denver, where he studied piano at an early age and became known as a child prodigy. Later he learned to play the organ and helped support himself by serving as organist and choirmaster in churches. He studied at Huntington Preparatory School in Boston and under Guy Maier at the University of Michigan from 1926 to 1930. He received the bachelor of music degree with highest honors from that university; subsequently, he studied in Europe with Artur Schnabel and Vladimir Horowitz.

Following his debut with the Philadelphia Orchestra under Leopold Stokowski in 1934, Frantz was signed by Columbia Concerts Corporation and began a long and brilliant career that took him from coast to coast in recitals and in appearances with most of the major orchestras in the United States. During this period he also taught two summer sessions at the University of Washington in Seattle and returned for further study at the University of Michigan. In 1934 he married Martha King of Detroit. They were separated five years later.

Frantz's eminence as a pianist attracted attention in Hollywood, and he appeared in several motion pictures. During World War II he served for a time as an intelligence officer in a West Coast fighter squadron but was given a medical discharge before the end of the war. In 1943 he joined the University of Texas music department. In spite of physical misfortunes that continued to plague him, he pursued his teaching until the time of his death and was recognized as one of the outstanding music teachers in the country. He inspired a large number of student pianists, some of whom won national and international acclaim; well-known professional pianists went to Austin to work with him. Some of his experiences and convictions about piano teaching were passed on to music teachers all over the United States through a series of articles in a publication of the National Piano Guild.

BIBLIOGRAPHY: Vertical files, Center for American History, University of Texas at Austin.　　*Kent Kennan*

French Music. Under the rubric "French music in Texas" one thinks first of Cajun music. The Francophone musical heritage of East Texas and southwestern Louisiana, however, is quite complex. At least four major French-speaking groups have left their musical imprint on Texas and the American Southwest over the past three centuries.

French exploration of Texas began as early as 1682. By 1685 La Salle had built the rudimentary Fort St. Louis near Matagorda Bay. But France was unable to establish a permanent presence along the Texas–Louisiana coastline until the founding of New Orleans at the mouth of the Mississippi River in 1718. Early in the eighteenth century, French settlers built a thriving port there, through which they could control the flow of goods up and down the Mississippi between the Great Lakes and the Gulf of Mexico. The descendants of these original French colonists, known as "white creoles," generally remained in New Orleans, where they developed a sophisticated urban culture. Their art, music, and literature largely reflected the high culture of their more aristocratic peers back in France.

Along with the trappings of European high culture, early French settlers brought black slaves to Louisiana. These bondsmen came from various regions in Africa and the Caribbean and consequently spoke a variety of languages. Over time, the slaves and their descendents, known as "black creoles," developed a common patois, or mixture of the French language with their own tongues. By the time the United States acquired New Orleans and the rest of the Louisiana Territory in the Louisiana Purchase (1803), thousands of former slaves living in the area had gained their freedom. These French-speaking free blacks soon spread across the region from New Orleans throughout southwestern Louisiana and into East Texas. With the constitutional abolition of slavery in 1865, thousands more Francophone African Americans moved westward into Texas. World War II and the attendant boom in the petrochemical industry, which affected the upper Gulf Coast from Houston to Port Arthur, brought another large influx of French-speaking blacks into the state during the 1930s and 1940s.

Throughout the eighteenth, nineteenth, and twentieth centuries, black creoles and their descendants had a profound impact on the musical development of Texas and the Southwest. They combined their African and French musical heritage with the dominant culture around them. They also added gospel, blues, and other musical influences, which had evolved out of the experiences of Southern slaves. Blending African rhythms, gospel, blues, Cajun, and country and western, French-speaking blacks in Texas and Louisiana concocted a new musical style by the 1940s known as "La La" or "Zydeco." The word *Zydeco*, derived from French *les haricots* ("kidney beans"), first appeared in print on sound recordings made in the Houston area during the immediate post–World War II era.

The Louisiana-born brothers Clifton and Cleveland Chenier were the first black Francophone musicians to popularize Zydeco on a national scale. They developed a customized metal washboard that could be worn over the chest and strummed with spoons or other metal objects to create a sharp, rhythmic sound. They added accordion, fid-

Castroville Brass Band, 1910. Castroville Public Library, Castroville, Texas No. ITC-81-641. French-speaking settlers who arrived in Central Texas in the mid-1800s brought with them European influences in music.

dle, and guitar to produce an energetic blend of blues and Cajun music, with lyrics sung both in French and English. Based in Houston for many years, Clifton Chenier, the "King of Zydeco," died in 1987. The Zydeco style is evidence of the broad and lasting impact of Francophone African-American music in Texas and throughout the country.

The most well-known French-speaking group that has left a distinct musical legacy in Texas and Louisiana is the Cajuns. The term *Cajun* is a derivative of the French *Acadien*, which denotes an inhabitant of the region known as Acadia in what is now Nova Scotia. French settlers began arriving in the future Maritime Provinces of eastern Canada in 1605. Most of those who settled in Acadia were from the northern and western coastal areas of Brittany and Normandy. Consequently, their music reflected both French and Celtic traditions. In the Treaty of Utrecht (1713), France ceded Acadia and other parts of Nova Scotia to the British. Since many of the French-speaking residents of Acadia refused to pledge an oath of allegiance to the British Crown, Great Britain began imprisoning, killing, and deporting Acadians. By 1755 British forces had expelled around 8,000 Acadians and confiscated their homes, farms, and businesses. Many sought refuge in New Orleans, with its large French-speaking population. But the authorities in New Orleans, fearful that these uprooted Frenchmen would bring poverty and disease into the city, directed the refugees to settle in the less populated bayous and swamplands of southwestern Louisiana. Except for limited interaction with local blacks and Indians, the Aca-

dians, or Cajuns, managed to live in relative isolation until the 1930s, when technology, industrialization, and highway development brought the region into closer contact with the outside world. Because of decades of cultural isolation, Cajuns were able to preserve much of their musical heritage well into the twentieth century.

During the nineteenth and twentieth centuries, thousands of Cajuns migrated westward into East Texas. Again, the rapid growth of the petroleum industry along the upper Texas coast was a factor. During the 1930s and 1940s it brought a huge influx of Cajuns into the Lone Star State. Cajun music soon blended with western swing, honky-tonk, and other forms of popular Texas music to produce such hits as "Corrina, Corrina" and "Jole Blon." Although Cajun music is often thought of as being a distinctly Louisiana-based music, many of the most influential Cajun musicians lived and recorded in East Texas. Cajun music and Cajun culture in general are now widely celebrated throughout the United States and the world.

The last major group of French-speaking people to settle in Texas arrived in the mid-1800s directly from France. The largest contingent, which settled in and around Castroville under the leadership of Henri Castro, was from Alsace, which straddles the border between Germany and France and consequently has a culture that reflects both strong German and French influences. The Alsatian immigrants who settled in Texas during the mid-nineteenth century performed a wide variety of music, ranging from the formal works of Europe's most noted composers to the rich and complex folk music of the working classes. Through their celebration and preservation of cultural traditions, these Francophones, along with all the others who made Texas their home, have contributed to the widely varied musical mosaic of the state.

BIBLIOGRAPHY: Chris Strachwitz and Pete Welding, eds., *The American Folk Music Occasional* (New York: Oak, 1970). "The Vieux Carré" (www.new-orleans.la.us/cnowrb/vcc/hisfq.html), on the Official City of New Orleans Website, accessed January 15, 2002.

Gary Hartman

Frizzell, Lefty. Country musician; b. William Orville Frizzell, Corsicana, Texas, March 31, 1928; d. Nashville, Tennessee, July 19, 1975; son of Naamon Orville R. C. and Adie (Cox) Frizzell. His father's occupation was listed as "roustabout" on Lefty's birth certificate, and the family lived in Texas, Oklahoma, and Arkansas as they followed the oilfields. In the late 1930s Lefty had a featured spot on a children's radio program broadcast from KELD. In his teens he worked country fairs, dances, bars, and clubs throughout North Texas. He also married a girl named Alice. By the time he was sixteen, he was making frequent appearances in the Eldorado, Arkansas, area. He was only twenty-two when he made his first recordings for Columbia Records in 1950.

By 1951 Frizzell was an established recording star, with four songs on *Billboard*'s Top 10 chart. Jimmie Rodgers was an early and lasting influence, even though Frizzell did not imitate him. He did however, record an album in tribute called *Lefty Frizzell Sings the Songs of Jimmie Rodgers*. After 1952 Frizzell's career hit a slump due to the emergence of rock-and-roll. His lack of hit records during this time did not hurt him, however, on the country-fair and package-show circuit, where he remained a popular attraction well into the 1960s. He got on the charts again with the single "Long Black Veil" in 1959.

In 1953 he moved to Los Angeles and became a regular on "Town Hall Party," a radio and TV show produced in Los Angeles. In 1964 Frizzell recorded "Saginaw, Michigan," another number-one national hit. His career total of Top 10 songs was thirteen, three of which made number one. His most successful recordings include "If You've Got the Money, Honey, I've Got the Time," "I Love You in a Thousand Ways," "Always Late," and "I Want to be with You Always." His unique style and musical phrasing carried Frizzell's popularity into the decades following his death, and his influence can be heard in the inflections of such singers as Willie Nelson and George Jones.

BIBLIOGRAPHY: Bill C. Malone, *Country Music U.S.A.* (Austin: University of Texas Press, 1968). Bob Millard, *Country Music: 70 years of America's Favorite Music* (New York: Harper Perennial, 1993). Irwin Stambler and Grelun Landon, *Encyclopedia of Folk, Country and Western Music* (New York: St. Martin's, 1969; 2d. ed., 1983). Vertical files, Center for American History, University of Texas at Austin.

Phillip L. Fry

Fuchs, Adolph. Lutheran minister, musician, teacher, and pioneer German settler; b. Gustrow, Mecklenburg, Germany, September 19, 1805; d. Goeth ranch, near Cypress

Lutheran Minister Adolf Fuchs, 1894. Courtesy of Frieda Fuchs, UT Institute of Texan Cultures at San Antonio, No. 68-695. Immigrant Fuchs made many contributions to music education and the German music heritage in Texas.

Mill, Blanco County, Texas, December 1885. Fuchs was educated at Jena, Halle, and Göttingen. After marrying Luise J. Rüncker on July 10, 1829, and serving as pastor in Kölzow, Mecklenburg, from 1835 to 1845, he immigrated, with his wife and seven children, to Texas. In honor of his departure A. H. Hoffmann von Fallersleben wrote a farewell song, "Der Stern von Texas" ("The Texas Star"). Fuchs settled at Cat Spring, where copies of Hoffmann's *Texanische Lieder* (*Texas Songs*) arrived. The book, partly inspired by the pastor, bore the false imprint "San Felipe de Austin Bei Adolf Fuchs & Co."

Finding himself unprepared to cope with pioneer conditions, Fuchs became a music teacher at Baylor Female College in Independence. He was given credit for founding the first state-supported public school in Texas. In December 1853 the family located on the Lüder grant near Marble Falls, Burnet County. In spite of hardships, Fuchs's love of freedom made him enjoy frontier life. A good singer and great lover of music, he wrote settings to many outstanding German poems and both the text and music of other songs; at his home he and his family and friends frequently gathered for sing-songs around his piano, one of the first west of the Colorado.

BIBLIOGRAPHY: Rudolph L. Biesele, *The History of the German Settlements in Texas, 1831–1861* (Austin: Von Boeckmann–Jones, 1930; rpt. 1964). Ottilie Fuchs Goeth, *Was Grossmutter erzählt* (San Antonio: Passing Show Printing, 1915; trans. Irma Goeth Guenther as *Memoirs of a Texas Pioneer Grandmother*, Austin, 1969; rpt., Burnet, Texas: Eakin Press, 1982). Vertical files, Center for American History, University of Texas at Austin. *Lota M. Spell*

Fulbright, Dick. Jazz musician; b. Richard W. Fulbright, Paris, Texas, 1901; d. New York City, November 17, 1962. Fulbright played both tuba and string bass, and worked with a number of notable groups during his career. After first touring with the Virginia Minstrels, forming part of the De Luxe Syncopators from 1926 to 1928, and playing for a season in Florida with pianist–composer Luckey Roberts, Fulbright moved to New York, where he worked with tenor saxophonist Bingie Madison. In 1931–32 he was with Elmer Snowden and then worked regularly with Teddy Hill until 1937, touring Europe with Hill during this last year. In 1939 he joined Zutty Singleton, and after 1947 he worked with Noble Sissle. Fulbright retired from music in 1958.

BIBLIOGRAPHY: John Chilton, *Who's Who of Jazz: Storyville to Swing Street*, Fourth Edition (New York: Da Capo Press, 1985). Barry Kernfeld, ed., *The New Grove Dictionary of Jazz*, Second Edition (New York: Grove's Dictionaries, 2002). *Dave Oliphant*

Fuller, Bobby. Rock-and-roll performer; b. Goose Creek, Texas, October 22, 1943; d. Hollywood, California, July 18, 1966. When Fuller was fourteen his family moved to El Paso, where he began his career in music. In the late 1950s he was playing drums in a local band called the Counts. They performed in shopping-center parking lots around the city and drew criticism from members of various El Paso churches, who called them "tools of the devil." By 1962 Fuller had teamed up with rhythm guitarist Jim Reese, drummer Dewayne Quirico, and bassist Randy Fuller (Bobby's brother) to form the Bobby Fuller Four. Bobby, as singer and songwriter, became the group's front man.

With the financial help of his parents, Fuller built a recording studio and established his own record label, Exeter, which released his first recording, "I Fought the Law." He also opened the Teen Rendezvous Club, a hot spot in El Paso. After the club burned down in 1964, the band moved to Los Angeles and began recording with Bob Keene of Mustang Records. Keene had been successful with Richie Valens, Buddy Holly, and the Big Bopper, who all died in the same plane crash in 1959. In June 1965 Fuller's band hit nationally with "Let Her Dance." The Bobby Fuller Four rerecorded "I Fought The Law," and it soared to the national Top 10. Fuller made his film debut as the costar of *Bikini Party in a Haunted House.*

The Bobby Fuller Four went on two national tours and, after completing some unfinished recordings in Los Angeles, decided to break up. The group released two albums during Fuller's life, *King of the Wheels* (1965) and *I Fought the Law* (1966); subsequently, more were released: *Live Again* (1984), *The Best of the Bobby Fuller Four* (1981), the *Bobby Fuller Tapes, Volume 1* (1983), *Memories of Buddy Holly* (1984), and *The Bobby Fuller Instrumental Album* (1988).

On July 18, 1966, Fuller was found dead at the wheel of his car in front of his Hollywood apartment. Though authorities ruled his death a suicide, some friends believed that he may have been murdered.

BIBLIOGRAPHY: Norm N. Nite, *Rock On: The Illustrated Encyclopedia of Rock n' Roll* (New York: Crowell, 1974–). *Penguin Encyclopedia of Popular Music* (New York: Penguin, 1990). Vertical files, Center for American History, University of Texas at Austin. *Robert M. Blunt*

G

Garibay, Randy Beltran. The "Chicano Bluesman"; b. Ramiro Beltrán Garibay, Palm Heights neighborhood, San Antonio, December 3, 1939; d. May 23, 2002 (buried in San Antonio); son of Isidro and Feliz Garibay. His parents were Mexican immigrants, and the family divided its time between home in the San Antonio barrio and a life as migrant workers traveling throughout the American Midwest.

Garibay began his musical career early when he joined vocal harmony groups as the lead singer. He first sang with the Velvets and then the Pharaohs while attending Burbank High School. The Pharoahs performed in Texas and Mexico and sang backup vocals for Doug Sahm on some of Sahm's earliest recordings, including "Crazy Daisy." After learning to play guitar on a Sears and Roebuck instrument given to him by his brother for his eighteenth birthday, Garibay left the vocals-only doowop group to play guitar for Sonny Ace and Charlie & the Jives.

He played in local San Antonio blues clubs, including the renowned Eastwood Country Club, before joining the Dell-Kings. The group started a road adventure that took them first to California, and then to a record-breaking 280-week stint as the house band at the Casbar Lounge of the Las Vegas Sahara Hotel. At the Sahara the group backed headliners such as Jackie Wilson, Judy Garland, and Sammy Davis Jr.

The band members, thinking the group's name dated, took the name Los Blues, and went on to play a nightclub circuit that extended from Hawaii to Madison Square Garden in New York City. They also backed rhythm-and-blues acts, such as Curtis Mayfield and the O'Jays. Calling Garibay the glue that held the Dell-Kings and Los Blues together, band leader Frank Rodarte said, "In his later life, what he did for the whole Chicano nation with his blues was take things a step further to a place that wasn't violent, to a place that sang about depression but with humor."

In 1974 Garibay found himself back in San Antonio, where he pulled out all the stops to play his "puro pinche blues" style that showcased his unique ability to play Texas blues with a Chicano twist—combining blues, jazz, country, doowop, and classic Mexican boleros. He and his band Cats Don't Sleep were fixtures on the Texas music scene, playing a variety of styles from blues to jazz, and performing everywhere from clubs to festivals. "He played with everybody. He was a significant part of San Antonio music. Everywhere he went, he was always from San Antonio," said Regency Jazz Band bassist and bandleader George Prado.

In his later years Garibay released three solo CDs, *Barbacoa Blues*, *Chicano Blues Man*, and *Invisible Society*. The title track of the first CD became Garibay's signature song. "Barbacoa Blues" became synonymous with the Chicano Bluesman. Garibay won the Pura Vida Hispanic Music Award in 1994 and 1995, as well as the 1996 West Side Rhythm and Blues Award, and was chosen to be the featured performer at the 1998 Chicano Music Awards. He was a touring artist with the Texas Commission on the Arts from 1999 until his death. In 2001, Chicano filmmaker Efrain Guiterrez used eight original Garibay songs for the soundtrack of his film *Lowrider Spring Break en San Quilmas."*

Randy Garibay died of cancer and was survived by his wife, Virginia Schramm Garibay, a son, Randy G. Garibay, and a daughter, Michelle Garibay–Carey. Garibay's musical legacy continued with his brother, Ernie, who assumed leadership of Cats Don't Sleep. Michelle Garibay-Carey carried on as lead singer of her own band, Planet Soul, in San Antonio.

BIBLIOGRAPHY: San Antonio *Express–News*, May 24, 28, June 14, 2002. *All Music Guide* (http://www.allmusic .com), accessed November 1, 2002. *Jackie Potts*

Garland, Red. Jazz pianist; b. William M. Garland, Dallas, May 13, 1923; d. Dallas, April 23, 1984. He began his musical training on the clarinet as a child and played the alto saxophone at Booker T. Washington High School, though he never graduated. He quit to join the army during World War II and took impromptu piano lessons from other servicemen at Fort Huachuca in Sierra Vista, Arizona. After leaving the army in 1944 he joined a band led by Buster Smith, and a year later was touring the southwestern and eastern United States with Hot Lips Page. After the tour ended in 1946 in New York, Red Garland began playing in night clubs.

He was part of one of the most exciting periods of jazz evolution. Much of the 1950s jazz now regarded as classic was built upon Garland's characteristic block chords. Until 1956 he continued playing in New York and Philadelphia with such famous musicians as Charlie Parker, Billy Eckstine, Coleman Hawkins, and Fats Navarro. He achieved his greatest fame, however, as a member of Miles Davis's Quintet from 1955 to 1958, and was sideman on several of Davis's recordings, including "Workin' and Steamin'," "Round About Midnight," and "Milestones." The music that the group produced in the mid-1950s began a new era of jazz.

After leaving Miles Davis's Quintet, Garland started his own trio, which performed for several years. He cut three albums as leader in 1957—*All Mornin' Long*, *Soul Junction*, and *High Pressure*. He returned to Dallas in 1965 because of his mother's illness and made few public appearances until the late 1970s, when he performed several times in New York and recorded a new album, *Red Alert* (1977). His last performance was at the Park Central Jazz Festival in Dallas in 1981. Garland and his wife, Lillie (Newsom), had two children.

BIBLIOGRAPHY: Austin *American–Statesman*, April 28, 1984. Dallas *Morning News*, April 24, 1984. Barry Kernfeld, ed., *The New Grove Dictionary of Jazz* (London: Macmillan, 1988). Leonard Lyons, *The Great Jazz Pianists* (New York: Morrow, 1983). *Lisa C. Maxwell*

Garlinghouse, Esther C. Jonsson. Concert pianist; b. Ishpeming, Michigan, August 22, 1901; d. Amarillo, April 25, 1982 (buried in Llano Mausoleum, Amarillo); daughter of Esther and Andrew W. Jonsson, Swedish immigrants. The family moved to Chicago, where Esther's father served as organist at the Swedish Lutheran Church. At the age of three or four, according to one story, Esther played on the piano by ear a chorale her father had played earlier at church. She studied music first with her father and at the age of eight was playing Bach, Haydn, and Mozart. She began to study music formally when she was nine. Her family moved to Amarillo about 1909, and Esther gave her first recital there before an audience in the Henderson Music Store. She spent much of her adolescence and young adulthood in Amarillo in the home of B. V. Blackwell, who by 1919 had become her guardian.

She attended the University School of Music in Lincoln (later absorbed by the University of Nebraska) in 1918–19 and 1919–20, studying with Sidney Silber. She reportedly earned a bachelor's degree in music at the school when she was seventeen, although there is no official record of her having done so. She then studied in New York with Milan Blanchet and Sigismund Stojowski; in London; in Paris with Nadia Boulanger; and in Vienna with Emil Sauer. Esther Jonsson made her professional debut in Paris with the Orchestre de la Société des Concerts du Conservatoire, with Philippe Gaubert conducting. In 1931 she became the first American to perform as a soloist at the Quarter-Century Mozart Festival in Salzburg (this may have been the festival held in January 1931, commemorating the 175th anniversary of the composer's birth and featuring students from the Salzburg Mozarteum conservatory). She was also reportedly the first American chosen as an "official soloist" at the Salzburg Festival, held later in 1931. A reporter in Salzburg noted her relaxed approach, commenting that she confined her practice to three or four hours a day, while other pianists practiced twice as long.

Jonsson studied in Salzburg for a year and assisted Dr. Bernhard Paumgartner, director of the Salzburg Mozarteum, during one of the summer schools there. Although she gave concerts in the United States and Canada, she became better known in Europe, where she toured extensively and won special acclaim for her playing of Mozart. Her concert career harmonized with an interest in international relations and a gift for languages. In addition to a reading knowledge of Greek, she spoke Swedish, German, French, and Italian.

By 1935 her tours of southern Europe had led to a fascination with the music of the Balkans. In 1938 her study of Slavic music took her to southern Serbia. Equipped with a recording machine and movie camera, she sought out the music of villages where the radio had not yet intruded. The expedition to such isolated communities, sometimes little known even to scholars, necessitated both guides and frequent travel by burro. Esther Jonsson's collecting efforts may have been inspired in part by the ambitious program of field recordings made in Yugoslavia by Milman Parry and Albert Bates Lord in the mid-1930s. She translated some of the folk music she studied during these years into piano compositions and incorporated her films and recordings in her concerts whenever she performed Balkan music for American audiences. She also published articles about Balkan music and began work on a book-length manuscript concerning that subject. She was performing in Greece when Italy invaded that country in October 1940. About 1946 she returned to Yugoslavia and made additional field recordings. Her music, which she deemed the "music of the people," was broadcast in London, Vienna, Paris, and New York. The National Broadcasting Company included her in the inaugural radio program of the Dance International Festival.

In 1941 Esther Jonsson married Arthur A. Garlinghouse, and by 1949 they were residing in Amarillo. Mrs. Garlinghouse became involved in civic and cultural affairs and in the 1960s fought renovation and highway construction that would significantly alter or destroy some older areas of the city. She was described as a modest, deeply religious woman. The Indiana University Archives of Traditional Music has several collections of field recordings that she made of Yugoslavian poems and Bulgarian and Yugoslavian music.

BIBLIOGRAPHY: Amarillo *Globe–Times*, April 27, 1982. Archives of Traditional Music, Folklore Institute, Indiana University, *A Catalog of Phonorecordings of Music and Oral Data Held by the Archives of Traditional Music* (Boston: Hall, 1975). Dallas *Morning News*, September 20, 1931. Esther Johnson, "The Peasant Sings," *Christian Science Monitor Weekly Magazine Section*, July 17, 1935. Vertical files, Center for American History, University of Texas at Austin (Music and Musicians Scrapbook).

H. Allen Anderson

Gary, John. Singer and stage and television star; b. John Gary Strader, Watertown, New York, November 29, 1932; d. Dallas, January 4, 1998; son of Harold Strader and Merle Dawson Harrington. Gary became a popular stage and television star during the 1960s because of his soulful, heartfelt singing style and three-octave range. His signature song, "Danny Boy," revealed his love for Irish tunes, but his singing repertoire included show tunes, country hits, and romantic ballads.

He began singing at age five with his older sister, Shirley, at amateur talent shows. At age nine, he won a three-year scholarship as a boy soprano to the Cathedral School of St. John the Divine in New York. At age ten he won two "Pins of Distinction" from the American Theater Wing and the Merchant's Seaman's Club for the Stage Door Canteen..

By Gary's twelfth birthday, his parents were divorced. After he toured the Southern States with Macon Conservatory pianist Frank Pursley, he went to live with his mother and three siblings in California. He attended North Hollywood Junior and Senior High and enrolled in Hollywood Professional School, while performing as a regular staff member on CBS / KNX radio. He also sang for tips as he worked as a waiter, doorman, and usher at various restaurants, hotels, and theaters. His stepfather, Bob Yale, became Gary's agent and manager and promoted his early career in Hollywood. As a teenager, Gary made stage and radio appearances with Lionel Barrymore, Paul Whiteman's Orchestra, Billy Wardell, Martha Tilton, Marie Wilson, Jack Cooper, George Jessel, Ken Murray's Blackouts, and others.

When he was seventeen, his voice finally began to crack and change. Consequently, he decided his singing career was over and joined the Marine Corps, in which he served as a military policeman and chaplain's assistant. But he began singing in military chapel services and found his voice had matured to a brilliant tenor with rich baritone flexibility. After being discharged from the service at age twenty, Gary met Bob McGimsey, who became his mentor and manager. Gary made "demo" recordings for songwriters such as Harry Ruby, Sammy Fain, Jimmy McHuch, Hoagy Carmichael, Johnny Mercer, Victor Young, and Henry Mancini. He performed regularly on Don McNeill's popular network radio show, Breakfast Club, and then began a steady career making television and stage appearances across America.

About 1962 he signed with RCA records. During Gary's affiliation with RCA, he recorded more than twenty albums; the first was *Catch a Rising Star*. He also recorded about twenty-five albums for various independent labels. He performed on the Tonight Show, the Ed Sullivan Show, the Bell Telephone Hour, Dick Clark's Bandstand, and the Danny Kaye Show. In the early 1970s, a summer-replacement program for Danny Kaye's CBS television show evolved into Gary's own syndicated television variety show, the John Gary Show, which ran for three years. Gary also sang in stage productions—*The Student Prince* and *Camelot*, for instance—at venues such as the Kansas City Starlight Theater, the Dallas Theater in the Round, and the Dallas Crystal Palace. Gary's popularity continued well into the 1990s, and he sang with numerous symphonies and at various concert halls, conventions, and special events around the world.

In 1971 he moved to Richardson, Texas, and married Lee Wilson. Gary also had children from previous relationships with Muriel Stafford Getz and Lois Reidy McDonnell. His family included four sons, two adopted sons, and seven stepchildren. Although Gary's singing talents made him famous, he excelled at many other interests throughout his life, such as boxing, archery, and underwater diving. Among his achievements are two published books of poetry and numerous published songs, including "Possum Song," "I'll Say It All Again," "One Red Rose," and "I'll Never Fall in Love Again."

He received many honors and awards, including the National Association of Recording Arts and Sciences "Most Promising Vocalist" award in 1963, mention in the California and United States congressional records, and numerous appearances as Grand Marshall at St. Patrick's Day parades throughout America. Though he scored no hit singles, some of his mid-1960s albums rose to the top twenty, including *The Nearness of You, Encore,* and *A Little Bit of Heaven*. Other popular albums by Gary include *Songs of Love and Romance* (Collector's Choice, 1994), *Ireland's Greatest Hits* and *The Very Best of John Gary*

(RCA, 1997), and *The Essential John Gary* (BMG Records, 2001).

In 1991 Gary was diagnosed with cancer, to which he succumbed in 1998. He died at Baylor University Medical Center in Dallas.

BIBLIOGRAPHY: Dallas *Morning News*, January 6, 1998; January 11, 1998. John Bush, "John Gary Discography," *All Music Guide* (http://www.websterrecords.com/artists/gary.html), accessed February 1, 2003. *John Gary Biography* (http://www.johngary.com/gary_bio2.html), accessed February 1, 2003.　　　*Cheryl L. Simon*

Gee, Matthew Jr. Trombonist; b. Houston, November 25, 1925; d. New York City, July 18, 1979. Music critic Leonard Feather considered him one of the "best and most underrated bop-influenced trombonists." Gee began, however, on trumpet and moved to baritone horn (an instrument on which he recorded with the Duke Ellington Orchestra in 1959), before settling by age eleven on the trombone. His father was a bass player, and his brother Herman was, like Matthew, a trombonist. Reportedly Gee took up the trombone after hearing Trummy Young, the trombone star with the Jimmie Lunceford Orchestra and later a member of the Louis Armstrong All-Stars.

Gee attended Alabama State College and then in New York performed with the Coleman Hawkins band before serving in the army during World War II. Following his tour in the service, he worked with Dizzy Gillespie in 1946 and with various name jazz figures during the early 1950s, among them Gene Ammons, Sonny Stitt, Count Basie, fellow Houstonian Illinois Jacquet, Lou Donaldson, and singer Sarah Vaughn.

In 1956 Riverside Records issued Gee's album entitled *Jazz by Gee* (reissued in 1996 as a CD), which includes fellow Texan Kenny Dorham on trumpet. This album exhibits Gee's finest work as a soloist. Unfortunately, as several commentators have noted, his later performances do not fulfill the promise of his early years. Critic Orrin Keepnews described Gee's style as "driving" and "plunging," with "in-tempo guttural throat sounds with which—in some unexplainable way—Gee occasionally seems to answer himself while playing!" Gee can be expressive as a ballad player, as well as being quite agile in producing turns and also darting phrases that are definitely in the bop tradition.

From 1959 to 1963, Gee was with the Duke Ellington Orchestra and can be heard on the 1960 Ellington album *Blues in Orbit*, which features two compositions by Gee: "The Swingers Get the Blues Too" and "The Swinger's Jump." The first of these is credited to Gee and Ellington, but Gee had already recorded "The Swingers Get the Blues Too" in 1956 on an Atlantic Records album entitled *Soul Groove*, featuring tenorist Johnny Griffin. Even here the trombonist's own solo work lacks the spirit and inventiveness of his other 1956 album, *Jazz by Gee*. As for Gee's solo performances on the Ellington album, he is most impressive on "The Swinger's Jump." Although the album cover does not indicate that the trombonist solos on this piece, his style is clearly recognizable and distinct from that of Booty Wood, the other trombone soloist on Gee's composition. Gee also solos on Ellington's "C Jam Blues."

In later years Gee made appearances with various small groups, including one with tenorist Paul Quinichette, but not much was heard from the trombonist to make his a vital name in the period of free jazz, or even for that matter of hard bop in the late 1950s and early 1960s. Nonetheless, Gee, along with Henry Coker, was probably the most important bop-inflected trombonist from Texas.

BIBLIOGRAPHY: Leonard Feather and Ira Gitler, *The Biographical Encyclopedia of Jazz* (New York: Oxford University Press, 1999). Orrin Keepnews, liner notes to *Jazz by Gee* (Riverside OJCCD-1884-2, 1996).

Dave Oliphant

George, Zelma Watson. Diplomat, social-program administrator, musicologist, opera singer, and college administrator; b. Hearne, Texas, December 8, 1903; d. Cleveland, Ohio, July 3, 1994; daughter of Samuel E. J. and Lena (Thomas) Watson. Zelma's father was a Baptist minister. She lived in Hearne, Palestine, and Dallas and briefly in Hot Springs, Arkansas, during her childhood. She later remembered the presence of a number of prominent black leaders who spoke at her father's church and visited her home in Dallas. W. E. B. DuBois, Booker T. Washington, Carter Woodson, Mary Branch Terrell, and Walter White were a few of the notable visitors who frequently discussed issues relating to black Americans in her presence.

Her family left Dallas when her father incurred the wrath of some white Dallas citizens for his assistance to black prisoners. Threatened by vigilantes, the family moved to Topeka, Kansas, where her father accepted another pastorate in 1917. After graduating from the Topeka public schools, she enrolled in the University of Chicago. Because the university would not permit her to reside in the dormitory with white women, her father accepted a pastorate in Chicago, and Zelma lived with her family while attending college. She received a bachelor's degree in sociology from the University of Chicago in 1924, studied the pipe organ at Northwestern University from 1924 to 1926, and was a voice student at the American Conservatory of Music in Chicago from 1925 to 1927. She received a master's degree in personnel administration from New York University in 1943 and a Ph.D. in sociology from New York University in 1954. Her doctoral dissertation, A Guide to Negro Music: Toward A Sociology of Negro Music, catalogued approximately 12,000 musical compositions either inspired or written by African Americans. She received honorary doctorates from Heidelberg College (Ohio) and Baldwin Wallace College in 1961 and Cleveland State University in 1974.

During the 1920s, after her graduation from the University of Chicago, Zelma Watson served as a social worker for the Associated Charities of Evanston, Illinois, and was a probation officer for the juvenile court of Chicago. From 1932 to 1937 she was dean of women and director of personnel administration at Tennessee State University in Nashville. She moved in 1937 to Los Angeles, where she established and directed the Avalon Community Center until 1942. With the assistance of a grant from the Rockefeller Foundation, she then moved to Cleveland, Ohio, where she researched her dissertation and began a lengthy career of civic involvement through membership in such organizations as the YWCA, the Council of Church Women, the Girl Scouts, the Conference of Christians and Jews, the League of Women Voters, the Fund for Negro Students, the Urban League, and the NAACP. She married Clayborne George of Cleveland, Ohio, in 1944; the couple had no children.

Beginning in 1949, Mrs. George performed in several stage presentations. She played and sang the lead role in Menotti's *The Medium*, an opera that ran for sixty-seven nights at the Karamu Theater in Cleveland and for thirteen weeks in New York City at the Edison Theater. After *The Medium* closed on Broadway, George received the Merit Award of the National Association of Negro Musicians. She also acted in Menotti's *The Consul* at the Cleveland Playhouse and performed the role of Mrs. Peachum in Kurt Weill's *The Three Penny Opera* at the Karamu.

During the 1950s she became involved with national and international political issues as an adviser to the Eisenhower administration. She toured with the Defense Advisory Committee on Women in the Armed Services from 1954 to 1957 and served in 1958 on the president's committee to plan the White House Conference on Children and Youth. She was on the executive council of the American Society for African Culture from 1959 to 1971, traveled to Europe and Asia through the Educational Exchange Program, and served as a member of the United States delegation to the United Nations in 1960. Beginning in the 1960s, she served as a speaker for the W. Colston Leigh Lecture Bureau, the Danforth Foundation, and the American Association of Colleges, usually addressing secondary schools, universities, civic clubs, and corporate employees.

Mrs. George attended a "Ban the Bomb" conference in Ghana in 1963 and attended the first World Festival of Negro Art with Marion Anderson and Duke Ellington at Senegal in 1966. Also in 1966 she became executive director of the Cleveland Job Corps Center for Women. She delivered the keynote address for the first Student International Security Council Meeting in 1969. President Richard Nixon named her to the Corporation for Public Broadcasting, where she worked in 1971–72. She won the Dag Hammarskjöld Award for contributions to international understanding in 1961, the Dahlberg Peace Award in 1969, and the Mary Bethune Gold Medallion in 1973. She received good-citizenship honors from various civic and academic organizations. An exhibit recognizing her achievements as an "outstanding Texan" was mounted at the Fort Concho Museum in San Angelo in 1974. Riding in a motorized wheelchair, she participated in a march against nuclear arms in 1982, when she was eighty-eight. Zelma George was a Baptist and a member of the Alpha Kappa Alpha sorority.

BIBLIOGRAPHY: Houston *Chronicle*, July 5, 1994. Rowena Woodham Jelliffe, *Here's Zelma* (Cleveland: Alpha Omega Chapter, Alpha Kappa Alpha Sorority, 1971). *Who's Who Among Black Americans*, 1985. Ruthe Winegarten, *Texas Women* (Austin: Eakin Press, 1985).

Paul M. Lucko

La Grange Band, ca. 1900. Courtesy Edward Gips. The German band tradition survives today in various Central Texas communities.

German Music. The earliest reference to music among Texas German immigrants dates from 1834, when the elder Robert Justus Kleberg imported a piano and music books to Harrisburg. In 1837 Mary Austin Holley enjoyed the informal singing of some Germans on a boat trip between Galveston and Houston. Two years later German musical soirées were held at Kessler's Arcade in Houston, and in 1840 Emil Heerbrugger gave recitals on violin, horn, and guitar, with piano accompaniment, at the Capitol.

With colonization by the Adelsverein after 1844, German music began to flourish in Texas, and German musicians became more influential, even in the centers where the population was not primarily German. Johann N. S. Menger was active in San Antonio as a piano teacher in 1847, and Franz Xavier Heilig became a music teacher for the city's public schools in 1853, to be joined later by Christoph Plagge and Henry Grossmann. Likewise Joseph Petmecky, and later Udo Rhodius, J. Messner, and William Besserer taught in Austin, and other Germans taught in Houston, Galveston, Dallas, and other cities. About 1879 Julius Weiss, from Saxony, went to Texarkana, where he taught a young student named Scott Joplin, destined to become "King of Ragtime."

Singing was among the earliest leisure activities, first with informal groups in Galveston, Houston, and New Braunfels in the mid-1840s, and then with formal male singing societies, including the San Antonio Männergesang-Verein (1847), New Braunfels Germania (1850), Austin Männerchor (1852), and Houston Männer-Gesangverein. In 1853 the societies held a *Sängerfest* (singers' festival) in New Braunfels and formed the Texas State Sängerbund (singers' league). The German singing societies ultimately became the prime promoters of serious music in Texas before World War I.

Other leagues served their respective locales: the Hill Country, Gillespie County, Guadalupe Valley, and South Texas. Singing societies existed at one time or another in roughly ninety Texas communities. The oldest surviving singing society is the Beethoven Männerchor (San Antonio), founded in August 1865. Mixed choruses were begun outside of church settings: the New Braunfels Concordia (1860), San Antonio Mendelssohn (1872), Houston Philharmonic Society (1872), and Austin Musical Union (1888), for instance. These often signaled increased participation by non-German Texans and wider musical education throughout the community.

Opera arrived early in Texas in one form or another; Emil Heerbrugger's 1840 Houston recitals contained overtures and potpourris of popular operatic airs. Musical immigrants brought opera scores and selections with them from Europe and often sang them around the family piano. Frederick Law Olmsted heard excerpts from Mozart's *Don*

Giovanni during a social gathering in Sisterdale in 1854, and operatic choruses were standard repertoire for singing societies before the Civil War. Weber's *Der Freischütz* (or extensive portions of it) was reputedly staged by the Casino Club in San Antonio in the late 1850s. Dallas saw a complete local production of Friedrich von Flotow's *Martha* with piano accompaniment in 1868 and again, with orchestra, in 1875. San Antonio opened its Grand Opera House in 1886 with Donizetti's *Lucrezia Borgia*, performed by the Emma Abbott Opera Company, and later witnessed Wagner's *Lohengrin* in the same theater. The final state *Sängerfest* (1916) before World War I included extensive selections from Wagner's *Die Meistersinger*, which was not performed whole in Texas until 1974.

Musical instruments among the Germans in early Texas were often of high quality: Heinrich Backofen, son of a prominent Darmstadt clarinet maker, brought "a whole chest" of instruments with him to Bettina in 1847. A piano trio consisting of the violinist Listich, cellist Scheliche and pianist C. D. Adolph Douai was active in San Antonio and New Braunfels in 1852–53. Bands ranged from a single fiddler playing for dances in the 1840s to full concert ensembles by the 1880s and were often connected with the conductor's teaching activities, either in school or private studio. The German band tradition survives today in the American Legion bands of Seguin and New Braunfels, as well as the Beethoven Concert Band of San Antonio. In the 1870s the Germans were responsible for the first symphony orchestras in Texas.

The Texas German population included a number of composers. Gottfried Joseph Petmecky (New Braunfels), Adolph Douai (San Antonio), Simon Menger (San Antonio), and C. Wilke (La Grange) all wrote works for male chorus in the 1850s. The last also composed and arranged the music for *Texas Fahrten*, a song pageant written by Friedrich Hermann Seele. Adolph Fuchs wrote and composed several songs in the 1840s and later. Menger wrote a few piano pieces, as did Gabriel Katzenberger and John M. Steinfeldt in the 1880s and 1890s. W. C. A. Thielepape of San Antonio left twenty-seven compositions dated from 1840 to 1899, and conductors Carl Venth and Arthur Claassen were already noted composers when they arrived in Texas during the decade before World War I.

BIBLIOGRAPHY: Theodore Albrecht, German Singing Societies in Texas (Ph.D. dissertation, North Texas State University, 1975). Theodore Albrecht, "Heinrich Backofen, Sohn: Musical Instrument Maker of Darmstadt and Bettina," *The Clarinet*, May 1976. Theodore Albrecht, "The Music Libraries of the German Singing Societies in Texas, 1850–1855," *Notes: The Quarterly Journal of the Music Library Association* 31 (March 1975). Ottilie Fuchs Goeth, *Was Grossmutter erzählt* (San Antonio: Passing Show Printing, 1915; trans. Irma Goeth Guenther as *Memoirs of a Texas Pioneer Grandmother*, Austin, 1969; rpt., Burnet, Texas: Eakin Press, 1982). Oscar Haas, *A Chronological History of the Singers of German Song in Texas* (New Braunfels, Texas, 1948). Hermann Seele, *Travels in Texas*, trans. Theodore Gish (Austin: Nortex, 1985). Lota M. Spell, *Music in Texas* (Austin, 1936; rpt., New York: AMS, 1973).   *Theodore Albrecht*

Gilley's. A nightclub in Pasadena, Texas; open from 1970 to 1990. The club, owned by Sherwood Cryer, had been previously called Shelly's. Cryer decided to reopen it in 1970 under the name Gilley's, with budding musician Mickey Gilley as partner. Gilley, who grew up in Ferriday, Louisiana, with cousins Jerry Lee Lewis and Jimmy Swaggart, wanted to call the club the "Den of Sin," but Sherwood insisted on naming it Gilley's, since Mickey Gilley himself was to be the headlining act.

Gilley's launched Mickey Gilley's career, for the club was an instant success. It filled to capacity nightly soon after the opening. It had a shooting gallery, showers for truckers, a rodeo arena with mechanical bulls, pool tables, punching bags, and a dance floor big enough for thousands. It had a 6,000-person capacity and is listed in the *Guinness Book of World Records* as the world's largest honky-tonk. Gilley's was open seven days a week, from 10 A.M. to 2 A.M. Its motto was "We Doze but We Never Close." Dramatic economic growth occurred along the Texas Gulf Coast in the late 1970s, especially in Houston. Many residents of Pasadena worked in the Houston-area petrochemical plants, and they used Gilley's as a place to socialize.

Loretta Lynn, Ernest Tubb, Emmylou Harris, and Roseanne Cash all played at Gilley's, along with many other famous country artists. Most performances were recorded live and archived, and the nightly shows were broadcast weekly on radio from 1977 to 1989. "Live from Gilley's" was carried nationally by over 500 stations. Thanks to Armed Forces Radio, the show was also broadcast around the globe.

In 1978 Aaron Latham published "The Ballad of the Urban Cowboy: America's Search for True Grit" in the September 12 issue of *Esquire* magazine. Cryer had urged Latham to write this article, based on Latham's experiences at Gilley's, in hopes that a movie would be made of the story. The movie *Urban Cowboy* began filming in 1979. Most of the movie was filmed inside Gilley's. It starred John Travolta and Debra Winger as the characters Bud and Sissy, who meet at Gilley's, marry, divorce, and then reunite.

Gator Conley, a regular at Gilley's, was considered the best dancer and mechanical bull rider; the director used him frequently throughout the movie. Conley stated, "A lot of people say the movie made Gilley's, but actually it was the other way around." *Urban Cowboy*, a box office hit, brought Gilley's into American pop culture and made the club one of Houston's main tourist draws. Even after the fad passed, Gilley's continued to draw crowds. The Academy of Country Music awarded Gilley's the title "best nightclub of the year" in 1984.

Eventually Mickey Gilley became frustrated because he believed that Cryer failed to maintain the place and present quality acts. Cryer refused to make major renovations over the years, and fans were complaining of dirty restrooms and a bad parking lot, among other problems. Gilley, who thought this reflected poorly on his name, sued to gain control of the club in 1988, claiming that Cryer had been keeping profits. The jury awarded Gilley the club and forced Cryer to pay Gilley $17 million. Cryer had to give up much of his real estate to pay the debt.

The club operated under Gilley briefly after the lawsuit, until the judge ordered it closed in 1989 due to loss of profits. Gilley rescued the tapes of the live shows before a suspicious fire burned the club down in 1990. The Pasadena school district has owned the lot since 1992. As of 2002 the property was still mired in tax liens, unpaid taxes amounted to more than the property was worth, and PISD was searching for a buyer. The restored Gilley's sign can be seen about a mile away at the Cowboy Ranch restaurant.

BIBLIOGRAPHY: Bob Claypool, *Saturday Night at Gilley's* (New York: Delilah / Grove Press, 1980). Robert Crowe, "Mickey Gilley," *All Music Guide* (http://www/all-music. com/cg/amg/dll), accessed January 16, 2003. Gregory Curtis, "Looking for Love," *Texas Monthly*, November 1998. Bill Porterfield, *The Greatest Honky-Tonks in Texas* (Dallas: Taylor, 1983). *Heather Milligan*

Gilliland, Henry Clay. Fiddler; b. Missouri, 1845; d. Altus, Oklahoma, April 21, 1924. With Eck Robertson, Henry Gilliland recorded the first country music record in 1922.

He had immigrated to Texas with his family in 1853. The Gilliland brothers were noted fiddle players in the frontier region near Weatherford. Gilliland enlisted in 1863 in the Second Texas Cavalry, Arizona Brigade, and remained in the Confederate service throughout the Civil War, seeing action in South Texas and during the Red River Campaign. After the war, he developed a reputation as an Indian fighter and Texas Ranger, and held numerous public offices in Texas and Oklahoma. He was also active in the affairs of various Confederate veterans' organizations, eventually obtaining the rank of lieutenant general in the United Confederate Veterans.

Gilliland won many many fiddle contests in North Texas during the late nineteenth and early twentieth centuries. He was a driving force behind the organization of the Old Fiddlers' Association of Texas (1901) and served for many years as its secretary. He deftly combined Confederate veterans' issues with fiddle contests and used the contests as a means to disseminate "Lost Cause" ideology. In 1910 Gilliland performed at the opening of the State Fair of Texas. The following year he tied for the title of world's championship fiddler at a contest held in Little Rock, Arkansas. Along with Jesse Roberts and the legendary Matt Brown, Gilliland toured northeastern Texas in a fiddling exhibition shortly after the championship contest.

In 1922 he attended the United Confederate Veterans' reunion in Richmond, Virginia. After the convention, he and Eck Robertson journeyed to the New York studio of Victor Records and recorded two sides, "Arkansas Traveler" and "Turkey in the Straw." The session resulted in the first recordings of what came to be called country music. Upon Gilliland's death, the magazine *Confederate Veteran* memorialized him as "the greatest fiddler of the world."

BIBLIOGRAPHY: Kevin S. Fontenot, "Country Music's Confederate Grandfather: Henry C. Gilliland," *Country Music Annual 2001* (Lexington: University Press of Kentucky, 2001). Henry C. Gilliland, *Life and Battles of Henry C. Gilliland for Seventy Years* (Altus, Oklahoma, ca. 1915). Bill C. Malone, *Country Music U.S.A.* (Austin: University of Texas Press, 1985). Charles Wolfe, *The Devil's Box* (Nashville: Country Music Foundation and Vanderbilt University Press, 1997). *Kevin S. Fontenot*

Gillis, Donald Eugene. Composer, conductor, musician, teacher, and producer; b. Cameron, Missouri, June 17, 1912; d. Columbia, South Carolina, January 10, 1978. He and his family moved in 1931 to Fort Worth, where Gillis attended Texas Christian University and studied composition with Keith Mixson. At TCU Gillis played trombone in and served as assistant director of the university band and wrote music for two musicals. He also played trombone in the staff orchestra of radio station WBAP from 1932 to 1935 and directed a symphony orchestra of his own at Polytechnic Baptist Church from 1935 to 1942. He earned a B.M. degree at TCU in 1935 and continued to serve on the faculty there until 1942. He also taught at Southwestern Baptist Theological Seminary during this period. He did graduate work in composition at North Texas State University in Denton in 1942 and was awarded his M.M. degree in 1943. He also attended Louisiana State and Columbia universities.

In 1942 Gillis became production director for radio station WBAP. In December 1943 he transferred to the NBC affiliate in Chicago. A year later he went to New York to become producer and scriptwriter for the NBC Symphony Orchestra, directed by Arturo Toscanini. Gillis produced several NBC radio programs, including "Serenade to America" and "NBC Concert Hour." After Toscanini retired in 1954 Gillis, serving as president of the Symphony Foundation of America, was instrumental in helping to form the Symphony of the Air, using members of the old NBC Symphony. He also produced the radio program "Toscanini: The Man Behind the Legend," which ran for several years on NBC after the Italian conductor's death. Other posts held by Gillis during his long and varied career include vice president of the Interlochen Music Camp in Michigan (1958–61), chairman of the music department at Southern Methodist University (1967–68), chairman of the arts department at Dallas Baptist College (1968–72), and composer-in-residence and chairman of the Institute of Media Arts at the University of South Carolina (1973–78). From 1968 on, Gillis was vitally interested in mixed media.

He composed prolifically in virtually all contemporary styles and genres. Much of his music emphasizes the comical, and his works often carry whimsical titles that convey the satire and humor of his music. One of his artistic goals was to interpret his American background musically. His music therefore draws on popular material, particularly emphasizing jazz, which Gillis viewed as a dynamic and vitalizing element in American music. He assimilated popular influences in a simple and straightforward style aimed at communicating with his audiences through an emphasis on clear, accessible, melodic writing. As a result of his popular appeal, his music has achieved considerable success and has been performed by a number of major orchestras, including the NBC Symphony and the Boston Pops.

His more than 150 works include ten symphonies; six string quartets; *The Panhandle*, a symphonic suite; *The Alamo*; *Symphony No. 5½*, "a symphony for fun," the world premiere of which was conducted by Toscanini; *Por-*

trait of a Frontier Town; *Alice in Orchestralia*; *Texas Centennial March*; *Amarillo—A Symphonic Celebration*; and *Toscanini: A Portrait of a Century*. Gillis also wrote three books: a humorous unpublished autobiography, *And Then I Wrote* (1948); a satirical conducting methodology, *The Unfinished Symphony Conductor* (1967); and an important textbook in the media field, *The Art of Media Instruction* (1973). Gillis's papers are housed at the University of North Texas in Denton.

BIBLIOGRAPHY: David Ewen, ed., *American Composers: A Biographical Dictionary* (New York: Putnam, 1982). Stanley Sadie, ed., *The New Grove Dictionary of Music and Musicians* (Washington: Macmillan, 1980).

Larry Wolz

Glenn, Lloyd. Blues pianist, writer, and arranger; b. San Antonio, November 21, 1909; d. Los Angeles, May 23, 1985. Glenn is best known as one of the pioneers of the "West Coast" blues sounds. At the age of nineteen he joined Millard McNeal's Melody Boys. The next year he moved to Dallas, where he played with the Royal Aces and later with the De Luxe Melody Boys. Throughout the 1930s and early 1940s, he played with a variety of jazz bands around San Antonio, including Don Albert and "Boots" Douglas and His Buddies.

In 1942 Glenn left the Lone Star State for California, where he worked at the Douglas Aircraft Factory. He joined the Walter Johnson trio in 1944, but left the next year to form his own group. Glenn accompanied T-Bone Walker on his classic 1947 hit "Call It Stormy Monday." That same year, he began to record his own songs for the Imperial label. In 1949 he signed with the Swing Time label, which was owned by Jack Lauderdale. After Swing Time's demise in 1954 Glenn recorded for Aladdin Records and returned to Imperial in 1962. A couple of his more popular cuts included "Twistville" and the 1962 record "Young Dale." He also played on several Lowell Fulson records in the 1950s and 1960s and wrote Fulson's number one hit, "Blue Shadows."

Glenn remained active throughout the 1960s and 1970s. He worked with T-Bone Walker and played with B. B. King on his *My Kind of Blues* and *Lucille* recordings. Toward the end of his career, he played at clubs in Los Angeles and made an appearance at the Hollywood Bowl. He also performed at the Monterey Jazz Festival and toured Europe with his musician son, Lloyd Glenn, Jr. He died of a heart attack.

BIBLIOGRAPHY: John Chilton, *Who's Who of Jazz: Storyville to Swing Street*, Fourth Edition (New York: Da Capo Press, 1985). Michael Erlewine, ed., *All Music Guide to the Blues* (San Francisco: Miller Freeman, 1999). Barry Kernfeld, ed., *The New Grove Dictionary of Jazz* (New York: Macmillan, 1988). Colin Larkin, ed., *The Guinness Encyclopedia of Popular Music* (New York: Guinness, 1998). Los Angeles *Times*, May 25, 1985. Tony Russell, *The Blues from Robert Johnson to Robert Cray* (New York: Schirmer, 1977). Robert Santelli, *The Big Book of Blues* (New York: Penguin, 1993). Frank Scott, *The Down Home Guide to the Blues* (Chicago: Cappella, 1991).

James Head

Glenn, Tyree. Jazz trombonist; b. Evans Glenn, Corsicana, Texas, November 23, 1912; d. May 18, 1974. Glenn played trombone and vibraphone with local Texas bands before moving in the early 1930s to Washington, D.C., where he performed with several prominent bands of the Swing Era. He joined Tommy Myles's band in 1934 and played with it until 1936.

After he left Myles, Glenn moved to Los Angeles and performed with several well-known entertainers, including Eddie Barefield, Lionel Hampton, Eddie Mallory, and Charlie Echols. He joined Cab Calloway in 1939 and was an important member of the band until he left it in 1946. From 1947 to 1951 he played with Duke Ellington's orchestra. During the 1950s Glenn did some radio, television, and acting work. In 1953 he joined Jack Sterling's New York daily radio show, with which he remained until 1963. After leaving radio, Glenn joined Louis Armstrong's band and played with it from 1965 until Armstrong died in 1971. He formed his own band after Satchmo's death and performed with it until shortly before he died.

Although Glenn primarily recorded with other bands, such as those of Ellington, Armstrong, and Sy Oliver, he also recorded albums of his own—*Tyree Glenn at the Roadhouse* (1958), *Tyree Glenn with Strings* (1960), and *Tyree Glenn at the London House* (1961). He also wrote "Sultry Serenade," which was recorded by Duke Ellington and Erroll Garner. Glenn died of cancer and was survived by two sons, Tyree Jr. and Roger, both musicians.

BIBLIOGRAPHY: Leonard Feather, ed., *The Encyclopedia of Jazz* (New York: Horizon Press, 1955). Leonard Feather, ed., *The Encyclopedia of Jazz in the Sixties* (New York: Horizon Press, 1966). Leonard Feather and Ira Gitler, eds., *The Encyclopedia of Jazz in the Seventies* (New York: Horizon Press, 1976). Colin Larkin, ed., *The Guinness Encyclopedia of Popular Music* (New York: Guinness, 1995). Eileen Southern, *Biographical Dictionary of Afro-American and African Musicians* (Westport Connecticut: Greenwood Press, 1982).

James Head

Glinn, Lillian. Blues singer and vaudeville performer; b. Hillsboro, Texas, ca. 1902; d. California (?), 19—? She moved to Dallas when she was in her twenties. Texas blues singer Hattie Burleson discovered her while she was singing in a Dallas church and encouraged her to pursue a musical career. Dallas entrepreneur R. T. Ashford, who later founded the Dallas Negro Chamber of Commerce, helped Glinn secure a recording contract with Columbia Records in 1927. She cut her first record for Columbia in December 1927, and over the next two years she recorded over twenty-two sides, including the popular tunes "Black Man Blues," "Doggin' Me," and "Atlanta Blues."

Glinn, who sang in a heavy contralto voice, was often accompanied by banjo, piano, and bass brass instruments. Her songs, often labeled "race music," revealed her life experiences in Dallas and the harsh realities of life on the streets. Her lyrics, some of which advised other women how to keep their men and how to handle unreliable lovers, often included strong sexual overtones. Between 1927 and 1929 Glinn became nationally known as a result of her recordings. On April 24, 1928, she cut her best-known record, "Shake It Down," in a New Orleans session. In April 1929 she recorded a session in Atlanta, probably accompanied by a white jazz band. Later that year, she recorded another session in Dallas that included the pop song "I'm Through (Shedding Tears Over You)."

Her musical career, unfortunately, was extremely brief. After recording for only two years, she gave up her "secular" work to return to the church. In the early 1930s she moved to California, where she married Rev. O.P. Smith and distanced herself from her former life.

BIBLIOGRAPHY: Alan B. Govenar and Jay F. Brakefield, *Deep Ellum and Central Track* (Denton: University of North Texas Press, 1998). Dallas *Morning News*, September 26, 1999. Colin Larkin, ed., *The Guinness Encyclopedia of Popular Music* (New York: Guinness, 1998). Dave Oliphant, *Texan Jazz* (Austin: University of Texas Press, 1996). Frank Scott, *The Down Home Guide to the Blues* (Chicago: Cappella, 1991). *James Head*

González, Balde. Singer, composer, and instrumentalist; b. Beeville, Texas, May 30, 1928; d. Houston, 1974. González was born blind, and when he was eight, his mother, María Delgado, sent him to the State School for the Blind in Austin. In the capital city he learned to play several instruments, including the violin and piano. He performed with a few of his classmates—mostly popular music at local parties.

In 1948, before finishing school, he returned to Beeville, where he formed his own orchestra, comprising a trumpet, alto and tenor saxophones, contrabass, trap drums, and piano. In 1949 he signed with Melco, a small recording company in Corpus Christi. He recorded boleros and foxtrots in a cosmopolitan style, singing in Spanish and English in a soft, soothing, baritone. By the early 1950s González had enlarged his band and signed with Ideal Records. The hits he composed included "Oye Corazón," "Qué me puede ya importar," and "Cuéntame tu vida."

His style of *orquesta*, an example of the *jaiton* or "high class" ensemble, emphasized an Americanized repertoire. In the 1960s, as his fame began to diminish, González pursued his musical career as a soloist by playing piano and singing in clubs in the Houston area. Without his orchestra, he relied on mainstream popular music. His choice of musical style and his avoidance of the ranchero orchestra genre associated with Beto Villa and Isidro López somewhat limited his popularity. Nevertheless, in 1985 he was inducted into the Tejano Music Hall of Fame, which recognized him for his "excellence in the Tejano music industry."

BIBLIOGRAPHY: Manuel Peña, *Música Tejana: The Cultural Economy of Artistic Transformation* (College Station: Texas A&M University Press, 1999). Manuel Peña, *The Mexican American Orquesta: Music, Culture, and the Dialectic of Conflict* (Austin: University of Texas Press, 1999). *Juan Carlos Rodríguez*

Gospel Music. Convention gospel music and community gospel singing are two variations of an American heritage with direct roots in colonial New England and indirect roots reaching to the Italian Renaissance. Community gospel singing is a folk phenomenon that allows individuals to reenact the process of community through artistic expression by singing religious hymns and reaffirming social bonds through the informal festival of a picnic among neighbors.

Gospel music was a major venue for creative folk expression in rural Southern agricultural communities during the late nineteenth and early twentieth centuries. The folk art form was spread by singing masters who toured rural America with evangelistic fervor teaching musical fundamentals to young audiences. Community singing and its more formal cousin, convention gospel music, also constituted the first instance of mass musical participation across geographic and cultural lines in American popular culture and presaged more modern forms of mass musical participation such as country and western music and rock-and-roll. Texas community singers still gather on weekends in towns around the state in a nondenominational setting to sing religious hymns.

Singings consist of two types, both of which employ four-part harmony. Each genre is further characterized through the use of shaped notes for musical notation. Shaped notes are a method of musical notation adapted for sight-singing choral arrangements. They reduce the tones of the scale to specific shapes such as circles, triangles, trapezoids, or squares. Those shapes represent relationships between the root note "do" and the subsequent notes of the melody. As an alternative notation to the usual type, shaped notes convey the tonal relationships of sound through shape in addition to positions on lines and spaces. Shaped-note music enables singers to move the root note, or key, up or down to fit individual vocal ranges.

The seven-shaped-note tradition is a nineteenth-century development from the original fasola, or four-note solmization, which was imported from the British Isles and proved popular in colonial America. The four-note system—or fasola—continues today under the name Sacred Harp music, which generally uses minor scales, relies on one songbook only, and groups singers by their voice parts. Sacred Harp melodies have been traced back 900 years to Medieval Europe, although the lyrics were subsequently changed or updated to reflect religious themes. Sacred Harp also relies on a similar set of republished songs and exhibits remarkable continuity over time. Sacred Harp is generally confined to the eastern parts of Texas and areas of the South.

Hymnody employing seven shaped notes attracts greater audiences and is popular statewide. It became a dynamic vehicle for gospel songwriters in the late nineteenth century and attracted a growing body of new compositions that demonstrated greater musical sophistication than their fasola cousins. Seven-shaped-note songbooks exhibit the musical versatility that appealed to young people at singing schools and was responsible, therefore, for the growing popularity of the tradition. The first Texas community singing using seven shaped notes reportedly occurred in December 1879. Itinerant teachers representing the A. J. Showalter Company of Dalton, Georgia—including company founder A. J. Showalter—ventured west to Giddings, Texas, and conducted a rural music school that lasted for several weeks. At least two individu-

Gospel Music Workshop of America, Austin Chapter, 1997. Photograph by Michael J. Young, courtesy Texas Folklife Resources. The Texas Folklife Resources concert "Texas Gospel Train" showcased the state's stellar contemporary performers. The Austin concert was a tribute to the veteran Austin gospel deejay Elmer Akins.

als from that initial school learned enough over the next year to continue as teachers of the seven-note method in Texas and were subsequently employed by the Showalter company.

Though community singings are relatively unstructured, convention gatherings display formal organization. Generally, a convention is a gathering of participants from several communities. Conventions occur on the county, regional, and state levels. In 1936, as community gospel music approached its peak popularity, singers from several southern states gathered at the behest of songbook publishers to stage the first national gospel-singing convention in Birmingham, Alabama. The national convention continues to this day, rotating among various small towns nationwide but usually staged in the South. In Texas, national conventions were staged at Plainview (1968) and Stephenville (1987).

A convention president manages the singing in a formal but sensitive manner. Individuals are called from the audience to lead the class or congregation. They choose the song and piano player, and lead the singing. Convention presidents try to allow all who want to lead a singing the opportunity to do so during gatherings, which typically occur on Saturday afternoon and evening and reconvene on Sunday. Convention singing depends on newly published convention books, which participants purchase to take home.

Without the support of songbook publishers, convention singing would not have achieved its widespread popularity. In early conventions—those taking place about 1900—

quartets demonstrated the musical ideals of harmonic gospel singing. Within a decade, songbook publishers, beginning with the Vaughn Music Company of Lawrenceburg, Tennessee, asked the better groups to represent their companies. While skillfully demonstrating the music form in its ideal, quartets were good advertising for songbook publishers.

The technique of using quartets as advertising was put into widespread use by the Stamps–Baxter Music and Printing Company in Dallas, which had a dozen quartets on the road in the 1930s. After World War II the Stamps Quartet Music Company was represented by more than thirty-five quartets in the South. In Georgia, Alabama, and Mississippi, some quartets aligned themselves with Texas music companies.

Gospel music and the ability to sing it were spread through the rural singing-school tradition, which depended on itinerant music teachers. Singing schools using the seven-shaped-note system spread rapidly in Alabama, Georgia, and Virginia after 1900; became common in East Texas during the World War I era; and reached widespread audiences in West Texas as the 1920s came to a close.

Local churches hosted annual community singing schools, rotating among denominations, although in West Texas the community itself put up funding for the school, which was usually supplied through an auction of baked goods. A typical ten-day singing school began at 9 AM and lasted until 3 or 4 in the afternoon. Teachers reviewed musical rudiments. If an individual worked hard, he could master the scale and direct a song at the end of the two-week session. Meanwhile, there was daily practice from the new convention books that the teacher provided. At the end of the session, the community was invited to hear the class in a recital. One sidelight of a community singing school was that churches developed choirs and the overall level of musical competence improved.

The gospel music movement peaked in the mid-twentieth century, largely through the influence of Texas-based musical publishing companies including Stamps–Baxter and the Stamps Quartet Music Company, both headquartered in Dallas. Other prominent twentieth-century songbook publishers included Vaughan Music Company in Lawrenceburg, Tennessee, and the Tennessee Music and Printing Company in Cleveland, Tennessee. It is not uncommon to find an individual who compiles songs, adds a few original compositions, and self-publishes smaller books. Quartets like J. D. Sumner and the Blackwoods became so successful financially that they purchased the Stamps Quartet Music Company. Similarly the Blackwoods and the Statesmen purchased the James D. Vaughn Music Company in 1964. The publishing end of the companies declined rapidly after the purchase, and rights to the Vaughn company were sold subsequently to the Church of God. Similarly, Zondervan, a religious publishing company in Michigan, purchased the Stamps–Baxter Music and Printing Company and eventually moved the operation to Michigan.

Radio was also a major factor in the spread of gospel music. One feature of the 1936 Texas Centennial celebration in Dallas was a series of radio studios in hexagonal glass booths at the fair grounds. Rural folk were fascinated. They had heard radio broadcasts but had never seen one. Stamps–Baxter quartets performed several live broadcasts at the state fair, and KRLD in Dallas, impressed with the reception, decided to try a noonday program in the fall of 1936. V. O. Stamps entreated listeners to write in if they liked the music. Within a week KRLD was deluged with mail. The KRLD broadcasts, sponsored by American Beauty Flour, became noontime staples in Texas. Eventually, live gospel singing expanded into the morning hours at 6:45 AM and occupied a 10 PM evening slot. At noon during the summertime, it was possible to walk down any street in Texas within broadcast range of KRLD and hear the Stamps Quartet singing.

By 1938 the Stamps–Baxter singing normals in Dallas became so popular that V. O. Stamps hosted an All Night Singing at the end of the three-week class session in June. KRLD carried the first broadcast, which was held in the Cotton Bowl. At midnight FCC limitations were lifted. KRLD turned up the wattage, and the broadcast went international. Soon, V. O. Stamps and his quartets were traveling to Del Rio and providing wire recordings to radio station XERA for international broadcast.

The singing school declined in popularity after World War II as people moved to urban centers. Convention gospel music was primarily a phenomenon of rural America. In this new audience milieu, quartets discovered they no longer needed sponsorship from songbook publishers and achieved popularity on their own as entertainment acts. The Statesmen Quartet added flourishes that entertained new audiences—exuberant singing, arm waving, hand clapping, and electric modification. Although this was alien behavior for traditional convention quartets, the new stage business attracted interest. The Statesmen became so popular that subsequent gospel quartets imitated their style.

Today, the seven-shaped-note tradition of gospel singing has become an isolated niche inside the greater market of gospel music. Although a national convention for gospel quartets attracts thousands of devotees and participants from across the United States during the course of a week, the National Singing Convention draws fewer than a thousand for a weekend meeting somewhere in the South. The trend parallels musical expression in modern America. Music has evolved from a communal folk activity in which many participated into an art that supports individual musical specialists who reach mass audiences through technological means such as radio and recordings. Convention gospel music and community singings still occur in Mineral Wells, Brownfield, Seymour, Stephenville, and dozens of other small Texas towns. The Four State Convention was held in Gladewater in 2002.

BIBLIOGRAPHY: *Precious Memories of Virgil O. Stamps* (Dallas: Stamps–Baxter Music and Printing Company, 1941). Southern Gospel Music (http://gospelsingingconventions.com/), accessed February 21, 2003. David H. Stanley, "The Gospel Singing Convention in South Georgia," *Journal of American Folklore* 95 (January–March 1982).   *Richard J. Mason*

Green, Clarence. Blues guitarist and band leader; b. Mont Belvieu, Chambers County, Texas, January 1, 1934; d. Houston, March 13, 1997. He was a versatile guitarist who should not be confused with the piano-playing blues singer Clarence "Candy" Green (1929–88) from nearby Galveston. Green, the guitar player, was a stalwart of the Houston scene who fronted a number of popular bands, the most famous being the Rhythmaires, between the early 1950s and his death.

The oldest son of a Creole mother, he grew up in Houston's Fifth Ward in the neighborhood known as Frenchtown. He had first started making music on homemade stringed instruments devised in collaboration with his brother, Cal Green, who later served as lead guitarist for Hank Ballard and the Midnighters and did studio work for Ray Charles and other stars (relocating permanently to California in the process). Clarence, however, opted to stay close to home all his life, choosing the security of full-time employment with Houston Light and Power, where he worked for twenty years.

Nevertheless, he found ample opportunity in the Bayou City to exploit his musical talents, both on stage and in recordings. He started out around 1951 or 1952 in a group that called itself Blues For Two. Throughout the next decade the band personnel changed often; some of the more well-known members, at various times, included fellow guitarists Johnny Copeland and Joe Hughes. Green went on to lead the High Type Five, the Cobras (not to be confused with the mid-1970s Austin-based band of the same name led by Paul Ray), and ultimately his most well-known ensemble, the Rhythmaires, which was a mainstay of the Houston scene for over thirty years.

Mixing blues, jazz, and soul music—and playing in all manner of venues, from small clubs in the old wards to grand corporate affairs downtown and in private mansions—the Rhythmaires are remembered not only for Green's precisely swinging performances on electric guitar, but also for the many female vocalists they developed and featured over the years, including Iola Broussard, Gloria Edwards, Luvenia Lewis (who married Cal Green but did not follow him to the West Coast), Trudy Lynn, Faye Robinson, Lavelle White, and others.

Starting in the late 1950s and continuing through the 1960s, Green also did regular session work as a guitarist at various studios, the most notable being Duke Records, where he backed artists such as Bobby Bland, Joe Hinton, and Junior Parker and released a few singles, including "Keep On Working," under his own name. In 1958 he had recorded his first single, "Mary My Darling," for the C & P label, which later leased it to Chicago-based Chess Records. In the following years he made numerous records for a variety of other small labels, including Shomar (which released his "Crazy Strings" in 1962), All Boy, Aquarius, Bright Star, Lynn, Pope, and Golden Eagle. His backing personnel on these tracks varied from session to session but occasionally included notable Texas blues musicians such as Henry Hayes, Wilbur McFarland, Teddy Reynolds, Ivory Lee Semien, and Hop Wilson.

However, Green did not always receive proper compensation for what happened to his many recordings, especially as they began to reappear on CD in the 1990s. In 1994 he became a co-plaintiff in a class-action lawsuit filed against one of his former producers on behalf of fifteen Houston blues musicians or their descendants. In March of 1997, just days before Green died of natural causes, a federal jury ruled in favor of the plaintiffs.

In the final months of his life Green was especially focused on performing gospel music in the context of religious worship, especially at the Frenchtown institution known as Buck Street Memorial Church of God in Christ, where he served as a deacon for many years. Green had a daughter, three sons, and several stepchildren.

BIBLIOGRAPHY: Alan Govenar, *Meeting the Blues: The Rise of the Texas Sound* (Dallas: Taylor, 1988). Sheldon Harris, *Blues Who's Who* (New Rochelle, New York: Arlington House, 1979). Houston *Chronicle*, March 15, 1997. Bill Wasserzieher, "The Houston Scene: Clarence Green," *Living Blues* 131 (January–February 1997). Roger Wood, *Down In Houston: Bayou City Blues* (Austin: University of Texas Press, 2003).   *Roger Wood*

Grierson, Al. Singer, songwriter, and "Poet Laureate of Luckenbach, Texas"; b. New Westminster, British Columbia, Canada, 1948; d. Gillespie County, Texas, November 2, 2000; eldest of eight children. Grierson grew up in British Columbia and Calgary, Alberta. As a singer and songwriter, he briefly used the name McKinney, after his picture was mislabeled in a songbook. In the 1970s he served as editor of the *Georgia Straight*, an alternative newspaper, in Vancouver.

Grierson's life took a dark turn when two of his brothers perished in a house-fire while still in their teens. His music and poetry reflect his wanderings through philosophy, mythology, literature, history and religion, as well as his life on the road. He worked on the railroad and carried the red "Wobblies" (International Workers of the World) card, took part in the peace movement of the 1960s, and lived for a time in England and Ireland.

Grierson's first wife was from Ireland. With his second wife, Claudia Stevens, to whom Grierson was married from February 1989 to February 1997, he had two daughters. Alan and Claudia met in a Buddhist monastery "in the shadow of Mount Shasta" in Oregon, where he lived for six years and became a Zen Buddhist monk. The two left the monastery to live together and have children. During their marriage Grierson started a small home business—a tofu chip factory. Folk singer and songwriter Utah Phillips wrote that the business failed because the chips were so unpalatable as to be almost inedible. Phillips also wrote, in a tribute to Grierson printed in *Performing Songwriter* magazine, that Grierson's older daughter was allergic to tofu. While living in Ashland, Oregon, Grierson became part of a group of writers called Camp California. He wore a rose tattoo, as part of a sort of loose society comprising "about twenty people," according to Utah Phillips.

From Oregon, Grierson moved to Texas in 1997 and took up residence in a school bus parked in a makeshift camp called Armadillo Farm just outside Luckenbach. There the peripatetic poet owned little besides his Guild guitar. He was, however, an enthusiastic e-mailer and his own Webmaster, according to singer-songwriter Anne Feeney, who at the time of his death was planning to record two of Grierson's songs. One of his songs, "Rick Blaine Retires to Luckenbach, Texas to Cultivate the Middle Way," which appears on his second album, speculates on what might have happened to the Humphrey Bogart character from the movie "Casablanca." In Grierson's fancy, Blaine moves to Luckenbach, becomes a hermit and studies Buddhism.

Grierson's festival appearances include the first Vancouver Folk Festival, the Napa Valley Festival, the High Sierra Fest, and, in Texas, the Kerrville Folk Festival. He was a two-time finalist in the Napa Valley Music and Wine Festival's emerging-songwriter showcase and a guest on National Public Radio's "River City Folk" program. The twenty-fourth annual Vancouver Folk Music Festival was dedicated to Al Grierson.

Al Grierson made only two recordings: *Things That Never Added Up to Me* (1995; all Grierson's songs except Jack Hardy's "The Zephyr") and *A Candle for Durruti* (1999). The title of his second album came from singer-songwriter Dave Van Ronk, who told Grierson a story about a friend of his who never passed a Catholic cathedral without stopping to light a candle in memory of Buenaventura Durruti, leader of the anarchist militia during the Spanish Civil War. Both albums are recorded with vocals, guitar, and harmonica by Grierson alone, on Grierson's own label, "Folkin' Eh!"

According to his wife, Grierson said it would take a crane to get him out of Texas. He died in a flash flood that swept him off the road when his pickup stalled three miles from Luckenbach, after a performance at a school. His body was found some two miles downstream the following day. Grierson's ashes are said to repose at the Buddhist monastery in Oregon.

His songs recorded by others include "The Resurrection," from his second album, recorded by singer–songwriter Ray Wylie Hubbard on his CD *Dangerous Spirits*; and "Sunday 'Way up Yonder," from his first album, recorded by performer–songwriter–folklorist Alan Wayne Damron on his CD *Texas Spirit Live*. The latter album was made in response to the request of numerous Texas teachers to promote appreciation for Texas history and culture.

BIBLIOGRAPHY: Austin *American–Statesman*, November 5, 2000. *A Web Site for Al Grierson* (http://www.surfnetusa.com/celticfolk/artists/algrierson.htm), accessed January 16, 2003.   *Jackie Jordan*

Gruene Hall. In Gruene, Texas; one of the oldest functioning dance halls in the state. Largely a tourist attraction today, Gruene (originally known as Goodwin) was settled in the mid-nineteenth century by German farming families. As the head of one of these families, Ernst Gruene moved with his wife and two sons to the area northeast of New Braunfels in 1872. The second of his two sons, Henry (Heinrich) D. Gruene, firmly established the family's presence in the area by acquiring enough cotton-producing land to support between twenty and thirty tenant-farm families. Before his death in 1920 he built the town's first mercantile store, cotton gin, lumberyard, and bank. He also provided land for a school and served for a time as postmaster. In 1878 he built the dance hall known today as Gruene Hall.

Henry Gruene's Dance Hall provided area residents a place for socializing and offered hard-working farm families a diversion from their difficult lives. A sign hanging over the bar proclaimed "Den feinsten Schnaps, das beste Bier, bekommt man bei dem Heinrich hier" (The best liquor, the best beer, you get at Henry's here). In addition to serving both "the best beer" and "dime-a-shot whiskey," and providing a venue for polka bands and square dancing, the hall often was used by traveling salesmen for displaying their wares. Gruene Hall also became a popular location for *Saengerfeste* (German singing festivals), high school graduation ceremonies, political elections, and both dog and badger fights. During Prohibition, Henry Gruene hung a sign in the bar that read, "Only Near Beer is Sold Here. Real Beer is Sold Near Here."

In the early part of the twentieth century, weekend dances usually began early on Saturday evenings. Typically, there would be a break at midnight for sandwiches and coffee, followed by more dancing until 5 A.M. The late Oscar Haas, a long-time resident of New Braunfels, remembered "those wonderful all-night dances at Gruene Hall—the long bar and the beer—the midnight supper—the children sleeping in the side room, as the parents danced until 5 A.M. . . the polkas, schottisches, waltzes, and the happiest of all, the ring-arounds."

Despite such joyous occasions, the residents of Gruene faced difficult times as well. In 1925 a boll weevil infestation devastated area crops. The Great Depression and the attendant decline in cotton prices nearly wiped out what was left of the town. In 1972 developers planned to raze the town, but a local architect, Chip Kaufman, convinced local authorities of the historical value of Gruene Hall and the other surviving buildings. In 1975 Gruene was added to the National Register of Historic Places. Two years later, San Antonio residents Bill Gallagher and Pat Molak used a $20,000 loan to purchase a number of local buildings, including the hall. Their plans for the hall involved very little structural change. They insisted on maintaining the vintage signs, stage, dance floor and forty-eight-star United States flag. Under its new ownership the hall began to attract the performers that have helped make it a musical landmark, as well as a destination for hundreds of music fans every Saturday night. George Strait, for example, played regularly at Gruene Hall in the 1970s and 1980s. Others who have performed there over the years include Kris Kristofferson, Lyle Lovett, Tish Hinojosa, Robert Earl Keen, Jr., Jerry Jeff Walker, Stevie Ray Vaughan, Jerry Lee Lewis, Don Walser, Chris Isaac, the Austin Lounge Lizards, and the Fabulous Thunderbirds.

BIBLIOGRAPHY: Joe Hammer, Schlaraffenland: Gruene, Texas (MS, Sophienburg Archives, New Braunfels, Texas). San Antonio *Express–News*, May 24, 1975; January 6, 1985. Seiedenschwara, Gruene, Texas: A Town that Tried to Survive (MS, Sophienburg Archives, New Braunfels, Texas). Connie Sherley, "It's Gruene, They Say!," *Texas Highways*, June 1989. Richard Zelade, *Hill Country: Completely Updated 4th Edition* (Houston: Texas Monthly Guidebooks, Gulf Publishing Company, 1997).
                                                Brandy Schnautz

Guadalupe Cultural Arts Center. A nonprofit arts organization dedicated to developing and promoting Latin-American and indigenous arts; located at 1300 Guadalupe, in the heart of San Antonio's Westside barrio. The center developed from Performance Artists Nucleus, Incorporated, which formed in 1979 to unite various Hispanic arts groups.

In the early 1980s Rolando Rios, Ralph Garcia, and other leaders of PAN determined that the organization needed a permanent facility close to the Hispanic community it wished to serve. The historic Teatro Guadalupe, which operated as the Westside's most opulent movie theater from 1940 until it fell into disrepair and was closed in 1970, presented an ideal site for an arts center. Councilman Bernardo Eureste persuaded the city to purchase the land where the theater was located and sublease the theater from developer William Schlansker, who raised $1 million for the theater's reconstruction. The Reyna–Caragonne architectural firm subsequently drafted reconstruction plans for the theater.

During this period of negotiation and construction PAN changed its name to Guadalupe Cultural Arts Center. The center, initially headquartered in Teatro Guadalupe and later in the Progreso Drugstore adjacent to the theater, sponsored art classes and performances throughout San Antonio. In the spring of 1984 the reconstruction of the theater was completed. The 410-seat facility, a hybrid of southwestern mission style and Art Deco ornamentation, is equipped for stage and screen presentations and includes a small art gallery. The offices, classrooms, and graphics department are located in the Progreso Drugstore. The two buildings provide a total of 20,000 square feet of space.

The Guadalupe Cultural Arts Center sponsors programming in six major areas: visual arts, music, literature, film, theater, and dance. With its major emphasis on education, the center offers a wide array of classes and workshops in visual arts, music, literature, theater, and dance on a year-round basis. Such artists as Valerio Longoria, Jorge Piña, and Kathy Vargas have taught the classes, which are offered at low cost.

The visual arts program organizes nine exhibitions annually, featuring local, national, and international artists. Each year the Guadalupe Cultural Arts Center sponsors the Juried Women's Art Exhibit and an arts and crafts bazaar called Hecho a Mano. The center has cosponsored two exhibitions with the San Antonio Museum of Art: Art Among Us / Arte Entre Nosotros (1986), an exhibition featuring Mexican folk art from San Antonio; and Influence: An Exhibition of Works by Contemporary Hispanic Artists Living in San Antonio, Texas (1987). The center has also organized exhibitions with San Antonio's Instituto Cultural Mexicano and Appalshop, a center devoted to Appalachian culture located in Whitesburg, Kentucky. The visual arts program supports local artists by making its facilities available to them and by offering technical assistance, special workshops, and round-table discussions for the exchange of information.

The center's Xicano Music Program presents performances in parks and at schools, churches, and other community centers. Since 1982 the music program has sponsored the annual Tejano Conjunto Festival in San Antonio, the largest festival of its kind in the United States. The seven-day event presents an average of forty conjuntos and features such major performers as Ruben Vela, Los Dos Gilbertos, Tony de la Rosa, and Esteban Jordan, along with emerging talents. Each year at the festival several pioneering performers are inducted into the Conjunto Music Hall of Fame.

The Guadalupe Cultural Arts Center offers a strong literature program, with frequent literary performances and annual residencies, in which several writers teach workshops, give public lectures and readings, and advise area writers and poets. Many prominent Hispanic writers have participated in the program in the past, including Norma Alarcón, Rolando Hinojosa, Raul Salinas, and Alurista. Since 1987 the center has sponsored the Inter-American Book Fair and Literary Festival, which features readings, workshops, public forums, and bookselling. Such prominent writers as Carlos Fuentes, Maya Angelou, Maxine Hong Kingston, Isabel Allende, Alice Walker, Oscar Hijuelos, and Robert Bly have appeared at the Book Fair.

The Guadalupe Cultural Arts Center's cinema program focuses on Spanish-language and Latino-theme films and videos. The center regularly presents series featuring films from Mexico, Brazil, Spain, Argentina, and other Latin-American countries. Since 1983 the center has sponsored San Antonio CineFestival, the country's longest-running Latino film and video festival, which began in 1975 under the sponsorship of Oblate College in San Antonio. The center's theater-arts program presents four plays annually, many of which are original works commissioned from established and aspiring playwrights.

The center places an emphasis on bicultural or bilingual productions. Productions by the center's resident acting company, Los Actores de San Antonio, are supplemented by performances mounted by major Hispanic theatrical troupes such as Teatro de la Esperanza of Santa Barbara, California. In 1991 the Guadalupe Cultural Arts Center began a Hispanic dance program in response to the dissolution of several folkloric dance companies in San Antonio. Together with the Instituto Cultural Mexicano, the center offers studio space and dance classes and plans to develop a professional dance company.

The Guadalupe Cultural Arts Center extends its services beyond the San Antonio community through the publication of Tonantzin, a periodical that includes artwork, poetry and short stories, critical essays on all aspects of Latino culture, reviews of books, movies, records, and art exhibitions, interviews, and listings of cultural activities. The literature and artwork of Hispanic women, children, and prisoners have been featured in past issues of the magazine, which the center has published several times a year since December 1983. Tonantzin means "our mother" in Náhuatl, the common language of the Aztec empire, and thus links the magazine and the center with the mestizo heritage of the Mexicanos, a source of pride to the Chicano movement. The center also publishes a monthly newsletter.

A board of no more than twenty-five directors oversees the long-term development of the Guadalupe Cultural Arts Center. Pedro Rodriguez, director of the center beginning in 1984, coordinated a staff of seventeen in 1991. The center supports artists and benefits students and the public by hiring artists, musicians, writers, and actors to oversee its programs and teach classes. Each year about 700 volunteers assist the center at various events and festivals. Funding for the center is provided by the city of San Antonio, the Texas Commission on the Arts, the Texas Committee for the Humanities, the National Endowment for the Arts, the Meadows Foundation, the Rockefeller Foundation, the Ford Foundation, the Ewing Halsell Foundation, and other corporate and private contributors. Membership fees and revenue from programs also provide financial support for the center, which operated on a budget of more than $2 million in 2000. As one of the largest community-based organizations dedicated to Latin-American cultural arts in the United States, the Guadalupe Cultural Arts Center received a Challenge Grant from the National Endowment for the Arts in 1986, and in 1987 won the Arts Organization of the Year award from the San Antonio Business Committee for the Arts. In January of 2002 the center was awarded a $1 million endowment grant by the Ford Foundation.

BIBLIOGRAPHY: Guadalupe Cultural Arts Center Archives, San Antonio. *Kendall Curlee*

Guenther, Heinrich. Teacher, politician, and musician; b. Zeitz, Saxony, March 9, 1821; d. New Braunfels, Texas,

April 8, 1870. Guenther sailed to Texas, probably in the 1840s with the colonists of the Adelsverein. After the death of Jean J. von Coll, Guenther married Coll's widow; they had six children. Guenther taught in the city school until 1858, when New Braunfels Academy superseded it. In 1854, as a delegate of the Politischer Verein of New Braunfels, Guenther was elected president of the annual Staats-Sängerfest in San Antonio on May 14 and 15. He served on a committee with a Dr. Nohl and Louis C. Ervendberg to formulate plans to stir up interest for a national convention of the Bund Freier Männer at St. Louis early in November 1854. He was also one of the first directors of the Germania, the first singing society in Texas, organized at New Braunfels on March 2, 1850.

BIBLIOGRAPHY: Rudolph L. Biesele, *The History of the German Settlements in Texas, 1831–1861* (Austin: Von Boeckmann–Jones, 1930; rpt. 1964). Edgar R. Dabney, The Settlement of New Braunfels and the History of Its Earlier Schools (M.A. thesis, University of Texas, 1927). New Braunfels *Zeitung*, December 17, 1852; April 29, July 1, 1853; May 19, 26, 1854; April 15, 1870; July 22, 1926.

Rudolph L. Biesele

Guinan, "Texas." Night-club, Wild West, vaudeville, and movie entertainer; b. Mary Louise Cecilia Guinan, near Waco, Texas, January 12, 1884, the daughter of Irish immigrants Michael and Bessie Duffy Guinan; d. Vancouver, British Columbia, November 5, 1933.

Mary Louise Guinan became one of the most colorful figures in American entertainment during the Prohibition era (1920–33). As a child, she learned to rope and ride broncos on her family's ranch outside of Waco. As a teenager, she combined her riding, roping, and shooting skills into a performance that won her acclaim at a local "frontier days" celebration and earned her the nickname "Texas." After winning a prized singing scholarship to the American Conservatory of Music in Chicago, she spent several years traveling and performing throughout the country in various Wild West shows. On December 2, 1904, she married John J. Moynahan, a Denver newspaper artist; their marriage ended within two years.

In 1906 she settled in New York City to work in theater and vaudeville. By 1908 she had established herself as a promising newcomer in vaudeville. She fashioned her stage appearance and her performances after some of the more daring female celebrities of the day, including Mae West and Lillian Russell. In 1917 she successfully transferred her singing, acting, riding, and roping skills to the silver screen. She soon became one of the few women to be offered prominent action roles in Hollywood westerns. By 1921 she had starred in several Western movies and founded her own company, Texas Guinan Productions.

In 1923 she returned to New York City to work on Broadway. With Prohibition in effect, hundreds of cabarets and nightclubs skirted the law by clandestinely offering booze along with musical entertainment. Texas Guinan became one of the most popular singers and performers in the underground New York City nightclub circuit. By displaying a brassy style and determined will, she was able to move from singer to master of ceremonies, an unusual role for women at this time. She was noted for greeting audiences each night with her trademark, "Hello, sucker!" Authorities frequently raided these establishments, and, on several occasions, the star was swept up in police dragnets. Throughout the remaining years of Prohibition, Guinan was embroiled in conflict with authorities over the matter of alcohol sales at the clubs where she performed.

Despite her busy and controversial life onstage in the nightclubs of New York City, she found the time to return to Hollywood to star in several more films. She also continued to tour throughout the United States and Canada. In 1931 she attempted to take her nightclub show to Europe, but her reputation preceded her, and the ship carrying her and her dancers was refused entry at every European country it called on. The debacle was later turned to Guinan's advantage when it became the basis for a successful revue entitled *Too Hot for Paris.* In November 1933, while touring in Vancouver, she died of complications from amoebic dysentery. She is buried in Calvary Cemetery, Queens, New York. She has been memorialized in several movies, including Phyllis Diller's portrayal of the so-called "Queen of the Nightclubs" in the 1961 Warner Brothers film *Splendor in the Grass.*

BIBLIOGRAPHY: Louise Berliner, *Texas Guinan, Queen of the Night Clubs* (Austin: University of Texas Press, 1993). Glenn Shirley, *"Hello Sucker!": The Story of Texas Guinan* (Austin: Eakin Press, 1989). *Gary Hartman*

Guion, David Wendel. Composer and musician; b. Ballinger, Texas, December 15, 1892; d. Dallas, October 17, 1981 (buried at Evergreen Cemetery, Ballinger); son of John I. and Armour (Fentress) Guion. His mother was an accomplished singer and pianist, and his father was a prominent judge. Guion's parents discovered his musical ability when he was five years old; consequently he started his musical education early. He studied first in nearby San Angelo, then at the Whipple Academy in Jacksonville, Illinois, and further at Polytechnic College in Fort Worth. His parents sent him to Vienna to study with Leopold Godowsky at the Royal Conservatory of Music. After the outbreak of World War I Guion returned to the states, where he began teaching and composing.

Throughout the 1920s and 1930s he composed and performed music that reflected his Texas heritage. For a time he hosted a Western-oriented weekly radio show in New York City, for which he wrote the scripts and music. But Guion, at one time himself an accomplished cowboy, became most famous for his arrangement of the cowboy song "Home on the Range," which was performed for the first time in his New York production *Prairie Echoes.* It became a favorite of President Franklin D. Roosevelt and the nation. In 1936 Guion was commissioned to write *Cavalcade of America* for the Texas Centennial celebration, and in 1950 he received a commission from the Houston Symphony Orchestra, for which he completed the suite *Texas* in 1952. His compositions number over 200 published works and include orchestral suites, ballet music, piano pieces, and secular and religious songs. His music has been performed around the world.

Guion was one of the first American composers to col-

Autographed publicity photo of David Guion by Apeda, New York, ca. 1920s. Texas State Library and Archives Commission. Guion wrote over 200 compositions that reflected his Texas cowboy heritage and is best known for his arrangement of "Home on the Range."

lect and transcribe folk tunes, including Negro spirituals, into concert music. He is well-known for his arrangements of "Turkey in the Straw" and "The Arkansas Traveler," as well as "The Yellow Rose of Texas," "The Lonesome Whistler," "The Harmonica Player," "Jazz Scherzo," "Barcarolle," "The Scissors Grinder," "Valse Arabesque," and the *Mother Goose Suite*. He was a master at musically representing the history and heritage of early Texas with such works as "Ride, Cowboy, Ride," "The Bold Vaquero," "Lonesome Song of the Plains," "Prairie Dusk," and the "Texas Fox Trot." A collection of his waltzes, "Southern Nights," was used in the movie *Grand Hotel*.

Guion was a member of the American Society of Composers, Authors, and Publishers; the Texas Composers Guild; and the Texas Teachers Association. In 1955 the National Federation of Music Clubs announced that Guion was one of America's most significant folk-music composers. Guion, a Presbyterian and a Democrat, had a teaching career spanning over sixty years. He influenced young musicians at numerous colleges and conservatories including Howard Payne University (which in 1950 awarded him an honorary doctorate in music), Fort Worth Polytechnic College, Fairmont Conservatory, Chicago Musical College, Daniel Baker College, and Southern Methodist University.

Upon his death, his large collection of furniture, glassware, music recordings, books, and memorabilia was donated to the International Festival–Institute at Round Top. The Crouch Music Library at Baylor University, the Dallas Public Library, and the Fine Arts Library at the University of Texas at Austin have portions of his archives.

BIBLIOGRAPHY: Sam Hanna Acheson, Herbert P. Gambrell, Mary Carter Toomey, and Alex M. Acheson, Jr., *Texian Who's Who*, Volume 1 (Dallas: Texian, 1937). Donna Bearden and Jamie Frucht, *The Texas Sampler: A Stitch in Time* (Austin: Governor's Committee on Aging, 1976?). Houston *Chronicle*, October 21, 1981. Vertical files, Center for American History, University of Texas at Austin.

James Dick

Guizar, Tito. Singer and actor; b. Federico Arturo Guizar Tolentino, Guadalajara, Jalisco, Mexico, April 8, 1908; d. San Antonio, December 24, 1999. Guizar immigrated to the United States in 1929 with his father and mother, José Guizar and Adele Tolentino. By the age of sixteen he had demonstrated a strong interest in music. In the 1920s he moved to New York and performed regularly in private clubs. He later became host for a bilingual CBS radio show, "Tito Guizar and his Guitar." In New York he married Mexican singer Carmen Nanette Noriega on August 5, 1931.

Around 1935 Guizar became one of the first Mexican actors to appear in Hollywood movies. In 1936 he returned to Mexico to play the lead in a movie entitled *Allá en el Rancho Grande*, which helped establish both his singing and acting careers. Back in Hollywood, he appeared in such movies as *The Big Broadcast of 1938*, *On the Old Spanish Trail* (1947), *Blondie Goes Latin* (1941), *Brazil* (1944), *The Gay Ranchero* (1948), and *Time and Touch* (1962). After his relatively brief American movie career, Guizar remained active in radio, TV, and records well into the 1980s. In all, he appeared in over forty Mexican films and fourteen American ones. His career, which included performing and composing music for film, theater, and television, spanned nearly seventy years.

His wife died in 1990. Guizar was ninety-one when he died, of respiratory failure. He was survived by three children, Nina, Lillya, and Tito Jr.

BIBLIOGRAPHY: *Who's Who*, 2001. Tito Guizar page in *Fuller Up, The Dead Musician Directory* (http://elvispelvis.com/titoguizar.htm), accessed January 16, 2003.

Jesse J. Esparza

Guthrie, Woody. Folk and protest singer; b. Woodrow Wilson Guthrie, Okemah, Oklahoma, July 14, 1912; d. New York City, October 3, 1967; son of Charles Edward and Nora Belle (Tanner) Guthrie. After Woody's mother was committed to a mental hospital, he followed his once-prosperous father to be with relatives in Pampa, where Woody lived from 1929 to 1937. An indifferent student, he dropped out of Pampa High School, but devoured books on psychology, religion, and Eastern philosophy at the local library and found a spiritual mentor in the Lebanese poet Kahlil Gibran. He supported himself by odd jobs, especially sign painting.

Performing with bands at night clubs and radio stations in the Panhandle, Guthrie found his calling—poet and lyricist—and his tools—his voice and his guitar—and began developing skills that later gained him a reputation as writer, cartoonist, and down-home philosopher. He married a Pampa girl, Mary Jennings, in 1933 and experienced the pain of the Dust Bowl and the Great Depression, which gave him subject matter for many songs. The most memorable song of Guthrie's Pampa years, "So Long, It's Been Good to Know You," was a response to the great dust storm of April 14, 1935. When that storm hit, some Pampans believed that the end of the world was upon them and that there was just time for final goodbyes.

Tired of dust and poverty, Guthrie left for Los Angeles in 1937 and found local fame on radio station KFVD, where, to fill hours of time on the air, he turned out lyrics at stream-of-consciousness speed, usually setting them to someone else's music. His listeners were often Okies, Arkies, and Texans who, in search of the American dream, had fled to the West Coast; there, Guthrie told them with biting irony, they would find it only if they brought "Do Re Mi." Some longed nostalgically for "The Oklahoma Hills" and all listened knowingly while Guthrie sang "Dust Bowl Refugee" and "I Ain't Got No Home in this World Anymore." Thrilled by the hydroelectric power flowing from massive New Deal dams on the Columbia River in Washington and Oregon, Guthrie composed "Roll On, Columbia," which celebrates the New Deal, and "Pastures of Plenty," which celebrates the nobility of nearby migrant laborers. Both were political statements. So was "This Land Is Your Land," written in 1940 to tell Guthrie's countrymen that America belongs to the many and not the few.

Although Guthrie was an inveterate wanderer, after 1940 he usually called New York City home. Many of the lyrics of this period, especially those for children, were light, singable, and fun, but others continued to strike with a populist rage against the putative faceless rich men of Eastern boardrooms, each with his "Philadelphia Lawyer" who drove farmers from their land, robbing with fountain pens instead of guns. John Steinbeck had immortalized (and greatly fictionalized) the victims in *The Grapes of Wrath*, and Woody Guthrie retold Steinbeck's story of angry impotence in "Tom Joad." Though singing about rejection and being down and out, Guthrie was rich and famous. The 1940s were the best years in his troubled life. He taped his songs for the Library of Congress. He performed on CBS radio shows. He published the first of several books, *Bound for Glory*, later made into a movie. He survived two German torpedoes in the United States Merchant Marine. And after he was divorced by Mary, he married Marjorie Greenblatt Mazia, an unlikely union of a farm-belt populist and a beautiful Jewish dancer in the Martha Graham company.

Happiness was not to last. By the early 1950s Guthrie's period of great productivity—he wrote perhaps a thousand songs—was over. It had lasted no more than sixteen years, from about 1937, when he left Pampa, to about 1953, when Huntington's disease, an incurable hereditary illness of the central nervous system which had killed his mother, put him in the hospital. He spent nearly all of his last fourteen years there, from 1953 until his death. Guthrie had three children with his first wife, Mary; four with Marjorie, including the singer Arlo Guthrie; and one with Anneke Marshall in their brief marriage. His body was cremated.

The protest singers of the 1960s canonized Woody Guthrie, seeing him as their forerunner and mentor. Bob Dylan was but one of those who went as pilgrims to his bedside. They loved the old lyrics that roasted the "establishment." They counted his Bohemian lifestyle as virtue and not vice. They envied him for being something they were not, a supposedly authentic man of the people whose lyrics had given voice to desperate migrants of the depression years. Pampans held their first annual Tribute to Woody Guthrie on October 3, 1992, which Governor Ann Richards proclaimed as Woody Guthrie Day in Texas. City officials dedicated a cast iron sculpture 150 feet long with the musical staff and notes of "This Land," and then named U.S. Highway 60, which crosses the Panhandle, the Woody Guthrie Memorial Highway.

BIBLIOGRAPHY: Austin *American-Statesman*, July 16, 1991. Joe Klein, *Woody Guthrie: A Life* (New York: Knopf, 1980). Richard Pascal, "Walt Whitman and Woody Guthrie: American Prophet–Singers and Their People," *Journal of American Studies* 24 (April 1990). *Penguin Encyclopedia of Popular Music* (New York: Penguin, 1990). Edward Robbin, *Woody Guthrie and Me: An Intimate Reminiscence* (Berkeley: Lancaster-Miller, 1979). *Texas Observer*, July 24, 1992. Mildred Tolbert, "Woody Guthrie Country: Pampa, Texas," *Greater Llano Estacado Southwest Heritage* 12 (Spring 1982). Keith Windschuttle, "John Steinbeck," *The New Criterion* 20 (June 2002).

Richard B. Hughes

Hall, Gene. Saxophonist, arranger, and music educator; b. Morris Eugene Hall, Whitewright, Texas, June 12, 1913; d. Denton, Texas, March 4, 1993; son of Benjamin Baxter and Leila G. (Cook) Hall. As a boy he studied the saxophone and played in church and later in a local combo called the Joy Makers. Hall performed with dance bands in the North Texas area in the 1930s and in 1934 began a two-year European tour with the Clarence Nemir Orchestra.

He graduated from North Texas State Teachers College in Denton, received an M.A. in 1942, and after playing with a number of bands in Texas and working in radio, began teaching at his alma mater in 1947. Hall established the first collegiate jazz degree, although it was referred to as a "dance band" major because of objections to the word *jazz*. He received his doctorate from New York University in 1954.

In a contest held in1959, Hall's North Texas State dance band was selected as the best in America among college groups by the American Federation of Musicians. Also in 1959 Hall developed a jazz program at Michigan State University, where he had accepted a teaching position. He later served as chairman of the music department at College of the Desert in Palm Desert, California, and at Stephen F. Austin State University in Nacogdoches, Texas. He was a principal mover in the formation in 1968 of the National Association of Jazz Educators and served as its first president. He was considered the dean of Stan Kenton workshops, both at North Texas State and later at Michigan State. His master's thesis, entitled *The Development of a Curriculum for the Teaching of Dance Band Music at a College Level*, became the basis for the first jazz degree, and the text, published in 1944, is still used today.

Hall received the Hall of Fame Award from the International Association of Jazz Educators in 1981. In 1992 he received the *Down Beat* Achievement Award for Jazz Education. He had three children with his first wife, Geraldine. Several years after her death, he married Marjorie Lynn.

BIBLIOGRAPHY: Michael Cogswell, "Gene Hall: In his own words," *Jazz Educators Journal* 25.3 (Spring, 1993). Barry Kernfeld, ed., *New Grove Dictionary of Jazz*, Second Edition (New York: Grove's Dictionaries, 2002).

Dave Oliphant

Hamblen, Carl Stuart. Country–western and southern gospel singer, songwriter, bandleader and radio–movie personality; b. Kellyville, Texas, October 20, 1908; d. Santa Monica, California, March 8, 1989; son of James Henry Hamblen, an itinerant Methodist preacher, and his wife, Ernestine. Much of his childhood was spent traveling throughout the state as his father's ministerial work decreed, but in West Texas, young Stuart was exposed to the lore and folk music of both the black field hands and cowboys working on area farms and ranches. Thus steeped in the "cowboy tradition," he learned to ride and rope and enjoyed some success during his teens as an amateur singer while working the rodeos. In 1925 he enrolled at McMurry State Teachers' College in Abilene, Texas, to study for the teaching field.

But music quickly became his passion. In 1926 Hamblen reportedly became radio broadcasting's first real "singing cowboy" after landing a spot on KAYO in Abilene. In 1929, after winning the fifty-dollar prize at a talent contest in Dallas, he journeyed to Camden, New Jersey, where he auditioned for the Victor (later RCA Victor) Recording Company. The Victor Studios recorded and released four of Hamblen's early compositions—"The Boy in Blue," "Drifting Back to Dixie," "When the Moon Shines Down on the Mountain," and "The Big Rock Candy Mountain #2"—in June of that year. Shortly afterward, Hamblen headed west for California, where he appeared on Los Angeles radio station KFI as "Cowboy Joe," possibly the earliest cowboy act airing in Los Angeles.

In 1930 Hamblen briefly joined the Beverly Hillbillies, an early radio country-and-western singing group then broadcasting over KMPC in Los Angeles. He made a couple of recordings with them, although not as a lead vocalist. The following year he formed his own band, a group that included singing cowgirl Patsy Montana, and launched his highly successful broadcasting career over KFWB in Los Angeles. Under various names and titles such as "Stuart Hamblen & His Lucky Stars," "King Cowboy's Woolly West Revue," and "The Covered Wagon Jubilee," his radio program remained immensely popular for the next two decades. In 1933 he met and married Suzanne (Suzy) Obee; they subsequently had two daughters.

In 1934 Hamblen was the first West Coast artist to sign with Decca Records, where he recorded with his own band for the first time. His initial disc, "Texas Plains / Poor Unlucky Cowboy," became only the second record issued by that fledgling company. A prolific composer, Hamblen was said to be able to turn out a tune within a matter of minutes. His catalogue of songs that he either wrote or co-wrote, beginning in the 1930s, included such hits as "My Mary," "Texas Plains," "Walking My Fortune," "Ridin' Ole Paint" and "Golden River." Subsequent recording sessions with Decca in 1934 and 1935 further enhanced Hamblen as a true pioneer in the country-and-western genre. Although he concentrated almost solely on his radio program over the next ten years, his recording career began anew in the mid-1940s with the West Coast–based ARA label. This subsequently led to lengthier contracts with Columbia, RCA, and Coral Records.

In the 1930s and 1940s, Hamblen appeared in several B-Western movies, usually cast as a villain, alongside such stars as Gene Autry, John Wayne, Roy Rogers, Wild Bill Elliott, and Bob Steele. During World War II his patriotism was clearly reflected in songs and recitations such as "Oklahoma Bill" and "They're Gonna Kill You." In addi-

Cover to sheet music "It Is No Secret (What God Can Do)," showing Stuart Hamblen, ca. 1950 (Dutchess Music Corporation, New York). Courtesy H. Alan Anderson. Hamblen was considered the first singing country and western cowboy in the history of radio broadcasting. In the 1950s to 1970s he wrote songs reflecting his Christian faith.

tion, Hamblen enjoyed hunting in the wilds with his prize hounds and also began breeding thoroughbred racehorses; in 1945 he became the first person to have a horse flown to a race when he transported his prize racer, El Lobo, from Los Angeles to Bay Meadows on Flying Tiger Airlines. El Lobo won the Burlingame Handicap and was flown back home the same day.

As the pressures of his public career mounted, Hamblen began gambling and became increasingly addicted to alcohol. His drinking binges occasionally landed him in jail for brawling and shooting out streetlights. He later confessed that he was the "original juvenile delinquent." But due to his radio popularity, his sponsors usually were able to bail him out, although his drinking problem increasingly affected his performances. All the while, he continued to turn out songs, including several of the honky-tonk variety that became popular among country musicians after World War II. Indeed, two of his most noted recordings in the late 1940s were "I Won't Go Hunting With You, Jake (But I'll be Chasin' Women)" and "Remember Me (I'm the One Who Loves You)," the latter also recorded by Ernest Tubb and Dean Martin.

Hamblen's wild, boozing lifestyle might have gone indefinitely had his praying, God-fearing wife not introduced him to the young upstart evangelist Billy Graham. She persuaded him to attend Graham's path-breaking tent revival campaign, which was being held at Washington and Hill Streets in Los Angeles. The day after, Hamblin gave his testimony over the radio and declared that he was "hitting the sawdust trail." That public testimony was allegedly a key factor in influencing William Randolph Hearst's decision to order his newspaper chain to "puff Graham." True to his word, Hamblen swore off alcohol and tobacco, sold his racehorses and dedicated his life to Christ. Many of his later songs such as "It Is No Secret (What God Can Do)," "His Hands," "This Ship of Mine," and "Open Up Your Heart (and Let the Sunshine In)" reflected his new-found faith, while others such as "Good Morning You All" and "Daddy's Cutie Pie" emphasized home and family. In 1954, while on a hunting trip in the Sierras, Hamblen and his party came upon the body of an old, dead prospector in his remote tumbled-down shack. That experience resulted in Hamblen's most famous country gospel tune, "This Ole House," which was subsequently popularized by Rosemary Clooney and made the 1954 Song of the Year. Jo Stafford, Red Foley, Elvis Presley, and Jimmy Dean also made top hits out of Hamblen's songs.

In the early 1950s, Hamblen's new radio show, "The Cowboy Church of the Air," was syndicated nationwide. But when he refused to air a beer commercial, the sponsors pulled the plug. That episode, in 1952, prompted the Prohibition party to recruit Hamblen to run for president of the United States on their ticket. When the final counts were in, Hamblen could truly boast that he had set a new record for votes for the Prohibitionists, though he ran fourth to Dwight D. Eisenhower.

For the next twenty years, Stuart and Suzy Hamblen hosted a local TV show and made nationwide tours to prisons, reformatories, and youth organizations, at which they presented the Gospel in their own, down-home country way through songs mixed in with cowboy stories rather than straight sermonizing. They also continued to support Billy Graham's ministry and made occasional appearances at the latter's crusades. Then in 1971, with the backing of KLAC manager Bill Ward, Hamblen returned to the radio airwaves. His country gospel stories and songs were again heard through the revived "Cowboy Church of the Air," which was produced at the Hamblen family's horse ranch near Los Angeles over the next decade. O their ranch the Hamblens raised their Peruvian Paso horses, which they featured in horse shows throughout the country and also in the annual Tournament of Roses Parade at Pasadena, California, on New Year's Day. One of their prize stallions, AEV Oro Negro, was three times U.S. National Champion of Champions.

In 1970 Stuart Hamblen was inducted into the Nashville Songwriters' Hall of Fame. Two years later the Academy of Country and Western Music honored him with its Pioneer Award for being the "first singing Country and Western Cowboy in the history of broadcasting." In 1974 he was given the Gene Autry Award for the enrichment of America's western musical heritage and received a star on Hollywood Boulevard's Walk of Fame. The Los Angeles City Council proclaimed February 13, 1976, "Stuart Hamblen Day." He received a Golden Boot Award in 1988.

Late in February 1989, Hamblen entered St. John's Hospital and Health Center in Santa Monica for surgery to remove a malignant brain tumor. Following the delicate operation he lapsed into a coma and died. In addition to his wife of fifty-five years and two daughters, he was survived by ten grandchildren and nineteen great-grandchildren. Following a memorial service at Rev. Lloyd John Ogilvie's Hollywood Presbyterian Church, at which Billy Graham was a guest speaker, he was interred in the Forest Lawn Cemetery in Hollywood Hills.

BIBLIOGRAPHY: Richard Carlen, *The Big Book of Country Music : A Biographical Encyclopedia* (New York: Penguin, 1995). *Encyclopedia of Country Music* (Oxford University Press, 1998). *Encyclopedia of Folk, Country and Western Music* (New York: St. Martin, 1969). *Encyclopedia of Popular Music*, Volume 3 (1998). Billy Graham, *Just As I Am* (New York: Harper–Collins, 1997). *Los Angeles Times*, March 8, 9, 1989. John Pollock, *Billy Graham: The Authorized Biography* (Minneapolis: World Wide Publications, 1969).
H. Allen Anderson

Hardee, John. Tenor saxophonist; b. Corsicana, Texas, December 20, 1918; d. Dallas, May 18, 1984. Hardee's was a musical family, and while still living at home, he formed part of Dan Carter's Blue Moon Syncopaters, a local group that also included Texas trombonist Tyree Glenn.

Hardee belonged to the Texas tradition of big-toned tenor saxophonists. He attended Bishop College in Marshall, but left school to tour with the Don Albert band from San Antonio during 1937–38. Afterwards he returned to Bishop and graduated with a music degree in 1941. While in the military and stationed in Nyack, New York, from 1941 to 1944, he played clarinet in various army bands, and during this time and after the war took part in jam sessions at New York's City's famed Minton's, as well as at venues on 52nd Street. After his discharge Hardee and his wife moved to Harlem. In 1946 he performed and recorded with Tiny Grimes. During his years in New York, Hardee played a number of famed venues including the Apollo Theater in Harlem and the "845" in the Bronx.

In the late 1940s he moved back to Texas and taught school in Wichita Falls until 1955, when he settled in Dallas. There he held a teaching position at Oliver Wendell Holmes High School until his retirement in 1976. He gave his last performance at the Nice Jazz Festival in France in 1975.

Hardee was reportedly inspired by swing-era tenorist Chu Berry of the Fletcher Henderson and Cab Calloway orchestras. The Texan's own solos have been characterized as "heated" and "strongly swinging," "completely without artifice," and also as "soulful" and "steeped simultaneously in raw power and gentle lyricism." In 1946 Hardee recorded for the prestigious Blue Note label, and in the year of his death, Mosaic Records reissued the Blue Note sides. By 2002 several of Hardee's recordings had been released on CD, including *Hardee's Partee: Forgotten Texas Tenor* (2002) and *The Definitive Black and Blue Sessions* (2002).

BIBLIOGRAPHY: Leonard Feather and Ira Gitler, *The Biographical Encyclopedia of Jazz* (New York: Oxford University Press, 1999). Dan Morgenstern, notes to *The Complete Blue Note Forties Recordings of Ike Quebec and John Hardee* (Mosaic Records, MR 4-107, 1984). Dave Oliphant, *Texan Jazz* (Austin: University of Texas Press, 1996). *Dave Oliphant*

Harper, Margaret Pease. Founder of the outdoor musical drama *Texas*; b. St. Paul, Minnesota, July 22, 1911; d. Amarillo, November 16, 1991 (buried in Dreamland Cemetery, Canyon); daughter of Rollin and Lena Alma (Mason) Pease. Margaret's father was a famed oratorio singer who performed in numerous historical pageants. She grew up in Evanston, Illinois, and received her bachelor's degree from the University of Arizona and her master's degree from the University of Chicago. Her professional experience included teaching, traveling as her father's accompanist, direction of activities at International House at the University of Chicago, and administration of the Colegio América in Callao, Peru.

She married Ples Harper in Tucson, Arizona, on June 1, 1939, and accompanied him to his post as cultural-exchange director for the United States government in Peru. Upon their return to the United States, Ples Harper accepted the position of chairman of the modern language department at West Texas State Teachers College in Canyon in 1946, and Mrs. Harper resumed her occupation as a piano teacher. She wrote *Meet Some Musical Terms: A First Dictionary*, published by the Fischer Company in 1959.

She also grew to love the Panhandle and recognized Palo Duro Canyon's potential as a site for an outdoor musical production. After discussing the idea with her husband and

William and Margaret Moore, and partly influenced by Allen Rankin's "His Theater is as Big as All Outdoors," which appeared in the July 1960 issue of the *Reader's Digest*, she wrote to the Pulitzer Prize–winning playwright Paul Green, suggesting that the geography and history of the Panhandle of Texas provide the ideal setting for a symphonic drama. Green immediately indicated his willingness to meet and discuss the project. Margaret Harper captured enough people's imaginations with her enthusiasm to make the theater and production a reality. She was elected the first president of the Texas Panhandle Heritage Foundation, which sustains the production *Texas*, and served as the public-relations director for the show from 1961 until 1985. Between its opening performance in July 1966 and its twenty-fifth season in 1991, *Texas* was attended by more than two million people.

In addition to her work with *Texas*, Mrs. Harper was a member of the team that founded the Lone Star Ballet, and served as its first president. She lectured across the country on a variety of arts-management topics and was the vice president of the Texas Tourist Council. Her many honors include induction into the National Cowboy Hall of Fame, the National Cowgirl Hall of Fame, and the Texas Hall of Fame for Women. She was Citizen of the Year in both Canyon and Amarillo, and she received the Distinguished Service Award from the Texas Division of the American Association of University Women. She was a member of Alpha Phi, Phi Kappa Phi, Phi Beta Kappa, and the Fine Arts Club of Canyon. She was also a member of the Presbyterian church in Canyon. The Harpers had two children.

BIBLIOGRAPHY: Amarillo *Sunday News–Globe*, November 17, 1991. Canyon *News*, November 21, 1991. Duane F. Guy, "An Amphitheater for the Panhandle," *Panhandle–Plains Historical Review* 51 (1978). *Paul Green's "Texas": A Musical Romance of Panhandle History* (25th Anniversary Souvenir Program, Palo Duro Canyon State Park, 1990). Carroll Wilson, "'Texas' and the Woman Behind It," *Accent West*, June 1980. *Claire R. Kuehn*

Hauschild Music Company. In Victoria; founded by George Hermann Hauschild in 1891. The company began by selling musical instruments and accessories but soon began publishing music. In 1893 Hermann and his eldest son, Henry John Hauschild, who managed the business, built the Hauschild Opera House. This building housed the music company and an auditorium in which silent movies, plays, vaudeville shows, and concerts were performed into the 1930s. The music company was one of the two earliest music publishers in the state (the first was Goggan of Houston). The first publication of the Hauschild Company was "The Ideal Polka" by Charles L. Streiber (1892).

Throughout its history the company was committed to publishing composers from the region. At least eight were Tejanos and seven were women, including one Hispanic. The Hauschild Company ended its publishing operations in 1922 due to the proliferation of similar businesses in the state. It maintained its appliance trade until 1981, when it liquidated its stock and closed down. The opera house was issued a historical marker by the Texas Historical Commission in 1984.

"Twentieth Century Waltz" by Leonora Rives–Diaz, 1901. Published by Hauschild Music Company. Courtesy Henry J. Hauschild, Victoria. Composer Rives–Diaz dedicated this piece to Henry John Hauschild, of the Hauschild Music Company, and his wife Laura Doehler Hauschild. Their wedding picture appears on the cover.

BIBLIOGRAPHY: Vertical files, Center for American History, University of Texas at Austin (under "Henry George Hauschild," "Henry J. Hauschild").

Teresa Palomo Acosta

Haywood, Cedric. Arranger and pianist; b Houston, December 31, 1914; d. Houston, September 9, 1969. Haywood worked in his hometown with the Milt Larkin band from 1935 to 1940. This band included such important figures as Illinois Jacquet and Arnett Cobb, both of whom joined the Lionel Hampton Orchestra after 1940, as did Haywood in 1941. Haywood rejoined Larkin in 1942 and in the same year performed with Sidney Bechet. He served in the army during World War II. From 1948 to 1951 he was a member of Illinois Jacquet's group, which in 1950 recorded Haywood's tune "Hot Rod." In 1952 Haywood worked with the Cal Tjader Quartet in California, and in 1955 he joined up with Kid Ory, touring Europe twice with this traditional trombonist. In the early 1960s Haywood worked with tenorist Brew Moore, after which he returned to Houston, where he led his own band from 1964 until his death.

BIBLIOGRAPHY: John Chilton, *Who's Who of Jazz: Storyville to Swing Street*, Fourth Edition (New York: Da Capo Press, 1985). Barry Kernfeld, ed., *The New Grove Dictionary of Jazz*, Second Edition (New York: Grove's Dictionaries, 2002).

Dave Oliphant

Hemphill, Julius. Saxophonist; b. Fort Worth, January 24, 1938; d. April 2, 1995. Hemphill, an integral part of the "loft jazz" scene in New York City, is regarded as one of the most experimental saxophonists of the modern era. He grew up around Forth Worth's blues and jazz clubs. Although he was from a family with a long religious and musical tradition, he was initially not interested in becoming a musician. This changed, however, when in high school he met John Carter, who taught him the clarinet.

Hemphill continued playing at North Texas State College before joining the United States Army Band in 1964. Four years later he moved to St. Louis and became involved in the Black Artists Group—an association of musicians, visual artists, and actors. The BAG was also involved in politics and helped organize a citywide rent strike in the early 1970s.

During this time Hemphill founded his own jazz label, entitled Mbari, through which he released his debut album, *Dogon, A.D.* Feeling constrained in St. Louis, he moved to New York, where he landed spots playing and recording with Anthony Braxton, Lester Bowie, and Kool and the Gang. On the side, he dabbled in combining dance, theater, and mixed media with jazz to produce an extravagant blend of both sound and vision. This experimentalism eventually culminated in his jazz opera, *Long Toungue*. In 1976 Hemphill formed the World Saxophone Quartet, which made several tours and recordings. His activities in the 1980s and 1990s tapered off as his diabetes worsened. Though he lost a leg toward the end of his life, he still managed to play occasionally.

BIBLIOGRAPHY: Colin Larkin, *The Encyclopedia of Popular Music* (London: MuzeUK Limited, 1998). Bill Shoemaker, "Julius Hemphill and the Theater of Sound," *Down Beat* 53 (February 1986). Miyoshi Smith, "Julius Hemphill," *Cadence* 14 (June 1988). Ludwig van Trikt, "Julius Hemphill Interview," *Cadence* 21 (June 1995). Ron Wynn, Michael Erlewine, and Chris Woodstra, eds., *All Music Guide to Jazz* (San Francisco: Miller Freeman, 1994).

Bradley Shreve

Hewitt, Helen (Margaret). Musicologist and music professor; b. Granville, New York, May 2, 1900; d. Denton, Texas, March 19, 1977. She received a thorough academic and musical education on the East Coast and in Europe. She attended Vassar (B.A., 1921) and the Eastman School of Music (Mus.B., 1925). In 1926 she traveled to France to study organ with Charles-Marie Widor and harmony with Nadia Boulanger at the American Conservatory, Fontainebleau.

Upon returning to the U. S., she continued her organ studies with Lynwood Farnam at the Curtis Institute in Philadelphia (1928–30) and earned graduate degrees at Union Theological Seminary (M.S.M., 1932) and Columbia University (M.A., 1933). After further European study with Heinrich Besseler at the University of Heidelberg, she completed the Ph.D. degree at Harvard University in 1938.

Hewitt began her teaching career at the State Normal School, Potsdam, New York (1925–28). She later taught at the Florida State College for Women (1938–39) and Hunter College (1942). She was appointed to the faculty at North Texas State University in 1942 and was one of the founders of the doctoral program in music there. She remained on the NTSU faculty until her retirement in 1969.

She was best known for her authoritative editions of two printed music incunabula by the renowned Venetian music printer Ottaviano dei Petrucci, *Harmonice musices odhecaton A* and *Canti B* (1502). Professor Hewitt was the compiler and editor of the first four editions of *Doctoral Dissertations in Musicology* (1952–65), published under the auspices of the American Musicological Society. She also translated *Die Orgelwerke Bachs* (Leipzig, 1948) by Hermann Keller (published as *The Organ Works of Bach*, New York, 1967) and authored numerous articles in musicological journals and festschrifts.

She received a number of high honors during her career. She was the first faculty member at NTSU to receive the Piper Professor Award for outstanding teaching. She was given a Guggenheim Memorial Fellowship for research in Paris in 1947, and Mu Phi Epsilon, an international honorary music sorority, honored her with its Elizabeth Mathias Award in 1972. Upon her retirement, Hewitt donated a notable collection of organ music to the NTSU music library. A variety of additional books, musical scores, recordings, and archival materials came to the library upon her death. Collectively, these materials are part of the Helen Hewitt Collection in the special collections of the music library at the University of North Texas.

BIBLIOGRAPHY: Hewitt Collection, University of North Texas music library. *The New Grove Dictionary of Music and Musicians*, Second Edition, Volume 12 (New York: Grove, 2001). Nicolas Slonimsky and Laura Kuhn, editors, *Baker's Biographical Dictionary of Musicians*, Centennial Edition (New York: Schirmer, 2001). Obituary, *The Diapason* 68.7 (June 1977). *Larry Wolz*

Hill, Z. Z. Blues singer; b. September 30, 1935; d. April 27, 1984; birthplace unknown. He was raised in Naples, Texas; his name, Arzell J. Hill Jr., may have been an adoptive name. He devised a combination of blues and contemporary soul styling, and helped to restore the blues to modern black consciousness. In 1954, at the age of nineteen, Hill went to Dallas, where he began his musical career by singing with a gospel quintet known as the Spiritual Five. He moved to California in 1963 and cut his first single, "You Were Wrong," in a garage studio the next year. The song reached the *Billboard* pop chart and stayed there for a week.

After a few other recordings that proved to be commercially unsuccessful, Hill continued to perform but did not make another album until 1972, when he signed with United Artists. He recorded three albums and six rhythm-and-blues singles with the label. In 1977 he signed with Columbia and recorded his best-selling hit, "Love Is So Good When You're Stealing It." In 1980 he signed with

Malaco Records. Two years later, he produced the album *Down Home Blues*, the title song of which became one of the most popular blues songs of the 1980s. The album sold well, remaining on *Billboard*'s soul album chart for almost two years. Hill produced his final album, *Bluesmaster*, in 1984. It comprised a mixture of soul and blues sounds.

In February of that year Hill was involved in a car accident. On April 23 he gave his last performance, at the Longhorn Ballroom in Dallas. He died four days later from complications stemming from a blood clot that had formed in his leg after the car accident.

BIBLIOGRAPHY: Dallas *Morning News*, April 28, 1984. April Frank Scott, *The Down Home Guide to the Blues* (Chicago: A Cappella, 1991). *Juan Carlos Rodríguez*

Hoffmann von Fallersleben, August Heinrich. German poet, scholar, librettist, and author of Texas lyrics; b. Fallersleben, Hannover, April 2, 1798; d. Corvey Castle, near Höxter, Westphalia, January 19, 1874. Though now largely remembered as the author of the anthem "Das Deutschlandlied" (known to Americans by the first line, "*Deutschland, Deutschland über alles*") and a number of children's songs, he was a highly productive writer and scholarly editor. While he was a student at the University of Göttingen (1816–19) he made the acquaintance of the Grimm brothers, whose influence, especially that of Jacob Grimm, shows in his own works and in his lifelong preoccupation with folk literature. After further studies in Bonn (1819–21), some travel, and a stay in Berlin (1821–23), Hoffmann obtained a position in Breslau (now Wroc?aw, Poland), where he stayed for twenty years (1823–43). He was at first a librarian, then was appointed to a professorship in German language and literature. He quickly had a long list of professional publications to his credit, along with successful collections of his own poetry.

Hoffmann was also an outspoken political liberal who supported the growing unrest in the various German lands. Once he published his supposedly "nonpolitical songs," *Unpolitische Lieder* (1840–41), which are in effect politically highly charged, the swift consequence was suspension, dismissal, and banishment from Prussian lands. But fame was now his.

Though he was not formally in exile, the next half dozen years of his life were rather unsettled, and it was at this time that Hoffmann's association with Texas began. In the fall of 1843 the poet befriended Gustav Dresel, who had recently returned from Texas. Not only Dresel's tales, but his Texas journal, intrigued Hoffmann. At Hoffmann's urging, the two men started readying the journal for print. Hoffmann was to edit the work and supply an introduction. Dresel's Texas journal was never published in Germany, for reasons not entirely clear; two publishers are known to have turned it down. While work on the journal was in progress, Hoffmann also befriended Adolf Fuchs just a few weeks before the Fuchs family sailed for Texas in late 1845. For their departure Hoffmann wrote his first poem about the Lone Star emblem, "Der Stern von Texas." During the following months Hoffmann came under a third influence, in the form of Hermann Ehrenberg's book on the Texas Revolution, which impelled him to complete his collection of thirty-one Texas songs, *Texanische Lieder* (1846). In order to circumvent censorship regulations, Hoffmann had the title page state that the book was written by German Texans and published in San Felipe, Texas, by "Adolf Fuchs & Co.," whereas it actually came out in Wandsbeck, Germany.

At about this time the Adelsverein, concerned about its rapidly tarnishing image, also approached Hoffmann, in part through Dresel, hoping apparently to enlist the poet as a prospective emigrant, and to that end made it known that its next settlement after Fredericksburg was going to be named Fallersleben. In November 1846 the society deeded him 300 acres of Texas land as a gift. But the town of Fallersleben was never founded, and the owner never took possession of his Texas acreage.

In 1852 Hoffmann again used Texas in his writing, this time as one of the settings in a three-act opera, *In beiden Welten* ("In Both Worlds," printed in 1868). He approached Robert Schumann, among other musicians, as a possible composer, but to no avail. Not until 1860, when he was employed as a nobleman's librarian, did Hoffmann truly settle down. Among his many late works the largest is his memoirs, *Mein Leben* (1868), volumes four and five of which are about his Texas connections.

BIBLIOGRAPHY: Fritz Andrée, *Hoffmann von Fallersleben* (1972). Max Freund, ed. and trans., *Gustav Dresel's Houston Journal* (Austin: University of Texas Press, 1954). August Heinrich Hoffmann von Fallersleben, *Gesammelte Werke* (8 vols., Berlin: Fontane, 1890–94).

Anders S. Saustrup

Hofner, Adolph. Pioneer of western swing music; b. Moulton, Texas, June 8, 1916; d. San Antonio, June 2, 2000 (buried in Mission Park South, San Antonio). Hofner's father was part German, and his mother was of Czech extraction. Adolph and his younger brother, Emil, grew up speaking Czech. The family moved to San Antonio in 1928, and Adolph and Emil (nicknamed "Bash") learned guitar and steel guitar, respectively. They played in polka bands as teenagers.

In the early 1930s Adolph and Emil teamed up with Simon Garcia to form a trio called the Hawaiian Serenaders. They landed a fifteen-minute spot on radio station KTSA, but the station pulled the plug on them halfway through their first broadcast. Adolph, whose smooth singing style earned him the nickname the "Bing Crosby of Country," first recorded with Jimmie Revard's Oklahoma Playboys, whom he and Emil joined in 1936. Subsequently, Hofner returned San Antonio and worked briefly as a mechanic. He resumed his musical career in the late 1930s with Tom Dickey and the Showboys, with whom he recorded "It Makes No Difference Now," but was fired for showing up late for a radio spot and resolved to form his own band.

Adolph Hofner and All the Boys began playing at clubs in San Antonio and around South Texas. They changed their name to the San Antonians for a recording engagement. Hofner recorded at various times for the Imperial, Columbia, RCA, Decca, and Sarg labels. His first recording success came in 1940, when "Maria Elena" became a

minor hit. He claimed to have been the first to record the classic "Cotton Eyed Joe" (1941), which has since become a standard.

During World War II he briefly changed his stage name from Adolph to Dolph to avoid association with Adolf Hitler. In 1945 he moved to California. For three years he and his nine-piece Texans played on the radio and at various Los Angeles–area nightclubs owned by promoter Foreman Phillips. After returning to San Antonio, Hofner renamed his band the Pearl Wranglers, after Pearl Beer, the sponsor of his radio show. Among those who played in Hofner's band at various times over the years were such well-known musicians as singer and guitarist Floyd Tillman and fiddler J. R. Chatwell. Throughout his career, Hofner switched effortlessly among western swing, honkytonk, the occasional Mexican standard, and polkas and waltzes, which he often sang in Czech. He continued to perform into the 1990s, though he was slowed by a stroke in 1993. He died of lung cancer. Hofner and his wife, Susan, had three children.

BIBLIOGRAPHY: San Antonio *Express–News*, June 3, 2000. Adolph Hofner website (http://www.geocities.com/~jimlowe/western/hofner.html), accessed October 24, 2001. *Martin Donell Kohout*

Hogg, Ima. Philanthropist and patron of the arts; b. Mineola, Texas, July 10, 1882; d. London, England, August 19, 1975 (buried in Oakwood Cemetery, Austin); daughter of Sarah Ann (Stinson) and Governor James Stephen Hogg. She had three brothers, William Clifford Hogg, born in 1875; Michael, born in 1885; and Thomas Elisha Hogg, born in 1887. Ima was named for the heroine of a Civil War poem written by her uncle Thomas Elisha and was affectionately known as Miss Ima for most of her long life. She was eight years old when her father was elected governor; she spent much of her early life in Austin. After her mother died of tuberculosis in 1895, Ima attended the Coronal Institute in San Marcos, and in 1899 she entered the University of Texas.

She started playing the piano at age three and in 1901 went to New York to study music. From 1907 to 1909 she continued her music studies in Berlin and Vienna. She then moved to Houston, where she gave piano lessons to a select group of pupils and helped found the Houston Symphony Orchestra, which played its first concert in June 1913. Miss Ima served as the first vice president of the Houston Symphony Society and became president in 1917. She became ill in late 1918 and spent the next two years in Philadelphia under the care of a specialist in mental and nervous disorders. She did not return to Houston to live until 1923.

In the meantime, oil had been struck on the Hogg property near West Columbia, Texas. By the late 1920s Miss Ima was involved in a wide range of philanthropic projects. In 1929 she founded the Houston Child Guidance Center, an agency to provide therapy and counseling for disturbed children and their families. In 1940, with a bequest from her brother Will, who had died in 1930, she established the Hogg Foundation for Mental Hygiene, which later became the Hogg Foundation for Mental Health at the University of Texas. In 1943 Miss Hogg, a lifelong Democrat, won an election to the Houston school board, where she worked to establish symphony concerts for schoolchildren, to get equal pay for teachers regardless of sex or race, and to set up a painting-to-music program in the public schools.

In 1946 she again became president of the Houston Symphony Society, a post she held until 1956, and in 1948 she became the first woman president of the Philosophical Society of Texas. Since the 1920s she had been studying and collecting early American art and antiques, and in 1966 she presented her collection and Bayou Bend, the River Oaks mansion she and her brothers had built in 1927, to the Museum of Fine Arts in Houston. The Bayou Bend Collection, recognized as one of the finest of its kind, draws thousands of visitors each year.

In the 1950s Miss Ima restored the Hogg family home at Varner Plantation, near West Columbia, and in 1958 she presented it to the state of Texas. It became Varner–Hogg Plantation State Historical Park. In the 1960s she restored the Winedale Inn, a nineteenth-century stagecoach stop at Round Top, Texas, which she gave to the University of Texas. The Winedale Historical Center now serves as a center for the study of Texas history and is also the site of a widely acclaimed annual fine arts festival. Miss Hogg also restored her parents' home at Quitman, Texas, and in 1969 the town of Quitman established the Ima Hogg Museum in her honor.

In 1953 Governor Allan Shivers appointed her to the Texas State Historical Survey Committee (later the Texas Historical Commission), and in 1967 that body gave her an award for "meritorious service in historic preservation." In 1960 she served on a committee appointed by President Eisenhower for the planning of the National Cultural Center (now Kennedy Center) in Washington, D.C. In 1962, at the request of Jacqueline Kennedy, Ima Hogg served on an advisory panel to aid in the search for historic furniture for the White House. She was also honored by the Garden Club of America (1959), the National Trust for Historic Preservation (1966), and the American Association for State and Local History (1969).

In 1968 Miss Hogg was the first recipient of the Santa Rita Award, given by the University of Texas System to recognize contributions to the university and to higher education. In 1969 she, Oveta Culp Hobby, and Lady Bird Johnson became the first three women members of the Academy of Texas, an organization founded to honor persons who "enrich, enlarge, or enlighten" knowledge in any field. In 1971 Southwestern University gave Miss Hogg an honorary doctorate in fine arts, and in 1972 the National Society of Interior Designers gave her its Thomas Jefferson Award for outstanding contributions to America's cultural heritage.

At the age of 93, Ima Hogg died of complications from a traffic accident that occurred while she was vacationing in England. Her funeral was at Bayou Bend. The major bequest in her will was to the Ima Hogg Foundation, a charitable nonprofit organization she established in 1964.

BIBLIOGRAPHY: Virginia Bernhard, *Ima Hogg: The Governor's Daughter* (Austin: Texas Monthly Press, 1984). James Stephen Hogg Papers, Center for American History, University of Texas at Austin. Louise Kosches Iscoe, *Ima Hogg* (Austin: Hogg Foundation for Mental Health, 1976). *Notable American Women: A Biographical Dictionary* (4 vols., Cambridge, Massachusetts: Harvard University Press, 1971–80). *Virginia Bernhard*

Holley, Mary Austin. Writer, musical enthusiast, lyricist, and composer; b. New Haven, Connecticut, October 30, 1784; d. New Orleans, August 2, 1846; daughter of Elijah and Esther (Phelps) Austin and cousin of Stephen F. Austin. Though largely known as an early writer about Texas, Mary Austin made plain her love of music in an 1804 letter to her future husband, Horace Holley, in which she wrote that the "appropriate province" of music "is to elevate and charm the whole circle of human feelings," and that "it serves…the great cause of virtue and happiness." This "letter from a lady to a gentleman who was thought not to be pleased with music" was published anonymously in the June 1821 issue of the *Western Review*.

On January 1, 1805, she married Holley, a minister. They were parents to a son, Horace, and a daughter, Harriette. From the fall of 1805 until 1808, Mrs. Holley studied music and languages at New Haven schools. She became musically adept in voice, piano, and guitar; later she studied the harp as well, and numbered the renowned Norwegian violinist Ole Bull among her friends.

In October 1831 she traveled to Stephen F. Austin's colony in Texas by way of the Brazos River. During this trip she composed and set to music her "Brazos Boat Song" (published by John Cole, Baltimore, 1832 or 1833). In 1838 Firth & Hall, New York, published "Brazos Boat Glee," composed, arranged, and dedicated to Henry Austin, Mary's brother, by the German-American composer Wilhelm Iucho, with words by Mary Holley. The lyrics to this song are similar but not identical to those of "Brazos Boat Song."

Mary Holley and her "Brazos Boat Song" inspired several Texas plays and songs with the same title. In 1934, Dallas playwright and author John William Rogers wanted to include this song in his *Westward People* (New York: Samuel French, 1935), a one-act play loosely based on her letters, but was unable to find a copy. Instead, Rogers wrote his own "Brazos Boat Song," with lyrics based on Holley's letters set to a barcarole-like melody. In 1936 Texas composer David W. Guion adapted and expanded on Rogers's song and arranged it for voice and piano. Guion's "Brazos Boat Song" (New York: Schirmer, 1936) was published as a special Centennial Edition and included an annotation describing Mary Holley's version as the "First Texas Song." In 1953, Ellen (Clayton) Garwood wrote *No Other Time for Austin: A Play in One Act about Stephen Austin and Mary Holley*. Although this play includes references to "Brazos Boat Song," a comparison of texts indicates that the source was "Brazos Boat Glee."

Mrs. Holley also wrote the lyrics to "The Texan Song of Liberty," a song inspired by the battle of San Jacinto. Her words were first published in the May 19, 1836, *Kentucky Gazette* with a note stating that they should be sung to the Scottish tune "Bruce's Address." Later that year, her friend Iucho set them to an original tune that was published by Dubois and Bacon in New York.

BIBLIOGRAPHY: Mattie Austin Hatcher, *Letters of an*

Early American Traveler, Mary Austin Holley: Her Life and Her Work, 1784–1846 (Dallas: Southwest Press, 1933). Mary Austin Holley Papers, Center for American History, University of Texas at Austin. Rebecca Smith Lee, *Mary Austin Holley: A Biography* (Austin: University of Texas Press, 1962). Kevin E. Mooney, Texas Centennial 1936: Music and Identity (Ph.D. dissertation, University of Texas at Austin, 1998). *Kevin E. Mooney*

Hollimon, Clarence. Blues, jazz, and R&B guitarist; b. Milton Howard Clarence Hollimon, Houston, October 24, 1937; d. Houston, April 23, 2000. Hollimon was widely acknowledged as one of the greatest guitarists in his musical genres. During the forty-six years of his professional career, he appeared on countless recordings produced in Houston as well as in other cities across the nation (including Austin, Los Angeles, New Orleans, New York, and Providence, Rhode Island), as well as in Germany.

With his wife—singer, pianist, and fellow recording artist Carol Fran—whom he married in 1983, Hollimon toured widely in the United States and abroad and performed at the 1996 International Olympics celebration in Centennial Park, Atlanta. He also received the Texas Black Caucus Entertainer of the Year award in 1987 and the Jazz Heritage Society's Guitarist of the Year award in 1989.

Hollimon initially dropped out of Wheatley High School, in the Fifth Ward of Houston, in 1954 to play guitar full-time with the famous blues orchestra led by Bill Harvey. The artists he backed on his first road tour included Clarence "Gatemouth" Brown and Willie Mae "Big Mama" Thornton. This affiliation with Harvey eventually led to an opening for Hollimon to work for the Duke and Peacock labels, owned by Don Robey. From 1957 to 1962 Hollimon proved to be a brilliant session guitarist, performing mainly under the direction of legendary producer Joe Scott. He provided guitar accompaniment for such blues singers as Bobby Bland, Joe Hinton, Junior Parker, and O. V. Wright, as well as gospel singers such as Rev. Cleophus Robinson and groups such as the Mighty Clouds of Joy, the Dixie Hummingbirds, and the Five Blind Boys.

Hollimon also worked during the late 1950s and early 1960s for artists not linked to the Duke and Peacock labels. He married and had two sons. Between 1956 and 1960 he intermittently toured and recorded (on the King label) with pianist Charles Brown, a Texas native who had moved to California. In 1964 he temporarily moved to New York to do session work at Scepter One Recording Studios. Among the pop singers he backed during his tenure there were Dionne Warwick and Maxine Brown. Following his return to Houston the next year, Hollimon assumed a salaried position as a Duke–Peacock studio guitarist, but he still worked locally during this period on other recording projects, including sessions with jazz band leader and saxophonist Arnett Cobb.

Throughout the later 1970s and early 1980s Hollimon's musical productivity waned, especially during a period of substance abuse. However, his relationship with Carol Fran helped him regain his former prowess. Though the two had initially met around 1958 in New Orleans at the famous Dew Drop Inn, it took a chance crossing of paths some twenty-five years later (at a blues jam in a Houston nightclub) to make them a couple. That union, which billed itself professionally as Fran & Hollimon, eventually evolved into what was likely the most widely traveled and recorded husband-and-wife blues duo in Texas history. During that time they not only played marquee concert halls in numerous cities overseas, as well as major festivals nationwide; they also logged hundreds of hours traveling around the Lone Star State to perform concerts and serve as artists-in-residence in programs sponsored by the Austin-based organization Texas Folklife Resources.

The couple recorded several CDs in the final decade of the twentieth century. Following Hollimon's featured guest role on the Grady Gaines disc *Full Gain* (1988), Fran & Hollimon first collaborated in the studio as contributors to the compilation *Gulf Coast Blues, Volume One* (1990), followed by appearances on Gaines's *Horn of Plenty* (1992); then they released their first full album as a team, *Soul Sensation* (1992), and its sequel, *See There!* (1994)—all on the Black Top label. In 2000 they released their final recording as a duo, *It's About Time*, on the JSP label.

Meanwhile, Hollimon remained in demand as a session guitarist during the final years of his life. He did studio work for various Texas blues singers, including his former Duke–Peacock colleague Lavelle White, who featured him prominently on her CDs *Miss Lavelle* (Antone's, 1994) and *It Haven't Been Easy* (Discovery, 1996). And Hollimon provided all the guitar work for the W. C. Handy Award–nominated 1999 CD *Rockin and Shoutin the Blues* (Bullseye Blues and Jazz) by Houston vocalist Jimmy "T-99" Nelson.

Hollimon was known to his closest friends and musical associates by the nickname "Gristle." He died of natural causes at home.

BIBLIOGRAPHY: Clarence Hollimon, with Carol Fran, "You Can't Fire Me & I Ain't Quittin'": interview, *Living Blues* 116 (July–August 1994). Houston *Chronicle*, April 26, 2000. Houston *Press*, October 21–27, 1999; May 4–10, 2000. Roger Wood, "Clarence Hollimon," *Living Blues* 152 (July–August 2000). Roger Wood, *Down In Houston: Bayou City Blues* (Austin: University of Texas Press, 2003). *Roger Wood*

Holly, Buddy. Rock-and-roll pioneer; b. Charles Hardin Holley, Lubbock, September 7, 1936; d. near Mason City, Iowa, February 3, 1959; youngest of four children of Lawrence and Ella (Drake) Holley. His father worked as a tailor and salesman in a Lubbock clothing store, and though Lawrence Holley did not play an instrument himself, he and his wife encouraged the musical talents of their children. Buddy made his debut at the age of five, when he appeared with his brothers in a talent show in nearby County Line and won five dollars for his rendition of "Down the River of Memories." At eleven he took piano lessons and proved to be an apt pupil, but quit after only nine months. After briefly studying the steel guitar, he picked up the acoustic guitar and taught himself to play. At Hutchinson Junior High School he befriended Bob Montgomery; the two formed a duo that performed country and what eventually was called rock-and-roll music.

Buddy Holly performing at the Alan Freed Big Beat Show, Waterloo Hippodrome, Waterloo, Iowa, 1958. Photograph by Dick Cole

In fall 1953 Holly, Montgomery, and bass player Larry Welborn earned a regular spot on Lubbock radio station KDAV's "Sunday Party" program. While attending Lubbock High School, Holly studied printing and drafting and worked part-time at Panhandle Steel Products. He apparently never doubted, however, that he would become a professional musician. In 1954 and 1955 he, Montgomery, and Welborn made a few demonstration recordings in Wichita Falls, hoping to land a recording contract, but in 1956 Decca offered Holly a solo contract. Decca was well-known as a country-and-western label and tried unsuccessfully to fit Holly into the country mold. After releasing two unsuccessful singles the company terminated Holly's contract.

Buddy returned to Lubbock still determined to make it big in the music business. In February 1957 he, Welborn (who was soon replaced by Joe B. Mauldin), drummer Jerry Allison, and guitarist Niki Sullivan went to independent producer Norman Petty's studio in Clovis, New Mexico, and adopted the name the Crickets. From this point Holly's career took off. Brunswick Records signed the Crickets, while Holly signed a solo contract with Brunswick's Coral subsidiary. The records put out under the Crickets' name had backing vocals, while those put out under Holly's name, with the exception of "Rave On," did not. The arrangement made no difference in their recording technique. All of the records included Holly's unmistakable vocal style, which incorporated hiccups, nonsense syllables, a wide range, and abrupt changes of pitch, and was described by one critic as playfully ironic and childlike. The first Crickets single, "That'll Be the Day," backed with "I'm Looking for Someone to Love," was released on Brunswick Records on May 27, 1957. The record eventually reached number three on the pop charts and number two on the rhythm-and-blues charts.

At first many listeners assumed that Holly and his band were black. In July 1957, when the Crickets flew east, they discovered that they had been booked on various package tours with black artists at such theaters as the Apollo in New York and the Howard in Washington, D.C. Their reception at the Apollo was chilly, until they launched the third day's show with a wild version of "Bo Diddley." The next few months were busy ones for Holly and his band. They appeared on television on "American Bandstand," "The Arthur Murray Dance Party," and "The Ed Sullivan Show" and on a number of package tours and concert bills with some of the most famous rock-and-rollers of the day. In late December, Holly's second solo single, "Peggy Sue," backed with "Everyday," reached number three on the pop and R&B charts. The Crickets' second single, "Oh Boy!," backed with "Not Fade Away," was released in October 1957 and sold close to a million copies. Niki Sullivan quit the band, and over the next few months the Crickets toured Australia, Florida, and Great Britain as a trio before Holly asked guitarist Tommy Allsup to replace Sullivan. Their third single, "Maybe Baby," backed with "Tell Me How," also cracked the Top 100.

In the summer of 1958 Holly met Maria Elena Santiago, a native of Puerto Rico who had gone to New York as a child to live with her aunt after the death of her mother. Maria was the receptionist at Peer-Southern Music when Holly and the Crickets stopped in for a business meeting. Holly asked her out that night and, over dinner at P. J. Clarke's, asked her to marry him. She accepted, and they were married on August 15 at Holly's home in Lubbock.

Things were not going well for Holly professionally in late 1958. His last few singles had failed to recapture the success of the early releases. In October, after another tour, he announced that he was moving to New York. Norman Petty, however, convinced Allison and Mauldin to stay in Clovis. Holly reluctantly agreed to the breakup of the Crickets and determined to carry on alone. In New York he took acting lessons and recorded several songs with strings and orchestral backing. In January 1959 he agreed to go on tour again as part of what was billed as the "Winter Dance Party." He was accompanied on the tour by Allsup, bassist and future superstar Waylon Jennings, and drummer Charlie Bunch. The tour promoters rather unscrupulously billed this group as the Crickets.

Holly and his band, along with Ritchie Valens, J. P. (the Big Bopper) Richardson, and several others traveled by bus through the midwestern winter. After a February 2 show in Clear Lake, Iowa, they were supposed to get back on the bus for a 430-mile trip to Moorhead, Minnesota, but Holly decided instead to charter a plane to fly him and his band to Fargo, North Dakota, just across the Red River of the North from Moorhead. When the other performers heard of his plans, they wanted to come, too, and Jennings and Allsup ended up giving up their seats to Richardson and Valens. The red Beechcraft Bonanza took off from Mason City, ten miles east of Clear Lake, at about 1:50 A.M. on the morning of February 3, 1959. The weather was cold, about eighteen degrees, with light snow, and the plane went down almost immediately; the wreckage was discovered later that morning eight miles from the Mason City airport. The pilot, Valens, Richardson, and Holly, who had been thrown twenty feet from the airplane, all died in the crash.

Shortly after Holly was buried in Lubbock, his widow suffered a miscarriage. (She later remarried and named the first of her three sons Carlos, after Holly.) Holly's last single, "It Doesn't Matter Anymore," backed with "Raining in My Heart," had been released on January 5 and entered the Top 100 on the day of his death.

Holly had an incalculable influence on rock-and-roll music. Performers who either recorded his songs or were influenced by his and his band's distinctive style, image, and instrumentation include the Beatles, the Rolling Stones, Bob Dylan, the Grateful Dead, Linda Ronstadt, Bruce Springsteen, and Elvis Costello. In 1971 the singer-songwriter Don McLean commemorated February 3, 1959, as "the day the music died" in his number-one single, "American Pie."

The city of Lubbock, however, was somewhat slower to recognize its most famous son. Not until the release of the movie *The Buddy Holly Story* in 1978 did the city begin to realize the tourism potential of Buddy Holly. In 1979 the city hosted a concert by Jennings and the Crickets to raise funds for a statue of Holly. The 8½-foot-tall bronze by Grant Speed, mounted near the Lubbock Memorial Civic Center, was unveiled in 1980. In 1983 the city turned the area around the statue into a "Walk of Fame" honoring

West Texas musicians. Three years later the city celebrated the fiftieth anniversary of Buddy Holly's birth with a concert featuring Bo Diddley and Bobby Vee, and in 1990 an auction of Holly memorabilia in New York raised more than $703,000. Actor Gary Busey, who portrayed the singer in *The Buddy Holly Story*, paid $242,000 for his guitar, and the Hard Rock Cafe paid $45,100 for a pair of Holly's distinctive black-framed glasses. The Buddy Holly Center, in Lubbock, opened in 2000. It houses the Buddy Holly Gallery, the Texas Musicians Hall of Fame, and the Lubbock Fine Arts Center. In 2002 Steve Richards recorded an unfinished song by Holly, "That Makes It Tough"—part of Holly's informal recordings *The Apartment Tapes*—for an album called *Southbound Train*.

BIBLIOGRAPHY: Dallas *Morning News*, August 14, 2002. John Goldrosen, *The Buddy Holly Story* (New York: Quick Fox, 1979). Lubbock *Avalanche–Journal*, October 26, 2000. Vertical files, Center for American History, University of Texas at Austin. *Martin Donell Kohout*

Hopkins, Lightnin'. Blues singer and guitarist; b. Sam Hopkins, Centerville, Texas, March 15, 1911; d. Houston, January 30, 1982; son of Abe and Frances (Sims) Hopkins. After his father died in 1915, the family (Sam, his mother, and five brothers and sisters) moved to Leona. At age eight he made his first instrument, a cigar-box guitar with chicken-wire strings. By ten he was playing music with his cousin, Texas Alexander, and Blind Lemon Jefferson, who encouraged him to continue. Hopkins also played with his brothers, blues musicians John Henry and Joel.

By the mid-1920s Sam had started jumping trains, shooting dice, and playing the blues anywhere he could. He served time at the Houston County Prison Farm in the mid-1930s, and after his release he returned to the blues-club circuit. In 1946 he had his big break and first recording—in Los Angeles for Aladdin Recordings. On the record was a piano player named Wilson (Thunder) Smith; by chance he combined well with Sam to give him his nickname, Lightnin'. The album has been described as "downbeat solo blues" characteristic of Hopkins's style. Aladdin was so impressed with Hopkins that the company invited him back for a second session in 1947. He eventually made forty-three recordings for the label.

Over his career Hopkins recorded for nearly twenty different labels, including Gold Star Records in Houston. On occasion he would record for one label while under contract to another. In 1950 he settled in Houston, but he continued to tour the country periodically. Though he recorded prolifically between 1946 and 1954, his records for the most part were not big outside the black community. It was not until 1959, when Hopkins began working with legendary producer Sam Chambers, that his music began to reach a mainstream white audience. Hopkins switched to an acoustic guitar and became a hit in the folk-blues revival of the 1960s.

During the early part of that decade he played at Carnegie Hall with Pete Seeger and Joan Baez and in 1964 toured with the American Folk Blues Festival. By the end of the 1960s he was opening for such rock bands as the Grateful Dead and Jefferson Airplane. During a tour of

Europe in the 1970s, he played for Queen Elizabeth II at a command performance. Hopkins also performed at the New Orleans Jazz and Heritage Festival. In 1972 he worked on the soundtrack to the film *Sounder*. He was also the subject of a documentary, *The Blues According to Lightnin' Hopkins*, which won the prize at the Chicago Film Festival for outstanding documentary in 1970.

Some of his biggest hits included "Short Haired Women / Big Mama Jump!" (1947); "Shotgun Blues," which went to number five on the *Billboard* charts in 1950; and "Penitentiary Blues" (1959). His albums included *The Complete Prestige / Bluesville Recordings*, *The Complete Aladdin Recordings*, and the *Gold Star Sessions* (two volumes). Hopkins recorded a total of more than eighty-five albums and toured around the world. But after a 1970 car crash, many of the concerts he performed were on his front porch or at a bar near his house. He had a knack for writing songs impromptu, and frequently wove legends around a core of truth. His often autobiographical songs made him a spokesman for the southern black community that had no voice in the white mainstream until blues attained a broader popularity through white singers like Elvis Presley.

Hopkins died of cancer of the esophagus. He was survived by his wife, Antoinette, and four children. His funeral was attended by more than 4,000, including many fans and musicians.

BIBLIOGRAPHY: Sheldon Harris, *Blues Who's Who: A Biographical Dictionary of Blues Singers* (New Rochelle, New York: Arlington House, 1979). Houston *Chronicle*, February 7, 1982. Stanley Sadie, ed., *The New Grove Dictionary of Music and Musicians* (Washington: Macmillan, 1980). Robert Santelli, *Big Book of the Blues: A Biographical Encyclopedia* (New York: Penguin Books, 1993). Eileen Southern, *Biographical Dictionary of Afro-American and African Musicians* (Westport, Connecticut: Greenwood, 1982). *Alan Lee Haworth*

Horton, Johnny. Singer; b. John Gale Horton, Los Angeles, April 30, 1925; d. Milano, Texas, November 5, 1960; son of John Lolly and Ella Claudia Horton. His parents moved back and forth from Los Angeles to East Texas during his early years. Johnny graduated from high school in Gallatin, Texas, and attended junior college in Jacksonville and Kilgore. He earned a basketball scholarship to Baylor University in Waco and went from there to Seattle University. After college, Horton worked in Alaska and California in the fishing industry.

In 1950 he began singing country music on KXLA, Pasadena, Texas, and then proceeded to Cliffie Stone's "Hometown Jamboree" on KLAC–TV. He joined the "Louisiana Hayride" in 1955 and performed under the name the Singing Fisherman. Companies he recorded with included Mercury, Dot, and Columbia. Horton was known for his versatility, but his specialty was honky-tonk. In 1956 he had his first hit, "Honky Tonk Man." His first number-one recording in the country was "When It's Springtime in Alaska," released in 1959. At that time both country and popular-music radio stations began playing his music.

He became famous for his saga songs, and influenced a

brief trend of popularity for these historical and patriotic numbers. He achieved national recognition when some of his songs made the popular hit parade. His more popular saga songs, including "The Battle of New Orleans" and "Sink the *Bismarck*," reached positions on both country and pop charts. Despite his crossover appeal, Horton remained entrenched in the country music scene and had only moderate success.

He died in an automobile accident while traveling to Shreveport, Louisiana. His wife, Billie Jean (Jones) Horton, became a widow for the second time, as she had been married previously to Hank Williams.

BIBLIOGRAPHY: *The Illustrated Encyclopedia of Country Music* (New York: Harmony Books, 1977). John Morthland, *The Best of Country Music* (Garden City, New York: Doubleday, 1984). Melvin Shestack, *The Country Music Encyclopedia* (New York: Crowell, 1979).

Jill S. Seeber

Houston Grand Opera. The Houston Grand Opera Association was incorporated in August 1955 as Houston's first permanent opera company. Its general director and conductor was Walter Herbert, a native of Germany, who had been instrumental in founding the New Orleans Opera in 1943. With the support of Edward Bing, a local opera singer and teacher, Mrs. Louis G. Lobit, and Charles Cockrell Jr., the opera was chartered by the Texas secretary of state with a board of directors, general manager, and conductor.

The first performances of the new company, in January 1956, were productions of Richard Strauss's *Salome* and Puccini's *Madame Butterfly*, staged in the Music Hall. Walter Herbert remained general director of the company through the 1971–72 season and made substantial contributions. Although he labored under severe financial limitations, he gave Houston good, occasionally superb, opera. Owing to the tastes of the Houston audiences, Herbert's repertory remained conservative, although he did occasionally present more adventurous operas such as Hans Werne Henze's *Young Lord*. Herbert also brought black artists to Houston to assume leading roles. He wanted to bring opera to as many people as possible and established opera workshops to give instruction in all phases of opera production; these resulted in some unusual summer productions. He also worked with theater groups in Houston to produce opera in a variety of settings.

As early as 1965 Herbert was named artistic director of the San Diego Opera. At first, he held the positions at San Diego and Houston simultaneously, but later became increasingly involved in the San Diego company. In 1969–70 he became full-time artistic director and conductor of the San Diego opera, sharing his Houston duties with his assistant, Charles Rosenkrans. During Herbert's years the Houston Grand Opera encountered considerable financial difficulties. It experienced a particularly difficult season in 1959–60 as a result of the failure of a maintenance fund drive.

Gradually, however, the Houston opera's financial stability improved; these improvements coincided with the work of David Gockley, who was hired in 1970 as business manager and promoted in 1972 to general director of the company. Due to Gockley's imaginative leadership, the growing sophistication of opera audiences, and booming financial support for the arts due to Houston's emergence as a petroleum center, the Houston Grand Opera rose to national and international prominence. By 1981 the company operated on an extremely sound financial basis. Its success was aided by gifts of corporations such as Armco Steel, Atlanta Richfield, Shell, and United Energy Resources. During the 1978–79 season Tenneco gave generously to the Houston Grand Opera, making it possible to tape the productions so that they might be heard coast-to-coast on the radio, as the New York Metropolitan and Chicago Lyric companies are heard.

Dating from the beginning of his association with the Houston company, Gockley showed a total commitment to opera, but opera as broadly defined. He aimed to present different kinds of opera to a diversified audience, in his own words combating "the image of opera as a medium for only the wealthy and elite." Under his direction the company expanded its repertory to include the less familiar works ranging from the Baroque era to the twentieth century. The company also encouraged contemporary opera and has staged several world and American premieres: Thomas Pasatieri's *The Seagull* (1974), Carlisle Floyd's *Bilby's Doll* (1976) and *Willie Stark* (1981), Leonard Bernstein's *A Quiet Place* (1987), and Philip Glass's *Akhnaten* (1984). In 1990, with a $1 million grant from the National Endowment for the Arts, Houston Grand Opera expanded its commitment to contemporary music theater with the formation of a ground-breaking new program, Opera New World. Opera New World is HGO's ongoing program to commission and produce new music theater works that hold appeal for audiences who may have felt culturally, socially or economically removed from the traditional American opera audience.

Although consistently giving opportunities to young singers, Gockley increasingly brought in major talents from around the world. There have been a number of important opera stars associated with the Houston Grand Opera. Particularly important is Beverly Sills, whose relationship with the Houston company predated her international career. Sills appeared several times with the Houston Grand Opera in the leading roles of Donizetti operas such as *Don Pasquale*, the *Daughter of the Regiment*, and *Lucrezia Borgia*. Also, Marilyn Horne appeared in the title role of Handel's *Rinaldo*, a part with which she is often associated, and John Vickers appeared in the title role of Britten's *Peter Grimes*. In addition to these performances, a number of internationally known opera singers have given concerts sponsored by the Houston Grand Opera. These include Luciano Pavarotti, Placido Domingo, Leontyne Price, Mirella Freni, and Renata Scotto. Gockley also engaged leading conductors, stage directors, and costume and set designers as the company's fame has grown.

Each spring at Miller Theater in Hermann Park, Houston Grand Opera gives fully staged performances of operas to the public at no charge. One of these productions, Scott Joplin's *Treemonisha*, presented in 1975, revealed a delightful American stage work, which went on to a major tour, a run on Broadway, a recording on the *Deutsche*

Grammophon label, and a television program on PBS in 1986. A production of Gershwin's *Porgy and Bess* was also recorded and brought the company its first Tony Award.

Among the more than two dozen world premier operas performed by the Houston Grand Opera are Carlisle Floyd's *Cold Sassy Tree* (2000), Mark Adamo's *Little Women* (1998), Steward Wallace and Michael Korie's *Harvey Milk* (1995), Noa Ain's *The Outcast* (1994), and John Adams and Alice Goodman's *Nixon in China* (1987). *Nixon in China* was performed at the 1988 Edinburgh Festival and won both an Emmy and a Grammy. Houston Grand Opera's *Show Boat* was performed in Cairo, Egypt, at the Cairo National Culture Centre in 1989, and the 1995–96 production of *Porgy and Bess* toured Japan.

In 1989 the Houston Grand Opera became the second opera company in the United States to establish an archives and resource center. The Grand Opera also established an Education and Outreach Department, which implemented community outreach programs, education programs for children and the general public, and the organization of STARS (Students Through Arts Reaching Success). STARS was formed to interest students in reading and writing and was cited by the Business Committee for the Arts in New York as a model arts education program.

After 1966 the Houston Grand Opera performed in Jesse H. Jones Hall for the Performing Arts. By 1981 money had been raised for a new facility. The Wortham Theater Center opened in 1987 at a cost of $72 million. The Wortham Center is one of only a few theaters constructed in the United States after World War II with the specific needs of opera in mind. Others include the Metropolitan Opera House, the Kennedy Center Opera House, and Indiana University's Opera Theater.

In 1984, Houston Grand Opera began using surtitles on all foreign language productions, becoming one of the first opera companies in the United States to do so. In 1995, the company began including Spanish-language synopses in its *Stagebill* program for Wortham Theater Center productions. In the fall of 2000, HGO initiated OperaVision, a "system of plasma and projection screens designed to improve sight lines to the stage for the Balcony and Grand Tier." OperaVision makes the entire stage visible to the entire audience, and also delivers special close-up shots taken by cameramen and by concealed cameras.

BIBLIOGRAPHY: Deborah Fowler, "State of the Arts," *Houston Magazine*, December 1988. Robert I. Giesberg, *Houston Grand Opera: A History* (Houston: Grand Opera Guild, 1981). "Houston Grand Opera: A History," 2003 (http://www.houstongrandopera.org/history/history.asp), accessed January 9, 2003. *Robert I. Giesberg*

Houston Symphony Orchestra. Began performing in 1913. Orchestral music in Houston dates from 1868, when Professor Stadtler led a small ensemble at the Exchange Saloon. Orchestras connected with German *Sängerfeste* from 1885 to 1913, a local Symphony Club by 1902, and a visit by Modeste Altschuler's Russian Symphony Orchestra in the 1912–13 season whetted local appetites for a permanent ensemble.

More than the other major orchestras in Texas, the Houston Symphony Orchestra began as a project of fashionable society, when civic leader and art patron Ima Hogg marshaled her forces to sponsor a concert on June 21, 1913. Under Julien Paul Blitz, the thirty-five-member orchestra played a diverse program, including Mozart's Symphony No. 39 and "Dixie." The concert was a success and built enthusiasm for continuing activity. Blitz was succeeded in 1916 by Paul Bergé, who remained until the orchestra disbanded in 1918 because of World War I.

The 1920s witnessed many guest orchestras touring through Houston until the HSO was reconstituted under Uriel Nespoli in 1931. His programs displayed his loyalty to Italian music, as well as his enthusiasm for Wagner; unfortunately, the budding orchestra was not yet up to the grandeur of sound that Wagner required. There was a brief rivalry during this period with the newly organized Philharmonic Society, and Nespoli's unfamiliarity with the English language and the workings of Houston society made his tenure a rocky one. Frank St. Leger then conducted the orchestra for three seasons. The orchestra at this time was hampered by the unevenness of talent among its members, some of whom were amateurs, and the poor quality of some of the instruments, which resulted from the orchestra's low budget.

In the spring of 1936 the symphony society amended its charter and became officially the Houston Symphony Society. Ernest Hoffmann, St. Leger's successor, began the 1936 season with renewed community support. Realizing the orchestra's limitations, he made moderate demands on it initially, but during his tenure he built the ensemble to major status. He was a model of thoroughness and extremely partial to the music of Richard Strauss. During World War II he organized numerous concerts for nearby army camps. On February 22, 1947, the orchestra played on NBC's national radio program "Orchestras of the Nation." An appearance on this program was a recognition of an orchestra's merit, and Burt Whaley, NBC national program director, claimed the Houston orchestra was one of the finest ever on the series. Despite these achievements, in 1947 the society asked Hoffmann to resign, feeling the conductorship needed new direction. This move caused a rift in the society and resentment on Hoffmann's part, and he finally relinquished his post at the end of the season under a cloud of ill-feeling.

During the following season the orchestra played under a number of guest conductors, among them Leonard Bernstein. Effrem Kurtz, the next conductor, served seven seasons, through 1953. He was allocated a much more generous budget, and under his direction the orchestra performed with more gloss and virtuosity, especially in the string and woodwind sections. However, the ensemble was not yet performing as a unit, and Kurtz received some less-than-enthusiastic reviews. Despite a brilliant procession of guest artists in 1949, among them Igor Stravinsky as guest conductor, audience attendance slipped throughout the early 1950s. Ferenc Fricsay brought with him a potential Deutsche Grammophon Gesellschaft recording contract in 1954, and conducted with great intensity but with uneven results. Because of his numerous demands, including plans for a new concert hall, he was released in mid-season, to be replaced by the ebullient and prestigious Sir Thomas Beecham.

In 1955 Leopold Stokowski arrived, loaded with charisma, exotic tastes, and exciting plans for several premieres each season, at which he often had the composers present. The orchestra bloomed under his direction. Although a segment of the audience did not appreciate his programming and some players resented his demands, under Stokowski the orchestra gained a new sense of its position and widened its coverage of new music. He left it more polished and confident, with a sharpened stylistic facility. Stokowski also made a number of recordings with the orchestra, including the *Carmina Burana*, Shostakovich's 11th Symphony, Gliere's *Ilya Mourometz*, and Wagner's *Parsifal*.

Sir John Barbirolli, who took the baton in 1961, maintained the orchestra's discipline, constructed stimulating programs, and built an enthusiastic audience, although his programs, like Stokowski's, included a fair percentage of modern music. Under his guidance the orchestra's playing grew richer and more imaginative in blend, yet he made few revisions to the ensemble. During the 1963–64 fiftieth anniversary season, Barbirolli took the orchestra on a tour of the eastern seaboard, passing through Washington, D.C., and culminating with a triumphant performance in New York that garnered unanimously good reviews, which rated the Houston Symphony among the major orchestras of the country. Barbirolli returned to an audience with renewed enthusiasm for the orchestra.

After decades in City Auditorium or the Music Hall, the HSO moved into the visually and acoustically fine Jesse H. Jones Hall for the Performing Arts in 1966. The new building brought a surge in audience attendance, but the more expensive hall also necessitated more frequent touring to generate income. With his health declining, Barbirolli became conductor emeritus in 1967; he continued as a guest conductor until his death in 1970.

André Previn brought youthful vigor from 1967 to 1969, with evenings almost equally divided between traditional and modern music. During his tenure, an annual young artists' competition was organized under the Houston Symphony Society's supervision. More and more, the orchestra came to be regarded as a regional, as well as a city, treasure. However, new and younger concertgoers were not attracted by the orchestra's young conductor as had been hoped, and the attendance of older patrons began declining.

Antonio de Almeida served as principal guest conductor before Lawrence Foster took directorship in 1971. Foster had high standards and was bent on enhancing and polishing the quality of the ensemble, although his detractors claimed he was moody, stiff, and even power-hungry. He expanded the company's repertoire and acquired an exclusive five-year recording contract. The 1970s, however, brought funding problems; deficits grew while audience attendance eroded, as the Houston Grand Opera and Houston Ballet rivaled the symphony.

The first Houston Symphony Marathon was held in 1977 on KLEF–FM, a fund-raiser designed to revive the orchestra's fortunes. In the early 1980s Sergiu Comissiona became artistic advisor, and then music director in 1984. In Houston's sagging economy, the orchestra continued to experience debt and labor problems until the symphony was broke and near collapse, despite a successful East Coast tour that included a performance at Carnegie Hall. However, a five-year planning effort by the Houston Symphony Society and Comissiona's leadership helped bring the orchestra out of debt; by 1985 the deficit had been greatly reduced and the orchestra once more promised to be a thriving major artistic force. Comissiona claimed his goal was to make music part of the daily life of the population. The 1983–84 seventieth anniversary season drew nearly a quarter million dollars by featuring a repertoire that drew heavily on the classic and romantic masters and featured a series of particularly fine guest pianists.

Christoph Eschenbach became music director of the orchestra in 1988. He and the Houston Symphony recorded for Virgin Classics and Pickwick International. In addition to its tours in the United States, the orchestra performed in the Singapore Festival of Arts in 1990, the Pacific Music Festival in Japan in 1991, and in Germany, Switzerland, and Austria in 1992. In 1993 Eschenbach and members of the orchestra formed a chamber-music ensemble called the Houston Symphony Chamber Players.

In 2000 Hans Graf took over direction of the orchestra and Eschenbach became conductor emeritus. The same year—a reflection of efforts to broaden the ensemble's appeal—Michael Krajewski became the full-time pops conductor. In the seasons that followed, the orchestra annually performed more than 160 classical, pops, educational, and family concerts that were attended by an estimated 300,000 people.

BIBLIOGRAPHY: Houston Symphony homepage (http://www.houstonsymphony.org/), accessed February 27, 2003. Oliver Daniel, *Stokowski: A Counterpoint of View* (New York: Dodd, Mead, 1982). Robert Lincoln Marquis, The Development of the Symphony Orchestra in Texas (M.A. thesis, University of Texas, 1934). Charles Reid, *John Barbirolli* (New York: Taplinger, 1971). Hubert Roussel, *The Houston Symphony Orchestra, 1913–1971* (Austin: University of Texas Press, 1972).

Theodore Albrecht

Howell, Tom. Jazz musician; b. Thomas Alva Howell Jr., Belton, Texas, May 6, 1906; d. July 5, 1989; one of five sons born to T. A. and Mamie Howell. In the year of his birth, the family moved to Cameron. Tom and all his brothers graduated from Cameron High School. Their mother was a church pianist, and their father had won a fiddlers' contest in 1900 in Comanche, Texas. Thomas senior began as a rancher in Lee County, ran a bicycle shop in Temple, and worked as a piano tuner and music-instrument repairman for Mary Hardin–Baylor College in Belton, before opening his own music store in Cameron and continuing in that business until his death in 1939.

Tom's older brother Hilton learned to play the piano from listening to a shoeshine man named "Teenus," who came in the back door of the music store, sat down at a piano, and played the blues by ear. All the Howell boys were self-taught, and Tom listened to Teenus for hours. By

1921 the four oldest boys were attending the University of Texas in Austin, where the two eldest organized the popular Howell and Gardner Band, a dance orchestra. Tom moved to Austin with his mother the same year and attended Austin High School. At fifteen he joined his four siblings in the Howell Brothers Moonshiner Orchestra, which played regularly for university dances and in the Central Texas area. The two youngest Howell brothers, Lee and Tom, took up music as a career while both were still completing their degrees. Lee on trombone and Tom on cornet were recorded with local bands, and their performances are strikingly impressive.

As the cornetist on a 1930 jazz recording made by Fred Gardner's Texas University Troubadours, Tom Howell was mistakenly identified in England as the legendary Bix Beiderbecke. Hearing Howell, one can understand why, for his playing is so much in the jazz style of Bix and approaches so closely his rich, ringing sound that it is uncanny. Howell is pictured in the 1929 volume of the university's *Cactus* yearbook as a member of the Hokum Kings, led by music director Steve Gardner. The Hokum Kings are credited in the *Cactus* with providing the best dance music by any local band and with being superior to better-known bands from larger cities. Recording in San Antonio but under the direction of Fred Gardner, the same group of university students performed four tunes; especially on the tune entitled "No Trumps," Tom Howell shapes and executes his solos as exceptionally fine hot jazz, while the rest of the group plays with great drive and finesse.

Tom Howell, along with his brother Lee, are present on two sides recorded in 1929 by Sunny Clapp, whose Band O' Sunshine, like the Texas University Troubadours, was recorded in San Antonio. The compact disc that reissues the Clapp recordings, *Texas & Tennessee Territory Bands*, does not list Tom and Lee among the personnel, but the discographies of Brian Dust and Tom Lord both include the two Howell brothers. It is clear that Tom Howell is present as one of the band's two trumpets, since on the tune "Do Me Like You Do" the lead trumpeter sings the lyrics of the song while Tom can be heard in his very decidedly Beiderbecke style playing obbligato behind the vocalist. That a Texas jazzman could play on a level approaching that of the legendary Bix was a remarkable feat and demonstrates the early achievements of little-known Texas musicians.

In later life, after retiring in 1968 as a special agent with the Internal Revenue Service, Tom Howell performed at times in San Antonio with various River City jazz groups. He was survived by his wife, Pat, and two children.

BIBLIOGRAPHY: *Jazz Records 1897–1942*, Volume 1, compiled by Brian Rust (London: Storyville, 1975). *Jazz in Texas 1924–1930* (Timeless Records, CBC 1-033, 1997). Tom Lord, *The Jazz Discography*, Volume 4 (West Vancouver, Canada: Lord Music Reference, 1992). Milam County Heritage Preservation Society, *Matchless Milam: History of Milam County* (1984). *Texas & Tennessee Territory Bands* (Retrieval Recordings, RTR 79006, 1997).

Dave Oliphant

Hunt, Jerry. Composer and performer; b. Waco, November 30, 1943; d. Canton, Texas, November 27, 1993. Hunt studied piano and composition at what is now the University of North Texas, briefly taught at Southern Methodist University, and worked as a pianist until 1969. He composed music for video and film production companies and served as technical consultant for audio and video instrumentation companies. He also performed regularly at the Kitchen in New York and headlined various New Music festivals throughout the United States and Europe.

Following a childhood interest in black magic and the occult, Hunt read underground magazines from secret societies and at fourteen became an initiate Rosicrucian. After a couple showed up at the family's door in response to ads placed by young Jerry in the local newspaper offering instruction "in the path of the infinite," his parents sent him to Galveston for psychological evaluation, but he was found to be well-adjusted. As an adult, Hunt became an atheist but remained fascinated by the occult, especially by the mystical system of alchemy and Tarot and by the Englishman John Dee.

Hunt is best-known for his performances, which he called "interrelated electronic, mechanic and social sound-sight interactive transactional systems." He was self-taught, yet was an avid inventor of musical technology, including electronic circuitry, computer software, and cybernetic systems, and was involved in the design of semiconductor integrated circuits. This knowledge allowed him access to the very early digital speech synthesis heard in *Transform (Stream)* (1977) well in advance of others in the field. His other recordings include "Lattice for pianoforte" (1979), "Fluud" (1989), "Babylon" (1990), and *Ground: Five Mechanic Convention Streams* (1992). The only available videotape of Jerry Hunt's performance style is *Four Video Translations*.

Hunt's work now reaches a larger audience because of the continuing sale of his CDs. However, recordings do not capture the power of his live performances, in which his unique personality was most apparent. Many have reported his appearance during performances as shaman-like or reminiscent of an exorcism. Hunt used a variety of electronic equipment, as well as homemade items and props, such as rattles, wands, and bells. His unorthodox performance style prompted one reviewer to say, "Our civilization makes us uncomfortable with this lanky figure from West Texas. Is he following any score? Are the electronics really doing anything? Clearly, this man is playing. Most probably, he is playing with us."

In the 1980s and early 1990s, Hunt collaborated on projects with such people as visual artist Maria Blondeel, performance artist Karen Finley, and composer and software designer Joel Ryan. Hunt's work with Karen Finley brought him into conflict with the National Endowment for the Arts, but her production was successfully completed anyway. Satirizing a television talk show, Finley and Hunt began "The Finley / Hunt Report" in 1992 by "discussing off-color subjects in the glib tones and smiley cadences television interviewers use for innocuous chatter."

Hunt lived in Texas his entire life and spent most of his last years in his self-built house on his family ranch. He committed suicide after a long battle with lung cancer and emphysema. Although during his life he was known only to a small group of followers, his music influenced a younger generation of electro-acoustic musicians, such as Gordon Monahan, Samm Bennett, and Laetitia Sonami. Multiple memorial performances have honored Hunt since his death. These include a performance at Experimental Intermedia in New York City in March 1994 with Joseph Celli, Karen Finley, and others, and in 1996 a virtual collaboration with Hunt by the composer and vocalist Shelley Hirsch. On October 24, 2002, Rodney Waschka performed "Keeping the Core Pure: In Memory of Jerry Hunt" at North Carolina State University.

BIBLIOGRAPHY: "Jerry Hunt: Composer" (http://www4.ncsu.edu/~waschka/hunt.html), accessed March 7, 2003. Paul DeMarinis, "Notes for Jerry Hunt 'Lattice' CD on CRI" (http://www.well.com/~demarini/hunt.html), accessed March 7, 2003. Michael Schell, *Unlikely Persona: Jerry Hunt (1943–1993)*" (http://www.jerryhunt.org/Jerry-Hunt/ huntmus.asp). *Lois Smith*

Hunter, Ivory Joe. Singer, songwriter, and pianist; b. Kirbyville, Texas, October 10, 1914; d. Memphis, Tennessee, November 8, 1974; son of a gospel-singing mother and a guitar-playing father, Dave Hunter. Ivory Joe Hunter took up piano as a child and by his teen years was playing gigs across Southeast Texas. He made his first recording, for the Library of Congress, under the pseudonym Ivory Joe White in 1933. Subsequently, he began hosting his own radio show on KFDM, Beaumont, where he later became program manger.

In 1942 he moved to California. Three years later he started his own label, Ivory Records, in Oakland and produced his first commercial hit, "Blues at Sunrise." Shortly afterwards, this label went out of business, but Hunter soon helped start another label known as Pacific Records. Ivory Joe recorded for many labels during his long career, including 4-Star, Excelsior, and King, before finding his professional home with MGM in 1949. During the 1950s he produced a number of hits, such as "I Almost Lost My Mind," "I Need You So" (1950) on the MGM label, "Since I Lost My Baby" (1956), "Empty Arms" and its flipside "Love's a Hurting Game" (1957), and "Yes I Want You" (1958) on the Atlantic label. After 1958 his career began to decline. He tried to keep his momentum going, however, by recording with several other labels, such as Dot, Vee-Jay, Capital, Smash, Paramount, Strand, and Veep.

Hunter changed along with the dramatic changes of the 1960s. With the waning popularity of rhythm-and-blues, he ventured into the country-and-western market. He had been using elements of this style of music for years. He soon moved to Nashville, Tennessee, where he performed at a variety of venues, including the Grand Ole Opry. In 1970 the Epic label attempted a comeback for him with a record entitled *The Return of Ivory Joe Hunter*, but the album did not have much commercial success.

Hunter's declining health brought mounting medical bills, which eventually drained his financial resources. He died of lung cancer at the age of 60. His reputation rests not only on his impressive string of hit records, but also on his influence, which extended to such important artists as Isaac Hayes and Ray Charles.

BIBLIOGRAPHY: Michael Erlewine, Vladimir Bogadanov, Chris Woodstra, and Cub Coda, eds., *All Music Guide to the Blues: The Expert's Guide to the Best Blues Recordings*, Second Edition (San Francisco: Backbeat, 1999). "Ivory Joe Hunter" (http://www.crl.com/~tsimon /hunter .htm), accessed May 1, 2002. Robert Santelli, *The Big Book of Blues: A Biographical Encyclopedia* (New York: Penguin, 1993). *Jarad Brown*

Hurley, Clyde Lanham Jr. Jazz trumpeter; b. Fort Worth, September 3 , 1916; d. Fort Worth, August 14, 1963; son of Clyde L. and Esther B. (Temple) Hurley. He first studied music with his mother, who was a professional pianist and vocalist. Influenced by early Louis Armstrong recordings, Hurley switched from piano to trumpet, worked with local bands, attended Texas Christian University in Fort Worth from 1932 to 1936 (playing for all four years in the school jazz band), and joined the Ben Pollack orchestra in 1937 when it was touring Texas.

He moved to California with the band. In the spring of 1939 he joined the Glenn Miller orchestra, and with Miller Hurley was recorded playing perhaps the orchestra's most famous solo, the one for trumpet on Miller's "In the Mood." Hurley also took other fine solos, including appearances on Miller recordings of "Stardust," "Glen Island Special" (a tune written by Texan Eddie Durham), and "Rug Cutter's Swing," as well as on "One O'Clock Jump," recorded at Carnegie Hall in 1939. In 1940 Hurley left Miller to join the Tommy Dorsey orchestra, and the next year he signed on with the Artie Shaw orchestra. During the rest of the 1940s he worked in Hollywood. He worked in the NBC television studios in the 1950s and later freelanced for various television, film, record, and radio companies. He was seen in many films, including *The Five Pennies* and *The Gene Krupa Story*. He had a wife and two sons.

BIBLIOGRAPHY: John Chilton, *Who's Who of Jazz: Storyville to Swing Street*, Fourth Edition (New York: Da Capo Press, 1985). Fort Worth *Star–Telegram*, August 16, 1963. *Dave Oliphant*

Hutchenrider, Clarence. Jazz saxophonist and clarinetist; b. Waco, Texas, June 13, 1908; d. New York City, August 18, 1991. Hutchenrider began his career playing tenor saxophone at age fourteen in his own band during high school. He played with Jack Gardner's outfit at the Adolphus Hotel in Dallas and other territory bands before joining Ross Gorman in 1928.

In the autumn of 1931, Hutchenrider became a member of the prestigious Casa Loma Orchestra, with which he was the featured clarinetist, although one of his finest solos was taken on baritone saxophone ("I Got Rhythm," 1933) and another fine outing on alto saxophone ("That's How Rhythm Was Born," 1933). The reedman was with the Casa Loma Orchestra until 1943, when he left due to lung illness, which also curtailed his career until the mid-1950s, when he began to play with several groups before forming in 1958 a successful trio that played through the early 1970s at several New York nightspots. He joined the Gully Low Band in 1982. In 1985 and 1988 Hutchenrider was

Walter Hyatt (right) and Deschamp "Champ" Hood, 1986. Photograph by Niles Fuller. Niles J. Fuller Photograph Collection, CAH; CN 11496.

interviewed by jazz trumpeter and critic Richard M. Sudhalter for the book *Lost Chords*. Hutchenrider was survived by his wife, Barbara, and two children.

BIBLIOGRAPHY: John Chilton, *Who's Who of Jazz: Storyville to Swing Street*, Fourth Edition (New York: Da Capo Press, 1985). Leonard Feather and Ira Gitler, *Biographical Encyclopedia of Jazz* (New York: Oxford University Press, 1999). Notes to *Casa Loma Orchestra: Stompin' Around* (HEP CD 1062, 1999). Dave Oliphant, *The Early Swing Era, 1930–1941* (Westport, Connecticut: Greenwood Press, 2002). Richard M. Sudhalter, *Lost Chords: White Musicians and Their Contribution to Jazz, 1915–1945* (New York: Oxford University Press, 1999).

Dave Oliphant

Hyatt, Walter. Singer and songwriter; b. Spartanburg, South Carolina, October 25, 1949; d. Florida, May 11, 1996. Hyatt's early musical influences included his attorney father, Simpson Hyatt, who sang such songs as "Darkness on the Delta" in the home for the family. The Hyatts listened to everything from classical music to Louie Armstrong; Walter's older brother, Buzz, favored rock-and-roll and rhythm-and-blues. Hyatt's favorite musical styles included British ballads, folk, and blues. He was also influenced by Carolina coastal music and bluegrass. Some of the most important musicians in his life were Bob Dylan, the Beatles, Elvis Presley, Django Reinhardt, Bob Wills, and Hank Williams.

When Hyatt began to play the guitar he experimented with blending jazz, black gospel, and pop music styles. By combining a variety of styles with increasingly sophisticated chord structures and a rich baritone voice, he soon developed a unique style. Hyatt formed Uncle Walt's Band, the group with which he achieved his greatest musical success, in Spartanburg in 1970. The acoustic trio included Deschamps "Champ" Hood and David Ball. In 1971 Hyatt moved the band to Nashville, where his unique melding of swing, country, and jazz made the group popular in the local club circuit. Singer–songwriter Willis Alan Ramsey persuaded Hyatt to move to Austin in 1973. There, Hyatt, Hood, and Ball attracted a following of musicians who appreciated the group's three-part harmonies and eclectic arrangements.

At the height of their popularity, Uncle Walt's Band appeared on "Austin City Limits" and produced four independent releases: *Uncle Walt's Band* in 1974, *An American in Texas* in 1980, *Uncle Walt's Band Recorded Live* in 1982, and *6-26-79* in 1988. In 1991 Sugar Hill Records re-released these four albums as a two-CD set entitled *The Girl on the Sunny Shore* and *An American in Texas Revisited*. Although the members of Uncle Walt's Band went their separate ways to pursue solo careers in 1983, they often played together until the early 1990s. They also performed in various combinations with other musicians. In 1976 Hyatt and Hood played with the Contenders, a Nashville folk-rock band. In 1989 Hyatt, Hood, and Ball reunited to play and sing backup on "Once is Enough," the closing song on Lyle Lovett's *Large Band* album. Hood and Ball also accompanied Hyatt on his solo albums in the early 1990s. Hyatt and Hood performed as a duo at the Kerrville Folk Festival in 1992. In October 1995 (coincidentally, on Hyatt's forty-sixth birthday) Hyatt, Hood, and Ball joined several other artists at Threadgill's Restaurant in Austin to record the live album *Threadgill Supper Session: Second Helpings*. A few other recordings featuring Hyatt's music include the *Kerrville 1980* album, the movie soundtrack from *Clay Pigeons*, James Hyland's 2000 CD release, and *The Contenders: Light from Carolina, Volume 1*.

Hyatt produced two major solo albums: the jazzy *King Tears*, coproduced by Lyle Lovett for MCA in 1990, and the swinging *Music Town*, for Sugar Hill Records, in 1993. He also had produced some independent recordings, including *Fall Through To You*, in the mid -1980s. Hyatt's voice has been described as sultry, at times creaky, but always as a versatile, soulful baritone. He played in a variety of Texas venues—the Waterloo Ice House in Austin, in Bryan–College Station, and at Corky's and Anderson Fair in Houston, as well as at Threadgill's, in the South by Southwest music conference (Austin), and the Kerrville Folk Festival. He also performed in the Boulder Theatre in Colorado, the Birchmere in Washington, D.C., Schubas in Chicago, and Uncle Pleasant's in Louisville.

By 1995 he had formed a new band called King Tears, named after his 1990 album. He and the four-piece band had been working on new album material in 1996, when Hyatt died. He was killed along with 110 other people in the crash of ValuJet flight 592 in the Florida Everglades. He left behind his wife of ten years, Heidi Narum Hyatt, two daughters, and a son. Texas singer–songwriter Lyle Lovett, one of Hyatt's biggest fans, adopted Uncle Walt's Band's swing and jazz combination. Before his debut on the national music scene, Lovett opened for Uncle Walt's band. Once Lovett became a success in his own right, he helped Hyatt produce *King Tears* and supported Hyatt as a solo performer by including Hyatt as his big band's opening act on the road. Other musicians influenced by Hyatt include Marcia Ball and Jimmie Dale Gilmore.

A Walter Hyatt bench beside Town Lake in Austin provides a memorial for Hyatt's many fans. After Hyatt's death many musicians participated in benefits, tributes, and memorials to him. Champ Hood, Sarah Elizabeth Campbell, Mandy Mercier, Toni Price, David Heath, Christine Albert, Erica Wheeler, Darcie Deaville, Bill and Bonnie Hearne, Jim Roonie, and Butch Hancock performed tributes on radio, at Waterloo Ice House, and at Threadgill's within days of the crash. Willis Alan Ramsey, B. J. Thomas, and Lyle Lovett sang at a benefit for Hyatt's widow and children at the Ryman Auditorium (the former location of the Grand Ole Opry) in May 1996. Ramsey and Lovett participated in a televised memorial to Hyatt on "Austin City Limits" in 1999. Lovett also paid tribute to his mentor and friend by recording four of Hyatt's songs on a double-CD set, *Step Inside This House* (1998). Also in 1998, the Austin City Council recognized Hyatt with a certificate of appreciation signed by Mayor Kirk Watson. Hyatt was inducted into the Texas Music Hall of Fame in 1998.

BIBLIOGRAPHY: Austin *Chronicle*, May 16, 1996. Dallas *Morning News*, May 13, 1996. Houston *Chronicle*, May 14, 1996.   *Cheryl L. Simon*

Ideal Records. One of the most influential regional recording companies for Mexican-American music during the post–World War II era; founded in 1946 by Armando Marroquín of Alice, Texas. Marroquín started recording local artists during the 1940s. Major record labels had begun reducing their involvement in the ethnic music markets, in part because of wartime shortages in shellac and other materials needed for making records. Frustrated with the major labels' pullout from the local Texas-Mexican music markets, Marroquín paid $200 for an acetate-disk recording machine and set up a makeshift studio in his living room. The first recordings he made were of Carmen y Laura (the former being his wife) and Narciso Martínez. Paco Betancourt, who owned the Rio Grande Music Company in San Benito, Texas, helped distribute the records. Marroquín also found distributors in the Los Angeles area. With very little competition from other labels, records sold very well, and the Ideal studio soon became a magnet for aspiring local musicians who previously had virtually no access to any major recording facilities.

Over the next few decades, Ideal Records helped resurrect or launch the careers of several important performers. Among the most successful of the Ideal artists were Narciso Martínez, Tony de la Rosa, Valerio Longoria, and El Conjunto Bernal, led by Eloy and Paulino Bernal. Perhaps the most influential musician to record for Ideal was Beto Villa, widely recognized as the "father" of *orquesta tejana*, a unique blend of traditional Mexican folk music with 1940s big-band swing. Hoping to push popular Mexican-American music in a new direction, Villa persuaded Marroquín to let him add more sophisticated instrumentation and musical arrangements to what had been a traditional conjunto band. Consequently, Villa was able to build a larger orchestra that combined Mexican-American folk-music traditions with the big-band sound that dominated the popular music scene during and after World War II. Despite Marroquín's initial apprehension, Villa's new sound quickly caught on and led to a booming *orquesta tejana* movement that influenced Mexican-American music for generations to come.

Ideal Records played a major role in shaping Tejano music in other ways as well. Ideal artist Narciso Martínez helped make the accordion a standard backup instrument for a variety of prominent vocal duets. Valerio Longoria was the first to make vocals a prominent feature of conjunto by integrating polka instrumentals with *ranchera* lyrics. Longoria also led the way in incorporating into conjunto modern drums and such popular dance steps as the bolero. Despite complaints from some that Marroquín exploited his artists by underpaying them, Ideal remained the largest and most influential regional Mexican-American music label in the Southwest until Marroquín founded a new company, Nopal Records, in 1960.

BIBLIOGRAPHY: Manuel Peña, *Música Tejana: The Cul-* tural Economy of Artistic Transformation (College Station, Texas: Texas A&M University Press, 1999). Manuel Peña, *The Texas-Mexican Conjunto: History of a Working-Class Music* (Austin: University of Texas Press, 1985).

Gary Hartman

International Festival–Institute at Round Top. In Fayette County; established by concert pianist James Dick in 1971. Dick, a performer with a distinguished career, was uniquely qualified for the task of creating a campus and organization to operate one of the major music festivals in the United States. He graduated from the University of Texas with special honors in piano in 1963 and was a student of pianist and pedagogue Dalies Frantz. Following graduation at UT, he received two Fulbright fellowships for study at the Royal Academy of Music in London and private study with Sir Clifford Curzon. Dick also was a major prizewinner in the Tschaikovsky, Busoni, and Leventritt international competitions and represented the United States on the juries of the Tschaikovsky Competition in Moscow and the Van Cliburn Piano Competition in Fort Worth. His concert tours take him throughout the United States and abroad each year.

The 1971 festival, a ten-day session with ten piano students, included two concerts. During its first five years the Festival–Institute leased facilities, but its master plan of development was soon established for programs and the future permanent campus. The first major facility, the Mary Moody Northen Pavilion, was acquired in 1973. It is the largest single-unit transportable stage in the world and was used for open-air concerts until 1983. It was later housed in the 1,200-seat Festival Concert Hall, on which construction began in 1980, until the permanent stage was completed in the Concert Hall in 1993. An abandoned school building and six acres of land east of Round Top, Texas, were acquired in 1973 for a future campus to be named Festival Hill.

Festival Hill grew gradually until it became a beautifully landscaped campus of more than two hundred lush and restored acres, located directly between nearby Houston and Austin. The Festival–Institute and its year-round operations moved to this site in the Bicentennial summer of 1976. The first historic structure moved to Festival Hill came from La Grange and was named the William Lockhart Clayton House at its new site. Built in 1885, it was renovated in 1976 for faculty, offices, teaching, and indoor concerts. It features some of the most commanding woodwork on Festival Hill, surpassed only by the splendid, acoustically amazing Festival Concert Hall. The Menke House, built in 1902, was moved to Festival Hill from Hempstead and renovated as a faculty and conference center in 1979. It houses the furnishings and collections of the late Texas composer David Guion, and its Gothic Revival ceilings and staircases make it a showcase of Texas carpentry. The historic sanctuary of the former Travis Street United Methodist Church of La Grange, built in 1883, was moved to Festival Hill in 1994, for restoration as a center for chamber music, organ recitals, lectures, and seminars. The Festival–Institute Museum and Library exhibits its art collections in the Festival Concert Hall and the restored historic houses. The Central Library includes the largest collection of valuable guidebooks to English country homes in the world. The David W. Guion Archives, which are being researched for eventual release as a biography on the life and times of this extraordinary Texan, and the Americana collection, as well as the Anders and Josephine Oxehufwud Swedish and European Collection, have unique hand-crafted galleries in the Festival Concert Hall. Other facilities have been built to house accommodations, practice, teaching, meeting, and seminar rooms for the festival and for year-round programs and conferences.

The two concerts in 1971 have grown into over thirty programs during June and July of each year. The August to April Concerts and other programs presented each season at Festival Hill bring the total number of year-round concerts to more than sixty. These include orchestral, chamber music, choral, vocal, brass, and solo performances. The repertoire extends from Baroque to contemporary music, including newly commissioned works. The first commissioned work, *Etudes for Piano and Orchestra* by Benjamin Lees, was nominated for the Pulitzer Prize. The Festival–Institute commissioned a new concerto for piano and orchestra, *Shiva's Drum*, by Dan Welcher as part of its twenty-fifth anniversary collection. James Dick performed the work with the Texas Festival Orchestra, conducted by Pascal Verrot of France.

Students from conservatories and universities in the United States and abroad pursue their musical studies at Round Top under the guidance of an international music faculty. Although the number of Festival–Institute alumni is in the thousands, the project manages to give each student the personal attention that has been a hallmark of its programs. It is both a festival and an institute, where students and faculty perform for appreciative and large audiences. Broadcasts of "Live From Festival Hall" over public radio stations extend the concerts and audiences of the Festival–Institute throughout the United States and Canada. Broadcasts of the Festival Concerts were presented throughout France beginning in 1994. The Festival–Institute presented the Texas premiere of Claude Debussy's only opera, *Pelléas et Mélisande*, with a French cast and conductor, Pascal Verrot, on the evening of July 6, 2002. This was the only performance of Debussy's venerable opera classic in all of North America in its centennial year, and was received with great media acclaim in the United States and abroad.

The campus is also used for conferences, meetings, and retreats. Major business groups, museum administrators, law firms, and numerous university and professional organizations have held conferences there. A series of distinguished museum lectures is presented at Festival Hill each year. The campus, famed for its gardens and rare trees, herbal collections, cascades, fountains, and unusual landscaping, is a destination for visitors from all over the world. An outreach program of public-service concerts featuring students and faculty who contribute their performances further extends the benefits of the Festival–Institute to the wider public. Former Festival–Institute students are found in the New York Philharmonic, the San Francisco Symphony, the Boston Symphony, the Cleveland Symphony, and on the faculties of major institutions both in the United States and abroad.

BIBLIOGRAPHY: Austin *American–Statesman*, May 25, 1991. Bryan–College Station *Eagle*, June 22, 1985. Houston *Post*, June 7, 1985.   *Richard R. Royall*

J

Jackson, Lil Son. Blues singer and guitarist; b. Melvin Jackson, Barry, Texas, August 16, 1915; d. Dallas, May 30, 1976. Jackson's father, Johnny Jackson, was a singer and musician who taught his young son to play the guitar; his mother, Ivora Allen, played gospel guitar. Lil Son grew up on his grandfather's farm listening to records of Texas Alexander, Blind Lemon Jefferson, and Lonnie Johnson. As a child he often sang and performed in the nearby Holiness church choir.

As a young adult during the Great Depression, he became dissatisfied with the harsh life of a sharecropper. After running away to Dallas he formed a spiritual group, the Blue Eagle Four. Throughout the 1930s the band played for local churches, parties, and family get-togethers. Jackson was drafted into the army during World War II and served with the Quartermaster Corps in England, France, and Germany. After the war he returned to work in Dallas, where he cut a cheap demo record that he sent to Gold Star Records owner Bill Quinn. Quinn signed Jackson to a record contract. Starting in 1948, Jackson cut several records for Gold Star and then for Imperial Records. A few of his recordings had some regional success in Texas and on the West Coast. His 1948 song "Freedom Train Blues" made the R&B Top 10.

In 1954 he was involved in a serious automobile accident. After recovering from his injuries, he retired from recording and performing to work as a mechanic in a scrapyard. In 1960, however, he was "rediscovered" by California producer Chris Strachwitz, who was on a field trip through Texas and Louisiana looking for talent. Strachwitz persuaded him to come out of retirement and record some of his old songs. Jackson recorded the album *Lil Son Jackson* for Strachwitz's Arhoolie label in 1960. He followed that up with another album in 1963 on the Houston-based Ames label. That album included newer versions of several of his older cuts, including "Gambling Blues," "Cairo Blues," and "Roberta Blues." Jackson retired permanently in the mid-1960s. He died of cancer and was buried in Lincoln Memorial Park Cemetery, Dallas.

BIBLIOGRAPHY: Lawrence Cohn et al., *Nothing But the Blues: The Music and the Musicians* (New York: Abbeville, 1993). Sheldon Harris, *Blues Who's Who* (New Rochelle, New York: Arlington House, 1979). Colin Larkin, ed., *The Guinness Encyclopedia of Popular Music* (New York: Guinness, 1998). Robert Santelli, *The Big Book of Blues* (New York: Penguin, 1993). Eileen Southern, *Biographical Dictionary of Afro-American and African Musicians* (Westport Connecticut: Greenwood Press, 1982).

James Head

Jacquet, Russell. Trumpeter; b. St. Martinville, Louisiana, December 4, 1917; d. Oakland, California, March 4, 1990. Jacquet's family moved to Texas when he was a child, and shortly thereafter he started playing the trumpet.

His father, who nurtured his children's musical development, played in local big bands and eventually formed a family band with his sons Russell, Illinois, and Linton. Russell and his brothers started their own group, the California Playboy Band, and played locally from 1934 to 1937.

Two years later Russell joined Ray Floyd's Orchestra, before entering Wiley College and, later, Texas Southern University. In 1940 he headed for Los Angeles to join the band of his brother Illinois. During this period Russell also led a band that played regularly at the famed Cotton Club. Though his band's extensive recordings included the well-known "Merle's Mood," Jacquet reached greater fame while playing for his brother. Several recordings and a tour of Europe with Illinois made Jacquet a household name among jazz enthusiasts. Eventually, however, Russell faded from the jazz scene. He taught in the Los Angeles public schools before moving to Oakland in 1959. He continued to play now and then with his brother and with other performers such as Ike and Tina Turner. He died of a heart attack.

BIBLIOGRAPHY: Jim Burns, "The Two Jacquets," *Jazz Journal* 19 (August 1966). Leonard Feather, *The Encyclopedia of Jazz* (New York: Horizon Press, 1960). Barry Kernfeld, ed., *The New Grove Dictionary of Jazz* (London: Macmillan, 1988).

Bradley Shreve

James, Harry Hagg. Jazz trumpet player and big-band leader; b. Albany, Georgia, March 15, 1916; d. Las Vegas, Nevada, July 5, 1983; son of Everett Robert and Maybelle (Stewart) James. James began his stage life as the circus contortionist in the Hagg Circus, which later became the Christy Brothers Circus. The gimmick was "the Youngest and Oldest Contortionists in the World," because young Harry worked with a seventy-year-old partner. He started his musical education with the drums at age four in the circus band. He learned to play piano and trumpet with his father, the circus bandmaster.

Though thought by many to be a native Texan, Harry James did not arrive in Texas until the 1930s, when he and his parents moved to Beaumont. There he played trumpet and led a band. In 1934 he toured as a trumpet player with Joe Gill. In 1935 he joined Ben Pollack's band, with which he made his recording debut early in 1936. Fame came later that year, when James joined Benny Goodman's orchestra. He made a name for himself with fiery trumpet solos and an appearance in the band's 1938 movie, *Hollywood Hotel*. After he started the Harry James Band in 1940, his hit song "You Made Me Love You" (1941) sold over a million copies. Other popular Harry James recordings included "Carnival in Venice" and "Flight of the Bumble Bee."

He had a great technique that showed off rich, brassy tones. A true virtuoso, Harry, along with his band, devel-

Harry James was a popular trumpeter and bandleader of the Big Band era. He appeared cameo or with Benny Goodman's band in many movies of the 1940s and 1950s. Duncan Scheidt Collection.

oped the boogie-woogie style for big-band swing. His romantic ballads, the key to his success, shot him to fame as a big-band leader. In 1941 a national poll voted his band the number-one dance band in the country. He appeared on radio shows for Danny Kaye, Coca-Cola, and Jack Benny, and also on his own series, sponsored by Chesterfield Cigarettes. Some of the famous musicians who performed with Harry James in the 1940s were Dick Haymes, Frank Sinatra, and Helen Forrest. Into the 1950s and 1960s Harry and the band were joined as well by Buddy Rich, Sam Firmature, Jack Perciful, and Ray Sims.

James continued to be popular, appearing cameo or with Benny Goodman's band in many movies, including *Two Girls and a Sailor* (1944), *Young Man with a Horn* (1950), *The Benny Goodman Story* (1955), and *Anything Goes* (1956). Still an active musician in the 1970s, he was quoted then as saying, "I don't look at people as changing, being old or being young. I just look down from the stand to see if people are having fun."

James was married first to Louise Tobin in 1935. That lasted until he met Betty Grable, whom he married in 1943. He and Betty moved to Las Vegas, where Harry played for many years. They were divorced in 1965. Afterward, he married Joan Boyd, a Las Vegas showgirl. He later married a fourth time. James had five children from his various marriages. He died of cancer at the age of sixty-seven.

BIBLIOGRAPHY: Charles Eugene Claghorn, *Biographical Dictionary of Jazz* (Englewood Cliffs, New Jersey: Prentice–Hall, 1982). Peter Gammond, *The Oxford Companion to Popular Music* (Oxford University Press, 1991). Roger D. Kinkle, *The Complete Encyclopedia of Popular Music and Jazz: 1900–1950* (4 vols., New Rochelle, New York: Arlington House, 1974). Vertical files, Center for American History, University of Texas at Austin. Leo Walker, *The Big Band Almanac* (Hollywood: Vinewood Enterprises, 1978).   *Alan Lee Haworth*

Jazz. As Ross Russell observes in his classic *Jazz Style in Kansas City and the Southwest* (1971), "the state of Texas, the largest and most populous in the Kansas City–Southwest area, [has] predictably yielded the greatest number of musicians and bands." Throughout the history of jazz, Texans have contributed to the important movements in this native American music, beginning with blues, ragtime, and boogie-woogie in the early years of the twentieth century and continuing with hot jazz in the 1920s, swing in the '30s, bebop in the '40s, cool, hardbop, and funk–soul in the '60s, and free jazz from the late '50s into the '60s, '70s, and '80s.

Not only have Texans participated at crucial moments in the development of jazz, either as composers, arrangers, or sidemen, but a number of Texas musicians have figured as outstanding soloists and as leaders of vital, innovative groups of their own. Although Texas was the home to a large number of territory bands, most of the significant performances by Texans were recorded outside the state, principally in Chicago, New York, Kansas City, and Los Angeles. Yet wherever Texans have traveled, they have always taken with them something of their own musical heritage.

Historian Gunther Schuller remarks that the Texas blues tradition is "probably much older than the New Orleans idiom that is generally thought to be the primary fountainhead of jazz." The transition between the early forms of black and white folk music and the blues is represented in Texas by the recordings from 1927 to 1929 of Henry "Ragtime Texas" Thomas, a "songster" who accompanied his versions of "rag" ditties, "coon" songs, minstrel or vaudeville tunes, and various square dances on both guitar and a reed instrument known as the quills. Thomas's "Texas Easy Street Blues" has been ranked "with the finest blues ever recorded"; his "Cottonfield Blues" employs the minor thirds and sevenths common to the form; his "Bull Doze Blues" is an instance of the Texas tradition of prison blues; and his "Railroadin' Some" draws on his own experience of riding the rods throughout Texas and the Midwest. All three of these sources—farm labor, prison life, and railroading—also inspired much of the blues of the two most famous male blues singers active in Texas in the 1920s, Blind Lemon Jefferson, the "King of the Country Blues," and Huddie "Leadbelly" Ledbetter, the "King of the Twelve-String Guitar," whose "enormous reservoir of music...with its powerful elements of the work song, the ring-shout, and the field-holler" furnished, as Marshall Stearns has observed, an "original mixture" to which "jazz and near-jazz returned again and again" and without which "jazz could never have developed." Jefferson's masterful sound and vocal phrasing—the latter consisting of long, unconventional lines—were matched by his instrumental work, as on his "Long Lonesome Blues," in which he performs so many inventive riffs on guitar that he "comes close to setting a blues record." Although recorded late in his career, Jefferson's songs contain the kinds of "carefully knit blues breaks" that were the basis of the greatest jazz. They inspired bluesmen in his own day and have influenced bluesmen ever since.

More closely associated with the practice of jazz was the work of a group of Texas female blues singers who recorded with a number of the early jazz giants, including King Oliver and Louis Armstrong. Three women singers from Houston—Beulah T. (Sippie) Wallace, Victoria R. Spivey and Hociel Thomas—were among the earliest successes in the field of urban blues, and Maggie Jones of Hillsboro also made a group of important recordings with major jazz musicians. All four of these figures, "in using some of the finest jazz musicians of the day as their accompanists,...made possible some of the earliest recorded jazz breaks by [such] great artists" as Armstrong, Oliver, Fletcher Henderson, Sidney Bechet, Johnny Dodds, Henry "Red" Allen, and J. C. Higginbotham. Sippie Wallace recorded with Armstrong in November 1924 and Maggie Jones with the trumpeter in December 1924, and on both occasions Armstrong was able to "stretch out" and develop many of the breaks that marked his revolutionary jazz style. Also performing with Wallace on a February 1925 recording with King Oliver was Sippie's brother Hersal Thomas (a Houston native as well), who as a teenager had already mastered a forward-looking form of blues piano, complete with tremolos and the kinds of rips associated with Armstrong's trumpet style and with the full-handed chords of Jelly Roll Morton's piano. As a team, Sippie and Hersal represented an outstanding example of urban blues, and together with Oliver and Armstrong the two Texans produced some of the classic blues recordings of the 1920s.

Even before the blues recordings by country and urban singers from Texas, another important ingredient in the jazz mix was furnished by Scott Joplin of Texarkana. From Joplin's ragtime—most notably his famous "Maple Leaf Rag" of 1899—jazz inherited the formal structure and the syncopated rhythms that lent the later music its special infectious appeal. Combined with the freer phrasing of the blues, with its spontaneous riffs and breaks, ragtime provided jazz with a patterned but driving design that made possible both form and freedom. Through Joplin's influence on Jelly Roll Morton, whose performances of Scott's "Original Rags" and "Maple Leaf Rag" are especially revealing, the ragtime composer has been credited in part with Morton's "invention" of jazz as early as 1902. Another Texas rag composer, Euday L. Bowman of Fort Worth, contributed a classic tune that served jazz musicians in the making of some of their seminal recordings. Louis Armstrong's 1927 recording of Bowman's "Twelfth Street Rag," according to jazz critic Martin Williams, was a precursor to the trumpeter's "beautifully free phrasing on [his] 1928 recordings with Earl Hines, *West End Blues* and *Muggles*." Williams remarks, "We are prepared for the later passionate melodies that swing freely without rhythmic reminders and for the double-time episodes that unfold with poise. We are prepared for a fuller revelation of Armstrong's genius." Likewise, the Count Basie recording of Bowman's rag from 1939 has elicited praise for the solos performed by tenorist Lester Young, which have been called "perhaps the very zenith of Lester's greatness....one can sense instantly the detachment of the aphorist and the presence of an original spirit." Still other outstanding performances of Bowman's rag include those by Bennie Moten from 1927, Duke Ellington from 1931, Fats Waller from 1935, Andy Kirk from 1940 (with Mary Lou Williams as arranger and pianist), and Sidney Bechet and his New Orleans Footwarmers from 1941 (with Everett Barksdale playing a Charlie Christian–inspired form of bop guitar). These recordings taken together trace the history of jazz from hot and swing to bebop and include both combos and big bands, as well as the distinctive styles of Ellington and Basie and the humorous touch of Fats Waller.

Boogie-woogie or barrelhouse-style piano, something of a hybrid form of blues and ragtime, also originated, according to some authorities, in Texas, in particular in the lumber camps and along the railroad lines of East Texas. The earliest recording to use the boogie-woogie "intermittent walking bass" was George W. Thomas's "The Rocks," recorded in February 1923. This composition by the older brother of Sippie Wallace and Hersal Thomas is also considered the first recording to employ the boogie-woogie structure, which is that of a twelve-bar blues. In general, boogie-woogie is highly percussive and is marked by a repeated left-hand bass played usually with eight beats to the bar; while "moving to the three blues-chord positions (C, F and G in the key of C)," the right hand improvises

John Handy played in California in 1964 and 1965 at the annual Monterey Jazz Festival. Photograph by William Russell, ca. 1959. William Ransom Hogan Jazz Archive, Tulane University.

over the continuous bass figure "in fascinating and varied polyrhythmic, polymetric patterns." Boogie-woogie further developed in the 1930s in Chicago at the hands of such figures as Meade "Lux" Lewis and Albert Ammons. However, boogie found its first major practitioner in Hersal Thomas, however, who influenced those later pianists by recording his own composition entitled "Suitcase Blues" in February 1925. In addition, Hersal and his brother George jointly composed "The Fives," which consists of a number of characteristic boogie-woogie bass patterns: stride ("in which a broken octave is interposed between the on- and off-beats in the left-hand part"), walking bass ("broken or spread octaves repeated through the blues progression" that "provide[s] the ground for countless improvisations"), and stepping octave chords. Both Lewis and Ammons asserted that "The Fives" "was instrumental in shaping 'modern boogie-woogie'." The influence of "The Fives," as well as "The Rocks," was such that every boogie-woogie player during the 1930s was judged by his performance of these pieces by the Thomases: "In those days if a pianist didn't know the *Fives* and the *Rocks* he'd better not sit down at the piano at all."

Territorial bands in Texas first promoted the careers of many of the early jazz musicians who later moved to Chicago, New York, and Kansas City. Among these were Eddie Durham of San Marcos; Budd and Keg Johnson, Oran "Hot Lips" Page, and Dan Minor of Dallas; Henry (Buster) Smith of Alsdorf; Herschel Evans of Denton; Carl Tatti Smith of Marshall; Joe Keyes of Houston; W. L. (Jack) Teagarden of Vernon; and Tyree Glenn of Corsicana. None of the bands in Texas, however, achieved a national reputation, with the possible exception of the Alphonso

Trent Orchestra in Dallas, which was composed almost exclusively of sidemen from other states. Only late in the 1930s did a Texan like Charlie Christian perform with the Trent band, but at that time Christian was playing bass rather than the electric guitar on which he subsequently made jazz history.

After touring with a number of white groups in Texas (among them R. J. Marin's Southern Trumpeters and Doc Ross and His Jazz Bandits), Jack Teagarden headed for New York, where in 1927 the trombonist immediately revolutionized the solo jazz conception of his instrument. After spending five years with the Paul Whiteman Orchestra in the mid 1930s, Teagarden formed his own band, which featured the trombonist himself and fellow Texan Ernie Caceres, a reedman from Rockport. Teagarden's brother Charlie was also was a fine swing-era trumpeter. Both Teagarden and Tyree Glenn became members of the Louis Armstrong All-Stars, the former with the first group in the 1940s and the latter with the final group in the late '60s. Glenn, following a stint in the early years with Eddie and Sugar Lou's band in Temple (based in Austin at another date when Lips Page was a member), traveled first to Los Angeles and then to the East Coast, where he performed with various groups before joining the Cab Calloway Orchestra in New York and later in 1946 the Duke Ellington Orchestra.

Most of the Texas musicians of the first generation of jazzmen ended up in Kansas City. The first to record there was Lammar Wright of Texarkana, who probably arrived as a teenager. On Bennie Moten's first recordings of 1923, Wright is considered the most outstanding musician of the Moten band, which cut two sides entitled "Elephant's Wobble" and "Crawdad Blues," with Wright delivering on the former an Oliver-inspired cornet solo in the same year that the King himself first recorded his music. Before joining the Moten band, guitarist–trombonist–composer–arranger Eddie Durham, trumpeter Lips Page, who was later billed as the "Trumpet King of the West," and altoist Buster Smith, who later became an important influence on saxophonist Charlie "Bird" Parker, were members of the Blue Devils, an Oklahoma commonwealth unit that so threatened the Moten band that the leader "raided" the Blue Devils and hired away Durham first and later Page. Smith too threw in with Moten, but not until after the Kansas City band recorded in 1932 for RCA Victor what is considered one of the all-time classic albums of early big band jazz. After Moten's sudden death in 1935, the band was reorganized by Count Basie and Buster Smith, and the trumpet section was composed of Lips Page, Joe Keyes from Johnson's Joymakers in Houston, and Carl Tatti Smith, who came by way of the Terrence Holder band and Gene Coy's Happy Black Aces from Amarillo. Dan Minor, who also had been with the Blue Devils and the Moten band, played trombone with the Basie orchestra. The Johnson brothers, Budd and Keg, also worked with the Happy Black Aces in the late 1920s before joining Jesse Stone in 1929 and heading for Kansas City, where the brothers joined the George E. Lee band, which at the time rivaled Bennie Moten's. In 1930 Keg left for Chicago, where he played trombone with the Ralph Cooper band at the Regal

Theatre and with the Clarence Moore band at the Grand Terrace Ballroom, along with pianist Teddy Wilson of Austin (later a star member of Benny Goodman's trio). After Budd arrived in Chicago in 1932, the brothers played in a combo with Wilson, and by 1933 all three were members of the Louis Armstrong orchestra. Both Budd on tenor saxophone and Keg on trombone take impressive solos on a recording with Armstrong of "Mahogany Hall Stomp." Later Keg became a sideman with the Cab Calloway Orchestra, along with fellow Texans Tyree Glenn, who doubled on trombone and vibraphone, and Lammar Wright. Meanwhile, brother Budd performed several roles with the Earl Hines band at the Grand Terrace Ballroom, serving as manager, composer–arranger, section leader, and soloist in the new "cool" style more closely identified with the work of tenorist Lester Young. Budd also figured prominently in the rise of bebop when, early in 1944, he organized the first bop record date with Coleman Hawkins and Dizzy Gillespie.

During the Swing Era of the 1930s, Eddie Durham contributed significantly to the bands of Jimmie Lunceford, Count Basie, and Glenn Miller, primarily as a composer–arranger but also with Lunceford and Basie as a trombonist and guitarist. It was Durham who first recorded on an amplified guitar, for a 1935 recording with Lunceford. Soon thereafter Durham reportedly introduced Charlie Christian of Dallas to the electric guitar. Christian, with his long-lined single-string solos, went on to establish this new instrument as a vehicle for jazz while with the Benny Goodman Orchestra (trumpeter Harry James of Beaumont having starred earlier with Goodman's band) and with Goodman's Sextet, as well as with after-hours groups devoted to the incipient bebop movement. Christian has been called the greatest jazz guitarist of all time. Another Texas guitarist, Oscar Moore of Austin, was a vital member of the Nat King Cole Trio during the 1940s and is considered one of the first important modern combo guitarists. Though not so important as a soloist on guitar, Durham recorded on this instrument as well as trombone for a historic recording with Lester Young in 1938, for which Durham served both as leader and arranger. Even before this, Carl Tatti Smith also performed with Lester Young on a 1936 session that marked the tenorist's recording debut, which included a rendition of "Oh, Lady Be Good" that influenced countless jazz musicians during the following decades. Yet another Texan to record with Young was Herschel Evans, who, after early work in the late 1920s with the Troy Floyd band of San Antonio, was featured in tandem with Lester as a tenor soloist in the Count Basie band. A later contingent of Texans to form part of the Basie organization included Buddy Tate of Sherman, Gene Ramey of Austin, Gus Johnson of Tyler, Henry Coker of Dallas, and Illinois Jacquet of Houston. Tate, who had been with Herschel Evans in Troy Floyd's San Antonio band (as well as with Eddie and Sugar Lou's Austin band and Andy Kirk's Twelve Clouds of Joy from Kansas City), took over the other tenor chair in the Basie band when Evans died in 1939. Jacquet, another Texas tenorist, got his start with the Milt Larkin outfit from Houston (considered probably the last of the great Texas

Ornette Coleman playing with the Prime Time ensemble in Fort Worth, October 2, 1983. Photograph by Jerry Hoefer/Star-Telegram. Special Collections Division, University of Texas at Arlington Libraries.

Corpus Christi jazz pianist Red Camp playing at the Kerrville Ragtime Festival, July 1973. Rod Kennedy Presents, Inc. Records, CAH; CN 11497.

tra, in which Houston altoist and blues singer Cleanhead Vinson is present. Also participating in the 1944 Williams session was trumpeter Harold "Money" Johnson of Tyler, who recorded with Duke Ellington between 1968 and 1972. In 1947, Gene Ramey was a member of Monk's first trio to record the pianist–composer's own music for Blue Note records, which between 1947 and 1952 produced what is considered Monk's "most powerful and lasting body of work" and "among the most significant and original in modern jazz." Also present for this Blue Note series was trumpeter Kenny Dorham of Fairfield, who performed in 1952 with Monk's sextet. Dorham had joined Charlie Parker as the replacement for Miles Davis in Bird's quintet from 1948 to 1952. Both Ramey and Dorham also took part in the first hardbop recordings, made in 1953 by what later became Art Blakey's Jazz Messengers, of which Dorham was a founding member. In addition, during the early to mid-1950s Ramey recorded not only in the last recording sessions of Lester Young's combo but participated in a 1950 Miles Davis recording date known as "the birth of the cool."

Other Texans active during the postwar period include Jimmy Giuffre, Gene Roland, and Harry Babasin of Dallas and Herb Ellis of Farmersville. These students from North Texas State University in Denton became members of several outstanding jazz groups, including the orchestras of Stan Kenton and Woody Herman, various ensembles formed in Los Angeles at such clubs as the Lighthouse and the Trade Winds, and such combos as those of Shorty Rogers and Oscar Peterson. Giuffre led a number of his own groups, notably his Trio, which included Jim Hall on guitar. Giuffre was a composer and multi-instrumentalist (clarinet, tenor, baritone) who also made his mark as an early exponent of so-called "third stream" music, a fusion of jazz and classical traditions. Meanwhile, two other Dallas jazzmen, Red Garland and Cedar Walton, were important members of two highly popular jazz ensembles: Garland as pianist for the original Miles Davis Quintet of the mid-1950s and Walton as pianist for the Jazz Messengers of the '60s.

At the end of the 1950s and during the first years of the '60s, three prominent members of the Charles Mingus Jazz Workshop were also Texans: tenorist Booker Ervin of Denison, altoist John Handy of Dallas, and trumpeter Richard Williams of Galveston. A fourth Texan to perform at times with the Mingus group was Leo Wright of Wichita Falls, who also worked with the Dizzy Gillespie big band. Handy later organized his own successful group, which at one time included Houston violinist Michael White. Two other Dallas products, tenorists James Clay and David "Fathead" Newman, were also active during this period, Clay on the West Coast with Red Mitchell's first recording group and Newman as a featured soloist with the Ray Charles big band. Both Clay and Leo Wright were students of tenorist John Hardee of Dallas, who in the '40s had recorded in New York for Blue Note.

At the end of the 1950s, jazz underwent its greatest revolution since the beginnings of the bebop movement some twenty years before. In 1958 Ornette Coleman of Fort Worth initiated what he labeled—through two of his

bands, which included two other notable members, Arnett Cobb on tenor and Eddie "Cleanhead" Vinson on alto). Jacquet starred with the Lionel Hampton orchestra in 1942, when he took one of the most famous solos of the war years on "Flying Home," then joined Basie in 1945. Bassist Gene Ramey and drummer Gus Johnson were at first members of another Kansas City band, that of Jay McShann, which featured at the time the early work of the great saxophonist Charlie Parker. After serving as timekeepers for Parker's revolutionary alto flights, Johnson joined Basie in 1948, and Ramey was with the Count briefly in 1953. Trombonist Henry Coker had been with Buddy Tate in the Nat Towles band in 1937 before moving to Hawaii. On returning to the States, Coker formed part of the Illinois Jacquet band in 1949 and then joined up with Basie in 1952.

During the 1940s and '50s, a number of Texas jazzmen participated in various developments in jazz that were associated with or grew out of the bebop movement. The first recording of Thelonious Monk's "'Round Midnight" dates from a 1944 session with the Cootie Williams orches-

albums from 1959 and 1960—the "Change of the Century" and "Free Jazz." As multi-instrumentalist (alto and tenor saxophones, trumpet, and violin), composer, and band leader, Coleman moved jazz away from a dependence on chord changes and based the music instead on what he called "harmolodics," a freer harmonic structure founded on a musician's melodic conception. Coleman was aided and abetted by a number of Texans who formed at one time or another members of his various groups. Many of his protégés were also natives of Fort Worth, where they attended I. W. Terrell High School, as did Ornette. Among these were tenorist Dewey Redman and drummers Charles Moffett and Ronald Shannon Jackson. (An earlier generation of Fort Worth musicians had included drummer Ray McKinley and tenorist Tex Beneke, both of the Glenn Miller orchestra. Beneke was featured by Miller as a tenor soloist and a singer, while McKinley took over as codirector at Miller's death in 1944.) Other followers of Coleman from Fort Worth who did not belong to his groups were altoist Prince Lasha and clarinetist John Carter, both of whom formed their own ensembles in California after Ornette had made his first recordings there before moving on to New York in 1959. Another Fort Worther influenced by Coleman was reedman Julius Hemphill, who became a founding member of the Black Arts Group in St. Louis and in 1976 of the World Saxophone Quartet. Still another member of a Coleman group was trumpeter Bobby Bradford of Dallas, who later joined with John Carter in the early 1970s to form the New Art Jazz Ensemble.

John Carter of Fort Worth brought the clarinet back to jazz as a viable instrument, after it had lost out to the saxophone following its heyday in the 1920s, '30s, and early '40s in the hands of such musicians as Barney Bigard and Benny Goodman. Performing with Bobby Bradford, with Houston pianist Horace Tapscott, and as a solo artist on an album entitled *A Suite of Early American Folk Pieces*, Carter recorded his own version of free jazz by means of his stratospheric, multiphonic clarinet. His most significant contribution, however, came in the 1980s with the five-album, five-suite recording of his "Roots and Folklore: Episodes in the Development of American Folk Music," a tracing of Afro-American history through jazz compositions mostly played by an octet featuring Carter on clarinet and Bobby Bradford on either cornet or trumpet. Carter's work brings full circle the Texas contribution to jazz history, especially in his fourth suite, entitled *Fields*. This penultimate section of "Roots and Folklore" includes a spoken narrative by Carter's great-uncle John, who talks of his life as a field hand in north central Texas while Carter and his group weave modern jazz in and around the uncle's words. John, as well as Carter's grandfather, had been a member of marching and dance bands and remembered Carter's great-great-grandfather as a virtuoso country fiddler at dances, suppers, wakes, funerals, and the traditional celebrations following the graveside obsequies of an earlier day. From the African diaspora to slavery, emancipation, segregation, and integration, Carter recounts the sad but inspirational story of jazz to which so many Texans have made a profound and lasting contribution.

BIBLIOGRAPHY: Dave Oliphant, "Eddie Durham and the Texas Contribution to Jazz History," *Southwestern Historical Quarterly* 96 (April 1993). Dave Oliphant, *Texan Jazz* (Austin: University of Texas Press, 1996). Sally Placksin, *American Women in Jazz: 1900 to the Present* (New York: Wideview, 1982). Ross Russell, *Jazz Style in Kansas City and the Southwest* (Berkeley: University of California Press, 1971). Gunther Schuller, *The Swing Era: The Development of Jazz, 1930–1945* (New York: Oxford University Press, 1989). Marshall W. Stearns, *The Story of Jazz* (New York: Oxford University Press, 1956). Martin Williams, *The Jazz Tradition* (New York: Oxford University Press, 1970).   *Dave Oliphant*

Jefferson, Blind Lemon. A seminal blues guitarist and songster; b. on a farm in Couchman, near Wortham, Freestone County, Texas, September 24, 1893; d. Chicago, December 1929; son of Alec and Clarissy Banks Jefferson. His parents were sharecroppers. There are numerous contradictory accounts of where Lemon lived, performed, and died, complicated further by the lack of photographic documentation; to date, only two photographs of him have been identified, and even these are misleading. The cause of his blindness isn't known, nor whether he had some sight.

Little is known about Jefferson's early life. He must have heard songsters and bluesmen, like Henry "Ragtime Texas" Thomas and "Texas" Alexander. Both Thomas and Alexander traveled around East Texas and performed a variety of blues and dance tunes. Clearly, Jefferson was an heir to the blues songster tradition, though the specifics of his musical training are vague. Legends of his prowess as a bluesman abound among the musicians who heard him, and sightings of Jefferson in different places around the country are plentiful.

By his teens, he began spending time in Dallas. About 1912 he started performing in the Deep Ellum and Central Track areas of Dallas, where he met Huddie Ledbetter, better known as Leadbelly, one of the most legendary musical figures to travel and live in Texas. In interviews he gave in the 1940s, Leadbelly gave various dates for his initial meeting with Jefferson, sometimes placing it as early as 1904. But he mentioned 1912 most consistently, and that seems plausible. Jefferson would then have been eighteen or nineteen years old. The two became musical partners in Dallas and the outlying areas of East Texas. Leadbelly learned much about the blues from Blind Lemon, and he had plenty to contribute as a musician and a showman.

Though Jefferson was known to perform almost daily at the corner of Elm Street and Central Avenue in Dallas, there is no evidence that he ever lived in the city. The 1920 census shows him living in Freestone County with an older half-brother, Nit C. Banks, and his family. Jefferson's occupation is listed as "musician" and his employer as "general public." Some time after 1920, Jefferson met Roberta Ransom, who was ten years his senior. They married in 1927, the year that Ransom's son by a previous marriage, Theaul Howard, died. Howard's son, also named Theaul, remained in the area and retired in nearby Ferris, Texas.

In 1925 Jefferson was discovered by a Paramount recording scout and taken to Chicago to make records.

Blind Lemon Jefferson, one of the earliest "classic blues" musicians, made seventy-nine records for Paramount Records in the 1920s. Courtesy Alan Govenar, Documentary Arts.

Though he was not the first folk (or "country") blues singer–guitarist, or the first to make commercial recordings, Jefferson was the first to attain a national audience. His extremely successful recording career began in 1926 and continued until 1929. He recorded 110 sides (including all alternate takes), of which seven were not issued and six are not yet available in any format. In addition to blues, he recorded two spiritual songs released under the pseudonym Deacon L. J. Bates. Overall, Jefferson's recordings display an extraordinary virtuosity. His compositions are rooted in tradition, but are innovative in his guitar solos, his two-octave vocal range, and the complexity of his lyrics, which are at once ironic, humorous, sad, and poignant.

Jefferson's approach to creating his blues varied. Some of his songs use essentially the same melodic and guitar parts. Others contain virtually no repetition. Some are highly rhythmic and related to different dances, the names of which he called out at times between or in the middle of stanzas. He made extensive use of single-note runs, often apparently picked with his thumb, and he played in a variety of keys and tunings.

Jefferson is widely recognized as a profound influence upon the development of the Texas blues tradition and the growth of American popular music. His significance has been acknowledged by blues, jazz, and rock musicians, from Sam "Lightnin'" Hopkins, Mance Lipscomb, and T-Bone Walker to Bessie Smith, Bix Beiderbecke, Louis Armstrong, Carl Perkins, Jefferson Airplane, and the Beatles. In the 1970s, Jefferson was parodied as "Blind Mellow Jelly" by Redd Foxx in his popular "Sanford and Son" television series, and by the 1990s there was a popular alternative rock band called Blind Melon. A caricature of Blind Lemon appears on the inside of a Swedish blues magazine, called *Jefferson.* He appears in the same characteristic pose as his publicity photo, but instead of wearing a suit and tie, he is depicted in a Hawaiian-style shirt. In each issue, the editors put new words in the singer's mouth: "Can I change my shirt now? Is the world ready for me yet?" Alan Govenar and Akin Babatunde have composed a musical, *Blind Lemon: Prince of Country Blues,* staged at the Majestic Theatre, Dallas (1999), and the Addison WaterTower Theatre (2001), and have also developed a touring musical revue, entitled *Blind Lemon Blues.*

Jefferson died in Chicago on December 22, 1929, and was buried in the Wortham Negro Cemetery. His grave was unmarked until 1967, when a Texas state historical marker was dedicated to him. In 1997 the town of Wortham began a blues festival named for the singer, and new granite headstone was placed at his gravesite. Among Jefferson's most well-known songs are "Matchbox Blues," "See That My Grave Is Kept Clean," "That Black Snake Moan," "Mosquito Blues," "One Dime Blues," "Tin Cup Blues," "Hangman's Blues," "'Lectric Chair Blues," and "Black Horse Blues." All of Blind Lemon Jefferson's recordings have been reissued by Document Records.

BIBLIOGRAPHY: David Evans, ed., *Journal of Black Music Research* 20.1 (Spring 2000). Alan Govenar, *Meeting the Blues* (New York: Da Capo Press, 1995). Alan Govenar and Jay Brakefield, *Deep Ellum and Central Track: Where the Black and White Worlds of Dallas Converged* (Denton: University of North Texas Press, 1998). Robert Uzzel, *Blind Lemon Jefferson: His Life, His Death, and His Legacy* (Austin: Eakin Press, 2002).

Alan Govenar

Jennings, Waylon. Singer and bass guitarist; b. near Littlefield, Texas, June 15, 1937; d. Phoenix, Arizona, February 13, 2002 (buried in Mesa, Arizona); son of William Albert and Lorene Bea (Shipley) Jennings. Waylon was born on the J. W. Bittner farm; his father was working there as a tenant farmer. The family later moved to Littefield, where the elder Jennings ran a produce store.

Waylon learned to play the guitar before the age of ten and became a DJ on a local radio station by age twelve. He dropped out of high school and moved to Lubbock in 1954. There he met Buddy Holly on the KDAV radio program "Sunday Party" in 1955. Holly became a mentor to Jennings, coaching him in music and, in 1958, producing Jennings' first single, "Jole Blon." In 1959 Jennings joined Holly's band, the Crickets, just in time for the group's final tour. Two weeks later, Holly died in the well-known plane crash that also killed Ritchie Valens and J. P. Richardson (the "Big Bopper"). Jennings had given up his seat to the Big Bopper.

He spent two years mourning the loss of his friend and then moved to Phoenix, where he resumed his musical career. After forming a band called the Waylors and playing with great regional success, he moved to Nashville in 1965 and, partly as a result of his success with the Waylors, was soon signed to RCA by Chet Atkins. Jennings's first Top 10 hit came the following year.

His success was due to his baritone voice and his ability to convey songs in a way that convinced the listener of his sincerity. He was also popular for his burly attitude; Jennings often dressed like a biker and, in fact, used members of Hell's Angels as bodyguards. He was focused on making different music from that of Nashville production studios. When they wanted to add studio musicians, string sections, and smooth background vocals to his recordings, he argued for the use of his touring band and a stripped-down sound. Jennings experienced considerable success as a country music recording star and used this as leverage against his recording label. In doing so, he was able to renegotiate his contract to allow him control over the production of his music.

Once he took control of the production, Jennings started to receive critical praise from outside the world of country music, and his influence and fame grew substantially. He turned his rebellious streak into performance by teaming up with Willie Nelson in the 1970s and forming the Outlaw movement of country music, a sub-genre that positioned itself against what it saw as Nashville's mechanistic approach to making country music. Jennings and Nelson's first Outlaw album, *Wanted: The Outlaws* (1976), was the first platinum album ever recorded in Nashville. It received the Country Music Association's award for Best Album, Best Single, and Best Vocal Duo of the Year, though Jennings may not have been there to receive the awards; he often refused to attend music-award shows, since he thought that artists should not compete among themselves.

The Outlaw movement, which became synonymous with Jennings and Nelson, influenced a new generation of country music performers, encouraging the direction of New Traditionalists (like Dwight Yoakum) in the 1980s and subsequently the alternative-country movement of the 1990s. Jennings also continued to record solo albums during this time. His 1977 album *Ol' Waylon* was the first country album by a solo artist to go platinum. His 1979 *Greatest Hits* went quadruple platinum, which was an unprecedented mark of success in the country music industry of that time.

In addition to his recordings, Jennings also gained notice through occasional film and television appearances. His only lead role in a movie was that of Arlin Grove in *Nashville Rebel* (1966), a largely autobiographical tale. He later appeared in the films *Travelin' Light* (1971), *Moon Runner* (1974), *Follow That Bird* (1985), and *Maverick* (1994), in addition to several made-for-TV movies. His most memorable work in television was his narration and singing the theme song for the hit show "The Dukes of Hazzard." Jennings forged yet another new direction in country music in the 1980s by forming the superstar performing group the Highwaymen with fellow country musicians Willie Nelson, Johnny Cash, and Kris Kristofferson.

Beginning in the 1980s, sales of Jennings' records slipped, the beginning of a continual decline in his commercial success. This was due to changing consumer tastes among country music fans in general, and also to his drug addiction. However, his popularity with his fans did not wane. His live shows continued to draw large crowds, and his recordings received critical praise throughout his life. In all, Jennings recorded more than sixty albums, earned thirteen gold records, and performed sixteen country songs that made it to the top of the Billboard charts. Although he did not write many songs himself, he is credited with creating a unique, gritty, edgy, and sparse sound that combined blues, rock-and-roll, and country music. Jennings was inducted into the Country Music Hall of Fame in October 2001.

He had serious and well-publicized health problems. He supported a $1,500-a-day cocaine habit before he quit cold-turkey in the early 1980s. Later, he underwent heart surgery and was diagnosed as diabetic. Circulatory problems caused by his diabetes led to the amputation of his left foot in 2001. Jennings was married four times: to Maxine Carroll Lawrence (four children), Lynne Mitchell (one child), Barbara Rood, and his sometime musical partner Jessi Colter (one child).

BIBLIOGRAPHY: Phil Hardy and Dave Laing, *The Faber Companion to 20th Century Popular Music* (London: Faber and Faber, 1990). Waylon Jennings, with Lenny Kaye, *Waylon: An Autobiography* (New York, Warner Books, 1996). Lubbock *Avalanche–Journal*, September 1, 1995; February 14, 16, 2002.　　*Cathy Brigham*

Jesse H. Jones Hall for the Performing Arts. In Houston. On June 1, 1962, John T. Jones Jr., the nephew of Houston philanthropist Jesse Holman Jones, announced that Hous-

ton Endowment, Incorporated, had offered to underwrite the construction costs for a performing arts hall in Houston. The Houston Endowment, a charitable foundation endowed by Jesse Jones and his wife, Mary Gibbs Jones, for the purpose of supporting charitable, educational, or religious undertakings, made possible the establishment of a home for the Houston Symphony Orchestra, the Houston Grand Opera Association, and the Houston Ballet Foundation.

The city council of Houston passed an ordinance accepting the offer made by John Jones on June 6, 1962, and, on December 4, 1962, the council passed an ordinance officially naming the prospective building the Jesse H. Jones Hall for the Performing Arts. On January 10, 1964, groundbreaking for the building took place. On October 20, 1965, the cornerstone was laid, and on October 2, 1966, the building became the property of the city of Houston. In 1967 the American Institute of Architects awarded the facility its Honor Award.

The site for the building was provided by the city, and the total construction cost was $7.4 million. The building occupied a full city block and consisted of a grand lobby decorated with sculpture by Richard Lippold, a minor lobby, and the main hall, which seated 2,912 and was renowned for its acoustics. A counter-weighted ceiling had panels that could be lowered to reduce seating capacity to 2,304. The stage measured fifty-five feet by 120 feet, the largest in the city in 1968. Other facilities included a room for performing artists to entertain friends and press, a rehearsal room, and offices for the administrative staff. The hall is renowned for fine acoustics.

In 1993 Jones Hall closed for several months to bring the building into compliance with the Americans with Disabilities Act. In 2003 Jones Hall remained the resident performance hall for the Houston Symphony and the Society for the Performing Arts. Houston Grand Opera and Houston Ballet Foundation moved to the Wortham Theater Center in 1987.

BIBLIOGRAPHY: *Jesse H. Jones Hall for the Performing Arts* (http://www.ci.houston.tx.us/cef/jones/), accessed March 3, 2003.

Jim Hotel. A jazz and blues venue in Fort Worth. Black millionaire William Madison "Gooseneck Bill" McDonald built the three-story, fifty-room hotel at 413 East Fifth Street in the late 1920s. He named the hotel after his second wife, Jimmie Strickland, and the Jim gained a reputation as the finest "Negro" inn in Fort Worth by the end of the 1930s. In 1934 Levi and Oscar Cooper purchased the hotel and built the environment that attracted jazz and blues enthusiasts. The Coopers hired T-Bone Walker to lead the house band that played in the hotel lobby, known by guests as the College Inn.

Although the hotel's check-in clientele remained strictly black, white music lovers headed for the Jim after midnight to listen to "real jazz" in the College Inn. They often stayed for early-morning jam sessions with such musicians as Louis Armstrong, Count Basie, Cab Calloway, Ray Charles, Billy Eckstine, Ella Fitzgerald, Lowell Fulson, Errol Garner, Woody Herman, Al Hibbler, Earl "Fatha"

Conjunto accordionist Santiago Jimenez y sus Valedores. Left to right: Ismael Gonzalez, Santiago Jimenez, and Manuel Gonzalez, San Antonio, ca. 1940s. UT Institute of Texan Cultures at San Antonio, No.82-85.

Hines, Billie Holiday, the original Inkspots, Louis Jordan, B. B. King, Andy Kirk, George E. Lee, Pigmeat Markham, Bennie Moten, Red Nichols and his Ten Pennies, the Andrews Sisters, King Oliver, Buddy Rich, Art Tatum, Sara Vaughn, Joe Venuti, Fats Waller, Chick Webb, Paul Whiteman, Mary Lou Willliams, Lester Young, and Trummy Young.

The Jim Hotel changed hands in the late 1940s, and a series of owners cared for the structure and its twenty-five-room annex, which included a dining room, a beauty salon, and a taxicab stand. During the early 1950s the place was renamed New Jim Hotel. It began to deteriorate and saw a declining quality of clientele over the next decade. In 1964 the structure was razed to make room for a freeway. A ramp, driveway, and parking lot now occupy the site where black–white crossover music found a foothold in segregated Fort Worth.

In 2001 the Fort Worth Historic Exhibit Committee approved the construction of a tribute to east downtown Fort Worth's black-owned business district. A bas-relief by Denton sculptor Paula Blincoe Collins, depicting such community icons as Goose-neck Bill McDonald and the Jim Hotel, was commissioned to stand at a covered walkway connecting the Fort Worth Intermodal Transportation Center's main building to the platform at the west end of the Fort Worth–Dallas rail.

BIBLIOGRAPHY: Fort Worth *Star–Telegram*, June 30, 1991; February 13, 1994; April 20, 1997; June 2, 1999; April 2, 2001. *Cheryl L. Simon*

Jimenez, Santiago Sr. Conjunto accordionist and songwriter; b. San Antonio, June 1913; d. San Antonio, December 18, 1984; son of Patricio Jimenez. The elder Jimenez, an accordionist and dance musician from Eagle Pass, Texas, encouraged his son Santiago to pursue music. By age eight Santiago had begun to play the accordion, and by the time he was twenty, he was playing music on live KEDA radio. In 1936 Jimenez released his first record, "Dices Pescao" / "Dispensa el Arrempujon," on Decca. The record was successful, and Jimenez became known for his inventive use of the *tololoche*, a Tejano contrabass that became prevalent in the conjunto music of the 1940s. Jimenez later recorded for Imperial, Globe, and Mexican Victor. His polkas "La Piedrera" and "Viva Seguin" (recorded in 1942) became well-known regional hits.

He was known for his use of the two-row button accordion even after new developments were made in accordion technology. His continued use of this increasingly old-fashioned instrument contributed to the traditionalist sound of his music in his later years. In the late 1960s Jimenez moved to Dallas and worked as a school janitor. He moved back to San Antonio in 1977 and started playing music again. He made some recordings with his son, Flaco, including *Santiago Jimenez con Flaco Jimenez y Juan Viesca* in 1980 for Arhoolie Records.

He was survived by his wife, Virginia, and six sons and two daughters. His sons Flaco and Santiago Jimenez Jr. carried on the tradition of his conjunto music.

BIBLIOGRAPHY: Manuel Peña, *The Texas-Mexican Conjunto: History of a Working-Class Music* (Austin: University of Texas Press, 1985). San Antonio *Express-News*, December 19, 1984. Vertical files, Center for American History, University of Texas at Austin.

Jill S. Seeber

Johnson, Blind Willie. Bluesman and virtuoso of the "bottleneck" or slide guitar; b. Marlin, Texas, ca. 1902; d. Beaumont, ca. 1950. Johnson was blinded at age seven. He taught himself to play the guitar and accompanied himself as he performed at Baptist Association meetings and churches around Hearne, Texas. At age twenty-five he married a young singer named Angelina, sister of blues guitarist L. C. "Good Rockin'" Robinson (1915–76). Angelina accompanied Johnson on some of his recordings for Columbia Records between 1927 and 1930.

Blind Willie made his professional debut as a gospel artist. He was known to his followers as a performer "capable of making religious songs sound like the blues" and of endowing his secular songs with "religious feeling." Johnson's unique voice and his original compositions influenced musicians throughout the South, especially Texas bluesmen. He sang in a "rasping false bass," and played bottleneck guitar with "uncanny left-handed strength, accuracy and agility." So forceful was his voice that legend has it he was once arrested for inciting a riot simply by standing in front of the New Orleans Customs House singing "If I Had My Way I'd Tear This Building Down," a chant-and-response number that stimulated great audience enthusiasm.

Johnson's celebrity career ended with the Great Depression, after which he continued to perform as a street singer but did no further recording. At his death he left behind a legacy of musical masterpieces, some of which have been rerecorded on Yazoo Records. His work includes such classics as "Nobody's Fault but Mine," "Dark Was the Night—Cold Was the Ground," "God Don't Never Change," "Mother's Children Have a Hard Time," "Bye and Bye I'm Going to See the King," "God Moves on the Water," "Jesus Make Up My Dying Bed," and "I Know His Blood Can Make Me Whole."

Self-taught Blind Willie Johnson began his career as a gospel singer and made a number of recordings for Columbia Records between 1927 and 1930. (*Texas Rhythm, Texas Rhyme: A Pictorial History of Texas Music,* Austin: Texas Monthly Press, 1984). Courtesy Larry Willoughby.

BIBLIOGRAPHY: Harold Courlander, *Negro Folk Music, U.S.A.* (New York: Columbia University Press, 1963). Alan B. Govenar, *Meeting the Blues* (Dallas: Taylor, 1988). Stanley Sadie, ed., *The New Grove Dictionary of Music and Musicians* (Washington: Macmillan, 1980). Eileen Southern, *The Music of Black Americans: A History* (New York: Norton, 1971; 2d ed. 1983). *Peggy Hardman*

Johnson, Budd. Influential in the development of modern jazz; b. Dallas, December 14, 1910; d. New York City, October 20, 1984. Johnson is credited with having organized the first bop jazz recording. His father was a choir director and cornetist who taught him piano at a young age. By Johnson's teenage years, he had switched to drums and was playing with his brother, Keg Johnson, in bands around town. Eventually the two started their own group, the Moonlight Melody Six. They later joined Gene Coy's Amarillo-based band, the Happy Black Aces.

Switching instruments again, this time to the saxophone, Johnson headed to Kansas City and then to Chicago, where he met and joined Louis Armstrong in 1933. During his stint in the Windy City he also met Earl Hines, and their musical relationship lasted nine years. By 1944 Johnson had moved to New York City, where he became involved in organizing and playing in smaller jazz combos. Along with Coleman Hawkins, Dizzy Gillespie, Woody Herman, and Billy Eckstine, Johnson became a pioneer of the emerging bop jazz style. He remained an integral part of American jazz throughout the 1950s. In 1956–57, he played with Benny Goodman, with whom he toured Asia, and in 1958 he formed his own septet and recorded *Blues a la Mode*. During the 1960s, Johnson played with Count Basie and Quincy Jones and rejoined Earl Hines. He also served as music director for Atlantic Records and started his own publishing company. In the 1970s and 1980s he taught music at Queens College and Stoneybrook University.

BIBLIOGRAPHY: Eddie Cook, "The Budd Johnson Interview," *Jazz Journal International* 37 (May 1984). Leonard Feather, *The Encyclopedia of Jazz*, New Edition (New York: Horizon Press, 1960). Dave Oliphant, *Texan Jazz* (Austin: University of Texas Press, 1996). Ron Wynn, Michael Erlewine, and Chris Woodstra, eds., *All Music Guide to Jazz* (San Francisco: Miller Freeman, 1994). *Bradley Shreve*

Johnson, Gus. Jazz drummer; b. Tyler, Texas, November 15, 1913; d. Denver, February 7, 2000 (buried at Fort Logan National Cemetery, Denver). Johnson grew up in Beaumont, Houston, and Dallas; he attended Booker T. Washington High School in Dallas. After learning how to play the drums from his next-door neighbor, Johnson was featured by the age of ten at the Lincoln Theater in Houston. At age eleven he played in local jazz and blues bands—most notably, McDavid's Blue Rhythm Boys.

After graduating from high school, he moved to Kansas City and enrolled in Sumner Junior College. He could not stay away from music, however, and decided to take up drumming full-time in Kansas City, where jazz was flourishing. He drummed in various acts before joining Jay McShann's band in 1938. Playing alongside McShann and Charlie "Bird" Parker, Johnson built a reputation as a solid percussionist. In 1941 he, McShann, and Gene Ramey performed and recorded as a trio. Johnson joined the military in 1943. After his discharge in 1945 he moved to Chicago and joined the Jesse Miller Band. He subsequently headed to New York City and began drumming for the legendary Count Basie.

Johnson recorded and toured extensively with Basie's band. Some of his best work is featured on the 1952 classic *Basie Rides Again*. Two years later an attack of appendicitis forced Johnson out of the band. Following a slow recovery, he climbed back behind the drum kit to support Lena Horne and, later, Ella Fitzgerald. Through the 1960s he played with numerous bands and was featured on hundreds of recordings. In 1969 he joined the World's Greatest Jazz Band, with which he recorded and toured throughout America and Europe. Three years later he and his old bandmates Jay McShann and Gene Ramey recorded the album *Going to Kansas City*.

Johnson subsequently moved to Denver and performed into the 1980s. In 1989 he developed Alzheimer's disease.

BIBLIOGRAPHY: John Chilton, *Who's Who of Jazz: Storyville to Swing Street* (New York: Da Capo Press, 1985). Gus Johnson, "In My Opinion," *Jazz Journal*, May 1964. Burt Korall, "The Great Drummers of Count Basie," *Modern Drummer*, April 1994. Dave Oliphant, *Texan Jazz* (Austin: University of Texas Press, 1996). Nathan W. Pearson, Jr., *Goin' to Kansas City* (Urbana: University of Illinois Press, 1987).

Johnson, Keg. Jazz trombonist; b. Frederic H. Johnson, Dallas, November 19, 1908; d. Chicago, November 8, 1967. Keg Johnson, the son of a choir director, was active in the jazz scenes of Dallas, Kansas City, Chicago, and New York City from the 1920s to the 1960s. Along with his better-known brother, Budd, he began his musical development under his father's supervision before studying with Portia Pittman, daughter of Booker T. Washington.

By Keg's teenage years he had settled on the trombone as his instrument of choice, and with his brother he began playing in such Dallas-area bands as the Blue Moon Chasers and Ben Smith's Music Makers. During the day, he worked with his father at the local Studebaker factory to supplement his music earnings. Later, he and Budd joined up with Gene Coy's Amarillo-based group, the Happy Black Aces, and toured the Southwest. In the late 1920s the two brothers moved to Kansas City, where they landed spots in various bands.

In 1930 Keg left for Chicago and joined Louis Armstrong's orchestra. He toured and recorded his first solo under Armstrong on the album *Basin Street Blues*. In 1933 he headed to New York and played with Fletcher Henderson and Benny Carter. The following year he joined Cab Calloway, whose band played regularly at the Cotton Club. After fifteen years with Calloway, Keg moved to Los Angeles, changed careers, and began house decorating and painting. His absence from music was brief, however, for by the late 1950s he was playing again in New York. He reunited with his brother to record the album *Let's Swing*, before joining forces with Ray Charles in 1961. Johnson died while on tour with Charles's orchestra.

BIBLIOGRAPHY: John Chilton, *Who's Who of Jazz: Storyville to Swing Street*, Fourth Edition (New York: Da Capo Press, 1985). Leonard Feather, *The Encyclopedia of Jazz*, New Edition (New York: Horizon Press, 1960). Colin Larkin, *The Encyclopedia of Popular Music*, Third Edition (London: MuzeUK Limited, 1998). Dave Oliphant, *Texan Jazz* (Austin: University of Texas Press, 1996).

Bradley Shreve

Johnson, "Money." Trumpet player; b. Harold Johnson, Tyler, Texas, February 23, 1918; d. New York City, March 28, 1978. Johnson began playing the trumpet when he was fifteen. During the early 1930s he was with Eddie and Sugar Lou's Tyler Hotel orchestra. He moved to Oklahoma City in 1936, and the next year became a member of the Nat Towles band before joining Horace Henderson.

In a career that spanned four decades, he performed in a variety of cities both American and foreign, joining some of the biggest jazz names on stage, including Cootie Williams, Count Basie, and Duke Ellington. Johnson took part in jam sessions in Oklahoma City with fellow Texan Charlie Christian and with Oklahoma City native Henry Bridges. He rejoined Towles in Chicago in 1944, but within the year he was working with Count Basie and sharing time between the bands of Cootie Williams and Lucky Millinder.

While Johnson worked most often in jazz combos, he also formed part of Bullmoose Jackson's rhythm-and-blues band, the Buffalo Bearcats, in 1949. Into the '50s Johnson recorded with several different band leaders, including Louis Jordan, Little Esther Phillips, Mercer Ellington, Cozy Cole, Buddy Johnson, Lucky Thompson, and Sy Oliver. He traveled the world, performing from Uruguay to Europe, playing in 1953 with Panama Francis in Montevideo, Uruguay, with a state department–sponsored tour of the USSR in 1966 with Earl Hines, and in Europe with Hines in 1968. He also played from time to time with Duke Ellington in New York in the late 1960s and became a regular Ellington band member in the early 1970s. Johnson can be heard on the album *Up in Duke's Workshop* (1969). Known for his sharp, active, and precise horn solos, Johnson complemented Ellington's original compositions. His last recording was with Buck Clayton in 1975.

BIBLIOGRAPHY: John Chilton, *Who's Who of Jazz: Storyville to Swing Street*, Fourth Edition (New York: Da Capo Press, 1985). Barry Kernfield, ed., *The New Grove Dictionary of Jazz*, Second Edition (New York: Grove's Dictionaries, 2002). Dave Oliphant, *Texan Jazz* (Austin: University of Texas Press, 1996). *Daniel Rendon*

Johnson, Willie Neal. Gospel singer, known as "Country Boy Johnson"; b. Tyler, Texas, August 25, 1935; d. Tyler, January 10, 2001; oldest of six children in a musical family. His mother, probably the most musically inclined person in the family, motivated her children to pursue their singing carriers by taking them to church and making them sing every Sunday. Willie started singing gospel in his early teens.

His first musical group, the Gospel Keynotes, included Ralph McGee, Charles Bailey, Rev. J. D. Talley, John Jackson, Lonzo Jackson, and Archie McGee. They recorded their first major hit, "Show Me the Way," on the Nashville gospel record label Nashboro Records. They received a Grammy nomination in 1980 for "Ain't No Stoppin' Us Now." Johnson also joined the Five Ways Of Joy gospel group. In 1985 the Gospel Keynotes signed with Malaco Records and changed their name to the New Keynotes. With Malaco, they recorded seven albums by 2002. Popular songs by the group include "I'm Yours, Lord." Their "Lord, Take Us Through" made the top twenty-five. The group was inducted into the Gospel Music Hall of Fame in Detroit and the American Gospel Quartet Hall of Fame in Birmingham, Alabama, in 1999. Johnson was survived by his wife, Captoria, three sons, five daughters, and his mother, Luretia.

BIBLIOGRAPHY: Tyler *Courier–Times–Telegraph*, January 16, 2002.
Willie Neal Johnson and the New Keynotes (http://www.afgen.com/willie_neal.html), accessed November 25, 2002. *Samantha Lange, Adrian McCall, Devin Solice, and Leighann Weggemann*

Jones, Dennis. Blues musician, known as Little Hat Jones; b. on a farm near the Sulphur River, Bowie County, Texas, October 5, 1899; d. Linden, Texas, March 7, 1981 (buried in Morning Star Cemetery, Naples, Texas); only child of Felix Jones and his wife. The family farm was purchased by Jones's grandfather, a former slave named George (some sources call him Dennis).

Jones was a talented, though little known, blues musician. He quit school at the age of thirteen, after his father became ill and several crops were destroyed, in order to help out on the farm. During this period his mother bought him his first guitar. Between 1916 and 1929, he probably worked as a menial laborer. He acquired his nickname at a construction job in Garland. Because Jones came to work with a hat from which half the brim had been cut off, his boss called him "Little Hat" Jones and even made out his paychecks this way.

In 1929 Jones was in San Antonio. He first recorded, for Okeh Records, on June 15 of that year, when he cut two records of his own, "New Two Sixteen Blues" and "Two String Blues," and played backup for Texas Alexander. Jones then made a contract with Okeh for three years and recorded "Rolled from Side to Side Blues," "Hurry Blues," "Little Hat Blues," "Corpus Blues," "Kentucky Blues," "Bye Bye Baby Blues," "Cross the Water Blues," and "Cherry Street Blues." He also played in such cities as New Orleans, Galveston, and Austin, and occasionally ventured into Mexico. He was influenced in his guitar playing by Blind Lemon Jefferson and played with T. Texas Tyler and Jimmie Rodgers.

In 1937 Jones settled in Naples, Texas, with his second wife, Janie Traylor, and worked at odd jobs. In the years before his death he was employed at the Red River Army Depot.

BIBLIOGRAPHY: Colin Larkin, ed., *The Encyclopedia of Popular Music* (New York: Grove's Dictionaries, 1998).

Little Hat Jones made his first recording on June 15, 1929, for Okeh Records. Courtesy Alan Govenar, Documentary Arts.

"George 'Little Hat' Jones," *Notables* (http://www.angelfire.com/tx3/nostalgia/Notables.html), accessed January 15, 2003.   *Jenny Odintz*

Jones, Maggie. Pianist and vocalist; b. Fae Barnes, Hillsboro, Texas, ca. 1900; death date unknown. This daughter of sharecroppers moved in the early 1920s to New York City,

where she began to perform in local clubs. Billed as the "Texas Nightingale," she also worked a circuit of traveling shows for the Theater Owners Booking Association, including performances at the Princess Theater in Harrisburg, Pennsylvania. On July 26, 1923, she became the first Texas singer to record a song. She recorded two more sides in August and followed those with two more cuts the following month. She continued to record for various labels, including Black Swan, Victor, Pathé, and Paramount. Some of her best-known songs are "Undertaker's Blues," "Single Woman's Blues," and "Northbound Blues."

She recorded with several musical legends between 1924 and 1926, including Louis Armstrong, Fletcher Henderson, and Charlie Green, and participated in a touring review in 1928–29. She was frequently forced to earn her living outside the world of music, however, and operated a dress store in New York for a time. In the early 1930s, she moved to Dallas and formed her own revue, which performed at such spots as the All-American Cabaret in Fort Worth. In the mid-1930s she disappeared from the music scene and from the written record.

BIBLIOGRAPHY: Virginia L. Grattan, *American Women Songwriters: A Biographical Dictionary* (Westport, Connecticut: Greenwood Press, 1993). Sheldon Harris, *Blues Who's Who* (New Rochelle, New York: Arlington House, 1979). Colin Larkin, ed., *The Guiness Encyclopedia of Popular Music*, Volume 4 (New York: Guiness, 1998).
James Head

Joplin, Janis Lyn. Blues and rock singer; b. Port Arthur, Texas, January 19, 1943; d. October 4, 1970; daughter of Seth Ward and Dorothy (East) Joplin. Janis grew up in a respectable middle-class home; her father was an engineer and her mother a Sunday school teacher. The future queen of nonconformity is remembered as a bright, pretty, and artistic little girl.

Signs of rebellion, however, against the religious, sexual, and racial conservatism of her environment were evident in junior high school, and by the time Janis graduated from Jefferson High School in Port Arthur in 1960, her vocabulary of four-letter words, her outrageous clothes, and her reputation for sexual promiscuity and drunkenness (signs of alcoholism were already apparent) caused her classmates to call her a slut. Bereft of friends, without dates for school dances, ashamed of her acned face and overweight figure, Janis responded with contempt and insults to cover the rejection that scarred her for the rest of her life.

In her junior year she found acceptance in a small group of Jefferson High beatniks who read Jack Kerouac and roamed the nightspots from Port Arthur to New Orleans, thus mining one of the motherlodes of American ethnic music. There were Anglo, African-American, Cajun, Mexican, and Caribbean sounds. There were the lyrics and rhythms of country and western, gospel, jazz, soul, and the blues. Janis did not read music, but at the roadhouses or at home listening to records of Odetta, Bessie Smith, or Willie Mae Thornton, she had an uncanny ability to imitate the sounds she heard. Out of imitation there slowly developed the timing, phrasing, inflections, and talent at evoking changing moods that were the Joplin trademarks.

She found Lamar State College of Technology at Beaumont no improvement over Port Arthur; she was a rebel and a "nigger lover" in both places. She fled to the University of Texas in Austin in the summer of 1962 to study art. Indifferent to classwork, she found soulmates at the Ghetto, a counterculture enclave, and got gigs around Austin, most importantly at Threadgill's, a converted filling station and late-night hangout for lovers of music and non-stop partying. The proprietor, country singer Kenneth Threadgill, offered Janis encouragement and lifelong friendship.

Janis craved such acceptance, but her nonconforming behavior often provoked rejection, as when university fraternity pranksters nominated her as their candidate in the annual Ugliest Man on Campus contest. Characteristically, she laughed to cover the hurt, and dreamed of San Francisco, where Beats and Hippies were not outsiders. She spent 1963 to 1965 in the Bay area and won attention from local audiences, until drugs became more important than singing and reduced her to an emaciated eighty-eight pounds. Her friends passed the hat and gave her a bus ticket home.

Parental care restored her health, and fear of relapse produced a period of sobriety. Business suits and bouffant hairdos announced conversion to the Port Arthur ethos. But Janis's mind was torn: Port Arthur was safe but dull. San Francisco offered both excitement and potential self-destruction. She made her decision after receiving an offer to audition for a new rock band, Big Brother and the Holding Company, and headed west in May 1966, toward four years of meteoric fame—and death at age twenty-seven.

"Imagine a white girl singing the blues like that!" they said of Big Brother's lead singer. And Joplin's belting of rock gathered huge swaying, clapping, shouting, and dancing audiences. For Janis a good audience was an audience in motion, and her body joined her voice in pleading for audience participation. She stopped the show at the Monterey Pop Festival in 1967 with "Ball and Chain." That triumph and the album *Cheap Thrills* (1968) elevated her to national stardom. A new manager, Albert Grossman, whose stable of stars included Peter, Paul and Mary and Bob Dylan, urged Janis to dump Big Brother for more versatile and disciplined support. The Kosmic Blues band was never satisfactory; the Full-Tilt Boogie band was.

Joplin's career now surged forward full tilt, driven by Southern Comfort booze, heroin, bisexual liaisons, compulsive work, and the hope that fame would bring inner peace. Success now meant concerts in Madison Square Garden, Paris, London, Woodstock, and Harvard Stadium; adulation in the New York *Times*; a guest appearance on the Ed Sullivan show; and a six-figure salary.

Janis was ready in August 1970 to confront the Jefferson High classmates who had called her a slut. Whether her primary purpose in attending the tenth-anniversary class reunion was revenge, a desire to be worshiped as a hero, or just a quest for acceptance is unclear. What is certain is that she left Port Arthur feeling further alienated from her classmates, her parents, and her hometown. When she died two months later, of an accidental overdose of heroin and alcohol, her newly drawn will required that her ashes be strewn over California soil.

The judgment of others has been far kinder to Janis Joplin than she was to herself. She has been called "the best white blues singer in American musical history" and "the greatest female singer in the history of rock 'n' roll." Those who missed her live performances must judge her from a relatively small number of albums, audiotapes, and videotapes. *Pearl*, an album recorded just before her death and featuring "Me and Bobby McGee," shows that Janis was growing musically almost to the moment of her death. The film *The Rose* (1979), starring Bette Midler, is not faithful in detail to Janis's life, but it captures her mesmerizing power on stage, in contrast to her utter powerlessness offstage to halt her relentless descent to self-destruction. Janis's sad life cannot be separated from her greatness; like Bessie Smith, the great Afro-American blues singer who also succumbed to alcohol and drugs, Janis Joplin's tortured soul gave her blues the authenticity of direct experience. After her death she was finally accepted in the hometown she both loved and ridiculed. In 1988 some 5,000 people from Port Arthur, tears in their eyes, sang "Me and Bobby McGee" as a bust of Janis Joplin was unveiled. It now sits in a Port Arthur library.

During the next three decades, various Joplin anthologies and live recordings were released as well as numerous biographies. In 1992 her sister, Laura Joplin, published *Love, Janis*, a collection of letters Janis wrote to her family beginning in 1963. A play with the same title and based on the book opened in Denver in 1995 and subsequently had a long run at the Zachary Scott Theater in Austin in summer 1997. The performance opened off Broadway in April 2001 and ran to January 5, 2003. Janis Joplin was inducted into the Rock and Roll Hall of Fame on January 12, 1995.

BIBLIOGRAPHY: *All Music Guide* (http://www.allmusic .com/), accessed December 12, 2002. Ellis Amburn, *Pearl: The Obsessions and Passions of Janis Joplin: A Biography* (New York: Warner, 1992). Austin *American–Statesman*, June 16, 1994; June 7, 2001. Myra Friedman, *Buried Alive: The Biography of Janis Joplin* (New York: Harmony, 1992). Laura Joplin, *Love, Janis* (New York: Villard, 1992). Vertical files, Center for American History, University of Texas at Austin. Larry Willoughby, *Texas Rhythm and Texas Rhyme: A Pictorial History of Texas Music* (Austin: Texas Monthly Press, 1984).

Richard B. Hughes

Joplin, Scott. Composer and pianist, called the "King of Ragtime"; b. probably at Caves Springs, near Linden, Texas, November 24, 1868; d. New York City, April 1, 1917 (buried in St. Michael's Cemetery, New York); son of Jiles and Florence (Givins) Joplin. His father, a laborer and former slave who possessed rudimentary musical ability, moved the family to Texarkana by about 1875. Encouraged by family music making, Scott, at age seven, was proficient in banjo and began to experiment on a piano owned by a neighbor, attorney W. G. Cook, for whom Mrs. Joplin did domestic work.

Janis Joplin has been called "the best white blues singer in American musical history." (*Texas Rhythm, Texas Rhyme: A Pictorial History of Texas Music*, Austin: Texas Monthly Press, 1984}. Courtesy Larry Willoughby.

Sheet music for one of Scott Joplin's compositions (John Stark & Sons, St. Louis). "The Entertainer" was used as the soundtrack for the 1973 movie *The Sting*. (*Texas Rhythm, Texas Rhyme: A Pictorial History of Texas Music*, Austin: Texas Monthly Press, 1984). Courtesy Larry Willoughby.

At about age eleven, young Joplin began free piano lessons from Julius Weiss (born in Saxony, ca. 1841), who also taught him the basics of sight reading, harmony, and appreciation, particularly of opera. Weiss lodged as family tutor for lumberman Col. R. W. Rodgers, and possibly introduced Scott to the same academic subjects he taught the Rodgers children. Indeed each of the Rodgers family learned a musical instrument, and young Rollin Rodgers became a lifelong opera enthusiast (the same subject that haunted Joplin in his later years) due to Weiss's encouragement. The second-hand square piano that Jiles Joplin bought for Scott probably came from the Rodgers home when the family bought a new instrument during Weiss's residence there. After Colonel Rodgers died in April 1884 and following the subsequent departure of Weiss, Joplin may also have left Texarkana. September 1884 seems to be a seminal month in his life, signifying either his departure from the border town or the date when he became an assistant teacher in Texarkana's Negro school. Some authorities believe that he remained there until about 1888, performing in Texarkana and area towns.

After several years as an itinerant pianist in brothels and saloons, Joplin settled in St. Louis about 1890. A type of music known as "jig-piano" was popular there; its bouncing bass and syncopated melody lines were later referred to as "ragged time," or simply "ragtime." During 1893 Joplin played in sporting areas adjacent to the Columbian Exposition in Chicago, and the next year he moved to Sedalia, Missouri, whence he toured with his eight-member Texas Medley Quartette as far east as Syracuse, New York, and, in 1896, into Texas, where he possibly witnessed the staged collision of two MK&T railroad trains near Waco—the "Crash at Crush." In 1897 he enrolled in Sedalia's George R. Smith College for Negroes, studying piano and theory. During this time he was an "entertainer" at the Maple Leaf Club and traveled to Kansas City, where in 1899 Carl Hoffman issued Joplin's first ragtime publications, including his best-known piece, *Maple Leaf Rag*. The sheet music went on to sell over a million copies.

Thereafter Joplin entered into an on-and-off arrangement with John Stark, a publisher in Sedalia and later in St. Louis and New York. In addition to his output of increasingly sophisticated individual rags, Joplin began to integrate ragtime idioms into works in the larger musical forms: a ballet, *The Ragtime Dance* (1899); and two operas, *The Guest of Honor* (1902–03) and *Treemonisha* (1906–10). Unfortunately the orchestration scores for both the operas were lost. A piano–vocal score and new orchestration for *Treemonisha* were later published.

When he moved back to St. Louis in 1901, Joplin renewed an acquaintance with Alfred Ernst (1867–1916), conductor of that city's Choral–Symphony Society, and possibly took theory lessons from him. The German Ernst noted, "He is an unusually intelligent young man and fairly well educated." Joplin had a strong conviction that the key to success for African Americans was education, and this was a common theme in his works. After further periods of residence in Sedalia, Chicago, and St. Louis, with a possible visit home to Texarkana, he followed publisher Stark to New York in 1907, using the city as a base for his East Coast touring, until he settled down there permanently in 1911, to devote his serious energies to the production of *Treemonisha*, mounted unsuccessfully early in 1915.

Joplin had contracted syphilis some years earlier, and by 1916 his health had deteriorated considerably, as indicated by his inconsistent playing on the piano rolls he recorded. He was projecting a ragtime symphony when he entered the Manhattan State Hospital, where he died. He was married twice: to Belle Hayden (1901–03) and Lottie Stokes (from ca. 1909); one daughter (born ca. 1903) died in infancy.

Joplin's works include his ballet and two operas; a manual, *The School of Ragtime* (1908); and many works for piano: rags, including *Maple Leaf*, *The Entertainer*, *Elite Syncopations*, and *Peacherine*; marches, including *Great Crush Collision* and *March Majestic*; and waltzes, including *Harmony Club* and *Bethena*. Throughout the latter half of the twentieth century, Scott Joplin's music won more critical recognition. His collected works were published by the New York Public Library in 1971, and his music was featured in the 1973 motion picture *The Sting*, which won an Academy Award for its score. In 1976 Joplin was posthumously awarded a Pulitzer Prize for *Treemonisha*, the first grand opera by an African American.

BIBLIOGRAPHY: Theodore Albrecht, "Julius Weiss: Scott Joplin's First Piano Teacher," *College Music Symposium* 19 (Fall 1979). Rudi Blesh and Harriet Janis, *They All Played Ragtime: The True Story of an American Music* (London: Sidgwick and Jackson, 1958; 2d ed., New York: Oak Publications, 1966). James Haskins and Kathleen Benson, *Scott Joplin* (Garden City, New York: Doubleday, 1978). Vera Brodsky Lawrence, ed., *The Collected Works of Scott Joplin* (2 vols., New York Public Library, 1971).

Theodore Albrecht

K

"Kat's Karavan." A rhythm-and-blues radio program broadcast from Dallas, 1953–67, on WRR AM. The program aired R&B music to a primarily white teenage audience with burgeoning interests in music previously off-limits to them because of contemporary race relations.

In the 1950s, white-owned radio stations across the country were just beginning to dabble in playing music made by blacks. Unsure of the commercial prospects of such a venture, many radio stations were reluctant to cross racial lines in their programming. "Kat's Karavan" defiantly played early R&B music performed by blacks, even though the show was hosted by and targeted to whites. The show was particularly influential because of its formatting, its personalities, the large region it broadcast to, and the number of famous musicians who came of age while listening to it.

"Kat's Karavan" showed strong support for local music acts such as the Nightcaps, who recorded their only album (*Wine, Wine, Wine*) at the WRR studio in 1959; the single of the same name was used as a promotional vehicle for the show. This album, which also included the song "Thunderbird," influenced upcoming local artists including Jimmie Vaughan, Stevie Ray Vaughan, and members of ZZ Top.

While promoting local music, Kat's Karavan also exposed its listeners to other musicians outside of the area, including John Lee Hooker and Muddy Waters; the show intended to expand the horizons of its listeners and inform them of the musical styles being created by black musicians.

The DJ personalities also contributed to the show's success. "Kat's Karavan" was co-hosted by Jim Lowe Jr. and Bill Carroll, both of whom provided comedy for the listeners and encyclopedic information about the music and the musicians. Lowe became such a well-loved figure in the Dallas area that, for forty years, he was the voice of the mechanical cowboy, Big Tex, at the State Fair of Texas.

"Kat's Karavan" was also successful because of the unique format used by its co-hosts. Lowe and Carroll divided the show up into two parts. Part 1 began at 10:30 each weeknight and centered on R&B vocal groups, and Part 2 began at 11:15 and focused on both electric and acoustic blues (New Orleans, Memphis, St. Louis, and Chicago styles). All these blues styles influenced the development of R&B. The show informed listeners of contemporary R&B developments and their historical backgrounds. Two rare segments of a 1961 broadcast of Kat's Karavan have been discovered and given back to WRR by a private collector.

BIBLIOGRAPHY: "Historical 1961 WRR Broadcasts Found" (http://wrr101.com/headlines/kats_karavan .shtml), accessed March 7, 2003. *Cathy Brigham*

Kelley, Peck. Jazz pianist; b. John Dickson Kelley, Houston, October 22, 1898; d. Houston, December 26, 1980; considered by many of his fellow musicians to be "the finest white jazz pianist of all time." He was one of nine brothers. Although his mother reportedly had a fine singing voice, the Kelleys were not particularly musical. A cousin, Charlie Dickson, was a pianist and popular Houston bandleader in the 1920s.

Peck was the only one of the nine brothers who showed much interest in the family's upright piano. He received his first instruction on the instrument from the teenaged daughter of a neighbor, but soon quit because she kept rapping his knuckles with a pencil when he made a mistake. His interest in the piano continued, however, and by 1919 he was reportedly playing with Jack Sharpe in the red-light district south of Buffalo Bayou. In the fall of 1921 he organized his own band, Peck's Bad Boys, which at various times during the decade included such notable musicians as Jack Teagarden, Pee Wee Russell, Wingy Manone, Snoozer Quinn, Johnny Wiggs, Leon Prima (the brother of Louis), and Leon Roppolo. The band played dances and fraternity parties around the Houston–Galveston area, and also performed at the Washington Hotel in Shreveport in 1926. In addition, Kelley played occasional solo engagements around Houston and provided accompaniment for silent films at several local theaters.

He studied harmony and musical theory with Aldrich Kidd in Houston in the mid-1920s. He also studied classical piano with his friend Patricio Gutierrez and possibly with Albino Torres. Kelley idolized Vladimir Horowitz, though jazz immortal Art Tatum was the pianist to whom his peers most often compared him. In late 1925 Kelley journeyed briefly to St. Louis, where he played with Frankie Trumbauer's orchestra, which also included former Bad Boy Russell and Bix Beiderbecke. Beginning in 1929 Kelley played with several local bands that performed at the Gunter Hotel in San Antonio, the Adolphus Hotel in Dallas, and the Hollywood Club in Galveston, and briefly in New Orleans. In 1931 he also had a regular gig at the cafeteria of the Rice Hotel, Houston.

As alumni of his bands moved on to other organizations and spread word of his talents, Kelley became a legend in jazz circles, but he stubbornly resisted the stardom that seemed his due. "I never liked to play for a living," he once said, "but I liked to play on the piano." He refused to leave Houston, turning down offers from Paul Whiteman, Tommy Dorsey, Jimmy Dorsey, Benny Goodman, Artie Shaw, and Rudy Vallee, among others. "If I was working with a top band," he reasoned, "it would be rehearse, record, broadcast, play, rush, hurry, with no time to myself." He also declined recording contracts from Decca and Okeh. One measure of his growing reputation came in July 1939, when an admiring article by John Hammond, "Peck Kelley Is No Myth," appeared in *Down Beat*. Kelley attracted more attention in February 1940, when *Collier's* ran an article titled "Kelley Won't Budge." He began an

Jazz pianist Peck Kelley (lower left) and the Bad Boys, mid-1930s. Duncan Scheidt Collection.

engagement in 1938 at the Southern Dinner Club, where he played off and on until late 1950. He joined the army in 1942 and was stationed in San Antonio. There he organized a band, but eye problems led to his discharge in March 1943, whereupon he found work in a Houston shipyard for the duration of World War II.

Plagued by deteriorating vision from cataracts and glaucoma, Kelley retired from the music business in 1950, although he reportedly spent hours practicing at home on a stringless piano—soundless so as not to disturb his neighbors. He had begun to show the symptoms of Parkinson's disease. He finally recorded informally, at the urging of friends, in 1951, 1953, and 1957. The 1957 session, recorded at the studios of radio station KPRC, was released as a double album in 1983. At a Houston gig in 1960, his old friend Teagarden invited Kelley to sit in, but Kelley, nearly blind, refused to play in public.

Kelley married in 1920, but he and his wife were divorced amicably two years later, reportedly over her refusal to attend a Christmas party at a movie theater where he had been working. In later years he lived with his nephew and his nephew's wife. Despite his lack of formal education, he was a dedicated reader of philosophy, and was especially fond of the essays of Ralph Waldo Emerson. "He was extremely modest," remembered his old friend Johnny Wiggs. "He just wanted to stay on in Houston and live a quiet life."

BIBLIOGRAPHY: Leonard Feather and Ira Gitler, *The Biographical Encyclopedia of Jazz* (New York: Oxford University Press, 1999). Dick Raichelson, notes to *Out of Obscurity: Peck Kelley and Lynn "Son" Harrell* (Arcadia LP 2018D).   *Martin Donell Kohout*

Kelly, Lawrence Vincent. Founder and general manager of the Dallas Civic Opera; b. Chicago, May 30, 1928; d. Kansas City, Missouri, September 16, 1974; son of Patrick James and Thelma (Seabott) Kelly. He was a student at Chicago Music College (1942–45) at the same time that he attended Loyola Academy, from which he graduated. He went to Georgetown University in Washington, D.C., and returned to Chicago in 1950 to assist in the family real estate business; upon his father's death he became business manager and later secretary–treasurer and director. He attended De Paul University Law School at night (1950–51), became a vice president and director of Dearborn Supply Company (1951–52), and established himself as an insurance broker in 1953.

In 1953 Kelly was a cofounder of the Lyric Theatre of Chicago, an opera company of which he was secretary–treasurer from 1953 to 1956 and managing director from 1954 to 1956. For two years, under his guidance, Chicago was the scene of "some of the most brilliant nights of opera seen in the United States," according to one writer. In June 1956, however, the founders of the company had a disagreement, and Kelly moved to New York City, where he stayed a year.

Considering where he might start a new opera company, he chose Dallas as a likely place. Through the efforts of music critic John Rosenfield, Kelly was brought to Dallas, and by March 1957 the Dallas Civic Opera was chartered. Kelly was general manager. In November 1957 the company presented soprano Maria Callas in a concert; she had been presented by Kelly in her American debut three years earlier in Chicago. That first season only one opera, Rossini's *L'Italiana in Algeri*, was mounted; the cast was headed by Giulietta Simionato, and the production was designed and staged by Franco Zeffirelli, who made his American debut in it. This production set a quality standard for the future of the company, and Kelly's subsequent pattern of originality established the Dallas Civic Opera internationally. Over the next seventeen years Dallas opera lovers saw the American debut of such singers as Teresa Berganza, Jon Vickers, and Joan Sutherland. Kelly also introduced a distinguished group of theatrical directors and designers, and the company had its own scenic department, which built productions for other companies as well. He was also a cofounder and director of the Performing Arts Foundation of Kansas City, Missouri.

Early in 1974 Kelly took on the job of acting manager of the Dallas Symphony Orchestra, which was in serious financial trouble. Several months later he became gravely ill and had to resign that position. He went to Missouri for treatment and died there. A requiem Mass was offered for him at Christ the King Catholic Church in Dallas on September 19, the day before he was buried in the family plot in Chicago.

BIBLIOGRAPHY: Dallas *Morning News*, October 12, 1958; May 19, September 17, 18, 22, 1974. Vertical files, Center for American History, University of Texas at Austin. *Who's Who in America*, 1968–69.

Eldon S. Branda

Kerrville Folk Festival. First held June 1 through 3, 1972, in the 1,200-seat Kerrville Municipal Auditorium; 2,800 fans from all over Texas and as far away as Colorado attended the thirteen-performer event. The festivals at Kerrville were a direct outgrowth of the Austin Zilker Park KHFI–FM Summer Music festivals (1964–68), the Chequered Flag folk-music club on Lavaca Street in Austin (1967–70), and the eight Longhorn Jazz festivals (1966–73), as well as the "live" and recorded programs of Austin folk artists produced on KHFI–AM–FM–TV during the 1950s, 1960s, and early 1970s. Performers included Allen Damron, Willis Alan Ramsey, Jerry Jeff Walker, Michael (Martin) Murphey, Townes Van Zandt, Kenneth Threadgill, Carolyn Hester, Frummox (Steven Fromholz and Dan McCrimmen), Rusty Wier, Three Faces West (including Ray Wylie Hubbard), Bill and Bonnie Hearne, Mance Lipscomb, Bill Neely, and others. Many of them emerged as national recording artists identified with the "Austin Sound."

The first Kerrville Folk Festival included many of the Austin artists as well as National Fiddling Champion Dick Barrett of Pottsboro and Peter Yarrow (of Peter, Paul, and Mary). The 1973 festival expanded to five concerts in three nights, and 5,600 people jammed the auditorium. Among the new performers were Willie Nelson and B. W. Stevenson. The success of the event led to a search for larger quarters, preferably an outdoor location. In December 1973 a sixty-acre plot was acquired nine miles south of Kerrville on State Highway 16 and dubbed the Quiet Valley Ranch to keep from frightening the neighbors. Work began immediately dozing thousands of cedar stumps and debris from a previous runaway fire. Construction began on a stage, a seating area, a concession stand, underground water and wiring, and 6,000 feet of deer-proof seven-foot fencing.

The facilities (except for camping facilities) were completed, outhouses rented, and the first outdoor festival held on the new stage on May 23–26, 1974; the schedule had been expanded to four nights. Asleep at the Wheel, Willis Alan Ramsey, Flaco Jiménez, and Chubby Wise were among the first-time performers, who drew a crowd of 6,000. Lucinda Williams was among the New Folk finalists. The gates were opened daily at 6 P.M., and the concerts started at 8. The nonprofit Kerrville Music Foundation, Incorporated, was established in 1975 to help beginning songwriters and, for many years, also promoted and worked to preserve such traditional art forms as country yodeling, harmonic and mandolin playing, and bluegrass music. While attendance was growing, a spirit also grew out of the warm ambience of the festival, which has been described as "spiritual optimism." The campfire singing in the now-developed campgrounds became a worldwide trade mark of the festival, which maintained its momentum in spite of seven years of heavy rains out of the first nineteen.

In 1980 crowds reached 13,000, and the festival expanded to eleven days for its tenth anniversary in 1981. The present expanded and cantilevered stage was built in three weeks by volunteers that year. In 1986 the festival celebrated its fifteenth anniversary with an eleven-day festival, a special documentary album, and a musicians' fifteen-day tour of nine states on behalf of the Texas Sesquicentennial as official state ambassadors. The next year the festival expanded to its present format of eighteen days, which includes three weekends.

By the 1990s, attendance had grown to 25,000. The program included an eighteen-day schedule of eleven six-hour evening concerts, New Folk Concerts with forty writers, Folk Mass celebrations, six two-hour children's concerts, and a four–day Festival of the Eagle honoring American Indians at a newly constructed and then expanded Threadgill Memorial Theater in the campgrounds. The festival has become America's largest and longest-running celebration of original songwriters and draws performers and fans from around the world. It remains a family affair with the same intimate atmosphere of the early years. By its twenty-second season in 1993 more than two dozen of its early "unknown" performers had earned national recording contracts, including Lyle Lovett, Nanci Griffith, Hal Ketchum, David Wilcox, John Gorka, Tish Hinojosa, Pierce Pettis, Cliff Eberhart, Darden Smith, Michael Tomlinson, Lucinda Williams, James McMurtry, David Massengill, Steve Earle, Robert Earl Keen Jr., Jon Ims, and the Flatlanders (including Joe Ely, Butch Hancock, and Jimmie Dale Gilmore).

Kerrville Folk Festival promoter Rod Kennedy, 1986. Photograph by Niles J. Fuller. The purpose of the festival, which began in 1972, was to help beginning songwriters and to promote and preserve traditional music. Niles J. Fuller Photograph Collection, CAH; CN 11495.

On October 1, 1999, ownership of the festival changed hands, as founder Rod Kennedy, now aged seventy, sold the event to Vaughn Hafner, of Dallas, and his investors. By the year 2000, festival attendance had grown to 30,000, and popular performers on the main stage included Jimmy La Fave, Trout Fishing in America, Eric Andersen, Katy Moffatt, Peter Rowan, Stacey Earle, Tom Prasada-Rao, Sara Hickman, the Chenille Sisters, Susan Werner, and the Limeliters, among hundreds of others. Rod Kennedy was scheduled to continue as producer through the year 2005.

BIBLIOGRAPHY: Rod Kennedy, *Music From the Heart: The Fifty-Year Chronicle of His Life in Music (With a Few Sidetrips!)* (Austin: Eakin Press, 1998). Vertical files, Center for American History, University of Texas at Austin (Kerrville Folk Festival, Music—Folk, Music Festivals).

Rod Kennedy

Keyes, Joe. Trumpeter; b. Houston, ca.1907; d. New York City, ca. November 6, 1950. Around 1928 Keyes began playing with Houston bands, including Johnson's Joymakers. In 1930 he was with Gene Coy's Black Aces from Amarillo and during that summer with Jap Allen's Kansas City unit, which accompanied Houston blues singer Victoria Spivey.

In 1931 Keyes played with singer Blanche Calloway before joining forces with the Kansas City band of Bennie Moten in 1932, in time for Moten's historic RCA Victor recording session that produced some of the most notable sides issued by any swing-era band. After Moten's death in 1934, Keyes became a member of the Count Basie orchestra, and was included on the group's early recordings in 1936–37. In 1937 Keyes left Basie and joined the band of fellow Texan Hot Lips Page. Three years later, he played with two other fellow Texans, guitarist Eddie Durham and reedman Buster Smith, with whom he had worked as a sideman both in the Moten and Basie bands.

Although rarely a soloist, Keyes was present on a number of seminal recordings. He can be heard most fully on a recording of "I Want a Little Girl," made in 1940 with Durham and Smith. In 1941 Keyes was briefly with the bands of Fletcher Henderson and Fats Waller. In 1943 he worked with Claude Hopkins' Wildcats Band, but in his last years he played very little due to a drinking problem. On November 6, 1950, his body was found floating in the Harlem River in New York City. His death was attributed to drowning, although some evidence suggested foul play.

BIBLIOGRAPHY: John Chilton, *Who's Who of Jazz: Storyville to Swing Street*, Fourth Edition (New York: Da Capo Press, 1985). Dave Oliphant, *Texan Jazz* (Austin: University of Texas Press, 1996). *Dave Oliphant*

Kidd–Key, Lucy Ann Thornton. Music college administrator; b Kentucky, 1839; d. September 13, 1916; daughter of Willis Strother and Esther (Stevens) Thornton. As a descendent of two old Southern families, she received a genteel education in the classics and fine arts at Georgetown, Kentucky, and married Dr. Henry Byrd Kidd of Yazoo, Mississippi. Financial reverses caused by the Civil War and the prolonged invalidism and death of her husband in 1876 or 1877 left her in debt and responsible for the support of three children. She took a job as assistant principal at a Kentucky girls' school and was presiding teacher of Whitworth College in Brookhaven, Mississippi, for ten years.

Her experience led Bishop G. D. Galloway to nominate her before the Southern Methodist Conference for the presidency of North Texas Female College in Sherman. The college was in debt and had been closed for two years when Mrs. Kidd arrived in Sherman in July 1888. She spent the remainder of the summer traveling in Texas and Indian Territory, canvassing at Methodist conferences for money and students. The college had no endowment, and its later record of financial stability reflected her astute management. She reopened the college in the fall with 100 students and watched the enrollment grow to a peak of 521 in 1908. By the beginning of her second year in office the college was able to purchase property adjoining the campus, thus beginning an extensive building and expansion program that continued throughout her tenure. Meanwhile, she married Methodist bishop Joseph S. Key in 1892 and was known thereafter as Mrs. Kidd–Key.

She devoted equal effort to enhancing the college's academic reputation. Under her direction North Texas Female College became the most renowned women's college in the Southwest, noted especially for its curriculum in the fine arts. She so expanded the music department that by 1893 the school had become North Texas Female College and Kidd–Key Conservatory of Music, and she traveled extensively in Europe and the United States to recruit distinguished musicians for the faculty.

Since she was a Southern lady of the old school, Mrs. Kidd–Key insisted on strict standards of propriety for her young women: they were chaperoned on visits to town, outgoing mail was subject to presidential inspection, and church attendance was mandatory. She admonished the students to be devout and ladylike and to cherish their future duties as wives and mothers above all other pursuits. She continued to direct the college until her death. The institution was renamed Kidd–Key College in her honor three years later.

BIBLIOGRAPHY: Ruth O. Domatti, "A History of Kidd–Key College," *Southwestern Historical Quarterly* 63 (October 1959). Sherman *Democrat*, September 13, 1916.
Judith N. McArthur

Kidd–Key College. At Sherman; founded in the late 1860s under the name Sherman Male and Female High School by Rev. William R. Petty, under the patronage of the North Texas Methodist Conference. In 1870 the trustees appointed by the conference bought land and built a two-story structure for the school, to which it moved from rented quarters in the Odd Fellows Hall. J. C. Parks succeeded Petty in 1872, and the following year the North Texas Conference acquired the deed to the school and began planning its change to a women's college. The institution formally became North Texas Female College in the fall of 1874. Presidents after Parks were W. I. Cowles, James Reid Cole, J. C. Parham, E. D. Pitts, and I. M. Onins. Lacking administrative stability and plagued by debts, the school was forced to close in 1886.

Two years later Bishop G. D. Galloway persuaded a stalwart widow, Lucy Ann Thornton Kidd, who was teaching at Whitworth College in Brookhaven, Mississippi, to move to Texas and reopen the school. She set about her task immediately, and North Texas Female College reopened in September 1888 with 100 students. From the beginning Mrs. Kidd's curriculum emphasized the fine arts, especially music. Upon her marriage to Bishop Joseph S. Key in 1892, she became Lucy Ann Kidd–Key, and the school became North Texas Female College and Conservatory of Music. The college eventually grew to include seven brick buildings, several cottages, and a gymnasium, after taking over the property of Mary Nash College (across the street) in 1905. Peak enrollments of more than 500 were reached before World War I. By 1910 the school owned 120 pianos and had a library of more than 1,000 volumes.

The conservatory was Mrs. Kidd–Key's primary interest. By hiring prominent teachers from Europe she extended the reputation of the school far beyond Sherman and built a music school of solid quality. Her most important appointment was that of Paul Harold von Mickwitz as head of the conservatory in 1897. Mickwitz, a Finnish pianist, was trained in Russia and Austria by Theodor Leschetizky. Other important teachers brought to the conservatory were pianists Frank Renard, Hans Rischard, Pet-

tis Pipes, and Bomar Cramer; singer Louis Versel; and violinists Jacob Schreiner and Carl Venth. The school gave artist diplomas in music and the bachelor of music degree.

By the eve of World War I, Mrs. Kidd–Key's policy of off-campus chaperonage, compulsory church attendance, and strict regulations regarding dress and ladylike demeanor appealed to fewer and fewer students and parents. The steady decline in enrollment was exacerbated by hard economic times and the opening of Southern Methodist University in 1915, with the consequent reduction of Methodist support for smaller schools. The college made several attempts at self-preservation. In 1917 it joined the Association of Texas Colleges as a first-class junior college, from which credit could be transferred to upper-level institutions. Although it had long been called by the name informally, North Texas Female College officially became Kidd–Key College and Conservatory in 1919, three years after Mrs. Kidd–Key's death.

Edwin Kidd succeeded his mother as president and served until 1923, when E. L. Spurlock took on the duties. When, in 1928, ill health forced Spurlock to resign, Kidd resumed the presidency with reluctance and made a last attempt at expanding the college. Despite a new administration building and auditorium, completely refurbished facilities, and heavy expenditures for new furniture, equipment, and landscaping, enrollments failed to rise. In 1930 Kidd–Key and neighboring Austin College attempted to weather the deepening depression by coordinating programs and sharing facilities. Kidd-Key eliminated its junior college and taught only home economics, religion, fine arts, and women's physical education. The cooperative venture prolonged the institution's existence by a few years, but complete withdrawal of Methodist support forced the college to close in 1935. The property reverted to creditors and was later sold to the city of Sherman in 1937 as a site for a municipal center. Nothing remains of the original buildings.

BIBLIOGRAPHY: Annie Laurie Connelly, The History of Kidd–Key College, Sherman, Grayson County, Texas (M.A. thesis, Southern Methodist University, 1942). Ruth O. Domatti, "A History of Kidd–Key College," *Southwestern Historical Quarterly* 63 (October 1959). Kidd–Key College Records, Southern Methodist University Archives, Dallas. Graham Landrum and Allen Smith, *Grayson County* (Fort Worth, 1960; 2d ed., Fort Worth: Historical Publishers, 1967).
Larry Wolz

Kincaide, Deane. Tenor saxophonist; b. Robert Deane Kincaide, Houston, March 18, 1911; d. St. Cloud, Florida, August 14, 1992. The Kincaide family moved to Decatur, Illinois, when Deane was still a child. During his youth, Deane learned a number of instruments, including piano and trombone, before concentrating on the tenor saxophone. After playing in a local band in Illinois, in 1932 he joined the band of trumpeter Wingy Manone in Shreveport, Louisiana. He returned to the Midwest in 1933 and worked in Chicago until 1935 with the Ben Pollack band, which also included Harry James of Beaumont.

Kincaide left Pollack, along with several other band members, to form the Bob Crosby Orchestra, in whose

Bluesman Freddie King at Armadillo World Headquarters, May 15, 1974. Photograph by Burton Wilson. King made the first major live album ever made in Austin at the Armadillo World Headquarters in 1971.

reed section he played until June 1936, when he became the band's staff arranger. In the spring of 1937 he left Crosby for the Woody Herman band, then returned to the Crosby outfit for several months before rejoining Manone for two months. From March 1938 to January 1940, Kincaide was with the Tommy Dorsey orchestra, and briefly thereafter worked with Glenn Miller. After serving in the navy air force from 1942 to 1945, he worked mainly as an arranger but also played in the band of Texan Ray McKinley from 1946 to 1950 and again in 1956.

As an arranger, Kincaide is best known for his neo-dixieland versions of "Royal Garden Blues" (1936), on which he is a featured tenor soloist; "South Rampart Street Parade" (1937), co-arranged with Bob Haggart; and "Milenberg Joys" (1939). Other well-known arrangements include "Hawaiian War Chant" (1938) and "Boogie Woogie" (1938), the latter a huge hit for Tommy Dorsey. In the later part of his life, Kincaide was active as an arranger for television. He was seen in a 1934 film entitled *Ben Pollack and His Orchestra*, which also featured Texas trombone star Jack Teagarden. Although the arranger–reedman left his home state at an early age, he worked with a number of Texans throughout his career, as well as arranging for bands other than those mentioned here, such as that of Benny Goodman. He retired in 1981. He was survived by his wife, Dorothy.

Bibliography. John Chilton, *Who's Who of Jazz: Storyville to Swing Street*, Fourth Edition (New York: Da Capo Press, 1985). Barry Kernfeld, ed., *The New Grove Dictionary of Jazz*, Second Edition, (New York: Grove's Dictionaries, 2002).   *Dave Oliphant*

King, Freddie. Blues musician; b. Freddie Christian, Gilmer, Texas, September 3, 1934; d. December 28, 1976 (buried in Hillcrest Memorial Park, Dallas); son of J. T. Christian and Ella Mae King. At the age of six he began playing guitar with his mother and an uncle, Leon King. He moved to Chicago when he was sixteen and developed his style under the influence of Lightnin' Hopkins, T-Bone Walker, B. B. King (not a relative), and others. Freddie claimed that Eddie Taylor and Jimmie Rodgers taught him how to use guitar picks.

He played in local clubs from 1950 to 1958 and in the latter year made his professional debut. In the 1950s King worked with the Sonny Cooper Band and Earlee Payton's Blues Cats making records for the Parrot label. In the 1960s he recorded under the Cotillion label with his own band. In 1970 he signed with Shelter Records, a company partly owned by musician Leon Russell. He recorded with such early greats as Muddy Waters, Sonny Cooper, and T-Bone Walker. In 1960 he also began touring the United States, Europe, and Australia, appearing in concert halls, night clubs, and at jazz and blues festivals. Some of his classic songs were "Have You Ever Loved a Woman," "Hide Away," and "Woman Across the River."

Like many blues artists in the late 1960s and early 1970s, King had close ties to rock-and-roll. Musicians such as Eric Clapton and Jeff Beck recorded his songs, and King toured with Clapton in the mid-1970s. In 1963 he returned to Texas and settled in Dallas. In 1971 he recorded the first major live album ever made in Austin, at Armadillo World Headquarters, known sometimes as "the House That Freddie King Built." He opened the club and returned periodically for fund-raisers. His recordings with Shelter Records brought him recognition throughout the state as a "top-notch Texas bluesman."

King married a woman named Jessie, and they had seven children. He died of bleeding ulcers and heart failure at the age of forty-two.

BIBLIOGRAPHY: Sheldon Harris, *Blues Who's Who: A Biographical Dictionary of Blues Singers* (New Rochelle, New York: Arlington House, 1979). Eileen Southern, *Biographical Dictionary of Afro-American and African Musicians* (Westport, Connecticut: Greenwood, 1982). Vertical files, Center for American History, University of Texas at Austin.   *Amy Van Beveren*

King Curtis. Saxophonist and guitarist; b. Curtis Ousley, Fort Worth, February 7, 1934; d. New York City, August 14, 1971. Ousley was raised in Mansfield by adoptive parents. As a child, he was fascinated by the music of saxophonists Lester Young and Louis Jordan, which he heard regularly on the radio. Hoping to encourage their son's musical interests, Curtis's parents gave him a saxophone when he was twelve. He honed his skills playing with his high school band and with a pop band he formed.

He moved to New York City in 1952 and subsequently played with Chuck Willis, Clyde McPhatter, the Coasters, the Alan Freed Band, and other groups. Throughout the 1950s he toured the United States and Europe with Lionel Hampton's band. During that time, Curtis mastered the guitar and learned to arrange music. He stopped touring in the early 1960s, moved back to New York, and soon became one of the best-known saxophone players of the 1960s. He played back-up for numerous singers, including Bobby Darin, Andy Williams, Sam Cooke, Connie Francis, Nat King Cole, the Coasters, and Buddy Holly.

Curtis formed his own group, the Noble Knights, in the early 1960s. He later changed their name to the King Pins. The group signed with Enjoy Records and recorded a number one R&B single, "Soul Twist," in 1962. In the 1960s, fifteen of Curtis's recordings made the pop charts. He recorded for Prestige and Capitol Records, and signed with the Atco label in 1965. He stayed with that label for the remainder of his career, making numerous records, including *King Curtis Plays the Great Memphis Hits*, *That Lovin' Feeling*, and *King Size Soul*. A couple of his songs, "Memphis Soul Stew" and "Ode to Billie Joe," recorded in 1967, were huge hits. Curtis had even more success in the late 1960s, when soul music became more popular. His record sales soared, and he became highly sought after for concerts and music festivals around the country and in Europe. He was at the apex of his career—producing Freddie King, directing Aretha Franklin, and working on a John Lennon album—when he was fatally stabbed outside his New York City apartment. He was survived by a son, Curtis Jr.

BIBLIOGRAPHY: Ed Decker, ed., *Contemporary Musicians*, Volume 17 (Detroit: Gale Research, 1995). Michael Erlewine, ed., *All Music Guide To The Blues* (San Francisco: Miller Freeman, 1999). H. Wiley Hitchcock and

Stanley Sadie, eds., *The New Grove Dictionary of American Music* (New York: Macmillan, 1986). Barry Kernfeld, ed., *The New Grove Dictionary of Jazz* (New York: Macmillan, 1988). Irwin Stambler, *Encyclopedia of Pop, Rock and Soul* (St. Martin's Press, 1977). *James Head*

Klaerner, Christian. Teacher, state librarian, and choral director; b. near Bayreuth, Bavaria, November 9, 1861; d. Austin, September 16, 1949 (buried at Memorial Park, Austin); son of Hans Adam and Elizabeth (Foerster) Klaerner. He attended the seminary at Bayreuth before 1880, when he immigrated to the United States and traveled via New York and Virginia to Houston, Texas. He taught school briefly at Nelsonville and from 1881 to 1887 taught at Frelsburg, where he married Emma Schneider on June 23, 1883, and organized a song and musical club.

Klaerner taught in Austin County from 1887 to 1891. After his first wife's death in 1886, he married Hedwig May at New Ulm on August 15, 1889. He taught in a Lutheran college at Brenham from 1891 to 1897, when he established the German-American Institute, a demonstration school in teaching methods, which he headed until he became county superintendent of Washington County in 1907. From 1915 to 1918 he was state librarian. He taught at Rogers Ranch from 1918 to 1924 and at Uhland from 1925 to 1931. Klaerner was director of a Brenham singing club from 1897 to 1915, of the Uhland choir from 1925 to 1931, and of the Saengerrunde Club at Austin from 1922 to 1949. He composed music for church and choir use and directed choirs at St. Martin's Lutheran Church and the First English Lutheran Church in Austin.

BIBLIOGRAPHY: Austin *American*, September 17, 1949. Mrs. R. E. Pennington, *History of Brenham and Washington County* (Houston, 1915). Vertical files, Center for American History, University of Texas at Austin.

Knox, Buddy Wayne. Musician, songwriter, and early rock-and-roll singer; b. on a wheat farm northeast of Happy, Texas, July 20, 1933; d. Bremerton, Washington, February 14, 1999; son of Lester and Gladys Knox. Buddy and his younger sister, Verdi Ann, grew up during the Great Depression and World War II years with relatives who often enjoyed singing and playing country, folk, and gospel music. At a young age Buddy showed his own knack for music, and in his teens bought his first guitar with money he had saved from a summer job with a surveying crew in New Mexico. After graduating from Happy High School, at which he lettered in football, in 1951, Knox enrolled at West Texas State College (now West Texas A&M) at Canyon. There he was active as a cheerleader and rodeo clown, took part in college drama productions, and in his senior year was elected vice president of his class. In addition, Knox and several of his college buddies began serenading the girls' dorms during after-curfew hours; soon Knox and his "Serenaders" received requests from adoring coeds to perform at dances and other campus functions.

Although he was working on a master's degree in accounting and already had prospects of a steady job with a major oil company, Knox's appetite for the music business was further whetted when he and Dumas natives Jimmy Bowen and Donald Lanier formed a three-man band, which later numbered four with the addition of Dave Alldred on drums. Calling themselves the Orchids, after the color of their matching shirts, the combo played area clubs and fraternity dances to help defray their education costs. When Elvis Presley performed at Amarillo during his path-breaking 1955 tour, Knox attended the concert and afterward met the upcoming "king of rock" backstage. Presley further encouraged the group to do some recording, declaring prophetically that rock 'n roll was "fixing to happen." From another aspiring young West Texas musician, Roy Orbison, Knox and the Orchids learned of Norman Petty's recording studio in Clovis, New Mexico.

In 1956, after scraping together sixty dollars, the group arranged with Petty to make their first studio recordings there. With Dave Alldred drumming on a cotton-stuffed cardboard box, Knox on lead vocals, and his sister Verdi and three other WTSC coeds as backup singers, the Orchids launched their session with "Party Doll," a song Knox had written at age fifteen in 1948. He later recalled that they did the song "at least 57 times before we got it right." But the effort paid off. The song was first issued locally on the Triple-D label, which was formed by Knox and his publisher, Chester Oliver, and named after KDDD Radio in Dumas. "Party Doll" subsequently became the first release on Roulette, a new record company formed by New York nightclub owner Maurice Levy. Knox's band became the Rhythm Orchids after executives of Gee Records in Harlem mistakenly assumed that the group was black. At any rate, Levy and Roulette Records signed up the hot new act from Texas, and in 1957 "Party Doll" soared to the top of the charts in the United States. At that same first session in Clovis, Jimmy Bowen had recorded another Knox composition, "I'm Stickin' With You," which rose to number fourteen on the charts, and Knox's Rhythm Orchids were among the guest performers invited to appear on the "Ed Sullivan Show" on April 7, 1957.

With his light tenor voice skimming over the insistent rhythms, Buddy Knox thus became the first in a line of young West Texas–born rock singers that included Orbison and Buddy Holly. It was Knox who reportedly coined the term "rockabilly" for his new sound, similar to straight rock-and-roll but with less instrumentation. In 1957–58, Knox and his Rhythm Orchids placed a total of eight songs on the charts that they recorded on the Roulette label, including "Rock Your Little Baby to Sleep," "Hula Love" (a Top 10 hit), and "Somebody Touched Me."

Knox appeared in the 1957 movie *Disc Jockey Jamboree*, along with other top rock stars of the day, and toured frequently with Alan Freed's package shows. Over time the Rhythm Orchids included several session guitarists, or some noted guest artist like Bobby Darin on the piano. Since Jimmy Bowen rarely played bass in the studio, Buddy Holly's Crickets were brought in on many sessions, including Holly himself on one song, "All For You." The last top-100 entry for Knox and the Rhythm Orchids was "I Think I'm Going to Kill Myself" in 1959, a controversial song that was banned on many radio stations. Knox was on tour, performing in a small Iowa town on the night of February 3, 1959, when the fatal plane crash that killed Buddy Holly,

Ritchie Valens and J. P. "The Big Bopper" Richardson occurred near Clear Lake, some thirty miles away.

Despite their almost phenomenal success, Knox and his band often found themselves grossly underpaid (compared to the large salaries of Fats Domino and other big-name performers) by the sometimes-shady Roulette executives. What was more, in the week that "Party Doll" hit number one, Knox was called into the U.S. Army Reserves for six months to fulfill his ROTC obligation. This turn of events forced the Rhythm Orchids to cancel proposed concert dates in Europe, including a scheduled performance at the London Palladium. Indeed, "Rock Your Little Baby to Sleep" was issued under the name of Lieutenant Buddy Knox. Knox also made a second appearance on the "Ed Sullivan Show" in uniform, sharing the billing with another celebrity Texan, actress Jayne Mansfield. While at Fort Hood, Texas, Knox renewed his friendship with Presley, who was also stationed there during his legendary army stint; later Presley invited Knox and his first wife, Glenda, to Graceland, the mansion in Memphis.

Soon after his release from the army, Knox saw the breakup of his Rhythm Orchids. All the original members eventually achieved success as solo artists. For his own part, Knox switched from Roulette to Liberty Records and later to United Artists, but with only minimal success. In 1960 he and Jimmy Bowen moved to Los Angeles. There Knox turned to "teen-beat" numbers such as "Lovey-Dovey (1960)" and "Ling Ting Tong (1961)," his last two big hits, with producer Snuff Garrett, another West Texas native. Garrett also produced Knox's recording of "She's Gone," which in 1962 became a minor hit in Great Britain. During the mid-1960s, Knox returned to his country roots, recording in Nashville for Reprise, and in 1968 had a fairly big hit with "Gypsy Man," composed by one-time Cricket Sonny Curtis. This led to movie appearances in *Travelin' Light* (with Waylon Jennings) and *Sweet Country Music* (with Boots Randolph and Johnny Paycheck, among others).

In 1970 Knox moved to Vancouver, British Columbia. There he set up his own Sunny Hill label, bought the rights to his record masters, and opened a nightclub called the Purple Steer. He also toured Europe with rockabilly revival shows during the 1970s and early 1980s. In his later years, Knox sprouted whiskers and dressed in gaudy country-and-western outfits, a stark contrast to the youthful, clean-cut image of his early career. In 1994 he released his last album, a compilation CD entitled *Hard Knox and Bobby Sox*. He also filed lawsuits in an effort to recover money owed him and the Rhythm Orchids by recording companies such as Roulette "that took us to the cleaners." In September 1994 he was inducted into the West Texas Walk of Fame in Lubbock. In 1997 he moved to Port Orchard, near Bremerton, Washington, where he worked only part of the year. That year he joined Bobby Vee, the Shirelles, and the Crickets at a tribute concert to mark the thirty-eighth anniversary of Buddy Holly's death.

Knox married twice after his divorce from Glenda. He had five children and three grandchildren. His oldest son, Wayne, became a successful musician and songwriter in the Nashville area. Knox died of cancer at Harrison Memorial Hospital in Bremerton. On March 6, 1999, a funeral service was held for him at the First United Methodist Church in Canyon, Texas.

BIBLIOGRAPHY: Buddy Knox's official website (www.buddyknox.com), accessed December 4, 2002. Ray Franks, "The Legend of the Other Buddy and His Party Doll," *Accent West*, July 1999. Colin Larkin, ed. *The Encyclopedia of Popular Music*, Volume 4 (1998). Lubbock *Avalanche–Journal*, September 4, 1994; February 17, 1999; February 27, 1999.	*H. Allen Anderson*

Kreissig, Hans. Pianist, music teacher, and conductor; b. Germany, 1856; d. Dallas, December 28, 1929. After training in England, Kreissig toured the Continent as piano accompanist of cornetist Jules Levy. At Christmas 1883 he traveled to Dallas with a touring London opera company, and in the spring of 1884 he established himself there as a teacher of piano and organ. For a time he directed choirs in Jewish synagogues and Catholic churches; his major secular conducting assignment was a male chorus, the Dallas Frohsinn. In December 1886 the Frohsinn offered Kreissig thirty dollars a month and a guarantee of twelve private students if he would remain in Dallas as conductor. He married a woman from the Dallas French colony, and the couple had at least one child.

In a concert in October 1887 Kreissig conducted the Frohsinn in Act I of Gounod's *Faust*, with Henry J. Frees at the piano. More elaborate instrumental music began to appear occasionally in Kreissig's concerts, with the new Dallas band featured at the winter 1887–88 offering. The chorus and its soloists were joined by an orchestra during a concert of March 1892 in which Kreissig conducted works by Franz von Suppé, Brahms, and others. A piano soloist played a march by Joseph Joachim Raff and a sonata by Beethoven. Eight years later, in May 1900, the orchestral movement had become strong enough in Dallas that Kreissig could form the first Dallas Symphony Orchestra, even though the Frohsinn performed in the new orchestra's first concert as well.

An ardent promoter of the arts, Kreissig trod the streets of Dallas, going from merchant to merchant and soliciting funds for his current musical projects, few of which, however, survived more than four or five seasons. In addition to the orchestra, he founded the Beethoven Trio and a slightly larger chamber group, the Phoenix Club. His longest association was with the Frohsinn; he remained its conductor, except for brief periods, until 1912. Over the years he took the chorus to singing festivals in San Antonio (1887), Houston (1902), Galveston (1909), and Austin (1911). After this period Kreissig virtually retired from public life and concentrated on piano teaching.

BIBLIOGRAPHY: Theodore Albrecht, German Singing Societies in Texas (Ph.D. dissertation, North Texas State University, 1975). Lilla Jean Brown, Music in the History of Dallas, Texas, 1841–1900 (M.A. thesis, University of Texas, 1947).	*Theodore Albrecht*

L

Landrum, Miriam Gordon. Pianist; b. Waco, November 25, 1893; d. Austin, January 2, 1967 (buried in Whitewright, Texas); daughter of Sam Houston and Mary Cutler (Dickey) Landrum and sister of Lynn Landrum. Both of Miriam's parents were painters. She attended public schools in Altus, Oklahoma, received a diploma from Kingfisher College in 1915, and attended the University of Texas in 1916–17. She studied piano with Gertrude Concannon, Charles Haubiel, Rudolph Ganz, and Frederic Emerson Farrar. In addition, she studied with Isidore Philippe in Paris and with Robert Casadesus at the American Conservatory at Fontainebleau, France. She also coached with Edwin Hughes and E. Robert Schmitt.

Landrum taught piano at Kingfisher College, at Radnor College in Nashville, Tennessee (1911–12), and at the University of Texas (1922–25). She cofounded the Austin chapter of the Music Teachers' Association in 1930 and helped to establish the Texas School of Fine Arts, which she jointly directed with Anita Gaedke. In 1942 she became sole owner and director of the school, a position she held until her death. She was a charter member of the National Guild of Piano Teachers and served as a member of its board of trustees. She wrote numerous educational articles and gave lecture recitals on piano literature and technique. She was active in many religious and cultural activities, including the founding of the Austin Symphony Orchestra.

Her skill as a teacher was reflected in the success of her pupils, many of whom won high ratings and first places in auditions sponsored by the National Guild of Piano Teachers. Landrum was elected Music Teacher of the Year by the Austin District Music Teachers' Association in 1962. She was a faculty member of the American College of Musicians and a member of the Austin and Texas chapters of the Music Teachers' Association, the National Guild of Piano Teachers, and the Mu Phi Epsilon, Delta Kappa Gamma, and Delta Zeta sororities. She was also a member of the Daughters of the American Revolution and the Albert Sidney Johnston chapter of the United Daughters of the Confederacy. Her hobbies included Bible archeology and genealogy.

BIBLIOGRAPHY: Austin *American–Statesman*, January 3, 1967. Ina M. O. McAdams, *Texas Women of Distinction* (Austin: McAdams, 1962). E. Clyde Whitlock and Richard Drake Saunders, eds., *Music and Dance in Texas, Oklahoma, and the Southwest* (Hollywood, California: Bureau of Musical Research, 1950). *Kendall Curlee*

Lanier, Sidney. Poet, critic, and musician; b. Macon, Georgia, February 3, 1842; d. Lynn, North Carolina, September 7, 1881 (buried in Greenmount Cemetery, Baltimore); son of Robert S. and Mary Jane (Anderson) Lanier. He graduated from Oglethorpe College in 1860 and at the outbreak of the Civil War joined the Macon Volunteers. He participated in several battles and later served as a scout and in the signal service. He was captured on November 2, 1864, and eventually imprisoned at Point Lookout, Maryland, where amid hardships he contracted tuberculosis. After his release in February 1865, he walked home; he arrived in Macon on March 15, desperately ill. These experiences, reflected in his antiwar novel *Tiger-Lilies* (1867), made the remainder of his life a battle against time, poverty, and ill health.

On December 19, 1867, Lanier married Mary Day; the couple had four sons. He practiced law with his father to support his family, and his health grew worse. In 1872 he left his family in Macon and traveled to San Antonio, Texas, via New Orleans, Galveston, Houston, and Austin. He wrote more than 100 letters from Texas, but apparently no poetry. He wrote three short essays: "The Texas Trail in the '70's" (a portion of which was printed under the title "The Mesquit[e] in Texas"), "An Indian Raid in Texas," and "The Mexican Border Troubles." All were published, under the pseudonym Otfall, in the New York *World* in 1872 and 1873. Lanier's long article "San Antonio de Bexar," with descriptions of places, peoples, and northers, and with historical accounts based on Henderson K. Yoakum's *History of Texas* (1856), appeared in the July–August, 1873, edition of the *Southern Magazine*.

Lanier left Texas in March 1873. After a stint as first flutist in the Peabody Orchestra of Baltimore, he wrote a cantata for the Centennial Exposition in Philadelphia (1876). He published a volume of poems in 1877, and in 1879 he gave lectures (published as *The Science of English Verse*, 1880) at Johns Hopkins University. The most important of his posthumously published works are *Poems of Sidney Lanier* (1884), *The English Novel and the Principle of its Development* (1883), *Music and Poetry* (1898), *Retrospects and Prospects* (1899), and *Shakespeare and His Forerunners* (two volumes, 1902). Lanier's interests were equally divided between music and literature. He is noted for his theory that the laws of music are identical to those of poetry, and that both are based on the physics of sound: duration, intensity, pitch, and tone color. His poem "The Marshes of Glynn," with its scene of the sea marshes near Brunswick, Georgia, reflects this theory.

BIBLIOGRAPHY: Charles R. Anderson, ed., *The Centennial Edition of Sidney Lanier* (Baltimore: Johns Hopkins University Press, 1945). Jane S. Gabin, *A Living Minstrelsy: The Poetry and Music of Sidney Lanier* (Macon, Georgia: Mercer University Press, 1985). Lincoln Lorenz, *The Life of Sidney Lanier* (New York: Coward–McCann, 1935). John S. Mayfield, *Sidney Lanier in Texas* (Dallas: Boyd Press, 1932). Edwin Mims, *Sidney Lanier* (Boston: Houghton Mifflin, 1905). Aubrey S. Starke, *Sidney Lanier: A Bibliography and Critical Study* (New York: Russell & Russell, 1964). George Stockton Wills, *Sidney Lanier: His Life and Writings* (Washington, D.C.: Southern History Association, 1899). *Ruth S. Angell*

Larkin, Milt. Jazz trumpeter and bandleader, aka Tippy Larkin; b. Milton Larkin, Navasota, Texas, October 10, 1910; d. Houston, August 31, 1996. Larkin was a self-taught trumpet player who, after working with Chester Boone's Band and Giles Mitchell's Birmingham Blue Blowers, formed his own unit in 1936 and opened in his hometown at the Aragon Ballroom. In subsequent years Larkin and his band toured the territories and performed in Kansas City, in Chicago at the Rhumboogie night club, and in New York at the famed Apollo Theatre.

Reportedly, the Larkin unit, which has been called "probably the last of the great Texas bands," could stand comparison with such name orchestras as those of Jimmie Lunceford and Cab Calloway. Certainly the Larkin band included top-notch sidemen in tenor saxophonists Illinois Jacquet and Arnett Cobb, who went on to make names for themselves as solo stars with the orchestra of Lionel Hampton. Other vital members of the Larkin band were saxophonist and vocalist Eddie Vinson and two pianist–arranger–composers, "Wild Bill" Davis and Cedric Haywood. Larkin refused to record during the period of his greatest success in the 1930s and early 1940s, as he was unwilling to accept the low wages offered to black musicians by record companies. He served in a military band during World War II.

After making a recording of "Chicken Blues" in 1946, Larkin led small groups that toured the country before landing a residency in 1956 at the Celebrity Club in New York. In 1977 he returned to Houston, where he remained active in the community and gave free performances at senior centers, hospitals, and children's wards. He also inspired the formation of the Milt Larkin Jazz Society, which promoted younger musicians. Larkin's trumpet playing can be heard on a 1947 Arnett Cobb album, entitled *Flower Garden Blues / Big League Blues*, which was reissued on CD by Delmark. Larkin was survived by his wife, Catherine, and four children.

BIBLIOGRAPHY: John Chilton, *Who's Who of Jazz: Storyville to Swing Street*, Fourth Edition (New York: Da Capo Press, 1985). Barry Kernfeld, ed., *The New Grove Dictionary of Jazz*, Second Edition (New York: Grove's Dictionaries, 2002). Dave Oliphant, *Texan Jazz* (Austin: University of Texas Press, 1996). *Dave Oliphant*

Lawndale Art Center. In Houston; founded in 1979 under the name Lawndale Art and Performance Center; a nonprofit organization dedicated to innovative art exhibitions, music, and performance art. The center was established principally to offer local artists and musicians a place to exhibit and perform. Lawndale became an important outlet for controversial art and performances by regional artists and a prototype for many other alternative art venues in Houston.

After a fire destroyed the University of Houston's art annex, the painting and sculpture studios were moved to a former cable factory at 5600 Hillman in the East End of Houston, where Texas sculptor James Surls, then a professor at the university, began organizing exhibitions and performances in 1979. The first Lawndale programs were planned and implemented independently of the University of Houston, although the university bore a substantial portion of the center's operating costs. Envisioned by Surls as a "place for artistic phenomena to happen," Lawndale helped to forge a sense of community among Houston artists. Surls and other University of Houston art professors involved with the project, including Derek Boshier, Gael Stack, Richard Stout, and John Alexander, shared ideas with young artists who profited from their expertise and from the opportunity to exhibit their work. Artists such as sculptor Sharon Kopriva, printmaker Melinda Beman, painter and Rome Prize–winner Bert Long, the Art Guys (a performance-art duo), and many other artists who have since established national reputations received their first exposure at Lawndale.

In the twenty-first century, Lawndale Art Center mounts more than twenty exhibitions annually. Historically, such shows as Women-in-Sight: New Art in Texas (1980), Latin Spirit of the '80s (1981), and The Eyes of Texas: An Exhibition of Living Texas Folk Artists (1980) demonstrated the center's commitment to exhibiting work by women, minority, and folk artists. Lawndale also organized exhibitions centered around such provocative themes as This Land: the State of Texas (1990), an exhibition of environmentally focused artworks commemorating Earth Day, and On the Balcony of the Nation (1990), an exhibition of new works by five artists from Northern Ireland, which Lawndale organized as a counterpoint to the Houston International Festival's Salute to the United Kingdom (1990). In the fall 2002 the center sponsored, among other projects, Latino writers reading their works; art associated with El Día de los Muertos, and a program entitled Crew, about the crew of the battleship *Texas*. Lawndale supplements visual-arts programs with performances and lectures by such artists as composer Phillip Glass, choreographer Lucinda Childs, poet Allen Ginsberg, jazz musician Max Roach, architect Paolo Soleri, and performance artists Laurie Anderson, Spaulding Gray, and Terry Allen.

Until 1989 the center was attached to the University of Houston, which provided warehouse space, paid for utilities, and paid the salaries of the directors, who also taught courses. The center depended on private donations to fund exhibitions, catalogues, and publicity. In 1988 the Texas Higher Education Coordinating Board ordered the University of Houston to sell some property, including the Lawndale annex, in order to build a new science and research center. Lawndale became a private, nonprofit institution in June 1989 and formally severed its financial relationship with the university two months later. In the summer of 1990 the governing board voted to close Lawndale while searching for a new location. The organization subsequently moved its offices from the old warehouse site to 1202 Calumet, with the intention of mounting programs in various sites around Houston. In 1993 the Lawndale Art Center moved to 4912 Main Street, in the Houston museum district—to a building built by Houston modernist architect Joseph Finger and opened to the public in 1930. The center has been praised in *Art in America* magazine as Houston's "most flexible, experimental venue."

BIBLIOGRAPHY: Rosanne Clark, "UH's Lawndale: Taking Risks with Art," *Houston*, March 1985. Jamey Gambrell, "Art Capital of the Third Coast," *Art in America* 75 (April 1987). Houston *Post*, June 13, 1989, July 11, 1990. Lawndale Art Center homepage (http://www.lawndaleart-center.org/Page/Home.htm), accessed December 5, 2002. Charlotte Moser, "Playing Cowboys and Artists in Houston," *Art News* 79 (December 1980).   *Kendall Curlee*

Ledbetter, Huddie. Singer and guitarist, known as Leadbelly; b. near Mooringsport, Louisiana, January 21, 1888; d. New York City, December 6, 1949 (buried at Shiloh Baptist Church, north of Shreveport); son of a black tenant farmer, Wess Ledbeter, and his half-Indian wife, Sally Pugho. Ledbetter attended public schools in Louisiana, then in East Texas after his family purchased a small farm near Boulder when he was ten.

Having learned to play the six-string guitar, he left home in 1901 to make his way as a minstrel, first on Fannin Street in Shreveport, and later in Dallas and Fort Worth. He spent summers working as a farmhand in the blackland counties east of Dallas and supplemented his income by singing and playing his guitar in saloons and dance halls during the winter. While working in Dallas, he met Blind Lemon Jefferson, and it was as his partner that Leadbelly first began to play the twelve-string guitar.

In 1918, under the name of Walter Boyd, Ledbetter was convicted of murder and sentenced to thirty years in the Texas penitentiary. Either prior to his sentence or during it, the musician received his famous nickname, Leadbelly. Some reports say that he got it for taking a gunshot in the stomach; others suggest that fellow inmates gave it to him for his hard work and fast pace on the chain gangs. In any case, it sounds like his surname. Pardoned in 1925 after having written a song in honor of Governor Pat Neff, Leadbelly again lived from odd jobs until 1930, when he entered the state prison in Angola, Louisiana, on a charge of assault with intent to murder. There his music attracted Texas folklorist John Avery Lomax and his son Alan. As a result of their intervention, Leadbelly was released from prison, and for several months he toured with the Lomaxes, giving concerts and assisting them in their efforts to record the work songs and spirituals of black convicts.

Soon after arriving in New York City with the Lomaxes, Leadbelly came to national prominence through his singing and unconventional background. Despite his growing musical reputation, he continued to have problems controlling his temper and found himself briefly incarcerated for assault in 1939 on Riker's Island. Ironically, his popularity was stronger in the white folk-music scene than the black blues field. His associates included Woody Guthrie, Pete Seeger, and Sonny Terry. His original songs, such as "Bourgeois Blues" and "Scottsboro Boys," reflected his politics. Leadbelly's most popular composition, "Goodnight Irene," achieved its greatest success when the Weavers recorded it in the early 1950s, after his death.

Ledbetter's association in 1905 with Margaret Coleman produced two children. In 1916 he married Eletha Henderson; the two were later divorced. He married Martha Promise, from Louisiana, in 1935. Ledbetter died of Lou Gehrig's disease. In 1988 Louisiana erected a historical marker at his gravesite. In 1980 the Nashville Songwriters

Association inducted him into its International Hall of Fame. That honor was followed in 1986 with membership in the Blues Foundation Hall of Fame, and in 1988 Leadbelly's work was honored by the Rock and Roll Hall of Fame.

BIBLIOGRAPHY: Moses Asch and Alan Lomax, eds., *The Leadbelly Songbook* (New York: Oak, 1962). Benjamin Filene, "Our Singing Country: John and Alan Lomax, Leadbelly and the Construction of the American Past," *American Quarterly* 43 (December 1991). Alan B. Govenar, *Meeting the Blues* (Dallas: Taylor, 1988). Sheldon Harris, *Blues Who's Who: A Biographical Dictionary of Blues Singers* (New Rochelle, New York: Arlington House, 1979). Gerard Herzhaft, *Encyclopedia of the Blues* (Fayetteville: University of Arkansas Press, 1979). John A. and Alan Lomax, *Negro Folk Songs as Sung by Lead Belly* (New York: Macmillan, 1936).   *Christine Hamm*

Lee, Sonny. Trombonist; b. Thomas Ball Lee, Huntsville, Texas, August 26, 1904; date and place of death unknown. Lee studied at a teachers' college and worked with Texas pianist Peck Kelley in Houston before continuing his studies in St. Louis, where as early as 1925 he worked with Frankie Trumbauer. He also worked with such orchestra leaders as Gene Rodemich, Vincent Lopez, and Paul Specht. From 1932 to 1936 Lee was with the Isham Jones Orchestra, and in 1936 he worked with Artie Shaw and recorded with the Charlie Barnet Orchestra. In 1937–38, Lee was with the Bunny Berigan Orchestra, with which in 1937 he recorded "Mahogany Hall Stomp." On this tune made famous by Louis Armstrong, Lee turns in a superb solo that shows his skilled handling of his instrument, somewhat under the influence of his fellow Texan Jack Teagarden. In 1938 Lee began an association with the Jimmy Dorsey Orchestra that lasted until 1946.

BIBLIOGRAPHY: John Chilton, *Who's Who of Jazz: Storyville to Swing Street*, Fourth Edition (New York: Da Capo Press, 1985). *An Introduction to Bunny Berigan: His Best Recordings, 1935–1939* (Best of Jazz 4021, 1995).
          Dave Oliphant

Lemsky, Frederick. Fife player at the battle of San Jacinto; b. in Europe; d. Galveston Bay, January or February 1844. Lemsky moved to Texas in February 1836, enlisted in the Texas army on March 13, 1836, and served in the company of William E. Howth and Nicholas Lynch. He was a musician in the army until December 31, 1836. He is said to have played "Come to the Bower" on the fife at the battle of San Jacinto.

Lemsky advertised in the *Telegraph and Texas Register* on January 27, 1838, offering his services as a music teacher and teacher of German and French. He was a charter member of the German Union of Texas, incorporated on January 21, 1841. In March 1842 the Brazos and San Luis Canal was being dug near the site of what is now the town of Oyster Creek in Brazoria County; Lemsky was the employer of thirty men digging there. The work lapsed for a while but may have begun again in late 1843.

In January or February 1844 Lemsky and a partner named Franke drowned when a "hard norther" capsized the barge on which they were hauling corn. Lemsky's body was recovered near Virginia Point, on the mainland side of Galveston Bay. According to the probate records in Brazoria County, "1 octave flute" and "1 keyed flute" were included in the inventory of his property. They were sold for $2.25 at auction in June 1844.

BIBLIOGRAPHY: James A. Creighton, *A Narrative History of Brazoria County* (Angleton, Texas: Brazoria County Historical Commission, 1975). Sam Houston Dixon and Louis Wiltz Kemp, *The Heroes of San Jacinto* (Houston: Anson Jones, 1932).   *Donald W. Pugh*

Lewis, William T. Jazz clarinetist and bandleader; b. Cleburne, Texas, June 10, 1905; d. New York City, January 13, 1971. Lewis grew up in Dallas and began his performing career playing in a Texas variety theater. He trained in the New England Conservatory of Music. While in the East he auditioned for and earned a place in the Will Marion Cook Orchestra. Soon thereafter he left Cook's group to join the Sam Wooding Band, which performed at the Nest Club in New York, and he traveled with the band to Europe. Beginning in 1925 Lewis toured South America, North Africa, and Europe with Wooding's Symphonic Syncopators. When the band broke up in 1931, he formed his own band, Willie Lewis and His Entertainers, with some members of the old group.

During the 1930s he was the first prominent black expatriate jazz bandleader in Europe. Lewis played alto and baritone saxophone as well as clarinet; he also performed as a singer. His shows featured such jazz musicians as pianist Herman (Ivory) Chittison, alto saxophonist Benny Carter, tenor saxophonist Frank (Big Boy) Goudie, and trumpet great Bill Coleman. While in Paris, Lewis and the Entertainers recorded for the French label Disques Swing.

Despite its success, the group disbanded in 1941, and Lewis returned to New York. During the 1940s and 1950s he faded from the jazz scene. He occupied himself briefly with acting, but earned his living primarily as a waiter in Harlem. His musical works include *Christopher Columbus* (1936), *Swinging for a Swiss Miss* (1937), *Happy Feet* (1941), and *Willie Lewis and His Entertainers* (1985), a compilation highlighting trumpeter Bill Coleman. In 1988 an additional compilation recording, *Willie Lewis in Paris*, was released.

BIBLIOGRAPHY: Barry Kernfeld, ed., *The New Grove Dictionary of Jazz* (London: Macmillan, 1988). *New York Times*, July 7, 1985. *New Yorker*, July 1, 1985.
                Peggy Hardman

Light Crust Doughboys. Western swing band; founded in 1931. Of all the western swing bands in the Fort Worth–Dallas area, the one that had the greatest and longest success was the Light Crust Doughboys, whose history covers more than half a century. In 1929 James Robert (Bob) Wills moved from West Texas to Fort Worth and formed the Wills Fiddle Band, a rather unimposing aggregation made up of Wills as fiddler and Herman Arnspiger as guitarist. In 1930 Milton Brown joined the band as vocalist, and in 1931 the Wills Fiddle Band—Wills, Arnspiger, and Brown—became the Light Crust Doughboys.

With help from friends and fans in Fort Worth, Wills persuaded Burrus Mill and Elevator Company to sponsor the band on a radio show by advertising the mill's Light Crust Flour. After two weeks of broadcasts, W. Lee O'Daniel, president of Burrus Mill, canceled the show because he did not like "their hillbilly music." However, a compromise, inspired by Wills's persistence and the demands of thousands of fans who used Light Crust Flour, brought the group back to the air in return for its members' agreement to work in the mill as well as perform. People listened at noon each day for a couple of licks on Bob Wills's fiddle and Truett Kimsey's enthusiastic introduction: "The Light Crust Doughboys are on the air!" Then the Doughboys sang their theme song, which began: "Listen everybody, from near and far if you wanta know who we are. We're the Light Crust Doughboys from Burrus Mill." This went over so well that it became the permanent salutation of the Doughboys.

So impressed was O'Daniel with the band's following that he became the announcer for the show and organized a network of radio stations that broadcast the Doughboys throughout Texas and most of Oklahoma. The Texas Quality Group Network, formed in 1934, included such radio stations as WBAP, Fort Worth; WFAA, Dallas; WOAI, San Antonio; KPRC, Houston; and KOMA, Oklahoma City. The show became one of the most popular radio programs in the Southwest.

In 1932 the original Doughboys began leaving the band. Brown left the show that year to form the Musical Brownies, and in 1933 O'Daniel had to fire Wills for missing broadcasts, especially because of drinking. In 1933 Wills organized the Playboys in Waco. Of all the early Doughboys, Wills was the most influential. The Light Crust Doughboys never departed from the fiddle-band style that Wills established in the band's formative years.

In October 1933 O'Daniel took a new and talented group of Doughboys to Chicago for a recording session with Vocalion (later Columbia) Records. O'Daniel, who deserves much credit along with Brown and Wills for the initial success of the Doughboys, continued as manager and announcer until the mid-thirties. In 1935, when Burrus Mill fired him after a series of disputes, O'Daniel formed his own band, the Hillbilly Boys, and his own flour company, Hillbilly Flour. O'Daniel used this band in his successful bid for the governorship in 1938.

The years between 1935 and World War II were the most successful in the long history of the Doughboys. By 1937 some of the best musicians in the history of western swing had joined the band. Kenneth Pitts and Clifford Gross played fiddles. The rhythm section consisted of Dick Reinhart, guitar; Marvin (Smokey) Montgomery, tenor banjo; Ramon DeArman, bass; and John (Knocky) Parker, piano. Muryel Campbell played lead guitar. At various times Cecil Brower played fiddle. Almost from the beginning, the Light Crust Doughboys enjoyed a successful recording career; their records outsold those of all other fiddle bands in the Fort Worth–Dallas area. Their popularity on radio had much to do with their success in recording. By the 1940s the Light Crust Doughboys broadcast over 170 radio stations in the South and Southwest. There is no way of knowing how many millions of people heard their broadcasts. Though the Doughboys played good, danceable jazz, the band was basically a show band whose purpose was to entertain. Their shows took the listeners' minds off the economic problems of the thirties and added joy to their lives.

In the early months of World War II members of the band went into either the armed forces or war-related industries. In 1942 Burrus Mill ended the Doughboys' radio show. The mill reorganized the band in 1946, but the broadcasts were never as appealing as they had been in the prewar years. The company tried various experiments and even hired Hank Thompson and Slim Whitman in the hope that somehow the radio show could be saved. By 1950 the age of television had begun, however, and the dominance of radio was over.

With its passing went the radio show that Texans had enjoyed since 1931. The Light Crust Doughboys were no longer "on the air." But the group's demise was only apparent, for in the 1960s the Doughboys' music was revived. In 1973 members of the band took part in the last recording session for Bob Wills in Dallas for the album *For the Last Time*. During the following decades leader Smokey Montgomery continued to keep the band going in some form. In the late 1980s the Light Crust Doughboys were the first inductees into the Texas Western Swing Hall of Fame. Burrus Mill still owned the Doughboy name in 1991, and throughout the 1990s the Doughboys continued to bring their music to new audiences. Art Greenhaw joined the group; as co-producer he added horns to their sound in 1993, thus bringing about a new type of "country jazz," influenced by the old swing sound. The Texas legislature declared the Doughboys the "official music ambassadors of the Lone Star State" in 1995.

The band received some national recognition when one of their 1930s jukebox classics was featured in the movie *Striptease* in 1996. By the late 1990s the Doughboys were also recording gospel music with James Blackwood on Greenhaw's independent record label, based in Dallas. Beginning in 1998 the group performed jointly with the Lone Star Ballet in Amarillo, the Texas Wind Symphony, the Dallas Wind Symphony, the Abilene Philharmonic, and other ensembles. They were inducted into the Rockabilly Hall of Fame in 2000 and continued to release material including the CD *Doughboy Rock* (2000).

After Montgomery's death in 2001, the Light Crust Doughboys played a fitting tribute at his funeral, held in the Hall of State in Dallas. Art Greenhaw became the band's leader and producer. The history of the Light Crust Doughboys was chronicled by John Dempsey in his book *The Light Crust Doughboys Are on the Air: Celebrating Seventy Years of Texas Music*, published in 2002. In 2003 the band won a Grammy for the CD *We Called Him Mr. Gospel Music: The James Blackwood Tribute Album*. The same year, the Doughboys were inducted into the Texas Cowboy Hall of Fame.

BIBLIOGRAPHY: Light Crust Doughboys website (http://www.heroeswest.com/doughboyfan/), accessed March 11, 2003. Art Greenhaw website (http://www.artgreenhaw.com), accessed March 10, 2003. Bill C. Malone, *Country*

Music U.S.A. (Austin: University of Texas Press, 1968). Charles R. Townsend, *San Antonio Rose: The Life and Music of Bob Wills* (Urbana: University of Illinois Press, 1976).   *Charles R. Townsend*

Lindhe, Vin. Multitalented musician; b. Chicago, ca. 1907; d. Dallas, November 3, 1986 (buried in Hillcrest Memorial Park, Dallas). Vin grew up in a Swedish neighborhood in Chicago, where as a child she showed a talent for music, especially piano playing. She earned a spot as a staff pianist for a Chicago radio station while a young woman and then joined a girls' trio and traveled the country on the theater circuit singing, playing, and arranging music.

In 1927 the trio visited Dallas to play the Majestic. While doing a promotion for the trio's show on WFAA radio, Lindhe was asked by the station to become staff pianist. She accepted and became a well-known radio personality in Dallas. At WFAA's studios at the Baker Hotel she played the piano and acted in several character roles on featured programs; she later said she "did everything but sweep the studio" for WFAA. During this same time, she did some acting and directing with the Dallas Little Theater and some occasional orchestra conducting at the Palace.

While playing the piano for a soloist at a local Rotary Club meeting she was noticed by S. A. "Roxy" Rothafel, who hired her in the 1930s, after she had moved to New York City, to work at Radio City Music Hall. In New York, Lindhe served as assistant conductor to Erno Rapee, the original music director at Radio City. She was also in charge of the men's vocal ensemble and prepared scripts for a weekly opera, as well as assisting Rapee with broadcasts he did for General Motors from Carnegie Hall. During World War II she moved to Cleveland, where she hosted her own radio show.

In 1949 she moved back to Dallas and returned to work for WFAA. She also worked as stage director for the new Dallas Lyric Theater and began playing at the Old Warsaw Restaurant, where, throughout the 1950s and 1960s, she delighted Dallas diners with her classical and popular performances on the grand piano.

She died at home and was eulogized at services in All Saints Episcopal Church. She apparently was briefly married but had no survivors.

BIBLIOGRAPHY: Dallas *Morning News*, September 21, 1969; November 4, 1986.   *Debbie Mauldin Cottrell*

Lipscomb, Mance. Guitarist and songster; b. Bowdie Glenn Lipscomb, in the Brazos bottoms near Navasota, Texas, April 9, 1895; d. Navasota, January 30, 1976 (buried at West Haven Cemetery, Navasota); son of Charles and Jane Lipscomb. Mance lived in the Brazos valley most of his life as a tenant farmer. His father was an Alabama slave who acquired the surname Lipscomb when he was sold to a Texas family of that name. Lipscomb dropped his given name and named himself Mance when a friend, an old man called Emancipation, died. Lipscomb and Elnora, his wife of sixty-three years, had one son, Mance Jr., three adopted children, and twenty-four grandchildren.

Lipscomb represented one of the last remnants of the nineteenth-century songster tradition, which predated the

Mance Lipscomb playing his guitar on the front porch of his home in Navasota, ca. 1960s. His wife, Elnora, is sitting behind him on the left. Lipscomb–Myers Collection, CAH; CN 07486.

development of the blues. Though songsters might incorporate blues into their repertoires, as did Lipscomb, they performed a wide variety of material in diverse styles, much of it common to both black and white traditions in the South, including ballads, rags, dance pieces (breakdowns, waltzes, one and two steps, slow drags, reels, ballin' the jack, the buzzard lope, hop scop, buck and wing, heel and toe polka), and popular, sacred, and secular songs. Lipscomb himself insisted that he was a songster, not a guitarist or "blues singer," since he played "all kinds of music." His eclectic repertoire has been reported to have contained 350 pieces spanning two centuries. (He likewise took exception when he was labeled a "sharecropper" instead of a "farmer.")

Lipscomb was born into a musical family and began playing at an early age. His father was a fiddler, his uncle played the banjo, and his brothers were guitarists. His mother bought him a guitar when he was eleven; he was soon accompanying his father, and later entertaining alone, at suppers and Saturday night dances. Although he had

some contact with such early recording artists as fellow Texans Blind Lemon Jefferson and Blind Willie Johnson and early country star Jimmie Rodgers, he did not make recordings until his "discovery" by whites during the folk-song revival of the 1960s.

Between 1905 and 1956 he farmed as a tenant for a series of landlords in and around Grimes County, including the notorious Tom Moore, subject of a local ballad. Lipscomb left Moore's employ abruptly and went into hiding after he struck a foreman for abusing his mother and wife. His rendition of "Tom Moore's Farm" was taped at his first session in 1960 but released anonymously (Arhoolie LP 1017, *Texas Blues, Volume 2*), presumably to protect the singer. Between 1956 and 1958 Lipscomb lived in Houston, working for a lumber company during the day and playing at night in bars where he vied for audiences with Texas blues great Lightnin' Hopkins, whom Lipscomb had first met in Galveston in 1938. With compensation from an on-the-job accident, he returned to Navasota and was finally able to buy some land and build a house of his own. He was working as foreman of a highway-mowing crew in Grimes County when blues researchers Chris Strachwitz of Arhoolie Records and Mack McCormick of Houston found and recorded him in 1960.

Lipscomb's encounter with Strachwitz and McCormick marked the beginning of over a decade of involvement in the folk-song revival, during which he won wide acclaim and emulation from young white audiences and performers for his virtuosity as a guitarist and the breadth of his repertoire. Admirers enjoyed his lengthy reminiscences and eloquent observations regarding music and life, many of which are contained in taped and written materials in the Mance Lipscomb–Glenn Myers Collection in the archives and manuscripts section of the Center for American History at the University of Texas at Austin. He made numerous recordings and appeared at such festivals as the Berkeley Folk Festival of 1961, where he played before a crowd of more than 40,000.

In clubs Lipscomb often shared the bill with young revivalists or rock bands. He was also the subject of a film, *A Well-Spent Life* (1970), made by Les Blank. Despite his popularity, however, he remained poor. After 1974 declining health confined him to a nursing home and hospitals. Arhoolie Records (El Cerrito, California) has released seven albums of material by Lipscomb: *Mance Lipscomb: Texas Songster and Sharecropper* (Arhoolie 1001); *Mance Lipscomb Volume 2* (Arhoolie 1023); *Mance Lipscomb Volume 3: Texas Songster in a Live Performance* (Arhoolie 1026); *Mance Lipscomb Volumes 4, 5,* and *6* (Arhoolie 1033, 1049, and 1069); and *You'll Never Find Another Man Like Mance* (Arhoolie 1077). *Trouble in Mind* was released by Reprise (R-2012). Individual pieces are included in other anthologies.

BIBLIOGRAPHY: Austin *American-Statesman*, February 1, 1976. Mance Lipscomb and A. Glenn Myers, *I Say Me for a Parable: The Life and Music of Mance Lipscomb* (Washington-on-the-Brazos, Texas: Possum Heard Diversions, 1981). Mance Lipscomb and A. Glenn Myers, *Out of the Bottoms and into the Big City* (Red Rock, Texas: Possum Heard Diversions, 1979). A. Glenn Myers, *Mance and His Music: Mance Lipscomb Speaks for Himself* (Washington-on-the-Brazos, Texas: Possum Heard Diversions, 1976). Vertical files, Center for American History, University of Texas at Austin. *John Minton*

Lomax, Alan. Musicologist; b. Austin, January 31, 1915; d. Safety Harbor, Florida, July 19, 2002; son of John Avery and Bess (Brown) Lomax. Alan attended the Choate School in Connecticut and spent a year at Harvard University, but enrolled at the University of Texas in Austin and graduated in 1936 with a philosophy degree. He married Elizabeth Lyttleton Harold the following year.

He pursued graduate studies in anthropology at Columbia University in 1939, but proved better suited to life on the road than in academia. His father, one of the founders of the Texas Folklore Society, had begun recording cowboy songs as a youth, and in 1933 Alan made his first trip as his father's traveling assistant, helping lug a 350-pound "portable" recording machine through the South and West. In Angola, Louisiana, the Lomaxes discovered and

recorded a prisoner named Huddie Ledbetter, who became better known by his nickname, Leadbelly. Alan Lomax also interviewed the New Orleans jazz pioneer Jelly Roll Morton in 1938; the resulting book, *Mister Jelly Roll* (1950), is considered a classic work on jazz. In the early 1940s, Lomax also made pioneering recordings of two other giants of American music: folk singer Woody Guthrie and blues singer McKinley Morganfield, who became better known as Muddy Waters.

The Lomaxes also collaborated on several influential publications, including *American Ballads and Folk Songs* (1934), *Negro Folk Songs as Sung by Leadbelly* (1936), *Cowboy Songs* (1937), *Our Singing Country* (1938), and *Folk Song: USA* (1946). The senior Lomax became curator of the Archive of Folk Song at the Library of Congress, and Alan joined him as assistant director in 1937. By the end of the 1930s, the two had recorded more than three thousand songs.

In 1939 Alan Lomax began a weekly program on CBS radio's "American School of the Air," and then became the host of his own show, "Back Where I Come From." In 1948 he hosted "On Top of Old Smokey" on the Mutual Broadcasting System and performed with Pete Seeger and Paul Robeson in support of Henry A. Wallace's unsuccessful presidential campaign.

In 1950, as his leftist political views became increasingly unpopular at home, Lomax moved to England. His fieldwork there helped inspire the skiffle craze of the late 1950s, which heavily influenced such groups as the Beatles. His recordings of British folk music were released as a ten-album set in 1961. He also made extensive field recordings of folk music in Spain and Italy that were issued in the eighteen-volume *Columbia World Library of Folk and Primitive Music* (1955).

By the time Lomax returned to the United States in 1957, the folk music revival was in full swing. His book *The Folk Songs of North America* was published in 1960, and he became a consultant to the annual Newport Folk Festival. He remained true to his leftist convictions, finally publishing *Hard Hitting Songs for Hard-Hit People*, originally compiled in the 1940s with his friends Guthrie and Seeger, in 1967. Despite his political views, however, Lomax was a musical conservative who had little use for such hybrid forms as folk-rock. In 1965, when the electrically amplified Paul Butterfield Blues Band performed at Newport, an outraged Lomax got into a fistfight with Bob Dylan's manager.

In 1962 he became a research associate at the Columbia University anthropology department and Center for the Social Sciences. He stayed at Columbia until 1989, when he moved to Hunter College and began developing the Global Jukebox, an interactive multimedia software program surveying the relationship between music, dance, and social structure. Lomax also became a champion of the notion of "cultural equity," a term he coined, which advocates making modern media technology available to traditional, local cultures. The Association for Cultural Equity, located at Hunter College, maintains the Alan Lomax Archive and organizes workshops and symposia.

Lomax wrote, directed, and produced the documentary

film *The Land Where the Blues Began* (1985) and *American Patchwork,* a five-part series shown on the Public Broadcasting System in 1990. He was awarded the National Medal of the Arts in 1986. In 1993 his book of memoirs, also called *The Land Where the Blues Began,* won a National Book Award. More recently, his recording of a Mississippi prisoner named James Carter singing a work song called "Po' Lazarus" was featured on the Grammy Award–winning soundtrack of the film *O Brother, Where Art Thou?* (2000).

Lomax retired in 1996 and moved to Florida. He died at Mease Countryside Hospital in Safety Harbor and was survived by a daughter and stepdaughter.

BIBLIOGRAPHY: Alan Lomax website (http://www.alanlomax.com/), accessed January 30, 2003. New York *Times,* July 20, 2002. *Martin Donell Kohout*

Lomax, John Avery. Folklorist; b. Goodman, Mississippi, September 23, 1867; d. Greenville, Mississippi, January 26, 1948; son of James Avery and Susan Frances (Cooper) Lomax. In August 1869 the Lomaxes set out for Texas in two covered wagons. They arrived in Bosque County before Christmas and settled on a farm north of Meridian. Young Lomax learned to do farm work and attended short terms of school between crops. As his home was located on a branch of the Chisholm Trail, he heard many cowboy ballads and other folk songs; before he was twenty, he began to write some of them down. In 1887 he had a year at Granbury College. With that training he taught for a year at Clifton and for six years at Weatherford College; he spent a summer in study at Eastman Business College, Poughkeepsie, New York, and three summers at Chautauqua. In 1895 he enrolled at the University of Texas, from which he graduated in 1897. He remained at the university as secretary to the president, as registrar, and as steward of the men's dormitory. In 1903–04 he taught English at Texas A&M. On June 9, 1904, he married Bess B. Brown; they had two sons and two daughters.

In 1906 Lomax received a scholarship at Harvard University, where Barrett Wendell and George Lyman Kittredge encouraged him to take up seriously the collection of western ballads he had begun as a youth. He collected by means of an appeal published in western newspapers and through his own vacation travel, financed in part by Harvard fellowships. In the back room of the White Elephant Saloon in Fort Worth he found cowhands who knew many stanzas of "The Old Chisholm Trail." A Gypsy woman living in a truck near Fort Worth sang "Git Along, Little Dogies." At Abilene an old buffalo hunter gave him the words and tune of "Buffalo Skinners." In San Antonio in 1908 a black saloonkeeper who had been a trail cook sang "Home on the Range." Lomax's first collection, *Cowboy Songs and Other Frontier Ballads,* was published in 1910.

From 1910 to 1925 Lomax was secretary of the Alumni Association (later the Ex-Students Association) of the University of Texas, except for two years, 1917–19, when he was a bond salesman in Chicago. He was active in the fight to save the university from political domination by James E. Ferguson. From 1925 until 1931 he was vice president of Republic National Company in Dallas. His first wife

died on May 8, 1931, and on July 21, 1934, he married Ruby R. Terrill. Lomax was one of the founders of the Texas Folklore Society and was president of the American Folklore Society.

In his collecting of folk songs, he traveled 200,000 miles and visited all but one of the forty-eight states. Often accompanied by his son, Alan, he visited prisons to record on phonograph disks the work songs and spirituals of black inmates. At the Angola prison farm in Louisiana, he encountered a talented black minstrel, Huddie Ledbetter, better known as Leadbelly. Upon Leadbelly's release from prison, Lomax took him on a tour in the North and recorded many of his songs. In 1919 he published *Songs of the Cattle Trail and Cow Camp*; it was republished in 1927 and in 1931. With his son, Lomax edited other collections: *American Ballads and Folk Songs* (1934), *Negro Songs as Sung by Lead Belly* (1936), *Our Singing County* (1941), and *Folk Song: U.S.A.* (1947). In 1947 his autobiographical *Adventures of a Ballad Hunter* (1947) was awarded the Carr P. Collins prize as the best Texas book of the year by the Texas Institute of Letters. Beginning in 1933 Lomax was honorary curator of the Archive of Folksong at the Library of Congress, which he helped establish as the primary agency for preservation of American folksongs and culture.

BIBLIOGRAPHY: Dallas *Morning News,* January 27, 1948. Vertical files, Center for American History, University of Texas at Austin. *Wayne Gard*

Long, Hubert. Country music promoter and talent agent; b. Poteet, Texas, December 3, 1923; d. September 7, 1972. Long grew up in Freer and Corpus Christi, Texas. He worked in the record department of a Corpus Christi dime store, and entered the production end of the music industry when he took a job at Decca Records in San Antonio. Long followed his Decca boss to RCA Victor in Houston, where he met music promoter Colonel Tom Parker. Parker put Long in charge of publicity for Eddy Arnold, whom Long is credited with having promoted to superstardom. This marked the real beginning of Long's career as a music promoter.

He came into his own professionally in the early 1950s, when, as manager of the "Louisiana Hayride," he signed Faron Young and Webb Pierce to management contracts. Long founded the Hubert Long Agency in 1952. He further increased his influence as a talent agent when he founded the independent talent agency Stable of Stars in 1955. Over the course of his career, he expanded his interests to include advertising, real estate, and the famous Moss Rose music publishing house, among other ventures.

Country music suffered in 1958, as rock-and-roll began to compete with it. Long and others sought to strengthen country music's presence in the commercial music market. On August 14, 1958, Long took part in a meeting that led to the chartering of the Country Music Association, an organization devoted to the promotion of country music. The CMA replaced the floundering Country Music Disc Jockey Association as the only non-profit group working to advance country music. Long served as secretary when the CMA opened in Nashville on December 8, 1958. He went on to serve as president of the CMA in 1968 and as chairman in 1972. Since its charter in 1958, the CMA has grown from 233 members to more than 6,000 in forty-three countries.

Whether he managed them, sold their songs, promoted their shows, or fought for them through the CMA, Hubert Long touched the lives of countless country musicians. The CMA posthumously elected him into the Country Music Hall of Fame in 1979.

BIBLIOGRAPHY: CMA World homepage (www.cma-world .com/organization/history.asp), accessed on November 1, 2002. Paul Hemphill, *The Nashville Sound: Bright Lights and Country Music* (New York: Simon and Schuster, 1970). "Hubert Long" (www.halloffame.org/hall/mem/hubert-long.html), accessed on November 5, 2002. Paul Kingsbury, *The Encyclopedia of Country Music* (New York: Oxford University Press, 1998). *Stacy's Music Row Report* (http:// www.geocities.com/Nashville/2851/new-cma.html), accessed on 11/5/2002.   *Adam Compton*

Long, Joey. Blues guitarist, singer, and songwriter; b. Joseph Earl Longoria, Zwolle, Louisiana, December 17, 1932; d. Houston, March 22, 1995 (buried in Houston); son of Earlene Leone and Fred Longoria. His parents were of Italian-French and Mexican-French extraction. When Joey was very young, the family moved to Merryville, Louisiana, and continued sharecropping during some of the bleakest years of the Great Depression. Along with his parents, six brothers, and one sister, Joey picked cotton, worked on the farm, and lived a hard rural life. When he was four years old, he developed polio. The disease left his legs weak and slightly deformed. For a time, until his legs became stronger, Joey's mother had to carry him on her back into the cottonfields.

Although Earlene played mandolin, young Joey's interest in music came from his friendship with Charlie Wiser, an old black sharecropper who lived down the road from the Longorias. Wiser taught Joey to play guitar, and, after working all one summer saving his money, Joey bought himself a guitar. He also learned to play the harmonica and sometimes sneaked out of the house at night to go out to the pasture and practice his music in the moonlight.

School records indicate that he attended school only through the third grade. At sixteen years of age he moved north to live with an uncle and work as a truck driver. By the early 1950s he moved back to Louisiana and started his music career, shortening his name to Joey Long and sometimes calling himself Curly Long. His musical roots were in the kind of country music and black blues he had heard in his youth from Charlie Wiser. The duo of Long and Sonny Fisher was one of the first groups to play rockabilly. In commenting on the rise of rockabilly in the late 1940s and early 1950s, historian Bill C. Malone observed that "[c]ountry music had long demonstrated its affinity for the stepped-up rhythms of black music," and rockabilly was thus a "successful fusion of 'rocking' black music and 'hillbilly' music," played and sung by white performers.

During the 1950s, Fisher and Long made appearances on "Louisiana Hayride" in Shreveport. The "Hayride," which first aired on radio station KWKH on April 3, 1948, provided "a forum for musical exposure," and served "as a launching ground for future stardom." Musical talents such as Elvis Presley, Webb Pierce, Johnny Cash, George Jones, and Hank Williams started their national touring careers on this program.

Long eventually stopped playing with Fisher. By the mid-1950s, he had married and moved his wife and baby son to Houston. He lived the rest of his life in Southeast Texas. The marriage ended in divorce, however, and Long's wife and son returned to Louisiana. At some time before his move to Houston, Long lived in New Orleans and performed with a variety of musicians, including singer Clarence "Frogman" Henry. He played lead guitar on Henry's hit recording of "Ain't Got No Home." Later, Long recorded with Ivory Joe Hunter of Beaumont, playing saxophone on "Since I Met You Baby." At one time, Long had a recording contract with Houston's legendary rhythm-and-blues producer Huey Meaux. Other Meaux artists included Freddie Fender, Doug Sahm, Lightnin' Hopkins, T-Bone Walker, and Dr. John.

Long made a living recording and performing in a variety of Houston-area clubs, such as the Cedar Lounge. He built a solid reputation as a multi-talented musician. His authentic, down-home, country blues sound, as well as his unique, flamboyant style, caught the attention of many young white artists who wanted to play the blues. Tary Owens, an Austin musician, folklorist, and record producer, believes that Long was the first non-black blues musician in Texas to play with black blues bands. Early in the 1960s, for example, Duke / Peacock recording artist Big Walter the Thunderbird invited Long to play lead guitar on a new recording, since guitarist Albert Collins had left the band shortly before the scheduled recording date. Big Walter's song "Nobody Loves Me" features Long on lead guitar.

A discography of Long includes such songs as "Something to Ease My Pain," "The Rains Came," "The Blues Just Walked In," and "If You See My Baby." Long also recorded and performed with numerous other artists, such as Papa Link Davis, King Ivory, T-Bone Walker, and Ikey Sweat. Sweat, known in Texas as the "King of the Cotton-Eyed Joe," was a close friend and performed with Long, off and on, for nearly twenty years, until Sweat's death in 1990. In 1978 Long released two albums, *The Rains Came* and *Flying High*, on the Crazy Cajun label.

From the 1950s through the mid-1960s, Long married five times and fathered three children. The marriages were short-lived, except for his last union, with Barbarella Windham, in 1966. This marriage lasted twenty-nine years, although it produced no children. Barbarella's personal reminiscences about her husband suggest that playing music was the all-consuming focus of Long's life. She has commented that Joey had little interest in managing the business side of his career nor in promoting himself outside of Texas. Long went to Europe only one time, to perform at the 1992 Blues Estefete in Utrecht, Netherlands, with band members Gary Dorsey and John Turner.

Long's involvement in the Texas music scene and his profound influence on a whole generation of Texas musicians is not widely recognized outside of the Houston area.

Valerio Longoria, 1988. Conjunto accordionist Longoria recorded more than 200 songs during his sixty-year career and was inducted into the Tejano Conjunto Music Hall of Fame in 1982.

Nevertheless, his playing style had a huge impact on musicians such as Johnny Winter and Billy Gibbons of ZZ Top. John Turner, who has also played with Johnny Winter, described Joey Long as the "godfather" of all white blues guitar players from Texas.

A mild stroke in the mid-1980s slowed Long down only slightly. Barbarella indicated that her husband refused to stop playing and would not follow the doctor's orders for medications and rest. The lifestyle typical of many musicians—late hours, alcohol, and drugs—no doubt contributed to Joey Long's sudden death from a heart attack and brain hemorrhage. He was survived by his wife and three children.

BIBLIOGRAPHY: *All Music Guide* website (www.allmusic .com), accessed January 24, 2003. "Joey Long" (http://rcs. law.emory.edu/res/comps/c/col1085.htm), accessed November 24, 2002. Rick Koster, *Texas Music* (New York: St. Martin's Press, 1998). Bill C. Malone, *Country Music, U.S.A.*, Second Edition (Austin: University of Texas Press, 2002). *Ruth K. Sullivan*

Longoria, Valerio. Conjunto musician; b. Clarksdale, Mississippi (some sources say Kenedy, Texas), on December 27 (some sources say March 13), 1924; d. San Antonio, December 15, 2000. Longoria was an accordionist, a composer, and the first conjunto musician to combine lyrics with the accordion sound. He is credited with being the first conjunto musician to experiment with octave tuning and to introduce drums and boleros to the conjunto repertoire.

Because he was the son of migrant farmworkers and worked as a child in the fields with his father, he rarely attended school. Nevertheless, he displayed an early talent for music. At age six, he was given his first guitar and learned to play the basics. A year later, his father bought him a two-row accordion for $10. Longoria began playing the instrument by imitating conjunto pioneer Narciso Martínez. By the 1930s he was playing at weddings and parties in Harlingen. At age eighteen he was drafted into the army and stationed in Germany. There he played the accordion at local nightclubs.

When he returned to the United States in 1945 he moved to San Antonio, where Corona Records recorded his first songs in 1947—the polka "Cielito" and the corrido "Jesús Cadena." During two years Longoria recorded several hits for the Corona label, including the *canción ranchera* "El Rosalito." He then signed with Ideal Records and stayed with that company for eight years, earning a fee of $20 a recording, compared to the Corona fee of $15.

With Ideal, Longoria established himself as one of the most innovative leaders of the new generation of conjunto musicians. In 1959 he moved to Chicago, where he recorded for Firma Records. Unfortunately, the company did not promote or distribute his recordings in Texas. Eight years later, Longoria moved to Los Angeles and signed with Volcán Records. Like Firma, Volcán did not market Longoria's music in Texas, a failure that caused his fame and fan support to fade.

Even though Longoria never duplicated his earlier success, he recorded more than 200 songs for several music labels in his sixty-year career. In 1982 he was among the first inductees into the Tejano Conjunto Music Hall of Fame. In 1986 he was recognized with the highest honor for a folk artist when he was awarded the National Heritage Award. In March 2000 he received a Lifetime Achievement Award at the San Antonio Current Music Awards. In October of that same year, the Guadalupe Cultural Arts Center, which had hired him in 1981 to teach accordion to young students on San Antonio's West Side, honored him with yet another Lifetime Achievement Award. Longoria had taught hundreds of students to play the accordion.

In June 2000 he was diagnosed with lung cancer, of which he subsequently died. He was buried in Mission Burial Park South, San Antonio. He was survived by his wife, Rebecca, and five sons, Valerio III, Alex, Juan, Flavio, and Valerio IV.

BIBLIOGRAPHY: Ramiro Burr, *The Billboard Guide to Tejano and Regional Mexican Music* (New York: Billboard, 1999). Manuel Peña, *The Texas–Mexican Conjunto: History of a Working Class Music* (Austin: University of Texas Press, 1985). Manuel Peña, *Música Tejana: The Cultural Economy of Artistic Transformation* (College Station: Texas A&M University Press, 1999). San Antonio *Express–News*, December 16, 2000.

Juan Carlos Rodríguez

"Louisiana Hayride." One of three major live-audience country music radio shows during the 1940s. (The others were the "National Barn Dance" out of Chicago and "Grand Ole Opry" from Nashville.) All three showcased major country performers and were huge successes in their parts of the nation. The Louisiana show was particularly important in Texas.

"Louisiana Hayride" was aired on KWKH, a radio station featuring hillbilly music. The station, founded in 1925, already had experience broadcasting regionally successful country music programs. But once it secured the authorization to broadcast with 50,000 watts, KWKH could reach a much larger audience than before. This was the opportunity that station announcer Horace "Hoss" Logan saw when he pitched the idea of another Saturday-night country music show to the station managers.

The "Hayride" was a larger venture than the station had previously attempted. The show aired for three hours on Saturday nights and was based on KWKH shows from the 1930s, including the station's variety shows and its regionally popular "Saturday Night Roundup." The "Louisiana Hayride" went on the air on April 3, 1948, and was immediately popular. It was well-attended locally, in part because of its huge success and its ability to draw major performers week after week, and also in part because of the low admission cost to attend the performances; admission at that 1948 premiere started at sixty cents for adults and half that for children, a rate that stayed the same for eleven years.

The show was popular also because it was broadcast to a huge area. Because of the wattage of KWKH, "Hayride" could be heard deep in Arkansas and as far west as New Mexico. Within a year, the show's popularity led various stations to work together to broadcast the program over even greater distances. By 1953, KWKH's parent company, the CBS Radio Network, had made a weekly Saturday-night radio slot for country music shows. CBS selected six programs, of which "Hayride" was one, and alternated them on this national Saturday-night show. The following year, as the Louisiana show's legendary performances continued, the program was picked up by the Far East Network of the Armed Forces Radio Service. The Louisiana program was now heard around the world.

The most obvious reason for its success was that it served as a stage for a phenomenal number of talented and popular performers. Careers were made on "Hayride" as early as the program's first year. Within its fourth month of broadcasting, the show served as the site of Hank Williams's debut. Williams performed regularly on "Hayride," as well as on other KWKH radio programs, and within months was the most recognizable and commercially successful country artist of the time. Williams left Shreveport to join the "Opry" in Nashville, thus starting a trend. Aspiring performers wanted to emulate the success Williams enjoyed and viewed the "Hayride" as their springboard to the "Opry." This was the path taken by many country artists over the years, including Webb Pierce, Faron Young, Kitty Wells, Slim Whitman, Jim Reeves, George Jones, and Johnny Cash. This movement was not the result of one radio program's being viewed as more prominent than the other. Rather, the surrounding towns provided different environments for career musicians. And while Shreveport was a hotspot of musical activity for aspiring musicians, it did not have the artist network, record companies, or publishing houses that Nashville did.

"Hayride" was not alone in featuring famous musicians, but no other radio program had the image it developed: this was the program that discovered country talent, the show where careers were made. So many future performers were started on "Hayride" that the program was known as the "Cradle of the Stars." Among these luminaries were many Texans, both seasoned performers and relative beginners, who began or enlarged their audiences on the show. They included, for instance, Charline Arthur, Johnny Carroll, Bob Luman, Johnny Horton, Howard Crockett, Jimmy Day, and Joey Long. Another Texan, Hubert Long, was manager of the "Hayride" in the 1950s.

Another prominent musician making his debut on the "Louisiana Hayride" was Elvis Presley, who appeared on the show in October of 1954, at the age of nineteen. He had been invited to the stage because of the success of his first single, "That's Alright Mama." Presley was the first musician on "Hayride" to sing rock-and-roll. He had tried to get on the "Grand Ole Opry" first, but had been rejected because the music he performed didn't match the show's image. When "Hayride" expanded its domain to include rock, it also widened its audience to include a younger, more rockabilly, crowd. When Presley moved on to Hollywood, and the course of popular music favored rock over country, this new, younger fan base for "Hayride" also left.

The show didn't survive the change in cultural taste that it had helped create. The post-Elvis "Hayride" started to plunge in popularity as country music audiences aged and teenagers continued to favor rock-and-roll. "Hayride" aired its final live show in 1960. The radio program was subsequently revived in various incarnations over the years, but never attained the success of its heyday.

BIBLIOGRAPHY: Joe Carr and Alan Munde, *Prairie Nights to Neon Lights: The Story of Country Music in West Texas* (Lubbock: Texas Tech University Press, 1995). Michael Luster, "Hayride Boogie: Blues, Rockabilly and Soul from the Louisiana Hill and Delta Country" (Louisiana Folklife Festival booklet, 1996). Bill C. Malone, *Country Music U.S.A.* (Austin: University of Texas Press, 1985).
Cathy Brigham

Lowery, Fred. The "king of whistlers"; b. Palestine, Texas, November 2, 1909; d. Jacksonville, Texas, December 11, 1984; son of William and Mary (White) Lowery. He lost his eyesight before he was two years old. His mother died shortly after his birth, and his father deserted him and his three older sisters, who were then raised by their Grandma Lucy White. In September 1917, at the age of seven, Lowery entered the Texas School for the Blind in Austin, where he was in attendance for the next twelve years.

His whistling career began with the encouragement of his piano teacher, Peggy Richter, and a bird imitator named Ernest Nichols. In May 1929, Lowery and Richter traveled to Chicago, where Lowery took lessons in acting at the American Institute to develop stage presence. In August of 1929 he had his first spot on a radio show, the "Farm and Home Hour." In November of that year he left the School for the Blind and moved into the home of Peggy Richter. Lowery continued to perform, and soon after a performance at the National Business Confidence Week, a Lions Club event, he received a letter inviting him to try out for a full-time job with the Early Birds on station WFAA, Dallas.

In 1932, entrepreneur and carnival pitchman Henry Murphy hired Lowery, along with the other Early Birds, for a six-month tour with Lignon Smith's band in Texas, Arkansas, Oklahoma, and Louisiana. They worked out a two-hour program with music and comedy called "Heads Up!" When this program ran out of money, Lowery returned to work at WFAA.

Despite some apprehension and self-doubt, in 1934 he moved to New York City to pursue his musical career. He joined the Vincent Lopez orchestra and, during the ensuing four years with Lopez, met and performed with many stars, including Bing Crosby, Mary Pickford, and Jack Dempsey. Toward the end of 1938, Lowery began working for Horace Heidt and his Musical Knights. After this stint,

he began touring solo. He had a radio show and hosted La Rue's Supper Club in Indianapolis in the early 1950s. From the 1960s into the early 1980s Lowery entertained schoolchildren at assembly programs.

In his career he also appeared with Steve Allen, Edgar Bergen, Jackie Gleason, Bob Hope, Stan Kenton, Ed Sullivan, and Paul Whiteman. His biggest-selling record was "Indian Love Call" (1939) which sold over two million copies. His autobiography, *Whistling in the Dark*, was published in 1983.

In 1932 Lowery began courting Gracie Johnston in Dallas. He had met her years earlier at a party he attended in Jacksonville, Texas. Fred and Gracie were married on December 20, 1940. Their only child, Fred M. Lowery, was born the next year. Lowery died at home in Jacksonville, and was survived by his wife and son.

BIBLIOGRAPHY: Fred Lowery, with John R. McDowell, *Whistling in the Dark* (Gretna, Louisiana: Pelican, 1983). "Whistling," *The Wild Scene* (http://www.wildscene.com/oddpop/whistle.html), accessed October 1, 2002. *Variety Obituaries*, Volume 10 (New York: Garland, 1988).
Alicia Leschper

Lucchese, Josephine. Opera singer; b. San Antonio, July 24, 1893 (some sources mistakenly say 1901); d. San Antonio, September 10, 1974; one of seven children of Sam and Frances (Battaglia) Lucchese. Sam Lucchese was a bootmaker. Josephine received her musical training entirely in the United States and primarily in San Antonio, where she graduated from Main Avenue High School. She took up the study of the mandolin at age six and the piano at age ten; at fifteen she began voice lessons with Virginia Colombati. Three years later she accompanied Mme. Colombati to New York, where she continued her studies and made her recital debut at Aeolian Hall on November 26, 1919. She made her operatic debut as Olympia in Offenbach's *Tales of Hoffmann* on September 22, 1920.

During the 1920s and 1930s Mme. Lucchese toured in the United States and Europe, giving both opera and concert performances and singing opposite such leading tenors as Tito Schipa and Giovanni Martinelli. Known in Europe as the "American Nightingale," Lucchese was an operatic success at a time when it was considered impossible to achieve an international reputation without having first studied in Italy. She was featured at the Teatro Nacional in Havana and appeared with opera companies in Berlin, Hamburg, Prague, New York, Chicago, San Francisco, and Philadelphia. She was especially acclaimed for her performances of such coloratura roles as Lucia di Lammermoor and Rosina in *The Barber of Seville*.

Lucchese returned to Texas at the close of her operatic and concert career and taught voice at the University of Texas from 1956 to 1968. After her retirement from the faculty, she continued to give private lessons to a few select students. She was twice married: first to her business manager, Adolfo Caruso, and later to Florentine Donato.

BIBLIOGRAPHY: *The Italian Texans* (San Antonio: University of Texas Institute of Texan Cultures, 1973). San Antonio *Light*, May 3, 1981.
Judith N. McArthur

Luckenbach General Store, February 1996. Luckenbach became a pop phenomenon when Waylon Jennings recorded his hit song "Luckenbach, Texas (Back to the Basics of Love.)"

Luckenbach, Texas. A scenic community in southeastern Gillespie County with strong musical associations. The site was settled in the late 1840s and early 1850s by German farmers, among them the brothers Jacob and August Luckenbach. Jacob was a veteran of the Texas Revolution. The pleasant setting is a mixture of caliche hills and bottomlands on Grape Creek, a tributary of the Pedernales River.

The first post office opened in 1854 under the name of South Grape Creek. Mrs. Albert Luckenbach, née Minnie Engel, established a store and saloon. A dance hall, a cotton gin, and a blacksmith shop were in existence by the late 1800s. A number of family cemeteries and a Catholic cemetery were also established. The growing population supported a primary school and a Methodist church. Residents in addition to Methodists included in roughly equal numbers Lutherans and Catholics. One local schoolmaster, Jacob F. Brodbeck, designed and tested an airplane in this

community, but a major demonstration flight in 1865 terminated in a crash.

Sometime in the later 1800s the post office closed. When it reopened in 1886, August Engel served as postmaster and renamed the town Luckenbach. William Engel became the next postmaster and opened the general store, which remains today in its original building. In 1896 the population was 150. It increased to a high of 492 in 1904 but declined dramatically in the first half of the twentieth century. From the 1920s to the 1950s Luckenbach had a population of twenty.

The dance hall was rebuilt by the early 1930s, and the new structure included a maple dance floor. During dances, William's wife, Anna Schupp Engel, often served homemade dishes on her own china plates. When William died in 1935, his sons assumed control of the family businesses, including the saloon and dance hall. One son, Benno

Engel, served as the new postmaster. The town's population was sixty in 1960 but shrank during the following decades to twenty-five. By 1967 the seven-grade school was consolidated with the Fredericksburg schools.

In 1971 Benno Engel sold Luckenbach to John Russell (Hondo) Crouch, from nearby Comfort. Kathy Morgan and Guich Koock also bought into the town as Crouch's partners. Styling himself the "mayor" and "Clown Prince of Luckenbach," Crouch, a former swimming champion, actor, and columnist, declared Luckenbach "a free state...of mind" and successfully turned the small community into a foil of the nearby "Texas White House"—Lyndon Johnson's place down the Pedernales at the LBJ Ranch. In 1973 singer–songwriter Jerry Jeff Walker recorded his best-selling album *Viva Terlingua* in Luckenbach. Frequent festivals—including an annual Mud Daubers' Day, an annual Hug-In, a women's chili cook-off, the Luckenbach Great World's Fair, and the Non-Buy Centennial Celebration (a take-off from the Republic of Texas Bicentennial in 1986), to which the Prince of Wales and Elizabeth Taylor were invited—brought tens of thousands of people to the pastoral setting.

Popularized in regional culture as the place where "Everybody is Somebody," Luckenbach achieved legendary proportions in 1977, the year after Hondo's death, when the Waylon Jennings hit song "Luckenbach, Texas (Back to the Basics of Love)" became a national favorite. The town attracted both professional and amateur musicians who enjoyed the laid-back, historic atmosphere. State historical markers for the Luckenbach school and town of Luckenbach were erected in 1982 and 1986, respectively. At the beginning of the new millennium the *Texas Almanac* gave the population of Luckenbach as twenty-five, even though the marker for tourists at the entrance to "old" Luckenbach gave the population as three. A Luckenbach Club continued to meet seasonally at the old school to maintain the grounds and to support what remained of a sense of community.

Luckenbach was the site of Willie Nelson's Fourth of July Picnic from 1995 through 1999. In December 2002 *Texas Monthly* listed the town in the "Top 25 Unusual Treasures of Texas." The dance hall continued to be a popular gathering place for area and visiting musicians. Although most road signs directing travelers to Luckenbach have been stolen as souvenirs, the determined visitor still can find the historic hamlet just a few miles east of Fredericksburg, on Farm Road 1376 south of U.S. 290.

BIBLIOGRAPHY: Don Hampton Biggers, *German Pioneers in Texas* (Fredericksburg: Fredericksburg Publishing, 1925). Gillespie County Historical Society, *Pioneers in God's Hills* (2 vols., Austin: Von Boeckmann–Jones, 1960, 1974). Annie Engel Knape, The Story of Luckenbach, Texas (MS, Sophienburg Archives, New Braunfels). Joe Nick Patoski, "Lookin' Back, TX," *Texas Monthly*, December 1990. Becky Crouch Patterson, *Hondo, My Father* (Austin: Shoal Creek, 1979). Vertical files, Center for American History, University of Texas at Austin. Richard Zelade, *Hill Country: Completely Updated 4th Edition* (Houston, Gulf Publishing Company, 1997).

Glen E. Lich and Brandy Schnautz

Luman, Bob. Guitarist and country and rockabilly singer; b. Robert Glynn Luman, Nacogdoches, Texas, April 15, 1937; d. Nashville, Tennessee, December 27, 1978; son of Joe and Lavine Luman. Luman was introduced to music by his father, who played the fiddle, guitar, and harmonica in local amateur bands. He received his first guitar at age thirteen. In high school in Kilgore, where the family had moved, he formed his own band. Luman was also a baseball star at Kilgore High School.

In 1955 he saw the South's newest singing sensation, Elvis Presley, an encounter that helped him determine his career interest. After failing a trial in professional baseball with the Pittsburgh Pirates, he dedicated himself full-time to music. In 1956 he won a talent contest held by the Future Farmers of America. This earned him a spot as a regular in the "Louisiana Hayride" in Shreveport. At the show, Luman formed the Shadows, a band that consisted of James Burton on guitar, James Kirkland on bass, and Butch White on drums. In 1957 he signed with Imperial Records and recorded "All Night Long" and "Amarillo Blues." That same year, he was televised on "Town Hall Party" in Los Angeles and appeared in the movie *Carnival Rock*, backing the film's featured artist, David Houston. A year later, after being released by the Imperial label, Luman signed with Capitol Records and recorded "Try Me" and "I know My Baby Cares." After a dispute with Capitol over changing his name, which he refused to do, Luman was dropped by the label. He then signed with Warner Brothers in 1959 and recorded "Class of '59" and "Loretta."

In 1960 he was drafted by the army, but not before he released the single "Let's Think about Living," which hit the Top 10 while he was in the service. Even though he never had another song on the pop charts, "Let's Think about Living" started a long string of country hits. After his discharge from the army in 1962, Luman moved to Nashville, where he married in 1964. He and his wife, Barbara, had a daughter in 1966. In 1965 Luman joined the "Grand Ole Opry" and toured regularly. He became a popular attraction in Las Vegas by mixing country and rockabilly in his live shows. He signed with Epic Records in 1968 and produced fifteen chart hits and four top-ten hits over the next ten years, including "Lonely Women Make Good Lovers" and "Still Loving You." He performed for the last time with the "Grand Ole Opry" on December 15, 1978. He died of pneumonia.

BIBLIOGRAPHY: Craig Morrison, *Go Cat Go: Rockabilly Music and Its Makers* (Urbana: University of Illinois Press, 1996).

Lyons, Lucil Manning. Music clubwoman; b. Raymond, Texas, September 11, 1879; d. Fort Worth, September 25, 1958; daughter of John W. and Charlie Ella (Burton) Manning. She graduated from George Peabody College for Teachers, Nashville, in 1899 and received the A.B. from the University of Nashville in 1900. After her marriage to John F. Lyons in October 1901 the couple moved about and settled in Fort Worth two years later. After succeeding Mrs. R. B. West as president of the fledgling Harmony Music Club in 1903, Mrs. Lyons helped bring music to Fort Worth under sponsorship of the club until 1926, at which time she continued as an independent concert manager. Under her presidency and management, Fort Worth, Dallas, Wichita Falls, and New Orleans hosted performances by Fritz Kreisler, Rachmaninoff, Paderewski, the New York Philharmonic, the Ballet Russe, and Caruso, as well as Will Rogers.

Mrs. Lyons organized the Texas Federation of Music Clubs and served as its first president from 1915 to 1917; she was secretary of the National Federation of Music Clubs from 1917 to 1921. She became the first woman honored with two terms as president of the national organization (1921–25) and subsequently served on its board until 1955. She organized and was first secretary of the Fort Worth Civic Music Association and served as the regional director of the Federal Music Project in Texas from its inception to its end (1936–41). In 1956 she was granted the Zonta Club Award for "outstanding contribution to the public." She was a Presbyterian and a Democrat.

BIBLIOGRAPHY: Sam Hanna Acheson, Herbert P. Gambrell, Mary Carter Toomey, and Alex M. Acheson, Jr., *Texian Who's Who*, Volume 1 (Dallas: Texian, 1937). Dallas *News*, September 26, 1958.   *Craig H. Roell*

M

Maas, Isabella Offenbach. Opera singer; b. Cologne, Germany, March 11, 1817; d. Galveston, February 19, 1891; daughter of the rabbi of Cologne. She was the older sister of composer Jacques Offenbach. She toured Europe with young Jakob (Jacques) and another brother, Julius, giving operatic performances. Samuel Maas first saw her performing in a cathedral that he visited on one of his many trips to Europe from Texas. They were married in the spring of 1844 in Cologne.

Isabella had an attack of yellow fever eight days after she and Samuel arrived in Galveston, where 200 out of a population of 2,500 had already died in the current epidemic. She lived to have four children. To Galveston she brought the civilizing influence of opera by continuing her singing, mainly among family and friends, and often at her son Max's home on a special stage he built for her in the attic. She also conducted concerts for the German Ladies Benevolent Society and the French Benevolent Society. Eventually, the Maases separated and Isabella moved into her daughter's home, across the street from Samuel's house. She was survived by sixteen grandchildren. Harry Levy, Jr., president of E. S. Levy and Company department store, was a great-grandson of Samuel and Isabella.

BIBLIOGRAPHY: Galveston *News*, February 20, 1891; January 11, 1897. Samuel Maas Papers, Center for American History, University of Texas at Austin. Natalie Ornish, *Pioneer Jewish Texans* (Dallas: Texas Heritage, 1989).

Natalie Ornish

McAuliffe, Leon. Western swing steel guitar player; b. Houston, March 1, 1917; d. Tulsa, September 20, 1988. McAuliffe grew up playing both Hawaiian and standard guitar. In 1933 he was hired to play for W. Lee O'Daniel's Light Crust Doughboys. Two years later he signed on with Bob Wills and his Texas Playboys and quickly gained national prominence. McAuliffe's signature song, "Steel Guitar Rag," also introduced the trademark phrase "Take it away, Leon," which Wills called out each time he introduced the song. The song, first recorded in 1936, has been recorded numerous times since and has become somewhat of an anthem for steel guitar players. The addition of guitarist Eldon Shamblin produced a dynamic combination and inspired another classic Wills song, "Twin Guitar Special."

McAuliffe joined the military in 1941, as did many of the other Playboys. Upon completion of his service, he moved to Tulsa to form his own band, the Cimarron Boys. This group recorded over 200 songs and was generally recognized as innovative and technically proficient.

By the 1960s, western swing had declined in popularity, and many western swing bands had broken up or changed their musical format. The style revived, however, beginning with the 1973 recording of *For the Last Time*, featuring Merle Haggard, Bob Wills, and most of the old Playboys. Wills, who had recently suffered a stroke, realized he was

Publicity photo of Leon McAuliffe, who played with both the Light Crust Doughboys and Bob Wills and his Texas Playboys. McAuliffe recorded his signature song, "Steel Guitar Rag," in 1936. Courtesy Jurgen Koop.

dying and hoped to complete one more album. Among those who returned for the session was Leon McAuliffe. The album's success encouraged the Playboys to tour again. Following a successful "Austin City Limits" taping in 1975 and a subsequent appearance at an Austin night spot, the Original Texas Playboys began to tour with McAuliffe at the helm. They did so successfully until the death of pianist Al Stricklin in 1986, at which time they disbanded. McAuliffe moved on to Rogers State College in Claremore, Oklahoma, and taught a course on the "Music Industry," which dealt primarily with business and legal issues.

BIBLIOGRAPHY: Jean A. Boyd, *The Jazz of the Southwest* (Austin: University of Texas Press, 1998).

N. D. Giesenschlag

McBride, Laura Lee Owens. Western swing vocalist; b. near the Canadian River in Oklahoma, ca. 1920; d. Bryan, Texas, January 25, 1989; daughter of Tex Owens and his wife, Maude. After Tex gave up his job as a mechanic to pursue a career as an entertainer, he landed a radio show in Kansas City and in 1934 wrote his most famous song, the country classic "Cattle Call."

Owens encouraged his daughter to perform. By the age of ten she was singing with her sister on their father's radio program and road shows. She formed her own band, the Prairie Pioneers, after her graduation from high school in Kansas City in 1938. The following year she married her father's guitarist, Herb Kratoska. The band moved to California, where they made thirteen movies with cowboy star Gene Autry.

Shortly thereafter Laura divorced Herb and moved to Tulsa. She went to work with a regrouped Pioneers, known as the Sons of the Range, on Tulsa station KVOO. Her spirited singing style was influenced by the big-band vocalists of the thirties and by her aunt, Texas Ruby Owens, who sang with Pappy O'Daniel's Hillbilly Boys. Laura's sassy vocalizing caught the attention of Western Swing giant Bob Wills, who was looking for a girl singer to perform with his Texas Playboys. Wills recruited her as the first woman to sing with the Playboys. She traveled with him to California, where they acted in B-grade westerns and toured the West Coast. She also married Cameron Hill, a guitar player with the Playboys. In 1943 and 1944 Laura Lee recorded two programs with Wills for the Armed Forces Radio Service. One of the numbers, "I Betcha My Heart I Love You," quickly became her signature song. She more than adequately traded jibes with the unrelenting Wills. During this period she toured briefly with Tex Ritter.

In 1945 Cameron Hill took a job playing with band leader Dickie McBride in Houston. Laura Lee followed her husband to Texas and sang with the McBride organization on KTRH. She divorced Hill and married McBride in 1946. They had a daughter, Sharon. Dickie McBride had celebrity status in East Texas, where he had performed with Cliff Bruner, Floyd Tillman, and Moon Mullican. Together, Dickie and Laura Lee developed a loyal following from Houston to western Louisiana and north to Dallas. In 1950 she returned to the Playboys for a brief time and rerecorded her classic, "I Betcha My Heart I Love You."

During the 1950s she continued to sing with her husband and held various other jobs, including managing a restaurant and selling real estate in Bryan. She also disc-jockeyed for a short period in the 1950s and worked occasionally with Hank Williams. After Dickie died in 1971, Laura Lee returned to singing and toured for eight years with Ernest Tubb. She also participated in numerous Texas Playboy reunions, particularly after Wills's death in 1975, just as the music gained a new appeal. She recorded an album of Western Swing classics, *The Queen of Western Swing*, for the Delta label in the 1970s. The album featured music by members of the original Texas Playboys.

Besides her singing career, Laura McBride managed Walter M. Mischer's resort in Lajitas, Texas, and Grandpa Jones's dinner theater in Mountain View, Arkansas. In 1980 she returned to the airwaves as a disc jockey in Farmington, New Mexico. In the 1980s she received numerous awards, including the title of official Texas State Ambassador and election to the Western Swing Hall of Fame in Sacramento, California. With her happy-go-lucky vocals Laura Lee McBride won a large following among Western Swing aficionados. Her performances with Wills in the 1940s opened the doors for women to perform on the road with the Western Swing bands—one of her major contributions to Texas music. She died of cancer.

BIBLIOGRAPHY: Bill C. Malone, *Country Music U.S.A.* (Austin: University of Texas Press, 1968). Charles R. Townsend, *San Antonio Rose: The Life and Music of Bob Wills* (Urbana: University of Illinois Press, 1976).

Kevin S. Fontenot

McGinty Club. A men's fun-making group that also contributed to civic development in the bustling frontier town of El Paso in the "wonderful nineties." Almost every historian of El Paso in that era has dealt favorably with it. A convivial group of El Paso men loved to gather at the assay office of Dan Reckhardt and O. T. Heckleman on San Francisco Street. Between them, "Reck and Heck" owned a guitar and a mandolin. The crowd joined them in singing songs of the day, the most popular being "Down Went McGinty."

One evening in 1889 found the gang singing and planning a desert picnic east of town. One member, "Peg" Grandover (so called because of his peg leg) was a painter, especially adept at painting signs. On the morning of the picnic, Peg showed up at the assay office, driving a buckboard adorned with signs reading "barbecued burro meat," "ice water" and, most important, "Hunting for McGinty." This was in answer to the expected question, "Where are you going?" and referred to a well-remembered phrase of the McGinty song, "Down went McGinty to the bottom of the sea. He must be very wet, for they haven't found him yet."

From this beginning, the McGinty Club soon sprang into full being. Reckhardt, a hearty 300-pounder who had been an oarsman at Columbia in his college years, was the only president the club ever had. Peg Grandover was involved in everything the club did. Without any firm rules and with a constitution that was largely a joke (it stated the club's purpose as "to put down liquor"), it nevertheless drew to its membership lawyers, three mayors, three prominent bankers, several judges, the manager of Myar's Opera House, a tax assessor, two physicians, and "almost everybody who was anybody." The club had over 300 members. It named as its "poet liar-ate" the poet-scout Capt. Jack Crawford, whose daughter later became Mrs. Dan Reckhardt.

The club enlisted the aid of the bandmaster from Fort Bliss, and throughout the nineties the McGinty marching band was a part of almost every civic endeavor. The club established "Fort McGinty" on a hill near the downtown area; its booming cannon would wake the town for the next big civic event. Long before El Paso dreamed of a chamber of commerce, the McGinty Club was the town's chief booster organization. The projects were endless. Among them were bicycle races made famous by the appearance of Miss Annie Londonderry, who had just completed a world tour by bicycle; the appearance of such theatrical lights as Edwin Booth, Lawrence Barrett, and Madame Luisa Tetrazzini at Myar's Opera House (Reckhardt bought two seats, both for himself, with the partition removed); the hometown baseball club, the El Paso

Browns; a United States Department of Agriculture experiment that used explosives in a valiant attempt to produce rain; a world's heavyweight championship boxing match; a reception for President Benjamin Harrison; a major railroad convention for the proposed White Oaks Railroad; and the volunteer fire department. The McGinty Club was never formally disorganized. It simply died out with the coming of a new and more sophisticated century. By the end of 1902 it was a glorious but fading memory.

BIBLIOGRAPHY: Conrey Bryson, *Down Went McGinty: El Paso in the Wonderful Nineties* (El Paso: Texas Western Press, 1977). C. L. Sonnichsen, *Pass of the North: Four Centuries on the Rio Grande* (2 vols., El Paso: Texas Western Press, 1968, 1980). W. H. Timmons, *El Paso: A Borderlands History* (El Paso: Texas Western Press, 1990).

Conrey Bryson

McGregor, John. Bagpiper and Alamo defender; b. Scotland, 1808; d. San Antonio, March 6, 1836. McGregor lived in early 1836 in Nacogdoches. He took part in the siege of Bexar and later served in the Alamo garrison as a second sergeant of Capt. William R. Carey's artillery company. It is said that during the siege of the Alamo, he engaged in musical duels with David Crockett, McGregor playing the bagpipes and Crockett the fiddle. McGregor died in the battle of the Alamo.

BIBLIOGRAPHY: Daughters of the American Revolution, *The Alamo Heroes and Their Revolutionary Ancestors* (San Antonio, 1976). Daughters of the Republic of Texas, *Muster Rolls of the Texas Revolution* (Austin, 1986). Bill Groneman, *Alamo Defenders* (Austin: Eakin, 1990).

Bill Groneman

McKinley, Ray. Big Band drummer; b. Raymond Frederick McKinley, Fort Worth, June 18, 1910; d. Key Largo, Florida, May 7, 1995. Ray's father, Ray Harris McKinley, deputy district clerk of Tarrant County and an editor of the *Daily Livestock Reporter*, encouraged his son's interest in music. By the age of nine young Ray was playing in the Fort Worth area.

At age fifteen he started touring with big bands such as Duncan Marion's Orchestra and the Tracy Brown Band. In 1932 he joined Smith Ballew's band, with which he earned a reputation as a steady, consistent drummer. Two years later, McKinley began playing for the notorious Dorsey Brothers, but after a row caused the brothers to break apart, he continued to play with Jimmy until 1939. Shortly thereafter, he formed an ensemble with Will Bradley, with whom he toured, recorded, and released hit singles such as "Beat Me Daddy Eight to the Bar" and "Celery Stalks at Midnight."

During World War II McKinley joined the Army Air Force and played with the Glenn Miller Band, traveling throughout Europe playing for the Allied troops. In 1944, after Miller and most of the band died in a plane crash, McKinley carried on as bandleader, holding the act together for the remainder of the war. Upon returning to America, he started his own big band, which included fellow Texans Curley Broyles and Ted Newman.

Although never very popular, McKinley was successful and played throughout the country. In 1956, Miller's

Drummer Ray McKinley began touring with big bands at age fifteen. During World War II he traveled throughout Europe playing for Allied troops with the Glenn Miller Band. Ray Bauduc Collection, William Ransom Hogan Jazz Archive, Tulane University.

widow asked him to head up a new Glenn Miller Orchestra. McKinley enlisted other jazz veterans, and soon they were playing all of the Glenn Miller classics and touring Europe, performing even in Communist Bloc countries. Despite his success, McKinley wanted to return to a career in which he headed his own act and stayed put. His band eventually landed a spot as the house band at the Riverboat in New York City. McKinley continued playing through the 1960s and 1970s and later retired to Key Largo.

BIBLIOGRAPHY: John Chilton, *Who's Who of Jazz: Storyville to Swing Street* (New York: Da Capo Press, 1985). Leonard Feather, *Encyclopedia of Jazz* (New York: Horizon Press, new ed., 1960). Fort Worth *Star-Telegram*, September 25, 1996. Colin Larkin, ed., *Encyclopedia of Popular Music* (London: MuzeUK Limited, 1998). Dave Oliphant, *Texan Jazz* (Austin: University of Texas Press, 1996).

Bradley Shreve

McKinney, Baylus Benjamin. Writer of gospel songs, teacher, and music editor; b. Heflin, Louisiana, July 22, 1886; d. Bryson City, North Carolina, September 7, 1952; son of James Calvin and Martha Annis (Heflin) McKinney. He attended Mount Lebanon Academy, Louisiana; Louisiana College, Pineville, Louisiana; Southwestern Baptist Theological Seminary, Fort Worth; Siegel–Myers Correspondence School of Music, Chicago, Illinois (B.M. 1922); and Bush Conservatory of Music, Chicago. Oklahoma Baptist University awarded him an honorary Mus.D. in 1942.

From 1918 to 1935 McKinney served as music editor for Robert Henry Coleman, songbook publisher in Dallas, and many of his works were originally published in Coleman's songbooks and hymnals. In 1919, after several months in the United States Army, McKinney returned to Fort Worth, where Isham E. Reynolds asked him to join the faculty of the School of Sacred Music at Southwestern Baptist Theological Seminary. He taught there until 1932, when he left the seminary due to its financial difficulties caused by the Great Depression. From 1931 to 1935 McKinney served as assistant pastor of Travis Avenue Baptist Church, Fort Worth, in charge of music. In 1935 he was named music editor for the Baptist Sunday School Board of the Southern Baptist Convention, Nashville, Tennessee, where he edited the popular *Broadman Hymnal* (1940). In 1941 he became secretary of the newly formed Department of Church Music of the Sunday School Board, a post he held until his death.

During McKinney's career he led music in numerous revivals, including those at the Buckner Orphan's Home (later Buckner Baptist Children's Home) in Dallas. He had a special relationship with the children there, who expanded his initials, "B. B.," to "Big Brother." He also taught in schools of church music in local Southern Baptist churches. Under his own name and pen names including Martha Annis, Otto Nellen, and Gene Routh, he composed words and music to 149 gospel hymns and songs, composed the music for 114 others, and arranged more than 100 works. Additionally, he contributed to several textbooks. He is included in the Gospel Music Hall of Fame.

McKinney married Leila Irene Routh on June 11, 1918. They had two sons. He died of injuries received in an automobile accident.

BIBLIOGRAPHY: *Encyclopedia of Southern Baptists* (4 vols., Nashville: Broadman, 1958–82). Robert J. Hastings, *Glorious is Thy Name: B. B. McKinney, the Man and His Music* (Nashville: Broadman, 1986). H. Wiley Hitchcock and Stanley Sadie, eds., *The New Grove Dictionary of American Music* (4 vols., New York: Macmillan, 1986). B. B. McKinney Collection, Roberts Library, Southwestern Baptist Theological Seminary, Fort Worth. Paul R. Powell, *Wherever He Leads I'll Go: The Story of B. B. McKinney* (New Orleans: Insight, 1974). William J. Reynolds, *Companion to Baptist Hymnal* (Nashville: Broadman, 1976). Terry Carel Terry, *B. B. McKinney: A Shaping Force in Southern Protestant Music* (Ph.D. dissertation, North Texas State University, 1981). *Michael Pullin*

McLendon, Gordon Barton. Radio programming innovator and sportscaster, nicknamed the Old Scotchman; b. Paris, Texas, June 8, 1921; d. at his ranch home near Lake Dallas, Texas, September 14, 1986; son of Barton Robert and Jeanette Marie (Eyster) McLendon. He grew up in Idabel, Oklahoma, and later graduated from Kemper Military Academy, Booneville, Missouri. He won a nationwide political-essay contest judged by journalists Arthur Brisbane, Henry Luce, and Walter Lippmann. McLendon later attended Yale University, where he studied Far Eastern languages, worked for the campus radio station, and served as business manager for the *Yale Literary Magazine*. World War II began just before he was to graduate from Yale. He accepted a commission in the United States Navy and worked as an interpreter, translator, and interrogator. Later he was reassigned to armed forces radio, where he earned a reputation as the "Bill Mauldin of the Pacific" for his colorful broadcasts, which reminded some listeners of the famous war cartoonist.

After the war he briefly attended law school at Harvard and then returned to Texas, where he bought an interest in radio station KNET, Palestine. He soon sold his interest in this station to establish radio station KLIF in the Oak Cliff part of Dallas. Since no other radio stations operating in Dallas then carried live baseball broadcasts, McLendon decided to do so. But without adequate funds to pay for the rights to live broadcasts, he paid people to sit in stadiums across the country and feed him play-by-play information about games via Western Union. To prerecorded sound effects and the information received through Western Union, McLendon joined his ability to ad lib and made routine games seem exciting.

As word of his baseball games spread, other stations sought to carry them. In 1947 McLendon and his father founded the Liberty Broadcasting System to carry them. With 458 radio stations in 1952, LBS was the second largest radio network in the United States. McLendon became well known for his "Game of the Day" broadcasts. For a time his broadcast partner was Hall of Fame pitcher Dizzy Dean. McLendon helped start such broadcasters as Lindsay Nelson, Jerry Doggett, and Don Wells. In 1951 he won a coveted award from *Sporting News* as America's Outstanding Sports Broadcaster. Meantime, baseball owners fumed. In a courtroom argument over dwindling attendance and rights to broadcast, McLendon settled out of court for $200,000 and discontinued his broadcasts.

The McLendon family built a communications empire that included radio stations across the United States. In addition to KLIF, McLendon owned KNUS–FM in Dallas, KOST in Los Angeles, WYSL–AM and FM in Chicago, WWWW–FM in Detroit, WAKY in Louisville, KABL in Oakland, KABL–FM in San Francisco, KILT in Houston, KTSA in San Antonio, and KELP in El Paso. He owned television station KCND in Pembina, North Dakota, which broadcast into Canada. For a time he owned Radio NORD, a converted fishing boat in the North Sea, which beamed into Sweden and other European countries. His broadcasting success was due to his vivid imagination and innovations. He is credited by most broadcast historians with having established the first mobile news units in American radio, the first traffic reports, the first jingles, the first all-news radio station, and the first "easy-listening" programming. He also was among the first broadcasters in the United States to editorialize. He introduced five-minute news broadcasts and pioneered in top-forty record presentations as a standard format for radio. McLendon especially attracted attention for his stern denunciations of French president Charles De Gaulle, whom he called "an ungrateful four-flusher" who could "go straight to hell."

McLendon and his family also owned drive-in and conventional movie theaters. In 1959 he made three "B" movies—*The Killer Shrews*, *The Giant Gila Monster*, and *My Dog Buddy*. A New York film critic described *The Killer Shrews* as one of the worst movies ever made. McLendon wrote and produced more than 150 motion-picture campaigns. From 1963 to 1966 he worked under an exclusive contract to promote movies for United Artists.

In 1964 the conservative McLendon entered politics, but lost to incumbent Ralph Yarborough, a liberal, in the Texas primary for the Democratic nomination to the United States Senate, receiving 419,883 votes to Yarborough's 520,591. In a spirited campaign, accompanied at times by such Hollywood luminaries as Chill Wills, John Wayne, and Robert Cummings, McLendon attacked foreign aid to Communist countries as well as federal aid to education. He also supported racial desegregation of public schools and equal voting rights for all races. McLendon entered the 1968 Texas Democratic gubernatorial primary but withdrew, possibly because of the large number of conservative candidates and the absence of Yarborough, who many believed would enter the race. McLendon said in his withdrawal statement that he could no longer support the Democratic party policies sponsored by President Lyndon Johnson. McLendon, who had traveled to Vietnam as a correspondent, criticized the Vietnam War and voiced fears that the conflict would lead to financial bankruptcy as well as involvement in other East Asian land wars.

The McLendon family sold radio station KLIF, Dallas, in 1971 to Fairchild Industries of Germantown, Maryland, for $10.5 million, then a record price for a radio station. By 1979 the family had sold all of its broadcasting properties, including fourteen radio and two television stations, worth approximately $100 million. McLendon became an authority on precious metals and wrote a book entitled *Get Really Rich in the Coming Super Metals Boom*, published in 1981. That year he also was executive producer of the feature film *Victory*, directed by John Huston and starring Sylvester Stallone and Michael Caine. He also authored a number of other books, including *How to Succeed in Broadcasting* (1961), *Correct Spelling in Three Hours* (1962), *Understanding American Government* (1964), and *100 Years of America in Sound* (1965). By 1985 *Forbes* magazine estimated McLendon's net worth at $200 million.

He will, however, be best remembered as a celebrated innovator of radio programming during the 1950s, when many people thought television had killed radio. Asked in 1980 what he learned from radio, McLendon responded: "That it all begins with creativity and programming. You can have the greatest sales staff and signal in the world, and it doesn't mean a thing if you don't have something great to put on the air."

McLendon was married in 1943 to Gay Noe, daughter of James A. Noe, former governor of Louisiana; in 1973 he married Susan Stafford, a syndicated columnist, radio talk-show host, and actress. McLendon was a member of the board of stewards of Highland Park Methodist Church in Dallas and the board of directors of the Dallas Symphony Orchestra, Texas chairman of the March of Dimes, and an honorary chairman of the Veterans of Foreign Wars Poppy Drive. In 1964–65 he served as a communications advisor to the United States Peace Corps. In 1971 he conducted a month-long all-expense-paid broadcasting course for nine minority-group members, including African Americans, Puerto Ricans, and Mexican Americans. He died of cancer and was survived by a son and three daughters. In 1994 he was inducted into the Radio Hall of Fame by the Museum of Broadcast Communications in Chicago.

BIBLIOGRAPHY: *Broadcasting*, September 22, 1986. Chicago *Tribune*, September 16, 1986. Dallas *Morning News*, September 16, 21, 1986; November 6, 1994. Dallas *Times Herald*, September 15, 1986. Gordon B. McLendon Papers, Southwest Collection, Texas Tech University. Vertical Files, Center for American History, University of Texas at Austin.

David Dary

Majestic Theatre. At 1925 Elm Street in downtown Dallas; restored and reopened on January 16, 1983, after having been closed for ten years. The Majestic is actually the third theater in Dallas to bear that name. The first was built on the corner of Commerce Street and St. Paul in 1905 by Karl St. John Hoblitzelle as part of his Interstate Amusement Company, a chain of vaudeville houses. It burned in 1916, and Hoblitzelle engaged renowned Chicago theater architect John Eberson to design its replacement. Until the new building was completed in 1921, the old Opera House at Main and St. Paul served as the second Majestic. Construction of the present Majestic Theatre, which cost nearly $2 million, was begun in February 1920. The cornerstone was laid on October 18 of that year. The cornerstone ceremony, with Mrs. Hoblitzelle officiating, was held on March 26, 1921. The Majestic, the flagship theater of Hoblitzelle's Interstate chain, opened on April 11, 1921.

The Majestic, a twentieth-century interpretation of the Renaissance Revival style, is five stories tall. Originally a large canopy projected over the entire first-floor elevation. A large marquee extended vertically from the fourth floor level over the canopy. In 1948 the canopy was enclosed by a new, larger marquee. A series of tripartite windows set into square and arched frames extends across the front elevation of the second through fourth stories. Square windows on the fifth story are framed by elaborate moldings. The structure is crowned by a cornice of applied ornament. The floors are divided by decorative panels, and large scored pilasters marked by sculptural ornament act as vertical terminating elements, while smaller scored pilasters divide the five bays.

The interior of the Majestic was originally divided into theater and office space, with 20,000 square feet of the upper four floors used as the headquarters of the Interstate Amusement Company chain. The opulent and baroque main lobby and the auditorium had decorative detailing of Corinthian columns, egg-and-dart molding, cartouches, and Roman swags and fretwork. The lobby was dominated by a magnificent black-and-white Italian-style Vermont marble floor and twin marble staircases. An ornate cage elevator, complete with a brass rail and carriage lamps on either side, served the two upper balconies. Adding to the "Roman gardens" theme of the theater were crystal chandeliers, brass mirrors, ferns, and a marble fountain copied from one in the Vatican gardens in Rome. During a remodeling in the late 1940s a concession stand was added to the lobby, and red carpet was laid over the marble floors. The 2,400-seat auditorium was dominated by a ceiling "sky" of floating clouds and mechanically controlled twinkling stars. The seating was laid out in the shape of a fan, with seats of woven cane, each with its own hat rack for the gentlemen. There was seating not only on the main floor, but also in two balconies. Large paintings were set into panels on the auditorium walls, along with intricate latticework. The stage was set back beneath an arch flanked by massive Corinthian columns, with an orchestra pit in front. Backstage were twelve dressing rooms, a loft to accommodate scenery, and a set of wooden lighting controls. The stage curtain was decorated with a classical scene.

Patrons at the Majestic were pampered by such amenities as a fantasy playroom called Majesticland—complete with a carousel and a petting zoo—where children were cared for while their parents watched the shows. Adjacent to this was the Land of Nod, a nursery with infant cribs, trained nurses, and free milk and crackers. A smoking lounge, furnished with wicker chairs and couches, was provided for gentlemen.

The Majestic originally offered seven vaudeville acts twice daily during the winter vaudeville season and movies during the summer. Beginning in 1922 and lasting until the mid-1930s, films were added to the regular vaudeville offerings. Among the many famous entertainers who appeared on the Majestic stage were Mae West, Jack Benny, Milton Berle, Bob Hope, George Burns, and Gracie Allen. Magicians Harry Houdini, Harry Blackstone, and Howard Thurston amazed Majestic audiences with their magic tricks. Ginger Rogers began her career at the Majestic. Appearances were also made there by Duke Ellington, Cab Calloway, John Wayne, James Stewart, and Joan Crawford. Movies gradually took over as the main attraction and were shown in the Majestic until July 1973, when it closed.

The Hoblitzelle Foundation gave the Majestic to the city of Dallas on December 31, 1976. The Oglesby Group in Dallas served as architects for its renovation. The present-day elegance of the Majestic begins with its exterior, where the original cast-iron marquee has been uncovered and repainted dark green and tan. The cream-colored terracotta facing has been repaired and cleaned. The main lobby echoes its original baroque splendor, with the black-and-white marble floor again revealed, and with decorative molding, egg-and-dart borders, acanthus leaves, and floor-to-ceiling mirrors in gilt frames. The original crystal chandelier was removed during an earlier remodeling; in its place hangs a chandelier salvaged from the old Baker Hotel, historically correct and in excellent proportion to its new setting. Throughout the theater, walls have been painted shades of gray with gold-leaf highlighting, and the carpeting is wine-colored. In the auditorium, the original Corinthian columns, balustrades, urns, and trellises have been repaired and repainted. New seats have been installed, and the number of seats has been reduced from 2,400 to 1,570, to allow for an enlarged orchestra pit, the conversion of the second balcony to house advanced sound and lighting systems, and the division of the first balcony into box seating. The stage itself has been given a resilient floor suitable for dance performances. Backstage, dressing-room space has been greatly expanded. In 1977 the Majestic Theatre became the first Dallas building to be listed on the National Register of Historic Places. In 1983 it received a Texas Historical Commission marker.

During the 1990s and into the new century the city of Dallas used the refurbished theater for shows that were unsuited to the much larger State Fair Music Hall. The Dallas Ballet made the restored Majestic its home, and the Dallas Opera, the Theatre Operating Company, and the City Arts Program division of the Dallas Park and Recreation Department maintained offices there. The Shakespeare Festival of Dallas, the Dallas Symphony Orchestra, and other local performing arts groups and some touring shows also used the Majestic Theatre.

BIBLIOGRAPHY: Dallas *Morning News*, January 9, 1983. Dallas *Times Herald*, January 23, 1983. Texas Historical Commission, National Register Files.

Shirley Caldwell

Mariachi Music. Although most people enjoy the atmosphere of *alegría* (joy) generated by a good mariachi group, few are familiar with the background of mariachi music in either Mexico or Texas. Today large mariachis with the traditional instrumentation of trumpets, violins, guitar, *vihuela* and *guitarrón* are easy to locate in all Texas cities, while smaller groups are ubiquitous entertainment in Mexican restaurants throughout the state.

The music they play can be quite intricate and has a colorful history covering the past 200 years. The story of the mariachi, especially its development before the twentieth century, is sketchy, but by piecing together various bits of information from historical records we can say that mariachis probably first appeared in the late 1700s as regional music groups in the small towns of Jalisco, Mexico. These groups, primarily folk string ensembles, often consisted of a harp, two violins, and a *vihuela* (a small five-string guitar with a rounded back). They played mostly local or regional *sones* (instrumental pieces), using a complex 6/8 meter. Changes came by the late 1800s, when vocals were added to many of the *sones* and the harp was slowly replaced by the bass *guitarrón*. This instrument, invented for the mariachis, is a much larger version of the *vihuela* with six bass strings; it produces a bass sound of great volume and is more portable than the harp.

Other changes came to mariachi instrumentation and repertoire in the twentieth century, such as the addition of the trumpet. A number of different versions account for this addition. According to Philip Sonnichsen, a noted scholar of Mexican music, the long-time popularity of the brass band in Mexico is behind it. "In small pueblos," he writes, "ensembles might well use whatever instruments were available: thus mariachis using flutes, clarinets and even trombones were known to exist." The trumpet, he states, was briefly introduced into the famous Mariachi Vargas in 1913 and the historic Mariachi Coculense de Cirilo Marmolejo in 1925.

By the 1930s trumpets were widely accepted as part of the modern mariachi ensemble, which thus acquired the ability to perform a wide variety of musical styles in addition to the regional *sones* of Jalisco. The versatile combination of strings, brass, a powerful bass, and the rhythm and harmony of the guitar and *vihuela* opened the door for commercial success. From the 1930s on, mariachis became the standard back-up bands for popular singers in Mexico.

In its customary modern form, a mariachi group must include violins, trumpets, guitar, *vihuela*, and *guitarrón*. The typical mariachi must be able to perform *sones*, polkas, waltzes, boleros (modern love ballads), *rancheras* (country "ranch" songs), and any other popular song that is requested and that people are willing to pay for. Since mariachis work primarily as "request bands," playing

San Antonio mariachis in traditional black and silver dress at Mission San José, 1988. Mariachi music originated in the late 1700s in the state of Jalisco, Mexico, and has become more popular in Texas since the 1940s with the influx of immigrants from central Mexico.

whatever a customer wants to hear, they are often paid on a per-song basis or for the amount of time they play. With their trademark black and silver regional dress, the *traje de charro* (Jalisco cowboy outfit), they have appeared in movies, on recordings, and on live radio with such Mexican stars as Pedro Infante, Jorge Negrete, Javier Solís, and more recently with *ranchera* (ranch-country) music greats such as José Alfredo Jiménez, Antonio Aguilar and Vicente Fernández. Through this exposure, mariachi groups and mariachi music have become the best-known Mexican musical style all over the world. Who can think of Mexican music without picturing a mariachi group?

The mariachi's historical uncertainties, however, are further reflected by the mystery surrounding the origins of the word itself. Some scholars have suggested that during the French occupation of Mexico in the 1860s, local groups who played at French wedding parties came to be known as "mariachis," a derivation of French *mariage*. Sonnichsen, however, cites a letter written by a priest in the state of

Nayarit as early as 1852 that refers specifically to "mariachis" and their music. Other stories offer further explanations: that the term comes from one of the local indigenous languages, that it comes from the name María, or that it is transferred from the name for a dance platform. Whatever the origin, the term is commonly used today to apply not only to the large musical ensemble, but to the musical style and to the individual musicians who play Mexican music, whether they are part of a large group or not.

Texas has a long tradition of musicians and *guitarreros* (guitar-playing singers that some might call mariachis) playing Mexican folk and popular music on request. In the 1920s and 1930s, La Plaza del Zacate or Haymarket Square in San Antonio was where the local populace went to hear such famous duos as Rocha and Martínez or the family of Lydia Mendoza sing popular Mexican tunes. Today this tradition continues in the same area, where many mariachi groups perform nightly at the well-known restaurant Mi Tierra. Besides the *guitarreros*, small *ad hoc* music groups called *orquestas típicas*, which probably spread from Central and Northern Mexico, existed in Texas by the turn of the century. In his book *The Texas-Mexican Conjunto: History of a Working-Class Music*, Manuel Peña writes about this tradition of string and wind ensembles among South Texas Mexican Americans. String *orquestas* and their *típica* variants, he states, were widely known in the state by the early twentieth century, though "makeshift ensembles...must have been in currency long before. These continued to exist until the 1930s, when better-organized wind orquestas, patterned after the American swing bands and featuring saxophones, trumpets and piano began to appear with increasing frequency." The presence of such groups, using an instrumentation and folk or popular song repertoire similar to that found in mariachi groups, may explain why the mariachi style caught on so easily in Texas.

From about 1930 through the 1950s, the mariachi style gradually became the national popular music of Mexico. Lagging a decade or so behind, mariachi music in Texas began to become popular between the 1940s and the 1960s with the constant influx of immigrants from central Mexico. The new arrivals, who had not grown up with the local Texas-Mexican conjunto or *orquesta tejana* musical styles, brought their own stylistic preferences with them. The popularity of mariachi music was also growing in the non-Hispanic population as more and more Texans visited tourist areas of Mexico. By the 1960s Spanish-language radio had proliferated over South Texas and could be found in major urban areas throughout the state. At that time stations in the Fort Worth–Dallas area played primarily mariachi music from Mexico rather than homegrown Texas-Mexican styles, partly because the area was largely populated by immigrants from central Mexico and also because of a prejudice against "lower-class" Texas-Mexican music (especially conjunto music).

The 1970s through the early twenty-first century saw continued growth in the popularity of mariachi music among all Hispanics as well as non-Hispanics in Texas so that conjunto, *orquesta tejana*, and mariachi have equal and sometimes overlapping followings. The three types of music seem to have somewhat separate territories, however. Whether in large ensembles with full instrumentation or in smaller quartets or trios of varied instrumentation, mariachi groups function as popular entertainment at restaurants, house parties, weddings, and other similar occasions They also play at churches on such occasions as the memorial of Our Lady of Guadalupe. Conjuntos and *orquestas*, on the other hand, play primarily at dance halls or at parties featuring dancing.

Some highly polished concert mariachi groups, patterned after Mexico's famous Mariachi Vargas de Tecalitlán, play nightclub and hotel shows in Mexico City, Los Angeles, and a few other large cities. Occasionally these types of mariachi groups can be found in Houston, San Antonio or Austin. Several websites list cities, venues, and names of mariachi groups performing, and many mariachi groups now have their own promotional websites. Continuing immigration from Mexico including musicians has also helped to swell the ranks of both average restaurant-style and concert-style mariachi groups in Texas.

Today mariachi groups are not only a standard feature of the Texas music scene but are also found within the school systems. Since the 1970s, mariachi has been offered as a musical ensemble course in many universities, colleges, and public schools. Contrary to old stereotypes of out-of-tune violins and blaring trumpets, today's players are usually well-trained; many hold degrees from university music departments. Both the University of Texas at Austin and Texas A&M University at Kingsville have offered mariachi ensemble study since 1977. Junior high and high school mariachi programs date from the late 1970s in Austin, San Antonio, and several South Texas towns, from the early 1980s in Fort Worth and Houston, and from the late 1980s in El Paso. International mariachi conferences and workshops for these students were held yearly in San Antonio for many years beginning in the 1970s, and in the 2000s similar conferences are held in San Antonio, Tucson, Arizona and many other cities throughout the Southwest.

Many of these conferences have traditionally hosted and still feature performances and instruction by current or former members of the Mariachi Vargas de Tecalitlán—probably the best-known concert-style mariachi in Mexico. These conferences and listings of college and school mariachi ensembles can also be found on several websites. The new generations of mariachi musicians produced by the schools and universities over the past thirty years have continued forming groups that have perpetuated the mariachi style throughout the state and that bode well to increase the popularity of mariachi music in Texas for decades to come.

BIBLIOGRAPHY: Dan W. Dickey, *The Kennedy Corridos: A Study of the Ballads of a Mexican American Hero* (Center for Mexican-American Studies, University of Texas at Austin, 1978). Juan S. Garrido, *Historia de la música popular en México (1896–1973)* (Mexico City: Editorial Extemporáneos, 1974). Patricia Harpole and Mark Fogelquist, *Los Mariachis* (Danbury, Connecticut: World Music Press, 1989). Manuel Peña, *The Texas-Mexican Conjunto: History of a Working-Class Music* (Austin, University of Texas Press, 1985). Philip Sonnichsen, *The Earliest Mariachi Recordings*, ed. Chris Strachwitz (El Cerrito, California: Folklyric Records, 1986). *Dan W. Dickey*

Marroquín, Armando. Tejano music recording businessman; b. Alice, Texas, September 12, 1912; d. July 4, 1990 (buried in Alice); son of Luciano and Anita (Solís) Marroquín. He grew up in South Texas and studied for two years at Texas A&I University in Kingsville. Afterwards, he worked for a time as a teacher in South Texas. On November 20, 1936, Marroquín married Carmen Hernández, who became part of the famous duet Carmen y Laura. The Marroquíns had two sons.

In Alice, Marroquín set up a jukebox business, but was frustrated by the lack of available Mexican-American records. In 1946 he started Four Star Records in the family's home, using the kitchen as a recording studio. Later he set up the house garage as the recording studio. One of the first Four Star recordings featured Carmen y Laura singing "Se me fue mi amor a la guerra" ("My Love Went Away to the War"). The flip side was entitled "Quisiera volar" ("I wish I Could Fly"). The record, which recalled wartime sentiments, was an immediate hit.

A few months later Marroquín and Paco Betancourt, a South Texas distributor for RCA and Columbia, established Ideal Records. They transported the recording studio to Reynolds Street in Alice, where they could work without interfering with the family's routine. Over the next decade Ideal Records helped establish a vital Tejano music industry, recording all the important Texas Mexican musicians, including Narciso Martínez, Chelo Silva, Valerio Longoria, Carmen y Laura, Paulino Bernal, and many more.

Marroquín was an enthusiastic entrepreneur, intent on popularizing the vocalists and musicians he recorded, so he organized road tours of Carmen y Laura, one of his most prominent groups. He set up and managed at least three tours in the Southwest and Midwest, the first in 1951, a second in 1954, and a third one in the late 1950s. According to Carmen Marroquín, Beto Villa and his orchestra accompanied them on some of the tours. She also recalled that, in some cases, they determined which cities to play, typically for only one night per city, by consulting a map of their route. They then selected their stops, often the next city on their route.

With the end of the tours, Marroquín and Betancourt parted ways, and Marroquín started La Villita, an open-air dance platform in Alice, where he featured top Tejano musicians. La Villita was later covered and transformed into a 700-seat ballroom. Marroquín also continued to work as a record producer, establishing his third and final company, Nopal Records, to record Tejano musicians through the 1970s, after which the Tejano music market waned.

In the 1980s Marroquín was struck with Alzheimer's disease. La Villita was closed during his illness. In 1991, after his death, he was inducted into the Conjunto Hall of Fame. After his death Carmen Marroquín reopened La Villita to host Tejano musicians and dances.

BIBLIOGRAPHY: Manuel Peña, *The Texas-Mexican Conjunto: History of a Working-Class Music* (Austin: University of Texas Press, 1985). *Tejano Conjunto Festival en San Antonio, 1991* (San Antonio: Guadalupe Cultural Arts Center, 1991). "Tejano Roots / Raíces Tejanas: The Women (1946–1970)," *Tejano Roots* (El Cerrito, California: Arhoolie Records, 1991). *Teresa Palomo Acosta*

Marsh, William John. Musician, composer, and teacher; b. Woolton, Liverpool, England, June 24, 1880; d. Fort Worth, February 1, 1971; son of James and Mary Cecilia (McCormick) Marsh. He attended Ampleforth College in Yorkshire and studied harmony, composition, and organ. He moved to Texas in 1904 and became a United States citizen in 1917. He was professor of organ, composition, and theory at Texas Christian University, as well as a choir director.

During his career as composer, teacher, and performer, Marsh published more than 100 works, mainly classical and sacred. He composed "O Night Divine," a Christmas song; *The Flower Fair at Peking* (1931), a one-act opera,

William Marsh, professor and choir director at Texas Christian University, published more than 100 works, including the state song, "Texas Our Texas." Texas State Library and Archives Commission.

reputedly the first opera to be composed and produced in Texas; the official Mass for the Texas Centennial; and the state song, "Texas, Our Texas" (1924), which John Philip Sousa once described as the finest state song he had ever heard. Marsh also composed numerous pageants, Masses, anthems, and cantatas.

In 1921–22 he won first prize in San Antonio for the best song by a Texas composer. In 1929 he won double first prizes in Dallas for vocal and piano compositions as well as the Texas Federation of Music Clubs choral prize. Marsh was chairman of the Texas Composers' Guild for twenty-seven years and a music critic for the Fort Worth *Star-Telegram*. In 1959 he received an award as Outstanding Senior Citizen of Fort Worth.

BIBLIOGRAPHY: *Daily Texan*, February 2, 1971. Lota M. Spell, *Music in Texas* (Austin, 1936; rpt., New York: AMS, 1973). Vertical Files, Center for American History, University of Texas at Austin. *Who's Who in America*, 1946–47.

Martin, Mary. Musical theater star; b. Maria Virginia Martin, Weatherford, Texas, December 11, 1913; d. Rancho Mirage, California, November 3, 1990 (buried in Weatherford); younger daughter of Preston and Juanita (Presley)

Martin. Her father was an attorney, and her mother was a violin teacher. Family and friends encouraged Mary to perform in local theater as a child, and she began taking voice lessons at age twelve. At sixteen she attended Ward Belmont Finishing School in Nashville for a few months. She married Benjamin J. Hagman, a Weatherford accountant, on November 3, 1930, and soon left school. The couple went back to Weatherford, where their son, the actor Larry Hagman of "Dallas" fame, was born in September 1931.

Mary Hagman subsequently opened a dance school in the town. She obtained a divorce from Hagman in 1935 and left Weatherford to try a performing career, billed as Mary Martin. She gained singing spots on national radio broadcasts in Dallas and at Los Angeles nightclubs but could not break into the feature-film industry. However, her performance at a California club impressed a theatrical producer enough that he cast her in a play in New York. Though that production never opened, she got a role in Cole Porter's production *Leave It To Me*. Martin's rendition of "My Heart Belongs to Daddy" soon endeared her to Broadway audiences.

The resulting national media attention provided her the entrée she had sought in Hollywood. Paramount Pictures signed her to appear in *The Great Victor Herbert* in 1939. During the next three years she starred in ten films on contract with that company. Between films she performed frequently on NBC and CBS radio programs, including "Good News of 1940" and "Kraft Music Hall." Martin met Richard Halliday, an editor and producer, at Paramount. They were married on May 5, 1940, and two years later, Halliday became Mary Martin's manager. The couple had one daughter.

Martin returned to New York in 1943, cast as Venus in *One Touch of Venus*, for which she won the New York Drama Critics Poll. In 1946, after touring with *Venus*, she appeared in *Lute Song*, a Chinese story adapted to showcase her talents. The following year she had the lead role in a touring production of Irving Berlin's musical *Annie Get Your Gun*. Upon returning to Broadway in 1949, she appeared with opera star Ezio Pinza in the Rodgers and Hammerstein hit *South Pacific*. She not only suggested material for songs in the show, but helped develop the choreography as well. The critics' poll favored her portrayal of Ensign Nellie Forbush, a plucky role that exploited her comedic talents.

In 1951 she moved to London for a two-year run of *South Pacific*. For the rest of the 1950s she divided her time between stage and television performances. In *The Skin of our Teeth* and *Annie Get Your Gun*, she offered televised portrayals built on her stage experience in the same roles. Likewise, she took the youthful character of Peter Pan, in the play of the same name, from a brief Broadway run to repeated NBC-TV presentations. Martin as Peter Pan was "an exact meeting of actress and character," a New York *Times* writer commented. Indeed, the actress called the sprite's role her favorite, perhaps because it featured her own optimism and love of adventure. Martin won Tony Awards for performances in *Peter Pan* and *The Sound of Music*. In the latter she played the leading character of Mary Rainer from 1959 to 1961. She also starred in a 1965–66 production of the musical *Hello, Dolly!* on a challenging tour for military audiences stationed in Asia. Later in 1966 she was back on Broadway, appearing with Robert Preston in *I Do, I Do*. She continued in this two-person musical for a 1968–69 North American tour as well.

Martin's stage career slowed during the 1970s, as she and her husband spent longer periods on their ranch in Brazil. He died there on March 3, 1973. She made a Broadway comeback in 1978 in the comedy *Do You Turn Somersaults?* In 1981 she hosted a public television series on aging, "Over Easy." After a debilitating automobile accident, she joined the musical actress Carol Channing in a 1986 touring production of *Legends*, portraying an aging actress.

Her lifetime achievements brought Martin a coveted award from the John F. Kennedy Center for the Performing Arts in Washington in 1989. She is credited with having advanced the significance of the performer in musical theater. She died at home of cancer and was cremated.

BIBLIOGRAPHY: Mary Martin, *My Heart Belongs* (New York: Morrow, 1976). New York *Times*, November 5, 1990. Alice M. Robinson et al., *Notable Women in the American Theatre: A Biographical Dictionary* (New York: Greenwood Press, 1989). *Sherilyn Brandenstein*

Martínez, Narciso. "Father" of the Texas-Mexican conjunto; b. Reynosa, Tamaulipas, Mexico, October 29, 1911; d. San Benito, Texas, June 5, 1992 (buried at Montmeta Memorial Park, San Benito). His parents immigrated to the United States the year of his birth and settled in La Paloma, near Brownsville, Texas. The family often migrated from one town to another doing farmwork, and Martínez received little formal education. As a child he often listened to *orquestas típicas*, regional musical groups made up of violin, flute, bass, and guitar, but he preferred the accordionists who also played in the Rio Grande valley. In 1928 he was married; he and his wife, Edwina, had four daughters.

Martínez took up the accordion the year he married, and became proficient enough to play at dances. He moved to Bishop around the same time and absorbed the accordion-playing traditions of the local Czechs and Germans during a three-year stay. He purchased his first new accordion, a Hohner, in 1930. In 1935 he switched from the one-row button accordion to the more versatile two-row button version and also began his productive association with Santiago Almeida, a talented *bajo sexto* (twelve-stringed bass guitar) player. Working together, the two established the accordion and *bajo sexto* as the basic instruments of the conjunto and became well regarded as a team. Their pairing led to Martínez's major innovation in the development of the conjunto. He emphasized the right-side melody and treble notes of the accordion, leaving the left-side bass notes to the *bajo sexto* player. Most other conjunto accordionists soon adopted this change.

In 1936 Martínez and Almeida started recording for Bluebird Records, a subsidiary of RCA. Their first record, "La Chicharronera" ("The Crackling"), became a big hit. After 1936 Martínez became the most prolific of the conjunto stylists, capable of recording up to twenty pieces in one session. He continued to record instrumental polkas,

Narciso Martínez began playing accordion and recording in the 1930s. He continued performing into the 1990s. His powerful and fast playing earned him the nickname "Hurricane of the Valley." Photograph by Al Rendon ©2003.

which were his most popular compositions, and other traditional forms such as *huapangos* and Bohemian redowas for the Bluebird label until 1940. Some of his early pieces were "La Parrita" ("The Little Grapevine"), "La Polvadera" ("The Dustcloud"), and "Los Coyotes," all of which reflected his close ties to his rural background.

In 1946 he began to record for Ideal. As the house accordionist for this company, he accompanied some of its artists, notably the duet Carmen y Laura. Martínez remained a popular performer throughout the 1940s and was nicknamed "El Huracán del Valle" ("The Hurricane of the Valley") for his fast-paced accordion-playing. His Bluebird and RCA recordings were also well received outside of Texas. In San Francisco, for instance, Basques relished his sound and eagerly bought his records. In the Blue Bird Cajun series, Martínez was billed as "Louisiana Pete." In the label's Polish series, Martínez and his band were marketed as "Polski Kwartet."

Despite his artistic ability, however, Martínez, like many other conjunto pioneers, never earned much money as a musician. Because Mexican Americans, his principal audience, could not afford to pay much, he had to take other jobs to support himself throughout his life, including work as a truck driver, field hand, and caretaker at the Brownsville Zoo. To support himself in the 1930s he often played at outdoor public dances throughout the Valley. He

also entertained at *bailes de negocio*, public "for-pay" dances where women earned money for their families by selling dances to men during the Great Depression. In the 1950s, with his popularity still growing, Martínez joined other Mexican-American performers on the Tejano dance-hall circuit. He also toured New Mexico, Arizona, and California, and even played in Chicago. A new generation of conjunto musicians emerged in the mid-1960s, and Martínez returned to work as a field hand in Florida. In 1968, however, he recorded for ORO Records, a Tejano label in McAllen.

Despite the subsequent emergence of other accordionists, Martínez maintained his importance as a conjunto innovator and received accolades for his work. In 1976, for instance, he was featured in *Chulas Fronteras* ("*Beautiful Borders*"), a documentary film about Texas-Mexican music. He was inducted into the Conjunto Music Hall of Fame in 1982 and was honored the following year with a National Heritage Award from the National Endowment for the Arts for his contributions to the nation's cultural heritage. The 1985 publication of Manuel Peña's *The Texas-Mexican Conjunto, History of a Working-Class Music* brought Martínez critical attention. In 1989 Arhoolie Records reissued some of his work; the new recording earned him a nomination for the Grammy Award for best Mexican-American recording of the year. In

1991 the San Benito Cultural Arts and Science Center was dedicated to him.

In January 1992 Martínez released *16 Éxitos de Narciso Martínez* ("*16 Hits of Narciso Martínez*"), his last recording, on the R y R Record label in Monterrey, Nuevo León. After he retired from his job at the Brownsville Zoo in 1977, he continued to play on weekends, traveling to engagements from his home in La Paloma. The annual Tejano Conjunto Festival in San Antonio also brought him before a new and larger audience. He was scheduled to appear at the event in May 1992 when illness forced him instead to enter the hospital, where he died. A funeral Mass was offered for him at Our Lady of Lourdes Catholic Church in La Paloma.

BIBLIOGRAPHY: Manuel Peña, *The Texas-Mexican Conjunto: History of a Working-Class Music* (Austin: University of Texas Press, 1985). *Teresa Palomo Acosta*

Mary Nash College. In Sherman; founded in 1877 as Sherman Female Institute by Jesse G. and Mary Louise Nash. The school, sponsored by the Baptist Church, started in a four-room house and soon moved to a larger campus. Its motto, taken from Psalm 144, was "That your daughters may be as cornerstones, polished after the similitude of a palace." The emphasis in the school in both its preparatory and college divisions was on language, music, and polite behavior.

Because of its music program the school was sometimes called Mary Nash College and Conservatory of Music. Its teachers and students were required to attend Bible studies and daily chapel services. Physical exercise—done in a ladylike manner—was considered important, and the campus included a large gymnasium. Instead of examinations, reviews were given to gauge a student's progress, since fear of examinations was thought to be too hard on girls. On February 7, 1896, Mary Nash died. The school was continued by her son, A. Q. Nash, and his wife. It closed in 1901, and the campus was sold to Kidd–Key College. Over the course of its existence Mary Nash College granted B.A., B.S., and B.Litt. degrees to 257 girls.

BIBLIOGRAPHY: Graham Landrum and Allen Smith, *Grayson County* (Fort Worth, 1960; 2d ed., Fort Worth: Historical Publishers, 1967). Donald W. Whisenhunt, *The Encyclopedia of Texas Colleges and Universities* (Austin: Eakin, 1986). *Lisa C. Maxwell*

Massey, Louise. Country and western singer; b. Midland, Texas, 1902; d. San Angelo, June 20, 1983. Labeled the "original rhinestone cowgirl" by later generations, she was known for her spectacular costumes and ladylike style on stage, and for recording in both English and Spanish. Her career, which lasted from 1918 to 1950, marked a time when women first became prominent in country music. She formed a band in 1918 with her father, husband, and two brothers. The band, based in Roswell, New Mexico, was called Louise Massey and the Westerners.

After playing local venues and touring the Texas area, the band auditioned for a music show, "The Red Path Chautauqua." The success of the audition led to a two-year tour of the United States and Canada. In 1930 the Westerners signed a five-year contract with CBS radio in Kansas City, Missouri. In 1934 their song "When the White Azaleas Start Blooming" was released; it sold three million copies. Other hit songs included "South of the Border (Down Mexico Way)" and "My Adobe Hacienda." The latter, cowritten by Massey and Lee Penny, had the distinction of being listed on both the hillbilly and the pop charts simultaneously, causing some to classify it as the first-ever "crossover" hit.

In 1938 Louise Massey began recording and singing for NBC programs in New York. She retired in 1950 to the Hondo valley in New Mexico. She and her husband, Milt Mabie, had one daughter, Joy. Louise Massey was inducted into the National Cowgirl Hall of Fame in 1982.

BIBLIOGRAPHY: Mary A. Bufwack and Robert K. Oermann, *Finding Her Voice: The Saga of Women in Country Music* (New York: Crown, 1993). *The Illustrated Encyclopedia of Country Music* (New York: Harmony Books, 1977). Vertical Files, Center for American History, University of Texas at Austin. *Robin Dutton*

Melody Maids. In 1942 Eloise Milam was asked to help arrange entertainment for a bond rally at the Jefferson Theater in Beaumont. As a private music teacher, she had a group of voice students, whom she presented as a choral group, all dressed in white. The newspaper insisted on having a name for the group, which called itself the Melody Maids. They became a self-sustaining, nonprofit organization consisting of teen-age girls, and were a great hit.

They began to travel from coast to coast singing for organizations, but mostly they performed at military bases and military hospitals. The group made four tours of Europe, several to England, three to the Far East, seven to the far North, four to the Caribbean, five to Mexico, seven to Hawaii, and four to Bermuda, Iceland, and the Azores. The girls financed some of the tours themselves by holding bake sales, style shows, and other fund-raisers. After 1956 all of the Melody Maid tours were financed by the Entertainment Branch of the Department of Defense. Of all the performers who traveled with the Entertainment Branch, the Melody Maids were requested the most. They sang for the troops at military bases and hospitals from 1942 to 1972.

The Melody Maids and Eloise Milam wore identical costumes. Their routines called for a variety of costume changes, depending on their location and the content of the show. The group had a book of rules for conduct and etiquette. This book, the Melody Maid "Bible," taught them how to act when presented to royalty and the correct way to present themselves at formal affairs. Milam always said she taught the girls morals, manners, and music, in that order. Many of the Melody Maids kept in touch and established a tax-exempt Melody Maid Foundation, which sponsored a $10,000 scholarship fund at Lamar University. There were around 1,500 Melody Maids through the years. The group received many awards. The Eloise Milam–Melody Maid Rose Room at the Julie Rogers Theater in Beaumont opened in 1990. Many scrapbooks, souvenirs, photographs, and other memorabilia are housed there. The room is open to the public by request.

Mamie Bogue

Mendoza, Leonora. Singer and composer; b. San Luis Potosí, Mexico; d. 1952. Leonora learned to sing from her mother who, some sources say, taught music in Rosita, Coahuila. She married Francisco Mendoza, also a musician from San Luis Potosí. They had eight children, several of whom performed with the family's troupe. Later, with her assistance, her three daughters became popular singers among Mexican Texans.

Leonora Mendoza passed on the repertoire she learned from her mother to her own children and in 1927–28 organized the family into a musical and performing troupe called La Familia Mendoza. The group performed traditional Mexican songs; Mrs. Mendoza played guitar, and other family members played violin, mandolin, and percussion. The group originally worked in restaurants and barbershops in the Rio Grande valley for small wages and tips. They sometimes "passed the hat" for money.

Around 1928 an advertisement in *La Prensa* seeking musicians to record songs drew the troupe to San Antonio, where they recorded twenty pieces for the Okeh label. For the recording project they called themselves Cuarteto Carta Blanca. With this recording, the Mendozas became part of the "race" recordings produced by such major recording businesses as the Victor Talking Machine Company, which ventured to San Antonio in the 1920s to put the music of Spanish-speaking musicians on double-sided discs. After recording the songs, for which they received $140, Leonora Mendoza, who was in charge of the family's shows, and her family moved to Detroit, where they stayed two years, performing for Hispanics in the Midwest. The group later returned to Texas and eventually staged its revue in the Plaza de Zacate in San Antonio to entertain shoppers.

La Familia Mendoza once again recorded music in the 1930s, with Leonora often singing the lead vocal and playing guitar. Because of the growing success of her daughter, Lydia, the family undertook tours throughout the Southwest and Midwest. Leonora organized and directed the shows, which consisted of music, skits, and comedy routines. Although her husband was opposed to educating their daughters, she taught all her children rudimentary reading and writing. However, none of her daughters ever received formal schooling.

In the early 1930s she and Lydia recorded several duets. Among them were two songs attributed to Leonora Mendoza: "Vale Más que Te Alejes" ("It Is Better That You Stay Away from Me") and "Desdichada de Tí" ("Disgraced by You"). When World War II started, La Familia Mendoza's touring came to a standstill due to gasoline and tire rationing. In San Antonio Lydia accompanied her daughters Juanita and María, as Las Hermanas Mendoza, on the guitar. She convinced Arturo Vásquez, the proprietor of Club Bohemia in San Antonio, to let them sing at his club. Later, she was able to set up a better arrangement at the Pullman Bar. Eventually the group also made records. The success of the women was great enough to help them purchase their first family home in San Antonio. After the war La Familia Mendoza's show, now expanded to include Lydia as a soloist and Juanita and María as Las Hermanas Mendoza, did a six-months-a-year tour throughout the Southwest for the next six years. Leonora Mendoza's death brought the group to an end.

BIBLIOGRAPHY: *Ethnic Recordings in America: A Neglected Heritage* (Washington: American Folklife Center, Library of Congress, 1982). "Lydia Mendoza, The Story behind the Recordings" (liner notes to *Lydia Mendoza, Part 1, 1928–1938*, Folklyric Records 9023, Texas-Mexican Border Music Series, Benson Latin American Collection, University of Texas at Austin). Philip Sonnichsen, liner notes for *Los Primeros Duetos Femininas, 1930–1955* (Folklyric Records 9035, Texas-Mexican Border Music Series, Benson Latin American Collection, University of Texas at Austin). Chris Strachwitz, liner notes for *Las Hermanas Mendoza, Juanita and Maria* (Arhoolie Records C-3017, 1981). *Teresa Palomo Acosta*

Menger, Simon. Piano teacher, choral conductor, and soap manufacturer; b. Johann Nicholaus Simon Menger, Stadtilm, Schwarzburg–Rudolstadt, Thuringia, June 6, 1807; d. San Antonio, May 1, 1892. Menger was a teacher in Germany for many years before immigrating to Texas as a member of Castro's colony. In October 1846 he and his family arrived at Galveston, where they remained for a short time. Menger then went to Indianola, Victoria, and New Braunfels; on January 1, 1847, he bought fifty acres in Hortontown. He farmed until June, when he moved to San Antonio to teach piano.

His offerings included methods and pieces by Ignaz Moscheles, Ferdinand Ries, Friedrich Wilhelm Kalkbrenner, John Field, and several other of the most progressive pedagogues of his own youth. In July 1847 he founded the San Antonio Männergesang-Verein, possibly the first formally organized male singing society in Texas. During this period he also composed "Grand Waltz" (August 30, 1847) and "Mis[s] Paschal Polka" (September 3, 1847), both for piano, as well as simple études for his piano students.

In 1850 Menger opened a soap and candle factory, which became his principal source of income. The business, San Antonio's first industrial enterprise, prospered, and after Menger's death it was taken over by his son Erich, who operated it until the end of World War I. Menger must have let his singing society lapse, for the Männergesang-Verein seems to have been reorganized on March 2, 1851. The following October it gave a concert under his direction at San Pedro Springs, in which the "Prayer" from Méhul's opera *Joseph* may have been sung. For its New Year's Eve concert Menger's chorus sang music by Rodolphe Kreutzer, Felix Mendelssohn, and other composers. The society continued to make progress under Menger until he resigned in early March 1853. Late the same year he composed a male chorus, "Deutscher Sang," for the New Braunfels Germania society, but Menger's public musical activities became fewer as his soap business prospered. He sang sporadically with the San Antonio chorus for another two years and afterwards essentially restricted his musical activities to teaching piano, primarily to family members. In 1867 he composed "Ida's Reward Waltz" for his youngest daughter.

The Menger Soap Works, located on the banks of San Pedro Creek, was restored in the early 1980s. It is considered a rare example of pre–Civil War industrial architecture and is believed to be the oldest industrial building extant in the state.

BIBLIOGRAPHY: Theodore Albrecht, German Singing Societies in Texas (Ph.D. dissertation, North Texas State University, 1975). *Theodore Albrecht*

Mgebroff, Johannes. Lutheran pastor, historian, and church music composer; b. Nikolaev, South Russia, July 18, 1868; d. Salem, Washington County, Texas, May 24, 1920; son of Gabriel and Katherine (Bishof) Mgebroff. He attended school in Russia and at Dorpat, Estonia, graduated from St. Chrischona, Switzerland, and was ordained to the Lutheran ministry in 1893.

The next year he moved to Texas, where he settled at Giddings and organized Martin Luther Church. He married Helene Kuemmel at Bartlett and was pastor of St. Peter's Lutheran Church at Walburg until 1898, when he moved to Salem, Washington County, where he remained the rest of his life. He was district archivist for Salem Lutheran Church, served on the board of the Lutheran College of Seguin, and was chairman of the Brenham Conference. As a result of his particular interest in the work of young people, he was called the "Father of the Texas District Luther League."

Mgebroff was editor of *Lutherische Gemeinde-Bote fuer Texas* (commonly cited as *Der Gemeinde-Bote*), and under the pen names of Hans Maler and of Freund he wrote plays, magazine stories, religious articles, and pamphlets. In 1902 Wartburg Publishing House of Chicago published his noted *Die Geschichte der ersten deutschen evangelisch-lutherischen Synode in Texas* (The History of the First German Evangelical Lutheran Synod in Texas). While writing a book on the history of famous Christian women of the world, he died at his home at Salem. He was buried in Salem Cemetery, which in 1984 was all that remained of the community.

BIBLIOGRAPHY: Max Heinrich, comp., *History of the First Evangelical Lutheran Synod of Texas* (Waverly, Iowa: Wartburg, 1928). Heinz Carl Ziehe, *A Centennial Story of the Lutheran Church in Texas* (2 vols., Seguin, Texas, 1951, 1954). *Jeanette H. Flachmeier*

Milam, Lena Triplett. Music teacher and pioneer in the development of community music in Beaumont; b. Sweet Springs, Missouri, October 19, 1884; d. Beaumont, November 8, 1984; one of four children of Henry Franklin and Amanda (Wheeler) Triplett. Lena attended school in Sweet Springs and later in Ennis, Texas. She received her teaching certificate from North Texas Normal School and taught two years at Baptist College in Lexington, Mississippi. In 1901 her family moved to Beaumont, Texas, where Lena's father had been hired as superintendent of schools; she followed in 1903. After teaching for two years she married Allen Barnes Milam and moved to Sulphur, Louisiana. In 1911 she returned to Beaumont with three children. She resumed teaching and in 1919 became music supervisor of the Beaumont schools, a position she held until her retirement in 1955. She received a B.S. degree (1936) and an M.M. degree (1942) from North Texas State Teachers College. In 1937 she was awarded an honorary doctorate of music by Southwestern University in Georgetown.

Under Mrs. Milam's direction the Beaumont High School Orchestra became well known throughout the state. She developed a music-appreciation program that involved the community as well as students. She was a charter member and president of the Music Study Club and an active member of the Woman's Club, the Altrusa Club, the American Association of University Women, the Business and Professional Woman's Club, and the Daughters of the American Revolution. She served as cochairman of the city's first Music Week celebration (1922) and helped develop the Beaumont Music Commission (1923) and the Beaumont Symphony Orchestra (1953). She also founded and directed the Schubert Ensemble, a group that gained considerable distinction for its community performances in the 1930s. In 1929 she organized the First Methodist Orchestra, an ensemble that became a regular part of the church's Sunday night services.

Lena Milam was president of the Texas Federation of Music Clubs from 1932 to 1934 and served on the organization's national board until her retirement in 1955. She often served as chairman of the music division of the Texas State Teachers Association and was on committees of the Texas Music Educators Association, the National Education Association, and the Texas Music Teachers Association. During the summer months she participated in workshops, attended conventions, and taught summer classes at various institutions. She frequently taught at the College of Industrial Arts and North Texas State Teachers College in Denton, the University of Texas in Austin, and the American Institute of Normal Methods in Auburndale, Massachusetts. She was the author of a graded music-workbook series published by the Steck–Vaughn Company of Austin. She wrote a *Handbook for Junior Clubs Counselors*, published by the National Federation of Music Clubs in 1954.

Beaumont recognized Mrs. Milam's contributions on many occasions. In 1935 the Rotary Club honored her as "Beaumont's Most Distinguished Public Servant." She was the 1944 recipient of the Golden Deeds Award conferred by the Exchange Club of Beaumont. She died a few days after her 100th birthday.

BIBLIOGRAPHY: L. Randolph Babin, Lena Milam, 1884–1984: Music Educator and Pioneer in the Development of Community Music in Beaumont, Texas (Ph.D. dissertation, Louisiana State University, 1987). Lena Milam Papers, Tyrrell Historical Library, Beaumont. *L. Randolph Babin*

Milburn, Amos. Rhythm and blues pianist, singer, and bandleader; b. Joseph Amos Milburn Jr., Houston, April 1, 1927; d. Houston, January 3, 1980. Milburn, called "the first of the great Texas R&B singers," began developing his talent at an early age. When he was five years old his parents rented a piano for his sister's wedding, and in less than a day young Amos had taught himself to play "Jingle Bells." His parents enrolled him in piano lessons, but Milburn jumped ahead by lingering outside local taverns and juke joints and imitating what he heard. In 1942 he lied about his age to enlist in the United States Navy. He spent just over three years in the Pacific Theater, where he entertained troops with his lively piano tunes.

Upon returning, he put together a band and played in clubs all over Houston and the surrounding suburbs. His music so impressed local fan Lola Cullum that she allowed him to practice on her baby grand piano and helped him to record "After Midnight." She then took the record and Milburn to Los Angeles, where she visited Eddie Mesner, president of Aladdin Records, in his hospital room and played the record for him. Mesner signed Milburn immediately.

Milburn began recording for Aladdin on September 12, 1946. In twelve years he recorded about 125 songs, most of them arranged by saxophonist Maxwell Davis. "After Midnight" sold over 50,000 copies. In 1949 Milburn was *Billboard*'s best-selling R&B artist. Davis, acting as sax soloist and producer, helped Milburn on seven of his biggest hits—"Chicken Shack Boogie," "In the Middle of the Night," "Hold Me Baby," "Bad Bad Whiskey," "Good Good Whiskey," "Vicious Vicious Vodka," "Let's Have a Party," "House Party (Tonight)," "Let Me Go Home, Whiskey," and "One Scotch, One Bourbon, One Beer." These songs and others made it to the top ten of *Billboard*'s charts in the early and middle 1950s.

Milburn's rocking, boogie-woogie piano style greatly influenced such younger stars as Fats Domino and Little Richard. Some of Milburn's songs, such as "Let's Rock a While" (1951) and "Rock, Rock, Rock" (1952), anticipated the mid-1950s rock-and-roll styles. Milburn ended his association with Aladdin in 1954. He continued to perform, often with such stars as Charles Brown and Johnny Otis. He toured the country, playing nightclubs in various cities, including Los Angeles, Cleveland, New York City, Dallas, Cincinnati, and Washington. He also recorded for labels such as Ace, King, and Motown. However, it is apparent that he had achieved his greatest success by 1953.

No stranger to alcohol, as his song titles suggest, Milburn was often ill. He suffered two strokes, lost a leg to amputation, and was an invalid for some time before his death.

BIBLIOGRAPHY: Alan Govenar, *Meeting the Blues* (Dallas: Taylor, 1988). Sheldon Harris, *Blues Who's Who: A Biographical Dictionary of Blues Singers* (New Rochelle, New York: Arlington House, 1979). Rick Koster, *Texas Music* (New York: St. Martin's Press, 1998). Robert Santelli, *The Big Book of Blues: A Biographical Encyclopedia* (New York: Penguin, 1993). *Carlyn Copeland*

Miller, Roger Dean. Musician and composer; b. Fort Worth, January 2, 1936; d. Los Angeles, October 25, 1992; son of Jean and Laudene (Holt) Miller. Roger's father died when the boy was one year old, and he was raised by relatives in Erick, Oklahoma. His schooling ended before graduation from high school. He spent a number of years on the road working at odd jobs and practicing on the guitar, banjo, and piano.

Miller had no formal training on any of these instruments and apparently never learned to read or write music. After service in the army, where he entertained troops in a Special Services country-music band and added the drum and fiddle to his repertory, he decided to live in Nashville until he could make it either as a songwriter or performer. In addition to part-time jobs, he played in back-up bands for entertainers such as Minnie Pearl and Ray Price. His first song to attract notice was "Invitation to the Blues," recorded by Price and by Patti Page. Miller soon had a contract as a drummer with the Faron Young organization, and other performers began singing his songs. In 1961 he first made the top-ten country charts as a performer with "When Two Worlds Collide," co-written with Bill Anderson. Nevertheless, he grew discouraged and moved to Hollywood to enroll in a dramatic acting course.

His singing career took off in California in 1964. "Chug-a-lug" and "Dang Me" were hits in both country and pop categories. The next year Miller scored a series of bestsellers: "King of the Road," "Engine, Engine No. 9," "Kansas City Star," and "One Dyin and a-Buryin'." He became associated with Andy Williams when Williams recorded Roger's "In the Summertime," and the well-known popular singer put Miller in his TV program in late 1965. NBC featured Miller in his own weekly variety show, which fared well in 1966 but subsequently lost out in the ratings and was cancelled.

Miller continued to perform in major venues through the rest of the decade, but never surpassed his production of songs during 1964–65. He earned eleven Grammy awards during this time, both as composer and performer in the categories of contemporary and country and western. The versatility of Roger Miller was seen one last time before the end of his career. In 1985 he received five Tony awards for his score to *Big River*, a musical based on *Huckleberry Finn*.

Miller married Mary Margaret Arnold on February 14, 1978. They had six children.

BIBLIOGRAPHY: Bob Millard, *Country Music: 70 years of America's Favorite Music* (New York: Harper Perennial, 1993). Irwin Stambler and Grelun Landon, *Encyclopedia of Folk, Country and Western Music* (New York: St. Martin's, 1969; 2d. ed., 1983). *Phillip L. Fry*

Minor, Dan. Trombonist; b. Dallas, August 10, 1909; d. New York City, April 11, 1982; known as "Slamfoot" Minor. He took part in the formative period of the Kansas City jazz era of the late 1920s and early 1930s. Thereafter, in the later 1930s and early '40s, he played with many significant musicians, including Count Basie, Cab Calloway, and Mercer Ellington.

Minor began his musical career in 1926 playing for a local church orchestra; later he joined the Blue Moon Chasers, a band that was active in and around Dallas. His first major professional work came with Walter Page's Blue Devils, with which he stayed from 1927 to 1929. He then joined a Texas band called the Blues Syncopaters, led by Ben Smith. In 1930–31 he worked with Earl Dykes, Gene Coy's Black Aces (from Amarillo), Lloyd Hunter's Serenaders, and the Dallas orchestra of Alphonso Trent. In 1931 Minor joined the Bennie Moten band.

When Count Basie formed his own band after Moten's death in 1934, Minor became a member of that first Basie unit. He remained with the Count from 1936 to 1941. While with Basie, he was included in the recordings of

Roger Miller, "Austin City Limits," ca. 1984. Courtesy Scott Newton/Austin City Limits. Miller first made the Top Ten country charts in 1961 and continued his success as a writer and singer in the mid-'60s with such hits as "Chug-a-lug," "Dang Me," "King of the Road," and "Engine, Engine No. 9."

"Gone with What Wind?" (1940) and "You Can't Run Around" (1940), among many other pieces. From 1941 to 1944 he was with the Buddy Johnson band. He also played with Cab Calloway during 1942. In 1945 Minor worked with Mercer Ellington, and at different times he also played and recorded with Lucky Millinder and Willie Bryant. After the 1940s he played freelance. He performed occasionally during the 1960s. Minor was not regarded primarily as a soloist, but rather as a vital section player who rarely took solos.

BIBLIOGRAPHY: John Chilton, *Who's Who of Jazz: From Storyville to Swingstreet* (New York: Da Capo Press, 1985). Leonard Feather and Ira Gitler, *The Biographical Encyclopedia of Jazz* (New York: Oxford University Press, 1999). Raymond Horricks, *Count Basie and His Orchestra: Its Music and Its Musicians* (London: Jazz Book Club, 1958). *New Grove Dictionary of Jazz*, ed. Barry Kernfeld (London: Macmillan, 1988). Ross Russell, *Jazz Style in Kansas City and the Southwest* (London: University of California Press, 1971). *Alex Daboub*

Moffett, Charles. Jazz musician; b. Fort Worth, September 11, 1929; d. New York City, February 14, 1997; son of Columbus Mark Moffett. Moffett was known primarily for his work with fellow Texan Ornette Coleman. His family attended daily services at a church where music was vital and his mother was the pianist. Moffett developed an interest in music that eventually led him to take up the trumpet. At the age of thirteen he played trumpet with Jimmy Witherspoon's band. In high school he joined the marching band, switched to drums, and continued playing on the local music scene.

He met Ornette Coleman during this period, and the two became close friends. After graduation Moffett served in the navy and became an accomplished boxer, but music remained his obsession. Upon being discharged from the navy he entered Huston–Tillotson College in Austin to study music. He graduated in 1953, married (with Coleman presiding as best man), and was hired as a music-education teacher at the public school in Rosenberg, Texas.

He had his first brush with fame when he spent a summer drumming for Little Richard. In 1961, beckoned by Coleman to New York City, Moffett began a successful yet rocky stint on the city's jazz scene. Although Coleman paid his band members well, work was sporadic, and Moffett supplemented his income by teaching. Musical differences eventually dissolved the partnership and subsequently led Moffett to Oakland, California, in 1968. After quickly gaining a reputation in Oakland by running a successful music club, he was named the city's music director. Two years later he was appointed principal of an alternative school in Berkeley. He subsequently worked at Berkeley High. He also organized a band—the Moffettettes—that included his children and several of their schoolmates. The band played throughout California and made several recordings.

In the 1980s Moffett and his family moved back to New York, where he took a job teaching mentally retarded children. He remained musically active, but never reached the prominence of his earlier years. He died of cancer. Moffett was married twice, in 1953 and 1959; he had one child by his first wife and four children by his second wife, Shirley. All five children became musicians.

BIBLIOGRAPHY: "Charles Moffett," *Down Beat*, May 1997. George Coppens, "Charles Moffett," *Coda*, August 1983. Leonard Feather and Ira Gitler, eds., *Encyclopedia of Jazz In the Seventies* (New York: Horizon Press, 1976). Bob Rusch, "The Charles Moffett Interview," *Cadence*, February 1997. *Bradley Shreve*

Montgomery, Marvin "Smokey." Banjo player; b. Marvin Dooley Wetter, Rinard, Iowa, March 17, 1913; d. June 6, 2001; older of two sons of Charles and Mabel Wetter. Marvin started singing in church at the age of six. When he was ten he learned to play chords on a banjo ukulele by accompanying his mother as she played the piano. He soon began to play a real banjo that his mother had bought for his younger brother.

His parents were divorced when he was thirteen, and to help make ends meet Marvin and his mother maintained a band that played at dances until he graduated from high school. Marvin went to Iowa State at Ames, studied industrial arts, and, with a cousin who also played banjo, made meal money by touring around southern Iowa playing for tips. In 1933 a traveling tent show from Texas came to Ames and held an amateur contest. Marvin entered but placed second to a little girl of five or six who won with a tap dance. The manager of the show, J. Doug Morgan, was impressed with Marvin's playing, however, and invited him to join the show two weeks later. Marvin packed his belongings and banjo when school let out, and his grandfather drove him to Grinell, Iowa, to join the show. As the tent show toured through Illinois and Iowa that summer, Marvin was asked to pick a stage name, since the name Wetter did not look good on a marquee. He liked Robert Montgomery, a popular movie actor, so he became Marvin Montgomery. The show traveled through Missouri that fall, to Texas that winter, back up to Iowa and Illinois the following summer, and in the fall of 1934 returned to Texas, where the performers took a break in Victoria for Christmas vacation. Montgomery, homesick for Iowa, bought a train ticket with the money he was able to save on the tour, and traveled until his money ran out in Dallas.

He arrived in Big D early in the morning and walked to the Adolphus Hotel, where he knew Blackie Simmons and his Bluejackets had an early-morning radio show on KRDL, which broadcast from the hotel. Montgomery auditioned for Simmons, who put him on the show that same morning. Simmons offered him a job playing at a party for the manager of KRDL that night. The party turned out to be a stag party, and after it was over, Marvin was no longer homesick for Iowa. At the party another player from a band called the Wanderers, who had a radio show on WFAA, offered him a job. Montgomery played banjo for the Wanderers until he joined the Light Crust Doughboys as "Junior" Montgomery in October 1935.

The extremely popular Doughboys had a radio show on WBAP and the Texas Quality Network. In 1936 they made two movies with Gene Autry, *Oh Susannah* and *The Big Show*, in which Montgomery played, rode a horse, and sang. In 1937 Marvin married his first wife, Kathleen. The Doughboys went off the air in 1942 as America fought World War II. Marvin spent the war in Fort Worth manufacturing six-inch shells for the U.S. Navy, using his industrial arts skills. In 1945 the Doughboys' radio show resumed, and the group began performing on WBAP–TV in 1948 as the Flying X Ranchboys. They were the first band to appear on television in Texas.

Marvin played so fast that his hand was blurred by the early television cameras, and the Doughboys changed his nickname from "Junior" to "Smokey" because his hand looked like smoke on the TV screen. The Light Crust Doughboys' radio broadcasts became more sporadic and eventually ceased as television grew in popularity in the 1950s, but Montgomery and the Doughboys continued playing at county fairs and other live events, as they did into the twenty-first century. Montgomery became the de facto leader of the Doughboys in the late 1940s. From 1948 to 1962 he was also the musical director of the "Big 'D' Jamboree," a weekly radio show syndicated nationally from Dallas that featured the biggest stars in country music. Montgomery and the Doughboys, the house band for these shows, performed under the name Country Gentlemen. Under the same name they backed Elvis Presley on one of his early tours.

As folk music became popular in the 1960s, Montgomery formed a group called the Levee Singers, who performed across the country, played shows in Las Vegas, and appeared on many popular television shows. Montgomery built the famed Sumet Studios in Dallas in 1962 with fellow Levee Singer Ed Bernet, and began a successful career producing pop music. In 1962 he produced and played piano on Bruce Channel's hit "Hey Baby," which earned a gold record. Later that year he also produced and played guitar and vibes on "Hey Paula" by Paul and Paula (Ray Hildebrand and Jill Jackson), the number two record in 1963, which also earned a gold record. Montgomery remained prominent in the Dallas–Fort Worth music and studio scene for many years after that and was part of Bob Wills's last recording session, organized by Merle Haggard in late 1973.

In the 1980s Montgomery formed a Dixieland group, Smokey and the Bearkats, which performed variously as a trio, a quartet, and quintet. They performed at many jazz festivals. Smokey was chosen to be the banjo player with the All World All Star Band in 1985. In 1989 he formed the Dallas Banjo Band, a thirty-plus-piece group that achieved renown by playing such works as Beethoven's Fifth Symphony. Throughout this period Smokey was still active with the Light Crust Doughboys. In April 1989 he was inducted into the Texas Western Swing Hall of Fame for introducing the Dixieland banjo to western swing in 1935. In October 1989 he was inducted into the Western Swing Society Hall of Fame in Sacramento, California, along with Gene Autry. The Western Swing Halls of Fame in Seattle and Nashville inducted him in 1991.

In the 1990s the Doughboys shifted their music towards gospel and released four Grammy-nominated albums late in the decade. Montgomery's first wife, Kathleen, died in 1992, after fifty-five years of marriage. With his second wife, Barbara, Montgomery and Art Greenhaw of the Doughboys wrote the music and lyrics for a program called "God Bless Amarillo (and All the Cowboys, Too)," which was performed by the Doughboys and the Lone Star Ballet in Amarillo in 1998. The Doughboys also released the songs on a CD. In 1997 Montgomery was made the first member of the National Four-String Banjo Hall of Fame in Guthrie, Oklahoma, and the Jazz Banjo Festival held there placed him in its Ring of Honor. In 2000 the Light Crust Doughboys and the Lone Star Ballet performed another program called "Gospel, Strauss and Patsy Cline," for which Montgomery had written the arrangements.

Though he still played every night and day, Montgomery had struggled with leukemia for some time. He died less than a month after his last performance with the Light Crust Doughboys. His funeral service was held at the Hall of State on the State Fair of Texas grounds in Dallas.

BIBLIOGRAPHY: Dallas *Morning News*, June 7, 10, 2001. John Mark Dempsey, *The Light Crust Doughboys Are on the Air: Celebrating Seventy Years of Texas Music* (Denton, University of North Texas Press, 2002). John Dempsey, "Marvin 'Smokey' Montgomery: A Life in Texas Music," *Journal of Texas Music History* 1.2 (Fall 2001). Lowell Schreyer, "The Marvin 'Smokey' Montgomery Story," *Jazz Banjo Magazine*, September–October, 2001.

Gary S. Hickinbotham

Moore, Alexander Herman. Blues pianist; b. in the part of Dallas known as Freedmen's Town, November 22, 1899; d. January 20, 1989 (buried at Lincoln Memorial Cemetery, Dallas). Because of the death of his father, Moore dropped out of the sixth grade to support his mother and two siblings. While working odd jobs, he learned to play the piano before entering the United States Army in 1916. He arrived at his unique sound during the 1920s by combining elements of various musical styles, including blues, ragtime, barrelhouse boogie, and stride. In the 1920s he acquired the nickname "Whistlin' Alex" for a piercing whistle he made with his lips curled back while playing the piano.

Moore was among the first of his peers to record in a studio. He recorded six tracks for the Columbia Company in Chicago in 1929. Although he made other recordings in 1937, 1947, and 1951, he had little regard for commercial endeavors. In addition to his piano engagements, he continued to work his day job until his retirement in 1965. Though he was soon forgotten in his native surroundings, he was rediscovered during the 1960s throughout the United States and Western Europe. In 1969 he toured with the American Folk Blues Festival in England and Western Europe, performing with such blues artists as Earl Hooker and Magic Sam. He also recorded a session in Stuttgart, Germany, in 1969, which produced the popular album *Alex Moore in Europe*.

During the 1970s and 1980s, Moore could be found at the Dallas YMCA playing dominos or at a local blues club playing his piano. In 1987 he was awarded a National Heritage Fellowship by the National Endowment for the Arts. He became the first African-American Texan to receive this honor. The state of Texas designated his birthday, Novem-

Alex Moore playing at the Southern House, a "White Patrons Only" club, Dallas, 1947. Courtesy Alan Govenar/Documentary Arts. Moore always worked a day job in addition to his piano engagements. In this photograph, still wearing his white work coat, he plays the piano while the Southern House owner and his wife dance in the background.

ber 22, 1988, "Alex Moore Day." That same year Moore celebrated his last record release, entitled *Wiggle Tail*, which was recorded live at a Dallas show. About his bachelorhood he remarked, "I say the reason why I never got married is I always been married to my piano—my piano's my wife, my girlfriend, my lady, my bed." He died of a heart attack.

BIBLIOGRAPHY: Sheldon Harris, *Blues Who's Who: A Biographical Dictionary of Blues Singers* (New Rochelle, New York: Arlington House, 1979). Vertical Files, Center for American History, University of Texas at Austin.

Randi Sutton

Moore, Johnny. Guitarist; b. John Dudley Moore, Austin, October 20, 1906; d. Los Angeles, January 5, 1969. Moore's father was a violinist. Moore began playing guitar for his father's string band in 1934. The family moved to the West Coast, where Moore joined a group called the Blazes, with whom he performed until 1942.

He soon formed his own band, the Three Blazers. Eddie Williams played bass, and Garland Finney played piano, although he left the following year to be replaced by Charles Brown. Brown, whom Moore had first seen at an amateur talent show, was not only a pianist but a singer as well. The Blazers began recording in 1944 for the Atlas label. Between 1945 and 1948, the group recorded extensively for Exclusive, Philo / Aladdin, and Modern. During this time the group became a household name with such hits as "Driftin' Blues," "Merry Christmas Baby," "Sunny Road," and "More Than You Know."

Moore's younger brother Oscar joined the group in 1947. He had previously been a part of Nat "King" Cole's Trio. Shortly after Oscar Moore joined the group, problems arose, and Brown left the Three Blazers. Moore tried to replace Brown with sound-alikes, but had only minimal success. One replacement vocalist, Billy Valentine, joined and took the group to the R&B charts with RCA Victor's "Walkin' Blues" in 1949. After recording for Victor, Moore's Blazers recorded for a number of Los Angeles labels. Two successful label recordings were "Dragnet Blues" on Modern in 1953 and "Johnny Ace's Last Letter" on Hollywood in 1955.

Moore and Brown were reconciled in the mid-1950s, and the original Three Blazers reunited. They recorded for Aladdin, Hollywood, and Cenco. By that time, Moore's style of guitar, which has been described as cool, sophisticated, and melodic, was out of favor with most R&B fans. Moore performed solos on recordings by Ivory Joe Hunter, Floyd Dixon, Charles Brown, and tracks with his own group. B. B. King lists Moore as one of the top ten guitarists of all time.

Moore recorded with various groups after the Three Blazers broke up, but was not professionally active for a number of years before his death, though he did teach young musicians. He died at home of kidney failure. He had only one kidney, and this complicated his ability to recover from a flu epidemic. No obituary was published upon his death.

BIBLIOGRAPHY: Dave Dexter Jr., "Dexter's Scrapbook," *Billboard*, March 8, 1969. *Down Beat*, March 6, 1969.

Colin Larkin, ed., *The Encyclopedia of Popular Music*, Volume 5 (London: MUZE UK, 1998).

Amy Cockreham

Moore, Oscar Frederic. Jazz guitarist; b. Austin, December 25, 1912 or 1916; d. Las Vegas, Nevada, October 8, 1981. Moore grew up in Phoenix and formed a guitar duo with his brother Johnny around 1934. He moved to Los Angeles within a few years and joined up with Nat King Cole in 1937. Except for a brief stint in the army in 1944, he remained with Cole until 1947, first recording in 1939 as part of the famed Nat King Cole Trio. During the '40s, Moore also recorded with Lionel Hampton (1940), Art Tatum (1941), and Lester Young (1946).

His solos on three tunes from Cole–Hampton recording sessions, "Central Avenue Breakdown," "Jack the Bellboy," and "Jivin' with Jarvis," all bear the influence of fellow Texas guitarist Charlie Christian, but also exhibit some of Moore's own distinctive styling. Most impressive is Moore's interplay with Nat King Cole in the Trio recordings, as on "What Is This Thing Called Love" and "Sweet Georgia Brown," from 1944 and 1945 respectively.

In 1947 the Moore brothers were together again, this time in Los Angeles as part of the Three Blazers, a group that remained active until the mid-1950s. During 1953–54, Moore recorded three albums, but then left music to become a bricklayer. He resumed his music career in the 1960s, but only performed occasionally. In 1965 he recorded an album, *Tribute to Nat King Cole*. Moore was survived by his wife, Sally, three sons, and one stepson.

Bibliography. Barry Kernfeld, ed., *The New Grove Dictionary of Jazz*, Second Edition (New York: Grove's Dictionaries, 2002). Dave Oliphant, *Texan Jazz* (Austin: University of Texas Press, 1996). *Dave Oliphant*

Moore, Tiny. Mandolinist and fiddler; b. Billy Moore, Energy, Hamilton County, Texas, May 12, 1920; d. Nevada, December 15, 1987. Moore's mother and grandfather taught him piano, fiddle, and guitar during his childhood. As an adolescent he backed his mother in her band and played with a group of friends known as the Clod Hoppers. After hearing Leo Raley play one of the first electric mandolins, Moore adopted the instrument. His first electric mandolin was built by Raymond Jones, a friend who lived in Port Arthur, Texas.

Beginning in 1937, Moore traveled the South playing mandolin in several bands. In Mobile, Alabama, he played in Lloyd Ellis's Jazz Trio, and in Rayne, Louisiana, he accompanied a Cajun band called the Rainbow Ramblers. He moved to Houston before 1943 and played in the Crustene Ranch Gang band, which regularly appeared on local radio stations.

Moore enlisted in the US Army Air Force and served from 1943 to 1945. After the war he joined western swing legend Bob Wills and His Texas Playboys. In 1946 and 1947, Wills and the Playboys recorded the *Tiffany Transcriptions*, in which Moore played electric mandolin and fiddle, and for which he arranged music. He also managed the Wills Point Ballroom in Sacramento, California, which was owned by Bob Wills. In 1950 Moore took a break from performing with Wills's traveling band and married Dean McKinney, another member of the Wills band. They had three children.

After his departure from the Texas Playboys, Moore settled in the Sacramento area and formed a western swing band with Bob's younger brother, Billy Jack Wills. The band played regularly at the Wills Point Ballroom and on local radio station KFRK. Moore arranged most of the music and played fiddle and his newly built Bigsby five-string electric mandolin. Billy Jack played drums, and a young Vance Terry played steel guitar in the ensemble. In 1954 the band broke up, but Moore continued to play with Bob and Billy Jack Wills at local venues throughout the decade. From 1956 to 1962 he also hosted and regularly performed on "Ranger Roy and the Anna Banana Show," a locally televised children's program.

In 1961 Moore opened the Tiny Moore Music Center, where he gave lessons on mandolin, fiddle, and guitar. He focused on teaching throughout much of the 1960s and wrote an instructional book called *Mandolin Method*. Moore played as a guest musician on numerous albums and was a member of Merle Haggard's band in the mid-1970s. In 1970 he recorded with Haggard on the album *Tribute to the Best Damn Fiddle Player in the World*, a salute to Bob Wills. In 1972 Moore recorded his first solo album, *Tiny Moore Music*. He regularly played with former members of the Playboys, such as Eldon Shamblin and Vance Terry, and frequently performed at music contests. In 1973 he played on Bob Wills's final recording, *For the Last Time*. Moore paired with fellow mandolinist Jethro Burns (of Homer and Jethro fame) and recorded a twin mandolin album called *Back to Back* in 1980.

Throughout Moore's career, jazz musicians heavily influenced him, especially the early work of legendary Texas jazz guitarist Charlie Christian. Moore taught dozens of guitarists and was a major influence on musicians such as Ken Fraizer and Bob Murrell. He frequented nightclubs from Texas to California to stay in touch with the jazz music scene. He had a fatal heart attack on stage while playing with the Cadillac Band at a club in Jackpot, Nevada.

BIBLIOGRAPHY: Jean Boyd, *The Jazz of the Southwest: An Oral History of Western Swing* Austin: University of Texas Press, 1998). Colin Larkin, ed. *The Encyclopedia of Popular Music*. (New York: Grove's Dictionaries, 1998). "Tiny Moore" (http://www.mandozine.com/special/elect-mando3.html), accessed November 20, 2002. "Tiny Moore" (http://www.texasplayboys.net/Biographies/moore.htm), accessed March 25, 2003.

Ryan A. Kashanipour

Morales, Felix Hessbrook. Entrepreneur, radio personality, and civic leader; b. New Braunfels, Texas, May 27, 1907; d. June 8, 1988 (buried in Morales Cemetery, Houston); one of ten children of Felix and Hillary (Hessbrook) Morales. He attended racially segregated schools during most of his childhood. After his father died Morales contributed to the family's income by working as a shoe-shine boy, selling newspapers, and later doing construction work at the dam at Gingham Mills. When he was still in his teens, he moved to San Antonio, where he delivered newspapers for the San Antonio *Light*, worked at his brother Andrew's funeral home, and managed his own six-cab taxi business. On March 12, 1928, he married Angeline Vera in San Antonio. They had one son.

In 1931 Morales sold the taxi business, moved to Houston, and with a $150 loan from his brother opened his first funeral home, at 2701 Navigation Street in the Second Ward. The first years were difficult because of the Great Depression, during which the Morales Funeral Home donated services to many poor families. Unable to purchase the equipment he needed, Morales built caskets himself, while Angie spent hours sewing clothes for the deceased. During these years Angie also served as an interpreter in court cases. After the depression the funeral home was moved to new, expanded facilities at 2901 Canal Street. In 1940 the family also purchased ten acres of land off Aldine Road for a cemetery. Both Felix and Angie returned to school and graduated from the Landig School of Mortuary Science, in 1936 and 1942 respectively, and received their state licenses as embalmers.

Now financially secure, Felix moved toward owning a radio station. He had previously produced his own show at a station in San Antonio. Before investing in a station in Houston, he studied the market, purchased time from radio station KXYZ, sold it to advertisers, and produced a Spanish-language radio program. At first the program aired for only one hour a week, from eleven to twelve each Saturday night; but over a period of years it became a nightly program of news, interviews, and both live and recorded music. Often, when musical groups failed to arrive for their scheduled performances, Felix picked up a guitar and played himself. The FCC, however, soon ruled that radio stations could not sublet time to outside purchasers, and so in 1942 Morales applied for a permit to operate his own station. Due to the war the application was delayed until 1946, and the permit was not granted until four years later. The station, KLVL–AM in Pasadena, officially went on the air on May 5, 1950, to celebrate both the Cinco de Mayo and Angie's birthday. During the first few years, the station operated only during the day, but the permit was eventually extended to authorize a seven-day, twenty-four-hour operation.

Radio Station KLVL, "La Voz Latina," became the first Spanish-language radio station to cover news for the Gulf Coast area and soon established a reputation for community service. Apart from various news, education, and music programs, KLVL produced such programs as "Yo necesito trabajo" ("I need a job"), during which unemployed persons called in and received job referrals. Angie Morales also produced a program entitled "Que Dios se lo pague" ("May God reward you") in which she asked her listeners to assist needy cases in the community. In 1954, KLVL collected more than $10,000 and eight carloads of food and clothing to help victims of the lower Rio Grande valley flood, prompting one man, Juan Francisco Hernández, to write a corrido in honor of the Morales family and KLVL. Because of its commitment to service in the community, the station was dubbed "*la madre de los Mexicanos.*"

Catering to Houston's large Hispanic community, KLVL

broadcast news and music from all over the Americas. Immensely popular were the daily *radionovelas,* or soap operas, as well as the dramatizations of historical events. The station also sponsored top stage shows from Mexico, which played at the Music Hall and Coliseum. Local social and civic clubs, such as the Club Cultural Recreativo México Bello and the various *sociedades mutualistas* (mutual-aid societies), advertised their news and social events on KLVL, as did schools and sports teams. Each day at noon, the programming was momentarily silenced so that Father Patricio Flores, later archbishop of San Antonio, could offer a prayer for peace. The Morales family also operated KLVL--FM, which was sold in 1969. In 1978 they opened an FM station in San Antonio, KFHM (for Felix H. Morales) at the market. The station, also known as "Big M" or "La Voz del Mercado," became the first bilingual radio station in the city. KHFM also continued the custom of sponsoring live performances of musical groups from the United States, Spain, and Mexico.

Morales was a member of the Texas Association of Broadcasters and the National Association of Broadcasters. In addition, he was a founding member of the League of United Latin American Citizens Council Number 60, a board member of Unión y Progreso Barrio Development of Houston, president of the Sociedad Unión Fraternal, and an honorary member of the Sociedad Mutualista Obrera Mexicana and the Club Cultural Recreativo México Bello in Houston, as well as the Asociación de Charros de San Antonio. He received numerous awards as a big-game hunter and fisherman, including the Houston Press's Outstanding Hunter award in 1959. He was also honored as one of 500 successful Hispanic businessmen in the nation. Scholarships have been established in his name in schools in Houston, Pasadena, Three Rivers, and New Braunfels. An elementary school in Pasadena was named for him in 1991.

Morales's son José, program director at KLVL and a well-known radio personality, assumed charge of the Felix H. Morales and Son Funeral Home. The Morales family owned homes in Houston and Three Rivers, as well as a ranch in Wentz.

BIBLIOGRAPHY: Houston *Chronicle,* June 10, 1988. Houston *Post,* August 5, 1973; June 10, 1988. Houston *Press,* June 8, 1963. *La Crónica* (Laredo), February 24, 1974. *Texas Catholic Herald,* September 27, 1968.

María-Cristina García

Morris, Harold. Composer and teacher; b. San Antonio, March 17, 1890; d. New York City, May 6, 1964; son of Harold and Nellie (Meyer) Morris. He earned his B.A. degree at the University of Texas. At the Cincinnati Conservatory he earned the degrees of master of music in 1922 and doctor of music in 1939. From 1922 to 1939 he taught at the Institute of Musical Art at the Juilliard School in New York City. In 1939 he joined the faculty of Teachers College at Columbia University.

In addition to teaching and composing, Morris made recital and lecture tours. He held the guest music lectureship at Rice Institute, Houston, in 1933. His lectures there were later published as *Contemporary Music* (1934). In 1939 and 1940 he gave lectures and recitals at Duke University.

Morris's compositions include three symphonies, piano and violin concertos and sonatas, chamber music, and solos. His works won the Juilliard Publication Award, the New York State and National awards of the National Federation of Music Clubs, the Publication Award of the National Association of American Composers and Conductors, the Philadelphia Music Guild Award, the Fellowship of American Composers Award, and the Award of Merit from the National Association of Composers and Conductors for service to American music. His original manuscripts are in the Texas Composers' Collection of the School of Fine Arts at the University of Texas at Austin. Morris was a founder of the American Music Guild. From 1936 to 1940 he served as United States director of the International Society for Contemporary Music. He was a life member of the National Association of American Composers and Conductors and served as its vice president. On August 20, 1914, he married Cosby Dansby; they had one daughter.

BIBLIOGRAPHY: *Alcalde* (magazine of the Ex-Students' Association of the University of Texas), December 1931, November 1940. E. Ruth Anderson, *Contemporary American Composers* (Boston: Hall, 1982). Lota M. Spell, *Music in Texas* (Austin, 1936; rpt., New York: AMS, 1973).

Alice C. Cochran

Morse, Ella Mae. Blues singer; b. Mansfield, Texas, September 12, 1924; d. Bullhead City, Arizona, October 16, 1999. Ella Mae Morse climbed to stardom at the age of seventeen with her 1942 hit single, "Cow Cow Boogie." She was the daughter of a husband-and-wife jazz combo. Her father, George Morse, was a British sailor turned Texan who played the drums; her mother, Ann, played the piano. They encouraged Ella Mae's musical development, and as a girl she sang with them in local performances.

Ella's parents split up, however, and she and her mother moved to Paris, Texas. There she met an elderly black guitarist who taught her how to sing the blues. Despite segregation, Ella and "Uncle Joe" would often sit at a local corner store and sing old blues classics for hours until her mother called her home. Mother and daughter moved to Dallas when Ella was twelve. Her mother, who recognized her vocal talent, allowed her to audition for Jimmy Dorsey's jazz and blues outfit a few months before her fourteenth birthday. Dorsey hired her as a regular singer, and this gave her her first taste of commercial success. The Dorsey band played regularly at the New Yorker Hotel and also appeared in live radio broadcasts.

When she and her mother moved to San Diego, Ella hooked up with another former Dorsey band member, Freddie Slack. With Slack she signed her first record deal with Capitol and released "Cow Cow Boogie." She soon followed this hit with others, such as "Mr. Five by Five," "House of Blue Lights," and "Milkman Keep Those Bottles Quiet." She supplemented her singing by a career in the movies during the late 1940s and early 1950s. After a brief dry spell, she had a comeback in 1952 with "Blacksmith Blues." In 1956 she appeared on the "Ed Sullivan Show" with a youthful Elvis Presley, who told her that he had learned to sing by listening to her records. The following year, she made her final recording.

Through the 1960s, 1970s, and 1980s, Ella occasionally performed, but she had traded in her role as singer for one as mother. She married three times and had six children; her third husband was Jack Bradford, a carpenter. Although her career was brief, her influence touched many rhythm-and-blues singers. Sammy Davis Jr. once said to her, "Ella, baby, I thought you was one of us." Ella responded, "I am."

BIBLIOGRAPHY: Austin *American–Statesman*, March 7, 1996. Leonard Feather, *The Encyclopedia of Jazz*, New Edition (New York: Horizon Press, 1960). Colin Larkin, ed., *Encyclopedia of Popular Music*, Volume 5 (London: MuzeUK, 1998). Spencer Leigh, "Ella Mae Morse," *Independent* (London), October 20, 1999.

Bradley Shreve

Mullican, Moon. "King of the Hillbilly Piano Players"; b. Aubrey Wilson Mullican, near Corrigan or Moscow in Polk County, Texas, March 29, 1909; d. Beaumont, January 1, 1967; son of Oscar Luther and Virginia (Jordan) Mullican. He lived on his family's eighty-seven-acre farm at Corrigan during his childhood and developed his musical skills on a pump organ his father purchased around 1917.

The elder Mullican, a deeply religious man, wanted his children to learn sacred music. Though Moon served as a church organist during his teens, he developed an interest in blues music and learned to play the guitar with instruction from a black farmer. Impressed also by pianists who performed in local juke joints, Mullican developed a distinctive two-finger right-handed piano style that became his trademark. Much to the chagrin of his father, he began to play for dances as a teenager and aspired to become a professional musician. When he was about sixteen years old he moved to Houston and worked as a piano player for establishments that some observers characterized as "houses of ill repute." Sleeping by day and working evenings, Mullican may have received his nickname for his nocturnal habits during this period. For a time in the 1930s he performed with his own band in clubs and on the radio in Southeast Texas and Louisiana.

Later in that decade and in the 1940s he became associated with bands that performed the western swing music made famous by Bob Wills. Mullican played and sang this music with the Blue Ridge Playboys, a band that included such pioneers as Pappy Selph, Floyd Tillman, and Ted Daffan; he later worked with Cliff Bruner's bands, the Texas Wanderers and the Showboys. While with Bruner, a former member of Milton Brown's Musical Brownies, Mullican sang the lead vocal on the classic "Truck Driver's Blues" in 1939. That same year he traveled to Hollywood, where he played a role in the movie *Village Barn Dance*. He also led the band that performed with James Houston Davis during the latter's successful campaign for the Louisiana governor's office in 1944.

By 1947 Mullican, who had made his first recording in 1931, had signed a contract with King Records of Cincinnati, Ohio. With King he recorded two songs, Harry Choates's "New Jole Blon" (1947) and "I'll Sail My Ship Alone" (1950), that sold over a million copies each. The King recordings, which numbered 100, featured Mullican's smooth vocals and a piano style that merged swing, blues, honky-tonk, Cajun, ragtime, pop, and country music. During his years with the King label (1947 to 1956), Mullican had great success with such best-selling recordings as "Sweeter than the Flowers" (1948), Huddie Ledbetter's "Goodnight Irene" (1950), "Mona Lisa" (1950), and "Cherokee Boogie" (1951), which he coauthored with W. C. Redbird. He was less successful commercially with "Foggy River," "Sugar Beet," "Well Oh Well," "Moon's Tune," "Good Deal Lucille," "You Don't Have to Be a Baby to Cry," "Rocket to the Moon," "A Thousand and One Sleepless Nights," and others. In some of the King recording sessions Mullican was accompanied by a rock-and-roll band that featured a saxophone player.

In 1949 he joined the cast of the Grand Ole Opry in Nashville, Tennessee, where he was probably the first singing piano player to perform as a solo act on a regular basis. He remained with the show until 1955. During his career he traveled and performed across the United States as well as in Europe and Vietnam and entertained with such well-known artists as Hank Williams, Ernie Ford, and Red Foley. At one stage in his career, Mullican had his own radio show on station KECK in Odessa. He also appeared as a guest on the ABC television program "Jubilee U.S.A." and entertained periodically on the "Big D Jamboree" in Dallas. Mullican, who in conjunction with partners owned several nightclubs in Texas, served as a supporting musician on more than 200 recordings by other performers. The legendary singer Jim Reeves was a member of a Mullican band that played in the Beaumont region during the late 1940s.

In 1958–59 Mullican recorded in Nashville for the Coral label, a subsidiary of Decca Records. His records for Coral were remakes of songs that he had previously performed for King, as well as such new releases as "Moon's Rock," "I Don't Know Why (I Just Do)," "Jenny Lee," "Sweet Rockin' Music," and "The Writin' on the Wall." Hoping to benefit from the ascendancy of rock-and-roll in the United States, Coral sought to incorporate this style with the more traditional honky-tonk, swing, and blues forms that had made Mullican a star. However, the Coral recordings achieved virtually no commercial success and little critical acclaim. Some observers believe that Mullican's strongest performances for Coral consisted of the songs that he performed in the more conventional country style, as opposed to the newer sound.

From 1960 to 1963 Moon was a member of Jimmy Davis's band. He recorded for several minor companies at various times in his career. He made his final hit record, "Ragged but Right," on the Starday label in 1961. He also recorded a few songs such as "Quarter Mile Rows," "Colinda," "Mr. Tears," "Make Friends," and "This Glass I Hold," for the Hall–Way label in Beaumont between 1962 and 1964. Though his health declined in the 1960s, when he underwent several illnesses, he continued to perform. He died of a heart attack. He and his wife, Eunice, who survived him, had no children.

Actor and western songwriter Audie Murphy (right) at a movie premier for *To Hell and Back*, San Antonio, ca. 1955. UT Institute of Texan Cultures at San Antonio, No. Z-1659.

Mullican's bobbing two-finger piano style influenced other musicians, including rock and country vocalist and pianist Jerry Lee Lewis and his cousin, Mickey Gilley. Lewis listened to Mullican's performances on records and over the radio and copied much of his piano style. According to a Lewis biographer, Mullican "raided jazz for rhythm to complement his country cadences." He "shouted his words and was far more interested in being heard than in being precise." Mullican once explained that "music don't count if it don't make the bottles bounce on the table."

The Nashville Songwriters' Association International posthumously inducted Mullican into the Songwriters' Hall of Fame in 1976. He had written such compositions as "Pipeliner Blues," "Moonshine Blues," "Cush Cush Ky-Yai," "That's Me," "My Love," "Heartless Lover," and "So Long." According to some sources, Mullican may have helped Hank Williams write "Jambalaya," a popular novelty song that described the French Cajun culture of Louisiana. Mullican also coauthored many songs with various composers. Among those were "Leaving You with a Worried Mind," "Triflin' Woman Blues," "I Was Sorta Wanderin'," "Southern Hospitality?," and "Don't Ever Take My Picture Down." Mullican's recordings have been preserved on numerous long-play compilations that include the King label's *Moonshine Jamboree* and *Moon*

Mullican Sings His All-Time Hits, as well as Bear Family Records' *Moon's Rock*.

BIBLIOGRAPHY: Jimmy Guterman, *Rockin' My Life Away: Listening to Jerry Lee Lewis* (Nashville: Rutledge Hill Press, 1991). Houston *Post*, January 2, 1967. Irwin Stambler and Grelun Landon, *Encyclopedia of Folk, Country and Western Music* (New York: St. Martin's, 1969; 2d. ed., 1983).   *Paul M. Lucko*

Murphy, Audie Leon. War hero, Hollywood actor, and songwriter; b. near Kingston, Texas, June 20, 1924; d. near Christiansburg, Virginia, May 28, 1971; one of twelve children of Emmett Berry and Josie Bell (Killian) Murphy.

At the time of his death Murphy was the most decorated combat soldier in United States history. He enlisted in the United States Army at Greenville, Texas, in June 1942, around the date of his eighteenth birthday. After basic infantry training at Camp Wolters, Texas, and advanced training at Fort Meade, Maryland, he was assigned to North Africa as a private in Company B, Fifteenth Infantry Regiment, Third Infantry Division. He later served as the commander of Company B. During his World War II career Murphy received thirty-three awards, citations, and decorations and won a battlefield promotion to second lieutenant. He received every medal that the United States gives for valor, two of them twice. On January 26, 1945, he was awarded the Medal of Honor for exceptional valor near Holtzwhir, France, where he was personally credited with killing or wounding about fifty Germans and stopping an attack by enemy tanks. After the war's end, Murphy also received several French and Belgian decorations for valor. He fought in eight campaigns in Sicily, Italy, France, and Germany; participated in two amphibious assaults, in Sicily and southern France; and was wounded three times. He was discharged from the United States Army at Fort Sam Houston, San Antonio, on August 17, 1945.

He subsequently pursued several careers—as a successful movie actor, a lyric writer for country and western songs, an author, and a poet. He appeared in forty-five motion pictures and starred in thirty-nine of them. His best known films were *The Red Badge of Courage* (1951), *To Hell and Back* (1955), *Night Passage* (1957, with James Stewart), and *The Unforgiven* (1960, with Burt Lancaster). In 1955 Murphy was selected one of the year's most popular Western stars by United States theater owners, and in 1957 he was chosen as the most popular Western actor by British audiences.

He wrote the lyrics for fourteen songs and collaborated on three instrumentals. Two of his songs, "Shutters and Boards" and "When the Wind Blows in Chicago," were recorded by such top-ranking vocalists as Dean Martin, Porter Wagoner, and Eddy Arnold. Both were in the top ten songs on the Hit Parade for several weeks. With David McClure, Murphy wrote the best selling book *To Hell and Back* (1949), the story of his World War II exploits, which went through nine printings and was made into a successful motion picture by the same name, starring Murphy.

In 1950 Murphy joined the Thirty-sixth Division of the Texas National Guard as a captain, hoping to fight in the Korean War. The division, however, was not called to active duty. Murphy remained with the Thirty-sixth "T-patchers" for several more years, eventually attaining the rank of major. In 1957 he was assigned to inactive status. He transferred to the United States Army Reserve in 1966, where he remained until his death.

Murphy married movie actress Wanda Hendrix in 1949, and their marriage ended in divorce two years later. In 1951 he married Pamela Archer, a stewardess for Braniff Airlines; they had two sons. Murphy was killed in an airplane crash, and his body was not found until three days later. Two funeral services were held for him on June 4, 1971, one at Hollywood Hills, California, and the other at the First Baptist Church in Farmersville, Texas. Murphy was buried with full military honors near the Tomb of the Unknown Soldier at Arlington Cemetery on June 7. An Audie L. Murphy Memorial is located at Farmersville, a statue of Murphy stands at the Veterans Hospital in San Antonio, and a collection of Murphy memorabilia is housed at Hill Junior College.

BIBLIOGRAPHY: Dallas *Morning News*, September 16, 1962. Don Graham, *No Name on the Bullet: A Biography of Audie Murphy* (New York: Viking Penguin, 1989). Harold B. Simpson, *Audie Murphy, American Soldier* (Hillsboro, Texas: Hill Junior College Press, 1975).

Harold B. Simpson

Música Norteña. *Música norteña* grew out of *música tejana*, or "Tex-Mex music," the music of Mexican Texans. The development of *música tejana* is in turn interwoven with the history of its people from the 1700s to the present.

Without moving from South Texas, Mexican Texans have successively been citizens of Spanish Texas, of Mexican Texas, of the Republic of Texas, of the Confederate States, and of the United States of America. As a result, over the course of two centuries their music has evolved from a blending of early Spanish and Mexican music, French-European dance music styles filtered through Mexico, and Mexican and American popular music. In a cultural sense, from the 1700s until the early 1900s, the Tejanos were a Mexican provincial people, living in an isolated frontier area. Despite the Anglo-American political and economic domination of the area beginning in the mid-1800s, Tejanos retained their cultural ties with northern Mexico. But subsequently, Tejanos migrated from the farms and ranchos of South Texas to the urban industrial centers in Texas and throughout the United States.

Through the process of urbanization, and due to increasing pressures to adapt to the dominant society, Tejanos incorporated aspects of Anglo-American culture, but they resisted becoming a totally colonized and absorbed people. They maintained a regional Texas-Mexican culture that is reflected in their musical styles. Little is known about the beginnings of *música tejana*. As settlement expeditions emanated from central Mexico in the 1700s and 1800s, Spanish, Creole, and mestizo soldiers and settlers brought their music and dances to the Texas frontier. There are many paintings and diary accounts of fandangos or dances held in San Antonio and South Texas through the 1800s, but they give little description of the sound of the music besides calling it "Spanish" or "Mexican." Small bands were composed of available local musicians who used whatever instruments were at hand. Violins and *pitos* (wind instruments of various types) usually provided the melody, and a guitar the accompaniment.

Historical information from the latter part of the century shows, however, that by the middle to late 1800s, Tejano musicians were playing Spanish and Mexican dance music less and were adopting a new European style that was trickling in from central Mexico. In the 1860s Maximilian, backed by his French army, ruled Mexico. In his court in Mexico City, and in garrisons throughout the country, the European salon music and dances of the time, such as the polka, waltz, mazurka, and schottische, were popular. These styles, disseminated from France, were taken up by the Mexican people in various parts of the country, but nowhere were they more enthusiastically embraced than in South Texas by the Tejanos. South Texas musical culture was similarly influenced by Germans who began immigrating to South and Central Texas in the 1840s. These German Texans also favored European salon music and dances. At times they would hire local Tejano musicians to play for their own celebrations. By the late 1800s, informal Tejano bands of violins, *pitos*, and guitars were almost exclusively playing European salon music for local dances. But taking root in this frontier area, far from its European and Central Mexican source, this music was

The Diaz Sisters, Clara, Lucy and Mary, played in Victoria and San Antonio. *Advocate Magazine*, Victoria *Advocate*, Victoria, Texas, June 1907. UT Institute of Texan Cultures at San Antonio, No. 92-196.

being thoroughly adapted to the Tejano taste. At the turn of the century the locally performed polkas, waltzes, and schottisches could truly be called Tejano or "Tex-Mex" rather than European.

One of the most unusual styles of *música tejana* to begin its development at that time is *música norteña* (music of the north), or "conjunto music," as it is often called. (*Conjunto* literally means "a musical group.") *Música norteña* embodied traits of Tejano music but also arose with the appearance of a relatively new instrument that was rapidly becoming popular among Tejanos on the farms and ranchos of South Texas. As a result, in the 1900s *música norteña* has become identified with the sound of the German diatonic button accordion. This instrument may have been brought and popularized by the Germans and Bohemians settling in Central Texas or by the Germans working in the mining and brewing industries in northern Mexico. Newspaper accounts show that by 1898 Tejanos in rural areas of the South Texas chaparral were playing their Texas-Mexican polkas, waltzes, schottisches, mazurkas, and redowas on a one-row, one-key accordion.

Norteña accordion music began as a solo tradition. The left-hand buttons of the instrument sound bass notes and chords, while the right-hand buttons give the consecutive notes of a simple scale. Since one person could play both melody and harmony on the accordion, it could substitute for a more costly band of musicians. Hence, partially for

economic reasons, but also because of its sweet vibrato, the accordion gradually replaced the violins and *pitos* as the preferred instrument for dance music in rural areas. But because it was played around the ranchos for laboring people, the button accordion became associated early with working-class Tejanos. As more of them moved from the ranchos to the cities, the instrument was heard in the houses and cantinas of the barrios.

By the 1930s the popularity of the *norteña* style was such that accordionists, paired with guitarists or *bajo sexto* (a type of twelve-string guitar known in various parts of Mexico with lower bass strings and a different tuning) players, began recording their own ranch-style Tejano polkas. Following the lead of the *guitarreros* (singing guitarists) who were making "ethnic records" for American recording companies, the developing conjuntos also began commercializing their style and bringing nostalgia for the rancho to the city.

Although accordion dance music had been popular for some thirty years in rural areas, two men, Santiago Jimenez and Narciso Martínez, were responsible for pioneering the *norteña* style on recordings and radio broadcasts in the 1930s. Because of their popularity in recordings, their styles became models for a generation of musicians. Jimenez had a smooth, fluid style of playing the polkas and waltzes that he composed, and he emphasized the bass notes and chords of his instrument. Expanding his conjunto, he utilized a guitarist for harmonic accompaniment and added a *tololoche* or upright bass for a stronger bass line. Martínez, however, had a faster, more ornamented style than Jimenez, and emphasized the treble tones of his accordion. Rarely using the bass notes or chords of his instrument, he delegated the harmonic accompaniment and bass line completely to his accompanying guitarist. Both musicians used the newer two-row, two-key model of accordion.

In the 1940s, incorporating the singing tradition of the *guitarreros* into their music, these pioneer accordionists began to add song lyrics with duet harmonies to their instrumental dance music. The typical lyrics of lost love, often framed in a rural setting, seemed to reflect the working-class Tejanos' tie with the past on the rancho. By the 1950s *música norteña* was crystallizing into a mature style as a second generation of accordionists came to popularity in the cantinas, clubs, and dance halls. The conjuntos utilized new technology in their music and made some innovations, but to please their public they basically maintained the Tejano style.

Tony de la Rosa, from Sarita, Texas, became an extremely popular performer in that decade. He used the more versatile three-row, three-key accordion and was one of the first to add a drum set to his conjunto. Playing in the larger dance halls, groups like his needed more volume, so amplification was used for the four instruments that by this time had become standard in the conjuntos: accordion, *bajo sexto*, bass, and drums. Rosa's *conjunto* was one of the first of scores of groups to perform on what became known as the migrant trail. In the 1950s and 1960s, many poor Tejanos moved from Texas to jobs in agriculture and industry from California to the Midwest, thinking that a change of residence might bring a change in fortunes.

Cities like Fresno, California, and Chicago, Illinois, accumulated large communities of transplanted Tejanos who would pay well to have conjuntos play for their weekend dances. After the late 1950s the *conjunto* of accordion, *bajo sexto*, electric bass, and drums, playing mostly polkas and *valses rancheras* (both with romantic lyrics), changed little, though its popularity grew. Flaco Jimenez, son of Santiago Jimenez, was the first to perform *norteña* music in concerts over the United States and Europe for general audiences and was enthusiastically received.

Through the late twentieth century the *norteña* style remained conservative and stable with minor refinements in electronic sound quality and recording techniques. This era is probably best represented by the style of accordionist Rubén Naranjo from the Corpus Christi area, who died in 1998. *Música norteña* has also had its own category for many years in the Grammy awards, and a perennial winner in the early 2000s was the long-popular group of Ramón Ayala y Los Bravos del Norte.

BIBLIOGRAPHY: Dan W. Dickey, *The Kennedy Corridos: A Study of the Ballads of a Mexican American Hero* (Center for Mexican-American Studies, University of Texas at Austin, 1978). Dan W. Dickey, "Tejano Troubadours," *Texas Observer*, July 16, 1976. Vicente T. Mendoza, *El corrido mexicano* (Mexico City: Fondo de Cultura Económica, 1954). Vicente T. Mendoza, *Lírica narrativa de México: El Corrido* (Mexico City: Universidad Nacional Autónoma de México, Instituto de Investigaciones Estéticas, 1964). Américo Paredes, Ballads of the Lower Border (M.A. thesis, University of Texas, 1953). Américo Paredes, El Corrido de Gregorio Cortez: A Ballad of Border Conflict (Ph.D. dissertation, University of Texas, 1956). Américo Paredes, *A Texas-Mexican Cancionero: Folksongs of the Lower Border* (Urbana: University of Illinois Press, 1976). Américo Paredes, *With His Pistol in His Hand: A Border Ballad and Its Hero* (Austin: University of Texas Press, 1958). Manuel Peña, *The Texas-Mexican Conjunto: History of a Working-Class Music* (Austin: University of Texas Press, 1985). Merle Simmons, *The Mexican Corrido as a Source of an Interpretive Study of Modern Mexico, 1870–1950* (Bloomington: University of Indiana Press, 1957). *Dan W. Dickey*

Musical Arts Conservatory of West Texas. In Amarillo; organized in 1929 as a private, coeducational institution offering courses from kindergarten to the fourth year of college. Previously, no institutional music education had been available in the Panhandle. Gladys M. Glenn, who served for many decades as the school's director, was the leading organizer, and James O. Guleke was on the first board of associate directors. The conservatory, following the guidance of the National Association of Music Schools, was accredited in 1939 by the State Board of Education, and its credits were accepted by all colleges with music departments. It was a charter member of the Texas Association of Music Schools and was incorporated in 1939; its first permanent home on Tyler Street was purchased in 1940.

During the conservatory's peak years, from 1950 to 1967, the faculty increased to twenty-two and the student enrollment to 600. In the late 1960s the school maintained a musical kindergarten, had elementary, junior high, and high school courses, and maintained a four-year college course leading to the B.Mus. degree and the B.F.A. degree in ballet. Over the years many of Amarillo's finest music teachers taught at the institution, and many world-renowned artists came as guest instructors. Several alumni of the ballet department, directed by Peggy Norman (beginning in 1961), went on to win scholarships in universities and the New York City Ballet.

The library contained several hundred volumes—books, music, and music and art magazines—as well as hundreds of recordings. Twenty-eight studies and two recital halls were available for conservatory activities. After 1970 the Musical Arts Conservatory concentrated on precollege students because by then most colleges had better music curricula as well as lower tuition. Competition from other private music schools also contributed to the decline of the institution, which closed around 1975.

BIBLIOGRAPHY: Clara Thornhill Hammond, comp., *Amarillo* (Amarillo: Autry, 1971; 2d ed., Austin: Best Printing, 1974).

N

Nail, Robert Edward Jr. Playwright, director, and creator of the *Fort Griffin Fandangle*; b. Wolfe City, Texas, September 13, 1908; d. Albany, Texas, November 11, 1968; son of Robert Edward Nail Sr. and Etta (Reilly) Nail. The family moved to Albany, Texas, in 1909. Despite a severe drinking problem, Bob Nail Sr. had an aptitude for business and was successful in a grocery and dry goods store and later in a feed and seed mill.

Young Bobby showed an early interest in drama and writing verse and graduated from Albany High School in 1926, the year a prolific shallow oilfield was discovered on the Cook Ranch, property of Nail's uncle W. I. Cook. He traveled in Europe after graduation. Influenced by the J. A. Matthews family, whose son Watt had graduated from Princeton University in 1921, Nail headed east to the Lawrenceville School in New Jersey, where an English professor, the famous Thornton Wilder, took an interest him and encouraged him. Bobby, by then called "Spike," had an outstanding record at Lawrenceville that included editorship of *Olla Podrida*, the yearbook, and managing editorship of the literary magazine. In the fall of 1929 he entered Princeton, determined to be a playwright. Among classmates such as Joshua Logan, Jimmy Stewart, Jose Ferrer, and Bill Reynolds, Nail served as the class poet and president of the Theatre Intime. He wrote several plays, one of which, *Time of Their Lives*, received unanimous acclaim. It was performed his senior year and pronounced "the maturest and best piece of undergraduate playwrighting to come out of Princeton," even when it was given a repeat performance in 1937. Nail graduated with Phi Beta Kappa honors in 1933.

Though others expected him to accompany others of his class to New York, a dean advised Nail to go home and see how he could help there. His father, overcome by alcoholism and devastated at the death of his sister, Mrs. Cook, had committed suicide the year before, and Bobby later told friends that he felt a duty to see about his mother. He returned to Texas and directed the Little Theater in Fort Worth from 1933 to 1935, the Dallas Theater in 1936, and the Abilene Little Theater. But the Great Depression militated against theater in Texas, so Nail returned to boomtime Albany to live with his mother. The Aztec Theater on Main Street, along with other new enterprises, reflected the Shackelford County oil boom.

Nail became head of the drama department at Albany High School in March 1938. Superintendant C. B. Downing encouraged the senior class to ask Bob to write and direct a colorful, fast-moving cavalcade portraying the history of Shackelford County. *Dr. Shackelford's Paradise* had a cast of 200 students; the band, the choral club, and the tumbling team took part. The spectacle, held on the football field, was such a success that the Albany Chamber of Commerce decided to hold a July performance with added adult participation, and to rename the show the *Fort Grif-fin Fandangle*. Bobby enlisted a talented young artist and music graduate from Baylor University, Miss Alice Reynolds, who had returned to Albany and set up a studio. For thirty subsequent years the two brought entertainment and music to West Texas of a polished quality not seen there before.

Bob wrote the beautiful finale song, "Prairie Land," for the 1939 show, and it has been the final piece of every show since. Alice incorporated classical themes into the musical interludes of the show, eschewing harsh, crude melodies for more soothing, sophisticated pieces. During the first years many traditional songs were used, but these were largely replaced by home-grown products, particularly the songs of James Ball, who, in combination with Bobby or Alice, wrote most of the show's most popular tunes. By the time of Nail's death, the *Fandangle* included mostly original songs. Nail wrote or assisted in writing the lyrics for "Let's Settle in this Country," "The Town of Fort Griffin," "Old Red-Eye," "Love Hovers over You," "There's a Night and a Day," "It's a Gully Washer," "My Love and I Will Marry," "Officer's Ball," "Four Little Girls," "Lonesome," "Work Is a Song," "Shank of the Evening," "You Can't Change Them Ways," "Think Twice," and "Kissin' Kin." He wrote both music and lyrics for several songs, including "Tall Tale," the rattlesnake song, "The Horse that I Ride," "Lottie's Song," and "Prairie Land."

Many saw directing as Nail's greatest skill, however, for he could evoke polished performances from ordinary people, especially young ones. He called the *Fandangle* the "People's Theater." Its elaborate props, along with Longhorn cattle borrowed from Fort Griffin and herded by real cowboys, resulted from the hard work of many individuals. Local welders and mechanics built the sets, steam calliope, stagecoach, and train, produced by G. P. Crutchfield, an engineer working in Albany for Marshall R. Young Oil Company of Fort Worth. The singers on stage came from all walks of life. Ordinary people showed themselves willing to pool their talents and be directed by Bob Nail, who received a small remuneration of $3,000 a year for only a few of the shows he directed. No one was paid in the earliest years, and the performers have never been paid.

Crutchfield and Nail's brother Bill both died in 1958, and the show was halted until 1964, when John Musselman, a young University of Texas graduate, returned home and became the producer. After two performances were held on the Musselman Ranch in 1964, Nail took forty *Fandangle* performers to Palo Duro Canyon State Park to inaugurate a new amphitheater built there for the show *Texas*. The crew returned eager for a *Fandangle* amphitheater. Rancher Watt Matthews, who had provided wagons, mules, and horses for performances, with other family members donated the site of the old railroad shipping pens just northwest of town, where the Prairie Theater was built in 1965.

The Ministerial Association of Albany, led by the First Baptist Church, asked Nail to write and direct a Christmas pageant in 1939. He did so, with Alice Reynolds's assistance. The pageant, the *Albany Nativity*, is presented on alternate years in the restored Aztec Theater, free to the public.

Several of Nail's one-act plays were published by the Samuel French Company. The first of these, *Antic Spring*, inspired by Thornton Wilder, made its premier at Albany High School in 1939. This is Nail's most popular play and has been presented thousands of times by high school classes around the nation. Nail's other plays include *The Young and the Miserable*, *The Real Princess*, *Joe*, *The Thing a Man Loves*, *Remember the Alamo*, *Love Errant*, *A Portrait of Nelson Holiday, Jr.* (for which Bill Overton wrote ten songs), *Touch of Fancy*, and *2,000 Nights in the Theatre*.

Nail raised funds early in World War II by staging entertainment for "Bundles for Britain." After the bombing of Pearl Harbor, though suffering from an ulcer, he volunteered for service. The army put him to work in the War Bond effort. Toward that end, he wrote "Letters from the Front" and "What's Your Name, Soldier?," two popular radio programs. He also wrote a successful play, *Men of Bataan*, patterned on the life of a boyhood friend, pilot and hero Edwin Dyess. For this Nail received the Legion of Merit from the War Department in 1943. During this time, he directed such well-known Hollywood stars as Robert Taylor, Jack Holt, Tyrone Power, and William Holden. Nail entered the army a private and attained the rank of captain. In 1946, though he received an offer to be associated with the Reeder Children's School of Theater and Design in Fort Worth, he returned to Albany to maintain the *Fandangle* and *Nativity*. These shows were not presented during the war years but were revived in 1947. They were stopped in 1951 when Nail had major abdominal surgery.

In order to ready the cast and publicize a revived *Fandangle*, Nail took small groups to do shows around the state. These shows he called "samplers." He did two samplers at Dyess Air Force Base, Abilene, and one in Austin highlighting Texas music brought together by the Fine Arts Commission. The biggest sampler went to the LBJ Ranch in 1967 for the entertainment of a group of Latin-American ambassadors, United States officials, and the White House press corps. A selected cast of about forty performed at the presidential ranch, where Cactus Pryor and Carol Channing introduced them to an appreciative audience.

In 1947 Nail was named Albany's outstanding citizen; in 1963 Albany set up a scholarship in his name still given today. In the late 1960s Nail established the Robert E. Nail Foundation to provide for the annual production of the *Fort Griffin Fandangle* and to preserve historical and archival materials of Albany. In 1966 the West Texas Chamber of Commerce honored him, and Governor John Connally named him to the first Fine Arts Commission of Texas. In 1968 he received an honorary doctorate from Hardin–Simmons University. The Texas legislature passed a resolution upon Nail's death. The *Fandangle* has been awarded honors, including the Coral H. Tullis Award from the Texas State Historical Association (1969). In 1970 Governor Preston Smith presented the *Fandangle* and the entire community with the annual Tourist Development Award. Lady Bird Johnson asked the *Fandangle* to return to the LBJ Ranch for a performance to benefit a grove of trees honoring her husband in Washington, D.C.

Nail was stricken at home by a fatal heart attack. Subsequent directors of the *Fandangle* have been James Ball, Marge Bray, and Betsy Black Parsons, who grew up performing in the show. In 1940 Bob Nail purchased the old county jail to use as a repository for his papers and photographs. His nephew Reilly Nail inherited the old jail building from his uncle and converted it into the Old Jail Art Center and Archives.

BIBLIOGRAPHY: Albany *News*, 45th Anniversary Fandangle Souvenir Edition, June 1983. Robert Nail Archives, Old Jail Art Center, Albany, Texas. Robert E. Nail, *The Fandangle: A People's Theater* (Albany, Texas: Fort Griffin Fandangle Association, 1970). Alice Reynolds, James Ball, and Robert Nail, *Fort Griffin Fandangle Favorite Songs*. Vertical files, Center for American History, University of Texas at Austin ("Fort Griffin Fandangle," "Robert E. Nail").
Shirley Caldwell

National Guild of Piano Teachers. The largest nonprofit organization of piano teachers in the United States; founded by Irl Allison Sr. to promote music appreciation through national piano-playing auditions. Allison, a pianist and music teacher, introduced an all-Southwest piano-playing contest in 1929 under the supervision of the National Bureau for the Advancement of Music. At the time, he was head of the music department at Hardin–Simmons University in Abilene.

The purpose of the tournament was to stimulate better teaching and to inspire pupils to self-development. Forty-six entrants, thirty-five of whom were Allison's own students, were rated on the basis of individual merit, not in competition with each other. In 1930 the tournament drew 100 contestants. By 1933 there were 400 contestants, and Abilene, Dallas, Tyler, Waco, Beaumont, San Antonio, Lubbock, El Paso, Albuquerque, Oklahoma City, and Shreveport had auditions. A Texas oilman donated $4,000 to the project, enabling Allison to expand the organization beyond the state.

In 1933 he moved the guild to New York City to gain prestige. The next year the first guild-sponsored national piano-playing contest was held in Steinway Hall in connection with National Music Week; it was open to students of elementary, high school, and college age. For the next eight years Allison traveled the country trying to interest music teachers in holding local contests under guild auspices. His wife, Jessie, remained in New York as secretary. By 1937 there were 150 guild centers nationwide. Monetary problems forced the Allisons back to Texas in 1943, but their move did not diminish the guild's growing reputation. By 1949 NGPT membership had risen to 26,000 teachers and pupils, with practically every major American city holding annual contests. Membership exceeded 70,000 by 1962. In the early twenty-first century the guild has grown to over 118,000 participants who enroll annually in international auditions, which are held in over 800 locations throughout the U.S. and abroad.

The basic aim of the guild is to establish attainable goals, honors, and cash awards for piano pupils of all grades and talent through noncompetitive evaluation in the Annual National Piano Playing Auditions. Pupils entering the auditions are heard and rated by qualified examiners who are members of the American College of Musicians, a guild-sponsored organization also founded by Allison. Student performance is graded on the order of conservatory tests, with emphasis on rhythm, tempo, tone, pedaling, interpretation, and technique. In addition to the auditions, the guild sponsors an annual composition contest and an international piano-recording competition, as well as giving awards to teachers for excellence. Allison also founded the Van Cliburn International Piano Competition.

The NGPT publicizes its members and events through *Piano Guild Notes*, published since 1951, and an annual yearbook. Membership includes the National Fraternity of Student Musicians, composed of the pupils of guild members who are enrolled in the auditions; active and associate teachers and retired teachers subscribing to the Guild Code of Ethics; and faculty, who usually hold degrees, serve as guild judges, and belong to the American College of Musicians. Allison's belief in the ennobling power of music contributed the guild motto: "May pleasure in piano playing be our goal, our guide the Golden Rule." The Guild is headquartered in Austin.

BIBLIOGRAPHY: Austin *American*, October 14, 1962. Austin *American–Statesman*, June 12, 1949. Guild homepage (http://www.pianoguild.com/1.html), accessed January 9, 2003. *The Guild Syllabus* (Austin: National Guild of Piano Teachers). *Texas Music News*, April 1933.

Craig H. Roell

Native American Music. The accounts of early Spanish and French explorers confirm that music was an important part of Native American ceremonial life. In 1535, the first chroniclers of Indian life in Texas, the shipwrecked Cabeza de Vaca and his party, were greeted by native people who shouted, clapped their thighs, and brought out gourd-and-pebble rattles to which they attached great importance. Almost 200 years later, in what is now northern Texas, the French explorer Bénard de La Harpe was treated to a ceremony that lasted twenty-four hours, "during which time their music did not discontinue for a moment." Spanish archives are replete with accounts of Coahuiltecan dances that lasted as long as eight days and were motivated by such diverse events as seasonal harvests, battles, astronomical phenomena, and the threat of disease.

Singing apparently accompanied most of the dances, with the human voice the dominant source of sound. The 1582 Rodríguez expedition to the area of modern-day Presidio, in far west Texas, described a festival in which the dancers raised their hands to the sun and sang "with much compass and harmony" so that three hundred men performed as one. Circa 1605, Spanish chronicler Pérez de Riba described another such communal celebration, or mitote, in which motets were sung in "the tone and rhythm that they use, the same way one pauses and then repeats the brief verses of a song when accompanied by an organ." In 1645, writing specifically about the mitotes of the native people in the vicinity of Monterrey, in the northern Mexican state of Nuevo León adjacent to Texas, Alonso De León commented that the people sang "in their own peculiar way," words with no meaning (to the Spanish listeners), but pleasing to the ear. He thought that the participants sang so harmoniously, with no discordant voices, that all together seemed to make but one voice. The same impression was voiced by Fray Francisco de Céliz, diarist of the Alarcón expedition to East Texas in 1718. During a welcoming ceremony, the Caddo men, women, and children were seated separately but sang "without disagreeing one point in their voices," making "a gentle although coarse harmony." That the same response was elicited from European observers so widely separated in time and space implies that Native American music, and especially singing, conformed to some uniform standard that transcended linguistic and social boundaries.

By the time European settlers colonized Texas, the indigenous populations had been decimated by internecine warfare and introduced diseases. Many of the named tribes that are thought of today as native were in fact immigrants, the Apache in the late seventeenth century, the Comanche in the eighteenth century, and the Alabama–Coushatta and the Kickapoo tribes in the nineteenth century. The Tiguas of far west Texas are closely related to the Pueblo people of the Southwestern United States, rather than any more easterly Texas groups. The Caddoan people, with their tribal headquarters in Oklahoma, trace their ancestry to prehistoric agriculturalists of East Texas and Louisiana as well as Oklahoma. Although descendants of other native peoples undoubtedly still live in South and West Texas, their cultural identity has been lost. Unlike the sedentary Caddos, the vast majority of the indigenous people were hunters and gatherers who lived highly mobile lives that limited their ability to make and transport large or complex musical instruments. The early demise of so many native cultures is reflected in the paucity of the written accounts of their ceremonies, including their music.

The archeological record provides rare examples of rhythm sticks, rattles, whistles, and flutes but is incapable of recreating the totality of musical performances or explaining how and when they were played. Another bias is introduced by the preservation factor; more instruments have been recovered from the dry caves of West Texas than from the rest of the state, where wooden objects tend to decay rapidly. Taken together, and viewed in the context of New World cultures as a whole, archeology and ethnography do substantiate the interaction between music and ritual that undoubtedly prevailed in Texas as well as the rest of North America.

Percussion Instruments. Most of the musical instruments known archeologically are classed as percussive and probably served to establish and maintain dance rhythms and to encourage the trance state essential to some ceremonies and rituals. Various types of rattles and rasps were apparently used by all of the indigenous people of Texas and neighboring areas.

Commonly, shaken rattles, like those described by

Comanche dancer Hanna Yellowfish, ca. 1910. Courtesy Panhandle Plains Historical Museum. Music, accompanied by singing and dancing, was an important part of Native American ceremonial life.

Cabeza de Vaca, were made of gourds, either dried with the seeds inside or perforated and filled with small pebbles, bits of quartz, seeds, or other hard objects that would collide with each other and the gourd when shaken. Alonso De León specified that the Nuevo León gourd rattles were perforated with many small holes and filled with the gravel-like detritus found around ant mounds. One of the more unusual fill materials detected archeologically is some 300 black drum teeth found in a coastal grave that also produced bone whistles. Gourds have the advantage of a fixed handle, but other containers are more durable. Turtle carapaces, filled with pebbles and transfixed by wooden handles or strung on cords, are not uncommon. Rare examples of rattlesnake rattler rattles were recovered from two children's graves in West Texas. The most intact specimen was made by attaching the tail skin and rattles of twenty-six snakes to the end of a wand made of an arrow shaft. These unusual artifacts may have been as much magical as musical, given their mortuary context. Animal skulls and basketry containers are reported from adjacent areas of Native America and may well have been utilized in Texas as well. The Caddos made hollow ceramic vessels that rattled although it is not clear that they were intended as musical accompaniment.

Suspended rattles are difficult to identify archeologically, as the cords or strings have often deteriorated. Again, the dry caves of West Texas provide examples of drilled mussel shells that were presumably suspended rattles. Four deer scapulae, or shoulder bones, still strung on a cord when first collected from a cave in Southwest Texas, are on exhibit at the Witte Museum in San Antonio. Modern kachina dancers are depicted with scapula rattles or using a scapula as a sounding stick, drawn across a rhythm stick or rasp. Scapulae seem to have been prized for their broad flat surfaces, which were sometimes painted with abstract designs, as well as for the dry clacking sound they produce on contact. The relationship between deer and music is furthered by reports of wooden sticks or antlers being struck together to imitate the sound of combative stags, which may or may not be music to the ear.

Deer hooves, mountain laurel beans, and snail or marine shells were strung on cords to be worn as ankle or wrist rattles or suspended from clothing to augment the cadence of the dance. The hard red beans of the mountain laurel tree, which were traded as far north as Canada, had a three-fold attraction. In addition to their percussive sound and vibrant color, mescal beans were ingested for their narcotic properties during rituals that required the participants to enter an entranced state.

Shell tinklers were supplanted in historic times by pieces of metal that were cut and fastened to the dancer's costumes. The Caddos count among their traditional paraphernalia hawk bells, a type of miniature pellet ball that was introduced to them by the Spanish. A very few copper bells from prehistoric contexts in far West Texas were probably obtained in trade from Mexican metallurgists. Nearing the end of their journey on the west coast of Mexico, Cabeza de Vaca's party was given a copper rattle that the natives said came from the north.

Rasps or rhythm sticks are one of the more durable

Ironwood rasp varnished with hematite, West Texas. (Illustration taken from Donny L. Hamilton, *Prehistory of the Rustler Hills, Granado Cave* [Austin: University of Texas Press, 2001]). Courtesy D. L. Hamilton, Texas A&M University.

types of percussion instrument and thus survive in the archeological record, especially in dry caves. Typically, rasps were made of bone or hard wood notched at intervals and played with a sounding stick. Possibly, the sound was augmented by resonating devices, such as gourds, bowls, or skulls. Spanish chroniclers in Mexico noted that rasps made of human femurs contributed a lugubrious note to human sacrifices and funerals. Alonso De León described the rasps that accompanied dances in Nuevo León as sticks made of *ébano* (hard wood) and other kinds of wood, with deep grooves, so that rubbing another stick vigorously over the grooves made a pleasant sound. A well-preserved ironwood rasp and a sounding stick from a burial cave in the eastern Trans-Pecos were varnished with hematite suspended in an emulsion of plant resin. Another, also from a mortuary context, is a combination of rasp and atlatl or spear thrower with notches cut into the shaft that serves as an elongation of the throwing arm, thus adding propulsive force.

Stereotypically, drums are linked with American Indian music, but they are virtually absent from the archeological record. One possibility is that drums were made of materials whose function is not evident once the instrument has been discarded or dismantled, much like the scapula or snail-shell rattles. An example is a turtle shell and antler tine in the Witte Museum in San Antonio. A Mayan mural painting illustrates a musician playing a turtle-carapace drum with just such an antler tine, providing a possible analogue for the Witte specimens. Historically, turtle or tortoise carapaces were scraped or rubbed rather than struck, aligning them with rhythm sticks or rasps rather than drums.

Early in the eighteenth century, Spanish military documents report that attacks against their forces in northern Mexico, near the Big Bend region of Texas, were accompanied by fife and drum, but the novelty suggests that these tactics may have been newly adopted from the Europeans. The Caddos count drums among their traditional instruments, describing both wet and dry variations. The Alarcón expedition of 1718 was feted at a welcoming ceremony in which the kettledrum and various timbrels accompanied the singing. The kettledrum was described as made of a large water-jug covered with a stretched and dampened skin. Wet drums are now antique kettles partly filled with water; presumably, in the past ceramic vessels served the same purpose. The diarist for the 1582 Rodríguez expedition to the pueblos along the Rio Grande mentioned a drum in the form of a tambourine, made by attaching skins to an unspecified vessel. Ethnohistoric accounts describe Apache drums as simple constructions: a piece of hide stretched over a pot or a gourd and struck with a stick. Pérez de Ribas mentioned that the Coahuiltecans had unusual little drums made of a special wood but his description ended there.

Several very recent Indian rock art sites, such as Meyers Spring, Bailando Shelter, and Hueco Tanks, show lines of animated dancers, some with hand-held objects that may be rattles or rasps. Circular objects beside or between the dancers could represent either drums or shields. According to the modern Tiguas, one round pictograph motif at Hueco Tanks symbolizes a drum. The Tarahumara Indians of northern Mexico, who are probably distantly related to the prehistoric people of South and West Texas, are well known for their commercial traffic in traditional drums. Thus, some form of drum was assuredly known by most of the Indians, but the instruments themselves have either not been found or not been recognized.

Wind Instruments. Archeologically, the most common wind instruments are whistles, usually made of the central shaft of bird long bones. The articular ends are removed or reamed to form a hollow tube with a round or rectangular air hole cut into one end. In some, asphaltum plugs inserted into the tube just below this hole channel the flow of air to achieve the desired sound. Caddoan eagle-bone flutes were reportedly used from about A.D. 1400 until the introduction of the Ghost Dance, circa 1880.

Along the upper Texas coast, bird-bone whistles, often made of whooping crane ulnas and incised with geometric designs, have been recovered in mortuary contexts that suggest a complex relationship between myth and music. In many American Indian religions, birds are icons for supernatural flight to the spirit world and bones, the most durable elements of the body, symbolize resurrection. Cranes, in particular, are mythological guardians or spirit guides, thus explaining their metaphorical role as funerary offerings. The rattles found with whistles in some graves add the element of percussion to the ensemble.

The humpbacked, flute-playing Kokopelli figures generally associated with the Pueblo cultures of the American Southwest provide evidence of yet another wind instrument. The mythological Kokopelli beguiled women with his haunting music and plied them with gifts carried in his backpack or hump. The pictographs and fragments of wooden or bone flutes found in dry cave deposits indicate that the flute was tubular and played vertically although transverse flutes were recovered from an East Texas site dating to around A.D 1000.

Pairs of reed cylinders, lashed together with twine and placed in an Archaic infant's grave, have been interpreted as a panpipe. Perforated shell discs in the same context were thought to be part of a bullroarer or chiringa, but that interpretation is questionable since no other archeological or ethnohistoric evidence for such an instrument exists.

Discussion. The Native American musical repertoire in Texas appears to be limited to percussion and wind instruments of relatively simple construction but of immense ceremonial importance. Ethnohistoric accounts of festivals describe marathon singing and dancing, thus emphasizing the importance of vocalization and percussion. The fact that most of the archeological examples of prehistoric musical instruments were recovered from mortuary contexts indicates their special relevance to ceremonial, supernatural, or spiritual events. Rattles, tinklers, and bells were designed to be worn or held by dancers participating in communal or sacred rites, while most of the other percussion instruments probably accompanied them. Cabeza de Vaca was told that gourd rattles were used for important events and could only be touched by their owners due to their supernatural powers. Rhythmic music, and especially percussion, has long been recognized as one means of attaining the altered states of consciousness that were an important part of many Native American religions. The Caddos have endeavored to preserve their traditional music, making records that are available to the general public. The Tiguas are closely related to other Pueblo people of the American Southwest who have also recorded many of their songs. The Kickapoos, however, are reluctant to discuss their music, which is handed down from generation to generation, thus maintaining its ceremonial importance.

BIBLIOGRAPHY: Álvar Núñez Cabeza de Vaca, *Cabeza de Vaca's Adventures in the Unknown Interior of America,* trans. Cyclone Covey (Albuquerque: University of New Mexico Press, 1983). Fray Francisco Céliz, *Diary of the Alarcón Expedition into Texas, 1718–1719,* trans. Fritz Leo Hoffman (Los Angeles: Quivira Society Publications 5, 1935). Clarence Debusk, An Appraisal of the Musicological Resources of the Pecos River Focus (Master's thesis, University of Texas, 1963). Alonso De León, *Historia de Nuevo León* (Monterrey, Nuevo León: Biblioteca de Nuevo León 1, 1961). Frances Densmore, *The American Indians and Their Music* (New York: Woman's Press, 1926). William B. Griffen, *Culture Change and Shifting Populations in Central Northern Mexico* (Tucson: Anthropological Papers of the University of Arizona 13, 1969). George P. Hammond and Agapito Rey, *The Gallegos Relation of the Rodriguez Expedition to New Mexico.* Historical Society of New Mexico Publications in History 4 (Santa Fe, 1927). William W. Newcomb Jr. and Forrest Kirkland, *The Rock Art of Texas Indians* (Austin: University of Texas Press, 1967). Andrés Pérez de Ribas, *History of the Triumphs of Our Holy Faith among the Most Barbarous and Fierce People of the New World* (1645), trans. Daniel T. Reff, Maureen Ahern, and Richard K. Danforth (Tucson: University of Arizona Press, 1999).

Solveig A. Turpin

Neely, Bill. Composer and singer of country blues music; b. Collin County, Texas, September 19, 1916; d. Austin, March 22, 1990 (buried at Capital Memorial Park, Austin). Neely, the son of sharecroppers, grew up in McKinney. At thirteen he met his greatest musical influence, country singer Jimmie Rodgers, who gave him his first guitar lesson. Because of the depression, Neely dropped out of

Bill Neely had his first guitar lesson from his greatest musical influence, Jimmie Rodgers. He played regularly at Threadgill's restaurant in Austin in the 1950s and released his only album, *Blackland Farm Boy*, in 1974. Photograph by Burton Wilson.

the eighth grade to look for work at the age of fifteen. He began working at Civilian Conservation Corps camps and traveling about the country on freight trains. Although he had begun composing his own music, his musical career was arrested for four years (1939–43) by service in the army. In 1943 he moved to Arizona.

In 1949 he moved to Austin, where he met musician Kenneth Threadgill. Before long, Neely was a regularly scheduled Wednesday-night act at Threadgill's restaurant, where he played for most of the 1950s. In 1968 he befriended another Austin musician, Larry Kirbo. The two played together for nearly twelve years, including special performances in programs hosted by the Smithsonian Institution, Washington, D.C. Neely also played with such notable musicians as Janis Joplin, Mance Lipscomb, and Pete Seeger. In 1974 he released his only album, *Blackland Farm Boy*. In December 1989 he traveled to Paris with three other Texas musicians to perform for two weeks at the House of World Cultures.

Besides performing onstage, Neely owned restaurants, worked as a hotel chef, and drove a truck for the state of Texas. He married Bobbie Hamilton in 1948. The couple had three daughters, a son, and a step-daughter. Neely died

of leukemia at home. His influence lives on in the work of such Austin artists as Dan del Santo, Alejandro Escovedo, and Nanci Griffith.

BIBLIOGRAPHY: Robyn Turner, *Austin Originals: Chats with Colorful Characters* (Amarillo: Paramount, 1982). Vertical Files, Center for American History, University of Texas at Austin. *Keith Huang*

Nelson, Harrison D. Songwriter and blues performer, known mainly as Peppermint Harris; b. Texarkana, Texas, July 17, 1925; d. New Jersey, March 19, 1999. Nelson was primarily associated with Houston during the defining years of his musical career. After first moving to the city in 1943 and starting to play blues professionally in 1947, at such venues as the Eldorado Ballroom, he invented the stage name "Peppermint" in response to the success of other local performers with catchy nicknames—friends such as Clarence "Gatemouth" Brown or Sam "Lightnin'" Hopkins, the latter of whom also helped him get his first chance to record (for the Gold Star label) in 1947 or 1948.

A subsequent session in 1949 or 1950 for the label known as Sittin' In With produced Nelson's (and the label's) first hit record, the song "Rainin' in My Heart," performed with a band led by noted Houston musician Henry Hayes. It also triggered confusion over Nelson's identity. Because the recording was produced as an afterthought following a day full of auditions by various musicians, the studio personnel had not been properly informed of Nelson's surname. They had overheard others calling him "Peppermint," and apparently later misunderstood someone's clipped pronunciation of his given first name, Harrison, to be a last name, Harris. Thus, they issued the record as a performance by Peppermint Harris, and its success led Nelson to keep the accidentally crafted pseudonym.

That combination of self-motivated creativity and susceptibility to forces beyond his control in some ways characterized Nelson's career as a bluesman, which involved recordings on over a dozen labels (including Aladdin, Money, Dart, Duke, and Jewel) and authorship of countless songs. Many of these compositions were reportedly sold outright for instant cash and therefore never properly credited to him. However, among titles for which Nelson did retain his rights as original songwriter is his greatest commercial success, "I Got Loaded." This 1951 Aladdin release occupied a spot on the Billboard Top Ten for six months and decades later was re-recorded by British rock star Elvis Costello. Among the many other songs to which Nelson retained his rights were "Think It Over One More Time," "As the Years Go Passin' By," "Whole Lot of Loving," and "Stranded in St. Louis."

In 1997 Nelson released a Peppermint Harris CD called *Penthouse in the Ghetto*, comprising various vintage tracks recorded in Houston in 1958, 1960, 1974, and 1975, with noted local musicians such as Clarence Green, Clarence Hollimon, Teddy Reynolds, and others. Nelson reportedly had earned a B.A. in English from the institution now known as Texas Southern University. His verbal adroitness was suggested by the album title and by the fact that, though he was a capable guitarist and musician, he is best remembered by his fellow musicians as a gifted lyricist. He lived in Sacramento, California, for the last decade of his life, before moving to New Jersey to be close to family members.

BIBLIOGRAPHY: Alan Govenar, *Meeting the Blues: The Rise of the Texas Sound* (Dallas: Taylor, 1988). Sheldon Harris, *Blues Who's Who* (New Rochelle, New York: Arlington House, 1979). Mike Leadbitter, *Nothing but the Blues* (London: Hanover Books, 1971). Roger Wood, "Peppermint Harris," *Living Blues* 146 (July–August 1999).

Roger Wood

Newbury, Mickey. Singer and songwriter; b. Milton Newbury Jr., Houston, May 19, 1940; d. Springfield, Oregon, September 29, 2002; son of Milton and Mamie Newbury. He attended Jefferson Davis High School in Houston, where one of his classmates and friends was Kenny Rogers.

In 1954 Newbury began singing as a tenor in a local doo-wop group called the Embers, who signed a recording contract with Mercury Records in 1956. When he was seventeen he taught himself to play guitar, absorbing influences from the folk, blues, country, rockabilly, jazz, and border music of the Houston music scene. He wrote songs and performed with the Embers until 1959, when he joined the U.S. Air Force. After three years of overseas duty in England he returned to Houston and resumed his songwriting career. Newbury worked at odd jobs and on shrimpboats in the Houston and Southeast Texas area, staying with friends and relatives until he moved to Nashville in the early 1960s.

Shortly after arriving in Nashville he met Willie Nelson and Kris Kristofferson, who recorded his songs and became his lifelong friends, along with fellow Houstonian Townes Van Zandt. Newbury's songwriting caught the attention of Wesley Rose, who signed him in 1964 to Acuff–Rose Music in Nashville. Country star Don Gibson sang the first Newbury hit song when he recorded "Funny, Familiar, Forgotten Feelings" in 1966, the first of twelve Newbury songs that he recorded.

In 1968 Newbury became the first and only songwriter ever to have number-one hits on four charts at the same time: easy listening, with Andy Williams's version of "Sweet Memories"; country, with "Here Comes the Rain" sung by Eddy Arnold; rhythm and blues, with Solomon Burke's "Time is a Thief"; and pop–rock, with "Just Dropped In (To See What Condition My Condition Was In)," recorded by Kenny Rogers and the First Edition. In 1969 "Sweet Memories" made the country charts when it was covered by Dottie West and Don Gibson. Around this time and the early 1970s B. B. King hit the charts with "Time is a Thief," Ray Charles recorded "Sunshine," and Jerry Lee Lewis had success with "She Even Woke Me Up To Say Goodbye." "Heaven Help the Child" won the "World Popular Song" contest at the Tokyo Music Festival in 1973. Willie Nelson made the charts with "Sweet Memories" in the early 1990s, a tribute to the timeless quality of Newbury's songs.

In 1969 Newbury married Susan Pack, a former Miss Oregon and member of the New Christy Minstrels. They moved to Oregon in 1974 and settled near Springfield in 1980. Newbury continued to write songs and record there in his own studio, releasing albums on his Mountain Retreat label. On October 12,1980, he was inducted into the Nashville Songwriters Association International Hall of Fame.

Newbury made over fifteen albums of his own during his career. On one of those albums, *Frisco Mabel Joy* (1971), he performed his arrangement of a trio of Civil War songs entitled "American Trilogy." The medley of "Dixie," "Battle Hymn of the Republic," and "All My Trials" became his best-known work and reached number twenty-six on the charts in 1971. Elvis Presley loved "American Trilogy" and closed his live shows with it until his death; it thus became the last song Elvis performed in public. Since then "American Trilogy" has been recorded by over 100 performers. Newbury's albums are full of mournful songs that are sometimes accompanied by a lonesome steam locomotive whistle. Willie Nelson and Waylon Jennings' hit version of Chips Moman's "Luckenbach, Texas" refers to "Hank Williams' pain songs, Newbury's train songs and 'Blue Eyes Crying in the Rain.'"

Newbury's songs have been recorded over 500 times by almost 400 performers in over fourteen countries, making him one of the foremost American popular songwriters.

Artists who have each recorded three or more Newbury songs include Don Gibson, Roy Orbison, Waylon Jennings, Joan Baez, Kenny Rogers, Jerry Lee Lewis, Tom Jones, Johnny Rodriguez, Willie Nelson, Roy Acuff Jr., Ray Charles, Brenda Lee, Dottie West, Buffy Ste. Marie, Eddy Arnold, Brook Benton, Don Cherry, B. B. King, Wayne Newton, and Perry Como.

Newbury struggled against emphysema for the last five years of his life, but continued to write and record while enjoying family life. Susan said of him, "He was a wonderful husband and father. He didn't put much stock in what the rest of the world did. He just took care of his family. We'd have kids, and he'd take the next year off to feed his family." Newbury made his last public performance at the Kerrville Folk Festival in 1998, but kept contact with his many fans via his website. He released his last CD, *Winter Winds*, in early 2002. He died in his sleep and was survived by his wife, his mother, three sons, and a brother.

BIBLIOGRAPHY: Eugene *Register–Guard*, October 1, 2002. Nashville *Tennessean*, September 30, 2002. Mickey Newbury obituary (www.guardian.co.uk/obituaries/story/0,3604,803302,00.html), accessed March 9, 2003. *All Music Guide* (www.allmusic.com), accessed March 9, 2003. New Oregon Archives Obit Report—Register–Guard 30 September 2002 (www.sos.state.or.us/piper-mail/or-roots/2002-September/000838.html), accessed March 9, 2003. Mickey Newbury homepage (www.mickeynewbury.com), accessed March 9, 2003.

Gary S. Hickinbotham

Nix, Hoyle. West Texas fiddler and bandleader; b. Azle, Texas, March 22, 1918; d. Big Spring, August 21, 1985; son of Jonah Lafayette and Myrtle May (Brooks) Nix. The family moved to Big Spring when Hoyle was one year old. His father was a fiddler and his mother a guitarist, and the couple often performed together at community gatherings. Nix was six years old when he learned his first fiddle tune. In addition to his parents' influence, the music of Bob Wills was also very important to his style. According to Nix, Wills was the finest fiddler he ever heard.

Nix and his brother Ben formed the West Texas Cowboys in 1946 and patterned the band after Wills's Texas Playboys. In 1954 the Nix brothers built a small dance hall on the Snyder highway just outside of Big Spring and named it the Stampede. Nix had already established a dance circuit in the area and was making regular appearances in other towns, including Abilene, Lubbock, Midland, Odessa, and San Angelo. The West Texas Cowboys cut their first recordings in 1949 for the Dallas-based Star Talent label. The initial Star Talent release, Nix's "Big Ball's in Cowtown," a folk-derived re-write, proved to be an enduring standard. He continued to record for small Texas record companies—Queen, Caprock, Bo-Kay, and Winston—in the 1950s and early 1960s. In 1968 Nix started his own label, Stampede, named after the dancehall.

During the late 1950s, the West Texas Cowboys grew to its largest size with nine members. The band at this time included former Texas Playboys Eldon Shamblin, Millard Kelso, and Louis Tierney. Nix had first shared a stage with Bob Wills in 1952 in Colorado City, Texas, and their two bands soon began touring together, splitting the playing time at each dance. After Wills disbanded the Texas Playboys in the early 1960s, he continued to appear with Nix on a fairly regular basis until his first stroke in 1969. The respect that Wills had for Nix was evidenced when he invited Nix and his son Jody to participate in what turned out to be Wills's final recording session, *For the Last Time*, in 1973.

Nix's last recordings were made in 1977 and released on Oil Patch. He was inducted into the Nebraska Country Music Hall of Fame in 1984, the Colorado Country Music Hall of Fame in 1985, the Texas Western Swing Hall of Fame in 1991, and the Western Swing Hall of Fame in 1991. He died after a short illness.

Nix married five times and had four children, Larry (1940), Jody (1952), Hoylene (1957), and Robin (1959). Larry joined his father's band in 1957 and played bass. When Jody signed on in 1960 as drummer and fiddler, the two siblings became the rhythm section of the West Texas Cowboys, a position they held for the next twenty-five years. Jody Nix took over leadership of the band as his father wanted, and with the younger Nix carrying on the show, Texans were assured of dancing to the music of a Nix fiddle well into the twenty-first century.

BIBLIOGRAPHY: Joe W. Specht, "An Interview with Hoyle Nix, the West Texas Cowboy," *Old Time Music*, nos. 34–36 (1980–81). Joe W. Specht, "Hoyle Nix," in Paul Kingsbury, ed., *The Encyclopedia of Country Music* (New York: Oxford University Press, 1998). *Joe W. Specht*

Oberdoerffer, Fritz. Musicologist and professor of music; b. Hamburg, Germany, November 4, 1895; d. Austin, December 8, 1979. Oberdoerffer attended school in Hamburg (1906–08) and Jena (1908–14). Following service in the German army in World War I, he studied at the University of Jena in 1919 and at the Leipzig Conservatory from 1920 to 1923, pursuing studies in music theory, music composition, and piano. In 1921 he was awarded the Robert Schumann Stipendium at Leipzig.

On February 14, 1925, he married Rosemarie Herschkowitsch. A daughter, Marianne, was born on February 11, 1926. By 1926 the family had moved to Berlin, where Oberdoerffer took advanced piano lessons from 1926 to 1929 from a famed Russian piano virtuoso, Leonid Kreutzer. In 1929 Oberdoerffer entered the Humboldt University of Berlin to undertake graduate study in music history and literature, philosophy, and German literature. Among his teachers were some of the most influential musicologists of the twentieth Century, including Arnold Schering, Johannes Wolf, Erich Moritz von Hornbostel, Curt Sachs, Georg Schünemann, and Friedrich Blume. Oberdoerffer completed his studies at the university in 1933 and received his Ph.D. in 1939. His dissertation, *Der Generalbass in der Instrumentalmusik des ausgehenden 18. Jahrhunderts* (*The Thorough-Bass in the Instrumental Music of the Late 18th Century*), was published by Bärenreiter Verlag in Kassel in 1939.

From his arrival in Berlin, through his years of graduate study, and into the years of World War II, Oberdoerffer earned a living by teaching and performing. He received a State Teacher Certificate for piano in 1927 and a State Teacher Certificate for music history in 1933. From 1926 to 1938 he taught piano and music history at various music conservatories in Berlin, including the Klindworth–Scharwenka Conservatory. He was also active in Berlin from 1926 to 1944 as a private instructor of piano, music theory, and music history; as a vocal coach; and as an accompanist and chamber music performer. From 1942 to 1945 (with an interruption from 1944 to the end of the war), he taught music history, ear training, and score playing at the Institute for Evangelical Church Music in Berlin–Spandau. Before the end of the war Oberdoerffer and his wife and daughter were compelled by the Nazis to work in a forced labor camp.

After World War II, Oberdoerffer was appointed chief of archive records, tapes, and the library of Radio Berlin, a position he held from 1945 to 1948. In 1949–50, he was employed as an editor with the C. F. Peters Corporation, a music publisher, in New York City.

He moved to Austin in 1950 to become a guest professor at the University of Texas. There, his duties included teaching courses in musicology, music history and literature, piano, and coaching. He remained a "guest" from 1950 to 1964, at which time he was given a permanent appointment and promoted to the rank of professor. From 1964 until his retirement in July 1974, he taught courses in musicology, music history and literature, and coaching.

In addition to his teaching responsibilities at UT, Oberdoerffer continued to pursue his research. He wrote an extended article on thorough-bass (*Generalbass*) for the eminent German music encyclopedia *Die Musik in Geschichte und Gegenwart*, as well as ten smaller articles for the same publication. He also published articles in leading scholarly journals such as *Acta Musicologica*, *Die Musikforschung*, and *Musica*, as well as articles in *Deutsche Tonkünstlerzeitung*, *Neues Musikblatt*, *American Music Teacher*, and *Texas String News*.

However, even in his research, he was never far from his passionate love of performance and from his commitment to making the music of seventeenth and eighteenth century Europe available for general performers. He worked tirelessly to produce modern performing editions of vocal and choral compositions, chamber music, and orchestral works of these centuries. His numerous editions include works by composers such as Melchior Vulpius (1570–1615), Heinrich Schütz (1585–1672), Johann Rosenmüller (1619–84), Christoph Bernhard (1628–92), Dietrich Buxtehude (1637–1707), Henry Purcell (1659–95), Louis–Nicolas Clérambault (1676–49), Antonio Vivaldi (1678–1741), Georg Philipp Telemann (1681–1767), Johann Sebastian Bach (1685–1750), Michael Haydn (1737–1806), and Wolfgang Amadeus Mozart (1756–91). His editions were published by Bärenreiter, Kassel–Wilhelmshöhe; Concordia Publishing House, St. Louis; Lienau, Berlin–Lichterfelde; C. F. Peters, New York; B. Schott's Söhne, Mainz; and Vieweg, Berlin–Lichterfelde.

In 1974, after twenty-four years on the faculty of the Department of Music at the University of Texas at Austin, Oberdoerffer retired. In recognition of his distinguished service, he was named professor emeritus.

BIBLIOGRAPHY: Vertical Files, Center for American History, University of Texas at Austin   *Charles A. Roeckle*

Ochs, Phil. Singer and songwriter; b. Phillip David Ochs, El Paso, December 19, 1940; d. Far Rockaway, New York, April 9, 1976. Like Bob Dylan and Joan Baez, Ochs was one of the most successful singer–songwriters to arise on the New York City folk-music scene in the 1960s. Plagued with depression throughout his short life, he wrote politically charged songs that became protest anthems of that decade. He strongly opposed the war in Vietnam and supported the civil-rights movement—two themes that dominated much of his music.

His father, Jacob "Jack" Ochs, was of Polish–Jewish descent and served as a medical officer in the U.S. Army. Phil's mother, Gertrude, a native of Scotland, had met Jacob while he was attending medical school at the University of Edinburgh. Like many military families, the Ochses moved often. After living in San Antonio and Austin, they moved to Far Rockaway, New York, where Phil began his music education on the clarinet. He considered taking up the drums, but the confines of the family's four-room apartment led his parents and the neighbors to encourage him to stick with the clarinet.

After the family moved to Columbus, Ohio, Ochs refined his musical skills at the Capital University Conservatory of Music. Although he was only sixteen, he was one of the primary soloists for the conservatory. He continued his education at Staunton Military Academy in Virginia, where he played in the school's marching band. In the evenings he would sit in his dorm room and listen to the local radio station, which introduced him to country music performers such as Faron Young, Ernest Tubb, and Lefty Frizzell. He also became enamored of rock-and-roll, particularly the music of Elvis Presley.

After finishing his time at Staunton, Ochs headed back to Columbus and enrolled at Ohio State University. He studied journalism and landed a job writing for the student paper, *The Lantern*—an experience that sparked his interest in politics. He also developed a liking for the folk music of Woody Guthrie, Pete Seeger, and the legendary Joe Hill and the Industrial Workers of the World, or "Wobblies," as they were called. Inspired by this music, Ochs learned the guitar and, along with his best friend, Jim Glover, formed a duo called the Sundowners.

Ochs left Ohio State without graduating, after which he worked in a club in Cleveland. There he opened for the Smothers Brothers and the Greenbriar Boys, among other feature acts. He then headed to New York City, where folk music was becoming increasingly popular. He began by playing at "hootenannies," the folkies' version of an open talent night. His reputation grew, and in 1963 he performed at the Newport Folk Festival. Shortly thereafter, his song "The Ballad of William Worthy" was featured on a folk-music album entitled *The Broadside Ballads, Volume 1*. In 1963 he married Alice Skinner; they had one daughter.

Through his music Ochs expressed his political and moral convictions; during the Christmas of 1963, for example, he headed to Kentucky to play for striking coal miners. The following year he joined the Mississippi Caravan of Music and traveled through the state, playing at black voter-registration drives. When the Caravan arrived in Mississippi shortly after the murder of three civil-rights workers, they faced hostile white opposition. This experience led Ochs to write the song "Here's to the State of Mississippi"—an indictment of bigotry and racism. Ochs's songs hit a nerve with a growing politically minded youth, and the Elektra Record Company signed him to a contract. His first album, *All the News That's Fit to Sing*, had only moderate success, but his second effort, *I Ain't Marching Anymore*, was hailed as a "folk classic."

Despite his newfound fame, Ochs still managed to write journalistic pieces for such publications as *Sing Out!* and *Boston Broadside*. Like his music, his writing expressed his political convictions. Because of his outspokenness, the FBI opened a file on him, classifying him as a "security matter." As United States military involvement in Vietnam grew, Ochs became more critical. His songs "White Boots Marching in a Yellow Land" and "Cops of the World" displayed his increasing disillusionment with America. He frequently played at anti-war demonstrations and was instrumental in the formation of the Yippie party. In 1968, at the Democratic National Convention in Chicago, he performed at a Yippie-sponsored rally in Lincoln Park. The violence that followed the rally pushed him into a deep depression. He contemplated quitting music, but instead responded by releasing the album *Rehearsals for Retirement*. A grim statement on war and peace, the album featured a backing band and orchestration—a departure from the pure "folk" of his earlier recordings.

In the 1970s Ochs's music became more eclectic, his lyrics less focused. In 1970 he released the album *Greatest Hits*, which, despite the title, contained only new material. He also traveled extensively, making treks through both South America and Africa. While staying in Dar es Salaam, Tanzania, he was attacked and strangled. This assault, which Ochs believed was politically motivated, left his vocal chords permanently damaged. With his music career now essentially over, he became even more involved in politics. In 1973, following Augusto Pinochet's coup d'etat in Chile, he organized a benefit concert for the country's refugees. The successful event featured Bob Dylan, Arlo Guthrie, Pete Seeger, and others.

In 1974 Ochs again became severely depressed. He continued to write on occasion, but was frustrated that his vocal chords never completely healed. He began to drink heavily, and his behavior became more and more erratic. He died by suicide.

BIBLIOGRAPHY: Marc Eliot, *Death of a Rebel* (New York: Franklin Watts, 1989). Colin Larkin, ed., *Encyclopedia of Popular Music* (London: MuzeUK Limited, 1998). Michael Schumacher, *There but for Fortune: The Life of Phil Ochs* (New York: Hyperion, 1996). Neal Walters and Brian Mansfield, eds., *Music Hound Folk: The Essential Guide* (Detroit: Visible Ink Press, 1998). *Bradley Shreve*

O'Daniel, Wilbert Lee. Governor of Texas, United States senator, and music factor, known as Pappy O'Daniel; b. Malta, Ohio, March 11, 1890; d. Dallas, May 12, 1969 (buried in Hillcrest Memorial Park); one of two children of William Barnes and Alice Ann (Thompson) O'Daniel. His father, a Union veteran, was killed in an accident soon after Wilbert's birth. Before the boy was five years old his mother remarried and went to live on a farm in Reno County, Kansas. O'Daniel was educated in the public schools of Arlington, Kansas, and completed the two-year curriculum at Salt City Business College in Hutchinson, Kansas, in 1908. At eighteen he became a stenographer and bookkeeper for a flour-milling company in Anthony, Kansas. Later he worked for a larger milling company in Kingman, rose to the post of sales manager, and eventually went into the milling business for himself. On June 30, 1917, in Hutchinson, he married Merle Estella Butcher; they had three children.

He moved to Kansas City in 1919, and then to New Orleans in 1921. In 1925 he moved to Fort Worth, where O'Daniel became sales manager of the Burrus Mills. He took over the company's radio advertising in 1928 and began writing songs and discussing religious subjects on the air. He hired a group of musicians and called them the Light Crust Doughboys. O'Daniel served as president of the Fort Worth Chamber of Commerce in 1933–1934. He organized his own flour company in 1935.

At the behest of radio fans, he filed for governor on May 1, 1938. During the Democratic primary campaign in one-party Texas, he stressed the Ten Commandments, the virtues of his own Hillbilly Flour, and the need for old-age pensions, tax cuts, and industrialization. While posing as a hillbilly, he acted under the professional direction of public-relations men. Accompanied by his band, the Hillbilly Boys, and the Bible, he attracted huge audiences, especially in rural areas. In the primary he smashed the other candidates and eliminated the usual necessity of a runoff. He had pledged to block any sales tax, abolish capital punishment, liquidate the poll tax (which he had not paid), and raise old-age pensions; but he reneged on all these promises. He unveiled a tax plan, secretly written by manufacturing lobbyists, that amounted to a multiple sales tax, but the legislature voted it down.

Solons laughed at the vaudevillian atmosphere of the O'Daniel administration, but most of his legislative opponents were defeated in their bids for reelection. O'Daniel won again in 1940, after divulging that he had wired President Franklin Roosevelt that he had confidential information about a fifth column in Texas. No one ever found the traitors. The governor and several Texas business leaders began attacking organized labor in the spring of 1941, but most of the provisions of the ensuing O'Daniel Anti-Violence Act were eventually discarded by the courts. O'Daniel began packing the University of Texas Board of Regents with people who wanted to limit academic freedom and ferret out alleged subversion on campus. These regents, along with those selected by his successor, Coke Stevenson, eventually fired University of Texas president Homer Rainey and provoked a nine-year censorship of UT by the American Association of University Professors. As governor, O'Daniel enjoyed little success in putting across his agenda. He was unable to engage in normal political deal-making with legislators, vetoed bills that he probably did not understand, and was overridden in twelve out of fifty-seven vetoes—a record. But he was able largely to counter his ignorance, his isolation, and his political handicaps with masterful radio showmanship.

O'Daniel ran for the Senate in a special election in 1941. He edged his leading opponent, New Deal congressman Lyndon Johnson, in a flurry of controversial late returns. After taking office in August, O'Daniel introduced a number of antilabor bills, all of which were defeated overwhelmingly. In running for reelection the next year, he faced former governors James Allred and Dan Moody. He charged that there was a conspiracy among Moody, Allred, the professional politicians, the politically controlled newspapers, and the "communistic labor leader racketeers" to smear and defeat him. Some prominent conservatives and conservative newspapers, embarrassed by O'Daniel, endorsed New Dealer Allred in the runoff. But posturing as a supporter of President Roosevelt, O'Daniel hung on to enough rural and elderly voters to win barely. During the war years he and Senator Tom Connally supported the Republican–Southern Democratic coalition more often (seventy-four votes) than any other Southern duo in the Senate. O'Daniel was the leading campaigner for the Texas Regulars, a third-party effort to siphon off enough Democratic votes in Texas in 1944 to deny Roosevelt a fourth term. The president carried Texas and was reelected despite O'Daniel's inflammatory "educational" broadcasts. O'Daniel was shunned and ineffective in the Senate. With public opinion polls giving him only 7 percent support in 1948, he announced that he would not run again since there was only slight hope of saving America from the communists.

He bought a ranch near Fort Worth, invested in Dallas real estate, and founded an insurance company. He attempted comebacks in the Democratic gubernatorial primaries of 1956 and 1958; in the campaigns he ranted about blood running in the streets because of the "Communist-inspired" Supreme Court decision desegregating the nation's schools. He failed to make the runoff on both occasions, although in 1956 he carried sixty-six counties with almost 350,000 votes. His contribution to music—paradoxically the most positive aspect of his career—was the Light Crust Doughboys and their own musical progeny.

BIBLIOGRAPHY: *Current Biography*, 1947. Fort Worth *Star–Telegram*, May 12, 1969. Frank Goodwyn, *Lone Star Land* (New York: Knopf, 1955). George N. Green, *The Establishment in Texas Politics* (Westport, Connecticut: Greenwood, 1979). Seth Shepard McKay, *W. Lee O'Daniel and Texas Politics, 1938–1942* (Lubbock: Texas Tech Press, 1944). Homer P. Rainey, *The Tower and the Dome: A Free University Versus Political Control* (Boulder, Colorado: Pruett, 1971).   *George N. Green*

Opera. Although opera had been previously heard in Texas, the first opera troupe did not come to the state until 1856, when the German Opera Company visited Galveston and performed opera acts in German at the Lone Star Hall. During this time, most of the opera performance in Texas took place in the southern part of the state; Galveston, Brownsville and Houston all saw touring opera companies perform. In 1871 the first real opera house, called the Tremont, was erected on Galveston Island, and by the end of the nineteenth century, Austin, Dallas, Fort Worth, and San Antonio all had established opera houses as well. These houses offered a variety of musical and theatrical venues including opera.

By the last quarter of the nineteenth century, North and Central Texas cities began to see more opera performances. The Dallas Opera House opened on October 15, 1883, on St. Paul and Main Streets with a production of Gilbert and Sullivan's *Iolanthe*. Although Dallas audiences heard *Martha* and *Il Trovatore* in 1875 at Field's Theater, the Dallas Opera House served as the primary performance venue for touring opera companies, musicians, and acting troupes in the Dallas area. Fort Worth audiences heard their first real opera in 1877, when the Tagliapietra Company staged Verdi's *Il Trovatore* and *La Favorita* at Evans Hall, located on the second floor of Evans' General Store. Additionally, the Opera House in San Antonio and three opera houses in Austin began to offer opera and theater performances for local audiences on a regular basis.

Itinerant opera performance continued to flourish during the last quarter of the nineteenth century and into the twentieth century. Helped by the railroad industry, touring opera companies, some with national reputations, began making their way to cities across Texas. Audiences in Dallas, Houston, San Antonio, Galveston, and Austin were hearing opera performances by reputable companies, such as the Faust Opera Company, the Carleton Opera Company, and Emma Abbott's troupe. In November 1901 the Metropolitan Opera Company debuted in Houston with a performance of Wagner's *Lohengrin*. Subsequently, Texas opera audiences also saw performances by the touring companies, including the Boston Opera Company, the Henry W. Savage English Opera Company, the Chicago Opera, and the NBC Opera Theatre.

Eventually, Texas opera aficionados realized that the state could support its own opera productions and opera companies. In 1945 San Antonio founded the first resident opera company in Texas. Max Reiter, who had established the San Antonio Symphony six years earlier, extended the symphony season to include a springtime opera festival. The first opera produced was *La Bohème,* starring Nino Martini and Grace Moore. The San Antonio Symphony continued to produce an annual opera season that included four different productions, one performance each given over two consecutive weekends. In these productions, nationally known talent filled leading roles and local talent filled the chorus.

Victor Alessandro became San Antonio's new music director after Reiter's death in 1950, and Peter Wolf of Dallas designed most of the sets for the company. Opera in San Antonio was performed in the San Antonio Municipal Auditorium, which seated nearly 6,000 people. The annual opera festival in San Antonio continued until 1983, when the program was terminated. The San Antonio Symphony continued to present concert versions of operas.

In 1997 Mark A. Richter, tenor and local businessman, founded Lyric Opera of San Antonio. The company, originally known as the Pocket Opera of San Antonio, opened its first season with Mozart's *The Impressario* in 1998. This production was performed at the San Pedro Playhouse and starred local artists. *Trouble in Tahiti* concluded the first season of San Antonio Pocket Opera. In its third season, the company began seeking national and local talent for its productions. The company was renamed Lyric Opera of San Antonio to reflect these changes, and the Lyric Studio, Lyric Opera's apprentice program, began. The fourth season included Puccini's *Madama Butterfly,* the company's first production sung in Italian with English subtitles. Lyric Opera's budget has grown to accommodate these changes, too. The $5,000 budget of the first season grew to almost $90,000 in the sixth season.

Fort Worth followed San Antonio, with its first production of resident opera in 1946. Founded by three local women, the Fort Worth Civic Opera Association opened on November 25 with a production of *La Traviata.* This company is the longest continually operating company in the state. Local opera productions prior to the formation

of the civic opera association included Gounod's *Faust* and Carl Venth's *Fair Betty* in 1917. Fort Worth audiences also attended operas performed by Texas Women's College in the 1910s and 1920s.

Rudolf Kruger directed the Fort Worth opera company from 1955 to 1982. Under his direction four operas were given each season, with two performances of each work. During Kruger's tenure the company was associated with such singers as Lily Pons, Placido Domingo, and Beverly Sills. Productions were performed in English, with the exception of *Lucia* with Lily Pons (1962), until the late 1960s, when more works were sung in the original languages. The company has striven to provide opportunity for local talent to perform, using professionals only in leading roles. Fort Worth Opera and the Opera Guild of Fort Worth continue this practice of community outreach with the Children's Opera Tour and the Marguerite McCammon Voice Competition respectively.

The third resident opera company in Texas, the Houston Grand Opera Association, was founded in 1955 and opened with *Salome* by Richard Strauss in January 1956. Walter Herbert was the company's first general director and served in that post until 1972. Houston Grand Opera has always seemed to provide audiences with unconventional repertoire and currently is one of the premiere opera houses in the world.

Following Houston, Dallas had its own resident opera company, the Dallas Civic Opera, by March 1957. Lawrence Kelly, formerly with the Chicago Lyric, was asked to be the general manager; Nicola Rescigno, artistic director for the Chicago Lyric, was asked to be musical director; Franco Zeffirelli was chosen to be set designer and stage director; and Jean Rosenthal became production manager. Maria Callas opened the opera's first season with a concert on November 21, 1957. Even though this famous temperamental diva was associated with the opening season, the company's first production, Rossini's *L'Italiana in Algeri,* starring Giulietta Simionato, was not a complete success. The skepticism of Dallas audiences waned, however, and Dallas Civic Opera became known as one of the top opera houses in the country. The company currently presents as many as six operas each season, with four performances each.

Many world and American debuts have occurred at Dallas Civic Opera. The company has produced over 100 different operas including the world premiere of Argento's *The Aspern Papers* in 1988 and the American premieres of Handel's *Alcina,* in 1960, Vivaldi's *Orlando furioso* (1980), and Monteverdi's *L'incoronazione di Poppea* (1963). Also, many singers have made their American debuts in Dallas as well. These include Joan Sutherland in *Alcina,* Luigi Alva, Teresa Berganza, Montserrat Caballe, Denise Duval, Placido Domingo, Gwyneth Jones, Magda Olivero, and Jon Vickers.

Although the Austin Civic Opera Company was in commission from 1927 to 1931, Austin's first resident opera company did not appear until 1986. The Austin Lyric Opera was founded by Walter Ducloux, musical director, and Joseph McClain, stage director, in 1986. The company's first production was Mozart's *Die Zauberflöte*

(1987). The company has generally performed three operas each season, at the Performing Arts Center at the University of Texas. The Austin Lyric uses both local and professional talent in its productions. In 1992 the company performed the American premiere of Rossini's *La pietra del paragone*.

Amarillo Opera, founded in 1988 by Mila Gibson, was the next professional opera company to be formed in the state. The company, which specializes in American folk opera, performs four or five operas annually. Amarillo Opera's season is split into two two-week sessions, and performances are generally held at the Amarillo Civic Center, which seats 2,300. The company utilizes both professional singers and local talent in its productions. Amarillo Opera has staged two premieres of operas by Gene Erwin Murray—*Whirligig* on August 22, 1990, and *Dear Doctor* on October 16, 1991.

El Paso Opera began as Opera à la Carte in 1992. Opera à la Carte performed opera excerpts for El Paso audiences. In 1993 the name was changed to the Opera Company, and in January 1994 the company produced its first complete opera. Puccini's *Tosca* was well received by El Paso audiences. In the 1997–98 season the El Paso Opera included Spanish-language supertitles in its productions of Mozart's *Don Giovanni* and Puccini's *La Bohème*. Both professional and local talent performs with the company.

Texas opera audiences can enjoy opera performances in many cities across the state. The Waco Lyric, the Abilene Opera Association, the Denton Light Opera Company, the Gilbert and Sullivan Society of Austin, and the Ebony Opera of Houston are some of the other opera companies that offer opera productions each year. In addition, numerous colleges and universities across the state present full-scale opera productions each year.

BIBLIOGRAPHY: Dallas Opera history (http://www.dallasopera.org/permapag/history.htm), accessed March 24, 2003. Ronald L. Davis, *A History of Opera in the American West* (Englewood Cliffs, New Jersey: Prentice Hall, 1965). Ronald L. Davis, "Stars over Texas," *Opera News*, November 14, 1964. Fort Worth *Star–Telegram*, November 12, 1964. Lota M. Spell, *Music in Texas* (Austin, 1936; rpt., New York: AMS, 1973). San Antonio Lyric Opera homepage (http://www.lyricoperasa.com), accessed March 24, 2003. *Christina H. Wilson*

Orbison, Roy Kelton. Rock-and-roll singer and songwriter; b. Vernon, Texas, April, 23, 1936; d. Hendersonville, Tennessee, December 6, 1988; son of Orbie Lee and Nadine Orbison. He grew up in Wink, a small West Texas oil town, where his father taught him to play the guitar at age six. Orbison dedicated himself to music as a young man, performing at school and on the radio. While attending Wink High School he formed a country music group called the Wink Westerners, which featured Orbison as lead singer and guitar player.

Only later, while attending North Texas State College—where he met fellow student and musician Pat Boone—did Orbison transform the Wink Westerners into his first rock-and-roll band, the Teen Kings. After two years of college he dropped out. The group played throughout West Texas and

Roy Orbison in a scene from the 1967 western comedy movie *The Fastest Guitar Alive* (*Texas Rhythm, Texas Rhyme: A Pictorial History of Texas Music*, Austin: Texas Monthly Press, 1984). Courtesy Larry Willoughby.

on a number of television shows. They also recorded "Ooby Dooby," which brought him to the attention of the Sun record label in Memphis. Orbison rerecorded the song for Sun, and in 1956 it became his first chart hit. It was made in the pioneering rock-and-roll style known as rockabilly—a frantic mixture of country music and rhythm-and-blues developed by Elvis Presley and Sun label owner Sam Phillips. Unlike Carl Perkins, Johnny Cash, and Jerry Lee Lewis, up-and-coming music stars who were also recording rockabilly on the Sun label, Orbison had little chart success. The Teen Kings dissolved, and Orbison left Sun.

Most of his early success was as a songwriter. "Claudette," a song written by Orbison and named after his first wife, was a hit in 1958 for the country and rockabilly duo the Everly Brothers. In 1959 Orbison joined the small Monument label in Nashville, which resulted in a string of international hit records from 1960 to 1966, including such classic rock-and-roll melodramas as "Only the Lonely" (1960), "Blue Angel" (1960), "Running Scared" (1961), "Blue Bayou" (1963), "It's Over" (1964), and "Oh, Pretty Woman" (1964). Elvis Presley once referred to Orbison as "the greatest singer in the world." Roy's hits in this period featured his trademark three-octave voice with its soaring, emotional splendor and his lush songwriting with its beautiful melodies, sophisticated studio production, and dark, brooding themes of love, loss, and longing. Wearing his trademark black clothes, slicked back hair, and dark glasses, the short, pale, shy performer with the overpowering voice played his hits around the world. In England in 1963 he headlined a tour that included the Beatles, then on the verge of international popularity.

Orbison's time at the top was brief. Claudette Orbison was killed in a motorcycle accident in 1966, and in 1968 two of his three sons were killed in a fire at his Nashville home. He married his second wife, Barbara, in 1969, and they had two more sons. Orbison underwent open-heart surgery in 1979. Although he continued to tour, this period of personal difficulty also saw his hit recordings dwindle. He experienced a revival of popularity in the late 1970s and 1980s, when such artists as Linda Ronstadt and Van Halen recorded some of his songs and he released new recordings of his classic hits. His 1980 recording of "That Loving You Feeling Again" with Emmylou Harris won a Grammy Award, and in 1987 his recording "In Dreams" was featured in the soundtrack of *Blue Velvet*, a popular movie. That same year Orbison was inducted into the Rock 'n' Roll Hall of Fame with a poignant introduction from Bruce Springsteen, whose monumental hit album of 1975, *Born To Run*, paid lyrical and stylistic homage to Orbison.

In 1988, the year of his death, Orbison's renewed popularity was confirmed in a critically acclaimed television special featuring his music performed by him and his musical heirs. He also released an album in 1988, *The Traveling Wilburys, Volume One*, featuring Orbison and his friends Bob Dylan, George Harrison of the Beatles, Tom Petty, and Jeff Lynne of the Electric Light Orchestra. The record was in the top ten when he died of a heart attack at his mother's home.

BIBLIOGRAPHY: Ellis Amburn, *Dark Star: The Roy Orbison Story* (New York: Carol, 1990). Alan Clayson, *Only the Lonely: Roy Orbison's Life and Legacy* (New York: St. Martin's Press, 1989). Jim Miller, ed., *The Rolling Stone Illustrated History of Rock & Roll*, revised and updated (New York: Random House / Rolling Stone Press, 1980). New York *Times*, December 8, 1988.

George B. Ward

Oscar, Gussie. Pianist, conductor, and controversial general manager of the Waco Auditorium; b. Calvert, Texas, 1875; d. Waco, February 7, 1950 (buried in Hebrew Rest Cemetery, Waco); daughter of Rudolph and Ella Oscar, the owners of Casimir's Opera House and the Grand Hotel. She was the youngest of three children. Although she was Jewish, she was educated in an Austin convent school. She first supported herself by playing the piano at weddings, churches, dances, and theaters, and toured with plays and orchestras. She always lived unconventionally, traveling unchaperoned, living in hotels instead of private homes, and socializing with entertainers and performers. She moved to Waco in 1905 and played in the orchestra for vaudeville and operettas at the Majestic Theater and the Waco Auditorium.

Waco had become a resort known for its artesian waters, and Gussie Oscar eventually settled permanently into the honeymoon suite of one of its fine new hotels, the Raleigh. By 1911 she was the conductor of an all-woman orchestra at the Majestic, and in 1913 she was May Irwin's accompanist on a tour of the Western states and Canada. Later she was one of few women elected to membership in the International Alliance of Theatrical Employees. After becoming manager of the Waco Auditorium in 1915 she brought nationally known performers to Waco, including Anna Pavlova, John Philip Sousa, Jascha Heifetz, Harry Houdini, Will Rogers, and the Marx Brothers.

She became controversial during the 1920s when, for financial reasons, she defied Waco's Sunday closing law and censorship board to schedule increasingly racy acts on Sundays. Arrests, including hers, and forced closings led to a boycott of Waco by touring companies and eventually to the closing of the auditorium in 1928. Nevertheless, Oscar booked acts at the Cotton Palace Coliseum and Waco Hall until her death.

BIBLIOGRAPHY: Patricia Ward Wallace, *A Spirit So Rare: A History of the Women of Waco* (Austin: Nortex, 1984).

Patricia Ward Wallace

Owens, Tex. Country music singer and songwriter; b. Doie Hensley Owens, Killeen, Texas, June 15, 1892; d. New Baden, Texas, September 9, 1962; son of Curcley Sly and Susan (Frances) Owens. He came from a large and musically talented family; one of his ten sisters, Ruby Agnes, also went on to country music fame as Texas Ruby. While he was still a teenager Owens performed in a traveling outfit, Cowdell's Wagon Show, which played throughout the Texas plains. Tex Owens and his wife, Maude, were married on June 16, 1916.

Owens spent his early years as a cowboy and oilfield worker in Texas. He later held a series of jobs in the Midwest, until his friends urged him to take his musical talents to radio in 1931. For the next ten years he co-hosted the popular "Brush Creek Follies," on KMBC in Kansas City, featuring his group, the Original Texas Rangers, and his two daughters Dolpha (Jane) and Laura Lee (Joy). Laura Lee later married country musician Dickie McBride and sang for many years with Bob Wills and His Texas Playboys. In 1935 Owens penned his biggest hit song, "Cattle Call," which he recorded for Decca Records. The song later became a hit recording for singer Eddie Arnold. Owens also hosted the "Boone County Jamboree" on WLW in Cincinnati and appeared on several other radio shows.

Though Owens went back to the oilfields during World War II, he later returned to entertainment as a movie cowboy. His postwar career was cut short, however, when a horse fell on him and broke his back during the filming of *Red River*, with John Wayne, in 1950.

BIBLIOGRAPHY: *The Illustrated Encyclopedia of Country Music* (New York: Harmony Books, 1977). Vertical Files, Center for American History, University of Texas at Austin.

John Wheat

Owens, William A. Folklorist, author, and professor; b. Pin Hook, Lamar County, Texas, November 2, 1905; d.

Nyack, New York, December 8, 1990; son of Charles and Jessie Ann (Chennault) Owens. His father died within a few days after Owens's birth, and the boy spent his early years helping his mother and his older brothers scratch a living from the worn-out red soil of Lamar County.

His education was spotty in his early years, for he was never able to go to school for more than a few months at a time, and, as he tells in his first volume of autobiography, *This Stubborn Soil* (1966), the school at Pin Hook was only open about three months a year. Owens learned to read and write, and when he met a poorly educated crosstie cutter who owned twenty-five books that he was willing to lend, young Bill read all the tiehacker's books and resolved to devote his life to reading and study.

At the age of fifteen he moved to Dallas to live with an aunt and work, on rollerskates, filling catalog orders at Sears and Roebuck's huge mail-order warehouse. Later, he found a job washing dishes for a Catholic school and saved enough money to attempt study at East Texas State Normal College in Commerce. Despite his lack of education, he made a high score on the entrance exam and was allowed into the college's high school program in 1920. These early years are detailed in *This Stubborn Soil*. The filmmaker James Lipscomb turned some of the early material from *This Stubborn Soil* into a PBS television program entitled *Frontier Boy*.

In the second volume, *A Season of Weathering* (1973), Owens tells of his years teaching school at Pin Hook and other East Texas schools beginning in 1928, working in the Kress store in Paris, taking courses at Paris Junior College, and ending up at Southern Methodist University in Dallas, where he took his bachelor's and master's degrees in 1932 and 1933 respectively. His master's thesis, published as *Swing and Turn: Texas Play Party Games* (1936), grew from all the years Owens had spent hearing and singing the old English and Scottish ballads that were a part of his East Texas heritage. "Play parties" were the dances of religious fundamentalists who forbade dancing to music unless it was without fiddles, guitars, and other instruments..

As Owens tells in his third volume of autobiography, *Tell Me a Story, Sing Me a Song* (1983), he spent much of the thirties collecting folksongs, teaching at Texas A&M, and completing his Ph.D. at the University of Iowa. Working partly on his own and partly for the Extension Division of the University of Texas, he recorded songs from East Texas to the Cajun Country of the Texas Coast to the Mexican border, using a second –hand Vibromaster recorder. The records were played with bamboo or cactus needles. Owens later worked closely with J. Frank Dobie, Walter Prescott Webb, and Roy Bedichek. Bedichek was the director of the Extension Service's Interscholastic League and Owens's employer for part of his time as a collector of songs. Owens's close relationship with "the old three" led to his publishing *Three Friends* (1969), a collection of letters that Dobie, Bedichek, and Webb wrote to one another. It also includes a running commentary by Owens on his relationship with the three men. A later book that grew from his folklore-collecting days was *Tales from the Derrick Floor: A People's History of the Oil Industry* (1970),

which he edited with Mody C. Boatright, Dobie's successor as secretary–editor of the Texas Folklore Society.

As Owens notes in *Tell Me a Story, Sing Me a Song*, he entered the University of Iowa in 1937 after he failed the entrance examination at the University of Texas. Encouraged by Professor Edwin Ford Piper, he took his folklore collection to Iowa and turned it into his dissertation, later published as *Texas Folksongs* (1950), a book still in print. He received his Ph.D. from the University of Iowa in 1941, and he claims that one of the influences on his writing there was the painter Grant Wood. Owens drove for Wood and learned from him something about cleanness and clarity of style.

In 1942 he joined the army as a buck private and was assigned to the intelligence branch. One of his postings was to Tulsa, Oklahoma, where because of the Tulsa race riots of 1921 the government feared that blacks might revolt against the United States. Owens's job was attend black churches in his capacity as a folklorist in order to take the temperature of African Americans about America's war effort. Needless to say, he found no disloyalty among blacks, and from his Oklahoma experience came his best novel, *Walking on Borrowed Land* (1954), the story of a black teacher from Mississippi who was hired to be principal of a segregated school in the "Little Dixie" section of Oklahoma. This book won the Texas Institute of Letters 1954 prize for best first novel by a Texas writer.

Owens served in the Philippines during the war and wrote of his experiences there in his fourth volume of autobiography, *Eye Deep in Hell* (1989). He was awarded the Legion of Merit. He joined the faculty of Columbia University in 1947 and remained there until his retirement in 1974. He was professor of English and dean of the summer session there for many years.

In addition to his collections of folklore and his four volumes of autobiography, Owens wrote the novels *Fever in the Earth* (1958), set at the Spindletop strike in 1901; *Walking on Borrowed Land* (1954); and the novelette *Look to the River* (1963). In 1985 he and Lyman Grant edited the letters of Roy Bedichek, Owens's old boss at the UT Extended Education Division and one of the Texans he most admired. Owens also wrote *Slave Mutiny: The Revolt of the Schooner Amistad* (1953), which provided much of the material for a Steven Spielberg film, *Amistad* (1997). In 1975 he wrote a family history, *A Fair and Happy Land*.

Owens married Ann Seaton Wood on December 23, 1946, and had two children—David, director of business systems for a large accounting firm, and Jessie Ann, dean of arts and sciences at Brandeis University. Jessie Ann Owens, a musicologist, provided the notations for her father's collections of songs and ballads. Owens lived the last years of his life in Nyack, New York.

BIBLIOGRAPHY: Bert Almon, "William Owens," *This Stubborn Self: Texas Autobiographies* (Fort Worth: TCU Press, 2002). James W. Lee, ed., *William A. Owens: A Symposium* (Denton: Trilobite Press, 1981). William A. Owens Papers, Cushing Memorial Library, Texas A&M University, College Station. William T. Pilkington, *William A. Owens* (Austin: Steck–Vaughn, 1968). *James Ward Lee*

P

Page, Hot Lips. Jazz trumpeter, singer, and bandleader; b. Oran Thaddeus Page, Dallas, January 27, 1908; d. New York City, November 5, 1954; son of Greene and Maggie (Beal) Page. Page's mother, a schoolteacher and musician, taught him the basics of music when he was a child. By the age of twelve he could play the clarinet, saxophone, and trumpet. He joined a local youth band, led by drummer Lux Alexander, that played at local venues around Dallas. Page attended Corsicana High School and Texas College (in Tyler), and worked for a time in the oilfields.

He began his professional touring career when he joined Ma Rainey's band in the 1920s. After leaving that group he toured with Walter Page's Blue Devils from 1928 to 1931. During the early 1930s he toured with Bennie Moten's band. In 1936 he joined Count Basie's band for a short stint and subsequently played with Artie Shaw. Page formed his own big bands in the late 1930s and early 1940s, often playing in New York, Chicago, Boston, and other cities. Between 1938 and 1954 he cut several tracks, including the 1938 record "Skull Duggery" on the Bluebird label. He recorded "Pagin' Mr. Page" in 1944 and "St. James Infirmary" in 1947. He recorded with numerous bands during his career, including those of Artie Shaw, Bennie Moten, and Eddie Condon.

In addition to recording, Page appeared on numerous radio and television shows in the 1940s and 1950s. In 1948 he performed on NBC's "Three Flames Show." He was featured on the CBS show "Adventures in Jazz" in 1949, and in 1951 he made an appearance with Pearl Bailey on the "Ed Sullivan Show." Page continued to be musically active in the late 1940s and early 1950s. He led his own bands on extensive tours and played in various venues in Europe, including the 1949 Paris Jazz Festival. From 1952 until his health began to deteriorate in 1953, he worked various jazz shows around the United States.

In October 1954 he suffered a heart attack. Seven days later he died of complications from pneumonia. He is buried in Dallas Cemetery. Page was married twice. He had one child with his first wife, Myrtle, and two children with his second wife, Elizabeth.

BIBLIOGRAPHY: John Chilton, *Who's Who of Jazz: Storyville to Swing Street* (New York: Chilton, 1972). Leonard Feather, ed., *The Encyclopedia of Jazz* (New York: Horizon Press, 1955). Sheldon Harris, *Blues Who's Who* (New Rochelle, New York: Arlington House, 1979). H. Wiley Hitchcock and Stanley Sadie, eds., *The New Grove Dictionary of American Music* (New York: MacMillan, 1986). Barry Kernfeld, ed., *The New Grove Dictionary of Jazz* (New York: MacMillan, 1988). Eileen Southern, *Biographical Dictionary of Afro-American and African Musicians* (Westport Connecticut: Greenwood Press, 1982).

James Head

Panther Hall. A live-music performance hall at the intersection of East Lancaster and Collard in Fort Worth; opened in 1961 by Bill and Corky Kuykendall as a bowling stadium. The 32,000-square-foot hall was soon converted from bowling to rock-and-roll, and then from rock-and-roll to country. *Country Music Reporter* photographer Wayne Beckham recalled, "It started off as rock 'n' roll, and even ol' Elvis played there, but then they decided to go country because they couldn't draw a big enough crowd."

Panther Hall gained statewide fame and exposure with a 6 P.M. Saturday television broadcast, "Cowtown Jamboree," which came before the live concert. The move to country music not only brought additional music fans to the hall at night, but also a large television audience on Saturday evenings. Channel 11, KTVT, an independent station at that time, aired "Cowtown Jamboree" as part of its Saturday evening lineup, which included other popular syndicated country shows such as the Wilburn Brothers, Charlie Louvin, and Porter Wagoner.

The Jerry Lee Lewis and Charley Pride show drew a crowd of 3,000 people. Other famous performers who played to the enormous dance floor at Panther Hall included Bob Wills, Loretta Lynn, Buck Owens, George Jones, Ray Price, Tanya Tucker, Johnny Rodriguez, Porter Wagoner, Dolly Parton, Johnny Cash, Lefty Frizzell, and even the Grateful Dead. Tanya Tucker made her first appearance there at the age of fourteen.

In Willie Nelson's autobiography (with Bud Shrake), *Willie: An Autobiography*, many colorful experiences of Willie's life and music take place at Panther Hall. In 1966 Willie recorded a live album entitled *Live Country Music Concert at Panther Hall* on RCA. The legendary and now rare album includes live versions of such classic hits as "My Own Peculiar Way," "Night Life," "Mr. Record Man," and "I Never Cared for You." Despite hosting many country legends, Panther Hall closed in 1973.

BIBLIOGRAPHY: Fort Worth *Star–Telegram*, December 20, 1999; February 11, 2001. "Willie Nelson Live at Panther Hall," *Rockzillaworld* (http://www.rockzilla.net/panther. html), accessed December 9, 2002.*Jahue E. Anderson*

Patek, Joe. Czech bandleader; b. Shiner, Texas, September 14, 1907; d. Victoria, Texas, October 24, 1987; youngest of six sons of John and Veronica Patek. His band, one of the best-known Texas Czech polka bands, had its origins with John Patek in the 1920s. When he was a boy in Czechoslovakia, John became an accomplished musician. In 1889, at the age of twenty, he immigrated to America and played in community bands. In 1920 he formed the Patek Band of Shiner. As the years went by, his sons took music lessons and joined the band.

In the early 1940s Joe took over the band, which he later renamed the Joe Patek Orchestra. It first recorded in San Antonio for the Decca label in 1937. The Pateks were unhappy with the results because Joe claimed the recording

In the 1930s famed trumpeter "Hot Lips" Page played with Bennie Moten, Count Basie, and Artie Shaw. Duncan Scheidt Collection.

director had rushed the band. After World War II the Patek Orchestra found success by recording for Martin, an independent San Antonio label. The best-known piece on the Martin label was "The Shiner Song," a newer version of an old Czech ballad, "Farewell to Prague." "The Shiner Song" became the unofficial Texas-Czech anthem. The band also recorded "Krasna Amerika" ("Beautiful America") and "Corrido Rock," which became popular in the Mexican-American community. In 1995 "The Shiner Song" received special recognition from the Texas Polka Music Association as an "all time favorite song." This was only the second time such an award had ever been given by the TPMA. From the time Joe Patek took over the band, it recorded more than twenty-four 78-RPMs, more than twenty-four 45-RPMs, and several tapes and LPs. One of the Pateks' most successful records was the "Beer Barrel Polka," which sold more than a million copies.

The success of his recordings helped make Patek one of the most popular Czech polka bandleaders in Texas. The band played in rural towns throughout Texas and in larger cities, such as San Antonio, Corpus Christi, Houston, Dallas, Fort Worth, and San Angelo, or wherever a dance or social function was held. Starting in the 1950s, the Joe Patek Orchestra was booked every weekend a year or more in advance. Their increasing popularity can be measured by the way the band members traveled. In the early years under Joe, they used two cars to carry all members and instruments. Then, in the mid-1940s, the band members rode in the back of a panel truck on long benches. In later years, a station wagon was used to pull a trailer for the band instruments. The trailer, decorated with Shiner Beer emblems, became a well-known symbol of the band on Texas highways.

The Patek Orchestra had its own hour-long radio show on KCTI, Gonzales, starting in the mid-1940s. The broadcast was done live every Sunday afternoon for several years from Bluecher Park in Shiner. In later years, because of the orchestra's busy schedule and longer trips, the broadcast known as the Patek Hour continued with recorded music until 1985.

Patek is credited for establishing a different style of Texas polka with its harder sound and emphasis on swing. This style, characterized by martial brass band arrangements, differentiated the Pateks and Texas polka from the polka bands in other parts of the United States.

The Joe Patek Orchestra retired after playing its last performance at the Annual Fireman's New Year's Eve Dance on December 31, 1982, at the American Legion Hall in Shiner. Hundreds of people packed the hall to hear this final performance. The last song the orchestra played was "The Shiner Song."

Joe Patek married Emily Novosad on May 21, 1934. They were married until Emily passed away in the early 1980s. They had seven children. Patek is buried in the Catholic cemetery in Shiner. He owned and operated a grocery store and meat processing plant in Shiner, both of which were still in business in 2003. The TPMA honored him posthumously in 1991 with its Lifetime Achievement Award for "development of a unique sound in Texas polka music." Joe Patek's Orchestra can be heard on the Arhoolie Records compilation CD *Texas Czech Bohemian–Moravian Bands, Historic Recordings 1929–1959*.

BIBLIOGRAPHY: "The Pateks—A Passion for Polka," *Texas Polka News*, May 2002. Mark Rubin, "Texas-Czech Bohemian and Moravian Bands: Historic Recordings 1929–1959," *Music City Texas* 55 (March 1994). Chris Strachwitz, notes to *Czech–Bohemian Bands: Early Recordings 1928–1953* (El Cerrito, California: Arhoolie Records, 1983). Victoria *Advocate*, October 15, 1989.

David DeKunder

Payne, Leon Roger. Country and western singer and composer; b. Alba, Texas, June 15, 1917; d. San Antonio, September 11, 1969 (buried in Sunset Memorial Park, San Antonio); son of Jesse and Gertrude (Murdock) Payne. He was blind in one eye at birth and lost the sight of the other in a childhood accident. He attended the Texas School for the Blind from May 17, 1922, until his graduation, on May 31, 1935.

Payne began his singing and composing career at a radio station in Palestine, Texas. He played the guitar and several other stringed instruments, and he sang, according to some critics, "in the soft, smooth style of Eddie Arnold." In 1948 his composition "Lifetime to Regret" established his reputation as a composer, and in 1949 he composed "I Love You Because" (a song inspired by his wife), which became a top hit and a standard in country and western music. His "You've Still Got a Place in My Heart" was first recorded in 1951, but its greatest success came in the 1960s, when Dean Martin and many others recorded it. Payne made many appearances on both the "Louisiana Hayride" in Shreveport and the "Grand Ole Opry" in Nashville. Other well-known singers who recorded Payne's songs were Elvis Presley, Glen Campbell, Don Gibson, Jim Reeves, and George Jones. Jones recorded an album of Payne's songs in 1971.

On August 16, 1948, Payne married Myrtie Velma Courmier, whom he met at the Texas School for the Blind. They had two children and reared two other children born to Velma in a previous marriage.

BIBLIOGRAPHY: Bill C. Malone, *Country Music U.S.A.* (Austin: University of Texas Press, 1968). Vertical Files, Center for American History, University of Texas at Austin.

Eldon S. Branda

Penn, William Evander. Baptist evangelist and hymn writer; b. Rutherford County, Tennessee, August 11, 1832; d. Eureka Springs, Arkansas, April 29, 1895 (buried in Eureka Springs Cemetery); son of George Douglas and Telitha (Patterson) Penn. He began his education at age ten and joined the Beachgrove Baptist Church on October 3, 1847. He attended one term each at the Male Academy, Trenton, Tennessee, and Union University, Murfreesboro, Tennessee. He read law at the firm of Williams and Wright and was admitted to the bar. Penn opened his law office in Lexington, Tennessee, about 1852. He married Corrilla Frances Sayle on April 30, 1856. They adopted two girls and a boy. One of the girls died as a child. Captain Penn was assigned to Andrew N. Wilson's regiment, Sixteenth Tennessee Cavalry, in the Confederate Army, and was captured on February 18, 1864, in Hardeman County, Tennessee. He was in a group that was exchanged for captured Union soldiers on April 7, 1865, after which he was assigned to a regiment and promoted to major. After the Confederate surrender, Penn signed his parole at Shreveport, Louisiana, on June 21, 1865.

He and his family moved in January 1866 to Jefferson, Texas, where he opened a law office. The Penns joined the Baptist Church at Jefferson, and later Penn was ordained a deacon. In January 1872 he was elected Sunday school superintendent of Jefferson Church. He attended the Texas Baptist Sunday School and Colportage Convention and was elected president in 1873 and 1874. At a Sunday school institute in July 1875 Rev. James H. Stribling, pastor at the Baptist church at Tyler, Texas, asked Penn to preach a revival there. He was later licensed to preach by the Baptist church at Jefferson. On December 4, 1880, at Broadway Baptist Church, Galveston, reverends W. W. Keep, J. M. C. Breaker, C. C. Pope, and W. O. Bailey ordained him.

Penn wrote hymns and published *Harvest Bells*, a hymnal, with J. M. Hunt in 1881. A second edition was published in 1886, and H. M. Lincoln and Penn published a third in 1887. Penn has been called the "Texas Evangelist," but he also led revivals in other states and in Scotland and England. The Penns moved to Eureka Springs, Arkansas, about 1887. Penn's health began to decline in 1892. He wrote the autobiographical part of *The Life and Labors of Major W. E. Penn* in 1892, but the book was not published until 1896, after his death.

BIBLIOGRAPHY: L. R. Elliott, ed., *Centennial Story of Texas Baptists* (Dallas: Baptist General Convention of Texas, 1936).   *Samuel B. Hesler*

Peters–Hacienda Community Hall. In Peters, Austin County, where Texas Anglo settlement started in the 1820s with the founding of Stephen F. Austin's first colony. German immigration to the area began shortly after the arrival of Friedrich Ernst in 1831. Ernst sent letters back to Germany, where his descriptions of the area were printed in newspapers and attracted other Germans to move to Texas. These immigrants established numerous fraternal associations devoted to literature, singing, marksmanship, agriculture, gymnastics, and mutual aid.

In the 1870s the county received its first railroad service when the Gulf, Colorado, and Santa Fe Railway extended its Galveston–Brenham main line through Wallis, Sealy, and Bellville. In the 1880s the same company built a branch line from Sealy to Eagle Lake through southwestern Austin County. Peters, a German community named for Albert Peters, an early resident, is situated on State Highway 36. During the community's early history, it had a post office established in 1883, stores, cotton gins, a church, a hospital, and two schools, Peters School and Hacienda School. These places no longer exist, and the post office was discontinued in the mid-1940s.

Peters Hall was built for the Peters–Hacienda Schuetzenverein (Shooting Club), an association organized in 1897. The Schuetzenverein was a traditional sportsman's club that German immigrants brought to Texas. Such societies date back to medieval Europe, where contests such as jousting and archery were held to keep everyone's skills honed, should the need for combat arise. Later these contests became more of a social activity, with shooting competitions, food, and, other activities, followed by a dance at night. In 1943 the hall's name was changed to Austin County Gun Club. In 1995 the hall was renamed Peters–Hacienda Community Hall.

The first structure associated with the Schuetzenverein was a dance platform in the Huff family pasture (1898–99), north of Highway 36 and near present Farm Road 331. In 1900 the Seigart family donated a plot of land to the organization at the corner of Peters–San Felipe and Trenckmann roads. At this site members of the organization built an eight-sided frame dance hall. The hall was designed with a center pole to support the shingled hip roof, a spacious floor for dancing, and a cupola to provide ventilation and air circulation in the crowded hall. Glass-paned windows let in light and air, and benches along the walls provided a place to rest or to watch the dancers.

Since its original construction, many changes have been made to the hall. In 1910 a stage with a roll-up curtain was built. Before this, bands had performed around the center pole. After the stage was constructed, the center pole was boxed in. In 1940 Houston Lighting and Power brought electricity to the area, making it possible to use an electric pump to provide water for inside restrooms. In 1958 a bar was built onto the hall, and in 1965 a butane system for heating was installed. In 1975 a kitchen, including a stove, refrigerator, and water heater, was added. In June 1977, three bays of the hall were enlarged by eighteen feet, providing space for tables and chairs and leaving the original dance floor open. In March 2001, a storm caused the top of the tree between the food booth and bar to fall onto the roof, which has since been repaired. The hall remains without air-conditioning.

Although Peters Hall was built for shooting competitions, dancing eventually became its main use. Dancing was an important social event for German residents, and often entire families would attend. In the early 1900s, ladies used swatches of their new calico dresses as tickets. At these early dances only men paid admission, but later both dancers and spectators were charged. Dances soon became a regular event held at the hall on the second Saturday of each month. One type of dance was the masquerade dance, at which prizes were awarded in such categories as most beautiful, most comical, and best couple. Also popular were the Christmas dances, in which Santa would make an appearance, and New Year's Eve dances. During the 1970s, locals organized a dance club, in which members paid a yearly rate and could attend any or all dances during the year. Bands that played for these dances included the Kreneks, Gaylen Ackley, the Countrymen, and the Sounds of Country. Dances were also held for the younger people of the community with music provided by the Emotions and Texas Pride.

An early event held at the hall was the May Fest, which included a parade, crowning of a king and queen, a barbecue, and dance. Later, an annual barbecue and dance were held on the second Sunday in July. This major fund-raiser was moved to Mother's Day in 1963 and featured such bands as the Country Playboys and Jimmy Heap and the Melody Masters. Today this annual celebration, the largest fund-raiser for the organization, consists of a raffle, cake-walk, auction, and barbecue dinner. Music is provided outside during the afternoon, and after the auction a free dance is held inside the hall. Today the hall survives on the money it receives from hall rentals and from its three major fund-raisers—the Sweethearts chili cook-off in February, the Mother's Day celebration in May, and Funday Sunday in September.

BIBLIOGRAPHY: Austin County Historical Commission, *Dance Halls of Austin County* (1993), Geronimo Treviño III, *Dance Halls and Last Calls: A History of Texas Country Music* (Plano: Republic of Texas Press, 2002).

Alicia Leschper

Petty, Norman. Record producer and piano player; b. Clovis, New Mexico, May 25, 1927; d. Lubbock, August 15, 1984 (buried in Clovis). Petty began playing piano when he was five and had a fifteen-minute show on KICA radio while he was still in Clovis High School. He organized his first group, the Torchy Swingsters, as a teenager. To improve their performance, he recorded their shows for play-back practice, thus beginning his interest in recording. In 1946, after his service in the United States Air Force, he went to work as staff announcer for KICA. He married his high school sweetheart, Violet Ann Brady, in 1948.

The same year, he moved across the state line into Texas, where he worked part-time as a recording engineer. He formed the Norman Petty Trio, in which he played organ, his wife played piano, and Jack Vaughn played guitar. Petty moved back to Clovis in 1954 and established a recording studio and a new label known as NorVaJak. The trio soon landed a recording contract with ABC–Paramount Records. Shortly thereafter, *Cashbox* magazine voted the trio the "Most Promising Group of 1954." By 1956 their recording of the Duke Ellington song "Mood Indigo" had sold a half million copies. In 1957 the trio's song "Almost Paradise" hit number eighteen and Petty won his first BMI Writers Award. Another Top Forty hit, "On the Alamo," followed, along with some lesser hits. Petty used the income derived from these songs to improve the studio.

He soon realized that he had the only recording studio in New Mexico and West Texas. Confident in his own technical abilities as both engineer and producer, he went public in 1955. He became one of the first independent producers of rock-and-roll, and one of its most successful. Roy Orbison's Teen Kings were among Petty's first customers. Through a leasing agreement with Roulette Records, the studio's first million-seller was Buddy Knox's "Party Doll," which went all the way to number one in 1957. The most famous of Petty's customers, however, was Buddy Holly, who, along with his band, the Crickets, drove ninety miles west from Lubbock, Texas, to cut a demo on February 25, 1957. Their rocking version of "That'll Be the Day," which rose to number one by September, won them a contract from the New York–based Coral/Brunswick label.

Holly was an innovator, and Petty, who quickly became Holly's manager, encouraged him to experiment with his music. Petty and his wife played on several of Holly's

recordings. In addition, Petty took credit for co-writing some of the group's hits. Whether he actually did co-write all the songs he is credited with has been questioned. However, this was a practice that was common in the music business at the time. In any case, Petty produced forty to fifty of Holly's songs at his studio in eighteen months. Nearly every one of these has since become a million-seller. In the fall of 1958, Holly split from Petty and went to live in New York City. After Holly died (in February 1959), Petty acquired the rights to some of Holly's unreleased tracks. Petty has been criticized for dubbing in parts of these songs and releasing them, but by doing so he managed to make some hit songs from tapes that had been intended only as demos. The Crickets continued recording in Petty's Clovis studio for a short time.

Petty continued to record other groups from the Southwestern United States. His most successful instrumental composition, "Wheels," was recorded by the String-A-Longs. It reached the top ten in 1961 and earned him another BMI Writers Award. Another band, Jimmy Gilmer and the Fireballs, had several Top Forty hits, including the Petty-produced number-one hit, "Sugar Shack," in 1963. In 1973 Petty, who had retained the rights to all items recorded by Buddy Holly, sold them to Paul McCartney, who purchased the entire Holly song catalog.

Petty continued to operate his famed Clovis studio until his death, of leukemia. He was working on a new Holly overdub project when he died. He had no children. Violet Petty died on March 22, 1992.

BIBLIOGRAPHY: Colin Larkin, ed., *The Encyclopedia of Popular Music* (London: MuzeUK, 1998). Patricia Romanowski, Holly George–Warren, and Jon Pareles, eds., *The Rolling Stone Encyclopedia of Rock and Roll* (New York: Rolling Stone Press, 1995).

Matthew Tippens

Phillips, Esther Mae. Jazz vocalist, pianist, organist, and trumpeter, known as Little Esther Phillips; b. Esther Mae Washington, Galveston, December 23, 1935; d. Carson, California, August 7, 1984; daughter of Arthur Jones and Lucille Washington. As a child she moved to California with her mother and grew up in the Watts area of Los Angeles. She was singing with the church choir when she was six and competing in local talent shows by the age of twelve.

Johnny Otis, a Los Angeles bandleader, discovered her when she competed in one of his club's talent contests. Otis signed Esther to a contract when she was fourteen. In 1949 she dropped out of school and joined his touring troupe. Little Esther made several hit recordings while touring with Otis from 1949 through 1952. When "Double Crossing Blues," recorded on the Savoy label in 1949, became a huge hit in 1950, she became the youngest R&B artist ever to reach number one on the national charts. She quickly followed this success with another number-one song, "Cupid's Boogie." Other Phillips songs that made the Top Ten included "Misery," "Deceivin' Blues," and "Wedding Boogie." When Otis's group disbanded in 1952, Little Esther went solo. Over the next few years, she recorded more than thirty sides. Only one, "Ring-A-Ding-Do," hit the charts. It charted at number eight in 1952.

Unfortunately, Little Esther's career was on the skids before she turned twenty because of her addiction to heroin. In 1954 she moved to Houston, where she remained virtually inactive musically until 1962. In 1963 she remodeled a country song, "Release Me," into a number-one rhythm-and-blues hit. She also made a 1965 appearance with the Beatles on a London BBC-TV program. In 1966 she had another hit record with "When a Woman Loves a Man." Her drug addiction, however, limited her activity for most of the 1960s.

But she rebounded in 1969 with recordings for Roulette and Epic, and with appearances at the Monterey Jazz Festival and on the "Johnny Carson Show." In the early 1970s she began to perform and record again for the Kudu label. Her live appearances and recordings helped rejuvenate her career by introducing her to a new generation of listeners. In 1972 Little Esther recorded the "biographical" record of her drug addiction, "Home Is Where the Hatred Is." She also recorded the successful albums *From a Whisper to A Scream* and *Alone Again Naturally*, both in 1972. In 1973 she was nominated for a Grammy Award for "Best R&B Performance by a Female Vocalist."

Although she continued to record and perform throughout the 1970s and early 1980s, she had very little further success. Little Esther died of kidney and liver failure.

BIBLIOGRAPHY: Lawrence Cohen, *Nothing But the Blues: The Music and the Musicians* (New York: Abbeville Press, 1993). Leonard Feather, *The Encyclopedia of Jazz in the Sixties* (New York: Horizon Press, 1966). Leonard Feather and Ira Gitler, eds., *The Encyclopedia of Jazz in the Seventies* (New York: Horizon Press, 1976). Sheldon Harris, *Blues Who's Who* (New Rochelle, New York: Arlington House, 1979). Colin Larkin, ed., *The Guiness Encyclopedia of Popular Music*, Volume 6 (New York: Guiness, 1998). Robert Santelli, *The Big Book of Blues* (New York: Penguin, 1993). Eileen Southern, *Biographical Dictionary of Afro-American and African Musicians* (Westport Connecticut: Greenwood Press, 1982). *James Head*

Phillips, Washington. Gospel musician; b. George Washington Phillips, probably in Freestone County, Texas, January 11, 1880; d. Freestone County, September 20, 1954; son of Tim and Nancy (Cooper) Phillips.

Phillips is known for unique gospel songs that influenced a generation of African-American singers. He is believed to have been a farmer and itinerant preacher before Columbia Records recorded him. His career lasted only from 1927 to 1929, but he managed to become one of the best-selling soloists in that short period. His first 78-rpm record, "Take Your Burden to the Lord," sold more than 8,000 copies in 1928.

Phillips's style comprises his solo tenor and the sounds of a harp-like instrument. Through the years, musicologists have opined that the accompaniment was a dolceola, an instrument invented about 1902 that is essentially a zither with a keyboard. However, neighbors and relations recalled a homemade boxlike instrument that Phillips had fashioned from the insides of a piano. In any case, the unique sound led to a music described as "gentle" and "ethereal." Phillips's songs were usually on moral themes.

For example, in "The Church Needs Good Deacons" he criticizes philandering deacons, and in "I Am Born to Preach the Gospel" and "Denomination Blues" he bemoans the state of bickering and competing Christian denominations.

Phillips recorded eighteen songs for Columbia Records in Dallas between December 1927 and December 1929. The onset of the Great Depression in the latter year brought about a drastic decline in field recorders in search of talent. After the 1920s Phillips returned to his Freestone County farm and lived with his mother in Simsboro. He produced and sold cane syrup, and traveled the area and preached. He continued to play his gospel songs for family and friends.

Phillips was buried in the Cotton Gin Cemetery in western Freestone County. In 1992 Yazoo Records released *I Am Born to Preach the Gospel*, a CD of his songs. Washington Phillips has often been confused with another man by the same name who was confined to the Austin State Hospital and died there on December 31, 1938.

BIBLIOGRAPHY: Austin *American–Statesman*, December 29, 2002. "Washington Phillips" (http://www.geocities.com/SunsetStrip/Venue/1006/phillipswash.html), accessed October 24, 2002. Alan Young, *Woke Me Up This Morning: Black Gospel Singers and the Gospel Life* (Jackson: University Press of Mississippi, 1997). *Mike Reaves*

Piano Manufacture. The great majority of pianos made in the United States in the nineteenth and early twentieth centuries—the golden era of American piano production—were manufactured in and distributed from New York, Boston, Chicago, and Cincinnati. Though Texas hosted hundreds of retail dealers selling a variety of piano brands, the state was not a manufacturing center of musical instruments. Alfred Dolge did not mention Texas in his comprehensive two-volume history, *Pianos and Their Makers*, published in 1911 and 1913.

Nevertheless, Texas manufactured some keyboard instruments. Undoubtedly, the most familiar Texas name was Thomas Goggan and Brothers, established in 1866 in Galveston. Less well known were K–L Piano Manufacturers of Texarkana, Arkansas, J. R. England of Houston (reed and pipe organs), and Harmon Organ Company of Dallas (reed and pipe organs). Information is sketchy at best regarding these firms; no manufacturing data is known.

More elusive still are dealer-stencil pianos bearing Texas names, giving the illusion that they were made in the state, though in fact they were not. Stencil pianos, common in the United States before World War I, were manufactured without brand name by major makers to be sold to dealers, who would in turn "stencil" their own name or some fanciful one on the pianos to sell as a second line to their name-brand stock. The quality of these pianos varied, and though their manufacture, distribution, and sale were accepted trade practices throughout the United States, they generally were regarded as inferior instruments. Among the known stencil instruments sold in Texas were "El Paso Piano Company" and "Shutes" piano (both in reality manufactured by Haddorff Piano Company, Rockford, Illinois, for the Shutes company of El Paso), "George Allen" pianos of San Angelo (made by M. Schultz Company, Chicago), and "Brooks–Mays" pianos (made for Brooks–Mays of Houston, manufacturer unknown). Not surprisingly, there were also pianos stenciled with names especially chosen to appeal to Texas-conscious consumers: "Alamo," "Indianola," and "Texas," and others. The manufacturers and dealers of these pianos are unknown; merely the names are preserved in trade literature both as testament to dealer ingenuity and as a caveat that they were stencil brands.

The American piano trade in the late twentieth century was troubled with a limited market and intense competition from Japanese and European firms. But this situation, coupled with the economic attractiveness of Texas, has put the state back in the industry. In the 1990s there were four piano manufacturers with offices in Texas, all of them German: August Forster Piano Company and Zimmermann Piano Company in Houston, and Bernhard Steiner Piano Company and Dietmann Pianos Limited in Dallas. Interestingly, the Whittle Music Company of Dallas now controls the name commonly associated with the invention and development of the first pianoforte in 1709—Bartolomeo Cristofori of Padua, Italy.

BIBLIOGRAPHY: *The Purchaser's Guide to the Music Industries, 1991* (Englewood, New Jersey: Music Trades Corporation, 1990). Craig H. Roell, *The Piano in America, 1890–1940* (Chapel Hill: University of North Carolina Press, 1989). *Craig H. Roell*

Pickens, Buster. Blues pianist; b. Edwin Pickens, Hempstead, Texas, June 3, 1916; d. Houston, November 24, 1964; son of Eli Pickens and Bessie Gage. As an itinerant musician in his early life, Pickens played in barrelhouses across the southern states. This helped him to shape his own blues piano style, which partook of the Texas idiom— what some would call "sawmill" piano.

After serving in the military in World War II, he returned to Houston and made his first record, accompanying the vocals of Texas Alexander along with guitarist Leon Benton. In addition, he performed regularly with Lightnin' Hopkins. He appears in some of Hopkins's records for Prestige / Bluesville in the early 1960s. The Lightnin' Hopkins Quartet included Lightnin' Hopkins on vocals and guitar, Donald Cooks on bass, Spider Kilpatrick on drums, and Pickens on piano.

He also made a solo album, *Buster Pickens*, in 1960, that showed his thorough knowledge of the Texas blues style. In 1962 Pickens appeared in the movie *The Blues*. His promising new career in the blues revival, however, was ended when he was murdered a few years later, at age forty-eight, as a result of a barroom dispute about a dollar.

BIBLIOGRAPHY: Sheldon Harris, *Blues Who's Who* (New Rochelle, New York: Arlington House, 1979). Houston *Post*, November 25, 1964. *Prestige Discography, 1962* (http://www.tgs.gr.jp/jazz/pr1962-dis/c/), accessed January 17, 2003. *Larry S. Bonura*

Pillot, Joseph Eugene. Playwright and song composer; b. Houston, February 25, 1886; d. June 4, 1966 (buried in Glenwood Cemetery, Houston); son of Teolin and Anna C.

(Drescher) Pillot. He attended the University of Texas and Cornell University with the intention of studying law, but gave up that pursuit to enroll in the New York School of Fine and Applied Arts. He worked for a while as an interior decorator in New York, then entered the workshop course in play-writing at Harvard. He continued there for several years, writing and working with the Boston Community Players. He also took a drama course at Columbia.

Pillot became a successful writer of one-act plays, many of which were widely produced on stage, radio, and television. His best known play, *Two Crooks and a Lady* (1918), was first produced at Harvard and has been called a model of construction; it has been republished and produced many times. His other plays include *My Lady Dreams* (1922), *Hunger*, and *The Sundial* (probably 1920s). His works have been included in many anthologies and handbooks on the technique of play-writing.

He was also a writer of songs, the most popular of which were "As a Snow White Swan" and "Let Not Your Song End." Most of Pillot's later writing was sacred music. He also wrote poetry. In 1955 he and artist Grace Spaulding John, in cooperation with the River Oaks Garden Club, produced a prose book, *Azalea*, the story of a real dog and two iron dogs that had guarded the Pillot residence in Houston for more than 100 years. In 1965 the family home was given to the Harris County Heritage and Conservation Society and moved to Sam Houston Park, where it was restored, furnished, given a historical marker, and opened to the public. Pillot was a member of the Poetry Society of Texas and the 1953 president of its Houston chapter. He never married.

BIBLIOGRAPHY: Grace Leake, "Eugene Pillot, Playwright," *Holland's*, May 1939. Vertical Files, Center for American History, University of Texas at Austin. *Who's Who in the South and Southwest*, 1961.

Julia Hurd Strong

Pisk, Paul Amadeus. Composer, conductor, pianist, musicologist, and teacher; b. Vienna, May 16, 1893; d. Hollywood, California, January 12, 1990; one of the many Austrian and German musicians who helped build music departments in American universities when they settled in the United States after fleeing the chaos of Europe in the wake of World War II.

Pisk was educated in Vienna during the final flowering of that city's musical culture in the early twentieth century. He studied musicology with Guido Adler at the University of Vienna and earned his Ph.D. in 1916. He also earned a diploma in conducting at the Vienna Conservatory in 1919. He was active as a music critic and editor and avidly promoted the performance of new music throughout his career. Pisk studied composition with Arnold Schoenberg and served as secretary of Schoenberg's important Society for Private Musical Performances (1918–21). He was also closely associated with the other composers of the Second Viennese School (Alban Berg and Anton Webern), and his compositions show their influence. Pisk's works extended to more than 130 opus numbers, most of it chamber music. His compositions are extremely chromatic, leaning toward atonality. In the tradition of Viennese classicism, his works are also structured around thematic development, although sometimes employing folk melodies.

Pisk was a founding member of the Austrian section of the International Society for Contemporary Music and served as its secretary (1922–34). He was director of the music department of the Volkshochschule in Vienna (1922–34) and taught theory at the New Vienna Conservatory (1925–26) and the Austro-American Conservatory near Salzburg (1931–33). By the early 1930s he had married a Viennese music teacher; they had two sons.

Because of his American contacts in the ISCM, Pisk visited the U.S. in the 1930s, and his works were performed in new-music concerts in New York. He emigrated to the U.S. in 1936. After a year in New York he took a position on the faculty at the University of Redlands, California (1937–51). His family joined him in the United States in 1939. He headed the music department in Redlands after 1948.

Pisk also taught at the University of Texas in the summers of 1945, 1947, and 1951. In 1951 he was appointed professor of music at UT and charged with building the Ph.D. program in musicology. His work in Austin brought national prominence to the UT music program. During his Texas years he co-authored (with Homer Ulrich) *A History of Music and Musical Style* (New York, 1963), a textbook, still in print, that traces the history of music through the music itself rather than events and lives of composers. In 1963, mandatory retirement rules at UT forced Pisk to retire. In honor of their distinguished professor and his seventieth birthday the College of Fine Arts at UT commissioned and published a festschrift of twenty-six essays by colleagues and musicologists from throughout the world: *Paul A. Pisk: Essays in His Honor* (Austin, 1966).

Not ready to retire, however, Professor Emeritus Pisk took up a position as visiting professor at Washington University in St. Louis. There he taught musicology until 1972, when, at the age of seventy-nine, he did finally retire. He moved back to California and settled in Los Angeles, taught, lectured, and continued his writing. Pisk was still active in 1983, when many friends and colleagues gathered to celebrate his ninetieth birthday. A chronic back ailment plagued his final years and confined him to his bed during the last year of his life. He died at his Hollywood home. His name is perpetuated by the Paul A. Pisk prize, awarded annually since 1991 by the American Musicological Society to recognize the most outstanding scholarly paper read at its annual meetings by a graduate music student. An important archive of his works is housed in the Center for American History at the University of Texas at Austin.

BIBLIOGRAPHY: Hanns-Bertold Dietz, "Obituary: Paul Amadeus Pisk (1893–1990)," *AMS Newsletter*, August 1990. *The New Grove Dictionary of Music and Musicians*, Second Edition (New York: Grove's Dictionaries, 2001). Nicolas Slonimsky and Laura Kuhn, eds., *Baker's Biographical Dictionary of Musicians*, Centennial Edition (New York: Schirmer, 2001). Vertical files, Center for American History, University of Texas at Austin.

Larry Wolz

Pittman, Portia. Musician and teacher; b. Portia Marshall Washington, Tuskegee, Alabama, June 6, 1883; d. Washington, D.C., February 26, 1978; only daughter of Booker T. and Fanny (Smith) Washington. Upon her mother's death in 1884, Portia's care came from nursemaids and two stepmothers. Already a fairly accomplished pianist by the age of ten, she entertained her family by playing spirituals and simple classical pieces. Her father arranged for her to attend New England's finest boarding schools, including Framingham State Normal School in Massachusetts in 1895. After grammar school she returned home to take classes at Tuskegee Institute (her famous father's school), and in 1901 she attended Wellesley College in Massachusetts. In New England she continued her piano studies and received a degree from the Bradford Academy (now Bradford Junior College) in 1905, the first black to obtain a degree from that institution.

Upon graduation Portia traveled to Berlin to study under Martin Krause, master pianist and former student of Franz Liszt. Complicating her time in Europe, however, were the persistent attentions of William Sidney Pittman, a Tuskegee student and teacher she had met in 1900. Now, five years later, Pittman determined to marry Portia, and persuaded her through a passionate correspondence. Portia sacrificed her piano studies, returned to the United States, and married Sidney Pittman on Halloween 1907, in the chapel of Tuskegee Institute.

Pittman decided that he and Portia should begin afresh in Washington, D.C. There he set up an architectural practice and built their home in Fairmont Heights, Maryland. Between 1908 and 1912 Portia gave birth to her three children. Nevertheless, she made her concert debut in a joint recital with Clarence Cameron White in May 1908 in Washington, and periodically toured on a concert circuit. Despite family happiness, money problems plagued the Pittmans. Sidney's architectural contracts dried up, and Portia began giving private piano lessons in order to maintain the family income.

Pittman's vanity was wounded by his wife's having to work as well as by her family's fame. He moved the family in 1913 to Dallas, where he thought Booker T. Washington's shadow would be less oppressive. They settled on Juliette Street. After Pittman's contracts again dropped off, partly because Dallas blacks who could afford his services preferred to hire white architects, financial difficulties again plagued Portia's life. On November 14, 1915, her father died. A fire in 1918 destroyed the Pittmans' second Dallas home on Germania Street, and they moved to Liberty Street. Improvement in the family's fortunes began at this time, however, and continued for nearly ten years. Pittman became the president of the Brotherhood of Negro Building Mechanics of Texas, and Portia began teaching music at Booker T. Washington High School in 1925. She also chaired the education department of the Texas Association of Negro Musicians.

In March 1927 the National Education Association held its annual convention in Dallas. Almost 7,500 teachers attended. A 600-voice choir from Booker T. Washington High School, under Portia's direction, sang a medley of popular and spiritual songs. It was the first time in history that a black high school group had appeared on the NEA program. Tremendous applause and cries of "encore" rose after the performance, and a spontaneous sing-along erupted as audience and choir together sang spirituals and folk songs. NEA president Randall J. Condon, a Los Angeles principal, judged the performance a "complete success." Later that summer Portia traveled to Columbia University in order to acquire academic credentials to allow her to continue teaching in the Dallas public schools.

In 1928 a violent quarrel between Pittman and his daughter, Fannie, culminated in his striking the girl. Portia packed, took Fannie, and left Pittman and Texas. She began teaching at Tuskegee that same year. Her classes included piano, public school music, glee club, and choir. Tuskegee had changed, however, since her father s death. The new administration demanded that all faculty members have academic degrees in order to teach. Lacking such credentials, Portia was removed from the faculty by 1939, but opened her own private music studio in her home in order to support herself. In 1944, at age sixty-one, she retired. She now dedicated herself to a campaign to have her father's Virginia birthplace preserved as a national monument. Before the success of that effort in May 1949, her efforts to memorialize her father bore fruit on May 23, 1946, when a bust of Washington was installed in the Hall of Fame in New York, and also on August 7, 1946, when President Harry Truman signed a bill "authorizing the minting of five million Booker T. Washington commemorative fifty-cent coins." Portia also oversaw the establishment of the Booker T. Washington Foundation to provide academic scholarships for black students. Though she had resolved to leave Texas behind her, she traveled to Dallas one last time to attend the funeral of her former husband, who died on February 19, 1958.

Although Portia suffered financial and health problems during the last years of her life, she remained interested in the ongoing effort of black Americans to acquire their civil rights. She was heartened by the heightened interest in black history during the 1960s and the assurance that her father would be remembered as a great African-American leader.

BIBLIOGRAPHY: Eileen Southern, *Biographical Dictionary of Afro-American and African Musicians* (Westport, Connecticut: Greenwood, 1982). Ruth Ann Stewart, *Portia: The Life of Portia Washington Pittman, the Daughter of Booker T. Washington* (Garden City, New York: Doubleday, 1977). *Peggy Hardman*

Poovey, Groovey Joe. Disc jockey, guitarist, songwriter, and rockabilly singer; b. Arnold Joseph Poovey, Dallas, May 10, 1941; d. Dallas, October 6, 1998; son of Bernice Arthor and Aligene (Tyler) Poovey. Joe, who embraced many nicknames in his career, was encouraged to become an entertainer by his father at age four. By age nine he was recording hillbilly music in a studio.

In 1953 he formed his own band, the Hillbilly Boys, and was performing on the broadcast country music show "Big D Jamboree." A year later, he became the DJ known as Jumping Joe Poovey on the weekly radio show "Hillbilly Lowdown." In 1955 he shared vocals with Earny Vandagriff in a recording of three Christmas-theme songs released by the Rural Rhythm label—"Be Bop Santa

Claus," "Atomic Kisses," and "Santa's Helper," a song written by Poovey's father.

That same year, after he first saw Elvis Presley perform, Poovey decided to drop the hillbilly sound and convert to rockabilly. He produced his first rockabilly record in 1957, the single "Move Around." He was given the nickname Groovey Joe Poovey by the DJ who introduced the song. A year later, with writer and producer Jim Shell as his writing partner, Poovey produced another hit, "Ten Long Fingers." He remained in the Dallas area as a local artist and as a DJ with the "Big D Jamboree" until its demise in 1960.

After that year, Poovey reverted to country music and began writing for such musicians as George Jones, Wynn Stewart, and Jimmy Patton. In 1966, under the name Johnny Dallas, he reached the *Billboard* chart with the hit "Heart Full of Love." Rather than producing follow-up hits, however, he worked full-time as a disc jockey in the Dallas–Fort Worth area. In 1975 Rollin' Rock Records released five previously unreleased songs that Poovey had produced in the 1950s. This helped reactivate his career, which he now pursued under the name Texas Joe Poovey. After "Ten Long Fingers" became a favorite among European fans, Poovey toured Europe in 1980 using his rockabilly style. He continued to record rockabilly material and performed throughout the 1980s and 1990s.

He died in his sleep of heart disease and was buried in Grove Hill Memorial Park, Dallas. He was survived by his wife, Peggy (Mitchell) Poovey.

BIBLIOGRAPHY: Craig Morrison, *Go Cat Go: Rockabilly Music and Its Music* (Chicago: University of Illinois Press, 1996.) *Juan Carlos Rodríguez*

Powell, Jesse. Tenor saxophonist; b. Smithville, Bastrop County, Texas, February 27, 1924; d. New York City, October 19, 1982. Powell was trained formally in music before he began his professional career at age eighteen, when he toured with fellow Texan Hot Lips Page during 1942–43. He played with Louis Armstrong in 1943–44, with the Luis Russell Orchestra in 1944–45, and replaced fellow Texas tenorist Illinois Jacquet in the Count Basie band for a tour of California in September 1946. At this time Powell also worked with blues singers Champion Jack Dupree and Brownie McGhee. In 1947 he was with the Curly Russell band, and then in 1948 he formed his own band in New York City. Also in 1948 Powell performed with trumpeter Howard McGhee at the first international jazz festival in Paris. In 1949–50, Powell was a member of the Dizzy Gillespie big band, with which he recorded a solo on "Tally Ho." In 1953 he formed his own jump-rhythm band, and in 1964 a Powell quintet played at Birdland in New York City, where the tenorist died. Powell was survived by his wife, Maxine, and two children.

BIBLIOGRAPHY: Barry Kernfeld, ed. *The New Grove Dictionary of Jazz*, Second Edition (New York, 2002). Dave Oliphant, *Texan Jazz* (Austin: University of Texas Press, 1996). *Dave Oliphant*

Price, Sammy. Blues and jazz pianist; b. Honey Grove, Texas, October 6, 1908; d. New York City, April 14, 1992. Although Price's style was steeped in the barrelhouse blues tradition, his first musical exposure came from church. After moving to Waco, where his father took a job at Braxo's Bakery, Sammy began cornet lessons at the age of seven under a Professor Cobb. Cobb told Sammy that he had no musical ability and urged him to quit music. But the boy rejected this advice and formed a band with some of his friends.

In 1918 he and his mother and brother moved to Dallas after his father deserted the family. Sammy studied piano under Booker T. Washington's daughter, Portia Pittman. He became engrossed in the new dance craze, the Charleston, and took first prize in a statewide Charleston competition. This in turn led to a spot in Alphonso Trent's band as a side dancer. In 1927 Sammy joined the Theater Owners' Booking Association music circuit and toured extensively. In 1930 he moved to musically fertile Kansas City, where he landed a job as leader of the house band at the Yellow Front Café.

In 1933 Price moved to Chicago and then Detroit, where he performed at the Chequers Barbecue. He moved to New York City in 1937 and played at the Café Society, the Famous Door, and the Downbeat before Decca Records hired him as the house pianist. At Decca he recorded with Trixie Smith and Sister Rosetta Tharpe, among others, and by the early 1940s he was leading his own "Texas Blusicians." After becoming involved in the Philadelphia Jazz Society, he was instrumental in organizing the first African-American jazz festival in Philadelphia.

In 1951 Price returned to Texas, where he started an undertaking company and two nightclubs. After moving back to New York in 1954, he toured Europe with the Blusicians and began a long partnership with trumpet player Henry "Red" Allen. Through the 1960s, 1970s, and 1980s, he continued recording and touring, both in Europe and in the United States. He also became heavily involved in politics and worked as a campaign supervisor for the Democratic party. He died of a heart attack.

BIBLIOGRAPHY: John Chilton, *Who's Who of Jazz: From Storyville to Swing Street* (New York: Da Capo Press, 1985). Leonard Feather, *The Encyclopedia of Jazz*, New Edition (New York: Horizon Press, 1960). Sammy Price, *What Do They Want? A Jazz Autobiography* (Urbana: University of Illinois Press, 1990). Ron Wynn, Michael Erlewine, and Chris Woodstra, eds., *All Music Guide to Jazz: The Best CDs, Albums, and Tapes* (San Francisco: Miller Freeman, 1994).   *Bradley Shreve*

Punk Rock. A music phenomenon of the 1970s and 1980s that had its roots in the late 1960s and early 1970s and continues to influence musicians today. Generally considered a reaction to mainstream rock-and-roll, punk, sometimes called "freak music," placed great emphasis on personal expression and anti-professional or amateur approaches to making and performing music.

Although most Texas punk music is represented by three-chord songs with a fast tempo and emphasis on the downbeat, the eclecticism of the genre permitted many different variations and styles. Influences ranged from garage rock and roots rock to electronic music, folk, soul, rhythm-and-blues, and even antithetical Top 40 pop music. Subject matter in punk songs is widely varied, though revisited themes are politics (usually leftist, though there were also right-wing sentiments), sex, and anti-establishment and anti-authoritarian sentiments.

Punk's more commercial, less angry face was new-wave, though the terms were often interchangeable and vague. Several new-wave acts from Texas caught brief national attention, such as Joe "King" Carrasco and the Crowns from Austin, and the Judy's from Houston. Punk includes numerous sub-genres, including "skate punk" (referring to punk's embrace of skateboarding), "hardcore," "cow-punk" (incorporating country and western themes and fashions), the less definable, experimental "art" punk, and other styles. Though punk's dates of popularity in Texas are debatable, several frames of reference are useful. Most fans learned about the genre from its East Coast movement and from widespread media coverage of early British punk. Many people count the "christening" events of Texas punk as the two dates played in the state in January 1978 by the seminal British group the Sex Pistols. The shows that occurred at two country and western venues (the Longhorn Ballroom in Dallas and Randy's Rodeo in San Antonio) featured opening acts from local bands and undoubtedly influenced the formation of many more.

A further nationally noted incident in Texas punk occurred in Austin on September 19, 1978, when Huns lead singer Phil Tolstead verbally abused a police officer investigating a noise complaint at the club. A small riot occurred, and six arrests were made. The event was covered in *Rolling Stone* the following week and cemented the state's punk rock reputation. Texas, specifically Austin, also gained international attention as the site for the filming of the Clash's *Rock the Casbah* video in 1982.

Punk rock as an "underground" movement faded by the mid-1980s as the music became more acceptable to mainstream audiences and the genre itself branched into multiple sub-genres. For most historical purposes, Texas punk rock's first wave flattened out around and after summer 1984, at the time of the Republican National Convention in Dallas and a nationally mobilized musical protest movement called Rock Against Reagan that encamped there briefly. While the punk-specific venues dwindled and interest in the earlier punk style waned, several early groups continued to perform, and younger musicians formed punk-influenced bands. Punk continues in spirit in the songwriting and performance styles of many bands.

The punk movement in Texas was often characterized by the "do it yourself" school of thought. Most musicians were self-taught and eschewed formal music training, though a handful were classically trained. Part of the appeal of untrained musicians and nonconformity in this musical form was the inventiveness and spontaneity that often resulted. Bands varied in instrumentation from traditional three and four piece rock combos to groups featuring electric violin, keyboards, synthesizers, unusual items such as blenders, and horn sections. Production values in recordings generally favored raw, live performances with little or no overdubbing, though there were exceptions.

Because of punk's publicly perceived notoriety as violent and antisocial, venues were few, and bands adapted quickly to playing in places as varied as house parties, Tejano bars (Raul's Club, Austin), gay bars (the Bonham Exchange, San Antonio), defunct fur vaults (the Vault, Austin), and warehouses. Besides these, the most famous venues of the 1978–1985 period around the state included Duke's Royal Coach Inn, Club Foot / Night Life, and Liberty Lunch (Austin); Tacoland (San Antonio); the Axiom and Rock Island (Houston); and Twilight Room, Studio D, and the Hot Klub (Dallas). Dozens of other establishments around the state opened and closed during this time, some of them open for only a few months. Perhaps Texas punk's most famous live recording was a split LP featuring the Big Boys and the Dicks of Austin, recorded over two nights at Raul's Club in September 1980.

Band names were chosen specifically to amuse, engage, and offend. Names such as Butthole Surfers, Toxic Shock, Sharon Tate's Baby, Millions of Dead Cops (BANG GANG), and the Dicks offered shock value, while the Big Boys, the Reactors, the Marching Plague, the Hugh Beaumont Experience, the Offenders, the Hickoids, the Nervebreakers, the Next, Really Red, the Mistakes, the Rejects, and the Stickmen With Rayguns took a more humorous approach. Punk groups hailed from throughout the state, including San Antonio (Butthole Surfers, Bang Gang, Marching Plague, Rejects), Dallas (Nervebreakers, Hugh Beaumont Experience, Stick Men With Rayguns), Houston (Really Red, the Judy's), and Austin (the Next, Offenders, Dicks, Reactors).

Until late in its life, the punk rock genre was largely ignored by the mainstream media in the state. Left to define and promote itself, the Punk movement was primarily fueled by an underground print media, small, independent record labels, record stores, and clubs. Writing about Texas punk mostly appeared in homemade, photocopied, and small-press magazines, known as "fanzines," in student newspapers at Texas colleges and universities, and later in local alternative arts and music guides in major cities. Very few locally recorded punk rock 45s, LPs, and audio cassettes were produced on labels with more than one artist.

In most cases bands produced and distributed their own music. Most groups pressed fewer than 1,000 copies, and today a number of them are highly collectible. A few bands, like the Big Boys and the Dicks, were lucky enough to have their music released or re-released on nationally known independent labels such as Touch and Go (Chicago) and SST Records (Los Angeles).

A punk rock circuit, however loosely defined, developed in the state, and nationally known punk acts toured Texas, such as Black Flag, Minor Threat, X, the Dead Kennedys, the Dils, and Fear. As with other musical movements in Texas, there were ancillary currents in literature, fashion, and the arts, manifested in many different forms throughout the state. The arts in Texas were deeply influenced by punk rock. From the collage art appearing on concert posters and in fanzines to photography, film and video, painting, sculpture, and serigraphy, many artists embraced a punk aesthetic or helped to describe it visually to the outside world. Punk rock fashion was as much an anti-statement as a statement. While many punks wore the trademark black leather jackets and ripped shirts and jeans of their band idols on the East Coast or in Britain, just as many others flouted anti-fashion by wearing grossly unfashionable polyester, work uniforms, and—in the hot Texas weather—Bermuda shorts (sometimes with cowboy or motorcycle boots). Women's fashions included school uniforms with fishnet stockings or combat boots, among other styles. Hair fashions, a major hallmark of punk fashion, included multicolored dyed hair, crew cuts, Mohawks, shaved heads, and Rockabilly-inspired pompadours.

BIBLIOGRAPHY: Austin *American–Statesman*, May 16, 1996. *Discography of Texas Punk, 1977–1983* (http://www.collectorscum.com/volume3/texas/), accessed March 14, 2003. *Live at Raul's* (Raul's Records, 1979). *Big Boys and the Dicks Recorded Live at Raul's Club* (Rat Race Records, 1981). George Gimarc, *Post-Punk Diary: 1980–1982*, ed. Bryan Ray Turcotte (New York: St. Martin's Press, 1997). *John H. Slate*

R

Radio. Broadcasting emerged in Texas on the campuses of the University of Texas and Texas A&M in College Station. In 1911 J. B. Dickinson, manager of the Texas Fiscal Agency at San Antonio, constructed wireless facilities at both schools to teach electrical engineering students about radio transmissions. As part of his experiments in high-frequency radio, University of Texas physics professor S. Leroy Brown built radio equipment and began broadcasting weather and crop reports from a physics laboratory on the UT campus in 1915.

During World War I, using the call letters KUT, the UT Division of Extension operated Brown's equipment to broadcast reports from the United States Marketing Bureau and Department of Agriculture. By March 1922 the station had combined with a second campus station (call letters 5XY) and with a 500-watt power rating was one of the best-equipped and most powerful stations in the nation. The usual broadcasts were from 8 to 10 P.M. three nights a week; programming consisted of music, lectures, and agriculture and marketing reports. In addition, a church service was aired on Sunday.

On November 24, 1921, possibly the first broadcast of a football game in the country aired from A&M via call letters 5XB, now WTAW. The station operated as a ham relay station at 250 watts. Originally, the station was to air the final score of the Texas–Texas A&M Thanksgiving game, but Frank Matejka, W. A. Tolson, and others decided to send a play-by-play account of the game via Morse Code. Student Harry Saunders and assistant coach D. X. Bible designed a set of abbreviations to fit every possible football situation and sent the list to every station that would broadcast the contest. The game aired over the ham relay stations; the Morse Code was deciphered and announced to fans over a public-address system.

One of the earliest broadcasting stations in the United States and the first in Texas was WRR, Dallas, owned by the city, which began broadcasting in 1920 with Dad Garrett as announcer. The station received a provisional license on August 4, 1921. During these early days of broadcasting, many small, homemade radio stations went on the air on a noncommercial basis, primarily for the amusement of the operators and their neighbors. By the end of 1922, the year that commercial radio broadcasting began in Texas and before there was a federal agency to regulate radio broadcasters, twenty-five commercial stations were in operation in the state. Among them were WBAP, Fort Worth; KGNC, Amarillo; WFAA, Dallas; WOAI, San Antonio; KFJZ, Fort Worth; KFLX, Galveston; and WACO, Waco.

Radio Station WBAP in Fort Worth established the basic format for country music variety show broadcasting (a format since taken over by Nashville's "Grand Ole Opry" and Chicago's "National Barn Dance") with a "barn dance" program that began on January 4, 1923, fea-

turing a fiddler, a square-dance caller, and Confederate veteran Capt. M. J. Bonner. As of January 1931, KFJZ in Fort Worth was the first station to broadcast the Light Crust Doughboys. The group, sponsored by Light Crust Flour, played popular ballads, blues, and jazz of the day and was considered a pioneer of the Western Swing sound. They eventually moved to WBAP, Fort Worth, a more powerful station, in late 1931. The broadcasts gained statewide popularity, and the Light Crust Doughboys radio program continued into the early 1950s.

WFAA in Dallas, operating on 150 watts, held many firsts in radio broadcasting in Texas. It was the first to carry programs designed to educate; first to produce a serious radio drama series, which was entitled "Dramatic Moments in Texas History" and sponsored by the Magnolia Petroleum Company; first to air a state championship football game; first to join a national network (1927); and first to air inaugural ceremonies, specifically those of Governor Ross Sterling in 1931. WFAA was the property of the Belo Corporation, publisher of the Dallas *Morning News*; Adam Colhoun, the first announcer, at times read to his listeners from that newspaper when there was nothing else to offer. Gene Finley was the first manager until Robert Poole replaced him in 1924. The station carried no newscasts; entertainment held top priority. Early programs carried the voices of the Early Birds, Eddie Dunn, Frank Munroe, Jimmie Jeffries, Pegleg Moreland, the Cass County Kids, and Dale Evans. The Folger Coffee Company, WFAA's first paying advertiser, sponsored the Bel Canta Quartet.

An early station in South Texas, WOAI in San Antonio, went on the air on September 25, 1922. Founded by G. A. C. Halff with an initial power of 500 watts, it was increased to 5,000 watts in 1925, considered powerful for the time. On February 6, 1928, WOAI joined the world's first network, the National Broadcasting Company. It eventually became a clear channel operating on 50,000 watts. WOAI was one of the first stations to employ a local news staff. One of its greatest achievements was a regular Sunday broadcast of "Musical Interpretations," featuring Max Reiter, conductor of the San Antonio Symphony Orchestra. Reiter also conducted the orchestra for NBC's nationwide "Pioneers of Music," originating from the municipal auditorium in San Antonio.

In Houston a radio club was organized in 1919 for amateur builders and operators of crystal sets, with James L. Autrey as president. The first local commercial station was WEV, owned and operated by Hurlburt Still. On May 21, 1922, the Houston *Post* broadcast a Sunday concert from the radio plant of A. P. Daniel, 2504 Bagby Street. Later that year the Houston Conservatory of Music sent out programs over station WGAB. In 1924 the Houston *Post–Dispatch* absorbed a station operated by Will Horwitz and established it as KPRC, which made its debut in May 1925. In November 1928 there were thirty-two broadcasting stations in Texas. Several new ones were licensed in the next few years. KXYZ, Houston, which had first broadcast on October 20, 1930, was taken over by Jesse H. Jones in 1932 and increased its power to 1,000 watts two years later.

In 1934 the state's four largest stations, WBAP in Forth Worth, WFAA in Dallas, WOAI in San Antonio, and KPRC of Houston, formed the Texas Quality Group Network. The stations were connected by telephone lines, established the capacity for simultaneous broadcasts, and commanded a combined night-time power of 101,000 watts. A major factor in the push to share programming was the popularity of the Light Crust Doughboys radio show. TQN also featured other regular programs such as "Riding with the Texas Rangers," sponsored by Kellogg, and the "Pepper-Uppers," sponsored by Dr Pepper. TQN eventually included stations in Oklahoma, Arkansas, and Louisiana and continued broadcasting into the 1950s.

When stations KPRC and KTRH installed one broadcasting plant for sending out waves simultaneously in 1936, the plant was the second of its kind in the world. Each station increased its power to 5,000 watts. KTRH became the Houston *Chronicle* station in 1937. In 1946 Raul Cortez established KCOR–AM in San Antonio. KCOR was the first Spanish-language and Hispanic-owned radio station in the United States. KNUZ / KQUE was also among the first radio stations to employ women and members of minorities—in 1948 the station hired the first female account executive and the first black disc jockey. Other KNUZ / KQUE firsts include a remote broadcast studio, helicopter reporting, wireless microphones, a computer traffic system, a full-dimensional FM antenna and a solid-state AM transmitter.

With the advent of television during the second half of the twentieth century the number of radio stations decreased. By 1971 the state had a combined total of 392 standard radio (AM) and frequency-modulation (FM) stations. During the next two decades there was an upswing, however In 1993 Texas had 311 AM and 420 FM radio stations with valid current operating licenses.

During the 1990s and into the twenty-first century a Texas-based communications company had a major impact on national and international radio markets. Clear Channel Communications, headquartered in San Antonio, traced its beginnings to 1972, when businessmen Lowry Mays and Red McCombs formed the San Antonio Broadcasting Company. They purchased KEEZ–FM and in 1975 acquired WOAI–AM. Through the 1980s and 1990s Clear Channel purchased radio stations in San Antonio, Austin, and Houston, other stations nationwide, and stations in Australia, New Zealand, and Mexico. The company, named by the *Wall Street Journal* as having the fifth best-performing stock in the 1990s, also acquired television stations, advertising billboards, and concert promotion companies.

By 1998 Clear Channel owned or programmed 204 radio stations. In 1999 the company bought Dallas-based AMFM, Inc., thereby making Clear Channel the largest radio-station operator in the nation, with some 830 stations. This growth reflected a trend of mass consolidation in the radio industry. In 2000 Clear Channel Communica-

tions, under CEO Lowry Mays, owned or had interests in 1,376 stations worldwide. Some smaller concert promoters and radio operators accused the company of monopolizing the industry, and in 2001 Clear Channel faced an anti-trust lawsuit by a Denver concert promoter. In 2002 Texas had 295 AM and 555 FM radio stations with valid current operating licenses.

BIBLIOGRAPHY: Bernard Brister, "Radio House: 'Forty-Acres' Gets an Airing," *Southwest Review*, Spring 1944. Clear Channel Worldwide (http://www.clearchannel.com) accessed December 14, 2002. John Mark Dempsey, *The Light Crust Doughboys are on the Air: Celebrating Seventy Years of Texas Music* (Denton: University of North Texas Press, 2002). Richard Schroeder, *Texas Signs On: The Early Days of Radio and Television* (College Station: Texas A&M Press, 1998). Vertical files, Center for American History, University of Texas at Austin. Bobby Wimberly, "WOAI: Texas Pioneer in Radio," *Junior Historian*, September 1952. WPA Writers Program, *Houston* (Houston: Anson Jones Press, 1942).

Ramey, Gene. Jazz bassist; b. Austin, April 4, 1913; d. December 8, 1984. Ramey attended Anderson High School and played trumpet in college. He also played sousaphone with George Corley's Royal Aces. In the early 1930s he played with the Moonlight Serenaders and Terence Holder's band before moving to Kansas City in 1932.

Ramey learned to play string bass from the famous Kansas City bassist Walter Page and was soon leading his own bands. During the 1930s he also worked with Oliver Todd's band and Margaret "Countess" Johnson. He played with Jay McShann off and on between 1938 and 1944. During this period Ramey worked closely with McShann's alto sax player, Charlie Parker, who became one of the most innovative jazz soloists.

Ramey moved to New York in 1944 and began playing with many of the era's most prominent bandleaders, including Luis Russell, Ben Webster, Coleman Hawkins, Charlie Parker, John Hardee, Eddie "Lockjaw" Davis, Miles Davis, Dizzy Gillespie, Oran "Hot Lips" Page, Tiny Grimes, Lester Young, and others. In the 1950s he played for Count Basie, Dorothy Donegan, Art Blakey, Eartha Kitt, and others. In the late 1950s he played numerous studio engagements as a freelance session bassist. In the 1960s he worked with Mugsy Spanier, Teddy Wilson, Dick Wellswood, Jimmy Rushing, and Peanuts Hucko, and toured in Europe with Jay McShann and Eddie "Cleanhead" Vinson.

In 1976 Ramey returned to Austin from New York and announced his retirement, but lessons to local bassists led to a few live shows. Soon he was again a full-time musician, although he talked of becoming a "gentleman farmer." During the late 1970s and early 1980s he helped promote jazz in Austin. He died of a heart attack.

BIBLIOGRAPHY: Austin *American–Statesman*, December 8, 1989. Doug Ramsey, "Bass Hit," *Texas Monthly*, May 1981. Ross Russell, *Jazz Style in Kansas City and the Southwest* (Berkeley: University of California Press, 1971).
Kharen Monsho

Charlie "Bird" Parker (left) and bassist Gene Ramey of Austin, 1940. Duncan Scheidt Collection.

Ramsey, Buck. Cowboy poet and singer; b. Kenneth Melvin Ramsey, New Home, Texas, January 9, 1938; d. Amarillo, January 3, 1998; son of David Melvin and Pearl Lee (Williams) Ramsey. David Ramsey nicknamed his son Buckskin Tarbox when he was born, and he always went by the name of Buck.

As a child, Ramsey attended a two-room schoolhouse in Middlewell, Texas. He came from a musical family and grew up singing four-part harmony in the Primitive Baptist Church. He also attended shaped-note singing schools. Buck was born with perfect pitch. He sang in the school choirs, and his music teachers used him as their tuning fork all through his school days. By the time he was in high school, he was singing with a band called the Sandie Swingsters.

Ramsey graduated from Amarillo High School in 1956 and entered Texas Technological College. He soon left school, traveled the United States, and worked in California and New York. In 1958 he returned to Texas and entered West Texas State College (now West Texas A&M University) at Canyon. During this time he started seriously cowboying and punched cattle around the Panhandle. He continued the cowboy life until the early 1960s, when injuries sustained in a riding accident left him paralyzed from the waist down and bound to a wheelchair. In the 1960s he worked as a newspaper reporter for the Amarillo *Globe–News*. He made an unsuccessful bid for the state legislature in the Democratic primary in 1974.

Over the years Ramsey cultivated his talent as a poet and musician. Through his writings and music he chronicled cowboy culture and eventually garnered a national reputation for preserving the traditions and lore of the cowboy life. Ramsey began resurrecting the old ranching and trail songs, performing and recording his versions to catalog them for posterity, and critics and colleagues regarded his contemporary cowboy poetry as some of the best in that genre. His recordings of the traditional cowboy songs "Rolling Uphill from Texas" (1992) and "My Home It Was in Texas" (1994) each won Western Heritage Wrangler Awards from the National Cowboy Hall of Fame. In 1993 his epic poem, *As I Rode Out on the Morning*, was published by Texas Tech University Press. The prologue, "Anthem," was highly acclaimed.

Ramsey's awards and achievements included a National Heritage Fellowship from the National Endowment for the Arts in 1995, Lifetime Achievement and Best Poetry Book awards from the Academy of Western Artists in 1996, and the Golden Spur Award from the National Cowboy Hall of Fame in 1997. His performances of cowboy poetry and songs were featured at the Smithsonian Institution in Washington and at the Gene Autry Western Heritage Museum in Los Angeles. In the late 1990s Ramsey began recording more than 150 traditional cowboy songs in an effort to preserve them.

He was survived by Bette Cave Ramsey, his wife of thirty-five years, and a daughter. In 2002 the Academy of Western Artists named their annual poetry book award the Buck Ramsey Award in his honor.

BIBLIOGRAPHY: "Buck Ramsey Best Cowboy Poetry Book Award" (www.cowboypoetry.com/buckramsey award. htm), accessed December 6, 2002. Buck Ramsey Houston *Chronicle* online obituary (www.chron.com/cgi-bin/auth/story/content/chronicle/metropolitan/98/01/06/obit-ramsey.2.0.html), accessed November 21, 2002. Vertical files, Center for American History, University of Texas at Austin.   *Susan Kouyomjian* and *Laurie E. Jasinski*

Recording Industry. Texas has been prominent in the history of the recording industry, although there has never been a recording center or record label in Texas comparable to those of New York, Los Angeles, or Nashville. The sales of so-called "cowboy," "hillbilly," and "ethnic" recordings in the 1920s and '30s bankrolled the growth of the recording industry in America. At the time, the recording companies considered the audience for "popular" music "lower-class," but it was certainly a larger and more profitable market than that for classical and operatic music recordings and remains so today. Texas was and is the source for much of that popular music.

The recording industry is an interdependent but not-always-harmonious mix of music, technology, marketing, and ego. A change in each of these elements affects the development of the others. In the earliest days of American recording the scarcity and expense of the requisite equipment, coupled with the technical knowledge necessary to operate it, limited the market for recordings mostly to the wealthy. As recording technology developed, the audience for recordings expanded, to the point where even the Mexican immigrant communities in South Texas had an average of 118 records for every 100 people by 1936.

The constant search for new songs and artists led the competing record labels to Texas because of the state's broad variety of musical scenes and styles. The popularity of these recordings spread the influence of Texan artists' musical styles across America and into the world at large.

Early recording pioneers. Thomas Edison made his historic first recording on a tinfoil-covered cylinder in 1877. Though originally intending only to record telegraph signals, he had invented a machine that could record intelligible audio. He then designed a commercial recorder to be used for dictation, but its real value turned out to be making and playing recordings for entertainment. Edison introduced the first commercial version of his cylinder recorder in 1887. In 1893 a team of Edison's engineers on a field trip made the first known recording in Texas, a performance of *Los Pastores* (the shepherds' songs of the Latino Christmas pageant) in a San Antonio hotel.

Piano rolls were also made at that time, and it was on these that one of the earliest recordings of the performances of a Texan were made. Ragtime innovator Scott Joplin made piano rolls of his compositions from 1896 until shortly before his death in 1917.

By end of the nineteenth century there were three major competing formats for recording audio, none of them electronic, and each of these systems had an associated label; all the labels were fierce competition with one another. Edison's lateral-groove cylinder system was utilized by Victor Records. Emile Berliner's "Gramophone," on the Brunswick label, used a zinc photo-engraved lateral-cut disc. Charles Tainter's "Graphophone," a vertical-groove cylinder-type recorder, was used by Columbia. Until the advent of electronic recording in the mid-1920s most recording systems funneled sound from the musicians into a trumpet-like horn, where the vibrations caused a needle to engrave a "groove" in a rotating wax-coated cylinder or disc. The mechanical limitations of these acoustically driven systems severely limited frequency response and were "scratchy," but the sheer novelty of listening to recordings created a great demand. The Columbia Phonograph Company was formed in 1889 to market the graphophone system for dictation, but soon found that music sold far better. Columbia produced its first record catalog in 1890, a list of Edison and Columbia recordings on cylinders.

One of Edison's star recording artists was Texan Vernon Dalhart. Dalhart sang operatic and popular compositions in New York, recording for Edison around 1915. Edison was constantly improving his cylinder recorder's design, and Dalhart was one of the artists whose recordings introduced the famous "Blue Amberol" cylinder that would last through many playings. Dalhart's recordings sold well enough, but his greatest success was in 1924 when his career, and Victor Records' business, were flagging, and by various accounts either he persuaded Edison or Edison persuaded him to record some "hillbilly" tunes. Dalhart set aside his vocal training and sang in a nasal twang a number of the songs he had heard in his youth. One of these recordings, "The Wreck of the Old 97," with "The Prisoner's Song" became the first million-selling country record in history, reviving both his career and Victor Records. Victor claimed that six million copies of the songs were eventually sold. Dalhart's hit recording of "Home On the Range" in 1927 established him as the first country music "star."

The first country music performer known to be commercially recorded was also a Texan, legendary fiddler Eck Robertson of Amarillo, who went to New York on his own in 1922 and persuaded RCA to record six of his hillbilly fiddle tunes. These recordings established the fiddle band tradition, and their popularity created a demand for hillbilly music as well as cowboy music.

Field recording. What we call country music today began with some of the earliest recordings made in Texas. John A. Lomax made enormously popular field recordings of Texas cowboy songs in 1908 that were published as *Cowboy Songs and Other Frontier Ballads* in 1910. Lomax had grown up in Texas and as a teenager wrote down the words to the songs he heard the cowboys sing. Funded by Harvard because his alma mater, the University of Texas, was not interested in his study of what they termed "tawdry, cheap and unworthy" cowboy music and lore, the location-recording pioneer had a portable recording rig and traveled by automobile to cities, towns, prisons, and ranches in Texas, where he recorded cowboys and others singing the old songs of the original American West. Because of his efforts songs like "Home on the Range," "The Streets of Laredo," "Bury Me Not on the Lone Prairie," and "Git Along Little Dogies" did not fade into obscurity, but rather became the musical identity of the Old West. Lomax and his son Alan went on to record throughout the southeastern United States in the 1930s for the Library of Congress Archive of American Folk Song.

One of their sessions at the Angola Prison in Louisiana brought Huddie Ledbetter, known as Leadbelly, to the attention of the world.

Though John Lomax, a co-founder of the Texas Folklore Society, is the earliest, most prolific and famous, there were other notable folklorists who recorded regional music in Texas. William Owens, from Pin Hook, Texas, traveled with a gramophone-type recorder that embossed aluminum discs that were played back with needles made of cactus thorns. Owens, who had taught at Texas A&M, recorded in East Texas and Louisiana in the mid-1930s for his doctorate from the University of Iowa. That institution was not interested in keeping his collection of recordings, but the University of Texas was (as he hoped), perhaps recognizing their initial mistake with Lomax. In 1941 J. Frank Dobie hired Owens as a folklorist and UT acquired Owens's collection. Owens continued to add recordings to the collection into the 1950s. Also recording in Texas in the 1940s for the Library of Congress were John Rosser Jr. and famous Texan folklorist John Henry Faulk. Another folklorist–recorder was Dallas attorney Hermes Nye. In the 1940s he recorded and at times performed on the radio some old Texas songs for national distribution.

Continuing the field-recording tradition, Chris Strachwitz's Arhoolie Records came from California to Texas beginning in the 1960s to record local musicians (including Lightnin' Hopkins). In 1960 Arhoolie made the first recordings of Mance Lipscomb, a sixty-five-year-old Navasota musician who had never been recorded previously. Lipscomb recorded for Arhoolie until just before his death in 1976, influenced countless musicians, and became famous for his varied stylistic repertoire, which included gospel, rags, ballads, and other traditional songs, as well as Texas-style blues.

In more recent years popular demand for these archival field recordings has diminished, probably because recordings are no longer a novelty to listeners, and because many more musicians are now able to record themselves. Even Arhoolie Records exists only because it has other sources of income than record and CD sales. However, field recordings can still have appeal, as evidenced by singer–songwriter Michelle Shocked, who achieved commercial success and critical acclaim with the release by Cooking Vinyl Records of a cassette recording of her singing off-stage by a campfire at the 1986 Kerrville Folk Festival.

The "race labels." Record companies in the 1920s noticed how well "ethnic" recordings were selling along with hillbilly music, and began to actively search for new artists and music for their "race labels" as well. Because there were few real studio facilities outside of New York and Chicago, major record labels of the time such as Victor, Columbia, Okeh, Brunswick, Vocalion, and American Record Company sent teams of engineers and equipment around the country (and the world) to record regional music. A regular destination for these teams was Texas.

Throughout the 1920s and 1930s recording sessions in Texas were held in hotel rooms, churches, office buildings, banquet halls, and radio stations, including WFAA, WRR, and KLIF in Dallas and WOAI in San Antonio. Finding suitable locations at that time was often difficult because of racial rules at hotels and other commercial locations, and because churches would not always approve of the music being recorded. There was also the need for room to store the twenty or more trunks of equipment and supplies necessary for a remote recording trip.

Recording onto wax-coated cylinders or thick beeswax discs presented a number of problems, especially in the Texas heat. The engineers would keep the wax on ice before and after recording. When electronic recording began in the mid-to-late 1920s, high temperatures also caused noisy crackling in the carbon microphones used at the time, so they were often kept on ice along with the wax until just before starting the recording. The record companies tried whenever possible to avoid summer sessions in Texas. The conditions at recording sessions were primitive by today's standards. Musicians usually were in one room, and the equipment and engineers were in another, so they could not see one another. The musicians had to wait quietly with no idea of what was going on until a yellow light went on, which meant "get ready!" When a green light came on, it was time to play, and there was no stopping because of mistakes. Needless to say, the process of cramming a group of musicians into a room without windows or air-conditioning did not always foster creativity, and reflected the inherent conflicts between achieving technical sonic excellence in recording and musical "groove" in performance that still exist today.

Artists recorded at these remote sessions were not always Texans, but the "race label" recordings are of note because they were virtually the only recordings done in Texas during this period. Among the major blues and gospel sessions, Victor records and a later subsidiary label, Bluebird, recorded in Dallas and San Antonio almost once a year from 1929 to 1941. Artists recorded in Texas by Victor include Hattie Hyde, Sammy Hill, Jesse "Babyface" Thomas, Bessie Tucker (Dallas, 1929), Jimmie Davis, Eddie and Oscar, Pere Dickenson, Ramblin' Thomas, Walter Davis, Stump Johnson (Dallas, 1932), Mississippi Sheiks, Bo Carter, Joe Pullum, Rob Cooper (San Antonio, 1934), Boots and His Buddies (San Antonio, 1936), Andy Boy, Walter "Cowboy" Washington, Big Boy Knox, Ted Mays and His Band (San Antonio, 1937), Bo Carter, Frank Tannehill (San Antonio, 1938), and the Wright Brothers (Dallas, 1941).

The Atlanta-based Okeh label made its first field trip to Texas in 1925. In Dallas they recorded Rev. Wm McKinley Dawkins, though this recording was for Sunshine Gospel Records. In 1928 and 1929 Okeh returned to record "Texas" Alexander, Lonnie Johnson, Troy Floyd and His Plaza Hotel Orchestra, "Little Hat" Jones, Lonesome Charlie Harrison, and Jack Ranger.

Columbia came to Dallas in 1927 and 1928, and recorded Washington Phillips, Lillian Glinn, Blind Willie Johnson, Billiken Johnson and Fred Adams, Coley Jones, Willie Tyson, William McCoy, Willie Mae McFarland, Hattie Hudson, Gertrude Perkins, the Dallas String Band, Laura Henton, Le Roy's Dallas Band, Franchy's String Band, Blind Texas Marlin, Bobby Cadillac, Mary Taylor, Baby Jean Lovelady, Emma Wright, Rev. J. W. Heads, Willie Reed, Charlie King, the Texas Jubilee Singers, Billiken Johnson and Neal Roberts, Otis Harris, and Jewell Nelson.

In late 1929 Columbia bought Okeh, one of a number of mergers in the recording industry brought about by the Great Depression. The joint Okeh–Columbia field trips to Texas took place in December 1929 and June 1930. Although records were released on both labels, only one recording team was sent. In Dallas and San Antonio they recorded many of their artists again, completing recordings for the Columbia label before recording for Okeh.

Brunswick and Vocalion preferred to record in New York or Chicago, but made field trips to Dallas in 1928, 1929, and 1930. Artists recorded there include Texas Tommy, Ben Norsingle, Ollie Ross, Hattie Burleson, Eddie and Sugar Lou's Hotel Tyler Orchestra, Bo Jones, Luis Davis, Sammy Price and His Four Quarters, Bert Johnson, Douglas Finnell and His Royal Stompers, Effie Scott, Perry Dixon, Jake Jones, Blind Norris, Gene Campbell, and Coley Dotson. Vocalion also had successful sales with Henry "Texas Ragtime" Thomas of Big Sandy. Brunswick later established an office in Dallas.

The American Record Corporation made perhaps the best known and influential of the race-label field recordings in Texas, the Robert Johnson sessions of 1936–37. ARC and its legendary producer Don Law recorded Texas Alexander at their first Texas session in San Antonio in April 1934. In September 1934 they returned to Fort Worth and San Antonio, where they recorded Perry Dixon and Alfoncy Harris. In 1935 they recorded Bernice Edwards, Black Boy Shine, and "Funny Paper" Smith in Fort Worth, the Dallas Jamboree Jug Band in Dallas, and J. H. Bragg and His Rhythm Five in San Antonio. In early 1936 Buck Turner (the Black Ace) recorded for ARC in Fort Worth. In November and December 1936 at the Gunter Hotel in San Antonio, Mississippi bluesman Robert Johnson recorded seventeen of the legendary twenty-nine songs, including "Cross Road Blues," that became both his legacy and a fundamental root of rock-and-roll. In June 1937 the remaining twelve songs of the twenty-nine were recorded at the Brunswick Records Building in Dallas, along with Black Boy Shine. Later that year ARC recorded Son Becky, Pinetop Burks, Dusky Dailey, Jolly Three, Kitty Gray, and Buddy Woods in San Antonio. In 1938 and 1939 ARC returned to record Kitty Gray, Buddy Woods, and Dusky Dailey. In 1940 ARC recorded the Wright Brothers Gospel Singers at the Burrus Mill Recording Studio in Saginaw, Texas. (This studio belonged to the Light Crust Doughboys.)

Other Texas R&B race-label musicians left the state to be recorded. Blind Lemon Jefferson, born near Wortham in Freestone County, was recorded by Paramount in Chicago from 1925 until 1929. He recorded his first national hit, "Long Lonesome Blues," in 1926 and went on to record over eighty songs for Paramount Records in Chicago and two for Okeh Records in Atlanta. He was the first country blues player to record commercially, and he was the most popular blues singer of the 1920s until his untimely death in 1929, twelve short years after he began performing with a tin cup at the corner of Elm Street and Central Tracks in the Deep Ellum district of Dallas. Jefferson's music has influenced countless musicians, from the first electric bluesman, T-Bone Walker, who combined Jefferson's acoustic guitar blues style with Charlie Christian's electric guitar style, to Bob Dylan, who recorded a Blind Lemon song, "See That My Grave Is Kept Clean," on his first album; and Jefferson Airplane, the band named for him.

T-Bone Walker made his first recordings in Dallas in 1929 for Columbia, but many of his major recordings in later years were made outside of Texas. In 1929 Columbia recorded "Whistlin" Alex Moore, one of the originators of the Texas boogie barrelhouse piano style, at its studio in Chicago. Okeh Records recorded Sippie Wallace (born Beulah Thomas in Houston) in Chicago and on a field trip to St. Louis (1926), where they also recorded jazz singer Victoria Spivey of Houston for the first time.

Mexican-American border music was also proving to have a profitable regional market, so some of the major race labels began recording Tejano artists. Most of the early recordings of Mexican-Americans were done in Los Angeles and Mexico. In the late 1920s some labels on their recording tours through Texas brought a few Tejano artists to their sessions in San Antonio, most notably accordionists Bruno Villareal and José Rodríguez, both from the San Benito area. The vocal duet of Pedro Rocha y Lupe Martínez, La Orquesta Típica and El Cuarteto Carta Blanca were also recorded in the late 1920s. In 1928 the great Lydia Mendoza made her first recording, for Okeh Records.

Recordings of Mexican-American music increased in the 1930s, with Tejano artists occupying more of the recording slots at the temporary studios in Texas. One of the Victor–Bluebird San Antonio sessions in 1934 recorded Octavio Mas Montes, Los Hermanos Chavarria, Gaytan y Cantú, Trio Texano, Pedro Rocha y Lupe Martínez, Bruno Villareal, Los Hermanos San Miguel, and Rafael Rodríguez. Also recorded at that session were the hillbilly band W. Lee O'Daniel and His Light Crust Doughboys and bluesman Texas Alexander. Lydia Mendoza left Okeh Records and began recording on the Bluebird label in 1934. An extremely popular singer worldwide, she recorded over 200 songs for them by 1940.

Accordionist Santiago Jiménez Sr. made his first recordings in San Antonio on the Decca label in 1936. He later switched to Victor because they paid $75 per recording and Decca only paid $21. Also in 1936, Narciso Martínez, accompanied by his *bajo sexto* player Santiago Almeida, of Skidmore, Texas, recorded twenty titles in one session. These recordings on the Bluebird label cemented the use of the *bajo sexto*, a Mexican double-coursed twelve-string bass guitar, as the preferred rhythm instrument with the accordion, replacing the traditional *tambora de rancho*, a drum that drowned out the accordion on recordings. Martínez had lived for a while near Corpus Christi among many Bohemians, Czechs, and Germans. He was among the first to blend the European and Mexican accordion styles, along with Camilo Cantú of Central Texas and Santiago Jiménez, who was doing the same in San Antonio. Martínez's recordings for Bluebird began the popularization of the conjunto style and were distributed worldwide. They were well received in many places, except Mexico

City, where music from "El Norte" was frowned upon at the time. Sadly, even though he is in the Conjunto Hall of Fame, Camilo Cantú was never recorded and his music is lost.

During the 1930s a clear difference in styles evolved between the border music of California and Texas. The popularity of the recordings from Texas helped to establish the Texan accordion–*bajo sexto* conjunto as a genre of its own. Contributing to this style was another San Antonio musician, Adolph Hofner, who recorded there for Okeh and Columbia. His band, Adolph Hofner and the San Antonians, played Western Swing mixed with Czech and German polkas.

Recording, radio, and western swing. When electronic recording began in 1925, there was some promise for expanding record sales, because discs were easier to replicate than cylinders. Electronics also brought about radio, however, and the expansion of commercial broadcast radio put a crimp in the growth of record sales in the early-to-mid 1920s. Radio was free and records were expensive, and the marketing relationship between the radio industry and record industry had not yet developed. Much of the recording in the 1920s was done at radio stations such as WOAI in San Antonio and WFAA in Dallas, where musicians would perform and be recorded on transcription discs for later broadcast. Transcription recording equipment was expensive, usually found only at the larger radio stations, and was not a consumer format, although some radios with built-in disc recorders were in the homes of wealthy people. The large transcription discs could be played only a few times, so copies of these are extremely noisy, but a few survive. The Great Depression further reduced the demand for records, which sold for about seventy-five cents, a fair amount of money in those days. However, the increasing use of jukeboxes created a market for records, and the major record companies that survived the depression saw their market expand in the 1930s, though prices of the 78-rpm records had dropped to about thirty-five cents each.

W. Lee O'Daniel's Light Crust Doughboys, a hillbilly precursor of western swing bands, was one of the first groups to exploit and be exploited by the powerful mix of radio and recording that began in the late 1920s. The popularity of their radio show on WBAP (Fort Worth) led to the creation of one of the first radio networks in America, the Texas Quality Network. The Light Crust Doughboys grew popular enough to afford their own recording studio in Saginaw, Texas, and may have been the first band in Texas to have its own studio. Though personnel in the band changed, the Light Crust Doughboys continued to record for decades, all the way into the twenty-first century. O'Daniel capitalized on the fame his band brought him by becoming governor of Texas and later a U.S. Senator.

Several members of the Light Crust Doughboys had a large impact on Texas music and recording after leaving the band. Milton Brown of Stephenville formed what is generally recognized as the first western swing band, Milton Brown and His Musical Brownies, in 1932. Brown made over 100 recordings for Victor and Decca before his untimely death in 1936. His blend of white hillbilly ("cow-

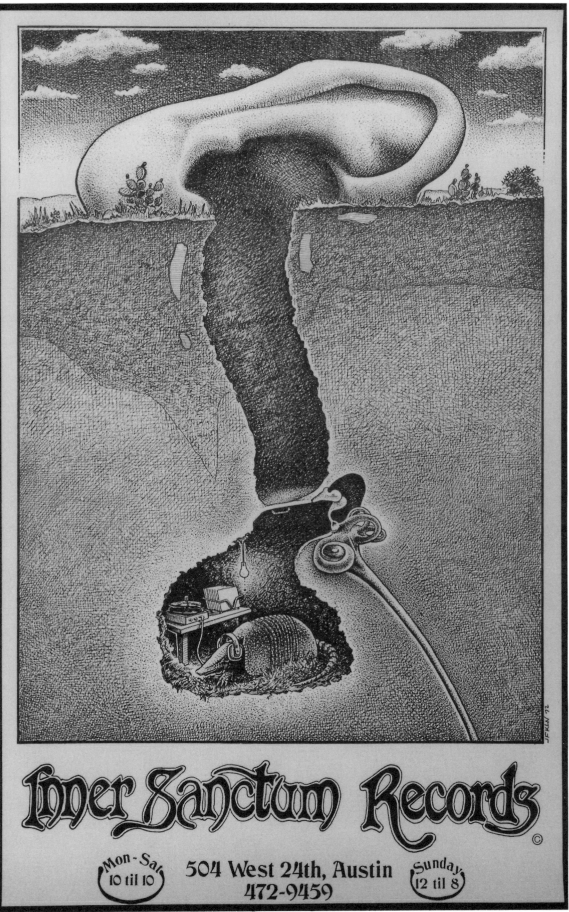

Inner Sanctum Records poster by Jim Franklin, 1972. Inner Sanctum was a popular record store located near the University of Texas campus, Austin. Courtesy George B. Ward.

boy square dance") music with blues and jazz and even polka and Mexican music became known as western swing. Bob Wills of Kosse, Texas, left the Doughboys in 1933 and formed the Texas Playboys, the most well known of the western swing bands, which often incorporated a horn section and played in a variety of styles. Wills and the Texas Playboys made their first recording in 1935, for American Record Company's other famous producer, Art Satherley. Marvin "Smokey" Montgomery, a long-time member of the Doughboys, became a successful record producer and studio owner in the decades after World War II.

Bill Boyd's Cowboy Ramblers, another top Western swing group of the 1930s, recorded the popular "Under the Double Eagle." Boyd, from Ladonia, Texas, first recorded his band for Bluebird in San Antonio in 1934, with a style and instrumentation that was more traditional than Wills's. The Cowboy Ramblers were also different in that they performed mostly in the recording studio and on the radio, rarely touring. They recorded over 200 songs for RCA–Bluebird and appeared in six Hollywood films in the 1940s.

In 1939 the Houston dance band Cliff Bruner and His Boys recorded "Truck Driver's Blues," written by East Texas musician Ted Daffan, a steel and electric guitar pioneer. This record was a hit for the Decca label and was the first song of the "big-rig truck-drivin'" genre of country music, which remained popular for decades. Moon Mullican, from Corrigan, was the vocalist.

World War II, the postwar era, and the rise of Texas record labels and recording studios. When World War II began, commercial recording in the United States slowed dramatically. The shellac used for discs was needed for the war effort, as was the beeswax used for the master recordings. In addition, a general strike by the American Federation of Musicians in 1942 prevented the labels from recording for two full years. The strike was called to seek royalties from the record companies for a fund to compensate musicians who lost work because of competition from recorded music. Until the strike, musicians were paid only a flat fee per recording, and were not compensated when their records were sold, played on jukeboxes, or broadcast on radio. By 1943, through an agreement with the AFM, this work stoppage induced the U.S. Army to produce its own records, called V-discs ("Victory-discs") for the entertainment of American soldiers. Texan jazz musicians Jack Teagarden and Oran "Hot Lips" Page recorded on V-discs, as did Bill Boyd, Bob Wills with the Texas Playboys, and Tex Ritter. Between 1943 and 1949 more than eight million of these vinyl twelve-inch records were manufactured. Most of the V-discs were destroyed after the war, in keeping with an agreement made with the AFM.

After the war, the American recording industry grew and changed. Innovations in materials and electronics developed during the war were adapted to commercial recording. Once again, Texas had a large role to play in the artistic, technical, and commercial areas of the recording industry. Technology derived from antisubmarine acoustic listening equipment was adapted to audio recording and record production. The development of the first working transistor by Texas Instruments in 1954 further improved

electronic designs, allowing higher fidelity with lower noise levels than vacuum tube circuitry, along with reduced size and heat levels. Although immediately after the war smaller labels often made new records of melted old ones, advances in plastics ended the use of shellac and led to discs that could have grooves much closer together, allowing longer playing times and eventually slower rotation speeds. Masters were no longer recorded on wax but rather on magnetic tape, a new medium developed from captured German tape recorders. The reviving American economy and the baby boom were creating a huge audience for recorded music and its consumer technology. Broadcast television began to have as much of an impact on the recording industry as radio did in the 1920s and '30s, and Hollywood had discovered the "singing cowboy." After the war, the large record companies did not resume their field recording trips. They were making large profits from national hits recorded at their studios and decided the extra expense of location recording did not justify the return from sales in regional markets. This was typically shortsighted on their part, but it opened the door for the growth of the Texas recording industry.

The postwar decade saw the rise of smaller regional labels to fill the void left by the larger companies. The cessation of location recording by the larger labels also created a need for recording facilities in Texas. Many GIs returned from the war with electronic skills, which they put to use by building recording studios. In the late 1940s studios and record manufacturing plants were built in Dallas, Houston, San Antonio, and even Alice and McAllen by entrepreneurial engineers and businessmen to facilitate recording for their record labels. The lack of commercially manufactured professional-grade audio-recording equipment meant many studio engineers had to design and fabricate their own microphone preamplifiers and mixing consoles until the 1970s, when designers such as Englishman Rupert Neve began producing high-quality manufactured equipment. Neve, widely regarded in the professional audio industry as its foremost designer, resides in Wimberley, Texas.

Houston and East Texas. One of the premier Texas studios of the period, ACA Studios, was built in the growing city of Houston in 1948 by Bill Holford Sr. after he left the service, where he had been a radio and sound-reinforcement technician. ACA (Audio Company of America) had its own label, ACA Records, but many other regional Texas labels hired Holford, including Peacock, Bellaire, "D" Records, Starday, and even the diminutive but no less significant Sarg Records label of Luling, Texas. (Sarg Records produced the first recordings of KBOP disc jockey Willie Nelson and San Antonio child prodigy Doug Sahm.) Known for the quality of his recordings, Holford was well liked and respected by such artists as B.B. King, Sonny Boy Williamson, Lightnin' Hopkins, Johnny Winter, Clarence Brown, Johnny Copeland, T-Bone Walker, Big Mama Thornton, Little Richard, and many other famous musicians who enjoyed recording at his studio.

Native Houstonian producer, label owner and songwriter Don Robey was one of the most important figures in Texan pop, jazz, gospel and R&B music. In 1949 Robey, a nightclub owner, was managing Clarence "Gatemouth" Brown, of Orange, Texas. In order to get Brown recorded, Robey started his own label, Peacock Records. The first successful black-owned record label, Peacock produced hits by Gatemouth Brown, Willie Mae "Big Mama" Thornton ("Hound Dog"), Floyd Dixon, Memphis Slim, and Marie Adams. Peacock also released progressive jazz recordings by Betty Carter and Sonny Criss. Robey bought the Duke label of Memphis, Tennessee, in 1952, adding Bobby Blue Bland, Roscoe Gordon, Junior Parker, and Johnny Ace to his roster of artists. In 1957 Robey started the Back Beat label and had hits by O.V. Wright, Joe Hinton, and country-rocker Roy Head of San Marcos. Robey built Peacock Studio in Houston in 1958, and added gospel artists to his R&B roster, including the Hummingbirds, who had a minor national hit with "Loves Me Like A Rock" and later backed Paul Simon on his recording of the song. Robey sold Duke–Peacock Records to ABC–Dunhill in 1973.

Houston became a major center of rhythm-and-blues and zydeco in the 1950s and '60s, giving rise to a number of record labels, studios, and record-manufacturing plants. Bill Quinn built Gold Star Studio there, where East Texas musician Harry Choates recorded his famous arrangement of "Jole Blon" for Gold Star Records in 1946. Moon Mullican's version of Choates's song on King Records a year later took the nation by storm. Quinn had started Gold Star to record country singers, but the label became known for its blues artists. In the 1950s J. P. "Big Bopper" Richardson recorded "Chantilly Lace," and Johnny Preston recorded "Running Bear" at Gold Star. Lightnin' Hopkins recorded his first songs at Gold Star. He would often stop in to record a song or two, sometimes written on the spot, when he needed cash. Gold Star was one of twenty labels on which Hopkins recorded. Thunder Smith, Lil Son Jackson, and Smoky Hogg also recorded at Gold Star.

Pappy Daily of Houston bought Bill Quinn's Choates masters in 1955, and released them on his independent "D" Records label. "D" Records started the commercial careers of the Big Bopper, George Jones, Willie Nelson, and George Strait and the Ace in the Hole Band. It ceased operations in 1975, but started up again in 2002. Daily's larger Starday label, established in 1952, was distributed by Mercury and is best known for releasing George Jones's first recordings. Daily sold Starday in 1957, and the label moved to Nashville.

Quinn's Gold Star Studio eventually became Sugar Hill Studio in 1971, purchased by legendary producer Huey Meaux who had earlier used it for his Crazy Cajun, Jetstream, Pacemaker, and other labels. It subsequently hosted many noted artists, some not on Meaux's labels, including Archie Bell and the Drells, Barbara Lynn, Clay Walker, the Who, B. J. Thomas, Sunny (Sonny Ozuna) and the Sunliners (the first all-Mexican-American band to appear on American Bandstand), Roy Head, the Sir Douglas Quintet with Doug Sahm and Augie Meyers, Freddy Fender (who had a hit with "Before the Next Teardrop Falls") Janis Joplin, Smash Mouth, Destiny's Child, and even the Rolling Stones. Tejano star Selena recorded her first album at Sugar Hill in 1983 for Freddie Records.

International Artist was a Houston label of the 1960s. It was run by Kenny Rogers's brother Lelan and recorded early psychedelic bands at Andrus Studios, most notably Austin's Roky Erickson and the 13th Floor Elevators, Bubble Puppy, and Gold Rush. The psychedelic scene provided contrast to the country music scene in Houston that centered around Mickey Gilley's Jones Recording Studio in North Houston, and later, Gilley's night club in Pasadena. Gilley built a new studio next to the club, where part of the soundtrack to the film *Urban Cowboy* was produced.

Tyler, Texas, also has a recording history. Studio recording there began in the 1960s, with facilities like Robin Hood Brian's Recording Studio, where ZZ Top, John Fred & His Playboy Band, David Houston, the Uniques, the Five Americans, Southwest FOB (later England Dan & John Ford Coley), Mouse & the Traps, Jon & Robin, and Gladstone, along with hundreds of other regional acts, recorded for larger labels such as Epic and Paula and smaller local labels such as Ty-Tex and Custom. LeAnn Rimes has recorded many songs, including Grammy-winning "Blue," at Rosewood Studio in Tyler. From a handful of studios after the war, by the twenty-first century there were over 150 listed studios in the Houston and East Texas area.

Dallas and Fort Worth. Dallas also had its share of recording business in the postwar period. Though there was still musical activity in Deep Ellum, much of the R&B recording of the time was done in Houston, but some small, musician-owned labels were established, including Timothy McNeally's Shawn label and Roger Boykin's Soul-Tex label. Country artists continued to record in Dallas, along with some rockabilly pioneers. Bill Boyd was recording at Jack Sellers Studios during the 1950s, where Eck Robertson had recorded a comeback try in the 1940s. Rockabilly pioneers Gene Summers, Johnny Carroll of Cleburne, Gene Vincent of "Be-Bop-A-Lula" fame (the "Lost Dallas Sessions"), Dallas's rockabilly pioneer Groovey Joe Poovey (later "Johnny Dallas") and Bob Kelly, who also owned Top Ten Studios in Dallas, all recorded at Sellers Studios.

Dallas studio owner Jim Beck discovered Lefty Frizzell. Beck, who recorded the singer from Corsicana in 1950, took the recordings to his friend Don Law, then with Columbia Records. Law came to Texas and recorded Frizzell singing "If You've Got The Money, I've Got The Time" which sold 2½ million copies in two months, thus launching Lefty's career. Also recording at Jim Beck's studio were George Jones, Ray Price, Floyd Tillman, and Marty Robbins. Beck was very influential with the major labels, and if not for his untimely death in 1958, Dallas might have gained the stature of Nashville as a country music recording center.

In nearby Fort Worth, producer "Major Bill" Smith's Josie Records label released several national hits in the 1960s, including Bruce Channel's hit "Hey Baby," Delbert McClinton and the Ron-Dels' "If You Really Want Me To I'll Go," Paul & Paula's "Hey Paula," and J. Frank Wilson and the Cavaliers' "Last Kiss."

Marvin "Smokey" Montgomery, of the Light Crust Doughboys, who produced "Hey Baby" and "Hey Paula," built the world-famous Sumet Studios in Dallas. Montgomery produced and recorded albums by the Doughboys and many other Texas bands there for decades. Still in operation today, Sumet Studios has seen many famous musicians from all over the world, including Helen Reddy, who recorded "I Am Woman" there in 1971.

In 1974, engineers Glen Pace and Phil York built Autumn Sound, the first twenty-four-track recording studio in Texas. Within a month of its opening, Willie Nelson recorded *Red-Headed Stranger* there. Willie's first number one hit as a singer, "Blue Eyes Crying In The Rain," was on that Grammy-winning album, and he went on to record three more platinum albums at Autumn Sound. Today the studio is called Audio Dallas. Dallas Sound Labs hosted Stevie Ray Vaughan for three albums in the 1980s and is still in open today as both a studio and recording school. Planet Dallas, Palmyra Studios, Indian Trail, and Deep Ellum Studios are among the 200 or more studios that are continuing the Dallas–Fort Worth and North Central Texas recording tradition in the twenty-first century.

West Texas and the beginnings of rock-and-roll. In West Texas during the 1950s, a new musical style was emerging that took the world by storm. Buddy Holly and the Crickets in 1957, and Buddy Knox and the Rhythm Orchids with Jimmy Bowen in 1956, recorded their first hit songs at Norm Petty's studio in Clovis, New Mexico, just across the state line. Roy Orbison also recorded there, as did Jimmy Gilmer and the Fireballs. There were some small studios in West Texas, like Bobby Peeble's Venture Recording Studio in Lubbock, where Holly recorded once in 1956, and Nesman Recording Studio in Wichita Falls, where Buddy recorded the acetates that led to his short-lived contract with Decca, but Petty's production skills and equipment quality were well known and in demand. The songs Holley and the Crickets recorded there, including "That'll Be The Day," were released on the Brunswick and Coral labels. Musicians such as Tommy Allsup, who built a studio in Odessa in the 1960s, met the need for studios in the region. Allsup had played lead guitar for Buddy Holly.

Long-time Lubbock saxophonist and four-track studio owner Don Caldwell, with the help of Lubbock banker–musician Lloyd Llove, built a multi-track studio where Texas artists such as the second-generation Maines Brothers, Joe Ely, Delbert McClinton, Butch Hancock, Terry Allen, and many others recorded and continue to record. Norm Petty required long-term contracts from his artists, and was known for sometimes keeping their royalties, so Caldwell's studio and Telephone Records label, which often allowed artists on the label to retain ownership of their material, was popular for many years. The studio still operates today. In El Paso, Bobby Fuller built a studio in 1962 and released on his own Exeter label the first recording of "I Fought the Law," which he later recorded again in Los Angeles. In West Texas and the Panhandle today there are at least three dozen studios.

South Texas and San Antonio. In South Texas, labels sprang up to present the music of Tejano and other artists abandoned by the major labels. In Alice, jukebox business owner Armando Marroquín was frustrated with the postwar lack of Tejano records from American labels. To supply his jukeboxes, Marroquín started Ideal Records at his home in 1946. He recorded his wife, Carmen, who sang with her sister Laura as Carmen y Laura, and released the recordings as mass-produced 78s. Marroquín was the first Mexican American to produce a conjunto record in the United States. Paco Betancourt, a record distributor from San Benito, partnered with Marroquín that year. They moved the studio to a building in Alice, where hundreds of recordings by artists including Narciso Martínez, Chelo Silva, Beto Villa's Orchestra, Valerio Longoria, Carmen y Laura, Juan López, Maya y Cantú of Nuevo Laredo, Paulino Bernal, Johnny Herrera and Linda Escobar were made over the next decade. In this decade Narciso Martínez made recordings in which he added vocal duets to the accordion conjunto, innovating yet another musical style. When a Mexican bolero singer, María Victoria, recorded one of Johnny Herrera's songs for RCA Victor in Mexico and the song became popular, the long-standing Mexican resistance to music from "El Norte" began to break down. Eventually a strong market for Texas music developed south of the border.

Ideal also recorded corrido singers such as Jesús Maya and Timoteo Cantú, reviving an old tradition of singing ballads about current events and politics that had gone dormant in the 1940s with the demise of the major labels' field trips. The partnership of Marroquín and Bentancourt ended amicably in 1959, with Marroquín starting Nopal Records in Alice and Betancourt moving Ideal to San Benito. Ideal opened a new studio and record-pressing plant in San Benito, where one of the singers on the label, Baldemar Huerta, also engineered at times. Baldemar, who recorded regional music at the time along with Spanish translations of American pop tunes, went on to popular music fame under the name Freddie Fender.

Arnaldo Ramírez founded Falcon Records in McAllen in 1948. With several subsidiary labels, including Bronco, ARV, Impacto, El Pato, and Bego, it became the largest of the conjunto labels. Many artists who recorded for Ideal recorded for Falcon, whose roster included Los Alegres de Terán, Chelo Silva, Lydia Mendoza, Dueto Estrella, Steve Jordan, and the woman duets of Hermanas Degollado, Rosita y Aurelia, Hermanas Cantú, Hermanas Mendoza, Hermanas Segovia, and Las Dos Marías. Musicians from Nuevo León, Mexico, also recorded for Falcon and Ideal as the cross-border exchange of musical styles increased.

In San Antonio, Manuel Rangel Sr., with a recording of Valerio Longoria, started the Corona label in 1948. He was soon followed by Hymie Wolf, who founded Rio Records. Rio had a relatively brief lifespan, but recorded many established artists of the period, including Pedro Rocha, Jesús Casiano, who was another pioneer conjunto accordionist, Juan Gaytán, Frank Cantú, Manuel Valdez, and Lydia Mendoza's sisters, Juanita and María. Some new artists who later became popular made their first recordings on Rio, including Fred Zimmerle, Valerio Longoria, Tony de la Rosa, Leandro Guerrero, Felix Borrayo, Frank Corrales, Los Pavos Reales, Pedro Ibarra, Los Tres Diamantes, Los Chavalitos, Conjunto Topo Chico, Conjunto San Antonio Alegre, a lower Valley accordionist who played in the Louisiana zydeco style of Clifton Chenier named Armando Almendárez, Alonzo and his Rancheros, and ranchera singer Ada García. Also making his debut on Rio in 1956 was Santiago Jiménez Sr.'s son Leonardo, better known today as the great Flaco Jiménez, who has recorded on many major labels. Flaco's younger brother, Santiago Jr., continues their father's musical tradition on Chief Records. Other San Antonio Tejano labels included Discos Grande, Lira, and Magda.

The Texas Top Hands owned Everstate Records, a small country label in the late 1940s and early 50s. San Antonio disc jockey Joe Anthony's R&B label, Harlem–Ebony, and Bob Tanner's TNT (Tanner 'N Texas) Records, which also had a studio and a record manufacturing plant in the city, were also important labels. Some other early studios in San Antonio were Jeff Smith's Texas Sound Studios, Abe Epstein Studio, and Eddie Morris' Studio. KENS Radio–TV studio was also used to record music; Adolph Hofner recorded there for Sarg Records in 1958. Blue Cat Studio opened in the late 1970s, and in the early 1980s Augie Meyers built CAM Studios. There are at least six dozen studios in the San Antonio area today.

By the 1960s a new generation of Tejano artists was emerging, as was the Chicano movement, and new labels were created to record their music. Roberto Pulido, with Los Clasicos, debuted on the Lago label. San Antonio's Sonny Ozuna, who blended Tejano with American pop as Sunny and the Sunliners, recorded on Joey Records, and bandmate Manny Guerra started his GC and Mr. G labels and built Amen Studios, still in operation after the turn of the century. In Corpus Christi, Freddie Records was started by Freddy Martínez Sr. to release his own recordings. Still in business today, the label added artists like Tony de la Rosa, Ramón Ayala, Little Joe y La Familia and Jaime de Anda y Los Chamacos, among others, and owns the Legends Studio. Hacienda Records, also formed in Corpus Christi, recorded the famous Los Hermanos Ayala and, later, Linda Escobar, La Tropa F, Mingo Saldivar, David Lee Garza, and accordionist Eva Ybarra. New artists include Victoria Galván and Albert Zamora. Hacienda Records also built the first twenty-four-track recording studio in South Texas in the late 1970s and is still a major South Texas studio. In Corpus Christi and the Valley today there are at least two dozen studios.

Austin and Central Texas. In the late 1950s Austin had a local label called Domino Records, which released records by George Underwood, Clarence Smith (later Sonny Rhodes) and the Daylighters, blues steel guitarist Sonny Rhodes, Ray Campi, the Slades, and Joyce Harris. Domino shut down in the early 1960s, leaving a few other smaller labels including jazz–funk keyboardist James Polk's Twink Records and Bill Josey's Sonobeat Records. Sonobeat built a small studio and made records released on other labels by Johnny Winter, Ray Campi, the Lavender Hill Express, James Polk, and others until it closed in the early 1970s. These labels faded away just as Texas saw the emergence of its own blend of folk, rock, and country musical styles variously called "alternative country," "progressive country" and "redneck rock."

A sizable scene of this genre sprang up in Austin, and the city's reputation for alternative country really caught on when Willie Nelson moved back from Nashville in the early 1970s. Willie, Waylon Jennings, Jerry Jeff Walker, Carolyn Hester, Steve Fromholz, B. W. Stevenson, and Ray Benson were joined by a new generation of progressive folk–country–rock musicians, including Alvin Crow, Michael Martin Murphy, Jimmie Dale Gilmore, Ray Wylie Hubbard, Butch Hancock, Rusty Weir, Gary P. Nunn, Walter Hyatt and David Ball (Uncle Walt's Band), Joe Ely, Junior Brown, Stephen Doster, Nanci Griffith, Lyle Lovett, and Robert Earl Keen, to name just a few. This influx of talent demanded good recording facilities. There were some small studios in the back of clubs like the Vulcan Gas Company and the Armadillo World Headquarters, but there were no real commercial studio facilities for recording in Austin until the 1970s, when several studios were built to serve the city's expanding music scene.

Willie Nelson built Pedernales Recording Studio for his Lone Star label at his estate outside Austin in the mid-1970s, where he has recorded most of his albums, including duets with Frank Sinatra, of which at least a dozen are platinum records. He later built Arlyn Studios at the Austin Opry House complex in the early 1980s. Eric Johnson, Stevie Ray Vaughan & Double Trouble, the Indigo Girls, and Little Joe y La Familia recorded gold records at Arlyn, in the company of major recording artists from around the country. Johnson and Little Joe now have their own studios. Odyssey Studio was opened in 1972 by a group of Austin musicians. It was remodeled and became Pecan Street Studios, the first Texas studio to be recognized by the Society of Professional Audio Recording Services. In 1981 Pecan Street Studios was rebuilt once more and as "Studio South" became the first automated studio in the Southwest. At the Studio South facility, FreeFlow Productions recorded numerous successful projects for major-label release and international distribution before it closed a few years later. Among these were projects by Carole King, Jerry Jeff Walker, Ry Cooder, Willie Nelson, Shake Russell, Joe Ely, Al Kooper, and the Lost Gonzo Band.

The Austin Recording Studio also opened in the early 1970s, and Asleep at the Wheel recorded several Grammy winners there before building their own studio. ARS is still in business. In the late 1970s Riverside Sound Studio opened; before it closed in the early 1990s, it recorded tracks for Stevie Ray Vaughan's *Texas Flood* (1983) and *Soul to Soul* (1985) albums, and Eric Johnson's *Ah Via Musicom* (1990), in addition to many albums for its Austin Records label. Electric Graceyland Studios and associated label Jackalope–Rude Records opened in 1978, and has produced recordings for Kimmie Rhodes, Alejandro Escovedo, Joe King Carrasco, Butch Hancock, Jimmie Dale Gilmore, Alvin Crow, the Leroi Brothers, Wes McGhee, Calvin Russell, Asleep at the Wheel, Ray Campi, and Willie Nelson. In the late 1980s the Hit Shack studio made the first of many albums for Texas artists, including Jerry Jeff Walker, Bill Carter, Chris Smither, Stephen Bruton, Sue Foley, Jerry Lightfoot, the Leroi Brothers, Charlie Sexton, Terry Allen, Hal Ketchum, Ian Moore, Alejandro Escovedo and others.

By the mid-1980s digital recording technology was making rapid gains, and more major labels such as WEA International, Sony Discos, and Arista Texas were recording in Texas. Fire Station Studios in San Marcos had the first digital multitrack in Texas, followed closely by Digital Services in Houston and Arlyn Studios in Austin. The first digitally recorded album released in Texas, Doug Sahm's 1989 *Juke Box Music* on the Antone's label, was recorded at the Fire Station and won an Indie, the award of the National Association of Independent Record Distributors and Manufacturers, in 1989. Other albums recorded there include the Texas Tornados' *Texas Tornados* (1990), which won a Grammy on the Warner Reprise label; Tish Hinojosa's Indie-winning albums, *Homeland* (1989) on A&M and *Culture Swing* (1992) on the Rounder Records label; and even a Lucha Villa record for WEA International in Mexico. The Fire Station became the home of the Sound Recording Technology program at Southwest Texas State University in the early 1990s. Today in the Central Texas region there are well over 200 studios. The sound archives in the Center for American History at the University of Texas at Austin holds one of the state's most extensive collections of music and the spoken word in all formats from early cylinders to the modern CD.

The "digital revolution" in recording technology that began in the 1980s dramatically reduced the cost of professional-quality recording equipment. Many more musicians began building their own project studios and started their own record labels. The rapid proliferation of studios and labels, coupled with the growth of the Internet as a low-cost digital distribution and marketing medium, is having an even more dramatic impact on the major-label recording industry than the advent of radio and television. Just over three decades ago, there were a few dozen studios and labels in Texas. Today, at the dawn of the twenty-first century, there are over 700 studios, and nearly that many record labels, listed with the Texas Music Office. Undoubtedly, many more unlisted private home studios exist across the state, and the trend towards releasing music on private labels shows no signs of slowing down.

BIBLIOGRAPHY: Arhoolie Records homepage (www.arhoolie.com), accessed March 1, 2003. Andrew Brown, liner notes to *Harry Choates—Devil in the Bayou* (Bear Family Records, BCD 16355). Andrew Brown, *The Sarg Records Anthology: South Texas 1954–1964* (Sarg Records, n.d.). Ronald Dethlefson, *Edison Blue Amberol Recordings, Volume II, 1915–1929* (Brooklyn, New York: APM Press, 1981). R. M. W. Dixon, John Godrich, and Howard Rye, *Blues and Gospel Records, 1890–1943*, Fourth Edition (Oxford: Clarendon Press, 1997). Cary Ginell and Kevin Coffey, *Discography of Western Swing and Hot String Bands, 1928–1942* (Westport, Connecticut: Greenwood Press, 2001). Alan B. Govenar and Jay F. Brakefield, *Deep Ellum and the Central Track* (Denton: University of North Texas Press, 1998). Pekka Gronow and Ilpo Saunio, *An International History of the Recording Industry*, trans. from Finnish by Christopher Mosely (New York: Wellington House, 1998). Frank Hoffman and Tim Gracyk, *Popular American Recording Pioneers 1895–1925* (New York: Haworth Press, 2000). Bill C. Malone, *Country Music USA*, third printing (Austin: University of Texas Press, 1993). Manuel H. Peña. *The Texas-Mexican Conjunto* (Austin: University of Texas Press, 1985). Jan Reid, *The Improbable Rise of Redneck Rock* (New York: Da Capo Press, 1977). Brian Rust, *The American Record Label Book* (New Rochelle, New York: Arlington House, 1978). Mark Sanders and Ruthe Winegarten, *The Lives and Times of Black Dallas Women* (Austin: Eakin Press, 2002). Richard Schroeder, *Texas Signs On* (College Station: Texas A&M Press, 1998). Steve Schoenherr, *Recording Technology History* (http://history.acusd.edu/gen/recording/notes.html), accessed March 1, 2003. Alan Sutton, *Directory of American Disc Record Brands and Manufacturers* (Westport, Connecticut: Greenwood Press, 1994). Vertical file, "Recording Studios," Center for American History, University of Texas at Austin. Larry Willoughby. *Texas Rhythm, Texas Rhyme* (Austin: Eakin Press, 1991). *Gary S. Hickinbotham*

Reeves, Jim. Country and popular singer; b. James Travis Reeves, Galloway, Texas, August 20, 1923; d. near Nashville, July 31, 1964; son of Tom and Mary (Adams) Reeves. After graduation from Carthage High School in 1942, Reeves attended the University of Texas and played for the university baseball team. He pitched briefly for Marshall and Henderson in the Class C East Texas League but retired from baseball in 1946 after a leg injury. In 1947 he was an announcer and disc jockey at KGRI in Henderson and began singing locally under the name Sonny Day.

Reeves recorded first in 1949 for Macy, a small Houston company, but had no real success until 1952, when he signed a contract with Abbott Records. His second Abbott recording, "Mexican Joe," brought him national popularity and led him in 1953 to employment as an announcer for KWKH, Shreveport, and subsequent appearances on the "Louisiana Hayride." After his second successful recording, "Bimbo," Reeves joined the Grand Ole Opry in Nashville, Tennessee, in 1955 and began recording for RCA Victor. His most successful recordings were "He'll Have To Go" and "Four Walls."

Reeves and his pianist, Dean Manuel, were killed when his private plane crashed near Nashville. He was buried in a two-acre memorial plot near Carthage, Texas, on the road to Shreveport. At the time of his death Reeves owned KGRI in Henderson and three music-publishing companies. He had made three European tours and two trips to South Africa, where he starred in a film, *Kimberley Jim*, which was released the year after his death. He was survived by his wife, Mary, whom he had married in 1946. They had no children. In 1967 Reeves was inducted into the Country Music Hall of Fame.

BIBLIOGRAPHY: Linnell Gentry, *A History and Encyclopedia of Country, Western, and Gospel Music* (Nashville: McQuiddy Press, 1961). Bill C. Malone, *Country Music U.S.A.* (Austin: University of Texas Press, 1968). Vertical Files, Center for American History, University of Texas at Austin. *Bill C. Malone*

Reis, Claire Raphael. Music promoter and author; b. Brownsville, Texas, August 4, 1888; d. New York City, April 11, 1978; daughter of Gabriel M. and Eugenie (Salamon) Raphael. She married Arthur M. Reis, president of Robert Reis and Company, on December 20, 1915. They

Country singer and Shreveport radio announcer Jim Reeves with young fan Gianfranco Spellman, Fort Polk, Louisiana, ca. 1953. Gianfranco Spellman Collection.

had two children. Claire was educated in France, Germany, and New York and studied music under Bertha Fiering Tapper at the Institute of Musical Art. From 1912 to 1922 she worked to found the People's Music League of the People's Institute in New York, an organization that provided free concerts for immigrants and public schools. She became licensed as a kindergarten music teacher and adapted Montessori teaching methods to music. In 1914 she helped establish the Walden School.

In 1923 Mrs. Reis and several contemporary composers established the League of Composers as an alternative to the International Composers' Guild. She was the league's executive director for twenty-five years, during which time she promoted many first performances and commissioned 100 new works; among the new artists she helped was Aaron Copland. In 1955 she published *Composers, Conductors and Critics*, which describes events and people from her experience in the league. She also wrote several articles, two catalogs for the International Society for Contemporary Music, and *American Composers of Today* (1947; revised and enlarged as *Composers in America: Biographical Sketches*, 1977). She was secretary of the board of directors of the New York City Center of Music and Drama.

Mrs. Reis helped found the Women's City Club and was a member of the advisory board for New York City of the WPA. She served on the advisory committee of music for

the 1939 New York World's Fair, and she was appointed by President Franklin Roosevelt to the New York Committee on the Use of Leisure Time. Among the awards she received were the National Association of American Composers and Conductors award for outstanding service (1945–46); the Laurel Leaf award of the American Composers Alliance (1963); a scroll from Mayor John V. Lindsay acknowledging her assistance in founding the City Center (1968); and the New York City Handel Medallion for "her outstanding contributions and dedicated efforts for cultural achievement" (1969).

BIBLIOGRAPHY: H. Wiley Hitchcock and Stanley Sadie, eds., *The New Grove Dictionary of American Music* (New York: Macmillan, 1986). New York *Times*, April 13, 1978. *Who's Who of American Women*, 1968–69.

Donna P. Parker

Reiter, Max. Director of the San Antonio Symphony Orchestra; b. Trieste, Italy, October 20, 1905; d. San Antonio, December 13, 1950. In 1915 his German-born businessman father and his Italian mother moved to Munich, where he continued his middle-school education and attended a university. He studied conducting with Bruno Walter and at the insistence of his father also earned a doctorate in law.

Reiter's first public appearance was in a concert in 1927 with the violinist Joseph Szigeti. In 1929 he became the first assistant conductor at the State Opera of Berlin. He conducted orchestras to glowing reviews in all the major cities of Italy, at the Mozarteum in Salzburg, at Munich, Budapest, and Warsaw, and in Russia. He conducted opera in Yugoslavia as well. In 1933, with the rise of Nazism, he left Germany and settled in Milan, where he became director of the orchestra. In 1937 in Merano he became acquainted with Richard Strauss, who arranged a symphonic suite of waltzes from the opera *Der Rosenkavalier* at Reiter's suggestion. The friendship between the two men later led Reiter to premiere many of Strauss's works with the San Antonio Symphony and in radio broadcasts.

After the Fascists staged an anti-Semitic demonstration outside of the hall in Rome where he was conducting in August 1938, Reiter left for the United States. Following a brief stop in Switzerland, he arrived in New York, only to find the city overcrowded with conductors, many of whom were European refugees. Reiter was advised by the Steinway family to go to Texas, which he believed to be one of the areas least affected by the Great Depression—more Steinway pianos per capita had sold in Texas than in any other state.

In Texas, Reiter first went to San Antonio, where, in spite of initial encouragement, he made little immediate progress in establishing an orchestra. He then traveled to Waco, where he gave a "demonstration concert," using an orchestra composed of Baylor University music faculty, student members of the Baylor orchestra and band, amateur musicians from Waco, and a few key players from the Dallas Symphony Orchestra. Inspired by the success of this concert, Waco citizens decided to form a symphony orchestra and engaged Reiter to conduct four concerts the following season.

In the meantime some of Reiter's supporters from San Antonio had attended the Waco concert and reasoned that Reiter would do even better in a city like San Antonio, which had a greater supply of talent and a long-standing tradition of supporting the arts. Reiter's supporters organized a similar demonstration concert in the Sunken Garden Theater in San Antonio on June 12, 1939. The event was a resounding success and led to the establishment of the Symphony Society of San Antonio, with Reiter as the orchestra's founding conductor and music director. Under his baton the San Antonio Symphony Orchestra, which began with amateur players as well as professional musicians, grew and prospered.

Reiter was invited to conduct with the NBC Orchestra, which was under the direction of Arturo Toscanini, and with the ABC Orchestra, among other distinguished appearances. The San Antonio children's concerts and the annual opera festival, with nationally acclaimed guest stars, were inaugurated under Reiter's leadership. In June 1946 Reiter married Pauline Washer Goldsmith, who had helped found the orchestra.

BIBLIOGRAPHY: Theodore Albrecht, "101 Years of Symphonic Music in San Antonio," *Southwestern Musician / Texas Music Educator*, March, November 1975. San Antonio *Express News*, October 11, 1964. San Antonio *Light*, October 6, 1963. *Lois G. Oppenheimer*

Reo Palm Isle. A dance hall in Longview, Texas; originally between Longview and Kilgore. Mattie Castleberry established Mattie's Ballroom in the East Texas woods in 1935. Born in oil-boom days, Mattie's Ballroom was an instant success. The boom brought big money to depression-era East Texas towns, leading to the rapid growth of dance halls and clubs such as Mattie's Ballroom, which catered largely to oilfield workers.

The music played at Mattie's and other such honky-tonk dancehalls had a strong danceable beat and lyrics derived from blue-collar life. Mattie's was a rustic building containing a dance floor, an orchestra pit, booths, and a giant revolving mirror ball above the center of the dance floor. Bands that frequented the ballroom during this era included Glenn Miller, Tommy Dorsey, Ted Lewis, Ozzie Nelson, Ella Fitzgerald, Jack Teagarden, Louis Armstrong, Paul Whiteman, Fred Waring and his Pennsylvanians, Jan Garber, Bob Wills, Gene Krupa, Glen Gray, and Herb Cook. The club employed hostesses, a practice that was common in dance halls at the time. Each girl charged a dime per dance. At one time the hall had forty such hostesses. Later, Mattie's Ballroom gained a reputation as a good place for couples to go dancing; the cover charge was fifty cents per couple.

World War II tightened the supply of gasoline and affected transportation. Mattie decided to move the dance hall closer to town and contacted Hugh Cooper about purchasing his Palm Isle Club (the current location, at Farm Road 1835 and Highway 31 in Longview). Mattie didn't have enough money to purchase the club, but her reputation preceded her, and Cooper allowed her to pay for the club in installments. There was no written contract between the two, and Castleberry paid her complete debt with no problems. She renamed the club Reo Palm Isle.

Mattie Castleberry died in Marshall, Texas, in August 1954. In 2003 the owners of the club were Max and Sharon Singleton. Over the years the Reo Palm Isle has provided a venue for many stars and ascending stars, including Elvis Presley, Waylon Jennings, David Frizzell, Boots Randolph, Loretta Lynn, Shelly West, Jerry Lee Lewis, Kenny Sarrett, Frenchie Burke, Willie Nelson, Joe Stampley, Jackie Ward, Johnny Paycheck, Alabama, Boxcar Willie, Hank Williams Jr., Ronnie Milsap, Lee Greenwood, Ricky Skaggs, Delbert McClinton, David Allen Coe, and Mickey Gilley. The club has a 3,000-square-foot dance floor, the largest in East Texas. Other features include pool tables, a mechanical bull, and a restaurant. Reo Palm Isle was rated the best dance hall in *Texas Monthly* magazine in 1976 and one of the state's top ten clubs in *Texas Highways*.

BIBLIOGRAPHY:; Bill C. Malone, "Texas Myth, Texas Music," *Journal of Texas Music History* 1.1 (Spring 2001). "The Reo Palm Isle: An East Texas Tradition for 67 Years" (http://www.thereo.com/), accessed November 23, 2002. Geronimo Treviño III, *Dance Halls and Last Calls: A History of Texas Country Music* (Plano: Republic of Texas Press, 2002). *Heather Milligan*

Reyna, Cornelio. Singer, songwriter, actor, and "godfather" of *norteño*–conjunto music; b. Cornelio Reyna Cisneros, Natillas, Coahuila, September 16, 1940; d. Mexico City, January 22, 1997. In Saltillo, Coahuila, at the age of sixteen, Reyna started his musical career by writing songs, singing, and playing the *bajo sexto* (twelve-string guitar).

He later moved to the border town of Reynosa, Tamaulipas, where he joined accordionist Juan Peña and formed Dueto Carta Blanca. While playing at the Cadillac Bar in Reynosa, Reyna met a fifteen-year-old accordion player named Ramón Ayala. In 1961 Reyna and Ayala teamed up to form the group Los Relámpagos del Norte, with Reyna as the lead singer. Two years later, while playing at a cantina in Reynosa, Los Relámpagos was discovered by Paulino Bernal, who signed the group with his newly founded Bego Records. Within a short time, Los Relámpagos became the premier conjunto attraction along both sides of the border. Reyna and Ayala were first in bridging the musical gap between the *norteño* and conjunto styles. They featured the accordion and *bajo sexto* as backing rhythms for corridos, polkas, and *rancheras*.

Throughout the 1960s and 1970s, Los Relámpagos dominated the *norteño*–conjunto scene with such hits as "Te Traigo Estas Flores," "Llora," and "Un Día con Otro." In 1971 the group split up, after recording more than twenty albums for Bego Records. Ayala went on to form his own group, Los Bravos del Norte. Reyna, as a soloist, began singing with mariachis and appeared in numerous Mexican films. By this time he had gained a reputation as a prolific songwriter with such compositions as "Mil Noches," "Callejón sin Salida," "Hay Ojitos," and "Me Caí de las Nubes." He appeared in more than thirty movies, some of which were based on his more popular songs. He also directed several films and starred with Antonio Aguilar, Pedro Infante Jr., Los Tigres del Norte, and other actors. Reyna later formed his own group, Los Reyes del Norte. In 1995 he and Ayala reunited as Los Relámpagos del Norte and produced the album *Juntos para Siempre*.

In 1997, while preparing to record a new album with Sony Music in Mexico City, Reyna became ill and died of complications from a bleeding ulcer. He was buried in Reynosa. He was survived by three sons and a daughter, from a series of marriages, including one to the well-known singer Mercedes Castro.

Alberto Reyna, known in the musical world as Cornelio Reyna Jr., was the only child who followed in his father's footsteps. In 1997 he released the Sony Discos album *Ayer y Hoy*, which included previously unreleased songs written by his father.

BIBLIOGRAPHY: Ramiro Burr, *The Billboard Guide to Tejano and Regional Mexican Music* (New York: Billboard, 1999). Manuel Peña, *Música Tejana: The Cultural Economy of Artistic Transformation* (College Station: Texas A&M University Press, 1999). Manuel Peña, *The Texas-Mexican Conjunto: History of a Working-Class Music* (Austin: University of Texas Press, 1985).

Juan Carlos Rodríguez

Reynolds, Isham Emmanuel. Church musician, teacher, composer, and conductor; b. Shades Valley (now part of Birmingham), Alabama, September 27, 1879; d. May 10, 1949 (buried in Greenwood Cemetery, Fort Worth); son of Winfield Pickney and Mary (Eastis) Reynolds. "Ike" or "Ikie," as he was called by his friends, attended Mississippi College, Clinton, Mississippi (1905–06), Moody Bible Institute (1907–08), and Chicago Musical College (1920), as well as doing individual study under private tutors in voice, theory, and composition. The Southern School of Fine Arts in Houston awarded him an honorary doctor of music degree in 1942. From 1906 to 1915 he worked with the Mississippi Baptist State Mission Board and Home Mission Board of the Southern Baptist Convention.

In May 1915 he was asked to be director of the new music department at Southwestern Baptist Theological Seminary; the department became the School of Sacred Music in 1921. This was the first church music school established by Baptists. The department began with the director, one piano teacher, and nine students, one of whom was Baylus B. McKinney. Reynolds served as director until poor health forced his retirement in 1945. In 1930, when the seminary was having financial difficulties, he offered his own resignation rather than ask one of his teachers to leave. His offer was not accepted. While at SWBTS he conducted schools of music in many states, associations, and local churches, taught at Ridgecrest Baptist Assembly (North Carolina), and influenced organizational activities of Southern Baptist music at state and convention levels. He also began the annual Christmas-season performance of Handel's *Messiah* at SWBTS.

I. E. Reynolds composed two sacred music dramas, four cantatas, miscellaneous anthems, hymns, and gospel songs. He authored five textbooks for his own classes as well as *A*

Manual of Practical Church Music (1925), *The Ministry of Music in Religion* (1928), *Church Music* (1935), *The Choir in the Non-Liturgical Church* (1938), and *Music and the Scriptures* (1942).

On July 18, 1900, he married Velma Burns, who died in 1906 along with an infant daughter. On July 17, 1912, he married Lura Mae Hawk, whom he called "Miss Lu." They had one daughter.

BIBLIOGRAPHY: *Encyclopedia of Southern Baptists* (4 vols., Nashville: Broadman, 1958–82). I. E. Reynolds Collection, Roberts Library, Southwestern Baptist Theological Seminary, Fort Worth. William J. Reynolds, "I. E. Reynolds: Southern Baptist Church Crusader," *Southwestern Journal of Theology*, Spring 1983.

Michael Pullin

Reynolds, Teddy. Blues pianist, songwriter, and singer; b. Theodore Reynolds, Houston, July 12, 1931; d. Houston, October 1, 1998; son of Ora Lee Reynolds Miles. Reynolds recorded numerous tracks but is most famous among blues aficionados for his studio work and touring with some of the top Texas-based artists of his generation, including Bobby Bland, Texas Johnny Brown, Johnny Copeland, Grady Gaines, Clarence Green, Peppermint Harris, Joe "Guitar" Hughes, B. B. King, and Phillip Walker.

Reynolds was raised by his maternal grandmother, Hallie Robinson, in the southeast Houston neighborhood known as the Third Ward. In an interview he reported that his father, also named Theodore, had played piano in "bootleg" houses in Houston. Teddy attended Blackshear Elementary School but discontinued his formal education in the fifth grade. He survived by working a variety of odd jobs until his mid-teens, when his skills on piano, which he had learned at his grandmother's house, earned him a chance to perform in a Third Ward nightclub called Shady's Playhouse (originally Jeff's Playhouse). He soon became a member of the house band there and formed key friendships with guitarists such as Johnny Copeland and Albert Collins, as well as with the man Reynolds always credited as his most significant music teacher, Henry Hayes, plus songwriting collaborator Joe Medwick and pianists Charles Brown and Amos Milburn.

In 1950 Reynolds first recorded in Houston, for the label called Sittin' In With. He provided the vocals for a regional hit single, "Cry Cry Baby," by Ed Wiley and His After Hours Band—and thereafter became known to many as Teddy "Cry Cry" Reynolds. He also released several other singles under his own name from those 1950 sessions, including "Why Baby Why," "Too Late to Change," "Walkin' the Floor Baby," and "Right Will Always Win." In 1958 he recorded for the Mercury label, playing piano on the first disc ("Rock and Roll Lily") ever made by Johnny Copeland, who reciprocated by contributing guitar to Reynolds' several Mercury singles, including "Puppy Dogs."

Reynolds's did his most prolific and enduring studio work as a regular session player at Duke and Peacock Records in Houston, which in the 1950s was the largest black-owned record company in the world. Starting in 1958 and lasting into the mid-1960s, he played piano or organ on classic sides by Bobby Bland and Junior Parker, with whom he toured constantly in a popular twin-bill revue for almost three years.

Throughout the 1960s he maintained residency in California, where he recorded his own singles for the Crown label and backed other artists on projects for various other small labels. During this era he also worked with other Duke–Peacock artists, such as Joe Hinton and Al "TNT" Braggs. In 1970 Reynolds played on the ABC–Dunhill album *Together for the First Time*, which united Bland with B. B. King.

While living in Los Angeles, he married a woman named Barbara. Apparently they had several children. In late 1970 Reynolds returned from the West Coast with his family to settle permanently in Houston. Sometime after their return, the marriage broke up. He married a second wife, Ester, and worked in the construction and oil-refinery service industries.

In 1986 he began to make music professionally again, joining Grady Gaines's reunited band, the Texas Upsetters. Recording with that group he contributed keyboards, vocals, and several compositions to the CDs *Full Gain* (1987) and *Horn of Plenty* (1992), and performed as featured artist on a compilation called *Gulf Coast Blues* (1990) and various others, all on the Black Top label. In 1991 Reynolds appeared singing and playing piano in a television commercial, so popular that it ran for many years thereafter, for Texas-based Blue Bell Ice Cream. Locally he performed with several groups through the mid-1990s, including the Quality Blues Band, led by his former Duke–Peacock session mate Texas Johnny Brown. Reynolds's final studio work appears on Brown's 1997 CD *Nothin' But the Truth*. In February 1997 he received an award from the Houston Blues Society.

BIBLIOGRAPHY: Alan Govenar, *Meeting the Blues: The Rise of the Texas Sound* (Dallas: Taylor, 1988). Houston *Press*, October 8–14, 1998. David Nelson, with Roger Wood, "Teddy Reynolds," *Living Blues*, March–April 1999. Teddy Reynolds, "I Got Somethin' for Everybody," interview by John Anthony Brisbin, *Living Blues*, March–April 1998. Steve Sucher, "The Houston Scene: Teddy Reynolds," *Living Blues*, January–February 1997. Roger Wood, *Down In Houston: Bayou City Blues* (Austin: University of Texas Press, 2003).

Roger Wood

Rinehart, Cowboy Slim. "King of Border Radio"; b. Nolan Arthur Rinehart, near Gustine, Comanche County, Texas, March 12, 1911; d. Detroit, Michigan, October 28, 1948. Rinehart made a career singing hillbilly songs and playing guitar on border radio programs. Big Bill Lister, rhythm guitarist and opening act for Hank Williams, fondly remembered listening to Rinehart in 1935 on Brady radio station KNEL, which also featured Bobby Kendrick's (a.k.a. Bob Skyles) family medicine-show band and the Skyrockets.

In 1936 Rinehart and the Skyrockets preformed on KIUM, Pecos. Soon afterward, Rinehart moved to the station that helped him become famous, XEPN near Eagle Pass. In 1937 XEPN of Piedras Negras, Coahuila, was one of the numerous border radio stations, unregulated by the United States government, that transmitted their programs into the U.S. Since these stations operated in Mexico, they could use very strong signals that reached as far north as Canada. This arrangement gave Rinehart an audience much larger than that of a conventional American radio station. He performed as part of the "Good Neighbor Get-together," a block of radio programming that included such musicians as Patsy Montana, the original Carter Family, Doc Hopkins, Russ Pike, and the Modern Pioneers. The show, which ran twice a day, also included Mainer's Mountaineers and Doc and Carl, as well as a future governor of Texas, W. Lee (Pappy) O'Daniel, who addressed political and economic issues and sang with the Hillbilly Boys.

Performing on XEPN gave Rinehart national popularity. He played and sang, often with Patsy Montana, with whom he went on tour to the East Coast. Hollywood movie producers invited him to audition for roles in westerns. Rinehart went to Hollywood, but turned down the offers, choosing instead to return to XEPN. He eventually ended up at XEG, Monterrey, Nuevo León, where he was very popular in 1946.

In addition to his influence on Big Bill Lister and others, Cowboy Slim Rinehart helped shape Ernest Tubb's career. Tubb attempted to convince Rinehart to follow his lead and record at Decca, but Rinehart was unwilling to go. There is some conflicting information as to why Rinehart never commercially recorded. One theory, offered by Lister, was that Rinehart was afraid records would hurt his business of selling songbooks to the border stations. A second explanation was offered by Dallas Turner, another border radio entertainer who was greatly influenced by Rinehart. Turner claims Rinehart held a great disdain for disc jockeys, whom he saw as the reason so many musicians lost their jobs. During Rinehart's time, it was these disc jockeys who were responsible for firing the live entertainment, since many radio stations were replacing studio performances with records.

Rinehart was killed in a car crash. One source says that he died with a record contract from Decca in his pocket; others state that he was on his way to a recording session at the time of the accident. In any case, he never made any commercial recordings. Most of what remains of the "King's" musical legacy is recordings of his radio broadcasts, principally those made at XEG.

BIBLIOGRAPHY: *American Gramophone & Wireless Co. Classic Country Catalogue* (http://members.aol.com/ AGW1886/cpioneers.htm), accessed November 24, 2002. *Big Bill Lister—History of a Country Music Pioneer* (http://www.bigbilllister.com/history.htm), accessed November 24, 2002. *Country and Western Music Shows* (http://members.shaw.ca/dougkosmonek/country.html), accessed November 24, 2002. "Dallas Turner Interview" (http://www.furious.com/perfect/dallasturner.html), accessed November 24, 2002. Gene Fowler and Bill Crawford, *Border Radio—Quacks, Yodelers, Psychics, Pitchmen, and Other Amazing Broadcasters of the American Airwaves* (Austin: University of Texas Press, 2002). Colin Larkin, *The Encyclopedia of Popular Music* (New York: Grove's Dictionaries, 1998).

Hugh O'Donovan

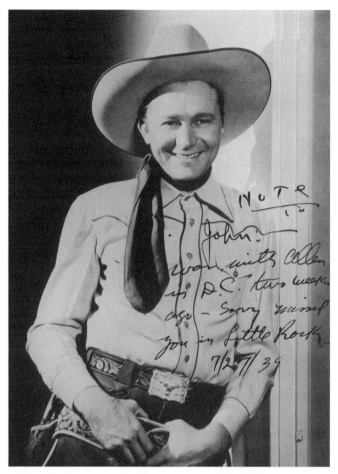

Tex Ritter, ca. 1939. John Lomax Papers, CAH; CN 06677. As a student at the University of Texas, Ritter studied authentic cowboy songs under the guidance of John Lomax and J. Frank Dobie. Later he went as a performer to New York, where his success on the radio led to movie contracts in Hollywood.

Ritter, Tex. Western singer and movie star; b. Woodward Maurice Ritter, Murvaul, Panola County, Texas, January 12, 1905; d. Nashville, January 2, 1974 (buried in Oak Bluff Memorial Park, Port Neches, Texas); son of James Everett and Elizabeth (Matthews) Ritter. Ritter's signature as a student at the University of Texas shows that he spelled his first name Woodard (not Woodward), and a delayed birth certificate filed in Panola County in 1942 also shows the spelling Woodard; however, all printed sources use the spelling Woodward. He moved to Nederland in Jefferson County, to live with a sister, and graduated from South Park High School in nearby Beaumont. He attended the University of Texas from 1922 to 1927, spending one year in the law school there, 1925–26.

As a student he was influenced by J. Frank Dobie, Oscar J. Fox, and John A. Lomax—who encouraged his study of authentic cowboy songs. Ritter, more interested in music, did not take a degree; for a time he was president of the Men's Glee Club at the university. He also attended Northwestern University for one year in 1929 before he began singing western and mountain songs on Radio Station KPRC in Houston in 1929.

The following year he was with a musical troupe touring the South and the Midwest; by 1931 he was in New York and had joined the Theatre Guild. His role in *Green Grow the Lilacs* (predecessor to the musical *Oklahoma*) drew attention to the young "cowboy," and he became the featured singer with the Madison Square Garden Rodeo in 1932. Further recognition led to his starring in one of the first western radio programs to be featured in New York, "The Lone Star Rangers." His early appeal to New Yorkers as the embodiment of a Texas cowboy, in spite of his roots in the rural southern music tradition, undoubtedly led to his first movie contract in 1936.

Tex appeared in eighty-five movies, including seventy-eight westerns, and was ranked among the top ten money-making stars in Hollywood for six years. Although his movies owed much to the genre begun by other singing cowboys such as Gene Autry, Ritter used traditional folk songs in his movies rather than the modern "western" ditties. Films such as *Arizona Frontier* (1940), *The Utah Trail* (1938), and *Roll Wagons Roll* (1939) earned him a reputation for ambitious plots and vigorous action not always found in low-budget westerns. Tex Ritter's successful recordings, which began with "Rye Whiskey" in 1931, included over the years "High Noon" (1952), "Boll Weevil" (1945), "Wayward Wind," "Hillbilly Heaven," and "You Are My Sunshine" (1946). "Ranch Party," a television series featuring Ritter, ran from 1959 to 1962.

He was married to Dorothy Fay Southworth on June 14, 1941; they were the parents of two sons. His younger son, John, became well-known through his television shows, "Three's Company" and "Hearts Afire." In 1964 Tex Ritter was elected to the Country Music Hall of Fame, only the fifth person to be so honored; he also served as president of the Country Music Association from 1963 to 1965. In 1970 he made an unsuccessful bid for the United States Senate from Tennessee. His funeral services were held in Nederland, Texas, near Port Neches.

BIBLIOGRAPHY: Johnny Bond, *The Tex Ritter Story* (New York: Chappell Music Company, 1976). *Comprehensive Country Music Encyclopedia* (New York: Times Books, 1994). *Movie Highlights of America's Most Beloved Cowboy, Tex Ritter* (Keokuk, Iowa: R. A. Tucker, 1971). Melvin Shestack, *The Country Music Encyclopedia* (New York: Crowell, 1979). Vertical Files, Center for American History, University of Texas at Austin.

Rives–Diaz, Leonora. Pianist and composer; place and date of birth and death unknown. Evidence suggests that she was American-born, possibly in the late 1860s or early 1870s, and perhaps in South Texas. Her early musical training showed "promise of a career as a piano virtuoso," but "a serious accident to her eyes" frustrated that ambition. Nevertheless, "her talent found vent in compositions of merit in the Mexican idiom," and in music publishing.

A Galveston and San Antonio music company, Thomas Goggan & Brothers, published two important compositions by Leonora Rives during the 1880s. The better known of these two, the "New Administration Grand March," was dedicated to President Grover Cleveland and published in 1885. The composer had taken up residence in Mission Valley, Texas, near Victoria, by 1885. She was "commissioned to compose a piece to commemorate the opening of the new capitol building in Austin." The formal dedication took place on "May 16, 1888, but the celebration started May 14 and continued through May 19 with major attractions each day." Copies of her composition, "State Capitol Grand Waltz," were available for sale as souvenirs at sixty cents each. "The *Austin Daily Statesman* printed over 10,000 copies, which were all gone by 11 A.M." The "Grand Waltz," dedicated to Governor Lawrence S. Ross, the first Texas governor to occupy the new Capitol, was performed on the evening of May 18 at the dedication ball, held in the Senate and House chambers. The governor and his wife led the grand march into the chambers with music playing from the second floor.

After moving to Mission Valley, Leonora Rives married another composer, Louis Felipe Diaz, both of whom had been publishing their works through the Hauschild Music Company in Victoria. The company was committed to publishing South Texas artists, male and female, from many ethnic backgrounds. Until 1922, Hauschild published compositions from German, French, Polish, English, Irish, and Mexican composers and arrangers. The numerous ethnic groups represented by Hauschild's music catalogues also attest to the variety of cultures in South Texas and the cross-pollination of musical styles that resulted.

Louis F. Diaz, who began his career as a sign painter, became one of "the most prolific composers of the nineties" in South Texas and "director of a small but excellent dance orchestra, consisting of himself and his sisters, Clara, Lucy, and Mary." Hauschild published at least fourteen compositions by Diaz, including "City of Roses" waltz (1899), "Margarita" polka and two-step (1899), and "The Paris Exposition " march (1889). In 1901 Leonora Rives–Diaz dedicated her work "Twentieth Century Waltz" to the honor of the marriage of her friends Laura and Henry John Hauschild, the eldest son of George Hermann and manager of the music company. Rives–Diaz published many other compositions, including "Without Thee I Cannot Live," "Southwest Texas Waltz," "Without Thee I Cannot Sing," and "I Cannot Help But Think of Thee."

No positive references have yet been found to her death date or burial location. The *Hauschild Musical Chronicle* states that Louis F. Diaz died in Galveston, but no year is recorded. The rich legacy of music from these two composers pays tribute to the enormous contributions of Hispanic culture to Texas music history.

BIBLIOGRAPHY: "Capitol Dedication Was A Gala Day in 1888," *Texas Public Employees*, August 1964 (vertical files, Austin History Center). Henry J. Hauschild, "The Hauschild Music Company and the Opera House," in Roy Grimes, ed., *300 Years in Victoria County* (Victoria, Texas: Victoria Advocate Publishing Company, 1968; rpt. Austin: Nortex, 1985). Henry J. Hauschild, *A Musical Chronicle from the Historical Scrapbooks* (Austin, 1999). Elizabeth Power Warden, *Through the Years with Music in a Little Texas Town: An Account of Music in Victoria, Texas* (Victoria: Victoria Advocate Publishing Company, 1943).

Ruth K. Sullivan

Roberts, Alice Bryan. Patron of the arts and musician; b. Talvotton County, Georgia, ca. 1870; d. Dallas, March 5, 1952 (buried in Grove Hill Memorial Park, Dallas); daughter of Henry Monroe and Alice (O'Neill) Bryan. When Alice was four, her family moved in a covered wagon to Dallas, where her father became a teacher and principal. She developed an early appreciation of music from her mother, who was a piano teacher and player. After completing high school in Dallas, she studied at the Cincinnati College of Music. She returned to Dallas and taught music at St. Mary's College and Ursuline Academy. In 1891 she married Jules D. Roberts, a Dallas businessman and civic leader.

As she continued teaching and lecturing on music, Mrs. Roberts also determined to improve the level of music appreciation in Dallas. With a desire to expose the growing frontier city to some of the world's finest artists, she established and became president of the St. Cecilia Choral Society in 1895. The society, the first such music organization in the state, struggled successfully to bring cultural performances to North Texas, long before the area was considered a regular touring stop for such events. The expense of attracting famous singers, dancers, and musicians was considerable.

After the society ceased to operate, Alice Roberts continued as an individual benefactor to sponsor cultural events. She arranged performances in Dallas of the Ballet Russe, Lillian Nordica, Walter Damrosch, Teresa Carreño, Harold Bauer, Anna Pavlova, Nellie Melba, and other famous groups and individuals, and thereby established a tradition of musical and artistic culture in the city that endured well beyond her death. While pursuing these endeavors, Mrs. Roberts also performed as a church soloist and directed choirs at numerous local churches.

She was preceded in death by her husband, and was survived by a daughter, a son, and several grandchildren. Her requiem Mass was offered at the Church of the Holy Cross.

BIBLIOGRAPHY: Sam Hanna Acheson, *Dallas Yesterday*, ed. Lee Milazzo (Dallas: Southern Methodist University Press, 1977). Dallas *Daily Times Herald*, March 6, 1952. John William Rogers, *The Lusty Texans of Dallas* (New York: Dutton, 1951; enlarged ed. 1960; expanded ed., Dallas: Cokesbury Book Store, 1965).

Debbie Mauldin Cottrell

Robertson, Eck. Legendary fiddler; b. Alexander Robertson, Delany, Arkansas, November 20, 1887; d. Borger, Texas, February 15, 1975. When he was three, Robertson's family moved to the Texas Panhandle and settled on a small farm outside Amarillo. In the nineteenth century his grandfather, father, and uncles often entered fiddlers' conventions. At age twenty-one his father quit fiddling to preach at a "Campbellite" church. Robertson decided to pursue a musical career and left home at age sixteen. He traveled with medicine shows, a major employer of country musicians at the time, through Indian Territory. In 1906 he married Nettie Levy, a childhood friend.

The couple settled near Amarillo, where Robertson worked tuning pianos for the Total-Line Music Company.

Pursuing his musical ambitions, he and Nettie performed in vaudeville theaters and fiddle contests in the Southwestern states. As a son of a veteran, Robertson attended Old Confederate Soldiers' Reunions annually. In Richmond, Virginia, at the 1922 reunion, he met fiddler Henry C. Gilliland, and the two performed at the opening ceremony for over 4,000 veterans. Upon realizing their complementary talents, Gilliland and Robertson traveled to New York in an attempt to record with the Victor Talking Machine Company.

Gilliland utilized his contact, Martin W. Littleton, who enabled the two to record what most country music historians consider the first commercial recordings of country music, on June 30, 1922. The duets included the famous "Arkansas Traveler" and "Turkey in the Straw." The following day, Robertson returned to the studio without Gilliland and recorded six additional tracks solo, including "Sallie Gooden," as well as two tracks that were never released. The Victor Company issued a limited release of "Arkansas Traveler" and "Sallie Gooden" in September 1922, but not until April 1923 was the disc in wide circulation. Two other records were released later in 1923 and 1924.

Robertson set the trend for future performers; fourteen Central Texas fiddlers succeeded him by recording commercially in the years shortly following his first recording. After a seven-year break in 1929, he recorded again with the Victor Company in Dallas, accompanied by his son Dueron, wife Nettie, daughter Daphne, and friend Dr. J. B. Cranfil. Success of the recording was limited because of the stock market crash and ensuing contract disputes with Victor. Robertson did, however, have something of a radio career in Texas, performing occasionally for WBAP in Fort Worth and other unknown stations.

In the 1930s and 1940s he lived in Panhandle, Texas, where family disasters occurred. Daphne died of pneumonia in 1931, and Dueron died in the war in 1944. In September 1940 Robertson recorded with the Sellers transcription studios in Dallas, with marginal success. Until his death he claimed that the Victor Company had treated him unfairly. Although Robertson never achieved fame or commercial success through his recording endeavors, he is remembered in country music history for being the first to record commercially.

BIBLIOGRAPHY: H. Wiley Hitchcock and Stanley Sadie, eds., *The New Grove Dictionary of American Music* (4 vols., New York: Macmillan, 1986). Bill C. Malone, *Country Music U.S.A.* (Austin: University of Texas Press, 1968). Vertical Files, Center for American History, University of Texas at Austin.   *Jill S. Seeber*

Robey, Don Deadric. Music entrepreneur; b. Houston, November 1, 1903; d. Houston, June 16, 1975 (buried in Paradise North Cemetery, Houston). A life-long passion for music led Robey into promotional work for ballroom dances in the Houston area. In the late 1930s he spent three years in Los Angeles, where he operated a nightclub called the Harlem Grill. After returning to Houston, he opened the famous Bronze Peacock Dinner Club in 1945. He booked top jazz bands and orchestras to play the club, which became a huge success.

Building from this venture, Robey opened record stores and a talent-management agency in 1947. The first client he signed was a twenty-three-year-old singer and guitarist named Clarence "Gatemouth" Brown. Dissatisfied with the way Aladdin Records was handling Brown, Robey decided to start his own record company in 1949; he named it Peacock Records after his nightclub. Over the years he added an impressive array of talent to his label, with artists including Memphis Slim, Marie Adams, Floyd Dixon, and Willie Mae "Big Mama" Thornton, whose 1953 recording of "Hound Dog" was later imitated by Elvis Presley. Robey added a gospel division to Peacock Records with artists such as the Dixie Hummingbirds, the Sensational Nightingales, and the Mighty Clouds of Joy. Peacock became one of the leading gospel labels in the United States. Robey added a second gospel label, Songbird, in 1963–64.

In August 1952 he formed a partnership with Duke Records owners David J. Mattis and Bill Fitzgerald. Less than a year later, in April 1953, Robey gained full control over both labels and established their headquarters at the Bronze Peacock Club. His acquisition of Duke brought recording rights to artists Johnny Ace, Junior Parker, Roscoe Gordon, and Bobby "Blue" Bland. Between 1957 and 1970, Bland recorded thirty-six songs that reached the Billboard R&B charts, thus becoming Robey's most consistently successful artist. A subsidiary label, Back Beat, was formed in 1957 and became a soul-music label in the 1960s. The talent roster on Back Beat included Joe Hinton, O.V. Wright, and Carl Carlton.

At the height of his music-promotion and recording success, Robey had more than a hundred artists and groups under contract to his various labels. Although controversial because of his shrewd business practices and dealings with artists, he is credited with substantially influencing the development of Texas blues by finding and recording blues artists. His music director, Joe Scott, helped define Texas blues through his distinctive arrangements.

Robey's business began to decline in the mid-1960s. He sold Peacock Records and the subsidiary labels to ABC–Dunhill on May 23, 1973, with the agreement that he would stay on as consultant and oversee the release of catalog materials, a position he held until his death. He was a leader in the United Negro College Fund Drive, a member of Douglass Burrell Consistory No. 56, Doric Temple No. 76, and Sanderson Commandery No. 2 K.T.; and a Century Member of the YMCA, NAACP, and Chamber of Commerce. He died of a heart attack and was survived by his wife of fifteen years, Murphy L. Robey, three children, three sisters, and seven grandchildren. The Masonic Lodge performed graveside services for him.

BIBLIOGRAPHY: David Edwards, "Don Robey's Labels" (http://www.bsnpubs.com/robey.html), accessed June 5, 2002. Alan Govenar, *The Early Years of Rhythm and Blues: Focus on Houston* (Houston: Rice University Press, 1990). Houston *Post*, June 18, 1975. Rick Koster, *Texas Music* (New York: St. Martin's Press, 1998). Robert Santelli, *The Big Book of Blues: A Biographical Encyclopedia* (New York: Penguin, 1993).   *Ruth K. Sullivan*

Rock-and-Roll. Texas musicians have profoundly influenced the development and evolution of rock-and-roll and the various branches of its musical tree—rockabilly, blues rock, Tex-Mex, psychedelia, and redneck rock. Some of the Rock and Roll Hall of Fame's most high-profile inductees, including Buddy Holly, Roy Orbison, and Janis Joplin, pioneered the direction of the musical idiom. The Hall has also honored other musicians, both native Texans and those who made a name in the Lone Star State, as early influences critical to the genre's development. These musicians include T-Bone Walker, Leadbelly, Robert Johnson, Charlie Christian, and Bob Wills and His Texas Playboys.

Rock-and-roll's historic roots lie in a fusion of several musical genres that came into prominence in the early decades of the twentieth century. Texans played major roles in pioneering these varied styles, including blues, jazz, and western swing. Blues guitarist Blind Lemon Jefferson from Freestone County, Texas, is credited as the first blues star. His recordings from 1926 to 1929 were the first blues records to be commercially successful and thus introduce what had been an African American music form to a national audience.

In the 1930s, "race labels" recorded many black blues musicians in Texas. Two landmark sessions in San Antonio (1936) and Dallas (1937) captured the only recorded legacy of guitarist Robert Johnson, the itinerant Delta bluesman from Mississippi. Many music historians and guitar aficionados credit these songs, which include his legendary "Cross Road Blues," for laying the fundamental groundwork for rock-and-roll. Another historic blues great, Huddie Ledbetter ("Leadbelly"), traveled to Texas where he played his twelve-string guitar with the likes of Jefferson in Deep Ellum. Field-recording pioneers John and Alan Lomax discovered his guitar prowess while he was incarcerated in the Louisiana State Penitentiary and thus brought his blues to the world. These early players inspired later guitarists like Sam "Lightnin'" Hopkins, Freddie King, and Albert Collins and their Texas blues sound, a highly improvisational style that encouraged a variety of personal playing techniques. The early bluesmen played an important role in the evolution of rock guitar. Legendary groups and players from the Beatles, the Rolling Stones, and Jefferson Airplane, to Eric Clapton, Jeff Beck, and Jimmy Page, all credit these blues players as major musical influences.

Texas jazz players also contributed significantly to the development of rock. In 1935 guitarist Eddie Durham of San Marcos was one of the first performers on the electric guitar, and he made the first jazz recording of the amplified instrument. Fellow jazzman Charlie Christian of Dallas further elevated the electric guitar as a lead instrument. Guitarist Aaron "T-Bone" Walker, born in Linden, forged the link to the modern electric guitar in the 1940s and established the instrument as the foremost soloing tool for rhythm-and-blues.

In Texas in the 1930s another musical sound, the interesting mix of jazz, hillbilly, boogie, blues, and country that became known as western swing, also influenced the beginnings of rock. Three bands were very representative of the catchy sound that caught on: the Light Crust Doughboys,

Milton Brown and His Musical Brownies, and Bob Wills and His Texas Playboys. Both Brown and Wills had originally played in the Light Crust Doughboys before forming their own groups, and radio presented a popular medium to reach a wide listening audience.

In the late 1940s and throughout the 1950s the "Big 'D' Jamboree" barn dance and radio program in Dallas cultivated local talent and recruited national acts. In additional to country performers, the show also explored new trends and presented a bluesy sound mixed with country and bluegrass (or hillbilly) music called rockabilly. "Big 'D' Jamboree" and its larger Louisiana counterpart, the "Louisiana Hayride," often featured one of the most visible rockabilly stars—a young Elvis Presley. Several native Texans, however, are recognized as groundbreaking rockabilly performers, including Charline Arthur, Dean Beard, and Johnny Carroll. In the mid-1950s Charline Arthur, born in Henrietta, Texas, headlined the "Big 'D' Jamboree." Her bold stage presence earned praise from Elvis, and music historians have credited her as a major precursor to rockabilly, but her aggressive manner and rowdy stage shows did not fit in with the times. Other rockabilly pioneers were Dean Beard of Coleman County and his West Texas band the Crew Cats, who recorded "Rakin' and Scrapin'" in 1956. That same year Johnny Carroll from Cleburne, a "Big 'D' Jamboree" and "Louisiana Hayride" favorite, recorded his "Crazy, Crazy Lovin'" for Decca in Nashville.

During the 1950s Houston record executive Don Robey gathered an impressive lineup of blues performers for his Duke and Peacock Records labels. One artist, Willie Mae "Big Mama" Thornton, recorded "Hound Dog" in 1953, and the song became a major rock-and-roll hit for Elvis in 1956.

The emergence of rockabilly as a new musical style and the steady output of blues recordings set the stage for the development of a new genre—rock-and-roll. The wind-blown plains of West Texas furnished a wealth of musical talent. In 1956 Happy, Texas, native Buddy Knox and his band, the Rhythm Orchids, which included Knox's classmate Jimmy Bowen, learned of Norm Petty's recording studio in Clovis, New Mexico, from another up-and-coming West Texas musician, Roy Orbison. The group recorded "Party Doll," and Knox subsequently became the first artist in rock to write and perform his own number-one hit with that song. Bowen's "I'm Stickin' With You," originally the flip side of "Party Doll," also got into the Top 20.

In early 1957 another West Texas rocker, Buddy Holly of Lubbock, ventured to Petty's studio. The tracks recorded by Holly and the Crickets resulted in the release of their first single, "That'll Be the Day," on May 27, 1957. The song soared to number three on the pop charts, and subsequent releases "Peggy Sue," "Oh Boy!," and "Not Fade Away" also met great success. The pioneering influence of Holly, an inaugural inductee into the Rock and Roll Hall of Fame (1986), on the development of rock-and-roll cannot be overstated. Holly wrote much of his own material, and his band, the Crickets, brought to the forefront the combination of guitars, bass, and drums as a viable self-contained musical combo. These two precedents set the standard for rock groups. Young fans, John Lennon, Paul McCartney, and other future British rockers saw Holly perform in England and were inspired to emulate him. His star shone brightly for less than two years, until he lost his life in a plane crash in Iowa on February 3, 1959. The Big Bopper, J. P. Richardson of the Beaumont area, also perished. His fun-loving single "Chantilly Lace" had been a hit in 1958. Another rising Texas musician and Holly's guitarist at the time, Waylon Jennings, was not on the plane. The crash, which killed the pilot, Holly, Richardson, and teenage star Ritchie Valens, marked the end of the first chapter of rock-and-roll, an event that songwriter Don McLean later so aptly proclaimed "the day the music died," in his anthem "American Pie" in 1971.

Texas rock-and-roll progressed, however, as the 1960s dawned. Singer–songwriter Roy Orbison carried the banner of the West Texas rockers throughout the early 1960s and, in fact, was one of the few American stars to hold his own on the charts against the rising Beatles. Born in Vernon, Texas, Orbison (in the band the Teen Kings) had made his own pilgrimage to Norm Petty's Clovis studio in the 1950s. His recording of "Ooby Dooby" caught the attention of Sun Records in Memphis, and in 1956 Orbison joined the ranks of a group of emerging rockabilly stars. He gained the reputation of a successful songwriter, but when he could not attract the interest of either Elvis or the Everly Brothers to record his "Only the Lonely," Orbison recorded it himself in 1960 and introduced to the world his soaring voice and a string of aching rock ballads that became his signature style. Rock-and-roll singers from Elvis to the Beatles to the later Bruce Springsteen heralded the dramatic voice of Orbison. Inducted into the Rock and Roll Hall of Fame in 1987, Orbison, like Holly, has shown incredible staying power, as evidenced by his popular comeback in the 1980s with Bob Dylan, George Harrison, Tom Petty, and Jeff Lynne as the Traveling Wilburys and his best-selling album *Mystery Girl* (1989) after his death in 1988.

Mexican-American rockers entered the national rock-and-roll scene in the early 1960s. In 1960 Baldemar Huerta, better known as Freddy Fender, had a hit with "Wasted Days and Wasted Nights." In 1962 a band from San Antonio called Sunny and the Sunliners became the first all-Hispanic group to play on "American Bandstand." Dallas's Trini Lopez had a hit in 1963 with an upbeat version of the folk song "If I Had a Hammer." This emergence of such Mexican-American performers hinted of musical influences adopted from the rich Mexican heritage of Texas.

In the early 1960s Major Bill Smith of Fort Worth produced a number of artists who had national hits. Ray Hildebrand and Jill Jackson, known as Paul and Paula and formed in Brownwood, had a number one song, "Hey Paula." Bruce Channel of Grapevine recorded "Hey! Baby." Denton's Ray Peterson scored a 1960 hit with "Tell Laura I Love Her," while Lufkin's J. Frank Wilson and the Cavaliers, a band formed in San Angelo, had a number-one smash with "Last Kiss" in 1964. Both songs were symbolic of the "teenage tragedy" subgenre of rock in the early 1960s. Another young Lubbock group, Delbert McClinton

and the Ron-Dels, recorded "If You Really Want Me To I'll Go." McClinton, who had cut his musical teeth on the Jacksboro Highway blues scene of Fort Worth, had established himself as a rising rockabilly–blues player and went on to sustain a lengthy musical career encompassing various styles. McClinton played harmonica on Bruce Channel's "Hey! Baby." A longstanding legend tells that it was McClinton who, while on tour with Channel in England, advised John Lennon on his distinctive harmonica technique—information that the Beatle subsequently immortalized in the harmonica solo of "Love Me Do."

When the Beatles burst upon the American music scene in 1964, their performances had an impact on the growing stable of Texas musicians. Savvy music producer Huey Meaux of Houston decided to jump on the "British Invasion" bandwagon but with a distinctively Texas flavor. The result produced one of the enduring bands in Texas rock history—the Sir Douglas Quintet. Meaux approached San Antonio musician Doug Sahm, whose musical legacy established him as a quintessential rock-and-roller. Formed in San Antonio in 1964, the Sir Douglas Quintet consisted of frontman Sahm, Augie Meyers on organ, Frank Morin on horns, Harvey Kagan on bass, and John Perez on drums. Their stylish suits and Beatle haircuts, mandated by Meaux, were designed to give the band an English flavor and thereby to capitalize on the British Invasion. Meaux had to "break" the band in England before it played in the U.S., but the group scored a major international hit in 1965 with "She's About a Mover." The song's infectious hook was the thin "con queso" line of Meyers's Vox organ. Reminiscent of an accordion fill, this reflected the Tex-Mex influence on the group. The band eventually moved to the budding rock scene of San Francisco and released other notable tracks, including "Mendocino" in 1969.

Other noteworthy bands of the mid-1960s hailed from Texas and also echoed their Tex-Mex musical traditions. Domingo Samudio (Sam Samudio) of Dallas led Sam the Sham and the Pharaohs, whose 1965 hit "Wooly Bully" topped the U.S. charts in 1965. They also enjoyed success with "Lil' Red Riding Hood." Question Mark and the Mysterians likewise tapped into their own queso organ hook, played by Frank Rodriguez of Crystal City, in their hit "96 Tears" in 1965.

Meaux also produced the early material of versatile vocalist Roy Head from Three Rivers, who later scored a number-two pop single in 1965 with his soulful "Treat Her Right." Houston native B. J. Thomas was also in the Meaux stable before moving on to pop and country stardom with such hits as "Hooked on a Feeling" and "Raindrops Keep Fallin' on My Head."

As Beatlemania swept the nation, Hollywood sought to capitalize on the British Invasion in the mid-1960s and introduced the Monkees. Bandmember Michael Nesmith was born in Houston and grew up in Dallas. Nesmith, considered the best musician in the quartet, also achieved other musical success. His song "Different Drum" was a hit for Linda Ronstadt and the Stone Poneys in 1967. He later went on to front his own country rock band in the 1970s and became a music video pioneer, winning the first Grammy given for a video in 1981.

West Texas gave forth another popular group, the Bobby Fuller Four from El Paso. The band had a national hit in 1966 with "I Fought the Law," a tune written by Sonny Curtis of the Crickets. Fuller's success was cut short by his suspicious "suicide" on July 18, 1966.

Psychedelic and its heavier variation, acid rock, emerged from both folk-rock and electric roots during the mid-to-late 1960s. Texas spawned its share of garage bands, known for their original compositions and free-form improvisation, and these psychedelic groups had both regional and national impact. Red Krayola emerged from Houston. The punky blues of Zakary Thaks came from Corpus Christi. Mouse and the Traps was born in Tyler. The Austin band Bubble Puppy recorded in Houston for Lelan Rogers (brother of Kenny Rogers) around 1967 and scored a national hit, "Hot Smoke and Sassafras." Lelon Rogers also produced another band—the 13th Floor Elevators. Formed in Austin in 1965, the 13th Floor Elevators commanded a devoted local following and created a potent combination when they added vocalist Roky Erickson to the lineup. His song "You're Gonna Miss Me" became a hit; it was from their 1966 album, *The Psychedelic Sounds of the 13th Floor Elevators*, released on Houston's International Artist label. A second LP, *Easter Everywhere* (1967), also had a strong showing. Musicologists have heralded Roky Erickson and the 13th Floor Elevators as pioneers of acid rock, but their overt drug use, also a trademark of the psychedelic culture, took its toll on the band and especially Erickson. Convicted twice for drug possession, Erickson opted for a sentence to the Rusk State Hospital over state prison in 1969. During his incarceration he was diagnosed with paranoid schizophrenia and treated with various drug therapies and electroshock. He was never the same after his release in 1972, and took years to return to some semblance of musical coherence.

Janis Joplin, another innovator and ultimately victim of the psychedelic counterculture, burst on the rock-and-roll scene in the mid-1960s. Born and raised in Port Arthur, Texas, she moved to San Francisco and joined the band Big Brother and the Holding Company. Her electrifying rendition of the song "Ball and Chain," which had also been recorded by one of Joplin's musical mentors, Big Mama Thornton, at the Monterey Pop Festival in 1967, immediately earned her and the band national acclaim. Rock critics praised Joplin as the greatest white blues singer, but an accidental heroine overdose ended her life on October 4, 1970. Her posthumous single "Me and Bobby McGee," penned by Texan Kris Kristofferson, reached number one on the charts.

The 1960s and early '70s saw many Texas-born musicians earning musical names for themselves outside of the state. The impressive list includes Billy Preston, who was born in Houston, Sylvester "Sly Stone" Stewart of Dallas, who performed in Sly and the Family Stone, and Houston native Johnny Nash, whose catchy "I Can See Clearly Now" reached number one in 1972. Mason Williams of Abilene won a Grammy for his pop instrumental guitar hit "Classical Gas" in 1968. Houston's Kenny Rogers and his pop group First Edition had a hit with "Just Dropped In To See What Condition My Condition Was In." Dallas-born

Stephen Stills found fame in the late 1960s in California as a member of Crosby Stills Nash and Young.

The 1970s ushered in the radio-popular genre of soft rock, with smoothly crafted, tight songs that inspired the term "California Sound." Notable Texans helped influence the California Sound. Seals and Crofts was one of the most popular mellow rock acts of the 1970s. Jim Seals, born in Sidney, Texas, and Dash Crofts of Cisco, played as teenagers with rockabilly star Dean Beard and the Crew Cats in the late 1950s. The two, along with Beard, moved to Los Angeles and joined the Champs, who had the instrumental hit "Tequila" in 1958. Eventually playing together as an acoustic duo, they hit it big with their song "Summer Breeze" in 1972. Seals's brother Dan achieved his own fame in the duo England Dan and John Ford Coley.

The Eagles, a hugely successful group of the 1970s, owe a lot of their success to two Texans. Drummer–vocalist Don Henley was born in Gilmer and played in a hometown band called Shiloh, before the group moved to California in 1969. Henley was one of the founding members of the Eagles in 1971, and his songwriting and distinctive voice helped propel the group to fame. Eagle associate J. D. Souther of Amarillo played in the Cinders, a Panhandle band of the early 1960s, before heading West. Souther wrote some of the Eagles' most memorable songs, such as "New Kid in Town" and "Best of My Love," and later recorded a hit of his own, "You're Only Lonely."

In the early 1970s the hard-edged sounds of rock and blues were still alive and well with Texas musicians. Brothers Johnny and Edgar Winter grew up in the Beaumont area and listened to the records of blues masters like Blind Lemon Jefferson and T-Bone Walker. Johnny attracted a massive audience with the release of *Johnny Winter* (1969), which showcased blues–rock guitar prowess, including a considerable penchant for slide guitar. Winter has established himself among aspiring guitarists as one of the modern blues greats. Brother Edgar achieved success as a keyboardist. Edgar's part jazzy, part rhythm-and-blues tunes earned him respect as an amazing multi-instrumentalist (he also played saxophone) and vocalist.

The early 1970s saw prolific output from a band formed in Fort Worth, Bloodrock, which issued six albums from 1970 to 1973. Their first three, released between February 1970 and March 1971, all went gold, and the second LP included a popular single, the morbid "D.O.A." Fort Worth guitarist and vocalist John Nitzinger, though not a formal member of the group, contributed many of Bloodrock's finer songs.

The band ZZ Top became the Lone Star State's most successful rock act of the 1970s. This threesome emerged from the ashes of the Texas psychedelic scene. Drummer Frank Beard and bassist Dusty Hill had played in the American Blues in Dallas, and guitarist Billy Gibbons performed in the noteworthy Moving Sidewalks in Houston. Evidently he had turned heads, because Jimi Hendrix, while appearing on the "Tonight Show," had praised Gibbons as the next hot young guitarist. Gibbons, Beard, and Hill came together in Houston in 1970 (after Gibbons had replaced two previous band members). They built a strong following with their touring and Southern-influenced, guitar-driven rock. Their third album, *Tres Hombres* (1973), went platinum on the strength of the hit "La Grange." Throughout the following decades, ZZ Top's continued popularity with releases such as their best-selling *Eliminator* (1983) attested to the band's popular appeal and staying power.

In the early 1970s Texas gave birth to a distinctive and unusual blending of country music and urban blues and rock that resulted in a hybrid style known variously as redneck rock or progressive country. The redneck rock movement began in Austin as Willie Nelson, Waylon Jennings, and a group of country and rocker songwriters congregated to create a burgeoning music scene. Nelson had rejected the slick commercial environment of Nashville and returned to his native Texas. The redneck rock movement inspired enthusiasm from both native Texans and Northern transplants in search of its laid-back, open-minded attitude. Rock and country musicians Joe Ely, Butch Hancock, and Jimmie Dale Gilmore formed the Flatlanders in rock's root town of Lubbock before each eventually moved to the Central Texas area.

Jerry Jeff Walker, B. W. Stevenson, and Michael Martin Murphey were three singer–songwriters who symbolized the redneck rock movement and garnered acclaim with big crossover hits. Walker, a transplanted Texan, penned "Mr. Bojangles," and the tune became a major radio hit for the Nitty Gritty Dirt Band in 1971. The big voice of Dallas native B. W. Stevenson belted out "My Maria," which went to number nine in 1973. Michael Martin Murphey's "Wild Fire" was a huge hit that went to number three on the charts in 1975. The outgrowth of this flourishing Austin redneck rock scene also led to the creation of the syndicated public television program "Austin City Limits," which brought numerous Texas country, blues, and rock musicians to a national audience.

The mid-to-late 1970s continued the tradition of Texan musicians gaining national and international fame. Players who had headed west in the 1960s included Steve Miller and Boz Scaggs, high school classmates in Dallas. During the 1970s each went on to success. Dallas native Marvin Lee Aday, better known as Meat Loaf, scored national hits with his musical theatrical flair, and his *Bat Out of Hell* (1977) became one of rock's biggest-selling albums.

The 1980s ushered in the national fame of Christopher Cross. Formed by San Antonio native Chris Geppert and consisting of some notable Austin-based musicians, Christopher Cross swept the Grammys with five awards, which included best new artist, album of the year—*Christopher Cross* (1980)—and three awards for the hit single "Sailing." The crisp recording and production of the songs earned Christopher Cross a place as one of pop music's biggest acts in the early 1980s.

The emergence of punk music and its mellower cousin new wave claimed its roots in the psychedelic bands of the 1960s, most notably Roky Erickson and the 13th Floor Elevators. Other musicians also adopted styles tinged with Tex-Mex nuances that harkened back to the influences of the Sir Douglas Quintet and Question Mark and the Mysterians. By the early 1980s punk bands performed throughout the state. The Judy's of Houston achieved moderate

success. Dallas contributed acts like the Nervebreakers, and Austin spawned the Big Boys and the Next. Austin-based musicians such as Joe Ely toured as the opener for the Clash, and Joe "King" Carrasco's high energy, Tex-Mex–flavored "nuevo wavo" was a perennial draw on the club circuit. One of the early punk Texas bands that has shown staying power is the Butthole Surfers. Trinity University students Gibby Haynes and Paul Leary formed the group in San Antonio in the early 1980s. Their screeching sounds and societal satire have evoked shock and loathing in some, but have also inspired a devoted cult following for two decades.

The 1980s saw the increasing recognition of the skill and versatility of a new generation of Texas guitarists. Numerous awards and polls in guitar magazines have heralded Austinite Eric Johnson as one of the technically best guitarists. He first turned heads as a member of the Austin jazz fusion group the Electromagnets, which also featured Stephen Barber, Bill Maddox, and Kyle Brock, in the mid-1970s. Word of Johnson's virtuosity continued to build as he worked as a session player for the likes of Carole King, Cat Stevens, and Christopher Cross. His first solo album, *Tones*, came out in 1986, followed by *Ah Via Musicom* in 1990.

Van Wilks is another formidable guitar player in the Central Texas area. Listeners have often compared the blues rock master to ZZ Top's Billy Gibbons, and he has toured with ZZ Top. Wilks released the album *Bombay Tears* in 1980 to critical acclaim. He and his band have also been the winners of many newspaper polls in recognition of their popular hard-rock style. Van Wilks and Eric Johnson teamed up in a memorable guitar duo performance of "What Child Is This" for the *Texas Christmas Collection* (1982).

The Vaughan brothers, Jimmie and Stevie, finally earned their long-sought national attention in the 1980s. Born in the Dallas area, the brothers had moved to Austin by the 1970s. Guitarist Jimmie Vaughan hit it big in the Austin-based blues group the Fabulous Thunderbirds, whose songs "Tuff Enuff" and "Wrap It Up" became national hits and featured videos on MTV in 1986. Jimmie's younger brother Stevie and his band, Double Trouble, stormed the blues rock scene with their release of *Texas Flood* (1983) and *Couldn't Stand the Weather* (1984). Musicians recognized Stevie Ray Vaughan as one of the great new guitarists. Vaughan, standing on the shoulders of the old Deep Ellum blues greats, influenced countless young players, and many guitar magazines and instructional books have analyzed his use of heavy-gauge strings and tuning to achieve his distinctively fat sound. His tragic death in a helicopter crash in 1990 cut short a remarkable music career.

Pop bands such as Timbuk 3 and Edie Brickell and the New Bohemians had their day in the sun in the mid-to-late 1980s. Timbuk 3's husband and wife duo, Pat and Barbara MacDonald, who had moved to Austin, wrote the very catchy "The Future's So Bright I Gotta Wear Shades" in 1986. The New Bohemians were an established band playing in Deep Ellum when they added art student and singer Edie Brickell in 1985. A revamped lineup signed with Geffen Records and released their debut, *Shooting Rubber-*

bands *At The Stars* (1989), which included the hit "What I Am." Brickell's airy vocal style and the band's hippie harkening image caught the public eye for a time. Both Timbuk 3 and Edie Brickell and New Bohemians were destined to be relegated to one-hit wonder status.

One of the biggest Texas acts of the 1990s consisted of legendary veteran rockers Doug Sahm, Augie Meyers, Freddy Fender, and conjunto accordionist Flaco Jimenez. The supergroup the Texas Tornadoes released its eponymous debut album with Warner Brothers in 1990. Once again the musicians relied heavily on their Texan-influenced roots, combining Tex-Mex conjunto rhythms with catchy lyric and melody hooks that had crossover appeal in the rock world. Throughout much of the 1990s the group toured nationally and internationally and were ready to embark on a new journey when Doug Sahm died on November 18, 1999. Sahm's career epitomizes Texas rock-and-roll, a meeting of cultures that borrows from the black blues greats, border-flavored Tex-Mex, and Texas cowboy and folk music, with some doowop thrown in.

The significant influence shown by notable rock pioneer Roky Erickson was honored in the 1990 Warner Brothers release of *Where the Pyramid Meets the Eye: A Tribute to Roky Erickson*, on which various rockers recorded his songs. Another noteworthy tribute album resulted in an unlikely, but compelling combination. *Twisted Willie* (1996) was a compilation of Willie Nelson's songs as performed by some of the nation's top grunge bands. The alternative rock scene of Seattle in the early 1990s nodded to the legacy of the Texas Outlaw, redneck rocker Willie Nelson.

The rise of female singer–songwriters in the rock industry in the mid-1990s also featured a Texas-born artist whose unlikely commercial path led to stardom. Dallas native Lisa Loeb secured a place in music history for achieving the first-ever number-one hit single without having a record deal. In 1994 her song "Stay," which was featured on the soundtrack of the film *Reality Bites*, bulleted up the charts. Subsequently, Loeb signed with Geffen and later participated as a featured artist on the Lilith Fair tour promoting female musicians in 1997.

Throughout the 1990s and into the new millennium, heavy metal bands (and their various subgenres such as death metal or thrash metal) have flourished in the Lone Star State. Arlington's group Pantera actually formed in the early 1980s but, after building an impressive following through several album releases and tours, came into their own in the 1990s. Their formidable album *Far Beyond Driven* entered the U.S. and U.K. charts at number one in 1994, and releases and tours throughout the 1990s have cemented the Texas group as a worldwide force. Other listeners, perhaps not familiar with thrash metal's blazing tempo and heavy atonal guitar riffs, got a taste of Pantera's style when the group wrote a brief metal theme song for the NHL team the Dallas Stars during their Stanley Cup season in 1999.

King's X, a band based in Houston, has garnered critical acclaim for its interesting and intricate blend of vocal harmonies, progressive rock elements, and metal tendencies. Their often spiritual and introspective lyrics border on the genre of Christian rock, as evidenced in their successful LP *Faith, Hope and Love* (1990). They have continued to release works through 2002.

The Central Texas band Sixpence None the Richer entered the music scene in the 1990s. After several years of obscurity, they finally got national recognition with their hit "Kiss Me" in 1999.

The hard-hitting rock band The Union Underground formed in San Antonio in 1996. By 1999 they signed with a subsidiary of Columbia Records, and their debut, *An Education in Rebellion* (2000), earned praise from critics as some of the best heavy metal of the day. Their recording and performance of the theme song for World Wrestling Entertainment's *RAW* show in 2002 brought the group to an even larger worldwide audience.

Another metal splash occurred for the Dallas quartet Drowning Pool in 2001. The group formed in the late 1990s and toured with alternative metal bands Sevendust and Kittie while peddling their demos. Eventually they signed to a major label, and the group's debut album, *Sinner* (2001), went platinum on the strength of the breakout single "Bodies." The band rode the wave of stardom as a major stage act on the Ozzfest tour, but suffered a great setback with the sudden death of singer Dave Williams in August 2002.

Texas rock-and-roll at the dawn of the new millennium continued to bring both veteran favorites and fresh faces, all classified under the broad umbrella of rock music. Veteran musician Delbert McClinton still toured heavily. Guitarists Eric Johnson, Jimmie Vaughan, and Van Wilks, as well their inspired protégés such as brothers Charlie and Will Sexton, participated in a vibrant scene. The Flatlanders, Ely, Hancock, and Gilmore, performed together again in 2002, and ZZ Top still appeared before packed audiences worldwide. The strength of Texas rock-and-roll also lies in the many regional and road bands playing at venues across the state. With the proliferation of home recording studios and the potential marketing exposure of the Internet, Texas rock-and-roll bands have increasing opportunities to present their music to new audiences.

BIBLIOGRAPHY: All Music Guide web site (), accessed March 25, 2003. *Discography of Texas Punk 1977–1983* (), accessed April 1, 2003. Alan B. Govenar, *The Early Years of Rhythm and Blues: Focus on Houston* (Houston: Rice University Press, 1990). Alan B. Govenar and Jay F. Brakefield, *Deep Ellum and the Central Track: Where the Black and White Worlds of Dallas Converged* (Denton: University of North Texas Press, 1998). Rick Koster, *Texas Music* (New York: St. Martin's Press, 1998). Colin Larkin, ed., *The Encyclopedia of Popular Music* (New York: Grove's Dictionaries, 1998). *Mike Lowell's San Antonio Band Trivia* (), accessed March 25, 2003. Margaret Moser et al., "A Brief History of Texas Garage Rock: One Two Three Faw!" (), accessed April 8, 2003. H. P. Newquist, "A Capsule History of the Blues," *Guitar*, June 1995. Joe Nick Patoski, "Roky Road," *Texas Monthly*, March 1995. Joe Nick Patoski, "Sex, Drugs, and Rock & Roll," *Texas Monthly*, May 1996. Jan Reid, *The Improbable Rise of Redneck Rock* (New York: Da Capo Press, 1977). Rock and Roll Hall of Fame and Museum homepage (), accessed

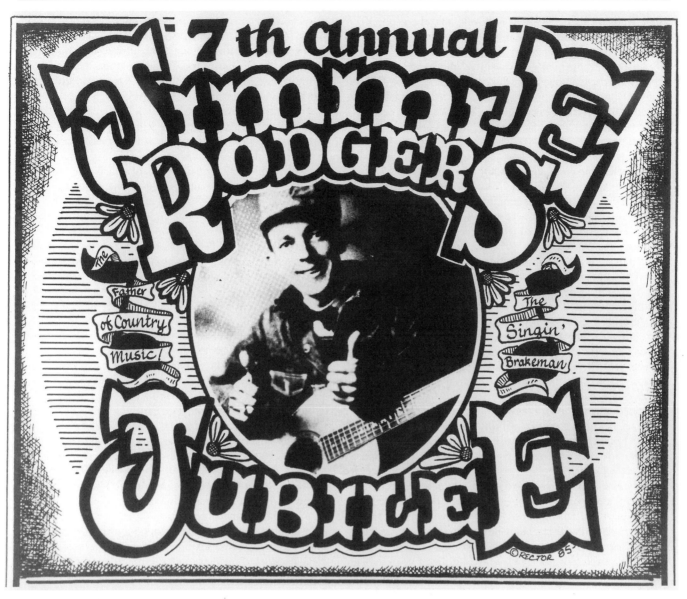

Poster advertising the 7th Annual Jimmie Rodgers Jubilee, September 17, 1988. The Kerrville event featured a yodeling contest and performances by many musicians who were influenced by Rodgers. Texas Poster Art Collection, CAH; CN 11499.

March 25, 2003. Barry Shank, *Dissonant Identities: The Rock 'N' Roll Scene in Austin, Texas* (Hanover, New Hampshire: University Press of New England, 1994). David Shutt, comp., *Journey to Tyme: A Discography and Interpretive Guide to Texas 1960s Punk/Psychedelia*, Second Edition (Austin: D. Shutt, 1984). Texas Music Office, Texas Grammy Winners list (), accessed March 29, 2003. *Texas Music*, compilation produced by John Morthland and James Austin (Los Angeles: Rhino Records R271781, R271782, R271783, 1994). Vertical file, "Music—Rock," Center for American History, University of Texas at Austin. Larry Willoughby, *Texas Rhythm, Texas Rhyme* (Austin: Eakin Press, 1991). *Laurie E. Jasinski*

Rodgers, Jimmie. The "father of modern country music"; b. James Charles Rodgers, Meridian, Mississippi, September 8, 1897; d. New York City, May 26, 1933 (buried in Oak Grove Cemetery, Meridian, Mississippi); son of Aaron W. and Eliza (Bozeman) Rodgers. His father was a railroad gang foreman, and Jimmie, whose mother died when he was four years old, grew up on the railroad. He started work as a water carrier at the age of fourteen and eventually became a brakeman. Working on railroads throughout the South, he learned songs from black railroad workers, who also taught him to play the banjo and the guitar. He was married to Carrie Cecil Williamson on April 7, 1920, and they had two daughters, one of whom died in infancy.

A severe case of tuberculosis, contracted in 1924, forced Rodgers to retire from the railroad, after which he went through a chain of odd jobs and migrations in the South and Southwest. He served a brief stint as an entertainer with a medicine show and for a while was a city detective in Asheville, North Carolina, where he had moved in search of a more healthful climate. He organized the Jimmie Rodgers Entertainers in Asheville, and the group performed on the local radio station, singing both popular and country music.

In 1927 Rodgers signed a contract with the Victor Talking Machine Company, and his records catapulted him to almost immediate fame. He made his first recording on August 4, 1927, in Bristol, on the Tennessee–Virginia border, recording "Sleep, Baby Sleep" and "Soldier's Sweetheart."

Rodgers introduced a new form to commercial hillbilly music, the blue yodel, heard best in the "Blue Yodel" series of twelve songs—"Blue Yodel No. 1," "Blue Yodel No. 2," etc. One of this series has remained one of the most popular of his songs and has become known as "T for Texas." Rodgers recorded 111 songs altogether and sold twenty million records between 1927 and 1933. He earned as much as $100,000 annually, but medical bills took most of it. Billed during his professional career as "America's Blue Yodeler" and the "Singing Brakeman," Rodgers, although unable to read music, enthralled radio, recording, and stage audiences with his performance of songs that seemed to catalogue the varied memories and experiences of small-town and rural Americans. His records included such songs as "The One Rose," "The TB Blues," "In the Jailhouse Now," "Any Old Time," "Carolina Sunshine Girl," and "The Yodeling Ranger" (composed shortly after Rodgers was made an honorary Texas Ranger in Austin in 1931). Rodgers's guitar technique and his famous blue yodel, as well as the informality of his presentation, were emulated by scores of young country-and-western singers—Jimmie Davis, Hank Snow, Gene Autry, Ernest Tubb, Hank Williams, Kenneth Threadgill, and others—whose success was a tribute to the country-singing star.

To seek relief from tuberculosis, Rodgers moved to the dry region of the Texas Hill Country and restricted himself to performances in the South and Southwest. During the last few years of his life he made most of his appearances in Texas. In 1929 he built a $50,000 mansion, Blue Yodeler's Paradise, in Kerrville, but left there to live in a modest home in San Antonio in 1932. He died in a hotel room in New York City while on a recording trip there. Jimmie Rodgers was the first person named, by unanimous vote, to the Country Music Hall of Fame in Nashville, Tennessee. He received this posthumous honor on November 3, 1961, less than a month before the death of his wife in San Antonio.

BIBLIOGRAPHY: Austin *American*, July 29, August 5, 1972. Bill C. Malone, *Country Music U.S.A.* (Austin: University of Texas Press, 1968). Carrie Williamson Rodgers, *My Husband Jimmie Rodgers* (Nashville: Ernest Tubb, 1935; rpt., 1953).

Roland, Gene. Jazz instrumentalist and composer; b. Dallas, September 15, 1921; d. New York City, August 11, 1982. Roland began studying the piano at age eleven. He eventually became proficient on a variety of instruments and developed into a noted arranger and composer. Taken at the age of eighteen with the big band sound, he switched his emphasis from piano to trumpet and taught himself to play in 1939. While attending North Texas State College in Denton from 1940 to 1942, he and three other Texas jazz musicians became friends and roommates. The three were Jimmy Giuffre, Herb Ellis, and Harry Babasin.

After leaving North Texas, Roland served in the Eighth Army Air Force Band, for which he created dance-band arrangements. In 1944 he made his way to California to join the Stan Kenton orchestra, in which he served as arranger, composer, trombonist, and trumpeter. He appeared with Kenton in the film *Artistry in Rhythm* (1944) and established himself as Kenton's first full-time arranger. Roland also composed songs for vocalist June Christy, probably the most famous of which was "Ain't No Misery in Me," and contributed to the arrangement of Kenton's first million-selling album, *Tampico*. Roland was rightly credited with helping to make Kenton's orchestra known across America.

For a brief period he was an arranger for Lionel Hampton and a trumpeter for Lucky Millinder before rejoining Kenton in the summer of 1945. In 1946 he split his time between arranging in New York and playing piano in Los Angeles with Zoot Sims, Herbie Steward, Jimmy Giuffre, Woody Herman, and Stan Getz. Woody Herman recorded Giuffre's piece "The Four Brothers," which Roland's experimentation with the sound of three tenors and baritone had helped make possible. In the late 1940s Roland played bass trumpet with jazz great Count Basie and wrote arrangements for Claude Thornhill and Artie Shaw.

In the early 1950s he had a chance to lead a twenty-six-piece band with some of bop's greatest musicians, including Dizzy Gillespie and Charlie Parker. This project unfortunately proved unsuccessful, and Roland returned to his arranger position with Kenton. He was an integral part of the Kenton orchestra during the next few years before rejoining Woody Herman to arrange sixty-five new numbers for the Herman Herd. Roland can be heard playing mellophonium and soprano saxophone in his original compositions recorded in 1961 for the Kenton album entitled *Adventures in Blues*. He toured with Kenton in 1973 and worked for the remainder of his career in New York playing piano, tenor sax, and trumpet, and arranging for his own big bands. He was survived by his wife, Charlotte, and two children.

BIBLIOGRAPHY: Leonard Feather and Ira Gitler, *Biographical Encyclopedia of Jazz* (Oxford University Press, 1999). *New Grove Dictionary of Jazz*, Second Edition (2002). Dave Oliphant, *Texan Jazz* (Austin: University of Texas Press, 1996).

Daniel Rendon

Rosenfield, John Jr. Journalist and critic; b. Dallas, April 5, 1900; d. November 26, 1966 (buried in Dallas); son of Max John and Jennie Lind (Kramer) Rosenfield. The younger Rosenfield attended Dallas public schools, the University of Texas, and Columbia University, where he graduated. He worked for the New York *Evening Mail*, first as a reporter, then as a motion-picture reviewer. Following brief employment as a publicity man for Paramount Pictures, he returned to Dallas in 1923 and joined the staff of the Dallas *Morning News*. Two years later he was asked by George B. Dealey, the founder of the *News*, to form an amusements department for the paper.

During his forty-one years as drama and music critic for

the *Morning News*, Rosenfield became a recognized cultural spokesman for the Southwest. He contributed widely to national periodicals, as well as writing his local column, "The Passing Show." His reviews were characterized by astute judgment, dashed with keen wit. Largely through Rosenfield's influence with wealthy Dallas families, the Margo Jones Theatre was able to secure the financial backing that enabled it to open in June 1947. The Southwest Theatre Conference twice voted Rosenfield its annual award (in 1955 and 1960), and the Screen Directors Guild cited him for distinguished motion-picture criticism in 1956. He was a member of Temple Emanu-El. He married Claire Burger in 1923 and was the father of one son. In 1957 he gave up his administrative duties with the Dallas *Morning News* but continued to write reviews until June 1966.

BIBLIOGRAPHY: Dallas *Morning News*, November 27, 1966. Dallas *Times Herald*, November 27, 1966. *Who Was Who in America*, Volume 4.   *Ronald L. Davis*

S

Sacred Harp Music. A religious folk music named for Benjamin Franklin White's *The Sacred Harp* (1844). Its old-time white spirituals are sung a cappella; the "sacred harp" is the human voice singing hymns to God. Sacred harp music, maintained primarily by religious fundamentalists, is sometimes called "fasola" music because of the names of its shape notes.

Sacred harp music had its beginnings in the late eighteenth century. The frontier preachers in the Southern Highlands and the Deep South found themselves with large congregations that wanted to sing praises to God but lacked music. As Charles Wesley said, "The devil had all the good tunes." The frontier preachers therefore took the old ballads—the English, Irish, Scottish, and Welsh folksongs—that had been a part of their culture for generations and put religious words to them. "The Ballad of Captain Kidd" became "Wondrous Love," and the Scottish air we call "Auld Lang Syne" became the tune of "Hark! From the Tombs."

A simpler type of religious song that was later incorporated into sacred harp was the camp-meeting song. This was a substitution song of one or two lines that was based on repetition. For instance, in a song with the unlikely title of "Cuba," the line "Go, preachers, tell it to the world" is repeated three times and then tagged with a final line, "Poor mourners found a home at last." The chorus is "Thro' free grace and a dying lamb," a line repeated three times and followed by "Poor mourners found a home at last." The song could be sung as long as the leader could think up substitutes for "preachers": "Christians," "Baptists," "brothers," and so forth.

Another influence on the development of sacred harp music was the singing school, a tradition that began in the eastern states in the 1770s and was still popular among the people of the South during the Second Great Revival of the early 1800s, which entered Texas in the mid-nineteenth century. All that a singing-school master had to have to start a school was a fair voice, a tuning fork, and some made-simple books. The book that had the greatest effect on sacred harp singing was *Easy Instructor, or A New Method of Teaching Sacred Harmony*, published by William Little and William Smith in 1801. The new method was the use of shape notes: a right triangle for fa, a circle for sol, a square for la, and a diamond for mi.

The singing master always led his pupils through the song first by singing the note names for the seven-note scale, which went back to pre-Elizabethan England (the full scale was fa, sol, la, fa, sol, la, mi, fa). When the pupils had the notation well in hand, they sang the words. This practice continues in present-day sacred harp singing. The singing master's other contribution to sacred harp music was the composition of songs, mainly "fuguing" ("fleeing") songs. These were popular in Britain over 300 years ago and later in singing schools of the American colonies;

their melodic lines were based on traditional rounds, each singing part beginning and repeating a set phrase at a different time, and all parts concluding together.

In 1844 B. F. White published his collection of revival songs, hymns, spirituals, and fuguing songs in a longways book titled *The Sacred Harp*. The book was notated in Little and Smith's shape notes, with each song divided into three or four singing parts, singing-school style. *The Sacred Harp* became the favorite hymn book for Southern fundamentalists and gave fasola music its name.

Although sacred harp all-day singings and dinner on the grounds are not as widespread as before World War II, singings regularly take place throughout East Texas. Though monthly singings were once held in almost every rural community in East and Central Texas, several annual singings are still held. The two that in the 1990s had the longest existence and largest meetings were the Southwest Texas Sacred Harp Singing Convention at McMahan, held on the first fifth Sunday in the spring, and the East Texas Sacred Harp Singing Convention in Henderson, organized in 1914 and held on the second weekend in August.

Sacred harp singings traditionally were (in some places, still are) a part of a community's homecoming celebration, of which the church and religion were major parts. At an all-day singing the main body of singers sits in blocks two or three deep and forms a hollow square, with the leader in the middle. Tenors sit at the south of the square and sing the melodies with the audience sitting and singing behind them. Across from the tenors are the altos. The basses sit in the west across from the sopranos, or trebles. The groups sing a cappella, with neither piano nor organ to trouble the sound of their harmonies. The secretary of the singing calls individual singers to lead their two songs. The leader, standing in the middle of the square, announces his first song by page number and top or lower "brace," if two songs happen to be on the same page. The "pitcher" or "keyer," usually among the tenors, sings the first note of all the parts, trying to pitch the song within the range of the singers. Pitch is relative, not absolute, so if the notes are too high, someone will probably remark that it is "sharp"; if it is too low, it is "flat." When the pitch is agreed upon, the singing begins. Faithful to the old singing-school tradition, the singers begin by singing the notes of their parts. When they have finished the solmizing, they move directly into the words of the song and never miss a beat. Sacred harp singing is strong and personal and purposeful, and the singers are singing for themselves and for the joy of the sounds they are making. They saw the air with their hands and pound out the beat with their fists, and the music is grand to hear.

The sacred harp sound is over 200 years old, much of it, and it differs from modern church music with its doleful minor chords and unusual harmonic patterns. Sacred harp songs emphasize the tonic and dominant chords while

Donald Ross (center) of Henderson, leads a group in Sacred Harp singing. Sacred Harp is a religious folk or gospel music, sung acapella, characterized by its use of shaped notes, minor keys, and unusual four-part harmonies. Photograph by Jane Levine, courtesy Texas Folklife Resources.

neglecting the subdominant and nearly all other ones. Many of them feature pentatonic melodies in minor keys. The songs were written during the hard times of the frontier, and their content often is a reminder that suffering is a natural and an endurable part of life. And, of course, they carry the message that when this difficult life is done there will be the life with God hereafter.

All-day singings usually begin at ten o'clock, although conventions might start earlier and last longer. The morning session has a ten-minute break at eleven o'clock and ends at noon. The women begin drifting out of the church before noon to get dinner spread. After dinner, singing resumes at one o'clock and lasts till three or later, with a two-o'clock break. Memorial songs are sung toward the end of the day in remembrance of those singers who have gone on to the heavenly choir. At the end of the singing, announcements of future singings are made and invitations are extended. Unspoken agreements exist among the singers to reciprocate attendance at each other's singings. A National Sacred Harp Convention is held annually in the summer in Birmingham, Alabama. It is sponsored by the Sacred Harp Publishing Company, which still publishes B.

Poster by artist Kerry Awn for the "Special Midnight Groovers Concert" featuring Doug Sahm and his friends, at the Ritz Theatre, Austin, November 1970. Courtesy George B. Ward.

F. White's *The Sacred Harp*, revised in the twentieth century by W. M. Cooper and others.

BIBLIOGRAPHY: Francis Edward Abernethy, *Singin' Texas* (Dallas: E-Heart Press, 1983). Lisa Carol Hardaway, Sacred Harp Traditions in Texas (M.A. thesis, Rice University, 1989). George Pullen Jackson, *The Story of the Sacred Harp: 1844–1944* (Nashville: Vanderbilt University Press, 1944). George Pullen Jackson, *White Spirituals in the Southern Uplands* (Chapel Hill: University of North Carolina Press, 1933). "Shape-note Hymnody," "Spiritual," *The New Grove Dictionary of Music and Musicians*, ed. Sadie Stanley (Washington: Macmillan, 1980). Benjamin Franklin White, *The B. F. White Sacred Harp* (12th ed., Troy, Alabama: Sacred Harp Book Company, 1988).

Francis E. Abernethy

Sahm, Douglas Wayne. Musician in several popular genres; b. San Antonio, November 6, 1941; d. Taos, New Mexico, November 18, 1999. Sahm was a musical prodigy who, at an early age, began playing music with a local band. He was singing on the radio at the age of five, and was so gifted that he could play the fiddle, steel guitar, and mandolin by the time he was eight years old. When he was thirteen he was invited to join the "Grand Ole Opry," but had to decline so he would not miss school. Sahm's career spanned over four decades and encompassed a variety of musical styles, including German polkas, blues, rock, and Tejano. In the 1950s he attended Sam Houston High School, San Antonio, where he formed several bands. In 1964 he helped found the Sir Douglas Quintet, an outlandish group of Texans who dressed up and pretended to be part of the so-called "British Invasion" of the mid-1960s. Sahm wrote the quintet's 1965 smash hit, "She's About a Mover," which made the Top Twenty chart. The group's second single, "The Rains Came," made the Top Forty. Sahm moved to San Francisco in 1966 and continued to record. He had some minor successes, including the single "Mendocino." The quintet broke up in 1971.

In the 1970s he moved to Austin and became a member of the "Cosmic Cowboy" scene, along with Willie Nelson and Jerry Jeff Walker. He was signed by Atlantic Records in 1973. With help from his friends Flaco Jimenez, Bob Dylan, and Dr. John, Sahm released the album *Doug Sahm and Band*, which included the song "Is Anybody Going to San Antone?" Later that year he released the album *Texas Tornado*. He continued making records throughout the 1970s and 1980s for different labels, including his popular 1974 album *Groover's Paradise* (Warner Brothers).

In 1989 Sahm teamed up with Freddie Fender, Flaco Jimenez, and Augie Meyers to form the Texas Tornados. The group produced a soulful mix of country, rhythm-and-blues, ballad singing, Texas rock-and-roll, and *conjunto*. They were signed by Reprise Records in 1990 and released their first album, *Texas Tornados*, later that year. The album, in both English and Spanish, was well received by fans and critics alike. It quickly charted on *Billboard*'s rock, Latin, and country charts. In 1991 the album won a Grammy. During the 1990s the Tornadoes toured and released several other successful albums, including *Hangin'*

on by a Thread and *Live from the Limo*. The Tornados were planning a 2000 European concert tour when Sahm was found dead of heart disease in his hotel room. He was married and divorced and had two sons, a daughter, and two grandchildren.

BIBLIOGRAPHY: Associated Press reports, November 19, 1999. Chicago *Sun-Times*, November 22, 1999. *The Guardian: World Reporter*, November 23, 1999. *The Independent—London*, November 29, 1999. Julia M. Robiner, ed., *Contemporary Musicians*, Volume 8 (Detroit: Gale Research, 1993).

James Head

Samaroff, Olga. Concert pianist, author, and teacher; b. Lucie Hickenlooper, San Antonio, August 8, 1882; d. New York City, May 17, 1948; daughter of Carlos and Jane (Loening) Hickenlooper. Soon after her birth, her father resigned his army commission and resettled the family, first in Houston and then (until 1900) in Galveston, where Lucie was tutored at the Ursuline convent.

Both her mother and her maternal grandmother, Lucie (Palmer) Grünewald, who had also been a concert pianist in the United States and Europe, recognized her ability very early in life. By age ten, Lucie had performed for musicians who recommended European training. With her grandmother Grünewald, she moved to Paris in 1894. A year later she won a scholarship to the Paris Conservatoire, the first American woman to do so. There she studied with Elie M. Delaborde. After graduation in 1897, she worked with the Russian pianist–teacher Ernst Jedliczka in Berlin and with Ernest Hutcheson in Baltimore. Over her relatives' protests around 1900 she married Boris Loutzky, a Russian civil servant, who took her back to St. Petersburg. For over three years she devoted her time to general music studies away from the keyboard and expanded her musical horizons. When Loutzky turned out to be cruel, she divorced him and began an earnest effort at a concert career.

To aid the effort, she changed her name from Hickenlooper to Samaroff around 1904–05, borrowed money from a wealthy Cincinnati relative for a concert debut, and acquired an enterprising manager. She became internationally successful and was admired for "tonal color, warmth, and intellectual control." She performed with the New York Symphony Orchestra in 1908 and with the Boston Symphony. A severe illness in 1910, and her subsequent marriage to neophyte conductor Leopold Stokowski in 1911, forced her again to take time out from touring. She was married to Stokowski during his leadership of the Cincinnati Symphony Orchestra (1909–12) and of the Philadelphia Orchestra (1912–1936). She pushed both of them toward recording, then a very new enterprise. She was the first American woman pianist to present all thirty-two Beethoven sonatas in recital. Samaroff and Stokowski were divorced in 1923.

Following an arm injury in 1926, Samaroff turned to teaching and writing for money and a stable life with her only child, Sonya Stokowski. In 1925 she accepted a position at the newly founded Juilliard Graduate School, and for many years was the only American-born member of the piano faculty. She also chaired the piano department of the

Julien Paul Blitz conducting the San Antonio Symphony Orchestra, ca.1917–18. Courtesy San Antonio Symphony Association, UT Institute of Texan Cultures at San Antonio, No. 74-1262.

Philadelphia Conservatory, beginning in January 1928. In addition, she served as a music critic for the New York *Evening Post* from 1926 to 1928.

For the next two decades (1928–48) she reigned as a powerful, demanding teacher. For her students she was able to obtain scholarships and patrons, arrange important social contacts with managers and conductors, and help secure employment during the depression years. She initiated and organized two programs—the Schubert Memorial Foundation (1928) and the Laymen's Music Courses (1932)—meant to provide professional performance opportunities for music students and educate audiences in music study. She published *The Layman's Music Course* (1935) and *An American Musician's Story* (1939). Her experiences in Russia and with Stokowski made her emphasize contemporary music and the importance of media attention at premieres.

Her most famous performing students—William Kapell, Eugene List, Raymond Lewenthal, Joseph Battista, Rosalyn Tureck, Alexis Weissenberg—usually made their careers specializing in contemporary or specific period literature. Samaroff's pedagogical method stressed artistic independence, the concept that each student was to work out his individual approach on a composition. She decried the artist–coach technique in which the teacher talked through or showed a student each part of a work. Consequently, her students' performances were quite varied.

In addition to her teaching, Samaroff was involved in numerous public activities related to music. During the Great Depression she helped organize the Musicians' Emergency Aid (later Musicians' Emergency Fund), and in

1935 she became one of twenty-five musicians chosen to help the Federal Music Project of the WPA plan work-relief programs. Her various awards included honorary doctor of music degrees from the University of Pennsylvania (1931) and the Cincinnati Conservatory of Music (1943). In 1944 President Roosevelt appointed her a member of the Advisory Committee on Music to the Department of State.

BIBLIOGRAPHY: Oliver Daniel, *Stokowski: A Counterpoint of View* (New York: Dodd, Mead, 1982). Donna Pucciani, Olga Samaroff: American Musician and Educator (Ph.D. dissertation, New York University, 1978).

Geoffrey E. McGillen

San Antonio Symphony Orchestra. The Germans of San Antonio had an Instrumental Verein as early as 1852 but did not form a full orchestra until the state *Sängerfest* of 1874. Orchestral life grew, and in the early 1900s San Antonio had some form of symphony orchestra. Noted musician and professor Julian Paul Blitz, for example, conducted a San Antonio orchestra from 1917 to 1922.

In the 1920s and 1930s, however, orchestral activity apparently declined, until Max Reiter, a young German conductor and refugee from European anti-Semitism, drummed up enough support for a trial orchestra concert in June 1939 at the Sunken Garden Theater for an audience of 2,500. Moved by the success of this concert, the Symphony Society of San Antonio formally incorporated. Reiter staged four concerts in the symphony's first season, engaging soloists such as pianist Alec Templeton and violinist Jascha Heifetz in order to attract large audiences. In addition, he commissioned the exiled Czech composer Jaromir Weinberger to write a *Prelude and Fugue on a Southern Folk Tune* for the new orchestra.

Season ticket sales grew, and by 1943–44 Reiter had placed the orchestra on a fully professional basis. He added a tour through the Rio Grande valley and children's concerts and began to lure the city's Hispanic population with a visit from Mexican composer–conductor Carlos Chávez, who conducted his own music. Spring 1945 witnessed the first Grand Opera Festival. Starting with performances of *La Bohème*, Reiter established a tradition of regular opera productions that achieved considerable financial and artistic success. On December 13, 1950, at the height of his artistic powers, Reiter died of a heart attack.

Within a short time, Victor Alessandro had been named his successor. Alessandro, born in Waco, had received his education from the Eastman School of Music and after graduation had gone on to conduct the Oklahoma Symphony, bringing it up to a remarkable level in only three years. As the conductor of the San Antonio Symphony, Alessandro built upon Reiter's foundations a far-reaching and varied program of his own, initiating a series of pops concerts and greatly expanding the role of the associated conductor, principal hornist George Yaeger. In 1961 Alessandro established the Rio Grande Music Festival, a week-long series of operas and concerts each spring. From his earliest years in San Antonio, Alessandro challenged his audiences with contemporary works and championed American music, especially by Texas and local composers.

Beginning in the late 1960s the orchestra gave its concerts in pairs, one performed at the Lila Cockrell (now HemisFair) Theater, the other at Trinity University. When Victor Alessandro died on November 27, 1976, much of the orchestra's growth, stability, and artistic integrity had been directly attributable to his quarter-century tenure. After a two-year search, François Huybrechts replaced Alessandro as the symphony's music director. After two seasons he was succeeded by Lawrence Leighton Smith, in 1980.

Under Smith the orchestra received greater exposure with its city-funded outreach program and increased touring in South Texas and Louisiana. In 1985 Smith resigned, and a search for a new musical director began. Sixten Ehrling served as artistic advisor, and guest conductors led many of the concerts. Financial difficulties forced the cancellation of the 1987–88 season before a new music director could be found. Many of the musicians of the San Antonio Symphony played for the newly formed Orchestra San Antonio until January 1988, when the San Antonio Symphony reinstated its season and assumed Orchestra San Antonio's remaining commitments. For the 1988–89 season Zdenek Macal served as artistic director and principal conductor. Christopher Wilkins was appointed music director designate in 1990 and assumed the post of permanent music director in 1992. In 1994 the symphony was given the first ASCAP / Morton Gould Award for Creative Programming and was recognized for its community-relevant programming by the American Symphony Orchestra League. In 1993–94 the orchestra included seventy-six musicians and performed more than 125 concerts in a forty-one-week season. The San Antonio Symphony had recorded for Mercury Records.

By the late 1990s the San Antonio Symphony faced more financial difficulties and was near bankruptcy on the eve of its sixtieth anniversary season in 1998. Donations from a number of area businesses and the Kronkosky Charitable Foundation helped save the orchestra. After the 2001–2002 season Christopher Wilkins was named music director emeritus, having completed eleven musical seasons. That same season, the symphony was honored with the Leonard Bernstein Award for Educational Programming. Larry Rachleff succeeded Wilkins as the symphony's seventh music director effective for the 2003–2004 season.

As of 2003 the San Antonio Symphony Orchestra consisted of 77 full-time musicians who performed over a 39-week season, and the organization had received a total of seven ASCAP awards. Additionally, the symphony also included a 120-member volunteer chorus, a 17-member volunteer board, and 20 full-time administrative staff positions. The symphony's primary concert venue since 1990 has been the Majestic Theater in downtown San Antonio.

BIBLIOGRAPHY: Theodore Albrecht, "101 Years of Symphonic Music in San Antonio," *Southwestern Musician / Texas Music Educator*, March, November 1975. Ronald L. Davis, *A History of Opera in the American West* (Englewood Cliffs, New Jersey: Prentice–Hall, 1965). San Antonio *Express–News*, January 18, September 6, 18, October 11, 1998; May 25, 2000. San Antonio Symphony website (http://www.sasymphony.org), accessed January 27, 2003. Hope Stoddard, *Symphony Conductors of the U.S.A.* (New York: Crowell, 1957). *Theodore Albrecht*

Schuetze, Julius. Judge, German-language newspaper publisher, and music teacher; b. Dessau, Anhalt, Germany, March 29, 1835; d. Austin, April 23, 1904; son of Heinrich and Louise (Seelman) Schütze. He arrived at Indianola, Texas, with his family in November 1852. His brothers Louis and Adolf had preceded him to Texas.

Julius lived in Yorktown and hauled freight between Indianola and other points. He also lived in Meyersville, where he founded the Texas Sängerbund, a German singing society. In 1854 he moved to San Antonio. There he taught speech and music and married Henrietta Heinz of Seguin, one of his music pupils. In 1858 he moved to Austin, where he taught at the German School.

Schuetze tutored the children of governors Sam Houston and Pendleton Murrah, studied law under Judge Wooldridge, and was admitted to the bar. Upon the death of his first wife he married Julia Ohrndorf, née Brügerhoff; Schuetze had ten children. In 1864 he moved to Bastrop, where he taught at the Orgains School. After the Civil War he became chief justice of Bastrop County. Judge Schuetze served in the Twelfth Texas Legislature as a federal tax collector and was an Indian agent with a tribe in Colorado. He was a Republican and worked actively against prohibition.

From 1870 to 1873 he and O. H. Dietzel published *Vorwärts* ("Forward"), a German-language newspaper, first in New Braunfels and later in Austin. In 1883 Schuetze again published *Vorwärts* in Austin. Like his father, who had been a silk grower in Germany, Schuetze raised silkworms, which he exhibited at the State Fair of Texas. His article "Seidenbau in Texas" ("Silk Farming in Texas") was published in the *Jahrbuch für Texas* in 1884. Schuetze was active in the Order of the Sons of Hermann, which he served as national president from September 1897 until his death.

BIBLIOGRAPHY: Austin *Statesman*, April 24, 25, 1904.

C. A. Schutze Jr.

Scott, Clifford. Saxophonist, vocalist, recording artist, and composer–arranger; b. Clifford Doneley Scott, San Antonio, June 21, 1928; d. April 19, 1993; youngest child of Grace and Harry L. Scott Sr. Clifford's mother died when he was six months old, and he was raised by his father and stepmother, Mattie Scott. His siblings included a brother, Harry, two sisters, Harriett and Marcy, and a step-sister, Katherine Dotson.

Clifford's father worked for the railroad but was also a talented musician who played violin and piano. He encouraged all of his children to appreciate music at an early age. According to Clifford's sister Marcy, they had a little family band. By the time he was six years old Clifford was playing music, and upon entering Douglass Middle School he was considered a musical prodigy, having learned the clarinet, violin, trumpet, tuba, and drums. Before he entered Wheatley High School the tenor saxophone had become his instrument of choice.

Scotty, as he was called by those who knew him, was able to meet many future world-renowned musicians who came through San Antonio. In the early 1940s when big-name musicians such as Zoot Sims and John Coltrane came to town and were stranded, they were able to stay with Scotty's family. At that time he was playing with Amos Milburn and the Alldin Chicken Shackers, a Houston group. He also played with George Abrams and the Cavaliers, an all-black orchestra.

Lionel Hampton went to San Antonio when Scotty was fourteen years old to perform at the Municipal Auditorium. He needed a saxophone player, and Scotty got the gig. Afterwards, Lionel asked Scotty's parents if he could join his group for a European tour. They agreed, on the condition that he return to graduate from high school, which he did in 1946.

Whenever Scott returned from touring, he would teach younger musicians in San Antonio. While traveling throughout Europe and the United States, Scotty learned from and performed with such famous musicians as Charlie Parker, Clifford Brown, Count Basie, Les McCane, and Quincy Jones. He also studied composition, arranging, and theory at the Hartnet Music School in New York. During this time Scotty performed and recorded with organist Bill Doggett and wrote the international hit song "Honky Tonk" (1956), which sold millions of copies. "Honky Tonk," Scotty's trademark song for the rest of his life, earned him the nickname "Mr. Honky Tonk."

During the 1950s and '60s Scotty played with such legendary stars as Little Richard, Ray Charles, and Fats Domino. He lived in Los Angeles in the 1960s, but in 1976 he returned to San Antonio permanently and continued to perform at local clubs. In 1992 he released the album *Mr.*

Honky Tonk Is Back in Town on the New Rose label.

Scott was presented the Carver Living Legend Award by the Carver Community Cultural Center of San Antonio. He was scheduled to perform at the center's jazz festival on the night he was to accept his award. Unfortunately, he had suffered a slight stroke the Monday before the performance and was hospitalized. Nevertheless, he surprised the audience by arriving for the performance via ambulance, and even though he was weak he gave a masterful performance to a standing ovation. Scotty continued to play around San Antonio until his death. He was survived by three sons and two daughters.

BIBLIOGRAPHY: All Music Guide (http://www.allmusic.com/), accessed February 21, 2003. San Antonio *Express–News,* April 20, 1993. *Karla Peterson*

Seele, Friedrich Hermann. Teacher, public official, writer, and cultural leader; b. Hildesheim, Hannover, Germany, April 14, 1823; d. New Braunfels, Texas, March 18, 1902; son of Jonas and Anna (Runge) Seele. Hermann Seele was educated at the Andrenaeum Academy in Hildesheim and subsequently immigrated to Texas.

After landing at Galveston on December 12, 1843, he joined the Adelsverein (a colonization society of German nobles) and arrived in May 1845 in the month-old city of New Braunfels, which became his home for the rest of his life. Pastor Louis Cachand Ervendberg, the spiritual leader of the New Braunfels colony, chose Seele to teach the colony's first school, and the community still remembers Hermann Seele as its first teacher. His law career began when he was elected the first Comal County district clerk in 1846. He was admitted to the bar on April 27, 1855. He was active on behalf of the Democratic party and opposed the American (Know-Nothing) party, a nativist, xenophobic, anti-Catholic movement. During the Civil War he served as adjutant and inspector general of the Thirty-first Brigade, Texas Militia, with the rank of major. Concurrently he served as mayor of New Braunfels. He married Mathilde Blum on January 25, 1862, and to them were born three sons and two daughters. From 1863 to 1865 Seele served in the Tenth Texas Legislature.

After the Civil War he turned his energies to education and served as a member of the board and faculty of New Braunfels Academy until 1879. In 1871 he organized the first state Teachers Conference, and when in 1872 the Texas State Board of Education mandated the formation of teachers' institutes, Seele's school served as a model. To Seele's influence is attributed the fact that Jacob Waelder was able to include in the Constitution of 1876 a section establishing independent school districts empowered to finance public schools through taxation.

In the fall of 1876 Seele, as attorney, had to give his full attention to the suit of the Veramendi heirs, who sought to gain title to the Comal tract, upon which New Braunfels is built. Seele, who had first joined in defending the New Braunfels citizenry in 1852 against the Veramendi claim, succeeded on April 23, 1879, in winning a decision in the citizens' favor in the United States Circuit Court. He became postmaster in New Braunfels on October 1, 1889, and served until February 28, 1895. He was a charter

member of the First German Protestant Church of New Braunfels. He was elected secretary of the congregation in 1845 and served until his death, when he was succeeded by his son Harry. On occasion Seele also served as lay preacher.

As a member of the Germania Singing Society he helped organize the first and subsequent *Sängerfeste* (singing festivals) throughout Texas. Seele's *Sängerhaus* (singers' hall), a thirty-by-eighty-foot brick structure built in 1855 beside the Comal River, was a center not only for singers but also for the New Braunfels Dramatic Society, in which Seele participated. He was also a writer of both verse and prose. He was regularly called upon for stanzas to grace birthdays, weddings, and other social and civic events.

In 1851 Ferdinand Jacob Lindheimer, the great Texas botanist, founded and edited the *Neu Braunfelser Zeitung.* Seele participated in the founding, contributed to the newspaper's columns, and later had editorial control. In 1936 his descendants privately published a collection of his writings, *Die Cypresse und Gesammelte Schriften.* An English edition, *The Cypress and Other Writings of a German Pioneer in Texas*, was published by the University of Texas Press in 1979.

After his death Seele was honored with a monument in Landa Park, New Braunfels, set up in 1936, the Texas Centennial year. In 1954 his portrait was included in a painting, *The Heroes and Heroines of Texas Education*, commissioned by the Texas Heritage Foundation. In 1976 a marker recounting his achievements was placed on the Sophienburg Museum and Archives grounds, and in Landa Park a large monument named him among the early settlers. The Sixty-fifth Texas Legislature designated April 14, 1977, Hermann Seele Day, and his church named its activities building the Seele Parish House.

BIBLIOGRAPHY: Rudolph L. Biesele, *The History of the German Settlements in Texas, 1831–1861* (Austin: Von Boeckmann–Jones, 1930; rpt. 1964). Oscar Haas, *History of New Braunfels and Comal County, Texas, 1844–1946* (Austin: Steck, 1968).   *Edward C. Breitenkamp*

Selena. Singer; b. Selena Quintanilla, Lake Jackson, Texas, April 16, 1971; d. Corpus Christi, March 31, 1995; daughter of Abraham and Marcella (Perez) Quintanilla Jr. Selena married Christopher Perez, guitarist and member of the band Selena y Los Dinos (slang for "the Boys") on April 2, 1992. They had no children. Selena attended Oran M. Roberts Elementary School in Lake Jackson and West Oso Junior High in Corpus Christi, where she completed the eighth grade. In 1989 she finished high school through the American School, a correspondence school for artists, and enrolled at Pacific Western University in business administration correspondence courses.

Her career began when she was eight. From 1957 to 1971 her father played with Los Dinos, a Tejano band. He taught his children to sing and play in the family band and taught Selena to sing in Spanish. They performed at the family restaurant, Pappagallo, and at weddings in Lake Jackson. After 1981 the band became a professional act. In 1982 the group moved to Corpus Christi and played in rural dance halls and urban nightclubs, where Tejano

Tejano music star Selena became popular in Texas in the 1970s and crossed into a broader Latino and Latin-American audience in the 1980s. Photograph by Al Rendon © 2003.

music flourishes. In her late teens Selena adopted fashions sported by Madonna.

Preceded by Lydia Mendoza and Chelo Silva, Mexican-American star vocalists of the 1930s, and by pioneer orchestra singer Laura Canales in the 1970s, Selena became a star in Tejano music. She won the Tejano Music Award for Female Entertainer of the Year in 1987, and eight other Tejano awards followed. By the late 1980s Selena was known as "*la Reina de la Onda Tejana*" ("the Queen of Tejano music") and "*una mujer del pueblo.*" Her popularity soared with annual awards from the Tejano Music Awards and a contract with EMI Latin Records in 1989. At the 1995 Houston Livestock Show and Rodeo, the band attracted 61,041 people, more than Clint Black, George Strait, Vince Gil, or Reba McIntire.

Selena y Los Dinos recorded with Tejano labels GP, Cara, Manny, and Freddie before 1989. Their albums include *Alpha* (1986), *Dulce Amor* (1988), *Preciosa* (1988), *Selena y Los Dinos* (1990), *Ven Conmigo* (1991), *Entre a Mi Mundo* (1992), *Selena Live* (1993), *Amor Prohibido* (1994), and *Dreaming of You* (1995). The band's popularity surged with *Ven Conmigo. Entre a Mi Mundo* made Selena the first Tejana to sell more than 300,000 albums. In 1993 she signed with SBK Records to produce an all-English album, but it was replaced with the bilingual *Dreaming of You*. The 1995 album became number one on the national *Billboard* Top 200 the week of its release.

Despite her success in the Spanish-language market, mainstream society largely ignored Selena until around 1993. In 1994 *Texas Monthly* named her one of twenty influential Texans and the *Los Angeles Times* interviewed her. The band won a Grammy in 1993 and was nominated for one in 1994. Also in 1993 and 1995, *Lo Nuestro Billboard* gave the band awards in four categories. Selena y Los Dinos was a cross-over act in Tejano, romance, cumbia, tropical, pop, rap, and salsa in Spanish and English; Selena was not only bilingual but biethnic. Before her death, the band sold more than 1.5 million records.

By the mid-1980s Selena had crossed into the national Latino and Latin-American market. A recording with the Puerto Rican band Barrio Boyzz furthered inroads into this area. Selena y Los Dinos began to acquire a following in Mexico (Matamoros) as early as 1986. Along with Emilio Navaira, Selena y Los Dinos attracted 98,000 fans in Monterrey, and thus popularized Tejano music in Mexico. In 1994 the band played in New York to a Mexican and Central American audience. The band was the first Tejano group to make *Billboard*'s Latin Top 200 list of all-time best-selling records.

Selena was also known to Latin-American television audiences. At the age of twelve or thirteen she was introduced on the Johnny Canales Show. She appeared on "Sábado Gigante," "Siempre en Domingo," "El Show de Cristina," and the soap opera "Dos Mujeres, Un Camino." She also made a cameo appearance in the 1995 film *Don Juan de Marco*. Advertisements also made Selena popular. Coca-Cola featured her in a poster, and she had a promotional tour agreement with the company. She had a six-figure contract with Dep Corporation and a contract with AT&T and Southwestern Bell. A six-figure deal with EMI Latin made her a millionaire. In 1992 she began her own clothing line. In 1994 she opened Selena Etc., a boutique–salon in Corpus Christi and San Antonio. At the time of her death she had plans to open others in Monterrey and Puerto Rico. A 1994 *Hispanic* magazine stated her worth at $5 million. Despite her wealth, however, she lived in the working-class district of Molina in Corpus Christi.

Selena considered herself a public servant. She participated with the Texas Prevention Partnership, sponsored by the Texas Commission on Alcohol and Drug Abuse (Dep Corporation) Tour to Schools, in an educational video. She was also involved with the D.A.R.E. program and worked with the Coastal Bend Aids Foundation. Her pro-education videos included *My Music* and *Selena Agrees*. She was scheduled for a Dallas–Fort Worth boys' and girls' club benefit. Selena taped a public-service announcement for the Houston Area Women's Center, a shelter for battered women, in 1993.

On March 31, 1995, Selena was shot fatally in the back by Yolanda Saldivar, her first fan club founder and manager of Selena Etc., in Corpus Christi. The *New York Times* covered her death with a front-page story, as did Texas major dailies. Six hundred persons attended her private Jehovah's Witness funeral. More than 30,000 viewed her casket at the Bayfront Plaza Convention Center in Corpus Christi. Hundreds of memorials and Masses were offered for her across the country; on April 16, for instance, a Mass was celebrated on her behalf at Our Lady Queen of Angels Church in Los Angeles. Her promotion agency, Rogers and Cowan, received over 500 requests for information about her. "Entertainment Tonight" and "Dateline NBC" ran short stories on her, and *People* magazine sold a commemorative issue. Spanish-language television and radio sponsored numerous tributes, typically half-hour or hour programs.

Selena's fans compared the catastrophe to the deaths of John Lennon, Elvis Presley, John F. Kennedy, and Pedro Infante. Songs, quilts, paintings, T-shirts, buttons, banners, posters, and shrines honored her. Radio talker Howard Stern of New York, however, snickered at her music and enraged her fans. Bo Corona, a disc jockey at a Houston Tejano radio station, asked him to apologize, and the League of United Latin American Citizens organized a boycott of his sponsors. Selena's death became part of the controversy over the Texas concealed-handgun bill. Her death also fostered greater awareness of Tejano music. According to superstar Little Joe, as a result of Selena's death "the word Tejano has been recognized by millions." Governor George W. Bush proclaimed April 16 "Selena Day." Selena's family founded the Selena Foundation.

BIBLIOGRAPHY: Clint Richmond, *Selena! The Phenomenal Life and Tragic Death of the Tejano Music Queen* (New York: Pocket Books, 1995). Geraldo Ruiz, *Selena, La Última Canción* (New York: El Diario Books, 1995). *Selena; Her Life in Pictures, 1971–1995, People,* Commemorative Issue, Spring 1995.   *Cynthia E. Orozco*

Selph, Pappy. Honky-tonk fiddler, a "founding father" of honky-tonk music; b. Leon Selph, Houston, April 7, 1914; d. Houston, January 8, 1999; son of Lee and Alvenie Selph. He began playing the violin at the age of seven, played with the Houston Youth Symphony when he was fourteen, and joined W. Lee O'Daniel's Light Crust Doughboys in 1931, when he was seventeen. Although O'Daniel paid Selph $20 a week to play for the band, the fiddler's primary duty was to teach the Doughboys, who could not read music, one new song a week to perform on their radio show. Bob Wills was one of his students.

When Wills moved to Waco to form the Texas Playboys, Selph joined him. He stayed with the Playboys until Wills moved the band to Tulsa in 1934, then moved back to Houston and formed his own band, the Blue Ridge Playboys. The group, which included legendary musicians Floyd Tillman, Moon Mullican, and Ted Daffan, signed with Columbia Records in 1938 and achieved some regional success with recordings that included "Give Me My Dime Back" and the classic "Orange Blossom Special." From the 1930s until World War II the Blue Ridge Playboys had their own national radio show on KPRC in Houston. The show was canceled at the outbreak of the war, when Selph enlisted in the navy. After the war he returned to Houston and joined the Houston Fire Department, where he worked for the next thirty years. After he retired

Shaw learned his "barrelhouse" piano style from musicians in the Fourth Ward, a Houston center of black entertainment. In the 1920s he worked the Santa Fe circuit, hopping freight trains on a tour. Photograph by Burton Wilson, March 1971.

in 1972, he formed another band, with which he toured the Soviet Union and served as a cultural ambassador for the State Department.

He continued to play local venues around Texas until his death. Selph and his wife, Inez, had two sons and two daughters. In 1996 he was inducted into the Texas Western Swing Hall of Fame.

BIBLIOGRAPHY: Dallas *Morning News*, January 11, 1999. Houston *Chronicle*, June 27, 1985; June 5, 1991; January 10, 1999. *The Independent—London*, January 16, 1999.   *James Head*

Shaw, Robert. Blues pianist; b. Stafford, Texas, August 9, 1908; d. Austin, May 16, 1985; son of Jesse and Hettie Shaw. His parents owned a 200-acre farm. The Shaws had a Steinway grand piano and provided music lessons for his sisters, but Shaw was not permitted to take piano lessons because his father was opposed to the idea. Years later he told an interviewer that he would "crawl under the house" to catch the musical strains coming from one of his sisters' piano lessons.

Shaw obeyed his father and worked alongside him in the family's cattle and hog business, but played the piano when the rest of the family was away from home and practiced the songs he heard on errands into town. Reportedly, the first song he learned was "Aggravatin' Papa Don't You Try to Two-Time Me." By the time he was a teenager, Shaw would slip away to hear jazz musicians in Houston and at the roadhouses in the nearby countryside. As soon as he was able, he sought out a piano teacher to take lessons and paid for them from his own earnings. In time, despite his father's opposition, he decided to pursue his ambition of becoming a jazz musician.

In addition to ragtime elements such as syncopation, the "barrelhouse" piano style that Shaw played employs a heavy, hard-hitting touch with fast release. The style was named for the barrelhouses, where it was performed—sheds with walls lined with beer and whiskey, an open floor, and a piano on a raised platform in a corner of the room. The back of the barrelhouse was also used as a bawdy house.

Shaw learned his distinct brand of piano playing from other musicians in the Fourth Ward, Houston, the center of black entertainment in the city. Clubs there hosted such important blues stylists as Lightnin' Hopkins. Famous dance bands of the era also appeared at the El Dorado and the Emancipation Park Dance Pavilion, two of the best dance halls in the Fourth Ward.

In the 1920s Shaw became part of an itinerant band loosely referred to as the "Santa Fe Circuit" because the musicians hopped Santa Fe freight trains to do their tours. Shaw played as far north as Chicago, but he mostly confined himself to Texas. He appeared as a soloist in the clubs and roadhouses of such Southeast Texas towns as Sugar Land and Richmond, the South Texas town of Kingsville during the cotton harvest, and the big cities of Houston and Dallas. When the Kilgore oil boom occurred in 1930, Shaw went there to play, and in 1932 he headed to Kansas City, Kansas, to perform at the Black Orange Cafe. In 1933 he had a radio show in Oklahoma City before returning to Texas, first to Fort Worth and then to Austin, where he took up permanent residence and opened a barbecue business. He later owned and operated a grocery store called the Stop and Swat in the predominantly black east side.

Shaw met Martha Landrum in Austin in 1936, and they married on December 22, 1939. They had no children. He had previously been married to a woman named Blanche, with whom he had a daughter, Verna Mae, and a son, William. For several decades after his marriage, Shaw ran his business in partnership with Martha. He was named the black businessman of the year in Austin in 1962.

He also continued to play his music privately and for people who dropped by the Stop and Swat. In 1967, seven years before his retirement from the grocery business, he returned to public musical performance, this time with a younger generation of followers and growing fame. With the revival of his career, as one of the few remaining "virtuoso" barrelhouse blues pianists of his period, Shaw played often in Austin and at the Kerrville Folk Festival. Over the following years he also performed in Amsterdam, in Frankfurt, and at the Berlin Jazz Festival. In addition he played at the Smithsonian Institute's American Folk Life Festival, the World's Fair Expo in Canada, the Border Folk Festival in El Paso, and the New Orleans Jazz and Heritage Festival.

Shaw also made at least one album, called *Texas Barrelhouse Piano*, recorded in Austin by Mack McCormick over a three-month period in 1963. It was originally released by McCormick's Almanac Book and Recording Company. Arhoolie Records, one of the country's best-known folk recording companies, later reissued the album. Shaw was also featured with the Preservation Hall Jazz Band during its appearance at the 1973 Austin Aqua Fest, and his fame spread widely enough in the next decade to earn him an invitation to participate in the Texas Commission on the Arts touring arts program between 1981 and 1983.

He was scheduled to take part in the Texas Music Tour in honor of the Texas Sesquicentennial in 1986, but died of a heart attack. After a funeral service at the Ebenezer Baptist Church in Austin, he was buried at Capital Memorial Gardens.

Some jazz critics have noted that Shaw's repertoire remained fresh throughout his career because he continued to practice his unique barrelhouse style during his thirty-year hiatus, unaffected by newer or more popular blues styles. Moreover, his commitment to his technique ensured that a unique black musical tradition remained intact. On May 27, 1985, two weeks after his death, the state Senate adopted a resolution to honor Shaw's many contributions to the state's musical heritage.

BIBLIOGRAPHY: Alan B. Govenar, *Meeting the Blues* (Dallas: Taylor, 1988). Robert Springer, "Being Yourself Is More Than Tryin' to Be Somebody Else," *Blues Unlimited*, March–April 1978. Vertical Files, Austin History Center. Vertical Files, Center for American History, University of Texas at Austin. *Teresa Palomo Acosta*

Silva, Chelo. Tejana singer; born Consuelo Silva, Brownsville, Texas, August 25, 1922; d. Corpus Christi, April 2, 1988; eldest daughter of seven children. As a teenager she started singing in school and at church, and by her late teens began performing with a local group, the Tito Crixell Orchestra. By 1939 she was well known in Brownsville and was invited to sing on a local radio show hosted by the young Américo Paredes. The two were married the same year, but the marriage ended in divorce some years later.

During the early 1940s, Silva continued to perform on radio and at the Continental Club, where she had begun her singing career. As a brilliant interpreter of the *canción romántica* style, she rapidly became popular. In 1952 she was signed by Discos Falcon in McAllen. With a more extensively marketed recording arrangement, her fame quickly spread throughout the Southwest. Soon the Mexican label Peerless began distributing her records all over Mexico, and she became an international star. Chelo eventually recorded more than seventy titles for Discos Falcon.

In 1955 she signed with Columbia Records and gained even more commercial exposure. She made a series of major hits, including "Está Sellado," "Sabes de Qué Tengo Ganas," "Amor Aventurero," and "Soy Bohemia." Accompanied by guitar trios, her distinctive low contralto had a melancholy quality well-suited to the *canción romántica*. Hailed as "la Reina de los Boleros," she continued to perform until the 1980s, touring extensively throughout Mexico, South America, and the United States. She also performed with notable figures of the *música ranchera* style, such as José Alfredo Jiménez, Javier Solís, and Lola Beltrán. She died of cancer.

BIBLIOGRAPHY: Ramiro Burr, *The Billboard Guide to Tejano and Regional Mexican Music* (New York: Billboard, 1999). Manuel Peña, *Música Tejana: The Cultural Economy of Artistic Transformation* (College Station: Texas A&M University Press, 1999). *Juan Carlos Rodríguez*

Sims, Frankie Lee. Blues singer and guitarist; b. New Orleans, April 30, 1917; d. Dallas, May 10, 1970; one of thirteen children of Henry and Virginia (Summuel) Sims. Sims was a first cousin to Lightnin' Hopkins and is said also to have been Texas Alexander's cousin.

He was a prominent member of the "Texas country blues movement" of the 1940s and 1950s. When he was a child his family moved to Marshal, Texas. Both of his parents were guitarists, and Frankie taught himself to play the instrument when he was only twelve. He ran away from home around 1929 to play for parties, dances, and other gigs in the Crockett–Centerville area. In the mid-1930s he attended Wiley College, in Marshal. After college, he taught elementary school in Palestine, Texas. Sims served with the U.S. Marines from 1942 to 1945. After the war he settled in the Dallas area, where he frequently worked with T-Bone Walker, Smokey Hogg, and others from the late 1940s well into the 1950s. He made his first recording in 1948 for Herb Rippa's Dallas-based Blue Bonnet Records.

Sims did not have much commercial success, however, until 1953, when he cut "Lucy Mae Blues," his only real hit. He continued to record extensively during the 1950s, primarily for Specialty Records, and later for Johnny Vincent's Ace and Vin labels. He displayed his rocking style on numerous cuts including "Walking with Frankie" and "She Likes to Boogie Real Low." He worked local venues in Dallas throughout the 1960s.

Unfortunately, due to numerous personal problems, he was not able to cash in on the 1960s blues revival. Sims died of pneumonia and is buried at Lincoln Memorial Cemetery, Dallas. He was married and left one son, Little Frankie Lee, also a musician.

BIBLIOGRAPHY: Lawrence Cohen, *Nothing But the Blues: The Music and the Musicians* (New York: Abbeville Press, 1993). Michael Erlewine, ed., *All Music Guide to the Blues* (San Francisco: Miller Freeman, 1999). Sheldon Harris, *Blues Who's Who* (New Rochelle, New York: Arlington House, 1979). Colin Larkin, ed., *The Guiness Encyclopedia of Popular Music*, Volume 6 (New York: Guiness, 1998). Robert Santelli, *The Big Book of Blues* (New York: Penguin, 1993).

James Head

Skyliner Ballroom. A night spot on "Thunder Road," the 3½-mile stretch of the Jacksboro Highway between Tiffin Hall's Mexican Inn and the Skyline Drive Motel in north Fort Worth. This strip sported eighteen restaurants, six liquor stores, seven nightclubs, and ten motels. The Skyliner Ballroom, one of the wildest and most colorful clubs on the strip, was established in the late 1930s when platinum recording artist George Campbell and his partner Gene Hames decided to open a club, both men wishing to get into the lucrative and burgeoning entertainment business on the north side of Fort Worth.

At its inception, the Skyliner Ballroom was by far the largest dance hall in Fort Worth, playing host to as many as 500 of the city's upper-income couples. The white stucco building held 2,500 square feet of maroon plastic dance floor, surrounded by blue carpeting, furnished with wine and rose colored couches and armchairs, all reflected by numerous mirrors, and decorated with a mural of the Fort Worth skyline at the entrance. Campbell's fourteen-piece black-tie orchestra serenaded the dancers. Many popular

big bands played at the club. One of the regular performers who packed the Skyliner with his elaborate musical acts was Denny Beckner.

Despite bringing prominent national acts to the club, such as Louis Armstrong, Hames and Campbell could not meet their overhead. The two partners eventually sold out to F. A. Florence, and Florence eventually sold out to W. D. Satterwhite. Satterwhite hired the Jewel Box Revue, a cast of female impersonators, to perform musical numbers in the club. Although business soon tripled with the addition of the female impersonators, so did fistfights, once the unwitting male patrons realized they were dancing and flirting with men.

In the 1950s Satterwhite also opened the Annex Club, a small gambling room run by gangsters Tincy Eggleston, Nelson Harris, and Howard Stripling. In addition to gambling, the Annex Club offered X-rated movies, strip shows, and other illegal activities. By 1954 Satterwhite sold the Skyliner club to Jimmy Levens and his partner, Emmett Spinks.

Levens hired Charlie Applewhite, a former actor from the Milton Berle Show, who became a regular headlining performer and singer at the Skyliner Ballroom. Levens also hired the famous stripper and dancer Sherry Lynn for late-night performances. Another famous dancer, Candy Barr, worked as a stripper at the Skyliner, but she eventually ended up in prison. Miss Barr was charged with possession of a small amount of marijuana, but many claim that the real reason she was sentenced to fifteen years in prison (she served three) is that she would not give information to authorities about her Las Vegas gangster boyfriend, Mickey Cohen.

Other notables who performed at the Skyliner Ballroom include Nick Lucas, who popularized "Tiptoe Through the Tulips" long before Tiny Tim. Sally Rand, Rudy Vallee, and Delbert McClinton also performed at the club. McClinton's band was the only white act to play Blue Monday nights at the Skyliner Ballroom as the backing band for headliners. He received a first-class tutelage from such masters of blues as Jimmy Reed, Howlin' Wolf, and Sonny Boy Williamson. McClinton claimed about his nights at the Skyliner, "I was at the right place at the right time and knew it."

After Levens died in 1966, the club closed and stood abandoned for three years. In April 1969, condemned by city inspectors, it was demolished.

BIBLIOGRAPHY: Ann Arnold, *Gamblers and Gangsters: Fort Worth's Jacksboro Highway in the 1940s and 1950s* (Austin: Eakin Press, 1998). "Delbert McClinton Biography" (http://www.urbanabusinessalliance.org/delbert_mcclinton.htm, accessed November 25, 2002.

Jahue Anderson

Smith, Buster. Jazz saxophone player; b. Henry Smith, Alsdorf, Texas, August 24, 1904; d. Dallas, August 10, 1991. His early musical influences were his mother, a church pianist, and his father, who played guitar. At age four, Buster was playing the organ with his brother, pianist Boston Smith; Buster played the keys and Boston stepped on the pedals. Soon thereafter, his grandfather gave away the family organ because he believed it would direct Buster to a life of sin. By the time Smith was eighteen, however, he had learned how to play organ, guitar, alto saxophone, and clarinet. He bought his first clarinet in 1922 for $350, which he raised by picking more than 2,000 pounds of cotton in five days.

At this time his family moved to Dallas, where Buster soon supported them by his music-making. He played alto saxophone and clarinet with the Voodie White Trio in Dallas. In 1923 he got a professional gig playing alto saxophone with medicine shows; he had to play very loudly because that attracted more customers. His loudness later added to his style. Oran (Hot Lips) Page's Blue Devils asked Buster to play alto saxophone with them in 1925, and fame followed. Smith played with Page, Lester Young, Count Basie, Jimmy Rushing, and Emir (Bucket) Coleman until 1933, when Page was replaced by Bennie Moten. They toured the Kansas City area and the Midwest playing jazz for a year.

Then the formation of the Buster Smith–Count Basie Band of Rhythm joined two of the jazz greats and originated a new technique of louder jazz. The sound came from Buster, who used a tenor saxophone reed in an alto saxophone to get a louder, fatter sound. Tenor saxophonist Lester Young played in the band with a baritone reed. This big sound was labeled the Texas sax sound. Smith's great influence in jazz and blues perpetuated the Texas sax sound. He taught Charlie Parker saxophone during the 1930s, and they had a relationship like father and son. He also aided an old friend from Dallas, Charlie Christian, who played in Benny Goodman's band. For an African American in the 1930s, Buster Smith received great respect from all musicians.

But by 1941 fame and touring were no longer his first priority. He returned to Dallas. Remaining active in the music scene, he wrote for jazz and blues bands, played often, and taught many young Texas musicians—T-Bone Walker, for example. By 1959 Atlantic Records had convinced Buster to record his first session in Fort Worth. Some of the songs from the session were "Kansas City Riffs," "Buster's Tune," "E Flat Boogie," and "September Song." It was his first 33 rpm record. His work was already available on 78 rpm records from the Blue Devils, Pete Johnson's Boogie-Woogie Boys, Eddie Durham, Snub Mosely, Bon and His Buddies, and the Don Redman Orchestra.

An auto accident in the 1960s disabled Smith so that he never played saxophone again. He turned to bass guitar to keep current in the music business in Dallas, where his musical influence was strong felt for years. He led a dance band until 1980 and died of a heart attack.

BIBLIOGRAPHY: John Chilton, *Who's Who of Jazz: Storyville to Swing Street* (London: Bloomsbury Book Shop, 1970; American ed., New York and Philadelphia: Chilton, 1972; 4th ed., New York: Da Capo Press, 1985). Eileen Southern, *Biographical Dictionary of Afro-American and African Musicians* (Westport, Connecticut: Greenwood, 1982). *Alan Lee Haworth*

Smith, Carl "Tatti." Trumpeter; b. Marshall, Texas, date uncertain; death date and place unknown. Although few recordings exist of Smith's performances, he played an important role during the Swing Era as a member of Count Basie aggregations, both the large orchestra and a sextet composed of Basie, tenorist Lester Young, bassist Walter Page, drummer Jo Jones, and blues shouter Jimmy Rushing. Smith's early career included work with the Terrence Holder band in Kansas City in 1931. Subsequently, from 1931 to 1934, Smith toured the West Coast with the Amarillo band of Gene Coy.

In 1936 Smith joined the Count Basie Orchestra and during that year was the nominal co-leader of a sextet, labeled Jones–Smith, Inc., which played in the first recording session for legendary tenorist Lester Young. Smith's trumpet solos on "Lady Be Good" and "Shoe Shine Boy" are outstanding examples of his artistry, which in many ways complements and even matches that of "President" Young. It was only owing to the fortuitous absence of Hot Lips Page, Smith's fellow Texan and Basie band member, who was suffering from a cracked lip, that Smith served as a substitute for Page on the famous Jones–Smith, Inc. recording session.

Smith left Basie the next year and performed with Skeets Tolbert's Gentlemen of Swing until 1940. During 1939 he also played with groups led by Hot Lips Page. In the 1940s Smith was briefly with several other bands, including that of Benny Carter. After World War II he left for South America, and during the late 1940s and into the 1950s he was playing with groups in Argentina and Brazil. No further information on this unique trumpeter has surfaced since his move to South America, and his whereabouts after the 1950s have not been reported in any reference works on jazz history.

BIBLIOGRAPHY: *Count Basie–Harry James: Basie Rhythm* (HEP Records 1032, 1991). Barry Kernfeld, ed. *The New Grove Dictionary of Jazz*, Second Edition (New York, 2002). Dave Oliphant, *Texan Jazz* (Austin: University of Texas Press, 1996). *Dave Oliphant*

Smith, John T. Blues guitarist and singer, known as "Funny Papa" Smith; b. East Texas, 1885–90; death date and place unknown. Smith helped develop and popularize the Texas blues guitar style during the late 1920s and 1930s. He is often compared to Blind Lemon Jefferson. Smith's style consisted of detailed melody lines and repetitive bass riffs, as well as what has been called "a surprisingly refined country blues vocal style." Some critics also found his style more sophisticated than that of other guitarists of his generation because of his unique use of alternating thumb picking. Others, however, noted his tendency to play out of tune.

As a young man, Smith worked at the Lincoln Theater in New York City. He also lived in Oklahoma for a while. He married in the 1920s and played at local dances, picnics, and fairs in Texas and Oklahoma, pairing frequently with bluesman Thomas Shaw. Though Smith played in the Dallas area during the 1920s and 1930s, he began his recording career in 1930 for the Vocalion label in Chicago. He recorded nearly twenty songs during 1930 and 1931, including "Howling Wolf Blues" (parts one and two), from which he took the pseudonym "The Howlin' Wolf." Smith's nickname, "Funny Papa," was erroneously printed as

"Funny Paper" on his first records. He is said to have frequently worn a stovepipe hat with his name stitched on it.

In the early 1930s he killed a man in an argument, reportedly over either a woman or a gambling disagreement. He spent the next few years in a Texas penitentiary. In 1935 he recorded some songs for the Vocalion label in Fort Worth, but they were never released. In 1939 he toured through Texas with blues singer Texas Alexander. Smith's subsequent whereabouts are not known. He is believed to have died in 1940.

BIBLIOGRAPHY: Alan Govenar and Jay Brakefield, *Deep Ellum and Central Track: Where the Black and White Worlds of Dallas Converged* (Denton: University of North Texas Press, 1998). Sheldon Harris, *Blues Who's Who: A Biographical Dictionary of Blues Singers* (New Rochelle, New York: Arlington House, 1979). Rick Koster, *Texas Music* (New York: St. Martin's Press, 1998). Robert Santelli, *The Big Book of Blues: A Biographical Encyclopedia* (New York: Penguin, 1993). *Carlyn Copeland*

Smith, Julia Frances. Composer, concert pianist, author, and advocate for women composers; b. Denton, Texas, January 25, 1911; d. New York City, April 27, 1989; daughter of James Willis and Julia (Miller) Smith, who were both musical and who encouraged their daughter's obvious musical talent. During her teens she studied with Harold von Mickwitz at the Institute of Musical Art in Dallas. In 1930 she earned a B.A. in music from North Texas State Teachers College, where she composed the school's Alma Mater.

She then moved to New York for further study and remained there. She studied piano and eventually composition at the Juilliard Graduate School (1932–39), where she earned a diploma. She also studied at New York University (M.A., 1933; Ph.D., 1952). From 1932 to 1942 she was pianist for the Orchestrette Classique of New York, a women's orchestra founded by Frederique Petrides. The group premiered several of her works. Smith studied composition at Juilliard after completing her master's degree at NYU, first with Rubin Goldmark and then with Frederick Jacobi. During her career she wrote in practically all musical forms for ensembles large and small. It was her success in writing in the larger forms and getting them performed, however, that set her apart from earlier women composers.

By 1934 she determined to write her first opera, *Cynthia Parker*, in honor of the coming Texas Centennial. Although the premiere of the work was delayed until 1939, it brought her to national prominence and was only the first of six operas she wrote. Many of her works incorporate folk melodies and dance idioms within a relatively conservative, tonal harmonic palette, although she was not afraid of dissonance. The accessibility of her work to a wide audience aided the success of her compositions.

On April 23, 1938, Julia Smith married Oscar A. Vielehr, an engineer and inventor who wholeheartedly supported his wife's career as a composer. Beginning in 1935 Smith took up a part-time teaching career, first at the Hamlin School in New Jersey. A few years later she taught at Juilliard (1940–42) and then as founder and head of the department of music education at Hartt College (1941–46). She also taught at Teachers College of Connecticut (1944–46).

The decade of the 1950s marked the beginning of her writing career with the publication of her revised doctoral dissertation: *Aaron Copland: His Work and Contribution to American Music* (New York, 1955). This book, the first detailed study of this important American composer, received critical acclaim. Smith also performed numerous lecture–recitals featuring Copland's piano works in succeeding years. She later published *Master Pianist: The Career and Teaching of Carl Friedberg* (New York, 1963) as a tribute to her teacher at the Juilliard School.

The decade of the 1950s also marked the beginning of Smith's vocal advocacy for the woman composer. In 1951 she spearheaded a New York recital of works by Marion Bauer. In the late 1960s she and Merle Montgomery planned a concert of chamber music by American women composers for the Musicians Club of New York, dedicating it to the National Federation of Music Clubs in honor of its efforts on behalf of women composers. This began her association with the NFMC and its programs. She was appointed chairman of American Women Composers, a post that led to the publication of her *Directory of American Women Composers* (Chicago, 1970), a pioneering work that appeared just as the women's movement of the 1970s was getting underway. She also chaired for the NFMC its Decade of Women Committee (1970–79) and in 1972 and 1973 arranged two thirteen-week series of national broadcasts of works by American composers, almost half of them women.

Although her work on behalf of other composers encroached, Smith still managed to continue her own composing career. She wrote a work for the inauguration of Lyndon B. Johnson in 1965 (*Remember the Alamo!*) and her final opera, *Daisy* (1973), based on the life of Juliette Gordon Low, founder of the Girl Scouts in the United States. In the end, however, her importance as an advocate for the plight of ignored women composers may have overshadowed her own career as a composer. Smith died while preparing to return from New York to Fort Worth for a performance of her opera *Cockcrow*.

BIBLIOGRAPHY: Christine Ammer, *Unsung: A History of Women in American Music*, Second Edition (Portland, Oregon: Amadeus Press, 2001). Jane Weiner LePage, *Women Composers, Conductors, and Musicians of the Twentieth Century*, Volume 2 (Metuchen, New Jersey: Scarecrow Press, 1983). *The New Grove Dictionary of Music and Musicians*, Second Edition (New York, Grove's Dictionaries, 2001). Nicolas Slonimsky and Laura Kuhn, eds., *Baker's Biographical Dictionary of Musicians*, Centennial Edition (New York, Schirmer, 2001). *Larry Wolz*

Snow, Robert Joseph. Musicologist and university professor; b. Indiana, 1926; d. Austin, June 9, 1998. Snow grew up in Crothersville, Indiana, and attended a Catholic seminary after graduating from high school. Studying primarily with Willi Apel, he completed B.M. and M.A. degrees at Indiana University. In 1968 he earned his Ph.D. at the University of Illinois, Urbana–Champaign, where he studied with Dragan Plamenac and Charles Hamm. His dissertation focused on a fifteenth-century manuscript from the Strahov Abbey in Prague.

Snow's early professional career included service as a church choir director and music adviser to the American Council of Catholic Bishops during the controversial post–Vatican II years of the late 1960s. He also served as an editor for the World Library of Sacred Music publishers in Cincinnati from 1958 to 1974. Snow held academic appointments at the University of Notre Dame, the University of Illinois, Duquesne University, and the University of Pittsburgh before being appointed to the faculty at the University of Texas at Austin, where he taught from 1976 until his retirement in 1996.

Although his scholarly studies ranged widely, Snow's greatest impact as a musicologist came from his study of sacred music of the Iberian Peninsula and Latin America during the sixteenth and seventeenth centuries, accomplished primarily during his years in Texas. He and Texas-born musicologist Robert M. Stevenson have been the principal promoters of interest in this music, which is important to the history and culture of the Southwest. Through their publications and subsequently through the research and publication of their students, these two musicologists have filled countless lacunae in the history of music in the Americas.

Snow published two books: *The 1613 Print of Juan Esquivel de Barahona* (Detroit, 1978) and *The Extant Music of Rodrigo de Ceballos and Its Sources* (Detroit, 1980). Perhaps most importantly, he prepared editions of the works of Portuguese composer Gaspar Fernandes (Lisbon, 1990) and Spanish composer Rodrigo de Ceballos (Granada, 1995). His crowning achievement as an editor of early music was *A New-World Collection of Polyphony for Holy Week and the Salve Service: Guatemala City, Cathedral Archive, music MS 4* (Chicago, 1996). Snow also wrote numerous articles for musicological journals and dictionaries and encyclopedias of music.

After his death a memorial festschrift of thirty-nine essays by his colleagues and students was published in 2002. Snow's large library and archives on Iberian music are now a part of the Centro de Investigación de Música Religiosa Española at Santiago de Compostela in Spain. This collection is housed in the Robert J. Snow Hall, along with a portrait of the musicologist by Rafael Romero commissioned by the center.

BIBLIOGRAPHY: David E. Crawford, "Robert J. Snow Obituary," *AMS Newsletter*, February 1999. David E. Crawford, ed., and Grayson Wagstaff, asst. ed., *Encomium musicae: Essays in Memory of Robert J. Snow* (Festschrift Series No. 17) (Hillsdale, New York: Pendragon Press, 2002).   *Larry Wolz*

South by Southwest. The short name for the South by Southwest Music and Media Conference and Festival, held annually in Austin. The festival began in 1987 and is produced by the Austin-based private company South by Southwest Inc. The internationally recognized event in March serves as a showcase for musicians and provides a forum for music-industry professionals.

Inspired by the successful New Music Seminar held in New York in the 1980s, Austinites Nick Barbaro, Louis Black, and Roland Swenson, all of the Austin *Chronicle*, and Louis Meyers, a band manager and musician, founded the event to promote the Austin music scene. At its inception the festival featured primarily local acts. In 1987, 700 registrants participated and approximately 200 bands performed at fifteen venues. In the 1990s the symposium continued to grow in participation and promotion. The four founders incorporated in 1991. In 1993 SXSW added film and interactive media events to an expanded schedule, and by 1994 the conference registered over 4,000 participants and showcased 500 musical acts at twenty-eight venues.

The five-day music portion of the festival includes meetings and panel discussions on such issues as independent record labels, technology and music, copyright laws, and artist promotion. Austin's night clubs, particularly along Sixth Street, host bands from all over the world. Many musicians hope to attract the attention of major record labels, while other players who have already brokered deals view the festival as a major vehicle for publicity.

The film and interactive media conference hosts workshops and special screenings that feature documentary films, music videos, animation, and other media presentations. All aspects of the Internet as well as trends in web design are examined. Trade shows profile the latest equipment, technology, and companies in film, music, and interactive media. In 2001 SXSW staff had organized 900 showcases playing at forty-eight venues, and in 2003 SXSW held its seventeenth festival over a ten-day period.

BIBLIOGRAPHY: Austin *American–Statesman*, March 16, 1994; March 17, 1999. *SXSW* (http://www.sxsw.com/), accessed March 18, 2003. Vertical files, Center for American History, University of Texas at Austin.

Laurie E. Jasinski

Southwestern Seminary School of Church Music. Originated in 1915, when Southwestern Baptist Theological Seminary in Fort Worth established a Department of Gospel Music and thus became the first Southern Baptist seminary to offer any type of church music training. The new department consisted of director I. E. Reynolds, a piano teacher, and nine students. It grew to five faculty members and sixty-one students by 1919, and the curriculum changed to provide a three-year course leading to a Bachelor of Gospel Music degree. By 1921 the department, with fifteen faculty members and 209 students, had become the School of Gospel Music at Southwestern Seminary. This name change was soon followed by the addition of the Master of Gospel Music degree program in 1922.

Since its inception, the School of Gospel Music had shared a building with the School of Theology, but it soon became clear that separate quarters were needed. Mrs. George E. Cowden answered this need with a gift of $150,000 in 1925. Cowden Hall was completed in 1926 at a cost of $335,000. At the same time, the title School of Gospel Music was changed to School of Sacred Music to reflect growing musical interests.

Unfortunately, this era of prosperity fizzled during the Great Depression of the 1930s. The music school faculty was reduced to nine and all salaries were halved, with merely 50 percent of that being paid in money. However, the school managed to continue functioning even under difficult circumstances and in 1941 was accepted as a member of the Texas Association of Music Schools.

Reynolds retired as director in 1945 and was succeeded by Ellis L. Carnett, who retired two years later. His replacement, J. Campbell Wray, reorganized and expanded the curriculum, established the Department of Music in Evangelism and the Department of Church Music Education, established a separate music library, and instituted an annual Church Music Workshop. Wray retired in 1956, when James McKinney became the first dean of the School of Sacred Music at Southwestern Seminary. In 1957 the school's name was changed once again, this time to School of Church Music. In addition to his work in vocal pedagogy, McKinney was instrumental in forming the Doctor of Music program (1961) and gaining accreditation for the school from the National Association of Schools of Music (1966). He also oversaw the addition of the $3.5 million Kathryn Sullivan Bowld Music Library in 1993 before his retirement in 1994.

Benjamin Harlan was chosen to succeed McKinney. In 2001, 192 students were enrolled in five degree programs including Diploma in Church Music, Master of Music, Master of Arts in Church Music, Doctor of Musical Arts in Church Music, and Doctor of Philosophy in Church Music. The degree programs encompass fourteen areas of concentration ranging from orchestral instruments to music in missions. The school's mission is "to provide quality music education for future and current church leaders."

BIBLIOGRAPHY: William J. Reynolds, *The Cross & the Lyre: The Story of the School of Church Music, Southwestern Baptist Theological Seminary, Fort Worth, Texas* (1994); "Isham Emmanuel Reynolds: Church Musician," *Baptist History and Heritage* (April, 1992). Sara Virginia Thompson, "A History of the School of Church Music, SWBTS" (Fiftieth Anniversary Address).

Hannah Williams

Spanish-Language Radio. First established in Texas through a radio brokerage system set up by Anglo radio station owners throughout the Southwest in the 1920s and 1930s. Through this system Hispanics, many with broadcasting experience in Mexico, could purchase blocks of radio time for Spanish-language programs. By 1939 this type of radio grew enough to allow the International Broadcasting Company of El Paso to produce Spanish-language programs featuring Mexican radio celebrities, which they sold to stations around the country.

By 1941 an estimated 264 hours a week of Spanish-language programs was broadcast in the combined states of Texas, Arizona, California, and New York. Although the broadcasters favored musical programming on their shows, they also provided information on community activities, immigration services, American citizenship, and Hispanic businesses in an attempt to meet the unique needs and interests of their audience.

During World War II a San Antonio radio broker, Raul Cortez, applied to the Federal Communications Commission for a license to operate his own radio station. His request was approved, and in 1946 he set up KCOR–AM, the first full-time Spanish-language radio station in the

United States owned and operated by a Mexican American. Cortez recruited the Tejano actor Lalo Astol to work as an announcer and program host for the station. Astol also developed a radio theater program known as "La Hora del Teatro Nacional" and later organized and directed a series of other radio dramas with Mexican-American actors from San Antonio. These programs, broadcast around the country, brought KCOR–AM much acclaim.

Despite this success, however, Anglo entrepreneurs continued to run the state's Spanish-language radio programs in the 1940s and 1950s. A small number of Hispanic radio emcees continued to work on a brokerage basis, but most became salaried employees of the stations. Moreover, most of the opportunities to host radio programs were limited to Mexican-born announcers because station owners considered Mexican-American Spanish substandard. Spanish-language radio programming continued to expand in the 1950s and 1960s, and Hispanic radio personalities were often well respected by their listeners. As a result, they routinely influenced their audience through their pronouncements and advice on a host of community-related topics.

In the 1970s new marketing techniques and the rise of specialized Spanish-language advertising companies promoted growth in Spanish-language radio. In addition, the number of Mexican Americans working in the medium grew. Station ownership, however, generally remained beyond their reach. The FCC's commitment in 1978 to increase minority ownership of the broadcast media helped them make gains. Mexican Americans owned thirteen Spanish-language stations in Texas in 1982 and about thirty-one in 1992. Nonetheless, ownership of Spanish-language radio stations in the state continued to be dominated by nonminority broadcasting enterprises.

Hispanic broadcasting companies have pursued the issue of control of radio in the courts. In 1990 the Supreme Court endorsed their struggle in *Astroline Communications Co. vs. Shurberg* and *Metro Broadcasting vs. FCC*. The court found that the FCC had an obligation to provide for "diversity" in broadcasting under the Communications Act of 1934. This idea had been challenged by nonminority broadcasters, who charged discrimination against their interests. Spanish-language broadcasters have formed their own associations over approximately the past five decades to pursue Latino business interests and civil-rights issues in radio. Cortez, for instance, organized the Sombrero Network, a chain of Spanish-language radio stations. Ed Gómez, one of the pioneers in Hispanic radio in the state, helped found the Spanish Radio Broadcasters of America in the mid-1970s. He was also involved in a later group, AHORA (the Alliance of Hispanic Broadcasters), which continued to advocate minority clout in radio.

Spanish-language radio still emphasizes musical programming, with newscasts limited to hourly relays. Some stations feature Tejano soloists, Texas-Mexican conjuntos, and orchestras, while others specialize in international Spanish-language hits. Talk radio, except for Christian preaching, came late to Spanish-language stations. The medium remains quite important to Mexican Americans. It holds a special value for those who do not speak

English, for whom the stations provide valuable news and information.

BIBLIOGRAPHY: Félix Gutiérrez and Jorge Reina Schement, *Spanish-Language Radio in the Southwestern United States* (Center for Mexican American Studies, University of Texas at Austin, 1979). Ana Veciana–Suárez, *Hispanic Media, USA: A Narrative Guide to Print and Electronic Hispanic News Media in the United States* (Washington: Media Institute, 1987). *Teresa Palomo Acosta*

Spell, Lota May. Teacher, musician, and author; b. Big Spring, Texas, February 2, 1885; d. Austin, April 3, 1972 (buried in San Antonio City Cemetery Number One); daughter of William Harold and Mildred Addie (Dashiell) Harrigan. Her father was a superintendent of railroads in Mexico with headquarters in Mexico City and Querétaro, and so she received her early education from tutors. She began her musical studies under August Schemmel, first in San Antonio and then at the Virginia Institute of Bristol, Tennessee, from 1898 to 1901, when Schemmel was director of music there. From 1902 to 1905 she attended the Grand Ducal Conservatory at Karlsruhe, Germany, where she completed her education in piano, harmony, and composition. Between 1905 and 1910 she performed as a pianist in Europe and Mexico. In 1910 she became an instructor in the Whitis Preparatory School of Austin, Texas. On September 8, 1910, she married Jefferson Rea Spell, a fellow student who later became a professor of Romance languages at the University of Texas; they were the parents of one daughter.

Mrs. Spell was head of the music department of Melrose Hall of San Antonio from 1910 to 1914, during which time she also completed course work at the University of Texas for the B.A. degree (1914). She received an M.A. degree in 1919 and a Ph.D. in English in 1923 from UT. She also studied at Columbia University and the University of Chicago in the summers of 1919 and 1920. From 1921 to 1927 she served as librarian of the Genaro García Library (now the Nettie Lee Benson Latin American Collection) of the University of Texas. In the mid-1930s she was employed by the state to identify historical sites for the Texas Centennial celebrations and to write inscriptions for the monuments placed on those sites.

She was a teacher of music history and appreciation at the Texas School of Fine Arts, associate editor of *The Musicale* (1929–33) and the *Southwestern Musician* (1933–47), editor of *Texas Music News* (1946–48), and a contributor to numerous musical journals, including *The Etude*. She was intensely interested in musical education, especially that of young children, and devoted much of her lifetime to developing training tools for teaching the young. From 1939 to 1971 she taught children at her studio in Austin. She prepared bulletins for the University Interscholastic League to encourage musical education in the state, including the valuable work *Music in Texas* (1936; later reprinted).

Lota Spell's knowledge of German, French, Italian, Latin, and Spanish, along with her interest in music, enabled her to do research in musical development throughout the western hemisphere, especially in the Southwest and Mexico, and this brought her wide recognition. Her articles appeared regularly in many important quarterlies and reviews, both musical and historical. She was generous in assisting others who were interested in these fields. Her research in Latin-American culture led to her book *Pioneer Printer Samuel Bangs in Mexico and Texas* (1963). She wrote articles on seventeenth-century Mexican poetess Sor Juana Inés de la Cruz and on nineteenth-century Mexican diplomat, dramatist, and theater impresario Manuel Eduardo de Gorostiza. At the time of her death she had completed manuscripts on Gorostiza and on Fray Pedro de Gante, one of the first music teachers in Mexico. A complete list of her numerous publications has yet to be compiled.

Her correspondence, along with that of her husband, was given to the Latin American Collection of the University of Texas at Austin. The valuable Spell library was purchased by the University of Texas in the early 1960s. Mrs. Spell was a member and officer of many music associations, and she was a fellow of the Texas State Historical Association.

BIBLIOGRAPHY: Mrs. Jefferson Rea Spell Papers, Center for American History, University of Texas at Austin. Vertical Files, Center for American History, University of Texas at Austin. *Nettie Lee Benson*

Frontispiece and title page to *Music in Texas: A Survey of One Aspect of Cultural Progress* (Austin, Texas, 1936) by music historian Lota May Spell. CAH; CN 11500.

Spivey, Victoria Regina. Blues singer and songwriter, known as Queen, Vicky, and Jane Lucas; b. Houston, October 15, 1906; d. New York City, October 3, 1976 (buried in Greenfield Cemetery, Hempstead, New York); daughter of Grant and Addie (Smith) Spivey. Her mother was a nurse, and her father had his own family string band. Victoria learned piano as a child and during her teens played at local parties in the Houston area. In 1918 she played in Lazy Daddy's Fillmore Blues Band and L. C. Tolen's Band and Revue in Dallas; in the early 1920s she worked with Blind Lemon Jefferson and others in gambling houses,

Victoria
Spivey with
Muddy
Waters, New
York, 1975.
Photograph ©
1995 Anton J.
Mikofsky.

"gay houses," and other clubs in Galveston and Houston.

Known for her "'mean' blues with a hard and nasal voice," she made her first recording with her own composition "Black Snake Blues" on the Okeh label in St. Louis, Missouri, in 1926. Her sisters Addie (Sweet Peas), Elton Island (the Za Zu Girl), and Leona were also singers who toured with her into the 1930s, working in vaudeville houses, barrelhouses, and theaters through Missouri, Texas, and Michigan. Vicky's popularity increased because of her role in the 1929 King Vidor film *Hallelujah*. She wrote most of her songs and recorded them between 1926 and 1937. She recorded or performed with Louis Armstrong, Henry Allen, Lee Collins, Lonnie Johnson, Memphis Minnie (Minnie Douglas Lawless), Bessie Smith, and Tampa Red (Hudson Whittaker).

After her first marriage to trumpeter Reuben Floyd, she married William (Billy) Adams, a dancer, and performed with him. She was married two other times. From 1952 to about 1960, she performed only occasionally and worked some as a church administrator. In the 1960s she organized her own successful recording company in New York, the Spivey Record Company. From 1963 to 1966 she contributed articles to *Record Research* and *Sounds and Fury*. In 1970 BMI awarded her the Commendation of Excellence "for long and outstanding contribution to the many worlds of music." Two daughters survived her.

BIBLIOGRAPHY: Donald Bogle, *Blacks in American Film and Television: An Encyclopedia* (New York: Garland, 1988). John Chilton, *Who's Who of Jazz: Storyville to Swing Street* (London: Bloomsbury Book Shop, 1970; American ed., New York and Philadelphia: Chilton, 1972; 4th ed., New York: Da Capo Press, 1985). Sheldon Harris, *Blues Who's Who: A Biographical Dictionary of Blues Singers* (New Rochelle, New York: Arlington House, 1979). *Jazz on Record: A Critical Guide* (London: Hutchinson, 1960; rev. ed., London: Hanover, 1968). Eileen Southern, *Biographical Dictionary of Afro-American and African Musicians* (Westport, Connecticut: Greenwood, 1982). Mary Mace Spradling, ed., *In Black and White* (Detroit: Gale Research, 1971; rev. ed., Kalamazoo Public Library, 1976; 3d ed., with suppl., Detroit: Gale Research, 1980, 1985). *Donna P. Parker*

Stamps, Virgil Oliver. Gospel singer and promoter; b. Upshur County, Texas, September 18, 1892; d. Dallas, August 19, 1940. V. O. Stamps helped make southern gospel music popular and widely available throughout East Texas and the southern United States. His father, W. O. Stamps, served for a time in the Texas legislature. After attending several music schools, the younger Stamps worked for the Tennessee Music Company in Texas from 1914 to 1917. He lived in Atlanta and Lawrenceburg, Tennessee, then returned to Texas in 1919.

In 1924 Stamps opened the V. O. Stamps Music Company in Jacksonville, Texas. His friend J. R. Baxter became his business partner, and they changed the name of the company to Stamps–Baxter in 1927. The company soon became the country's premier gospel music business. Its activities included songwriting, publishing, and sponsoring musical groups and radio broadcasts. Baxter oversaw the operations east of the Mississippi River, while Stamps ran the operations in the western United States from his Dallas headquarters.

Stamps–Baxter helped bring gospel music into the mainstream by broadcasting it nationally on radio and by encouraging its performance in public. Stamps and his quartet started a noonday radio program on KRLD radio, Dallas, in 1936. The program brought him, the company, and gospel music increasingly into public view, and was so successful that it produced a boom in Stamps–Baxter's publishing operations. Success also attracted the best gospel singers and songwriters to the company, such as the Blackwood Brothers and Albert Brumley. Stamps died of heart disease not long after his success was assured. Thousands attended his funeral.

BIBLIOGRAPHY: Bill C. Malone, "Albert Brumley," in *Encyclopedia of Southern Culture*, ed. Charles Reagan Wilson and William Ferris (Chapel Hill: University of North Carolina Press, 1989). *Precious Memories of Virgil O. Stamps* (Dallas: Stamps–Baxter, 1941). Charles K. Wolfe, "Blackwood Brothers" and "Gospel Music, White," in *Encyclopedia of Southern Culture*, op. cit. *N. D. Giesenschlag*

Stamps–Baxter Music and Printing Company. Founded in 1924 by V. O. Stamps, who subsequently entered into partnership with J. R. Baxter, Jr., a former employee of A. J. Showalter. The partners had become close friends over a period of years, during which they represented competing music-publishing companies. Though their personalities were quite different, they were said to complement each other. Dwight Brock, who later became part owner of the Stamps–Baxter Company, described Stamps as the promoter and Baxter as the businessman. They were partners and sole owners of the business. Stamps served as president, with his office in Jacksonville, Texas, and later in Dallas. Baxter, as vice president, opened an office in Chattanooga, Tennessee. A third office was later opened in Pangburn, Arkansas.

From its inception, Stamps–Baxter enjoyed success unprecedented in the publication of gospel music. In addition to Stamps's ability to attract major songwriters to his company, line up the best quartets, and hire the most gifted instructors to conduct music schools, the company operated a radio station and published one of the industry's leading magazines. As an increasing number of quartets came under the management of the company, the Stamps Quartet Music Company was formed, with headquarters in Dallas. The popularity of the Stamps Quartet was aided by the daily Stamps broadcast on station KRLD. Through these broadcasts the company's singing schools, singing conventions, and published materials were successfully promoted. The Stamps–Baxter singing "normals," classes in which shaped-note music was taught, became so popular that the company began hosting an All Night Singing, broadcast on KRLD, at the end of the June class. The first of these events was held in the Cotton Bowl and was broadcast internationally.

The leadership of the company changed in 1940 upon the sudden death of Stamps. Baxter became president and manager, and Frank Stamps, brother of V. O., was made vice president and sales manager. Intending to maintain the company's previous level of success, Baxter pushed forward new ideas for publication and implemented a subscription plan originally conceived by V. O. Stamps. Though the years during World War II were difficult, the company continued to be profitable. In 1943 the Pangburn office turned profits of 25 percent above the previous year. By the end of the war the Stamps Quartet Music Company was represented by more than thirty-five quartets singing and promoting the music published by Stamps–Baxter.

But the singing school declined in popularity after the war, and interest in conventional gospel music shifted to the rural population. Quartets soon found that they no longer needed the support of the publishing companies and began to promote themselves, capitalizing on the public's demand for entertainment. In 1945, for reasons unknown, Frank Stamps left the company and formed his own rival business. With the Stamps–Baxter Music Company, Frank had served as manager of all radio stations and of the well-known Stamps Quartet. In addition, he was vice president in charge of sales and had made many business contacts, which he retained to the benefit of the new company. Fourteen other former Stamps–Baxter employees joined him. With his resignation, he retained control of the radio programs, which had been established by V. O. Stamps, as well as the name of the Stamps Quartet. As a result, the public was confused, and many unwittingly gave support to the new, rival company, being unaware of the change that had taken place.

By the following year, however, Stamps–Baxter had recovered from the effects of Frank's departure sufficiently to begin expanding again by purchasing the assets of Samuel W. Beazley and Son, based in Chicago. The company continued under the leadership of J. R. Baxter until his death in 1960, when his wife, "Ma" Baxter, became sole owner and manager of Stamps–Baxter Music and Printing Company. Under her leadership the company expanded and built a new office building in Dallas. When Mrs. Baxter died in 1972, she willed the company to four employees: Lonnie B. Combs, Clyde Roach, Videt Polk, and Dwight Brock. As Brock, Roach, and Combs were nearing retirement age when they inherited the company, the group decided to make a deal with the Zondervan Corporation of Grand Rapids, Michigan, to carry on the work of Stamps–Baxter. In the arrangement, the name Stamps–Baxter Music and Printing Company was retained, as was the staff of writers. The company's magazine, *Gospel Music News*, continued uninterrupted, with P. J. Zondervan, the new company president, assuring readers in his introductory article that the Zondervan Corporation was committed to reaching "everyone on the earth with the gospel of our Lord Jesus Christ...through Stamps–Baxter Music."

BIBLIOGRAPHY: Shirley L. Beary, The Stamps–Baxter Music and Printing Company: A Continuing Tradition, 1926–1976 (D.M.A. dissertation, Southwestern Baptist Theological Seminary, 1977). *Precious Memories of Virgil O. Stamps* (Dallas: Stamps–Baxter, 1941).   *Greg Self*

Steinfeldt, John Mathias. Musician, composer, and teacher; b Ankum, near Hanover, Germany, August 18, 1864; d.

February 28, 1946 (buried in St. Mary's Cemetery, San Antonio); son of Henry and Sophia (Zimmerman) Steinfeldt. When Steinfeldt was ten his family immigrated to Cincinnati, Ohio, where he attended public schools. He received an art scholarship to the Cincinnati School of Design, studied piano and harmony in the College of Music in Cincinnati, and attended Dayton College in Dayton, Ohio. He also studied music in New York and Paris.

He moved to San Antonio in 1887, became assistant organist at San Fernando Cathedral, and was organist at the Jewish Temple Beth-El and the First Baptist Church. A few years after his arrival, he became organist at St. Mary's Catholic Church, a position he held for more than fifty years. In 1920 he founded the San Antonio College of Music, where he taught piano and pipe organ; he also held classes in Eagle Pass and Laredo. He appeared several times as a soloist with the San Antonio Symphony Orchestra and the Chicago Symphony. Among his compositions were a number of concert pieces, *The Song of the River* (a chorus for women's voices), and *Missa Maria Immaculata* or *Mass in G*, the dedication Mass for the new St. Mary's Church. Steinfeldt was awarded a prize by the Texas Federation of Music Clubs for his San Antonio–inspired composition *La Concepción*.

He was married to Vivia May Ripley on July 10, 1893, in San Antonio. They were the parents of four children. Upon his death, a requiem Mass was offered for him at St. Mary's Cemetery.

BIBLIOGRAPHY: Ellis A. Davis and Edwin H. Grobe, comps., *The New Encyclopedia of Texas* (4 vols., 1929?). San Antonio *Evening News*, March 1, 1946. San Antonio *Express*, March 1, 1946. St. Mary's Church *Bulletin*, San Antonio, September 1924. *Who's Who Among the Women of San Antonio and Southwest Texas* (San Antonio: Fenwick, 1917).

Stevenson, B. W. Singer; b. Louis Charles Stevenson, Dallas, October 5, 1949; d. Nashville, Tennessee, April 28, 1988. He attended Adamson High School in Oak Cliff, where his peers included Michael Martin Murphey, Ray Wylie Hubbard, and Steve Fromholz. Under the name Chuck Stevenson he sang with a few local bands until he graduated in 1967 and went to North Texas State University in Denton on a voice scholarship. Operatic singing did not appeal to him, and he left the music program after a year. He subsequently attended Cooke County Junior College and served a stint in the U.S. Air Force.

Stevenson returned to Dallas, playing local clubs when he could and working odd jobs. He went to Austin in 1970 to look for work but found none. He then went to Los Angeles to try to sell his songs, but the LA labels also passed him by. Sometime in this period his long-time girlfriend left him unexpectedly, and, heartbroken, he wrote some of his best ballads. A representative from RCA who was in Los Angeles heard his songs and signed him in 1971.

Stevenson's first album on RCA was recorded in Chicago and released in 1972. The record included one of his songs that is very popular with his fans today, "On My Own," but RCA did not promote any songs on the album that were written by Stevenson. This was the first misstep in a long series of blunders in producing and marketing his music and voice. Stevenson's talent lay in his ballads and mournful tunes of lost and unrequited love, of which "On My Own" is a beautiful example, but RCA released as a single not one of them but Stevenson's recording of a song about songwriting written by Michael Martin Murphey. The single went nowhere, but "On My Own," along with a more sincere Murphey tune, "Five O'clock in the Texas Morning," got the attention of the Austin music scene, and Stevenson was welcomed back as a brother in the progressive country movement. RCA had given him the moniker "Buckwheat," and the name stuck. "Buck," as his friends called him, became a regular at the Armadillo World Headquarters and other clubs around Austin, often singing with Kenneth Threadgill, Jerry Jeff Walker, Ray Wylie Hubbard, and other stalwarts of the Austin "redneck rock" era.

RCA had no interest in the Austin music scene and took Stevenson to LA for his next recording, *Lead Free* (1972). This album had an LA sideman sound rather than a band sound, thematically jumped from Pennsylvania to Mexico to Memphis and to Jackson, Mississippi, and also produced no hits. For the third album RCA's producer found a song in the ABC–Dunhill reject pile called "Shambala," written by Danny Moore. It was perfect for Stevenson's voice, and he was climbing the charts with it as a single when ABC–Dunhill realized its potential and quickly released a version of it by Three Dog Night, even though RCA had negotiated a "lock" on the song. As Three Dog Night was very popular at the time, its cover of the tune quickly eclipsed Stevenson's and knocked him off the charts. This unscrupulous move generated some sympathetic press for Stevenson, but not much else until RCA released "My Maria," written by Stevenson and Danny Moore as a vehicle to show off Stevenson's powerful and distinctive voice. "My Maria" went to number nine on the pop charts for weeks in 1973 and was the most commercially successful of Stevenson's recordings, although he felt it was far from his best work. Nevertheless, it had a compelling sound, so much so that it became the number one *Billboard* "Country Song of the Year" when Brooks and Dunn covered it in 1996.

The misguided attempts to package Stevenson as something other than what he wanted to be, a Texas musician, continued with the next album on RCA, *Calabasas* (1974), and with subsequent albums from Warner Brothers and MCA. *Calabasas* was critically acclaimed, but its over-produced sound was difficult to reproduce on stage, and although Stevenson toured extensively to promote it, his heart was not in it. He grew discouraged and, already fond of food and drink, began to drink excessively. Warner Brothers and MCA also attempted to categorize him as a pop musician on the next five albums that he recorded, with fewer and fewer of his songs on the records. By the time his ninth major-label album was released in 1980 and Stevenson was free of his contracts, the progressive country scene had faded. Although he returned to Texas for a while, there were no further recording opportunities available to him. He spent much of the 1980s in Los Angeles but occasionally played in clubs in Dallas and Austin, trying to find a label that would allow him to be himself.

Stevenson returned to Texas once again in 1987 and went into the studio on his own. He recorded some new songs and some old ones, including "On My Own." This was the first time his songs were recorded the way he wanted them produced, and the first time all but one of the songs on an album were his. Willis Alan Ramsey produced some of them with Austin musicians, and the Muscle Shoals Rhythm Section played on others. Many of Buck's old friends joined him on some tracks, including Willie Nelson, Jerry Jeff Walker, Steve Fromholz, Christine Albert, Johnny Gimble, Mickey Raphael, Bobby Rambo, John Inmon, and Stephen Bruton. Stevenson was finally happy with and proud of one of his albums, his tenth. Though the record, called *Rainbow Down the Road*, was beautiful, the initial attempts to get major labels interested in it were unsuccessful.

Before the album was completed, however, Stevenson fell ill, in February 1988. At first he thought he had the flu, but the diagnosis was endocarditis, an inflammation of his heart that was eating away one of its valves. In April he went to the VA hospital in Nashville for a valve-replacement operation. The replacement was successful, but Stevenson never woke up from the anesthetic. He left his wife, Jan, and their three children. B. J. Thomas sang at his funeral at Laurel Land Memorial Park in Dallas, where Stevie Ray Vaughan also rests.

Just before the operation, Stevenson's manager and friend, Harry Friedman, had promised that he would personally see to it that the new record would be released and on the shelves in record stores. After much effort, with the last overdubs and mixing done after Stevenson's death, *Rainbow Down the Road* was released as a CD on Amazing Records in 1990 (not 1970 as some catalogs indicate). Out of print today, it is a sought-after collector's item, a hint of what might have been. The much-beloved Buck Stevenson, the man with "a voice as big as Texas," never got to hear it.

BIBLIOGRAPHY: Dallas *Morning News*, April 29, 1998; May 4, 1988; December 9, 1990. Jan Reid, *The Improbable Rise of Redneck Rock* (New York, New York: Da Capo Press, 1977)   *Gary S. Hickinbotham*

Stricklin, Al. Jazz pianist; b. Alton Meeks Stricklin, Antioch, Texas, January 29, 1908; d. Johnson County, Texas, October 15, 1986 (buried at Rose Hill Cemetery, Cleburne); son of Zebedee Meeks and Annie (Benton) Stricklin. He began playing piano at age four but never "had a paid lesson." The principal musical influence in his formative years was jazz. He claimed, "I never heard anything like country music. Jazz was all I ever tried to play." The greatest impact on Al Stricklin's career was the noted jazz pianist Earl "Fatha" Hines.

Stricklin's background in jazz made him ideal for the Bob Wills band because Wills played music for dancing, and the jazz idioms Stricklin learned were basic to dance music and dance bands. The "first commercial group" Stricklin played with was called the Rio Grande Serenaders. It was a standard Dixieland band with trumpet, trombone, clarinet, drums, banjo, and Al playing piano. After he graduated from Grandview High School in 1927,

Stricklin spent two years at Weatherford Junior College. In Weatherford he played with both the Rio Grande Serenaders and another jazz band called the Texans. After two years at the junior college he entered Baylor University, not to study music, but to major in history. It was music, however, that helped pay his way through the Baptist university. First, he began giving private lessons to aspiring piano players through what he called a "short method," an infamous method frowned on by the school of music. The short method did not earn Stricklin enough money to pay expenses at Baylor; so he began playing in a jazz band called the Unholy Three. When Samuel P. Brooks learned the Unholy Three had played for dancing at the Knights of Pythias Hall, "he suspended the band from the university." "Dean Alan" interceded for them, and "Dr. Brooks let us back in," Stricklin remarked.

In 1930 Stricklin was the assistant program director at radio station KFJZ in Fort Worth. A frightened secretary cried out one morning, "Mr. Stricklin, will you please come in here a moment." He rushed into the reception room and saw "three guys standing there, and they were hungry looking, and they needed a shave. One of them had something in a flour sack; the other one had a guitar strapped across his back, hanging over his back like he was carrying a rifle or something." Stricklin was almost as startled as the secretary. "It was Mr. Bob Wills," he said, "with his fiddle in a flour sack." Wills asked Stricklin for an audition. Wills and his band then performed on KFJZ. "They called two days later from the post office and said there was so much mail for the station one man couldn't carry it, better bring a pickup or something." Stricklin had given Wills a break, and when the management of the Aladdin Lamp Company learned of the success of the Wills Fiddle Band on KFJZ, the firm sponsored the band under the name Aladdin Laddies over WBAP, a much more powerful station.

Ironically, Stricklin did not take Wills seriously and actually thought the music was intended as comedy. He left Fort Worth to become principal and sixth and seventh grade teacher in Island Grove, Texas. By 1934 he was back in Fort Worth playing piano with a dance band called the Hi Flyers. Tommy Duncan had tried to double on piano and vocals ever since Wills moved his Texas Playboys to Tulsa, Oklahoma, in 1934. But Duncan admitted that he "only banged on [the piano] and didn't know what [he] was doing." During a trip to Fort Worth in August of 1935, Wills visited the Cinderella Roof, where Stricklin was performing with the Hi Flyers, and offered Stricklin a job. Later that month Stricklin wrote Wills, and Wills wrote back with an offer of thirty dollars a week.

In a few days the jazz pianist, who had never played in a western band, joined Bob Wills and His Texas Playboys. Other than the frontier fiddle music Wills often performed, Stricklin said, "There was no difference in playing with Bob and jazz bands I'd played with. Since I was the first piano player Bob ever worked with, I set the style for piano players in western swing bands. Bob didn't want the piano to play melody." When he told "the piano to tear it up, you went into orbit. I played hokum, we called it. I can't play the same way twice. I write as I go. To save my life I can't play the same way twice. You compose and create as you play. When Bob Wills gave me a chorus, I played jazz," Stricklin concluded.

The style set by Stricklin between 1935 and 1941 became the style every other Wills pianist followed. Stricklin was in the Bob Wills band during what the pianist called the "glory years" of the band. He played in Wills's first recording session for Columbia Records (now CBS Records) in September of 1935 and in all of the other recording sessions Wills made through 1941. In all, Stricklin played piano on over 200 Wills recordings, including the recording that made Bob Wills and His Texas Playboys national musical figures, "New San Antonio Rose" (1940).

When World War II began, the big orchestras like Glenn Miller's, Harry James's, and Bob Wills's began to break up. Stricklin left Wills in May 1942 to take a job with North American Aircraft. When the war was over, he thought of joining Wills in Hollywood, but he "married in 1943 and decided to settle down." With the "exception of a few little jobs," he was out of music for the next thirty years. He thought his musical career was over. It would have been, but United Artists asked Wills to get some of his former Texas Playboys together and record a double album. Wills asked Al to play in that historic session. It was historic for several reasons: because it turned out to be Wills's last recording session, because the album sold more copies than any other in Wills's career, because the National Academy of Recording Arts and Sciences awarded a Grammy to the album, and because it helped to bring on a revival of western swing.

When that session was over, Stricklin again thought his musical career had ended. But record companies such as Capitol encouraged the musicians who played in Wills's last session to form a group called the Bob Wills Original Texas Playboys, to make recordings and public appearances. Wills's widow, Betty, gave her blessing to the project, and the Original Texas Playboys had nearly ten years of remarkable success. They became very popular; western swing underwent a revival that continues to the present, with many young popular artists performing Bob Wills songs and playing in the Wills style. The Bob Wills Original Texas Playboys actually got much higher guarantees for their appearances than Wills himself, though they could never draw the crowds he drew.

Honors were heaped upon Al Stricklin and the Bob Wills band. The Smithsonian Institution invited the Original Texas Playboys to play a tribute to Bob Wills in one of its halls in Washington. The house was packed. While the band was in Washington, the State Department invited the group to play a show and a dance at an international gathering in Geneva, Switzerland, in 1983. People from many nations of the world danced to Bob Wills's music as Al Stricklin played that happy, jazzy background and lilting jazz choruses for such Wills classics as "Faded Love," "Take Me Back To Tulsa," "Maiden's Prayer," and, of course, "San Antonio Rose." When the band returned home, it was named the band of the year by the Country Music Association. In 1985 Stricklin and the Playboys were in the movie *Places In The Heart*, playing all the music except the hymns. Other honors received were Instrumental Group of the Year in 1977 by the Country

Music Association and Touring Band of the Year, 1978, by the Academy of Country Music. Stricklin was also a chronicler of his music. In 1976 he published his personal memoirs in a volume entitled *My Years With Bob Wills*. Stricklin is in the Country Music Hall of Fame.

Much of his personal life is obscure, however. He was married when in Tulsa and had a daughter. This wife died, and Stricklin writes in his book about receiving unrequested financial help from Bob Wills for her funeral, but her name is not mentioned. He had a son by his second wife and may have had two daughters. But Al Stricklin will be remembered for what he did best—playing western swing in the Bob Wills band. He played almost to the end; his last appearances were just a few months before his death.

BIBLIOGRAPHY: Ruth Sheldon, *Hubbin' It: The Life of Bob Wills* (Kingsport, Tennessee: Kingsport Press, 1938). *Texas Ragg*, November 1983. Charles R. Townsend, *San Antonio Rose: The Life and Music of Bob Wills* (Urbana: University of Illinois Press, 1976). Vertical Files, Center for American History, University of Texas at Austin.

Charles R. Townsend

Stubblefield, Christopher B. Sr. Lubbock restaurateur and music patron; b. Navasota, Texas, March 7, 1931; d. Austin, May 27, 1995; son of Christopher Columbus and Mary Stubblefield. Stubblefield, known as "C.B.," "Stubb," or "Stubbs," loved music and people. He also loved to cook. "I want to feed the world" was one of his favorite lines. When he opened Stubb's Bar-B-Q in Lubbock in 1968, his special blend of barbecue, music, and charisma attracted local and major musicians, and his rickety barbecue shack became the center of Lubbock's live-music scene.

Stubb's father was a Baptist preacher. After the family moved to Lubbock in the 1930s, Stubb spent his youth picking cotton and working in local hotels and restaurants. In 1947 he married Cleola Ruth Harris; the couple had three children. Stubb spent several years in the U.S. Army. As a gunner in the all-black Ninety-sixth Field Artillery during the Korean War (1950–53), he was wounded twice. His army career also foreshadowed his later life: he cooked, played music over the field radio to entertain his buddies in the trenches, and supervised food preparation for thousands of soldiers.

After being discharged, Stubb returned to Lubbock and bought a small, dilapidated building at 108 East Broadway. He hung signs reading "There Will Be No Bad Talk or Loud Talk in this Place" and loaded the corner jukebox with his favorite music, the blues. He made his own special sauce and, clad in overalls and a cowboy hat, tied a white apron around his 6½-foot frame and smoked chicken, ribs, beef brisket, and sausage in a hickory pit outside the back door.

When guitarist Jesse Taylor recognized the potential for a music venue in Stubb's quaint establishment, he talked Stubb into letting him build a stage. To the stage the young West Texas talent came: Taylor, Joe Ely, Jimmie Dale Gilmore, Terry Allen, Butch Hancock, and others. Many played their first gigs at Stubb's. Although Stubb couldn't pay them (they played for tips), he nurtured them with

kindness, and encouragement, along with heaping plates of barbecue and sides and sometimes a bed for the night. Stubb's Bar-B-Q became a musicians' hangout where Sunday night jam sessions became a tradition. The well known to the unknown, performers of blues, rock, country or folk—all were welcome on Stubb's tiny stage, and all were touched by the generous barbecue chef who espoused love and happiness. Soon, pictures of Stubb and his friends in the music industry decorated the walls.

Legend has it that Stevie Ray Vaughan drew inspiration from Stubb's jukebox and later recorded many of the songs he heard there. A pool game in Stubb's back room, in which Tom T. Hall and Joe Ely used a white onion for a cue ball, stimulated Hall to write his song "The Great East Broadway Onion Championship of 1978." Muddy Waters, John Lee Hooker, George Thorogood, Willie Nelson, Johnny Cash, Linda Ronstadt, and Emmylou Harris were among myriad others who performed at Stubb's. Stubb himself took the microphone occasionally to volunteer his rendition of "Summertime."

Stubb's Bar-B-Q drew a diverse crowd until 1984, when the restaurateur ran into financial problems, shut down his East Broadway location, and followed his West Texas friends to Austin. There he served barbecue at the blues club, Antone's, before opening his own barbecue and live-music place at 4001 Interstate 35 North in 1986. In 1989 Stubb closed the Austin location. Later, with business partners, he started to market his sauce and other products, which are now sold nationwide through Stubb's Legendary Kitchen in Austin.

On the day of his death, Stubb's partners bought the historic building at 801 Red River Street in Austin to continue his barbecue and live music tradition. Stubb died of congestive heart failure and related problems. In 1996, Stubb, who always described himself as "just a cook," became one of the first two inductees into Lubbock's Buddy Holly Terrace, which honors locals who have made significant contributions to the arts. When the Lubbock Arts Alliance decided to erect a life-size bronze statue of Stubb at his original East Broadway barbecue site, his musician friends played memorial jams to raise money for the project. The statue, sculpted by Terry Allen, was dedicated in 1999. Stubb's Bar-B-Q restaurants continued to operate in Austin and Lubbock.

BIBLIOGRAPHY: Austin *American–Statesman*, May 28, 1995; March 11, 12, 1996. Austin *Chronicle*, January 25, 1985. *Stubb's* (www.stubbsbbq.com/), accessed November 26, 2002. Stubblefield file, Southwest Collection, Texas Tech University, Lubbock, Texas. Vertical File, Center for American History, University of Texas at Austin.

Mary Beth Olson

Sudduth, James. Band director and composer; b. Crosbyton, Texas, October 19, 1940; d. Lubbock, December 3, 1997; son of Mr. and Mrs. Claude L. Sudduth. He earned his bachelor's and master's degrees at Texas Tech, where he also met his wife, Lynda, in 1959. Sudduth began his professional career with the Lubbock Independent School District. He finished it as director of bands at Texas Tech, a post he attained in 1981 and held until his death. Between the ISD and Tech, he worked as director of bands at Southwest Texas State University in San Marcos, and as an assistant professor of music and director of the marching band at Northwestern University.

In his supervisory role at Tech he oversaw the entire band program. He also conducted the university's nationally acclaimed Symphonic Band and directed the Texas Tech Band and Orchestra Camp, one of the largest youth music camps in the nation. Sudduth also taught arranging and conducting at both the graduate and undergraduate level. His arrangements, transcriptions, and compositions, for both marching and concert band, numbered more than 300. Many of them were published.

Omicron Delta Kappa and Mortar Board honored Sudduth in 1982 for outstanding service to Texas Tech. The next year he participated in the National Intercollegiate Band. Phi Mu Alpha Sinfonia Fraternity of America awarded him the National Citation of Excellence by in 1985 for outstanding contributions to music. Sudduth was guest conductor of the Lubbock Symphony Orchestra at Ballet Lubbock's performances of Tchaikovsky's *Nutcracker* from 1987 through 1993. In addition, he conducted the Lubbock Youth Symphony Orchestra in 1992 and led several of the Lubbock Symphony Orchestra's pops concerts. In October 1988 he became the first American to guest-conduct the Seoul Wind Ensemble in Seoul, South Korea. In May 1993 he conducted the Texas Tech University Symphonic Band at Carnegie Hall. In 1995 he received the Distinguished Service to Music Medal, the highest honor that can be bestowed by Kappa Kappa Psi / Tau Beta Sigma National Honorary Band Fraternity.

James and Lynda Sudduth had two sons. Sudduth died at home at age 57 after a lengthy illness.

BIBLIOGRAPHY: *The Foot'n A Half News* (publication of the Texas Tech Band Alumni Association), December 1997. "Goin' Band from Raiderland" (http://www.goinband.org/history2.htm), accessed January 3, 2003. James Sudduth obituary, Lubbock *Avalanche–Journal*'s Red Raiders.com (http://www.redraiders.com/news/97/12/04/james_sudduth.htm), accessed January 3, 2003.

Larry S. Bonura

Sweat, Isaac Payton. Singer and instrumentalist, known as Ikey Sweat; b. Port Arthur, Texas, July 19, 1945; d. Richmond, Texas, June 23, 1990. Ikey was born into a musical family. The nephew of country musician Moon Mullican, he became heir to Mullican's writing and publishing catalog. Mullican, as well as Sweat's other uncles and his own father, Dawdie Sweat, traveled through Texas towns to play country music in dance halls.

Sweat began playing instruments at an early age, beginning with the banjo and then learning guitar and bass. He played in rock bands throughout high school and, after graduation, enrolled as a pre-med student at Lamar University, where he planned to minor in music. The conflict of musical nights with educational days led him to drop out of school in order to concentrate on music. In the 1960s he became the bass player for the nationally renowned blues musician Johnny Winter. Sweat continued to play for Winter's bands (first the Crystaliers, later renamed the Coast-

liners) occasionally in the 1970s and 1980s. A product of the times, Sweat dabbled with psychedelic rock before returning to country music, a genre he found nearest to his heart. Although he played ably in other genres, whenever he sang, he sang country music.

He had his first major success in the early 1980s with a vocal cover of Al Dean's instrumental standard, "Cotton Eyed Joe." The song was popular, especially where people performed the eponymous dance. It was so popular, in fact, that Sweat became known as "Mr. Cotton Eyed Joe." He performed regularly until his death. After returning from a show in Houston, Sweat was found shot dead in his garage. The case is still unsolved. Sweat had a wife, Sharon, and three children.

BIBLIOGRAPHY: Houston *Post*, June 26, 1990.

Cathy Brigham

Symphony of Southeast Texas. A Beaumont symphony orchestra that had performed for fifty seasons as of 2003. It was long a dream to have a symphony in Beaumont. When the Beaumont Music Commission was founded in 1923, its constitution listed eight objectives, including the foundation and maintenance of the Beaumont Symphony Orchestra. The Symphony of Southeast Texas, as the orchestra is now called, contracted about sixty-five musicians in 2002. It has showcased great popular performers such as trumpeter Al Hirt and great classical artists, including Andre Previn, Van Cliburn, Isaac Stern, and has provided distinguished music for East Texans since its founding.

The desire for a symphony in Beaumont bore fruit after the Houston Symphony performed there on January 18, 1950. The next morning a steering committee was formed to lay plans for and arouse interest in a Beaumont symphony. Between 1950 and 1952, committees were formed, procedures determined, and concerts by other symphonies were held. A test performance was held on October 23, 1952, to determine if there was an adequate group of musicians to have an orchestra. The concert, which was deemed a success, was conducted by Jay Dietzer. The Beaumont Symphony Orchestra was officially founded and held its first performance on May 12, 1953.

Dietzer was conductor during the challenging early years of 1953 to 1957. He had previously conducted orchestras in other Texas cities, including San Antonio, New Braunfels, and Abilene. He recruited musicians from all walks of life to form the symphony.

Edvard Fendler was conductor of the symphony from 1957 to 1970. A native of Germany, Fendler was a noted scholar of musical compositions. He spoke English, French, German, Spanish, and Dutch. He had served as music director and conductor of the National Symphony Orchestra of Guatemala, and as the conductor of the symphony at Mobile, Alabama.

Joseph B. Carlucci, conductor of the symphony from 1971 to 1990, had not only impeccable credentials, including a degree from Yale University and a doctorate from the Eastman School of Music, but personal qualities of charm and diplomacy. He dramatically increased attendance at concerts by broadening the programming to include not only classical music but other genres, including jazz. Like conductors throughout the country, Carlucci held outdoor "Pops" concerts. He forged an ongoing and mutually beneficial relationship between the symphony and Lamar University, from where he recruited students and faculty to play in the orchestra.

When Carlucci retired at the end of the 1990 season, Diane M. Wittry was chosen from among many candidates to become music director and conductor beginning with the 1991–92 season. This graduate of the University of Southern California brought a new look and personality to the symphony—based not least on the fact that she was a woman. In an article in *Newsweek*, she explained that even in 1994, the 300 United States orchestras had only fifteen to twenty woman conductors. Under her guidance the symphony greatly expanded educational programming. New programs included Adopt-a-Musician, in which musicians travel to schools to give students in grades kindergarten through fifth grade the opportunity to meet musicians personally, ask questions, and witness a brief performance by a professional musician in a small group setting. The Side-by-Side program allows talented high school and even middle school children to perform next to professional musicians in the symphony. Today the symphony performs eight educational concerts for approximately 10,000 students from over ninety Southeast Texas schools.

During Wittry's tenure, in 1992, the name of the orchestra was changed from Beaumont Symphony Orchestra to Symphony of Southeast Texas. The name change reflected that musicians in the orchestra, and the audience itself, come from throughout Southeast Texas.

Christopher Zimmerman became music director and conductor of the symphony in 2001. Zimmerman, a native of London, is a graduate of Yale University. He made his professional debut with the Royal Philharmonic Orchestra and the London Symphony, and subsequently played with the Royal Liverpool Philharmonic. In 1989 he co-founded and became music director of the London Chamber Orchestra.

In 2000 the Symphony of Southeast Texas became affiliated with the Southeast Texas Youth Symphony, a full orchestra founded in 1983 for area young musicians. The youth symphony plays two full concerts a year and performs several times at community events. On October 26, 2000, the Symphony of Southeast Texas Chorus made its debut with the youth ensemble.

One of the keys to the success of the Symphony of Southeast Texas has been the support of the Symphony League of Beaumont. This group, originally organized as the Beaumont Symphony Women's League in 1955, has sold tickets, procured advertising, arranged lavish social affairs, and raised vast sums of money for the symphony. One of its most successful fundraisers was the "Symphony of Trees," which from 1979 until the late 1990s featured not only beautifully decorated trees in a wide array of themes, but parties, parades, shops, fireworks and children's activities. The league's best-known project is a debutante program that began in 1962. During its seven-month season, which includes trips, parties, balls, and a formal presentation at the symphony, high school girls and their escorts hone their manners and social skills. The league sponsors a shorter program for eighth-grade girls and boys called the Symphony Belles and Junior Escorts. The Symphony League of Beaumont educational projects include the Youth Guild, in which high school students learn more about music and assist with special events. The league also sponsors an annual String Competition, in which the area's young string students meet and compete. Prizes are awarded in several categories based on age and experience, with two grand prizes awarded for private study.

BIBLIOGRAPHY: Dr. Joseph B. Carlucci Scrapbooks, Symphony League Scrapbooks, and Vertical Files (under Symphony of Southeast Texas), Tyrrell Historical Library, Beaumont, Texas. Symphony of Southeast Texas website (www.sost.org), accessed December 16, 2002.

Penny Clark

T

Tapscott, Horace. Black activist and musician; b. Houston, April 6, 1934; d. Los Angeles, February 27, 1999. Tapscott spent the first decade of his life in the predominantly black Third Ward of Houston. His mother, Mary Lou Malone, played piano in a neighborhood church choir and had been a member of a jazz quartet that performed throughout East Texas and Louisiana in the 1920s. Horace met his father, Rev. Robert Tapscott, only once, when he was about six.

He grew up in a rich musical environment. As a child he knew musicians Amos Milburn and Floyd Dixon, who dated his sister, and among his kindergarten classmates was Johnny "Guitar" Watson. Tapscott's mother nurtured his musical abilities. By the age of six he had become a competent pianist, and his mother bought him a trombone when he was eight. In 1943 the family moved to Los Angeles, where Horace's stepfather, Leon Jackson, worked in the shipyards.

Once again the youngster found himself surrounded by music. He went to elementary school with Jamesetta Rogers, who later became famous as the rhythm-and-blues singer Etta James, and at Lafayette Junior High School he studied under Percy McDavid, who had taught Illinois and Russell Jacquet and Arnett Cobb in Houston; in Los Angeles, McDavid led a band that included future jazz legends Charles Mingus and Eric Dolphy. At Lafayette, Tapscott also met his future wife, Cecilia, whom he married in 1953 and with whom he eventually had five children (he also fathered five other children with four other women). He led a band at Jefferson High School, where his fellow students included musicians Jesse Belvin and O. C. Smith, and once won $200 in a talent contest at a local theater by playing "Marie" on the trombone.

After a brief stay at Los Angeles City College, Tapscott enlisted in the U.S. Air Force and served from 1953 to 1957, mostly at Fort Warren Air Force Base in Cheyenne, Wyoming. During his military service he switched back to the piano; after his discharge, he entered the LA jazz scene. He played with Lorez Alexandra and later with Lionel Hampton, primarily as a trombonist, from 1958 to 1961. Tapscott also was briefly a member of Motown Records' West Coast band, which backed popular Motown acts such as the Supremes.

In the early 1960s he grew dissatisfied with the commercialism of the music industry and increasingly interested in issues of black cultural awareness and radical politics. In response, he founded the "Pan Afrikan Peoples Arkestra," also known as the Ark, a collective group with an everchanging lineup dedicated to preserving and developing African-American musical traditions. He also founded the Underground Musicians Association, which later changed its name to the "Union of God's Musicians and Artists Ascension" (UGMAA). This organization provided a community center that preserved the Afro-American musical tradition and promoted cultural and musical education. It also distributed free food to families in Watts and made available meeting space for black radicals such as Stokely Carmichael and H. Rap Brown. The Ark was known for playing free outdoor concerts in south central Los Angeles, and often spontaneously loaded the UGMAA truck with equipment and offered unscheduled performances in local parks and on street corners. Tapscott taught a course at the University of California at Riverside on "Black Experience in the Fine Arts." He also helped set up the UGMAA Fine Arts Institute and briefly hosted a public television show, "The Store Front." The group's radical politics—it also played benefits for Angela Davis and for local Black Panther leader Geronimo Pratt—helped draw the attention of the FBI, which placed it and Tapscott under surveillance.

Perhaps unsurprisingly, given his dedication to radical causes, Tapscott's recording career got off to a relatively late start. In 1969 the Horace Tapscott Quintet released *The Giant Has Awakened*, a call for black consciousness and black liberation, on the Flying Dutchman label. His first solo album was *Songs of the Unsung* (1978), on the Interplay label. In that year, he suffered a cerebral aneurysm and almost died; nevertheless, he eventually released fourteen albums, including eight albums of solo piano called *The Tapscott Sessions* (on the Nimbus label), over the next six years. Tapscott and the Ark continued performing into the 1990s. His last recordings were *Among Friends* (on Jazz Friends Productions), recorded live in France with the Tapscott Simmons Quartet in 1995, and *Thoughts of Dar es Salaam* (on Arabesque Jazz), both released in 1999. Tapscott died of cancer. UGMAA still existed in 2002.

BIBLIOGRAPHY: Clora Bryant et. al., eds., *Central Avenue Sounds: Jazz in Los Angeles* (Berkeley: University of California Press, 1998). Aaron Cohen, "Papa's Optimism: The Final Interview," *Down Beat* 66 (May 1999). "Quiet West Coast Giant Reawakens," *Down Beat* 45 (December 1978). Ian Stewart, "Horace Tapscott," *Musician*, November 1979. Horace Tapscott, with Steven Isoardi, ed., *Songs of the Unsung: The Musical and Social Journey of Horace Tapscott* (Durham, North Carolina: Duke University Press, 2001). *Bradley Shreve*

Tate, Buddy. Tenor saxophonist; b. George Holmes Tate, Blue Creek Community (near Sherman), Texas, February 22, 1915; d. Chandler, Arizona, February 10, 2001. Tate, one of the great tenor saxophonists of the swing era, began his professional career in the late 1920s playing around the Southwest in bands led by Terence Holder, Andy Kirk, and Nat Towles. Although he began playing alto saxophone, he quickly developed into a formidable tenor sax player.

For a brief period in 1934 he played with the Count Basie Band, which was still relatively unknown at that time. Although this particular Basie band lasted only a short time, Tate came back to play with Count Basie in

1939 after the sudden death of saxophonist Herschel Evans, a good friend of Tate's. Evans and Tate had played together in Troy Floyd's San Antonio band. Tate later told writer Stanley Dance about a premonition concerning Evans's death. "I dreamed he had died, and that Basie was going to call me. It happened within a week or two. I still have the telegram."

Tate's first recording date with Count Basie came on March 19, 1939, when the orchestra cut an arrangement of "Rock-a-Bye Basie." Tate's favorite recording with Basie was his May 31, 1940, work on "Super Chief." Bringing his own sound to the Basie Orchestra, Tate formed a saxophone duo with Lester Young, which was comparable to the previous Young–Evans team. Tate's style influenced other tenor saxophonists, among them Texan Illinois Jacquet, Sonny Rollins, and Eddie "Lockjaw" Davis. During his ten years with the Count Basie Band, Tate carried on the fine Texas tenor tradition Basie favored. Some have described the Basie band in these ten years as the greatest jazz band of all time.

By the late 1940s, postwar economic pressures forced Count Basie to make changes in the lineup. Tate decided to leave the band, hoping to tour less and perform closer to his home in New York. He played for bandleader Lucky Millinder, for trumpeter Hot Lips Page, and in ex-Basie singer Jimmy Rushing's Savoy band in the early 1950s. Eventually Tate secured residency for his own band in 1953 at the Celebrity Club on 125th Street in Harlem, a position he held for twenty-one years. He continued to record, toured with swing trumpeter Buck Clayton, and, in 1975, briefly co-directed a band with saxophonist Paul Quinichette at the West End Café in New York. He also led a group at the Rainbow Room with drummer Bobby Rosengarden. In 1981 Tate was seriously scalded in a hotel shower, but recovered and soon resumed his performance schedule. He worked with saxophonist Jim Calloway, pianist Jay McShann, vibraphonist Lionel Hampton, a band called the Statesmen of Jazz, and another band with Illinois Jacquet, billed as the Texas Tenors. Tate's final recording appearance came when he was invited to play with saxophone star James Carter on his 1996 CD, Conversin' With the Elders.

Tate spent his retirement years in Massapequa, New York. Just a few weeks before his death, he moved to Phoenix, Arizona, to live with his daughter Georgette. He was survived by two daughters, both of Phoenix, and many grandchildren.

BIBLIOGRAPHY: John Fordham, "Buddy Tate," London Guardian, February 12, 2001. Kenny Mathieson, "Swinging Texas Tenorman Was Basie Star" (http://www.jazz house.org/gone/lastpost.php3?edit.htm), accessed November 12, 2001. Dave Oliphant, Texan Jazz (Austin: University of Texas Press, 1996). Ben Ratliff, "Buddy Tate, Saxophonist for Basie's Band, dies at 87" (http://elvis-pelvis.com/buddytate.htm), accessed November 12, 2001. Vertical file, Center for American History, University of Texas at Austin.   Ruth K. Sullivan

Taylor, Johnnie Harrison. Singer; b. Crawfordsville, Arkansas, May 5, 1938; d. Dallas, May 31, 2000. Taylor

grew up in West Memphis, Arkansas, but spent much of his adult life in Texas. Inspired by gospel and blues music, he recorded with a doo-wop group called the Five Echoes during the early 1950s While still a teenager, he joined such gospel groups as the Melody Masters, the Highway QCs, and the Texas-based Soul Stirrers, in which he replaced Sam Cooke as lead singer. The Soul Stirrers, formed in Trinity around 1932, are considered the founders of modern gospel, an urbane, secularized variation of rural church music. One of their innovations was to have a fifth member sing a powerful lead while the others sang the usual four-part harmonies.

In 1963 Taylor was signed to Cooke's Sar label, where he recorded the hit single "Rome Wasn't Built in a Day." Although by that time he had found secular music more lucrative, Taylor's vocal style continued to reflect his strong religious roots. Sar folded after Cooke's death in 1964, and Taylor signed with Stax Records in Memphis in 1966. There he recorded his biggest hit to that time, "Who's Making Love?," which went to number one on the R&B charts in 1968 and sold a million copies. This was followed by a string of bestsellers, including "Take Care of Your Homework," "I've Got to Love Somebody's Baby," "Steal Away," and "Cheaper to Keep Her." Although such big names as Otis Redding, Booker T & the MGs, and Sam & Dave all recorded with Stax, Taylor was that label's all-time best-selling artist.

During the early 1970s Taylor continued to score with top-ten R&B singles, including his second number one in 1971, "Jody's Got Your Girl and Gone," and his third in 1973, "I Believe in You (You Believe in Me)." When Stax folded in 1975, Taylor went to Columbia Records, where, in 1976, he had the biggest hit of his career, "Disco Lady." The song was the first single ever to be certified platinum for two million copies. Eargasm, the album from which the single came, was banned by many radio stations because it was considered too suggestive. Nevertheless, the record's success demonstrated that Taylor's sexually charged soul music appealed to popular audiences. Because the single was released in the middle of the 1970s disco era, Taylor found himself incorrectly tagged as a disco artist, a label he disavowed.

Temporarily unable to generate additional success, he left in 1982 for Beverly Glen Records, where he climbed back onto the charts with the single "What About My Love?" His final stop (1984) was at Malaco Records, where he made well-received albums throughout the late 1980s and 1990s, such as This Is Your Night, Wall to Wall, and Gotta Get the Groove Back. Although his career had waned considerably, Taylor continued to tour across the country and draw respectable crowds in various R&B venues. During his long career he incorporated blues, soul, pop, and funk into his repertoire. He scored eleven top-forty hits on the Billboard pop chart, and recorded about twelve albums for Stax alone. He was living in Duncanville, Texas, when he died of a heart attack. He was survived by his wife Gerlean and four children.

BIBLIOGRAPHY: H. Wiley Hitchcock and Stanley Sadie, eds., The New Grove Dictionary of American Music (London: MacMillan Press, 1986). Living Blues, September–

October 2000. Julia Rubiner, *Contemporary Musicians: Profiles of the People in Music* (Detroit: Gale Research, 1994). Robert Santelli, *The Big Book of Blues* (New York: Penguin, 1993). Stax Records, "Johnnie Taylor: Biography," *Johnnie Taylor Special Memory Page* (http://staxrecords.free.fr.jtaylor.htm), accessed March 10, 2001. Jeff Stevens, "The Philosopher of Soul, Johnnie Taylor, dies at 62," *Blue Soul Scene: Obituaries* (http://www.globaldialog.com/~jeff61/taylor60.htm), accessed March 10, 2001.   *Scott Jordan*

Teagarden, Charlie. Jazz trumpeter; b. Charles Teagarden Jr., Vernon, Texas, July 19, 1913; d. Las Vegas, Nevada, December 10, 1984; son of Charles and Helen Teagarden. Charlie spent most of his career in the shadow of his brother, Jack. Although the Teagarden parents both played instruments, Helen was the more accomplished musician; she sang, read music, and played piano, guitar, and horn. She taught her children to read music and performed professionally as a pianist.

After Charles Sr. died of influenza in 1918, Helen moved her family to Chappell, Nebraska, where she played at theaters during silent movies and taught music. She then moved the family to Oklahoma City. There her children, Jack, Norma, Charlie, and Clois, started their music careers playing in local bands. Charlie played trumpet expertly in big bands and Dixieland combos. His playing style was often compared to that of Red Nichols—a pleasant, effective sound.

Teagarden worked as a Western Union messenger when he first left school. Later, he played with Herb Book and his Oklahoma Joy Boys, and then he toured with Frank Williams and his Oklahomans. In 1929 the Oklahomans folded in New York, and Teagarden joined Ben Pollack's Orchestra. He left Pollack in September 1930 and played for a year with Red Nichols.

On October 22, 1931, he participated in a recording session with the Eddie Lang–Joe Venuti All-Star Orchestra, which was led by Benny Goodman and included Charlie's brother, Jack. Among the numbers recorded at that session were "Beale Street Blues," "After You've Gone," "Someday Sweetheart," and "Farewell Blues." According to jazz critic Gunther Schuller, Charlie's solo on "Beale Street" stood "unequalled as a fine example of white blues trumpet-playing for many years."

Teagarden played with Roger Wolfe Kahn in 1932 and with Paul Whiteman from 1933 to 1940. During the decade of the thirties he did freelance studio work. Also, from 1936 to 1940, he played with Jack and saxophonist Frankie Trumbauer in a jazz trio called the Three T's, as well as other band combos under Jack's leadership. By this time, Charlie had earned the nickname "Little 'T'" to Jack's "Big 'T.'" During the 1940s, Teagarden alternately played with his brother in Jack Teagarden's Big Band and led his own bands or played in theater orchestras for performances such as Ethel Waters's show *Cabin in the Sky* (1941).

In late 1942 Teagarden enlisted in the Ferry Command Service. Upon demobilization, he played freelance in Los Angeles entertainment and recording studios. He and Jack played with Harry James in 1946, and they shared the leadership role in Jack's jazz combo until Charlie joined Jimmy Dorsey's Original Dorseyland Jazz Band in 1948. Charlie again played with Ben Pollack and Jack, and he did studio work with Jerry Gray, while leading his own trio with Ray Bauduc and Jess Stacy in the early 1950s. Teagarden appeared on a daytime TV show and did studio work with Bob Crosby in Hollywood throughout much of the mid-to-late 1950s.

He moved to Las Vegas in 1960 and led a combo that played regularly in the Cinderella Club at the Silver Slipper, while he continued to freelance, doing relief band work on the Strip. In 1963 Charlie, Jack, Norma, and Helen Teagarden recorded together at the Monterey Jazz Festival. The same year, Charlie was elected to the executive board of the Local 369 Musician's Union; he became an assistant to the union president in 1968 and gave up his active music occupation for a career in politics. Teagarden and his wife, LaNora, had one son.

Teagarden worked with many musicians during his forty-year music career, including Drew Page, Carson Smith, Henry Cuesta, Billie Holiday, Art Karle, Larry Binyon, Babe Russin, Art Miller, Arthur Schutt, Shirley Clay, Eddie Lang, Carl Kress, Harry Goodman, and Allan Reuss. His trumpet can be heard on such albums as Fats Waller's *You Rascal You* (1929), Billie Holiday's *Billie Holiday: The Legacy Box* (1933) and *Quintessential Billie Holiday* (1933), *Bing Crosby and the Andrews Sisters* (1939), Jimmy Dorsey's *Dixie by Dorsey* (1950) and *America's Premier Dixieland Jazz* (1998), Benny Goodman and Jack Teagarden's *B. G. & Big Tea in NYC* (1929), Benny Goodman's *1931–1933, 1934–1935*, *Best of Big Bands* (1989) and *Permanent Goodman, Vol. 1* (2000), and Cole Porter's *Stars of the 30's* (1991). Teagarden can also be heard on numerous other titles by Billie Holiday and Benny Goodman, as well as on titles by Ethel Waters, Red Nichols, Pete Fountain, Lionel Hampton, Woody Herman, Alex Hill, George Wettling, and Paul Whiteman. He appears on most of Jack Teagarden's titles and his own 1962 recording, *The Big Horn of Little "T"*, and a recent release, *Live at the Royal Room Hollywood* (2000).

BIBLIOGRAPHY: Whitney Balliett, *American Musicians: 56 Portraits in Jazz* (New York: Oxford University Press, 1986). John Chilton, *Who's Who of Jazz: Storyville to Swing Street*, Fourth Edition (New York: Da Capo Press, 1985).Leonard Feather and Ira Gitler, *The Encyclopedia of Jazz in the Seventies* (New York: Horizon Press, 1976). Richard Hadlock, *Jazz Masters of the Twenties* (New York: Collier, 1965). Roger D. Kinkle, *The Complete Encyclopedia of Popular Music and Jazz: 1900–1950* (New Rochelle, New York: Arlington House, 1974). *The New Grove Dictionary of American Music* (New York, Macmillan, 1986).
                                    Cheryl L. Simon and Roy G. Scudday

Teagarden, Cubby. Drummer and occasional singer, also called Cub; b. Clois Lee Teagarden, Vernon, Texas, December 16, 1915; d. California, 1969; son of Charles and Helen (Geinger) Teagarden. Cubby played and sometimes sang in bands with his sister, Norma, and his brothers, Jack and Charlie. His first professional job, around 1930, was in the balcony of a drugstore in Dallas, where he played two-hour afternoon sessions, six days a week, with his brothers and Drew Page; the performers received merchandise credit.

Starting in 1939, Cubby played with Jack Teagarden's Big Band. He also played with the Oklahoma Symphony, and with his own band. He performed with such musicians as Charles McCamish, Casper Reardon, Clint and Carl Garvin, Hub Lytle, Mark Bennett, Herb Quigley, Terry Shand, Art Saint John, John Van Eps, Art Miller, Allan Reuss, Jose Gutierrez, Frankie Trumbauer, Charlie Spivak, Ernie Caceres, and Benny Goodman. His drums and some vocals can be heard on various Jack Teagarden LPs, such as *Stars Fell on Alabama: 1931–1940* (1990) and *Big T* (1994). Cubby Teagarden left the music world after 1948 and worked for the General Telephone Company in Long Beach, California.

BIBLIOGRAPHY: Whitney Balliett, *American Musicians: 56 Portraits in Jazz* (New York: Oxford University Press, 1986). "Big Bands Database Plus Homepage: Jack Teagarden Orch," *The Great American Big Bands Biographies* (http://www.nfo.net/.WWW/t1.html), accessed January 31, 2003. John Chilton, *Who's Who of Jazz: Storyville to Swing Street* (Philadelphia: Chilton, 1970). Drew Page, *Drew's Blues: A Sideman's Life with the Big Bands* (Baton Rouge: Louisiana State University Press, 1980). Leonard Feather, *Encyclopedia of Jazz* (1960).

Cheryl L. Simon

Jazz musician Jack Teagarden, 1920. Duncan Scheidt Collection.

Teagarden, Jack. Jazz musician; b. Weldon Leo Teagarden, Vernon, Texas, August 20, 1905; d. New Orleans, January 15, 1964 (buried in Los Angeles); son of Charles and Helen (Geinger) Teagarden. Jack was also known as Jackson T., Mr. T, and Big Gate. His father, an amateur cornet player, worked in the oilfields, and his mother was a local piano instructor and church organist. All four Teagarden children became prominent musicians. Jack was given piano lessons when he reached the age of five. He took up the baritone horn for a time but switched to trombone when he was seven. He and his mother played duets (trombone and piano) as background to the silent films at a Vernon theater. In 1918, after his father's death, the family moved to Chappell, Nebraska, where he and his mother again worked in the local theater. The following year the family moved to Oklahoma City.

At sixteen Teagarden first played the trombone professionally, at a concert near San Antonio as a member of Cotton Bailey's dance and jazz band. Later the same year (1921) he joined Peck Kelley's Bad Boys in Houston. Visiting band leader Paul Whiteman heard the group there and offered Teagarden a position in his New York orchestra. For several years, however, Jack continued to play with Texas groups. About 1923 he briefly attempted to enter the oilfield business in Wichita Falls but soon gave up the venture and returned to music.

He made his first trip to New York in 1926 as a performer on the eastern tour of Doc Ross's Jazz Bandits. The next year he went to the city on his own. He originally planned to join Whiteman's ensemble but happened to hear Ben Pollack's band first. After two months with the Tommy

Gott Orchestra, Teagarden secured a position in Pollack's organization, where he beat Glenn Miller for the seat of first trombone. He made his first recording in 1927 as a member of the Kentucky Grasshoppers, an offshoot of Pollack's group. Teagarden later recorded with many of America's jazz greats, including Red Nichols, Benny Goodman, and Louis Armstrong. He performed with Eddie Condon, Bix Beiderbecke, Paul Whiteman, the Dorsey brothers, Bob Crosby, Eddie Lang, Peck Kelley, and others. He was considered by many to be the greatest jazz trombonist of his era, but his style was so unusual that others did not follow his example.

In 1933, after a brief stint in Mal Hallett's band, Teagarden signed on with Paul Whiteman's orchestra, with which he played for five years. In 1939 he formed his own band; it was musically innovative but not financially successful and was disbanded in 1947. He teamed up with Louis Armstrong's All-Stars for some classic recordings in the late 1940s and formed the Jack Teagarden All Stars Dixieland band in 1951. The All Stars toured Europe and Asia in 1957–59 as part of a government-sponsored goodwill tour.

Teagarden's playing style was lyrical and seemingly effortless. He did not follow the traditional Dixieland "tailgate" treatment of his instrument. Upper register solos, the lack of a strict solo beat, and the use of lip trills were some of his characteristics. Having grown up in an area with a large black population, he developed an early appreciation of black music, especially the blues and gospel. He was one of the first jazz musicians to incorporate "blue notes" into his playing. He was also among the first white jazz musicians to record with black players. Teagarden was an excellent singer and developed a respected blues vocal style. In addition, he was an inventor who redesigned mouthpieces, mutes, and water valves and invented a new musical slide rule. He also started using Pond's Cold Cream and Pam cooking lubricant on his trombone, something many trombonists emulated.

Teagarden appeared in the movies *Birth of the Blues* (1941), *The Glass Wall* (1953), and *Jazz on a Summer's Day* (1959). He was an admired recording artist, featured on RCA Victor, Columbia, Decca, Capitol, and MGM discs. As a jazz artist he won the 1944 *Esquire* magazine Gold Award, was highly rated in the Metronome polls of 1937–42 and 1945, and was selected for the *Playboy* magazine All Star Band, 1957–60. Teagarden was the featured performer at the Newport Jazz Festival of 1957. *Saturday Review* wrote in 1964 that he "walked with artistic dignity all his life," and the same year *Newsweek* praised his "mature approach to trombone jazz."

Teagarden was married first to Ora Binyon in San Angelo in 1923; they had two sons before they were divorced. In the 1930s he was married to and divorced from, successively, Clare Manzi of New York City and Edna "Billie" Coats. Teagarden married Adeline Barriere Gault in September 1942; they had three children and raised a foster child. Early in 1964 Teagarden cut short a performance in New Orleans because of ill health. He briefly visited a hospital, then was found dead in his room at the Prince Monti Motel. The cause of death was bronchial pneumonia, which had followed a liver ailment.

BIBLIOGRAPHY: John Chilton, *Who's Who of Jazz: Storyville to Swing Street* (London: Bloomsbury Book Shop, 1970; American ed., New York and Philadelphia: Chilton, 1972; 4th ed., New York: Da Capo Press, 1985). Dallas *Morning News*, January 16, 17, 1964. H. Wiley Hitchcock and Stanley Sadie, eds., *The New Grove Dictionary of American Music* (4 vols., New York: Macmillan, 1986). *Newsweek*, January 27, 1964. Ross Russell, *Jazz Style in Kansas City and the Southwest* (Berkeley: University of California Press, 1971). Jay D. Smith and Len Guttridge, *Jack Teagarden* (London: Cassell, 1960; rpt., New York: Da Capo Press, 1976). *Charles G. Davis*

Teagarden, Norma. Jazz pianist; b. Vernon, Texas, April 28, 1911; d. California, June 5, 1996; daughter of Charles and Helen (Geinger) Teagarden. Norma studied piano with her mother and often performed with her brothers Jack, Charlie, and Clois.

She started her career in music in Oklahoma City around 1926. She moved to New Mexico in 1929 and played in various "territory" bands until 1935, when she moved back to Oklahoma City and started her own band. She moved to Long Beach, California, in 1942 and again led her own band. From 1944 to 1947 and from 1952 to 1955, she toured with Jack Teagarden's band. When she was not leading her own band or performing with her brothers, she worked with such jazz greats as Ben Pollack,

Matty Matlock, Ada Leonard, Ted Vesley, Pete Daily, and Ray Bauduc.

Norma Teagarden married John Friedlander in 1955 and settled in San Francisco in 1957. She remained active on the traditional jazz scene, playing alongside jazz artists such as Turk Murphy, Kass Malone, Dick Cary, Fred Greenleaf, Walter Page, Carl Kress, Pee Wee Russell, Edmond Hall, Jimmy McPartland, Leonard Feather, Kenny Davern, and Eddie Condon. In 1963 she joined her brothers Jack and Charlie and her mother at a recorded performance at the Monterey Jazz Festival.

Norma's piano can be heard on Eddie Condon's *Town Hall Concerts, Volume 7* (1944) and Jack Teagarden's *Meet Me Where They Play the Blues*, *Jazz Great*, and *Club Hangover Broadcasts* (1954), *100 Years from Today* (1963), *Big T Jump* (1995), *Jack Teagarden 1944–1947*, and (the second) *Meet Me Where They Play the Blues* (1999). Norma Teagarden Friedlander died of cancer.

BIBLIOGRAPHY: Whitney Balliett, *American Musicians: 56 Portraits in Jazz* (New York: Oxford University Press, 1986). Chuck Huggins, "Norma Teagarden," *Riverwalk Profiles Online* (http://www.riverwalk.org/profiles/norma.htm), accessed February 3, 2003. Roger D. Kinkle, *The Complete Encyclopedia of Popular Music and Jazz: 1900–1950* (New Rochelle, New York: Arlington House, 1974). *Cheryl L. Simon*

Tejana Singers. Texas women singers of Mexican descent. Such singers have played major roles as interpreters of Tejano music. When *música norteña* developed in the late 1920s and early 1930s, women sang in its early recordings, and they have remained involved in both Texas-Mexican conjunto and *orquesta* music since then.

Only a few references to women singers occur in standard sources, and only Lydia Mendoza, the earliest recognized Tejana singer, has received much attention. The Arhoolie Record Company releases *Los Primeros Duetos Femininas, 1930–1955* and *Tejano Roots, The Women* brought belated attention to Tejana singers' achievements and provided a summary of their work. These recordings were compiled from original recordings for Tejano labels, and for many years the texts that accompany them formed the few written accounts of significant Tejana singers.

Lydia Mendoza, known as *la alondra de la frontera* ("the lark of the border"), made her first recording in 1928 as a member of her family-based Cuarteto Carta Blanca, which Leonora Mendoza, her mother, managed. In her four-decade career as a soloist, she usually accompanied herself on a twelve-string guitar and was considered a uniquely artful and dramatic interpreter of Spanish-language songs. Among her most famous singles were "Mal Hombre" ("Cold-hearted Man"), a song she said she got off a chewing-gum wrapper from Monterrey, Nuevo León, and "Delgadina," which expressed a critical view of a father's questionable intentions toward his daughter. Lydia Mendoza was honored in 1982 with a National Heritage Award from the National Endowment for the Arts, inducted into the Texas Women's Hall of Fame in 1985, and became the first Tejana admitted into the Conjunto Hall of Fame in 1991. Juanita and María Mendoza, Lydia's sisters, had important careers as Las Hermanas Mendoza, a duet that their mother also managed. María had originally been part of the family's Cuarteto Carta Blanca.

During World War II the Mendoza family stopped touring due to tire and gasoline rationing, so Leonora acquired singing jobs for Juanita and María at the Club Bohemia in San Antonio and accompanied them on the guitar. When the Mendozas resumed touring after the war, Las Hermanas Mendoza found greater popularity as a duet. They recorded for nearly all the Spanish-language recording labels of the day, including Falcón, Alamo, Sombrero, and Imperial. Leonora Mendoza died in 1952, and Las Hermanas Mendoza subsequently undertook only a few more tours; the duet broke up when María married. Juanita, however, continued to work as a soloist at La Casita Nightclub in San Antonio through the 1970s. María died in 1990.

When Armando Marroquín and Paco Betancourt established Ideal Records in 1946, Marroquín's wife, Carmen Hernández Marroquín, and her sister, Laura Hernández Cantú, became an important duet known as Carmen y Laura. They brought fame to the new recording company with their war-time hit, "Se Me Fue Mi Amor" ("My Love Went Away"). Carmen y Laura, like Las Hermanas Mendoza, toured extensively in the Southwest and in Kansas and Illinois in the 1950s. Their recording career lasted into the late 1970s. The famous Alice-based duet collaborated on numerous occasions with Narciso Martínez, the "father of conjunto," and Tejano orchestra leader Beto Villa. The pair made many records for Ideal and were among the first Tejana singers to introduce blues, swing, and boleros to their repertoire.

Other Tejana recording artists who worked as duets or trios were Las Hermanas Segovia, Las Hermanas Guerrero, Las Hermanas Cantú, Las Hermanas Góngora, Las Rancheritas, Hermanitas Parra, "Las Preferidas" Hermanas Sánchez, Hermanas Peralta, Marcela y Aurelia, and many other groups about whom little is known except the titles of their records. These groups recorded for such Tejano labels as Ideal, Falcón, Azteca, Globe, Río, and Corona. Some of them remained popular for many years.

Besides singing in ensembles, Tejanas have also had significant careers as soloists. Chelo Silva, Delia Gutiérrez, Rosita Fernández, Juanita García, and Beatriz Llamaz were some of the most famous. Chelo Silva was born in Brownsville and later worked there as a singer at the Continental Club. In 1941 William A. Owens recorded her in his music-collecting project on the Texas-Mexico border. She was married for a while to folklorist Américo Paredes. She made her recording debut in 1954 on the Falcón label and became the most popular Texas-Mexican female singer along the border during the second half of the decade. In addition, she pursued an active career throughout the United States as well as in Mexico. She died of cancer on April 2, 1988.

Rosita Fernández was born in Monterrey, Nuevo León, Mexico, and started singing as a youth in the 1920s with her uncles, the Trío San Miguel of San Antonio. In 1932, after winning a singing contest sponsored by a local radio station, she became a soloist. Principally as an interpreter of boleros and *rancheras*, she was featured with the Eduardo Martínez and Beto Villa Orchestras. In her more than fifty years as an entertainer, she sang for many presidents of both the United States and Mexico. She was best known in Texas for her twenty-six years as the star performer at the Fiesta Noche del Río in San Antonio.

Delia Gutiérrez, born in Weslaco, started singing at eight years old with the *orquesta* headed by her father, Eugenio Gutiérrez. She also recorded for the Ideal and Falcón labels. In addition to her work as a soloist, she collaborated with Laura Hernández Cantú of Carmen y Laura on numerous recordings. Juanita García won a talent show in 1950. Her prize, a contract with Falcón, launched her career. In the early 1960s Beatriz Llamaz, who apparently recorded some 100 songs, became quite popular on tours throughout the Southwest. She retired in the early 1980s but by the end of the decade was once again recording music.

Many Tejanas were also part of male-female duos, including Victor y Lolita (Falcón records), and Martín y Malena (Azteca records). Most of the Tejana singers working in the 1980s and early 1990s have also become popular in the conjunto, bolero, and *ranchera* styles. Laura Canales grew up in Kingsville, where she first performed in 1974 with the famous Conjunto Bernal. By the early 1990s, after suffering several setbacks, she had formed a new group, Laura Canales y los Fabulosos Cuatro. Jean Le Grand, born in California but reared partly by relatives in Laredo, also heads her own group and is an attorney. Other important contemporary Tejana singers include Patsy Torres, Selena, Janie C. Ramírez, and Lisa López.

BIBLIOGRAPHY: Austin *America--Statesman*, July 14, 1990. Lydia Mendoza, *Lydia Mendoza: A Family Autobiography*, comp. Chris Strachwitz and James Nicolopulos (Houston: Arte Público Press, 1993). Lydia Mendoza (http://www.worshipguitars.org/lydiamendoza/), accessed February 19, 2003. Manuel Peña, *The Texas-Mexican Conjunto: History of a Working-Class Music* (Austin: University of Texas Press, 1985).   *Teresa Palomo Acosta*

Tejano Conjunto Festival. An annual music event in San Antonio, first organized by the Guadalupe Cultural Arts Center in 1982. The festival has become nationally known for its presentation of the Texas-Mexican Conjunto, a musical form developed by Texas-Mexican working-class musicians, beginning with Narciso Martínez.

Initially, the festival occurred over a few days in May, but it was later expanded to a full week. It features many hours of live entertainment, in which dancing by the audience is encouraged. Several dozen traditional, popular, and progressive conjuntos led by such established musicians as Fred Zimmerle, Roberto Pulido, and Esteban Jordán, have appeared at the event each year. Musicians from Northern Mexico, the origin of conjunto, have also participated in the festival, and the organizers have occasionally (1989 and 1992) included Cajun and Zydeco accordionists. In addition, such female conjunto musicians as Eva Ybarra, Lupita Rodela, and Laura Canales have also performed at the festival.

The festival program has often been divided into differ-

"Queen of Norteña" Lydia Mendoza, earliest recognized Tejana singer. Photo © by Chris Strachwitz (www.arhoolie.com).

ent areas to accommodate the many conjunto playing techniques. Some have been set aside for groups that represent the roots of conjunto, while others feature groups that embody the best of San Antonio, or bands that have a new conjunto sound through the addition of a synthesizer or such instruments as the saxophone. The annual Tejano Conjunto Festival poster competition and accordion student recitals complement the occasion. Other activities to celebrate landmarks in the conjunto tradition have also become part of the festival.

The Conjunto Hall of Fame, established in 1982, has inducted twenty-nine musicians, including one woman. In addition, at the 1986 gathering, which marked the golden anniversary of recorded conjunto music, Narciso Martínez, who made his first record in 1936, was recognized. On many occasions the city of San Antonio has proclaimed May "Conjunto Music Month" and hosted special performances by various conjunto artists, including Valerio Longoria, a veteran conjunto innovator, on the steps of City Hall.

An annual special edition of *Tonantzin*, the quarterly publication of the Guadalupe Cultural Arts Center, serves as the official festival program, often featuring special articles on conjuntos. Since its founding over a decade ago, the Tejano Conjunto Festival has grown in popularity, drawing a varied and large audience from around the country.

BIBLIOGRAPHY: *The Guadalupe Cultural Arts Center Presents the Eleventh Annual Tejano Conjunto Festival en San Antonio, 1992* (San Antonio: Guadalupe Cultural Arts Center, 1992). *Tejano Conjunto Festival en San Antonio, 1991* (San Antonio: Guadalupe Cultural Arts Center, 1991). *Tejano-Conjunto Music Festival*, 2003 (http://www.2camels.com/destination14.php3), accessed February 19, 2003. *Teresa Palomo Acosta*

"Texas, Our Texas." State song of Texas, adopted by the Forty-first Legislature after a statewide contest (1929). The music was originally written in 1924 by William J. Marsh of Fort Worth, and the lyrics were written by Marsh and Gladys Yoakum Wright. Alaska's statehood in 1959 necessitated the only change that has been made in the lyrics—modifying the line "largest and grandest" to "boldest and grandest." The Seventy-third Legislature again adopted "Texas, Our Texas" as the state song in a 1993 law.

BIBLIOGRAPHY: Vertical Files, Center for American History, University of Texas at Austin (under "Songs" and "William J. Marsh"). *Charles A. Spain Jr.*

Texas Association of Music Schools. Organized in November 1938, with twenty-five colleges represented; in 2003 its membership included ninety-five college and university departments and schools of music. William E. Jones, the first president, served from 1938 to 1942, and Grady Harlan was secretary from 1938 to 1948.

Both the Commission on Fine Arts, appointed by the Texas Association of Colleges (established in Austin, 1937), and a Symposium on the College Music Curricula at the Texas Music Teachers Association convention (Waco, June 1938) revealed the need for improved standards in music education that led to the beginnings of the

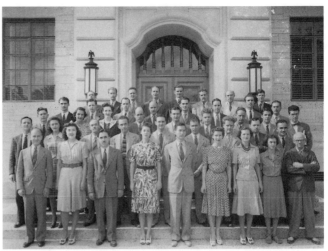

Dean E. William Doty (fourth row, far left) with the University of Texas College of Fine Arts faculty standing outside the Music Building, ca. 1942. Photograph by University Studio, Austin. Courtesy Martha Doty Freeman.

association. The first convention was held in December 1939 in San Antonio. The twenty-six institutions represented at this meeting are considered the charter members. Over a period of many years, E. William Doty, in his dual capacity as dean of the College of Fine Arts at the University of Texas and leader in both the Texas Association of Music Schools and the National Association of Schools of Music, persistently fought for the establishment of standards in music schools throughout the state.

From as early as 1898 the number of schools offering music instruction had rapidly increased. These schools searched for means to improve quality of instruction, to establish standards for course offerings, and to set criteria for weighting of credit. The problems they sought to solve included the lack of cooperative leadership and the inability of students to transfer credit between institutions, both obstacles to the establishment of academic standards for music in Texas higher education. The association has provided member schools a forum for discussion of major issues relating to music in higher education in Texas. It has enhanced research and development of music in higher education, encouraged music in general education, and fostered cooperation among institutions and public understanding of music education.

The association's early years were devoted to organizational policies. Its code of ethics, promulgated in 1938, has made a distinctive difference in music education in the state and country. In place of rivalry and competition, cooperative teamwork and fraternity prevail. In 1945 the association turned its efforts toward the music curricula and sought to establish minimum standards for courses, faculty, facilities, resources, and libraries. A culminating achievement of the Commission on Cooperation in Higher Education was the publication in 1982 of the *Transfer Curriculum in Music for Texas Colleges and Universities*. Upon publication and distribution on four continents of the bibliographic tool *Books on Music: A Classified List*, by Michael Winesanker, the association gained worldwide recognition.

Any department or school of music in a Texas colleges or university holding membership in the Association of Texas Colleges and Universities or accredited by the Southern Association of Colleges and Universities may apply, be nominated by the Commission on Academic Standards, and be elected to membership at the annual meeting of the association. One director of the association must represent a private institution, another a public college or university, and the third a two-year school. The association's official address has been at Tarleton State University since 1948. Don Morton served as executive secretary from 1948 to 1976.

BIBLIOGRAPHY: L. W. Chidester, "The Curriculum of TAMS as Related to Four-Year College," *Southwestern Musician*, October 1947. Frederick Eby, *The Development of Education in Texas* (New York: Macmillan, 1925). William Charles Martin, The Texas Association of Music Schools (Ed.D. dissertation, George Peabody College for Teachers, 1956). TAMS website (http://www.tmea.org/085_Tams/index.htm), accessed February 15, 2003.

Christian A. K. Rosner

Texas Centennial Music. Music written for the celebration of the Texas Centennial in 1936. The event inspired amateur and professional Texan as well as non-Texan composers to write original music on Texas themes. The various genres of Texas Centennial music include popular and art songs, film music, operas, and a Mass. In addition to music written specifically for the Texas Centennial, arrangements and reissues of previously composed songs were published in 1936 as "Special Centennial Editions."

Texas Centennial songs can be divided according to such types as praise songs, cowboy songs, advertisement songs, bluebonnet songs, and love songs. Despite such classification, virtually all of the texts praise the state and its heroes while paying tribute to such Texas themes and images as cowboys, bluebonnets, longhorns, the Alamo, and the state's independence from Mexico.

The composers of these songs were generally one of three types: Texas (professional) composer, Texas Federation of Music Clubs member, and non-Texan composer. Although the performance medium could vary, the majority of the songs were written for a single voice or a small group of singers, accompanied by either a piano or guitar. The most common musical structure is a four-measure instrumental introduction followed by a strophic setting of two or three verses and a chorus in the key of C, F, or G major.

Both Texan and non-Texan firms issued Centennial music. Publishers such as Cross & Winge of Los Angeles, C.C. Birchard of Boston, Shapiro, Bernstein of New York, and Schirmer of New York primarily published works by established composers with reputations that extended beyond the boundaries of Texas, such as Oscar J. Fox, David Guion, and Tim Spencer. Most of the songs composed by Texas Federation of Music Clubs members, whose talents were rarely recognized outside of their particular district, were published privately by the composers themselves.

Anthologies of Texas music published in association with the Texas Centennial include *The Music Hour: Texas Centennial Edition,* compiled by a board of consultants in Texas (including Texas music historian Lota May Spell) and the editors of *The Music Hour*, Osbourne McConathy et al. (New York: Silver, Burdett, 1935); *Songs Texas Sings,* compiled by the Public School Division of the Texas Department of Publicity for Centennial Celebrations (Dallas, Texas: Turner, 1936); *Centennial Songs of Texas* and *Texas Frontier Ballads, 1836–1936,* compiled by Virgil O. Stamps (Dallas, Texas: Stamps–Baxter, 1936); and *10 Homeland Songs,* a collection of original songs by Naomi Ollre (Gonzales, Texas, 1936).

Three western films based on Texas subjects were released in 1936 and had direct ties to the Centennial: *The Big Show* (Republic), starring Gene Autry and filmed partly on location at the Exposition in Dallas; *The Texas Rangers* (Paramount), intended to be an official recognition of the Centennial; and *Ride, Ranger Ride* (Republic), of which the title song, recorded by the Sons of the Pioneers, was approved by Texas governor James Allred as the official "Ranger–Texas Centennial Song."

Four operas based on a mixture of Texas history and fiction were composed specifically for the Centennial: Samuel E. Asbury's *San Jacinto Cycle* (unfinished); Theophilus Fitz's *Tejas* (1932–33); Carl Venth's *La Vida de la Misión* (1935); and Otto Wick's *The Lone Star* (1935). None of these operas was produced in 1936. Among several Centennial contributions by Texas state song composer William J. Marsh is a *Centennial Mass* that was performed at the Exposition in Dallas.

BIBLIOGRAPHY: Kevin E. Mooney, Texas Centennial 1936: Music and Identity (Ph.D. dissertation, University of Texas at Austin, 1998). Kenneth B. Ragsdale, "The 1936 Texas Centennial Exposition: Music's Spectacular Showcase," *Southwestern Musician Texas Music Educator* 55.2 (September 1986) and 55.3 (October 1986).

Kevin E. Mooney

Texas Federation of Music Clubs. Formed to aid communication and cooperation among Texas musical organizations and to promote music in the state. Although various municipal music clubs were founded in the late nineteenth century, until 1915 they remained independent organizations or were affiliated with the music department of the Texas Federation of Women's Clubs.

Prompted by TFWC Music Department chairman Louise Pace of Corsicana, and by members representing the Music Festival Association and the National Federation of Music Clubs, which had been established at Chicago in 1893, the Texas Federation of Music Clubs was organized on November 12, 1915, in Brownwood, Texas, during the annual meeting of the TFWC. For her efforts Pace was offered the presidency, though she declined in order to study music in New York. At her request the office was extended to Lucil Manning Lyons, president of the Fort Worth Harmony Club. Twenty-two Texas music clubs composed the nucleus of the new organization, which then joined the National Federation of Music Clubs. Membership was open to all Texas musical organizations, from choral societies and festival associations to music study clubs. Among the original standing committees were Community Music, Public School Music, Contests, Scholarships, and the Artist Bureau for recital scheduling.

The new organization held its first annual convention in May 1916 at Waco, where the New York Philharmonic Orchestra provided the program. Ima Hogg was named second vice president. Fifty delegates attended, representing thirty Texas clubs, whose combined membership was about 1,000. By 1918, the year TFMC was chartered under Texas law, forty-eight clubs were enrolled. "Texas Bluebonnet blue" was adopted as the organization's color, with the flower as its emblem, which was designed into a pin by Tiffany and Company jewelers of New York.

During its first thirty years the Texas Federation of Music Clubs distinguished itself with music education and appreciation campaigns and with the promotion of musical therapy and musical performance. The organization achieved particular recognition for these efforts during the Great Depression, during both world wars, and in public education. During World War I the federation assisted the Red Cross, YMCA, and YWCA in providing musical entertainment for Texas army camps and scheduling musical benefits using Texas artists. TFMC also aided the war effort by encouraging the public's singing of patriotic songs, campaigning for sales of liberty bonds, contributing to the Texas War Work Council to establish and maintain canteens in Texas and France, and donating sheet music, musical instruments, phonographs, records, and player-piano rolls to Texas military installations.

Postwar effort involved bolstering the "Americanization" movement through music, a reflection of the national trend toward isolation, which inspired federation-conducted singsongs statewide each Armistice Day and contributed Texas support for the establishment of a national conservatory of music, envisioned to prevent the need for promising Texan and other American artists to study in Europe.

The number of affiliate clubs grew to seventy-seven by 1920. By the time of the administration of Minnie Cox Hambrick (1921–23), TFMC was involved in Music Settlement work to the underprivileged, vocational instruction of the blind, and furnishing music and instruments to and organizing concerts in charitable institutions, schools, and prison camps. The Texas Federation, like its national counterpart, promoted American music (though specifically by Texas composers), National Music Week and the Music Memory Contest (which were nationally concerted public-awareness campaigns), and music appreciation courses in the public schools.

Partly because of TFMC support, Texas cities began giving credit in public school for private music study. Under Hambrick's administration Texas led all other states in service and won awards for the most consistent growth. In 1923 the federation had divided the state into seven districts and had increased its number of committees to seventeen, including Public School Music, Industrial Music to promote musical activities in industry, Municipal Opera, Pageantry and Folk Dancing, the Texas Composer's Guild to promote Texas music, a state symphony orchestra, state festivals, and the Traveling Music Library. By 1928, 320 clubs were affiliated with TFMC.

On February 1, 1928, *Texas Music News* premiered as the federation bulletin under Mrs. James L. Price's administration, with Mrs. Charles G. Norton as editor. This publication replaced a small newsletter that Mrs. R. J. Skiles had issued at her expense during her presidency (1923–25) and made unnecessary the continuation of a two-page column of TFMC news printed in *The Musicale*.

By 1929 federation activities were so numerous and its organization so large that it withdrew as a dues-paying department of its parent organization, the Texas Federation of Women's Clubs. An official seal was adopted, consisting of a Lone Star surrounded by a wreath of oak leaves atop an appropriate bit of music—"*Texas Our Texas*," composed by William J. Marsh, chairman of the federation's Texas Composer's Guild. TFMC efforts already had persuaded the state legislature to adopt Marsh's "sufficiently dignified" tune (as one federation president called it) as the state song.

With the onslaught of the Great Depression many clubs were forced to disband, but the federation remained active even in the dismal years of 1932–34. Its goal was to maintain musicians in order to "conserve American cultural traditions now threatened with annihilation," and to encourage music as a morale lifter in hard times. Texas continued to lead in the number of federated clubs as the TFMC sponsored radio programs featuring musical artists, donated musical instruments and radios to schools, and gave concerts in rural areas.

Supporting the campaign of the National Federation of Music Clubs to keep music and allied arts "in their rightful places in the 'New Deal'," TFMC helped to implement the Federal Music Project in Texas, thereby giving employment and opportunity to many unemployed musicians. In 1933 the federation added International Music Relations to its Department of American Music and adopted a Department of Motion Pictures with its Education Department, which sponsored many films and sought the production of superior music scores as a permanent requisite of motion-picture production. TFMC also sponsored numerous radio programs during the depression; sixty-five programs were presented from Paris and Longview in 1938 alone.

For the Texas Centennial in 1936 the Texas Federation of Music Clubs established a board to select Texas music appropriate for Centennial use. More than 300 manuscripts were submitted statewide, and the chosen pieces became "official Centennial music." In connection with the Federal Music Project, TFMC's 459 affiliate clubs helped to carry out musical events throughout the Centennial celebrations in each district, a highlight being the Texas Centennial Pageant at Dallas, which depicted "in drama, in color, in the dance, in song, the hardships, struggles, joys, and achievements" of Texas history. Throughout the Centennial each district of TFMC presented artistic programs, aiming "to spread the Gospel of Music throughout the entire State." Additionally, as a Centennial goal the federation sought to retain the hundreds of young Texans who sought collegiate musical training outside the state by establishing a fine arts department at the University of Texas. In large part because of what one Texas senator called TFMC's "zealous and persistent" petitioning of the governor, state legislature, and board of regents, the university founded its College of Fine Arts and Music Department at the Austin campus in 1938.

In the late 1930s Texas joined the national organization in promoting international understanding through music as an "antidote for the current war mania." During World War II, the antidote having failed, the Texas Federation of Music Clubs, together with other organizations, sponsored "Americanism Week" and the "Loyalty through Music Crusade." In 1941 TFMC established a Defense Department, which throughout the war aided USO entertainment, contributed funds to the Red Cross, and donated phonographs, records, radios, music, and musical instruments to military bases in Texas. At the suggestion of the U.S. State Department, the TFMC promoted Latin-American music to promote good relations with American allies to the south. Homefront club activities included production of music in the war industries, twilight musicals, park concerts, radio broadcasts, folk festivals, weekly community sings and dances for enlisted men, army-federation shows, and war bond drives.

TFMC also worked closely with the Joint Army and Navy Recreation Committee and helped to sponsor 700 shows for 245,000 men. The federation was named by the war department as the source from which post commanders should secure musical equipment, since the music industries were then producing war materials. The federation also conducted or encouraged musical therapy in military hospitals and prisoner-of-war camps. By February 1945 TFMC had music-rehabilitation programs in three of the four Texas VA hospitals, four of the five general hospitals, and in many camp and field hospitals, in addition to supplying musical instruments to hospitals ships and trains.

For its war service activities TFMC was awarded the national organization's highest honor in 1945, a prestigious supplement to a reputation that already included the formation of the first juvenile music club in the United States and the origin of National Music Week, both traceable to the Dallas district; Lucil Lyons as the first two-term national president; and the premiere of the Department of College and University Work, which was adopted by the national federation.

For some time after the war the federation continued to lobby for music in hospital therapy and as always encouraged local music-making and music education in the public schools. Nevertheless, TFMC membership and activities diminished significantly in the post–World War II era. Although the federation increased the original seven districts designated in 1928 to twelve by 1961 in order to equalize the number of counties in each district and to decrease the travel time of district presidents, the total number of clubs dropped to 156 in 1955 and continued to fall thereafter. Records indicate that TFMC activities in the 1950s and 1960s did not maintain the civic, artistic, or political impact that characterized the first thirty years of the organization's history, a reflection of the cultural changes brought on with the rise of movies, radio, and especially television, and other forms of alternative entertainment.

Throughout the 1970s and 1980s, however, affiliated clubs in the twelve districts continued to promote musical programs as well as award scholarships. By the mid-1980s this promotion also focused on commemorating the Texas Sesquicentennial. The official publication of TFMC, *The Musical Messenger*, announced both regional events and news of the National Federation of Music Clubs.

At the annual state convention in Del Rio in March 1990, the Texas Federation of Music Clubs celebrated its Diamond Jubilee. The NFMC honored TFMC with several awards of merit for that same year.

During the 1990s and into the twenty-first century TFMC continued to sponsor twelve annual Texas Junior music festivals for the twelve districts, which awarded scholarships to young musicians. The organization sponsored a triennial Festival of Texas Composers concert series. Individual clubs still practiced music therapy in nursing homes and hospitals, promoted festivals, and gave scholarships.

BIBLIOGRAPHY: Mrs. James Hambrick, "Early History of the Texas Federation of Music Clubs," *Texas Music News*, November 1939. Lota M. Spell, *Music in Texas* (Austin, 1936; rpt., New York: AMS, 1973). Texas Federation of Music Clubs Archives, Center for American History, University of Texas at Austin. *Craig H. Roell*

Texas Folklife Festival. Grew out of ideas formed in 1968, when the University of Texas Institute of Texan Cultures took part in the Smithsonian Institution's National Folklife Festival in Washington, D.C. Inspired by the success of the national event, the Institute of Texan Cultures began planning a Texas festival.

Under the leadership of the exhibits director, O. T. Baker, the country's first statewide folklife festival was held in September 1972, as an extension of the educational programs of the Institute of Texan Cultures. A major thrust was to preserve and display the ethnic traditions and pioneer skills that had helped to form the Lone Star State. Essential initial funding was provided by the Moody Foundation of Galveston, the Houston Endowment, and the Ewing Halsell Foundation of San Antonio. Hundreds of individuals, as well as various fraternal, ethnic, social, religious, professional, commercial, and industrial organizations, provided goods, services, and equipment. The San Antonio Hotel Association and the H. B. Zachry Company, general contractors, provided other essential services.

Since the first year the festival has been entirely self-supporting. In addition, food and beverage sales have provided millions of dollars to participating groups to help sustain their ethnic and cultural programs. The Texas Folklife Festival has been held every year since 1972 on the Institute of Texan Cultures grounds at the HemisFair '68 plaza in San Antonio. Paid admissions that first year totaled $63,565, and many more were admitted free the first two nights because some of the food booths ran short of food. Some 2,000 participants and staff provided entertainment, demonstrated skills, served food, or worked in other program areas.

In 1973 the festival was caught in the middle of Hurricane Delia, and after the first three years the festival was moved to early August to avoid the September rains. Begin-

Matachines drummer Florencio Ortiz, from Dolores, performing in a matachin dance–drama, ca.1990s. Ortiz is part of a group, Los Matachines de la Cruz de la Ladrillera, that was invited to the American Folklife Festival in Washington, D.C. in 1968. Photograph by Jane Levine, courtesy Texas Folklife Resources.

ning in the year 2000, the festival was moved from August to June to avoid the hottest part of the summer. In the years when bad weather has interfered, the activities have simply moved onto the covered veranda surrounding the institute building. Since 1972 the festival has continued to grow.

BIBLIOGRAPHY: Institute of Texan Cultures website (http://www.texancultures.utsa.edu/public/index.htm), accessed February 3, 2003. *Texas Folklife Festival, September 7–10, 1972* (San Antonio: University of Texas Institute of Texan Cultures, 1972).   *Art Leatherwood*

Texas Folklife Resources. A private, nonprofit organization founded in 1984 and dedicated to the preservation and celebration of the traditions and folkways of Texas; headquartered in Austin. Through exhibitions, concerts, and other programs, TFR sponsors the celebration of traditional Texas culture in communities across the state. The organization also seeks out and documents folk artists and others living and working throughout Texas whose industry relates to traditional culture. Through these and other means, TFR seeks to perpetuate Texas folklife today and preserve it for future generations.

One aspect of the organization's mission focuses on the fieldwork within Texas communities necessary for uncovering and documenting all types of traditional practices. TFR also offers Apprenticeships in the Folk Arts, a program that has granted more than fifty awards since 1987. Since 1992, in conjunction with the Texas Commission on the Arts, TFR has sponsored Touring Traditions, a program that organizes performances in communities across the state. The TFR Community Residency Program allows communities across Texas to host traditional musicians for weeklong programs.

TFR also sponsors the Texas Country Roots audio documentary series, which includes interviews and musical selections that explore the music of the state. Narrated by singer Jerry Jeff Walker, the series includes thirteen 8_-minute segments with such titles as *Fiddlin' Around* and *Honky-Tonk Heroes*. The series is available at no cost to radio stations, arts organizations, and educational institutions for non-profit use only. TFR has also sponsored the Texas Master Series of performances at the historic Paramount Theatre in Austin. The organization operates a gallery at its Austin headquarters. The founding director of the TFR, Pat Jasper, was succeeded by Martha Norkunas in 2002.

BIBLIOGRAPHY: Austin *Chronicle*, 21.51 (August 23, 2002). Texas Folklife Resources website (http://www.main.org/tfr/index.html).   *Brandy Schnautz*

Texas International Pop Festival, 1969. The first major rock festival in Texas; held August 30 through September 1, 1969, at the Dallas International Speedway in Lewisville; produced in part by Angus Wynne III of Wynne Entertainment. The Texas festival was held only two weeks after the legendary Woodstock festival in Woodstock, New York. It was unusual in the wide variety of musical acts it attracted.

With a budget of only $120,000, the promoters booked twenty-six of the biggest names in blues, rock-and-roll, and psychedelic rock. Janis Joplin, Sam and Dave, Sly and the Family Stone, Santana, Canned Heat, the Grass Roots, B. B. King, Chicago Transit Authority, Tony Joe White, Spirit, Johnny Winter, Sweetwater, Ten Years After, Freddie King, and a virtually unknown British band, Led Zeppelin, all performed during the three-day festival. The musical acts were not paid much to perform; Led Zeppelin and Janis Joplin were paid the most—$10,000 each. Some major groups that wanted to perform could not get in to play. A band from Michigan, Grand Funk Railroad, was allowed to perform only after the members agreed to play free and pay their own expenses.

The festival was extensively advertised through radio and newspaper and was promoted at Woodstock. Consequently, enthusiasts from all over the United States, and from numerous foreign countries, poured into Lewisville to pay the admission fee of $6.50 a day. Although the promoters anticipated a crowd of over 200,000, actual attendance for the three days was more like 120,000. The festival lost money, but was generally considered a success by those who attended. The promoters created a "carnival-like" atmosphere that featured booths catering to "flower children." Astrologers, painters, artists, craftsmen, and leather workers; sellers of incense, T-shirts, jewelry, and candles; and food vendors all peddled their wares. Most who attended the festival camped on the adjacent 10,000-acre lakefront. At night, many of the performers joined the campers and played without charge. Initially, police and local authorities were concerned about drug usage and traffic problems on nearby Interstate 35. Although there were a few drug overdoses and problems associated with the intense heat, in general the festival ran very smoothly. The primary complaint from local residents was that the festival participants swam naked in Lake Lewisville.

BIBLIOGRAPHY: Dallas *Morning News*, August 7, 29, 30, 31, 1969.   *James Head*

Texas-Mexican Conjunto. An important type of musical ensemble developed by Texas-Mexican working-class musicians, who adopted the accordion—the main instrument in conjunto music—and the polka from nineteenth-century German settlers in northern Mexico.

The conjunto grew out of the cultural links between Texas and northern Mexico at the end of the nineteenth century, when inexpensive one-row accordions became readily available. Tejano musicians took up the accordion as a solo instrument and used it at rural social events such as the fandango, a combination of dancing, eating, gambling, and other merriment, which remained a part of Tejano working-class life to the end of the nineteenth century. In the late 1890s the musicians began to pair the accordion with the *tambora de rancho* (a homemade goatskin drum) and later the *bajo sexto* (the twelve-string guitar).

Narciso Martínez has been called the "father" of the modern conjunto for promoting the accordion and the *bajo sexto* and for his unparalleled creativity as an accordionist. Martínez, also known as "*el huracán del valle*" ("the hurricane of the Valley") for his musical virtuosity, became a wizard of the two-row accordion in the 1930s. Santiago Jiménez Sr., of San Antonio, was another outstanding accordionist of this formative period. He contributed one innovation to the conjunto by adding a *tololoche* (contrabass), which, however, did not become a standard feature of the ensemble until the 1940s and was replaced with the electric bass in the late 1950s. Valerio Longoria, one of the foremost conjunto musicians of the 1940s and 1950s, combined his vocal talent with his accordion playing, and his repertoire increased interest in accordion-accompanied singing. Tejana singers also came to the fore in the 1930s with Lydia Mendoza. Female duets, which were popular by the early 1950s, were often accompanied by the increasingly popular accordion. One record featured Martínez on accordion with Mendoza and the famous Tejana duet Carmen y Laura as vocalists.

The vocals Longoria incorporated were called *canciones rancheras* ("ranch songs"). They became standard features of the conjunto. *Rancheras* are still sung in the slow (waltz) or fast (polka) tempo. Longoria shaped the modern conjunto in several other ways. He added the bolero, previously considered a part of "genteel" music because of its regal pace. This addition resulted in more intricate singing because vocalists in the bolero were required to use harmony and rhythm with more acumen. Also, the conjunto audience's acceptance of the bolero signified growing musical sophistication. Longoria altered the accordion's reeds to give it a distinctive *sonido ronco* ("hoarse sound") and was the first to use drums in the ensemble, a change considered the most radical innovation in conjunto music. With these alterations, as well as the addition of amplification, the modern conjunto was established as a four-instrument band: accordion, *bajo sexto*, electric bass, and drums.

Since the 1960s the Texas-Mexican conjunto has grown in prominence among Hispanics throughout the state, particularly in Austin, San Antonio, Alice, and Corpus Christi. Conjuntos headed by Paulino Bernal, Roberto Pulido, Rubén Vela, and Leonardo (Flaco) Jiménez gained stature during this era. A few innovations have occurred. Paulino Bernal and Esteban Jordán have imbued their conjuntos with their unique personal styles. Bernal augmented his group's sound by including three-part vocals, and Jordan, who has criticized conjuntos for their rigid attachment to the traditional polka approach, has blended other musical forms, including jazz, into his playing style. By 1990 he was considered the leading individual experimenter in the new conjunto sound. Other recent groups, such as Inocencia and Emilio Navaira and Río, have taken Jordán's vision to heart and added saxophones, keyboards, and synthesizers to their sound. The result, called *conjuntos orquestal*, have gained popularity and have performed in the Tejano Conjunto Festival in San Antonio.

In recent years the Texas-Mexican conjunto has drawn more general interest. Flaco Jiménez, the son of Santiago Jiménez, has played in Europe. He has also added the conjunto beat to other popular music by teaming up with other musicians, including the Texas Tornadoes. Their "Soy de San Luis" received a Grammy in 1991. Conjunto thus found new audiences. The conjunto's distinctively rousing delivery of its trademark *música alegre* ("happy music") has seemingly transcended ethnic and language barriers. The annual Tejano Conjunto Festival and the Conjunto Music Hall of Fame have also increased its prestige.

Since 1982 the Hall of Fame has recognized the achievements of twenty-seven conjunto musicians or promoters, including Narciso Martínez, Tony de la Rosa, and Juan Viesca. In 1991 it inducted Lydia Mendoza. Although the role of women in conjuntos has been mostly limited to singing, accordionists Eva Ybarra and Lupita Rodela garnered critical and public recognition. Many major conjunto musicians have worked alongside their audience as fieldworkers or common laborers, composing and playing music in their free time, often for meager compensation. *Música alegre* brought cheer. Some made their careers playing the "taco circuit," the public dances organized along the roads that Texas-Mexican cottonpickers followed to the harvests.

Although individuals propelled conjunto music to new stages, the conjunto phenomenon emerged from a collective folk tradition to which many individuals contributed. By 1990 the Texas-Mexican conjunto had emerged as a distinct musical form that, like the corrido and *orquesta*, was the product of a few acclaimed and countless uncelebrated border musicians.

BIBLIOGRAPHY: Joe Nick Patoski, "Squeeze Play," *Texas Monthly*, August 1990. Manuel Peña, *The Texas-Mexican Conjunto: History of a Working-Class Music* (Austin: University of Texas Press, 1985). *Teresa Palomo Acosta*

Texas Music. The first magazine of its kind, a quarterly devoted to celebrating and perpetuating the music of

Texas; first issued in the winter of 2000 under the editorship of Stewart Ramser. The mission of the magazine is three-fold: to entertain its readers, to showcase popular artists as well as those with potential to rise, and to relate the history of Texas music through interviews and articles. The magazine also reviews recent releases and showcases acts appearing throughout the state.

According to the "Letter from the Publisher/Editor" in the magazine's first issue, the idea for the publication grew out of Ramser's own experiences. In locations as varied and remote as Paris and Hawaii, he was able to hear live artists and bands whose attraction was not only their talents, but also their connections to the Lone Star State. In accordance with the editor's vision, *Texas Music* is not limited to showcasing only country-and-western or other genres of music typically associated with Texas. Instead, the magazine attempts to include all types of Texas music and musicians. In addition to the published magazine format, *Texas Music* maintains its own regularly updated website, which includes additional band and venue profiles, clips from songs, interviews, music news, trivia, and a chat room.

BIBLIOGRAPHY: *Texas Music* website (www.texasmusiconline.com), accessed June 5, 2002.

Brandy Schnautz

Texas Music Museum. A nonprofit organization established in Austin in 1984 as part of the Texas Sesquicentennial Project. It includes an archive, a museum, and a variety of exhibits on the history of music in Texas. Emphasizing the great cultural variety of Texas as reflected through the state's music, the museum "conducts research, collects photographs, artifacts, and documents relating to all aspects of Texas music and provides exhibits to other museums, schools, libraries, history centers, and other public facilities throughout the state." It houses an extensive collection of exhibits and archives focusing on the music of American Indians, Mexican Americans, Anglo Americans, African Americans, German Americans, and Czech Americans, which provides a wealth of information on conjunto, Tejano, country and western, ragtime, jazz, gospel, classical, and a variety of other musical forms.

The Museum also sponsors musical performances and educational seminars. The Texas Music Museum is endorsed by the Texas Music Association, the Texas Music Educators Association, and the Texas Music Teachers Association. Its headquarters is on East Eleventh Street, but most of its exhibits are at various other sites around Austin.

BIBLIOGRAPHY: "Our Mission," brochure produced by the Texas Music Museum, Austin. Texas Music Museum website (http://members.tripod.com/~texasmusicmuseum/), accessed June 5, 2002. *Gary Hartman*

Texas Star Inn. On the Bandera highway in Leon Valley, Texas, just northwest of San Antonio; a music venue established in 1946 as a beer joint and motorcyclists' hangout. Today the former Texas Star is a popular barbeque restaurant known as Grady's. Its main entry is filled with antiques and autographed photos of country musicians

Poster advertising an event sponsored by the Texas Music Museum: "An Evening of Texas Barrelhouse Blues Piano," November 1987. Texas Poster Art Collection, CAH; CN 11522.

who played at the inn or ate at the restaurant. The two-story building, constructed of Texas limestone blocks and sporting a Texas Star neon sign in the shape of Texas, has long been a landmark.

The place was originally a mom-and-pop operation run by Mama Aselee Mattie and Papa Frank Klein, who purchased it in 1952. Papa Klein was a singer and guitarist, and his Texas Star Playboys, a group that included young Larry Nolen, called the inn home until the early 1960s. The Texas Star Playboys appeared on KEYL television, now KENS in San Antonio, from 1951 to 1953, during the early days of TV. The Texas Star was a place in the finest Texas tradition, where one could go for food, drink, and "down home" music. Texas singer Johnny Bush, who later wrote Willie Nelson's hit "Whiskey River," got his first professional job at the Texas Star in 1954. After going on to a successful singing and songwriting career, Bush returned to the inn in 1984 to celebrate his many years in music. Many other famous musicians played at the inn over the years, including Willie Nelson, Ray Price, Faron Young, and Roger Miller. Miller, Nelson, and Bush were all in Ray Price's band at one time.

The Texas Star also provided a venue for local talent. Jim Noblett, of the Cactus Rose Band, reminisces about jamming with Johnny Bush there. Noblett also met his future bride, Linda Jo McMillan, at the inn when she was singing with Keith Fillmore's band. San Antonio has long been a military town, and many servicemen and women found good food, drink, and music at the Texas Star Inn. For many the nightclub was an introduction to a real Texas honky-tonk.

The inn was sold in 1979 to Polly Herschberger, Gene Pilton, and Dodie Sullivan. In the mid-1980s, Polly and Lorene Lucky bought it. Parts of the movie *Waltz Across Texas* were filmed there. The dance hall ceased operation in 1993 and became Grady's Bar-B-Que restaurant, a place where recorded country music still plays all the time. Grady's has live entertainment on weekends.

BIBLIOGRAPHY: Bill Porterfield, *The Greatest Honky Tonks in Texas* (Dallas: Taylor, 1983). San Antonio *Express News*, May 9, 2002. Texas Music Resources, *Honky Tonk Texas, U.S.A.* (http://www.honkytonktx .com/), accessed February 20, 2003. Geronimo Treviño III, *Dance Halls and Last Calls: A History of Texas Country Music* (Plano, Texas: Republic of Texas Press, 2002).

James Kent Cox

Texas State Sängerbund. An association of German singing societies. After a successful Fourth of July celebration in 1853, the New Braunfels Germania male singing society invited similar organizations from Austin, San Antonio, and Sisterdale to a state *Sängerfest* (singers' festival), held in New Braunfels on October 15 and 16, 1853. Each group sang a cappella separately and joined together for works by Felix Mendelssohn and Heinrich Marschner.

At the second *Sängerfest*, held in San Antonio in May 1854, when the societies formed the Texas State Sängerbund (Deutsch–Texanischer Sängerbund or German–Texan Singers' League), participation extended to singers from Coletoville, La Grange, Indianola, and Victoria. The next year's and each succeeding *Sängerfest* before the Civil War (New Braunfels, May 1855, October 1856, and October 1858; Fredericksburg, May 1859) brought added members or increased musical sophistication. In 1860 the first participating mixed chorus (male and female) contributed excerpts from Franz Joseph Haydn's *Creation*.

The Civil War disrupted plans for an 1861 *Sängerfest* in Austin, for which orchestral participation had been planned, and the festivals did not begin again until September 1870 in San Antonio, on a more modest scale. There was a *Sängerfest* in New Braunfels in May 1873. The festival in San Antonio in October 1874 was a milestone. An orchestra of symphonic proportions, conducted by Professor Müller, participated in the public concert. When San Antonio hosted the state festival again in 1877 because New Braunfels could no longer afford the burden, the city added an enlarged orchestra of nearly forty musicians under Emil Ludwig Zawadil. Mixed choruses and massed choruses began to take some of the emphasis from individual singing societies, but each local group had an opportunity to sing at the banquet.

Not to be outdone, Austin imported the orchestra of the National Theater of New Orleans from St. Louis, Missouri, for the April 1879 *Sängerfest*. With the addition of out-of-state musicians and non-Germanic politicians to speak, the festivals now became more oriented to the entire community rather than primarily to the German element.

When distant and wealthy Galveston invited the singing societies for a *Sängerfest* of two massive concerts in May 1881, the choruses of the New Braunfels–Fredericksburg area felt disfranchised and seceded from the state Sängerbund to found their own West-texanischer Gebirgs-Sängerbund (West Texas Hill Country Singers' League), which has held modest but musically and socially satisfying festivals for more than a century. While hosting the state festival in May 1883, Dallas added a third concert and an English-language chorus to the program for the first time and attracted audiences of up to 4,500 for the performances.

At that time the festivals, held at two-year intervals, began to rotate among Houston, San Antonio, Austin, Galveston, and Dallas. With minor variations this practice continued until 1916. The number of concerts ranged up to five for each festival; choruses of school children began to participate; the massed male choruses and larger mixed choruses shared with the orchestra and imported soloists (often of world fame) the increasingly sophisticated content of the festival concerts, while individual male choruses were almost totally relegated to the jovial *Kommerse*.

Wherever held, the festivals became the impetus for expanded musical activity on the purely local level, while they themselves ceased to be the sole property of the Germans as progressively more outsiders participated in the concerts and attended them. During World War I, the *Sängerfeste* ceased when German Texans were suspected of "Hunnish" collaboration. They began again in 1921 and have continued on a modest scale resembling the social and musical meetings of the early 1870s: individual choruses from San Antonio, Dallas, Austin, and Houston; massed choruses; a band concert; and an evening dance to celebrate a rich German heritage in Texas.

BIBLIOGRAPHY: Theodore Albrecht, German Singing Societies in Texas (Ph.D. dissertation, North Texas State University, 1975). Theodore Albrecht, "The Music Libraries of the German Singing Societies in Texas, 1850–1855," *Notes: The Quarterly Journal of the Music Library Association* 31 (March 1975). Oscar Haas, *A Chronological History of the Singers of German Song in Texas* (New Braunfels, Texas, 1948). Edward Schmidt, *Eine kleine Geschichte des Gesanges in Westtexas und des Gebirgs-Sängerbundes* (Fredericksburg, Texas, 1906). Moritz Tiling, *History of the German Element in Texas* (Houston: Rein and Sons, 1913). *Theodore Albrecht*

Texas Top Hands. One of the state's oldest continuously performing western-swing bands; debuted in 1945 with Clarence J. "Sleepy" Short on fiddle, George Edwin "Knee-High" Holley on string bass, Walter Kleypas on piano and accordion, and William Wayne "Rusty" Locke on steel guitar. Manager Johnny H. "Curly" Williams played acoustic guitar. The Top Hands had an early-morning spot on WOAI radio, which was at that time a 50,000-watt clear-channel station in San Antonio.

The group had performed since 1941 under the name Texas Tumbleweeds. Then Bob Symonds, the former man-

The Texas Top Hands standing beside their tour bus in front of radio station KONO in San Antonio, ca. 1950. UT Institute of Texan Cultures at San Antonio, No. Z-1361.

ager of the Tumbleweeds, came home from a stint with the Marines in World War II. When he filed a lawsuit to reclaim his band name, the group changed its name over a weekend, appearing under the old name on Friday and showing up Monday morning as the Texas Top Hands, the name that they still retain.

They traveled to New York in 1946 to record for Savoy and to back singer–songwriter "Red River" Dave McEnery on his Continental recording sessions. With McEnery, the Top Hands made several film shorts in 1947. That year they also co-starred in a ground-breaking movie filmed near San Antonio. The film, *Echo Ranch*, departed from the usual Hollywood westerns of the day in that it used no artificial scenery but was shot in natural outdoor settings. San Antonians made up the entire cast. Present-day Top Hands manager Ray Sczepanik owns a copy of the film.

In 1949 the Top Hands began recording on their own label, Everstate, on which they subsequently produced more than fifty recordings. The first—"Bandera Waltz" by O. B. "Easy" Adams—became a regional smash and remains a dance hall classic. The lament rode for fifty-two weeks at the top of the Hillbilly Hit Parade on KMAC. Slim Whitman, Ernest Tubb, Rex Allen, Jimmy Wakely, Adolph Hofner, David Houston, and nine other performers have recorded the song.

Tired of seven-night-a-week performing, with the Top Hands and with a band of his own, Kleypas left the band in 1952. Rusty Locke then managed the band until 1955, when he formed his own group. That left Easy Adams as

leader until 1979, when he suffered a heart attack. Ray Sczepanik replaced him and still leads the band. Locke later rejoined and played with the group for several years.

The Top Hands backed Hank Williams at his last Texas concert, on December 22, 1952, at the Macdona Shooting Club, near San Antonio; Williams died a few days later. The Top Hands have opened for or backed other well-known singers such as Webb Pierce, Tex Ritter, Moe Bandy, Johnny Rodriguez, Jerry Lee Lewis, George Morgan, Jackie Ward, and Mel Tillis. During the early 1950s, while the band played over radio station KABC, Gene Autry, William Boyd (known as Hopalong Cassidy), Wild Bill Elliot, Chill Wills, and other movie stars appeared with the band.

The Top Hands became known throughout Texas for their many appearances at local festivals and rodeos. They were the only band to perform at the first Poteet Strawberry Festival in 1948. On April 1, 1997, Locke, age seventy-seven, returned to the festival, where he sang "Milk Cow Blues" and "Westphalia Waltz." Other appearances include the State Fair in Dallas (1955), where the show was broadcast live. Again, the Top Hands were the only band to perform. They also appeared at the Fort Worth Fat Stock Show, the Central Texas Fair in Temple, the Stompede and Rodeo in Bandera, Buccaneer Days in Corpus Christi; the Oil Show in Odessa, the Wool Show and Rodeo in San Angelo, the Stockman's Ball in Laredo, the Peanut Festival in Floresville, the Watermelon Jubilee in Stockdale, the Horse Show and Fair in Junction, the rodeo in El Paso, and the Pecos Rodeo (where they were a regular act from 1950 to 1976). In their heyday they performed twenty-five to thirty evenings a month. Among notable Texans in their audiences, they entertained Allan Shivers, Beauford Jester, Bill Clements, and John Connally. Their road trip in early 1949 promoted the first San Antonio Stock Show and Rodeo, at which they also performed. The band returned for the show's thirty-fifth anniversary under the direction of Ray Sczepanik. In 1955 the Top Hands were selected to represent the Lone Star Brewery.

The Texas Top Hands were inducted into the Texas Western Swing Hall of Fame on May 9, 1992, in Austin. Former members of the band include Johnny Bush (drummer), Charlie Harris (guitarist), and Buck Buchanan (fiddler), all of whom later became members of Ray Price's Cherokee Cowboy Band. The band had several releases on the Melco label in the mid-1960s and three for TNT in the early 1960s. In early 2003, Kleypas and Locke were the only two surviving members of the original band. Kleypas lived at Canyon Lake with his wife, Lucille, with whom he had celebrated more than sixty wedding anniversaries. Lucille is credited with naming the Top Hands. (A "top hand" is the best worker on a ranch.) Locke lived with his wife, Cora, in Kirby, a suburb of San Antonio, where he owned and operated a television repair shop. Both Kleypas and Locke still make occasional guest appearances.

BIBLIOGRAPHY: "American Folk Music," *Billboard Encyclopedia of Music 1946-1947* (Cincinnati: Billboard, 1947). Paul Kingsbury, ed., *Encyclopedia of Country Music* (New York: Oxford University Press, 1998). Duncan McLean, *Lone Star Swing* (New York: Norton, 1997). "Texas Top Hands" (http://www.jerryconnell.com/music/artists/tophand/maintoph.htm), accessed November 21, 2002. *J. E. Jordan*

Thielepape, Wilhelm Carl August. Engineer, musician, and mayor of San Antonio; b. Wabern, Hesse, Germany, July 10, 1814; d. Chicago, August 7, 1904; son of Werner Philipp and Elisabeth (Thompson) Thielepape. He graduated from a *Gymnasium* in Kassel, attended the university in either Göttingen or Bonn, and during the 1840s was active as an engineer at Berlin, Bielefeld, and Schwelm. Among his earliest *Lieder* are songs dedicated to Mathilde Gössling, whom he married in 1841.

In 1850 Thielepape settled in Indianola, Texas, where he established himself as a surveyor; he moved to San Antonio in 1854. He sang tenor in the Männergesang-Verein (men's singing society) and soon became its assistant conductor. His professional activities included architecture, engineering, teaching, photography, and lithography, the last with abolitionist newspaper editor Adolph Douai. In 1855 Thielepape surveyed the townsite of Uvalde. In 1857 he designed the San Antonio Casino, a 400-seat auditorium and social center used by the famed Casino Club, and possibly helped plan the Menger Hotel. On April 2, 1858, he was among the organizers of the city's German-English School. He moved to New Braunfels in 1859 to design the Comal County Courthouse. Like many Union sympathizers of German origin, Thielepape probably spent part of the Civil War in Eagle Pass and Mexico. He was among those who raised the Union flag over the Alamo on July 21, 1865. He founded the Beethoven Männerchor shortly thereafter and conducted the chorus at the Casino on October 14.

Thielepape was appointed Reconstruction mayor of San Antonio on November 8, 1867. He supervised an administration that built bridges, laid macadam streets, strengthened the public schools, and provided for the eventual arrival of the railroad. Throughout these years he continued to conduct and compose and founded a singing school. On March 12, 1872, he was removed from office, but he remained active in the community until, in April 1874, he turned his chorus over to Andreas Scheidemantel and moved to Chicago to participate in the building boom that followed the Chicago Fire.

Even in retirement, Thielepape continued to compose; he wrote his last song in 1899. His compositions, influenced by Mendelssohn and Spohr, included *Lieder*, six duets for soprano and tenor, and incidental music for Ludwig Anzengruber's play *Der Meineidbauer*, all with piano accompaniment; and one unaccompanied male chorus, *Der Wind und der Wellen Lied.*

BIBLIOGRAPHY: Theodore Albrecht, German Singing Societies in Texas (Ph.D. dissertation, North Texas State University, 1975). Theodore Albrecht, San Antonio's Singing Mayor: W. C. A. Thielepape, 1814-1904 (MS, University of Texas Institute of Texan Cultures, San Antonio).

Theodore Albrecht

Thomas Goggan and Brothers. The first music house in the state; in Galveston and San Antonio. Irishman Thomas S. Goggan moved to Texas in 1866 with a complete stock of musical instruments and opened his original retail store at the corner of East Market and Twenty-second Street in Galveston.

Goggan attended St. Edwards University in Austin and Springhill College in Mobile, Alabama. He married Euginia Mangum, daughter of Uvalde rancher W. A. Mangum. The company motto was "Everything in Music." According to what may be his first advertisement in the Dallas *Herald* in 1866, "Thos. Goggan, Dealer in Sheet Music, Music Books, and all kinds of Musical Instruments...has a very extensive stock of goods in his line. Persons wishing music or musical instruments cannot do better than to give him a call." Similar ads list Goggan as a retail agent for Peters, Webb and Company pianos, Mason and Hamlin organs, and the fine line of Chickering and Sons pianos.

In 1868 Goggan was the authorized agent for the *U.S. Musical Review.* An extensive advertiser, he also circulated his company name throughout the 1870s by sending the latest sheet music "hits" to major Texas newspapers such as the Dallas *Herald*, which in turn would announce the titles to the public and thank the Goggan firm for its patronage. Although the Galveston store remained the company headquarters, Goggan eventually established sales branches over much of the state, shipping pianos and other musical instruments by wagon and ox-team. By 1870 he had taken into business a brother, John, and the firm—now called Thos. Goggan & Bro.—was listed in ads as being the authorized dealer for Knabe as well as Steinway and Sons pianos, "The name of either being a guarantee to themselves and need no puffing," Goggan wrote about the high quality of his merchandise. But the firm did not rely solely on the prestige of name brands for sales. As another ad headed "Pianos! Pianos! Pianos!" put it, "Remember—you can buy any make of Piano at Goggan's Music Store at ten percent below Factory prices."

A branch was opened in San Antonio about 1883, and the firm's name changed to Thomas Goggan & Bros., when Goggan took into business a younger brother, Mike, born about 1854 in County Kerry, Ireland. Mike Goggan assumed charge of the San Antonio store, which grew in importance as a center of distribution, especially because El Paso and Amarillo were good markets for the firm. The San Antonio store, called Goggan Palace of Music, was located at Broadway and Travis in the early twentieth century, and sold radios, phonographs, records, sheet music, and string and wind instruments, as well as all manner of pianos, from uprights and grands to player and reproducing pianos. The piano brands sold were nationally famous: Steinway and Sons, A. B. Chase, Schumann, Weber, Aeolian, Duo-Art, and also "Goggan." The store used the slogan, "Tell the Truth and Shame the Devil," and was a meeting place for many music celebrities.

By 1885 Goggan ads announced the firm as the "largest piano house in Texas" and the "oldest music house in Texas." Nevertheless, the company's history is sketchy. City directories indicate the San Antonio store changed addresses at least twice, though the Galveston headquarters apparently remained at its original location. According to his obituary in the San Antonio *Express* (November 27, 1914), Mike Goggan left the company and established himself in independent business after the deaths of his brothers (Thomas, ca. 1903, and John, date unknown), by which time the family firm had been incorporated and he had severed his connection with it. The *Texas State Gazetteer and Business Directory* for 1914–15 identifies *Mrs.* John Goggan as president of Thomas Goggan & Bros., Incorporated, with Thomas S. Goggan (perhaps a son) as vice president and secretary. The directory also listed Mike Goggan's Musical Goods, located at 225 E. Houston in San Antonio.

There is no doubt that Thomas Goggan & Bros. was a reputable and extensive dealer of musical instruments, but it is unclear whether the firm ever manufactured pianos. Available city directories for Galveston and San Antonio show addresses for sales offices and showrooms, but not for a factory. Alfred Dolge did not mention the Goggan firm in his comprehensive two-volume history, *Pianos and Their Makers*, published in 1911 and 1913. *Pierce Piano Atlas*, the most reliable trade compendium of serial numbers for all American pianos manufactured, contains the name Thomas Goggan & Bros., but with no serial numbers, a lack that usually means the firm was not a manufacturer.

Yet the company advertised "Goggan" pianos for sale. It is likely that the Goggans took advantage of an accepted trade practice quite common in the years before World War I—that of stenciling the dealer's name on a "nameless" piano manufactured for this purpose by an independent company—much as grocery chains sell generic merchandise under their own house labels. If the "Goggan" piano was a stencil, it most likely was manufactured by the Aeolian, Weber Piano and Pianola Company of New York, since this huge conglomerate supplied most of the various brands of instruments that the Goggan brothers sold and was a giant producer of "nameless" pianos available for dealers to stencil and sell as their own brand.

Nevertheless, there are rare individual pianos still extant that display "Thos. Goggan & Bros. Texas" apparently *cast* into the iron string-plate (instead of just being stenciled on the fall board or on the plate). This evidence suggests two alternatives to stenciling (especially given that Mike Goggan was a noted campaigner against stencil pianos, which were often of questionable quality). Either the firm did indeed manufacture pianos at some point, or it purchased made-to-order parts (i.e. string-plates, cases, keys, actions, sounding boards, etc.) from the numerous piano supply houses located in the North and Northeast and *assembled* the "Goggan" piano rather than actually making it. This was also a common trade practice, and unlike stenciling, usually resulted in instruments of at least medium quality. Nevertheless, piano production figures for the Thos. S. Goggan & Bros., if any, remain unknown, a conundrum made further elusive by Alfred Dolge's and the *Pierce Piano Atlas*'s silence on the matter.

BIBLIOGRAPHY: Albert Curtis, *Fabulous San Antonio* (San Antonio: Naylor, 1955). Ellis A. Davis and Edwin H. Grobe, comps., *The New Encyclopedia of Texas* (4 vols., 1929?). Craig H. Roell, *The Piano in America, 1890–1940* (Chapel Hill: University of North Carolina Press, 1989). San Antonio *Express*, November 27, 1914.

Craig H. Roell

Thomas, George Washington Jr. Composer, publisher, and boogie-woogie pianist, aka Clay Custer; b. Little Rock, ca. 1883; d. Chicago, March 1930; oldest of George and Fanny Thomas's thirteen children. Thomas grew up in Houston, where his father was a deacon at Shiloh Baptist Church. The Thomas family was exceptionally musically talented. The children, including George Jr., often sang in their father's church choir, and they learned to play the piano and organ at an early age. When George Jr. got a little older, he worked as a pit-pianist in local Houston theaters and soon became known as an accomplished musician. Other musically talented members of the Thomas family included his younger sister, Sippie Wallace, and Bernice "Moanin'" Edwards, who was raised in the Thomases' household. George taught his younger brother Hersal to play the piano. George and Hersal, both pioneers of the boogie-woogie piano style, helped to popularize the blues in Chicago during the 1920s.

In 1914 George became a partner of Clarence Williams, and they formed a publishing business in New Orleans. George soon became successful publishing, composing, and performing in the New Orleans Storyville district, a mecca of blues and jazz music that was also well-known for its red-light activities. The Storyville district attracted exceptionally talented young musicians, including George's friends Louis Armstrong and King Oliver.

After the Storyville district was shut down in 1917, George moved his business to Chicago. In the early 1920s, his younger sister and brother—Sippie and Hersal—joined him. By that time, George had established himself in the city's music business, and his connections enabled him to find work for them in the music industry. George composed an estimated 100 songs, including the popular "Houston Blues," the smash 1922 hit "Muscle Shoals Blues," and the 1916 tune "New Orleans Hop Scop Blues," which is considered the "first twelve-bar blues" song "published with a boogie-woogie bass line." George and Sippie composed several well-known songs, including "Shorty George Blues" and "Underworld Blues." Possibly his best work, however, was composed with Hersal. In 1922 he and Hersal published a classic composition, "The Fives," inspired by the sounds of railroad travel. This song became synonymous with the boogie-woogie style of music played in Chicago during that decade. It was often said that pianists were required to know how to play "The Fives" in order to get work there.

George was fatally injured when a Chicago streetcar hit him in 1930. His daughter Hociel was also a very successful blues singer.

BIBLIOGRAPHY: Lawrence Cohn, *Nothing But the Blues: The Music and the Musicians* (New York: Abbeville Press, 1993). Sheldon Harris, *Blues Who's Who* (New Rochelle, New York: Arlington House, 1979). Daphne Duval Harrison, *Black Pearls: Blues Queens of the 1920s* (New Brunswick: Rutgers University Press, 1988). Colin Larkin, ed., *The Guiness Encyclopedia of Popular Music*, Volume 7 (New York: Guiness Publishing, 1998). Dave Oliphant, *Texan Jazz* (Austin: University of Texas Press, 1996). Robert Santelli, *The Big Book of Blues* (New York: Penguin, 1993).   *James Head*

Thomas, Henry. An early exponent of country blues, known as Ragtime Texas Thomas; b. Big Sandy, Texas, 1874; date and place of death unknown. Thomas was one of nine children of former slaves; the family sharecropped on a cotton plantation in the northeastern part of the state. He learned to hate cotton farming at an early age and left home as soon as he could, around 1890, to pursue a career as an itinerant "songster." Derrick Stewart–Barker has commented that for his money Thomas was the best songster "that ever recorded."

Thomas first taught himself to play the quills, a folk instrument made from cane reeds that sounds similar to the *quena* used by musicians in Peru and Bolivia; later, he picked up the guitar. On the twenty-three recordings he made in 1927–29, he sings a variety of songs and accompanies himself on guitar and at times on the quills. His accompaniment work on guitar has been ranked "with the finest dance blues ever recorded." According to Stephen Calt, "its intricate simultaneous treble picking and drone bass would have posed a challenge to any blues guitarist of any era."

The range of Thomas's work makes him something of a transitional figure between the early minstrel songs, spirituals, square dance tunes, hillbilly reels, waltzes, and rags and the rise of blues and jazz. Basically his repertoire, which mostly consists of dance pieces, was out of date by the turn of the century, when the blues began to grow in popularity. Thomas's nickname, "Ragtime Texas," is thought to have come to him because he played in fast tempos, which were synonymous for some musicians with ragtime. Five of Thomas's pieces have been characterized as "rag ditties," among them "Red River Blues," and such rag songs have been considered the immediate forerunners and early rivals of blues.

Out of Thomas's twenty-three recorded pieces, only four are "bona fide blues," so that he has been looked upon as more of a predecessor rather than a blues singer as such. One commentator has claimed that Thomas's blues are original with him and that other musicians seem not to have performed his pieces. However, Thomas's "Bull Doze Blues" ends with the four-bar "Take Me Back," a Texas standard of the World War I era, which Blind Lemon Jefferson had recorded around August 1926 as "Beggin' Back." It would seem, then, that Thomas's blues represent many traditional themes and vocal phrases. For example, his "Texas Easy Street Blues" includes the verse made famous by Jimmy Rushing and Joe Williams in their 1930s to 1950s versions of the Basie-Rushing tune, "Goin' to Chicago": "When you see me comin', baby, raise your window high." Another well-known phrase found in this same Thomas piece is "blue as I can be." But perhaps most indicative of Thomas's transitional place between the early black music and jazz is his "Cottonfield Blues," which contains several standard blues themes: field labor, the desire for escape, and the role of the railroad in providing a freer lifestyle.

Thomas took to the rails to escape from a life of farm work, and made a living by singing along the Texas and Pacific and Katy lines that ran from Fort Worth and Dallas to Texarkana. In "Railroadin' Some," he supplies his itinerary, which includes such Texas towns as Rockwall, Greenville (with its infamous sign, "Land of the Blackest Earth and the Whitest People"), Denison, Grand Saline, Silver Lake, Mineola, Tyler (where Thomas was last active in the 1950s), Longview, Jefferson, Marshall, Little Sandy, and his birthplace, Big Sandy. Texas communities are not the only ones cited in this song, for Thomas traveled into the Indian Territory, as he still called it, to Muskogee, over to Missouri and Scott Joplin's stomping grounds of Sedalia, and on up to Kansas City, then into Illinois: Springfield, Bloomington, Joliet, and Chicago, where he attended the 1893 Columbian Exposition, as did Joplin. William Barlow calls this piece the most "vivid and intense recollection of railroading" in all the early blues recorded in the 1920s. The cadences in this early rural blues "depict the restless lifestyle of the vagabonds who rode the rails and their boundless enthusiasm for the mobility it gave them."

Thomas's recordings represent a wide variety of sources for his Texas brand of country music, dating back to a time before the blues became popular and before they subsumed many other popular song forms. This perhaps accounts for the fact that three of Thomas's songs—"Fishing Blues," "Woodhouse Blues," and "Red River Blues"—are not really based on the blues but may have taken the name as a way of capitalizing on the form's growing popularity.

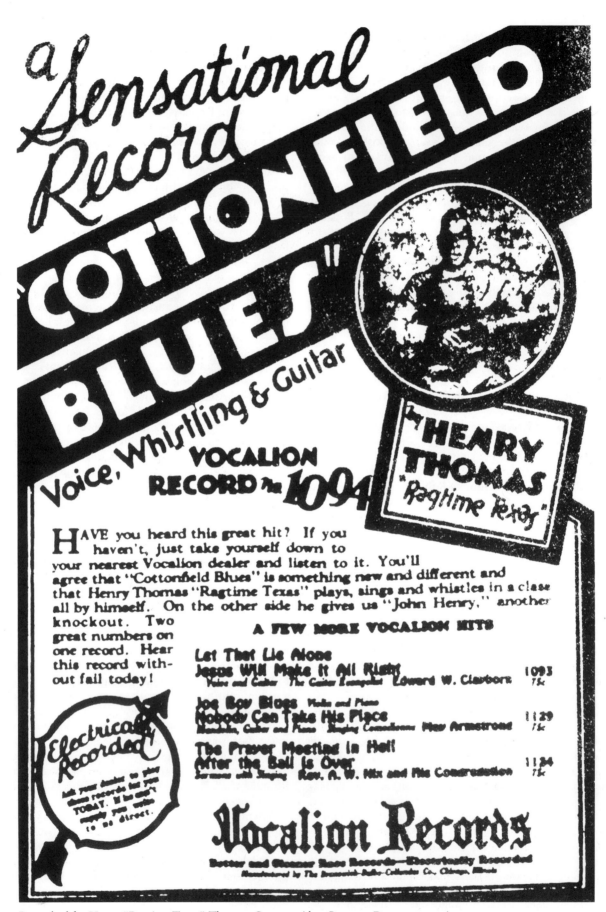

Record ad for Henry "Ragtime Texas" Thomas. Courtesy Alan Govenar, Documentary Arts.

According to Stephen Calt, both "Fishing Blues" and "Woodhouse Blues" are of vaudeville origins, while "Red River Blues" has been related melodically to "Comin' Round the Mountain," published in sheet music form in 1889 but deriving from an earlier spiritual.

The importance of Thomas's recordings as something of a compendium of the popular song forms of the late nineteenth and early twentieth centuries—from spiritual to "coon song," from "rag" song to blues—is enhanced by the similar range of instrumental techniques found in his work with guitar and quills. In a sense, then, Henry Thomas represents a vital link between the roots of black music in Africa, nineteenth and twentieth century American folksong (including spiritual, hillbilly, "rag," and "coon"), and the coming of the blues—all of these contributing in turn to the formation of jazz in its various forms, which are reflected in the varied approaches to rhythmic, tonal, and thematic expression practiced by "Ragtime Texas" decades before he made his series of recordings from 1927 to 1929.

BIBLIOGRAPHY: William Barlow, "*Looking Up at Down*": *The Emergence of Blues Culture* (Philadelphia: Temple University Press, 1989). Samuel Charters, *The Blues Makers* (New York: Da Capo Press, 1991). Samuel Charters, *The Country Blues* (London: Jazz Book Club, 1961). Sheldon Harris, *Blues Who's Who: A Biographical Dictionary of Blues Singers* (New Rochelle, New York: Arlington House, 1979). Derrick Stewart–Barker, "Record Reviews," *Jazz Journal* 28 (May 1975). *Dave Oliphant*

Thomas, Hersal. Child prodigy pianist; b. Houston, 1910; d. Detroit, Michigan, July 3, 1926; one of thirteen children of George and Fanny Thomas. The paterfamilias, George Sr., was a deacon at Shiloh Baptist Church, where his children often sang in the choir and played the piano and organ. The Thomas family was exceptionally talented musically. Hersal's older brother George was a publisher and composer whose tunes included "New Orleans Hop Scop Blues" and "Muscle Shoals Blues." In addition to composing, George was an accomplished pianist who taught Hersal to play. Although George was twenty-five years older than his youngest brother, Hersal's skills were so exceptional that he quickly surpassed his brother in musical accomplishment. The most famous member of the Thomas family, however, was Hersal's older sister, the sensational blues singer Beulah "Sippie" Wallace.

Hersal's life was intertwined with Sippie's. When he was a small child, he performed with her on Houston streetcorners for tips. In 1915 Hersal and Sippie moved to New Orleans to live with their brother George. They performed in New Orleans clubs and worked at theaters throughout the South. In 1923 the two moved to Chicago to work with their brother George and their niece, blues singer Hociel Thomas. Although Hersal was still a teenager, his musical talents quickly became much in demand around the city. In addition to playing in local venues, he toured with Louis Armstrong, Joe "King" Oliver, and Sippie. Hersal also backed his niece, Hociel, on most of her recordings. In 1925, at the age of fifteen, he recorded "Hersal Blues" and the piano classic "Suitcase Blues." At the age of sixteen,

while performing at Penny's Pleasure Inn in Detroit, he contracted food poisoning and died.

BIBLIOGRAPHY: David Dicaire, *Blues Singers* (Jefferson, North Carolina: McFarland, 1999). Colin Larkin, ed., *The Guiness Encyclopedia of Popular Music*, Volume 7 (New York: Guiness, 1998). Robert Santelli, *The Big Book of Blues* (New York: Penguin, 1993). *James Head*

Thomas, Hociel. Blues and jazz singer and boogie-woogie pianist; b. Houston, July 10, 1904; d. Oakland, California, August 22, 1952. Hociel belonged to a well-known musical family. George Thomas, her father, was a renowned pianist, composer, and author. Her mother was Octavia Malone Thomas. Her aunt, Sippie Wallace, was a legendary blues singer, and her uncle Hersal Thomas was a child-prodigy pianist. Hociel also counted among her relatives the influential vocalist Victoria Spivey.

She and her young uncle Hersal were raised by Sippie after they moved to Chicago from New Orleans in the early 1920s. Both women became vaudeville blues stars during the mid-1920s. Hociel toured extensively throughout that decade, once with Louis Armstrong. She also recorded at length in 1925–26 after the Okeh label moved to Chicago. Her recordings included the popular "Shorty George Blues" and "Tebo's Texas Boogie." Her teenage uncle backed her on piano.

After Hersal died in 1926 at the age of sixteen, Hociel was so devastated that she gave up music for the next twenty years. She moved to Oakland, California, around 1942. When she resumed her career in the mid-1940s, she played the piano on her own recordings in the boogie-woogie style that Hersal had taught her. Mutt Carey backed her on trumpet. She retired permanently in 1950, after a vicious fight with her sister. When the sister died shortly after the confrontation, Hociel was charged with murder. Although she was acquitted, she was permanently blinded by the fight. She was married to Arthur Tebo and had one child. After Hociel died of heart disease, Sippie Wallace raised her child, as she had raised Hociel.

BIBLIOGRAPHY: Lawrence Cohen, *Nothing But the Blues: The Music and the Musicians* (New York: Abbeville Press, 1993). Virginia L. Grattan, *American Women Songwriters: A Biographical Dictionary* (Westport, Connecticut: Greenwood Press, 1993). Colin Larkin, ed., *The Guiness Encyclopedia of Popular Music*, Volume 7 (New York: Guiness, 1998). *James Head*

Thompson, May Peterson. Opera star; b. Oshkosh, Wisconsin, date unknown; d. Austin, October 8, 1952 (buried in the State Cemetery, Austin); one of nine children of a Methodist minister. She began singing at the age of four in church meetings and later joined her sister Clara, an accomplished organist, to give recitals and concerts. She began her formal training at the Chicago Conservatory of Music and then traveled to Europe, where she raised money for her voice studies by teaching English and singing concerts. After spending two years in Florence, she went to Germany, where she was reduced to eating bread and water and was near starvation after a companion absconded with her funds. Nevertheless, she managed to

Willie Mae "Big Mama" Thornton moved to Houston in 1948. Although she did not stay in Texas very long, she contributed greatly to the Texas blues tradition. She wrote and recorded "Ball and Chain," a song that was later recorded by Janis Joplin and became a big hit in the 1960s. Photograph © Jerry Hausler. Blues Archive, Special Collections, University of Mississippi Libraries.

secure the tutelage of a singing master in Berlin and gave a command performance before Kaiser Wilhelm II. Weakened by a severe illness, she was advised to seek a milder climate, and thus set her sights on the Opéra Comique in Paris. After her arrival there in 1913, she studied under tenor Jean de Reszke, for whom she worked as an accompanist.

When World War I broke out, she returned to the United States to pursue a career in opera. After a six-week tour through her home state, in which she gave twenty-six concerts, she went back to Paris and was offered the lead in *Manon* at the Opéra Comique. She performed the role in rented costumes and makeup borrowed from Mary Garden. When the United States entered the war in 1917, Peterson visited and performed at various army camps. In 1918 she signed a six-year contract with the Metropolitan Opera of New York, where she sang with Enrico Caruso and John McCormack. Among her favorite roles were Micaela in *Carmen* and Mimi in *La Bohème*. Her golden voice and personality soon won her international fame as the "Golden Girl" of opera. Even then, she continued giving benefit concerts for the Methodist Church during the off-season. She made several records on the Vocalion label and was one of the first American artists to sing on radio.

In 1921 Emil Myers arranged to have May Peterson appear in concert at the First Methodist Church in Amarillo. The local civic committee selected attorney Ernest O. Thompson to be her escort. A romance ensued, and the two were married on June 9, 1924, in Bronxville, New York. Afterward they returned to Amarillo to a glittering reception held in the ballroom of the Amarillo Hotel, which Thompson had built and owned. May Thompson retired from the opera after her marriage, but she continued doing concert tours for several years. In 1925 she sang in the first musical festival to be staged at the Amarillo Municipal Auditorium, and she regularly assisted with local musical programs. In 1932, after Thompson was appointed to the Railroad Commission, the couple moved to Austin, where Mrs. Thompson became a leading figure in musical circles. The Thompsons had no children. On October 1, 1952, May Thompson suffered a cerebral hemorrhage at their summerhouse in Estes Park, Colorado, and lapsed into a coma. She was flown back to Austin, where she died in Seton Infirmary without regaining consciousness.

BIBLIOGRAPHY: Amarillo *Daily News*, October 9, 1952. James Anthony Clark, *Three Stars for the Colonel: A Biography of Ernest O. Thompson* (New York: Random House, 1954).
H. Allen Anderson

Thornton, Willie Mae. Blues singer and songwriter, known as Big Mama Thornton; b. Montgomery, Alabama, December 11, 1926; d. Los Angeles, July 25, 1984; one of seven children. Her father was a minister, and her mother sang in the church. The church's early musical influence helped her win first place in an amateur singing show. Sammy Green of Atlanta saw her there, and she went to play with his "Hot Harlem Review." In 1948 she moved to Houston, where she lived for a few years. She sang and wrote songs for performances in the local clubs.

Thornton only stayed a while, but she was influenced by Texas, and she contributed heavily to the Texas blues tradition. Willie Mae, Little Esther, and Mel Walker were a package show for Johnny Otis in the early 1950s. They became well known and traveled to New York to play the Apollo in 1952. Willie Mae, as the opening act, sang the Dominos' hit "Have Mercy Baby," among others. She was a huge success and headlined the show the next night at the Apollo. The nickname "Big Mama" came from somebody after the first show, and it stuck. She was a large, tall woman, and the name also suited her vocal tension and coarseness.

In 1951 Don Robey signed Thornton to his Peacock Records label. Jerry Lieber and Mike Stoller wrote "Hound Dog," and Willie Mae recorded it. Big Mama flew from Houston in 1953 back to New York for Peacock–Duke records' "Hound Dog" sessions. The B-side was "They Call Me Big Mama," and the single sold almost two million copies. She received a lifetime total of $500 for the song, even though Elvis Presley went on to make "Hound Dog" a rock-and-roll classic three years later. In a similar occurrence, Big Mama wrote and recorded "Ball and Chain," which became a hit for her. Janis Joplin later recorded the piece, and it became a huge success in the late 1960s.

Thornton left Houston in the early 1960s and moved to the San Francisco Bay area. She toured with shows in America and Europe and played at the Monterey Jazz Festival throughout the 1960s and 1970s. Her style captured the attention of many fans through the years because she was rough and beautiful and crazy yet controlled in her singing. Many companies recorded her work, such as Arhoolie Records, which released *Big Mama Thornton in Europe* (1966) and *Big Mama Thornton with the Chicago Blues Band* (1967). On the latter, Muddy Waters, Lightnin' Hopkins, and Otis Spawn appeared. In 1968 *Ball and Chain* compiled separate blues songs by Willie Mae, Hopkins, and Larry Williams. In the early 1970s Big Mama recorded *Saved* for Pentagram Records and *She's Back* for Backbeat Label. Vanguard Records caught her twice in the latter half of the decade in two penitentiaries with *Jail* and again with *Sassy Mama!* She appeared again in New York in 1983 at the Newport Jazz Festival with Muddy Waters, B. B. King, and Eddie "Cleanhead" Vinson. The show was captured by Buddha Records on *The Blues—A Real Summit Meeting*.

After Big Mama died of a heart attack, her sensitive, down-to-earth voice was heard in a posthumous album, *Quit Snoopin' 'round My Door* (Ace Records, United Kingdom). She was inducted into the Blues Foundation Hall of Fame in 1984.

BIBLIOGRAPHY: Virginia Grattan, *American Women Songwriters* (Westport, Connecticut: Greenwood Press, 1993). Sheldon Harris, *Blues Who's Who: A Biographical Dictionary of Blues Singers* (New Rochelle, New York: Arlington House, 1979). Gerard Herzhaft, *Encyclopedia of the Blues* (Fayetteville: University of Arkansas Press, 1979). Robert Santelli, *Big Book of the Blues: A Biographical Encyclopedia* (New York: Penguin Books, 1993).
Alan Lee Haworth

Threadgill, Kenneth. Country singer and tavern owner; b. John Kenneth Threadgill, Peniel, Texas, September 12, 1909; d. Austin, March 20, 1987; ninth of eleven children of Rev. John Threadgill. His father ministered between Hunt County and New Mexico. The family moved to Beaumont, and then in 1923 to Austin, where Kenneth attended Austin High School and subsequently met his future mentor and idol, Jimmie Rodgers. Threadgill worked at the Tivoli Theater in Beaumont and heard Rodgers sing. Backstage, Rodgers heard Threadgill imitating his yodeling and was impressed. Threadgill incorporated yodeling into his country singing act later in his life to make a unique style that fans loved.

In 1933 he moved to Austin and began working at an old service station on North Lamar Boulevard. By December, Threadgill had bought the establishment and changed it to Threadgill's Tavern, which still sold gas and food but operated with the first beer license in Austin after the repeal of Prohibition. At that time Threadgill did not allow dancing because he would have had to pay an extra tax on a dance hall that served beer. He and his wife, Mildred (Greer), ran the restaurant and tavern until World War II, when they closed for a few years. Though Threadgill was classified I-A by the army, he worked as a welder for the war effort, and the enlistment officer deferred him in ninety-day stretches until the war ended. Meanwhile, the music did not completely stop. Hank Williams came through Austin and managed to fit in an extra show at the Dessau Dance Hall, northeast of Austin in Dessau. Hank was late, so Kenneth was asked to sing a few Hank Williams songs in the meantime. As Hank walked into the hall, Threadgill was singing "Lovesick Blues." Hank came on stage to finish the show, and the two laughed together afterward.

Threadgill's Tavern opened again after the war. Due to the small size of the establishment, which seated about forty-five, the place was packed on weekends when Kenneth Threadgill and his Hootenanny Hoots played. Wednesday nights became the hot time for university students and local residents to congregate for beer, country music, yodeling, and the "Alabama Jubilee," the song that would usually get Kenneth to dance his patented shuffle. At midweek such disparate characters as goat ropers, university Greeks, hippies, and average Joes could relax together at the hootenanny.

On one occasion Julie and Chuck Joyce, two musicians from the Hootenanny Hoots, were driving around Austin and saw a small band, hippies with instruments, on the side of the road. They pulled over and invited them to come to Threadgill's. Since the show was usually in an impromptu, open-microphone style, Janis Joplin, one of the hippie musicians, shyly stepped on the stage before shouting "Silver Threads and Golden Needles." Her voice was a dull shriek that night, most reports say. Nonetheless, she became a close friend of Kenneth and Mildred. One night, in jest, she got two free Lone Star beers from Kenneth for not singing. She loved Threadgill's Tavern and frequented the establishment. Kenneth always swore that Janis did not get her start at his tavern, but rather started herself.

In 1970 a huge concert in the park near Oak Hill was held to celebrate Threadgill's birthday. Bar-B-Que, beans, and beer were consumed in massive quantities by Threadgill's fans. Janis Joplin, who had been in Hawaii the day before, canceled a $15,000 show to fly to Austin. She and Threadgill sang and danced for the crowd. Three months later Janis died of a drug overdose after promising Kenneth that they would be seeing each other much more often in the future. Threadgill's birthday picnic was recorded in the *Congressional Record* when Congressman J. J. Pickle commended the "Father of Austin Country Music" as a legend.

Threadgill was a unifier of Austin's past and present. He was quiet on the national scene until his first movie soundtrack and album in the early 1980s, when he and Willie Nelson appeared together and sang in *Honeysuckle Rose*. For the soundtrack, Threadgill sang "Coming Back to Texas" and "Singing the Yodeling Blues." He received $3,000 for acting and $4,000 for the songs; he afterward sold almost two million copies of the soundtrack. In September 1981 he released Kenneth Threadgill and the Velvet Cowpasture's first album, *Long-Haired Daddy*. The title describes the man, who had long white hair, horn-rimmed glasses, huge sideburns, and a rotund belly. Wearing a cowboy hat, he would stand on stage, lean back with his hands on his belly, and yodel like a bird. He had a baritone voice with a high falsetto. As for his lyrics, he sang about social stability with boundless optimism. Some of his topics were World War II, his hard-working father, patriotism, and Texas. His early influences were Jimmie Rodgers ballads and Al Jolson movies, which were apparent in his singing and dancing. Some of his best-known songs were "Silver-Haired Daddy of Mine," "There's A Star-Spangled Banner Waving Somewhere," "T for Texas, T for Tennessee," and "It Is No Secret What God Can Do."

Mildred died in 1976, and Threadgill sold the tavern in the early eighties. He died of a pulmonary embolism at Brackenridge Hospital. The tavern is now Threadgill's Restaurant.

BIBLIOGRAPHY: Vertical Files, Center for American History, University of Texas at Austin.

Alan Lee Haworth

Tilley, Wesley Hope. Musician and early filmmaker; b. Springfield, Illinois, December 23, 1885; d. Austin, June 24, 1972; son of Joseph Edgar and Millee (Davis) Tilley. After graduation from high school in Springfield, he studied music privately in St. Louis, Missouri. He and his brother Paul were among the pioneers of filmmaking in Texas. In 1910 they were producing silent movies in Houston, and in 1911 they moved to San Antonio, where they formed the Satex Film Company. They made one-reel silent films and showed them on a screen at night in front of the Alamo.

Though their attempt at filmmaking in San Antonio was successful enough, the Tilleys moved to Austin in 1913. With assets of $25,000 they reestablished the Satex Film Company and added a finishing plant for processing motion-picture film. The Satex Company was the only company manufacturing silent films south of St. Louis at that time and the first film company in the United States to make three-reel movies. But that same year the company

THREADGILL

Tavern owner and singer Kenneth Threadgill had the first beer license in Austin after Prohibition. His tavern was often packed by a motley audience that showed up to hear country music, and to see Threadgill dance and hear him yodel. Courtesy George B. Ward.

The Alphonse Trent Orchestra was the first African-American house band at the Adolphus Hotel in Dallas in the 1920s and 1930s. Duncan Scheidt Collection.

folded because of financial difficulties, even though it had made six movies and released them nationally. Tilley later joined the Hagenbeck Circus band and toured with them for two years in Germany, after which he returned to Austin and taught music. During World War I he taught code, construction, and radio electronics for the United States Army Air Corps in Austin.

Tilley was director of the Ben Hur Shrine band in Austin for thirty-eight years and served as secretary–treasurer for the Federation of Musicians Local 433 in Austin from 1943 to 1964. On January 31, 1920, he married Helen Grist of Austin. They had one son.

BIBLIOGRAPHY: Austin *American–Statesman*, May 25, 1941. James R. Buchanan, "A Look at the Texas Film Industry," *Texas Business Review* 46 (January 1972).

James R. Buchanan

Trent, Alphonse. Jazz band leader; b. Alphonso E. Trent, Fort Smith, Arkansas, August 24, 1905; d. Fort Smith, October 14, 1959. Trent was one of the great Texan jazz legends of the 1920s. Influenced as a child by the music of Fletcher Henderson and W.C. Handy, he formed his first band in 1923. Soon, however, he moved to Little Rock to study music at Shorter College. With this grounding, he landed a job in Eugene Crook's Synco Six, an experience that encouraged him to form another group of his own.

After moving to Texas, this new ensemble became the first African-American band to play weekly at the Adolphus Hotel in Dallas. Some people did not look favorably upon a black band that played for a white audience, and soon the band received threats from the Ku Klux Klan. But Trent and company persevered and became one of the most well-known acts in Dallas. Though much of their popularity was attributed to their fine jazz technique, weekly radio broadcasts by WFAA from the hotel also increased their influence and expanded their popularity in the surrounding area. The band made several recordings in 1928 and again in 1930 and 1933.

Trent temporarily retired in the early 1930s, but his band continued under his name. After he returned to music, the group toured the Southwest. During this period Trent met and took under his wing the young Charlie Christian, who later carved his own niche as one of the great jazz guitarists. Although Trent's band played widely in the Southwest, it did not tour the East Coast, where big national acts garnered much of their support. Its regional nature limited its reputation. Eventually, Trent retired from touring and moved back to Fort Smith.

BIBLIOGRAPHY: John Chilton, *Who's Who of Jazz: Storyville to Swing Street* (New York: Da Capo Press, 1985).

Ernest Tubb, "Austin City Limits," ca. 1978. Courtesy Scott Newton/Austin City Limits. As a regular performer on the "Grand Ole Opry," Tubb popularized Texas honky-tonk music in the 1940s.

Leonard Feather, *The Encyclopedia of Jazz*, New Edition (New York: Horizon Press, 1960). Colin Larkin, ed., *Encyclopedia of Popular Music*, Volume 7 (London: MuzeUK Limited, 1998). Dave Oliphant, *Texan Jazz* (Austin: University of Texas Press, 1996).   *Bradley Shreve*

Tubb, Ernest Dale. Singer; b. Crisp, Texas, February 9, 1914; d. Nashville, September 6, 1984 (buried in Hermitage Memorial Gardens, Nashville); son of Calvin and Ellen Tubb. He was reared by other relatives in Ellis County. As a teenager, Tubb took a job in San Antonio as a soda jerk, learned the guitar on his own, and landed an unpaid job at KONO radio station. During this time he was befriended by Carrie Rodgers, widow of Jimmie Rodgers, a major influence on Tubb's singing. She helped him obtain a recording contract with RCA Victor in 1936. In 1940 Tubb signed with Decca Records and began commercially promoting himself and his records through association with a flour company.

Known as the "Gold Chain Troubador," Tubb was earning only $75 a week in salary and not selling many records. He was almost ready to leave the music scene and take a job in the defense industry when he recorded "Walking the Floor Over You," a million-record seller that paved the way to Hollywood. He made several movies, joined the Grand Ole Opry in 1943, and remained a regular performer there for over forty years. With his band, the Texas Troubadors, Tubb began a performance schedule that eventually took a serious toll on his health and his personal life as well. He was married to Lois Elaine Cook on May 26, 1934; they were divorced in 1948, a year when Tubb had three songs on the *Billboard* top-ten charts. By 1949 the hits numbered seven: "Blue Christmas," "Don't Rob Another Man's Castle," "Have You Ever Been Lonely," "I'm Bitin' My Fingernails and Thinking of You," "Slipping Around," "Tennessee Border No. 2," and "Warm Red Wine." Tubb married Olene Adams Carter ("My Tennessee Baby") in June 1949. They had five children.

During his career Ernest Tubb recorded more than 250 songs and sold 30 million records. He was elected to the Country Music Hall of Fame in 1965. He owned a record store in Nashville and was known for his generosity to unknown artists who later became famous, including Hank Williams, Hank Snow, and Loretta Lynn. As a singer, Tubb was unique but not necessarily great, perhaps because of his change in voice from the tenor yodels of Jimmie Rodgers to a granite baritone not always on key. "I don't care whether I hit the right note or not. I'm not looking for perfection of delivery—thousands of singers have that. I'm looking for individuality," he told an interviewer. A Tubb concert or dance in his later years would include "Waltz Across Texas," "There's a Little Bit of Texas," "Filipino Baby," "Let's Turn Back the Years," "Little Ole Band of Gold," and "Thanks (Thanks a Lot)." He traveled in a customized bus and always ended a performance by flipping his insignia, THANKS, on the back side of his guitar. His fan club was in attendance in most Texas cities, and Tubb knew many families personally. "To me, country music is from your heart and soul. It's your LIFE," he said in 1980.

He was often credited with the electric amplification of instruments, which he was not the first to try, but when he did go electric he soon personified the folksy and rowdy music, known as Texas honky-tonk, that was beginning to sell records and attract people to dance halls in the 1940s. He seldom varied from a basic ensemble for his touring band, which always featured guitars. "Keep it low to the ground," he would tell the band, and he delivered all the vocals. He never appeared in public without a tailored Western suit and ten-gallon hat, a feature that helped erase "hillbilly" from "country and western." He has been credited as being a major influence both on both his musical peers and on younger players. He played himself in the 1980 movie *Coal Miner's Daughter*.

BIBLIOGRAPHY: Austin *American–Statesman*, September 7, 1984. Bill C. Malone, *Country Music U.S.A.* (Austin: University of Texas Press, 1968). Irwin Stambler and Grelun Landon, *Encyclopedia of Folk, Country and Western Music* (New York: St. Martin's, 1969; 2d. ed., 1983). Vertical Files, Center for American History, University of Texas at Austin.   *Phillip L. Fry*

Tubb, Justin Wayne. Singer and songwriter; b. San Antonio, August 20, 1935; d. Nashville, Tennessee, January 24, 1998; eldest son of country superstar Ernest Tubb and his wife, Elaine. He started his career in country music by singing on KGKL radio in San Angelo when he was four years old, and debuted on the "Grand Ole Opry" five years later.

Justin's interest in country music was complicated by his father's prominent role in the business. Never intending to ride on Ernest's coattails, Justin worked hard to distance himself from his father. Although he wrote a song that Ernest recorded, he seldom presented himself as Ernest's son. Nevertheless, while enrolled at the University of Texas in 1952 pursuing a degree in journalism, Justin formed a country band and played at some Austin-area venues. His college career suffered at the expense of his interest in country music and he dropped out from the university.

He then moved to Nashville and got a job as a DJ at WHIN, Gallatin, where he was able to perform his own songs on the air. This exposure led to a contract with Decca, but the singles Tubb released did not have great success. His lighter duets were better received. By 1954 he made it on the country charts with two duets with Goldie Hill ("Looking Back to See" and "Sure Fire Kisses"). A year later, at age twenty, he was made a member of the "Grand Ole Opry," the youngest person ever to be inducted into membership. Tubb had a few recordings of his own that enjoyed success, including "I Gotta Go Get My Baby" and "Take a Letter Miss Gray," but he was more successful as a songwriter. He penned many hit songs for other performers, including "Keeping Up with the Joneses," "Love Is No Excuse," and "Lonesome 7-7203." Ultimately, six of his songs won awards.

Part of the reason Justin Tubb's singing and songwriting career paled in comparison to his father's is that both Ernest and Justin Tubb favored one style of country performance and country songwriting, a style often described today as "traditional." By the time Justin's career was established in his mid-thirties, this traditionalist style was

Before World War II B. K. Turner recorded six songs and had a rhythm-and-blues radio show on KFJZ in Fort Worth. He did not record again until 1960, when Arhoolie Records recorded him. Photo © by Chris Strachwitz (www.arhoolie.com).

already passé. Although he never again reached the success he had in his early twenties, he made his mark in the 1970s by artistically protesting the decline of traditional country music, especially with his song "What's Wrong with the Way That We're Doing It Now?" The song was well-received when it debuted on the "Grand Ole Opry," and also did well as a recording.

While Justin never wanted to capitalize on his father's hard work, the two worked cooperatively, especially when Ernest was ill. During the 1960s, Justin worked with Ernest on various business projects. Also, towards the end of his own life, Justin completed an album of duets with his father, using recordings Ernest had made before his death. The album, *Just You and Me Daddy* (1999), was released after Justin's himself died unexpectedly. Tubb was survived by his wife, Carolyn McPherson Tubb.

BIBLIOGRAPHY: Michael Erlewine, *All Music Guide to Country: the Experts' Guide to the Best Recordings in Country Music* (San Francisco: Miller Freeman, 1997). Colin Larkin, *Encyclopedia of Popular Music* (New York: Grove's Dictionaries, 1998). Bill C. Malone, *Country Music, U.S.A.*, revised edition (Austin: University of Texas Press, 1985). *Nashville Scene*, February 12, 1998.

Cathy Brigham

Turner, Babe Kyro Lemon. Blues guitarist, known as Black Ace or B. K. Turner; b. Hughes Springs, Texas, December 21, 1907;. d. Fort Worth, November 7, 1972; son of J. T. and Della Lee (Lewis) Turner. B. K. was raised on the family farm. His early interest in music began at his church and soon led him to build his own guitar and teach himself to play. In the late 1920s he played locally and grew in popularity.

During the early 1930s he toured East Texas dance halls and juke joints with teenager Andrew "Smokey" Hogg and Oscar "Buddy" Woods, a Hawaiian-style guitarist. (A Hawaiian-style guitarist plays with the instrument flat on his lap.) Influenced by Woods, Turner bought a National Style 2 squareneck tricone steel guitar. With the guitar on his lap and fretting with a glass medicine bottle, he played what one music critic called "Hawaii meets the Delta," smooth and simple blues.

In 1936 Turner recorded six songs, including his signature "Black Ace," with Smokey Hogg and pianist Whistling Alex Moore for Decca Records in Chicago. Also beginning in 1936, he had a radio show on KFJZ–Fort Worth playing blues and R&B. During his last year on the radio, Turner appeared in the 1941 film *The Blood of Jesus*, an African-American movie produced by Spencer William. In 1943 he was drafted into the army. He did not return to music until 1960, when Arhoolie Records owner Chris Strachwitz approached him in Fort Worth and asked to him to record for his label. Turner found his guitar without strings in the attic, and, although he had not played since the early 1940s, he recorded seventeen new tracks for Strachwitz.

His performance in a 1962 documentary, *The Blues*, was his last public music appearance. He died of cancer. Turner was married to a woman named Minnie, and they had one child.

BIBLIOGRAPHY: Larry Benicewicz, "The Arhoolie Record Story," *Blues Art Studio Journal* 1999 (www.bluesartstudio.at), accessed May 8, 2002. Matthew Block, "Chris Strachwitz, Arhoolie Records and Traditional Blues Field Recordings" (www.delmark.com/rhythm.arhoolie.htm), accessed May 8, 2002. Al Handa, "The National Steel Guitar, Part Four" (www.nationalguitars.com/part4.html), accessed May 12, 2002. Sheldon Harris, *Blues Who's Who* (New Rochelle, New York: Arlington House, 1979).

Katherine Walters

Turner, Grant. Disc jockey; b. Jesse Granderson Turner, Abilene, Texas, May 17, 1912; d. Tennessee, October 19, 1991. Turner was a DJ for the Nashville radio station WSM's Grand Ole Opry for the majority of his career. His fascination with radio began in childhood, as he built and listened to his own radio crystal sets. He also developed a love for country music as a child, especially after seeing legendary country singer Jimmie Rodgers perform at a local radio station. Turner did his first radio announcing in 1928 on KFYO in Abilene, and he also performed on the program "Ike and His Guitar." He attended Hardin–Simmons University in Abilene and studied journalism, worked for local newspapers after graduation, and was later employed by the Dallas *Morning News*.

After Turner's early interest in radio resurfaced, he was able to work as an announcer for several Texas stations, including KFYO in Abilene, where, for a dollar a day, he hosted and performed songs under the nickname Ukulele Ike. He also worked at KRRV in Sherman and KFRO in Longview. In 1942 he left Texas for a job at WBIR in Knoxville, Tennessee, as an early-morning disc jockey.

Soon after, he auditioned with WSM and moved to Nashville.

His new job started on June 6, 1944, D-Day, when the Allies invaded France. He was first assigned to announce one segment of the Grand Ole Opry that was sponsored by Crazy Water Crystals, but he was quickly asked by George D. Hay, Opry master of ceremonies and mentor to Turner, to assist with all segments. Turner's style has been described as easygoing and efficient, one that conveyed the friendly atmosphere of the Opry to all who listened. He was just as well known for his commercials as he was for his introductions of the cast.

Known as the "Dean of the Opry Announcers," Turner was also thought of as the "Voice of the Grand Ole Opry" by millions of fans. He was inducted into the Country Disc Jockey Hall of Fame in 1975 and into the Country Music Hall of Fame in 1981. The Opry's rules stated that all employees had to retire at the age of 65. However, Turner was so popular with listeners that the management allowed him to continue well beyond this. He died of heart failure just hours after finishing a Friday evening broadcast, and is buried in Williamson Memorial Gardens, Franklin, Tennessee.

BIBLIOGRAPHY: Country Radio Broadcasters, "DJ Hall of Fame Inductee" (http://www.crb.org/2003/awards/dj/turner.html), accessed January 31, 2003. Fred Dellar, Allan Cackett, and Roy Thompson, *The Harmony Illustrated Encyclopedia of Country Music* (New York: Harmony, 1987). Ron Lackman, *The Encyclopedia of American Radio: An A–Z Guide to Radio from Jack Benny to Howard Stern* (New York: Facts on File, 2000). Ron Lackman, *Same Time, Same Station* (New York: Facts on File, 1996). Colin Larkin, ed., *The Encyclopedia of Popular Music* (London: MuzeUK, 1998). Abilene *Reporter–News*, July 4, 1999.
Amy Cockreham

U

University of North Texas College of Music. In Denton; one of the nation's premier institutions for musical training and education. Prominent alumni include Harry Babasin, Gene Roland, Jimmy Giuffre, Bob Belden, Lou Marini, Conrad Herwig, Jim Snidero, and Norah Jones. In 1947 North Texas State Teachers College (as the current University of North Texas was then named) became the first university in the world to offer a degree in jazz, and over the years the university has solidified its reputation as one of the preeminent institutions for the study of that genre.

From the beginning, music was a part of the UNT curriculum. A "Conservatory Music Course" was offered as part of the university's initial "Nine Full Courses" in 1890. The complete course in music, lasting forty-four weeks, required private lessons that had to be paid for, in addition to regular school tuition. These classes ran at a rate of $200 for the complete course, while regular tuition for a forty-week school year was only $48. President Joshua C. Chilton himself taught the first classes in the history of music and the theory of sound. John M. Moore, a Dallas Methodist bishop and teacher of mathematics and engineering courses, taught the classes in voice culture and harmony. Mrs. E. J. McKissack was also a teacher of music and may have served as the director of the music conservatory. Between 1917 and 1919 the school purchased land for the construction of expanded campus facilities. Included in the purchase was the former residence of past president Joel S. Kendall. This two-story frame house, known as Kendall Hall, became the Music Hall and served the department in various capacities until 1940.

Music-oriented activities played an important role in the extracurricular life of early North Texas students. As early as 1897, an Orchestra Club and a Mandolin and Guitar Club were organized. By 1920, extracurricular activities, including choral clubs, had become so distracting to many students that a point system was instituted in order to limit participation in them. In 1925, when motion pictures first came to the campus, a student pit orchestra was formed in order to provide music for the films. Faculty member Floyd Graham, who organized the orchestra, saw it as a means of providing income to the students who participated. Extracurricular musical clubs of the day also included the College Choral Club, Girls' Glee Club, Men's Glee Club, College Band, and College Orchestra.

The year 1938 was one of the most important in the development of the North Texas music program. Under the auspices of President W. J. McConnell, the music department was greatly expanded. Dr. Wilfred C. Bain was appointed to head the department, and under his leadership, several new initiatives were taken, including an enhanced degree program. The school began offering five degrees in music: bachelor of science in music education, bachelor of music in music education, bachelor of arts in applied music, bachelor of arts with a theory major, and a band master's certificate. At this time, an a cappella choir, which appeared on WFAA radio, was formed, and the college had a marching band, a symphony orchestra, a college band, and a stage band called "Fessor Floyd Graham and His Aces of Collegeland."

McConnell and Bain's plans for an improved music school immediately paid off. On December 17, 1939, the National Association of Schools of Music admitted North Texas as an associate member, the first such accreditation for the college in a discipline other than teacher training. In 1940 the association granted North Texas institutional membership, with Bain serving as the association's national vice president.

In 1940 the music program's success was rewarded with funds for expanded facilities. The board of regents voted in May to provide $70,000 for the construction of a combination male dormitory and music hall. Revenue from the fees charged the dorm residents was used to repay bonds sold to generate the construction funds. The three-story music facility opened in March 1941. Although the new building contained classrooms and practice rooms as well as a broadcasting studio, it still did not house the entire music department, which had practice rooms and studios spread throughout the campus.

In 1945, when the institution became North Texas State College—a name that reflected broader offerings than mere teacher training—an administrative reorganization gave the school of music its own dean. The Jazz Age also came to North Texas in the 1940s. Former students such as Harry Babasin, Gene Roland, and Jimmy Giuffre began making a name for themselves in the West Coast music scene. Famed bandleader Stan Kenton also began recruiting North Texas musicians for his orchestra. In 1942 Bain asked M. E. Hall, a graduate student in music, to write his thesis on proposals for a dance-band music-degree program at the university. Hall's work became the basis for the world's first university degree in jazz. The dean of music, Walter H. Hodgson, asked Hall to head up the founding of the new program in 1947. Of central importance to the program was the formation of a practice band—or "lab" band—for which students were given credit for participation. The Two O'Clock Lab Band, named for the time at which it met, became the first of these.

In 1959, renowned multi-instrumentalist and arranger Leon Breeden succeeded Hall as the head of the jazz program. Breeden moved the practice time of the Two O'Clock Lab Band up an hour, giving it the name it has today, the One O'Clock Lab Band. Under Breeden's leadership, the program earned nearly fifty national awards for individual and group performance. The One O'Clock Lab Band has shared the stage with musical greats, including Duke Ellington and Stan Getz, and has even toured abroad. Two albums cut by the band, *Lab '75* and *Lab '76*, were nominated for Grammy awards, the first such college band albums to be granted this honor.

In 1963 the music program once again championed innovation in musical technique with the establishment of the Electronic Music Center, formed by composer Merrill Ellis. A Merrill Ellis Intermedia Theater was opened in the new Music Building in 1983, and in September of that year the program was renamed the Center for Electronic Music and Intermedia. CEMI's key components involve experimentation with electroacoustic composition and the incorporation of various intermedia such as dance and visual-projection systems. In 1981 the program played host to more than 400 participants at the Seventh Annual International Computer Music Conference.

As a complement to the music program, the University of North Texas maintains one of the largest music libraries in the United States. It includes more than 135,000 volumes of material and over 100,000 recordings. Many of the musical scores in the collection date to the earliest history of music publishing, and the recorded media range from Edison cylinders to the latest digital renderings. One of the centerpieces of the Music Library is the Stan Kenton Collection. At his death, bandleader Kenton left his entire orchestra library to North Texas, a collection made up of some 2,000 manuscripts.

In 1988 North Texas once again changed its name, this time from North Texas State University to University of North Texas. As the school has expanded into a university system, the music program has expanded with it. The UNT School of Music became the College of Music in 1995. The college maintains one of the finest performance halls in Texas—the Murchison Performing Arts Center. It offers degrees in a variety of different disciplines, and has more than forty performance ensembles that give about a thousand concerts a year. In 2003 the UNT College of Music—one of the largest schools of its kind in the United States—was staffed by about 100 full-time faculty members and 100 adjunct faculty and teaching fellows.

BIBLIOGRAPHY: William W. Collins Jr., "Making Music," *North Texan Online*, Spring 2001 (http://www.unt.edu/northtexan/archives/p01/feedback.htm), accessed February 3, 2003. Robert S. LaForte and Richard L. Himmel, *Down the Corridor of Years: A Centennial History of the University of North Texas in Photographs, 1890–1990* (Denton: University of North Texas Press, 1989). Kenneth Lavender, *Treasures of the University of North Texas Libraries* (Denton: University of North Texas Libraries, n.d.). Dave Oliphant, *Texan Jazz* (Austin: University of Texas Press, 1996). James L. Rogers, *The Story of North Texas* (Denton: University of North Texas Press: 2002). University of North Texas College of Music homepage (http://www. music.unt.edu/), accessed March 20, 2003. University of North Texas College of Music, "About the UNT College of Music" (http://www.unt.edu/pais/insert/umusi.htm), accessed September 30, 2002. University of North Texas Music Library, "Stan Kenton Collection" (http://www.library.unt.edu/music/kenton/default.htm), accessed April 9, 2002. *Jerry C. Drake*

The Alamo City Highlanders performing at the Texas Folklife Festival, 1979. UT Institute of Texan Cultures at San Antonio, No. TFF-BW-79-29. The institute, located on the HemisFair '68 grounds, sponsors educational exhibits and events focused on the history and culture of ethnic groups that settled in Texas.

University of Texas Institute of Texan Cultures. Established by the Fifty-ninth Legislature on May 27, 1965; an educational center in San Antonio, dedicated to promoting understanding of the state's varied ethnic makeup. The original mission was to develop and implement an appropriate plan for the state's participation in HemisFair '68; to plan exhibits related to the history of Texas, its development, resources, and contributions; and to design and construct a building suited to housing these exhibits, giving due consideration to its utility for state purposes after the fair.

The importance of this project was indicated by the allocation of additional revenue by the Sixtieth Legislature, bringing the total investment to $10 million. The institute, a permanent state agency located on HemisFair grounds in San Antonio, was designed to study the ethnic groups that settled in Texas. While not a museum, the institute displayed relics, artifacts, and personal memorabilia, but only those that had a direct connection with telling the story of the people in each ethnic group. The exhibits made use of sound, color, movement, and atmospheric design.

R. Henderson Shuffler guided the research projects and formed the original staff. The institute's continued function is to bring together, on loan, fragments of Texas history collections from museums and archives throughout the state, to produce filmstrips and slide shows on segments of Texas history, and to publish historical pamphlets and books. ITC was put under the University of Texas System effective June 5, 1969, and its official title became the University of Texas Institute of Texan Cultures at San Antonio. In February 1973 the institute became, more specifically, a part of the University of Texas at San Antonio.

The institute was funded by biennial legislative appropriations, grants, contributions, and funds generated by the sale of publications, audiovisuals, other products, and the rental of the institute's facilities. In addition to maintaining 50,000 square feet of exhibits featuring twenty-seven cultures and ethnic groups, the institute hosts the Texas Children's Festival, Pioneer Sunday, the Texas Folklife Festival, and other events. The Institute also sponsors traveling exhibits, performances, and lectures and hosts *LIFETIMES: The Texas Experience,* a radio program featuring information and entertainment related to Texas people and places. In 1999 the ITC welcomed almost 230,000 visitors.

BIBLIOGRAPHY: Homepage of the Institute of Texan Cultures (http://www.texancultures.utsa.edu/new/info/infocontent.htm), accessed February 11, 2003.

David C. Tiller

Valery, Joseph Jr. Blues singer and guitarist, known as Little Joe Blue; b. Vicksburg, Mississippi, September 23, 1934; d. Reno, Nevada, April 22, 1990; finished his career in Texas. He had five brothers and two sisters. The family home was across the river in Tallulah, Louisiana, and it was there that Joe spent the first seventeen years of his life and began to work, now in agriculture, now in the local fish market.

In 1951 he moved to the Detroit area, where he obtained employment in the Lincoln–Mercury plant in Wayne. It was at this time that he began to be interested in music. However, he volunteered for the army in 1953 and spent the next three years in the service, part of the time in Korea. When he left the army he returned to Detroit and got work in the Ford plant.

As music became more important to him, he appeared as a vocalist in talent shows and in some of Detroit's small clubs and bars, and eventually formed his own small group. He married in 1958 and had two children (Angela and Joseph Devone); however the marriage ended in divorce and he moved to Reno, Nevada, where his sisters lived. There he formed another band and played in local clubs. In 1961 he moved to Los Angeles to live with his aunt. He worked on construction or demolition sites or in car-washes, but at nights and on weekends he appeared in local clubs.

This led in 1963 to his first recording, a single for the small Nanc label. A session for Kent followed in 1964, but nothing was issued. However, in 1966 producer Fats Washington (who gave him the stage name Little Joe Blue) got him a session for Mel Alexander's Movin' label, at which he recorded "Dirty Work Going On." He attracted the attention of Chess Records in Chicago, who leased the Movin' single and re-issued it on their Checker label, providing Little Joe Blue with his only appearance (for just one week at Number 40) in the R&B charts. Still, he was now a national rather than a local name and was from this time on able to make his living from music.

Valery also began now to play the guitar as well as sing. Further sessions, in Los Angeles in 1966 and in Chicago in 1967, produced three more singles on Checker, but they were not as successful. The tracks recorded in his final session for Chess (in 1967) remained unissued, as did those from a session for Kent in the same year. In 1968 Fats Washington introduced him to Jewel Records in Shreveport, and over the next four years Jewel issued five Little Joe Blue singles and an LP, recorded at sessions held variously in Los Angeles and Shreveport. In 1971 Valery also had an LP on Mel Alexander's Space label; from it singles were issued on Space, Sound Stage 7, and Kris.

At this time he went to live in Richmond, California. He had appeared at Fillmore West in San Francisco as early as 1968, but he began to consolidate his popularity with white blues fans with appearances at the Berkeley and Ann Arbor blues festivals in 1971, at the San Francisco Blues Festival in 1974 (two tracks from that show were issued on a Soul Set single), and again at the Berkeley and San Francisco festivals in 1975 (one title from the latter appearance was issued on a Solid Smoke LP). But most of his performances were still in the clubs and bars of Northern California and the Southern states. Singles on Elco and Miles Ahead, both produced by Miles Grayson, also appeared in the mid-seventies.

In 1975 Valery toured Europe with a package show called American Blues Legends '75; a couple of titles were recorded in London by Big Bear records. He made later trips to Europe in 1982 as part of the San Francisco Blues Festival (three tracks were issued on a Paris Album LP) and in 1986 with the Chicago Blues Festival '86 (recordings made in Holland have appeared on a Black & Blue CD), but these and a tour with the James Brown Revue in 1975 were highlights of a career largely played out in the black clubs of the West Coast and the South. Joe continued to record with reasonable regularity: singles on Kris, Platinum City, and Misipy (the last with Dino Spells), an LP and a spin-off single on Empire, and two LPs (each of which gave birth to a single) for Leon Haywood's Evejim label kept his name before his public.

In 1977, after a period in Kansas City, Missouri, he made his base in Dallas. He performed regularly throughout Texas. Eventually he moved back to Reno, where he died of stomach cancer. It would not be unfair to describe Little Joe Blue as a journeyman blues singer. Although by no means a star—and peripheral as a Texan—he was able to maintain a full-time career in music for over thirty years because he was always able to provide his African-American audience with the kind of show they wanted. He is often unfairly described as a B. B. King imitator, but his records show a fine singer who was always able to find good songs to record. He never found it necessary to compromise his basic style to win a wider audience, and as a result his work has an integrity that more popular bluesmen have sometimes lost.

BIBLIOGRAPHY: Daniel Ray Bacon, "Little Joe Blue," *Juke Blues* 20 (Summer 1990). Dallas *Morning News*, November 28, 1985. Norman Darwen, *Blues & Rhythm* 52 (May–June 1990). Lee Hildebrand, "Little Joe Blue," *Blues Unlimited* 66 (October 1969). Sheldon Harris, *Blues Who's Who* (1979). Keith Tillman, "Little Joe Blue," *Blues Unlimited* 53 (May 1968). Bez Turner, "Little Joe Blue," *Blues Unlimited* 114 (July–August 1975).

Ray Astbury

Van Cliburn International Piano Competition. A world-class performance contest for young professional pianists held every four years in Fort Worth. The competition was originated by Irl Allison Sr., who formed the Van Cliburn Foundation for the purpose.

Allison had long supported excellence in piano playing—as a pianist, as a piano teacher, and especially as the founder of the National Guild of Piano Teachers. This organization sponsors the National Piano Playing Auditions, a program that brings professional musicians to cities and towns all over the country to judge the performance of students. The occasion for the founding of the Cliburn Foundation was Van Cliburn's winning the Tchaikovsky Competition in Moscow in 1958; victory in this contest is one of the most coveted and prestigious achievements to which a young pianist can aspire. When Cliburn won, he was widely hailed as a major cultural ambassador whose influence would help to nullify the Cold War.

Cliburn's fame was Allison's opportunity. At a dinner in Fort Worth, Allison and Mrs. Grace Ward Lankford brought together a group with interest in supporting young artists through an annual contest to be held in Fort Worth. They got the Chamber of Commerce and the local piano teachers involved. Allison announced the contest in 1958, and the first competition was held in 1962.

The contest is in effect a final competition in which thirty or so of the world's best young pianists compete. Contestants cannot be older than twenty-nine. Before they come to Fort Worth, they have already won the right to do so in preliminary competitions in their own countries. In 2001, after six preliminary screenings in the Netherlands, Hungary, Russia, New York, and Chicago, 137 musicians were invited to Fort Worth for a seventh and final screening. The 137 were trimmed down to thirty after each played a solo recital judged by a panel of professional musicians and music educators. These thirty competed in the Cliburn Competition per se. Twelve of them advanced to the semifinals, and from the semifinals six emerged as finalists. Usually three medals are awarded to the winners of the final contest, but on occasion ties have been rewarded with dual medals; in 2001, for instance, the jury bestowed the gold medal on two performers.

Over the years the performance required of contestants has varied. Originally, all were required to play the same commissioned work by an American composer, as well as chamber works performed with local professionals and concertos performed with the Fort Worth Chamber Orchestra and the Fort Worth Symphony Orchestra. In 2001—the most recent contest in the quadrennial series—the contestants had a choice from several American works chosen by the jury. The Cliburn Competition has rightly been noted for supporting American composers, some of whom have been brought to prominence through the contest.

For several decades the opening performances of the contest took place at Ed Landreth Hall on the Texas Christian University campus, with the final rounds occurring at the Tarrant County Convention Center. In 2001 the contest was moved to the new Bass Concert Hall in downtown Fort Worth. That year the monetary award for the gold medal winner was $20,000—double the amount of the first competition in 1962. The other benefits of winning, however, amount to far more. These include publicity and, most importantly, a big round of concert-management services through which the winners acquire a busy schedule of performances.

Logistics for the contest are formidable. They include transportation of contestants and judges, the lodging of contestants with host families, the acquisition and distribution of music to orchestra and jury members (sometimes the selected works are not published yet, and in these cases manuscripts must be photocopied), and many other demands. A "pit crew" of piano tuners is essential.

Perhaps the most famous of the Cliburn gold medalists is Radu Lupu (1966), originally from Romania and now resident in London; though others have been quite successful. The most famous "nonwinner" is said to be Barry Douglas of Northern Ireland, who finished third in the 1985 contest but later won the Leeds Competition in England and became a quite successful concert pianist. The youngest winner of the competition was Alexei Sultanov of Uzbekistan, who was only nineteen when he took the gold medal in 1989. Catastrophically, a mere eleven years later a series of strokes quelled his "fiery virtuosity" and canceled his career. Stanislav Ioudenitch, one of the gold medal winners in 2001 (the other was Olga Kern of Russia), had to drop out of the 1997 contest because he burned his hand with boiling water. The 2001 contest also featured the first brother–sister contestants, Koreans Jong Hwa Park and his younger sister, Jong-Gyung Park.

The Cliburn Foundation has greatly enlarged its activities since 1958. It added a film festival to the 2001 competition. Chief among the foundation's other recent new activities is an International Piano Competition for Outstanding Amateurs, which began in 1999 and since 2000 has been held every two years. This contest is open to serious musicians who make their living at something besides music. Participants have included a massage therapist, a news producer, an astrologer, doctors, lawyers, housewives, and computer specialists.

The Cliburn naturally has its detractors. Some say that the structure itself, of chosen contestants performing in a high-stakes contest before an ad hoc panel of professional judges and the glaring eye of the media, leads to rewarding empty virtuosity. Others, however, say that real virtuosity is never empty, but is a product of heart as well as head and hand. Press coverage fell off slightly for the 2001 competition, though the New York *Times* music critic—the most prominent defector—allows that the *Times* might not skip future Cliburns. Although an affair as big as the Cliburn could hardly be without flaws, the spectacular contest continues to bring together large audiences and first-rate talent, and to enrich both Fort Worth and the state of Texas.

BIBLIOGRAPHY: Dallas *Morning News*, February 21, April 4, April 10, May 25, May 29, June 1, June 5, June 6, June 11, 2001; June 4, November 15, 2002. Van Cliburn Foundation homepage (www.cliburn.org/), accessed April 2, 2003.
Roy R. Barkley

Van der Stucken, Frank Valentine. Composer and conductor; b. Fredericksburg, Texas, October 15, 1858; d. Hamburg, Germany, August 16, 1929 (buried in Hamburg); son of Frank and Sophie (Schönewolf) Van der Stucken. His father had immigrated to Texas from Antwerp, Belgium, with Henri Castro and married in Fredericksburg on December 23, 1852. The elder Van der Stucken, a freight contractor and merchant who served as a captain in the

First Texas Cavalry during the Civil War and in 1864 was chief justice of Gillespie County, returned to Antwerp with his family in 1866.

Young Frank's musical education began when he was eight. He studied violin with Émile Wambach from 1866 to 1876 and composition and theory with Pierre Benoit. By age sixteen he had completed two major original works: a *Te Deum* for solo voices, chorus, and orchestra produced in St. Jacob's Church in Antwerp and an orchestral ballet presented at the Royal Theater in the same city. After a visit to Wagner's Bayreuth Festival in 1876, Van der Stucken settled in Leipzig, Germany, for two years of study with Carl Reinecke, Victor Langer, and Edvard Grieg. Grieg was the first of a number of important composers to befriend the young composer and conductor. From 1879 to 1881 Van der Stucken traveled throughout Europe and met and worked with Giuseppe Verdi, Emmanuel Chabrier, and Jules Massenet. He met his future wife in Paris in 1880. He was appointed *Kapellmeister* of the Breslau Stadttheater in 1881 and, as part of his duties, composed incidental music for Shakespeare's *The Tempest* in 1882. The next year, Franz Liszt sponsored a complete program of his works at Weimar, including his symphonic prologue to Heinrich Heine's *William Ratcliff.*

Van der Stucken returned in 1884 to America, where he succeeded Leopold Damrosch as director of the New York Arion Society, a male chorus founded in 1854. During his tenure with the chorus, which lasted until 1895, the society became the first American musical organization to tour in Europe. Van der Stucken also worked with other German male choruses in the *Sängerbund* movement, establishing festivals and training large numbers of singers in this country. During his first years in New York, he also established his reputation as a champion of music by American composers. In April 1885 in New York City he conducted the first concert in this country devoted exclusively to works by American composers, and in 1889 he conducted the first European concert with an entirely American program at the World Exposition in Paris. In 1895 he moved to Cincinnati to become the first conductor of the Cincinnati Symphony Orchestra, a post he held until 1907. He was also director and dean of the Cincinnati College of Music from 1897 to 1903 and musical director of one of the oldest music festivals in the United States, the Cincinnati May Festival, from 1906 to 1912 and 1923 to 1927.

After 1907 he lived in Germany and worked throughout Europe, where he was in great demand as a conductor of festivals. Except for work at the May Festival, he returned to the United States only occasionally. He gave his farewell symphonic concert in the hall of the Royal Society of Zoology in Antwerp on March 23, 1927. His last trip to his native country was in October 1928 for celebrations of his seventieth birthday in New York and Cincinnati.

As a composer, Van der Stucken followed the precepts of the Liszt–Wagner school of programmatic music. He wrote colorful orchestral and choral works as well as many songs. His major works include an unproduced opera, *Vlasda* (1891); *The Tempest*; and several symphonic works: *Pax Triumphans, William Ratcliff, Louisiana,* and *Pagina d'Amore.* He was a member of the American Institute of Arts and Letters and was named Officier de l'Instruction Publique by the French government and Chevalier de l'Ordre Leopold and Officier de la Couronne by King Albert of Belgium. An international music festival named for the composer was inaugurated in Fredericksburg in 1991. Van der Stucken and his wife had four children.

BIBLIOGRAPHY: *Baker's Biographical Dictionary of Musicians. The Biographical Dictionary of Musicians,* 1940. Stanley Sadie, ed., *The New Grove Dictionary of Music and Musicians* (Washington: Macmillan, 1980).

Larry Wolz

Van Zandt, John Townes. Singer and songwriter; b. Fort Worth, March 7, 1944; d. Smyrna, Tennessee, January 1, 1997 (buried in Dido Cemetery, Tarrant County); son of Harris William and Dorothy (Townes) Van Zandt. The Van Zandts were a wealthy family whose ancestors were among the founding families of Forth Worth. The law school building at the University of Texas at Austin, Townes Hall, bears the mother's family name. Van Zandt attended a private school in Minnesota and later the University of Colorado. Instead of law school and a future in the family oil business, he opted for a rootless life as a roaming singer and songwriter.

Once claiming that he wanted to know what it was like to fall, he sat on his fourth-floor balcony during a party and leaned slowly backward until he dropped. He came through without injury, but his family submitted him for psychiatric evaluation. The doctors diagnosed him as a "schizophrenic–reactionary manic depressive" and gave him insulin shock therapy, which is said to have erased his childhood memories and left him without any attachment to his past. Despite emotional and psychological problems, Van Zandt eventually wore such labels as "poet laureate of Texas," "premier poet of the time," "the James Joyce of Texan songwriting" and "the best writer in the country genre." He was married three times: to Fran Petters (1965–70; one son); to a woman named Cindi (1978–83); and to Jeanene Munselle (1980–94; one son and one daughter). All of the marriages ended in divorce.

Van Zandt was greatly influenced by Elvis Presley, Lightnin' Hopkins, Woody Guthrie, Hank Williams, and the early work of Bob Dylan. At the age of fifteen, he started playing the guitar after seeing Elvis on the "Ed Sullivan Show." He wrote songs about his experiences in life, including alcoholism, depression, and life on the road. He wrote in a narrative style, and his songs often were autobiographical. His best-known piece, "Pancho and Lefty," made popular through a duet with Willie Nelson and Merle Haggard, speaks of life on the road and hope for redemption. Van Zandt did not live to see his own songs succeed much, but his influence on other singers and songwriters was profound. Such performers as Lyle Lovett, Nanci Griffith, Emmy Lou Harris, Kris Kristofferson, and Steve Earle fell under his influence. Earle proclaimed him "the best songwriter in the whole world." Van Zandt's influence even extended to the grunge rock band Mudhoney. He joked that he "was the mold that grunge grew out of." He engendered the same devotion in a small but loyal following of fans that some have called "cult-like"

Townes Van Zandt, called by some the "poet laureate of Texas," wrote songs about the hard experiences of his own life. He influenced many of his contemporary singers and songwriters. Photograph by Niles J. Fuller. Niles J. Fuller Photograph Collection, CAH; CN 11494.

and "quasi-religious." Van Zandt died of an apparent heart attack after having hip surgery the previous week. His death came forty-four years to the day after that of his idol Hank Williams. He was survived by three children.

BIBLIOGRAPHY: Austin *American Statesman*, January 3, 1997. Austin *Chronicle*, 16.19 (January 1997). Rick Koster, *Texas Music* (New York: St Martin's Press, 1998).

John McVey

Vaughan, Stevie Ray. Blues musician and guitar legend; b. Oak Cliff, Dallas, October 3, 1954; d. August 27, 1990; son of Jim and Martha Vaughan. Stevie's exposure to music began in his childhood, as he watched his big brother, Jimmie, play guitar. Stevie's fascination with the blues drove him to teach himself to play the guitar before he was an adolescent.

By the time Vaughan was in high school, he was staying up all night, playing guitar in clubs in Deep Ellum, a popular alternative nightspot in Dallas. In his sophomore year he enrolled in an experimental arts program at Southern Methodist University for artistically gifted high school students, but the program did not motivate him to stay in school, and he dropped out before graduation in order to play music full-time.

In 1971, at the age of seventeen, Stevie moved to Austin, in an attempt to become involved in the music scene. Over the next few years he slept on pool tables and couches in the back of clubs and collected bottles to earn money for new guitar strings. He played in various local bands such as Cobra and Nightcrawlers, but recognition outside of Austin eluded him. Finally, in the late 1970s, Vaughan formed Triple Threat with Lou Ann Barton, Chris Layton, and Jackie Newhouse. This group evolved into Double Trouble, with Tommy Shannon and Reese Wynans replacing Newhouse and Barton.

By the early 1980s the group had built a solid following in Texas and was beginning to attract the attention of well-established musicians like Mick Jagger, who in 1982 invited Vaughan and the band to play at a private party in New York City. That same year Double Trouble received an invitation to play at the Montreux Jazz Festival in Switzerland. They were the first band in the history of the festival to play without having a major record contract. The performance was seen by David Bowie and Jackson Browne, and Stevie gained even more acclaim as a talented and rising young musician. Browne invited Vaughan to his Los Angeles studio for a demo session, at which Stevie recorded some tracks for his 1983 debut album, *Texas Flood*. Bowie had Vaughan play lead guitar on his album *Let's Dance* and join him on his 1983 tour.

Vaughan's fame immediately soared. The band signed a record contract with CBS / Epic records and came to the attention of veteran blues and rock producer John Hammond Sr. *Texas Flood* received a North American Rock Radio Awards nomination for Favorite Debut Album, and *Guitar Player Magazine* Reader's Poll voted Stevie Best New Talent and Best Electric Blues Guitarist for 1983. A track off the album also received a Grammy nomination for Best Rock Instrumental performance.

Vaughan's subsequent albums met with increased popularity and critical attention. Double Trouble followed *Texas Flood* with *Couldn't Stand the Weather* (1984), *Live Alive* (1985), and *Soul to Soul* (1986). All of the albums went gold and captured various Grammy nominations in either the blues or rock categories. Throughout the 1980s Vaughan and his band also became consistent nominees and winners of the Austin *Chronicle*'s music awards and *Guitar Player Magazine*'s reader's polls. In 1984, at the National Blues Foundation Awards, Vaughan became the first white man to win Entertainer of the Year and Blues Instrumentalist of the Year. At the Grammys that year he shared in the Best Traditional Blues honors for his work on *Blues Explosion*, a compilation album of various artists.

Although he rapidly gained prestige and success in the music world, Stevie also lived the stereotypical life of a rock-and-roll star, full of alcohol and drug abuse. On his 1986 European tour he collapsed and eventually checked into a rehabilitation center in Georgia. He left the hospital sober and committed to the Twelve Step program of Alcoholics Anonymous. Following his recovery, he released his fifth album, *In Step*, in 1989. It won him a second Grammy, this time for Best Contemporary Blues Recording. In 1990 Vaughan collaborated with Jimmie Vaughan, his brother and founding member of the Fabulous Thunderbirds, on *Family Style*, which was released after his death. This last album brought Stevie's career total of Grammys to four. After his death Epic records released two more albums of his work, *The Sky is Crying* (1991) and *In the Beginning* (1992).

Stevie married Lenny Bailey in 1980, and they divorced in 1986, when he was at the low point of his struggle with drug and alcohol abuse. At the time of his death, he had a girlfriend, Janna Lapidus. Vaughan died in a helicopter crash on the way to Chicago from a concert in Alpine Valley, East Troy, Wisconsin. The location of the concert was difficult to reach, so many performers stayed in Chicago and flew in before the show. Dense fog contributed to the pilot's flying the helicopter into the side of a man-made ski mountain. All on board were killed instantly. Over 1,500 people, including industry giants such as Jackson Browne, Bonnie Raitt, and Stevie Wonder, attended Stevie's memorial service in Dallas. He is buried at Laurel Land Memorial Park in South Dallas. The city of Austin erected a memorial statue of Stevie Ray Vaughan on November 21, 1993. It is located on Town Lake, near the site of his last Austin concert.

BIBLIOGRAPHY: Keri Leigh, *Stevie Ray: Soul to Soul* (Dallas: Taylor, 1993). Joe Nick Patoski and Bill Crawford, *Stevie Ray Vaughan: Caught in the Crossfire* (Boston: Little, Brown, 1993). Vertical Files, Center for American History, University of Texas at Austin.

Robin Dutton

Venth, Carl. Violinist and composer; b. Cologne, Germany, February 16, 1860; d. San Antonio, January 30, 1938; son of Carl and Fredericka (von Turkowitz) Venth. In 1878 he entered the Cologne Conservatory to study violin. In 1879 he made his first concert tour through Holland and went to Paris as a concertmaster of the Opéra Comique.

Venth arrived in America in 1880 and after a concert tour from Boston to St. Louis became concertmaster at

Blues musician Stevie Ray Vaughan performing during the 1984 season of "Austin City Limits." Courtesy Scott Newton/Austin City Limits. The city of Austin erected a memorial statue of the legendary guitarist on the south shore of Town Lake, near the site of his last Austin concert.

Rudolph Bila's concerts in New York. He was a member of the orchestra of the Metropolitan Opera House from 1884 to 1888, when he organized the Venth Violin School in Brooklyn. Between 1889 and 1897 he led the Seidl Orchestra and the Euterpe Orchestral Society and organized the Brooklyn Symphony Orchestra and the Venth Quartet. On July 13, 1897, in Brooklyn, he married Cathinka Finch Myhr of Norway. He was concertmaster of the St. Paul Symphony in 1906 but returned to New York in 1907 to organize the Venth Trio.

Sometime between 1907 and 1912 Venth moved to Texas as director of the violin department at Kidd–Key College at Sherman. In 1912 he directed the Frohsinn Chorus and conducted the Symphony Orchestra at Dallas. He became dean of the school of fine arts at Texas Woman's College in Fort Worth, where he conducted the choral club and was president of the Music Teachers' Association. From 1931 to 1938 he was head of the music department of the University of San Antonio. Venth's published music included 100 piano and violin pieces and songs.

BIBLIOGRAPHY: Fort Worth *Star-Telegram*, January 30, 1938. Frank W. Johnson, *A History of Texas and Texans* (5 vols., ed. E. C. Barker and E. W. Winkler [Chicago and New York: American Historical Society, 1914; rpt. 1916]). Goldie Capers Smith, *The Creative Arts in Texas: A Handbook of Biography* (Nashville: Cokesbury, 1926).

Venting, Albert Sobieski. Pastor, teacher, musician, and hymnologist; b. Omaha, Nebraska, February 6, 1883; d. Waco, June 13, 1965; buried in Cleburne; son of Count Adolf Sobieski of Crasaw, Poland, and Willie Mae (Ellyson) Sobieski, of Richmond, Virginia. His father was a representative of the Polish government, and his mother was an artist. After Willie Mae Sobieski died in childbirth, the count attempted to care for the child alone, but found he could not. At age two, Albert was turned over to some friends of his father to be cared for. When he was five, his father died. When he was fourteen, his foster mother died and the boy learned that she was not his real mother.

The same year, Albert was converted by the preaching of Dr. Richard Venting, a Baptist minister from England who was the pastor of First Baptist Church, Council Bluffs, Iowa. Afterward, Albert felt called to preach the Gospel, but his foster father was not favorable toward religion. In 1897 Venting adopted Albert. After graduating from high school in Council Bluffs, Albert attended William Jewel College in Liberty, Missouri (1899–1901). The pastor wanted his adopted son to experience the English education he had received, so in 1901 Albert moved to England, where he attended Harley College in London (1901–03) and Mansfield College, Oxford (1904). Albert Venting came to Texas in 1908 as pastor of East Henderson Baptist Church in Cleburne. In 1916 he entered Southwestern Baptist Theological Seminary, where he received a Th.M. degree (1920), a Th.D. (1924), and a B.Mus. (1931).

Venting was trained as a violinist very early in life; his foster father was a member of the Philharmonic Symphony Orchestra of New York. Albert was playing violin at age five and at age twelve was going with his foster father to orchestra practice. However, after his conversion, his training took him in the direction of religion and philosophy. He became a Baptist minister in 1900 and continued as such, at least part-time, until his death. He also taught religion and philosophy classes at Southwestern Baptist Theological Seminary from 1921 to 1937. His love for music and musical training was evident there, as one of his most popular courses was "Religion and the Fine Arts." He also influenced I. E. Reynolds, the dean of the music school at Southwestern. Venting introduced many of the songs from English hymnody to Reynolds. He was also instrumental in the change of name of the music school at Southwestern from School of Gospel Music to School of Sacred Music.

Concurrent with his teaching at Southwestern Seminary, Venting also pastored several churches: Seminary Hill Baptist Church in Fort Worth (now Gambrell Street Baptist Church), 1923; Tabernacle Baptist Church in Fort Worth, 1929–31; and First Baptist Church in Cleburne, 1933–47. Later, he quit pastoring in an official capacity, but taught a "Business Men's Bible Class" at Broadway Baptist Church in Fort Worth (1952–65), where he influenced the lives of many influential business leaders. In 1952, after Venting retired, Baylor University in Waco asked him to form a Department of Sacred Music within the School of Music. He remained on its faculty until his death, of heart disease. His funeral was held on June 15, 1965, at Broadway Baptist Church in Fort Worth.

BIBLIOGRAPHY: Fort Worth *Star–Telegram*, June 14, 1965. Enid E. Markham, "A Lonesome Place Against the Sky," *Baylor Line*, July–August, 1965. William J. Reynolds, *The Cross & the Lyre: The Story of the School of Church Music, Southwestern Baptist Theological Seminary, Fort Worth, Texas* (Fort Worth: School of Church Music, SWBTS, 1994). Vertical file, Archives and Special Collections Department, Roberts Library, Southwestern Baptist Theological Seminary, Fort Worth.

Michael Pullin

Villa, Beto. Saxophonist and "father" of the *orquesta Tejana*; b. Falfurrias, Texas, October 26, 1915; d. Corpus Christi, November 1, 1986. Beto's father, Alberto Sr., was both a tailor and a musician, and strongly encouraged his son to learn to read music. In 1932, while in high school, Beto formed a band called the Sonny Boys, which performed at local festivals and school dances. Four years later, he got his first full-time gig in Freer, Texas, at a dance hall known as the Barn.

For the next several years he played in primarily Anglo dance halls, where he learned to imitate popular American swing bands. Although Villa appeared to be well on his way to establishing a musical career, in 1940 he opened a meat market with his father-in-law. After serving in the U.S. Navy during World War II (he played in a band for enlisted personnel), he returned to Falfurrias and opened up the Pan American and La Plaza dance halls. While still working in his meat shop, he occasionally performed music on the weekends. He soon realized that he could earn more money performing in one weekend than he could working all week as a butcher. So he turned his attention increasingly toward becoming a full-time musician.

By 1946, Villa had developed the idea of merging Mexican-American music and more mainstream popular music by combining the urbanized *orquesta* with a *ranchero* style, thereby giving it an *arrancherado orquesta* sound. In that same year, he approached his friend, Armando Marroquín, founder of the new record company Discos Ideal, to ask Marroquín to help make a record that would capture the sound of this new musical style Villa had created. The partnership led to Villa's recording of his first singles on a 78-rpm acetate disc, which included a polka entitled "Las Delicias" and a waltz called "¿Porqué te Ríes?" With broader exposure through these new recordings, Beto Villa y su Orquesta quickly became popular in dance halls throughout South Texas. In 1948 the band scored its first hit, "Rosita." Other hits soon followed, such as "Las Gaviotas," "La Picona," "Tamaulipas," and "Monterrey." "Monterrey," a polka in which Villa teamed up with conjunto accordionist Narciso Martínez, demonstrated Villa's musical versatility and determination to blend together a variety of musical styles.

By 1950, Villa's band had grown to include as many as twelve members at a time, capable of handling a broad range of instrumental combinations, as well as more complex musical arrangements. In trying to make his *orquesta* more sophisticated than rival bands, he went so far as to fire members who did not learn to read music. For a period of twelve years, Beto Villa y su Orquesta toured throughout the United States, recorded over a hundred singles on 78 rpm, and produced over a dozen LPs for Discos Ideal. Villa also recorded *ranchera* singles with Lydia Mendoza and the duo Carmen y Laura.

In 1960, Villa stopped touring because of health problems. During his career, he created a new musical style for Mexican Americans, the *orquesta Tejana*, which helped them express both their *ranchero* (country) and *jaitón* (cosmopolitan) identities. In 1983, three years before his death, Villa was inducted into the TMA Hall of Fame.

BIBLIOGRAPHY: Ramiro Burr, *The Billboard Guide to Tejano and Regional Mexican Music* (New York: Billboard, 1999). Manuel Peña, *Música Tejana: The Cultural Economy of Artistic Transformation* (College Station: Texas A&M University Press, 1999). Manuel Peña, *The Texas–Mexican Conjunto: History of a Working-Class Music* (Austin: University of Texas Press, 1985).

Juan Carlos Rodríguez

Villareal, Bruno. Accordionist; b. La Grulla, Texas, October 6, 1901; d. Waco, November 3, 1976. According to stories told by Narciso Martínez, "father" of Texas-Mexican conjunto music, during the 1930s Villareal lived on a *ranchito* three miles from Santa Rosa, at the north end of the lower Rio Grande valley. Although he was half blind, he walked every day into town to play his accordion for whatever money was offered. At times, he was also hired out to play at *bailes de negocio* or other kinds of celebrations. Villareal was nicknamed "El Azote del Valle" (the Scourge from the Valley) and is today still remembered by people as far north as Amarillo, where he once played in the streets with a tin cup attached to his piano accordion, an instrument he used from the late 1930s onward. He originally played a two-row button accordion, but switched to a piano accordion later in his career. In the early 1930s, conjunto players such as he used the left-hand bass and right-hand treble chord elements of the accordion.

Villareal was among the first accordionists to become popular in South Texas through phonograph records, and he made the first recording of the accordion in 1928. By the 1930s, often backed by a *bajo sexto* (twelve-string bass guitar), he was an acknowledged master. During this time *música norteña* or conjunto became the music of choice among the Mexican-American working class. This music enjoyed a great popularity in the area known to Mexicans as *el Norte*, the region bounded by South Texas and the Mexican states of Nuevo Leon, Tamaulipas, and Coahuila.

Villareal apparently was the first accordionist to secure a long-term relationship with a major label. The Okeh label recorded him on June 12, 1930, and continued to do so for the next several years. Consequently, he is generally recognized as the first conjunto accordionist on records. His style was traditional, with almost equal emphasis on melody and bass. Villareal and fellow accordionists José Rodríguez and Jesús Casiano relied heavily on their left-hand, bass-and-chord elements for the accordion sets. This set them apart from Narciso Martínez, who began almost immediately to de-emphasize that side of the accordion in favor of more marked and better articulated melody lines at the treble end.

After World War II, Mexican-American music continued to evolve, and the accordion continued to play a central role. However, as some accordionists, such as Narciso Martínez and Santiago Jiménez, grew in popularity, others such as Jesús Casiano, who were unwilling or unable to meet new musical challenges, all but disappeared from the commercial market. One of the saddest cases was that of Villareal, who was reduced to near beggary until sympathetic relatives finally took him in.

BIBLIOGRAPHY: Arhoolie records, *Music Excerpts, Liner Notes, and Photos* (www.lib.utexas.edu/benson/border/arhoolie/arhoolie1.html), accessed January 29, 2003. Manuel H. Peña, *The Texas-Mexican Conjunto: History of a Working-Class Music* (Austin: University of Texas Press, 1985).

Elsa Gonzalez

Vincent, Louella Styles. Author and composer; b. Louisa Gabriella Styles, Fayetteville, North Carolina, September 5, 1853; d. Fort Worth, April 25, 1924 (buried in Meridian Cemetery, Meridian, Texas); daughter of Carey Wentworth and Fannie Jean (Evans) Styles. Her father founded the Atlanta, Georgia, *Constitution*. Louisa combined her given names to form the name Louella. She studied music and literature at Andrew Female Academy in Cuthbert, Georgia, and Augusta Female Seminary in Staunton, Virginia, before marrying James Upshur Vincent, a teacher, attorney, and journalist, on September 28, 1875. The Vincents lived in Canton and later Brunswick, Georgia, before moving in 1881 to Texas, where Carey Styles had accepted a position with the Galveston *News*.

The Vincents and their two sons lived in Galveston, Jonesboro, and Glen Rose before settling in Meridian in 1886. There Louella and James established a private academy; he served as principal, and she taught music. In 1890 the family moved to Stephenville and shared a house with Louella's parents. James became owner and manager of the Stephenville *Empire*, and Louella gave private lessons in vocal and instrumental music. She wrote music and poetry and established a United Daughters of the Confederacy chapter named for her elder son, who had died in 1886. With her mother, she became a charter member of the Twentieth Century Club in 1901; the two women made their interest in poetry and southern literature the emphasis of the club's programs.

Although they were never divorced, Louella and James had separated by the late 1890s, and Louella tried to turn a profit from writing and lecturing in order to ease her financial position. She published poems in regional magazines, tried unsuccessfully to find a publisher for a comic opera she had written, and with her son, Upshur, as her manager, lectured on the Chautauqua circuit in Georgia, Alabama, Arkansas, and Colorado. In 1905 she fulfilled a lifetime dream by founding and editing *The Southerner*, "Louella Styles Vincent's magazine of the South," a literary journal to which she and her mother were the heaviest contributors. Upshur Vincent published *The Southerner* from his printing house in Strawn and served as his mother's business manager; the magazine went through only four issues before the breakdown of Louella's health and Upshur's finances resulted in its demise.

Mrs. Vincent moved to Dallas late in 1905 and in July 1908 began publication of the *Dallas Clubwoman*, a weekly chronicle of society and church activities. She followed it with the short-lived *Texas Clubwoman* in 1909; both magazines served as showcases for her poetry. When her son became editor and publisher of the Dallas *Jeffersonian* in 1909, her verses were displayed prominently as one of the paper's regular features. She published "My Lowlier Lot" in the *Texas Review* in 1921 and submitted "Sonnets of Our City, Dallas" to the Poetry Society of England.

Louella Vincent was a charter member of the Dallas Women's Forum and the Texas Congress of Mothers, served two years as state secretary of the United Daughters of the Confederacy, and held memberships in the Poetry Society of Texas and the Poetry Society of England. When she died at her son's home in Fort Worth, she left three volumes of poetry, fifty musical compositions (half a dozen of which had been published), and five volumes of partially edited prose.

BIBLIOGRAPHY: Imogene Bentley Dickey, *Early Literary Magazines of Texas* (Austin: Steck–Vaughn, 1970). C. Richard King, "Louella Styles Vincent: Texas Editor and Author," West Texas Historical Association *Yearbook* 47 (1971). James Upshur Vincent Collection, Center for American History, University of Texas at Austin.

C. Richard King

Vinson, Eddie. Blues saxophonist and vocalist, known as "Mr. Cleanhead"; b. Houston, December 18, 1917; d. Los Angeles, July 2, 1988. Vinson was nicknamed "Cleanhead" after he destroyed his hair while trying to straighten it with lye. His grandfather was a violinist; his father, "Piano" Sam Vinson, and mother, Arnella Session, were both pianists.

As a child, Eddie sang in church choirs. While still attending Jack Yates High School in Houston, he developed his saxophone talents so impressively that he was asked to tour with Chester Boone's Territory Band in the summers. After graduating from high school in 1935, he became a full-time member of Boone's band. Milton Larkin assumed control of the band in 1936, and Vinson spent the next four years touring the South and Midwest with the group. He was strongly influenced by two other noted members of the band, guitarist T-Bone Walker and Arnett Cobb. While touring with Larkin, Vinson was also introduced to Big Bill Broonzy, who taught him how to "shout the blues."

Vinson moved to New York in 1941 and joined Cootie Williams's orchestra for a short time. In 1942 he made his first recording, the blues tune "When My Baby Left Me," on the Okeh label. He achieved notoriety while singing the blues on several of Williams's hit recordings, including "Cherry Red," "Is You Is," "Things Ain't What They Used To Be," and "Somebody's Got To Go." In addition to recording, Vinson also toured with Williams's band for the next three years. He formed his own big band in 1945 and, over the next several years, recorded extensively for different labels, including Capitol, Mercury, King, and others. Some of his best-known cuts were recorded with his own sixteen-piece band. He had some success with "Kidney Stew Blues," "Cleanhead Blues," "Old Maid Boogie," and "Tune Up."

By the late 1940s, however, his popularity had waned, and he moved back to Houston in 1954. He toured and briefly recorded with Count Basie's band in 1957. By that time, according to jazz historians, Vinson had lost much of his "falsetto voice," his recordings tended to be "grainy," and he sounded "hoarse," In the early 1960s he moved to Los Angeles, where he worked with the Johnny Otis revue. In addition, he recorded with Cannonball Adderley's band on the Riverside Records label. For the next two decades, Vinson continued to record. He cut several hybrid jazz and blues albums, including *Eddie Vinson and a Roomful of Blues* on the Muse label, and *Live at Sandy's*. On many of his recordings he sang with a "jump-blues" Texas style. Many of his sexually explicit songs, including "Oilman Blues," "Some Women Do," and "Ever-Ready Blues," were deemed too raunchy to be played on the radio.

Although many of Vinson's songs did not get air time, he remained popular on the international music-festival circuit throughout the 1970s and 1980s. He toured Europe and performed at various jazz and blues festivals in the United States until shortly before his death. Vinson was married to Bernice Spradley and had three children. He is considered a "mainstream" bluesman who never compromised his style.

BIBLIOGRAPHY: Leonard Feather and Ira Gitler, eds., *The Encyclopedia of Jazz in the Seventies* (New York: Horizon Press, 1976). Sheldon Harris, *Blues Who's Who* (New Rochelle, New York: Arlington House, 1979). Colin Larkin, ed., *The Guiness Encyclopedia of Popular Music*, Volume 7 (New York: Guiness, 1998). Dave Oliphant, *Texan Jazz* (Austin: University of Texas Press, 1996). Robert Santelli, *The Big Book of Blues* (New York: Pen-

Eddie "Mr. Clean-head" Vinson, blues saxophonist and vocalist, made his first recording in 1942 and formed his own big band in 1945. He recorded with his own band, as well as with Cootie Williams, Count Basie, and Cannonball Adderly. Benny Joseph Collection.

The Vulcan Gas Company was a popular night-spot on Congress Avenue in Austin for counterculture music and psychedelic light shows. Photograph by Burton Wilson.

guin, 1993).   *James Head*

Vulcan Gas Company. A popular Austin night club located at 316 Congress Avenue; opened October 27, 1967, and closed around July 1970, one month before the opening of Armadillo World Headquarters. Houston White, Gary Maxwell, Don Hyde, and Sandy Lockett originally opened the club, and Jim Franklin joined them in October 1967. Franklin, a noted poster artist, lived in the building—winters on the ground level behind the office, and summers in a loft near a skylight that opened onto the roof.

The club featured original "counterculture" music accompanied by psychedelic light shows. Musicians who played at the Vulcan include Doug Sahm, Angela Strehli, Stevie Ray Vaughn, Johnny Winter, and groups such as the Conqueroo, 13th Floor Elevators, Shiva's Headband, and Canned Heat. The Vulcan became a venue for musicians of various styles who refused to perform Top 40 pop tunes.

A platform suspended along the east wall of the building held eight slide projectors, three overhead projectors, and other special-effects equipment. Light-show and liquid-projection effects converted the stage, situated in the north-

Johnny Winter Trio (left to right: Johnny Winter, Uncle John Turner, and Tommy Shannon) at the Vulcan Gas Company, August 2, 1968. Photograph by Burton Wilson.

west corner, to a "living canvas." Special-effects artists used clock crystals filled with colored oil and original artwork to enhance the mood according to the type of music being performed. Although the Vulcan is commonly associated with hippie blues, it also served as a model for other Austin music venues, such as the Armadillo World Headquarters, that were later established by some of the people associated with the Vulcan Gas Company, including Jim Franklin and Eddie Wilson.

The Vulcan Gas Company closed, in part, due to its location on a crowded stretch of Congress Avenue. Young people who were not willing to pay the $1.50 cover charge would gather around the doorway and listen from the street. Some people bought marijuana from street dealers. Consequently, the Vulcan became associated with the illegal use of drugs and alcohol and rowdy street crowds. At times, Austin police officers would form a line in front of the Vulcan and make a sweep across the street and into the club, arresting suspects along the way.

Many stories are associated with the Vulcan. Besides its

intriguing hole-in-the-wall entrance from H&R Block off of Fourth Street, the Vulcan sat atop a cistern that provided echo effects for experimenting musicians. The Vulcan's storefront windows often were covered by drapes that allowed people outside to peep through slits and holes to view strange window dressings featuring provocative mannequins, artwork, and lighting. After the Vulcan's popularity as a hangout for hippies made it increasingly unpopular with local authorities, Franklin became convinced that he could save the club only by changing its name; the name he chose was Armadillo Gas Company. Although the plan was not successful, the armadillo, a regular feature in Franklin's posters, became the mascot of the Vulcan's successor, Armadillo World Headquarters, in 1970.

BIBLIOGRAPHY: *Austin Business Journal*, December 24, 1999. Dallas *Morning News*, August 8, 1987. Rush Evans, *Armadillo World Headquarters* (http://www.gogo.net/ awhq/indexarmdilo.htm), accessed July 23, 2002. Houston *Chronicle*, August 18, 1988.   *Cheryl L. Simon*

Walker, T-Bone. Blues musician, also known as Oak Cliff T-Bone; b. Aaron Thibeaux Walker, Linden, Texas, May 28, 1910; d. Los Angeles, March 16, 1975 (buried at Inglewood Cemetery, Inglewood, California); only son of Rance and Movelia (Jamison, Jimerson) Walker. Looking for a better future for her son, his mother left her husband and moved to Dallas, where Aaron attended Northwest Hardee School through the seventh grade. His mother played guitar, and his stepfather, Marco Washington, played bass and several other instruments. Family friendship with Blind Lemon Jefferson and Huddie Ledbetter familiarized him with the blues from infancy. T-Bone was recruited to lead Jefferson around the Central Avenue area, and he absorbed the legendary musician's style. While still in his teens, Walker met and married Vida Lee; they had three children.

Walker was a gifted dancer who taught himself guitar. Around 1925 he joined Dr. Breeding's Big B Tonic medicine show, then toured the South with blues artist Ida Cox. In 1929 in Dallas he cut his first record, "Wichita Falls Blues," under the name Oak Cliff T-Bone, using the name of his Dallas neighborhood. Around 1930, after winning first prize in an amateur show promoted by Cab Calloway, Walker toured the South with Calloway's band and worked with the Raisin' Cain show and several other bands in Texas, including those of Count Biloski (Balaski) and Milt Larkin. He also appeared with Ma Rainey, a great figure in blues history, in her 1934 Fort Worth performances.

In 1935 Walker moved to Los Angeles, where he quickly made a name for himself singing and playing banjo, and then guitar, for black audiences in two popular nightclubs, Little Harlem and Club Alabam. Crowds of fans were attracted to his acrobatic performances, which combined playing and tap dancing, and in 1935 he became the first blues guitarist to play the electric guitar. The Trocadero Club in Hollywood, where Walker had become sufficiently well known to appear as a star, welcomed integrated audiences after his 1936 performances. From 1940 to 1945 he toured with Les Hite's Cotton Club orchestra as a featured vocalist; he recorded the classic "T-Bone Blues" with Hite in New York City in 1940. Walker used a fluid technique that combined the country blues tradition with more polished contemporary swing, his style influenced by Francis (Scrapper) Blackwell, Leroy Carr, and Lonnie Johnson. He was subsequently billed as "Daddy of the Blues."

He also toured United States Army bases in the early 1940s and, recruited by boxing champion Joe Louis in 1942, went to Chicago, where he headlined a revue at the city's Rhumboogie Club so successfully that he returned year after year. In the mid-1940s he became a band leader, signed a recording contract with the Black and White label, and turned out some of the best titles of his long recording career, including "Stormy Monday." Many of his songs reached the Top Ten on the Hit Parade. In the 1950s he recorded under the Imperial label and worked for Atlantic

Clarence "Gatemouth" Brown (left) and "T-Bone" Walker (*Texas Rhythm, Texas Rhyme: A Pictorial History of Texas Music*, Austin: Texas Monthly Press, 1984). Courtesy Larry Willoughby. Walker was the first blues guitarist to play the electric guitar. He made his first record in Dallas in 1929. In the 1950s many of his songs, including "Stormy Monday," made the Hit Parade Top Ten.

Records. In 1955 he underwent an operation for chronic ulcers.

In the early 1960s T-Bone joined Count Basie's orchestra, appeared in Europe with a package called Rhythm and Blues, U.S.A., and played at the American Folk Blues Festival and Jazz at the Philharmonic. This began a new phase of his career as a blues legend, during which he appeared before largely white audiences. He was a regular attraction abroad, where his recordings made him a great favorite, and he was a participant on television shows and at jazz festivals in Monterey, California; Nice, France; and Montreaux, Switzerland. In Europe he recorded a Polydor album entitled *Good Feelin'*, which won the 1970 Grammy for ethnic–traditional recording. Among his other albums are *Singing the Blues*, *Funky Town*, and *The Truth*.

As an artist and performer, Walker was accurately evaluated by blues authority Pete Welding as "one of the deep, enduring wellsprings of the modern blues to whom many others have turned, and continue to return for inspiration and renewal." Among those he influenced were B. B. King, Pee Wee Crayton, Eric Clapton, Albert Collins, and Johnny Winter. Many titles from Walker's more than four decades of recording have been reissued. Walker died of a stroke, and his funeral at the Inglewood Cemetery was attended by more than a thousand mourners.

BIBLIOGRAPHY: John Chilton, *Who's Who of Jazz: Storyville to Swing Street* (London: Bloomsbury Book Shop, 1970; American ed., New York and Philadelphia: Chilton, 1972; 4th ed., New York: Da Capo Press, 1985). Helen Oakley Dance, *Stormy Monday: The T-Bone Walker Story* (Baton Rouge: Louisiana State University, 1987). Stanley Dance, *The World of Count Basie* (New York: Scribner, 1980). Sheldon Harris, *Blues Who's Who: A Biographical Dictionary of Blues Singers* (New Rochelle, New York: Arlington House, 1979). Per Notini, notes to *T. Bone Walker: The Invention of the Electric Guitar Blues* (Blues Boy LP, BB-304, 1983). Jim and Amy O'Neal, "Living Blues Interview: T-Bone Walker," *Living Blues*, Winter 1972–73, Spring 1973. Arnold Shaw, *Honkers and Shouters: The Golden Years of Rhythm and Blues* (New York: Macmillan, 1978). *Helen Oakley Dance*

Wallace, Sippie. Blues singer, also known as the Texas Nightingale; b. Beulah Thomas, Houston, November 1, 1898; d. Detroit, November 1, 1986; one of thirteen children of Fanny and George W. Thomas Sr. Her father was a deacon at Shiloh Baptist Church. Beulah was nicknamed Sippie in grammar school because, she said, "My teeth were so far apart I had to sip everything." As a child she began singing and playing the organ at her father's church. But on summer nights she would steal away from her home, follow the ragtime sounds of the traveling tent-show bands, and listen to the blues singers through a flap in the canvas tent. On one of her many visits, some of the performers asked her to fill an opening in the chorus line, and her career began.

As the tent shows expanded and grew more elaborate, Beulah found more opportunities to perform. When one of the shows moved from Houston to Dallas, she traveled with it. By 1916 she was acting in plays, dancing in the chorus line, doing comedy routines, serving as a snake charmer's assistant, and singing solo ballads. Later that year she moved to New Orleans to work with her older brother George, who was a pianist, songwriter, and publisher. Jazz and ragtime were flourishing, and Sippie found

Eighty-six-year-old Sippie Wallace at the New Orleans Jazz and Heritage Festival, 1985. Photograph © by Michael P. Smith.

herself surrounded by young musicians, many of whom later became legends. Rehearsals in the Thomas house included King Oliver, Louis Armstrong, Sidney Bechet, Clarence Williams, and Johnny Dodds.

In 1923 she moved to Chicago and, with George's help, met Ralph Peer, then general manager of Okeh Records. Three months after her first record was pressed with Okeh, she was on top of the black record industry, a star with a national reputation. Her songs, such as the classics "Mighty Tight Woman" and "Woman Be Wise," spoke with earthy directness about love and relationships. Her brother, noted pianist Hersal Thomas, and her second husband, Matt Wallace, both passed away in 1936. This sudden severing of two of her own relationships prompted her to settle in Detroit and return to singing gospel music.

Victoria Spivey, another Texas artist, persuaded Wallace to return to performing popular music in the 1960s. The "tough-minded" lyrics of some of Wallace's songs transcended the blues era in which they were written and appealed to feminists of the 1970s, when a young singer named Bonnie Raitt initiated renewed interest in Wallace. Raitt's debut album in 1971 included two Wallace songs, and during the 1970s and 1980s the two women recorded and toured together. Wallace subsequently made an album, *Sippie*, in 1983 (Atlantic Records). She wrote seven of the ten songs on the release, which was nominated for a Grammy. In 1985 the eighty-six-year-old Wallace appeared at the annual Austin Music Festival in Manor, her first Texas performance since her departure sixty-three years before.

Sippie Wallace is said to have possessed "qualities of shading and inflection in her singing that marked the classic blues artist." She was known as the last of the blues shouters and ranked among such blues greats as Bessie Smith, Ma Rainey, Ida Cox and Alberta Hunter. She died on her eighty-eighth birthday.

BIBLIOGRAPHY: John Chilton, *Who's Who of Jazz: Storyville to Swing Street* (London: Bloomsbury Book Shop, 1970; American ed., New York and Philadelphia: Chilton, 1972; 4th ed., New York: Da Capo Press, 1985). Sheldon Harris, *Blues Who's Who: A Biographical Dictionary of Blues Singers* (New Rochelle, New York: Arlington House, 1979). Houston *Post*, November 3, 1986. *Jazz on Record: A Critical Guide* (London: Hutchinson, 1960; rev. ed., London: Hanover, 1968). *Newsweek*, November 17, 1987. New York *Times*, November 4, 1986.   *Donna P. Parker*

Walton, Mercy Dee. Pianist; b. Waco, August 30, 1915; d. Murphys, California, December 2, 1962; son of Fred and Bessie (Wade) Walton. His parents worked on farms in the bottomlands of the Brazos River, and Mercy Dee was destined for a similar life when at the age of thirteen he began to learn to play the piano, inspired by the music he heard at local house parties. The greatest influence on him was the unrecorded Delois Maxey, but other (equally unrecorded) Texas pianists also made some contribution: Son Brewster from Waco, Pinetop Shorty, Willy Woodson, Sonny Vee and "Big Hand" Joe Thomas in Fort Worth, Son Putney in Dallas, and Bob Jackson in Marlin—all little more than names now—and the Grey Ghost (Roosevelt T. Williams)

who emerged from obscurity only after Mercy Dee's death. All of these men followed the same pattern of life, wintering in the cities and touring through the state during harvest time.

In the late thirties Mercy Dee moved to California, where he worked on farms up and down the Central Valley while performing in local bars and clubs for the region's black farmworkers. In 1949 he recorded for the Fresno-based Spire label and had an immediate hit with "Lonesome Cabin Blues," which reached number seven in the R&B charts. This success attracted the attention of the larger Los Angeles–based Imperial label, which signed him and recorded two sessions of twelve titles in 1950. No hits emerged, however, and by 1952 he was recording for Specialty, another Los Angeles label. His first track for them, "One Room Country Shack," was a hit in 1953, reaching number eight on the R&B charts.

This success led to a great change in his career; he had, for a while at least, become a nationally known artist, and he worked with various package shows touring the country. But his two other Specialty issues were less successful and he was dropped by the label. A recording for the small Rhythm label in 1954 had little impact, but in 1955 he recorded for the Flair label, part of the Modern Records stable in Los Angeles. These recordings were much more in the R&B style but did nothing to restore Walton's career to the heights of "One Room Country Shack." He returned to his earlier situation of supplementing his earnings from music with agricultural work and settled in the Stockton, California, area.

In 1961 he came to the attention of Chris Strachwitz, owner of the Arhoolie label. A series of sessions that year with sympathetic backing by guitarist K. C. Douglas, harmonica player Sidney Maiden, and drummer Otis Cherry produced albums on the Arhoolie and Bluesville labels. Soon afterwards Walton suffered a cerebral hemorrhage and died in hospital. He was a fine piano player in the barrelhouse style and a strong if not terribly expressive singer. His main claim to fame lies in his lyrics, which are largely based on his own experiences and those of his primary audience and are full of witty and striking ideas.

BIBLIOGRAPHY: Hank Davis, "Mercy Dee Walton," *Living Blues* 77 (December 1987). Bob Groom, "Mercy Dee," *Blues-Link* 4 and 5 (1974). Sheldon Harris, *Blues Who's Who: A Biographical Dictionary of Blues Singers* (New Rochelle, New York: Arlington House, 1979). Chris Strachwitz, "Tribute to Mercy Dee Walton," *Rhythm & Blues* 61 (July 1963).   *Ray Astbury*

Watson, Johnny. Guitarist, pianist, and vocalist, known as "Guitar" Watson; b. Houston, February 3, 1935; d. Yokohama, Japan, May 17, 1996. His father, a pianist, taught young Johnny to play. When Johnny was eleven, his grandmother gave him his grandfather's guitar. Watson eventually decided the guitar would be his instrument after watching Gatemouth Brown perform.

The Watsons moved from Houston to Los Angeles in the early 1950s, and Johnny joined the Chuck Higgins Band as its pianist. After switching to the guitar, he developed his style when he toured with New Orleans bluesman

Guitar Slim in the early 1950s. In order to be heard in the loud juke joints where they played, both men learned to pull on the strings of their guitars with their bare fingers to increase their volume. Watson also developed his flamboyant "bad-boy" stage act in the early 1950s. Wearing trademark sunglasses and a hat, he often played the guitar while standing on his head, or played it with his teeth or feet. His style, outrageous for the 1950s, was a generation before its time. It influenced countless younger guitarists, including Eric Clapton, Frank Zappa, and Jimi Hendrix.

Watson recorded his first single, "Space Guitar," in 1954. In another of his innovations that was years ahead of its time, he pioneered the use of feedback and reverberation. Unfortunately for him and for Federal Records, the public of the early 1950s, before rock-and-roll, was not prepared for his kind of music, and the record did not sell very well. He had greater success in 1955 with his song "Those Lonely, Lonely Nights," recorded on the Modern label. This recording hit the rhythm-and-blues top ten. In 1957 Watson recorded "Gangster of Love," a song that Steve Miller turned into a huge hit in the late 1960s. Watson toured with the group Olympics, and later with Little Richard, in the late 1950s. He made the charts again in 1962 with his song "Cuttin' In," which hit number six.

He achieved his greatest success in the 1970s, when he released seven hit albums. "Ain't That a Bitch," recorded on DJM Records, went gold. In the mid-1970s he made "Master Funk," "Funk Beyond the Call of Duty," and "A Real Mother for Ya." In addition to these recordings, Watson also performed on selected Frank Zappa albums and played solo on Herb Alpert's *Beyond*. During the late 1970s and 1980s he continued to tour and record, but with less success than in the mid-1970s.

Watson made a comeback in the 1990s. He toured with the O'Jays, and, in 1994, recorded his first album in fourteen years, *Bow Wow*. In 1995 it was nominated for a Grammy for best contemporary blues album. Watson also received a Pioneer Award from the Rhythm & Blues Foundation in 1995. While performing onstage at the Yokohama Blues Café in Japan, he collapsed and died of a heart attack. He was survived by his wife, Susan, a son and a daughter, and his mother, Wilma.

BIBLIOGRAPHY: Chicago *Sun–Times*, February 6, 1995. *Guardian* (London), May 20, 1996. Colin Larkin, ed., *The Guiness Encyclopedia of Popular Music*, Volume 6 (New York: Guiness, 1995). Los Angeles *Times*, May 21, 1996. *Orange County Register*, May 18, 1996. Jon Pareles and Patricia Romanowski, ed., *Rolling Stone Encyclopedia of Rock & Roll* (New York: Rolling Stone Press / Summit Books, 1983). Seattle *Times*, May 18, 1996. Washington *Post*, May 20, 1996.   *James Head*

Webb, Jitterbug. Guitarist, vocalist, composer–arranger; b. Willie E. Webb Jr., San Antonio, September 28, 1941; d. October 31, 1997; only child of Guidie Bell Evans and Willie E. Webb Sr.

Webb, a San Antonio blues legend, received the nickname "Jitterbug" from his grandmother because as a small child he was very energetic and jumped around a lot. His mother played piano. When he was nine, she encouraged

him to take trumpet and guitar lessons, but he liked the saxophone best. Jitterbug grew up singing in the youth choir at the West End Baptist Church in San Antonio, but like his mother he enjoyed other music such as blues and jazz.

He got his start as a teenager listening to black stars who performed in San Antonio—Louis Armstrong, Louis Jordan, Lionel Hampton, and Lester Young, among others—and performing with local musicians such as saxophonist Spot Barnett. Jitterbug formed his own band, the Five Stars, in 1955; with them he played the guitar and sang. The group became popular in San Antonio during the late '50s, playing in such places as nightclubs, military bases, and dance halls. In 1956, when Webb was fifteen, the group recorded two songs for Don Robey's Duke–Peacock Records in Houston. About 1958 he was hired by a San Antonio band, Charlie and the Jives. In the early 1960s the Five Stars began to travel outside of Texas. Jitterbug met Ike Turner, sat in with Ike and Tina Turner on a show they were performing in Los Angeles, and, after playing the whole show, was hired on the spot as their lead guitarist. Thereafter, Jitterbug played lead on the show until Ike appeared, and then he would switch to rhythm guitar.

He later returned to San Antonio and began playing locally again. In 1968 he received a call from former band-members of Ike Turner's who were appearing in Houston under the name Sam and the Good-Timers and was asked to join them. After returning to the West Coast with them he began working with Johnny Otis. At this time Jitterbug recorded with Lowell Fulson and Charles Brown for Savoy Records and was offered a job by Little Richard, but decided to stay with the Good-Timers.

While playing with the Good-Timers at the Soul'd Out Club in Los Angeles, the group was spotted by the Monkees, who hired them to tour with the British group in 1970. Jitterbug was able to tour foreign countries and appear on the "Tonight Show" with Johnny Carson, the "Joey Bishop Show" with Lou Rawls, and "Music Scene," hosted by David Steinberg. After his stint with the Monkees, Jitterbug joined the Johnny Otis Revue and toured Europe twice.

He returned to San Antonio again in the early 1980s. He continued to play music on the weekends but also opened a bar called Bug's Pub, a liquor store called Webb's Liquors, and a dry-cleaners called Deli-Care Cleaners. In 1987 he formed a band, the Super Crew, in which he combined young and veteran musicians. Jitterbug also began writing his own songs at this time—"That's The Way Life Is," "I'm So Happy," and "Life Goes On Without You," for instance.

During the April 1994 Fiesta San Antonio, Jitterbug was crowned Blues King and received a proclamation from the city of San Antonio signed by the mayor. He died of cancer.

BIBLIOGRAPHY: Jitterbug Webb homepage (http://www.netexpress.com/users/chips/jitter.htm), accessed January 7, 2003. *Living Blues*, March–April 1998.   *Karla Peterson*

Webster, Katie. Pianist, organist, "electric blues" vocalist, and harmonica player; b. Kathryn Jewel Thorne, Houston, 1936 or 1939; d. League City, Texas, September 5, 1999;

known as the "Swamp Boogie Queen." Her father, Cyrus, was a ragtime pianist before becoming a Pentecostal preacher, and her mother, Myrtle, played classical piano. The Thornes attempted to shield their young daughter from the evils of rhythm-and-blues music by locking up their piano when Katie was not taking her classical piano lessons. The girl, however, sneaked an old radio into her bedroom to listen to her favorite blues artists, Fats Domino, Little Richard, and Sam Cooke, on WLAC Radio, Nashville.

In the early 1950s she moved to Beaumont to live with more open-minded relatives. Her new-found freedom allowed her to pursue a boogie-woogie musical career in Lake Charles, Louisiana, while she finished high school. Within a couple of years, she had married Earl Webster. The union lasted only five years; after it, she never remarried.

Katie Webster had a long and very productive musical career, beginning with considerable popularity as a session pianist around Lake Charles. She blended a traditional boogie-woogie beat with barrelhouse rhythms to create her own style of "swamp blues." She played the piano on more than 500 recordings, primarily for Excello and Eddie Shuler's Goldband Records. She worked with such influential musicians as Guitar Jr., Lightnin' Slim, Lazy Lester, Lonesome Sundown, Juke Boy Bonner, Hop Wilson, and Ashton Savoy.

In 1964, while Otis Redding was playing at the Bamboo Club in Lake Charles, he asked the Swamp Boogie Queen to sit in with his band. Redding was so impressed by her talent that he asked her to join his tour. Katie Webster subsequently toured with Redding's band until he was killed in a plane crash in Lake Michigan in 1967. Webster, who was eight months pregnant, had overslept and missed the flight. She was so devastated by Redding's death that she gave up touring. In 1974 she moved to Oakland, California, to care for her ailing parents. Although she played at a few local venues, she was not very active musically during the 1970s.

In the late 1970s, her old friend Eddie Shuler re-released two of her albums, thus helping to launch her comeback. Katie made the first of sixteen European tours in 1982, wowing the audiences with her boogie-woogie piano. She played at numerous prestigious jazz and blues festivals during the 1980s and 1990s. She did not have any significant solo recording success, however, until the late 1980s, when she signed with Alligator Records. With guest appearances by Robert Cray, Kim Wilson, and Bonnie Raitt, she cut three well-received albums: *The Swamp Boogie Queen* (1988), *Two Fisted Mama* (1990), and *No Foolin* (1991). In the acclaimed *No Foolin* she displayed her powerful blues vocals and her skillful piano solos.

In 1993 Webster suffered a stroke, which hindered the use of her left hand and damaged her eyesight. Although she regained some use of her hand and played at a few festivals and other gigs, her musical career was essentially over. She moved back to Texas in the mid-1990s to live with two of her daughters. She died of a heart attack at her daughter's home. She left behind two sisters, three brothers, two daughters, eight grandchildren, and 12 great-grandchildren.

BIBLIOGRAPHY: Boston *Globe*, August 13, 1989. Michael Erlewine, ed., *All Music Guide To The Blues* (San Francisco: Miller Freeman, 1999). Sheldon Harris, *Blues Who's Who* (New Rochelle, New York: Arlington House, 1979). Houston *Chronicle*, August 8, 1995; September 8, 1999. Colin Larkin, ed., *The Guiness Encyclopedia of Popular Music*, Volume 7 (New York: Guiness, 1998). London *Daily Telegraph*, August 10, 1999. Los Angeles *Times*, March 7, 1986; August 9, 1999. Robert Santelli, *The Big Book of Blues* (New York: Penguin, 1993). *James Head*

Weiss, Julius. The German music professor who gave Scott Joplin, the King of Ragtime, his earliest formal music education; b. Saxony between June 4, 1840, and June 3, 1841; place and date of death unknown. Weiss was one of an inestimable number of itinerant German musicians who prepared the cultural soil in Texas for later development of symphony orchestras and opera companies. His approximate birthdate is extrapolated from the 1880 United States census and contemporary recollections.

Nothing is known conclusively about his education, but that he was a well-educated man is attested by the subjects other than music in which he tutored in Texarkana (German, astronomy, mathematics). He taught both piano and violin and had extensive knowledge and enthusiasm for opera, a fact that probably indicates some conservatory background in his training as well. No precise date can be determined when Weiss made his way to the U.S., but he was in St. Louis by the late 1870s, when Col. Robert W. Rodgers hired him to be a music teacher and live-in tutor for his six children in Texarkana, Texas. Rodgers was a successful lumbermill owner and businessman in Texarkana.

Weiss arrived in Texarkana between August 1877 and December 1878. He remained in the town until shortly after Rodgers's death in 1884. In Texarkana, Weiss befriended the young Scott Joplin and taught him piano, ear training, and harmony, and introduced him to the world of classical music, especially opera. Weiss probably helped the Joplins get the Rodgers family's old square piano when the lumberman bought a new one. According to recollections of his wife, Joplin fondly remembered his old German music teacher in later years. He even sent Weiss money after moving to New York in 1907. Weiss was surely the inspiration for Scott Joplin's quest to continue his musical education in later years and to use his ragtime style in conjunction with such larger musical genres as ballet and opera. The influence of mid-nineteenth-century German operatic style and forms is especially noticeable in Joplin's opera, *Treemonisha*, a work with which he was occupied in the last years of his life.

The straitened circumstances of the Rodgers family after the death of Colonel Rodgers forced Weiss to leave Texarkana. Nothing is known about his whereabouts until about 1895, when he appears in Houston as junior partner in W. C. Stansfield & Co., a store selling pianos, organs, and sheet music. By 1897 the partnership had dissolved and Weiss was listed in the city director as simply a music teacher. His fortunes declined further by the end of the century, and in the 1900–01 city directory he is listed as being with Perkins and Buchanan, operators of gambling establishments in the city. Ironically, Weiss was probably playing piano at gambling joints, making a living as Joplin did during his formative years. Weiss disappears from the Houston city directories at this point, and no record of his death has yet been located.

BIBLIOGRAPHY: Theodore Albrecht, "Julius Weiss: Scott Joplin's First Piano Teacher," *College Music Symposium* 19.2 (Fall 1979). Larry Wolz, "Roots of Classical Music in Texas: the German Contribution," in *The Roots of Texas Music*, ed. Lawrence S. Clayton and Joe W. Specht (College Station: Texas A&M University Press, 2003).

Larry Wolz

Wells, Henry James. Jazz trombonist and vocalist; b. Dallas, 1906; death information unknown. Wells studied music at Fisk University in Nashville and at the Cincinnati Conservatory. As a trombonist and vocalist he recorded with two of the important bands of the Swing Era, Jimmie Lunceford and Andy Kirk. In 1926 he was with the Boston Serenaders from Memphis, and from 1929 to 1935 he was with the Lunceford Orchestra. Featured regularly by the Kirk Orchestra as a vocalist, he soloed on trombone on a number of Lunceford recordings, including "Jazznocracy" (1934).

During this time he also worked with the Cab Calloway and Claude Hopkins bands. He joined up with Andy Kirk's Twelve Clouds of Joy in 1936 and remained with this group until 1939, when he left to form his own big band, which soon folded. Wells worked then with Gene Krupa and Teddy Hill, and in September 1940 he rejoined the Kirk Orchestra. After serving in World War II, he returned to work briefly with Kirk before joining Rex Stewart's band in 1946, after which he was a member of Sy Oliver's band until 1948. In the 1960s Wells was active in music in California, but during that same decade he disappeared from the records.

BIBLIOGRAPHY: John Chilton, *Who's Who of Jazz: Storyville to Swing Street*, Fourth Edition (New York: Da Capo Press, 1985).

Dave Oliphant

Wick, Otto. Composer, conductor, teacher, and arranger; b. Krefeld, Germany, July 8, 1885; d. Kyle, Texas, November 19, 1957. Wick received his musical education in Germany at the conservatory in Krefeld and at the university in Kiel. In 1905 he came to America to study composition and conducting with Vassily Ilyich Safonoff, the conductor of the New York Philharmonic.

His professional life was centered in New York until July 1935, when he moved to San Antonio. From 1919 to 1921 he was the first conductor of the Manhattan Opera House, under the management of Mrs. Oscar Hammerstein. His compositions for the stage include *Matasuntha*, a music drama in three acts; *The Moonmaid*, a light opera; *Alles für die Kunst* (For Art's Sake), an operetta in one act; and *The Lone Star* (1935), an American folk opera in three acts composed for the Texas Centennial in 1936. Wick also held positions as conductor and arranger for the Individual Film Company with Paramount; conductor, composer, and arranger with the National Broadcasting Company, New York; and guest conductor with the New York Civic

Orchestra. His great love of vocal music is evidenced by his role as conductor of various choral groups, including the Choral Society in Buffalo, New York, the Brooklyn Singers, and the New York Liederkranz Society; and, in San Antonio, the Beethoven–German Club Choir.

From 1937 until his death, Wick served as the musical conductor and general director of the San Antonio City-Wide Easter Sunrise Association. His works for orchestra include *The Gulf of Mexico*(1949), a symphonic poem inspired by William H. Prescott's *Conquest of Mexico*. Wick taught at the New York College of Music in New York City, where he received an honorary doctorate for excellence in music education (1933). In Texas, he was dean of music at the University of San Antonio (formerly San Antonio Female College) for four years and taught for three years at Trinity University.

In 1922 he married the soprano Elsa Diemer (1894–1993). They had three sons and one daughter. En route to a choral concert in Austin, Wick was stricken by a fatal cerebral hemorrhage.

BIBLIOGRAPHY: Kevin E. Mooney, Texas Centennial 1936: Music and Identity (Ph.D. dissertation, University of Texas at Austin, 1998). Otto Wick Papers, Center for American History, University of Texas at Austin Festival–Institute at Round Top.

Kevin E. Mooney

Wiley, Dewey Otto. The "Father of Texas Bands"; b. Alexander, Texas, April 17, 1898; d. Lubbock, December 30, 1980 (buried in Lubbock); one of nine children of George W. and Caroline (Martin) Wiley. Dewey spent his childhood in Graham and began his music education when his brother Jack gave him a violin for which he had traded a horse. Wiley learned to play the instrument through a mail-order method from the United States School of Music. During high school he studied under Carl Venth, then dean of music at what is now Texas Wesleyan University in Fort Worth. Wiley attended Midland College, where he taught violin, played football, and conducted the college orchestra. He married Willie Ruth Cole on January 1, 1921, while in school. The couple had three children.

At Simmons College in Abilene, Wiley directed the orchestra, taught violin, and in 1922 became the band director. He selected the cowboy uniforms for the Hardin–Simmons Cowboy Band, which toured the United States and Europe in 1930. He became the band director at Texas Technological College in Lubbock in the spring of 1934. One of his first and most lasting contributions to music included starting a summer band school. He also began the first high school band clinic for students. This program, started in 1934, continues each fall at Texas Tech. Part of his innovations included bringing nationally recognized band directors to the clinics and band schools.

Wiley served as secretary, treasurer, and later president of the Texas Music Educators Association. After he retired from Texas Tech he became the first executive secretary of TMEA. He was also a member of the American Bandmasters Association and editor of *Texas Music Educator* and *Southwestern Musician* when the two were combined. Before his involvement in TMEA, Texas high school music was a limited extracurricular activity. Afterward, Texas bands had a national reputation of excellence. Wiley received an honorary doctor of music from the Southwestern Conservatory in 1947. He retired from Texas Tech in 1959 and died at his home of heart disease.

BIBLIOGRAPHY: Hugh Anderson, "The Contributions of Professor Dewey O. Wiley to the School Band Movement in Texas," *Southwestern Musician and the Texas Music Educator*, February 1964. Phi Beta Mu National Bandmasters Fraternity, "Know Your Honorary Life President," *School Musician Director and Teacher*, February 1975. Charles A. Wiley, "Pete: Some Highlights in Memories of My Dad," *Southwestern Musician and the Texas Music Educator*, March 1981.   *Bill West*

Wilkerson, Don. Tenor saxophonist; b. Donald A. Wilkerson, Moreauville, Louisiana, July 6, 1932; d. Houston, July 18, 1986. Wilkerson was raised in Houston, and over the years the Bayou City remained his base of operations. He began playing alto sax in high school but later switched to tenor sax. Fellow Houstonians Illinois Jacquet and Arnett Cobb were among his acknowledged musical influences.

In the late 1940s and early 1950s he worked and toured with a variety of other Texans—Milt Larkin, T-Bone Walker, Amos Milburn, and Charles Brown. He also recorded with Milburn and Brown. While on the West Coast he jammed with the likes of Dexter Gordon and Wardell Gray.

In 1954 Wilkerson joined the Ray Charles band, and his hard-blowing tenor sax sound can be heard on several of Charles's hits from this period, including "I Got a Woman," "This Little Girl of Mine," and "Hallelujah, I Love Her So." Wilkerson's recording debut under his own name came in 1960 for Riverside Records. The title of the album, *The Texas Twister*, was most appropriate. Three more "soul jazz" albums followed on Blue Note Records in 1962 and 1963. *Elder Don, Preach Brother!*, and *Shoutin'* offered Wilkerson an opportunity to conjure up the sounds of his adopted state with original compositions such as "Lone Star Shuffle," "Camp Meeting," and "The Eldorado Shuffle." He even slipped in a version of Bob Wills's "San Antonio Rose." Clearly, Wilkerson never left his Southwestern musical roots far behind.

After another stint with the Ray Charles band in the early 1960s, he confined most of his activities to the Houston area. He traveled to New York City in 1982 to play on a B. B. King album, *B. B. King in Blues 'n' Jazz*, but he seldom recorded on his own during the last two decades of his life. Nevertheless, Wilkerson remained a vital contributor to the local music scene as mentor and friend to many musicians, including Earl Theodore Dunbar, Ed Soph, and Shelley Carrol.

Bibliography: Orin Keepnews, notes to *The Texas Twister* (Riverside OJCCD-1950, 2001). Bob Porter, notes to *Texas Tenors* (Prestige PRCD-24183, 1997). Barry Kernfeld, ed., *The New Grove Dictionary of Jazz*, Second Edition (New York: Grove, 2002). Dudley Williams, Joe Goldberg, Robert Levin, notes to *Don Wilkerson: The Complete Blue Note Sessions* (Blue Note 24555, 2001). Robert Wilonsky, notes to *Shelly Carrol with Members of*

the Duke Ellington Orchestra (Leaning House BB-003, 1997)   *Joe W. Specht*

Willet, Slim. Songwriter, disc jockey, record producer, and television personality; b. Winston Lee Moore, Victor, Texas, December 1, 1919; d. July 1, 1966; son of Luther and Fannie Moore. The Moore family moved to Clyde, and Willet graduated from Clyde High School in 1935. He married Jimmie Crenshaw in Clyde in 1938. They had two sons, Ted and Tim.

After serving a brief stint in the U.S. Army during World War II, Willet returned to the Abilene area and later entered Hardin–Simmons University. While working as student manager of the school radio station, he adopted the ironic pseudonym Slim; he was far from slender. He took the name Willet from his favorite comic strip, "The Willets." Upon graduation from Hardin–Simmons in 1949, he went to work for radio station KRBC as an advertising salesman and disc jockey. He had already begun writing songs, including "Pinball Millionaire," which was recorded by both Hank Locklin and Gene O'Quin.

Willett began his recording career in 1950 with the Dallas-based Star Talent label. He formed the Hired Hands, and his first release, his own "I'm a Tool Pusher from Snyder" (later changed to "Tool Pusher on a Rotary Rig"), was one of the songs with which he became most associated. In 1952 he recorded "Don't Let the Stars Get in Your Eyes." Released nationally on Four Star Records, the song reached number one on *Billboard*'s country and western chart, and at one time there were four versions of "Don't Let the Stars Get in Your Eyes" in the C&W Top 10. Perry Como also took the song to the top of *Billboard*'s pop chart.

At the height of his popularity, Willet was making regular guest appearances on the "Big 'D' Jamboree" in Dallas, the "Louisiana Hayride" in Shreveport, and the "Town Hall Party" in Compton, California. Although he never had another hit to match "Don't Let the Stars Get in Your Eyes," he continued to write and record. In 1956 he formed the Edmoral and Winston labels to release not only his own recordings but also those of area performers such as Dean Beard, Hoyle Nix, Curtis Potter, Darrell Rhodes, and Jimmy Seals. Willet even dabbled with the emerging rockabilly sounds of the day and recorded some sides under the name Telli W. Mils, the Fat Cat ("Telli W. Mils" is "Slim Willet" spelled backwards). In 1962 he released *Texas Oil Patch Songs*, an album devoted to life in the oilfields.

While continuing with his radio activities, Willet set up an advertising agency to handle local promotional ventures. In this capacity, he booked Elvis Presley's first appearance in Abilene in 1955. Willet was also a pioneer in live television as host of the "Big State Jamboree" on KRBC–TV. The weekly variety-show format provided exposure for many area performers, including the young Larry Gatlin. Willet left his disc jockey job at KRBC in 1957 and joined radio station KNIT. In 1964 he became general manager of KCAD, one of the few full-time country music radio stations in the state.

The combination of radio, recordings, and television made Willet well known in the Abilene area. He apparently died of a heart attack. He was elected to the Country Music Disc Jockey Hall of Fame in 1994.

BIBLIOGRAPHY: Abilene *Reporter–News*, December 24, 1995. Dick Grant, "Slim Willet: Smell That Sweet Perfume," *Rockin' Fifties*, June 1998. Joe W. Specht, "Slim Willet," in Paul Kingsbury, ed., *The Encyclopedia of Country Music* (New York: Oxford University Press, 1998).

Joe W. Specht

Williams, Richard Gene. Trumpet player; b. Galveston, May 4, 1931; d. November 5, 1985; known as "Notes" Williams. Williams started playing the tenor saxophone at an early age, but switched to the trumpet during his teenage years. He played in the Galveston area before enrolling in the music program at Wiley College, Marshall, Texas. After completing his degree in 1951, he enlisted in the U.S. Air Force and served diligently over the next few years.

In 1956, upon being discharged, he joined Lionel Hampton and toured Europe with Hampton's band. After spending three years on the road, Williams settled in New York City and received a master's degree from the Manhattan School of Music (1961). He also became a regular player with Charles Mingus's Jazz Workshop.

Williams devoted himself to playing full-time in New York, where he rose to prominence. In 1960 he recorded his only solo album, *New Horn In Town*. Through the 1960s and 1970s he played with Max Roach, Quincy Jones, Duke Ellington, and fellow Texan Booker Ervin. He toured Europe and Japan and recorded with Thad Jones and Mel Lewis in the late 1960s. In the early 1970s he was in Europe, where he occasionally led his own quartet. He recorded as a sideman several times in the later 1970s and was a member the Mingus Dynasty (1982) and co-leader of a quintet with Harold Vick (1980). Williams also played on Broadway and for the Orchestra U.S.A. He died of cancer.

BIBLIOGRAPHY: Barry Kernfeld, ed., *New Grove Dictionary of Jazz* (New York City: Macmillan, 1988). Dave Oliphant, *Texan Jazz* (Austin: University of Texas Press, 1996). *Variety*, December 4, 1985. *Bradley Shreve*

Willie Nelson's Fourth of July Picnic. Since the 1970s the Fourth of July and Texas music have been synonymous with Willie Nelson's Fourth of July Picnic. The country music extravaganza began in 1973 and was inspired by a country music festival that took place outdoors on a ranch near Dripping Springs, Hays County, in March 1972. Willie Nelson, one of the performers, and some of his business associates decided to organize a one-day event for July 4, 1973. Eddie Wilson, owner of Armadillo World Headquarters in Austin, promoted the concert, which was held at the same ranch in Dripping Springs. Musicians in addition to Nelson included Kris Kristofferson, Rita Coolidge, Charlie Rich, Waylon Jennings, and Tom T. Hall. Organizers soon realized that their plans were incomplete: the lack of sanitation, electricity, and parking space became obvious as an estimated 30,000 to 50,000 fans jammed two caliche backroads to the site. As understaffed health-care volunteers treated cases of heat exhaustion, security personnel tried to keep the stage clear and contended with intoxicated fans.

In spite of the first picnic's shortfalls, Nelson and promoters made plans to stage a bigger and improved Independence Day concert for the next year. In 1974 the picnic was actually a three-day festival that took place outdoors at the Texas World Speedway in College Station. Waylon Jennings, Jimmy Buffett, Leon Russell, Michael Martin Murphey, and Jerry Jeff Walker were among the lineup of musicians that attended. From this time on, Willie's picnic established itself as an annual event.

In 1975, 90,000 people descended upon the hamlet of Liberty Hill in Williamson County to hear Nelson and the Charlie Daniels Band, Delbert McClinton, the Pointer Sisters, and Kris Kristofferson. The Texas Senate proclaimed July 4 Willie Nelson Day. Ironically, the overcrowding problems of the previous picnics had also prompted the Texas legislature to pass the Texas Mass Gathering Act, and Williamson County officials charged Nelson with violating that law. Throughout the 1970s however, the picnics continued at various sites—Gonzales, the Cotton Bowl in Dallas, the Austin Opry House, and the Pedernales Country Club. Musicians included Doug Sahm, Emmylou Harris, Ray Wylie Hubbard, Ernest Tubb, and other semi-regulars such as Leon Russell and Kris Kristofferson.

After 1980 and a successful concert at which over 90,000 fans heard Merle Haggard, Asleep at the Wheel, Ray Price, Johnny Paycheck, and others at Nelson's Pedernales Country Club, Nelson and his organizers announced the discontinuation of the event, but in 1984 the picnic began anew and in the succeeding years was held at various venues around Austin. The 1986 concert also doubled as Farm Aid, which Nelson orchestrated in the mid-1980s to raise money for America's farmers. John Mellencamp, Neil Young, Stevie Ray Vaughan, Joe Ely, and the Fabulous Thunderbirds were among the musical acts that played Nelson's picnics.

By the 1990s the on again–off again picnic had become more subdued. A modest crowd of 15,000 cheered on performers at Zilker Park, Austin, in 1990. The Highwaymen, which featured Nelson, Kristofferson, Johnny Cash, and Waylon Jennings, headlined the concert. Nelson's next festival—in 1993—was a scaled-down affair at the Backyard in Austin, with about 3,000 people in attendance.

From 1995 to 1999 Willie's Fourth of July Picnic took place in the Hill Country town of Luckenbach. Logistical and county permit problems kept the concert from taking place there in the early twenty-first century. The 2000 event occurred at Southpark Meadows in Austin. Even though organizers cancelled the picnic, planned for Luckenbach, in 2001 and 2002, residents of that town sought to host future Fourth of July Picnics.

BIBLIOGRAPHY: Austin *American–Statesman*, June 22, 1995. William C. Martin, "Growing Old at Willie Nelson's Picnic," *Texas Monthly*, October 1974. Don Roth and Jan Reid, "The Coming of Redneck Hip," *Texas Monthly*, November 1973. *Laurie E. Jasinski*

Willing, Foy. Western singer; b. Foy Willingham, Bosque County, Texas, 1915; d. Nashville, Tennessee, June 24,

Willie Nelson's first Fourth of July Picnic, Dripping Springs, Texas, 1973. Photograph by Burton Wilson.

1978. As a teenager, Willingham sang solos on radio and performed with a local gospel chorus. From 1933 to 1935 he worked in radio in New York City, then returned to Texas to continue his musical career. In 1940 he moved to California. There, in 1943, he took over as leader of the Riders of the Purple Sage, a designation inspired by Zane Grey's romantic western novel of the same name. Other members at the time included Jimmie Dean and Al Sloey. Over the next nine years, the group included Scotty Harrell, Johnny Paul, Billy Leibert, Paul Sellers, Jerry Vaughn, Neely Plumb, and Freddy Travers.

The Riders of the Purple Sage soon became one of the most popular singing groups during the "Singing Cowboy" craze of the 1930s to1950s. During that era, dozens of groups, such as the Cowboy Ramblers and the Lone Star Cowboys, dressed in gaudy western attire and performed highly romanticized "cowboy" songs based on Hollywood's version of life on the open prairie. Foy Willing and the Riders of the Purple Sage performed on numerous radio shows. Willing appeared in some twenty-seven movies, including eleven with the Riders of the Purple Sage. The group recorded for various prominent labels, including Capitol, Decca, Columbia, and Majestic, and had several major hits, including "Cool Water" and "Ghost Riders in the Sky." Willing disbanded the group in 1952, although the members reassembled occasionally to perform. Willing continued to write and record songs and appear at western film festivals until his death.

BIBLIOGRAPHY: Fred Deller, ed., *The Harmony Illustrated Encyclopedia of Country Music* (New York: Harmony, 1986). Bill C. Malone, *Country Music U.S.A.* (Austin: University of Texas Press, 1975). Bill O'Neal, *Tex Ritter: America's Most Beloved Cowboy* (Austin: Eakin Press, 1998). *Gary Hartman*

Wills, Bob. Western musician; b. James Robert Wills, near Kosse, Limestone County, Texas, March 6, 1905; d. May 13, 1975 (buried in Memorial Park, Tulsa, Oklahoma); the first of ten children of John and Emmaline (Foley) Wills. In 1913 the family moved to Hall County, where they settled on the Ogden Ranch, between Memphis and Estelline. In the early 1920s they moved to a combination farm and ranch between the Little Red River and the Prairie Dog Town Fork of the Red River.

In Hall County Wills learned to play the violin; in 1915 he played at his first dance. He played for ranch dances in West Texas for the next fourteen years, and his life and career were greatly influenced by that environment. During that time he brought together two streams of American folk music to produce western swing. He had first learned frontier fiddle music from his father and grandfather, but he also learned blues and jazz from black playmates and coworkers in the cottonfields of East and West Texas. He played fiddle music with the heat of blues and the swing of jazz; his new music could as properly have been called western jazz as western swing.

In 1929 Wills moved to Fort Worth, where he performed on several radio stations, organized a band that became the Light Crust Doughboys, and worked for a future governor of Texas and United States senator, W. Lee O'Daniel. In 1934 Wills moved to Oklahoma, where he made radio and musical history with his broadcasts over Station KVOO. During his years in Tulsa (1934–43) he and his new group, the Texas Playboys, continued to develop the swinging western jazz he had pioneered in West Texas, adding drums and a horn section of brass and reeds. Wills's recording of his composition "New San Antonio Rose" (1940) made him a national figure in popular music. He went to Hollywood that year and made the first of his nineteen movies.

He joined the army in December 1942. After World War II he had his greatest success, grossing nearly a half million dollars during some years. In 1957 he was elected to the American Society of Composers, Authors, and Publishers. In 1968 he was elected to the Country Music Hall of Fame, although he never thought of his music as "country."

Wills was married and divorced several times between 1935 and 1941. On August 10, 1942, he was married to Betty Anderson, and they remained married until his death; they had four children. Wills had two children by former marriages.

In 1969 the governor and legislature of Texas honored Wills for his contribution to American music, one of the few original music forms Texas and the Southwest have produced. The day after the ceremonies in Austin, Wills had the first in a series of crippling strokes. By 1973 his health had improved to the extent that he could lead some of his former Texas Playboys in a recording session for United Artists. The album, *For the Last Time: Bob Wills and His Texas Playboys*, sold more copies than any other in Wills's career and was awarded a Grammy Award by the National Academy of Recording Arts and Sciences, the highest achievement of any recording in the history of western swing.

BIBLIOGRAPHY: Ruth Sheldon, *Hubbin' It: The Life of Bob Wills* (Kingsport, Tennessee: Kingsport Press, 1938). Charles R. Townsend, *San Antonio Rose: The Life and Music of Bob Wills* (Urbana: University of Illinois Press, 1976).   *Charles R. Townsend*

Bob Wills on the set of his KFJZ television program in Fort Worth in the early 1960s. Courtesy Joe Carr.

Wills, Johnnie Lee. Guitar and banjo player; b. Limestone County, Texas, 1912; d. Tulsa, 1984; son of John and Emmaline Wills and younger brother of Bob Wills. In 1913 the family loaded their possessions into two covered wagons and moved across the state to Hall County, in the Texas Panhandle. Johnnie Lee soon established his position within the musically talented Wills family. At the outset of the Great Depression, he got a job as a truck driver for Burrus Mills and Elevator Company of Fort Worth, which sponsored Bob Wills and the Light Crust Doughboys. When Johnnie Lee was fired over a dispute with his foreman, Bob hired his younger brother to play tenor banjo in the group, though manager W. Lee "Pappy" O'Daniel objected. Bob and several members of the band eventually left the Lightcrust Doughboys to form the Texas Playboys.

Johnnie Lee remained a member of the Texas Playboys until 1940, when he began performing with his own band, Johnnie Lee Wills and His Boys. The group became quite popular throughout North Texas and Oklahoma and included many of the same well-established musicians that were part of the Texas Playboys, such as Jesse Ashlock and Joe Holley. In 1940 Johnnie Lee Wills and His Boys began recording for Bullet Records. With the songs "Rag Mop" and "Peter Cottontail," the band gave Bullet its two all-time best-selling country hits. Johnnie Lee went on to record for RCA, Decca, and other labels, and for several years he ran the popular nightclub Stampede in Tulsa, Oklahoma.

357

BIBLIOGRAPHY: Fred Deller, ed., *The Harmony Illustrated Encyclopedia of Country Music* (New York: Harmony, 1986). Charles Townsend, *San Antonio Rose: The Life and Music of Bob Wills* (Urbana: University of Illinois Press, 1976).   *Gary Hartman*

Wilson, Dooley. Actor and musician; b. Arthur Wilson, Tyler, Texas, April 3, 1894; d. 1953. Wilson's career spanned more than forty years. He began at age twelve with performances in vaudeville as a minstrel player and culminated in 1951 with a television role. During the 1920s he led his own band, in which he performed as a singing drummer, on a nightclub tour of Paris and London. He returned to the United States in 1930 and gave up his drums for an acting career. He performed with Orson Welles and John Hausman in Federal Theater productions and then landed a Broadway role in the musical *Cabin in the Sky.*

Wilson made his film debut in 1939. Although his roles were primarily supporting ones, he made film history as Sam, the pianist–singer in *Casablanca* who performs "As Time Goes By." Director Hal Wallis wanted a woman for the role but chose Wilson instead, although Wilson "couldn't sing or play piano." The director allowed Wilson to sing, but the piano playing was dubbed. Wilson was under contract to Paramount and on loan to M-G-M. His film credits include *Keep Punching* (1939); *My Favorite Blonde, Night in New Orleans, Take a Letter Darling,* and *Cairo* (1942); *Casablanca, Two Tickets to London, Stormy Weather,* and *Hither and Hither* (1943); *Seven Days Ashore* (1944); *Triple Threat* and *Racing Luck* (1948); *Free for All* and *Come to the Stables* (1949); and *Passage West* (1951).

In 1945 he had a prominent role in the New York musical *Bloomer Girl.* He also acted in "Beulah," one of the first television series starring black actors, in 1951. He was on the board of directors of the Negro Actors Guild of America. He died shortly after his retirement.

BIBLIOGRAPHY: Donald Bogle, *Blacks in American Film and Television: An Encyclopedia* (New York: Garland, 1988). Thomas Cripps, *Slow Fade to Black: The Negro in American Film, 1900–1942* (New York: Oxford University Press, 1977). Otto Friedrich, *City of Nets* (New York: Harper and Row, 1986). Ephraim Katz, *The Film Encyclopedia* (New York: Crowell, 1979). Peter Noble, *The Negro in Films* (London: Skelton Robinson, 1948). David Ragan, *Who's Who in Hollywood, 1900–1976* (New Rochelle, New York: Arlington House, 1976).   *Peggy Hardman*

Wilson, Hop. Blues singer, guitarist, and harmonica player; b. Hardy Wilson, Grapeland, Texas, April 27, 1921; d. Houston, August 27, 1975; one of thirteen children of Charlie and Alma Wilson. Wilson grew up in Crockett, Texas, where his family moved while he was very young. When he was a child, he was strongly influenced by recordings of Blind Lemon Jefferson, which inspired him to learn the guitar and harmonica.

Wilson's nickname was derived from his ability to play the harmonica, or "harp," which he pronounced "hop." He played in local venues around Crockett when he was a

teenager and worked at other odd jobs throughout the 1930s and early 1940s. He was drafted in 1942 and served with the army until he was discharged in 1946. After returning to Crockett, he played local gigs while working in non-music-related jobs until the early 1950s. In the mid-1950s he joined drummer "King" Ivory Lee Semien, and for the next several years they worked clubs in East Texas and Louisiana.

Wilson had a short recording career. He cut several tracks with Semien on the Goldband label in 1958. In 1960 he switched to the Ivory label, which Semien owned. Wilson recorded several tracks during 1960 and 1961. From 1961, the year in which he made his final recordings, until the mid-1970s, he also performed in Houston clubs, bars, and restaurants. Although he was virtually unknown outside of Houston, he was a local sensation who influenced numerous modern guitarists. Wilson is best known for his work on the eight-string Hawaiian steel guitar, which he helped popularize throughout the South during the 1940s and 1950s. He played the instrument in the country-and-western style on a stand or in his lap. His unique slide stylings had a significant influence on a variety of guitar players, including L. C. "Good Rockin" Robinson, Sonny Rhodes, Jimmy Vaughn, and Johnny Winter.

Wilson was married to a woman named Glendora. He died of brain disease and was buried in Mount Zion Cemetery, Grapeland.

BIBLIOGRAPHY: Michael Erlewine, ed., *All Music Guide To The Blues* (San Francisco: Miller Freeman, 1999). Sheldon Harris, *Blues Who's Who* (New Rochelle, New York: Arlington House, 1979). Colin Larkin, ed., *The Guiness Encyclopedia of Popular Music*, Volume 8 (New York: Guiness, 1998). Robert Santelli, *The Big Book of Blues* (New York: Penguin, 1993).   *James Head*

Wilson, John Frank. Singer, known as J. Frank Wilson; b. Lufkin, Texas, December 11, 1941; d. October 4, 1991; son of a railroad engineer. Wilson became a one-hit wonder in the early 1960s when he was the lead singer of the hit song "Last Kiss." He and the Cavaliers, his own band, recorded Wayne Cochran's teenage-death melodrama, which rose to the top of the American pop charts in 1964. The lugubrious song was the last exemplar of a genre that flourished in the early 1960s. "Last Kiss" remained on the charts for twelve weeks.

Wilson had listened carefully to Buddy Holly and Elvis Presley. After graduating from Lufkin High School in 1960, he joined the U.S. Air Force and was stationed at Goodfellow Air Force Base, San Angelo. He joined the Cavaliers (guitarist Sid Holmes, bassist Lewis Elliott, saxophonist Bob Zeller, and drummer Ray Smith), a group that had formed in San Angelo in 1955; moved to Memphis in the early 1960s; and returned to San Angelo in 1962. Wilson enhanced the group's appeal and enlarged its audience. The Cavaliers and J. Frank Wilson became a popular attraction at area clubs.

In 1962, at the Blue Note in Big Spring, record producer Sonley Roush heard Wilson and the Cavaliers perform. At Ron Newdoll's Accurate Sound Recording Company on Tyler Avenue in San Angelo, the group recorded Cochran's song. Newdoll and his production company, Askell Productions, produced the recording and acquired ownership of the masters, with royalties, in exchange for the group's right to use the studio. Major Bill Smith, a recording executive in Fort Worth who had produced Bruce Channel's "Hey! Baby" and Paul and Paula's "Hey Paula," signed Wilson and the Cavaliers to record the song on the Josie label. The record was released in June 1964, entered the charts on October 10, and reached number two on the Billboard Top 40 charts on November 7. The album sold over 100,000 copies the first few months. Wilson and the Cavaliers earned a gold record for "Last Kiss."

On October 22 Roush was killed in a car wreck in which Wilson was severely injured. The press whooped up the connection between the accident and the lyrics of "Last Kiss," which is about a teen-aged girl who dies in the arms of her boyfriend after a car accident. Wilson was touring again within a week of the crash. On "American Bandstand"—and on crutches—he lip-synced "Last Kiss" and introduced a new single, "Six Boys," produced by Smith with studio musicians. Wilson and Josie Records put together a new group under the name Cavaliers, although the original Cavaliers were continuing to perform with Lewis Elliott as leader and James Thomas as vocalist. Wilson recorded with session musicians. He continued as a single act, traveling with Jerry Lee, the Righteous Brothers, the Animals, and other well-known performers until he bottomed out from alcoholism.

He made records and performed into the 1970s, but without much income or effect. On the tenth anniversary of the "Last Kiss" success, he was working in Lufkin as a nursing-home orderly for $250 a week. The depressed one-hit singer attempted marriage eight times and sank into alcohol addiction. Suffering from seizures and diabetes, he died in a nursing home not long before his fiftieth birthday. In 2000, VH1 fans voted "Last Kiss" number three in the all-time Top 10 cover songs. The song received a BMI 2-Million air-play award. In 1999 "Last Kiss" once again became a hit when the rock group Pearl Jam released its version. Lufkin was building a "Last Kiss Museum" in 2002.

BIBLIOGRAPHY: Austin American–Statesman, June 7, 1999. AVGuide.com (http://www.avguide.com/film_music/music/music_c8.htm), accessed February 10, 2003. "The Incredible Saga of J. Frank Wilson and the Cavaliers" (http://www.cicadelic.com/jfrank.htm), accessed February 10, 2003. Vertical Files, Center for American History, University of Texas at Austin.   Larry S. Bonura

Wilson, Teddy. Jazz pianist; b. Theodore Shaw Wilson, Austin, November 24, 1912; d. New Britain, Connecticut, July 31, 1986; second son of James and Pearl Wilson. In 1918 the family moved to Tuskegee, Alabama, where Wilson's mother worked as a librarian and his father taught English at Tuskegee Institute. Wilson studied piano and violin at the institute; he also played the E-flat clarinet and oboe in the school band.

Wilson attended Talladega College for a year, but moved to Detroit in 1929 to earn his living as a musician. He played in a band with Speed Webb in the Detroit area from 1929 to 1931. In 1931 he moved to Chicago, where he had the good fortune to play alongside Erskine Tate, Louis Armstrong, and Jimmy Noone. He joined the Benny Carter band in 1933 and made several recordings. Wilson's big break came in 1936, when he began touring with Benny Goodman and Gene Krupa. This trio was one of the first interracial groups to perform in the United States. Though crowds cheered Wilson on the bandstand, he still had to stay at the "colored" hotels. Between 1935 and 1939 he also performed with soloists from the Count Basie and Duke Ellington bands, as well as with vocalist Billie Holiday. During this time he recorded on the Brunswick label.

He formed his own band and worked with CBS studios in the 1940s and 1950s, and he taught piano at the Juilliard School of Music from 1945 to 1952. He also appeared in The Seven Lively Arts and in the movie The Benny Goodman Story (1956). Wilson brought to jazz an elegance and sophistication that it had not previously enjoyed. He drew elements from Fats Waller, Earl Hines, and Art Tatum, blending and refining them into his own unique sound. His subtle and disciplined style provided an effective contrast when he accompanied artists like Billie Holiday, who usually sang just outside the beat. Characteristics of Wilson's music included short, single-note phrases, tenth chords in the left hand, and a wonderfully provocative use of dissonance. His talent at improvisation enabled him to produce intricate counterpoint lines that complemented whatever soloist he was performing with.

He rejoined Benny Goodman's group for tours of Scandinavia in 1952, England in 1953, Australia in 1960, and Europe in 1965; several trips to Japan in the 1970s; and a concert at Carnegie Hall in 1982.

BIBLIOGRAPHY: Austin American-Statesman, August 1, 1986. Charles Eugene Claghorn, Biographical Dictionary of Jazz (Englewood Cliffs, New Jersey: Prentice–Hall, 1982). Barry Kernfeld, ed., The New Grove Dictionary of Jazz (London: Macmillan, 1988). New Yorker, July 19, 1982. Vertical Files, Center for American History, University of Texas at Austin.   Vivian Elizabeth Smyrl

Wolf, Sidney Abraham. Rabbi and musician; b. Cleveland, Ohio, December 8, 1906; d. Corpus Christi, February 18, 1983; eldest child of immigrant wholesale grocers Israel and Sophie Wolf. Sidney Wolf began taking piano lessons at age seven. By age thirteen, he was the youngest member of a musical combo performing at fraternity parties and wedding receptions. Soon after, his parents bought him his first pair of trousers, lest his knickers betray his youth. His high marks while he was a high school senior at the Cleveland Jewish Center in 1923 and 1924 won him several books on Jewish law and lore. Gradually, he made up his mind to become a community-oriented rabbi, a spiritual leader who would blend music with religion.

Wolf enrolled in 1924 at Hebrew Union College, the Reform Jewish seminary in Cincinnati. Because of his musical training he was invited to play the organ and teach in the religious school in a small congregation in Hamilton, Ohio. During his senior year he served that same congregation as student rabbi. He enjoyed stints at roadside honky-

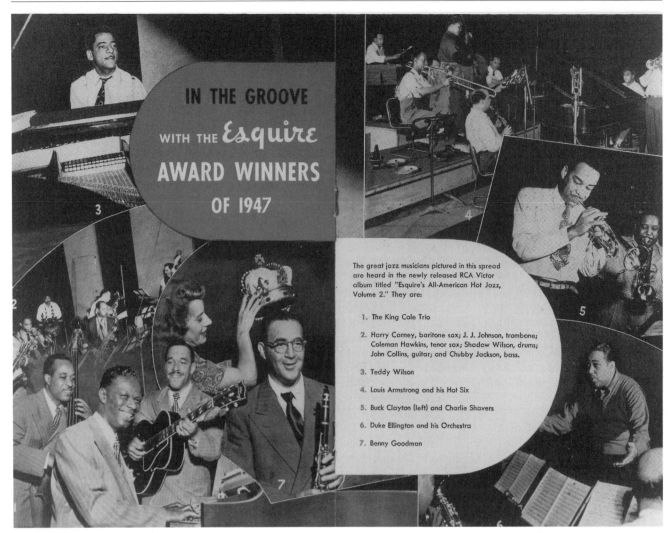

IN THE GROOVE
WITH THE *Esquire*
AWARD WINNERS
OF 1947

The great jazz musicians pictured in this spread
are heard in the newly released RCA Victor
album titled "Esquire's All-American Hot Jazz,
Volume 2." They are:

1. The King Cole Trio

2. Harry Carney, baritone sax; J. J. Johnson, trombone;
   Coleman Hawkins, tenor sax; Shadow Wilson, drums;
   John Collins, guitar; and Chubby Jackson, bass.

3. Teddy Wilson

4. Louis Armstrong and his Hot Six

5. Buck Clayton (left) and Charlie Shavers

6. Duke Ellington and his Orchestra

7. Benny Goodman

Brochure for RCA, "In the Groove with the Esquire Winners of 1947," featuring Teddy Wilson (upper left). Bill Boyd Papers, CAH; CN 11491. Jazz pianist Wilson performed with celebrities such as Benny Goodman, Gene Krupa, and Count Basie.

tonks, taught himself to play the saxophone, and organized impromptu concerts in the seminary dormitory. The dormitory's "bumming room" was also the setting for musicales during which Wolf and several members of the Cincinnati Symphony Orchestra joined other student musicians. While a rabbinical student, Wolf won a scholarship to the Cincinnati Conservatory of Music, where he studied piano, organ, theory, and harmony. His rabbinical curriculum included undergraduate classes at the University of Cincinnati; there, in 1929, he earned a B.A. in German. In his unpublished memoirs the rabbi noted that his foreign-language skills proved invaluable when he was poring through German music journals to research his rabbinical thesis. That thesis explored the life and impact of German Jewish musician Louis Lewandowski (1821–94), a choral director and composer who popularized organ accompaniment of traditional Jewish prayers. Wolf aspired to lead a congregation with a choir and pipe organ performing music in the style of Lewandowski.

But the rabbi's timing was off. Ordained in May 1932, at the height of the Great Depression, he became eligible for a pulpit when times were hard and congregations were not calling. Wolf received but one offer: a three-month trial at Temple Beth El in Corpus Christi, a congregation formed in 1928 with seventy families who worshiped in a makeshift wooden "shack." According to the rabbi's memoirs, the synagogue, located at Eleventh and Craig streets, had "burlap curtains" rather than interior walls, a pot-bellied stove, and, most disappointing, "a pump organ which wheezed more than giving forth some semblance of musical sound."

Literally and figuratively, Corpus Christi was at the time a cultural desert compared to musical centers like Cincinnati and Cleveland. The South Texas county seat in which Wolf made his new home had 30,000 residents and no formal musical organizations. The best pipe organ in town was the Wurlitzer at the Palace Theater. There were, however, scattered musicians who met informally to play chamber music and enjoy one another's company. Among the young rabbi's possessions was an extensive collection of classical records. To listen to these recordings, he met Sunday afternoons with his Episcopal colleague, Rev. William

Capers Munds, who had a phonograph. Other music lovers joined the two clergymen at these music appreciation sessions and were enlightened by the rabbi's insights. Before listening to a recording, Wolf explained the background of the composer and the nuances of each selection.

During the next dozen years, the rabbi tried to organize a local symphony orchestra. The town, however, was not large enough before World War II and the construction of Corpus Christi Naval Air Station to support such an effort. Finally, in 1945, when Corpus Christi Junior College (now Del Mar College) hired Dr. C. Burdette "Bud" Wolfe to establish a campus music department, the circumstances were right. The professor encouraged area musicians to form a part-time symphony. The success of such an endeavor, however, would depend upon raising sufficient money to pay the musicians, to underwrite acquisition of musical scores, to advertise and to print programs and tickets. The rabbi assumed the fundraising role and became the founding president of the Corpus Christi Symphony Society. With the first $6,500 in contributions, the symphony was launched. The initial concert was performed on December 10, 1945, in the city's largest hall, the 600-seat auditorium at Corpus Christi High School (now Roy Miller High School).

That inaugural season, the sixty-three-member orchestra presented four concerts with two additional performances for children. Ralph Thibodeau, former music critic at the Corpus Christi *Caller–Times*, recalled, "The orchestra did not have a regular concert schedule. They would rehearse and rehearse and then when they were ready, they would put an ad in the paper announcing the next concert." The repertoire remained traditional: Stravinsky was too avant-garde for the audience, but Bach proved popular. Handel's *Messiah* featured choral responses alternately sung in Spanish and English. During the orchestra's second season, the symphony performed Prokofiev's *Peter and the Wolf*, narrated by Rabbi Sidney Wolf and conducted by Dr. C. Burdette Wolfe. The newspaper referred to the performance as "Peter and the THREE Wolfs." In those early years the rabbi often substituted during rehearsals for guest pianists. He also served as the symphony's program annotator and radio promoter. The Corpus Christi Symphony Orchestra continues to enrich the cultural life of the region. Wolf also chaired the local chapter of the American Guild of Organists.

Music played a role in each of Rabbi Wolf's marriages. He met his first wife, Sarah Phillips, in 1931 when her parents invited rabbinical students to their Cincinnati home to listen to recorded classical music. His first sight of his bride-to-be, during Tchaikovsky's Fourth Symphony, found him falling in love. Sidney and Sarah were married in June 1933. She joined him in Texas but returned to Cincinnati in January 1936 to give birth to their son, Phillip. Her sad death from pneumonia six days after their son's birth left the young rabbi disconsolate. The infant remained with his maternal grandmother while the rabbi returned alone to the Texas Gulf Coast.

The rabbi's second wife, Bertha (Bébé) Rosenthal, a native of Chantilly, France, was, like the rabbi, an accomplished pianist. She lived in Lafayette, Louisiana, with her equally musical mother and sisters. At the suggestion of mutual friends, Wolf wrote Bébé. After an exchange of several letters, he boarded a Southern Pacific Railroad train to Lafayette. It was quickly apparent that the two were meant to be together. They were married in 1938. Three months later, they journeyed to Cincinnati to reclaim Sidney's son. The boy, Pinney, as he was called, now had a mother and would soon have a sister, Joanne (1940), to share his growing years. Sidney and Bébé's home was always awash in music. Local musicians from Del Mar College would join them to play quartets or listen to piano duos with Sidney on one piano and Bébé on the other.

During Rabbi Wolf's forty-year tenure at Temple Beth El, the congregation built a Moorish-style temple on the same property that was once the site of the wooden shack that had greeted the rabbi when he arrived. Music was always an important element of worship services. Cantatas, as well as piano recitals and duets by the rabbi and his wife, were performed in the sanctuary on many occasions.

Another kind of music rang out from the pulpit of Temple Beth El when in the early 1950s Wolf began inviting black ministers to preach each February during Brotherhood Month. The student choir from the black Solomon M. Coles High School, under the direction of Beulah Smith, became part of that tradition. Gospel hymns were added to the Friday Sabbath services in an era that predated the civil-rights movement. Historian Hollace Ava Weiner writes extensively about the rabbi's impact on civil rights in *The Quiet Voices: Southern Rabbis and Black Civil Rights, 1880s to 1990s* (University of Alabama, 1996).

That stunning interracial innovation was in addition to the annual joint Thanksgiving service begun in 1935 by Rabbi Wolf and his colleague Reverend Munds. The ecumenical Thanksgiving service, which alternated between the Church of the Good Shepherd and the synagogue, featured the clergymen preaching from one another's pulpits and was featured in the November 30, 1936, issue of *Time* magazine. Reaching across all divides and creating harmony was a keystone of the rabbi's pragmatic philosophy.

When Wolf retired from the pulpit in 1972, he joined the teaching staff at Del Mar College and instituted a music-appreciation class under the Continuing Education Department. Four years later, when he passed age seventy and was forced into mandatory retirement, Jo Ann Luckie, coordinator of the college's Senior Citizens Education Program, seized the opportunity to have the rabbi continue his music-appreciation classes as a volunteer instructor. He continued in this capacity from 1977 to 1982. These well-attended free classes focused on coming programs of the Corpus Christi Symphony. Students enrolled in the rabbi's course arrived to find him seated at the piano ready to accompany his lectures with musical excerpts.

When the rabbi was diagnosed with cancer and ceased teaching in 1982, 100 of his former students launched a scholarship fund in his honor to assist a deserving music student every year at Del Mar College. Additional contributions to this fund from Temple Beth El and the Church of the Good Shepherd helped it reach the goal of $5,000. A Sidney A. Wolf Orchestra Scholarship has been awarded annually since 1982. Mayor Luther Jones proclaimed November 10, 1982, "Rabbi Sidney Wolf Day" in Corpus Christi. Wolf demonstrated that music could enhance religious worship, traverse cultural divides, and enrich his community. He died of cancer and is buried at Seaside Cemetery in Corpus Christi.

BIBLIOGRAPHY: Corpus Christi *Caller–Times*, November 4, 1945; January 25, 1970; May 20, 1978; November 10, 1982; January 2, 2000. Fort Worth *Star–Telegram*, April 10, 1994. Hortense Warner Ward, *A Century of Missionary Effort: The Church of the Good Shepherd, 1860–1960* (1960). Sidney A. Wolf and Helen K. Wilk, *Our Golden Years—A History of Temple Beth El, 1928–1983* (Corpus Christi, 1984). *Helen K. Wilk*

Wright, Lammar. Cornet and trumpet player; b. Texarkana, Texas, June 20, 1905 or 1907; d. New York City, April 13, 1973. Wright attended Lincoln High School in Kansas City. By 1923 he was a member of the Kansas City band of Bennie Moten, which recorded for the Okeh company in that first significant year of jazz recording. Influenced by the great New Orleans trumpeter Joe "King" Oliver, Wright has been praised as the "best player" in the Moten band. His style has been described as full of searing, stabbing immediacy.

Wright remained with Moten until 1927, after which he joined the Missourians, a group that had been featured at the Cotton Club in New York. Between 1928 and 1930 he recorded with the Missourians. In 1930 the band was taken over by singer Cab Calloway. Continuing with Calloway as the lead trumpet in the vocalist's very popular orchestra, Wright performed a number of outstanding solos and remained with the group until January 1940. He subsequently performed with a number of other groups, including Don Redman, Claude Hopkins, Cootie Williams, Lucky Millinder, Sy Oliver, and the George Shearing big band.

Both of Wright's sons, Lamar Jr. and Elmon, were members of the Dizzy Gillespie big band in the late 1940s. Lammar Wright worked as a teacher and studio musician in the 1950s and 1960s, and appeared in the film *The Night They Raided Minsky's* in 1968.

BIBLIOGRAPHY: John Chilton, *Who's Who of Jazz: Storyville to Swing Street*, Fourth Edition (New York: Da Capo Press, 1985). Barry Kernfeld, ed., *The New Grove Dictionary of Jazz*, Second Edition (New York: Grove, 2002). Ross Russell, *Jazz Style in Kansas City and the Southwest* (Berkeley: University of California Press, 1971). Gunther Schuller, *Early Jazz: Its Roots and Musical Development* (New York: Oxford University Press, 1968). *Dave Oliphant*

Wright, Leo Nash. Alto saxophonist and flutist; b. Wichita Falls, Texas, December 14, 1933; d. Vienna, Austria, January 4, 1991; son of Mel Wright. His father played trombone with the San Antonio band Boots and His Buddies in the late 1930s and had a musical association with the father of tenorist Booker Ervin.

After beginning studies with his father, Wright was later taught by Texas tenorist John Hardee and attended Huston–Tillotson College in Austin and San Francisco State University in California. He played with Saunders King in San Francisco and with Charles Mingus in New York. In 1959 he joined the Dizzy Gillespie Quintet, with which he recorded on February 9, 1961, at the Museum of Modern Art (*An Electrifying Evening with the Dizzy Gillespie Quintet*, reissued by Verve on CD in 1999). Of his experience with Gillespie, Wright commented in a 1961 interview that "when you're working with the giants, you've got to improve. It is a challenge to play with a master. You've got to learn discipline, get down to business. I'm still in school." Under his own name, Wright recorded an album entitled *Blues Shout* (Atlantic, 1960), which includes on trumpet Texan Richard "Notes" Williams. Williams returned the favor by including Wright on the album *New Horn in Town* (Candid, 1960).

Wright left Gillespie in 1962, free-lanced in Scandinavia during 1963–64, then settled in Berlin. There he was a member of the Radio Free Berlin Studio Band. Around 1968 he moved to Vienna. In 1978 he appeared with another fellow Texan, pianist Red Garland, on the album *I Left My Heart* (Muse). Wright's performance of "Body and Soul" in this album is a masterpiece of alto saxophone artistry. His style has been described as combining the tonality of Johnny Hodges, star altoist in the Duke Ellington Orchestra, with the lines of bebop genius Charlie Parker, and as embodying "an inherent blues feeling." Wright retired from music in 1979 but returned to perform in 1986 with the Paris Reunion Band.

BIBLIOGRAPHY: Leonard Feather and Ira Gitler, *The Biographical Encyclopedia of Jazz* (New York: Oxford University Press, 1999). Interview with Dan Morgenstern, *Metronome* magazine, December 1961. Dave Oliphant, *Texan Jazz* (Austin: University of Texas Press, 1996). *Dave Oliphant*

Wurstfest. An annual celebration of food and music, held on the Wurstfest grounds beside Landa Park in New Braunfels. The fest commemorates the German heritage of the city and the surrounding region. German foods and musical traditions have played an important role in the cultural life of New Braunfels since it was founded by German settlers in 1845. In 1961 the mayor issued a proclamation setting aside one Saturday in November to celebrate the town's cultural heritage. This celebration came to be known as Wurstfest and has increased in popularity among both residents and tourists every year since. In 1963 attendance was estimated at 10,000. The event moved into the Wursthalle in 1967, and attendance reached 150,000 in 1974. By 2002 the festival had expanded from a single weekend event to a ten-day extravaganza.

Wurstfest visitors are treated to a variety of German and German-inspired dishes, including sauerkraut, *kartoffel* "puffers" (potato pancakes), strudel, bread pudding, funnel cakes, pretzels, and pastries. The ubiquitous sausage, including bratwurst and knackwurst, is perhaps the most popular food item of all. Beer is the drink of choice for many visitors, but nonalcoholic beverages are available. The Wursthalle, the largest of the music venues on the fairgrounds, hosts both traditional and modern bands. German polka music is especially popular, but traditional Mexican-American and country-and-western performers also draw large crowds, both in the Wursthalle and in smaller tents throughout the grounds.

The Wurstfest also provides area craftsmen and artists an opportunity to sell their wares. The Hummel and Sophienburg museums and the Museum of Texas Handmade Furniture host special events during Wurstfest to introduce tourists to German culture. The tour of Conservation Plaza offers visitors a taste of the old city with its restored buildings, and the Heritage Market and Exhibit presents exhibits on the city's history that draw thousands of visitors. In addition, Wurstfest stages dramas produced by the city's Circle Arts Theater, the Tour de Gruene bicycle classic, the Wurstfest Five-Mile Run, and the Wurstfest Regatta, featuring more than 200 sailboats on nearby Canyon Lake. In 2001 the new attraction was the Wurstfest Review variety show, staged in the Wursthalle.

Since its inception, Wurstfest has raised millions of dollars for community projects. The celebration is directed by a board of more than 200 "*Opas*," or honorary "grandfathers." These directors are members of the nonprofit Wurstfest Association, dedicated to promoting local business and tourism and preserving German heritage. The annual celebration is held in early November, rain or shine.

BIBLIOGRAPHY: San Antonio *Express News*, November 8, 1999. Sophienburg Archives, New Braunfels. *Texas Highways*, November 1975.   *Brandy Schnautz*

"Yellow Rose of Texas." A song about how a slave named Emily Morgan allegedly helped win the battle of San Jacinto, the decisive battle in the Texas Revolution, on April 21, 1836. According to legend, Emily was a mulatto slave owned by Col. James Morgan, of Washington-on-the-Brazos, who was kidnapped by soldiers under the orders of Mexican general Santa Anna. She was reportedly brought to Santa Anna's tent, where she entertained him sexually throughout the day of the battle. The distracted general supposedly failed to put his troops on alert, and when the battle began, the Texans caught the Mexicans by surprise.

In fact, however, "Emily Morgan" was a free-born black woman named Emily D. West, who worked as a housekeeper at the New Washington Association's hotel. No evidence supports the story of a tryst with Santa Anna.

One of the earliest versions of "The Yellow Rose of Texas" dates back to the first administration of Sam Houston, who became president of the Republic of Texas in 1836. A handwritten manuscript of the song, now in the A. Henry Moss Papers in the Center for American History at the University of Texas at Austin, was allegedly delivered to one E. A. Jones. This early version, possibly written around the time of the battle of San Jacinto, tells the story of a black man who yearns for his sweetheart. During that era, "yellow" was used to describe people of mixed-race origins, especially mulattoes, and the rose was a common symbol of young womanhood. Because the song was poorly written and full of spelling errors, at least one scholar believes that it could have been composed by an uneducated person, possibly one of Morgan's slaves.

The first published edition of the song was copyrighted by Firth, Pond and Company of New York on September 2, 1858. This edition states that the song and chorus were arranged and composed for vaudeville performer Charles H. Brown by someone with the initials of "J. K." The lyrics are almost identical to those in the handwritten manuscript. During the Civil War the song became popular with Confederate soldiers, though some of the lyrics were changed. A version sung by troops under the command of Gen. John B. Hood, for instance, later recorded in *The Dell Book of Great American Folk Songs*, substituted "soldier" for "darky," and added a reference to a recent military defeat: "The gallant Hood of Texas played hell in Tennessee."

Such modifications aside, the song remained relatively unchanged throughout the late nineteenth and early twentieth centuries. In 1930, Texas composer David Guion transcribed the song from memory, inserting his own distinct melodic effects while taking care to preserve the song's character. Guion's version of the "Yellow Rose" became popular, and a second transcription of the song was released in 1936 to commemorate the Texas Centen-

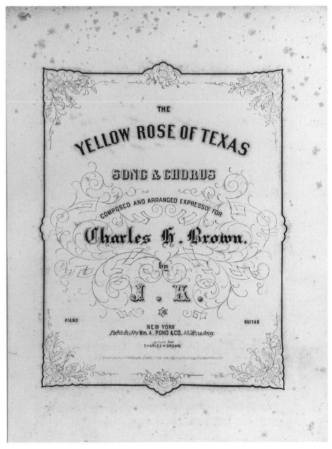

Sheet music cover for "The Yellow Rose of Texas," published in 1858 by William A. Pond & Co., New York. Texas State Library and Archives Commission.

nial. By World War II the former "Negro folksong" had become a standard, and was popular with military personnel serving overseas.

The song became even more popular in 1955, when Mitch Miller recorded it. Arranged by Don George and recorded for Columbia Records, this new version was tailored to the tastes of the dancing audience at the time. Miller retained some phrases from the original song manuscript, but eliminated some of its folk elements. In 1956 John W. Schaum arranged a boogie-woogie transcription. This version of the song was suitable for elementary piano students, and, over the years, its appeal extended to people of all ages.

BIBLIOGRAPHY: Martha Anne Turner, *The Yellow Rose of Texas: Her Saga and Her Song* (Austin: Shoal Creek, 1976).   *Juan Carlos Rodríguez*

Z

Ziegler, Samuel Peters. Painter, printmaker, musician, and educator; b. Lancaster, Pennsylvania, January 4, 1882; d. April 7, 1967; son of Christian and Mary R. (Peters) Ziegler. Ziegler worked as a hotel clerk to finance his education at the Philadelphia Musical Academy and the Pennsylvania Academy of Fine Arts. He studied under William Merritt Chase, Hugh Breckenridge, and Thomas Anshutz at the Academy of Fine Arts, and in 1912 won a Cresson European Traveling Scholarship that funded six months of travel to art centers in England, France, Belgium, Holland, Germany, and Italy. He returned in 1913 for a final year of study at the PAFA and subsequently operated a private studio. While living in Pennsylvania Ziegler married Cora Amanda Kresge; they had four sons and one daughter, and raised a foster daughter.

In 1917 Ziegler accepted a position on the fine arts faculty at Texas Christian University. There he taught cello and music theory until 1919, when he became head of the art department at Texas Women's College (later Texas Wesleyan College) in Fort Worth; in 1925 he returned to TCU as head of the art department, a position he held until 1953. During his years at TCU Ziegler became known for his paintings and prints featuring Fort Worth and neighboring ranches and oilfields. He made a series of lithographs depicting Fort Worth's growth and development over a period of years; he also completed a series of paintings, etchings, and crayon drawings of the petroleum industry in the Southwest.

Ziegler's talent began to be recognized in the middle to late 1920s, when he won a series of prizes in competitive exhibitions. He won first prizes in portrait and figure painting at the West Texas Exposition in San Angelo (1924–26), the Bailey Gold Medal at the State Fair of Texas in Dallas (1924), first prize in still life at the Texas Art League exhibition in Nashville, Tennessee (1927), and first prize in lithography, Southern States Art League Exhibition (1929). The Museum of Fine Arts, Houston, mounted a solo exhibition of his work in 1931, which was followed by a another solo exhibition in the Elisabet Ney Museum in Austin. In 1933 etchings by Ziegler depicting Texas landscapes, industries, and night views of Fort Worth skyscrapers were sent on request to colleges in Missouri, Illinois, and Wisconsin. The following year he painted a mural for the public schools of Fort Worth, *The Development of Aviation*, in which members of his family represented the stages of development towards aviation.

Ziegler was a member of the American Federation of Arts, the American Artists Professional League, the Southern States Art League, the Texas Fine Arts Association, and the Fort Worth Art Association. From 1925 to 1938 he served on the Fort Worth City Art Commission. He also played cello in the Fort Worth Symphony Orchestra and the Pro Arte String Quartet.

He earned two degrees at Texas Christian University, a bachelor of arts (1924), and a master of education (1951). He retired as professor emeritus in 1953. Samuel Ziegler's work is represented in the collections of the Modern Art Museum of Fort Worth, the Carnegie Library in Fort Worth, and Texas Christian University.

BIBLIOGRAPHY: Peter Hastings Falk, ed., *Who Was Who in American Art* (Madison, Connecticut: Sound View, 1985). Frances Battaile Fisk, *A History of Texas Artists and Sculptors* (Abilene, Texas, 1928; facsimile rpt., Austin: Morrison, 1986). Fort Worth *Star–Telegram*, April 8, 1967. Peggy and Harold Samuels, *The Illustrated Biographical Encyclopedia of Artists of the American West* (Garden City, New York: Doubleday, 1976). *Texas Outlook*, March 1937. *Kendall Curlee*

Zydeco. A type of music that evolved from an acoustic folk idiom known as la-la, dating back to the 1920s and unique to black Creoles originally from rural southwest Louisiana. The modern form emerged in southeast Texas in the late 1940s and 1950s among immigrants from this ethnic group, who came to cities such as Houston and Beaumont to find employment. There they fused old Louisiana French music traditions with urban blues and R&B to create a distinctive sound.

In zydeco the primary lead instrument is the accordion, and the fundamental cadences come from the polyrhythmic manipulation of hand-held metal utensils such as spoons scraped for percussive effect against the surface of a washboard (known in French as *le frottoir*). But since the 1950s zydeco instrumentation has included standard drums, electric bass, electric guitar, and even piano, organ, saxophone, and trumpet. Zydeco singing—plaintive vocalizing in a blues style—typically combines English and French.

Singer and accordionist Amédé Ardoin (1898–ca. 1950) is generally recognized as the most influential figure in the early development of Creole music. This native Louisianan made seminal la-la recordings, heavily influenced by traditional white Cajun music played at a regular, measured tempo, between 1929 and 1934. These included a session on August 8, 1934, at the Texas Hotel in San Antonio for the Bluebird / Victor company.

In subsequent years, la-la increasingly came to highlight Afro-Caribbean rhythms, in which accents shifted to various beats. The role of the washboard became more pronounced, laying the trademark "chanka-chank" foundation over which a featured accordionist would perform. And the repertoire began to expand beyond old-style French songs to encompass urban sounds and more technologically advanced instruments. These innovations occurred especially in Houston, where the black Creole immigrant population was concentrated in the Fifth Ward neighborhood known as Frenchtown, which was incorporated in 1922.

The origins of the word *zydeco* have been traced to a French lyric that surfaced first in various Creole folk songs in Louisiana: "*les haricots sont pas salé*" (roughly, "the snapbeans are not salted"). *Zydeco* derives from the first two words, "*les haricots.*" Among various attempts at making an English spelling correspond to the black Creole pronunciation, *z-y-d-e-c-o* eventually prevailed, under the influence of Houston folklorist Robert Burton "Mack" McCormick. He formalized the now-standard spelling in his transcription of lyrics for a two-volume 1959 record album, on the 77 Records label, called *A Treasury of Field Recordings.* McCormick originally intended for the term to apply only to the fusion of Texas blues and Creole la-la that he heard in Frenchtown.

The first two recordings to use variants of the term *zydeco* to refer to a style of music and dancing (as opposed to the original French sense referring to a vegetable) were produced in Houston. One was issued around 1947 on the song erroneously titled "Zolo Go" by bluesman Lightnin' Hopkins on Gold Star Records, and the second appeared in the 1949 recording of "Bon Ton Roula" by rhythm-and-blues performer Clarence "Bon Ton" Garlow on Macy's Records.

The key event in the movement of black Creole music into the public venues of Houston occurred at Irene's Café on Christmas Eve 1949, when accordionist Willie Green played an impromptu concert that drew large crowds and established the zydeco sound as a form of popular entertainment. Soon after that, the owner of Johnson's Lounge in Frenchtown decided to cease booking big bands and to feature Creole accordion music performed by stalwarts such as Lonnie Mitchell, who later assumed operation of the club. Eventually the lease reverted to Johnson's heir, Doris McClendon, who rechristened the lounge the Continental Zydeco Ballroom, the city's (and probably the state's) premier venue for the music throughout the latter half of the twentieth century.

One black Creole who moved to Texas in 1947 and became part of the Frenchtown scene was Clifton Chenier (1925–1987), generally acknowledged today as the "King of Zydeco"—the musician most responsible for popularizing the music. Among Chenier's innovations were the employment of the large piano-key chromatic accordion, which has a wider musical range than the traditional diatonic instrument, and the invention of the modern washboard vest, which expanded the musical possibilities for percussion beyond the limitations of the previously handheld household utensil. In 1964 at the Gold Star studio in Houston, Chenier recorded the classic song "Zydeco Sont Pas Salé," in which the producer abandoned the French phrase *les haricots* for the potent new word.

Since then, with southwest Louisiana, southeast Texas has remained a hotbed of zydeco culture—home to recording and touring artists such as Chenier, Wilfred Chevis, Step Rideau, and Brian Terry. Contemporary zydeco continues to evolve, incorporating progressive elements of various styles of popular music, especially including rock and hip-hop.

BIBLIOGRAPHY: Houston *Press*, September 2–8, 1999. John Minton, "Houston Creoles and Zydeco: The Emergence of an African-American Urban Popular Style," *American Music* 14.4 (Winter 1996). Nicholas R. Spitzer, "Zydeco," *Encyclopedia of Southern Culture*, ed. Charles Reagan Wilson and William Ferris (New York: Anchor, 1991). Chris Strachwitz, booklet for *Zydeco: Volume One, The Early Years, 1949–62* (Arhoolie CD 307, 1989). Lorenzo Thomas, "From Gumbo To Grammys: The Development of Zydeco Music in Houston" *Juneteenth Texas: Essays in African-American Folklore*, ed. Francis E. Abernethy, Patrick B. Mullen, and Alan B. Govenar (Denton: University of North Texas Press, 1996). Michael Tisserand, *The Kingdom of Zydeco* (New York: Arcade, 1998). Roger Wood, "Black Creoles and the Evolution of Zydeco in Southeastern Texas" in *The Roots of Texas Music*, ed. Lawrence Clayton and Joe Specht (College Station: Texas A&M University Press, 2003). Roger Wood, "Doris McClendon," *Living Blues*, March–April 1998. Roger Wood, "Southeast Texas: Hot House of Zydeco," *Journal of Texas Music History* 1.2 (Fall 2001). *Roger Wood*

AUTHOR INDEX

Abernethy, Francis E., 105–7, 278–79, 281

Acosta, Teresa Palomo, 134–35, 203–8, 287–88, 293–94, 307–10, 315

Albrecht, Theodore, 1–2, 17, 52, 118–19, 144–45, 168, 171, 180, 208–9, 282–83, 317, 319

Allen, Martha Mitten, 47

Anderson, H. Allen, 115, 131, 133, 179–80, 323, 325

Anderson, Jahue E., 239, 289

Angell, Ruth S., 181

Arhos, Damon, 10–11

Astbury, Ray, 336, 350

Babin, L. Randolph, 209

Barkley, Roy R., 336–37

Benson, Nettie Lee, 294

Bernhard, Virginia, 137–38

Berry, Margaret C., 99

Bickley, Charles, 4, 45

Biesele, Rudolph L., 128

Bishop, Constance M., 33–34

Blunt, Robert M., 113

Bogan, Patrick Henry Jr., 89, 91

Bogue, Mamie, 207

Bonura, Larry S., 84–85, 245, 300–301, 358–59

Branda, Eldon S., 16, 173–74, 241

Brandenstein, Sherilyn, 204–5

Breitenkamp, Edward C., 284–85

Brigham, Cathy, 20–21, 61–62, 161–62, 172, 191–92, 301, 330–31

Brown, Jarad, 12–13, 69–70, 147

Bryson, Conrey, 197–98

Buchanan, James R., 326, 328

Caldwell, Shirley, 200–201, 223–24

Christian, Garna L., 50

Christman, Bobby, 41–42

Clark, Penny, 301–2

Clayton, Lawrence, 108

Cochran, Alice C., 217

Cockreham, Amy, 215, 331–32

Compton, Adam, 188–89

Copeland, Carlyn, 209–10, 290–91

Cottrell, Debbie Mauldin, 58, 60, 184, 268

Cox, James Kent, 78, 316–17

Crawford, Bill, 30–32

Curlee, Kendall, 126–27, 181, 182–83, 365

Daboub, Alex, 60–61, 210, 212

Dance, Helen Oakley, 348–49

Dary, David, 199–200

Davis, Charles G., 46, 306–7

Davis, Ronald L., 276–77

DeKunder, David, 5, 239, 241

Dick, James, 128–29

Dickey, Dan W., 63–65, 201–3, 220–22

Drake, Jerry C., 22–23, 333–34

Dutton, Robin, 207, 340

Esparza, Jesse J., 74, 129

Fitts, Susan Love, 23–24

Flachmeier, Jeanette H., 209

Fontenot, Kevin S., 30, 120, 196–97

Fowler, Gene, 30–32

Frantz, Joe B., 50

Fry, Phillip L., 112, 210, 330

García, María-Cristina, 216–17

Gard, Wayne, 188

Gay, Wayne Lee, 57–58

Geary, Lynnette, 23

Giesberg, Robert I., 143–44

Giesenschlag, N. D., 196, 296

Gonzalez, Elsa, 94, 343

Govenar, Alan, 24–28, 159, 161

Green, George N., 233–34

Groneman, Bill, 198

Hamm, Christine, 183

Hardman, Peggy, 42, 164–65, 184, 246–47, 358

Hartman, Gary, 17, 45–46, 65–68, 92, 110–12, 128, 150, 316, 355–58

Haworth, Alan Lee, 20, 142, 152, 154, 289–90, 325, 326

Head, James, 2–3, 30, 87–88, 121–22, 152, 167, 178–79, 239, 243–44, 281, 286–89, 314–15, 320–21, 323, 344–46, 350–52, 358

Heide, Jean M., 18–19

Hellinger, Linda, 75

Hesler, Samuel B., 241–42

Hickinbotham, Gary S., 212–13, 230–31, 253–62, 297–98

Hooks, Michael Q., 7–8

Huang, Keith, 228–29

Hughes, Richard B., 129–30, 167–68

Jasinski, Laurie E., 48–49, 253, 270–75, 292, 355

Johnson, John G., 62

Jones, Nancy Baker, 69

Jordan, J. E., 125–26, 317–19

Jordan, Scott, 304–5

Kashanipour, Ryan A., 5, 215–16

Kennan, Kent, 110

Kennedy, Rod, 174–75

King, C. Richard, 343–44

Kleiner, Diana J., 14–15, 81, 101–2

Kohout, Martin Donell, 38–39, 41, 95, 97, 137, 139–42, 172–73, 187–88

Kouyomjian, Susan, 253

Krause, Tanya, 21–22, 38

Kreneck, Thomas H., 95

Krenn, Michael L., 46–47

Kuehn, Claire R., 134

Lange, Samantha, 166

Leatherwood, Art, 313–14

Lee, James Ward, 237–38

Leifeste, Linc, 34–35, 74–75

Leschper, Alicia, 192, 242–43

Lich, Glen E., 193–94

Looper, Lance, 89

Lucko, Paul M., 49–50, 117, 218–19

Malone, Bill C., 262

Mason, Richard J., 122–24

Maxwell, Lisa C., 78–79, 114–15, 207

McArthur, Judith N., 71–72, 175–76, 192

McCall, Adrian, 166

McGaughey, Janet M., 83–84

McGillen, Geoffrey E., 281–82

McVey, John, 338–40

Milligan, Heather, 119–20, 264

Minor, David, 29, 97, 99

Minton, John, 185–87

Monsho, Kharen, 58, 80, 84, 251–52

Mooney, Kevin E., 138–39, 311, 353

Moore, Michael Douglas, 10

Morawski, Michael S., 43–44, 82–83

Nance, Joseph Milton, 10

Odintz, Jenny, 166–67

O'Donovan, Hugh, 70–71, 266

Oliphant, Dave, 5, 7, 43, 57, 63, 69, 86–87, 102, 107–8, 113, 116–17, 131, 133–34, 135, 145–48, 154–59, 175, 176, 178, 182, 183, 215, 247, 290, 321, 323, 353, 362

Olson, Mary Beth, 300

Oppenheimer, Lois G., 263–64

Oren, Amanda, 91–92

Ornish, Natalie, 196

Orozco, Cynthia E., 285–86

Palmer, Jack, 75–77

Parker, Donna P., 262–63, 294–96, 349–50

Pease, S. W., 108, 110

Perez, Joan Jenkins, 42

Peterson, Karla, 91, 284, 351

Potts, Jackie, 48, 114

Pugatch, William, 47–48

Pugh, Donald W., 183–84

Pullin, Michael, 15–16, 198–99, 265, 342

Reaves, Mike, 35, 244

Rendon, Daniel, 166, 276

Roberts, Jeremy, 81

Rodríguez, Juan Carlos, 44, 62–63, 86, 92–93, 122, 136, 190–91, 247, 264–65, 288, 342–43, 364

Roeckle, Charles A., 232

Roell, Craig H., 3–4, 100, 194–95, 224–25, 244–45, 311–13, 319–20

Rosner, Christian A. K., 310–11

Royall, Richard R., 150–51

Saustrup, Anders S., 137

Schnautz, Brandy, 14, 72–73, 126, 193–94, 314, 315–16, 362–63

Schuller, Tim, 29–30

Schutze, C. A. Jr., 283–84

Scudday, Roy G., 19–20, 305

Seeber, Jill S., 80–81, 142–43, 163–64, 268–69

Self, Greg, 16, 296–97

Shreve, Bradley, 14, 57, 81–82, 83, 94–95, 100–101, 135, 152, 165–66, 198, 212, 217–18, 232–33, 247–48, 303, 328, 330, 355

Simon, Cheryl L., 1, 4, 32–33, 41–42, 61, 102–3, 115–16, 162–63, 305–6, 307, 346–49

Simpson, Harold B., 219–20

Slate, John H., 15, 248–49

Smith, Lois, 77–78, 146–47

Smyrl, Vivian Elizabeth, 359

Solice, Devin, 166

Spain, Charles A., Jr., 310

Specht, Joe W., 16–17, 231, 354–55

Spell, Lota M., 112–13

Standifer, Mary M., 13

Stoeltje, Beverly J., 103–5

Strickland, Kristi, 44–45

Strong, Julia Hurd, 245

Sucher, Steve, 82

Sullivan, Ruth K., 39–41, 189–90, 267–68, 269, 303–4

Sutton, Randi, 213–15

Swann, Lelle, 2

Thonhoff, Robert H., 28–29

Tiller, David C., 334–35

Tillis, Kirvin, 8

Tippens, Matthew, 62–63, 243

Townsend, Charles R., 85–86, 184–85, 298–300, 356–57

Turner, Elizabeth Hayes, 17–18

Turpin, Solveig A., 225–28

Van Beveren, Amy, 178

Wallace, Patricia Ward, 237

Walters, Katherine, 331

Ward, George B., 236–37

Weeks, Tresi, 8–9

Weggemann, Leighann, 166

West, Bill, 353–54

Wheat, John, 7, 237

Wilk, Helen K., 359–62

Williams, Hannah, 292–93

Williams, Stephen G., 58

Wilson, Christina H., 71, 234–36

Wolz, Larry, 19, 35–38, 120–21, 136, 176, 245–46, 291–92, 337–38, 352–53

Wood, Roger, 94, 124–25, 139, 229–30, 265–66, 365–66

Zachry, Juanita Daniel, 68

SUBJECT INDEX

Page numbers in boldface refer to main article on topic. Page numbers in italics refer to photographs and other illustrations.

A&M record label, 262
Abbott, Emma, 235
Abbott Records, 262
ABC–Dunhill record label, 27, 259, 266, 269, 298
ABC Orchestra, 264
ABC–Paramount Records, 243
Abe Epstein Studio, 261
Abilene Little Theater, 223
Abilene Opera Association, 236
Abilene Philharmonic, 54, 185
Abrams, George, 284
ACA Studios, 258
Accordionists, 163–64, 190–91, 205, 221, 256, 260, 308, 315, 343, 366
Accurate Sound Recording Company, 358
Ace, Johnny, 27, 259, 269
Ace, Sonny, 114
Ace in the Hole Band, 5, 48–49, 68, 75, 259
Ace Records, 210, 289, 325
Ackley, Gaylen, 242
Acuff, Roy, 38, 44, 231
Acuff-Rose Music, 230
Adams, Fred, 255
Adams, Marcus, 91
Adams, Marie, 27, 259, 269
Adams, O. B. "Easy," 318
Adams, William, 296
Aday, Marvin Lee, 273
Adderley, Cannonball, 82, 344
Adler, Guido, 245
Adolph Hofner and All the Boys, 137
Adolph Hofner and the San Antonians, 256
African American festivals, 104
After Hours Band, 265
Aguilar, Antonio, 202, 265
AHORA (Alliance of Hispanic Broadcasters), 293
Akins, Elmer, 1
Alabama (band), 264
Alabama–Coushatta Indians, 225
Aladdin Lamp Company, 299
Aladdin Records, 35, 39, 70, 121, 142, 210, 215, 230, 269
Alamendárez, Armando, 260
Alamo City Highlanders, 334
Alamo pianos, 245
Alamo record label, 308
Alarcón, Norma, 127

Alarcón expedition, 225, 227
Albert, Christine, 149, 298
Albert, Don, 98, 102, 121
Alessandro, Victor Nicholas, 1–2, 54, 100, 235, 283
Alexander, Birdie, 2
Alexander, John, 182
Alexander, Lux, 239
Alexander, Mel, 336
Alexander, "Texas," 2, 26, 27, 142, 152, 159, 166, 245, 255, 256, 288, 291
Alexandra, Lorez, 303
All Boy record label, 125
Alldin Chicken Shackers, 284
Alldred, Dave, 179
Allen, Gracie, 201
Allen, Henry, 154, 248, 296
Allen, Jap, 175
Allen, Steve, 192
Allen, Terry, 182, 260, 261, 300
Allende, Isabel, 127
Alley, Alvin, 3
Alley, Shelly Lee, 2–3, 3, 31, 50, 74
Alley Cats, 3, 74
Allied record label, 49
Alligator Records, 62, 352
Allison, Irl Sr., 3, 3–4, 56, 224–25, 336–37
Allison, Jerry, 141
Allred, James, 234, 311
All Stars, 306
Allsup, Tommy, 141, 260
All the Pretty Horses, 5
All World All Star Band, 213
Almanac Book and Recording Company, 288
Almeida, Antonio de, 145
Almeida, Laurindo, 14
Almeida, Santiago, 205, 256
Alonzo and his Rancheros, 260
Alpert, Herb, 351
Alphonse Trent Orchestra, 328
Altschuler, Modeste, 144
Alurista, 127
Alva, Luigi, 56, 235
Amarillo Opera, 236
Amarillo Symphony, 54
Amazing Records, 298
Ameche, Don, 97
Amen Studios, 261
"American Bandstand," 141
American Blues, 45, 272
American Blues Legends '75, 336

American College of Musicians, 4, 47
American Federation of Musicians, 258
American Folk Blues Festival, 213
American Folk Life Festival, 288
American Folklore Society, 188
American Music Guild, 217
American Musicological Society, 246
American Record Company, 254, 255, 258
American Recording Corporation, 80
Ames record label, 152
Ammons, Albert, 32, 155
Ammons, Gene, 7, 58, 116
Amster, Pearl, 4
Andersen, Eric, 175
Anderson, Bill, 210
Anderson, Ivie, 38
Anderson, Laurie, 182
Anderson, Lynn, 21
Anderson, Marian, 117
Anderson Fair Retail Restaurant, 4
Andrews Sisters, 163
Andrus Studios, 259
Angelou, Maya, 127
Anhalt Hall, 5
Animals, 359
Annex Club, 289
Annis, Rev. J. T. L., 19
Annis, Martha, 199
Anshutz, Thomas, 365
Anthony, Joe, 261
Antone, Clifford, 5
Antone's Nightclub, 5, 27, 300
Antone's Records, 5, 262
Apache Indians, 225
Apollo record label, 58
Applewhite, Charlie, 289
Aquarius record label, 125
ARA record label, 131
Archia, Tom, 5, 7, 35
Archie Bell and the Drells, 259
ARC records, 44
Ardoin, Amédé, 365
Arhoolie Records, 27, 30, 49, 61–62, 164, 186, 187, 206, 241, 254, 288, 307, 325, 331, 350
Arhos, Bill, 10–11
Arista Texas record label, 261

Aristocrat record label, 7
Arlyn studios, 261, 262
Armadillo Gas Company, 347
Armadillo World Headquarters, 6, 7, 67, 178, 261, 298, 346, 347
Armed Forces Radio Service, 191, 197
Armstrong, Louis, 14, 32, 33, 41, 43, 116, 121, 147, 148, 154, 155, 156, 161, 162, 165, 167, 183, 247, 264, 289, 296, 306, 320, 323, 350, 351, 359
Armstrong, Robert Wright, 7–8
Army musicians, 15, 47–48, 53, 57, 79, 81, 133–34, 135, 173, 183–84, 198, 276
Arnold, Eddy, 188, 220, 230, 231, 237
Arnspiger, Herman, 39, 184
Arrington, Joseph Jr., 8
Art Guys, 182
Arthur, Bettie Sue, 9
Arthur, Charline, 8–9, 44, 191, 270
Arthur, Dottie, 8, 9
Arthur, Jack, 9
Arthur, Mary, 9
Art patrons. *See* Patrons for music and art
ARV record label, 260
Asbury, Samuel Erson, 9–10, 311
Ashford, R. T., 121
Ashlock, Jesse, 10, 22, 23, 35, 39, 357
Askell Productions, 359
Asleep at the Wheel, 38, 48, 49, 67, 174, 261, 355
Asociación de Charros de San Antonio, 217
Association for Cultural Equity, 187
Astol, Lalo, 293
Astroline Communications Co. vs. Shurberg (1990), 293
Atco record label, 178
Atkins, Chet, 9, 11, 161
Atlantic Records, 58, 116, 147, 165, 281, 290, 348, 350, 362
Atlas record label, 215
Audio Dallas, 260
August Forster Piano Company, 245

Austin, Gene, 12
Austin, Henry, 138
Austin, Stephen F., 242
Austin
  Antone's Nightclub, 5, 27
  Armadillo World Headquarters, 7, 67, 178, 261, 298, 346, 347
  "Austin City Limits," 10–11, 38, 196, 273
  Austin Outhouse, 103
  blues, 5, 27
  Broken Spoke, 10, 37, 38
  Continental Club, 27
  opera, 56, 234–36
  punk rock, 248, 249
  Raul's Club, 249
  recording industry, 27, 261–62
  Soap Creek Saloon, 67
  Symphony Orchestra, 4, 47, 55, 56, 83, 181
  Threadgill's, 148, 149, 168, 326
  Vault, 249
  Victory Grill, 27, 33
  Vulcan Gas Company, 261, 346–47
"Austin City Limits," 10–11, 38, 196, 273
Austin Civic Opera Company, 235
Austin Lounge Lizards, 126
Austin Lyric Opera, 56, 235–36
Austin Opry House, 261
Austin Outhouse, 103
Austin Quartet Association, 1
Austin Recording Studio, 261
Austin Records, 261
Austin Symphony Orchestra, 4, 47, 55, 56, 83, 181
Autrey, James L., 250
Autry, Gene, 12, 12–13, 44, 66, 80, 131, 197, 212, 213, 267, 276, 311, 318
Autumn Sound, 260
Aves, Dreda, 13, 55, 60
Axiom, 249
Ayala, Ramón, 261, 264
Azteca record label, 308
Aztec Theater, 223

Babasin, Harry, 14, 158, 276, 333
Babatunde, Akin, 161
Baca, Frank, 14
Baca, Joe, 14
Baca, John, 14
Baca, L. B., 14
Baca, Ray, 14
Bacas of Fayetteville, 14, 73
Back Beat record label, 27, 259, 269, 325
Backofen, Heinrich, 119
Bad Boys, 306
Baez, Joan, 142, 231
BAG. See Black Artist Group (BAG)
Bagpipe music, 198
Bailey, Charles, 166
Bailey, Cotton, 306
Bailey, James A. "Gus," 14–15
Bailey, Joseph Weldon, 15
Bailey, Mollie Arline Kirkland, 14–15
Bailey, Pearl, 91, 239
Bailey, W. O., 242
Bain, Wilfred C., 333
Baker, Chet, 14
Baker, Norman, 31
Baker, O. T., 313
Ball, David, 11, 148, 261
Ball, James, 108, 223, 224
Ball, Marcia, 7, 33, 49, 149
Ballard, Hank, 124
Ballet, 56, 134
Ballet Russe, 268
Ballew, Smith, 15, 198
Band directors, 7, 17, 300–301, 353–54
Bandleaders, 15, 17, 34–35, 39–42, 50, 82, 100–101, 102, 124–25, 131–33, 152–54, 182, 184, 209–10, 231, 239, 241, 328. See also Conductors
Band O' Sunshine, 146
Bandy, Moe, 21, 318
Banjo players, 212–13, 357–58
Barbara K, 103
Barbaro, Nick, 292
Barber, Stephen, 273
Barbirolli, Sir John, 54, 145
Barclay, William Archibald, 15–16
Barefield, Eddie, 121
Barksdale, Everett, 155
Barlow, William, 321
Barnes, H. M., 91
Barnet, Charlie, 14, 183
Barnett, Billy Bob, 21
Barnett, Spot, 91, 351
Baromeo, Chase, 16, 55
Barr, Candy, 289
"Barrelhouse" blues, 87–88
Barrett, Dick, 174
Barrett, Lawrence, 197
Barrett, Leonora, 68
Barrio Boyzz, 286
Barrow, Clyde, 71
Barrymore, Lionel, 116
Barton, Lou Ann, 49, 340
Bartz, Ben, 58
Bar X Cowboys, 50, 74

Basie, Count, 32, 44, 58, 60, 86, 97, 116, 155, 156, 158, 162, 165, 166, 175, 210, 239, 247, 251, 276, 284, 290, 303–4, 321, 344, 348
Bassist, 251–52
Battista, Joseph, 282
Bauduc, Ray, 305, 307
Bauer, Harold, 268
Bauer, Marion, 291
Baxter, Don, 31
Baxter, Gordon, 50
Baxter, J. R., 16, 296, 297
Baylor Female College, 24, 112
Baylor University, 54
Beach, Amy, 36
Beach Boys, 21
Beard, Dean, 16–17, 17, 270, 272, 354
Beard, Frank, 272
Beatles, 45, 66, 141, 148, 161, 187, 237, 244, 270, 271
Beaumont, Jess, 71
Beaumont High School Orchestra, 209
Beaumont Music Commission, 209, 301
Beaumont Symphony of Southeast Texas, 209, 301–2
Bechet, Sidney, 32, 41, 135, 154, 155, 350
Beck, Carl, 17, 18
Beck, Jeff, 178, 270
Beck, Jim, 259
Beckham, Garland Wayne, 17
Beckham, Wayne, 239
Beckmann, Albert, 18
Beckner, Denny, 289
Becky, Son, 255
Bedichek, Roy, 238
Beecham, Sir Thomas, 54, 145
BeeHive record label, 58
Beers, Iola Barns, 17–18
Beethoven–German Club Choir, 353
Beethoven Hall, 17, 18, 52
Beethoven Männerchor, 17, 18–19, 52, 118
Beethoven Trio, 180
Bego Records, 92, 260, 264
Behr, Arthur, 28
Behr, Jennie von, 28
Behr, Oscar, 28
Behr, Ottmar Jr., 28
Behr, Ottmar von, 28
Beiderbecke, Bix, 146, 161, 172, 306
Bel Canta Quartet, 250
Belden, Bob, 333
Bell, Archie, 259
Bell, T. D., 27, 33
Bell, Vince, 4

Bellaire Records, 258
"Bell County March," 24
Belle Plain College, 19, 54
Bells of Joy, 88
Belo Corporation, 250
Beltrán, Lola, 288
Belvin, Jesse, 303
Beman, Melinda, 182
Benedict, Harry Y., 99
Beneke, Tex, 19–20, 159
Bennett, Mark, 306
Bennett, Samm, 147
Benny, Jack, 154, 201
Benoit, Pierre, 338
Benson, Ray, 49, 86, 261
Benton, Brook, 231
Benton, Buster, 61
Benton, Leon, 245
Berg, Alban, 56, 245
Berganza, Teresa, 56, 174, 235
Bergé, Paul, 144
Bergen, Edgar, 97, 192
Berhnard Steiner Piano Company, 245
Berigan, Bunny, 15, 183
Berkeley Folk Festival, 187
Berle, Milton, 201
Berlin, Irving, 85
Berliner, Emile, 253
Bernal, Eloy, 92, 150
Bernal, Paulino, 92, 150, 204, 260, 264, 315
Bernal Christian Records, 92
Bernal Records, 92
Bernet, Ed, 213
Bernhardt, Sarah, 18
Bernstein, Leonard, 84, 144
Berry, Chu, 134
Besseler, Heinrich, 136
Besserer, William, 53, 118
Betancourt, Paco, 150, 204, 260, 308
Beverly Glen Records, 304
Bible, D. X., 250
Bigard, Barney, 159
Big band music, 152–54, 198, 305–6
Big Bopper, 20, 75, 113, 141, 161, 180, 259, 271
Big Boys, 249, 273
Big Brother and the Holding Company, 168, 272
Big Cypress Boys, 77
"Big 'D' Jamboree," 9, 20–21, 33–34, 43, 44, 213, 218, 247, 270, 354
Big Walter the Thunderbird, 189
Bila, Rudolph, 342
Bill Naizer Brass Band, 72
Billy Bob's Texas, 21–22
Biloski, Count, 348

Binyon, Larry, 305
Birmingham Blue Blowers, 182
Black, Clint, 21, 68, 86
Black, Louis, 292
Black Aces, 210
Black and Blue record label, 58
Black and White record label, 348
Black Artist Group (BAG), 135
Black Arts Group, 159
Black Boy Shine, 255
Black Flag, 249
Blackie Simmons and the Blue Jackets, 22–23
Blackouts, 116
Blackstone, Harry, 201
Black Swan record label, 167
Black Top record label, 139, 266
Blackwell, Francis (Scrapper), 348
Blackwood, James, 185
Blackwood Brothers, 124, 296
Blaker, Clay, 5, 78
Blakey, Art, 82, 158, 251
Blanchet, Milan, 115
Bland, Bobby, 27, 91, 125, 139, 265, 266, 269
Blank, Les, 187
Blanton, Jimmy, 69
Blazes, 215
Bledsoe, Jules, 23, 56
Blind Melon, 161
Blind Texas Marlin, 255
Blitz, Flora, 24, 24
Blitz, Julien Paul, 23–24, 24, 144, 282, 282
Blondeel, Maria, 146
Bloodrock, 272
Bluebird Records, 34, 40, 77, 82, 205, 206, 239, 255, 256, 258, 365
Blue Bonnet Records, 289
Blue Cat Studio, 261
Blue Devils, 86, 156, 210, 239, 290
Blue Eagle Four, 152
Bluegrass music, 43–44
Blue Islanders, 74
Blue Jackets, 22–23
Bluejackets, 212
Blue Moon Chasers, 165, 210
Blue Moon Syncopaters, 133
Blue Note Records, 134, 158, 354
Blue Ridge Playboys, 74, 218, 286
Blues, 24–28, 25, 26, 32. *See also* Rhythm-and-blues music
    Antone's Nightclub, 5, 27, 300

Armadillo World Headquarters, 7, 67, 178
"Austin City Limits," 10–11
"barrelhouse" blues, 87–88
Cheatham Street Warehouse, 48–49
Chicano twist to, 114
country blues, 228–29, 321–23
documentaries on, 27
Eldorado Ballroom, 93–94
guitarists, 30, 62, 69–70, 124–25, 139, 142, 152, 159–61, 164, 166, 178, 183, 189–90, 229–30, 288–91, 331, 336, 340, 348, 351, 358
Jim Hotel, 162–63
pianists, 32–33, 38–39, 87–88, 121, 213–15, 245, 247–48, 265–66, 287–88, 350
promoters, 61
recording industry, 26–27
rock-and-roll and, 270, 272, 274
saxophonist, 344
singers, 2, 29–30, 61, 89, 102–3, 121–22, 136, 142, 148–49, 152, 159–61, 167–69, 183, 189–90, 217–18, 265–66, 288–91, 294–96, 304, 323, 325, 336, 340, 344, 349–52, 358
songwriters, 32, 62–63, 102–3, 121, 148–49, 189–90, 229–30, 265–66, 294–96, 320–21, 325, 351
"swamp blues," 351–52
Blues According to Lightin' Hopkins, 142
Blues Boy Willie, 61
Blues Cats, 178
Blues For Two, 124
Blues Specialists, 33
Blues Syncopaters, 210
Bluesville record label, 350
Blume, Friedrich, 82
Bly, Robert, 127
Blythe, Arthur, 63
Boatright, Mody C., 238
Bob and Earl duo, 42
Bobby Blue Band, 259
Bobby Fuller Four, 113, 272
Bob Strong Orchestra, 14
Boerne Village Band, 28, 28–29
Bogan, Patrick Henry Sr., 89, 90
Bo-Kay record label, 231
Boles, John, 29
Bollin, Zuzu, 27, 29–30
Bon and His Buddies, 290
Bone, Ponty, 49

Bongo Joe, 61, 61–62
Bonham Exchange, 249
Bonner, Juke Boy, 30, 30, 352
Bonner, Moses J., 30, 250
Bono, 5
Boogie Chillen, 89
Boogie-Woogie Boys, 290
Boogie-woogie pianists, 32–33, 155, 320–21, 323, 351–52
Book, Herb, 305
Booker T & the MGs, 304
Booker T. Washington Foundation, 247
Boone, Chester, 58, 182, 344
Boone, Pat, 236
Booth, Edwin, 197
Boots and His Buddies, 63, 82, 121, 255, 362
Bop music, 116–17, 156
Border Folk Festival, 104, 286
Border radio, 30–32, 266
Borrayo, Felix, 260
Boshier, Derek, 182
Bosner, Paul, 11
"Bossa nova" jazz, 14
Boston Serenaders, 353
Boulanger, Nadia, 115, 135
Boulez, Pierre, 84
Bowden, Iola, 47
Bowen, Jimmy, 179, 180, 260, 270
Bowie, David, 340
Bowie, Lester, 135
Bowman, Euday Louis, 32, 155
Bowser, Erbie, 32–33, 33, 88
Boxcar Willie, 33–34, 264
Boy, Andy, 255
Boyd, Bill, 48
Boyd, Jim, 34–35
Boyd, John, 35
Boyd, William Lemuel, 34–35, 35, 258, 259, 318
Boykin, Roger, 259
Boze, Calvin, 35
Bradford, Bobby, 45, 159
Bradley, B. G., 33
Bradley, Will, 198
Bragg, J. H., 255
Braggs, Al "TNT," 266
Branch, Bill, 31
Brant, Albert, 22
Braxton, Anthony, 135
Bray, Marge, 108, 224
"Brazos Boat Song," 138
Breaker, J. M. C., 242
Breckenridge, Hugh, 365
Breeden, Leon, 333
Bres, C. M., 31
Brewer, Clyde, 3
Brewster, Sam, 350
Brian, Robin Hood, 259
Brickell, Edie, 273–74

Bridges, Henry, 166
Bright Star record label, 125
Brinkley, John R., 31
Brisbane, Arthur, 199
Britain, Radie, 35–36, 56
Brite, Al, 105
Britt, Elton, 50
Brock, Dwight, 296, 297
Brock, Kyle, 273
Brodbeck, Jacob F., 193
Broken Spoke, 10, 37, 38
Broken Spoke Company, 38
Bronco record label, 260
Bronze Peacock Dinner Club, 269
Brooks, E. X., 29
Brooks, Garth, 11, 21, 86
Brooks, Samuel P., 299
Brooks, Tommy, 63
Brooks and Dunn, 298
Brooks–Mays, 245
Broonzy, Big Bill, 344
Broussard, Iola, 125
Brower, Cecil, 35, 39, 41, 184
Brown, Charles, 38–39, 139, 210, 215, 265, 351, 354
Brown, Charles H., 364
Brown, Clarence "Gatemouth," 229, 258, 259, 269, 348, 350
Brown, Clifford, 284
Brown, Durwood, 39
Brown, Gatemouth, 26, 27, 49, 70, 82, 91, 139
Brown, Howard, 63
Brown, H. Rap, 303
Brown, James, 58
Brown, Jewel, 58
Brown, Junior, 261
Brown, Matt, 120
Brown, Maxine, 139
Brown, Mel, 5
Brown, Milton, 2, 10, 23, 26, 39–40, 40, 41, 48, 66, 71, 74, 86, 184, 218, 256, 270
Brown, S. Leroy, 250
Brown, Texas Johnny, 82, 265, 266
Brown, Tracy, 198
Brown, Wylbert, 99
Browne, Jackson, 340
Brownskin Models Revue, 41
Brownwood, 54
Broyles, Curley, 198
Brumley, Albert, 296
Bruner, Cliff, 3, 39, 40–41, 48, 50, 74, 86, 197, 218, 258
Brunswick Records, 14, 15, 26, 89, 141, 253, 254, 255, 260
Brusilow, Anshel, 54
Bruton, Stephen, 261, 298
Bryant, Willie, 212

Bubble Puppy, 259, 272
Buchanan, Buck, 319
Buckner, John Edward, 41
Buckner, Teddy, 32
Buddha Records, 325
Buddy Holly Center, 142
Buddy Holly Story, 141, 142
Buffalo Bearcats, 166
Buffalo Booking Agency, 27
Buffett, Jimmy, 10, 355
Bullet Records, 9, 357
Bunch, Charlie, 141
Burden, Omega, **41–42**
Bureau, Allyre, **42**, 56
Burke, Frenchie, 264
Burke, Solomon, 230
Burkes, D. C., 24
Burks, Pinetop, 27, 255
Burleson, Hattie, 26, 121, 255
Burnett, T Bone, 89
Burns, George, 201
Burns, Jethro, 216
Burns, William Orville, 41
Burrus Mill and Elevator Company, 184, 185, 233–34, 357
Burrus Mill Recording Studio, 255
Burton, James, 194
Busey, Gary, 38, 142
Bush, George W., 286
Bush, Johnny, 316, 317, 319
Buster Smith–Count Basie Band of Rhythm, 290
Butler, Roy, 1
Butterfield, Billy, 43
Buttermilk Records, 4
Butthole Surfers, 249, 273
Büttner, Armin, 7
Butts, Robert Dale, 95, 97
Byrd, Bobby, **42**
Byrdland Attractions, 42

C & P record label, 125
Caballe, Montserrat, 56, 235
Cabeza de Vaca, 225, 227, 228
Caceres, Emilio, 43, **43**
Caceres, Ernesto, 43, 156, 306
Cactus Music and Video, 75
Cactus Rose Band, 316–17
Caddo Indians, 225, 227, 228
Cadillac, Bobby, 255
Cadillac Band, 216
Cadillac Bar, 264
Cain, Trummy, 30
Caiola, Al, 32
Cajun Classics record label, 49
Cajun music, 49–50, 111, 308, 365. *See also* Zydeco
Caldwell, Don, 260
Caldwell, Fred, 87
Calhoun, Fred "Papa," 39
California Playboy Band, 152

California Sound, 272
Callahan, Alma, 43
Callahan, Homer, **43–44**
Callahan, Walter, 43–44
Callahan Brothers, 31, 44
Callas, Maria, 55–56, 174, 235
Calloway, Blanche, 175
Calloway, Cab, 44, 121, 134, 156, 162, 165, 182, 201, 210, 212, 348, 353, 362
Calloway, Jim, 304
Calt, Stephen, 321
Calvin Boze All-Stars, 35
Calvin Boze Combo, 35
Calway, Brian "Hash Brown," 29
Camp, Red, *158*
Campbell, Dorothy, 33
Campbell, Gene, 255
Campbell, George, 289
Campbell, Glen, 241
Campbell, Muryel, 184
Campbell, Robert L., 7
Campbell, Sarah Elizabeth, 103, 149
Campi, Ray, 261
CAM Studios, 261
Canales, Laura, 92, 285, 308
Candid record label, 362
Canned Heat, 62, 314, 346
Cantagrel, François J., 42
Cantú, Camilio, 256
Cantú, Frank, 260
Cantú, Laura Hernández, 308
Cantú, Timoteo, 260
Capitol Records, 81, 147, 178, 194, 299, 307, 344, 356
Caprock record label, 231
Cara record label, 285
Carey, Mutt, 323
Carey, William R., 198
Carl, William, 16
Carlton, Carl, 269
Carlucci, Joseph B., 301–2
Carmen y Laura, 92, 150, 203, 204, 206, 260, 308, 315, 343
Carmichael, Hoagy, 116
Carmichael, Stokely, 303
Carnett, Ellis L., 293
Carpenter, Mary Chapin, 11
Carr, Leroy, 348
Carrasco, Joe "King," 49, 248, 261, 273
Carreño, Teresa, 268
Carrol, Shelley, 354
Carroll, Bill, 172
Carroll, Johnny, 44, 45, 191, 259, 270
Carson, Johnny, 351
Carter, Amon G., 22
Carter, Benny, 41, 60, 165, 184,

290, 359
Carter, Betty, 259
Carter, Bill, 261
Carter, Bo, 255
Carter, Clarence, 61
Carter, Dan, 133
Carter, Goree, 27
Carter, James, 188, 304
Carter, John, **44–45**, 135, 159
Carter Family, 31, 77
Cartwright, Acquilla, 8
Caruso, Enrico, 325
Cary, Dick, 307
Casa Loma Orchestra, 147
Cash, Johnny, 9, 11, 20, 67, 162, 189, 191, 236, 239, 300, 355
Cash, Rosanne, 10, 11, 119
Casiano, Jesús, 260, 343
Casner, "Lost John," 103
Cass County Kids, 250
Cassion, S. B., 84
Castleberry, Mattie, 264
Castro, Henri, 337
Castro, Mercedes, 265
Castroville Brass Band, *111*
Cats Don't Sleep, 114
Cavaliers, 259, 271, 284, 358, 359
CBS/Epic records, 340
CBS Radio Network, 191
CBS Studios, 359
C.C. Birchard, 311
Ceballos, Rodrigo de, 292
Cedar Lounge, 189
Céliz, Fray Francisco de, 225
The Cellar, **45**
Cellar Dwellers, 45
Celli, Joseph, 147
Cello, 14
Cenco record label, 215
Center for American History, 27, 36
Center for Texas Music History, **45–46**
Central Plains College and Conservatory of Music, **46**
Chabot, Frederick Charles, **46–47**
Chambers, Iola Bowden, **47**
Chambers, Sam, 142
Champs, 17, 272
Chance, John Barnes "Barney," **47–48**, 56
Channel, Bruce, 20, 213, 259, 271, 359
Channing, Carol, 205, 224
Charles, Ray, 10, 11, 57, 58, 60, 70, 74, 94, 124, 147, 158, 162, 166, 230, 231, 284, 354
Charlie and the Jives, 114, 351

Charlie Fisk Orchestra, 14
Charlottes, 87
Chase, William Merritt, 365
Chatfield, F. W., 19
Chatwell, J. R. "Chat the Cat," 41, **48**, 137
Chávez, Carlos, 283
Cheatham Street Warehouse, **48–49**
Checker, Chubby, 91
Checker record label, 336
Chenier, Cleveland, 110–11
Chenier, Clifton, 5, 82, 110–11, 260, 366
Chenille Sisters, 175
Cherokee Cowboys, 78, 319
Cherry, Don, 231
Cherry, Otis, 350
Chess Records, 125, 336
Chevis, Wilfred, 366
Chicago Opera, 235
Chicago Transit Authority, 314
Chief Records, 261
Child, Francis James, 106
Children's Opera Tour, 235
Children's songs, 76, 106
Childs, Lucinda, 182
Chilton, Joshua C., 333
Chittenden, William Lawrence, 68
Choate, Boone, 92–93
Choates, Harry H., 27, **49–50**, 218, 259
Choral music. *See also* Gospel music
    Beethoven Männerchor, 17, 18–19, 52, 118
    composers, 119
    conductors, 17, 52, 80, 108, 179, 180, 208–9
    German music, 17, 18–19, 52, 118, 128
    Melody Maids, 207
    Tejana Singers, 307–8
Christian, Ben, 50
Christian, Charles, 25, 50, 51, 86, 155, 156, 166, 215, 216, 256, 270, 290, 328
Christian, Elwood (Elmer), 50
Christman, Bobby, 42
Christy, June, 276
Chulas Fronteras (Beautiful Borders), 206
Church music, 16, 209, 241–42, 245, 265, 292–93, 297, 342. *See also* Sacred Harp music
Cimarron Boys, 196
Cinders, 272
Circus, 12, 14–15, 86, 152, 328
Cisneros, Henry, 65
Claassen, Arthur, 17, 18, **52**, 119

Clapp, Sunny, 146
Clapton, Eric, 11, 178, 270, 348, 351
Clarinetists, 44–45, 84–85, 102, 147–48, 184
Clark, Donald, 20
Clark, Guy, 11, 67
Clark, Jubal, 103
Clark, Roy, 21
Clark, W. C., 27
Clarke, Kenny, 107
Clash, 248, 273
Classical music, 52–57. *See also* Music schools; Opera; Orchestras
  composers, 23, 35–36, 56, 217, 245–46, 291, 342
  International Festival–Institute at Round Top, 129, 150–51
  pianists, 4, 35–36, 56, 110, 115, 180, 181, 245–46, 281–82, 291, 336–37
  string player, 23–24
  Van Cliburn International Piano Competition, 4, 55, 56, 150, 336–37
Clay, James Earl, 57, 158
Clay, Shirley, 305
Clay, Sonny, 41, 57
Clayton, Buck, 41, 97, 166, 304
Clear Channel Communications, 251
Clements, Bill, 319
Cleveland, Grover, 267
Cliburn, Rildia Bee O'Bryan, 57–58
Cliburn, Van, 53, 56, 57, 337
Cline, Patsy, 9, 67, 78
Clod Hoppers, 215
Clooney, Rosemary, 133
Club Bohemia, 208
Club Cultural Recreativo México Bello, 217
Club Foot/Night Life, 249
Clubs. *See* Dance halls; Music organizations; Nightclubs
Cntenders, 148
Coasters, 178
Coastliners, 301
Cobb, Arnett, 7, 35, 58, 59, 94, 97, 102, 107, 135, 139, 158, 182, 303, 344, 354
Cobb, Elizabeth, 58
Cobras, 124
Cochran, Wayne, 358
Cockrell, Charles Jr., 143
Coe, David Allen, 21, 264
Coffman, Wanna, 39
Cohen, Leonard, 10
Cohen, Mickey, 289
Cohron, Lenore, 55, 58, 60
Coin record label, 9

Coker, Henry, 60–61, 117, 156, 158
Cole, Cozy, 166
Cole, James Reid, 176
Cole, Nat King, 86, 156, 178, 215
Coleman, Bill, 184
Coleman, Emir (Bucket), 290
Coleman, Gary B. B., 61
Coleman, George, 61, 61–62
Coleman, Ornette, 44, 57, 157, 158–59, 212
Coleman, Robert Henry, 198
Colhoun, Adam, 250
Colleges. *See* Music schools; *and specific colleges*
Collins, Albert, 27, 62, 63, 82, 189, 265, 270, 348
Collins, Carr, 31
Collins, Carr P., 188
Collins, Lee, 296
Collins, Paula Blincoe, 163
Collins, Siki, 102
Colombati, Virginia, 192
Colquitt, Oscar Branch, 15
Coltrane, John, 57, 284
Columbia Phonograph Company, 254
Columbia Records, 14, 15, 26, 52, 74, 76–77, 85, 89, 112, 121, 131, 136, 138, 142, 164, 184, 213, 244, 254, 255, 256, 259, 274, 286, 288, 299, 304, 307, 356, 364
Comanche Indians, 225
Combs, Lonnie B., 297
Comissiona, Sergiu, 145
Como, Perry, 231, 354
Composers
  advocate for women composers, 291
  band music, 47–48, 300–301
  blues, 32, 62–63, 102–3, 121, 148–49, 189–90, 229–30, 265–66, 294–96, 320–21, 325
  choral music, 119
  church music, 209, 265, 297
  classical music, 23, 35–36, 56, 204, 217, 245–46, 291, 342
  conjunto music, 163–64, 264–65
  country and western music, 74–75, 97, 108–10, 210, 219–20, 230–31, 237, 241, 330–31, 354–55
  country blues, 228–29, 321–23
  electronic music, 94, 146–47
  folk music, 23, 102–3, 129–30, 148–49, 232–33

German music, 319
gospel music, 16
honky-tonk music, 284
jazz, 32, 44–45, 97, 276
movie music, 92
operas, 23, 94, 137, 171, 204, 353
orchestral works, 35–36, 120–21, 128–29, 297, 337–38
ragtime music, 168, 170–71
rockabilly music, 20, 236, 247
rock-and-roll, 236–37
songs, 23, 42, 70–71, 125–26, 136–37, 138, 204, 245, 338–40
swing music, 86–87
Tejano music, 122
truck-driving songs, 74–75
"Twelfth Street Rag," 32
waltzes, 267–68
western swing, 85–86
Computer music, 94, 146–47
Condon, Eddie, 306, 307
Condon, Randall J., 247
Conductors, 1–2, 17, 23–24, 52, 84–85, 120–21, 179, 180, 208–9, 237, 300–301, 337–38, 340, 342, 353–54. *See also* Band directors; Bandleaders
Conjunto Bernal, 308
Conjunto Hall of Fame, 204, 206, 256, 307, 310, 315
Conjunto music, 65, 92, 95, 126–27, 127, 150, 163–64, 163, 190–91, 203, 205–7, 260, 264–65, 274, 281, 308, 310, 315, 315, 343. *See also* Música norteña
Conjunto San Antonio Alegre, 260
Conjuntos orquestal, 315
Conjunto Topo Chico, 260
Conlee, John, 21
Conley, Gator, 119
Connally, John, 1, 87, 224, 319
Connally, Tom, 234
Conqueroo, 346
Considérant, Victor P., 42
Continental Club, 27
Cooder, Ry, 261
Cook, Herb, 264
Cook, W. I., 223
Cook, Will Marion, 184
Cooke, Sam, 178, 304, 352
Cooking Vinyl Records, 254
Cooks, Donald, 245
Cooley, Spade, 40
Coolidge, Rita, 355
Cooper, Dana, 4
Cooper, Hugh, 264

Cooper, Jack, 116
Cooper, Leroy, 29
Cooper, Levi, 162
Cooper, Oscar, 162
Cooper, Ralph, 156
Cooper, Rob, 27, 255
Cooper, Sonny, 178
Copeland, Johnny "Clyde," 27, 62, 62–63, 82, 124, 258, 265
Copland, Aaron, 263
Coral/Brunswick record label, 243
Coral Records, 131, 218, 260
Corley, George, 63, 251
Cornet player, 362
Corona, Bo, 286
Corona Records, 190, 260, 308
Corpus Christi Symphony Orchestra, 361
Corrales, Frank, 260
Corridos, 63–65, 92–93
Cortez, Gregorio, 64, 92–93
Cortez, Raul, 251, 293
Cortina, Juan Nepomuceno, 92
Costello, Elvis, 141, 230
Cotillion record label, 178
Cotton, James, 5
Cotton Club orchestra, 348
"Cottonfield Blues," 321, 322
Cotton Palace Coliseum, 237
Count Basie. *See* Basie, Count
Country and western music, 65–68, 107. *See also* Fiddlers; Western swing
  Armadillo World Headquarters, 7, 67
  Billy Bob's Texas, 21–22
  blues, 228–29, 321–23
  Broken Spoke, 10, 37, 38
  Cheatham Street Warehouse, 48–49
  composers, 74–75, 108–10, 210, 219–20, 230–31, 241, 354–55
  cowboy music, 12–13, 44, 50, 66, 68, 95–97, 107, 108–10, 128–29, 131–33, 207, 267
  guitarists, 161–62, 194, 357
  journalist, photographer, and publisher, 17
  "Louisiana Hayride" radio program, 9, 20, 21, 44, 50, 71, 78, 142, 188, 189, 191–92, 194, 241, 262, 270, 354
  Outlaw movement, 161–62
  Panther Hall, 239
  performers, 33–34, 43–44, 80–81, 112, 131–33, 142–43, 207, 210, 237, 253, 262, 267, 275–76, 301, 326,

330–31, 355–57
pianist, 147
progressive country, 7, 10–11, 67, 261, 273, 281, 297–98, 338–40, 355
promoter and talent agent, 188–89
radio, 131–33, 184–85, 191–92, 218, 250, 267
singer-songwriters, 147, 230–31, 237, 241, 330–31
Country Disc Jockey Hall of Fame, 332
Country Gentlemen, 213
Countrymen, 242
Country Music Association, 21, 188–89
Country Music Hall of Fame, 262, 267, 276, 330, 357
Country Music Reporter, 17
Country Playboys, 243
Country Ramblers, 48
Counts, 113
Cowboy festivals, 104
Cowboy music, 12–13, 44, 50, 66, **68**, 95–97, 107, 108–10, 128–29, 131–33, 207, 253, 254, 258, 267, 274, 356. *See also* Country and western music
Cowboy Ramblers, 34–35, *35*, 258, 356
Cowboy Records, 44
Cowboys' Christmas Ball, **68**
"Cowboy's Lament," *109*, 110
Cowdell's Wagon Show, 237
Cowden, Mrs. George E., 292
Cowles, W. I., 176
Cox, Ida, 348, 350
Coy, Ann, 69
Coy, Eugene, **69**, 156, 165, 175
Coy, Gene, 210
Cramer, Bomar, 176
Cranfil, J. B., 269
Crawford, Jack, 197
Crawford, Joan, 201
Crawford, Roberta Dodd, 69, **69**
Cray, Robert, 63, 352
Crayton, Pee Wee, 27, **69–70**, *70*, 348
Crazy Cajun record label, 189, 259
Creole music. *See* Zydeco
Crew Cats, 270, 272
Crickets, 141, 161, 179, 180, 243, 260, 270
Criss, Sonny, 259
Cristofori, Bartolomeo, 245
Crixell, Tito, 288
Crockett, David, 198
Crockett, Howard, **70–71**, 191

Crofts, Dash, 17, 272
Crook, Eugene, 328
Crosby, Bing, 192
Crosby, Bob, 176, 178, 305, 306
Crosby Stills Nash and Young, 272
Cross, Christopher, 273
Cross & Winge, 311
Crouch, John Russell (Hondo), 194
Crow, Alvin, 38, 49, 78, 261
Crowell, Rodney, 67
Crown record label, 266
Crustene Ranch Gang band, 215
Crutchfield, G. P., 108, 223
Cruz, Sor Juana Inés de la, 294
Cryer, Sherwood, 119
Crystaliers, 301
Crystal Spring Ramblers, 71
Crystal Springs Dance Pavilion, 39–40, 71
Cuarteto Carta Blanca, 208, 256, 307, 308
Cuesta, Henry, 305
Cullum, Lola, 210
Cummings, Robert, 200
Cuney-Hare, Maud, 71–72
Cunningham, Henry Sr., 71
Cunningham, Mary, 71
Cunningham, "Papa" Sam, 71
Curtis, Cricket Sonny, 180
Curtis, King, 58
Curtis, Sonny, 272
Curzon, Sir Clifford, 150
Custom record label, 259
Czech festivals, 104
Czech music, 14, 72, **72–73**, 239, 241

Daffan, Ted, 3, 50, **74–75**, 218, 258, 286
Daffan Records, 75
Dahlke, Noema, 24
Dailey, Dusky, 255
Daily, Bud, 75
Daily, Don, 75
Daily, Mike, 75
Daily, Pappy, 20, 75, 259
Daily, Pete, 307
Dalhart, Vernon, 55, 66, **75–77**, 254
Dallas, Johnny, 247, 259
Dallas
"Big 'D' Jamboree," 9, 20–21, 33–34, 43, 44, 213, 218, 247, 270, 354
blues, 26–27
The Cellar, 45
Deep Ellum, 26, 57, 78–79, 83, 159

Empire Room, 27
Frohsinn, 180
High School Orchestra, 2
Majestic Theatre, 200–201, 237
Opera, 55–56, 173–74, 235
punk rock, 249
radio, 250, 251, 256
recording industry, 26, 254, 255, 256, 258, 259–60, 270
Rose Ballroom/Room, 26–27
Symphony Orchestra, 24, 52, 54, 174, 180, 201, 263
Dallas Ballet, 201
Dallas Banjo Band, 213
Dallas Blues Society, 27, 29
Dallas Civic Opera, 235
Dallas Jamboree Jug Band, 255
Dallas Lyric Theater, 185
Dallas Opera, 55–56, 173–74, 201, 235
Dallas Opera House, 234
Dallas Sound Labs, 260
Dallas Stars, 274
Dallas String Band, 255
Dallas Symphony Orchestra, 24, 52, 54, 174, 180, 201, 263
Dallas Theater, 223
Dallas Wind Symphony, 185
Dameron, Tadd, 107
Damron, Alan Wayne, 126
Damron, Allen, 174
Damrosch, Leopold, 52, 338
Damrosch, Walter, 268
Dance, Stanley, 304
Dance halls. *See also* Nightclubs
Anhalt Hall, 5
Broken Spoke, 10, 37, 38
Crystal Springs Dance Pavilion, 39–40, 71
Czech music, 72–73
Double Bayou Dance Hall, 82
Gruene Hall, 126
Peters–Hacienda Community Hall, 242–43
Reo Palm Isle, 264
Skyliner Ballroom, 289
Daniel, A. P., 250
Daniels, Charlie, 355
Darin, Bobby, 178, 179
Dart record label, 230
Dave Clark Five, 42
Davern, Kenny, 307
Davila, Manuel Gonzales Sr., 77–78
Davis, Angela, 303
Davis, Art, 34, 35
Davis, Eddie "Lockjaw," 58, 251, 304
Davis, Frank, 58
Davis, James Houston, 218

Davis, Jimmy, 41, 218, 255, 276
Davis, Luis, 255
Davis, Maxwell, 210
Davis, Mel, 33
Davis, Miles, 57, 58, 82, 114, 158, 251
Davis, Papa Link, 189
Davis, Pluma, 94
Davis, Sammy Jr., 58, 61, 114, 218
Davis, Skeeter, 78
Davis, Tyrone, 91
Davis, Walter, 255
Davis, Wild Bill, 58, 182
Davries, Madame Herman, 69
Dawkins, William McKinley, 255
Dawson, Ronnie, 20
Day, Bobby, 42
Day, Jimmy, 78, 191
Day, John, 19
Daylighters, 261
Dead Kennedys, 249
Dealey, George B., 276
Dean, Al, 301
Dean, Billy, 22
Dean, Dizzy, 199
Dean, Jimmy, 66, 75, 133, 356
DeArman, Ramon, 184
Deaville, Darcie, 149
Decca Records, 15, 40, 41, 44, 50, 81, 86, 89, 137, 141, 164, 172, 188, 218, 237, 239, 248, 256, 258, 260, 266, 270, 307, 330, 331, 356, 357
Deep Ellum, 26, 57, **78–79**, *79*, 83, 159
Deep Ellum Studios, 260
Deep South Productions, 103
Deerfield, 45
Degüello, **79–80**, *80*
Delaborde, Elie M., 281
De la Rosa, Tony, 127, 150, 221, 260, 261, 315
De León, Alonso, 225, 227
Dell, Richard, 35
Dell-Kings, 114
Del Santo, Dan, *10*, 229
Delta Records, 197
De Luxe Melody Boys, 121
DeLuxe record label, 49
De Luxe Syncopators, 113
Dempsey, Jack, 192
Dempsey, John, 185
Denton Light Opera Company, 236
Denver, John, 86
Derailers, 38
Destiny's Child, 259
Deutsch Texanischer Saengerbund (German Texas Singers

League), 18
DeWitty, Virgie Carrington, 80
Dexter, Al, 80–81
Diaz, Louis Felipe, 268
Diaz, Rafaelo, 55, 60, 81, 81
Diaz Sisters, 221
Dick, James, 56, 150
Dickenson, Pere, 255
Dickenson, Vic, 60
Dickey, Tom, 137
Dickinson, J. B., 250
Dicks, 249
Dickson, Charlie, 172
Dick the Drummer, 53, 81
Diddley, Bo, 91, 142
Dielmann, Leo M. J., 18
Dienger, Karl, 28
Dietmann Pianos Limited, 245
Dietzler, Jay, 301
Digital Services, 262
Diller, Phyllis, 128
Dils (band), 249
Dimitrova, Ghena, 56
Disc jockeys, 20, 31, 35, 74,
    87–88, 172, 247, 331–32,
    354–55
Discos Falcon. See Falcon
    Records
Discos Grande, 261
Discos Ideal. See Ideal Records
Disques Swing record label, 184
Dixie Chicks, 38, 68
Dixie Hummingbirds, 139, 269
Dixie Serenaders, 57
Dixon, Floyd, 215, 259, 269,
    303
Dixon, Perry, 255
DJM Records, 351
DJ Screw, 74
Dobie, J. Frank, 238, 254, 267
Dobson, Richard, 4
Documentaries, 1, 27, 39, 86,
    103, 142, 206, 331
Documentary Arts, 27
Dodds, Johnny, 154, 350
Dodo Marmarosa Trio, 14
Doggett, Bill, 94, 284
Doggett, Jerry, 199
Dolge, Alfred, 244, 320
Dolphy, Eric, 303
Domingo, Placido, 56, 143, 235
Domínguez, Rosa, 31
Domino, Fats, 11, 91, 180, 210,
    284, 352
Domino Records, 261
Dominos, 325
Donaldson, Lou, 116
Donegan, Dorothy, 251
"Doo-wop" style, 42, 114
Dorati, Antal, 54
Dorham, Kenny, 81–82, 116,
    158

Dorsey, Gary, 189
Dorsey, Jimmy, 15, 172, 183,
    198, 217, 305, 306
Dorsey, Tommy, 15, 43, 147,
    172, 178, 198, 264, 306
Doster, Stephen, 261
Dot Records, 71, 142, 147
Dotson, Baby, 87
Dotson, Coley, 255
Doty, William E., 310, 310
Douai, Adolf, 18, 119, 319
Double Bayou Dance Hall, 82
Double Trouble, 261, 273, 340
Doughboys. See Light Crust
    Doughboys
Douglas, Barry, 337
Douglas, Boots, 63, 82, 121
Douglas, K. C., 350
Douglas Finnell and His Royal
    Stompers, 255
Downing, C. B., 108, 223
Draeger, Hans-Heinz, 82–83
Drake, Prebble, 57
Dranes, Blind Arizona, 83
Dr. Breeding's Big B Tonic medi-
    cine show, 348
Dream Machine, 45
D Records, 49, 75, 258, 259
Dresel, Gustav, 136
Drifters, 91
Drisko, Ruth, 1
Drought, H. P., 100
Drowning Pool, 274
Drummers, 53, 61–62, 69, 81,
    165, 198, 305–6
DuBois, Charlotte Estelle,
    83–84
Ducloux, Walter, 56, 235
Dudley, Sherman H., 84
Dueto Carta Blanca, 264
Dufalo, Richard, 84–85
Duke–Peacock Records, 189,
    259, 265–66, 270, 325, 351
Duke Records, 27, 125, 139,
    230, 259, 269
"Dukes of Hazzard," 162
Dukes of Rhythm, 62
Duke's Royal Coach Inn, 249
Dunbar, Earl Theodore, 354
Duncan, Catherine Jean, 24
Duncan, Tommy, 85–86, 299
Dunn, Bob, 39, 41, 86
Dunn, Eddie, 250
Dupré, Marcel, 36
Dupree, Anna, 93
Dupree, Champion Jack, 247
Dupree, Clarence, 93
Durante, Jimmy, 97
Durawa, Ernie, 48
Durham, Allen, 86
Durham, Clyde, 86
Durham, Eddie, 25, 26, 86–87,

87, 97, 147, 156, 175, 270,
    290
Durham, Joe, 86
Durham, Roosevelt, 86
Durham Brothers Band, 86
Durst, Albert Lavada, 27,
    87–88, 88
Dust, Brian, 146
Duval, Denise, 56, 235
Duvivier, George, 58
Dyess, Edwin, 224
Dykes, Earl, 210
Dylan, Bob, 67, 130, 141, 148,
    168, 233, 237, 256, 271,
    281, 338

Eagles, 39, 272
Ealey, Robert, 89
Earle, Stacey, 175
Earle, Steve, 174, 338
Early Birds, 192, 250
East Texas Sacred Harp Singing
    Convention, 278
East Texas Serenaders, 89–91,
    90
Eastwood Country Club, 91,
    114
Ebell, Eugene, 28
Eberhart, Cliff, 174
Eberson, John, 200
Ebner, Erhard, 28
Ebony Opera of Houston, 236
Eccentric Harmony Six, 57
Echols, Charlie, 121
Eckstine, Billy, 114, 162, 165
Eddie and Oscar, 255
Eddie and Sugar Lou's Hotel
    Tyler Orchestra, 156, 166,
    255
Eddie Lang–Joe Venuit All-Star
    Orchestra, 305
Eddie Morris' Studio, 261
Edens, Roger, 56, 91–92
Edison, Thomas, 253, 254
Edison Records, 76
Edmoral record label, 17, 354
"Ed Sullivan Show," 116, 141,
    168, 179, 180
Education in music. See Music
    educators; Music schools
Edwards, Bernice, 255, 320
Edwards, Gloria, 125
Eggleston, Tincy, 289
Ehrenberg, Hermann, 136
Ehrling, Sixten, 283
Eisenhower, Dwight, 117, 133,
    138
El Conjunto Bernal, 92, 150
Elco record label, 336
"El Corrido de Gregorio
    Cortez," 64, 92–93
Eldorado Ballroom, 93–94, 229

Eldorado Records, 9
Eldridge, Roy, 7
Electric Graceyland Studios,
    261
Electromagnets, 273
Electronic music, 56, 94,
    146–47
Elektra Record Company, 233
Elizabeth II, Queen, 142
Ellington, Duke, 32, 44, 60, 69,
    116–17, 121, 155, 156, 158,
    166, 201, 243, 333, 355,
    362
Ellington, Mercer, 166, 210,
    212
Elliot, Wild Bill, 318
Elliott, Lewis, 358, 359
Ellis, Herb, 14, 158, 276
Ellis, Lloyd, 215
Ellis, Merrill, 55, 56, 94, 334
Elmore, Randy, 42
El Paso
    Border Folk Festival, 104
    Opera, 236
    Symphony Orchestra, 54
    Teen Rendezvous Club, 113
El Paso Opera, 236
El Paso Piano Company, 244
El Paso Symphony Orchestra,
    54
El Pato record label, 260
Ely, Joe, 7, 27, 31, 174, 260,
    261, 273, 274, 300, 355
Embers, 230
Emerson, Ralph Waldo, 173
EMI Latin, 286
Emilio, 78
Emmons, Buddy, 78
Emotions, 242
Empire record label, 336
Empire Room, 27
Engel, Anna Schupp, 193
Engel, August, 193
England Dan & John Ford
    Coley, 259, 272
Engle, Benno, 193–94
Engle, William, 193
Enjoy Records, 178
"Entertainer," 170, 171
Entrepreneur. See Music entre-
    preneur
Epic Records, 147, 194, 244,
    259, 340
Erickson, Roky, 259, 272, 273,
    274
Ernst, Alfred, 171
Ernst, Friedrich, 242
Ervendberg, Louis Cachand,
    128, 284
Ervin, Booker, 29, 94–95, 158,
    355
Eschenbach, Christoph, 54, 145

Escobar, Eligio Roque, **95**
Escobar, Linda, 95, 260, 261
Escovedo, Alejandro, 229, 261
Estrella, Dueto, 260
Eubank, Lillian, 58
Eureste, Bernardo, 126
Evans, Clarence (Nappy Chin), 27
Evans, Dale, 66, **95–97,** 96, 250
Evans, Hershel, 86, **97–99,** 98, 102, 155, 156, 304
Evans, Joseph, 4
Evans Hall, 234
Evejim label, 336
Everly Brothers, 236, 271
Everstate Records, 261, 318
Excello record label, 352
Excelsior record label, 147
Exclusive record label, 215
Exeter record label, 113, 260
"Eyes of Texas," **99**

Fabulosos Cuatro, 308
Fabulous Thunderbirds, 89, 126, 273, 340, 355
Fagan, Ellis, 39
Fain, Sammy, 116
Falcon Records, 260, 288, 308
Fandangle. See Fort Griffin Fandangle
Fantasy record label, 58
Farm Aid, 355
Farnam, Lynwood, 135
Faulk, John Henry, 254
Faulkner, Roy "Lonesome Cowboy," 31
Faust Opera Company, 235
Fear (band), 249
Feather, Leonard, 116, 307
Federal Music Project (FMP), 54, 100, *101,* 282, 312
Federal Records, 351
Fender, Freddie, 67, 189, 259, 260, 271, 274, 281
Fendler, Edvard, 301
Ferera, Frank, 76
Ferguson, James E., 188
Ferguson, Ma, 31
Ferguson, Maynard, 107
Fernandes, Gaspar, 292
Fernández, Rosita, 308
Fernández, Vicente, 202
Ferrer, Jose, 223
Fessor Floyd Graham and His Aces of Collegeland, 333
Festival of Texas Composers, 313
Festivals
    African American festivals, 104
    Border Folk Festival, 104

cowboy festivals, 104
    Czech festivals, 104
    folk festivals, 103–5, 174–75, 313–14
    International Festival–Institute at Round Top, 129, 150–51
    Italian festivals, 104
    Kerrville Folk Festival, 104, 174–75, 231, 254, 288
    Mexican American festivals, 104
    Native American festivals, 104
    Oktoberfest, 5
    South by Southwest, 292
    Tejano Conjunto Festival, 207, 308, 310, 315
    Texas Folklife Festival, 29, *103,* 104, 313–14, 335
    Texas International Pop Festival 1969, 314–15
    Wurstfest, 104, 362–63
Fevertree, 4
Fiddlers, 2–3, 10, 30, 40–41, 48, 50, *103,* 105, 106, 120, 215–16, 231, 268–69, 286–87, 357
Fields, Ernie, 95, **100–101**
Field's Theater, 234
Fiesta Noche del Rio, 308
Fifth Ward, Houston, **101–2,** 124, 365
Fihn, Peter, 28
Fillmore, Keith, 317
Films. *See* Documentaries; Movies
Fine Arts Commission of Texas, 224
Finley, Gene, 250
Finley, Karen, 146, 147
Finnell, Douglas, 255
Finney, Garland, 215
Fireballs, 260
Fire Station Studios, 262
Firmature, Sam, 154
First Edition, 272
Fischer, Alfred, 28
Fisher, Fritz, 28
Fisher, Sonny, 189
Fisk, Charlie, 14
Fitz, Theophilius, 311
Fitzgerald, Bill, 269
Fitzgerald, Ella, 33, 58, 162, 165, 264
Five Americans, 259
Five Blind Boys, 139
Five Careless Lovers, 89
Five Echoes, 304
"Fives," 155
Five Stars, 351
Five Ways Of Joy, 166
Flatlanders, 174, 273, 274

Florence, F. A., 289
Flores, Patricio, 217
Floyd, Ray, 152
Floyd, Reuben, 296
Floyd, Troy, 63, 97, *102,* **102,** 156, 255, 304
Flutist, 362
Flying Dutchman record label, 303
Flying X Ranchboys, 213
Flyright record label, 30
FMP. *See* Federal Music Project (FMP)
Foley, Blaze, **102–3**
Foley, Red, 9, 103, 133, 218
Foley, Sue, 261
Folk festivals, **103–5,** 174–75, 313–14
"Folkin' Eh!" record label, 125
Folk music, **105–7**
    Anderson Fair Retail Restaurant, 4
    Armadillo World Headquarters, 7, 67
    "Austin City Limits," 10–11
    Cheatham Street Warehouse, 48–49
    collectors, 115, 187, 188, 237–38, 254
    festivals, 103–4, 174–75
    Kerrville Folk Festival, 104, 174–75, 231, 254, 288
    rock-and-roll and, 274
    singers, 102–3, 129–30, 148–49, 232–33, 267
    songwriters, 23, 102–3, 129–30, 148–49, 232–33
Foose, Jonathan, 33
Ford, Ernie, 218
Ford, Gerald, 61
Ford, Henry, 78
Ford, Jimmy, **107–8**
Ford, Mary, 74
Forrest, Helen, 154
Fort Griffin Fandangle, **108,** 223–24
Fort Worth
    Billy Bob's Texas, 21–22
    The Cellar, 45
    Crystal Springs Dance Pavilion, 39–40, 71
    Jim Hotel, 162–63
    New Bluebird Nite Club, 89
    opera, 55, 234, 235
    Panther Hall, 17, 239
    radio, 250, 251
    recording industry, 255, 259–60
    Skyliner Ballroom, 289
    Symphony Orchestra, 55, 337
Fort Worth Chamber Orchestra,

337
Fort Worth Civic Music Association, 195
Fort Worth Civic Opera Association, 235
Fort Worth Harmony Club, 311
Fort Worth Opera, 235
Fort Worth Opera Association, 55
Fort Worth Symphony Orchestra, 55, 337
Foss, Lukas, 84
Foster, Lawrence, 145
Fountain, Pete, 305
Four Star Records, 147, 203–4, 354
Fourth of July Picnic, 355
Fowler, Kevin, 21
Fox, Oscar Julius, 100, **108–10,** 267, 311
Fox Four Sevens, 17
Foxx, Redd, 58, 91, 161
Fraizer, Ken, 216
Fran, Carol, 139
Fran & Hollimon, 139
Franchy's String Band, 255
Francis, Connie, 178
Francis, Panama, 166
Franklin, Aretha, 178
Franklin, Jim, 7, 257, 346, 347
Franklin, Larry, 42
Franklin, Major Lee, 41, 42
Frantz, Dalies Erhardt, 110, 150
Freddie Records, 259, 261, 285
Freed, Alan, 178, 179
Freedom record label, 27
FreeFlow Productions, 261
Frees, Henry J., 180
Freivogel, Hans, 28
French Benevolent Society, 196
French music, 52, 110–12. *See also* Cajun music; Zydeco
Freni, Mirella, 143
Fricke, Janie, 21
Fricsay, Ferenc, 144
Friedheim, Arthur, 57
Friedman, Harry, 298
Frizzell, Lefty, 3, 20, 44, 66, 71, 112, 233, 239, 259, 264
Frohsinn, 180
Fromholz, Steven, 4, 174, 261, 297, 298
Frontier Centennial, 22–23
Frummox, 174
Fuchs, Adolph, *112,* **112–13,** 119, 136
Fuentes, Carlos, 127
Fulbright, Dick, **113**
Fuller, Bobby, **113,** 260
Fuller, Randy, 113

Fuller Family Gospel Singers, 103
Full-Tilt Boogie band, 168
Fulson, Lowell, 2, 27, 70, 121, 162, 351

Gabriel, Charles H., 16
Gaedke, Anita, 181
Gainer, Garland, 41
Gaines, Grady, 27, 139, 265, 266
Gaines, Ken, 4
Gallagher, Bill, 126
Galloway, Bishop G. D., 175, 176
Galván, Victoria, 261
Galveston, 17–18
Gante, Fray Pedro de, 294
Garber, Jan, 264
García, Ada, 261
Garcia, Buddy, 41
García, Juanita, 308
Garcia, Ralph, 126
Garcia, Simon, 137
Garden, Mary, 325
Gardner, Fred, 146
Gardner, Jack, 147
Garibay, Ernie, 114
Garibay, Randy Beltran, 114
Garibay-Carey, Michelle, 114
Garland, Judy, 91, 114
Garland, Red, 58, 114–15, 158, 362
Garlinghouse, Esther C. Jonsson, 115
Garlow, Clarence "Bon Ton," 366
Garner, Erroll, 121, 163
Garrett, Dad, 250
Garrett, Danny, 7
Garrett, Snuff, 180
Garrett, Vernon, 61
Garvin, Carl, 306
Garvin, Clint, 306
Gary, John, 115–16
Garza, David Lee, 261
Gatlin, Larry, 21, 55, 68, 354
Gatlin Brothers, 21, 55
Gaubert, Philippe, 115
Gaytán, Juan, 260
Gaytan y Cantú, 256
GC record label, 261
Geddins, Bob, 30
Gee, Herman, 116
Gee, Matthew Jr., 116–17
Geeks, 45
Gee Records, 179
Geezinslaw Brothers, 38
Geffen Records, 273, 274
Gentlemen of Swing, 290
George, Don, 364

George, Helen, 89
George, Luann, 108
George, Zelma Watson, 55, 117
George Allen pianos, 245
Geppert, Chris, 273
German festivals, 104
Germania Singing Society, 128, 285
German Ladies Benevolent Society, 196
German music, 17, 18–19, 28–29, 53, 112–13, 118, 118–19, 126, 127–28, 136–37, 220–21, 242–43, 256, 284–85, 315, 317, 319, 337–38, 362–63
German Opera Company, 234
Getz, Stan, 276, 333
Gibbons, Billy, 190, 272, 273
Gibran, Kahlil, 129
Gibson, Don, 230, 231, 241
Gibson, Mila, 236
Gilbert and Sullivan Society of Austin, 236
Gilewicz, Walter, 4
Gill, Joe, 152
Gillespie, Dizzy, 61, 70, 81, 116, 158, 165, 247, 251, 276, 362
Gilley, Mickey, 119–20, 219, 259, 264
Gilley's, 119–20
Gilliland, Henry Clay, 30, 120, 269
Gillis, Donald Eugene, 56, 120–21
Gilmer, Jimmy, 243, 260
Gilmore, Jimmie Dale, 3, 68, 149, 174, 261, 273, 274, 300
Gimble, Johnny, 10, 48, 89, 298
Ginsberg, Allen, 182
Giuffre, Jimmy, 158, 276, 333
Gladney, L. L., 46
Gladstone, 259
Glass, Phillip, 182
Gleason, Jackie, 192
Glenn, Gladys M., 222
Glenn, Lloyd, 121
Glenn, Lloyd Jr., 121
Glenn, Tyree, 121, 133, 155, 156
Glinn, Lillian, 26, 121–22, 255
Global Jukebox, 187
Globe record label, 3, 164, 308
Glover, Henry, 8
Glover, Jim, 233
Gockley, David, 55, 143
Godowsky, Leopold, 128
Goggan, John, 320
Goggan, Mike, 320

Goggan, Thomas, 56, 244, 267, 319–20, 319–20
Goggan Palace of Music, 320
Gold, Julie, 11
Goldband Records, 30, 352, 358
Golden, Ed, 93
Golden Eagle record label, 125
Goldman, Jack "Tiger," 44
Goldmark, Rubin, 291
Gold Rush, 259
Gold Star Records, 27, 142, 152, 229, 366
Gold Star Studio, 259, 366
Gómez, Ed, 293
Gomez, Johnny, 43
Gonzalez, Arturo, 32
González, Balde, 122
Gonzalez, Ismael, 163
Gonzalez, Manuel, 163
González, Victor, 92
Goodman, Benny, 14, 41, 43, 50, 152, 154, 156, 159, 165, 172, 178, 290, 305, 306, 359
Goodman, Harry, 305
Goodson, Steve, 26
Gordon, Dexter, 354
Gordon, Roscoe, 259, 269
Gorka, John, 174
Gorman, Ross, 147
Gorostiza, Manuel Eduardo de, 294
Gospel Keynotes, 166
Gospel music, 107, 122–24, 123
  composers, 16, 80, 198–99
  promoters, 1, 296
  publishers, 16, 296–97
  radio programs, 1, 124
  singers, 83, 131–33, 166, 244, 296
Gospel Music Hall of Fame, 199
Gott, Tommy, 306
Goudie, Frank (Big Boy), 184
Govenar, Alan, 161
GP record label, 285
Grady's Bar-B-Que Restaurant, 316–17
Graf, Hans, 145
Graham, Billy, 133
Graham, Floyd, 333
Graham, Gordon, 68
Grainger, Percy, 4
Grand Funk Railroad, 314
"Grand Ole Opry," 9, 20, 21, 33, 34, 191, 192, 194, 218, 241, 250, 262, 281, 330, 331, 332
Grandover, "Peg," 197
Grant, Lyman, 238

Grass Roots, 314
Grateful Dead, 7, 141, 142, 239
Graves, Sam, 22
Gray, Glen, 264
Gray, Jerry, 305
Gray, Kitty, 255
Gray, Linda Esther, 56
Gray, Spaulding, 182
Gray, Wardell, 354
Grayson, Miles, 336
Green, Cal, 27, 124, 125
Green, Charlie, 167
Green, Clarence, 27, 124–25, 230, 265
Green, Pat, 21, 68
Green, Paul, 134
Green, Sammy, 325
Green, Willie, 366
Greenbriar Boys, 233
Greenhaw, Art, 185, 213
Greenleaf, Fred, 307
Greenwood, Lee, 264
Greer, Harry, 50
Gregory, Bobby, 77
Grey, Zane, 356
Grey Ghost, 27, 33, 88, 350
Grieg, Edvard, 338
Grierson, Al, 125–26
Griffin, Johnny, 58, 116
Griffith, Nanci, 11, 174, 229, 261, 338
Grimes, Tiny, 134, 251
Grimm, Jacob, 136
Gross, Clifford, 184
Grosser, Alvin, 28
Grosser, Fritz, 28
Grosser, Harry, 28
Grossman, Albert, 168
Grossmann, Henry, 118
Gruene, Ernst, 126
Gruene, Henry (Heinrich) D., 126
Gruene Hall, 126
Guadalupe Cultural Arts Center, 126–27
Guenther, Heinrich, 127–28
Guerra, Manny, 261
Guerrero, Leandro, 260
Guinan, "Texas," 128
Guinn, Ed, 33
Guion, David Wendel, 56, 66, 100, 128–29, 129, 138, 150–51, 311, 364
Guitarists
  bass guitar, 161–62
  blues, 30, 62, 69–70, 124–25, 139, 142, 152, 159–61, 164, 166, 178, 183, 189–90, 229–30, 288–91, 331, 336, 340, 348, 351, 358
  country and western music,

161–62, 194, 357
electric guitar, 25, 50
jazz, 50, 86–87, 139, 215
rhythm-and-blues, 139, 215,
350–51
rockabilly, 44, 194, 247
slide guitar, 164
and songster, 185–87
soul music, 178–79
steel guitarists, 74–75, 78, 86,
196, 358
"Texas style" guitar, 25,
41–42, 63
western swing, 196
Guitar Jr., 352
Guitar Slim (Eddie Jones), 94,
351
Guiterrez, Efrain, 114
Guizar, Tito, **129**
Guleke, James O., 222
Gully Low Band, 147
Gurwitz, Arthur B., 99
Guthrie, Arlo, 130, 233
Guthrie, Woody, 66, **129–30**,
183, 187, 233, 338
Gutiérrez, Delia, 308
Gutiérrez, Eugenio, 308
Gutierrez, Jose, 306
Gutierrez, Patricio, 172
Guy, Buddy, 11

Hacienda Records, 261
Hackett, Bobby, 43
Haddix, Travis, 61
Haddorff Piano Company,
244–45
Hafner, Vaughn, 175
Haggard, Merle, 3, 20, 21, 86,
103, 196, 213, 216, 338,
355
Haggart, Bob, 178
Hagman, Larry, 205
Hahm, Shinik, 54
Hahn, Carl, 18
Halen, Van, 237
Halff, G. A. C., 250
Hall, Edmond, 307
Hall, Gene, **131**
Hall, Jim, 158
Hall, M. E., 333
Hall, Tom T., 300, 355
Hallett, Mal, 306
Halliday, Richard, 205
Hall–Way Records, 218
Hamblen, Carl Stuart, **131–33**,
132
Hambrick, Minnie Cox, 312
Hames, Gene, 289
Hamilton, Grace, 54
Hamman, Cloet, 89, 90, 91
Hammond, John, 50, 172, 340
Hampton, Gladys, 58

Hampton, Lionel, 32, 41, 58,
81, 97, 107, 121, 135, 158,
182, 215, 276, 284, 303,
304, 305, 351, 355
Hancock, Butch, 4, 149, 174,
260, 261, 273, 274, 300
Hancy, W. C., 328
Hander, Amalia, 81
Handy, John, 155, 158
Hanson, Howard, 1
Happy Black Aces, 156, 165,
175
Hardee, John, **133–34**, 158,
251, 362
Hardy, Jack, 125
Harlan, Benjamin, 293
Harlan, Grady, 310
Harlem–Ebony record label,
261
Harmonica players, 30, 351–52,
358
Harmon Organ Company, 244
Harmony Music Club, 194–95
Harney, Greg, 11
Harper, Margaret Pease, **134**
Harper, Ples, 134
Harpo, Slim, 61
Harrell, Mack, 55
Harrell, Scotty, 356
Harrell, Mrs. W. A., 16
Harris, Alfoncy, 255
Harris, Charlie, 319
Harris, Emmylou, 11, 119, 237,
300, 338, 355
Harris, Joyce, 261
Harris, Nelson, 289
Harris, Otis, 26, 255
Harris, Peppermint, 229–30,
265
Harrison, Benjamin, 198
Harrison, George, 237, 271
Harrison, Lonesome Charlie,
255
Harry James Band, 152
Harte, Roy, 14
Harth-Bedoya, Miguel, 55
Harvey, Bill, 139
Hauschild, George Hermann,
134
Hauschild, Henry John, 134,
268
Hauschild, Laura, 268
Hauschild Music Company,
134–35, 135, 268
Hausman, John, 358
Hawkins, Coleman, 114, 116,
165, 251
Hawkins, Erskin, 33
Hay, George D., 332
Hayes, Henry, 125, 230, 265
Hayes, Isaac, 8, 147
Hayes, Roland, 69

Haymes, Dick, 154
Haynes, Don, 19
Haynes, Gibby, 273
Haywood, Cedric, **135**, 182
Haywood, Leon, 336
Head, Roy, 259, 271
Heads, J. W., 255
Hearne, Bill and Bonnie, 4, 149,
174
Hearst, William Randolph, 133
Heath, David, 149
Heathercock, John, *105*
Heavy metal music, 274
Heckleman, O. T., 197
"Hee Haw," 34
Heerbrugger, Emil, 118
Hegwood, David, 91
Heidt, Horace, 192
Heifetz, Jascha, 237, 282
Heilig, Franz Xavier, 118
Hemma-Ridge Mt. Boys, 4
Hemphill, Julius, **135**, 159
Henderson, Fletcher, 134, 154,
165, 167, 175, 328
Henderson, Horace, 166
Henderson, Joe, 82
Henderson, Lynn, 50
Henderson, Nat Q., 102
Hendl, Walter, 54
Hendrix, Jimi, 272, 351
Henley, Don, 272
Henley, Jimmy, 41
Henry, Clarence "Frogman,"
189
Henry W. Savage English Opera
Company, 235
Henton, Laura, 255
Herbert, Walter, 55, 143, 235
Herbst, Clint, 28
Herbst, Kenneth C. Sr., 28
Herbst, Kenneth Jr., 28
Herman, Woody, 158, 163, 165,
178, 276, 305
Hermanas Cantú, 260
Hermanas Degollado, 260
Hermanas Mendoza, 260
Hermanas Peralta, 308
Hermanas Segovia, 260
Herman Herd, 276
Hermanitas Parra, 308
Hermann, George, 268
Hernández, Juan Francisco, 216
Herndon, Ty, 21
Herrera, Johnny, 260
Herschberger, Polly, 317
Herwig, Conrad, 333
Herzog, Roman, 28
Hess, Benny, 3
Hester, Carolyn, 174, 261
Hewitt, Helen (Margaret),
135–36
Heywood, Cedric, 58

Heywood, Eddie, 60
Hibbler, Al, 163
Hickman, Holt, 21
Hickman, Sara, 175
Hickoids, 249
Hicks, Dan, 4
Hicks, Johnny, 20
Hicks, Spec, 33
Hi-Flyers, 48, 299
Higginbotham, J. C., 154
Higgins, Chuck, 350
High Type Five, 124
Highwaymen, 355
Highway QCs, 304
Hijuelos, Oscar, 127
Hildebrand, Ray, 213, 271
Hill, Alex, 305
Hill, Cameron, 197
Hill, Dusty, 45, 272
Hill, Goldie, 330
Hill, Joe, 233
Hill, Rocky, 45
Hill, Sammy, 26, 255
Hill, Teddy, 353
Hill, Z. Z., **136**
Hillbilly Boys (O'Daniel), 184,
197, 234
Hillbilly Boys (Poovey), 247
Hillbilly Flour, 184, 234
Hillbilly music, 43–44, 191,
218–19, 253, 254, 256, 266,
270
Hines, Earl, 155, 156, 163, 165,
166, 298, 359
Hinojosa, Rolando, 127
Hinojosa, Tish, 126, 174, 262
Hinton, Joe, 125, 139, 259,
266, 269
Hired Hands, 354
Hirsch, Shelley, 147
Historial research, 9–10, 46–47.
See also Music history
Hite, Les, 348
Hit Shack studio, 261
Hobby, Oveta Culp, 138
Hoblitzelle, Karl St. John, 200
Hoblitzelle Foundation, 201
Hodges, Johnny, 362
Hodgson, Walter H., 333
Hoffman, Carl, 171
Hoffman, Rudolph, 4
Hoffmann, Ernest, 144
Hoffmann von Fallersleben,
August Heinrich, 112,
136–37
Hofner, Adolph, 48, 50, 73,
137, 256, 261, 318
Hofner, Emil, 137
Hogg, Ima, 54, 56, **137–38**, 312
Hogg, James Stephen, 15
Hogg, Smoky, 27, 259, 289,
331

Hokum Kings, 146
Holden, William, 224
Holder, Terence, 63, 156, 251, 290, 303
Holford, Bill Sr., 258
Holiday, Billie, 163, 305, 359
Holley, George Edwin "Knee-High," 317
Holley, Joe, 357
Holley, Mary Austin, 56, 138–39
Hollimon, Clarence, 139, 230
Holly, Buddy, 20, 67, 113, 139–42, 140, 161, 178, 179, 180, 243, 260, 270–71, 358
Hollywood Flames, 42
Hollywood record label, 215
Holmes, Sammy, 63
Holmes, Sid, 358
Holt, Jack, 224
"Home on the Range," 128
Homer and Jethro, 20
Honky-tonk music, 8–9, 21–22, 37, 38, 48–49, 66, 80–81, 284, 286–87
    Billy Bob's Texas, 21–22
    Broken Spoke, 38
    Cheatham Street Warehouse, 48–49
    composers, 284, 330
    fiddlers, 286–87
Hood, Adelyne, 77
Hood, Champ, 103
Hood, Deschamps "Champ," 11, 148, 148, 149
Hood, John B., 364
Hood's Texas Brigade, 15
Hooker, Earl, 213
Hooker, John Lee, 5, 31, 172, 300
Hootenanny Hoots, 326
Hope, Bob, 192, 201
Hopeful Gospel Quartet, 11
Hopkins, Carl, 42
Hopkins, Claude, 175, 353, 362
Hopkins, Joel, 142
Hopkins, John Henry, 142
Hopkins, Lightnin', 2, 27, 31, 61, 70, 79, 82, 89, 142, 161, 178, 186, 189, 229, 245, 254, 258, 259, 270, 288, 289, 325, 338, 366
Hopper, Jack, 90
Horace Heidt and his Musical Knights, 192
Horace Tapscott Quintet, 303
Hornbostel, Erich Moritz von, 82
Horne, Lena, 165
Horne, Marilyn, 143
Horowitz, Vladimir, 172
Horton, Big Walter, 5

Horton, Jimmy, 142–43
Horton, Johnny, 66, 71, 78, 191
Horwitz, Will, 31, 250
Hot Klub, 249
Houdini, Harry, 201, 237
Houston, David, 194, 259, 318
Houston, Sam, 283, 364
Houston
    Anderson Fair Retail Restaurant, 4
    blues, 27
    Bronze Peacock Dinner Club, 269
    Cedar Lounge, 189
    The Cellar, 45
    Ebony Opera, 236
    Eldorado Ballroom, 93–94, 229
    Fifth Ward, 101–2, 124, 365
    Jesse H. Jones Hall for the Performing Arts, 54, 144, 145, 162
    Lawndale Art Center, 182
    Opera, 143–44, 235
    punk rock, 249
    radio, 250–51
    recording industry, 27, 258–59, 262
    rhythm-and-blues, 259
    Symphony Orchestra, 24, 54, 128, 137, 144–45, 301
    Third Ward, 93–94
Houston Conservatory of Music, 250
Houston Grand Opera, 55, 143–44, 235
Houston Symphony Orchestra, 24, 54, 128, 137, 144–45, 301
Howell, Hilton, 145
Howell, Lee, 146
Howell, Tom, 145–46
Howell and Gardner Band, 146
Howell Brothers Moonshiner Orchestra, 146
Howlin' Wolf, 289, 290
Hubbard, Herbert (Blues Boy), 27
Hubbard, Ray Wylie, 126, 174, 261, 297, 298, 355
Hubert Long Agency, 188
Hucko, Peanuts, 251
Hudson, Hattie, 255
Huerta, Baldemar, 260, 271
Huffmeister, H. T., 13
Hugh Beaumont Experience, 249
Hughes, Joe, 27, 41, 62, 82, 94, 124, 265
Humming Bird record label, 49
Hummingbirds, 259
Huns, 248

Hunt, Jerry, 56, 146–47
Hunt, J. M., 242
Hunt, Walter "Pee Wee," 32
Hunter, Alberta, 350
Hunter, Ivory Joe, 70, 147, 189, 215
Hunter, Lloyd, 210
Hunter, Long John, 33
Hurley, Clyde Lanham Jr., 147
Hurley, Miller, 147
Hurok, Sol, 23
Huston, John, 200
Hutchenrider, Clarence, 147–48
Hutchinson, Ernest, 4, 16, 281
Huybrechts, François, 54, 283
H. W. Daily, Inc., 75
Hyatt, Walter, 11, 148, 148–49, 261
Hyde, Don, 346
Hyde, Hattie, 255
Hyland, James, 148
Hymns. See Church music

Ibarra, Pedro, 260
Ichiban Records, 61
Ideal Records, 92, 122, 150, 190–91, 204, 206, 260, 308, 343
Impacto record label, 260
Imperial Records, 9, 70, 121, 137, 152, 164, 308, 350
Improvisation Chamber Ensemble, 84
Ims, Jon, 174
Indianola pianos, 245
Indian Trail, 260
Indigo Girls, 11, 261
Infante, Pedro, 202, 265, 286
Ink Spots, 33, 163
Inmon, John, 298
Inner Sanctum Records poster, 257
Inocencia, 315
In Old Santa Fe, 13
Institute of Texan Cultures, 334–35
International Artist record label, 259, 272
International Broadcasting Company, 293
International Composers' Guild, 263
International Festival–Institute at Round Top, 129, 150–51
International Hot Timers, 31
International Piano Competition for Outstanding Amateurs, 337
International Society for Contemporary Music, 217, 246, 263
Internet, 262, 274, 292

Interplay record label, 303
Interstate Amusement Company, 200
Ioudenitch, Stanislav, 337
Irby, Jerry, 75
Irma record label, 30
Ironwood rasp, 227
Irwin, May, 237
Isaac, Chris, 126
Italian festivals, 104
"It Is No Secret (What God Can Do)," 132, 133
Iucho, Wilhelm, 138
Ivory, King, 189
Ivory Records, 147, 358

Jackalope–Rude Records, 261
Jackson, Bob, 350
Jackson, Bullmoose, 166
Jackson, Jill, 213, 271
Jackson, John, 166
Jackson, Johnny, 152
Jackson, Lil Son, 25, 27, 89, 152, 259
Jackson, Lonzo, 166
Jackson, Ronald Shannon, 159
Jackson, Shot, 78
Jackson, Wanda, 20
Jackson 5, 42
Jack Teagarden's Big Band, 305, 306
Jacobi, Frederick, 291
Jacquet, Illinois, 7, 35, 58, 60, 97, 102, 116, 135, 152, 156, 158, 182, 247, 304, 354
Jacquet, Linton, 152
Jacquet, Russell, 35, 81, 152, 303
Jagger, Mick, 340
Jaime de Anda y Los Chamacos, 261
Jama record label, 42
"Jamboree". See "Big 'D' Jamboree"
James, Costello, 38
James, Etta, 94, 303
James, Harry Hagg, 97, 152–54, 153, 156, 176, 299, 305
James, Jesse, 49–50
James Brown Revue, 336
Jasper, Pat, 314
Jazz, 154–59, 165
    Armadillo World Headquarters, 7, 67
    "Austin City Limits," 10–11
    bandleaders, 82, 102, 182, 184, 239, 328
    bassist, 251–52
    "bossa nova" jazz, 14
    clarinetists, 44–45, 102, 147–48, 184

composers, 32, 44–45, 97, 276
Dixieland jazz, 41
drummer, 165
Eldorado Ballroom, 93–94
electric steel guitarist, 86
guitarists, 50, 86–87, 139, 215
Jim Hotel, 162–63
"loft jazz," 135
musicians, 14, 113, 145–46, 212, 276, 303, 306–7
pianists, 32–33, 57, 69, 114, 172–73, 243–44, 247–48, 298–300, 307, 359
pizzicato jazz cello, 14
rock-and-roll and, 270
saxophonists, 58, 94–95, 97, 102, 107, 135, 147–48, 176, 178, 247, 289–90, 303–4, 354, 362
singers, 239, 243–44, 323, 353
trombonists, 116–17, 121, 165–66, 183, 210, 212, 353
trumpeters, 41, 81–82, 147, 152–54, 166, 175, 182, 239, 243–44, 290, 305, 355, 362
violinists, 43
Jazz Bandits, 306
Jazz Banjo Festival, 213
Jazz Heritage Society of Texas, 58
Jazz Messengers, 82, 158
Jazz Messiahs, 57
Jazz Pickers, 14
Jazz Prophets, 82
Jazz Workshop, 355
Jedlicaka, Ernst, 281
Jefferson, Blind Lemon, 2, 25, 26, 29, 79, 142, 152, 154, 159–61, 166, 183, 186, 255–56, 270, 272, 290, 294, 321, 348, 358
Jefferson Airplane, 142, 161, 256, 270
Jeffries, Jimmie, 250
Jenkins Music Company, 32
Jennings, Waylon, 21, 67, 86, 141, 161–62, 180, 194, 230, 231, 261, 264, 271, 273, 355
Jericho, Richard "Jerry," 50
Jesse H. Jones Hall for the Performing Arts, 54, 144, 145, 162–63
Jessel, George, 116
Jessie James and His Gang, 49–50
Jester, Beauford, 319
Jetstream record label, 259
Jewel Box Revue, 289

Jewel Records, 230, 336
J. H. Bragg and His Rhythm Five, 255
Jiménez, Flaco, 49, 164, 174, 222, 261, 274, 281, 315
Jiménez, José Alfredo, 202, 288
Jiménez, Santiago Jr., 164, 261
Jiménez, Santiago Sr., 77, 163, 163–64, 221, 256, 315, 343
Jimmie Rodgers Entertainers, 275–76
Jimmie Rodgers Jubilee, 275
Jimmie's Joys, 15
Jimmy Gilmer and the Fireballs, 243
Jimmy Heap and the Melody Masters, 243
Jimmy Joy Orchestra, 14
"Jive-talk," 87
Joe "King" Carrasco and the Crowns, 248
Joe Patek Orchestra, 239, 241
Joey Records, 261
John, Dr., 189, 281
John, Grace Spaulding, 245
John Fred and His Playboy Band, 259
Johnson, Alfred (Snuff), 27
Johnson, Bert, 255
Johnson, Billiken, 255
Johnson, Blind Willie, 164, 164–65, 186, 255
Johnson, Budd, 155, 156, 165, 166, 212
Johnson, Clifton "Sleepy," 39, 40, 85
Johnson, Conrad, 94
Johnson, Eric, 49, 261, 273, 274
Johnson, Evelyn, 27
Johnson, Gus, 156, 158, 165
Johnson, Jack, 84
Johnson, Keg, 155, 156, 165–66
Johnson, Lady Bird, 4, 138, 224
Johnson, Lewis, 99
Johnson, Lonnie, 2, 26, 152, 255, 296, 348
Johnson, Lyndon B., 194, 200, 234, 291
Johnson, Margaret "Countess," 251
Johnson, Marvin, 35
Johnson, "Money," 158, 166
Johnson, Pete, 290
Johnson, Robert, 26, 255, 270
Johnson, Stump, 255
Johnson, Walter, 121
Johnson, Willie Neal, 166
Johnson's Joy Makers, 131, 156, 175
"Jole Blon," 49, 111, 161
Jolly Three, 255

Jolson, Al, 326
Jon & Robin, 259
Jones, Anna Maxwell, 18
Jones, Bo, 255
Jones, Coley, 255
Jones, Dennis "Little Hat," 2, 26, 166–67, 255
Jones, E. A., 364
Jones, Eddie, 94
Jones, George, 66, 75, 112, 189, 191, 239, 241, 247, 259
Jones, Gordon, 71
Jones, Gwyneth, 56, 235
Jones, Isham, 183
Jones, Jake, 255
Jones, James, 33
Jones, Jesse Holman, 162
Jones, Jo, 290
Jones, John T. Jr., 162
Jones, Luther, 362
Jones, Maggie, 154, 167
Jones, Norah, 333
Jones, Quincy, 165, 284, 355
Jones, Raymond, 215
Jones, Thad, 355
Jones, Tom, 231
Jones, William E., 310
Jones Hall for the Performing Arts, 162–63
Jones Recording Studio, 259
Jones–Smith, Inc., 290
Jonsson, Esther, 115
Joplin, Janis Lyn, 55, 56, 167–68, 169, 229, 259, 270, 272, 314, 325, 326
Joplin, Scott, 53, 118, 143–44, 155, 168, 170, 170–71, 171, 253, 352, 353
Jordan, Barbara, 102
Jordan, Dooley, 27
Jordán, Esteban, 127, 308, 315
Jordan, Louis, 35, 163, 166, 178, 351
Jordan, Steve, 260
Josey, Bill, 261
Josie Records, 259, 359
Journal of Texas Music History, 46
Joy, Jimmy, 14
Joyce, Chuck, 326
Joyce, Julie, 326
Joy Makers, 131, 156, 175
J. R. England (piano manufacturer), 244
Judy's, 248, 273
Juke, Guy, 7
Juke Jumpers, 29, 89
Julie Rogers Theater, 207
Jury, Donald K., 21

Kagan, Harvey, 271
Kahn, Roger Wolfe, 305

Kallinger, Paul, 31
Kapell, William, 282
Karayanis, Plato, 56
Karle, Art, 305
"Kat's Karavan," 172
Katzenberger, Gabriel, 119
Kaufman, Chip, 126
Kaye, Danny, 116, 154
Kazanoff, Mark, 33
Keen, Robert Earl Jr., 21, 68, 126, 174, 261
Keene, Bob, 113
Keep, W. W., 242
Keepnews, Orrin, 116
Keillor, Garrison, 11
Kell, Reginald, 54
Kelley, Peck, 172–73, 173, 183, 306
Kellner, Murray, 76–77
Kelly, Bob, 259
Kelly, Lawrence Vincent, 55–56, 173–74, 235
Kelso, Millard, 231
Kemp, Hal, 15
Kendall, Joel S., 333
Kendrick, Bobby, 266
Kennan, Kent, 47
Kennedy, Claude "Benno," 102
Kennedy, Jacqueline, 138
Kennedy, John F., 65, 106, 286
Kennedy, Rod, 175, 175
Kenny Rogers and the First Edition, 230
Kenton, Stan, 158, 192, 276, 333, 334
Kentucky Grasshoppers, 306
Kern, Olga, 337
Kerrville Folk Festival, 104, 174–75, 231, 254, 288
Kersands, Billy, 84
Ketchum, Hal, 174, 261
Keyes, Joe, 86, 155, 156, 175
Kickapoo Indians, 225, 228
Kidd, Aldrich, 172
Kidd, Edwin, 176
Kidd–Key, Lucy Ann Thornton, 175–76
Kidd–Key College, 24, 54, 176, 207, 342
Kilpatrick, Spider, 245
Kimsey, Truett, 184
Kincaide, Deane, 176, 178
King, Albert, 5
King, B. B., 5, 10, 11, 58, 91, 121, 163, 178, 215, 230, 231, 258, 265, 266, 314, 325, 336, 348, 354
King, Ben E., 8
King, Carole, 261, 273
King, Charlie, 255
King, Freddie, 61, 62, 177, 178, 270, 314

King, Leon, 178
King, Saunders, 362
King Curtis, **178–79**
King Pins, 178
King Records, 8, 81, 139, 147, 210, 218, 219, 259, 344
Kingston, Maxine Hong, 127
King's X, 274
King Tears, 148
Kinlay, Kent, 48–49
Kirbo, Larry, 229
Kirk, Andy, 32, 86, 155, 156, 163, 303, 353
Kirk, Rahsaan Roland, 58
Kirkes, Walter, 34
Kirkland, James, 194
Kirkwood, Pat, 45
Kitt, Eartha, 251
Kittredge, George Lyman, 188
K–L Piano Manufacturers of Texarkana, 244
Klaerner, Christian, **179**
Klare, Edwin, 71
Kleberg, Robert Justus, 52–53, 118
Klein, Mama Aselee Mattie, 316
Klein, Pappa Frank, 316
Kletzki, Paul, 54
Kleypas, Walter, 48, 317, 319
Klink, Al, 19
Knight, Tim, 50
Knox, Big Boy, 255
Knox, Buddy Wayne, **179–80**, 243, 260, 270
Knox, Gertrude, 68
Knox, Wayne, 180
Koock, Guich, 194
Kool and the Gang, 135
Kooper, Al, 261
Kopriva, Sharon, 182
Kord, Major, 31
Kosmic Blues band, 168
Krajewski, Michael, 145
Kratoska, Herb, 197
Krause, Martin, 246
Kreissig, Hans, **180**
Kreneks, 242
Kress, Carl, 305, 307
Kris record label, 336
Kristofferson, Kris, 38, 67, 126, 162, 230, 272, 338, 355
Kronkosky Charitable Foundation, 283
Kruger, Rudolf, 55, 235
Krupa, Gene, 14, 19, 264, 353
Kryl Concert Band, 7
Kudu record label, 244
Kurtz, Effrem, 144
Kuykendall, Bill, 239
Kuykendall, Corky, 239

La Familia Mendoza, 208

La Fave, Jimmy, 175
Lago record label, 261
La Grange Band, *118*
La Harpe, Bénard de, 225
Lancaster, Byard, 63
Landrum, Miriam Gordon, **181**
Lang, Eddie, 305, 306
Langer, Victor, 338
Lanier, Donald, 179
Lanier, Sidney, 18, **181**
Lankford, Grace Ward, 337
La Orquesta Típica, 256
Larkin, Milt, 7, 35, 58, 93–94, 102, 107, 135, 156, 158, **182**, 344, 348, 354
Las Dos Marías, 260
Lasha, Prince, 159
Las Hermanas Cantú, 308
Las Hermanas Góngora, 308
Las Hermanas Guerrero, 308
Las Hermanas Mendoza, 208, 308
Las Hermanas Segovia, 308
"Las Preferidas" Hermanas Sánchez, 308
Las Rancheritas, 308
"Lasso of Time (The End of the Trail)," 36
Last of the Blue Devils, 86
Lateef, Yusef, 48
Lathan, Aaron, 119
La Tropa F, 261
Lauderdale, Jack, 121
Lavendar Hill Express, 261
La Villita, 204
Law, Don, 255, 259
Lawless, Minnie Douglas, 296
Lawndale Art Center, **182–83**
Laws, Hubert, 8
Laymen's Music Courses, 282
Layton, Chris, 340
Lazy Daddy's Fillmore Blues Band, 294
Leadbelly, 25, 79, 154, 159, 183, **183**, 187, 188, 218, 254, 270, 348
League of Composers, 263
League of United Latin American Citizens, 217, 286
Leary, Paul, 273
Leatherwood, Tim, 4
LeBlanc, Leroy "Happy Fats," 49
Ledbetter, Huddie "Leadbelly," 25, 79, 154, 159, **183**, 187, 188, 218, 254, 270, 348
LeDeux, Chris, 21, 22
Led Zeppelin, 314
Lee, Brenda, 231
Lee, George E., 156, 163
Lee, Jerry, 359
Lee, Johnny, 357

Lee, Robert E., 99
Lee, Sonny, **183**
Lees, Benjamin, 151
Legendary Blues Band, 61
Legends Studio, 261
Le Grand, Jean, 308
Leibert, Billy, 356
Leland, Mickey, 102
Lemsky, Frederick, **183–84**
Lennon, John, 178, 271, 286
Leonard, Ada, 307
Leroi Brothers, 261
Le Roy's Dallas Band, 255
Leschetizky, Theodor, 176
Lester, Henry, 89
Lester, Lazy, 352
Lester, Shorty, 89
Levee Singers, 213
Levens, Jimmy, 289
Levine, Larry, 25
Levy, Heniot, 35
Levy, Jules, 180
Levy, Maurice, 179
Lewandowski, Louis, 360
Lewenthal, Raymond, 282
Lewis, Brenda, 55
Lewis, Jerry Lee, 9, 119, 126, 219, 230, 231, 236, 239, 264, 318
Lewis, Luvenia, 125
Lewis, Meade "Lux," 155
Lewis, Mel, 355
Lewis, Ted, 264
Lewis, William T., **184**
Liberty Lunch, 249
Liberty Records, 30, 180
Library of Congress, 130, 147
Lickona, Terry, 11
Lieber, Jerry, 325
Light Crust Doughboys, 22, 23, 40, 48, 52, 85, **184–85**, 196, 212–13, 234, 250, 251, 255, 256, 259, 260, 270, 286, 357
Lightfoot, Jerry, 261
Lightnin' Slim, 352
Lilith Fair, 274
Limeliters, 175
Lincoln, H. M., 242
Lindbergh, Charles, 36
Lindhe, Vin, **185**
Lindheimer, Ferdinand Jacob, 285
Lindsay, John V., 263
Lippmann, Walter, 199
Lippold, Richard, 162
Lipscomb, James, 238
Lipscomb, Mance, 26, 31, 161, 174, **185–87**, *186*, 229, 254
Lira record label, 261
List, Eugene, 282
Lister, Big Bill, 266

Liszt, Franz, 52, 57
Little, William, 278
Little Esther, 325
Littlefield, Little Willie, 27
Little Joe y La Familia, 261, 286
Little Richard, 91, 210, 212, 258, 284, 351, 352
Little Theater, 223
Littleton, Martin W., 269
Litton, Andrew, 54
Llamaz, Beatriz, 308
Llove, Lloyd, 260
Lloyd, Mitt, 21
Lloyd, Thomas, 21
Lobit, Mrs. Louis G., 143
Locke, William Wayne "Rusty," 317, 318, 319
Lockett, Sandy, 346
Locklin, Hank, 50, 75, 354
Loeb, Lisa, 274
Logan, Horace "Hoss," 191
Logan, Joshua, 223
Lomax, Alan, 68, 183, **187–88**, 254, 270
Lomax, Mrs. John, *105*
Lomax, John Avery, 68, 108, 183, **188**, 254, 267, 270
Londonderry, Annie, 197
Lonesome Sundown, 352
Lone Star Ballet, 134, 185, 213
Lone Star Boys, 48
Lone Star Cowboys, 356
Lone Star Hall, 234
"Lone Star Jamboree," 20
Lone Star record label, 261
Long, Bert, 182
Long, Hubert, **188–89**, 191
Long, Joey, **189–90**, 191
Longhorn Ballroom, 248
Longoria, Valerio, 92, 127, 150, 190, **190–91**, 204, 260, 310, 315
Longview, Reo Palm Isle, 264
López, Isidro, 122
López, Juan, 260
López, Lisa, 308
Lopez, Trini, 271
Lopez, Vincent, 183, 192
Lord, Albert Bates, 115
Lord, Tom, 146
Lorenz, Dewitt J., 24
Los Aguilares, 78
Los Alegres de Terán, 260
Los Blues, 114
Los Bravos del Norte, 264
Los Chavalitos, 260
Los Clasicos, 261
Los Dinos, 285
Los Dos Gilbertos, 127
Los Hermanitos Bernal, 92
Los Hermanos Ayala, 261
Los Hermanos Chavarria, 256

Los Hermanos San Miguel, 256
Los Pastores, 253
Los Pavos Reales, 260
Los Relámpagos del Norte, 264, 265
Los Reyes del Norte, 265
Lost Gonzo Band, 261
Los Tigres del Norte, 65, 265
Los Tres Diamantes, 260
Lot, Little Daddy, 33
Louis, Joe, 58, 348
Louise Massey and the Westerners, 207
"Louisiana Hayride," 9, 20, 21, 44, 50, 71, 78, 142, 188, 189, 191–92, 194, 241, 262, 270, 354
Louvin, Charlie, 239
Lovelady, Baby Jean, 255
Lovett, Lyle, 4, 10, 11, 68, 126, 148, 149, 174, 261, 338
Low, Juliette Gordon, 291
Lowe, Jim Jr., 172
Lowe, Linda, 4
Lowery, Fred, 192
Lubbock Symphony Orchestra, 301
Lucas, Nicas, 289
Lucchese, Josephine, 55, 192
Luce, Henry, 199
Luckenbach, August, 193
Luckenbach, Jacob, 193
Luckenbach, Minnie, 193
Luckenbach, Texas, 125–26, 193, 193–94
"Luckenbach, Texas (Back to the Basics of Love)," 194, 230
Luckie, Jo Ann, 361
Lucky, Lorene, 317
Ludwig, Emil, 71
Luman, Bob, 191, 194
Lunceford, Jimmie, 58, 86, 116, 156, 182, 353
Lupu, Radu, 337
Lynn, Barbara, 82, 259
Lynn, Loretta, 119, 239, 264, 330
Lynn, Sherry, 289
Lynn, Trudy, 125
Lynne, Jeff, 237, 271
Lynn record label, 125
Lyons, Lucil Manning, 100, 194–95, 311, 313
Lytle, Hub, 306

Maas, Isabella Offenbach, 55, 196
Macal, Zdenek, 54, 283
McAuliffe, Leon, 196, 196

McBride, Dickie, 41, 75, 197, 237
McBride, Laura Lee Owens, 196–97, 237
McBride, Roy, 39
McCamish, Charles, 306
McCane, Les, 284
McCarthy, Albet, 102
McCartney, Paul, 243, 271
McClain, Joseph, 235
McClendon, Doris, 366
McClinton, Delbert, 31, 259, 260, 264, 271, 274, 289, 355
McClure, David, 220
McCombs, Red, 251
McConathy, Osbourne, 311
McConnell, W. J., 333
McCormack, John, 325
McCormick, Robert Burton "Mack," 187, 288, 366
McCoy, William, 255
McCraklin, Jimmy, 63
McCrimmen, Dan, 174
McDavid, Percy, 303
McDavid's Blue Rhythm Boys, 165
MacDonald, Pat, 103, 273
MacDonald, Barbara, 103, 273
McDonald, William Madison "Gooseneck Bill," 162, 163
McElheny, Bruce, 4
McEnery, Red River Dave, 77, 318
McEntire, Reba, 11
McFarland, Wilbur, 125
McFarland, Willie Mae, 255
McFay, Monk, 60
McGee, Archie, 166
McGee, Ralph, 166
McGhee, Brownie, 247
McGhee, Howard, 7, 247
McGhee, Wes, 261
McGimsey, Bob, 116
McGinty Club, 197–98
McGraw, Tim, 21
McGregor, John, 198
McHuch, Jimmy, 116
McHugh, Jimmy, 12
McIllhenny, John W., 19
McIntosh, Tom, 84
McKinley, Ray, 159, 178, 198, 198
McKinney, Baylus Benjamin, 198–99, 265
McKinney, James, 293
McKissack, Mrs. E. J., 333
McLean, Don, 141, 271
McLemore, Ed, 20, 44
McLendon, Gordon Barton, 199–200
McLin, Claude, 7

McMillan, Linda Jo, 317
McMurtry, James, 174
McNeal, Millard, 82, 121
McNeally, Timothy, 259
McNeill, Don, 116
McPartland, Jimmy, 307
McPhatter, Clyde, 178
McShann, Jay, 158, 165, 251, 304
Macy's Records, 27, 366
Maddox, Bill, 273
Maddox, Rose, 20
Madison, Bingie, 113
Magda record label, 261
Magic Sam, 213
Maiden, Sidney, 350
Maines Brothers, 260
Majek Orchestra, 73
Majestic Records, 356
Majestic Theatre, 200–201, 237
Malaco Records, 136, 166, 304
Mallory, Eddie, 121
Malone, Bill, 89, 189
Malone, Kass, 307
Malone, Mary Lou, 303
Mance Lipscomb–Glenn Myers Collection, 187
Mancini, Henry, 116
Mandolin, 215–16
Mandrell, Barbara, 68
Männergesang-Verein, 208, 319
Manone, Wingy, 172, 176, 178
Manny record label, 285
Mansfield, Jayne, 180
Manuel, Dean, 262
"Maple Leaf Rag," 171
Marcela y Aurelia, 308
Marchessi, Blanche, 69
Marching Plague, 249
Marcus, Stanley, 56
Margo Jones Theatre, 277
Marguerite McCammon Voice Competition, 235
Mariachi Coculense de Cirilo Marmolejo, 201
Mariachi music, 201–3, 202
Mariachi Vargas de Tecalitlán, 201, 203
Marin, R. J., 156
Marini, Lou, 333
Marion, Duncan, 198
Markham, Pigmeat, 163
Marroquín, Armando, 92, 150, 203–4, 260, 308, 343
Marroquín, Carmen, 204, 260, 308
Marsh, William John, 55, 56, 204, 310, 311, 312
Martin, Bill "the Mailman," 1
Martin, Dean, 133, 220, 241
Martin, Fats, 91

Martin, Mary, 29, 56, 204–5
Martinelli, Giovanni, 192
Martínez, Eduardo, 308
Martínez, Freddy Sr., 261
Martínez, Lupe, 256
Martínez, Narciso, 77, 92, 150, 190, 204, 205–7, 206, 221, 256, 260, 308, 310, 315, 343
Martini, Nino, 235
Martin record label, 241
Martín y Malena, 308
Marx, Wilhelm, 17
Marx Brothers, 237
Mary Nash College, 207
Mary record label, 49
Massengill, David, 174
Massey, Guy, 76
Massey, Louise, 207
Mata, Eduardo, 54
Matejka, Frank, 250
Matlock, Matty, 307
Matthews, John Alexander, 108, 223
Matthews, Watt, 223
Mattie's Ballroom, 264
Mattis, David J., 269
Mature, Anthony, 42
Mauldin, Joe B., 141
Maxey, Delois, 350
Maximilian, 220
Maxwell, Gary, 346
Maya, Jesús, 260
Maya y Cantú, 260
Mayes, Floyd "Texas Pete," 27, 82
Mayfield, Curtis, 114
Mayfield, Percy, 82
Mays, Curly, 91
Mays, Lowry, 251
Mays, Ted, 255
Mbari record label, 135
MCA Records, 58, 68, 148, 298
Meat Loaf, 273
Meaux, Huey, 189, 259, 271
Medwick, Joe, 265
Melba, Nellie, 268
Melco record label, 122, 319
Mellencamp, John, 355
Melody Boys, 49, 121
Melody Maids, 207
Melody Masters, 304
Melton, Dave, 50
Memphis Minnie, 296
Memphis Slim, 5, 259, 269
Mendoza, Francisco, 208
Mendoza, Juanita, 208, 260, 307–8
Mendoza, Leonora, 208, 307, 308
Mendoza, Lydia, 31, 202, 208, 256, 260, 285, 307, 309, 315, 343

Mendoza, María, 208, 260, 307–8
Mendoza, Vicente, 64
Mengelberg, Wilhelm, 23
Menger, Erich, 208
Menger, Johann N. S., 118
Menger, Simon, 18, 119, **208–9**
Menger Soap Works, 208–9
Men of the West, 35
Mercer, Johnny, 116
Mercier, Mandy, 103, 149
Mercury Records, 20, 62, 71, 75, 142, 230, 259, 265, 283, 344
Mercy Baby, 27
Merlick, Joe, 73
Merman, Ethel, 91
Mesner, Eddie, 39, 210
Messner, J., 118
Metro Broadcasting vs. FCC (1990), 293
Metropolitan Opera Company, 235
Mexican American festivals, 104
Mexican Victor record label, 164
Mexico. *See also* Conjunto music
  border radio, 30–32, 266
  conjunto, 315
  corridos, 63–65, 92–93
  degüello, 79–80
  mariachi music, 201–3
Meyers, Augie, 48, 49, 259, 261, 271, 274, 281
Meyers, Louis, 292
Mgebroff, Johannes, **209**
MGM record label, 147, 307
Mickwitz, Paul Harold von, 4, 176
Midland-Odessa Orchestra, 54–55
Midler, Bette, 168
Midnighters, 124
Mighty Clouds of Joy, 139, 269
Milam, Eloise, 207
Milam, Lena Triplett, **209**
Milburn, Amos, 82, **209–10**, 265, 284, 303, 354
Miles Ahead record label, 336
Milhaud, Darius, 84
Military musicians. *See* Army musicians
Miller, Art, 305, 306
Miller, Charles, 47
Miller, Glenn, 15, 19, 43, 86, 101, 147, 156, 159, 178, 198, 264, 299, 306
Miller, Jesse, 165
Miller, Mitch, 364
Miller, Roger Dean, 56, 66, 75,

210–11, *211*, 316
Miller, Steven, 273, 351
Millinder, Lucky, 166, 212, 276, 304, 362
Millions of Dead Cops (BANG GANG), 249
Mills, Irving, 12
Mills, J. M., *105*
Mils, Telli W., 354
Milsap, Ronnie, 264
Milt Larkin Jazz Society, 182
Milton Brown and His Musical Brownies, 10, 23, 39–40, 41, 48, 71, 86
Mingus, Charles, 82, 94, 95, 303, 355, 362
Mingus Dynasty, 355
Minick, Billy, 21
Minick, Pam, 21
Minor, Dan, 155, 156, **210**, 212
Minor Threat, 249
Minotis, Alexis, 56
Minstrel shows, 7, 15, 84, 99
Mischer, Walter M., 197
Misipy record label, 336
Mississippi Sheiks, 2
Mistakes, 249
Mitchel, Red, 57
Mitchell, Giles, 182
Mitchell, Lonnie, 366
Moats, Jack, 3
Modernaires, 19
Modern Mountaineers, 48
Modern Records, 70, 215, 350, 351
Moffatt, Katy, 4, 175
Moffett, Charles, 159, **212**
Moffettettes, 212
Molak, Pat, 126
Moman, Chips, 230
Monahan, Gordon, 147
Money record label, 230
Monk, Thelonious, 82, 158
Monkees, 271, 351
Montana, Patsy, 31, 266
Monterey Jazz Festival, 244, 305, 307, 325
Montes, Octavio Mas, 256
Montgomery, Bob, 139, 141
Montgomery, Marvin "Smokey," 22, 184, 185, **212–13**, 258, 259–60
Montgomery, Merle, 291
Montreux Jazz Festival, 340
Monument record label, 236
Moody, Dan, 234
Moog, Robert, 94
Moonlighters, 44
Moonlight Melody Six, 165
Moonlight Serenaders, 251
Moore, Alexander Herman, 27, **213–15**, *214*, 256, 331

Moore, Brew, 135
Moore, Clarence, 156
Moore, Danny, 298
Moore, Earl Vincent, 100
Moore, Ella B., 26
Moore, Garry, 43
Moore, Grace, 55, 235
Moore, Ian, 261
Moore, John M., 333
Moore, Johnny, 38–39, **215**
Moore, Margaret, 134
Moore, Oscar Frederic, 156, **215**
Moore, Tiny, **215–16**
Moore, Tom, 186
Moore, Walker, 100
Moore, William, 134
Morales, Andrew, 216
Morales, Angie, 216
Morales, Felix Hessbrook, **216–17**
Morales, José, 217
Morales Funeral Home, 216, 217
Moreland, Pegleg, 250
Morgan, Emily, 364
Morgan, George, 318
Morgan, James, 364
Morgan, J. Doug, 212
Morgan, Kathy, 194
Morganfield, McKinley, 187
Morin, Frank, 271
Morlix, Gurf, 103
Morris, Harold, 56, **217**
Morris, Joe, 29
Morris, W. T., 92–93
Morse, Ann, 217
Morse, Ella Mae, **217–18**
Morse, George, 217
Morton, Don, 311
Morton, Jelly Roll, 24, 57, 155, 187
Mosaic Records, 134
Mosely, Snub, 290
Mosley, T. B., 16
Moss Rose music publishing, 188
Moten, Bennie, 32, 86, 155, 156, 163, 175, 210, 239, 290, 362
Motion pictures. *See* Movies
Motown Records, 210, 303
Mountain Retreat record label, 230
Mouse and the Traps, 259, 272
Movies. *See also* Documentaries
  actors and singers, 12–13, 15, 23, 29, 44, 85, 95–97, 113, 128, 129, 131–33, 162, 179, 205, 212–13, 217, 219–20, 220, 267, 358

on Buddy Holly, 141, 142
composers of music for, 92
filmmakers, 199, 265, 326, 327
folklorists, 238
musical supervisors and composers of music for, 92
musicians in, 14, 35, 41, 110, 147, 152, 154, 178, 212–13, 218, 237, 245, 262, 265, 267, 286, 296, 299, 307, 318, 326, 330, 331, 356, 357, 358, 359, 362
nightclubs and, 317
recording industry and, 259
soundtracks of, 60, 114, 142, 148, 171, 237, 274, 326
South by Southwest, 292
Texas Centennial, 311
Texas locations for, 5, 21–22, 38, 119
Moving Sidewalks, 272
Movin' record label, 336
Mr. B's Records, 61
Mr. G record label, 261
M. Schultz Company, 245
MSNC. *See* Music Supervisors' National Conference (MSNC)
Muddy Waters, 187, 295, 300, 325
Mudhoney, 338
Mullican, Moon, 20, 41, 49, 50, 74, 197, **218–19**, 258, 259, 286, 301
Munds, William Caper, 360–61
Munger, Robert S., 78
Munnerlyn, Henry, 91
Munnerlyn, John, 89, *90*, 91
Munroe, Frank, 250
Murphey, Michael Martin, 67, 174, 261, 273, 297, 298, 355
Murphy, Audie Leon, 219, **219–20**
Murphy, Henry, 192
Murphy, Turk, 307
Murrah, Pendleton, 283
Murray, Ken, 116
Murrell, Bob, 216
Murrin, Steve, 21
Muscle Shoals Horns, 103
Muscle Shoals Rhythm Section, 298
Muse record label, 58, 344, 362
Museums
  Texas Music Museum, 316
  University of Texas Institute of Texan Cultures, 334–35
Musical Arts Conservatory of West Texas, 36, **222**
Musical Brownies, 10, 23,

39–40, 41, 48, 71, 86, 184, 218, 256, 270
Musical dramas
  composers, 210
  Fort Griffith Fandangle, 108, 223–24
  performers, 204–5, 267, 358
  Texas, 134, 223
  Texas Centennial Pageant, 312
Música norteña, 220–22, 264–65, 307–8, 343
Music as historical narrative, 9–10
Music critic, 276–77
Music educators, 2, 15–16, 23–24, 45, 47, 54, 80, 83–84, 110, 112–13, 131, 135–36, 180, 198–99, 204, 217, 232, 245–47, 265, 281–84, 291–92, 294, 297, 352–54. *See also* Music schools; Piano teachers
Music Educators National Conference, 83–84
Music entrepreneur, 269
Music festivals. *See* Festivals
Music history, 45–46, 71
Music in Texas (Spell), 294, 294
Music Makers, 165
Musicologists, 56, 82–83, 117, 135–36, 187–88, 232, 245–46, 291–92
Music organizations, 17–18, 194–95, 197–98, 224–25, 310–14, 317
Music patrons. *See* Patrons for music and art
Music publishers, 16, 17, 32, 56, 75, 123, 124, 134–35, 198–99, 267–68, 296–97, 320–21
Music schools. *See also* Music educators; University of Texas at Austin; *and other specific universities*
  administrator of, 175–76
  Belle Plain College, 19, 54
  Central Plains College and Conservatory of Music, 46–47
  jazz degree from North Texas State Teachers College, 131
  Kidd–Key College, 24, 54, 176
  Mary Nash College, 207
  Musical Arts Conservatory of West Texas, 36, 222
  Negro Fine Arts School, 47
  Southwestern Seminary School of Church Music, 265, 292–93
  Texas Association of Music

Schools, 310–11
  University of North Texas College of Music, 54, 55, 56, 60, 85, 94, 131, 136, 146, 158, 333–34
Music stores, 86, 319–20
Music Study Club, 209
Music Supervisors' National Conference (MSNC), 2
Music Teachers' Association, 181
Musselman, John, 223
Mustang Records, 113
Myers, Emil, 325
Myles, Tommy, 121

Nail, Reilly, 224
Nail, Robert Edward Jr., 108, 223–24
Naizer, Bill, 72
Nanc record label, 336
Naranjo, Rubén, 222
Nash, Johnny, 8, 272
Nashboro Records, 166
National Association of American Composers and Conductors, 217
National Association of Jazz Educators, 131
National Association of Music Schools, 222, 310, 333
National Association of Schools of Music, 83
National Barn Dance, 20, 191, 250
National Bureau for the Advancement of Music, 224
National Cowgirl Hall of Fame, 207
National Education Association, 209, 246–47
National Federation of Music Clubs, 47, 129, 195, 217, 291, 312
National Four-String Banjo Hall of Fame, 213
National Fraternity of Student Musicians, 4, 225
National Guild of Piano Teachers, 3–4, 47, 56, 181, 224–25, 337
National Music Week, 209, 224, 312, 313
National Piano Playing Auditions, 225, 337
National Sacred Harp Convention, 279
National Theater of New Orleans, 317
Native American festivals, 104
Native American music, 52, 225–28

Navaira, Emilio, 286, 315
Navarro, Fats, 107, 114
Neal, Mark, 38
Neely, Bill, 26, 174, **228–29**, 229
Neff, Pat, 183
Negrete, Jorge, 202
Negro Fine Arts School, 47
Nellen, Otto, 199
Nelson, Earl, 42
Nelson, Harrison D. (Peppermint Harris), 27, 94, **229–30**
Nelson, Jewell, 255
Nelson, Jimmy, 27
Nelson, Lindsay, 199
Nelson, Ozzie, 264
Nelson, Willie, 7, 10, 11, 17, 21, 22, 38, 46, 48, 49, 67, 75, 78, 86, 103, 112, 161–62, 174, 194, 230, 231, 239, 258, 259, 260, 261, 264, 273, 274, 281, 298, 300, 316, 326, 338, 355
Nemir, Clarence, 131
Nervebreakers, 249, 273
Nesman Recording Studio, 260
Nesmith, Michael, 271
Nespoli, Uriel, 144
Neurotic Sheep, 45
Neve, Rupert, 258
Nevitt, Chuck, 29
New Art Jazz Ensemble, 45, 159
New Bluebird Nite Club, 89
New Bohemians, 273–74
Newbury, Mickey, 230–31
"New Deal" Band, 14
Newdoll, Ron, 358–59
Newhouse, Jackie, 340
New Keynotes, 166
Newman, David "Fathead," 29, 57, 158
Newman, Roy, 86
Newman, Ted, 198
Newport Folk Festival, 187, 233
Newport Jazz Festival, 307, 325
Newton, Wayne, 231
New-wave music, 248, 273
Next, 249, 273
Nichols, Ernest, 192
Nichols, Lem, 33
Nichols, Red, 163, 305, 306
Nightcaps, 172
Nightclubs. *See also* Dance halls
  Antone's Nightclub, 5, 27, 300
  Austin Outhouse, 103
  Billy Bob's Texas, 21–22
  The Cellar, 45
  Cheatham Street Warehouse, 48–49

Continental Club, 27
Eastwood Country Club, 91, 114
Eldorado Ballroom, 93–94
Empire Room, 27
Gilley's, 119–20
Jim Hotel, 162–63
New Bluebird Nite Club, 89
Rose Ballroom/Room, 26–27
Texas Star Inn, 316–17
Victory Grill, 27, 33
Vulcan Gas Company, 261, 346–47
Nitty Gritty Dirt Band, 273
Nitzinger, John, 272
Nix, Ben, 231
Nix, Hoyle, **231**, 354
Nix, Jody, 231
Nix, Larry, 231
Nixon, Richard, 117
Noble Knights, 178
Noblett, Jim, 316–17
Nocturne Records, 14
Noelte, Albert, 36
Nohl, Dr., 128
Nolen, Larry, 316
Noone, Jimmy, 359
Nopal Records, 92, 204, 260
Nord Amerikanischer Saengerbund (North American Singers Association), 19
Nordica, Lillian, 268
Noriego, Carmen Nanette, 129
Norkunas, Martha, 314
Norman, Peggy, 222
Norman Petty Trio, 243
Norris, Blind, 255
Norsingle, Ben, 255
North Texas Female College, 175–76
North Texas State University. *See* University of North Texas College of Music
Norton, Mrs. Charles G., 312
NorVaJak record label, 243
Nunn, Gary P., 5, 11, 38, 49, 261
Nye, Hermes, 254

Oberdoerffer, Fritz, 56, 232
Oberstein, Eli, 19
Ochs, Jacob, 232–33
Ochs, Phil, **232–33**
O'Daniel, Wilbert Lee "Pappy," 31, 39, 40, 41, 184, 196, 197, 233–34, 256, 286, 357
Odetta, 167
Odin, Bishop Jean Marie, 53
Odyssey Studio, 261
Offenbach, Jacques, 196
Offenbach, Julius, 196
Offenders, 249

Ogilvie, Rev. Lloyd John, 133
Ohre, Adel aus der, 36
Oil Patch record label, 231
O'Jays, 114, 351
Okeh Records, 2, 14, 15, 26, 83, 166, 167, 172, 208, 254, 255, 256, 296, 323, 343, 344, 350, 362
Oklahoma Joy Boys, 305
Oklahomans, 305
Oklahoma Playboys, 137
Oktoberfest, 5
Old Fiddlers' Association, 30, 120
"Old Gray Mare," 15
Old Gray Mare Band, 7, 15
Old Warsaw Restaurant, 185
Oleanders, 102
Oliphant, Dave, 19
Oliver, Joe "King," 154, 163, 320, 323, 350, 362
Oliver, Paul, 25
Oliver, Sy, 121, 166, 353, 362
Olivero, Magda, 56, 235
Ollre, Naomi, 311
"Ol' Man River," 23
Olmsted, Frederick Law, 118–19
Olympics, 351
O'Malley, D. J., 107
Omar and the Howlers, 49
101 Ranch Brass BAnd, 86
One O'Clock Lab Band, 333–34
Onins, I. M., 19, 176
Opera, 55–56, 85, 118–19, **234–36**
  Austin Lyric Opera, 56, 235–36
  composers, 23, 55, 94, 137, 171, 204, 291, 353
  Dallas Opera, 55–56, 173–74, 201, 235
  Fort Worth opera, 55, 234, 235
  Houston Grand Opera, 55, 143–44, 235
  light opera, 56
  singers, 13, 16, 23, 55, 58, 60, 69, 76, 81, 117, 192, 196, 323, 325
  Texas Centennial, 291, 311
O'Quin, Gene, 354
Orbison, Roy Kelton, 9, 10, 179, 231, 236, **236–37**, 243, 260, 270, 271
Orchestras. *See also specific orchestras*
  Abilene Philharmonic Orchestra, 54
  Amarillo Symphony, 54
  Austin Symphony Orchestra, 4, 47, 55, 56, 83, 181

composers of orchestral works, 35–36, 120–21, 128–29, 297, 337–38
conductors, 1–2, 17, 23–24, 52, 84–85, 120–21, 180, 237, 337–38, 340, 342, 353
Dallas Symphony Orchestra, 24, 52, 54, 174, 180, 201, 263
El Paso Symphony Orchestra, 54
Fort Worth Symphony, 55
high school orchestra, 2
Houston Symphony Orchestra, 24, 54, 128, 137, 144–45, 301
Midland-Odessa Orchestra, 54–55
Plano Symphony Orchestra, 54
Richardson Symphony Ochestra, 54
San Antonio Symphony Orchestra, 1, 24, 52, 54, 55, 235, 250, 263–64, 282–83
Symphony of Southeast Texas, 209, 301–2
Orchestra San Antonio, 283
Orchids, 179
Organists, 15–16, 110, 243–44, 297, 351–52
Organizations. *See* Music organizations; *and specific organizations*
Original Dorseyland Jazz Band, 305
Original Texas Playboys, 10, 11, 196, 299. *See also* Texas Playboys
Original Texas Rangers, 237
Ormes, Alberta "Bertie," 84
ORO Records, 206
Orquestas típicas, 203, 205, 307
Orquesta tejana, 122, 150, 203, 342–43
Ortiz, Florencio, 314
Ory, Kid, 41, 135
Oscar, Gussie, **237**
Otis, Johnny, 42, 70, 210, 243, 325, 344, 351
O.T. record label, 49
Ousley, Curtis. *See* King Curtis
Overton, Bill, 224
Owens, Buck, 66, 239
Owens, Calvin, 94
Owens, Tary, 33, 189
Owens, Tex, **237**
Owens, Texas Ruby, 197, 237
Owens, William A., **237–38**, 254, 308
"Ozark Jubilee," 9

Ozuna, Sonny, 261
Ozzfest tour, 274

Pace, Glen, 260
Pace, Louise, 311
Pacemaker label, 259
Pacific Records, 147
Page, Drew, 305, 306
Page, Hot Lips, 7, 86, 114, 155, 156, 175, **239–40**, 240, 247, 251, 258, 290, 304
Page, Jimmy, 270
Page, Patti, 210
Page, Walter, 210, 239, 251, 290, 307
Palm Isle Club, 264
Palmyra Studios, 260
Palo Duro Canyon State Park, 223
PAN. *See* Performance Artists Nucleus, Incorporated (PAN)
Pan Afrikan Peoples Arkestra, 330
Panhandle Cowboys and Indians, 86
Pantera, 274
Panther Hall, 17, **239**
Pappy O'Daniel's Hillbilly Boys, 31
Paramount Records, 26, 147, 159, 161, 167, 255
Parchman, Mary, 91
Paredes, Américo, 64, 64, 93, 288, 308
Parham, J. C., 176
Paris, James B., 80
Parisotti, Luigi, 23
Paris Reunion Band, 362
Park, Jong Hwa, 337
Park, Jon-Gyung, 337
Parker, Bobbie June, 91
Parker, Bonnie, 71
Parker, Charlie "Bird," 14, 81, 82, 107, 114, 156, 158, 165, 251, 252, 276, 284, 290, 362
Parker, John W. "Knocky," 22, 23, 35, 184
Parker, Junior, 27, 125, 139, 259, 266, 269
Parker, Colonel Tom, 9, 188
Parks, Chester, 54
Parks, David, 103
Parks, J. C., 176
Parrot record label, 178
Parry, Milman, 115
Parsons, Betsy Black, 224
Parthé record label, 167
Parton, Dolly, 38, 239
"Party Doll," 179, 180
Patek, Joe, **239**, **241**

Patek Band, 239
Patriotic songs, 23
Patrons for music and art, 17–18, 56, 137–38, 268, 300
Patsy and the Buckaroos, 3
Patton, Jimmy, 247
Paul, Johnny, 356
Paul, Les, 74
Paul, Pamela Mia, 85
Paul and Paula, 213, 259, 271, 359
Paula record label, 259
Paumgartner, Bernard, 115
Pavarotti, Luciano, 143
Pavlova, Anna, 237, 268
Paycheck, Johnny, 180, 264, 355
Payne, Benny, 32
Payne, Leon Roger, **241**
Payton, Earlee, 178
Peabody, Charles, 24
Peabody, Thomas, 24
Peacock Records, 27, 101, 139, 258, 259, 269, 325
Peacock Studio, 259
Pearl, Minnie, 210
Pearl Jam, 359
Pearl Wranglers, 137
Pecan Street Studios, 261
Peck's Bad Boys, 172, 173
Pedernales Recording Studio, 261
Peeble, Bobby, 260
Peer, Ralph, 350
Peerless record label, 288
Pellum, Ray, 9
Peña, Juan, 264
Peña, Manuel, 203, 206
Penn, William Evander, **241–42**
Penny, Lee, 207
Pentagram Records, 325
Peppermint Harris. *See* Nelson, Harrison D.
Perciful, Jack, 154
Percussionists, 61–62. *See also* Drummers
Perez, John, 271
Perez, Ruben, 92
Pérez de Riba, 225, 228
Performance Artists Nucleus, Incorporated (PAN), 126
Performance halls. *See* Theaters and performance halls
Perkins, Carl, 20, 161, 236
Perkins, Gertrude, 255
Person, Houston, 58
Peter, Paul and Mary, 52, 168
Peters, Albert, 242
Peters–Hacienda Community Hall, **242–43**
Peterson, Oscar, 158
Peterson, Ray, 271

Petmecky, Joseph, 118, 119
Pettis, Pierce, 174
Petty, Norman, 141, 179, **243**, 260, 270, 271
Petty, Tom, 237, 271
Petty, Rev. William R., 176
Pharaohs, 114
Philadelphia Jazz Society, 248
Phil/Aladdin record label, 215
Phillips, Esther Mae, **243–44**
Phillips, Johnnie, 91
Phillips, Little Esther, 166
Phillips, Sam, 17, 236
Phillips, Utah, 125
Phillips, Washington, **244**, 255
Philo Records, 39
Phoenix Club, 180
Pianists
   band and orchestra music, 135, 237
   blues, 32–33, 38–39, 87–88, 121, 213–15, 245, 247–48, 265–66, 287–88, 350
   boogie-woogie, 32–33, 155, 320–21, 323, 351–52
   child prodigy pianist, 323
   classical music, 4, 35–36, 56, 110, 115, 180, 181, 245–46, 281–82, 291, 336–37
   country and western music, 147
   hillbilly music, 218–19
   jazz, 32–33, 57, 69, 114, 172–73, 243–44, 247–48, 298–300, 307, 359
   ragtime music, 168, 170–71
   rhythm-and-blues, 147, 209–10, 350–51
   Van Cliburn International Piano Competition, 4, 55, 56, 150, 336–37
   and vocalist, 167
Piano competitions, 4, 55, 56, 150, 336–37
Piano Guild Notes, 4
Piano manufacture, **244–45**, 320
Piano sales, 319–20
Piano teachers, 3–4, 57–58, 181, 208–9, 224–25, 246–47, 281–82, 297, 352–53. *See also* Music educators
Pick, Paul, 47
Pickard Family, 31
Pickens, Buster, **245**
Pickford, Mary, 192
Pickle, Jake, 1, 87, 99, 326
Pierce, Bruce, 22
Pierce, Webb, 20, 31, 78, 188, 189, 191, 318
Pillot, Joseph Eugene, 56, **245**

Pilton, Gene, 317
Piña, Jorge, 92, 127, **190–91**
Pinza, Ezio, 205
Piper, Edwin Ford, 238
Pipes, Pettis, 176
Pisk, Paul Amadeus, 56, **245–46**
"Pistol Packin' Mama," 80
Pittman, Portia, 165, **246–47**, 248
Pittman, William Sidney, 26, 78, 246
Pitts, E. D., 176
Pitts, Kenneth, 184
Pizzetti, Ildebrando, 1
Pizzicato jazz cello, 14
Plagge, Christoph, 118
Planet Dallas, 260
Plano Symphony Orchestra, 54
Plantation Orchestra, 57
Platinum City record label, 336
Playboys. *See* Texas Playboys
Play party, 106
Plumb, Neely, 356
Poetry Society of Texas, 245
Pointer Sisters, 7, 355
Polk, James, 261
Polk, Videt, 297
Pollack, Ben, 147, 152, 176, 305, 306, 307
Polydor record label, 348
Poole, Robert, 250
Poovey, Groovey Joe, **247**, 259
Pope, C. C., 242
Pope record label, 125
Porter, Cole, 205, 305
Portley, Lilly, 101
Potter, Curtis, 354
Powell, Bud, 107
Powell, Jesse, **247**
Power, Tyrone, 224
Prado, George, 114
Prairie Pioneers, 197
Prairie View A&M, 54, 71, 80
Prairie View Collegians band, 35, 38
Prasada-Rao, Tom, 175
Prather, William L., 99
Pratt, Geronimo, 303
Prescott, William H., 353
Preservation Hall Jazz Band, 288
Presley, Elvis, 9, 17, 20, 31, 44, 50, 78, 86, 133, 142, 148, 179, 180, 189, 191–92, 194, 213, 218, 230, 233, 236, 239, 241, 247, 264, 269, 270, 271, 286, 325, 338, 354, 358
Prestige/Bluesville record label, 245
Prestige Records, 58, 95, 178

Preston, Billy, 272
Preston, Johnny, 20, 259
Preston, Lew, 89
Preston, Robert, 205
Previn, André, 54, 145
Price, Big Walter, 27
Price, Mrs. James L., 312
Price, Leontyne, 56, 143
Price, Ray, 20, 38, 66, 67, 78, 86, 210, 239, 259, 316, 319, 355
Price, Sammy, 2, **247–48**, 255
Price, Toni, 149
Pride, Charley, 17, 239
Priest, Micael, 6, 7, 37
Prima, Leon, 172
"Prisoner's Song," 76, 77
Producers, 74, 75, 91–92, 120–21, 354–55
Progressive country, 7, 10–11, 67, 261, 273, 281, 297–98, 338–40, 355
Progressive record label, 58
Promoters, 1, 61, 75, 188–89, 262–63, 296
Pryor, Cactus, 224
Prysock, Arthur, 8, 58
Prysock, Red, 58
Publishers. *See* Music publishers
Puckett, Riley, 43
Pueblo Indians, 225, 228
Pulido, Roberto, 261, 308, 315
Pullman Bar, 208
Pullum, Joe, 255
Punk rock, **248–49**, 273
Pursley, Frank, 115
Putney, Son, 350

Quality Blues Band, 266
Queen record label, 231
Question Mark and the Mysterians, 271, 273
Quigley, Herb, 306
Quiline Publishing, 42
Quinichette, Paul, 117, 304
Quinn, Bill, 27, 49, 152, 259
Quinn, Snoozer, 172
Quirico, Dewayne, 113

R&B. *See* Rhythm-and-blues music
"Race music," 121–22, 254–56
Rachleff, Larry, 54, 283
Rader, Ryan, 103
Raderman, Lou, 76
Radio, 250–51
   big band music, 154
   "Big 'D' Jamboree," 9, 20–21, 33–34, 43, 44, 213, 218, 247, 270, 354
   bilingual radio program, 129
   border radio, 30–32, 266

Cajun French radio stations, 49
classical music, 24, 263
country and western music, 50, 131–33, 142, 184–85, 191–92, 218, 250, 267
Czech music, 73, 241
disc jockeys, 20, 31, 35, 74, 87–88, 172, 247, 331–32, 354–55
fiddlers on, 30
gospel music, 1, 124, 133, 296, 297
"Grand Ole Opry," 9, 20, 21, 33, 34
jazz, 102, 121, 239, 328
"Kat's Karavan," 172
"Live from Festival Hall," 151
"Louisiana Hayride," 9, 20, 21, 44, 50, 71, 78, 142, 188, 189, 191–92, 194, 241, 262, 270, 354
personalities, 1, 97, 130, 131–33, 185, 216–17, 233–34, 237, 266, 293
producers, 120
programming innovator, 199–200
recording industry and, 254, 256, 258
rhythm-and-blues, 172, 304
rock-and-roll, 272
Spanish-language radio, 77–78, 203, 216–17, 251, 293–94
Tejano radio, 77–78
Texas Federation of Music Clubs and, 312
Texas Quality Network, 80
vocalists, 95, 97, 116
western swing, 22, 34, 39, 41, 50, 184–85, 317
Radio Hall of Fame, 200
Raeburn, Boyd, 14
Raglin, Junior, 69
Ragtime music, 155, 168, 170–71
Rainbow Ramblers, 215
Rainey, Homer, 234
Rainey, Ma, 239, 348, 350
Rains, George, 33
Raitt, Bonnie, 5, 10, 11, 39, 340, 350, 352
Raley, Leo, 41, 215
Rambo, Bobby, 298
Ramey, Gene, 156, 158, 165, 251–52, 252
Ramírez, Arnaldo, 260
Ramírez, Janie C., 308
Ramón Ayala y Los Bravos del Norte, 222
Ramser, Stewart, 316

Ramsey, Buck, 253
Ramsey, Willis Alan, 148, 149, 174, 298
Rand, Sally, 22, 23, 289
Randolph, Boots, 180, 264
Randy's Rodeo, 248
Rangel, Manuel Sr., 260
Ranger, Jack, 255
Rankin, Allen, 134
Ransleben, Guido, 19
Rapee, Erno, 185
Raphael, Mickey, 298
Rap music and rapping, 8, 74, 87
Raul's Club, 249
Raven, Eddy, 21
Ravens, 35
Rawls, Lou, 351
Ray, Paul, 124
Raye, Collin, 22
Raymond, Rose, 4
RCA/RCA Victor, 9, 12, 19, 26, 40, 42, 77, 116, 131, 137, 156, 161, 175, 188, 205–6, 215, 254, 258, 262, 297–98, 307, 330, 357
Reactors, 249
Really Red, 249
Reardon, Casper, 306
Reckhardt, Dan, 197
Recording industry, 26–27, 253–62. *See also specific recording companies*
  African Americans and, 182, 254–56
  Austin, 261–62
  blues, 26–27, 255, 259
  conjunto music, 256, 260
  country and western music, 259
  cowboy music, 254
  Dallas, 254, 255, 256, 258, 259–60, 270
  early pioneers of, 253–54
  field recordings, 187, 254, 258, 270
  gospel music, 259
  hillbilly music, 254, 256
  Houston, 258–59, 262
  music entrepreneur, 269
  post–World War II rise of, 258
  producers, 75, 243, 256, 354–55
  punk rock, 249
  race labels, 121–22, 254–56
  rhythm-and-blues music, 259, 261
  rockabilly music, 259
  rock-and-roll, 260
  San Antonio, 253, 254, 255, 256, 258, 260–61, 270
  Tejano music, 150, 203–4,

256, 260–61
western swing music, 258
Redbird, W. C., 218
Redding, Otis, 304, 352
Reddy, Helen, 260
Red Krayola, 272
Redman, Dewey, 159
Redman, Don, 290, 362
Redneck rock, 7, 10–11, 67, 261, 273, 274, 297–98
Reed, Jimmy, 5, 94, 289
Reed, Willie, 26, 255
Reeder Children's School of Theater and Design, 224
Reese, Della, 91
Reese, Jim, 113
Reeves, "Big Six," 41
Reeves, Jim, 20, 31, 66, 78, 191, 218, 241, 262–63, 263
Regency Jazz Band, 114
Reinecke, Carl, 338
Reinhardt, Django, 148
Reinhart, Dick, 184
Reis, Arthur M., 262–63
Reis, Claire Raphael, 262–63
Reiter, Max, 1, 54, 55, 235, 250, 263–64, 282–83
Rejects, 249
Religious music. *See* Church music; Sacred harp music
Renard, Frank, 176
Rendezvous record label, 42, 100–101
Reno, Johnny, 89
Reo Palm Isle, **264**
Reprise Records, 180, 187, 281
Rescigno, Nicola, 235
Reszke, Jean de, 325
Reuss, Allan, 305, 306
Revard, Jimmie, 137
Reyna, Cornelio, **264–65**
Reyna, Cornelio Jr., 265
Reynolds, Alice, 108, 223
Reynolds, Bill, 223
Reynolds, Isham Emmanuel, 16, 198, **265**, 292, 342
Reynolds, Teddy, 125, 230, **265–66**
Rhodes, Darrell, 354
Rhodes, George, 58
Rhodes, Kimmie, 103, 261
Rhodes, Sonny, 261, 358
Rhodius, Udo, 118
Rhythmaires, 124, 125
Rhythm-and-blues music, 42. *See also* Blues
  Eldorado Ballroom, 93–94
  guitarists, 139, 215, 350–51
  "Kat's Karavan" radio program, 172
  pianists, 147, 209–10, 350–51
  recording industry, 259

saxophonist, 5–6
singers, 147, 209–10, 243–44
songwriter, 147
Rhythm Orchids, 179, 180, 260, 270
Rhythm record label, 350
Rice University, 54
Rich, Buddy, 154, 163
Rich, Charlie, 355
Richards, Ann, 130
Richards, Steve, 142
Richardson, J. P. *See* Big Bopper
Richardson Symphony Ochestra, 54
Richter, Mark A., 235
Richter, Peggy, 192
Rideau, Step, 366
Riders of the Purple Sage, 356
Righteous Brothers, 359
Riley, Jeannie C., 66
Rimes, LeAnn, 21, 68, 259
Rinehart, Cowboy Slim, 31, **266**
Rio Grande Music Company, 150
Rio Grande Serenaders, 298, 299
Rio Records, 260, 308
Rios, Rolando, 126
Rippa, Herb, 289
Rischard, Hans, 176
Ritter, John, 267
Ritter, Tex, 38, 66, 197, 258, 267, **267**, 318
Rivers, Ella, 82
Rivers, Manuel Jr., 82
Riverside Records, 344, 354
Riverside Sound Studio, 261
Rives-Diaz, Leonora, 56, 135, **267–68**
Roach, Clyde, 297
Roach, Max, 82, 182, 355
Robbins, Marty, 21, 44, 259
Robert Reis and Company, 262–63
Roberts, Alice Bryan, **268**
Roberts, Jesse, 30, 120
Roberts, Luckey, 113
Roberts, Neal, 255
Robertson, Daphne, 269
Robertson, Dueron, 269
Robertson, Eck, 66, 120, 254, 259, **268–69**
Robertson, Nettie, 268, 269
Robeson, Paul, 187
Robey, Don Deadric, 27, 139, 258–59, **269**, 270, 325, 351
Robin Hood Brian's Recording Studio, 259
Robinson, Angelina, 164
Robinson, Rev. Cleophus, 139
Robinson, Faye, 125
Robinson, L. C. "Good

Rockin'," 164, 358
Robison, Carson, 76–77
Rocha, Pedro, 256, 260
Rocha and Martínez, 202
Rockabilly music, 8–9, 16–17, 20, 44, 179–80, 185, 189, 194, 236, 247, 259, 270
Rock Against Reagan, 248
Rock-and-roll, 270–75
  Armadillo World Headquarters, 7, 67
  Cheatham Street Warehouse, 48–49
  "Louisiana Hayride" and, 192
  performers, 17–980, 113, 139–42, 167–69, 236–37, 358–59
  recording industry, 243, 260
  record producer, 243
  redneck rock, 7, 10–11, 67, 261, 273, 274, 297–98
  songwriter, 236–37
  Texas International Pop Festival, 1969, 314–15
Rock and Roll Hall of Fame, 237, 270
Rock Island, 249
"Rocks," 155
Rodarte, Frank, 114
Rodela, Lupita, 308, 315
Rodemich, Gene, 183
Rodgers, Carrie, 330
Rodgers, Jimmie, 3, 26, 31, 34, 43, 66, 77, 85, 112, 166, 178, 186, 228, 275, **275–76**, 326, 330, 331
Rodgers, Robert W., 352
Rodgers, Rollin, 171
Rodney, Red, 107
Rodriguez, Frank, 271
Rodriguez, Johnny, 5, 67, 231, 239, 318
Rodríguez, José, 256, 343
Rodriguez, Pedro, 127
Rodríguez, Rafael, 256
Rodríguez expedition, 225, 228
Rogers, Ginger, 201
Rogers, Jamesetta, 303
Rogers, John William, 138
Rogers, Kenny, 55, 68, 230, 231, 272
Rogers, Lelan, 259, 272
Rogers, Roy, 44, 96, 97, 131
Rogers, Shorty, 158
Rogers, Will, 13, 237
Roland, Gene, 158, 276, 333
Rolling Stones, 141, 259, 270
Rollin' Rock Records, 247
Rollins, Sonny, 304
Ron-Dels, 271
Ronstadt, Linda, 141, 237, 271, 300

Roonie, Jim, 149
Roosevelt, Franklin D., 128, 234, 263, 282
Roppolo, Leon, 172
Rose, Billy, 22, 23
Rose, Wesley, 230
Rose Ballroom/Room, 26–27
Rosenfield, John Jr., 174, 276–77
Rosengarden, Bobby, 304
Rosenkrans, Charles, 143
Rosenthal, Jena, 235
Rosewood Studio, 259
Rosita y Aurelia, 260
Ross, Doc, 156, 306
Ross, Donald, 279
Ross, Lawrence S., 268
Ross, Ollie, 255
Rosser, John Jr., 254
Rothafel, S. A. "Roxy," 185
Roulette Records, 179, 180, 243, 244
Rounder Records, 63, 262
Round Top Institute. See International Festival–Institute at Round Top
Roush, Sonley, 358, 359
Routh, Gene, 199
Rowan, Peter, 175
Rowe, James, 16
Royal Aces, 63, 121, 251
Royal Gospel Quartet, 1
Ruby, Harry, 116
Ruby, Jack, 29, 45
Ruffcorn, Roger, 4
Rural Rhythm record label, 247
Rush, Otis, 5
Rushing, Jimmy, 251, 290, 304, 321
Russel, Leon, 178
Russell, Bad Boy, 172
Russell, Calvin, 261
Russell, Curly, 247
Russell, Leon, 355
Russell, Lillian, 128
Russell, Louis, 247, 251
Russell, Pee Wee, 172, 307
Russell, Rosalind, 29
Russell, Ross, 154
Russell, Shake, 4, 261
Russin, Babe, 305
Ryan, Joel, 146
R y R Records, 207

Sachs, Curt, 82
Sacred Harp music, 106–7, 122, 278–79, 279, 281
Sacred Harp Publishing Company, 279, 281
Sahm, Douglas Wayne, 5, 48, 49, 114, 189, 258, 259, 262,

271, 274, 280, **281**, 346, 355
Saint John, Art, 306
Saldivar, Mingo, 261
Saldivar, Yolanda, 286
Salinas, Raul, 127
Sam & Dave, 304, 314
Sam and the Good-Timers, 351
Samaroff, Olga, 56, **281–82**
Sammy Price and His Four Quarters, 255
Samoiloff, Lazar, 23
Sam the Sham and the Pharaohs, 271
Samudio, Domingo, 271
Samuel French Company, 224
Samuel W. Beazley and Son, 297
Sam Wooding Band, 184
San Antonio
    Beethoven Hall, 17, 18, 52
    Beethoven Männerchor, 17, 18–19, 52, 118
    Bonham Exchange, 249
    The Cellar, 45
    Choir Club, 108
    Club Bohemia, 208
    Eastwood Country Club, 91, 114
    Guadalupe Cultural Arts Center, 126–27
    Lyric Opera, 55, 235
    mariachi music, 202–3
    opera, 234–35, 283
    Opera House, 234
    Pullman Bar, 208
    punk rock, 249
    radio, 250, 251, 256
    recording industry, 253, 254, 255, 256, 258, 260–61, 270
    Symphony Orchestra, 1, 24, 52, 54, 55, 235, 263–64, 282–83
San Antonio Choir Club, 108
San Antonio College of Music, 24
San Antonio Lyric Opera, 55, 235
San Antonio Pocket Opera, 235
"San Antonio Rose," 85
San Antonio Symphony Orchestra, 1, 24, 52, 54, 55, 235, 250, 263–64, 282, 282–83
Sanders, Don, 4
Sandie Swingers, 253
Sängerfeste, 285
San Marcos
    Center for Texas Music History at Southwest Texas State University, 45–46
    Cheatham Street Warehouse, 48–49
    recording industry, 262

San Pedro Playhouse, 235
Santa Anna, Antonio López de, 364
Santa Fe Group, 27
Santana, 314
Sante Fe Circuit, 288
Sarg Records, 137, 258, 261
Sar record label, 304
Sarrett, Kenny, 264
Satellites, 42
Satex Film Company, 326, 328
Satherley, Art, 80, 258
Satterwhite, W. D., 289
Sauer, Emil, 115
Saunders, Harry, 250
Savoy, Ashton, 352
Savoy (band), 304
Savoy Records, 243, 318, 351
Saxophonists, 5, 7, 19, 57, 58, 94–95, 97, 102, 107, 131, 133–34, 135, 147–48, 176, 178–79, 247, 284, 289–90, 303–4, 342–43, 344, 354, 362
SBK Records, 286
Scaggs, Boz, 273
Scarborough, Elmer, 48
Scepter One Recording Studio, 139
Schaefer, Alfred, 18
Schaum, John W., 364
Scheffrahn, Lia, 29
Scheffrahn, Rudolf, 29
Scheidemantel, Adreas, 319
Schemmel, August, 294
Schicht, Otto, 28
Schiedemantel, Andreas, 18
Schipa, Tito, 192
Schirmer, 311
Schlansker, William, 126
Schoenberg, Arnold, 56, 245
Schools of music. See Music educators; Music schools
Schrader, Henry, 28
Schreiner, Jacob, 176
Schubert Ensemble, 209
Schubert Memorial Foundation, 282
Schuetze, Julius, **283–84**
Schuller, Gunther, 19, 43, 154, 305
Schumann-Heink, Madame Ernestine, 13
Schünemann, Georg, 82
Schutt, Arthur, 305
Scott, Clifford, 91, **284**
Scott, Effie, 255
Scott, Harold, 41
Scott, Joe, 139, 269
Scotto, Renata, 143
Screwed Up Click, 74
Screwed Up Record and Tapes

record label, 74
Sczepanik, Ray, 318, 319
Seals, Jimmy, 17, 272, 354
Seals and Crofts, 272
Second Great Revival, 278
Seeger, Pete, 142, 183, 187, 229, 233
Seele, Friedrich Hermann, 119, **284–85**
Selena, 78, 259, 285, **285–86**, 308
Selena y Los Dinos, 285–86
Sellers, Jack, 259
Sellers, Paul, 356
Sellers Studio, 259
Selph, Pappy, 3, 50, 218, **286–87**
Semien, "King" Ivory Lee, 125, 358
Sensational Nightingales, 269
Serafin, Tullio, 60
Serenaders. See East Texas Serenaders
Serenaders, 210
Session, Arnella, 344
Setapen, James, 54
Sevendust and Kittie, 274
77 Records, 366
Sex Pistols, 248
Sexton, Charlie, 49, 261, 274
Sexton, Will, 49, 274
Shad, Bob, 27
Shadows (band), 194
Shady's Playhouse, 265
Shakespeare Festival of Dallas, 201
Shamblin, Eldon, 196, 216, 231
Shand, Terry, 306
Shannon, Tommy, 340, 347
Shapiro, Bernstein, 311
Sharon Tate's Baby, 249
Sharpe, Jack, 172
Shaw, Artie, 86, 147, 172, 183, 239, 276
Shaw, Robert, 27, 287, **287–88**
Shaw, Thomas, 290
Shawn record label, 259
Shearing, George, 362
Sheiks, Mississippi, 255
Shell, Jim, 247
Shelter Records, 178
Shelton Brothers, 31
Sheppard, Morris, 15
Shiloh, 272
Shine, Black Boy, 27
Shirelles, 180
Shiva's Headband, 346
Shivers, Allan, 138, 319
Shocked, Michelle, 254
Shomar record label, 125
Short, Clarence J. "Sleepy," 317
Shorty, Pinetop, 350

Showalter, A. J., 16, 122–23, 296
Showboat, 23
Showboys, 218
Shrake, Bud, 239
Shuffler, R. Henderson, 334
Shuler, Eddie, 352
Shutes piano, 244
Silber, Sidney, 115
Sills, Beverly, 143
Silva, Chelo, 204, 260, 285, 288, 308
Silver, Horace, 82
Simionato, Giulietta, 55, 174, 235
Simmons, Blackie, 22–23, 212
Simmons, Brownie, 22, 23
Simmons, Jewel, 27
Simon, Paul, 259
Sims, Frankie Lee, 27, 288–89
Sims, Ray, 154
Sims, Zoot, 276, 284
Sinatra, Frank, 154, 261
Sinclair, John Lang, 99
Singers. *See* Choral music; Opera; *and specific types of music, such as* Blues
Singleton, Max, 264
Singleton, Sharon, 264
Singleton, Shelby, 20
Singleton, Zutty, 113
Sinistre, Lenora, 71
Sir Douglas Quintet, 259, 271, 273, 281
Sissle, Noble, 113
Sittin-In-With record label, 27, 229
Sixpence None the Richer, 274
Skaggs, Ricky, 264
Skiles, Mrs. R. J., 312
Skyliner Ballroom, **289**
Skyrockets, 266
Slack, Freddie, 217
Slades, 261
Slide guitar, 164
Sloey, Al, 356
Sly and the Family Stone, 272, 314
Smalley, I. H. "Ike," 94
Smash Mouth, 259
Smash record label, 147
Smith, Ben, 165, 210
Smith, Bessie, 161, 167, 296, 350
Smith, Beulah, 361
Smith, Bob, 31
Smith, Boston, 289
Smith, Buster, 27, 29, 86, 114, 155, 156, 175, **289–90**
Smith, Carl "Tatti," 69, 155, 156, **290**
Smith, Carson, 305

Smith, Clarence, 261
Smith, Darden, 174
Smith, Fred, 33
Smith, "Funny Papa," 2
Smith, "Funny Paper," 255, 290–91
Smith, Jeff, 261
Smith, John T., 255, 289, **290–91**
Smith, Jon, 103
Smith, Julia Frances, 55, 56, **291**
Smith, Lawrence Leighton, 54, 283
Smith, Lignon, 192
Smith, Lonnie, 101
Smith, "Major Bill," 259, 271, 359
Smith, O. C., 303
Smith, Preston, 224
Smith, Ray, 358
Smith, Stuff, 48
Smith, Trixie, 248
Smith, William, 278
Smith, Wilson "Thunder," 142, 259
Smith Ballew Orchestra, 15
Smither, Chris, 261
Smith Music Group, 21
Smokey and the Bearkats, 213
Smothers Brothers, 233
Sneed, Adolphus, 29
Snidero, Jim, 333
Snow, Hank, 20, 50, 75, 276, 330
Snow, Robert Joseph, 52, 56, **291–92**
Snowden, Elmer, 113
Snyder, Shake, 91
Soap Creek Saloon, 67
Sociedad Mutualista Obrera, 217
Sociedad Unión Fraternal, 217
Society for Private Musical Performances, 245
Soileau, Leo, 49
Sokoloff, Nikolai, 100
Soleri, Paolo, 182
Solís, Javier, 202, 288
Solomon, Ervin, 41
Solomon, Norman, 41
Solomon, Vernon, 41
Solti, George, 54
Sombrero Network, 293
Sombrero record label, 308
Sonami, Laetitia, 147
Sonet record label, 30
Songbird record label, 27, 269
Song Is Born, 14
Songwriters. *See* Composers
Sonnichsen, Philip, 201, 202
Sonny Boys, 342

Sonobeat Records, 261
Sons of the Pioneers, 38, 311
Sons of the Range, 197
Sony Discos record label, 261
Sony Music, 265
Soph, Ed, 354
Soul music, 8, 178–79
Soul Note record label, 58
Soul Stirrers, 304
Soul-Tex record label, 259
Sounder, 142
Sounds of Country, 242
Sousa, John Philip, 18, 204, 237
South by Southwest, **292**
Southeast Texas Youth Symphony, 302
Souther, J. D., 272
Southern Melody Boys, 82
Southern Methodist University, 54, 176
Southern Music Company, 99
Southern Thunder, 21
Southern Trumpeters, 156
Southwestern Baptist Theological Seminary, 16
Southwestern Historical Quarterly, 10
Southwestern Seminary School of Church Music, **292–93**
Southwestern Territory Band, 35
Southwestern University, 47
Southwest FOB, 259
Southwest Texas Sacred Harp Singing Convention, 278
Southwest Texas State University
    Center for Texas Music History, 45–46
    Sound Recording Technology program, 262
Southwest Theatre Conference, 277
Space record label, 336
Spanier, Mugsy, 251
Spanish-language music, 52, 63–64, 208, 220–22, 308. *See also* Conjunto music; Mexico; Tejano music
Spanish-language radio, 77–78, 203, 216–17, 251, **293–94**
Spanish Radio Broadcasters of America, 293
Spawn, Otis, 325
Spears, Billie Jo, 67
Specht, Paul, 183
Specialty Records, 289, 350
Spell, Lota May, **294**, 311
Spells, Dino, 336
Spencer, Tim, 311
Spielberg, Steven, 238
Spinks, Emmett, 289

Spinks, Walter, 4
Spire record label, 350
Spirit, 314
Spiritual Five, 136
Spivak, Charlie, 306
Spivey, Addie (Sweat Peas), 296
Spivey, Elton Island (Za Zu Girl), 296
Spivey, Leona, 296
Spivey, Victoria Regina, 154, 175, 256, **294–96**, 295, 323, 350
Spivey Record Company, 296
Springsteen, Bruce, 7, 141, 237, 271
Spurlock, E. L., 176
Square-dance music, 106
SST Records, 249
Stable of Stars, 188
Stack, Gael, 182
Stacy, Jess, 305
Stafford, Jo, 133
Stampede record label, 231
Stampley, Joe, 21, 264
Stamps, Frank, 297
Stamps, Virgil Oliver, **296**, 297, 311
Stamps, V. O., 16, 124
Stamps, W. O., 296
Stamps-Baxter Music and Printing Company, 16, 107, 123, 124, **296–97**
Stamps Quartet Music Company, 123, 124, 296, 297
Stanwyck, Barbara, 29
Starday record label, 75, 218, 258, 259
Starnes, Jack, 75
Star record label, 49
Star Talent record label, 231, 354
Statesmen of Jazz, 304
Statesmen Quartet, 124
Stax Records, 304
St. Cecilia Choral Society, 268
Steagall, Red, 86
Stearns, Marshall, 154
Steel guitarists, 74–75, 78, 86, 196
"Steel Guitar Rag," 196
Steinbeck, John, 130
Steinberg, David, 351
Steinberg, William, 84
Steinfeldt, John Mathias, 56, 119, **297**
Steinfelt, Benjamin, 24
Ste. Marie, Buffy, 231
Stencil pianos, 244–45, 320
Stephen F. Austin State University, 131
Sterling, Jack, 121
Sterling, Ross, 250

Stern, Howard, 286
Stevens, Cat, 273
Stevenson, B. W., 174, 261, 273, 297–98
Stevenson, Coke, 234
Stevenson, Robert M., 292
Steward, Herbie, 276
Stewart, Jimmy, 201, 223
Stewart, Rex, 353
Stewart, Sylvester "Sly Stone," 272
Stewart, Wynn, 247
Stewart–Barker, Derrick, 321
Stickmen With Rayguns, 249
Still, Hurlburt, 250
Stills, Stephen, 272
Sting, 171
Stitt, Sonny, 58, 116
St. Leger, Frank, 144
Stockard, Ocie, 39
Stojowski, Sigismund, 115
Stokowski, Leopold, 54, 110, 145
Stoller, Mike, 325
Stompin' Six, 57
Stone, Jesse, 156
Stoneman, Ernest, 43
Stone Poneys, 271
Storyville record label, 30
Stout, Richard, 182
Stowe, Harriet Beecher, 23
Strachwitz, Chris, 27, 61, 152, 187, 254, 331, 350
Strait, George, 5, 10, 21, 22, 38, 48, 68, 75, 86, 126, 259
Strand record label, 147
Strauss, Richard, 263
Street performer, 61–62
Strehli, Angela, 27, 346
Streiber, Charles L., 134
Streisand, Barbara, 67
Stribling, James H., 242
Stricklin, Al, 85, 196, **298–300**
String-A-Longs, 243
Stripling, Howard, 289
Strong, Bob, 14
Stubblefield, Christopher B. Sr., 300
Stubb's Bar-B-Q, 300
Studio D., 249
Studio South, 261
Sudduth, James, 56, 300–301
Sudhalter, Richard M., 148
Sugar Hill Records, 148
Sugar Hill Studio, 259
Sullivan, Dodie, 317
Sullivan, Ed, 116, 141, 168, 179, 180, 192
Sullivan, Niki, 141
Sultanov, Alexei, 337
Sumet Studios, 213, 259, 259–60

Summers, Gene, 259
Sumner (J. D.) Quartet, 124
Sundowners, 233
Sunliners, 259
Sunny and the Sunliners, 261, 271
Sunny Hill record label, 180
Sunnyland Slim, 5
Sun Records, 17, 236, 271
Sunset Entertainers, 32
Sunset record label, 57
Sunshine Gospel Records, 255
Super Crew, 351
Supremes, 303
Sureshot record label, 42
Surls, James, 182
Susskind, Walter, 54
Sutherland, Joan, 56, 174, 235
Swaggart, Jimmy, 119
"Swamp blues," 351–52
Swanson, Gloria, 29
Sweat, Isaac Payton, 189, 301
Sweetwater, 314
Swenson, Roland, 292
Swing music, 19–20, 86–87, 102, 156, 158. *See also* Western swing
Swing Time record label, 121
Symonds, Bob, 317–18
Symphonic Syncopators, 184
Symphony League of Beaumont, 302
Symphony of Southeast Texas, 209, 301–2
Symphony orchestras. *See* Orchestras
Symphony Society of San Antonio, 264, 282
Synthesizer, 94
Szigeti, Joseph, 263

Tacoland, 249
Tainter, Charles, 253–54
Talent agents, 17, 188–89
Talley, Rev. J. D., 166
Tampa Red, 296
Tank, Black, 87
Tannehill, Frank, 255
Tanner, Bob, 261
Tapper, Bertha Fiering, 263
Tapscott, Horace, 159, 303
Tapscott Simmons Quartet, 303
Tarahumara Indians, 228
Tate, Buddy, 94, 97, 102, 156, 158, 303–4
Tate, Erskine, 359
Tatum, Art, 163, 172, 215, 359
Taylor, Eddie, 5, 178
Taylor, Eric, 4
Taylor, Jesse, 300
Taylor, Johnnie Harrison, 304–5
Taylor, Little Johnny, 61

Taylor, Mary, 255
Taylor, Robert, 224
Taylor, Spencer, 21
Teagarden, Charlie, 156, 305, 307
Teagarden, Cubby, 305–6, 307
Teagarden, Helen, 305
Teagarden, Jack, 43, 86, 155, 156, 172, 173, 178, 183, 258, 264, 305, 306, 306–7
Teagarden, Norma, 305, 307
Teen Kings, 236, 243, 271
Teen Rendezvous Club, 113
Tejana Singers, 307–8, 315
Tejano Conjunto Festival, 127, 207, 308, 308–10, 310, 315
Tejano Conjunto Music Hall of Fame, 191
Tejano music, 77–78, 122, 126–27, 150, 163–64, 203–4, 220, 256, 285–86, 288, 307–10, 342–43. *See also* Conjunto music; Música norteña
Tejano radio, 77–78
Telephone Records, 260
Television
    actors and vocalists, 115–16, 162
    "American Bandstand," 141
    "Austin City Limits," 10–11, 38, 196, 273
    blues, 266
    Bongo Joe on, 61
    country and western music, 213, 216, 218, 239, 316
    cowboy music, 267
    "Ed Sullivan Show," 116, 141, 168, 179, 180
    "Elmer Akins: Radio Man" documentary, 1
    filmed at Billy Bob's Texas, 21–22
    folk music, 238
    "Gospel Train" program, 1
    "Hee Haw," 34
    jazz, 239, 303
    John Gary Show, 116
    musical arranger for, 178
    orchestra, 43
    personalities, 354–55
    radio and, 251
    recording industry and, 258
    rock-and-roll music, 237
    "Roy Rogers Show," 97
    singers, 115–16, 205, 210, 217–18
    Tejano music, 286
Temple, Shirley, 29
Templeton, Alec, 282
Ten Years After, 314
Territory Band, 344

Terry, Brian, 366
Terry, Clark, 107
Terry, Sonny, 183
Terry, Vance, 216
Tetrazzini, Luisa, 197
Texajazzers, 15
Texanischer Gebirgs Saengerbund (Texas Hill Country Singers League), 18
Texans, 48
Texas, 134, 223
"Texas, Our Texas," 204, 310, 312
Texas A&M University at College Station, 54, 55, 250
Texas A&M University at Kingsville, 203
Texas Association of Broadcasters, 217
Texas Association of Music Schools, 222, 293, 310–11
Texas Association of Negro Musicians, 246
Texas Blusicians, 248
Texas Centennial music, 99, 128, 291, 311, 312, 364
Texas Christian University, 54, 120, 147
Texas Composers' Collection, 217
Texas Composers' Guild, 204
Texas Cowboy Hall of Fame, 185
Texas Cowboys, 50
Texas Federation of Music Clubs, 100, 195, 204, 209, 311–13
Texas Federation of Women's Clubs, 311, 312
Texas Folklife Festival, 29, *103*, *104*, 313–14, 335
Texas Folklife Resources, 27, 139, 314
Texas Folklore Society, 187, 188, 254
Texas Frontier Centennial, 22–23
Texas Houserockers, 82
Texas Instruments, 258
Texas International Pop Festival 1969, 314–15
Texas Jazz and Blues, 58
Texas Jubilee Singers, 255
Texas Medley Quartette, 171
Texas-Mexican conjunto, 65, 92, 95, 126–27, 127, 150, 163–64, *163*, 190–91, 203, 205–7, 260, 264–65, 274, 281, 307, 308, 310, 315, 315, 343
Texas Music, 315–16
Texas Music Association, 316

Texas Music Educators Association, 209, 316, 353
Texas Music Museum, *316*, **316**
Texas Music Office, 262
Texas Music Teachers Association, 2, 47, 54, 108, 209, 316
Texas Playboys, 22, 38, 48, 85–86, 91, 184, 196, 197, 215–16, 231, 237, 258, 270, 286, 299, 357. *See also* Original Texas Playboys
Texas Polka Music Association, 241
Texas Pride, 242
Texas Quality Group Network, 184, 251, 256
Texas School of Fine Arts, 181, 294
Texas Sesquicentennial, 28, 174, 313, 316
Texas Sound Studios, 261
Texas Star Inn, **316–17**
Texas Star Playboys, 316
"Texas State Barn Dance," 20
Texas State Historical Association, 10
Texas State Old Time Fiddlers Association, 41
Texas State Sängerbund, 52, 118, 283, **317**
Texas State Teachers Association, 2, 209
"Texas style" guitar, 25, 41–42, 63
Texas Tech University, 24, 54, 300–301, 353
Texas Tenors, 304
Texas Top Hands, 261, **317–19**, *318*
Texas Tornados, 262, 274, 281, 315
Texas Troubadors, 330
Texas Tumbleweeds, **317–18**
Texas University Troubadours, 146
Texas Upsetters, 266
Texas Wanderers, 41, 48, 74, 86, 218
Texas War Work Council, 312
Texas Western Swing Hall of Fame, 185, 213, 231, 287, 319
Texas Wind Symphony, 52, 185
Texas Women's College, 235
Thames, Johnny, 48
Tharpe, Sister Rosetta, 248
That Rhythm . . . Those Blues, 39
Theaters and performance halls
 Beethoven Hall, 17, 18
 Jesse H. Jones Hall for the

Performing Arts, 54, 144, 145, 162–63
 Little Theater, 223
 Majestic Theatre, 200–201, 237
 Panther Hall, 17, 239
 Peters–Hacienda Community Hall, 242–43
 Reo Palm Isle, 264
 Skyliner Ballroom, 289
 Waco Auditorium, 237
Theatre Intime, 223
Theatre Operating Company, 201
Thibodeau, Ralph, 361
Thielepape, Wilhelm Carl August, 18, 119, **319**
Third Ward, Houston, 93–94
13th Floor Elevators, 259, 272, 273, 346
Thomas, B. J., 67, 149, 259, 271, 298
Thomas, Gates, 24
Thomas, George Washington Jr., 27, 155, **320–21**, 323, 349
Thomas, Henry, 154, 159, 255, **321–23**, *322*
Thomas, Hersal, 27, 154–55, 320, 321, **323**, 350
Thomas, Hociel, 154, 321, **323**
Thomas, James, 359
Thomas, Jesse, 26
Thomas, Jesse "Babyface," 255
Thomas, Jimmie, 42
Thomas, Joe, 350
Thomas, Ramblin', 255
Thomas, Willard "Ramblin," 26
Thomas Goggan and Brothers, 56, 244, 267, **319–20**
Thomason, Benny, 41
Thompson, Clara, 323
Thompson, Ernest O., 325
Thompson, Hank, 20, 31, 50, 66, 185
Thompson, Lucky, 166
Thompson, May Peterson, 55, **323**, 325
Thornhill, Claude, 276
Thornton, Willie Mae "Big Mama," 62, 139, 167, 258, 259, 269, 270, 272, 324, 325
Thorogood, George, 300
Threadgill, Kenneth, 168, 174, 229, 276, 298, **326**, 327
Threadgill, Mildred, 326
Threadgill's, 148, 149, 168, 326
Three Blazers, 38–39, 215
Three Dog Night, 298
Three Faces West, 174

Thurstone, Howard, 201
Tierney, Louis, 231
Tigua Indians, 225, 228
Tilley, Wesley Hope, **326**, **328**
Tillis, Mel, 318
Tillman, Floyd, 3, 20, 38, 41, 50, 66, 74, 75, 137, 197, 218, 259, 286
Tilton, Martha, 116
Timbuk 3, 273–74
Tiny Moore Music Center, 216
Tiny Tim, 289
Tipica Orchestra, *101*
Tippin, Aaron, 22
Tjader, Cal, 135
TNT (Tanner 'N Texas) Records, 261
Todd, Oliver, 251
Tolbert, Skeets, 290
Tolen, L. C., 294
Tolson, W. A., 250
Tolstead, Phil, 248
Tom Dickey and the Showboys, 137
Tomlinson, Michael, 174
Tommy, Texas, 255
Tommy Duncan and His Western All Stars, 85
Tonantzin, 127
Top Ten Studios, 259
Torch record label, 29
Torchy Swingsters, 243
Torres, Albino, 172
Torres, Patsy, 308
Toscanini, Arturo, 120, 264
Total-Line Music Company, 268
Touch and Go record label, 249
Towles, Nat, 60, 158, 166, 303
Toxic Shock, 249
Traveling Wilburys, 237, 271
Travers, Fred, 356
Travis, Randy, 86
Tremont, 234
Trent, Alphonse, 155–56, 210, 248, **328**, 330
Treviño, Geronimo, 5
Treviño, Rick, 21, 68
Tribute record label, 49
Trinity University, 16
Trío San Miguel, 308
Trio Texano, 256
Triple-D record label, 179
Triple Threat, 340
Triplett, Kevin, 103
Trombonists, 60, 63, 86–87, 116–17, 121, 165–66, 183, 210, 212, 353
Trout Fishing in America, 175
Troy, Henry, 84
Troy Floyd and His Plaza Hotel Orchestra, 102, 255
Troy Floyd Shadowland Orches-

tra, 102, *102*
Truck-driving songs, 74–75
Truman, Harry, 247
Trumbauer, Frankie, 172, 183, 305, 306
Trumpeters, 41, 81–82, 147, 152–54, 166, 175, 182, 239, 243–44, 290, 305, 355, 362
Tubb, Ernest Dale, 3, 8, 21, 38, 49, 66, 78, 119, 133, 197, 233, 266, 276, 318, 329, 330, 331, 355
Tubb, Justin Wayne, 330–31
Tucker, Bessie, 255
Tucker, Tanya, 10, 17, 67, 239
Tureck, Rosalyn, 4, 282
Turner, Babe Kyro Lemon, 26, *331*, **331**
Turner, Big Joe, 27, 82, 91, 94
Turner, Buck, 255
Turner, Dallas "Nevada Slim," 31, 266
Turner, Elsa, 108
Turner, Grant, **331–32**
Turner, Ike, 91, 152, 351
Turner, Joe, 70
Turner, John, 189, 190, 347
Turner, Tina, 91, 152, 351
Turrentine, Stanley, 58
Tuttle, Wesley, 44
"Twelfth Street Rag," 32
Twelve Clouds of Joy, 32, 86, 156, 353
"Twentieth Century Waltz," *135*
Twilight Room, 249
Twink Records, 261
Two O'Clock Lab Band, 333
Tyler, T. Texas, 166
Tyson, Willie, 255
Ty-Tex record label, 259

Ulrich, Homer, 246
Uncle Ezra and the Boys, 22
Uncle Tumpie and the Boys, 22
Uncle Walt's Band, *11*, 148, 149, 261
Underground Musicians Association, 303
Underwood, George, 261
Unholy Three, 299
Union of God's Musicians and Artists Ascension (UGMAA), 303
Union Underground, 274
Unión y Progreso Barrio Development of Houston, 217
Uniques, 259
United Artists, 136, 180, 299, 357
United Negro College Fund Drive, 269

Universal Attractions, 58
Universities. *See* Music schools; *and specific colleges*
University of Houston, 182
University of North Texas College of Music, 54, 55, 56, 60, 85, 94, 131, 136, 146, 158, **333–34**
University of Texas at Austin
  Center for American History, 27, 36, 262
  classical music program, 54, 55
  "Eyes of Texas," 99
  faculty, 2, 16, 83–84, 110
  folk music, 254
  mariachi music, 203
  musicologists, 232, 246, 292
  O'Daniel and, 234
  radio, 250
  students, 13, 15, 47, 146, 150, 168
University Choral Society, 108
University of Texas Institute of Texan Cultures, 313, **334–35**
University professors. *See* Music educators
Uptown Records, 87
Urban Cowboy, 119

Vagabonds, 86
Valdez, Manuel, 260
Valens, Richie, 20, 113, 141, 161, 180, 271
Valentine, Billy, 215
Valery, Joseph Jr., **336**
Vallee, Rudy, 172, 289
Van Cliburn International Piano Competition, 4, 55, 56, 150, 225, **336–37**
Vandagriff, Earny, 247
Van der Stucken, Frank Valentine, **337–38**
Vandiver, John, 4
Van Eps, John, 306
Vanguard Records, 325
Van Katwick, Harold, 16
Van Ronk, Dave, 125
Van Zandt, John Townes, 4, 11, 49, 67, 103, 174, 230, **338–40**, *339*
Varèse, Edgard, 56
Vargas, Kathy, 127
Vásquez, Arturo, 208
Vaudeville, 84, 121–22, 128, 201
Vaughan, Jimmie, 27, 89, 172, 273, 274, 340, 358
Vaughan, Stevie Ray, 5, 7, 11, 27, 49, 63, 89, 126, 172, 260, 261, 273, 298, 300, **340**, *341*, 346, 355

Vaughn, Jack, 243
Vaughn, Jerry, 356
Vaughn, Sara, 58, 116, 163
Vaughn Music Company, 124
Vault, 249
V-discs, 258
Vee, Bobby, 142, 180
Vee, Sonny, 350
Vee-Jay record label, 58, 70, 147
Veep record label, 147
Vela, Rubén, 127, 315
Velvet Cowpasture, 326
Velvets, 114
Venth, Carl, 56, 119, 176, 235, 311, **340**, 342, 353
Venting, Albert Sobieski, **342**
Venting, Richard, 342
Venture Recording Studio, 260
Venuti, Joe, 10, 163
Verrot, Pascal, 151
Versel, Louis, 176
Vesley, Ted, 307
Vick, Harold, 355
Vickers, Jon, 56, 143, 174, 235
Victoria, María, 260
Victor Records, 15, 30, 34, 66, 76, 120, 167, 253, 254, 255, 256
Victor Talking Machine Company, 208, 269, 276
Victory Grill, 27, 33
Victor y Lolita, 308
Viesca, Juan, 315
Villa, Beto, 122, 150, 204, 260, 308, **342–43**
Villa, Lucha, 262
Village Boys, 48
Villareal, Bruno, 256, **343**
Vilonat, 13
Vincent, Gene, 259
Vincent, Johnny, 289
Vincent, Louella Styles, **343–44**
Vincent, Upshur, 344
Vin record label, 289
Vinson, Eddie, 27, 58, 94, 107, 158, 182, 251, 325, **344–46**, *345*
Vinson, Sam, 344
Violinists, 43, 340, 342. *See also* Fiddlers
Virdel, C. M., 19
Virginia Minstrels, 113
Vliet, R. G., 31
Vocalion Records, 2, 3, 26, 57, 184, 254, 255, 290, 322, 325
Volcán Records, 191
Voodie White Trio, 290
V. O. Stamps Music Company, 296

Vulcan Gas Company, 261, 346, **346–47**, *347*

Waco Auditorium, 237
Waco Hall, 237
Waco Lyric Opera, 236
Waelder, Jacob, 284
Wagner, Jacob, 18
Wagoner, Fred, 30
Wagoner, Porter, 220, 239
Wakely, Jimmy, 44, 318
Walden, Boot, 87
Walker, Alice, 127
Walker, Clay, 259
Walker, Jerry Jeff, 5, 38, 49, 67, 126, 174, 194, 261, 273, 281, 298, 314, 355
Walker, Mel, 325
Walker, Philip, 265
Walker, T-Bone, 25, 26, 27, 29, 41, 61, 62, 70, 82, 91, 94, 121, 161, 162, 178, 189, 256, 258, 270, 272, 289, 290, 344, 348, **348–49**, 354
Wall, Chris, 5, 38
Wallace, Henry A., 187
Wallace, Matt, 350
Wallace, Sippie, 27, 154–55, 256, 320, 321, 323, 349, **349–50**
Waller, Fats, 32, 155, 163, 175, 305, 359
Wallis, Hal, 358
Walser, Don, 38, 78, 126
Walter, Bruno, 263
Walton, Cedar, 158
Wambach, Émile, 338
Wanderers, 212
Ward, Bill, 133
Ward, Jackie, 264, 318
Wardell, Billy, 116
Warfield, William, 56
Warford, Claude, 23
Waring, Fred, 264
Warner Brothers, 44, 194, 274, 298
Warwick, Dionne, 139
Waschka, Rodney, 147
Washington, Dinah, 58
Washington, Fats, 336
Washington, Walter "Cowboy," 255
Waterloo Ice House, 148, 149
Waters, Ethel, 305
Waters, Muddy, 5, 31, 172, 178
Watson, Johnny, 27, 94, 303, **350–51**
Watson, Kirk, 149
Watson, Mercy Dee, 350
Watts, Jim, 33
Way-Beck Talent, 17
Waylors, 161

Wayne, John, 200, 201, 237
WEA International record label, 261
Weavers, 183
Webb, Chick, 163
Webb, Jitterbug, 91, **351**
Webb, Speed, 41, 359
Webb, Walter Prescott, 238
Webern, Anton, 56, 245
Webster, Ben, 69, 251
Webster, Katie, **351–52**
Weems, Ted, 15
Wehe, Heinrich, 5
Wehle, Billy, 12
Weinberger, Jaromir, 283
Weiner, Hollace Ava, 361
Weir, Rusty, 261
Weiss, Julius, 53, 118, 171, **352–53**
Weissenberg, Alexis, 282
Weizsäcker, Richard von, 28
Welborn, Larry, 141
Welcher, Dan, 151
Welcome to the Club: The Women of Rockabilly, 9
Welding, Pete, 348
Welles, Orson, 358
Wells, Don, 199
Wells, Henry James, **353**
Wells, Kitty, 9, 191
Wellswood, Dick, 251
Wendell, Barrett, 188
Werner, Susan, 175
Wesley, Charles, 278
West, Dottie, 230, 231
West, Emily D., 364
West, Mae, 128, 201
West, Shelly, 264
Westerners, 207
Western swing, 2–3, 10, 22–23, 34–35, 39–41, 46, 50, 66, 71, 85–86, 86, 89–91, 137, 184–85, 196–97, 213, 231, 256, 258, 270, 299, 300, 317–19, 357
West-texanischer Gebirgs-Sängerbund, 317
West Texas Cowboys, 231
Wettling, George, 305
Whaley, Burt, 144
Wheat, John, 27
Wheeler, Erica, 149
Whistler, 192
White, Barry, 8
White, Benjamin Franklin, 106, 278, 279, 281
White, Butch, 194
White, Clarence Cameron, 246
White, Houston, 346
White, James, 38
White, John, 60
White, Lavelle, 125, 139

White, Michael, 158
White, Tony Joe, 314
Whitely, Ray, 44
Whiteman, Paul, 22, 116, 156, 163, 172, 192, 264, 305, 306
Whitley, Smiley, 48
Whitman, Slim, 185, 191, 318
Whittaker, Hudson, 296
Whittle Music Company, 245
Who, 259
Wick, Otto, 18, 56, 311, **353**
Widor, Charles-Marie, 135
Wier, Rusty, 174
Wiggles, Miss, 91
Wiggs, Johnny, 172, 173
Wilburn Brothers, 239
Wilcox, David, 174
Wildcats Band, 175
Wilder, Thornton, 223, 224
Wild West shows, 128
Wiley, Dewey Otto, **353–54**
Wiley, Ed, 265
Wilke, C., 119
Wilkerson, Don, 94, **354**
Wilkerson, Wayne, 4
Wilkins, Christopher, 54, 283
Wilks, Van, 273, 274
Willet, Slim, 16, 17, **354–55**
William, Spencer, 331
Williams, Andy, 178, 210, 230
Williams, Clarence, 320, 350
Williams, Cootie, 158, 166, 344, 362
Williams, Daniel Huggins, 89, 90, 91
Williams, Dave, 274
Williams, Don, 67
Williams, Eddie, 215
Williams, Frank, 305
Williams, Hank, 20, 50, 78, 148, 189, 191, 197, 218, 219, 266, 276, 318, 326, 330, 338, 340
Williams, Hank Jr., 264
Williams, James Clifton, 47
Williams, Joe, 321

Williams, Johnny H. "Curly," 317
Williams, Larry, 325
Williams, Lester, 27
Williams, Lucinda, 4, 5, 103, 174
Williams, Martin, 155
Williams, Mary Lou, 32, 155, 163
Williams, Mason, 272
Williams, Nat, 33
Williams, Richard Gene, 158, **355**, 362
Williams, Roosevelt T. *See* Grey Ghost
Williams, Steve, 42
Williams, Tex, 40
Williamson, Sonny Boy, 258, 289
Williamson, Sonny Boy II, 62
William Specht Spring Branch Band, 5
Willie Lewis and His Entertainers, 184
Willie Nelson's Fourth of July Picnic, 194, **355**, *356*
Willing, Foy, **355–56**
Willis, Chick, 61
Willis, Chuck, 178
Wills, Billy Jack, 216
Wills, Bob, 3, 10, 11, 17, 23, 26, 32, 39, 40, 40, 50, 66, 71, 85–86, 91, 148, 184, 185, 196, 197, 213, 215, 216, 218, 231, 237, 239, 258, 264, 270, 286, 298, 299, 300, 354, **356–57**, *357*
Wills, Chill, 200, 318
Wills, Johnnie Lee, **357–58**
Wills Fiddle Band, 39, 184, 299
Wills Point Ballroom, 215, 216
Wilson, Dick, 69
Wilson, Dooley, **358**
Wilson, Eddie, 347, 355
Wilson, Hop, 125, 352, 358
Wilson, Jackie, 29, 58, 114

Wilson, John Frank, 259, 271, **358–59**
Wilson, Kim, 27, 352
Wilson, Marie, 116
Wilson, Teddy, 97, 156, 251, **359**, *360*
Wilson, U. P., 89
Winding, Kai, 107
Wink Westerners, 236
Winston record label, 231, 354
Winter, Edgar, 272
Winter, Johnny, 190, 258, 261, 272, 301, 314, 346, 347, 348, 358
Wise, Chubby, 174
Wiser, Charlie, 189
Witherspoon, Jimmy, 212
Wittry, Diane M., 302
Wolf, Hymie, 260
Wolf, Peter, 55, 235
Wolf, Sidney Abraham, **359–62**
Wolfe, C. Burdette "Bud," 361
Wolfman Jack, 31
Wonder, Stevie, 340
Wood, Booty, 116
Wood, Grant, 238
Wooding, Sam, 184
Woods, Buddy, 26, 255, 331
Woods, Cora, 91
Woodson, Willy, 350
World Saxophone Quartet, 135, 159
World's Greatest Jazz Band, 165
"Worried Blues," *160*
Wray, J. Campbell, 293
Wright, Elmon, 362
Wright, Emma, 255
Wright, Gladys Yoakum, 310
Wright, Lammar, 156, **362**
Wright, Lammar Jr., 362
Wright, Leo Nash, 158, **362**
Wright, O. V., 139, 259, 269
Wright, P. T., 84
Wright Brothers Gospel Singers, 255
Wurstfest, 104, **362–63**
Wynans, Reese, 340

Wynette, Tammy, 103
Wynne, Angus III, 314
Wynne Entertainment, 314

X (band), 249

Yaeger, George, 283
Yale, Bob, 115–16
Yanaguana Society, 46
Yarborough, Ralph, 199, 200
Yarrow, Peter, 52, 168, 174
Yates, Herbert, 97
Yazoo Records, 164, 244
Ybarra, Eva, 261, 308, 315
Yellowfish, Hanna, 224
"Yellow Rose of Texas," 129, 364, **364**
Yoakum, Dwight, 162
York, Phil, 260
Young, Ben, 19
Young, Faron, 67, 78, 188, 191, 210, 233, 316
Young, Lester, 7, 32, 86, 155, 158, 163, 178, 215, 251, 290, 351
Young, Neil, 355
Young, Trummy, 116, 163
Young, Victor, 116

Zakary Thaks (band), 272
Zamora, Albert, 261
Zappa, Frank, 7, 361
Zawadil, Emil Ludwig, 317
Zeffirelli, Franco, 55, 56, 174, 235
Zeller, Bob, 358
Ziegler, Samuel Peters, **365**
Zimmerle, Fred, 260, 308
Zimmerman, Christopher, 302
Zimmermann Piano Company, 245
Zondervan, P. J., 297
Zondervan Corporation, 297
Zydeco, 93–94, 110–11, 259, 308, **365–66**
ZZ Top, 21, 45, 89, 172, 259, 272–73, 274